NIGHTSHADE;

OR

CLAUDE DUVAL,

THE DASHING HIGHWAYMAN.

BY THE AUTHOR OF "JANE BRIGHTWELL."

WITH SIXTY ILLUSTRATIONS.
DRAWN BY F. GILBERT.

LONDON:
JOHN DICKS, 313, STRAND; AND ALL BOOKSELLERS.

INDEX TO THE ENGRAVINGS.

No.
1. Claude Duval Rescues Lucy Everton . . . . . . *See Page* 7
2. Claude Duval Stops the Noblemen on the Heath 18
3. The Governor of Newgate Makes a Discovery 23
4. Claude Duval Carving his Name on Newgate Stone 26
5. The Marchioness of Queensberry Accepts Claude as a Partner in the Dance . . 40
6. Duval Discovers the Dead Body of the Strange Lady 48
7. Claude Duval Presents his Sword to the King 52
8. The King Directs the Prince to be Removed 63
9. Duval Escapes from the Bow Street Runners 68
10. Duval Escapes Pursuit in the Crowd 74
11. Duval Disables Mossy Pendell's Servant 84
12. Mossy Pendell Visits Lucy Everton at Newgate 89
13. Duel Between Duval and Mossy Pendell 103
14. Lucy Everton is Conducted to the Old Bailey 107
15. Nightshade Disposes of Mr. Swallow 115
16. Duval and Lady Dominick at the Palace Ball 124
17. Duval Surprises the Marquis of Harcourt 130
18. Duval Receives the Pardon of Lucy Everton 139
19. The Discovery of Lord Horlop 145
20. Duval Rescues Marion Marley 154
21. The Conspirators Salute the Prince 167
22. Danger Threatens the Young Prince 169
23. The Rendezvous.—Plot and Counterplot 181
24. Duval Throws Muckles into the Thames 188
25. St. Ives Warns Duval of his Danger 197
26. Duval Releases the Stuart Princess from the Tower 203
27. Duval and his Party in General Everton's Vault 210
28. Duval and St. Ives in the Royal Gardens at Kew 220
29. The King Taking the Poisoned Cup 230
30. The Princess Produces a Pardon for Claude Duval 236
31. Claude Duval Rescues Constance Lascelles 243
32. The Stuart Princes Conveyed to the Tower 255
33. Claude Duval Makes Acquaintance with Dick Turpin 263
34. The Duchess of Cleveland Makes a Declaration of Love 270
35. The Stuart Princess Again Rescued from the Tower 277
36. The Duke of Montrose Made Prisoner 282
37. Alice Assaulted by Mossy Pendell 292
38. Claude Duval Accosts the Old Lady and her Niece 301
39. Duval Excites the Jealousy of the Duchess of Cleveland 306
40. Jabez Overwhelmed with Terror 315
41. The Removal of Dick Turpin's Body 323
42. Duval Conceals himself in the Corridor 335
43. Duval Seeks the Shelter of the Astrologer's Room 342
44. St. Ives Welcomes his Bride 347
45. Nina Restored to Charles Lennox 358
46. Duval Saves the Young Wife from Outrage 362
47. Mossy Pendell Enters the Trap 374
48. Duval in the House of Mourning 379
49. Duval Alarmed by a Spectre in the Forest 386
50. St. Ives Rescues Eva St. Clair 392
51. Eva St. Clair in Deep Meditation 405
52. Mrs. Joyce Plays the Eavesdropper 412

INDEX TO ENGRAVINGS.

No.		
53.	St. Ives at the Feet of Eva St. Clair	See Page 420
54.	Claude Duval in the Duchess of Cleveland's Opera Box	429
55.	Mrs. Maurice Releases Duval from the Closet	435
56.	Duval and Blossom Obtain Seats in the Mail Coach	443
57.	The Discovery of Agnes in the Meadow	451
58.	The Mysterious Family in the "House to Let"	458
59.	The Duel in the Palace	472
60.	The Murder of the Lord in Waiting	476

INDEX.

	PAGE
Chapter I. Claude Duval Rescues a Prisoner and Gains a Wife	1
,, II. Claude Duval Calls for his Boots, his Hat, and his Horse	4
,, III. Claude Duval Surprises both Friends and Foes	6
,, IV. Claude Duval's Name Changes the Current of Lord Horlop's Thoughts	10
,, V. Claude Duval Personates a High Official, and Baffles the Officers	12
,, VI. Claude Duval Finds Lucy Everton a Haunted Home	15
,, VII. Claude Duval Decides an Important Wager on Hampstead Heath	17
,, VIII. Claude Duval Escapes from the Officers	20
,, IX. Claude Duval Takes an Anxious Look into Newgate	22
,, X. Claude Duval Sacrifices All for Love, and yet Saves Himself	24
,, XI. Claude Duval dances a Cotillon with the Marchioness of Queensberry	27
,, XII. Claude Duval Hears Lucy Everton's Story from her Own Lips	29
,, XIII. Claude Duval meets with a Strange Adventure on Bagshot Heath	32
,, XIV. Claude Duval Fights a Duel with Lord Horlop	35
,, XV. Claude Duval Finds Himself in the Secret Chamber of Camden House	37
,, XVI. Claude Duval Visits the Masked Ball at Queensberry House	39
,, XVII. Claude Duval Throws himself on the mercy of the Duchess of Cleveland	42
,, XVIII. Claude Duval Pursues the Spectre Horseman in the Green Park	44
,, XIX. Claude Duval Finds Himself in Intimate Connexion with Royalty	47
,, XX. Claude Duval is the Means of Saving the King's Life	50
,, XXI. Claude Duval Makes a Compact with the King of England	52
,, XXII. Claude Duval Seeks Shelter in the Thieves' Ken in Westminster	54
,, XXIII. Claude Duval Finds himself in a Perilous Situation in Westminster Abbey	58
,, XXIV. Claude Duval Meets with a Severe Trial on his Return to Hampstead Heath	60
,, XXV. Claude Duval Discovers the Ingratitude of Kings, and is Apprehended at the Palace	62
,, XXVI. Claude Duval is Disappointed in his Estimate of King George	64
,, XXVII. Claude Duval Finds that Gratitude is not Extinct in the Breasts of all Men	67
,, XXVIII. Claude Duval has an Encounter with Colonel Jessop	70
,, XXIX. Claude Duval Pays a Visit to the Opera House, and Meets the Duchess of Cleveland	72
,, XXX. Claude Duval Returns the Letters to the Duchess of Cleveland	75
,, XXXI. Claude Duval Pays a Visit to Camden House	77
,, XXXII. Claude Duval Makes an Ally of a Police-Officer	79
,, XXXIII. The Midnight Rendezvous.—The Bereaved Heart	82
,, XXXIV. Claude Duval Encounters Great Danger in the Palace at Kew	85
,, XXXV. Claude Duval Stops a Coach, and Finds it Contains only a Ghostly Company	87
,, XXXVI. Lucy Everton is Visited by Mossy Pendell in Newgate	88
,, XXXVII. Claude Duval Determines to Ransom Lucy Everton	91
,, XXXVIII. Claude Duval has Two Adventures on the Road	94
,, XXXIX. Duval Enters the Vestibule of Newgate, but his Plans are Interrupted	96
,, XL. Claude Duval Meets with a Friend in Need	98
,, XLI. Claude Duval Robs the Oxford Mail, and Encounters an Enemy	101
,, XLII. Claude Duval has a Duel with Mossy Pendell	103
,, XLIII. Lucy Everton is Again Placed in the Dock	106
,, XLIV. Lucy's Danger, and a Voice from the Dead	108
,, XLV. Claude Duval is Recognised in the Witness for the Defence	111
,, XLVI. Claude Duval Makes himself the Almoner of the City Remembrancer	112
,, XLVII. Nightshade Takes a Novel Leap, and Frightens Mr. Swallow	116
,, XLVIII. Claude Duval Visits the Thieves' "Keep" in Covent Garden	118
,, XLIX. Swallow Makes a Compact with Claude Duval	120
,, L. Claude Duval Succeeds in his Desire to Attend the King's Ball	123
,, LI. Claude Duval Receives Good Advice from the Duchess of Cleveland	125
,, LII. Claude Duval is in Great Peril at St. James's Palace	127
,, LIII. Claude Duval Escapes from the Palace	130
,, LIV. Claude Duval Visits the Duchess of Cleveland	132
,, LV. Claude Duval Overhears a Strange Plot Concocted	134
,, LVI. The Majesty of England Finds himself in a Fix	136

		PAGE
Chapter LVII. Lucy is Released from Newgate	.	139
,, LVIII. Claude Duval and Lucy Make Good their Retreat	.	141
,, LIX. The Hut in the Wood.—The Dying Man	.	144
,, LX. Claude Duval and Blossom Meet with a Strange Adventure	.	147
,, LXI. Claude Duval Releases a Prisoner, and Gets the Better of Mr. Muckles	.	149
,, LXII. Claude Duval Seeks the Daughter of the Steward of the Grange	.	151
,, LXIII. Mr. Marley, by the Aid of Claude Duval, Recovers his Lost Child	.	152
,, LXIV. Blossom Learns some Satisfactory Intelligence Respecting Mossy Pendell	.	155
,, LXV. The Adventure with the Oxford Mail	.	158
,, LXVI. The Oxford Mail Pursues its Journey without the Aid of the Guard's Horn	.	160
,, LXVII. Claude Duval has Another Reckoning with Mossy Pendell	.	163
,, LXVIII. The Banqueting Hall.—The Conspirator's Plot	.	166
,, LXIX. Claude Duval Becomes an Actor, when he Intended only to be a Spectator	.	168
,, LXX. Claude Duval's Offer to the Young Prince	.	171
,, LXXI. Claude Duval Meets with a Surprise	.	173
,, LXXII. Claude Duval Refuses Overtures from the House of Stuart	.	179
,, LXXIII. Claude Duval Finds that his Confidence in St. Ives is not Misplaced	.	181
,, LXXIV. Mr. Pilkington is Placed Hors de Combat for the Present	.	183
,, LXXV. Claude Duval Makes an Expedition to Old Westminster Bridge	.	187
,, LXXVI. Mr. Swallow is Compelled to Answer a Few Questions	.	189
,, LXXVII. Claude Duval and St. Ives are in a Perilous Position	.	191
,, LXXVIII. Claude Duval Accompanies the Duchess of Cleveland to the Prime Minister's	.	195
,, LXXIX. Claude Duval and Lucy Make some Important Discoveries in the Valise	.	198
,, LXXX. Claude Duval is Received by the Deputy Governor of the Tower	.	200
,, LXXXI. Claude Duval and Mr. St Ives Pay a Visit to Harcourt House	.	205
,, LXXXII. The Search in the Vault at St. Paul's	.	208
,, LXXXIII. A Little Party Imprisoned in a Vault in St. Paul's Cathedral	.	211
,, LXXXIV. Mossy Pendell Finds Things do not Turn Out as he Desires	.	213
,, LXXXV. The Stuart Princess Undertakes a Perilous Enterprise	.	216
,, LXXXVI. Sir Charles Wilton Meets with his Match in Claude Duval	.	219
,, LXXXVII. Claude Duval has an Adventure on the Road	.	221
,, LXXXVIII. The First Secretary to the Russian Embassy is Placed in a Dilemma	.	224
,, LXXXIX. The Royal Banquet, and what Happened at It	.	227
,, XC. The Earl of Bute is Compelled to Recognise Claude Duval as a Friend	.	229
,, XCI. Claude Duval is Compelled to Become a Jacobite for a Time	.	233
,, XCII. Lucy Receives a Mysterious Visit at Farnborough House	.	237
,, XCIII. Claude Duval and Blossom Cry "Stand and Deliver" on the Road	.	239
,, XCIV. Claude Duval Rescues Constance Lascelles from her Foes	.	242
,, XCV. Mrs. Cumberpatch Receives Sir John's Confession	.	245
,, XCVI. Constance Lascelles Finds that she is not Friendless	.	246
,, XCVII. St. Ives Makes Another Attempt to Convey the Stuart Princess from England	.	250
,, XCVIII. Claude Duval and St. Ives are Arrested on Board the Dutch Galliot	.	252
,, XCIX. The Stuart Princess, with Duval and St. Ives, is Conveyed to the Tower	.	254
,, C. Blossom Meets with an Unexpected Friend	.	258
,, CI. Claude Duval and Blossom Seek an Adventure on the Road	.	260
,, CII. Claude Duval Makes Acquaintance with Dick Turpin	.	262
,, CIII. Dick Turpin Establishes his Toll-Bar for the Benefit of His Majesty	.	264
,, CIV. A Scene of Confusion at the Old Bedford Head	.	267
,, CV. The Duchess of Cleveland Makes an Unexpected Communication to Duval	.	269
,, CVI. Duval and Blossom Attempt the Rescue of St. Ives and the Stuart Princess	.	271
,, CVII. Claude Duval Makes some Prisoners in the Tower	.	274
,, CVIII. Claude Duval and his Friends Reach Traitors' Gate in Safety	.	277
,, CIX. Claude Duval and Blossom Meet with an Acquaintance	.	279
,, CX. Claude Duval Cancels a Debt of Honour	.	282
,, CXI. Claude Duval Makes a Terrible Discovery	.	284
,, CXII. Claude Duval and Blossom Find Themselves in an Uncomfortable Position	.	286
,, CXIII. Claude Duval Pays Another Visit to the Neighbourhood of Camden House	.	288
,, CXIV. Mossy Pendell Makes Known his Wishes	.	291
,, CXV. Mossy Pendell Makes a Mistake	.	293
,, CXVI. General Everton is Liberated	.	296
,, CXVII. Claude Duval Seeks Excitement in the Park	.	298
,, CXVIII. Duval has Reason to Reproach himself	.	301
,, CXIX. Claude Duval Flies from Temptation	.	303
,, CXX. Claude Duval Meets with an Adventure	.	306
,, CXXI. Duval Robs the Oxford Mail	.	308
,, CXXII. Claude Duval Attacked by a Highwayman	.	310
,, CXXIII. Duval Makes a Terrible Discovery	.	313
,, CXXIV. Claude Overhears a Fearful Disclosure	.	316
,, CXXV. Duval Obtains Possession of a Casket	.	318
,, CXXVI. Preparations for the Execution of Dick Turpin	.	320
,, CXXVII. Dick Turpin is not Deserted by his Friends	.	322
,, CXXVIII. The Dead Restored to Life	.	325
,, CXXIX. Duval and Lucy Take Up their Abode in Camden House	.	327

INDEX.

		PAGE
Chapter CXXX. Claude Duval Pays a Visit to the Lord Chamberlain		330
,, CXXXI. Claude Duval Finds Himself in Comfortable Quarters		332
,, CXXXII. Claude Duval Finds Himself in a Perilous Situation		334
,, CXXXIII. Claude Duval Succeeds in Escaping from the Palace		336
,, CXXXIV. Claude Duval Becomes a Second in a Duel		339
,, CXXXV. Claude Duval Meets Unexpectedly with an Old Friend		341
,, CXXXVI. Claude Duval Robs an Old Gentleman		343
,, CXXXVII. A Wedding at the Chapel Royal		347
,, CXXXVIII. Claude Duval Pledges Himself to Unravel a Mystery		349
,, CXXXIX. Treachery and the Iron Coffer		351
,, CXL. Nina Endeavours to Make her Escape from the Corinthian Temple		355
,, CXLI. Claude Duval Rescues Nina, at Great Peril to Himself		357
,, CXLII. Claude Duval Robs the Portsmouth Mail		359
,, CXLIII. Claude Duval Stops a Post-Chaise, and Releases a Prisoner		362
,, CXLIV. Lucy Makes a Strange Communication to Claude Duval		363
,, CXLV. Claude Duval Succeeds in Frightening the Dutch Envoy		366
,, CXLVI. The Two Plotters Defeated by Claude Duval		368
,, CXLVII. Claude Duval Encounters Mossy Pendell Once Again		371
,, CXLVIII. Claude Duval Enacts a New Character		373
,, CXLIX. Claude Duval Succeeds in Baffling Mossy Pendell		375
,, CL. Claude Duval Enters a House of Mourning		378
,, CLI. The Dead Restored to Life		380
,, CLII. Claude Duval and Dick Turpin Stop the Oxford Mail		382
,, CLIII. Claude Duval Meets a Spectre Statue		385
,, CLIV. Claude Duval Exorcises the Ghost		388
,, CLV. An Old Acquaintance Makes his Appearance		390
,, CLVI. The Broken Chaise		392
,, CLVII. St. Ives Rescues Eva St. Clair from Imminent Danger		395
,, CLVIII. A Night of Tumult and Anxiety		397
,, CLIX. The Innocent are Made Happy Again		399
,, CLX. St. Ives Encounters Two Old Acquaintances		402
,, CLXI. St. Ives Listens not to his Better Angel		404
,, CLXII. The Desolation of a Young Heart		406
,, CLXIII. Claude Duval and Lucy Entertain the Stuart Princess		408
,, CLXIV. St. Ives' First Interview with Eva After the Accident		411
,, CLXV. St. Ives Induces Eva to Write to him		413
,, CLXVI. The Stuart Princess Makes a Confidante of Lucy		415
,, CLXVII. Duval and Mossy Pendell Meet near Hampstead Heath		417
,, CLXVIII. Eva St. Clair and St. Ives have Another Interview		420
,, CLXIX. Shows that St. Ives Forms a Good Resolution		422
,, CLXX. A Happy Re-union		424
,, CLXXXI. Eva St. Clair Receives the Reward of Virtue		427
,, CLXXXII. Duval is Betrayed by the Duchess of Cleveland		429
,, CLXXXIII. Claude Duval Meets with a Strange Adventure		431
,, CLXXXIV. Duval Finds Himself in an Awkward Position		433
,, CLXXXV. Claude Duval Defends Mr. Maurice		436
,, CLXXXVI. Duval Tries to Gain the Confidence of Mrs. Maurice		438
,, CLXXXVII. Mrs. Maurice Makes a Startling Confession to Claude Duval		439
,, CLXXXVIII. Duval Makes Acquaintance with Mr. Knight, Attorney-at-Law		442
,, CLXXXIX. Mr. Knight Does not Seem Disposed to Carry Out his Threats		445
,, CXC. Claude Duval and Blossom Succeed in Disposing of a Troublesome Person		447
,, CXCI. Duval has a Narrow Escape		449
,, CXCII. Claude Duval and Dick Turpin Chastise a Villain		451
,, CXCIII. In which Claude Duval Overhears a Private Conversation		454
,, CXCIV. A Singular Person is Introduced to the Reader		455
,, CXCV. Claude Duval Determines to Watch Over Adelina		458
,, CXCVI. The Prince of Wales Solves some of the Mysteries of the "House to Let"		460
,, CXCVII. Frederick, Prince of Wales, takes Counsel		462
,, CXCVIII. Claude Duval is Made Acquainted with some of the Jacobite Plots		465
,, CXCIX. Duval Consents once More to Take Part in Jacobite Plots		467
,, CC. Frederick, Prince of Wales, is Challenged to Single Combat		470
,, CCI. St. Ives Persuades the Stuart Family to Quit the Precincts of the Palace		472
,, CCII. Duval and St. Ives Witness a Horrible Murder		475
,, CCIII. Claude Duval and St. Ives Visit St. Germains.—Conclusion		477

NIGHTSHADE;

OR, CLAUDE DUVAL, THE DASHING HIGHWAYMAN.

CLAUDE DUVAL RESCUES LUCY EVERTON.

CHAPTER I.

CLAUDE DUVAL RESCUES A PRISONER AND GAINS A WIFE.

"SAVE me! save me! Will no one save me? I am innocent of this crime which is laid to my charge. It is hard to die for that which never in thought, word or deed can cling to me in the shape of guilt. Save me, oh, save me!"

With a wild rapidity of utterance that would not be stayed.

With a shrieking vehemence which no human power could conquer.

No. 1.—NIGHTSHADE.

Wringing her hands and dashing back from her pale, blanched face the luxuriant hair, that seemed, in that moment of pain and degradation, to form a veil for the lovely face it belonged to, stood a young girl.

Scarcely past the age of childhood.

A young English maiden.

Such an one as is loved and cherished and made much of.

The idol of a house.

The cherished jewel of every heart.

A creature to speak gently to—a sunshine—an angelic presence, such as might wean the soul from all degrading thoughts and aspirations.

A fair young English girl.

She stood upon a scaffold.

She was brought out to die.

To die a death at once of horror and degradation—to be held up as a spectacle to the twice three thousand eyes bent upon her, beneath the fleecy clouds and scattered blue of a fair April sky.

To die by the hands of the common executioner, with a name which should be given over to execration when the light in those sweet eyes should be quenched for ever in the gloom of the grave.

"Save me! save me! I cannot, must not die! My trial was a mockery—a delusion! I am not guilty! Help, help, I cry to all! to earth—to heaven! Mercy, mercy! Is there no justice among men, or pity in heaven? I am not guilty! I am not guilty!"

"Stop her mouth!" growled a ruffianly voice; "stop her mouth, I say! This must not be, Mr. Sheriff."

"She was given leave to speak."

"Yes. To make a last speech and confession—but this is a defiance. Stop her mouth!"

"I dare not, Mr. Mossy Pendell; I dare not! Look at the people! Did you ever see such faces in your life? Look at their eyes! I told you how it would be! There now! there now!"

A roaring cry came from a thousand throats.

That was the cry that had been evoked from all those hearts by the shrieking appeal of the young girl.

That young girl brought out to die!

Oh, what a mockery was the April sunshine, as it mingled its golden hues with her fair hair.

The scene was old Bloomsbury Fields. The bright green spring grass spread a delicate carpet for miles around. The trees and hedges were bursting with new vegetation, and many a forest bird—the like of which has long since retired from the busy haunts of the great city, which has gathered within its long arms all those once fair fields to its great wilderness of bricks and mortar — hid themselves deep in bush and brake.

The second George was on the throne of these realms, and human life was of but little account.

"Help!" shrieked the girl again, as she saw the sympathetic movement of that myriad of upturned faces around her. "Help! Save me! Not because I am brought out here to die, but because I am innocent! You have children of your own, many of you! I see young faces among you, and I call upon them for aid! Save me! for the love of all that is merciful and just, save me from this terrible death! I am not guilty—not guilty—not guilty!"

The voice of the young creature became hoarse and appalling.

There was a spot of blood upon her lips.

The human agony of the fair face seemed to strike upon every heart there present as with a tangible blow.

Strong stalwart men fainted.

Mothers—for there were even such as spectators of that terrible scene—clasped their children to their breasts and shrieked aloud.

The Sheriff, whose duty it was to superintend that execution, turned white as his own cravat and ruffles and trembled palpably.

He stood by his carriage steps, and by his side was a man, tall beyond all ordinary tallness, with a face of such cadaverous malignity, that no one could look upon him without a shudder.

That was Mossy Pendell.

"By heaven and the other place!" he shouted, "we shall have a rescue! Look to your men, Mr. Muckles; you are the chief officer on the ground. Look to your men, and close round the scaffold. The people are already half mad with pity, and soon they will be wholly so with rage."

"Look to yourself, sir!" replied the officer, savagely. "Look to yourself, sir; for if the people's rage should come, I would not be in Mr. Mossy Pendell's shoes for the best estate in all England."

A terrible shout came from the crowd.

Crawling up upon the scaffold through an orifice in its centre, came something that looked scarcely human.

A shock of red hair.

A distorted countenance, boasting of but one eye.

A twisted trunk and legs that did not seem to belong to it.

The yell of execration came again, and the hangman—yes, that was the hangman—bent and cowered before the storm.

"Now, my dear, really——"

That was the way he addressed the young girl.

He placed one of his ugly, paw-like hands upon her neck.

She cast him from her with a shudder, and he fell grovelling at her feet.

"Too late! too late!" she shrieked. "Are you to feel for me, and is it to be too late to save me? What sympathy is this, that lets the victim perish? I call upon you to save me, and you answer me with shrieks and cries! Help! help! I say again! Not that I am young and that it is hard to die, but because I am innocent of the crime of which they have declared me guilty! Save me! save me! I tell you all that this is murder, and you are all murderers that can look on and see me perish without raising a hand to rescue me!"

These appeals exercised a powerful influence upon the assembled crowd.

The vast concourse swayed to and fro in an agitated fashion; and closer—closer still around the scaffold pressed the multitude.

It was in vain that the ordinary force of police-officers strove to keep the people from passing up to the very posts that supported the platform of death.

In a few seconds more those very officers themselves formed but units of the crowd, and were utterly helpless.

In fact, they found that their own safety was concerned in affecting an obscurity very foreign to their natures.

Then, the few authorities who were mounted, saw that affairs were getting serious.

One man, in a semi-military uniform, made a motion with his hand; and, in as compact a body as they could preserve, a party of what was then called the King's Light Horse began to press up from a distance towards the scaffold.

Simultaneously with that military movement ensued another.

A company of the Foot Guard, who had rested on their arms in a hollow of the ground not far from the back of old Montague House, formed in regular compact order, and slowly began to drive stragglers before them as they too approached the scaffold.

The terrified Sheriff retreated into his carriage

Some clouds stretched themselves over the face of the fair blue sky.

A sudden chill came through the atmosphere, and one of those remarkable changes which are the characteristics of an April day in England appeared about to ensue.

A few large, heavy drops of rain fell upon the upturned faces of the crowd.

It was a moment of perplexity.

A moment of indecision to the people.

A moment of despair to that young, fair creature, who was brought out to die in all her innocence and all her beauty on that morning of April smiles and tears.

The spectacle presented by the whole assemblage—by the terrible apparatus of death—and by the movement made by the civil and military authorities, was now strange and interesting in the extreme.

Up to that moment the people had the case in their own hands.

It only required an active movement of one or two adventurous spirits, and the innocent victim would be torn from the hands of the law.

If, however, the company of the Foot Guard, and the small party of the King's Light Horse, should succeed in hemming in the scaffold, all hope of rescue would be at an e..

The crowd saw it.

The girl on the scaffold saw it.

She made a last appeal.

"Help—help, again! Save me—save me! Help, ere it be too late! Take me among you and save me! You cannot have come here to see me die!"

A suggestive swinging movement among the crowd, which wafted as if in waves towards the foot of the scaffold some of the foremost of the throng, was the response to this appeal.

And the foremost of all was a tall man, having the appearance of a grazier or a well-to-do farmer.

He wore a broad-brimmed slouched hat, and a white frieze coat of ample dimensions.

This man, either from accident or design, kept himself in front of the crowd, and soon reached the very foot of the scaffold.

A strange movement now took place immediately in this man's vicinity; and it appeared as if some eight or ten persons were violently intent upon congregating themselves around him; although, to look at them, no one could suppose for a single moment that any community of feeling or interest could be among them.

One was attired as a sailor.

Another wore the rags of a beggar in the last stage of destitution.

A third had the unmistakable costume of a butcher.

Others of these men were in the ordinary costume of the half-shabby race of civilians who hover between want and a sufficiency, probably, for the next four-and-twenty hours.

The pertinacity with which these men fought their way onward was very great.

And yet it was done with a good-humoured exercise of strength and movement of the shoulders which would scarcely be resented.

Bit by bit, too, inch by inch, almost, a large waggon, drawn by four huge Flemish horses, had been making its way on the outskirts of the crowd in a most singular fashion.

Commencing its route where there were but few people to interrupt it, this waggon was drawn round the place of execution in a circle.

But it was a circle which narrowed each moment perceptibly, until at last the huge horses, and the great lumbering vehicle, with its enormous canvass covering, had insinuated themselves into the very midst of the throng.

So dexterously had this been done, that people found themselves entangled with the waggon and its horses before they could form the slightest suspicion of its presence.

It seemed to many as if this great vehicle had suddenly dropped from the clouds, so quietly did they find themselves hemmed in and jammed against each other by its ponderous wheels and sides.

And so the waggon neared the scaffold.

The King's Light Horse began to be impatient.

They were a small party of only twelve men and a sergeant.

The latter was a choleric man, and imprudently he used the flat of his sabre upon the heads of several of the crowd to force himself a passage.

For an instant a conflict ensued between the people and the troopers, which the latter had the good sense to prevent from being sanguinary, by allowing themselves to be effectually impeded by the people.

The impetuous sergeant was dismounted by the summary process of being dislodged from his saddle by a jerk of one of his legs, which no horseman could resist.

The company of foot soldiers halted on a little eminence.

And then the girl shrieked again for help, as she gazed about her and saw all these little changes rapidly effected like the mysterious changes of a kaleidoscope.

What did they portend to her?

A chance of life, or a greater certainty of death?

The executioner evidently thought the latter.

He crawled along the planking of the scaffold like some loathsome reptile.

He caught at the skirt of the dress of the young girl.

He spoke again in that same croaking voice which had before made her shudder.

"Now, my dear, time's up! What's the use of making a bother about what must be?"

"No, no!" she shrieked. "Time is passed! I will not die! I cannot; or if I must, let me meet death in any shape but this! Help—help—help!"

The tall man in the white frieze coat scrambled up on to the scaffold.

A roaring shout arose from the crowd, for they seemed to think that now something was about to be done which would gratify the interest they felt in the young criminal.

It was a weight off every heart to see that somebody was at all events commencing a course of action of a more practically defiant character to the authorities than mere yells and outcries.

The first movement of this tall and stalwart man was a highly popular one.

With one hearty kick he sent the executioner rolling from the scaffold among the crowd.

The fate of the hideous wretch seemed to be certain.

He was tossed from hand to hand like a human football.

Then some of these strangely assorted men who had gathered round the tall stranger in the slouched hat and the frieze coat laid hands on the half-fainting wretch, and tossed him back again on to the boards of the scaffold.

He rolled along until he reached that opening in its floor from which he had emerged, and then, dropping through it, disappeared into comparative obscurity and safety.

The tall man standing upon the scaffold glanced about him like some general on an eminence marshalling his forces.

And then, notwithstanding the frieze coat, the slouched hat, the coarse leather leggings he wore, and the hob-nailed boots, every one there present felt that he was not what he appeared, but that he had come forth to play some strange part in the exciting drama of that day.

"Friends all," he cried "do you wish this young girl to die?"

"No!" was shouted from every throat.

A bright smile was on the lips of the stranger.

Then that fair young creature on the scaffold understood, in the midst of her bewilderment of head and brain, that let his power to aid her be what it might, he came as a friend.

With a shriek of joy she sank to his feet.

She clung frantically to the skirts of that coarse frieze coat.

"Save me—save me! Heaven will bless you for the act! Save me—save me! I am innocent! Indeed I am innocent!"

"Hush!" whispered the stranger.

"Oh, no—no! Let me yet speak to you! Perhaps you are not quite sure that I am innocent; but I call heaven to witness—to witness by some visible sign—if it be but a gleam of sunshine, to my perfect innocence!"

A cloud swept aside, and right on to the scaffold, gilding into beauty even the rough garments of that grazier looking-man, came a broad beam of golden sunlight.

"You are answered," he said; "although the token was not needed."

"And you will save me?"

"When you were a little child, perchance amid the storms of winter you slept in peace, happiness, and security in some pretty cot, over which hovered a mother's love?"

"Yes—oh, yes!"

"You are as safe here, then, as you were in that happy time when no harm could reach you, while so fenced in by boundless affection. Hush!—do not cling to me, but let me act!"

The girl released him from her frantic hold.

She still knelt upon the rough planks of the scaffold.

Her overcharged heart found relief in a gush of tears.

She felt assured that that man would save her, although how he was to accomplish the feat was past comprehension.

CHAPTER II.

CLAUDE DUVAL CALLS FOR HIS BOOTS, HIS HAT, AND HIS HORSE.

"Arrest that man! What does he do upon the scaffold? Arrest him! Ten guineas from my own pocket to the officer who makes him a prisoner!"

Mossy Pendell spoke in tones of rage.

"Arrest him yourself, Mr. Pendell," growled Muckles, the chief officer. "Don't you see the Light Horse have come to a standstill, and how are we to persuade the people to give us free passage?"

"Is the girl to escape, then?"

Muckles shrugged his shoulders.

"I can do nothing," he said, "until reinforcements arrive. I have sent a messenger to the King's Mews, and we shall soon have plenty of help."

Pendell burst into a ferocious laugh.

"Bravo, Muckles! you're the man after all, and it will be a sad pity if the murderess of General Everton escape justice. What is that waggon doing yonder?"

Muckles shook his head.

"It's a mystery to me, Mr. Pendell, but I have watched it for these ten minutes, and it has been getting into the crowd by going round in a circle, or rather in a kind of cork-screw fashion. Another turn, and it will be at the foot of the scaffold."

"Muckles, the girl must hang, or there is no justice in England."

"I've nothing to do with justice," replied Muckles, drily. "It's my duty, as the Sheriff's chief officer on this occasion, to see that the execution takes place, and I mean to do so."

"But the people?"

"Bah! let them bawl themselves hoarse till the troops come from the King's Mews, and then we shall see another complexion put on the affair."

"And that waggon?"

"It is driven by some fool who probably is too bewildered to know where he is going."

"Behold! still that man upon the scaffold."

"I see him."

"Who and what is he?"

"I know not—and it matters not, except that he is doing you good service, Mr. Mossy Pendell."

"Me service?"

"Certainly! you want Lucy Everton hanged, and he is kindly putting off the time till the troops arrive from the King's Mews, by talking some mountebank rubbish to the crowd."

"Ah! look! look! I don't know that."

Mossy Pendell clutched the officer's arm with the energy of a vice.

The tall man on the scaffold had not been idle during this time.

Again he spoke to the people.

"Convinced of the innocence of this young girl—although she has been duly convicted of the murder of her uncle, General Everton—we all want to save her."

"All! all!"

"There was but one man in all England who it seemed to her had the courage to attempt her rescue, and she sent to him a ring."

"Yes! yes!" shrieked Lucy Everton. "There was one man who saved me a year since from a great danger, and on that occasion he gave me a ring which I was to send to him if ever I required his aid. I did send it. The ring was to be placed in the crevice of an old oak on Hampstead Heath. There was one who, in the dreary prison-house of Newgate, swore so to place it."

"He did so," said the stranger in the frieze coat.

Lucy uttered a cry of joy.

"Then he will still come to save me; but it is late, oh! it is late, and moments now are hours of agony and danger!"

"Hush! Fear nothing."

The stranger turned to the crowd again.

"Good people all, if you would save this young creature from the shameful death which perjury and false witnesses have prepared for her, you will let my waggon get a little nearer, for you see I am careful of my Flanders horses."

"Bring it along! bring it along! Make way! make way there! It's his waggon: he's a grazier from the marshes in Essex. He'll take the girl home in the waggon, and make a farmer's wife of her. Hurrah! hurrah! Bring it along!"

"And, gentlemen all," added the stranger, "you will be so good as to keep those few sensible dragoons of his Majesty's Light Horse at a respectful distance."

There scarcely needed this intimation to the crowd, for the dozen mounted men were so completely seperated and hemmed in, that for their own lives' sakes, they were compelled to be passive spectators of whatever might happen.

"As regards the company of foot yonder," continued the mysterious stranger, "I may tell you, all in confidence, that they are merely waiting for reinforcements from the King's Mews."

A tremendous yell of anger arose from the crowd.

"But as we don't intend to wait, and as I come here with the full intention of rescuing this young girl, and taking her with me, perhaps—as I feel myself among friends—it would look like a want of confidence not to let you know who I am."

There was a tone of high-bred courtly banter about the manner in which the seeming grazier spoke, that was exceedingly fascinating to the crowd.

He was cheered vociferously, and as each moment the waggon approached nearer and nearer to the scaffold, it was evident by the quick, keen movement of his head and eyes, that not the minutest change of circumstances escaped his observation.

From afar off came the light tap of a drum.

"That's kind," he said. "The reinforcements from the King's Mews have started, and we have no time to lose."

Every eye of that vast assemblage was fixed upon this mysterious man, as now he slowly stepped to the front of the scaffold, and took off the slouched hat which hitherto had concealed the whole upper part of his face.

A profusion of glossy black hair, in natural wavy masses, descended nearly to his shoulders, and as he shook it back from a brow which was certainly one of the finest, the smile that sat upon his lips was irresistibly engaging.

Lucy Everton uttered a shriek of joy

"It is he! It is he! I know him now! It is he, and I am saved!"

"Hush again! Poor suffering one," said the stranger, in low tones, "do not impede me, for we have yet much to do."

The tears that Lucy Everton shed now were those of joy and happiness.

What faith she must have had in that one man, to suppose that he could save her from all the power and all the myrmidons of the law!

The distant tap of the drum, now a little more distinctly, announced the route of the reinforcements from the King's Mews.

"We have ten minutes yet," said the mysterious stranger.

As he spoke, he unbuttoned the frieze coat from its close contact with his neck, and dashing it aside, he rapidly stripped it off and flung it from the scaffold, when it was caught by one of those men who had so closely surrounded him.

The metamorphosis in the stranger's appearance was something truly astonishing.

In the frieze coat he had looked a big, burly, and somewhat shabby man about the middle age; and although this latter supposition had been dissipated by the removal of the slouched hat, that effect was nothing in comparison with what now startled the senses of the immense throng of persons whose eyes were now all fixed upon him.

The stranger now appeared as a tall slender young man, attired in such startling contradiction to his first appearance, that he is worth a brief description.

A coat of rich crimson maroon velvet, loaded with gold lace.

A cravat of the most superb texture.

Ruffles of great value.

A vest of pearl-coloured satin—the buttons of which sparkled with precious stones.

A long, straight court sword, the hilt of which was either of gold, or richly gilt.

This was the kind of courtly rich apparition who emerged from beneath the frieze coat, and which bore as much resemblance to the rough-looking grazier he had first been taken for, as the most gorgeous sparkling butterfly does to the grub from which it owes its origin.

A shout of applause and a general clapping of hands arose from the delighted throng about the scaffold.

The elegantly attired stranger now slightly stooped, and removed the coarse leather leggings; at the same time that he knocked from his feet his heavy hobnailed shoes that had formed so characteristic a portion of his previous costume.

"Blossom!" he shouted.

"Yes, Captain!" responded a voice; and to the surprise of the crowd, a man in the costume of a very smart groom looked out from the tail of the waggon, which by this time was not twenty feet from the scaffold.

"My boots, Blossom."

"Yes, Captain."

From hand to hand a pair of tall horseman's boots reached the stranger, who, with all the deliberation and ease of a man in his own dressing-room, drew them on.

The mob raised another wild clamour of applause.

The costume was perfect.

The tall bright boots—the whole dress, so complete in its details, and so rich in its fabric—made this mysterious stranger look quite a picture of courtly grace and manly beauty.

"Blossom!" he cried again, when the shouts and clapping of hands had subsided—"my hat!"

An elegant hat of black felt, looped by a diamond, was handed up to the scaffold.

"Ah!" cried the stranger, as he gracefully placed it on his head; "our friends from the King's Mews are near at hand, and it is time for us to go."

"Mr. Sheriff," roared the man who was named Mossy Pendell,—"Mr. Sheriff, I call upon you to do your duty. Do you not see that there is something going on, which will defeat justice? John Muckles, I call upon you too."

"Peace, Mr. Pendell," replied the officer of police. "What is the use of you calling? We can do nothing. All those drums and fifes, which are now each moment becoming plainer, ring through Bloomsbury Fields."

"Then I myself will adventure," cried Pendell, in a voice of passion. "Twenty guineas each to every man who follows me!"

Several of the mounted police officers, allured by the bribe, put their horses in motion to follow Mossy Pendell, who, before he started, thumped heavily upon the roof of the Sheriff's coach with the heavy loaded handle of his riding whip.

"Mr. Sheriff! Mr. Sheriff! we are going to try to vindicate the law, and it is your duty to accompany us."

"It may be my duty," said the Sheriff, looking from the coach window, while anger and fear struggled for mastery in his countenance,—"it may be my duty, but it is not my pleasure, and I shall wait for the reinforcements from the King's Mews."

One straggling horseman of the dragoons had managed to get himself clear of the crowd, and with his accoutrements disordered, and his horse looking scared and frightened, he made his way towards the carriage of the Sheriff, and the little throng of mounted constables.

"Hilloa, you sir!" shouted Mossy Pendell. "If you are a good shot with your carbine, you may may do better service yet than all your comrades, by bringing down that man on the scaffold."

"Yes," said the soldier, sulkily, "and get pulled limb from limb for my pains. The people are half mad, and what care I if the girl hangs or not?"

"Lend it me, then."

The trooper laughed as he flung himself from his

horse, and commenced re-arranging some of the innumerable straps and buckles of his uniform.

"Take it, and welcome; but don't draw me into a mess."

"Is it loaded?"

"You may swear to that."

Mossy Pendell stooped to the saddle of the dragoon and unhooked the carbine.

He then by a rapid movement of his horse placed himself exactly behind the Sheriff's carriage.

He was then just of a height to make use of the edge of that roof as a resting-place for the carbine.

"Hold! hold, Mr. Pendell!" cried the Sheriff: "don't fire! We shall all be sacrificed to your indiscretion, whether you hit or miss."

"I will try my fortune."

Affairs on and about the scaffold had not stood still while Mossy Pendell was thus taking measures for the destruction of the mysterious and courtly personage who had come to the rescue of Lucy Everton.

Standing calmly near the extreme verge of the rough, uneven platform from which so much youth and beauty were to be dashed into eternity, the distinguished looking gentleman in the crimson maroon coat ran his eyes over the vast multitude, smiling lightly and gaily as if nothing were amiss.

He gave a slight inclination of his head in the direction of the advanced fifes and drums from the King's Mews.

"Good friends all," he said, "the air of Bloomsbury Fields will not for many minutes longer agree with my constitution."

A torrent of advice, in every possible tone that the human voice was capable of assuming, burst from all parts of the crowd.

"Off with you! Off while you may! Take the girl off, and we'll make a lane for you! Don't stay to be picked up by the guard! Off with you; there are choice hiding places in old Clerkenwell! Make way for him! Make way for him! He's some great lord, after all who, loves a pretty face! We'll make way for your honour, and good luck to you!"

The courtly personage waved his arm for silence.

"My very excellent friends, on an occasion like this I prefer horse exercise. Ah! there is less time to spare than I expected."

A rattling roll from the brass drums of the approaching infantry smote upon the ears of the crowd.

The elegant unknown on the scaffold turned abruptly towards the Sheriff's carriage.

"Fire, Mr. Mossy Pendell," he cried, "or you may be too late."

The movements of this great enemy to Lucy Everton had not for a single instant escaped the eagle glance of her handsome champion.

Mossy Pendell, upon hearing himself thus addressed, uttered a cry of alarm, and it was probably more an involuntary act than one intended at the moment, by which he pulled the trigger of the carbine.

A puff of white smoke.

A loud report.

A whistling bullet, that embedded itself deeply in one of the upright posts of the scaffold, were the results of this attempt to demolish the man who had become a popular idol in the space of ten minutes.

A roar of execration burst from the crowd, which in one mighty surge moved in the direction of Pendell, the Sheriff, and the group of half-terrified police officers who had been for some time enforced spectators of the strange rescue that was taking place.

The horses in the Sheriff's carriage likewise, unaccustomed to such alarming noises, apparently from the carriage behind them, became restive, and plunged and reared in an alarming fashion.

Then Lucy Everton's protector spoke aloud, and his voice rang like a clarion from one end of the vast space to the other.

"One moment, good friends," he cried. "That man will keep, for do you not see that he has been wrenched from his horse, and clings in desperation to the back of the carriage? It is now necessary that we should part, and it is more necessary still that this young girl and I should not be pursued instantly. We are about to take our way to Hampstead Heath. Ah, a strong party, by my faith!"

Scattering the outskirts of the crowd before them by a vigorous charge, appeared a couple of companies of the troops who had heralded their approach by the clamour of the brass drums.

"Blossom!" shouted the mysterious stranger.

The smart-looking groom re-appeared from beneath the awning of the waggon.

"Yes, Captain."

"My horse, Nightshade!"

CHAPTER III.

CLAUDE DUVAL SURPRISES BOTH FRIENDS AND FOES, AND GALLOPS FROM BLOOMSBURY FIELDS.

THE effect of this cool and apparently impracticable order from the mysterious and gallant-looking personage for his horse, upon the crowd, was immense.

Vociferous cheers greeted what seemed to be a piece of bravado.

The few cool and calculating heads among them might now doubt if this person had in any way the power of saving the young girl from the terrible death that seemed to await her, but to the vast majority the cool assurance of the gentleman in the velvet coat was perfectly enchanting.

"My horse, Nightshade!"

"Yes, Captain."

Another ringing cheer burst from the crowd.

"By your leave, gentlemen," added the mysterious stranger; and taking from his pocket as he spoke a pair of elegantly chased silver spurs, he with great grace of movement slipped them into the sockets in the heel of his boot.

"My horse, Nightshade! Quick, Blossom, quick!"

The crowd was awed into silence.

There was no levity about this man.

Not the ghost of a smile sat upon his finely chiselled lips as he in this manner called for a horse, which it would seem must either descend from the clouds or come up to him from the earth.

But the mystery was soon solved.

A large portion of the awning of the huge waggon was flung aside by the smart and agile groom.

The gentleman in the velvet coat caught Lucy Everton in his arms, swinging her lightly and gracefully on one side out of the reach of a possible danger.

Then from the waggon there leaped, like some glossy black apparition, a horse of singular beauty.

Leaped right on to the very scaffold.

Leaped through the intervening space, as if by some strange effort of volition, that carried the creature exactly wherever it wished to go, as though it had possessed wings.

Lightly the horse made good its footing upon the loose woodwork in a crouching attitude, and then drawing itself up until its long slender limbs were straight as mountain saplings, the creature rested its head upon the shoulder of its master with a mute caress.

Then the hearts of all present were taken by storm.

Cheers, shouts, cries and sobs burst from the multitude, and if that noble-looking steed and its courtly master had been something really more than human, they could not have more moved the great soul of the multitude about them.

The mysterious stranger flung his arm over the arched neck of his gallant steed.

"Ho, Nightshade!" he said. "My brave Nightshade, we shall have a short gallop, but a sharp one!"

He sprung to the horse's back.

Then Lucy Everton, with a cry that had some alarm mingled in it, wound her fair arms about the mane of the horse.

"Me too!" she cried. "Take me too! You will not desert me now?"

"Now, nor ever!" was the reply.

The tap of the drums ceased.

A man on foot had reached the advancing troops, and with furious gesticulations he had addressed the officer in command.

"Make ready! Present!" cried the officer in ringing accents.

"Ah!" said the gallant stranger; "it seems these people are in earnest."

A shriek of dismay proclaimed that the crowd saw what was about to happen.

"A hail-storm! A hail-storm!" cried the mysterious stranger. "Down, Nightshade, down!"

The horse doubled its long slender legs beneath him, and rolled lightly to his side.

The rider lay like some bright saddle-cloth over the black, glossy hide of the sagacious and obedient creature, and with one arm around the slender waist of Lucy Everton, he brought her down with him to the floor of the scaffold.

"Fire!"

The rattling discharge of musketry that followed must have been fatal to everything in life that had projected three feet above the scaffold floor but neither the gallant stranger in the velvet coat, nor Lucy Everton, nor that coal-black steed, who had obeyed voice and hand with such exactitude, sustained the slightest injury.

"Dear Lucy," he whispered, "one word while death thus hurtles over us. Will you be mine?"

"Yours?"

"Yes, my wife! Not the partner of my heart, but its sole possessor. Here, in this moment of peril, I put to you the question commonly breathed amid sylvan scenes of beauty, or in the quietude of some happy home. Will you be mine?"

Lucy looked into the bright eyes that were fixed upon her.

There was a flush in her face and a flutter at her heart.

The willing words flew to her lips.

"I will!"

"Then, dear girl, you shall know who and what I am before you confirm this consent by another word. And now we must be off. Up, Nightshade, up! Off and away! Emulate the storm-clouds as they career before the face of heaven! Let the loud south wind chase you in vain! Up and away, Nightshade! Up and away!"

The horse was on its feet in an instant.

Its mysterious rider rose with it.

"Spring, Lucy, spring!" he cried.

With his left arm he gave the young girl but slight assistance as she sprung behind him on the horse.

"Cling to me! cling to me! I may have much to do. Leap, Nightshade, leap!"

The horse crouched for a spring.

The mob parted right and left, like some ocean wave cleft by the keel of some mighty ship.

The black horse, with its double burden, leaped from the scaffold.

The hurrah that burst from every lips echoed far and near over that waste of fields now so densely populated.

For about three times its own length only was there space for the horse to proceed, but that short open route ever presented itself, as with a swinging half-gallop the creature sped its way.

The outskirts of the crowd were gained in two minutes.

There was a grassy knoll, near the topmost portion of which grew two small Oriental-looking cedars.

At three bounds the black horse reached the top of the knoll.

Then the mysterious stranger faced his steed to the people, and with a flush of excitement and joy upon his countenance, he raised his hat some half a foot from his head.

"Gentlemen all," he said, "we will not part company without an introduction. Your names, perhaps, being so numerous, would be tedious to mention, so I will take you all for Englishmen, who love justice and a pretty girl."

"Yes—yes!" shouted a thousand voices. "And a brave and gallant gentleman, too! Good fortune to you and yours!"

"That's kind; but as I am only one person, I can give myself a name, if you wish to hear it."

"Name—name! Who are you? Name—name!"

A smile lit up the stranger's face.

With the rim of his hat he dashed further back the heavy masses of his dark hair.

"*I am called Claude Duval!*"

Another of those roaring shouts burst from the crowd, which indicated extreme satisfaction.

They had all heard of Claude Duval.

The dashing and daring highwayman.

The finished gentleman.

The slayer of a thousand hearts.

The romantic hero of adventures almost past the bounds of credibility, and yet to the truth of which the highest in the land were willing to testify.

The great Claude Duval! Only believed in by many as a myth, because his depredations upon road and heath were confined to the great and the rich, neither of which classes of the social commonwealth were likely to be largely represented in such a throng.

Bowing gracefully upon his horse, until his own raven hair mingled with the mane of his gallant steed, the great highwayman spoke again:—

"Yes! I am Claude Duval; and already I can see that my name is at once an anger and a terror."

He pointed with his hat towards the disordered throng of police officers who were shrinking back irresolutely from the path he had taken.

Duval laughed.

"Off again, Nightshade! And yet one moment, good friends all: this is my horse, named Nightshade from his coat and mane, black as a thunder-cloud and sleek as satin. I have made a friend and companion of the creature, and so awakened all its rarer and nobler instincts. It is of Arab breed, full of chest, thin of flank, a small head, and slender neck; the creature loves me, and but that this day I have acquired the love of another dearer than a wilderness of Night shades, this four-footed friend of mine was nearly all the world to me. Farewell to all! and it may be that you again will hear of Claude Duval."

The horse shrunk down, as though seized with some sudden pang.

It was but a habit of the creature preparatory to the rush it was about to make forward in obedience to an impulse of its master.

The rush was made.

In two minutes more Claude Duval and his horse, with Lucy Everton clinging to him, and her long loosened tresses streaming in the wind, were out of sight amid the trees that skirted Bloomsbury Fields to the north.

* * * * * *

There is a gloomy, painted chamber in Camden House, Kensington— that house of many memories and associations, which has so recently succumbed to the great destroyer, fire!—that house which has witnessed the revelries of the second Charles.

That house, which, passing through many mutations, became an interesting study, even to the present generation, before it lay, as it now lies, a heap of shapeless ruins.

In that dim, painted chamber, on what has been a state bed, lies a man.

He is past the prime of life.

His white hair streams upon the pillow.

His face is pale with grief, with care, and with ill health.

The apartment has been at one time luxuriantly furnished.

But everything was fading to decay, and the bright colours which at one time had made the tapestries and the painted ceiling gay and beautiful, had all sobered down to one dead, dingy level.

By a great effort, the elderly man who was lying on the state bed raised himself on one arm and looked about him.

He spoke feebly.

"What is this? What is the meaning of all this? What mysterious slumber is this which seems for ever to sit upon my senses. I awaken for a brief half-hour, and crave for food. I eat, I drink, and then with difficulty I totter again to this bed, and the mysterious sleep comes over me. Why do I lead this life? What is the meaning of it? Where is Lucy? Where is my dear niece Lucy, the idol of my heart? Come to me now, child of my adoption. Come to me, and be happy in the consciousness of your dear uncle's love. I have chased your cousin Mossy Pendell from the house, and he can no longer insult you, or impose upon my goodness. You shall not be compelled to wed his dissolute companion, Lord Horlop. Lucy—Lucy, come to me—come to me!"

It was evident that this elderly man, whose tones words, and manner bespoke him a gentleman, was making great efforts to resist the overpowering desire to sleep again.

Thrice he let his head droop upon the pillow, and closed his eyes, but as often as he did so a confused murmuring sound in the lower part of the house partially aroused him.

He looked up.

He made an effort to leave the state bed.

Folding around him an old faded dressing-gown which had once been of the costliest brocade, he tottered across the floor of the room, holding to various articles of furniture as he went, to sustain his trembling limbs.

The room was of a strange shape.

It was long but very narrow.

Perhaps from end to end it might be thirty feet, but its utmost width did not exceed eight.

It was crescent-shaped, and indeed presented so eccentric an appearance that it could only be accounted for by being what it really was, a secret apartment, constructed round the curved end of one of the principal chambers of the house, and only having the width between that curved end and the outer wall.

There was a dim stained glass window, which looked out into the gardens of Camden House.

It was towards this that the weak, tottering man proceeded.

With difficulty he raised himself sufficiently to look through the stained glass.

It was a crimson pane through which he gazed, and all the trees, and all the shrubs, the flowers, the gravel pathways, and the sky, appeared of a blood-red tint.

But there were other objects which speedily attracted the attention of this mysterious personage.

Winding along the principal gravel path of the garden, came a funeral *cortege* of great pretensions.

The plumes of feathers—the numerous attendants, with black staves—the hearse, with all its gloomy trappings and paraphernalia, drawn by its six sleek black horses—the carriages that brought up the rear of the procession, and the busy, bustling crowd of officials that always haunt an obsequies of such consequence—made up what, to the eyes of this invalid, was a bewildering pageant.

It was not the less bewildering that he saw it through that ruddy glass, which cast over the whole that strange red tint.

Slowly the whole procession wound its way past one of the wings of the house, and faded from before his eyes, as though it had been the vision of a dream.

There was one carriage, however, that immediately followed the hearse, which attracted all the gazer's attention.

It was a well-appointed chariot, with some arms emblazoned on the panel.

"What is this?" cried the man with the white hair. "What is this? What can it mean? That is my coach—those are my arms upon its panels—my horses draw it! What can it mean? Am I a madman, or am I General Sir George Everton? Stop!—stop! Look up, some one, and tell me who and what I am!"

With all the feeble force that remained to him, this afflicted man strove to break the stained glass window.

His feeble strength was unequal to the task.

The framework was of massive lead, and the panes of glass were but small.

But still he struck upon them so as to produce an audible sound, and as he did so he still cried out feebly, "Help me!— help me! Explain all this to me! What does it mean? And who and what am I?"

A heavy hand was laid upon his shoulder.

The feeble man uttered a cry, and in turning abruptly round, lost his precarious footing and half fell to the floor.

"Well, well," said a voice, "how fares it with you?"

Sir George Everton looked up shudderingly.

"Fiend! wretch!" he murmured; "dare you return to this house, from which you have been expelled with ignominy?"

"Ha, ha!"

"Dare you, I say, return hither—you, Mossy Pendell—you, who I forbid even to cross the threshold of Camden House again?"

"I do not return to it, uncle—I never left it."

"Oh, help me heaven! Where is my strength—where my memory—where my energy? Help! help! Will no one help me to outface this villain? Help! help!"

The feeble man dragged himself across the floor, until by the assistance of a chair he rose again to his feet.

Mossy Pendell—for it was indeed he—stood with his arms folded, looking on with perfect indifference.

"Hark you, uncle!" he said. "I saw you looking through yonder window! Whether it was a red, a blue, or a yellow view of outward events that you took, I know not—that will depend upon the particular pane of glass you chose to look through, but you saw a funeral procession."

CLAUDE DUVAL STOPS THE NOBLEMEN ON THE HEATH.

"I did—I did!"

"Ha, ha! you would like to know, perchance, whose it was?"

"No, no—I ask you nothing, Mossy Pendell, but to rid me of your presence."

"Nevertheless, I will tell you. Look at me. Do you not see this suit of sober black—rich and costly, but still complete in its mourning fitness?"

"What—what then?"

"I wear it for my dear deceased uncle, General Sir George Everton."

"For me? For me?"

"Yes, you are dead, and this day you will be buried with great pomp and circumstance in the family vault of the Evertons beneath old St. Paul's."

The elderly gentleman clasped his brow with both hands, and tottered towards the bed.

But he had not strength to reach it.

He only succeeded so far as to clutch one of the rich tapestry curtains, and then he sunk to the floor, either in a swoon or a deep sleep.

No. 2.—NIGHTSHADE

Mossy Pendell stepped at once to a particular part of the panelling in one of the walls. He touched a spring, and a long, narrow opening appeared.

"Come in, Horlop," he cried; "but be sure you close the other panel well behind you."

"It is done," said a voice; and there stepped into this singular crescent-shaped apartment, a tall, rakish-looking young man, extravagantly attired according to the prevailing fashion.

"What now, Mossy? What is to be the next move, you complicated rascal?" he said, as with an indolent air he flung himself into the first chair he came to.

The tall, rakish-looking young man took a jewelled snuff-box from his pocket, and throwing the lid open, smelt at its contents.

"Horlop," said Pendell, "this indifference of yours is affectation. If I am a complicated rascal, what are you?"

"Eh?"

"I say, what are you, my Lord Horlop?"

"'Pon soul, I believe Mossy is in a passion."

"Pshaw, my lord, this is nonsense. It is necessary that we should consult as to what is next to be done —for at present all is abroad again."

"As how, Mossy? As how? 'Pon soul, you'll bring yourself to an untimely end with all these starts and agitations. What's amiss now? 'Pon soul, you get more complicated every day."

"What's amiss is simply this. The girl is not hanged."

"Not hanged! Ah! that's a pity; and yet it's a thousand shames to hang any one so young and tender, except round a fellow's neck. Ha, ha, ha! Not so bad that for so early in the day—is, it Mossy?"

"You jest, my lord, at everything; and for all I know, we are in a worse position than ever we were."

"Indeed!"

"Yes—for everything seems to fail with us; while you are as careless and as heedless as ever."

"Granted; but everything, you say, has failed, while you have been as designing, as anxious, and as miserable as any roundabout involved rascal could make himself."

"My lord," said Mossy Pendell, angrily. "These taunts and reproaches come with an ill grace from you to me, and I will not endure them."

"Ha, ha!"

"No, I say I will not endure them. We are in the same boat."

"Stop! stop! 'Pon soul, you make a fellow seasick to talk of boats. Just say what's happened, and make an end of it. I have an appointment for chocolate at one with the fair Barbara Millington."

Mossy Pendell dropped his voice almost to a whisper. "You know, my lord, that the only plan for recruiting your exhausted finances was by means of a wealthy marriage; and you made a bargain with me that if I could procure for you the hand of my cousin, Lucy Everton, who would assuredly inherit the whole of her uncle's vast property, we should share the——the——"

"Plunder, Mossy, plunder. Call it plunder."

"Yes—we were to share everything."

"No, no—'pon soul, no - not the lady."

Pendell gave a slight stamp on the floor, of impatience.

"Hear me out, my lord—hear me out. Lucy would not listen to you for a single moment, and therefore it became necessary to take strong measures to make her your own. You and I, with the assistance of some of those dissolute fellows that hang about the Cock-pit, and the Tennis Court by the Haymarket, seized her one evening as she returned from the Countess of Lichfield's 'Drum.' She was detained a whole night at your lordship's rooms in St. James's, and then offered a Fleet marriage to patch up her reputation."

"'Pon soul," said Lord Horlop, "you have a wonderful memory, Mossy. I dare say that all happened, but there was no reputation to patch up, for the girl was locked up in one of the guard chambers of St. James's Palace."

"I know—I know," exclaimed Pendell, impatiently. "She escaped us at the Fleet, and by her beauty and tears actually moved the hearts of the ruffianage of that place, so that we had a difficulty to escape with our lives, and she found her way home, unharmed and in security, to her uncle."

"Wonderfully true!" said Lord Horlop, as he again smelt at the snuff-box.

"From that moment we were both forbidden this house."

"Just so."

"But as I know a secret mode of entrance into it, I did not give up the game as lost; and now, but for an unfortunate accident this morning, I should have been heir-at-law to sixty thousand a year."

"Ah!" said Lord Horlop, as he yawned and stretched himself—"there is always some unfortunate accident that keeps fellows out of sixty thousand a year."

CHAPTER IV.

CLAUDE DUVAL'S NAME CHANGES THE CURRENT OF LORD HORLOP'S THOUGHTS.

"HUSH!" said Pendell.

He pointed to the apparently slumbering form of George Everton.

Slowly, and uttering moaning sounds, the suffering elderly gentleman struggled to his feet.

Acting on a sign from Pendell, Lord Horlop retired with that villanous personage behind a portion of the thickly hanging tapestry.

"I must live. I will try to live yet, for Lucy's sake. I will try to live yet."

On a side table was laid a repast, some dried fruits, some wine, some small loaves of bread, and a few light confections, such as might well tempt any one to partake of them.

With trembling hands Sir George Everton poured himself out some of the wine.

"Yes," he murmured, "yes—some of my own wine —my own Moselle. I know it well—I know it well. That cannot harm me."

He drank the wine.

He staggered backward till he reached the bed, and fell upon it with a deep sigh.

"He will sleep now," said Mossy Pendell, as he emerged from behind the tapestry—"he will sleep now for at least twelve hours. He gets feebler day by day."

"'Pon soul," said Lord Horlop, "it's almost a pity to save him up."

"I may want him. You know, my lord, that after we had both been turned from this house with ignominy and scorn, I took my measures—not only for revenge, but for the accomplishment of our purposes in another way."

"No doubt—no doubt! You always were an intricate scoundrel."

"Pshaw, my lord, pshaw! such epithets are useless. I took care that a powerful narcotic should be administered to General Everton, and that it should seem to have been given to him by Lucy. He fell into a deep sleep, which looked so like death, that an ignorant apothecary from the neighbourhood proclaimed it to be such. I then had him removed to this apartment; or rather, I may say, I removed him myself for I could trust no one. You and I, then, my lord, purchased of the sexton of All Hallows, a corpse, as nearly resembling in age as possible my uncle, Sir George, and that we placed in the state bed of the green chamber. That corpse has been to-day buried with great pomp and circumstance, as the mortal remains of my uncle."

"Stop—stop! 'Pon soul, I don't like to hear about corpses, and we will take all that for granted."

"Be it so. Lucy, however, still remained as an obstacle to my becoming possessed of my uncle's fortune, since he had made a will, and duly lodged it with his man of business, appointing her his heiress. The accusation, however, against her of having poisoned her uncle, I took care to surround with so many circumstances of apparent proof, that she was duly convicted of this seemingly atrocious crime, and was to have suffered the penalty of death this morning at Tyburn."

Lord Horlop nodded.

"But, being a felon, her property, assuming that she could ever claim under the will of the man she had murdered—which is, I understand, a moot point in law—would revert to the Crown; and, in that case, your lordship's interest would obtain a surrender from the King, and we divide between us the sixty thousand a-year."

"'Pon soul, that's about it; and since the girl is hanged, and not about my neck—since she preferred a rope to the noble arms of the Right Hon. Viscount Horlop—why I suppose all we have to do is to divide the plunder; and some of these days, you can give an over-dose of what you call your narcotic to the old General here, and bury him in earnest."

"There is a difficulty."

"Ah!"

"Yes; Lucy lives. She has been rescued, even from the scaffold."

"Rescued!"

"Yes, in the most audacious manner."

"By whom?"

"The notorious—the celebrated—the madly courageous Claude Duval."

Lord Horlop turned white, and the jewelled snuff-box fell from his nerveless hand.

"Claude Duval!" he gasped.

Mossy Pendell must have had some latent humour in his composition; for, flinging himself into a chair now, he got up a very good imitation of the gay, careless manner of Horlop, as he said, "Yes, 'pon soul, Claude Duval."

"Confusion!"

"Yes, that's it. Lucy is in the hands of Claude Duval, the great highwayman—the ladies' man—handsome, brave, insolent, and daring; and what will become of us now I know not."

"The Stadt-holder!"

"What?"

"His Majesty's Virginian settlements."

"Eh?"

"The other end of the world, or the centre of it. I tell you, Mossy Pendell, that if Claude Duval takes this matter up, the air of England will be as much too hot to hold me as though it had changed into the fiery breath of a furnace. We shall meet again to-night. Farewell—I must think—think—a process I don't like, but I must think!"

As he spoke, Lord Horlop hastily opened that narrow concealed door in the wainscot, and disappeared without uttering another word to his companion in iniquity, Mossy Pendell.

"This is something more than strange!" exclaimed Pendell; "never before have I seen Horlop so moved. But I, too, must think, or all is lost. This escape of Lucy's from the scaffold drives me to despair, and I must recover her, or good-bye to all the hopes of fortune to Mossy Pendell."

He approached the bed on which his uncle, the General, was lying.

A deep sleep had come over the aged man.

"Good!" said Pendell; "the dose of the narcotic in that one glass of wine that he has drunk was a good one; he will sleep now for many hours; and, on every occasion that he does so, some portion of his strength and life become dissipated. And yet I know not whether I may not require him now rather to live than to die. I must think—I must think; and in the meantime lie thou there, General Sir George Everton."

With a bitter laugh, Mossy Pendell turned from the room, leaving it by the same means that Lord Horlop had availed himself of.

A deep stillness then reigned in that secret chamber, only faintly now and then broken by the heavy breathing of the slumbering man who had become the victim of his nephew's grasping and avaricious spirit.

* * * * * *

"Halt we a moment!" cried Claude Duval, as his horse, Nightshade, with its double burden, reached the brow of that first hill on the road to Hampstead, to the left of which stands the white-fronted cottage, once the residence of Steele, the essayist; and to the right, the ancient hostel known as the "Load of Hay," then a notorious resort for knights of the road.

"Halt we a moment, fair Lucy Everton! Look back, dear girl, upon that London we have now left far behind us, and tell me if you see signs of pursuit, or if you hear a single cry of danger on this balmy air?"

"I am saved—I am saved!" cried Lucy. "I am saved by you! and if the devotion of a life—that life which now surely belongs to you, since but for you, by this time, it would have been quenched for ever——"

"No, Miss Everton," interrupted Claude Duval. "I am but a wild, wayward fellow, but the heart and feelings of a gentleman still linger in my breast. It was the impulse of a moment that made me ask you to be mine on the scaffold when the bullets of the guard were whistling over us."

"And I promised."

"You did: but I release you from the promise. No, Miss Everton, it shall never be said that Claude Duval took such an advantage, even where his heart had garnered up its choicest treasure. I—I release you, Miss Everton—you are free!"

"With all your heart?"

"No: it is not with all my heart that I release you; it is because I feel I ought to do so; and she who becomes the wife of Claude Duval must not be in the position when the question is asked her, to fancy the word 'No' will step between her and her life. Miss Everton, I again say that you are perfectly free. I am your humble servant; or, perhaps, what is better, your attached friend. Say to me where you would wish to go, and my horse Nightshade shall carry you fleet as yonder clouds that skim over this fair April sky. You hear me, Miss Everton?"

"You called me Lucy!"

"I—I did not mean it—it was disrespectful."

"Not if I call you Claude?"

"But—but you won't—you don't! Oh, Miss Everton—Lucy, dear Lucy—there, I will dismount—I will leave you to yourself—take the reins in your hand. One touch, and Nightshade will carry you off wherever you wish, far beyond pursuit."

"Claude!"

"Again, again!—she calls me Claude again!"

"I have no home—I have no friends. My good old uncle, Sir George Everton, is no more. I am proscribed and branded as one not fit to live, and yet I am innocent. Tell me—tell me before I add another word—that you believe me innocent!"

"I do; as truly as that I believe we stand upon the solid earth, and that there is a heaven above us."

"Then I am yours, and yours only, Claude. The promise I made you on the scaffold, I here, in safety and security, ratify."

"No, no!" cried Duval,—"no, no!"

"You say no to me?"

"One moment, dear girl—you know not whom and what I am!"

"Yes—you are gallant and brave; you are my preserver!"

"And I am Claude Duval! Have you never heard that name, Lucy?"

A flush came over the face of the young girl.

"Ah, I perceive that you have heard it! You have been told something of me—perhaps that there is a price upon my head—that I am a fugitive from justice. And the thought will recur to you that Claude Duval, the highwayman, is no fitting husband for the gently-nurtured Lucy Everton."

"No thought recurs to me," she replied, "but that you have saved me."

As she spoke, she stretched out both her hands towards him.

He clasped them in his, and looked with fervent affection in the face of the girl.

"Mine—mine!" he cried; "and for ever! My fate looks dark and stormy at this present time; but floating in imagination, I seem to see an airy coronet which I may yet place upon your brow."

"I seek for nothing but your dear affection. Take me with you, Claude; I trust you with all my heart."

"Yes, Lucy, as my *wife* I will take you with me; and, in order that it may be so, we will seek yonder spire. Look how it peeps up from among the trees."

"It is the old church of Hampstead; but we cannot be married in this fashion, Claude."

"Fashion!" cried Duval as he glanced at his dress.

"Nay, I did not mean that; but there are forms and ceremonies. Do you not know, Claude, that we must be asked in church, or procure a license from the Bishop?"

"Lucy!"

"I listen to you, Claude."

"Will you be content if your hand is placed in mine, fairly and honestly, at the altar, by a true and veritable clergyman, who shall perform the ordinary ceremony without the asking or the Bishop's license?"

"Ah, Claude! that can only be done with those wretched Fleet marriages, as they are called: and you would not take me to such a place, even to call me yours."

"No, Lucy; but we'll extend the privileges of the Fleet to Hampstead Church. So on we go again. Forward, Nightshade—forward!"

It was well that Duval lingered no longer on that rural eminence, for even as Nightshade, still with its double burden, galloped fleetly over the level bit of ground before reaching Red Lion Hill, a party of horsemen emerged from Pancras Vale, and with shouts, and cries, and animated gestures, proclaimed that they saw the fugitives.

"We are pursued," cried Lucy.

"Possibly," replied Duval, "but not caught. Fear nothing; I have been pursued the greater part of my life, and I am not likely now to allow myself to be captured, when it has a hundred times increased in value."

The pursuers' horses had not the remotest chance in an actual race with Nightshade.

By the time they had breasted the first hill, Claude Duval had galloped into the little village, which it then was, of Hampstead.

He made his way direct to the old church.

"Leap, Nightshade—leap, leap!"

The rough stone paling of the churchyard was cleared at a bound.

"Murder, murder! Mercy upon us! What's this? A mad horse, and two mad people on his back! Help! Murder! Mercy upon us, as I'm a sinner!"

The beadle of Hampstead Church happened just to have opened the door of that edifice from the inside as Claude Duval alighted within a dozen paces of him.

"Capital!" shouted Duval. "We shall win the wager."

"Wager, sir?"

"Yes, a hundred guineas and a gold cup. You shall have the guineas, and I will keep the cup. Open the door—out of the way!"

"Goodness gracious, sir! you're not going to ride full gallop into the church?"

The beadle still stood in the doorway; but, as he saw Nightshade preparing for a leap, he raised a shout of terror, and stooped low down.

There was a clatter and a rush, and Nightshade, still with its double burden, flew like an arrow over the beadle's back right into the church.

CHAPTER V.

CLAUDE DUVAL PERSONATES A HIGH OFFICIAL, AND BAFFLES THE OFFICERS AT HAMPSTEAD CHURCH.

DUVAL dismounted instantly.

The beadle was running off on all-fours.

"Halt, my good friend! We shall want you to play the father."

"Murder, murder! I can't! I never played the father in all my life."

"It's time you began," cried Duval; and jerking the beadle round as he spoke, he guided him into the church, instead of away from it.

"Stop him—stop him! A highwayman—a highwayman! It's a thousand pounds reward! Claude Duval—Claude Duval! Stop him—stop him!"

"Ah!" cried Duval, "the plot thickens. There are our friends from Pancras Vale."

Half-a-dozen mounted officers of the police, with Muckles, the chief constable of Bow Street, at their head, came dashing down Church Street.

Duval made his arrangements instantly.

He caught the unfortunate and mystified beadle by the collar, and propped him up against a pew. In another moment he had taken from him his ample blue official coat, with its gold lace cuffs and edging, and its ample capes.

With the celerity of a harlequin, Duval slipped this garment over his own light and agile form.

The huge cocked hat of the beadle he pressed low upon his brows.

"That ought to do," he said. "Ah, this is better than ever!"

Reposing in a corner was the long official staff of the beadle, with a gilt ball and cross at the end of it.

Duval had just time to seize it as a thundering appeal came at the door.

"Open—open! He came this way! Open—open! Is any one in the church? Open in the name of the law!"

Bang, bang, bang! went the constables' staves against the old oaken door.

"We are lost!" ejaculated Lucy.

"I think not," said Duval. "Lead the horse on one side, and keep out of sight, if you love me. Ah, Lucy! we commence our wedded life with peril, but it may be none the less sweet."

"Open—open!"

The clamour at the church door continued.

"Certainly, gentlemen—certainly," cried Duval.

He opened the door just sufficient to thrust out the beadle's staff violently into the face of Muckles, and to show some portion of the official coat and hat.

"Idiot!" roared the officer.

"Yes, gentleman, I am an idiot. I've been an idiot a matter of forty year in this parish, and that's why I was made the beetle."

"Knock the fool down—brain him!"

Duval fenced rather skilfully with the beadle's staff, and dealt another of the officers such a crack on the side of the head with it, that he retired at once from the contest in disgust and discomfiture.

"It's brawling in the church," cried Duval. "Fifty pounds penalty, and a month in the stocks. Get away, all of you, and be quiet, while I runs up to the belfry and rings a halarm."

"Let me speak to the fool," said Muckles. "Have you seen a man in a crimson velvet coat and a hat and feather, mounted on a black horse, with a young girl behind him?"

"A crimson man," said Duval, "with a black horse behind him, mounted on a feather! What do you mean, stupid?"

"The fellow's an idiot!"

"I told you I was, and the father of a family, too. What do you mean by coming here, and talking of young girls and black men with crimson feathers? You're worser a good deal than that fellow on the mad horse that gallopped past a little while ago, and cried out, 'Hurrah for Claude——' somebody or something —I don't like to say it on the porch of the blessed church."

"He means Duval. Was it Duval?"

"It was that, or the name of the t'other gentleman, only spelt a little different."

"This is important information," cried Muckles. "We might have questioned this born natural for half-an-hour, and not got so much from him. Duval has evidently passed this way, and if so he has made for the Heath. Forward, comrades—forward! We may have him down yet with a long shot."

"I don't think it is very likely," said Claude, as he closed the church door. "Now, Mr. Beadle, there is your coat and hat, and many thanks for the use of them. Nay, Lucy dearest, do not look so pale; Claude Duval's time has not come yet, and he has many adventures by road and heath to go through before the grim hand of death closes upon him. But we will not talk gloomily. There—sit there, my sweet girl, and believe that all will yet be well. Stop, sir!"

The beadle was slowly making his way towards the door.

"Have mercy upon me!"

"Come here."

"Yes, your majesty—yes. Ha, ha! It's a fine day, with a little rain, but nothing to speak of. 'Happy is the corpse that the sun rains upon, and happy is the bride'-——That's not it. 'Sacred to the memory of Mrs. Plumming——'"

The intellect of the beadle was fast fading away, but Claude Duval partially restored it by seizing him by the hand, and placing on the broad palm a guinea.

"Do you comprehend that?"

"Bless us all!"

"And that—and that—and that?"

A guinea accompanied each word.

"A gentleman," said the beadle, "as is a gentleman."

"There, there—I know all that. I want you to go to the clergyman of this church, and tell him that a lady and gentleman are here, desiring to see him on particular business."

"And a 'oss."

Duval laughed.

"Come, Mr. Beadle, that is not so bad for you; and now understand me. This is a twenty guinea job. Go to your clergyman, and open your mouth just wide enough to deliver my message, and no wider. If you add another word I'll skin you alive; but be discreet, and the twenty guineas are yours."

The beadle drew a long breath.

"I'm not quite such a fool, sir, as I look."

"I thought not. Be off with you. Lucy dearest, let me see a smile upon your lips. Have I the privilege to kiss away those tears that glisten in your eyes? Ah, yes! and yet you tremble. Believe me, the danger has passed away."

"Oh, Claude—Claude! all this tumultuous life is so new to me. And yet what horrors I have passed through this last fortnight! A trial, a condemnation, the expectation of a painful and disagreeable death!"

Lucy clasped her hands over her face.

"Think not of it!" cried Duval. "Let it pass away like the visions of some troubled dream. Hush! I hear a footstep! Nightshade, come hither. Who knows but you are as worthy an occupant of this family pew as ever sat in it?"

The door creaked open, and a quiet, gentlemanly-looking man in black walked into the church, followed by the beadle.

"Who is it wishes to see me?" he said, mildly.

"I, sir," cried Claude,—"I and this young lady. We both wish to see you if you are, as I presume, the clergyman of this church."

"I am."

"Then, sir, I put a case of conscience and of morals to you. We wish to be married. Accident has thrown us together in such a fashion that we must cling together—she to me for protection to her life, although she is as innocent a creature as ever breathed the air of heaven—and I to her because I love her, and am perhaps the only man in all this kingdom who can save her. We have not been asked in church—we have no license from your bishop—but, as I say, we must cling together; let us do so with as much holiness and as much ceremony as we may. Marry us, sir, and let us feel that in all essentials we have pledged ourselves to each other at heaven's altar, although some previous little ceremonies may have been omitted."

"I dare not!"

"Say not so, sir! I am a man who dares much, and often what is wrong. Now, sir, I call upon you to dare do something that is right!"

"I should incur great censure! I cannot do it!"

"Oh, sir, there are reasons!"

"Twenty reasons," murmured the beadle.

The clergyman shook his head.

"Well, Lucy," said Duval, "you see how I have striven to make our union honest. Come, then, with me, and as the dear sister of Claude Duval——"

"Of whom?" cried the clergyman.

"Claude Duval, the highwayman, with a thousand pounds reward upon his head!"

"And yet with good enough in him to speak to me as he has done? I will marry you!"

"Bless you all!" said the beadle. "I'm a father. I'm a family man as well as a beadle. I'll run and get your gown, sir. Shall I ring the bells, Mr. C. D.?"

"Hold!" said the clergyman, as the beadle was darting out of the church. "The surplice is in the vestry, and I sha'l require no more. This ceremony will be imperfect; but better that than none at all."

In ten minutes more Lucy leant upon the arm of Claude Duval, as much his wife as so strange a marriage could possibly make her.

"A thousand thanks!" cried Duval. "It may be, sir, that we shall both come to you under happier auspices; and, in the meantime, think as gently as you can of Claude Duval, the highwayman."

As Duval spoke, he threw a heavy purse to the beadle; and, turning to the family pew, he called out, "Nightshade—Nightshade, hoy!"

The obedient horse trotted out from his place of concealment.

The clergyman shook his head.

"You are a strange mixture, Claude Duval," he said, "of good and bad thoughts and impulses. Be gone now, lest some danger assail you; and I pray to heaven that the day will come when a feeling for some better mode of life will dawn upon you."

"Thanks! still thanks!" cried Duval. "I know you mean me well."

"Fire!" shouted a voice. "Now we have him!"

A sudden report, a blaze of light, and a puff of white smoke into the church, followed this exclamation.

From a window at the back a man's head and arm projected into the sacred edifice, and Claude Duval

"Come, Lucy," said Duval; "we are shut in by a thousand trees. This little estate of Boscowan, in addition to its ghostly reputation, has no known owner; and has been for many a year deserted."

"Except by you, Claude!"

"As you say, Lucy; and now you can see the house, or such a bit as is left to be seen by the trailing plants and wild vines, that have run riot over it from chimney-pot to basement."

"Oh, this is delightful!" cried Lucy, as she clasped her hands. "This house is the very romance of beauty!"

Claude reflected the smile of pleasure that was upon her face, as, opening a small door, three-parts concealed by ivy, he led her into the mansion.

Lucy drew back with alarm.

A subdued murmur, like the shout of many voices from a distance, came upon her ears.

"Fear nothing," said Duval; "they are friends of mine."

He placed a whistle to his lips, and blew one long, wailing sound.

Immediately all was as still as the grave in the old house.

"We are now in the ancient hall," said Claude. "Yonder staircase will lead you to a suite of rooms in which you will find much of the remains of former magnificence."

"Am I to go alone?"

"In your own house?" smiled Claude.

"If you desire it."

"Fear nothing, Lucy; no human footstep but yours and mine will ascend these stairs. They are rough spirits that I have here as companions, but they stand in awe of me; and my slightest wish becomes a law they never dream of breaking."

"Shall I not obey you now, Claude, on this my first day of promise so to do?"

He held her in his arms a brief moment, and then whispered to her with emotion.

"Go, Lucy, and arrange your new home as you would wish it. This brief April day is passing away, and already the shadows of the tall trees are lengthening upon the Heath. I have some work to do, but will rejoin you before the moon has climbed a third of its height in the blue sky."

Claude Duval watched the retreating form of Lucy as she slowly ascended the ancient staircase of the mansion, now and then pausing, as she did so, to look back and wave her hand to him.

Then, when she had wholly disappeared, he sighed deeply.

"I fear—I fear," he said, "that I may not make her happy; and yet the wish to do so is surely one half the battle. But I have work upon the Heath to-night, and already it is getting shadowy."

He looked out at the little door by which they had entered the mansion.

A white mist was gathering in the lower portions of the Heath, and a silvery brightness in the eastern horizon proclaimed the approach of the moon, which was then nearly at its full.

Duval then opened a door in the hall, and traversed two or three apartments.

He descended three steps, and rapped in a peculiar fashion at a strong oaken door.

The moment before he so rapped, a murmur of voices had come upon his ears.

Now, however, all was still, and the door itself creaked open as if from no human agency.

Duval passed through it.

The place to which it led was dim and ecclesiastical-looking; and had, in fact, in Catholic times, been an old chapel attached to the mansion.

The floor was deeply littered with straw.

A table, with some rude benches, occupied the centre of the chapel, and on that table burnt a lantern, shedding a dim sepulchral light about it.

But nothing human appeared to be in the place.

Duval advanced to the table, and struck it with his clenched hand.

"Are all here?" he asked.

"All!" replied a voice.

"Blossom returned?"

"Returned!" was the answer.

"One hour hence, then, see that the shadows show well upon the whitened wall, and now appear."

Various small openings in the walls of the chapel were now made manifest by the opening of concealed doors, through which emerged eight men, each bearing a lantern.

"Welcome, Captain!" they shouted. "Hurrah for the road and the heath! We were getting rusty!"

"You have done me good service to-day," said Duval. "I know you do not love this place, with its melancholy shades and sighing night wind; so, after this night, I no longer require you here. We will meet again in the old house in West Street, Smithfield; but you must play the shadows for the special benefit of a couple of lords from the Court, who have laid a wager to cross the Heath thrice to-night in defiance of Claude Duval!"

"It shall be done, Captain—it shall be done!"

"To your posts, then, all of you! I can see the moon's edge over the furze-bushes on the Heath!"

As he spoke, Duval left the place; and making his way rapidly to the outside, where he had left Nightshade, he mounted, and keeping his way through the thick growth of underwood, which the gardens presented in all directions, he finally leaped a low paling; and as the moonlight shone in brilliant beauty over the verdant scene, he was fairly on the Heath.

Duval then took off his hat, and dexterously made such alterations in its shape, that it assumed a very common, slouching appearance.

Taking off his elegant and richly-trimmed crimson velvet coat, he turned the sleeves inside out, and put it on in that fashion, when it presented all the appearance of a dull, grey, ordinary garment, such as some person of neither fashion nor repute might wear.

Duval then bent low in the saddle, and listened.

"Good!" he cried—"they come! I hear the tramp of horses' feet."

There was a well-trodden road across the common, and on to that Duval soon made his way in a right line without heeding either chasm or bush in his way, for Nightshade leaped both with unerring instinct.

Claude listened again.

From the direction of London there came evidently the sound of horses' feet, as well as the faint echo of voices.

"Now, Nightshade, boy!" said Duval, as he patted his sagacious steed on the neck—"now, Nightshade, lame—lame—lame—lame, Nightshade,—lame, boy!"

This was a trick Duval had taught his horse.

It was to show lameness.

Nightshade lifted up one fore-foot, as though all its tendons were stiffened, and brought it down again in a limping fashion.

Claude Duval began to sing, in a droning voice,—

"'Oh, it's my delight, on a shiny night,
To ride by the light of the moon.'

Woa, Dobbin, woa! Pluck up a spirit, do, and let's get past the haunted house! Don't you look, Dobbin, and I won't! Bless us! I wouldn't see them shadows on the walls of Boscowan Gardens for my best cow—that I wouldn't!"

"Hilloa, you fellow!—hilloa!" cried an imperious

THE GOVERNOR OF NEWGATE MAKES A DISCOVERY.

voice. "Who may you be, and where are you going?"

A couple of horsemen, well mounted, galloped up, one on each side of Claude Duval.

CHAPTER VII.

CLAUDE DUVAL DECIDES AN IMPORTANT WAGER ON HAMPSTEAD HEATH.

"SAVE you, gentlemen!" cried Claude,—"save you, gentlemen, and a pleasant evening!"

"And who may you be, fellow?"

"A poor man, your worships!"

"We didn't ask you if you were poor or rich but do you live hereabouts?"

"Can your Grace doubt it?" said the other. "Look at his lame horse. It's a hop and a jump, and could not carry him a mile, if it were to die for it!"

Both the gentlemen laughed.

"Come, my friend," said the first speaker, "we don't want to hurt your feelings, or those of your elderly nag; but do you live on the Heath?"

"Save us! no, sir! I live at Northend—right away yonder."

"You are a bold man!"

"I, your honour! It don't become the likes of me to be bold!"

"Oh, I mean, to trust yourself on a horse with three legs only!"

Both the gentlemen again laughed.

"He does well enough for I!" said Duval, humbly.

"Very likely—very likely!" cried one of the horsemen. "But tell me, my honest fellow—assuming you to be such,—did you ever hear of Claude Duval, the great highwayman?"

"Bless you, sir! don't speak of him here, on Hampstead Heath!"

"And why not?"

"Because, sir, it ain't quite safe!"

"Not safe?"

"No, sir. Claude Duval is here, there, and everywhere; and sometimes when you least expect it, he's close at hand!"

"Hark ye, my friend!" said the gentleman who had been called "your Grace,"—"I rather suspect you know more of this Claude Duval than you would like to own to; and if you do, and should happen to see him, you can tell him that two gentlemen have had a wager, that, in defiance of himself and any gang he may have at his heels, they will cross and re-cross Hampstead Heath three times to-night, and dare him to interfere with them."

"It don't need no telling," said Duval.

"What do you mean by that?"

"Because, you see, sirs, he's sure to find it out of himself; and as for having a gang at his heels when there's only two men to attack, Claude Duval is not very likely to do so."

To the astonishment of the two gentlemen, the apparently lame horse of the ignorant farmer they thought they were speaking to suddenly made a tremendous leap forward, and facing about, confronted them both in the clear moonlight that now spread its radiance right over the Heath without the slightest appearance of lameness or decrepitude.

"Halt!" cried Duval. "Your money or your lives; or both, if you prefer it, gentlemen!"

As he spoke, he drew his holster pistols, and letting the reins drop upon the neck of Nightshade, who stood still as a statue, he presented a weapon at the head of each of the noblemen.

The suddenness of this movement was so great, that neither of the horsemen had time to make the least show of resistance.

Simultaneously, however, they cried, in excited accents, "Who—who—who can you be?"

"Who should I be but Claude Duval? Come, gentlemen, you have lost your wager, and it becomes your rank and condition to lose it with a good grace!"

"Villain!"

"Scoundrel!"

"Come, come, gentlemen, no hard words, or the reply to them may come in such a shape as will be specially uncomfortable! My pistols are loaded, my fingers on the triggers; and, at times, gentlemen, I am apt to be short of temper!"

One of the noblemen then muttered some very unaristocratic imprecations.

The other one spoke more mildly.

"I have no difficulty," he said, "in believing you to be Claude Duval; and I presume we must admit our defeat. We will turn back, and go our way, while you go yours."

"Not so fast, Marquis!"

"Marquis! You know me?"

"Perfectly well. You rejoice in the title of Marquis; while your companion is one of England's oldest Dukes!"

"It matters not," cried the Duke, "who and what we are! We have no desire to meet so inglorious a death as that from the pistol of a highwayman!"

"Precisely so," replied Claude; "but you will allow me to state that, according to the terms of your wager with Prince Frederick of Wales——"

Both the noblemen started, and looked at each other in surprise.

"You were," added Claude, "to come to the Heath with your watches and purses, as usual. If you returned with them, you were to win your wager; otherwise, you lose it!"

"Confusion!" muttered the Duke.

"The fellow is in league with the fiend himself!" said the Marquis.

"And so, gentlemen," added Duval, "I will trouble you for those same watches and purses, or you will be so good as to take the consequences!"

"And those consequences?"

"Will be a couple of pistol-shots, which will leave two interesting vacancies in the House of Lords! Quick, sirs! I will parley with you no longer. You made a wager, and you have lost it! Pay it like gentlemen and men of honour!"

Nightshade made a dart forward, which brought him close to the two noblemen; so close, indeed, that the barrels of Claude's pistols touched their breasts.

The Duke turned pale.

It was a paleness that was manifest even in the moonlight.

With a trembling hand, he presented his watch to Duval.

"Be so good," said Claude, "as to drop it in this side pocket, in the skirt of my coat. You see, gentlemen, my hands are both engaged; and although my horse is sagacious enough to be lame when I wish him, I have not yet taught him to take purses and watches."

The Duke, with a very bad grace, dropped his massive watch and seals into the pocket indicated by Claude Duval.

"Now, your Grace, the purse, if you please!"

The purse followed the watch.

The Marquis now laughed outright.

He was a higher-hearted man, and of a gayer disposition, than the Duke.

"Claude Duval!" he cried, "you are a brave fellow; and if I had known half as much of you as I know now, I should have had no such wager as that which has brought us to Hampstead Heath to-night! You shall have my watch and purse with pleasure; and there they are."

"No, Marquis," said Claude, "you shall win, and my Lord Duke here shall lose."

As he spoke, Claude removed the pistol from its dangerous proximity to the breast of the Marquis, and replaced it in the holster of the saddle.

"Beware!" cried the Marquis.

Claude smiled.

"I am well armed, Claude Duval; and have now the opportunity of reversing our relative situations."

The Marquis took from his saddle a beautifully ornamented and silver-mounted pistol, which he presented full at the face of Claude Duval.

Still Claude smiled.

"Now," said the Marquis, "I can win my wager in a canter, and cry 'Stand and deliver!' to the highwayman."

"There is no danger," said Claude. "The Marquis of Harcourt is not the man to be outdone in generosity, even by a highwayman on Hampstead Heath!"

"Shoot him—shoot him!" cried the Duke. "Shoot him, Harcourt! The fellow's a fool as well as a highway robber!"

"No, my Lord Duke; no fellow is a fool who trusts to the honour and generosity of the Marquis of Harcourt!"

As he spoke, the Marquis returned the pistol to his saddle.

"You are mad, Harcourt,—you are mad!" cried the Duke. "You had the fellow at your mercy!"

"That was just it, your Grace. But the reason that I had him at my mercy was because he trusted me. There, Claude Duval, there is my watch, and there is my purse. Take them both, and welcome. I shall not be ashamed, now, to own that I lost my wager on Hampstead Heath, and that I found Claude Duval, the highwayman, something more."

"Something more, Marquis?" cried the Duke. "What do you mean?"

"I mean that I found him a man of honour; and henceforth he must be called Claude Duval, the gentleman highwayman. And now, your Grace, the sooner we get to town, the better, and own our defeat."

"This is intolerable!" cried the Duke. "One would think that you, Harcourt, were a highwayman yourself."

"If ever I should be," laughed the Marquis, "let me be such an one as we have met to night. Farewell, Claude Duval, the gentleman highwayman."

The Marquis slightly raised his hat; and then, facing his horse towards London, he galloped from the Heath.

The Duke hesitated a moment; and then, instead of raising his hat, he gave it a blow on the crown, which thrust it nearly right down to his eyes.

"Claude Duval," he said, "I hope we shall meet again."

"I hope not," said Duval; "for I am not partial to indifferent company."

"You shall bitterly repent to-night's work."

Duval laughed.

The Duke glared about him as though desirous of taking so accurate an observation of the spot that it should ever live in his memory.

"Your Grace," said Duval, "seems enamoured of this pretty picturesque eminence on Hampstead Heath."

"I wish to note it well," said the Duke, speaking with bitterness; "because after your execution at Tyburn, I mean to have you brought here and hung in chains as a terror to other evil doers."

"Another wager!" cried Duval.

"A what?"

"A wager, my Lord Duke. I bet you this watch and seals which you have recently handed to me, that you shall hang in chains here on this spot on Hampstead Heath before twelve months are over."

The Duke made no reply, but bending low in the saddle, he stuck his spurs savagely into his horse's flanks, and galloped from the Heath.

Claude Duval hummed a gay tune as he took off his hat and re-arranged it in its ordinary fashion.

He turned his coat again, and presented in the moonlight the richly-dressed figure which we have previously described.

Patting the neck of his noble and sagacious horse, while the moonlight fell in a flood of silver radiance about him, Claude Duval at that moment, on Hampstead Heath, looked something more than mortal.

The chimes preceding the striking of ten o'clock from the old steeple of Hampstead Church, came gently and musically upon the night air.

"Ah!" said Duval; "so late? There will be few visitors upon the old Heath to-night."

He took from his pocket the Duke's watch, and glancing at it, saw the hour.

Even as he did so, a harsh grating sound came upon his ears, accompanied by the cracking of a whip; and he felt confident that some vehicle was crossing the Heath.

"More sport!" cried Duval, as he leaped Nightshade over several clumps of furze-bushes which impeded his view of one of the lower roads that wound in a sinuous fashion amid the sandy knolls and prominences of the common.

A coach, drawn by four horses, and driven by a couple of postilions, was slowly making its way forward.

The heavy vehicle swayed from side to side as sometimes one wheel, and sometimes another, sunk deep down in the soft sand of the Heath.

"This looks promising," said Duval. "Ah! they come to a stand-still. The postilions whip the horses—the wheels are in a deep ruck! By Jove! there they go!"

The heavy coach slowly swayed to one side, and then went over with a crash.

"Forward, Nightshade—forward! Here is more adventure than we looked for!"

A succession of leaps and scramblings over furze-bushes and up sand-heaps, brought Duval to the side of the vehicle.

A sharp, shrill scream from its interior betokened a feminine presence there; and some hoarse cries, in more masculine tones, warned Duval that it was not a lady alone to whose rescue he had proceeded.

The carriage-lamp, on the side where it had fallen, was crushed on the sand; but the other cast a brilliant light about it, which was all the more necessary on that spot, inasmuch as, bright as were the moonbeams generally over the Heath, a clump of tall Norway pine trees cast a broad shadow over that spot.

"Help! help!"

"Murder!"

"Where are we now?—where are we now?"

"Postilions, you shall smart for this!"

"Zounds, sir! how could I help it? The old Heath's full of holes and corners!"

"Help! help!"

"Permit me," said Claude Duval, as he wrenched open the door of the coach that was uppermost, and assisted in the extrication of a lady from the prostrate vehicle.

"Oh, save me—save me!" she cried; "I am shaken to death! Was ever anything so unfortunate, and so indelicate, too! I declare I was thrown right into the arms of the Major, and I prefer yours vastly!"

As the lady spoke, she clung round the neck of Claude Duval with a pertinacity he found it impossible to resist.

A shout was then raised by both the postilions.

One of them seized Nightshade by the bridle.

The other clutched Duval round the waist.

And, scrambling from the interior of the coach, so that his head and arms were clear of the open doorway, a man appeared with a pistol in each hand, which he presented full in the face of Claude Duval.

"You are my prisoner!" he yelled. "You are my prisoner! And it is a choice of death or Newgate! Come out, Mr. Pendell—come out!—we have him! Ha, ha, ha! Claude Duval captured at last! Come out, Mr. Pendell, and bear witness that I am entitled to the thousand pounds reward! Hold on, my men—hold on—he's a slippery customer, but I think we have him now."

"So, so!" said Duval; "that's you, Mr. Muckles!"

"It is, and resistance is death!"

"Do you think me a fool, Mr. Muckles? Cannot you nab a fellow without making all this fuss about it?"

"You give in then, Claude Duval?"

"Certainly not—but I am taken in! And whom may this lady be who clings round my neck with such affection?"

"Ha, ha! It's not a lady at all. It's young Jem Sharples, the Governor's son at Newgate."

"Oh, indeed!"

"He's a lively youth, ain't he, Claude Duval?"

"Very!"

The lively youth uttered such a succession of roaring yells at this moment, that the Heath echoed with them.

Duval with his right hand had made a clutch at the feminine head dress that he wore, and wrenched it off, taking with it a fair handful of the lively youth's hair by the roots.

The operation was almost as bad as being scalped.

"What's the matter?" said Duval.

"Oh!—oh!—oh! Murder!—murder!"

"Nonsense—nonsense! You showed me your way of playing an affectionate part, and that is mine! Now, Mr. Muckles, what's your pleasure?"

"Newgate!" roared Muckles.

"Well, I am not deaf! If Newgate it must be, Newgate be it."

"Now look you, Claude Duval—here are five of us!"

"Oh, I see! One—two—three—four—five!"

"And upon the slightest attempt to escape, we shall be quite justified in shooting you!"

"Exactly! I await your pleasure, Mr. Muckles."

"Dismount!"

"Precisely—precisely!"

Duval dismounted with such celerity, that in swinging his leg over Nightshade's back, he caught the man who held him by the bridle so terrible a blow about the region of the jaw with his heel, that Nightshade was instantly liberated, while the man roared with pain.

"Off, and away!" cried Duval. "Off, Nightshade, off!"

The horse did not require a second order, but gathering itself up for a terrible spring, it fairly cleared the prostrate coach, and, in three seconds, disappeared over the Heath.

CHAPTER VIII.

CLAUDE DUVAL ESCAPES FROM THE OFFICERS.

"FIRE!" shouted Muckles. "Shoot the horse! There's not its equal in all England; but don't let it escape! Fire—fire! I have it—it's a long shot, but a true one!"

"Not yet!" said Duval, as, by a sudden movement, he flung up the arm of the officer, and the pistol was harmlessly discharged in the air. "Not yet! My horse is not a highwayman, whatever I may be!"

"You have foiled me," said Muckles, "and I'm glad of it; because I intend that horse for myself, and I might have killed it with a hasty shot."

Muckles himself, with a couple of his men, kept so close to Claude Duval, that escape, unless some better opportunity should present itself, was quite out of the question.

With a great deal of difficulty, the coach was righted, and then Muckles, with a mock courtesy, which set very ill upon him, bowed to Claude Duval.

"We mean to treat you as a gentleman," he said, "since you give yourself the airs of one, and you shall actually go to Newgate in your own coach and four!"

"Perhaps," said Duval; "but I would advise you not to make too sure."

"He meditates an escape!" cried Muckles; "and I would have you all look to it, my men. You will not do such another night's work as this in a hurry; and if Claude Duval is not lodged in in Newgate, we shall be the contempt of the profession!"

"Slip the bracelets on him!" growled one of the men.

"Hold!" cried Duval. "Mr. Muckles, you know me, and I know you. If you attempt to put your bracelets, as you call them, upon me, I will make a solemn determination that, if I live, I will take the first opportunity of blowing your brains out; while, if I die, and if it be permitted for the spirits of another world to haunt this, I will make your life a burden to you, and you shall knew no peace!"

"Let him alone," said Muckles. "We are enough of us to guard him well. Let him alone, and put him into the coach."

Claude Duval was hustled into the vehicle, and Mr. Muckles, with one of his myrmidons, rode inside with him.

The two postilions mounted their horses, and the young man who had played the part of the distressed female rode outside.

Did Claude Duval despair under these circumstances?

Certainly not.

He had made a resolution, and before the coach was well clear of Hampstead Heath, he proceeded to carry it into execution.

"Mr. Muckles," he said, "you are not alone, or I might have something to say to you more interesting than even your thoughts of the thousand pounds offered as a reward for my capture."

Muckles looked uneasy.

"You would try to bribe me, Duval," he said; "but it won't do; your time has come!"

"I think not; but since you are so incorruptible, I tell you once and for all you are like a man who has fortune in his grasp, and casts it from him for a toy."

Perhaps Mr. Muckles, had he been really alone with Claude Duval, would have listened with more interest to what he had to say; but he was compelled to assume a kind of heroic virtue, which, in good truth, he was far from feeling, in consequence of the presence of his brother constable in the coach.

"I tells you what it is, Mr. Muckles," growled this man; "I feels uneasy."

"May we venture to inquire what about?" asked Duval.

"About you."

"Me? Is that possible? Why, my good friend, except the natural uneasiness about his own ugliness, that a fellow like you is likely to feel, I do not see any cause for your mental perturbation."

"I ain't good at fine words," answered the constable, "but I tells you what it is, Mr. Muckles; Claude Duval will play upon you some slippery trick yet before you get him to London, and I advise that you put the bracelets on him at once."

"I will—I must, and will!" cried Muckles; "unless, Duval, you will give me your word of honour as a gentleman not to escape."

"I give you my word of honour," said Claude, emphatically, "that I will not make the slightest attempt to escape."

"Then I am satisfied; so hold your tongue, Swallow."

"Well, Mr. Muckles, if you're pleased, I am."

"We are all delighted," said Duval. "I do not see how we could be otherwise in the sweet society of a Swallow. I have objected, Mr. Muckles, to your iron bracelets, but perhaps you are not aware that the handcuffs were never yet forged that could keep my wrists together, if I chose to release them."

"Indeed!"

"Indeed, and in truth! It was a trick taught me by a blacksmith at York."

"A trick worth knowing," said Muckles.

"Well worth knowing, both for and against; and since you have behaved with some courtesy this night, I will show it you. Come, beautiful Swallow, out with the darbies, for I have heard them clanking in your pocket."

"He's up to some game, I knows!" growled Swallow; "and I wouldn't be showed any of his tricks!"

"Why, you suspicious dog," cried Duval, "have I not given my word of honour not to make the slightest attempt at escape?"

"He has—he has!" said Muckles; "and that is sufficient."

Swallow, still grumbling in an undertone to himself, produced the handcuffs.

"Now, you would fancy," said Duval, as with a quick movement he took the iron manacles from the hand of Swallow,—"you would fancy that when once these were locked round a man's wrist, no effort of his own could escape them."

"I feel pretty sure of that," replied Muckles.

"And I am quite sure of it," growled Swallow.

"Yet," said Duval, "I shall be able to show you both how even I, Claude Duval, can get clear of these steel bracelets. It is as pretty a trick as ever was show. Hold up your hands, Swallow."

"Me?"

"Yes, to be sure!—who else?"

"I thought you was to put 'em on yourself, and show us how you could wriggle out of 'em."

"Why, you stupid, Swallow, that is not worth the seeing; I want to show Mr. Muckles how to do it."

"Oh!"

"Don't be an idiot, Swallow. Hold up your hands, and let Claude Duval show us the trick. It may be worth the knowing some day."

"To be sure it will," said Duval. "All useful knowledge is sure to come in, if we do but live long enough."

Swallow was still reluctant to be the subject of the experiment; but, in obedience to his chief, he held up his great coarse hands, and placed the wrists together.

"Now, you see," said Claude Duval, as with great dexterity and delicacy of touch he fastened the handcuffs on the wrists of Swallow,—"now, you see, my friend Muckle, that this great ugly fellow is properly secured, and, before we go any farther, I would just ask him if he can get out of that without assistance."

"How should I?" growled Swallow. "They're about the strongest pair of handcuffs we have, and a trifle too small for me beside!"

"Good!" said Duval. "Now, under ordinary circumstances, Muckles, your key would be required to release Swallow."

"It would."

"Well, now for the conclusion of the trick. You sit there, and I sit here; Swallow is properly handcuffed and helpless; and if you, by word, cry, or movement, attempt to give the least alarm, I will scatter your brains about the lining of the coach, and your little career will come to an untimely end!"

As he spoke, Duval had plunged his hand into a breast pocket, and produced a small, double-barrelled pistol, which he held in close proximity to the eyes of the astonished and bewildered Muckles.

"I knowed it—I knowed it!" cried Swallow,—"I knowed he was up to some game of the sort!"

"I will trouble you to be quiet, ugly," added Duval. "You must perceive, with half an eye, that the pistol has two barrels; and if I accommodate Mr. Muckles with the contents of one, the other will be quite at your service."

"Done brown!" said Swallow.

"Not quite!" exclaimed Muckles.

During the last half-minute he had furtively plunged his hand into one of his capacious coat pockets, from which he now drew a pistol, and clashing its barrel across that of the weapon which Claude Duval presented at his head, he spoke in a tone of triumph.

"Blaze away!—blaze away! and if brains are to be scattered about, there'll be two lots of them!"

"Muckles," said Duval, "you are a brave fellow, and I have more respect for you now than even I had before!"

"Blaze away, Duval!—blaze away, if it must be so!"

"Certainly not; it would be unfair."

"What do you mean?"

"You forget."

"Forget what?"

"That that is the pistol you fired a short time since at my horse, and you have not had time to reload it."

Muckles dropped his hand, and let the pistol fall to the floor of the coach.

"Done brown again!" said Swallow. "I knowed it! It was sure and sartin! Down brown again!"

"Claude Duval," said Muckles, "you gave your word of honour that you would not make the slightest attempt to escape."

"Nor do I mean," said Duval.

"Ah!"

"Stop; don't call out till you hear what I have to say. I shall keep my word to the letter: I shall not make the *slightest* attempt to escape, which, in my situation would be perfectly ridiculous, since I mean to escape actually."

"Done brown again!" said Swallow.

Muckles bit his lips till the blood came.

"Good night!" said Duval.

He reached his hand from one of the coach windows and opened the door; and, before the bewildered Muckles could decide upon any course of action, Duval leaped out from the vehicle, and sped over the moonlit Heath like a shadow.

"After him—after him!" shouted Muckles. "I will lose my head yet on Hampstead Heath, before I will lose Claude Duval! After him, I tell you! I will and must have him! Drive on—drive on! You may surely now see him speeding across the Heath!"

The two officers who played the part of postilions had only began to suspect that something was amiss when the carriage door was opened, and Claude Duval leaped out.

They were speedily confirmed in that supposition now by the furious outcries of Muckles.

He dashed down the front window of the coach, and projecting his head out of it in that direction, he roared and yelled to the postilions.

Then making a leap himself from the vehicle, he ran on to the highest bit of ground he could see in the immediate vicinity, and glared about him over the moonlit Heath like some enraged tiger who had just been baulked of a victim.

"There! there!" he shouted. "I see him now!—I see him by yonder clump of trees! This way—this way! Bring the coach round! Follow swiftly! I will lead you the way, and we shall have him again!"

"Hoy! hoy, Mr. Muckles!" shouted Swallow.

"What now?" asked Muckles, impatiently, as he ran by the side of the coach, with his hand on the door-handle.

"Well, Mr. Muckles, I don't think I shall be much use, even if we do overtake him again, while I'm in limbo in this kind of way!"

"What do you mean?"

"The darbies."

"Idiot that you were to get them on! You deserve to wear them for the remainder of your life!"

"Thank you for nothing, Mr. Muckles; but it seems to me, if I wear them for the remainder of this night, you will have but a poor chance of nabbing Claude Duval!"

Muckles, upon consideration, seemed to be of the same opinion, for he called to the postilions to stop; and then, as Swallow projected his manacled hands out of the coach window, Muckles, with his key, released him from the handcuffs.

"Ah!" cried Swallow, with a long breath of relief, "I feels all the more comfortable now!"

"Hush! hush! Not a word, on your life!"

"Eh?"

"Be quiet, Swallow—be quiet! Make way for me! No, on second thoughts, I won't get into the coach! Look there!—what does that mean?"

"What—what, Mr. Muckles?"

"There, to the right, just coming out from among the trees! Is Claude Duval mad, or does he think himself a match for us all, now that he is mounted on his horse Nightshade?"

Into a broad patch of moonlight, from amid the deep shadow of a clump of trees on the Heath, there emerged a mounted figure.

Its identity could not be doubted for an instant.

No horse could look like Nightshade.

No rider could surely look like Claude Duval.

The costume, too, was exact.

The crimsom velvet coat, with its rich gold facings.

The tall boots, with their silver spurs.

The hat, looped with its jewel.

Yes, that this was Claude Duval, even as he had been in that coach with him and Swallow, Muckles had not the shadow of a doubt.

Moreover, he knew every point of Nightshade, for had he not had every opportunity of feasting his envious eyes upon the rare proportions of that gallant steed, on the occasion of the interrupted execution of Lucy Everton?

"Halt, halt!" cried Muckles, in subdued tones, to the postilions. "He is coming this way. Let us see what he is about."

The coach stopped.

"Look, Swallow—look!"

"I sees him, Mr. Muckles."

"Who is it?"

"Why, our customer, of course—Claude Duval."

Muckles seemed to want this confirmation of the evidence of his own senses, and having received it, he at once dodged round the coach, and began, in a flurried sort of way, to reload the only pistol he possessed, the empty condition of which had placed him so much at the mercy of Claude Duval.

The gallant-looking horseman who had emerged from the wood approached the coach at a swinging trot.

"Well," growled Swallow, "we've been done brown, but he seems as if he wanted to be done browner still!"

"Hush!" said Muckles. "Not another word! Let him come on!"

The horseman reached the side of the coach.

"Hilloa!" he said. "Who are you, and whither are you bound?"

No one answered.

"Are you all deaf, or struck dumb by some amazement? Answer me! Have you seen anything happen on the Heath? That—that in which, I mean, some one's liberty has been concerned?"

"Rather!" shouted Muckles.

At the same moment, he fired his pistol right at the head of the horseman.

The graceful-looking hat flew off, but no further injury seemed to be done.

Before, however, the supposed Claude Duval could make a movement in self-defence, Mr. Swallow, from the coach, perpetrated rather a clever manœuvre.

Leaning out as far as he could from the window, he caught the bridle of Nightshade, shouting, as he did so, "I have him, Mr. Muckles—I have him! Hurrah! It's all right now!"

It was not quite all right, though, for Nightshade backed, and Swallow came through the window of the coach like a harlequin, only the movement was not entirely by his own consent.

At the same moment, the rider of Nightshade rapidly dismounted, although the object of that movement seemed quite inadequate to its importance.

It was only for the purpose of picking up the hat, which had been struck from his head by the bullet of Muckles.

By this time, both the postilions had flung themselves from their horses; and both Muckles and Swallow, surprised at the whole occurrence, threw themselves bodily upon him whom they supposed to be Claude Duval.

"Nabbed at last!—nabbed at last!" shouted Muckles.

"It looks like it," said Swallow, "unless we're done brown in some sort of way."

"You mistake," said the horseman in the crimson velvet coat. "I know not for what or whom you take me, since my errand here is merely to seek information if you have a prisoner, or know of any party of officers who have taken a prisoner on the Heath to-night."

"He's a *haltering* of his voice," said Swallow; "but it's Claude Duval, for all that!"

CHAPTER IX.

CLAUDE DUVAL TAKES AN ANXIOUS LOOK INTO NEWGATE.

By this time, the dismounted horseman had looked into the coach, and saw that it was vacant.

"I am answered," he said; "I need trouble you no longer. I am not Claude Duval."

"And this, perhaps, is not his horse Nightshade?" said Muckles. "Ha, ha! We shall see! If you are not Claude Duval, there are two of you, and either one is a good nab for one night's work! The darbies, Swallow—the darbies! We'll try them on him this time!"

The horseman in the crimson velvet coat now seemed to be fully aware of his danger.

"No, no," he cried; "this must not be! It were well to exchange life for life, but an aimless capture must not—shall not be! Hold off, I say! I am not so helpless as I look!"

By a sudden effort, the horseman freed himself from the grasp of the officers about him, and retreating step by step, presented a couple of pistols full in their faces.

The two postilions shrunk back.

Even Swallow and Muckles hesitated to advance in face of such imminent danger.

It was possible that this mysterious personage might have escaped, had it not been that across the Heath, at this moment, there came a party of five or six mounted men.

"Help! help! I call upon you in the King's name!" shouted Muckles. "Help! help! A highwayman—a highwayman!"

The party of horsemen paused.

"In the King's name!" again cried Muckles; "and you will have a portion of the reward!"

These last words seemed to turn the scale completely in his favour, as regarded the feelings of the mounted men on this occasion.

As they came dashing up towards the spot, they showed themselves to be post-boys, as they were called, although men in age.

Their routes, after leaving London, lay in different directions, but it was quite common for them to pass over Hampstead Heath in a body, for mutual protection.

"Blaze away, now!" cried Swallow. "You can't do much harm!"

Bang! bang! went both the pistols of the supposed Claude Duval.

One bullet went through the panel of the coach.

The other, after striking one of the lamp-irons, diverged to the roof, through which it actually passed, and wounded the lively youth who had played the part of the distressed female on Duval's first apprehension.

The yell of pain and dismay that he uttered seemed for the instant to confound the gentleman in the crimson velvet coat.

The moment of hesitation was fatal.

The post-boys were on the spot.

Muckles threw himself forward again, and grasped the stranger by the arm.

"You are my prisoner, Claude Duval!" he cried. "You have given us some trouble to-night, but you shall give us no more!"

"Claude Duval!" cried the post-boys,—"is this Claude Duval?"

"Ah, to be sure!" said Swallow; "and he's done brown at last!"

The post-boys raised a cheer, for more than once, Duval, to their great personal terror, had eased individuals of their party of the mail-bags; and his very name was a something that made their blood run cold to think of.

"In with you, Duval, in with you!" said Muckles, as he held the coach door open. "In with you; for after all, you shall sleep in Newgate to-night."

"The darbies?" said Swallow. "There you are! Don't they go on comfortably? And now you can show us the nick of getting them off if you can."

The prisoner was hustled into the coach.

Once, and once only, he raised a cry.

"Help, Claude, help!"

What could it mean?

Nightshade was with difficulty yoked to one of the leading horses of the coach.

"Forward!" shouted Muckles. This is the best night's work ever was done on old Hampstead Heath. Forward, all of you, to Newgate! To Newgate!"

"No!" said the prisoner; "hold yet a moment—you know not what you do. Now who am I?"

"We know quite well enough you are Claude Duval, the ladies' highwayman. But as we don't happen to belong to the fair sex, why, you see, we have neither pity nor commiseration for you."

"You make a great mistake," said the prisoner, "and if I convince you that I am not Claude Duval, you have no warrant or right to apprehend me."

"Not the least! Ha, ha!—not the least!" said Muckles; "and if you do succeed in proving that to me, I'll let you go at once."

"Let me think—let me think!"

The prisoner pressed his hands for a moment over his face.

"Pshaw!" cried Muckles; "you can't think yourself out of your name. Drive on, postilions! To Newgate—to Newgate!"

"Be it so," said the prisoner; "it is better."

He shrunk back into a corner of the coach, and with both his manacled hands pulled his hat lower still upon his brow.

In something under three-quarters of an hour the coach halted at the grim portal of Newgate.

"Look to him, Swallow, look to him!" said Muckles, with an air of exultation. "I must see the Governor, and get a proper receipt, or we may miss our reward."

The arrival of the vehicle at that time of the night, coming at such a pace, and halting at the gate of Newgate, produced rather a sensation in the hall of the prison.

The warders on duty crowded to the wicket with curious faces.

"Who is it, Muckles—who is it? What's the game?"

"Claude Duval!"

The name had quite a magical effect.

A cheer arose from every throat.

It was the first time the redoubtable highwayman had ever been fairly brought across the threshold of the prison.

The wardens made a kind of lane for him to pass through; and with their peculiar views of criminality, they paid the prisoner quite as much attention and respect as they would have accorded to the monarch himself had he chosen to visit Newgate.

"Welcome, welcome, Claude Duval! Welcome to the old Stone Jug! You shan't have the worst crib in it. Welcome, welcome! You're the sort of customer we like, for you're sure to come on a high horse."

Coming on a high horse to Newgate meant with a pocketful of money.

And that was a period when money purchased anything in the great metropolitan prison, even to escape from its gloomiest cells, for the most hardened malefactor.

Muckles kept a good clutch upon his prisoner's sleeve, as the short flight of steps were ascended that led to the vestibule of the prison.

Swallow held him by the skirt of his coat as he followed.

And so the party found their way within the walls of Newgate.

The Governor's night-bell had been rung, and that individual, in his dressing-gown, made his appearance.

"Claude Duval, if you please, Mr. Governor," said Muckles. with an air of exultation.

"Ah, indeed, Mr. Muckles! A most important capture. I think his Majesty's Government offers a thousand pounds reward."

"Just so, sir."

"Then you and your companions have made a good night's work of it. Well, Duval, we will contrive to find you a lodging in old Newgate."

"On what charge?" said the prisoner

"Oh, only highway robbery! I fancy you will have to take your trial for stopping his Royal Highness Frederick Prince of Wales close to Kew Gardens, and stealing from him eight hundred guineas. I rather think, Mr. Duval, that will be sufficient for your business."

"I know not," said the prisoner, "why you call me Mr. Duval. I certainly have heard that name—since who has not? My wrists are manacled, and it is with difficulty I can lift off my hat, but——"

"Don't trouble yourself," said the Governor; "we will do it for you."

He lifted off the prisoner's hat.

There was a moment's pause, and then from a dense mass in which it had been gathered on the top of the prisoner's head, there fell on to the neck and shoulders of the supposed Claude Duval a quantity of fair and beautiful hair.

The condition of the redundant locks was certainly confused and disordered, but there was no mistaking the feminine character of them, nor of the face they surrounded.

The Governor stepped back aghast.

Muckles fell with a groan into the arms of a gigantic turnkey who happened to be behind him.

"Done brown again!" shouted Swallow.

The effect upon the wardens of Newgate was rather peculiar.

The vestibule of the prison resounded with whistling, since it was by long-drawn sounds of that description that the majority of them chose to testify their astonishment.

"You see," added the prisoner, "that I am not Claude Duval!"

"Then who," cried the Governor, "in the name of all that's—hem!—are you?"

"That is my business," said the prisoner, as she—for we must now call this representative of Claude Duval by the feminine pronoun—lightly stroked the artificial moustache she wore.

"Perhaps you will kindly say," she added, "upon what pretence I—whom none of you know at all, and who you cannot have any charge against—am detained in Newgate."

"Done brown again!" ejaculated Swallow.

Muckles made a savage blow at him, but Swallow ducked and avoided it, and as Muckles's arm was a long one, the blow fell exactly upon the most prominent feature of the face of the Governor.

A scene of confusion immediately ensued.

The Governor swore roundly, and ordered Muckles into custody.

The turnkeys with difficulty suppressed their laughter, and the representative of Claude Duval, whom we may as well call by her right name, Lucy Everton, slowly made her way to the wicket gate.

"Stop her, stop her!" cried Muckles. "I don't know who she is, but I charge her with obstructing me in my duty, and in aiding and assisting the escape of a felon."

"This is strange," said Lucy. "I doubt if there be another officer in the police of all England who would condescend to charge a girl with obstructing him in his duty, with five companions at his heels."

"That's all very well," replied Muckles; "but I charge her, and will hold to it."

"And I fancy," said one of the turnkeys, "that I have seen her somewhere before."

A faint flush came over the face of Lucy.

This was all she dreaded.

Her detection as the Lucy Everton who had been taken out to die, and had been so gallantly rescued by Claude Duval.

"And I, too," said another of the turnkeys. "I am certain I have seen her somewhere.

A lantern was held up so as to cast its full rays upon the face of the young girl.

She stood the scrutiny well.

And there were many reasons why she should not be recognised.

The male costume she wore, in the first place, made her look not nearly so tall as when in her own proper feminine dress.

Her hair—although its colour could not be concealed—hung about her face and neck totally different from that in which it had been worn by the Lucy Everton they knew.

The false moustache likewise that graced her upper lip gave quite a different expression to the face.

The turnkeys gazed at her for some time in silence. Then they shook their heads.

"I've seen her somewhere."

"So have I."

"And I too."

"Where?" cried the Governor. "Are you all idiots? Where have you all seen her?"

No one could answer that question.

A slight smile crossed the lips of Lucy Everton.

It was a smile of triumph.

She had passed successfully through the dangerous ordeal to which she had been subjected.

It was a smile of exquisite beauty, and lighted up the fair face like a gleam of bright sunshine.

But what means the sudden change?

The parted lips.

The blanched cheek.

The look of dismay.

"Fly—fly!" she shrieked. "Fly, and leave me! I am not in danger! Fly, Claude, fly!"

Over the wicket gate of Newgate, from the steps beyond, gazed a pair of anxious eyes, that belonged to a face flushed with heat and excitement.

The face and the eyes were Claude Duval's.

CHAPTER X.

CLAUDE DUVAL SACRIFICES ALL FOR LOVE, AND YET SAVES HIMSELF.

"Away, away!" shrieked Lucy once more, and then she had no longer the power of utterance.

A choking sensation came over her.

She could only point to the face that peered over the wicket gate of Newgate.

And that face did not disappear.

Its owner would not fly, although thus adjured to do so.

What had Claude done, then, that he should fly instantly upon sight of her to whom he had surrendered up his whole heart of love.

Did he not come to seek her there? And should he fly now that he had found her?

No, no! A thousand times, no!

He rapped at the wicket gate.

Then Lucy, in her despair, found breath to speak again. Her voice was hoarse and all unlike its ordinary tones; and still she counselled flight.

"Fly—fly! Save yourself! Let not all this terror—all this anxiety—all this danger be in vain! Fly! if you love me, fly!"

The appearance of Claude Duval at the wicket-gate—the terrified, agonized expression of Lucy's fear—the cries of despair with which she counselled him to save himself—all occupied not a tithe of the time they have taken in the recording.

The eyes of all the officers and warders were directed to the wicket.

A suspicion seized Mr. Muckles of the truth.

He flew to "the lock," as it was technically called, and threw the little barrier open.

"Lost—lost!" shrieked Lucy. "Oh, this is cruel—cruel—too cruel!"

Claude Duval stepped into the vestibule of Newgate.

He, too, was attired in a crimson velvet coat—he too, had tall horseman's boots with silver spurs, and his hat was likewise looped with a diamond.

Alas, poor Lucy!

It was the arrival of Nightshade without its rider at the haunted house on Hampstead Heath which had convinced her that some great danger was hovering about Claude Duval, or some calamity had actually fallen upon him.

And, from his wardrobe in the suite of rooms to which he had directed her, she had easily found an exact counterpart of the dress he wore.

Gratitude, love, devotion nerved her with power of purpose and strength of action.

She had sallied forth on the Heath to save him, and we have seen what has come of the perilous adventure.

And now Muckles knew his man.

With a yell of triumph he rushed forward, and cast his arms around Duval.

"Again I have him! Again I have him!" he cried. "This is the true Claude Duval! Close the wicket—close the wicket! Ha, ha! It's a good night's work yet!"

"Claude—Claude!" cried Lucy; "is this kind?"

"It is right!" said Duval. "Gentlemen all, I perceive there has been some mistake here. In this young lady you thought you had captured Claude

CLAUDE DUVAL CARVING HIS NAME ON THE NEWGATE STONE.

Duval. Look at me, and choose which you will have as the prisoner of that name, so that you liberate the other."

"Claude Duval! Claude Duval!" was the universal cry among the turnkeys and warders of Newgate. "This is Claude Duval!"

They crowded about him.

"If you please, gentlemen," said Duval, "give me room to breathe; and, at the same time, give this young lady space to leave Newgate."

"No, no!" cried Lucy. "For you, or with you!"

"Hush!" said Duval; "do not unman me. Go while you may—and be assured I am with you still!"

"With me still?"

"Yes, the better part of me—all my heart and all my love!"

"I cannot—I cannot!" cried Lucy, as she wrung her hands. "Oh, what a night is this! How foolish I have been!"

"Hush!"

"Claude—Claude, I did it for the best!"

No. 4.—NIGHTSHADE.

"And the best is ever well done. Go—go!"

"But how mistaken have I been! You cannot—you never will forgive me!"

"I don't feel quite certain," said the Governor of Newgate, "that this person who has been masquerading as Claude Duval ought to be let go so easily."

"Be content, Mr. Governor," said Duval; "it is not often such a night's work as this will come into Newgate. Clear the way, and let her go at once. You cannot have a charge against her."

"And you stay?" said Lucy.

"Oh, I am Claude Duval!"

"And you exchange yourself for me?"

"As you tried to do for me!"

Lucy clasped her hands.

"It is not too late—it is not too late! The law wants a victim—let it have one—and one at a time I am——"

"Silence!" cried Duval.

"I am——"

"I command you!"

Lucy dropped her hands.

Claude imperiously waved his hand to the wicket gate.

"Go!"

"I obey."

She turned and looked at him.

He made two steps towards her.

With a cry, she sprung into his arms.

Another moment, and she was gone—gone into the night air—disappearing before the astonished eyes of the warders before they could well comprehend the nature of the scene, with all its doubts, its fears, its wild emotions, and its unbounded affections, that had taken place about them.

It was Muckles who then rushed towards the wicket with a shout, as a new idea struck him.

"Two birds!" he cried. "Two birds with one stone; and both killed—ha, ha! I know her now! By all the bolts and bars of old Newgate, it's Lucy Everton!"

"Lucy Everton?" cried the warders, in chorus.

Claude Duval was just in time to catch Muckles by the back of the neck, and flung him with tremendous force to the other end of the vestibule.

"Peace!" he cried. "A prudent man never pushes his triumph too far. Be content all of you. I am Claude Duval, and the roof of Newgate is over my head!"

"Done brown again!" said Swallow.

Muckles sat up upon the cold stone floor, looking bewildered by his fall.

"I'll see him hanged!" he said; "and that's one comfort; and I shall have the thousand pounds reward!"

"Oh, dear, no!" said Duval.

"No!"

"Certainly not! The thousand pounds reward is for the capture of Claude Duval!"

"And here you are!" shrieked Muckles, as he made a rush towards Claude upon his hands and knees.

"Yes; here I am, that is perfectly true; but *I gave myself up!*"

* * * *

In ten minutes from these last ominous words that fell from his lips, and which had proved the destruction of all the hopes of Mr. Muckles, the constable, Claude Duval was in one of the deepest cells of Newgate.

A narrow habitation.

Six feet wide, and twelve in length.

The walls cold and slimy with damp.

The floor only of beaten earth, from which exhaled a perpetual noisome atmosphere.

It was Swallow and a couple of the warders of the prison who put Claude into this unsavoury abode.

"There you is: though I don't mind owning we're done brown at last, 'cos we don't get the reward."

"Now, Mr. Duval," said one of the warders; "how do you like this crib?"

"Not at all."

"I thought as how you wouldn't. A gentleman like you, as has spangles in his pocket, ought to have a better lodging; and it's only good enough for a poor devil as don't know the meaning of the word garnish."

"But I do!" said Duval. "Here are twenty guineas. I'm afraid they may get tarnished in Newgate!"

"That's your sort!" said the warder.

"It's halves, Billy—it's halves!" said Swallow.

"Not at all—you be a Bow Street runner; and we warders of Newgate always divides the garnish among us!"

"Done brown again!" said Swallow.

"Come on, Mr. Duval," added the warder. "I dare say we shall be able to find a better lodging than this for you in the Stone Jug."

"Stop a bit!" said Claude; "it may reconcile some poor devil who has no money in his pocket to this cell, if he thinks it was once occupied by Claude Duval. Lend me one of your big keys!"

"What for?"

Claude laughed.

"I mean to leave my mark behind me."

Curiosity induced the turnkey to lend him the key.

Upon the soft stone of the side of the cell, which many years of damp had disintegrated, the celebrated prisoner wrote, as he chanted, the following four lines:—

"When Claude Duval was in Newgate thrown,
He carved his name on the Newgate stone;
And when in the morning for me they call,
'I'll have vanished away,' said Claude Duval."

The turnkey rubbed his head.

"Well!" he said; "I've seen no end of poetry in my time—copies of verses—last dying speeches—confessions, and such like things; but I never did read anything half so clever as that—and all out of his own head too!"

"Don't be a fool!" growled Swallow. "Don't you hear he's a going to wanish!"

"Well, and if he does? A man as can write such poetry as that, has a right to vanish!"

"We shall all be done brown," said Swallow, "as sure as eggs and Barcelony nuts!"

The warders were men of their word, and Duval found himself in a rather comfortably-furnished apartment, which, although the walls were of stone, was palatial in comparison to the cell he had just left.

"Pay me a visit," whispered Claude to Swallow, as he passed him, "and I'll tell you where some of my swag lies hidden on Hampstead Heath."

"You will?"

"I swear it!"

"Then I don't feel half so done brown as I was!"

In about half an hour after Claude had been in his new cell, a key was cautiously turned in the lock of the door.

The gleam of a lantern shot into the place.

"It's me!" said Swallow.

"Come in!"

"All's right, Muster Duval! You see, it's very different with a poor fellow like me and Muster Muckles. He does things in a wicious sort of way; but when I'm done brown, I owns to it, and there's an end of it! You're sure to be hanged, which, in course, you knows as well as I can tell you; so it won't do you no harm to ease your mind about any swag you've got hid about in holes and corners!"

"That's what I thought," said Claude; "and as you seem an honest sort of fellow——"

"Oh, wery—wery!"

"I made up my mind to tell you. Ah, me!—ah, me! My heart is heavy about poor Nightshade!"

"About who?"

"My horse!"

"Oh, he's all right! He's at the inn opposite, and I daresay is making himself comfortable!"

"I rejoice to hear it; and yet I fear that some rascal, envying his speed and noble qualities, will take him away, and perhaps ill-use him!"

"They can't! He won't be given up unless somebody goes over with a red waistcoat and a constable's staff to fetch him!"

"A red waistcoat?"

"Yes; like mine."

"And a staff?"

"To be sure! This sort of thing."

"Oh, ah! I see now."

"Well, now, Muster Duval, about the swag?"

"Hush!"

"Eh?"

"Hist!"

"Whist!"

"I thought I heard some one!"

"It couldn't be! There isn't a soul near us, by ever so far; and leave me alone for a bit of management. We may speak up, for nobody can hear us. Bless your heart, Joskins, the head warder, has had his second pint of purl, and is fast asleep, with his hand on the lock."

"But you don't want to stay in Newgate all night?"

"Not I! He'll let me out when he sees my red waistcoat and top-coat, and I calls out the right word, which is 'Keys.'"

"And you are quite sure no one is within hearing?"

"Quite, Muster Duval!"

"Then," said Claude, "I am perfectly astonished that you should venture here, thinking me such an intolerable fool as not to take you by the throat, and dash your brains out against that stone wall!"

"Murder! murder! Mur—mur——"

"Silence! or you are a dead man!"

Swallow lay at the feet of Duval, having reached the ground with a force that nearly deprived him of consciousness.

"It may be," said Duval, "that there is no one within hearing, but I will have no outcry! Your life is in your own hands, because it is in mine! Decide! Shall it be death or submission?"

Claude put his foot upon the breast of the officer.

"Done brown again!" said Swallow. "I ought to have knowed it!"

"You would have known it, but you were blinded by your cupidity!"

"My what?"

"Pshaw! I waste words upon you!"

Claude stooped, and a short rummage in the pocket of Swallow produced a stout cord, with which Duval managed to pinion him in such a fashion that he was quite helpless.

"Stay!" said Duval, when he had accomplished this, on the spur of the moment. "I had quite forgotten. I must have the red waistcoat."

Swallow was effectually subdued, and made not the least resistance while Duval denuded him of the red waistcoat, the broad-skirted top-coat, and a rather gaudy cravat he wore, as well as of his top-boots.

"Now, Mr. Swallow," said Duval, "for your own sake, I shall properly secure you! It will be nothing against you that you were scarcely a match for Claude Duval! And as for the reason that brought you here, you must find one for yourself!"

"It's shabby," said Swallow—"it's shabby!"

"What is?"

"You said—you swore you'd tell me where the swag was."

"And so I will!"

"Oh!"

"You will go to Hampstead Heath, and, walking eighty steps, exactly to the north from the stone which records the murder of Colonel Richards, you will come to an ancient sycamore tree. Climb it, and you will find, at some fifty feet from the earth, that the stem is hollow, like the shaft of a chimney."

"That'll do!" said Swallow. "I ain't a going down. I'm done brown again!"

"And if you were to go down," added Duval, "you would find nothing. I promised to tell you where the swag *was*, not where it will be half a dozen hours hence!"

"Browner than ever!" growled Swallow. "I ain't fit to live; so good night to you, Claude Duval!"

CHAPTER XI.

CLAUDE DUVAL DANCES A COTILLION WITH THE MARCHIONESS OF QUEENSBERRY.

DUVAL was a head taller than Swallow.

That made a little difficulty in the way of disguise, but it was not an insurmountable one, especially when we consider that the only light by which he could be seen would be that dimly and artificially cast by the lanterns of the warders in the vestibule of Newgate.

Besides, Duval could stoop a little; and if the man on the lock had indeed taken his second pint of purl, it was not probable that he would be in a good condition to be critical about the accurate particulars of the personal appearance of one who bore the outward semblance of an officer of the police.

Duval took care that the red waistcoat should be prominent enough; and he likewise carried the small staff with the gilt crown at the end of it in his hand.

The usual three warders were lolling upon the wooden benches of the vestibule of Newgate as Duval reached it.

They looked up, but lazily.

The man on the lock was humming a drowsy sort of tune, and, at long intervals between the whiffs, smoking a pipe.

Duval felt that confidence, and an entire absence of all hesitation, would be the principal elements of success; and striving to imitate, as well as he could, the thick, growling voice of Swallow, he cried out, "Keys! keys!"

"Well, you needn't make such a row!" said the man on the lock.

"All's right!" cried Duval.

"Ah, yes; it's all right to you that's going out of the blessed Jug, but it's all one to us poor warders as if we was put in for cracking a crib, or crying 'Stand and deliver!' on the highway!"

"I'll send you in another drop of purl!" said Duval

"Will you, though? All's right—be quick!"

Click! went the key in the lock, and the wicket gate swung open.

Claude Duval was at liberty.

With what a keen relish he inhaled the first breath of the cool, pleasant night air, burdened even as it was with the exhalations of the Old Bailey and the region of Newgate Market in its immediate vicinity.

Half a dozen strides took him to the opposite side of the way.

Then he glanced over at the grim stone walls of the great prison from which he had just emerged.

"Good-bye to Newgate," he said, "I hope for many a day; and if I am fortunate enough to get possession of Nightshade, all will yet be well!"

Then there was a faint cry.

Some one rushed towards him.

"Claude! Claude!"

A pair of arms was flung about him, and he knew the voice to be that of his own Lucy.

"Here still, Lucy?" he said.

"Where you are, yes, for ever and for ever!"

"Oh, how imprudent you have been!"

"Blame me—kill me—but let me cling to you still!"

"Cruel Lucy! Wherefore should I blame the true love which begets such heroism? But this is no place for us. Let us hasten to our home, for I long again to hear the night wind among the tall trees on Hampstead Heath!"

"Yes, Claude; let us away—let us away! And although on foot, we shall soon reach our destination!"

"I hope we shall not go on foot. Nightshade, I am

credibly informed, occupies a stall in these stables close to us. We will get him out, if it be in the power of mortal man to do so!"

Claude, as he spoke, rung the bell at the entrance of the stable-yard which had been indicated by Swallow.

Again and again, though, he had to ring it before any attention was paid to the summons; and then, as a voice from within called out "Who's there?" in sleepy accents, the great clock of St. Paul's struck the hour of three.

"Open! open!" cried Claude Duval. "I'm an officer from Newgate, and come for the highwayman's horse. Open! open!"

"How do I know that? You may be the highwayman himself."

"Stuff, man — stuff! He's safe enough in the Stone Jug. Open, and be quick about it, or you'll get yourself into trouble!"

The ostler grumblingly opened the gate, and when he saw the well-known red waistcoat, and the little staff of authority, he made no further scruples.

"I'm glad to get rid of the brute!" he said. "He won't eat, and he won't drink. He has given me two kicks, and made one grab at me with his teeth."

Duval laughed.

"Hilloa!" said the ostler; "he seems to know you."

The moment Nightshade was liberated from his stable he trotted up to Duval, and performed a trick which had been taught him, and which consisted in lifting up a fore-foot, and placing it lightly upon the breast of his master.

"He ought to know me," said Claude, as he led Nightshade into the Old Bailey. "Mount, Lucy — mount!"

"Lucy!" said the ostler, as he held up his lantern. "Who's Lucy? Is there two of you?"

"Yes," said Claude, when both he and Lucy were on Nightshade's back, "there are two of us. This is a dear friend of mine, and I am Claude Duval!"

The ostler dropped the lantern.

"Thieves! thieves! Fire! Murder! Fetch the blunderbuss!"

"Good night!" said Duval; "and when next you have a highwayman's horse in your care, you had better look to it more carefully than you have to this one."

Duval gave the rein to Nightshade, and they trotted down the Old Bailey, towards Ludgate Hill.

They still heard the ostler calling out "Thieves!" and "Fire!" and so immediately opposite as he was to the wicket gate of Newgate, it was not possible but that his outcries must create some alarm.

A loud and startling report then came upon the night air.

The ostler had procured the blunderbuss he spoke of, and at a venture fired it off in the direction whence Claude had proceeded.

The only effect in the discharge, however, was nearly to demolish a watchman, who, hearing the uproar, had just turned the corner from Ludgate Hill and began to spring his rattle.

By this time Claude and Lucy were nearly at Temple Bar.

They intended to make their way through Soho towards the North Road, but before they passed St. Mary's Church, in the Strand, a couple of horsemen in rather gaudy liveries dashed by them.

At a short distance further a travelling carriage appeared, of which these two horsemen were the outriders.

The carriage had but two horses, which were ridden by a lad in the dress of a postilion.

"Lucy," whispered Claude, "do you recollect who you are?"

"Who I am, Claude?"

"Yes; the wife of a highwayman; and, as this is the highway, you know, and there is a carriage, is not the inference rather obvious?"

"But, Claude, is it not possible to forsake this mode of life?"

"No, Lucy; I am what I am and ever shall be."

As he spoke, he dashed up to the side of the carriage.

"Halt!" he cried; and the boy postilion, with an appearance of fright, drew up his horses.

Duval stooped from Nightshade, and looked in at the carriage window.

A couple of ladies occupied it.

One was a portly female, wrapped up in a profusion of velvets and furs.

The other was rather a slim young girl, whose principal effort appeared to be in that carriage to give as much room as possible to her portly companion.

"Madam," said Claude, addressing the lady with the furs, "I am in want of some money and jewels for a particular purpose."

"Thieves!"

"No, madam, only one. The gentleman I have with me on my horse is but a spectator. I will trouble you for your watch and purse, and I fancy that must be a diamond necklace I see glittering around your fair neck, although it scarcely adds to your beauty."

"Thieves!" again said the lady, but it was in a very mild, temperate tone of voice.

"And yet, after all," added Duval, "I may be mistaken, for now I look closer, it is so difficult to distinguish the sparkle of the jewels from your bright eyes that no one but a jeweller could detect the difference."

"Thieves!" said the lady again, but it was in a whisper.

"Dear aunt," said the young lady on the opposite side of the carriage, "let us proceed. Oh, pray let us proceed!"

"Tell me who you are," said the lady with the furs; "although I think I could name you."

Duval smiled.

"And I, madam," he said, "can name you."

"Indeed!"

"Yes, you are the Marchioness of Queensberry; but as my time is somewhat precious, I would fain receive from you these little keepsakes I have mentioned, and no longer expose myself to destruction in heart and brain from the battery of your charms!"

"Take this purse, and be content," said the Marchioness. "If one is to be robbed on the highway, it is a comfort to be so by a gentleman!"

Claude weighed the purse in his hand, and guessed its contents to be valuable.

"Tell me," said the Marchioness — "for I can now name you as Claude Duval, — is it true that on Ealing Common you robbed, and then danced a cotillion with, that odious little baby-faced Duchess of Cleveland?"

"I had that honour."

"Pooh! Honour, indeed!"

"And, madam," added Claude, with a smile, "if your ladyship will alight, I shall have great pleasure in repeating the dance here in the Strand. It is a time in the morning when we shall have but few spectators; a couple of drowsy watchmen, perhaps, or some belated wayfarer, who may prop himself against a door, and fancy himself in the midst of a dream of strange import!"

"Oh, aunt, do not think of such a thing!" said the young lady.

"That odious little Cleveland," muttered the Marchioness, "is always telling the story, and getting a gang of men about her to listen to it, because they know she picks out one of them as an illustration, and dances the cotillion with him!"

"Fight her with her own weapons, madam!" said

Claude. "Put it in your power to say that you, too, have been stopped on the highway, and forced to dance with Claude Duval!"

"Viewing it in that light," said the Marchioness "and to make her ridiculous, I think——"

"Aunt! aunt!" expostulated the young lady; "how can you be so absurd?"

"Absurd, Dorinda! Perhaps you would like a box on the ears!"

Claude felt that the frolic must be carried out, and hastily dismounting from Nightshade, he whispered to Lucy, "Fear nothing—fear nothing! These things are part of the reputation of Claude Duval!"

"Good gracious!" cried the Marchioness, "what are you doing?"

Claude began to take off his top-boots, but they were the top-boots of Mr. Swallow, which had been quite sufficiently capacious to be drawn on over his own.

He next flung Swallow's coat on to the pavement, and the cravat and waistcoat after it.

"Now, madam," said Duval, "you will recognise better your most humble servant, who sometimes has the enviable distinction of being called the ladies' highwayman!"

"Ah, me!" said the Marchioness. "Alas! it's a sad thing for poor me to be taken out of my coach in the middle of the night to dance with the celebrated Claude Duval! But it can't be helped, I suppose. Dorinda, you stay where you are; and when that odious little Cleveland tells her story again, you can bear witness how Duval would insist upon this cotillion."

"Nay," said Duval, "we will make two couples! My young friend here is a charming dancer. Nightshade, be still!"

Lucy uttered a remonstrance; but Duval, in a rapid whisper, told her it would be safer if she were to engage the Marchioness's niece likewise in the dance.

"Now, Nightshade!" cried Duval.

As he spoke, Claude began to nod his head, and whistle and stamp with one of his feet.

Nightshade had been taught to imitate these manoeuvres, with the exception of the whistling; and keeping pretty regular time, the creature beat with one of its fore-feet upon the roadway, nodding its head, and bending its arched neck, as if to the cadences of a tune.

"This is at once beautiful and astonishing," said the Marchioness, ' and beats that odious little Cleveland to nothing!"

The dance began.

The Marchioness's niece was half dragged from the coach, and compelled to take part in the extemporaneous ball.

The boy postilion looked petrified with astonishment; and half a dozen watchmen, who strolled up from different quarters of the neighbourhood, kept at a respectful distance, holding up their lanterns, and not knowing what to make of it.

"Bravo! bravo!" cried Claude; "your ladyship dances divinely!"

With great dexterity, Duval slipped ring after ring from the Marchioness's fingers.

He unclasped the necklace from her neck.

He took even the ear-rings from her ears, and every time he committed one of these depredations, the Marchioness uttered a faint scream.

Then there came the clatter of horses' feet.

The two outriders, missing the carriage from behind them, were returning.

"Our cotillion is over," said Claude Duval. "Allow me, madam, to hand you to your carriage."

The two outriders reined in their horses, and looked on the scene with unqualified amazement.

The Marchioness had one foot upon the carriage step, and in three minutes more the strange episode in her history and in that of Claude Duval would have been over.

An interruption, however, took place in the harmony of the proceedings, as from the neighbourhood of Temple Bar there came at furious, headlong-speed, a mounted man.

"Stop him! stop him! A thousand pounds reward for Claude Duval, the highwayman, dead or alive! dead or alive! Stop him! stop him!"

It was Muckles, the officer.

"Ah!" said Duval, "it seems that we shall have warm work. Mount, Lucy, mount!"

"Oh, this fatal delay!" exclaimed Lucy.

"Do not call it fatal. All will be well."

The two outriders took the alarm.

The shouts and cries of Muckles, and the manner in which he pointed towards Claude Duval, sufficiently opened their eyes to the real facts of the case.

"Halt!" cried Duval. "Mr. Muckles, I have no desire to do you an injury, but if you advance another step, you are a dead man."

"Ha! ha!" laughed Muckles. "Ha! ha! You have no pistols, Claude Duval. You will find your horse's holsters empty, and the pair you had with you we took care to ease you of at Newgate. Ha! ha! You have no pistols. Forward, my men, forward! and we shall have him yet, and the thousand pounds reward likewise, for this time he don't give himself up."

"Nor has he any need!" shouted a voice; "for if he has no pistols, I have plenty, and to spare."

From behind the Marchioness of Queensberry's carriage, a man scrambled right up on to the roof, and presented a pair of large horse pistols full in the face of Muckles.

"Blossom!" ejaculated Duval.

"Yes, Captain! I am here, and half a dozen of our fellows are just by the corner of the churchyard yonder."

"Done brown again!" roared a voice; and Swallow, who had run all the way from Newgate without his coat or boots, fell back in a state of despair into a doorway.

"Good night, Mr. Muckles!" cried Claude Duval. "Marchioness, I have the honour of bidding you good night, and wishing you a pleasant journey! Forward, Blossom! Where's your horse!"

"Here, Captain! At the back of the coach."

"Cowards! wretches!" cried Muckles to the two outriders; "we are yet three to two, and here are half a dozen watchmen! Help! Thieves! Highwaymen! Seize them! seize them!"

"Blossom, blow a whistle."

Loudly and shrilly the notes echoed round St. Mary's Church, and from the narrow thoroughfare at one side of it there emerged seven mounted men.

"The game's up!" muttered Muckles, as he dashed his hat into the roadway.

"Good night again," said Duval; "and now off and away in earnest."

Duval's men gathered about him.

They raised a cheer, which awakened many a deep sleeper in the houses of that part of the Strand, and then at a brisk trot they dashed up a little court at the end of Drury Lane, and disappeared from before the eyes of the bewildered watchmen, outriders, and constables.

CHAPTER XII.

CLAUDE DUVAL HEARS LUCY EVERTON'S STORY FROM HER OWN LIPS.

"TELL me, Claude," said Lucy, as she sat in the ancient bower chamber of the haunted mansion on

Hampstead Heath,—"tell me how you came to know me and to love me?"

"I heard your story obscurely," replied Claude, "and I was a partial spectator at your trial."

"Ah, Claude! could I but have guessed such kindly eyes were bent upon me! But you did not believe me guilty?"

"Not for a moment. There was a mystery in the whole transaction, which, although it was past my powers of solution, I felt had a meaning and an explanation, if one could come at them. However, Lucy, I made my determation."

"To save me!"

"Yes—having acquitted you in my own heart, I from that moment cared nothing for the verdicts of judges and juries. I determined to save you, and, thank heaven, succeeded."

Lucy shuddered.

Her thoughts had flown back to that terrible morning when she was conducted to Bloomsbury Fields to die.

"Oh, Claude! Claude!" she cried. "Even yet there are some strange things connected with the accusation against me that I cannot fathom."

"Tell me what you can of them, Lucy, and we will endeavour by our joint efforts to come to some conclusion concerning them."

"You know, Claude, that my uncle, General Sir George Everton, resided at Camden House, and his kindness to me was more that of a parent to a child than aught else. He loaded me with favours—was never weary of listening even to all my girlish caprices, and he made no secret of the fact that I was to become his heiress."

"And he judged wisely and well, my Lucy. But tell me of this man, Mossy Pendell. Is he in truth your cousin?"

"I am constrained to believe so. He was in the army for awhile, as I was told, but leaving it for some inexplicable cause, he threw himself upon the generosity of General Everton, who, when appealed to in that fashion, always responded with an open hand."

"Then he was not at first a resident of your uncle's house?"

"Oh, no, Claude! I had been more than a year the idol of my poor uncle's heart before Mossy Pendell's arrival at Camden House. At first he appeared to treat me with marked distinction and respect, but from some instinctive loathing, I shrunk from him."

Lucy shuddered as she spoke.

"He then tried caresses, and I threatened to complain to my uncle."

"The villain," said Duval. "When next we meet I will treat him to a caress of such a character that he shall hardly require another."

"Heed him not—heed him not, Claude! If ever there breathed a mortal man immeasurably beneath your contempt, that man is Mossy Pendell."

"Nay, Lucy, such reptiles must be crushed. But proceed with your story. What happened next?"

"Mossy Pendell introduced a friend of his—one Lord Horlop—to Camden House."

"Lord Horlop? I fancy I have heard the name as that of a dissolute son of some Court nobleman."

"My good uncle, with his unsuspicious nature, was hospitable to every one, and received Lord Horlop kindly; nor did I discover the reason of his presence, until one day he audaciously demanded my hand in marriage."

"Ah!" said Claude. "I fancy I shall have something to say to Lord Horlop likewise."

"I rejected him firmly and decisively, and then my cousin, Mossy Pendell, who appeared to have been listening in an adjoining room, stepped into the apartment where we were, and used these remarkable words: 'The orphan girl who can refuse the hand of a nobleman like Lord Horlop, would be quite capable of committing a great crime and suffering for it on the public scaffold!'"

"Those words had a meaning, Lucy."

"They had, although at the time they were uttered they were perfectly inexplicable to me. I hesitated long whether to inform the General of all that had taken place, and I did not do so until goaded to it by another circumstance that would have made longer silence on my part almost criminally weak."

"And what was that?"

"Lord Horlop, assisted by Mossy Pendell, my cousin, made an attempt one evening after the General had retired to rest, to force me into a carriage they had in waiting, but my cries alarmed the household, and I informed my uncle of the outrage, who, from that moment forbade them both the house?"

"You were then free from the persecutions of these heartless men?"

"I thought myself so, but Mossy Pendell showed such a world of repentance, and shed so many tears, that I interceded with my uncle for his forgiveness, and he returned apparently penitent and subdued."

Claude shook his head.

"A wolf, Lucy, although it may be cowed for a time, should never be trusted."

"I found so, for within one little week after that time, being at one of those entertainments called a drum given by a lady of quality, who was an old and dear friend of the General's, the coach which was conveying me home was assailed by Lord Horlop and his myrmidons, and to my own terror and alarm, as well as those of my uncle, I was kept from Camden House the whole night, and then offered a Fleet marriage, as Lord Horlop insolently said, to patch up what would be my wounded reputation."

"The worse than villain!"

"But I escaped them even then. There was no wounded reputation, Claude, to patch up by an union with such a man, and after that event my uncle was implacable against them both."

Claude drew a long breath.

"Let me live in hope," he said, "that this same Lord Horlop and I may yet meet face to face."

"Heed him not! heed him not! But let me tell you all. My poor uncle fell dangerously-ill. His physicians could give no name to his malady. There was a woman in the house in the capacity of a sick-nurse, who you may remember appeared at my trial."

"I remember her well. She gave the most dangerous evidence against you, and was named Mrs. Antrobus."

"She was; and you will remember, Claude, how she swore that upon weak pretences I persuaded her to leave my uncle's room, and that upon her return she found some suspicious liquid in a teacup, which she treasured up and produced after my uncle's death."

"I remember—I remember!"

"The physicians declared the liquid to be a virulent poison, and as a phial containing some more of the decoction was found in my own writing desk, it needed but little else to convince judge, jury, and the world that I was a murderess. Oh, Claude! I knew nothing of that poison, that phial, that cup, and that decoction, until they were all produced as terrible evidence against me."

Lucy trembled and sobbed convulsively.

"You shall tell me no more!" cried Claude. "I know enough, and more than enough. All the mystery of this hideous villany shall yet be brought to light, or my name is not Claude Duval."

"Alas!" said Lucy; "it is too late."

"Say not so, Lucy. It may be too late to undo the

evil that has been accomplished, but it is not too late for retribution upon the evil doers."

The day was sunny and beautiful on the old Heath of Hampstead, and to see Claude Duval and Lucy wandering about those luxuriant gardens—long neglected by the hand of man, and left to their own wild will—one might have imagined they were two persons who had cast from them all the cares and anxieties of the bustling world, and determined for a happy future to live but for each other.

And then the shadows of evening came.

Lucy clung more fondly to the arm of her lover—her husband.

"Oh, Claude, Claude!" she cried; "if you could only forsake this mode of life how happy we might be in the humblest cottage that ever afforded a shelter to true and gentle hearts."

Duval shook his head.

"It may not be, Lucy. I was born for a life like this, or for higher flight still; and some day, dear one, when better leisure serves, I will tell you how and why it was I took to the road."

"Leisure, Claude? What leisure like the present?"

Duval glanced in the direction of the western sky.

The sun had just dipped below the horizon, leaving behind it a path of gold, crimson, and every gorgeous combination of colour that can be imagined.

"My time has come!" he said. "I have business on Bagshot Heath to-night, but shall return by one o'clock."

Lucy sighed.

"Oh, what a life is this, so full of danger!"

"I have ceased to regard it as such, Lucy. At first I thought my career was full of hair-breadth escapes, but now I have ceased to think so, and counsel you to fear nothing, but to look to my arrival in safety with perfect confidence."

' I will strive to do so," said Lucy mournfully.

"Behold this little silver horn," said Duval; "it looks but a toy, and yet it can produce most exquisite notes."

He blew twice upon it, and the long mournful sounds produced were of the highest musical quality.

"I know, Lucy," he said, "you will be waiting and watching for me, and when you hear one of these notes you will be sure that I have arrived."

"I shall listen for it," said Lucy, "until fancy will almost produce it upon the night air."

There was now a rustling among the branches of a neighbouring tree, and Blossom, leading Nightshade by the bridle, made his appearance.

"Shall I accompany you, Captain?"

"No, Blossom, this is one of my nights alone. Look for me at one, and leave the iron gate on the latch. Lucy, farewell! Hark! there is eight o'clock. Five hours will soon pass away, when I shall return, I hope, with a good account of my night's adventures."

It was quite evident from this enforced gaiety of manner that Claude Duval rather dreaded a sentimental leave-taking on these occasions when he went forth to the road.

He wished to make such proceedings common-place occurrences; and now springing upon the back of Nightshade, and waving his arm, he trotted from the gardens of the old mansion at a rapid pace, and crossed the Heath.

Duval was in full costume, such as we have seen him in on previous occasions; but being slim, tall, and lithe of figure, he had the advantage of being able to put one dress on over another without looking in the least extraordinary as regarded bulk.

On this occasion he wore a great coat, such as substantial yeomen or gentlemen farmers might put on.

And where the skirts of the great coat terminated he wore an artificial pair of "tops," such as belonged to top-boots, and which gave him the appearance of wearing those rather clumsy feet apendages.

His hat was of plain black beaver, and he carried a riding whip in his hand with a heavy thong, the handle ornamented with silver.

Thus equipped and attired, Claude Duval presented anything but a threatening aspect, and anybody might have met him on the road without taking the least alarm at his appearance.

Immediately upon getting clear of Hampstead Heath, he made the best of his way across the country to that celebrated resort of highwaymen, Bagshot.

But Duval had no special adventure in view; he merely intended to take the chances the heath or the road might afford to him.

Heavy banks of clouds after sunset had come up from the west, and the sky was now so greatly obscured, that although the moon must have risen, its influence through the vapoury shroud that rolled between it and the earth was only sufficient to produce a hazy dim kind of twilight.

The Heath then looked boundless as Claude Duval reached it, and the silence was so profound of the apparently desolate spot, that Duval, perhaps for the first time in his life, felt that shrinking dislike to absolute solitude that is so incidental to human nature.

A dim white mist, too, seemed to be rising from the earth, and although this might be considered in some respects propitious to the proceedings of a knight of the road, yet in others it was specially perplexing.

"Halt, Nightshade!" said Claude, as he patted the neck of his steed. "I know not if it has been quite wise of us to venture forth to-night on to this desolate heath, for we seem to be the only living things in its vast expanse. Ah! What is that?"

Something dashed so close past the eyes of Claude Duval that he involuntarily jerked the bridle of Nightshade, causing the well-trained animal to execute a leap that would have unhorsed a less skilful rider than the celebrated highwayman.

Then Duval laughed.

"It was but a bat," he said, "that brushed my cheek with its leathery wings—it was but a bat, after all! How silent and desolate the Heath is! If this mist rises any higher I shall lose sight of the tree-tops, and hardly find my way off it in time to keep my word with Lucy."

A bright speck of light, apparently about two or three hundred yards in advance of him, appeared through the darkness of the air.

Duval bent low in his saddle to watch it.

The light moved over the surface of the Heath, not exactly in a straight line, but in that sort of manner which it would present if carried by some person picking their way among the furze bushes and stunted vegetation of the common.

Duval kept his eyes fixed upon this moving light which ast so limited a radiance about it, that he could see nothing of the person who carried it.

In fact, a kind of superstitious fear began to creep over him, that it was not carried by mortal hands at all.

But Claude Duval was the last man to be the slave of such fancies as these, and he soon discarded the irrational supposition.

He put Nightshade to a gentle walk, and in such a direction that if the bearer of the light continued the same course he was pursuing, Claude must inevitably meet him at a point not very far distant.

But the light suddenly paused.

It then moved lower and became stationary, and as it cast about it a strange halo through the white mist, Duval, to his surprise, saw that it shone upon some object—human figure or otherwise—of preternatural height.

Then there came some shrieking, horrible cries upon the night air.

Some of those cries were articulate, and evidently expressed the intense agony of some bereaved soul.

"This one—this one!" cried the voice—"this one, the best beloved of all—this one to meet with such an end! This one so fair, and once so good! Crows and ravens picking at his eyes, and I not able to save him!"

Shrieks and cries that contained no element of human sense about them, succeeded these few wildly uttered words.

Duval felt a cold chill at his heart.

Slowly, however, he advanced—keeping Nightshade to the same walking pace, and in three minutes more he was sufficiently near to the light and to the objects it shone upon to come to a just conclusion in regard to them.

There was a tall, upright post erected on the Heath.

A cross piece at right angles, supported by a strong spur of wood, sufficiently indicated what the erection was.

A gibbet!

A gibbet from which hung in chains a human form!

A ghastly semblance of humanity, encircled in that cage-like structure, which was calculated to hold together for as long a time as possible the rotting, decaying bones and muscles of a malefactor, who the genius of the law at that period thought it wise to present swinging and creaking to the air of heaven as a warning to evil doers.

At the foot of the gibbet was placed the lantern.

Crouching down by the side of the lantern, and swaying to and fro, and uttering shrieks and cries of mortal agony, was a human form.

CHAPTER XIII.

CLAUDE DUVAL MEETS WITH A STRANGE ADVENTURE ON BAGSHOT HEATH.

IT was the position of the light on the ground at the foot of the gibbet, and shining through that white mist which had risen up, after sunset, from the surface of the Heath, which gave so lurid and supernatural an appearance to the whole scene.

But Claude Duval could not be otherwise than somewhat shocked at the aspect of that terrible object on the gibbet, which seemed to typify the probable fate that might befall all persons in his career.

Often and often, too, had he traversed Bagshot Heath, but his eyes had never lit upon this spectacle, which probably arose from two causes.

In the first place, the spot on which the malefactor was hung in chains was remote from all the roads and bridle-tracks across the common.

Secondly, Claude Duval had never sought that region, except in the dusk of the evening, or the absolute darkness of the night.

Nightshade seemed to recoil from the spectacle on the gibbet; and it was with difficulty Duval could keep the creature with its face towards the ghastly sight.

For a few moments there was a pause in the wild ejaculations and outcries of the crouching figure.

Then she spoke again.

We say she, for by this time Claude Duval had seen enough of the costume of the wretched creature to be assured that it was a woman who thus, in the silence of the night, uttered such wailing cries at the feet of the dead.

"Who will save him now—who will save him now? Will the false brother do so? No, no—a thousand times, no! He will leave him to suffer for the crimes he never committed! I offered myself to the hands of the executioner, but he would not have me! Oh, save him from the hawks and kites, or, in mercy, heaven, let me go mad, and fancy that he still lives!"

It would be quite impossible for any words to express the agony of tone in which these expressions were uttered.

Claude Duval listened to them with profound pity.

"Hilloa! hilloa!" he shouted. "Why are you here alone upon the Heath? And who is it whose death you mourn upon that ghastly gibbet?"

The wretched woman uttered a shriek of dismay.

She immediately extinguished the lantern she had carried to that lonely spot.

And then, as far as regards Claude Duval, the gibbet, with its swinging malefactor, and the woman who mourned so bitterly at its foot, alike disappeared as though they had been visions conjured up by his fancy.

The white mist, that had risen up from the surface of the Heath, had materially thickened and increased, so that every object was shrouded in it that did not stand at least eight or ten feet above the surface of the ground.

"Listen to me," cried Claude Duval. "I am a friend, if you are willing that I should be such; and whether you want a friend or not, at all events you have nothing from me to fear."

There was no reply.

Duval dismounted from Nightshade, and, leading it by the bridle, he made his way, as nearly as he could guess, in the direction of the gibbet.

But by some reason he missed it.

After a fruitless search of some few minutes he gave it up.

Passing his hand over his eyes, he muttered to himself, "Am I but half awake, and is all this but a dream? Often and often as I have been upon the common, I have seen nothing of such a spectacle as that which has met my eyes to-night."

Duval mounted Nightshade again.

He patted the faithful friend and companion of his night's adventure on the neck.

"Nightshade, we shall have to return home without booty to-night. This white mist seems inclined to deepen to a fog."

But even as Claude Duval spoke, some change seemed to be taking place in the atmosphere around him.

It was suddenly getting lighter, and a bright tinge began to pervade it.

Then he felt certain that the mist was dissipating.

A brisk wind careered over the Heath.

The white vapour curled itself up as though by some word of command; and as the moon looked down upon the earth, through a broad rift in the clouds above, the atmosphere on the common became perfectly clear and transparent, so that every tree, every bush, every wild flower, and every blade of grass were distinctly visible.

"Ah, Nightshade!" cried Duval; "we shall yet have sport to-night!"

He turned his horse's head towards the eastern sky as he spoke, and then he started to find that he was within three or four feet only of the gibbet.

A glance around him showed that he had reached, accidentally, a very wild and desolate portion of the Heath, which he had never before seen.

Then he looked up at the dead man swinging in his chains.

The figure looked preternaturally long as it there hung swinging in the night air.

NIGHTSHADE; OR, CLAUDE DUVAL, THE DASHING HIGHWAYMAN.   33

THE MARCHIONESS OF QUEENSBERRY ACCEPTS CLAUDE AS PARTNER IN THE DANCE.

And full on to the dead face fell the bright moonbeams.

Duval started.

What was there in that face that came upon him like a recollection?

Still and ghastly in death, as they were, he felt certain that he had looked upon that face, or its living likeness, somewhere recently, but he could not at the moment sufficiently collect his scattered senses to remember where the features had met his eyes.

The hair was of a very peculiar colour.

A kind of blue-black, which, once seen, could not readily be forgotten.

A cold sort of sneer sat upon the face of the dead.

It seemed as if that expression must have been familiar to the living man, and that he had died with it stamped upon his features.

"There is some mystery in all this," said Claude Duval, "which time may develop. Farewell, for the present, unhappy wretch! Whatever your crimes may have been, this is a ghastly retribution!"

No. 5.—NIGHTSHADE.

Nightshade made some uneasy gestures, and began to paw the ground.

Well did Duval know the acute senses of his horse, and that these motions were indicative of the fact of some living thing approaching on the common.

A faint noise, as of the tread of horses' feet and the roll of carriage-wheels over one of the rough roads, in a few seconds more came to the ears of Duval.

Like two great blazing eyes, he saw two carriage-lamps coming rapidly across the Heath.

"We shall have some sport, Nightshade," he said; "and my name is not Claude Duval if I do not say 'Stand and deliver!' to these people, be they whom they may."

The carriage rapidly approached; and as it neared him, Duval saw that it was a pair-horse travelling chariot, with several imperials and boxes strapped to it, and driven, as was then the custom, by a postilion.

Duval tightened his rein, and, feeling his feet well in the stirrups, was about to dash forward, and call upon the postilion to halt, when he was spared the trouble by the vehicle suddenly coming to a standstill.

"Idiot!" shouted an angry voice from the interior of the carriage. "Idiot! where have you driven to now? You are off the track, for I can feel the wheels are on the turf."

"I couldn't help it, my lord," replied the frightened postilion. "The near horse has been dragging his way all over the Heath."

"Use your whip—use your whip!"

"It's no use, my lord. I must get down and change the horses to different sides."

"Fool! Am I to be detained because you don't know how to harness your cattle? I have half a mind to alight, and lay your own whip about your lazy shoulders."

"It's not my fault, my lord," said the postilion, sulkily. "I didn't harness the cattle."

"Be quick about what you have to do. This is most provoking, to be detained in the middle of Bagshot Heath, and on just such a night, too, as would suit some of those gentry of the road to cry 'Stand and deliver!' in."

"I can't help it, my lord."

"Don't answer me, scoundrel! You should help it!"

Duval smiled to himself.

"At all events," he thought, "when I attack his lordship, I shall not have much to fear from any active assistance the postilion may render him."

The change in the relative position of the horses was being rapidly effected, and then Duval became aware that there was another person in the carriage beside the imperious lord who had spoken so furiously to the postilion.

"I am frightened to death!" said a female voice.

"Which is not of the slightest use," cried my lord, snappishly.

Duval quietly trotted up to the side of the carriage.

The lady uttered a scream.

His lordship an oath.

Duval looked in at the open window.

"A fine night, my lord," he said, "as you remarked, for some of those gentry on the road who say, 'Stand and deliver!' I have the honour to be one of them."

"Take that, then!"

Bang!

A pistol-shot passed so closely before the eyes of Duval that they almost seemed singed with the heat of the bullet.

"Ah!" said Claude; "that was not so bad!"

The lady screamed, and flung herself upon his lordship.

"Help, help! Murder! We shall be killed! Give him some money, and let him go! Oh, my Lord Horlop, I thought you were one of the best of tempers."

"My lord who?" cried Duval. "Is this Lord Horlop?"

"I am Lord Horlop, fellow; and if this old woman will only let my arm go, I have another pistol-bullet at your service!"

"Old woman!" shrieked the lady. "Gracious heaven! has it come to this, and only six hours married?"

"Hands off, I say!" shouted Horlop—for it was, indeed, that mendacious nobleman. "Hands off, I say! and let me get my other pistol!"

"Alas, alas! I see it all now!" cried the lady. "In my old age I have shown more than the folly of youth. I have married this man, who now casts me off with contempt. Oh, this is dreadful—dreadful!"

"Well, madam," said Horlop, "since marriages are made in heaven, you must be content to believe that this one is perfectly right and proper. You married me for my title. You are sixty-seven, and I thirty-one. I married you for your sixty thousand pounds—settled on yourself, it is true, but with a reversion to me at your death, and the sooner that event comes off the better. Don't claw hold of me in this fashion! Where's my other pistol?"

"If you stir hand or foot, my lord," said Duval, "I will blow your brains out with as little compunction as I would those of a mad dog!"

Duval imparted an emphasis to these words by thrusting the muzzle of a pistol exactly against the temple of Lord Horlop.

"What hinders me," added Duval, "from relieving this unfortunate lady of a brutal husband, and at the same time avenging Lucy Everton?"

"Lucy Everton!" ejaculated Lord Horlop.

"Yes. Does not that name appal you?"

"Confusion!"

"Yes, my Lord Horlop, to your confusion you have met her avenger, even here upon Bagshot Heath."

Horlop trembled.

"I suppose I am to be murdered here, in cold blood," he said.

"No, my lord. My blood is hot enough when I think of your conduct to a young, defenceless girl, abandoned by one who should have been her natural protector, but who, on the contrary, aided you in your villanous purposes."

"I know not what you mean," said Horlop, gloomily.

"Perhaps your lordship has no such acquaintance, then, as Mossy Pendell?"

Horlop started.

He was, however, still more surprised by an exclamation that immediately came from the lips of Claude Duval, and which seemed to bear no relation whatever to the subject upon which they were conversing.

"Ah!" cried Duval; "now I recollect well. The malefactor on the gibbet is the likeness, in all respects, of Mossy Pendell."

The elderly lady in the carriage now began to wring her hands, and moan bitterly.

"Take comfort, madam," said Duval. "The next best thing to have preserved your liberty and money from such a man as this is to recover both, and I have a quarrel with my Lord Horlop which may bring about that desirable end."

"He means to murder me," said Horlop.

"Oh, spare him!" said the lady. "Bad and wicked as he is, oh, spare his life!"

"He has already aimed at mine," said Duval; "and shot for shot would be but fair play. I waive that consideration, however, since he fired at me in my capacity of a highwayman; and now, in that capacity, I say, my lord, your watch, money, and such valuables as you may have about you."

"Take them."

"That is well."

"Take all, and be off!"

"The highwayman is satisfied."

"Then the sooner the highwayman takes himself away, the better."

"He is gone."

"Gone?"

"Yes; the highwayman of Bagshot Heath is gone, but the avenger of the insulted Lucy Everton remains. And now, my Lord Horlop, if you be a peer and a gentleman, I insult you, and challenge you to mortal combat!"

As he spoke, Duval took off one of his gloves, and struck Lord Horlop twice in the face with it.

This indignity was responded to by a yell of rage.

"Let me out—let me out! Get away from the door, and let me out! I will soon take signal vengeance for all this!"

DECEMBER 1933

OFFICIAL ORGAN HAPPY HOURS BROTHERHOOD

(Courtesy of INLAND PRINTER)
A THRILLER OF THE OLD DAYS GONE BY.
The above is a reproduction of the De Witts Nightshade Series, a yellowback of the 1860's. It is a four color wood cut of the first No. of Nightshade. (De Witss NightShade Series, article inside.)

VOLUME THREE   NUMBER TWENTY-FIVE

Reckless Ralph's Dime Novel Round-Up

THIS IS IT

Size 6 x 9, 4 pages, or more, every month. Full of news and articles and data on 5c & 10c novels and their writers.

Price 10c per copy - $1.00 per Year

Advertising Rates

Per Half Inch	30c	of 25 words
Per Inch	50c	
Quarter Page	$1.50	
Half Page	2.75	
Full Page	5.00	

Four consecutive insertions for the price of three

RALPH F. CUMMINGS
Grafton, Mass. U. S. A.

"Certainly, my lord! Here, postilion!"
"Yes, sir."
"Open the door for his lordship"

The postilion obeyed, and Lord Horlop sprung out upon the Heath.

There was just a faint suspicion on the min do Claude Duval that Lord Horlop might take to his heels and flee.

But such was not the case.

There was either some genuine physical courage in this man's disposition, or anger at that moment took the place of it.

"Now, Mr. Highwayman!" he cried. "Dismount, and we will see if I cannot rid Bagshot Heath of such a pest as you."

"Still, Nightshade—still!" said Duval, as he hastily dismounted, and turned towards Lord Horlop.

The bright moonbeams now fell full upon the face and figure of Duval, so that Lord Horlop had no difficulty in taking a good view of him, and to some extent calculating the chances of a personal encounter.

The tall, slim, graceful figure.

The easy carriage, and that appearance of nervous agility which characterized Claude Duval, convinced Lord Horlop that he had entered upon an adventure of considerable danger.

Duval deliberately took off the overcoat he wore, and as he was doing so Lord Horlop thought he saw an opportunity of putting an end to the contest at once without personal risk.

He suddenly drew his sword and dashed forward at Duval.

But the latter was too quick for him.

Leaping on one side, he disentangled himself from the overcoat and flung it full in the face of Lord Horlop, who, for a few seconds, was entangled with it, and at the mercy of Claude.

But the latter disdained to take such an advantage, and coolly placing himself upon his guard, he drew his sword, saying as he did so, "Now, my lord, that all preliminaries are arranged, we can proceed to business, which on this occasion, so far as I am concerned, is combined with a large amount of pleasure."

CHAPTER XIV

CLAUDE DUVAL FIGHTS A DUEL WITH LORD HORLOP.

LORD HORLOP glanced at Claude Duval like an enraged tiger.

There can be no question but that he would gladly have taken the life of the man who so coolly and calmly braved him and forced him to account at the sword's point for his misdeeds.

The manner, too, in which Claude had taken his attempted assassination while off his guard fil'ed Lord Horlop with a thousand fears.

No man, without the most abundant confidence in himself, could possibly act as Claude Duval did.

It was an exhibition of the extremest confidence in the result of the encounter.

It was as if Duval had said, "I know perfectly well my own powers, and what will ensue from this conflict, that I can put up with anything antecedent to it."

But there was no escape.

Horlop was brought to bay.

There, upon that desolate common, as though fate had hurried him forward to a terrible destiny, he faced the man who was to avenge the wrongs of Lucy Everton.

Horlop whispered to himself in low tones, "I shall be killed—my time has come!"

He took that strange, wandering look about him that men will do when they think they are bidding farewell to the world for ever.

There was the coach, with that wretched woman in it who had sold herself to the unprincipled nobleman for the mere glitter of a name.

There was the boy-postilion with mouth and eyes wide open, indicative both of the alarm and interest he felt in the transaction.

The affair was something for that boy to speak of in after life, when time had furrowed his cheek and whitened his hair.

And there, creaking to and fro upon its gibbet hideously, was the body of the malefactor.

The clouds parted right and left, and left the moon in its full radiance, to shine down upon the scene.

There was a short pause.

"Now, my lord," said Claude Duval; "we waste valuable time."

"Have at you, then!" cried Horlop, with a feeling of desperation. "I will, at least, rid society of you!"

This was a boast.

A mere effort at bravado.

He had no notion in the world of being able to rid society of Claude Duval, but believed that his own last hour had come; and he only fought with the desperate feeling of a man who knew that, do what he might, he could not make things worse.

The swords clashed together.

And now the lady in the carriage, in the excitement and terror of the moment, began to scream "Murder!"

The post-boy took the alarm, and added his screams to hers.

And so, amid the echoing tumult of these shouts, Lord Horlop and Claude Duval fought.

The combat was a brief one.

It lasted but a few moments.

Horlop relied—if he relied upon anything—on a long-practised skill as a fencer.

But Duval had the same skill, and with it a strength of arm and suppleness of wrist far superior to anything that Lord Horlop could bring to bear upon the contest.

Suddenly Horlop half sunk to the earth.

His sword had flown from his grasp, and lay some distance from him on the green turf.

The man was not deficient in physical courage, but at such a moment human nature is weak.

"Mercy!" he ejaculated.

Claude Duval stayed his hand.

"If I were to show you such mercy as you would exhibit in a similar occasion to this, my sword blade would pass through your heart; but, as it is, my Lord Horlop, we shall meet again!"

Duval turned from the half-prostrate man, and was in the act of returning his own sword to the scabbard.

Horlop seized the opportunity, and making a spring towards his own weapon, he raised it from the grass, and before Duval could disengage his sword again from its half-way progress into its sheath, Lord Horlop, with a yell of rage and satisfaction, made a furious lunge at him.

Ripping up the crimson velvet coat of his adversary.

Carrying with it a piece of the embroidered waistcoat.

Grazing the skin of Claude Duval, just over the region of the heart, and causing a sudden effusion of blood that looked dangerous, although it was not so in reality, Lord Horlop's sword seemed to have done all the mischief he intended.

"Ah!" cried Claude Duval, "that was a treacherous thrust!"

Horlop drew back his sword-arm to repeat it.

But that instant of time was sufficient to enable Duval to put himself on his guard.

His drawn sword was in his hand again.

Scarcely knowing, then, whether he were seriously wounded or not, he rushed upon Horlop, who but feebly defended himself.

The swords clashed together for a few seconds, and then the bright blade of Claude Duval's weapon passed right through the breast of the dissipated and treacherous nobleman.

With a half-stifled cry, Lord Horlop fell backwards.

He rolled over twice upon the green turf of the common, and then lay profoundly still, with his eyes fixed as though intently gazing at the moon.

Duval stepped up to the coach.

"Madam," he said, "you are a widow!"

The lady screamed "Murder!"

"Nay, be thankful," said Duval; "for under ordinary circumstances, my Lord Horlop must have outlived you, and what would have been your existence as the wife of such a man?"

"Wretch!—villain!" cried the lady.

"Madam!"

"I hope I shall live, and it will only be with the hope of seeing you hanged!"

"This is gratitude and thankfulness," said Duval; "and I have but one consolation, which is truth, that I did not fight this man in your quarrel, but in my own."

"Villain! I will give an alarm, and I here offer ten thousand pounds for your capture!"

"A large sum, madam; and if I am ever particularly in want of money, I shall almost feel inclined to give myself up at such a price. As it is, however, I bid you farewell, and leave you under the more fortunate circumstances, if you would but think so, of having the companionship of the dead Lord Horlop instead of the living one."

Duval turned to the direction where he had left his horse.

"Ho, Nightshade! Nightshade! This way, boy!"

The creature trotted up to him.

Duval placed his hand on the saddle, and was about to mount, when, with shouts and cries—apparently with no other object than to encourage each other—there came over the heath a strong party of mounted men, making directly for the coach and its immediate neighbourhood.

"Hoy! hoy!" cried the post-boy; "this way! this way! Murder! murder! Hoy! hoy!"

"My lad," said Duval, "if you value your insignificant existence, you will hold your tongue."

"I can't hold my tongue!" said the boy. "He promised me a guinea; and I shan't get it now—'cos why? You've been and gone and killed him!"

"Is that all?"

"Yes; and enough too!"

"I'll give you five. Hold your tongue."

The post-boy was as quiet as a mouse.

Duval picked up the hat of Lord Horlop, which lay close to the carriage.

"Away, Nightshade, away!" he cried; and he flung the hat towards a clump of young pine trees some short distance off.

Nightshade galloped away in that direction; and Duval knew that when he chose to recover his steed he would find it, as it had been trained to do, keeping watch and ward over the hat.

"Now, madam," said Duval, as he leaped into the carriage. "I shall trouble you to help me play a part which will not be attended with any difficulty."

"I play a part?"

"Yes, madam; unless your affection for the deceased Lord Horlop is so great that you would rather join him in another and a better world."

"Would you murder me?"

"Murder, madam, is an ugly word; but I may have to kill you for self-preservation."

The lady screamed.

"Hush!"

The horsemen surrounded the carriage.

"Hilloa!" cried one; "what is all this? What is amiss upon the heath?"

"We have been attacked by a highwayman," said Duval; "but I rather think he has got the worst of it."

"Indeed, sir! Where is he?"

"Don't call me sir; I will trouble you to say your Grace."

"I beg pardon, your Grace. I am an officer of the police, and my name is Muckles. We are on the look-out for the notorious highwayman, Claude Duval."

"I don't think you need look far, then."

"Indeed!"

"Hilloa, fellows! when you speak to me, say your Grace."

"I beg pardon again, your Grace; but where is this Claude Duval?"

"Hurrah! hurrah! hurrah!" shouted another voice; "he's settled at last! Here he lies, Mr. Muckles!"

"Ah! what is that you say, Swallow?"

"Here he is, Mr. Muckles! here he is! You may see him in the moonlight. No, you won't."

As chance would have it, at that instant a dense black cloud swept over the face of the moon.

All was darkness on Bagshot Heath but for the carriage lamps, and some of the hand-lanterns carried by the officers in their waist-belts.

"This is unfortunate," said Duval; "because I wished you to identify the rascal. I have had some trouble with him; and there he lies."

"Pick him up! pick him up!" cried Muckles. "I should know him among a thousand."

"We must be humane," said Duval, "even to such a man. Bring him into the coach. I am quite sure my wife will make room for him."

"Wretch! monster!" cried the lady, who since the death of Lord Horlop seemed inclined to take his part so furiously, and to look upon Claude Duval as his most unjustifiable murderer.

"Exactly so," said Claude Duval; "he is a wretch and monster; but still, let us be humane, for the breath of life may yet linger within him."

The officers raised the body of Lord Horlop.

As they opened the coach-door on one side, to place it within, Duval quietly got out at the other.

He ran fleetly across the common towards the clump of trees where he knew he should find Nightshade.

Another moment, and he was in the saddle.

"Hilloa, Mr. Muckles!" he cried; "if you want Claude Duval, he is here; but as he happens to be mounted on his horse Nightshade, he has no objection to a race over Bagshot Heath, for any stakes you like to mention."

Muckles raised a shout of rage and alarm.

"Done brown again!" cried Swallow. "I knowed it, Mr. Muckles, I knowed it! Done brown again!"

Duval did not wait to hear what further took place among the officers; but, putting Nightshade to speed, he galloped over the common in the direction of town.

He felt that there was no further sport to be had upon the heath on that night, and, indeed, he wished for a short time to be left him before he redeemed his promise by returning to Hampstead Heath, in order that he might make an effort to discover who was in possession of Camden House.

It was not a very long gallop across the country to Kensington.

Upon arriving at the then pretty little royal village, Duval put up his horse at a famous old hostel called "The Crown and Sceptre," where he knew by experience, not only that no questions would be asked as to who and what he was, but that none would be answered on the same subject.

On foot he made his way to the ancient residence that had once been the happy home of Lucy Everton, and her uncle, the General.

The whole house seemed shrouded in darkness.

Duval slowly paced completely round its boundary walls, and could not discover the faintest ray of light from any of its windows.

The lateness of the hour might easily account, however, for that; but Claude had an irresistible curiosity to make his way into the gardens of that mansion which had for so long been the home of one now so near and so dear to him.

That there was some great mystery connected with this mansion, Claude Duval could not doubt for a moment; but what it was, surpassed all his powers of conjecture.

And had he been asked at that time what motive or ground of action he had for making his way into those gardens he would have been indeed at a loss to reply.

His presence there was one of those impulsive or instinctive actions such as come over men, from reasons which they are not able to give even to themselves, but which, in the result, turn out to be perfectly well founded.

The mysterious gloom of the mansion, and the sighing of the night wind among the tall trees that surrounded it, reminded him something of his own home on Hampstead Heath.

"Why should I linger here?" he said. "I have no memories connected with this spot; and although it has been the home of Lucy, it cannot have been a happy one."

He turned towards the wall again, intending to make his way from the premises; but as he did so, a strange, faint cry came upon his ears.

It might have been a night bird for all he knew.

Or it might be the echo of some very distant sound indeed, which, travelling through the still air, reached that quiet spot.

But it was sufficient to make Claude Duval pause.

He turned and looked up at the house again, and as he did so, it seemed to stand out in bolder relief against the night sky.

Those black clouds, which had shrouded the moon and produced such a cavernous darkness on Bagshot Heath had not entirely passed away, but had thinned sufficiently to enable a faint glow of moonlight to penetrate them.

Hence the house looked higher, and Claude Duval, for the first time, was able to come to a very accurate conclusion about its shape and size.

But still, why was he lingering there?

Again he asked himself the question, and again he moved towards the portion of the wall by which he had entered the grounds.

As he did so, he saw a shadow fall across the path nearest to him.

Duval shrunk back close to some bushes, which entirely concealed him, and then he felt convinced he was not alone in the gardens of Camden House, for he heard a footstep rapidly approaching.

Whoever the intruder upon that solitude was, he evidently felt no uncertainty about his route, nor was he careful to conceal his presence, for he crunched the gravel of the garden path under his feet with a steady tread.

The figure was tall, but there was something ungainly in the gait which came familiarly to the eyes of Duval.

He was certain he had seen that man somewhere, and it wanted but some tone, look, or movement, to enable Claude to thoroughly to identify him.

The man paused and looked up at the house.

"All alone at last!" he said. "I have succeeded in clearing the place of all the servants, and now the time has come for action. Surely the fear of death will do something, even with a man so near the termination of his mortal career."

These few words were quite sufficient to enable Claude Duval to name this person, who was in the garden at so unseemly an hour.

"Mossy Pendell!" he said to himself. "It is Mossy Pendell!"

CHAPTER XV.

CLAUDE DUVAL FINDS HIMSELF IN THE SECRET CHAMBER OF CAMDEN HOUSE.

WITHOUT uttering another word, Pendell moved towards the house.

Duval followed him as cautiously as he could, so as, at the same time, to keep him in sight, and yet not expose himself to observation.

Pendell disappeared for a few seconds round an angle of the house, but Duval was quickly on his heels, and he saw him opening a low door, which evidently, from the difficulty he had in moving the lock, was not often used as a means of entrance into the premises.

Claude would fain have followed him, but the moment Mossy Pendell succeeded in opening this door, he passed through it, and closed it instantly from the inner side.

The determination of Claude Duval to make his way into Camden House was now so firm and distinct, that he did not hesitate in at once seeking for means to carry it into execution.

That the lower windows and the lower door would in all probability be too well secured to permit him to force them, Claude Duval concluded, but he thought it quite possible to effect an entrance through some of the windows of the upper storey.

And to one so active and agile as Claude Duval, the difficulty was not so great as it might appear.

Clambering roses, and dense masses of variegated ivy found a home in front of this old mansion; and although, no doubt, for many a long year their stems had been lithe and tender, such was not now the case, and they had grown into trees of sufficient strength to repay, in some measure, the obligation of support they had long received from the ancient mansion.

Claude Duval clambered up to the nearest window on the upper floor.

A touch opened it, and he found himself beneath the roof of Camden House; at all events, within five minutes of the time when Mossy Pendell had made his way through the little disused door.

Duval listened.

Listened to catch the slightest sound that might be within the mansion.

He heard a door slammed shut.

Then all was still.

Still as the grave for the space of about five minutes, when there came a peculiar cry, which, to Duval's apprehension, had very much the same tone about it as the sound he had heard in the garden.

But still the cry was too indistinct for him to take upon himself to say from which direction it came.

The suggestion of distress, however, which it bore to his mind, induced him to adopt the most energetic means to discover its origin.

All he could do was to go as quickly as possible from room to room of the mansion, in the hope of finding some solution to the mystery that was evidently connected with it.

Duval emerged from the apartment in which he was on to a staircase, and almost immediately that he did so, a flash of light came across his eyes, and looking over the gilt balustrade, he saw below Mossy Pendell, commence the ascent of the stairs, and bearing a light.

Nothing had happened, then, as yet.

Duval had succeeded in interrupting the villain in whatever might be his intention in Camden House; but in order to discover those intentions, it would not be wise to encounter him.

To keep a watchful eye upon him would surely not be difficult, especially as he, Mossy Pendell, could not have the slightest suspicion but that he was alone in Camden House.

That is to say, alone with the victim of his plots and plans.

Alone with General Everton, his uncle, whom he was endeavouring to make the victim of his cupidity and his ambition.

Claude Duval stepped back into the room again from which he had just emerged.

Mossy Pendell reached the head of the stairs, and passed onward along the corridor which immediately presented itself, and which went the whole depth of the house.

He paused at a door on his right hand, opened it gently, and entered a room, which shrouded him from the sight of Duval.

But the latter was quickly after him, and pausing at the door of that apartment, Claude listened for a few seconds, and hearing nothing, he pushed at it gently, and stepped into the room.

It was vacant.

The light that Mossy Pendell had carried stood upon table, but although there seemed to be no other entrance or mode of exit from that apartment but the one at which Claude Duval had just entered, Mossy Pendell was not there, but had disappeared, as though he had been some unsubstantial presence that had reached its destination, and had then exhaled into thin air.

This mystery was not long in endurance.

For a third time the strange wailing cry, as if of mental or bodily suffering, came upon the ears of Claude Duval.

But its echoes were now quenched by the loud tones of Mossy Pendell.

"Peace!" he cried. "You ask for life in vain while you refuse the simple means by which it can be granted to you."

"For your own sake—for the sake of your own immortal welfare," moaned a voice, "do not add crime upon crime! Mossy Pendell, only tell me that Lucy is alive and unharmed, and I will forgive you all!"

Duval's heart beat with emotion.

Who could it be who thus spoke in such terms of affectionate solicitude of Lucy?

Of his Lucy?

Was not the only person beside himself who would have done so silent in the grave?

He listened still.

"You entreat in vain!" cried Pendell. "The only mode of escape from death is the one I propose to you. Sign this will which I now produce to you, and which leaves your property to me (I will manage that it be put in proper train to answer every purpose),—sign it, I say, and you shall be free; but refuse to do so, and your life is forfeit, while I, as heir-at-law of all your estates and properties, get easy possession of them."

"You are not my heir-at-law," was the reply. "And if you were, Lucy is co-heiress with you, for do you not both stand in the same relation to me? Moreover, your conduct to me has been such that my will is already made in her favour. Murder me, and you do but pave the way for her inheritance."

Claude Duval heard all this with such astonishment, that he might well be excused for doubting if he were in his waking senses.

The speech that he had just heard was one that ought to have been made by Lucy's uncle, General Everton; and yet was not General Everton dead; and had not Lucy herself been accused of his murder, and brought out actually to suffer death on the infamous charge?

"This is a dream—this is a dream!" said Duval, as he pressed his hands over his eyes. "This can be nothing but a dream, compounded of the story I have heard from Lucy, and my own imagination in regard to the guilt of Mossy Pendell, and the murder of her uncle."

There was another mystery, too, connected with the whole affair, which might well assist in inducing a belief in the mind of Claude Duval that he was the victim of some delusion, and that was the strangely distinct manner in which the voices came upon his ears, at the same time that he felt confident no one was present in that apartment but himself.

Pendell spoke again.

"I promise you perfect freedom. I promise you likewise an income, which will be sufficient to enable you to pass the remainder of your years in peace and comfort."

"And if I still refuse?" asked the wailing voice.

"I swear by all that men hold sacred, you shall not live till morning."

Claude Duval might wonder where the voices came from, but he could have no doubt about the direction from which they proceeded.

He crept close to the wall of the room which separated the secret chamber where poor General Everton was a prisoner from that apartment.

He passed his hand over that wall.

A portion of it slightly moved.

It was the tall, artfully concealed door in the panel which Mossy Pendell had not thought it worth while to pull close shut after him.

"Murder!" shrieked the wailing voice.

"Take your death," cried Pendell, "since you will have it!"

"Help—help!"

"There is no help for you in this world; and as I do not believe in another, I may say there is no help at all."

Duval pushed the narrow panelled door wide open.

"Your faith fails you both ways!" he cried loudly. "Mossy Pendell, there is help here for your victim, although there may be none hereafter for you!"

Pendell uttered a shriek of dismay.

As Claude Duval stood in the doorway of that concealed apartment, his back was towards the light on the table in the outer room, so that his whole figure was thrown into bold relief notwithstanding that his face was in shadow, and it might have been difficult at the moment actually to recognise him.

Duval was too intent upon frustrating the evil intentions of Mossy Pendell, to notice that an old white-haired man fell in a swoon nearly at his feet, as he stepped into that narrow chamber.

Then Pendell made an effort to escape, but it only required for Claude Duval to put out an arm, and he was arrested.

"Villain!" cried Duval; "this night I have already

executed summary justice upon your associate in crime, Lord Horlop. I scarcely hoped for the pleasure of ridding the world of two such fiends within so short a time."

Pendell sunk to the floor.

The action was so sudden that he wrenched himself from the grasp of Claude Duval, and availing himself of his momentary freedom, he scrambled to the door of the apartment, and was out on to the corridor before Duval could determine what to do.

That determination, however, was, of course, to pursue him; and it was sufficiently quickly formed to bring Claude sharply upon the heels of the fugitive.

As chance would have it, Mossy Pendell rushed into the very apartment that Duval had entered by the window which he had opened from without.

That window still swung idly open in the night air.

Frantic with fear, Pendall took but one leap, and passed through the opening into the garden.

Duval was scarcely inclined to follow him, and paused for a few seconds to note which way he went.

"Hold!" he cried, "or I fire!"

A shout of fear, and half of derision, came from Mossy Pendell, and he was so fast disappearing among the trees, that Duval saw the necessity of instant pursuit if he would not wholly lose him.

To leap from the window was one thing, and a reckless, hazardous thing, likewise; but to descend by means of the rose and ivy stems was not difficult.

Duval was quickly in the garden, but Mossy Pendell had disappeared, and the ten minutes search in it was perfectly fruitless.

Vexed and chagrined that he had allowed the villain to escape him, Duval hastened back to the house.

By the same route which he had pursued in leaving it, he made his way to the same chamber again.

The light still burned on the table in the outer room, but upon raising it and taking it with him into the narrow, unsuspected apartment beyond, Duval was surprised to see that it was perfectly untenanted, and there was no one for him either to save or to sympathise with.

"Speak!" he cried; "if any one requiring aid is concealed in this place. I am no enemy. Speak, and be assured I come as a friend, to assist and to save."

All was still.

Again and again did Claude Duval, with the idea upon his mind that there might be some hiding-place that escaped his observation, call upon that whitehaired man, whoever he might be, to declare himself.

There was no response to these repeated invitations, and then after half an hour spent in rambling from room to room in Camden House, Duval saw from one of the eastern windows that dawn was rapidly approaching.

He left the old mansion regretfully, and recovering his horse, he made the best of his way to Hampstead Heath, determined to relate to Lucy the interesting events of the night, or to consult her, perhaps, calmer judgment in regard to them.

A long slant ray of morning light shone upon the the old tree tops as Duval reached that home which, since it had been adorned by the presence of Lucy, was no longer desolate nor melancholy.

With surprise, not unmingled with some portion of superstitious terror, did Lucy hear of what had hapapened at Camden House.

The description of the white-haired man who had called for help tallied so well with her remembrance of her uncle, that the whole affair became a wonder and a surprise, admitting of no rational explanation.

Was not that uncle in his grave?

Had not even she, Lucy, been accused of his murder?

Had there ever arisen, since those calamitous events until now, the slightest doubt of his decease?

Lost in a maze of conjectures, she could only, over and over again, talk of the matter to Claude Duval, and pray for some solution of the strange, inexplicable mystery.

CHAPTER XVI.

CLAUDE DUVAL VISITS THE MASKED BALL AT QUEENSBERRY HOUSE.

An afternoon sun glances sweetly amid the old trees in the garden of Duval's Hampstead home.

Lucy is resting on his arm, and Duval is carelessly, although with some amount of curiosity, examining the contents of a pocket-book which he had possessed himself of from her ladyship of Queensberry, on the occasion of that remarkable cotillion in the Strand.

He took a card from it.

"Behold, Lucy!" he said. "Here is a card of invitation to a masked ball at Queensbury House!"

Lucy looked up in his face.

"You have not said it, Claude; but you mean to go."

Duval smiled.

"Shall I own," he said, "that I have the greatest desire to show myself at that assembly, although I must confess that the life I like best is that upon the road? Give me a cloudy sky, and the green turf beneath my horse's feet. I prefer all that to the sickly life of gilded saloons, whatever might be the profit of attaching myself to their fashionable frivolities."

"Then why go to this masked ball, Claude? It seems to me that to you it must be full of danger."

"Perhaps. But then, you know, danger is the atmosphere in which I live and breathe; so, for once, let me proceed to it, if for no other purpose than to hear what the great fashionable world has to say of Claude Duval."

Lucy no longer opposed Claude's disposition to this adventure; but she made him promise that he would return betimes, after having satisfied himself in regard to what was the current gossip of the day, both in respect to himself, and to her escape from an ignominious death.

Duval rode to town between eight and nine o'clock in the evening, for the fashionable entertainments at that period commenced at a much earlier hour than they do now, however they might be protracted into the small hours of the morning.

On this occasion, Duval took his man Blossom with him; and upon reaching the neighbourhood of Queensberry House Duval gave him his final instructions.

"You will put up the horses, Blossom, anywhere in this neighbourhood you think proper; but by one o'clock in the morning see that you be in waiting for me just within the palings of the Green Park, yonder."

"All right, Captain; you won't have to look for me twice."

"That I well know. And now, farewell for the present."

Masked balls at that period were a fashionable entertainment still, although they were certainly in their decadence.

The very high nobility and cream of the aristocracy of the country were beginning to repudiate that species of entertainment, which could not but carry with it a great amount of vulgarity.

Some very notable and scandalous intrigues likewise

had been concocted and carried out at these masked balls; so that the fashion for holding them was gradually descending in the scale of society.

This one at Queensberry House was the last ever held beneath the roof of that mansion.

And, as we see at present, when a drawing-room or levee is held at St. James's Palace there are Court suits to be hired in the immediate neighbourhood; so, when a masked ball at the time of which we write was held in one of the great houses of London, costumes, masks, disguises, and dominos could be hired to any extent in the immediate vicinity of the place of meeting.

Claude Duval repaired to one of these places, and over the complete highwayman's dress he wore he placed what was called a domino, which merely consisted of a cloak with sleeves that reached from the throat to the heels, completely shrouding whatever dress was worn beneath, and forming, with the assistance of a mask, a much more perfect disguise than any costume—properly so called—could produce.

Many of these dominos were so made that they could be turned with ease, looking quite perfect upon either side, and presenting at the same time a total dissimilarity of colour.

Duval took care that the one he provided himself with possessed that convenience.

His next step was to hire a sedan chair, of which there were numbers to be had at every turning; and taking care to keep in his hand the card of admission he had accidentally become possessed of, he gave orders to be carried at once to Queensberry House.

The crowd was immense.

The reputation of the Queensberry family did not stand very high, but inasmuch as the vast majority of persons who frequented such entertainments were themselves of doubtful character, there was no hindrance to the saloons of the lordly mansion being excessively crowded.

It was with great difficulty that Claude Duval's sedan chair reached the entrance hall.

Once there, however, there was no further obstruction.

His ticket of admission was hastily glanced at, and then torn in two, one half being flung into a basket ready there for the reception of such fragments, and the other being handed back to him.

This precaution was taken in case of any of the masks wishing to retire or change their dominos, and then requiring admission again to the saloons.

Up the grand staircase into the principal ball-room of the mansion Duval made his way, not without some difficulty, for the thoroughfare was crowded with maskers.

The sight that met his eyes upon fairly entering the brilliant saloon transcended anything he had imagined in the way of brilliancy and effect.

At least six hundred persons were there present, in every variety of costume that all the varied climes of the world could suggest.

There was no difficulty in mingling in such a throng and being wholly unobserved, but, as chance would have it, Duval trod on the skirts of a domino worn by a gentleman who turned round rather fiercely to question him.

The gentleman was masked, but Duval had no difficulty in recognising the tones of the Duke of Montrose, with whom he had had the adventure on Hampstead Heath, when accompanied by the Marquis of Harcourt.

"You are clumsy, sir!" said the Duke.

"Very, sir," said Duval.

"You admit it, sir?"

"It would be so rude to contradict your Grace."

"Ah, you know me?"

"Who can mistake those dulcet tones?"

"Pshaw, sir! you rather exceed the license even of a masquerade."

"And you fall short of it," said Duval; "for you have not the wit to keep yourself concealed."

"Sir," said the Duke, in tones of anger, "if it were not that a quarrel in such a place as this is quite out of the question, I should feel inclined to have one with you; but since by some accident you know who I am, it is but fair that I should know you."

"I have no objection."

"Well, sir—your name?"

"I am Claude Duval, the celebrated highwayman!"

The Duke of Montrose stamped on the floor passionately.

"Stuff, sir!" he said. "That is a silly jest."

Duval laughed, and the Duke, after darting at him a furious look through the eye-holes of his mask, abruptly left him and mingled with the throng.

"I find," said Duval, to himself, "that the best way of concealing who I really am, is to proclaim myself by my real name, which no one will believe. I need not have troubled myself about this domino, and will get rid of it, for in my actual costume as Claude Duval, I shall only be considered to be supporting an excellent character at the masquerade."

There was no real difficulty in getting rid of his domino.

Various small apartments opened from the grand saloon in which refreshments were laid, but as the evening was yet young they had not been resorted to by any of the company.

It was a daring thing for Claude Duval to do, but he made his way into one of these little apartments, and loosening the string that held the domino round his neck, he let it slip from him, stepping out of it as it lay upon the floor, fully attired in that rich and fanciful costume which we have described sufficiently minutely before.

From his coat pockets Duval took a pair of pistols, and, releasing one button of his vest, he thrust them in so that their butts only were visible.

From another pocket he took a coiled-up riding-whip, and then carefully adjusting his mask upon his face, he certainly presented in the most striking manner the character of a highwayman who might just have dismounted from his horse.

"Don't mention it," he whispered to the first mask he met after coming out of the room in which he had effected this little transaction,—"don't mention it; but I am Claude Duval, the highwayman!"

"Capital!" said the mask.

In less than five minutes it was rumoured throughout the whole saloon that one of the best personations at the ball was that of Claude Duval, the celebrated and gallant ladies' highwayman.

Duval found himself the observed of all observers; and as it was certainly not difficult for him to play his own part, he gathered great credit for his supposed ability.

A clapping of hands now announced the commencement of a dance.

A burst of music resounded through the saloon; and Duval, stepping up to a lady attired as Juno, gallantly requested her hand in the figure that was about to commence.

"Indeed," said the lady, "I have reason to refuse Claude Duval, since I have had a remarkable adventure with him."

Claude almost regretted, at the moment, that he had addressed this lady, for he felt confident that she was none other than the Marchioness of Queensberry herself.

But there was no retreat.

She clung to his arm, and Duval was forced to lead her into the throng of dancers.

DUVAL DISCOVERS THE DEAD BODY OF THE STRANGE LADY.

A faint scream came from a lady in a domino, who, with her partner, a knight in steel armour, was immediately opposite to Duval and the Marchioness of Queensberry in the dance.

"The lady is unwell," said Duval.

"Oh, no," said the Marchioness; "it is her odious affectation!"

"Indeed!"

"Yes; and if it were right to do so, I could tell you who she is, notwithstanding her mask.

"I have almost a right," said Duval, "to know who everybody is, since I so honestly and openly declare who I am!"

"Oh, nonsense!"

"Nay, I speak but the truth, when I declare myself to be Claude Duval, the highwayman!"

"You support the character excellently; but I think you are the young Earl of Sefton."

"Indeed, no; but nevertheless you will much oblige me if you will tell me who the lady really is in the yellow domino opposite."

"If you must know," said the Marchioness, lowering her voice to a whisper, "it is that odious little piece of affectation, the Duchess of Cleveland!"

"Ah, indeed!"

The dance at this moment commencing, prevented any further remarks, for our ancestors used to dance in earnest, and not merely lazily drag through a quadrille, as is the present fashion.

The figure was over.

But the Marchioness still clung to the arm of her highwayman partner.

"I, too, have had an adventure with the veritable Claude Duval!"

"Is that possible?"

"Yes. I was in my travelling chariot, at rather a late hour, in the Strand, when I was actually stopped by him; and he had the assurance to inform me, with a great many flourishes that I need not repeat to you, how enamoured he was of me; and how, on that very evening, he had risked his liberty and life purely for the purpose of dancing a cotillion with me as his partner."

"Ah!" said Duval, "the fellow is deceitful."

"I hardly think so."

"Yes, he would say all that merely for the purpose of robbing you."

"Indeed, sir, you are mistaken."

"Nay; when I play a part, I am never mistaken about any of its details. I seem to know everything that Claude Duval would do."

"No!"

"Yes; what is more wonderful still, I seem to know everything that he has done!"

"Then, perhaps," said the Marchioness, who was a little amused and a little angry,—" then, perhaps, you will tell me exactly what did happen on the occasion I refer to in the Strand!"

"Let me see!" said Duval, affecting to be in deep thought—"let me see! Oh, yes, I see it now! There is a travelling carriage, in which sits the Marchioness of Queensberry——"

"Ah!"

"And a young lady with rather a pale face, and her hair in ringlets——"

The Marchioness started.

"The carriage is driven by a boy postilion, and it is stopped near to Somerset House!"

"Good gracious!" exclaimed the Marchioness. "You must either be Claude Duval or the——"

"Don't mention him, my lady; and as for being Claude Duval, I have been assuring everybody that I am that very personage ever since I came into this saloon!"

"You amaze and confound me; and yet I cannot believe that you are playing a part, and I believe you to be now the Chevalier de Evremont!"

"Madam, I assure you I am Claude Duval!"

"If I thought you were——"

"What then?"

"I should instantly give you into charge of the constables!"

"Oh, no, madam; having once honoured me with your hand in a cotillion, you could not do such an ill turn to your partner! But to convince you that I am indeed Claude Duval, I will tell you that, on that delightful occasion in the Strand, a certain pocket-book was taken from you!"

"It was—it was! But I can easily comprehend now, that, in order to play your part here well to-night, you have either bribed the postilion who drove my carriage to give you all these particulars, or you have them from my niece, Lady Olive St. Clair!"

"You are very incredulous, Marchioness!"

"There you are wrong, too—I am not a Marchioness!"

"It is so rude to contradict a lady; but if you are not the Marchioness of Queensberry, then I admit that I am not Claude Duval! However, as you will not believe the latter assertion, I must prove it to you! Pocket-book, come hither!"

"Eh?"

"Pocket-book, come hither!"

In one of the pockets of his coat Duval had that very identical pocket-book in which he had found the ticket for admission to the masked ball.

The Marchioness of Queensberry leant upon his left arm, but Duval, insinuating his right hand into his pocket, grasped the book, and flinging it dexterously behind his back up into the air, it seemed to descend as if from the ceiling in front of himself and the Marchioness, when Duval caught it.

"There, my lady," he said. "Are you convinced now?"

The Marchioness uttered a loud scream.

She slipped from the arm of Duval to the floor, and he seized the opportunity of immediately mingling with the throng around them.

There was a rush of maskers of all sorts, ages, and conditions in that direction.

The Marchioness of Queensberry had fainted, and for about five minutes the greatest confusion reigned in the saloon.

Duval stepped into the recess of a window.

"Why am I here?" he said. "What good do I do in this place? I have frightened a woman, and, as yet, heard nothing of what I wish to learn!"

"And what may you wish to learn?" said a voice.

A gentlemanly-looking man, attired in a very old Court suit, was taking a pinch of snuff, and quietly looking at Duval from a few paces distant.

"I wish to learn," said Duval, "what has become of Lucy Everton, and what the impression is in high quarters concerning her future fate."

"The impression," said the gentleman, "certainly is that she will be hanged yet for the murder of her uncle, the General; and as for her rescue by Claude Duval, that only adds one to the catalogue of his offences, all of which he will have to expiate upon the scaffold?"

"When he is caught," said Duval.

"He is caught."

"Indeed!"

"Yes. Do you know me?"

"I have not that honour."

"The character, then, that I support at this masquerade is that of Philip St. Ives."

"Philip St. Ives! And who may he be?"

"A gentleman, but who has thought proper to allow his Majesty's Government the benefit of his services as a detective of great criminals and great crimes."

"Well, sir?"

"You are detected. Claude Duval, I arrest you in the name of the King!"

"Excellent!" said Duval; "we shall produce quite a sensation. Of course, I appear to yield!"

"Appear to yield?"

"Yes; I keep up my character, and you yours. I want to go home, as I am rather tired of this affair. It will be a capital incident of the ball, and make a paragraph in the *Mercury* of to-morrow morning, of how well the character of a detective police-officer was sustained by one gentleman, and that of Claude Duval by another."

"But I am a Government detective!" cried St. Ives in a loud tone.

"Very well, sir," roared Duval, at least an octave higher; "and I am Claude Duval!"

St. Ives collared him.

"Capital!" said Duval. "Mind my cravat."

"Come on, sir—come on! Constables! constables! Where are the constables on duty? This is the notorious Claude Duval!"

"I am—I own it," said Duval. "I am at length taken and defeated. I am Claude Duval, and this is Mr. St. Ives, the celebrated detective."

"Bravo! bravo! bravo!" shouted a hundred voices. "Bravo! by Jove! that's well done."

"And so natural," said the ladies.

The detective dragged Duval out from the recess into the middle of the saloon.

CHAPTER XVII.

CLAUDE DUVAL THROWS HIMSELF UPON THE GENEROSITY OF THE DUCHESS OF CLEVELAND.

EVERY action that had been taking place among that large assemblage of persons was now suspended, in order that universal attention might be directed to what was supposed to be an admirably acted drama by two gentlemen, one of whom personated Claude Duval, the highwayman, and the other Mr. St. Ives, the celebrated detective of the police.

Rage, impotence, and fury took possession of St. Ives.

He seemed to see in this admirable manœuvre of Claude Duval's snatched from him all the credit that he would otherwise have obtained by that important capture.

In vain he tried to silence the bravos and plaudits that greeted him on every side.

"I tell you all," he roared, "that this is really Claude Duval!"

"Yes," cried Claude, "and I tell you all that this is really Mr. St. Ives!"

"Bravo—bravo! Hurrah! Capital! Well done! Nothing could be finer! Who are they? It is quite the feature of the masquerade! Bravo—bravo!"

St. Ives would not quit his hold of Claude Duval; and, as the latter forced his way towards the doors of the saloon, the detective was compelled to accompany him.

Fearful, however, of losing his prisoner, St. Ives kept calling out for assistance.

"I call upon you all in the King's name to assist me. Gentlemen, this notorious highwayman will escape, unless you lend me your aid."

Upon this, another round of applause absolutely shook the saloon, and St. Ives saw that it was quite hopeless to contend against the fixed idea present in every one's mind, that he and Duval were two gentlemen only playing a part.

The staircase was reached.

There was still a hope on the part of the detective that he might carry out the arrest, for he knew that there were a couple of constables in the hall below.

"Help—help!" he cried. "An arrest—an arrest!"

"Certainly," said Duval.

As he spoke, he closed with Mr. St. Ives, and thrusting him backward down the staircase, he flung him right into the arms of a man who rushed across the hall to receive him.

"Who is it?" shouted this man.

It was the voice of Muckles, the Bow Street officer.

"Claude Duval!" cried Duval himself.

"Ah! no—a mistake! You are——"

"That individual—I know it! How do you do, Mr. Muckles?"

Duval turned, and in two or three bounds reached the saloon again.

He trod upon the skirts of a lady's dress.

It was the wood-nymph, who had been declared by the Marchioness of Queensberry to be no other than the young and lovely Duchess of Cleveland.

Duval took the fact upon trust, for the lady was masked; and having seen her but once before, he was not sufficiently acquainted with her general appearance to come to a conclusion with regard to her identity.

A bold reliance, however, upon the generosity of the Duchess might yet save him.

She was remarkably short and *petite* in figure, so that Duval had to stoop low to whisper in her ear.

"Madam, I am really that unfortunate Claude Duval, who, hunted by his enemies, throws himself this night upon your generous mercy."

"Ah!" cried the Duchess; "I know that voice."

"I am blessed in the recollection," said Duval. "It is the same voice that thanked you for condescending to dance with him one moonlight night."

"I have told the story," said the Duchess, "a hundred times, and with all the more pleasure that it has been a source of constant irritation to the Marchioness of Queensberry."

"How these women hate each other!" thought Duval. "Yes," he whispered again; "I know it is so. But if you will take my arm, and say that you know me to be young Lord Adderley, you may save me."

"What—my cousin?"

"Yes, I am aware that Lord Adderley is your cousin, and such being the case, your word would be taken for my identity.

"But really——"

"Do not, I implore you, force me to apply to the Marchioness of Queensberry for that merciful consideration which I would fain owe to one so infinitely fairer and more lovely."

"I will do it."

"Then I am safe."

"You are a wicked, impudent man!"

"Alas! I know it."

"There he is—there he is!" shouted St. Ives. "Come on, Muckles—follow me! There's your man!"

"I see him," replied Muckles. "Come on, Swallow—follow me!"

"I'm here, Mr. Muckles."

The whole three made a rush forward; but the Countess of Cleveland uttered two piercing shrieks, in a high tenor voice, and clung only the more closely to Claude Duval.

"What is the meaning of all this?" she cried.

"The meaning, madam," said St. Ives, "is that whoever you may be, you now rest on the arm of a highwayman."

"A highwayman?"

"Yes, madam. That is Claude Duval."

The Duchess of Cleveland burst into a shrill laugh.

It was evident that Mr. St. Ives had not the least idea of her quality.

"Mr. Muckles," he said, "keep the door; and now, madam, whoever you are, don't obstruct me in my duty."

"Your duty, sir?"

"Yes, madam, my duty."

"Do you know who I am?"

"I neither know nor care, madam; but it is quite evident you are a good friend to Claude Duval; and so, I suppose, you are some lady from the Mint, or St. Giles's, to whom he is to pass his plunder."

The Duchess raised her little person to its utmost height.

"Gentlemen all," she said, "since I am to be insulted in this manner by a vulgar constable, it becomes necessary that I shou'd call upon you for help!"

"Shame! shame!" shouted several young men. "Shame! shame! Turn the fellows out; we don't want constables here!"

St. Ives began to be hustled.

"At your peril, all of you!" he cried. "At your peril! I declare that man to be Claude Duval, the highwayman, and I arrest him!"

"This Claude Duval?" screamed the Duchess.

"I have said it!"

"This gentleman?"

"No, madam—that highwayman!"

"Ha, ha, ha! Ho, ho, ho! Why this is Lord Adderley, the cousin of the Duchess of Cleveland!"

"Madam, you either mistake, or tell a wilful falsehood!"

"Man!"

"I say, madam, that this is no more Lord Adderley, the cousin of the Duchess of Cleveland, than you are the Duchess of Cleveland herself."

"Indeed!" said the little Duchess, as she again drew herself up to the height of her small figure, and twitching off her mask at the same moment, she exhibited to the hundreds of eyes that were bent upon her, the well-known features of the little beauty of the Court, the Duchess of Cleveland herself.

St. Ives fell back, treading unmercifully upon the toes of Muckles.

There was a profound silence for a few seconds, which was broken by one voice calling out in half-frantic tones, "Done brown again!"

"I'll do you brown!" cried Muckles, as he turned upon Swallow, and caught him by the throat.

Some twenty or thirty gentlemen rushed now to the aid of the Duchess, and St. Ives was effectually separated from his prey.

"Imprudent man!" whispered the Duchess; "what could tempt you to risk your destruction by coming here?"

"A magnet!"

"A what?"

"A magnet of attraction!"

"I do not understand you."

"Its other name is Cleveland."

The Duchess shook her head.

"This must not be; it is necessary that you should take your departure at once, as I cannot undertake to be your champion, and to save you from your crimes and indiscretions."

"I have encountered some danger," said Duval, "but I am sufficiently repaid since I have had the happiness of again beholding one who——"

"Hold!" said the Duchess. "I must not, and will not hear such expressions. Step this way, and you will be in safety."

"Into this dark room?"

"Yes; it is surely better than the lightest cell in Newgate."

"Infinitely!"

"At its further extremity you will find a door that leads to the back staircase of Queensberry House; avail yourself of it, and escape at once."

"Farewell!" said Duval; "and while memory holds a seat in this distracted globe——"

"Silence!" cried the Duchess; "I can hear a tumult in the saloon, and, in another minute, it may be too late even for me to save you."

Duval made his way across the dark apartment, and found the door that had been mentioned to him.

A flight of dimly-lighted stairs lay beyond it, which he descended rapidly, and found himself in the midst of a throng of the female servants of Queensberry House, who were listening to the music, and endeavouring to catch what glimpses they could of the gay scene that was taking place above.

At sight of so brilliant an apparition as Claude Duval alighting among them, there was, of course, a great commotion.

"Ladies," said Duval, as he lifted his hat, "ladies, I beg you will not be alarmed!"

"Oh, dear! who is it?" cried every voice, in chorus.

"Nay, do not fly from me; I am one of the most harmless of individuals, which you will easily believe when I mention to you that I am Claude Duval, the highwayman."

There was a scream and a rush to escape; but Claude Duval caught one of the damsels before she could leave the spot; and arresting her progress, spoke to her in his gentlest tones.

"I am rather a stranger in this part of the house; be so good as to show me the way into the street, and I shall be for ever your debtor."

"Oh, murder! and are you really Claude Duval?"

"I am."

"That danced with the Duchess of Cleveland?"

"The same."

"And then with the Marchioness of Queensberry?"

"Exactly. But my crowning exploit was kissing pretty Mary, one of the household of Queensberry House."

"Gracious Providence! Don't do it again! My name is Jane!"

"I must!" said Claude; "as the first seems to have been a mistake! And now show me the way into the street, for my life hangs upon a thread!"

"Oh, dear, yes—this way—this way! His life hangs upon a needle and thread!"

The pretty housemaid soon escorted Duval into the open air, and he made his way as quickly as he possibly could towards the Green Park, where he hoped to find Blossom awaiting him with Nightshade, although the hour had certainly not come when he had ordered their presence there.

Westminster clock struck eleven.

The night was still young; but Claude Duval had had quite enough of the crowded saloons of Queensberry House.

The cool, fresh, open air was infinitely grateful to him; and when he reached the railings, through which he could look into the Green Park, he drew a long breath of intense relief, that he had escaped so well from the perils that had environed him.

He could see nothing of Nightshade, however.

The splashing of the fountain which then existed in an obscure corner of the Green Park, came distinctly upon his ears; and, as the gate was closed, he proceeded leisurely to climb over it, convinced that, by some excuse or another, Blossom would make his way within the enclosure to meet him.

Before Duval could descend on the other side of the gate, there came a flaring light from several links across the road.

"There he is! There he is!" shouted a voice. "There he is, getting over a gate into the Park!"

"Fire!"

Bang! went a pistol-shot.

The bullet hit one of the iron bars of the gate, and flattening itself out to the size of a penny piece, fell harmlessly to the ground.

"Thank you, Mr. St. Ives!" said Duval. "We shall meet again."

He ran some distance across the soft turf, and then paused to look around him as well as he could in the darkness.

A black-looking object was at a short distance from him.

Was it a horse?

Duval ran forward.

"Blossom! Nightshade!"

"All right, Captain; here you are!"

"Then all is right indeed! How did you get into the Park, Blossom? for I scarcely considered the difficulty of doing so when I desired you to be here."

"It's easy to leap the low wall by the Birdcage Walk, Captain."

"True, true; but you are so much before your time."

"I hope that is better, Captain, than being one minute beyond it; and Nightshade has been quite amusing himself by nipping off the short, sweet grass of the Park here."

The flare of the links carried by Claude Duval's pursuers still gleamed through the gate of the Green Park; but no one seemed inclined to risk the consequences of pursuing the daring highwayman into the darkness of the open space beyond.

CHAPTER XVIII.

CLAUDE DUVAL PURSUES THE SPECTRE HORSEMAN IN THE GREEN PARK.

"CAPTAIN," said Blossom, "let us get out of this as quick as we can. You know I am not afraid of mortal man; but I don't want to meet the ghost on its round."

"The what?" exclaimed Duval.

"Why, Captain, have you never heard that at twelve o'clock, in St. James's Park, every night, a spectre horse and spectre horseman move down the Mall and disappears close by the clump of trees that they say were planted by Queen Elizabeth?"

"What absurdity!" exclaimed Duval; "but, should there be a chance of meeting this spectre, I would fain take that route."

"Nay," said Blossom; "I would rather attack flesh and blood, even on the chance of a stray bullet or two; and, if I might advise, Captain, the sooner we get out of this place the better."

"Peace!" cried Duval; "I hear some one coming!"

It was quite evident that Blossom entertained a lively fear of the supposed supernatural being who was said to haunt St. James's Park at that midnight hour.

And, perhaps, Claude Duval was not himself altogether free from such impulses and sensations. Curiosity, however, was a powerful motive in his organization.

He determined, at least, to remain in the Park until the old Abbey clock of Westminster had struck the hour of midnight.

That time was not far distant; and, shrouded by the trees, Duval and his men got, by degrees, accustomed to the dim obscurity of the night air, and felt perfectly certain nothing could pass them without observation.

Suddenly Blossom grasped the arm of Duval.

"Look, Captain, look! what is that?"

The object that presented itself, coming down the Mall, was not in any way alarming to look at; but it was the perfectly silent mode of its progression which gave it a supernatural character.

It seemed to be a horseman; and it appeared but reasonable and rational to suppose that the horse's feet would make some sound upon the hard roadway.

Such, however, was not the case; for, although the supposed horseman came on with surprising quickness, not the slightest sound of the animal's feet could be heard.

Another singularity of the whole appearance likewise was the exceeding smallness of both horse and rider.

Claude Duval certainly looked on with some amazement as this apparition—if apparition it were—passed him and Blossom.

"There, Captain, there!" cried Blossom, almost panting for breath, in the excitement of the moment,—"there, Captain, you see it now, and there can be no further doubt about it.!"

"I see something!"

"The apparition!"

"So you say, Blossom; but I have my doubts. Let us follow it!"

"Not for worlds, Captain; it's unlucky!"

"For whom?" laughed Duval; "the apparition, or for us?"

"For us, or for any one who goes after it!"

"Very well, Blossom, I will take my chance; and, having no desire to bring ill-luck upon you, I will follow it alone."

Duval did not wait for any further remonstrances from his man Blossom, but, urging Nightshade forward, he made a dash after the singularly small horse and rider.

The apparition came to a dead stand-still, and this was an occurrence which more convinced Duval than ever of the terrestrial character of the appearance.

"Halt!" he cried,—"halt!"

An odd sort of sound, which certainly was suggestive of alarm, came from the small rider on his small steed; and then the seeming apparition darted forward with increased speed.

Under ordinary circumstances, Nightshade would very quickly have put an end to the chase, but the silent horse and rider had but a couple of hundred yards to go before it reached the iron railings that divided St. James's Park from Spring Gardens.

At that spot, suddenly, and without any apparent means of doing so, the singular object disappeared.

Claude Duval reined in Nightshade, and looked warily about him.

And now there were but two circumstances which Duval considered to be singular, and requiring explanation.

One of these circumstances was the perfect silence with which the small horse—if horse it were—had succeeded in traversing the Mall.

The other was the mysterious disappearance at the iron railings, as much before his eyes as it could be said to be in the darkness that reigned about the spot at that hour of the night.

There was but one trivial circumstance which still impressed Duval with a conviction that some trick was in the whole affair.

That circumstance was just this.

At the moment of the disappearance of the supposed apparition, he had heard, or fancied he had heard, a slight sound like the closing of an iron gate.

Dismounting rapidly from Nightshade, Duval cautiously examined the railings, close to which the spectre horseman had disappeared.

There was an iron gate.

One of those gates that led into a garden at the back of a tall, gloomy-looking house that abutted upon the Park.

That garden was very small, however; there did not seem to be any hiding-places in it of sufficient importance to conceal even so small a horse as that ridden by the apparition.

Claude's speculations, however, upon the mysterious occurrence were quickly put an end to by events that called upon all his courage, and all his vigilance, to encounter.

As he stood by Nightshade, various noises from different parts of the Park convinced him that he certainly no longer held it alone with his follower, Blossom.

From the direction of the Horse Guards, as well as from Buckingham House, at the other end of the long Mall, the tramp of horses' feet could be heard rapidly approaching.

Duval mounted instantly, and upon the principle that danger, if boldly met, loses one half its peril, he rode up the Mall—not ostentatiously exhibiting himself, but keeping the middle of the way, so that no one could say he betrayed the slightest anxiety for concealment.

In five minutes' time, he was in the midst of a party of horsemen, who, coming to an abrupt halt, began questioning him in many voices.

"One at a time, gentlemen, if you please," said Duval. "What do you require of me?"

"Your money or your life!" was the quick reply.

"The lantern—the lantern!" cried another.

"Ay, ay!" shouted a third; "this should be a rich spark by the texture of his coat."

Duval was somewhat surprised at these expressions in such a place; and, when the light of a lantern gleamed upon his face, it wore an expression of more amused surprise than fear.

"Now, sir!" said one of the party of horsemen; "whoever you are, please to make short work with us. We have possession of the Park for the next two hours, and let no one pass up and down the Mall without a heavy toll."

"Indeed!"

"Yes," said another; "and so heavy an one that it can only be paid by watch, pocket-book, rings, purse, and every article of value you have about you."

"Ah!" said Duval quietly; "I begin to understand. You are footpads!"

"Footpads! Do we not ride as good horses as any gentlemen in the land?"

"Oh, no!" said Duval. "You are mounted on them, it is true, but I can very well perceive that none of you can ride. You are footpads, from Westminster, and should the patrol from the Horse Guards come among you, your chance would be small indeed."

"We don't want advice, but plunder."

"Listen!" said Duval.

The thieves—for such they were—all turned instinctively in the direction to which he pointed.

At a quiet trot across the broad, open space in front of the Horse Guards, was approaching the night patrol, whose duty it was to go round the Park between the hours of twelve and one.

"Now, gentlemen," said Duval, "what do you think of your position?"

"It's off and away, that's all!" cried one who appeared to be a leader. "But we have not done with you yet. Now, sir! Is it to be a bullet, or are we to part good friends?"

Duval lifted his hat, and spoke in an imperious tone.

"I might leave you all," he said, "to your fate; and know not, exactly, why I should not do so. Your haunt is in Western House."

"Ah! He knows us!"

"Yes; and you should know me, but that your eyes are blinded by a thousand fears."

That the footpads were in some state of confusion was evident by the manner in which they impeded each other as they crowded round Claude Duval.

"A plant! a plant!" cried one. "He only seeks to betray us! We are detained until the patrol will be upon us!"

"Hush!" said Duval. "Listen!"

From the neighbourhood of the Green Park, and from Buckingham House, from Spring Gardens, and from the Birdcage Walk, came unmistakable indications in the way of sound that the Park was being guarded and surrounded on all sides by the authorities.

"We are lost," said one of the footpads, "and are fallen into a trap!"

"Then down with this fellow!" cried another; "for he is at the bottom of this mischief!"

"No," said the one who had previously spoken; "I will have no violence while there is a doubt in regard to who this gentleman is; but I promise him that if he is a spy upon us, I will hunt him out, for I shall know him again among a thousand."

"That speech," said Duval, "has saved you all. I am convinced from what I see and hear that the Park is completely surrounded. Will you trust to me to save you?"

There was a momentary pause on the part of the footpads, and then they replied, with one voice, "We will—we will!"

"It is wisely decided," said Duval. "Wait here for me, and I will rejoin you in a few seconds."

The military patrol from the Horse Guards had by this time made their way over three parts of the open space before that ancient building.

"Halt!" cried Claude Duval, as he proceeded to meet them at a canter—"halt!"

The tone was one of such great authority, that the military patrol came to a standstill.

"Is this party commanded by an officer?" asked Duval, in the same high, curt tones.

"No, sir," replied a voice; "I am a sergeant."

"Then take your orders from me."

"I don't know that, sir!"

"You don't know that, knave? Is a general officer and a peer of the realm to be thus spoken to?"

"Beg pardon, General! I did not know——"

"Let it pass—let it pass! You will continue your route in this direction no further. A strong party of footpads, or highwaymen—I know not which—are in the Park. You will take your way round by the Birdcage Walk, and I will meet you, with my escort, going in the other direction."

"Yes, General!"

"You will recollect that the password of the night is 'St. George.'"

"Beg pardon, General; but our captain said it was 'Cornet.'"

"It is altered. See that you forget it not!"

Claude Duval saw the flash of the sergeant's sword as he saluted him, and then turning his troops in the direction indicated by the supposed General, the mystified non-commissioned officer trotted off towards the Birdcage Walk.

Duval immediately made his way back to the party of footpads.

"Follow me!" he said; "and do so without hesitation, or you are lost. We shall be able to leave the Park by the small gate at Pimlico; and once out of it, the sooner you separate yourselves the better. Blossom! Blossom! Ho, Blossom!"

"Here, Captain!"

"He's a captain, you see," murmured some of the footpads. "Don't trust him!"

"It is over," said Duval. "I force my services on no men; but when you relate this story, and how you have been all captured in the Park, do not lay the blame upon Claude Duval."

"Stoop, Captain—stoop!" shouted Blossom.

Duval did so, right down to his horse's neck.

The action was not a moment too soon; for a rattling volley from the carbines of the military patrol at this moment whistled over his and Blossom's head, wounding some of the footpads, and creating intense confusion among them.

By a natural impulse, and without dictating the movement to each other, Duval and Blossom urged their horses into one of the side avenues of the Park.

They proceeded at a gallop, then, towards Spring Gardens, and succeeded in passing the patrol.

But their perils were by no means over, since every gate of the Park was strongly guarded by the military.

"It's a trap, Captain—it's a trap!" murmured Blossom.

"But not for us."

"I hope not. Ah, Captain, look there! I knew we should have no luck if once we clapped eyes on the spectre of the Mall!"

Close to the iron railings at which it had disappeared before, stood that small, supernatural horse and horseman.

"Not so," said Duval. "We will convert this into good, instead of evil, fortune."

"Stand, Nightshade—stand!"

Duval almost flung himself from the saddle, in his haste to dismount.

He made a rush towards the spectre horseman; but before he could reach the spot on which it stood, the object had disappeared again, and again came upon the ears of Duval the unmistakable sound of the closing of an iron gate.

"Blossom!"

"Yes, Captain!"

"I am determined to dive to the heart of this mystery. No one will interfere with you, if you remain here in the Park with the horses."

"I don't know that, Captain."

"Ah, a better plan still! Ride in here. The gate has yielded to my touch. We shall be in good quarters, let what will happen in the Park of old St. James's to-night."

By shaking at a part of the iron railings through which the small mysterious man and horse had disappeared, Duval succeeded in opening a gate; and as Blossom had taken the reins of Nightshade, he quietly trotted in on his own horse, leading the sagacious steed of Claude Duval by his side.

Then Claude closed the gate.

It made exactly the sound he had heard before.

"Good!" he said. "We shall this night come at the mystery of this much-dreaded spectre of St. James's."

CHAPTER XIX.

CLAUDE DUVAL FINDS HIMSELF IN INTIMATE CONNEXION WITH ROYALTY.

The garden adjoining the house was very small, but it was densely wooded.

There was no difficulty in exploring its length and width in a few seconds, and yet, while unexplored, it might have afforded shelter for half-a-dozen horses with ease.

Duval was a little surprised, however, to find no traces of the small steed ridden by the supposed spectre.

Blossom seemed rather rejoiced than otherwise at this new perplexity.

"You see, Captain," he said, "it was a ghost, after all!"

"And the ghost of a horse," rejoined Duval.

Blossom was silenced, but far from being convinced.

They both paused now for a few minutes, listening to the tumult going on in the Park between the patrol and the footpads.

"They must take their chance," said Duval. "I had a kind of fellow-feeling for them, and might have saved them."

"They are nothing to us, Captain," said Blossom; "our place is on the road. A cloudy sky, and a springy turf beneath our horses' feet, or, may be, a dusty or muddy roadway, where, in the shadow of the tall trees, we can cry, 'Stand and deliver!' to every horseman or every vehicle that passes!"

"You get quite poetical, Blossom," said Duval; "but I can well understand what you mean. You reproach me for lingering here among houses and gardens, and for troubling myself about masked balls and entertainments in gilded saloons. And you are right, Blossom; for those are not my vocations, and I shall not affect them much. Nevertheless, let us carry out this adventure, and then I mean to set up a toll bar upon Hounslow Heath. Keep close with the horses!"

Blossom retired, with Nightshade and his own horse, amid some tall thickets, the luxuriant topmost growth of which grew higher than the horses' heads, and effectually concealed them.

Duval then, on foot, advanced towards the house, which seemed all in profound darkness and repose.

Scanning it attentively from attic to cellars, Duval, owing to the absence of the slightest ray of light from any of its windows, began to doubt the propriety of interfering with the quietude of its inhabitants.

And yet he felt an almost irresistible curiosity to discover the mystery of the small horseman.

There was a flight of stone steps leading from the garden to a door, the upper part of which was glazed.

But the darkness inside the house was too profound to enable Duval to gain any information by looking into the hall.

If however, through that channel of investigation he could gain no information, his ears were open to impressions which soon produced an effect upon him.

Some strange, half-stifled cries came from the interior of the house.

Duval tried the door, but found it fast.

It was not difficult, however, to break one of the panes of glass in the upper portion of it, and that, too, with perfect security to his hands, inasmuch as he now wore the buff leather riding-gloves that usually formed a rather conspicuous part of his costume.

The door was secured by a bolt on the inside, which Duval was now enabled to remove, and in another moment he stepped into the hall.

The air in the house was warm and close, and Duval felt confident that he was not alone in the place, for the indistinct murmur of voices came upon his ears.

Suddenly a door opened.

It was the door of a room to the right hand of the hall.

"I am quite sure," said a voice, "I heard something."

"Your Royal Highness is mistaken," replied another. "A gust of night-wind from the Park always shakes the glass-door."

"It may be so, but he is late."

The door in the hall was closed again.

Duval was left to his conjectures.

Who could that be who was called his Royal Highness, and who, at such a time of night, was in so obscure and unregal a mansion?

There was but one person in the realm entitled to such a prefix to his name.

That was Frederick, the Prince of Wales, son of George the Second, the then reigning monarch, and father to George the Third, who was then in his nonage, and residing in the Palace at Kew.

It is well known that this Frederick, Prince of Wales, dying before his father, left the throne of England as an inheritance to his son George, who in very early life succeeded his grandfather, George the Second.

Unless, then, some person was named Royal Highness who had no right to the appellation, Claude Duval felt that he must certainly be beneath the same roof as Frederick Prince of Wales.

The dissensions and bad feeling between the royal father and son were matters of notoriety; and, indeed, it had been reported, perhaps from the excessive malice of the enemies of both, that there was nothing the King wished so ardently as the death or banishment of his son and heir; and there was nothing the son and heir devoted himself to so strenuously as to make a vacancy for himself on the throne of England.

Duval crept noiselessly along the hall of the house until he came to the door which had been recently opened.

He applied his ear to the panel and listened.

There came the murmur of voices, but he could not distinctly catch the words that were spoken.

As he leant lightly, however, against the door, it yielded a little, and so noiselessly that, although it opened perhaps for the space of an inch, the persons within the apartment took no notice of the circumstance.

Duval was then able to hear everything that passed, although the two persons in that room spoke in low tones.

"Ten thousand a-year," said one, "from the Privy Purse, secured to you under my hand and seal, so that there can be no doubt whatever of your receiving the sum regularly."

"And the barony, your Royal Highness?"

"Well, the barony, too, if you insist upon it. Ab

I suppose worse men have been made barons than an accomplished valet."

"May I suggest to your Royal Highness not to speak so loud?"

For a few seconds now there was silence in that room, and then the voice which belonged to the person addressed as his Royal Highness took up the subject of discourse.

"This will be a good night's work for you," he said. "Ten thousand a-year, a barony, and the good word of the King—for, of course, I shall never forget your services."

"I am all gratitude, your Royal Highness, and devotion; and, indeed, I almost feel that I ought to say your Majesty."

"That would be a little premature."

"For an hour, perhaps."

"Hush! I thought I heard a sound above. Do you think she is moving?"

"Certainly not—the potion is too strong; and if she moves again, your Royal Highness, it will be in a better or a worse world than this."

"Well, I was tired of her; and if she can be made thus useful at the termination of her career, it is better than well."

A faint cry came from the apartment above.

"Fool!" cried his Royal Highness; "you have but half done your work!"

Duval had but just time to step aside, when the door of the room was flung open.

A gleam of light streamed into the hall, and his presence there would most infallibly have been discovered were it not that he was able to slip behind a statue into a half-circular niche that had been made for its reception.

Two men came out into the hall.

One was clinging to the other, in order to keep him back.

"Hands off!" cried the foremost of the two—"hands off! This is too familiar!"

"I crave your Royal Highness's pardon, but would urge you not to interfere. You hear now that all is still."

The faint cry that had arisen from one of the upper rooms was not repeated.

"All is over!" said the person who had been addressed as a valet.

"You think so?"

"I feel certain of it. I, too, heard the cry, and am convinced, from its character, that it was her last."

The Royal Highness, as he was called, had, up to this point, his back to Claude Duval, but now, as he turned, and a gleam of light fell upon his face from the room, Claude recognised him at once as the veritable Frederick Prince of Wales, so well known and so widely execrated for his vices.

But what could all this mean?

Was it a plot against the life of the King?

And, if so, how was it possible to carry it out in that obscure house in Spring Gardens, while the monarch most likely slept soundly beneath the regal roof of St. James's?

But Duval was not left long to conjecture.

Events succeeded each other with tolerable rapidity in that house.

The Prince of Wales and the valet retired again to that room from whence they had emerged, and as the door swung shut the idea came across the mind of Claude Duval that he would like to make his way to the upper apartments of the house, and, if possible, see if murder had there really done its work.

Treading lightly across the hall, he ascended the thickly-carpeted staircase.

A statue on the landing carried a lamp, the glass surrounding which was of amber colour, shedding a golden tint upon all surrounding objects.

Duval had his choice of several doors on this landing, but he opened the first one that presented itself, and stepped into a bedchamber—small, certainly, in its proportions, but furnished with a reckless prodigality of expense that made it a perfect and gorgeous picture to look upon.

It was lit by a hanging lamp, shadowed by stained glasses of rose colour.

And such was the glitter and profusion of the costly articles of furnishing in that apartment, that Duval, although not usually a person liable to a confusion of ideas, was some seconds before he discovered the human occupant of the apartment.

Half-lying on the floor, and half-supported upon a chair, over which her arms were flung, and to the gilt rail at the back of which one hand was convulsively clutched, appeared a female form.

A very rich robe of purple brocade was clasped around the neck of this mysterious personage by a jewel of great price.

From the long floating hair that streamed right down to the rich carpet on the floor of the room, Duval might conjecture that this person was young.

But that could only be conjecture, inasmuch as the face was hidden on the soft yielding cushion of the chair.

Did the lady sleep?

And was that sleep real or feigned?

Surely it was scarcely possible for it to be so profound as not to be broken by Claude Duval's entrance into the room.

Or was it, indeed, true that the fair being whom he saw before him had uttered her last cry.

Treading as lightly as foot could fall, with that instinctive feeling that men have in the presence of the dead, Duval advanced towards the chair.

"Madam!" he said. "Madam!"

There was no movement—no response.

He touched one of the fair, round arms that clung to the chair.

That touch even failed to arouse the sleeper.

Then Duval felt a desire to ascertain if it were death or repose that he saw before him, which overcame all scruples, and he raised the head of the lady from the chair cushion.

One glance was enough.

The face was very fair.

The bloom of youth had but lately rested upon it.

But now, notwithstanding the reflection of that crimson light which would have imparted a glow of health even to the palest and most sickly features, Duval needed no voice to tell him that he looked upon the face of the dead.

He let the head droop again upon the chair.

He gazed around him upon that apartment as if in search of the invisible cause of the catastrophe that had overtaken one so beautiful, and so slightly on the threshold of existence.

There was no apparent cause, unless it could be found in some amber-coloured wine that half-filled a crystal decanter of great beauty, and a small portion of which appeared to have been poured into a tall glass, the stem of which was adorned with jewels.

Not the world's wealth would have tempted Claude Duval to place that amber wine to his lips.

But what was he to do?

That was the question.

Had he sufficient information to enable him to act, and if so, what was his action to be?

Was this fair young girl poisoned by the connivance of his Royal Highness Frederick Prince of Wales, and if so, what, in the history of human emotions, could be the motives for such an act?

CLAUDE DUVAL PRESENTS HIS SWORD TO THE KING.

Had the Prince alluded to her when he spoke of being tired of some one?

If so, that might certainly be a natural enough conclusion.

But wherefore take her life?

What so easy to do as he had done twenty times before, viz., cast her off to sink or swim in the great ocean of society as fortune pleased.

Was he the man to scruple at such an act?—and if he were, was murder the only refuge from it?

These ideas and suppositions rushed through the brain of Claude Duval.

But not for long was he left in that solitary apartment with the dead, to form conjecture upon conjecture in regard to what had led to the commission of the crime.

Something was happening below which seemed likely to bear a relation to what had already happened abov

A shrill whistle sounded; not from the garden adjoining the park, but from the other direction, that is to say, from the usual entrance door of the house, which was in the narrow street portion of Spring Gardens.

Duval hurried to the landing-place on the top of the stairs, and listened.

He heard a door opened and shut.

He heard a heavy footstep.

Then there was a croaking voice, accompanied by a short, dry cough, and a few words floated up to the ears of Claude Duval.

"Well, Norris, well? Is—is all well?"

"All, your Majesty."

"Hush! hush! You strangely forget, Norris; on all these little expeditions, we are not Majesty, but simply a Sir Fugleton Mace."

"I am mindful of your Majesty's wishes; but as we are so perfectly alone here, I ventured to speak as my respect indicated."

"Alone?—alone? Not perfectly alone, I hope, Norris?"

"No, your Majesty, there is one in this house who,

No. 7.—NIGHTSHADE.

I hope, will duly appreciate the honour that your Majesty has done her."

"Of course—of course!" cried the King: "we hope the time will never come in this realm when any one will fail to appreciate the honour we do them!"

The King slightly coughed as he spoke.

The valet replied in that soft, oily tone in which such persons as he are in the habit of addressing those greatly above them in wealth and station.

"I trust and hope that in all this transaction I shall deserve your Majesty's commendation. I have run some risks; for, as your Majesty may be well aware, his Royal Highness Prince Frederick is of a hasty disposition."

"A hasty disposition?" roared the King, losing all caution in the pasion that beset him,—"a hasty disposition? By jove! are not we of a hasty disposition likewise? Don't speak to us of hasty dispositions!"

"I most humbly crave your Majesty's gracious pardon; and if I might, in the most respectful manner suggest to your Majesty not to speak quite so loud."

"Hem! True, we are incautious. But for the future, Norris, you will understand that the only person in this realm really entitled to have a hasty disposition is ourselves."

"That is a truth, your Majesty, which will never be absent from the recollection of the most humble of your servants."

It is needless to say that Claude Duval listened to this conversation with the greatest possible surprise.

Over and over again he asked himself if it were possible that this person whom he heard speaking in the hall, and addressed as "Your Majesty," could really be the King of England.

Frequent opportunities had presented themselves to Claude Duval to see the monarch both in public and in private.

The peculiarity of voice which characterized George the Second was well known to him; and if this mysterious personage in the hall of that house in Spring Gardens were not the King, the resemblance certainly was very great.

Duval crept as far as prudence allowed him down the staircase, in order to catch every word that might be uttered in the hall.

"Well, Norris, well?" said the King, as he kept up the short, dry cough which had become habitual to him. "Well, Norris, we are here; what next?—what next?"

"If your Majesty will condescend to proceed to the upper floor, there will be two surprises."

"Two surprises! What mean you?"

"Your Majesty will be surprised to find a certain person so much more beautiful than even your imagination could paint her; and she, again, cannot but be flattered as well as surprised by the singular honour conferred upon her by your Majesty's attentions."

"Ha! ha!"

The King laughed sardonically.

"Upon our word, Norris, you become quite a courtier. It is really wonderful how you improve; and, but that we find you particularly handy in the service of Frederick, we should take you into our own household at once. Up those stairs, say you?"

"If your Majesty will be so good, I will do myself the honour to follow with a light."

"Do so—do so."

"By elevating it thus, at arms length above your Majesty's head, I throw its rays upon the path before you."

"Good!—good!"

The King commenced the ascent of the stairs.

Claude Duval found that the position he occupied on the landing on the first-floor was no longer tenable by him, unless he would be discovered.

Were he to retire into any of the other rooms, the doors of which presented themselves on all hands, he would lose the chance of further elucidating the mystery of that house.

There was no resource, then, but to make his way again into the chamber of death, where the soft roseate artificial light fell upon the face of one who been beautiful in life, and who, even with the awful shadow of the fell Destroyer upon her, was not yet stripped of all the charms which had belonged to her.

There was but little time to lose.

Duval cast a hasty glance about him, and then darted behind one of the heavy silken window curtains that fell in massive folds to the rich carpet covering the floor.

CHAPTER XX.

CLAUDE DUVAL IS THE MEANS OF SAVING THE KING'S LIFE.

FROM his place of concealment Duval commanded a sufficiently good view of the whole apartment to take cognizance of whatever might ensue within it.

Accustomed to adventure, and of sufficient strength of nerve to encounter any ordinary change or variety in human fortune, it was impossible even that Claude Duval could look on unmoved upon that mingled scene of death and gorgeous beauty.

It was a strange scene.

The apartment, so full of every luxury in the way of convenience and adornment which the genius of the age could suggest.

The soft, beautiful light, blending all things into an harmonious glowing colour, which seemed the very type of health and happiness.

And all for what?

For death!

What was he, Claude Duval, but an interloper there? A strange, and unexpected visitor. While the real inhabitant of that palatial apartment was the still nerveless form of that girl, who, in all the pride of her youth and beauty, had become but as a clod of the valley.

And what could England's King want there?

Did he come to look upon the dead, in order that it might read him a moral lesson of the vanity of human greatness?

Alas, no!

Far different were the motives that brought the sensual George the Second to that mysterious house in Spring Gardens at such an hour of the night.

Duval heard his short, dry cough upon the staircase as he ascended, followed by Norris the valet.

He heard him pause at the door of the apartment.

He saw the door gently opened.

"Is this the room?" asked the King.

"It is, your Majesty," replied the valet; "and now that we are thus far, permit me to say that the fair young creature who inhabits this house is heartily tired of the caprices and the brutalities of a certain person."

"Ah! Say you so?"

"Even so, your Majesty; and, overcome by fatigue, have reason to believe that she sleeps."

"Ha! ha! Sleeps?"

"Yes, your Majesty; and——Ah! can I believe my eyes?—she has not even retired to rest, but seeks for a brief repose, half upon the floor, and half resting upon yonder chair. Alas! this is very sad!"

"Hem! Norris."

"Your Majesty?"

The King turned full upon the valet, and slightly inclined his head.

It was the kind of movement with which he was always in the habit of ending an interview.

Norris took the hint at once, and bowed to the very floor.

He backed out of the room.

He closed the door, the lock of which shut with a silvery sound.

The King took off his hat and placed it upon a marble side-table.

He advanced three paces into the room, and then, as was usual with him, prefacing what he had to say with one of his short, dry coughs, he spoke.

"Madam—that is to say, beautiful being—chance has enabled me to cast my eyes upon your loveliness; and, favoured by Fortune, I was informed that you resided here, guarded by a dragon—a monster in the shape of a man. I cannot help presuming that the tone in which I speak is sufficient, in the silence of this place, to break your slumbers."

The King paused.

He coughed again.

He advanced three paces more towards the chair on which half-reposed the lifeless body of the beautiful girl whose ears were for ever deaf to all the flatteries of this world.

Again the fair dead face had fallen upon the chair-cushion from which Claude Duval had gently raised it.

The abundance of beautiful hair streamed down to the floor, where, tinctured by the coloured ray that came from the lamp, it looked more than mortally lovely.

The King became enthusiastic.

He forgot even his habit of coughing, and as he stooped and raised in his hand one of the long tresses, he spoke hurriedly, and with more real emotion than Claude Duval would have thought him capable of.

"Awake! awake!" he cried, "lovely unknown!—awake to the knowledge that kind Fortune has brought to your feet one who can load you with every earthly benefit. Awake! awake!"

The still form moved not.

"How is this?" added the King. "Can it be that fatigue and exhaustion have reached such lengths that now, when Nature demands repose, no external sounds can break it? Yet I must see that face. Again I must feast my eyes upon the loveliness without a fear!"

He dropped on one knee.

He placed one arm around the still form that rested on the chair.

"No alarm," he said,—"no alarm; nothing but serenity—nothing but joy. I have the wealth of power, and the power of wealth."

He raised the girl's head.

He turned the face towards him.

His enamoured eyes rested on it for a moment; and then, as Duval, almost losing caution in the interest of the scene, stepped half-way from behind the curtain, the expression in the King's face changed to one of ghastly terror.

"Dead!" he shrieked.

He seemed paralyzed with affright.

In vain he tried to disencumber himself of the still form he held in his arms.

In vain he tried to struggle to his feet

He fell backwards.

"Help—help! Norris! Treason! Death—death! It is death that enchains me—not beauty!"

The valet rushed into the room.

"Great heaven!—what is this? Did your Majesty call?"

"Help! help!"

The King had made a vigorous effort.

He half scrambled to his feet, and, staggering across the room, he fell, in a strangely huddled-up fashion on a distant couch, holding his arms out before him as though he would repel some terrible object from approaching.

"Dead!" he cried. "The girl is dead. She don't sleep. Yes, she does sleep; but it is the sleep of death. I faint, Norris, I faint! I hate death and the dead. I hate even the sick and sickness. Help! help! Wine! Is there no wine here?"

"Oh, your Majesty!" cried Norris, clasping his hands with a loud clap, "this is dreadful! He must have killed her! Some savage blow; or—or——That is to say, he must have killed her!"

"Let me go! Let me be off! Your arm, Norris, your arm; once in a way, your arm. Let me leave this place!"

"Ah, yes."

"Yes, what? Why do you exclaim yes?"

"Your Majesty is faint."

"And sick—sick, Norris!"

"Your Majesty mentioned wine. Behold! here is some, the quality of which looks unexceptionable. His Royal Highness, the Prince, is a connoisseur. His rich Spanish wines are the talk of the Court; and this I recognise at once, by its sparkle and its rare brilliancy, to be some of that old sherry he got from the Infanta."

"At once, Norris, at once!"

The valet poured out a sparkling tall glass of the amber-coloured wine.

He knelt on one knee, and was in the act of bending it to the King, when he held up the other hand in signification of alarm.

"Hush!"

"Hush, what?"

"Did your Majesty hear nothing?"

"Nothing."

"Yet it was a door. I hold your Majesty's safety dearer than my life. I will proceed below and reconnoitre."

"No—no!"

"Hush! There again! What if it be the Prince?"

"The fiend!"

Norris placed the wine on a small table near the couch on which half lay the King, and with a cautious, gliding movement he made towards the door.

"Hold, Norris, hold! I cannot stay here with a dead person. I shall faint!"

"Your Majesty, here's the rare old sherris; and if there be danger below, no one shall approach this room except over the corpse of the most faithful of your servants."

"No!" cried the King,—"no! Are you going to be dead too? Is this house to be a vault—a grave—a charnel-house? Help! Treason! We will raise the neighbourhood!"

"For mercy's sake, your Majesty—your life's sake—for the sake of this great realm—I implore you—I implore you!"

Norris made excited gestures as he still approached the door, and finally passed through it, leaving the King alone with the dead.

Alone, too, with the living Claude Duval, who had been an amazed spectator of all that had taken place, and who was beginning now to understand that the whole affair could be nothing less than a plot, which comprised the death of the King, and the elevation of Frederick Prince of Wales to the throne of England.

The door was closed.

A profound stillness reigned in the house.

The King looked about him with a strange, scared expression of countenance, and he spoke in low tones, for even his cold and selfish nature was sufficiently human that it could not wholly shake off respect for the dead.

"What is the meaning of it all? Why, oh, why did we ever look upon the beauty of that girl with longing eyes? Why have we suffered ourselves to be cajoled into this house, to be made faint and sick with such a sight? Norris! Norris! Where is the knave gone? There is luxury and beauty here; expense too. Ah! there is the Infanta's sherris! A draught of that—a deep draught—may take the chill from our heart, and perhaps compose the—the agitation—yes, agitation of our royal nerves."

The King reached out his hand for the tall glass.

Claude Duval drew his sword.

The King raised the glass to the light.

Sparkling and beautiful looked the treacherous draught within it—that draught which there could not be the slightest doubt was poisoned to saturation.

"Yes, the Infanta's wine. I have heard of it, and they refused it to me. I have heard that Frederick had it. And if I were not now in the presence of that poor still form, who so disagreeably puts me in mind of the fact that the day may come when even a king must die, I would dri—I would drink to his confu——"

The King finished his speech with a yell.

The tall glass of sherris was at his lips.

Claude Duval, with one stride, had emerged from behind the silken curtain.

There was a flash of the long, bright sword-blade in the soft roseate light of the apartment, and the point of the weapon just catching the glass an inch above its stem, shivered it to fragments, and sent the sherris that it had contained in a splashing stream on to the rich carpet at the King's feet.

The yell that the King had uttered was all the sound that he had breath to produce.

Gathering up his legs quickly, in a most unkingly fashion, on to the couch, he glared at Claude Duval with as much astonishment and terror as though the dead girl herself had suddenly risen and confronted him with the breath of life at her lips.

Duval bowed with courtly grace, and reversing his sword, presented the hilt towards the King.

"But for the hit which has given your Majesty some annoyance and much surprise," he said, "there would have been a royal funeral and a coronation in England —the sherris was poisoned!"

The King uttered a strange sound, between a sigh and a groan, and sank back upon the couch, completely unnerved and nearly insensible.

Duval darted behind the curtain again, and almost at the same moment the door was flung open, and Norris, with Frederick, the Prince of Wales, at his heels, appeared upon its threshold.

The valet carried a wax light in his hand, and he trembled so excessively that, if anything could have imparted an idea of the ludicrous at such a moment, it would have been the manner in which that wax light was waved to and fro in the agitated hand of the valet.

"Is it over?" said the Prince.

"You heard!" gasped Norris.

"I heard a cry!"

"It was his!"

"How do I know?"

"His last! Do you not remember—oh! do you not remember, we heard his last cry! And was not this its twin resemblance?"

"Ah! then I am——"

"K—K—King of England!"

The Prince laughed.

He turned his back upon the valet, who still, with his eyes fixed upon the distant couch whereon lay the King, was heedless of the actions of the Prince.

The latter was slowly drawing his sword from its scabbard, to which it seemed to cling rather tightly but he at length succeeded in freeing the entire blade, and turning sharply upon Norris, he shortened his arm, as he exclaimed: "One more, and the business of this night is complete! Thus I pay at one stroke the heavy debt that Frederick the First of England owes to Norris the valet!"

The wax light dropped from the hands of the murdered wretch.

He flung his arms up in the air as the bright sword passed through him, and then, without the slightest cry, he fell at the feet of the Prince.

"Now I live!" exclaimed Frederick; "I am rid of the false and frail fair one, of whom I was weary—of the King, who barred my way to advancement, and was something less than father, more than enemy— and of you, poor tool, who thought to play so fine a game with partners who might use you for a time, but who were sure to crush you when that time had passed away. Ha, ha! Ring, joy-bells! Blaze illuminations! Roar cannon, for Frederick the First, King of England!"

CHAPTER XXI.

CLAUDE DUVAL MAKES A COMPACT WITH THE KING OF ENGLAND.

DUVAL's impulse—and it was a most natural one under the circumstances—was to rush forward from his place of concealment, and, by a few words, put an end to the self-glorification of the Prince of Wales.

Indeed, it was with the greatest difficulty that he restrained this impulse.

But his better reason told him it would be far better to remain where he was, and allow things to take their course.

What could he do by issuing forth at such a moment?

The crime that had been contemplated was frustrated; and, small as was the sympathy of Claude Duval with George the Second, he could not but look with greater horror still upon the conduct of the Prince of Wales.

Keeping close, then, behind the curtain, he allowed the Prince to say his say, although he would certainly have interfered had he seen him on the point of making any active demonstration towards the couch on which lay the King, either actually in a swoon induced by fear, or with sufficient presence of mind to affect to be in that condition.

Twice the Prince approached two steps towards the couch.

No doubt he wished to make assurance doubly sure, and to convince himself that the path to the throne was indeed cleared of the incumbrance of his father.

And each of these times Claude Duval moved slightly from his place of concealment; but as the Prince paused Duval paused likewise.

Then the Prince turned upon his heel.

"It is over!" he said. "What need I further interfere. It is over! Let those discover him who will, I have but to wait! The plot is a good one, and has succeeded! The dead body of the King will be found here, accompanied with the corpse of this frail and fair delusion. Let Norris take the blame of the transaction, for it may be assumed that, before he drew his last breath, the King has had time sufficient to discover his treachery and avenge it."

And stepping over the dead body of the valet, the Prince of Wales left the apartment.

The moment the door was closed, Claude Duval came forth from his hiding-place, and made his way towards the couch on which lay the King.

At first Duval was himself in doubt whether the King retained sufficient consciousness to be aware of his real position.

The royal eyes were closed.

The sound of Duval's voice, however, acted as a charm to open them.

"I have the honour to assure your Majesty that all is safe."

The King looked at Duval suspiciously.

"And you?" he said,—"who may you be?"

Duval was annoyed at the tone of the question, and he replied curtly, "I am the man who has saved your Majesty's life, however slight you may consider the obligation."

The King uncoiled his legs, so to speak, from their huddled-up position on the sofa, and placed them on the floor.

"Remiss!" he cried,—"very remiss; but you are like all the rest!"

"I do not know your Majesty's meaning."

"I mean that you all do things by halves, and when the real period for action comes, you leave undone that which is of the greatest importance."

"I differ from your Majesty. Surely that which was of the greatest importance was done, and lies here in glittering fragments at your feet."

Duval meant the pieces of broken glass which were scattered on the carpet.

The King made an impatient gesture.

"That is well—that is well! But when Frederick was here, a man like you might, in a moment, have rid me of the incumbrance of my life."

Duval understood him.

"No, your Majesty; vengeance I leave to you."

The King coughed in his peculiar fashion.

"And," added Duval, "if I may speak my true mind on this question, I must say that, in interrupting the commission of this crime, which would have made you its victim, I only obeyed the common instincts of humanity."

By this Duval meant to imply that he had no special inclination to save the life of the King as an individual.

George the Second was quite acute enough to understand him.

Perhaps he had a better opinion of his preserver from this blunt sincerity than he would have had from the most courtly phrases and adulation.

"Assist us," he said. "We will not say that you have concluded your night's work until we are safe at St. James's."

The King leant on the arm of Duval, and, making as circuitous a route as he could, passed the two dead bodies that were in the apartment, and gained the top of the staircase with an evident feeling of relief.

They descended in silence.

The King turned towards the door in the hall which led into Spring Gardens, but Duval suggested the route through the Park.

"Here is another door," he said. "which conducts us to the small shrubbery, from which a gate opens to the Park, and as it is much the nearer route your Majesty will probably prefer it."

"Be it so—be it so. We have the key of the garden-gate of the Palace."

The little shrubbery was soon gained, and Duval cried out loudly to Blossom.

"Follow!" he said, "all is well!"

The King held Claude's arm with a tight grip.

"Who is that?" he cried. "To whom did you speak?"

"To a friend of mine who has charge of my horse."

"Who, then, are you? Your name—quality—condition?"

The Park was gained, and as the royal eyes, through the gloom of the night, could see dimly the square turrets of St. James's Palace, confidence and courage seemed to be restored.

"I am one," said Duval, "who wishes for the present to preserve an *incognito*."

"Ah!"

"But, at the same time, if your Majesty should preserve the remembrance of this night's adventure, and at the same time entertain a desire to return in any way the service I have rendered you, I leave it to you to adopt some mode by which I can approach you to ask a possible favour, if the time should come for me to desire it."

The King hesitated.

Duval saw him looking at his hand, and then with some reluctance he drew from his finger a ruby ring.

"Take this," he said. "There is a peculiar device engraven upon it which cannot be mistaken or imitated. Upon its production you may depend that our royal memory will not fail us in recalling the events of this night. But say, sir, whoever you be, have you any doubt whatever in your mind that Frederick intended to poison us?"

"None whatever."

The King coughed again, as he muttered in low tones to himself, "It will only be, then, a just retribution. A rattlesnake has fangs from which is emitted venom. If one attacked me, and I had poisonous fangs, I would bite the snake! Ha! ha! Eugh!"

The garden-gate of St. James's Palace was reached, and the King, taking a small key from his pocket, opened a narrow green door.

"Farewell!" he said: "we shall not forget."

Another moment and Duval was alone amid the silence and darkness of the Park, with nothing to remind him of the remarkable adventure he had gone through, but the King's ruby ring, which, after trying on to various fingers, he found at last one of them to fit sufficiently close to be safe.

"It is well!" said Duval. "The time may come when I may even have to apply to this false and fickle specimen of monarchy, for now life has assumed to me a better charm, and in the love of Lucy I find a reason for its preservation. Ho! Blossom! Whither away so fast?"

In the gloomy shadows of the old trees close to the garden wall of the Palace, Blossom ran the chance of passing Duval with the horses.

He pulled up now hastily, and in a tone of exultation he called out, "Captain!—Captain!—I have found out the secret!"

"What secret?"

"All about the Spectre Horseman!"

"Indeed?"

"Yes, Captain, and here it is."

These words were quite inexplicable to Claude Duval, nor could he divine what object it was that Blossom flung down at his feet, and at which he saw, even in the obscurity of the night air, the two horses looking with alarmed and curious eyes.

"What is it, Blossom?"

"A hobby-horse, Captain! Don't you know?—it is one of those affairs of paste-board and horse-hair such as used to be in the old games. A man fixes it on him, and races along on his own feet with apparently a horse's head before him and his haunches behind. I found the whole affair in the garden."

"Then so ends," said Duval, "the mystery of the spectre horseman of St. James's Park."

"And so ends the career of Claude Duval, the highwayman!" shouted a voice. "Drop, my men!—drop! and we shall have him before he can mount his famous horse. Nightshade!"

From the old elm trees around, there dropped on to

the Mall of the Park some ten or a dozen men, and so sudden and unexpected was the movement, that it would have been no great stretch of fancy to imagine those old trees had grown so strange a fruit which had been shaken from their branches by the night air.

Duval had one foot in the stirrups of Nightshade, and it was well for him that such was the case, or otherwise, in the darkness, he could scarcely have been expected to mount his horse.

The emergency of the occasion, however, lent him all that coolness and decision which were so characteristic of him.

"Fire, Blossom!—fire!" he cried.

Even as he spoke, he was in the saddle.

Blossom obeyed his injunction immediately by discharging his two holster-pistols.

The flashes lit up the night air, and considerable confusion was produced among the officers.

It was St. Ives, the detective, who then cried out in his loudest voice.

"Why cast away your life, Claude Duval? Surrender—and there may yet be a thousand chances for you."

"A tempting offer!" replied Claude; "but I prefer my liberty!"

"Close on him—close on him!" shouted Muckles. "We must have him to-night, dead or alive!"

Several of the officers clung to the bridle of Nightshade.

Then Duval gave his sagacious steed one of those impulses to action which were well understood between them, because they had been the subject of laborious practice.

Nightshade commenced kicking, plunging, and biting in the most furious manner.

"The horse is mad!" was the cry of the officers.

"Not so mad," said Duval, as he dealt heavy blows about him with his riding whip,—"not so mad, but it knows a friend from a foe. Forward! Off and away, Nightshade! Off and away!"

The horse was free.

Some one who had made pertinacious attempts to fling Duval from his saddle, by twisting at his foot, received a kick that sent him prostrate.

"Forward, again!" shouted Duval. "Let those follow me that dare!"

"Fire!" was the response from Mr. St. Ives.

Duval bent low in the saddle.

A rattling discharge of pistol-shots immediately ensued, but they had little other effect than to light up the scene, and give Duval an idea.

Those flashes fell right across the Mall.

They revealed for a moment the rough wooden paling that surrounded the centre of the Park, which was then nothing but a wilderness, with a stagnant kind of ditch occupying its middle portion.

It might be supposed that Duval would seek safety from the speed of his horse alone, and in that case a gallop round the Park to the gate of Birdcage Walk might answer the purpose.

But he knew he could depend upon Nightshade.

Three bounds took him across the Mall, and then a leap cleared the wooden palings, and Duval and his steed were within the enclosure of the Park.

For a fleeting moment, and amid the excitement of the scene that had taken place, Duval forgot Blossom.

It was not his habit to forget those who accompanied him, but the whole affair was one of those surprises during the action of which every one must to a certain extent look to himself.

But hardly had Nightshade alighted on the green turf of the enclosure of the Park, when Duval was mindful of the safety of his follower.

"Blossom!" he shouted.

"Here, Captain!"

"Fire!" again cried St. Ives.

There was another rattling discharge, and some of the bullets crashed through the wooden palings, behind which Duval was now in tolerable security.

Twice, then, Blossom put his horse to the leap.

Twice the animal swerved, and in the darkness hesitated to rise to the palings.

"Hold!" cried Duval; "clear aside!"

He backed Nightshade close to the rotten wooden fence.

One touch to the flank of the well-educated steed, and Nightshade's heels shot out with a force that few obstacles could withstand.

The palings yielded.

A wide gap appeared.

"Follow now!" shouted Duval. "Keep close to me, Blossom. I know your horse can swim, if it cannot leap."

The distance across the turf and rank weedy vegetation of that inner portion of the Park to the stagnant canal in its centre was but short, and in a few seconds Nightshade, with Duval, had plunged into the water.

Blossom's horse followed readily enough.

Then they both heard St. Ives and Muckles raving at their men for allowing their prey to escape.

They heard, too, the gallop of horses' feet.

"Quick, Blossom—quick!" said Duval, "or they will be round the Park yet before we can get over the enclosure."

The canal was passed over.

Some scrambling and kicking on the opposite bank enabled both the horses to get a firm foothold.

Blossom's horse then, encouraged by the immediate proximity and example of Nightshade, no longer hesitated at the leap of the opposite paling, and they both alighted in safety in the Birdcage Walk.

The gate leading into Westminster was closed.

A man stood against it with both his arms extended, and as Duval and Blossom approached, he cried out in tones of exultation, "No you don't—you don't get out here! This is a trap, my fine fellows!"

"Open the gate!"

"Ha, ha! Not a bit of it! A trap—a trap!"

Duval drew one of his pistols, and fired at once.

He purposely levelled an inch or two above the man's head, but the effect upon the exultant individual was immediate.

The gate-keeper dropped, with a yell, to his hands and knees; and in that posture made extraordinary speed into his lodge.

A massive key was in the gate, which Duval could turn without dismounting.

"Follow me, Blossom!" he said, "and lock the gate after you. If the Park is a trap, it will do for the cats as well as the mice."

The sound of hard galloping up the Birdcage Walk, from the direction of Pimlico, came now unmistakably on the ears of Blossom and Duval, as the former hastily closed the gate, and locked it on the outer side.

CHAPTER XXII.

CLAUDE DUVAL SEEKS REFUGE IN THE THIEVES' KEN IN WESTMINSTER.

"HALT a moment, Blossom," cried Duval.

Claude's faithful follower drew rein instantly.

"What do you hear now?"

"Nothing, Captain."

"Has the pursuit, then, ceased?"

"No—hardly so; and I should say that St. Ives and Muckles, with their men, have got out of the Park lower down, and mean to intercept us in Westminster."

Hardly had these words escaped the lips of Blossom, than, with shouts and outcries, down the street now so well known as Great George Street, but which was then rather a dingy, narrow thoroughfare, the party of mounted officers appeared.

"This is past jesting," said Duval. "These fellows seem bent upon my capture."

"Or your death, Captain."

"I will foil them yet. Follow me, Blossom, and fear nothing. This close pursuit could not have happened in a place better for me than Westminster."

There was a narrow court close at hand, with two posts at its entrance, which might have been supposed sufficiently close together to prevent the passage of a horseman.

Duval, however, instantly dismounted, and with some dexterity led Nightshade through the posts, and Blossom following his example, they not only evaded the onslaught of the officers, but placed a serious obstacle in their way.

"Surrender!" cried St. Ives; "we will and must have you!"

"Yes!" added Muckles, "surrender, Claude Duval, and you shall have the best of treatment."

"And if you don't surrender," added a voice, "we're down brown, that's all I can say."

Duval laughed.

"That was Swallow!" he cried. "Follow me, Blossom, and fear nothing. I will show you one of the refuges of the Knights of the Road in Westminster."

While the officers were impeding each other in their attempts to pass the posts at the end of the court, Duval and Blossom rode on.

They passed through a long, narrow street, which opened on to a much wider thoroughfare, but of much shorter dimensions.

"Now listen again," said Duval.

They both paused, and the sounds that met their ears from several quarters in that ancient suburb of Westminster, were all indicative of danger.

"Stop them! Stop them! Stop them! Highwaymen! Highwaymen! A thousand pounds reward! Stop them! Stop them! Dead or alive! Dead or alive!"

The springing of constables' rattles sufficiently indicated the general alarm that was spread through all the watch of the ancient suburb.

"Blossom," said Duval, "what do you think of all this?"

Blossom wiped the perspiration from his brow as he replied.

"I fancy luck's against us, Captain."

"Why so?"

"It seems to me that the whole of Westminster is up in arms, and that, turn which way we will, we shall only run into the hands of a throng of foes."

"Then, Blossom, we will seek a throng of friends. Did you ever hear of Western House?"

"I heard you mention it in the Park, Captain; and I have heard of it before as the great haunt of all the footpads in Westminster."

"It shall be our refuge. Follow! Ah! our foes approach."

The confusion of voices sounded nearer still.

"Close in! Close in! Guard the narrow streets! Let no one pass! A highwayman!—a highwayman! A thousand pounds reward for the great Claude Duval!"

"Lost!" said Blossom.

"Exactly so," replied Duval; "that is to say, they will lose us."

As he spoke he paused in the centre of the street in which they were, and, after looking cautiously about him, walked Nightshade right on to the pavement.

Pursuing his course thus upon the footway, Duval came to a particular house, with a large wooden cellar flap in front of it, such as are to be found covering the underground portion of most inns and public-houses.

The house was a huge, dingy looking pile, without the slightest light in any of its windows.

Duval paused upon this wooden cellar flap, and hastily dismounting, he cast one arm over the neck of Nightshade, while with the heel of one of his boots he struck nine times upon the thick wood-work immediately beneath him.

To the surprise, and somewhat to the consternation of Blossom, Claude Duval began to disappear from his sight.

By some mysterious and hidden means, the square of heavy beams and floor-boards slowly descended, carrying with it both Duval and Nightshade.

"Hold, Captain, hold! What am I to do?"

"No one will molest you! It is me they seek. Make the best of your way to Hampstead, and say that it may be the morning's light only that will see me at home from the pursuit, and take that to help you!"

Something was flung up from the subterranean recess; and as the wooden platform rose into its place again, the something, whatever it was, fell with a sullen thud upon it.

Blossom was greatly alarmed, and had hastily dismounted.

He picked up the object that had been cast towards him, and found it to be a constable's staff, which, amid the darkness of the night, would give him an air of authority, and enable him immediately to affect to join in the pursuit of Claude Duval.

We must leave Blossom, however, to whatever good or evil fortune that might befall him, while we follow our hero into the mysterious cavernous recess where he had made his way.

The platform of wood descended about twelve feet, touching at that depth the ground, so that Duval was easily enabled to lead Nightshade off it, and leave it at liberty to ascend again.

The place was in total darkness.

And, for a few seconds, a stillness, as if of the grave, was in and about it.

Then a voice spoke in deep, hollow accents.

"Who seeks sanctuary?"

"Claude Duval!"

There was a sudden exclamation.

Then there came the flash of a light, and a tall, ungainly-looking figure stood a few paces from Duval.

It was only for a few seconds that the light flashed between these two persons, and then it was either extinguished or a slide placed before it.

"Who disclosed the secret of this place?" was the next question asked of Duval.

"Richard Turpin."

"It is well! What seek you?"

"A few hours' rest. The whole of Westminster swarms with my enemies, and I was nearly hunted to the death!"

"Follow, and fear nothing!"

A faint light, not much larger than a star, appeared at a considerable distance off; and Claude Duval, understanding that he was to follow that light, did so unhesitatingly.

He had proceeded about twenty paces, when another voice broke the stillness about him, by exclaiming, "Shall he turn to the right or to the left? Does this new-comer consort with the living or with the dead?"

"Let him speak for himself," said the first voice.

"The living, then, certainly," said Claude Duval. "I am of the earth—earthy; and as for the dead, with all possible respect for them, I have no desire whatever for their company!"

"To the left, then!" said the voice.

Duval turned Nightshade's head in that direction, and still followed the star, which shifted so as to suit the new route he was pursuing.

A confused, murmuring sound, that might have been mistaken for the dim echoes of many voices a long way off, now came upon his ears.

Duval listened intently, in the endeavour to discover some precise words from out the chaos of sounds; but as easy would it have been to mould into intelligible language the rushing wind, or the roar of the sea, as those indistinct expressions.

The star then suddenly paused in its progression, and only remained sufficiently long visible to enable Duval to see an old oaken Gothic door, which barred his further progress.

At that door Duval knocked nine times, even as he had done upon the platform in the street above.

It was immediately opened.

The sight that met his eyes then was a strange one.

It seemed to him, at the first moment, as if he saw innumerable stars shining through some thick cloud.

That, however, was but a momentary delusion of the senses.

The thick cloud resolved itself into a heavy blanket, which still blocked up the doorway.

The innumerable stars were but small holes perforated over its entire surface, through which gleamed light.

A complete roar of many sounds.

A rattling of jugs, mugs, and glasses.

The unmistakable odour of tobacco.

All came through these crevices in the blanket, which, being now bodily flung aside, disclosed to Duval one of the strangest scenes his eyes had ever lit upon.

A large, vaulted apartment, of low pitch in the roof, and supported upon clusters of heavy, squat-looking columns, contained a strange, motley assemblage of some sixty or seventy people, whose various professional pursuits might well be guessed at a glance by so accurate an observer as Claude Duval.

The footpad.

The prowling day-thief, in the guise of a beggar.

The daring burglar, with half-shut eyes, blinking at the lights, and planning with a comrade the mode of entrance to some "crib" which was to be "cracked," according to art, on the ensuing evening.

The highwayman who had lost his horse, and upon whose head such a price was set that it was well for him to lie concealed for a time.

All these, and many other specimens of the criminal population of London, held high carousal in that singular apartment which Duval had reached so mysteriously.

"Claude Duval!" shouted the voice of one who seemed to act as major-domo on the occasion.

The announcement startled the motley crew, and each man sprang to his feet.

Duval stood by the head of Nightshade, and slightly lifted his hat.

He was a celebrity.

The cheer that burst from every throat made the air ring again, and went far towards extinguishing the many odds and ends of lights that were stuck in every crevice and cranny of the stonework in and about the columns.

"Hurrah for Claude Duval! Three cheers! Hip, hip, hip!—hurrah!"

"Gentlemen all," said Duval, "I claim your hospitality! Westminster is all alive with the watch; and Mr. St. Ives, with his man, Muckles—he being again followed by his underling, Swallow—make the old streets and alleys too hot to hold me and my horse, Nightshade."

"Welcome, welcome!—a thousand welcomes! Hurrah! Take a drink, Duval! Out of this!—out of this! No—out of this! Get out, you sneaking pad! Do you think a gentleman like Duval would drink out of a pewter pot? Here's a silver flagon that belonged to the Dean of Westminster! Drink, Duval, drink!"

Twenty hands were extended towards him with proffers of refreshment.

Then one voice called out, in stentorian accents, "Silence, all, in the ken!"

Every tone was hushed.

The oaken door had been closed; and now there distinctly sounded upon its panels a similar demand for admission to that which Claude Duval had made.

Nine knocks

"A pal!" cried the voice. "Open!"

The door was opened.

The heavy blanket was flung aside.

An aged man tottered into the ken.

There was blood upon his face, and he shook, either with fear or decrepitude.

He fell to the floor a few paces in front of Nightshade, and as he did so with a clanking sound, he released from beneath his arm a bag, from which rolled various articles of gold and silver plate.

"I've done it—I've done it at last!" he cried. "I was a prig and a footpad in my youth, but got into bad company, and became honest. I was a butler thirty years to Lady Westle, and I've robbed the pantry at last, and here's the swag!"

A roar of satisfaction came from the assembled thieves, and he who had called for silence with such authority, and had been so promptly obeyed, called out. "Give him a drink! It's the prodigal come back, and we'll bag the plate as his footing!"

"What?" cried the old man, as he spread his shivering hands over his booty, "all of it?—all of it?"

"To be sure! clear the way! Hoist him up here, and let's have a look at him!"

"Gentleman all!—gentleman all!—I'm rather infirm. Let me sit down in this corner; and yet, ha! ha! the sight of you all makes me feel quite young again. I was cast for death once—thirty-eight years ago—but reprieved. And who may this great gentleman be with his beautiful horse? Ha! ha! I, too, had a horse once. I cried stand and deliver on Hounslow Heath."

A strange sound pervaded the assembly.

It was a faint echoing breath from a bugle-horn.

It blanched every cheek.

It struck terror into every heart.

Duval looked about him in amazement.

"What is amiss?" he asked.

"A spy!"

"Ah!"

"Yes, comrades," cried the man who was in authority, and who had as yet given his orders freely, "that is a signal to us that there is a spy among us. The horn is blown by one who keeps good watch and ward. Look to the door, Mackheath; let that be your post. Silence all, now, and we shall know more about it."

"I think I can tell you," said the old man who had brought the plate, "for even as I descended from the street by the trap, I saw a suspicious person lurking about, and that was what put me in such a tremor."

"There cannot be the slightest doubt of it," exclaimed Claude Duval; "only if I were inclined to tremors—which I am not—it is a person here who would place me in them, and not outside."

"Here?" cried twenty voices at once.

THE KING DIRECTS THE PRINCE TO BE REMOVED.

"Yes!" added Duval, as he advanced half a dozen paces, and lifted his hat again; "I have this time the honour, and it is now a pleasure likewise, to salute an old acquaintance."

He fixed his eyes on the old man who had brought the plate.

The attention of the assemblage in that strange ecclesiastical-looking apartment was now directed to this personage.

A storm of questions assailed Duval.

He waved his hand for silence.

The old man cowered down before him, and in a voice half of entreaty and half of supplication, cried out, "Yes. I understand it all. I shall be absent only five minutes, and then I will bring such information as will be worth its weight in gold!—yes, in gold!"

He made a movement towards the door.

Duval touched Nightshade on the neck, and pointed to the old man.

The horse looked threateningly, and exhibited his teeth.

No. 8.—NIGHTSHADE.

"Let me pass! let me pass! The animal is vicious!"

"Patience!" said Duval, "and before you go let me have the pleasure of saluting you in your real name?"

"No—no."

"Which is——"

"Mercy!"

"Mr. St. Ives!"

Even as he spoke, Duval stepped forward, and with one impetuous action he slipped from the head of the old man the well-contrived grey wig, and cast it at his feet.

A roar of execration burst from the assembled thieves, for they all recognised in the person thus disclosed to them the well-known St. Ives, the detective officer, who had brought so many of their fraternity to the gallows, and who was the favourite aversion of every evil-doer in London.

And now that the officer saw that he was detected, he drew himself up to his full height, and strove to put on an air of courage.

It was his only chance.

And yet how poor a one.

"I am St. Ives," he said, "and it will be the worst hour's work that any man here ever did to attempt to lay a hand upon me."

As he spoke, he took from his pocket a very elegant silver staff, at the end of which was the gilt crown, symbolical of his authority.

"Clear the way here!" he added. "Any one who hinders me, does so at his own peril."

St. Ives was a bold man.

He calculated upon the surprise of the moment, and under some circumstances he might have been successful.

Some of the thieves hesitated.

Even Duval had some sensation of admiration for the courage of a man whose life hung upon a thread.

CHAPTER XXIII.

CLAUDE DUVAL FINDS HIMSELF IN A PERILOUS SITUATION IN WESTMINSTER ABBEY.

DUVAL stepped aside.

He patted the neck of Nightshade.

He was willing that St. Ives should make his escape, provided the thieves, housebreakers, and footpads in the ken would permit him.

And the detective officer might probably have added that one adventure to the list of the extraordinary escapades he had gone through, if he would but have been moderate in his triumph.

If he had but let well alone, all might have been well with him; but, mentally intoxicated for the moment by the success he was achieving, St. Ives thought he would carry out an adventure that would hand down his name to all posterity.

He turned sharply to Claude Duval.

He placed his hand upon his shoulder.

"I arrest you, Claude Duval; and do not leave this place, except with you as my prisoner!"

"This is too much!" said Duval, "you have taken the one step, Mr. St. Ives, from safety to destruction."

As Claude spoke, he snatched the staff from the hand of St. Ives, and flung it to the other end of the vaulted apartment.

The officer made a grasp at Duval's collar, but, missing him, fell upon all-fours.

The action was ludicrous.

All the effect which the courage of St. Ives had had vanished.

There was a roar of laughter, and that was rapidly succeeded by execrations and menaces.

The unhappy officer was tossed from hand to hand like a weed upon the ocean.

Duval then raised his voice above all the uproar, in the hope yet of saving the life of the shrinking wretch.

"Make him confess!" he said, "the reason of his presence here, and what he was about to do—after which, let him go!"

"I do confess," said St. Ives. "Hear me! hear me! I was lurking alone in the street above, and saw the descent of Claude Duval and his horse on the wooden platform. In the darkness, I succeeded in following; but under the present circumstances, I give my solemn pledge and oath that I will not reveal——"

What St. Ives would further have added was drowned in a shout of rage.

"The barrel! the barrel!" cried many voices.

Duval leant upon the neck of Nightshade, and wondered what was next to ensue.

A small barrel, such as might have contained a couple of gallons of liquid was produced.

It was set on end on the long, rough table that ran down the centre of the apartment.

As many hands then as could lay hold of him lifted up St. Ives and seated him on the barrel.

With many complicated folds of several long ropes that were produced for the occasion, the unfortunate detective, and the barrel likewise, were securely fastened to the table.

What could all this mean?

Was it merely some ridiculous farce for the purpose of playing upon the fears of the man who had made himself so obnoxious to that unlawful fraternity?

Duval could hardly look upon it as anything else; but he soon found that the whole affair had a much more fearful significance.

A hole was roughly bored in the side of the barrel.

There trickled out of it a black streak of something which lay in a little heap upon the table.

One glance was sufficient to let Claude Duval see what that substance was.

Gunpowder!

The fate of the detective was too fearful to contemplate.

Several of the thieves commenced making a train of the powder along the whole length of the table, and connecting that again by a piece of string with the floor.

Another ancient Gothic door was opened at the further extremity of the vaulted room, through which the visitors to the ken began to make their way.

"Hold, all of you!" cried Duval. "Let me advise you. This will be a foolish act, as well as a cruel and desperate one. Let me ask of you the favour of this man's life?"

"No!" was the universal shout.

In another moment every light was extinguished, and it was with some difficulty that Duval could lead Nightshade by the bridle towards the door, through which nearly all the thieves had made their escape.

St. Ives uttered two or three cries of despair.

Then he was profoundly silent.

The real courage of the man must have been great, and Duval felt an almost irresistible desire to make an effort to save him.

But he thought of his own home.

He thought of the light of love that was there awaiting him.

He was himself but young; and why should he run the fearful risk of quenching his early life in the endeavour to save a man who, after all, had placed himself in his present position in the effort to drag him, Duval, to death upon the scaffold.

No.

If ever there were an occasion when self preservation became a law, surely this was the one.

Duval felt eagerly before him for the low Gothic door by which the thieves had escaped.

It had partially closed, but he thrust it open and passed through it.

His feet struck against some stone-work.

A flight of stairs.

Under ordinary circumstances, this would have been an obstacle that must either effectually have barred his progress, or forced him to abandon his horse.

But Duval could depend upon Nightshade, even in such an emergency as that.

Going slowly up the stone staircase backward, Duval held the rein of Nightshade with both hands.

The creature stumbled against the first step, and then, with its rare sagacity, divining what it was, began slowly to ascend after its master.

"Fire the train!" cried a voice.

"No!" said Duval. "Pause while yet you may, and do not commit an act that in its vice and barbarity will far transcend anything that——"

There was a rumbling sound.

A cry!

A muffled report, and then the strong odour of gunpowder came upon the senses of Duval.

Nightshade snorted, and pressed quickly up the staircase.

There was a faint light at the top of it which disclosed another arched door, through which Duval passed, leading his horse.

He gazed about him with the most intense surprise, and it was some few minutes before he could convince himself that he was actually within the old Abbey of Westminster, and that the tall, groined arches which rose towering above his head, the marble paving on which he trod, and the tombs and monuments about him, belonged to that celebrated edifice.

The door closed behind him with a clang.

A small oil lamp stood upon a tomb, resting on the breast of an armed knight.

It shed out a faint lustre about it, but even that was sufficient to chase away some of the darkness, and enable Duval, with wonder and admiration, to gaze about him.

The silence was profound.

All that motley, lawless crew, that had held high revel in the ken, had disappeared.

Whither had they gone?

Duval spoke.

"Am I alone, or is there no one here to guide me from this place to the outer air?"

In faint, dreary echoes his own voice only was returned to him; and as he listened, the few words he had uttered appeared to be whispered from cloister to cloister—aisle to aisle, by invisible beings throughout the whole length and breadth of the Abbey.

A feeling of superstitious awe crept over him.

He had an intense desire to leave the place.

Lifting the little lamp from the tomb, he held it above his head, and leading Nightshade by the bridle, he slowly paced down the long nave of the Abbey, in the hope of finding some means of egress.

A rattling sound awakened the echoes of the ancient pile.

There was a murmur of voices, and Duval paused, for he felt certain that from without an attempt was being made to open one of the ponderous doors of the old structure.

"The villains must be concealed in the Abbey," said a voice; "and Mr. St. Ives is murdered."

These words were a sufficient indication to Duval that they were no friends of his who sought admission to the Abbey, and he felt the necessity of immediately providing in some way for his own safety.

There was a huge old Gothic tomb close at hand, which seemed as if it had been destined at one time to carry a statue or some of those cumbrous allegorical devices in marble which deform, rather than adorn, the old Abbey.

It was but a poor chance, but a romantic idea came over the mind of Claude Duval that he might, for a few seconds, at least, play the part of the missing statue.

If this suggestion were to be carried out, it must be at once, for the door of the cathedral had yielded to the key which was energetically applied to its lock, and a broad gleam of light from several lanterns shone into the nave.

Duval felt how desperate was the resource he projected.

And yet to adopt any other were certain destruction.

To attempt to fly from before those pursuers, without any knowledge or means of getting out of the Abbey, would be to invite capture, for the sound of Nightshade's feet upon the marble floor would necessarily be a guide to his whereabouts, and bring his foes upon him.

It was but a leap, and the experiment could be tried.

Another moment, and Claude Duval on Nightshade had taken his place on the vacant monument.

The space on which the horse had to stand was but small.

It was somewhat slippery, too, and uneven, for the marble had been worked into an imitation of rocks, no doubt with some special purpose connected with the general design.

Duval putted the neck of his steed.

"Peace, Nightshade! Peace! quiet! quiet!"

Nightshade was as still as a statue.

Duval himself scarcely drew breath, and as the light from the lanterns flashed upon him, he felt all the peril of his situation.

Well he knew, however, that it was a principle of human nature to assume, without particular inquiry, that which we believe we are fully assured of.

It was not likely, then, any of those persons visiting the Abbey, and intent upon his capture, would pay much attention to the monuments.

In that case, he might escape detection, notwithstanding the colour of his clothing, and the life-like appearance both of himself and Nightshade, would not stand a moment's investigation.

It was with a perfect rush that Muckles, closely followed by Swallow, and a whole posse of constables and watchmen, made their way into the Abbey.

"Seize him! Seize him!" cried Muckles. "Take him dead or alive! It is Claude Duval! Dead or alive! Dead or alive, I say!

The lanterns and links were held aloft, and by the many cross lights they exhibited, tended rather to confuse than to illuminate objects within the Abbey.

Muckles and his assistants scarcely expected to find Claude Duval near the entrance, and taking a cursory view about them, they rushed onwards in a confused throng.

That was Duval's opportunity.

Perhaps his only one.

He at once dismounted, and leaping lightly from the tomb, he held Nightshade by the bridle, assisting the horse with all his strength to step down on to the marble pavement with the least possible noise.

The footfall of Nightshade scarcely awakened an echo in the old Abbey as Duval then led him to the open door.

They were free.

Claude was in the saddle.

He placed his hand trumpet-like to his mouth, and shouted aloud, "Good night, Mr. Muckles!"

There was a yell of rage from the interior of the Abbey, and as Duval gave the reins to Nightshade and galloped off, he heard the unmistakable voice of Swallow.

"Done brown again, Mr. Muckles! Done brown again!"

In about a minute Duval was in Whitehall.

How still the night was, and how utterly and entirely deserted were the streets!

It was just that hour before the dawn when London, if ever really in repose, was at its quietest.

"Home! home!" cried Duval, as he inhaled, with great satisfaction, the pure night air. "Home! home! I have surely had adventures enough for this night, and would fain hear the light morning air making pleasant music among the tree-tops of Hampstead Heath."

Nightshade seemed to catch pleasantly that word home, and at a pace which, had there been any pursuit, would have soon left it far behind, he left the streets of London, and by the old North Road took his way to the beautiful suburban abode of Claude Duval.

No sooner had the horse and its rider emerged upon the heath, than Duval was a little startled by a horseman dashing out from the shadow of some trees with a loud "Hurrah!"

Duval reined in Nightshade, for he was busy with his own thoughts, and at the moment had not recognised the voice of Blossom.

"Hurrah, Captain! hurrah! The sight of you chases the night away, and makes sunshine of the old heath!"

"Blossom?"

"Yes, Captain. All's right. I see you have escaped. You were sure to do so; and yet I could not but feel anxious at seeing you disappear beneath the surface of the ground in that odd fashion at Westminster."

"It was an odd fashion."

"Yes, Captain; and I was afraid something serious would happen."

"Something serious has happened, but not to me."

"Then we won't mind about it. All's well that ends well."

"How are affairs at home?" asked Duval. "No alarm, I hope?"

"Well, to tell the truth, Captain, I've not had the courage to go there. You would not have me with you down that ugly trap in Westminster, so I was compelled to leave you; but for, all that, I could not make up my mind to put in an appearance at our mansion on the heath alone."

"Then I am anxious," said Duval. "I do not know how it is, but for the last half-hour a feeling of dread and anxiety—a kind of foreboding of evil has come across me, which I cannot account for."

"It is nothing, Captain—it is nothing. I have ridden round the estate, and all is perfectly quiet. If there had been the slightest sound of alarm, I must have heard it."

"Come on!" was Duval's brief reply. "Follow me, quickly!"

CHAPTER XXIV.

CLAUDE DUVAL MEETS WITH A SEVERE TRIAL ON HIS RETURN TO HAMPSTEAD HEATH.

THREE minutes ride across the heath would bring Claude Duval and Blossom to a small gate in the park palings surrounding the estate, which he, Duval, had taken possession of.

Deserted as had been those grounds and mansion on account of some absurd ghost story, Duval, with the assistance of Blossom and his men, had so far improved upon popular rumour, that there was not the slightest chance of their being disturbed in holding possession of the property.

And now Duval heard that light morning air, which he had pictured to himself as being so delightful, sighing and moaning among the old tree-tops.

His feelings, however, had now undergone a change, and every sound seemed to come upon his ears as a kind of confirmation of some disaster.

"This is folly and nervousness," he muttered to himself. "I want sleep, when all these fancies will pass away."

He hastily dismounted.

"Take Nightshade, Blossom. He must want both rest and food."

"All's right, Captain! I follow the old trooper's maxim, 'Look to your horse first, and then to yourself.'"

"Good night, Blossom! good night! or rather good morning, for I see there is a brightening colour in the east, and we shall soon have the dawn upon us."

Duval took the shortest possible route to the mansion, making his way by main force through some of the tangled brushwood and undergrowth of the beautiful vegetation that surrounded it.

He entered by a low door, leading from what was called the home garden, and darting up a narrow flight of steps, he called aloud upon the name of Lucy.

"Here—here at last!" he said. "The truant has returned, Lucy! Speak to me! Let me hear by one word that all is well!"

There was no reply.

The door at the top of the staircase, which usually was flung open by Lucy in her haste to welcome him, remained closed.

Duval paused.

He clung to the balustrades of the stairs.

A sickening feel came over him, which he strove to chase away by the most likely supposition in the world.

"She sleeps! Of course she sleeps, and well it is that it should be so! How selfish I was to suppose for a single moment that through this night, which must have been a long and weary one to her, she should know no repose! She sleeps! She sleeps!"

He opened the door.

He trod softly on the carpeted room.

That was not the chamber in which he expected to find Lucy.

There was an inner one—the door of which was partially open, and through which gleamed a light.

Duval, with long strides, for the horseman's boots he wore creaked as he trod, crossed the outer room.

"Lucy!"

A glance was sufficient.

The chamber was empty.

There was an overturned chair.

A broken mirror.

The coverlet of the bed streamed upon the floor, and through one half of the casement, which was swinging to and fro, the early morning air came in gusty puffs.

"Lucy!" he cried again.

The cry would have been sufficient to have awakened her who loved him had she been there present, in the deepest swoon.

Nay, in the agony of its supplication, it might almost have reached the ears of death.

But there was no response.

The half-opened casement creaked ominously, and then as Duval, almost stifled with apprehension and unable to utter another word, cast his alarmed glance in every corner of the apartment, he heard the wild birds without begin their morning song.

The night-light in the chamber began to pale and slowly fade away, as the morning dawn approached.

By a great effort, then, Duval shook off the despondency that was gathering at his heart, and as the necessity for action became more apparent he recovered from the wild despair which seemed about to take possession of him.

He flew to the window.

He gazed anxiously out, but nothing met his eyes save the tree-tops and the wide expanse of heath beyond them.

He rested his hand on the sill of the window.

It was cold and damp.

Claude directed his eyes towards it.

There was blood both upon his hand and upon the woodwork of the window, and upon the vine leaves that clustered about it.

Then a cry, half of rage and half of terror, burst from the lips of Claude, and drawing his sword, he stood in the centre of that chamber with the feeling at his heart as though he could defy a world in arms for the rescue of the being so dear to him.

For the first time he seemed to feel as if he fully appreciated the beauty and gentleness of the fair young girl he had rescued from death.

She seemed peculiarly to belong to him, to be his own, since but for him she must have passed away into the shadow of the tomb and been known no more.

He stamped furiously upon the floor.

"Help! help!" he cried. "Blossom! Blossom! Help, my men all! Help—help, I say!"

All was still.

Then Duval blew the whistle he carried with him shrilly and clearly.

Three notes of alarm.

A hasty footstep approached.

"Captain! Captain!"

There was a rush up the staircase.

Bearing several lights in their hands, Blossom and some of Duval's men appeared.

"I am robbed!" cried Duval,—"cheated! betrayed! Where is Lucy?"

Blossom looked amazed.

The consternation that sat upon the face of Duval's men was too real to be doubted.

"Heard you no alarm?" he added. "Is it possible that this abduction could have taken place amid the silence of the night, and none of you know aught of it?"

The men shook their heads.

"Kill us, Captain, if you think we could in any way betray you!"

"No—no!" exclaimed Duval. "I do not doubt you. I have enemies enough to accomplish a feat like this, without looking for its perpetrators among my friends."

"Tell us what to do, Captain," cried Blossom, "and we will do it with a right good will!"

Duval clasped his hands over his face for a few minutes in silence.

He was in deep thought; and yet what a whirl of ideas passed through his mind!

It took him some time before he could sufficiently concentrate his faculties, so as to come to anything like a clear decision in regard to his course of action.

Then he spoke calmly.

"Blossom!"

"I am here, Captain, at your service."

"Nightshade must be content with the rest he has had already. Let him be saddled, and await me at the wicket."

"It shall be done; and I have but one request to make to you."

"I anticipate it, Blossom. It is that you should come with me, but I think it necessary to leave you here in command. I may perhaps be near at hand, and if during my absence you should get any intelligence of Lucy, put a light in the window of the belfry turret at the top of the house, and it may hasten my return."

Blossom and Duval's men now thought that he was a little distraught, for instead of leaving that apartment by the way he had entered it, he began clambering from the window.

His object was, if possible, to take the same route from the mansion that Lucy had been enforced to take, in the hope that by so doing he might make some further discoveries with regard to the mode of her capture.

There was no great difficulty in descending from that window to the garden beneath, for the stems of the old ivy, that grew up against the house, were thick enough to form a natural, though somewhat intricate, ladder.

Something light and gauzy flapped in the morning air against Duval's face.

It was a piece of torn net or lace, and he felt no doubt whatever but that it had been torn from the dress of Lucy.

Nay, he began to remember that she had worn some lace ornament about her neck, and from the presence of this shred of it he, not unnaturally, came to the conclusion that she had been sitting up for him.

It was something of a relief to think that that was the case.

She had not been dragged from her slumbers in the dead, small hours of the night.

That was something.

Duval reached the garden without making any further discoveries.

Hastening to the small gate in the oak paling, he found Blossom with Nightshade.

"To you, Blossom," he said, as he instantly mounted, "to you I confide the task of making an accurate search throughout the grounds of the mansion. I will ride over the heath, and see if good fortune will permit me to discover the route by which Lucy has been taken."

The tone in which Claude Duval spoke was so full of anxiety and almost despair, that Blossom could find no words in which to reply to him.

Waving his hand then, Duval rode off.

But he had no fixed purpose, except it was that he meant to leave no spot of the heath unsearched.

The morning light was rapidly gaining strength, and Duval just emerged from one of the hollows of the heath, when he came upon a squalid-looking creature in the faded attire of a gipsy.

Reining in Nightshade, he called to her aloud.

"Speak, my good woman, and your words shall be worth their weight in gold if you can inform me who has been on the heath last night, and who has left it."

"One—two—three!" said the woman.

"What mean you?"

"Two hawks and a dove! But their gold was bright and red!"

"Ah!—I comprehend you!"

"Yes,—bright and red was their gold, and tunefully the guineas clink together. What music is like to that?"

"You shall have more gold," cried Duval; "only give me information worth it, and you will not think me a niggard!"

He held out several gold pieces to the woman as he spoke, and eagerly clutching them, she thrust into his hand a folded paper.

"It is all there!—it is all there!" she said. "I can tell you no more!"

With far greater speed then than she seemed capable of exerting, she hobbled from the spot, and Duval opening the paper, read it eagerly.

The written words were but few:—

"Should this fall into the right hands, he will understand it when he is told to seek her who is lost at Camden House, on the next midnight that shall darken the heavens."

Duval sighed deeply.

He gazed hopelessly around him.

The gipsy woman had fled, and he stood alone upon the heath.

"Till midnight!—till midnight!" he said, "and this is but early dawn. How can I endure the terrible delay?"

As he spoke, a strange booming noise came upon the morning air.

The noise was repeated at regular intervals.

"Guns!" exclaimed Duval. "Why do they fire at such a time?"

At almost a racing pace, a horseman, in a scarlet jacket, carrying a leather despatch box, appeared upon the heath.

"Halt!" cried Duval. "Whither so fast?"

It was but a mere lad who was thus riding northward, and he waved his arm to signify that he must not be stayed.

Duval, however, quietly took one of his pistols from the saddle of Nightshade, and presented it at him as he cried out, "Lead will fly swifter than your horse. Stop, I order you, and tell me why you make such post haste across the heath?"

The boy in the scarlet jacket drew up affrighted.

"Don't shoot a poor fellow, sir. I'm only the cross post-boy!"

Boom! boom! boom! came the echo of the guns from afar off.

"Tell me," added Duval, "what has happened in London, that such a salute is fired so early?"

"Bless you, sir, don't you know? The King's dead and the other King's alive; and so, you see, they've had out the guns in the Park, and are blazing away to let everybody know it; and I am sent post-haste to my Lord Mansfield, who, I take it, is to get to St. James's Palace as soon as possible."

"Indeed!"

"Oh! it's all true, sir; and I hope you'll let me go now, or I shall get into trouble."

"Go—go!"

The boy galloped off with a right good will.

"What can all this mean?" thought Duval. "Is it possible that, despite all that I saw pass before my eyes at that house in Spring Gardens, the Prince of Wales has really compassed the destruction of the King? If that be the case, of little use is this ruby ring, which was to be my passport to the royal favour."

Duval held still the small piece of paper in his hand which he had received from the gipsy.

Again glancing at it, he saw that there was some writing on the back which had hitherto escaped his observation.

He read it eagerly:—

"She whom you seek is not at Camden House, although you will find those there who will give you information of her. Any attempt, however, to seek that place before the hour indicated will be her instant destruction."

"Fiends!" exclaimed Duval. "Why do they torture me thus?"

At any other time, and upon any other occasion, how completely he would have laughed to scorn the threats contained in that paper, but now that his feelings and affections were so deeply concerned he felt almost the shrinking timidity of a child.

A sudden idea then struck him.

"Surely it is not possible that such ingratitude can always be the vice of monarchs, neither can it be within the region of belief that the King can be no more. I left him in life at that mysterious house in Spring Gardens! Why should I not seek him, and at once put an end to all peril on Lucy's account, by claiming as my sole reward for all I have done safety for her?"

Perhaps the idea was more romantic than wise, but Claude Duval was in no frame of mind to be exceedingly critical upon what might suggest itself to him.

At a gallop he took his route to London, only pausing in the Oxford Road for the purpose of purchasing a cloak, such as an officer of distinction might wear, and which was quite sufficient to conceal his highwayman's apparel.

There was a small inn yard not very far from Marlborough House, where, although reluctant to do so, he left Nightshade.

Wrapping his cloak, then, about him, so that nothing appeared but his boots and his embroidered collar, with part of the scarlet cuff of his coat, he made his way to the Palace of St. James's.

An extraordinary scene of bustle was there taking place.

Carriages were arriving in numbers, containing the great officers of state, and many officers who had hastily donned their uniforms were thronging on foot towards the royal residence.

The guards were doubled at the gateway of St. James's.

So many official personages, however, in all sorts of costumes, were making their way into the precincts of the Palace, that Duval had not the smallest difficulty in reaching the Colour Court.

Three sides of that court were lined with troops.

A crowd of officers and officials occupied its centre.

In and out of one of the doors leading to the private apartments of the Palace persons were continually passing.

The occasional roll of drums signified that some member of the royal family now and then made an appearance.

Duval spoke to an elderly officer who was leaning on his sword, and who he thought had a sour and discontented expression of countenance, which would lead him to give as rough and unvarnished an account of what all the bustle was about as possible.

CHAPTER XXV.

CLAUDE DUVAL DISCOVERS THE INGRATITUDE OF KINGS, AND IS APPREHENDED AT THE PALACE.

"CAN you inform me, sir," asked Duval of the elderly officer, "the meaning of all this excitement and tumult in and about the Palace?"

The old man curled his grey moustache and smiled sardonically.

"It is all grief, sir," he said—"grief!"

"I must confess I do not understand."

"Oh, it is not necessary to understand; but all these fine gentlemen you see here, who are thronging to the royal residence, are overcome with grief at the death of the King. Look at that one, sir, grinning like an ape, and adjusting his sword-knot. Yesterday, if the King had had a pain in his little finger, that man would have shed tears, so no wonder he is so overcome at his death."

A general movement among the throng of officers in the Colour Court at this moment seemed to signify that something of importance was about to take place.

A brilliantly dressed gentleman, all silks and satins, with his hair powdered to a nicety and a glittering Court sword by his side, came out of the doorway we have already noticed.

"Now, look there!" cried the officer. "Look at that bird of gay plumage! Only yesterday he was dressed in a sober suit of brown. Look at him now!"

Duval did look.

He could hardly believe his eyes, for in this gaily bedizened personage he recognised a man of the name of Hempson, who was well known as the barber generally in attendance on the Prince of Wales.

This person advanced to the throng of officers with a written paper in his hand.

"Gentlemen," he said, "I am commanded by his Majesty King Frederick the First to thank you for your dutiful love and attention, and to request your attendance in the Throne Room."

"To be showed!" cried the old officer.

There was a general laugh, and the gaily bedizened barber looked the picture of indignation.

Duval himself had a shrewd guess that this man Hempson must have had some hand in the diabolical plot of the Prince against his father, and that hence he appeared in such a jackdaw plumage.

The officers in a body moved towards the doorway, and Duval, amid the throng, was unquestioned by the couple of the Yeomen of the Guard on duty immediately within the Palace.

Along a corridor hung with pictures.

Up a staircase richly covered with a tapestry carpet.

Through one of the long galleries, and then into an ante-room, Duval proceeded, accompanied by some twenty gentlemen in uniform.

"Halt, gentlemen!" cried a voice.

An officer of the Palace Guard stood with his drawn sword in his hand at a pair of folding doors.

A couple of Yeomen had crossed their halberts at that spot, and Duval could very well believe that beyond it was the Throne Room.

What was to be the end of all these mysterious proceedings Claude could hardly guess, and there were moments when he was ready to suppose the Prince Frederick had really succeeded in taking the life of his father, the King, notwithstanding he (Duval) had seen that latter personage apparently in safety from the house in Spring Gardens to the Palace.

There was little time, however, for conjecture or speculation upon the events that were taking place.

Some signal was made from the other side of the folding doors.

The Yeomen uncrossed their halberts.

The officer with the drawn sword stepped aside.

The doors were flung open.

A heavy curtain, with a rush and rattle upon its rings, was drawn aside.

The Throne Room was fully exhibited.

A number of officers of state were already within it.

Standing about two paces in front of the throne, was Frederick, the Prince of Wales.

He looked pale and ghastly.

His attire was a complete suit of black velvet, with, on his breast, a star that blazed with such magnificence that it was almost dazzling and painful to behold.

Slowly the throng of officers, accompanied by Duval, entered the royal presence.

The Prince then made a slight inclination of his head towards a man in ecclesiastical costume at his right hand.

This man advanced, and spoke in soft, mellifluous accents.

"I am commanded by his Royal Highness, formerly Prince of Wales, but now Frederick the First of England, to make a painful communication to the attached servants of his Majesty. A mysterious billet has been received, stating that his Majesty King George the Second was lying dead at a house in Spring Gardens, and with great grief and consternation, his Royal Highness, formerly Prince of Wales, but now King Frederick the First of England, has verified the terrible truth of the statement. Every inquiry will be instituted to discover if the King's death be due from a visitation of heaven or the malice of his enemies, and in the meantime I call upon you, gentlemen, to cry 'God bless King Frederick the First!'"

There was a blank look upon the faces of all present.

If this communication meant anything at all, it certainly signified that the King was murdered.

And now Claude Duval began to see light through the transaction.

There could be no doubt that the Prince of Wales, on the preceding evening, had left that house in Spring Gardens with the full conviction that his father was no more.

The King, too, with the cunning incidental to his nature, had doubtless hidden himself in the Palace of St. James's, in order to await events and see what his exemplary son would do.

That this was the true explanation of all that was taking place, Duval did not doubt for a moment.

He only waited in intense anxiety and curiosity for the termination of the plot.

A look of bitterness and rage came over the face of Frederick the Prince at the complete stillness which followed the request of the ecclesiastical personage to cry God bless him.

"Gentlemen," he said, "we shall know how to discriminate between friends and foes, and we shall regret that so much Jacobitism still lingers in the land."

He waved his arm as a signal that the audience was over.

Then the dense stillness that reigned in the Throne Room was broken by a mysterious noise.

Three sharp taps appeared to be given on the other side of one of the tall mirrors that extended from the floor to the ceiling.

Frederick clutched at one of the arms of the throne for support.

The tall mirror moved.

A slight cough was heard.

"Way for the King!" shouted a voice.

In his usual costume, and carrying the gold-headed cane he commonly had with him, George the Second stepped into the Throne Room.

A yell of fear burst from the lips of Frederick the Prince, and he fell forward flat upon his face.

"Thanks, gentlemen all!" said the King. "We are exceedingly well—in fact, were never better in our lives."

The ecclesiastical personage who had taken so prominent a part in favour of the Prince retreated backwards, with his mouth open, and his eyes preternaturally extended.

He stumbled over the Prince, and made not the least attempt to rise.

The King approached, and slightly tapped them with his walking-stick, as he said. "We give an audience to the French Envoy at twelve. Remove this carrion!"

The look of malignant triumph on the face of the King—for such, indeed, was the character of the expression—was to Claude Duval most revolting.

Majesty, on this occasion, seemed far more intent upon the enjoyment of its triumph, than amenable to those feelings which one would have supposed the case capable of evoking.

"Remove that carrion!" repeated the King.

He touched Frederick Prince of Wales again with the walking-cane, to intimate the special carrion he alluded to.

The officer of the Yeomen of the Guard gave an order.

From the ante-room came the measured tread of armed men.

"Halt!"

A company of the Yeomen of the Guard paused at the entrance of the Presence Chamber.

"Remove that carrion!" said the King, a third time.

The very utterance of the words seemed to give him singular pleasure.

Then the officer of the guard, lowering the point of his sword, spoke in a tone of humility and quiet remonstrance.

"Your Majesty alludes to his Royal Highness the Prince of Wales?"

The King again tapped the prostrate form of the

Prince with his walking-cane, and gravely inclined his head.

"Yeomen, advance," said the officer, "and remove this——"

"Carrion!" added the King, as he turned upon his heel; and gently swaying the walking-cane by the middle, he made his way back again to the throne.

Frederick Prince of Wales either was, or thought it good policy to seem to be, completely crushed by the turn affairs had taken.

He kept his eyes resolutely shut.

He allowed his limbs to hang listlessly and nervously which way they would.

It was with a good deal of difficulty—so limber and limp did he appear—that the Yeomen of the Guard could lift him from the floor.

They did so with a sort of half respect, half fright.

"May it please your Majesty," said the officer, "where is it your royal pleasure that the Prince should be bestowed?"

Up to this moment, the King had preserved an icy cold exterior.

True, his lips were white.

True, there was a saffron-like hue upon his countenance.

A bloodshot expression about his eyes, and a nervous twitching of his hands, which betrayed the raging passion that was within him.

But, up to this time, he had succeeded in subduing all outward expression of feeling, so far as words were concerned.

When this question, however, was propounded by the officer of the Yeomen, all self-control seemed to leave the King, and it was with something of a roar that he shouted the answer.

"To the Tower!"

The Court looked at each other uneasily.

"To the Tower!" roared the King again. "To the Traitors' Gate, and only out to a scaffold!"

The officer bowed low.

The Prince of Wales, indeed, might have been past human vengeance, for all sign or token that he gave of the smallest intelligence of what was going on.

Perhaps nothing was, after all, better contrived for the purpose of baffling the King than this perfectly inert submission of the Prince.

Probably Frederick guessed as much.

Had he resisted.

Had he attempted the least justification of his conduct, the King might have roared the Palace down in the rage of his accusations.

But what was to be done with the man who shut his eyes, and surrendered himself to circumstances, in so perfectly limp and helpless a condition as that assumed by Frederick Prince of Wales?

He was carried out.

The ecclesiastical personage crawled after him.

And then the great officers of State, and the personal attendants of the monarch, felt a sensation of relief.

No one spoke, however.

No one seemed exactly to know what to say that would be most acceptable to royalty on that occasion.

Then the King put on a sardonic smile, which sat with a most ugly expression upon his countenance.

"My lords all," he said, "we will take it that joy strikes you dumb; and assume that this, our resuscitation, is an event that will make this day ever blessed in your memories."

Slightly raising his hat, he executed a half-bow.

Turning abruptly, then, towards a door that led to the private apartments of the Palace, George the Second would in another moment have disappeared, had not Claude Duval felt that his time to speak had come, and that if he now hesitated, the object for which he had risked so much would be lost.

He stepped forward.

"Your Majesty!"

The King turned abruptly, and glared at him.

Duval lightly dropped on one knee, and presented to the eyes of the astonished King the ruby ring that had been given him in the Park.

CHAPTER XXVI.

CLAUDE DUVAL IS DISAPPOINTED IN HIS ESTIMATE OF KING GEORGE.

A LOOK of great curiosity sat upon the faces of the courtiers.

The King was near-sighted, and had to stoop forward a little to see what it was that Duval presented to him.

"A ring belonging to your Majesty."

"Ah!"

"Probably your Majesty recognises it?"

"Certainly! The jewel is our own."

"Your Majesty will likewise remember the circumstance under which your most humble servant became possessed of it?"

"Perfectly!"

The King held out his hand, and took the ring.

As he put it on his finger, Duval thought—although the King was never noted for personal comeliness—that he never before had looked so positively apish and ugly.

"Perfectly!"

"Then, your Majesty, sooner than I thought it possible, I have the favour to ask which this ring was to be the forerunner of."

"Favour, man? What favour? We think any of our subjects sufficiently honoured and sufficiently repaid, for restoring to us a lost trinket, by this personal interview."

"Your Majesty!"

"What now?"

"Is it possible you do not know me?"

The King shook his head.

"Is my voice—are my features so soon forgotten?"

"We never saw you, man, in our lives before; and these interrogatories and presumptions become intrusive."

The King turned abruptly.

Duval sprang to his feet.

"Put not your faith in princes!" he cried.

"Treason!" said the King. "My Lord Mansfield, surely that is treason? Who knows this man?"

"None in this presence," said Duval, "half so well as King George the Second."

"And yet another sufficiently," said a voice.

A tall man, in very superb courtly costume, stepped forward.

"Ah, Montrose!" said the King. "What do you know of him?"

"Nothing," cried another gentleman, interposing, and grasping the arm of the Duke of Montrose,—"nothing that, as gentlemen, we ought not to know."

"Marquis," said the Duke, "act for yourself. I, for my part, have no fine-drawn sympathies with highwaymen."

"So, so, my Lord Harcourt!" cried the King; "it seems you know something of this personage. But we will leave you, my lords and gentlemen, to settle the question of his identity among you."

A door hastily opened.

The King darted through it.

Click! went the lock; and Claude Duval found that royal gratitude was a dream, and that all he had ever heard of George the Second of England was fully

DUVAL ESCAPES FROM THE BOW STREET RUNNERS.

verified by the reception he had himself received after actually being the means of saving the King's life.

A glance at the two gentlemen, who began to use high words to each other on his account, had at once sufficed to let Duval know that they were none other than the Duke of Montrose and the Marquis of Harcourt, with whom he had had the adventure on Hampstead Heath.

They were now fully carrying out their respective characters.

The Marquis was all generosity.

The Duke malevolently revengeful.

"Guard! guard!" he cried. "I denounce this man as a criminal! Guard! guard! This is an intrusion into the royal presence, at once insolent and suspicious!"

"Fly, while you can!" cried the Marquis of Harcourt. "My Lord Duke, I hold you answerable to me for your conduct on this occasion."

"When you will, and how you will, Marquis; but, on my own authority, I order the arrest of that man!"

No 9.—NIGHTSHADE

Duval flung off his cloak.

He drew his sword.

"There are times," he said, "when personal liberty is dearer than life itself, and this is one of them."

As he spoke, he dashed from the Throne Room, past the velvet curtain, into the outer apartment.

A burly Yeoman of the Guard strove to stay his progress with his halbert; but the impetuosity of the career of Claude Duval was such that, dashing full against him, both Yeoman and halbert rolled on the floor together.

It was only by a great effort that Claude hindered himself from inflicting some serious wound upon this man with his drawn sword.

He slightly stumbled over him.

Regaining his feet, then, he crossed the ante-room at a bound.

"Treason!—treason! Guard—guard! Stop him! Stop him!"

The Duke of Montrose had found adherents.

He was of high rank and immense fortune, and there

were many persons about the Court who were always ready to adopt either his hatreds or affections, and shape their line of conduct to his will.

And now, as it happened, the fall of that burly Yeoman of the Guard was quite a providence to Claude Duval.

Lying prostrate, the man still retained hold of his halbert, and with considerable confusion of ideas as to what was taking place, he thought his best plan was to continue on the offensive as long as possible.

The halbert made terrible havoc among the legs of the courtiers, as the Yeoman, still lying upon his back, made lunges and sweeps with it as though he were in the midst of some *mêlée*, and that was the only way of keeping off his enemies.

The curious antique combination of steel pikes and hatchet heads at the end of the halbert presented anything but an agreable prospect to those who came in contact with it.

Shouts, and cries, and admonitions—not unmingled with a liberal sprinkling of oaths—resounded in the ante-chamber.

Each moment seemed a life to Claude Duval.

He rushed down the gallery of royal portraits with the speed of light.

He swung himself down the very balustrade of that staircase, so richly covered with its velvet tapestry.

He reached the small circular hall where a bewildered Yeoman was on duty.

"You are wanted above," cried Duval. "Something happened to the King."

"The—the—new King?"

"No; the old one."

"But he his dead, sir."

"Yes; to conscience and to memory. Fly; you are wanted above! Leave your halbert with me. I hold guard in your place."

"But——"

"Another moment, and you are too late."

"Did Colonel St. Vincent, sir, give the order?"

"Thrice over!"

The Yeoman surrendered his halbert, and rushed up the stairs.

Another moment, and Claude Duval was in the court-yard.

"Stop him! Seize him! A highwayman! A robber! By order of the King! Seize him! Seize him! Guard! Guard! Take him dead or alive!"

The sentinel in the Colour Court brought his musket to the charge.

There was a confused rush of the reserved guard from the gloomy barrack room under the gateway.

Duval had but one chance.

He might possibly pass the sentinel, and make his way under the cloisters by that route to the Park.

He attempted it.

"Fire!" cried a voice.

Duval looked askance to see where it came from.

A window of the Palace was open, and the Duke of Montrose was gesticulating fiercely from it.

The sentinel fired.

But he aimed at Duval.

There was the safety.

The old flint and steel musket at that period never killed, except by accident.

The ball flew wide of its mark, and striking a projecting iron pipe, obeyed at once, with admirable precision, the laws of projectiles, by darting off at an angle, and breaking a pane of glass of the very window out of which the Duke of Montrose was looking, and within a couple of inches of his head.

The Duke retired with precipitation.

But Duval was surrounded.

Escape was out of the question.

He might kill a man—perhaps two men.

But what then? He would be still a prisoner.

With a deep sigh, he lowered his sword point.

"That is well done," said an officer of the guard; "a brave man knows when to surrender."

"To-morrow!—to-morrow!" cried Duval, "only till to-morrow! On my honour—my conscience—my soul—my life, I will be here to-morrow; but only let me go to-day!"

"Absurdly impossible!" said a voice. "You are my prisoner."

Duval dropped his sword.

He was not superstitious, but surprise and consternation sat upon his countenance as he recognised in this person who had stepped out from beneath the cloisters, no other than St. Ives, the detective.

The man who he thought had perished in the thieves' ken, at Westminster.

The man who, to all appearance, had met with that fearful death by gunpowder, as the penalty of his intrusion into the councils of the lawless, and who had assembled beneath the old Abbey.

But there he was.

Just as usual.

Without the least evidences of having gone through any such trial.

Calm, self-possessed, and smiling.

"St. Ives!" ejaculated Duval.

"Yes; and I arrest you, Claude Duval, for highway robbery. Now, at least, you are my prisoner, without evasion."

"Alive?"

"Oh, yes; certainly alive. Captain Ponsonby, you know me as an officer of the police?"

"Certainly, Mr. St. Ives!"

"Then you have no hesitation in surrendering this man to my keeping. He is a notorious highwayman."

"Faith, certainly not!" said Captain Ponsonby, as he sheathed his sword. "Some one called treason from the Palace window, or I should not have interfered."

"Claude Duval," said St. Ives, "I am alone, but I can summon plenty of assistance, and if I feel compelled to do it I will. Moreover, I will have you manacled like a common felon, as you are, and conveyed to Newgate in the first coach I can procure; but if you will give me your word not to attempt to escape, we may manage matters otherwise."

"I will resist," said Duval, using the words of Ferdinand, in the "Tempest"—"I will resist till mine enemy have more power."

A kind of frenzy had seized upon Duval.

The pang of not being able to keep his appointment at Camden House on that night, to seek for Lucy, was more than he could bear.

He closed with St. Ives instantly.

"Help, help, gentlemen all! The fellow will throttle me!"

Duval was overpowered by superior numbers, and despite all his resistance, handcuffs were put upon his wrists, and, amid a dense throng of the officials and domestics of the Palace, together with every idle passenger who passed that way, pale, excited, and his apparel torn, he was led out into St. James's Street.

The tumult in the Colour Court.

The discharge of the musket.

The cries and shouts of the courtiers and attendants of the Palace had made up a chorus of discords fully sufficient to arrest the attention of every passing passenger.

A number of people had assembled at the Palace gate, who were only kept from rushing into the Colour Court by the Guard.

And when Claude Duval appeared, flushed at moments and then deadly pale, the sympathies of the multitude were with him.

"He's the same man," cried a voice, "that saved the girl at Tyburn!"

"They want to hang him for it!" cried another.

"Rescue!—rescue!" shouted a dozen voices.

A faint smile crossed the lips of Claude Duval.

"It seems, Mr. St. Ives," he said, "that your triumph will not be so easy!"

"It shall be complete," replied St. Ives. "A coach!—a coach, there! A coach, constables!—a coach!"

Several men separated themselves from the crowd, producing constables' staves, and surrounded Duval and St. Ives.

A coach was hastily procured from a stand in Pall Mall.

"Now, Mr. Duval," said St. Ives, "as Captain Ponsonby says, 'a brave man knows when to submit.' Please to step in!"

Duval did so.

St. Ives sprang after him.

The constables crowded to the door, and with one voice proffered their services.

"No," cried St. Ives; "he is my prisoner, and mine only. I will have the glory of taking Claude Duval to Newgate, or the shame of failing to do so."

The officers fell back.

"Drive on!" cried St. Ives.

The coach, with many lurches to and fro, got into motion.

"To Newgate!" shouted St. Ives, in an excited tone.

The crowd burst into a roar of execration.

Again many voices cried out, "Rescue!—rescue!" and a rush was made at the horses' heads to stop them, while several of the more courageous of the mob tried to open the coach doors.

St. Ives had seated his prisoner at the back of the coach.

It was the place of honour, although probably Claude Duval at that time scarcely appreciated it.

Sitting, then, with his back to the horses on the opposite seat, the officer produced his pistols, and resting one on the lower framework of each window, he cried in loud tones, "I blow the brains out of the first man who interferes with me in my duty!"

No one seemed to like exactly being the victim on the occasion, and the mob fell back.

"Drive on, coachman!" cried St. Ives. "It's a guinea fare to Newgate."

The coach rattled down Pall Mall.

By the time it passed Vanbrugh House the fickle multitude had deserted it, and no one would have supposed that that unpretending vehicle contained so celebrated a person as Claude Duval.

St. Ives drew up both the windows.

He took off his hat and wiped the perspiration from his brow.

"Duval!"

"St. Ives!"

"You are my prisoner!"

"News, that!" said Duval.

St. Ives fumbled in his pocket.

He produced the key of the handcuffs.

There was a strange twitching motion about his mouth, and a blinking of his eyes as he spoke.

"Claude Duval, I am going to ruin and delight myself!"

Click! went the lock of the handcuffs.

They fell with a sudden dab to the floor of the coach.

St. Ives took hold of his pistols by the barrels.

He held the stocks close to Claude Duval.

"Take them!" he said. "The only plan is to shoot me and escape."

Duval looked incredulous.

He pushed the pistols aside.

"Mr. St. Ives, are you mad, or am I in a dream?"

"Neither, Claude Duval! But do you think I could take the man to Newgate, knowing that from thence he would only be taken to death, who made so kindly and heroic an effort to save my life?"

Duval opened his eyes wide with astonishment.

"You were in danger, I tell you!" added St. Ives.—"in mortal danger, as you stood in the Colour Court of St. James's Palace. There were no means of saving you but those which I adopted. I have saved you — you are free!"

"Is this credible?"

St. Ives clasped his hands over his face.

He gasped convulsively for a moment, and then looked at Duval with a smile.

"A ruined and delighted man," he said, "I shall live somehow! Farewell to all this mode of life and its prospects! But why do I speak thus to you Duval? I do not wish you to carry away a pang with you. Take the liberty I give you, and leave me to my own resources!"

The coach had turned into the Strand.

It was nearly half-way to Newgate.

"Hold!" cried Duval. "You held me, St. Ives, a short time since with manacles of steel, but now you hold me in a bondage I dare not escape from! We will go to Newgate!"

CHAPTER XXVII.

CLAUDE DUVAL FINDS THAT GRATITUDE IS NOT EXTINCT IN THE BREAST OF ALL MEN.

St. Ives looked at Duval in silence for some few seconds.

He seemed to wish to speak, and yet the words he would have uttered died away upon his lips.

Duval had settled himself in the corner of the coach, and was not at all prepared for the sudden action which St. Ives conceived and carried out.

Opening the coach door suddenly, the officer made but one spring into the roadway.

"Farewell!" he cried. "We shall meet again! I have paid my debt! Farewell!"

St. Ives ran, as though he were in fear of pursuit, down one of the narrow streets of the Strand, and Claude Duval was left sitting bewildered in the coach, with the door flapping to and fro, as the old crazy vehicle rocked uneasily on its springs.

"Hoy! halt!" he cried.

The coachman pulled up.

Duval leaped out and closed the door.

"Here is your guinea, my friend, and so good day!"

Duval walked calmly away, leaving the coachman gazing into the vehicle, through the front window, and wondering what was the meaning of the whole transaction.

And there, down the Strand in the open face of day, walked Claude Duval in his full costume of a highwayman, surrounded by so many dangers that it was something wonderful he reached the length of Northumberland House without being questioned.

An empty sedan chair presented itself most providentially to his observation.

"A chair, yer honour?"

"Yes."

Duval was in the chair, and had pulled down the little fluttering silk curtains, just as he saw a man come sauntering round the corner from Whitehall, who, had he been a moment sooner, might have succeeded in undoing all that St. Ives had done for the preservation of Claude Duval.

It was Muckles, the officer.

Three or four paces behind him was Swallow.

The poles of the sedan chair almost brushed them as it passed along.

"I knowed it!" Duval heard Swallow say. "I knowed it, Mr. Muckles! We shall always be done brown, and no mistake!"

"Where to, yer honour?" cried one of the chairmen.

A feeling of curiosity induced Muckles to incline his head forward to listen to the answer from within the chair.

It came in so admirably an imitated female voice that the chairman started at the seeming transformation of his fare.

"Number twenty-two, St. James's street!"

Muckles drew back.

"Some lady shopping," he said.

The chairmen looked at each other, and seemed inclined to question the transaction, but Duval spoke again in a low voice.

"A guinea each!"

The words were magical.

The sedan chair was lifted and carried off at a sharp trot.

"Yes," said Swallow; "that's my opinion, Mr. Muckles. Whatsomedever and wheresomedever we has anything to do with Claude Duval, we shall be done brown, and no mistake!"

The danger was over.

Duval breathed more freely.

If he could but reach the stable where Nightshade was put up, and place his foot in the stirrup, he would believe that all that morning of excitements and dangers had indeed dissipated, leaving but a dreamy recollection behind them.

One—two—three sounded the Palace clock of St. James's.

The corner of the street was reached, down which was the stable-yard where Nightshade was put up, therefore Duval halted the sedan chair and, giving a cautious glance from its window, he alighted.

"Your honour said a guinea a-piece for us!"

"There they are! The guineas are gold, you see; but if you do not take up your sedan, and trot back to the Strand from whence you took me, without looking once behind you, I will treat you to a baser metal—an ounce of lead each."

St. Ives had flung his pistols on the coach seat when he left it, and Duval had possession of them.

The sight of them was quite sufficient for the chairmen, and they rushed down St. James's Street with the sedan as though the enemy of mankind were at their heels.

"Three o'clock!" said Duval. "Nine hours till midnight, before which, according to the mysterious billet I have received, it will be useless to visit Camden House. What will become of me? How can I endure the suspense? Home! No, I have no home now, since it is robbed of its chiefest ornament! It is but a wreck—a ruin—and I feel as if the air of any of its chambers would stifle me. I must seek for some excitement or go mad. That ungrateful King! For what did I save his life? St. Ives, too; how strange his conduct. No—no; we do not all reap as we sow, or the gratitude of the King should have been ten times as vivid as that of St. Ives!"

Thus communing with himself and making strange gestures in the street, to the astonishment of the few chance passengers who passed him, Duval reached the stable.

A curious crowd was around its entrance.

What could it mean?

Duval forced his way in.

"My horse, ostler!"

"There he is! There he is!" shouted a dozen voices.

"That's him! That's him!"

Duval drew back a step.

"Come out—come out! Here he is!"

The stable door in which Nightshade had been put, was flung open.

It needed but a glance from Duval to see that not only Nightshade was there, but several men, who from their top-boots and red waistcoats could be none other than Bow Street runners.

"Seize him! seize him! Shut the outer gate! It's Claude Duval, the highwayman!"

"Nightshade!"

The horse saw his master.

"Nightshade!"

The creature heard the well-known voice that had trained him from a foal.

One plunge was sufficient to free him from the grasp of the officers, and he was by the side of Duval.

The stirrups were dashing about in wild commotion; but Duval scarcely needed their aid, as he twined one of his hands in the long, silken mane of Nightshade.

"Fire!"

Duval had half mounted.

Some pistols bullets whistled harmlessly over his head.

There was a yell of affright from some one at the yard entrance.

Duval was mounted.

Two leaps took him into the street, and the second one was over the prostrate figure of Swallow, who had just arrived, and whose hat had been blown from his head by one of the pistol-shots.

"Done brown again!" were the last words Duval heard, as the heels of Nightshade, catching Swallow lightly about the middle of his back, sent him rolling over and over several yards down the stable entrance.

In twenty minutes more, Claude Duval was on the Western Road, gently patting the neck of Nightshade, and proceeding at a walking pace, in the shadow of some tall and beautiful trees that lined the roadway.

Were the excitements and dangers of that day really over?

We shall see.

There was a little roadside inn—an old, semi-ecclesiastical-looking mansion, which had lost its character, and become a hostelry.

Beautifully embowered in trees, and looking picturesque even through its present vulgarity, the place was a tempting one to stop at.

Duval drew rein.

A few dozen more paces, and he stood at the door of the little hostel; but the rapid beat of horses' feet on the road behind him induced him to pause to see who was approaching at such headlong speed.

A gentleman in a rich riding-cloak.

Mounted on a chesnut horse of evident great value.

Altogether, both man and steed presented most emphatically the appearance of wealth and aristocracy.

The gentleman drew rein at the door of the inn, and hastily dismounting, he asked some hurried question, which seemed to be replied to in the affirmative—for, with a nod of gratification, he crossed the threshold and disappeared.

A boy led the chesnut horse along the garden-path, which probably led to the stables of the establishment.

Duval dismounted, and, leading Nightshade by the bridle, he thought he could not do better than follow the boy with the chesnut horse, since he had half made up his mind to remain at that house until the day should have passed away, and the night sufficiently advanced to warrant him in starting on his expedition to Camden House.

"Hilloa, boy! Does this lead to the stables?"

"Yes, measter, it does."

"Whose horse is that?"

"I mustn't tell. It be Colonel Jessop's; but it's a secret, and he'll wallop I if I tells!"

"Very good. So! you have a goodly range of stables here. And whose horse may this be with a side-saddle?"

"I mustn't tell that, neither. That be a secret. It be the Duchess of Cleveland's."

"Is that possible?"

"No, it bean't possible, because it be a secret; and I be main good at secrets—you don't get nothin' out of I! I keeps myself to myself, and listens at all the key-holes; and when I finds out somethin', I says nothin'; but I seed the Colonel a-stampin', and a-ragin', and a-threatenin' the poor lady like an old bull in the paddock when he sees the beadle on a Sunday with his fine coat and hat on. But I says nothin'—not I! Mum's the word, and you get nothin' out of I!"

"Very good," said Duval. "I see you are a discreet youth."

"And who may you be, sir? I won't tell, if so be as you don't want I?"

"Smith."

"Eh?"

"Smith, I tell you!"

"Thankee, sir. Smith! He be Smith."

The boy, without paying any more attention to Duval, went off immediately to communicate to everybody in the inn that the new arrival was Mr. Smith, on the principle that nobody got "nothin'" out of him.

"The Duchess of Cleveland here, and apparently holding a clandestine meeting with Colonel Jessop, one of the most well-known *roues* of the Court! What can it mean?" thought Claude Duval.

But that was a day of mysteries.

Firstly, there were those singular occurrences at the Palace of St. James's, which had culminated in an instance of ingratitude on the part of the King, which we will suppose human nature to be rarely capable of.

Then there was the something more than mysterious re-appearance of St. Ives, the detective.

That had still to be explained; although Claude Duval had little doubt, when he put the circumstances together in his own mind, that the pretended barrel of gunpowder in the thieves' ken contained, in reality, but a small portion of that combustible.

His feeling towards the Duchess of Cleveland was certainly one of gratitude.

Without her assistance, he must have fallen into the hands of his enemies on the occasion of the masked ball at Queensberry House.

Could he do anything, now, to return that obligation? Or would the kindest thing he could possibly do be to leave that roadside inn, and banish from his mind the memory of the fact that the young and charming Duchess held there an assignation with the notorious Colonel Jessop?

More than once, Claude Duval was in the act of taking this view of the case; but something—he knew not what—restrained him; and after seeing to the accommodation and comfort of Nightshade, he made his way into the inn.

Duval's costume was so like that of a military officer, that, in a country place, it might easily be mistaken for such.

In the streets of London, it was rather sensational, although at that period variety and eccentricity of costume were by no means so rare as at present.

This arose from the habit that official personages then had of wearing what may be called uniforms in private life.

The officer in the army seldom appeared without his scarlet coat.

Those of the navy likewise affected their uniform.

A lawyer, a Churchman, a physician, in fact, a member of any of the superior professions, could then be detected at a glance.

The effect was picturesque.

It has remained for the present age to reduce everything to a dead level of uniformity.

When Claude Duval, therefore, entered the little roadside inn, he might pass either as a highwayman or an officer in the army, but in either case his demand for a private room was promptly acceded to.

He was shown into an old-fashioned wainscoted apartment on the first-floor, and the pint of canary he had ordered being placed before him, he was left to his own reflections.

Those reflections were soon disturbed by a half scream, apparently coming from some one in the adjoining apartment.

The tone of the cry brought with it a kind of memory, which convinced Duval that he was in the immediate proximity of the Duchess of Cleveland, and that the sound came from her lips.

Still he shrunk from interference.

Was it an intrigue?

Was she in some manner the victim of this Colonel Jessop?

Did she require a friend's arm to aid her, or would the appearance of any one on the scene with whom she was acquainted be resented as a most gratuitous interference?

These considerations made Duval irresolute.

He listened intently in the direction from whence the cry had come, and examining the wall on that side of the room, he found an old deep cupboard.

Its door was locked.

The woodwork, as well as the lock, however, were both frail, and Duval had no difficulty with the point of his sword in wrenching the door open.

The back of that cupboard was only separated from the adjoining room by one thickness of the wainscoting which formed the wall.

Everything that took place, therefore, in that next apartment came to the ears of Duval with such startling distinctness, that for a moment he recoiled from being an eavesdropper on the occasion.

The Duchess was speaking.

It was her tone of voice—evidently one of distress—which encouraged Duval in listening to what she had to say.

"This transcends all persecution. Why do you torture me in this fashion? Over and over again I have paid you at the sacrifice of all the means I had in my power, and as often have you promised to restore to me those letters which, four years ago, when a mere girl, I was prevailed upon to write to you."

"Prevailed upon?" replied a male voice, in mocking accents. "You were delighted with me four years ago."

"I did not know you!"

"Ha! ha! You knew me well enough to pour forth on paper, in the most fervid and impassioned words, your attachment."

"It may have been so—it was so—but times are changed. The period of youth and indiscretion which then induced me to have boundless faith in human nature, has passed away. I know you now, Archibald Jessop, and I demand of you but two things."

"And they?"

"They are forgetfulness, and a return of those letters which you should never have possessed."

"Good!" cried the Colonel; "but as I do happen to possess them, they are the luckiest throw of fortune's dice that ever happened to me. I have had ill luck. The gaming table has gone against me, and I have lost all, while you have advanced in honour, dignity, and wealth. The remnant of my fortune consists of those letters. They are a mine containing rich ore, which, from time to time, I bring to the surface and turn to gold."

"This is infamous!"

"Give it what name you like, Duchess, it is profitable. Your income is some twenty-two thousand per annum."

"Alas! alas!"

"Ha, ha! A fine thing to cry alas for!"

"And what do you demand?"

"Share those thousands with me, and those letters will not see the light of day."

"I do not comprehend you."

Claude Duval heard the Duchess weeping.

He had sheathed his sword, but now he loosened it in its scabbard, and a flush of indignation crossed his brow.

CHAPTER XXVIII.

CLAUDE DUVAL HAS AN ENCOUNTER WITH COLONEL JESSOP.

There was a pause of some few seconds in the chamber where so singular an interview was taking place between the beautiful Duchess of Cleveland and the notorious Colonel Jessop.

From the sound of footsteps it appeared that the Colonel was pacing the room to and fro.

Then he suddenly paused, and spoke in harsh, stern accents.

"You say you do not understand me. I will make myself clear and comprehensible. Upon receiving annually one-half your income, I will undertake that those letters—forty in number—which, if produced, would cover you with ridicule and contempt, and render your position, both public and social, untenable, shall never see the light."

"Still," replied the Duchess, "I cannot understand you. Do you mean you will restore me the letters?"

"Certainly not!"

"Then you claim half my income in perpetuity merely on your promise of keeping them secret?"

"Exactly so!"

"Infamous!"

"Call it by what name you please. I am not particular to terms."

"Villain!"

"Please yourself, Duchess; but those expressions come but with an ill grace from your charming lips!"

"Oh, that I were a man!"

"What then?"

"I would wrest those letters from you, and at the same time rid society of such a monster."

The Colonel laughed sardonically.

"There is a man here," said Duval to himself, "who will probably accomplish that feat before you are a quarter of an hour older, Colonel Jessop."

The indignation of Duval was great, and had he consulted the impulse of the moment, he would then and there have made his way into the adjoining apartment and defied the Colonel.

There was one point, however, upon which he desired further information.

That was whether the letters so earnestly required by the fair Duchess of Cleveland were actually there and then in the possession of Colonel Jessop or not.

If they were, the transaction would be easy.

If not, a contest with the Colonel could lead to no good result, and would only, in fact, put him on his guard.

It was, then, very strange that this very point on which Duval required information should turn up to be the one next in question between the Duchess of Cleveland and her persecutor.

"Put an end," she cried, "to all this cruelty at once! There was a time when you pretended to love me. At that time those letters were written. You could have had no object in being so completely false as to extort them from me without a shadow of the feeling you pretended possessed you."

"Indeed, Duchess! That is your opinion?"

"It is. And I now call upon you by the memory of that feeling, to restore me those letters!"

"I have named my terms, and I call upon you, Duchess, by the memory of those terms, to accede to them."

"You are too false, too untrue, even if I felt inclined to accede to them, to trust you."

"What mean you? It is no trust. You have but to pay me money."

"But the letters may be destroyed or lost."

"Not so."

"I may be terrifying myself at a shadow."

"You shall see the substance. The letters are in my possession. I was prepared for this incredulity, because it was natural. I have the letters here."

The poor Duchess had cherished a hope that the letters might not really be in existence; but as Colonel Jessop took a packet from his pocket, and held it before her tearful eyes, that hope vanished.

"Are you satisfied?"

"Both satisfied and destroyed. And yet——"

She made a feeble snatch at the letters.

Colonel Jessop laughed, and held them higher than her reach.

"No, Duchess, your strength hardly suffices to wrest from me that which I wish to retain. Accede to my terms, and the letters shall never see the light, and even should I die they will be in some place of security, where no mortal eye can see them or hand rest upon them. I will give you four-and-twenty hours to consider my proposition. You will then meet me here again; and I have not the smallest doubt but that you will say yes to my terms."

"I cannot."

"You will. But if, by any possible perversity, you hold out beyond that period, you will hear of these letters as the talk of the town, the scandal of the Court, and the destruction of its celebrated beauties. What is that?"

The room had been rapidly darkening as Colonel Jessop spoke, and a peal of thunder appeared to shake the old inn to its foundations.

"A storm!" he cried. "Ha, ha! What care I? Duchess, you will have a wet riding-habit before you reach town; but according to the arrangement I laid down you had better leave this inn somewhat before me, and we shall not be seen upon the road together. Moreover, I require some refreshment, for these interviews make me thirsty, and there is as fine sherris in the cellar of this old inn as the kingdom can present. Can I offer you anything, Duchess?"

"No, no!"

"Then I have the honour of bidding you good day."

With a sob, the Duchess left the apartment.

A brutal laugh burst from the lips of Colonel Jessop.

"Men and women call me fickle," he said; "but I am constant to one thing, and the only thing that has ever bound my slippery soul—my own interest. And now for the sherris!"

He rang the bell violently, and was soon deep in the contents of that old Spanish wine, which then, before the Genius of Adulteration had raised its head, was to be had in far greater perfection in England than in the present day.

Not a word of all this had escaped Claude Duval.

The storm without lasted some twenty minutes, producing considerable darkness; and, as the evening was creeping on apace, that darkness of the tempest soon mingled with the twilight, and the outline of all objects began to get dim and confused.

Duval issued from the inn, and quietly making his way to the stable where Nightshade was resting, he mounted without troubling any of the persons connected with the hostel.

A leap over two hedges brought him into the high road.

The trees, bushes, roadway, were all saturated with moisture, for the storm having passed away had been succeeded by a small, drizzling rain.

Within view of the inn door, although at some little distance townward, up the road, there was a narrow lane.

Only wide enough for a horse and another to pass him, this lane was shadowed over by tall trees, whose tops so completely intermingled with each other that even at noonday they would have cast an impenetrable shadow beneath them.

There Duval hid himself.

It was only necessary to go a few paces down this lane in order to be completely secluded from all observation.

But he kept his eyes upon the inn door.

And there, with the only sound that came upon his ears being the pattering of the rain drops from leaf to leaf of the tall intermingling trees overhead, he waited for Colonel Jessop.

Half an hour elapsed.

Then the chesnut horse was brought round to the inn porch.

The Colonel appeared, drawing on his gloves.

His gait seemed slightly unsteady.

It was quite evident he had fully appreciated the excellence of the sherris, and had indulged himself with huge potations of it.

In the stillness of the night, notwithstanding the patter of the rain, Duval could hear that the tones in which the Colonel spoke were thick and uncertain.

"Out of the way, scoundrel!" he cried. "Let the stirrups be. Do you think I want a lazy groom about my horse gear?"

Duval saw him then mount.

It was evident that Colonel Jessop was a good horseman, and probably was well accustomed to ride, even after partaking of so large a dose of sherris as upon this occasion.

He touched his horse with the spurs.

The creature gave a demi-vault, which would have unhorsed a less practised equestrian.

"Woa, Damsel! woa!" cried the Colonel, as he drew rein sharply.

Another moment, and he was off at a sharp trot towards London.

"Now, Nightshade," said Duval, as he patted his horse's neck, "we shall have a race for it, for Colonel Jessop's horse is fretted and out of humour, and so soon as it hears another one at its heels, I'll wager it is off at a gallop."

Claude Duval's prediction was fulfilled to the letter.

The Colonel was well mounted, although his horse was a trifle small for him, and could scarcely be expected to keep up any great speed beyond a mile or two.

It was no match for Nightshade, who flew over the ground like an apparition.

Duval passed the Colonel, and did not relax his speed until half a mile ahead of him.

Then he turned and slowly walked his horse back.

Colonel Jessop had relaxed his speed, after Nightshade and his rider had passed him like an apparition, and was approaching at an easy trot.

The rain fell fast, and the road, with all its accompaniments, had a dim and murky look.

Claude Duval came to a halt exactly in the middle of the way.

"Halt!" he cried.

Colonel Jessop saw but a dim shadowy figure before him, having the outlines of a horse and rider, but those so faintly defined through the misty veil of rain that was falling, that it was quite out of his power to come to any conclusion in regard to their particular appearance or quality.

"Halt!" cried Duval again.

"Who dares cry 'Halt!' to me on the King's highway?"

"Your master."

"Insolence! Clear the road, or take the consequences either of folly or madness."

Duval moved not.

Colonel Jessop was a man of prompt action.

The dark roadway was instantly lit up by the flash of a pistol shot, and Duval, although he felt that the bullet had missed him, had a kind of consciousness of a very narrow escape.

His first impulse was to return the shot.

But a second thought decided him not to do so.

He drew his sword, and bounded up to the Colonel.

He hoped by the suddenness of his attack to master him before he could possess himself of his weapon. But, for once, Duval met his match in his rapidity of action.

Colonel Jessop was on the defensive, and the sword blades rung together as the horses met with rather a rude shock.

Duval was a perfect swordsman, but this was the first time in all his life that he had fought an equestrian combat.

The Colonel fought well, and one unlucky blow, alighting clean and fair upon the hat of Duval, very nearly put an end to the contest.

Indeed, if the hilt of the Colonel's sword had not turned a little in his hand, so that it came partially flat-bladed down upon Duval's head, there is no knowing what the consequences might have been.

As it was, Claude was stunned for the moment.

It was with difficulty he parried a thrust at his neck, which was the next offensive movement of Colonel Jessop.

Then Duval had the advantage.

The Colonel either overreached himself a little in the saddle, or his horse swerved backward.

With his left hand, Duval caught the wrist of the Colonel's sword arm.

The grip was a tremendous one.

"Forward, Nightshade!"

Duval's horse made a leap.

Colonel Jessop was as fairly lifted from his saddle as though he had fallen into the hands of some piece of machinery adapted for that purpose.

But Duval could not hold him by the wrist, and he fell on to the damp roadway.

"Surrender," cried Duval, "lest worse come of it!"

"Villain!" cried the Colonel; "chance has befriended you. This comes of being tardy to match. Now, fellow, what is it you want?"

With great majestic grace the Colonel struggled to his feet, and then began adjusting his cravat and ruffles, as if nothing particular had occurred.

"Is it a fair surrender?" said Duval.

"What otherwise? You would soon run me down, and I have no inclination for a race."

"I will not trust you, Colonel Jessop."

"Ah, you know me?"

"I do."

"And why not trust me?"

"Because you are treacherous. Yet surrender your sword, and I will take my chance of you having pistols or loaded arms about you."

The Colonel's horse had taken to its heels, and was by this time a good mile from the spot.

"As for my sword," said Jessop, "it lies somewhere about this spot, and I can only make you welcome to its sheath. I am a officer and a gentleman, and you may take my word that I shall attempt no further aggression. I fancy a transfer of my purse to your pocket will end our acquaintance. You fence very well, indeed."

"You have other valuables?"

"I have but the ring I wear, and which, doubtless you have seen, is an old acquaintance, which I would not willingly part with. If, however, you must have it, I will redeem it at my lodgings in Pall Mall, for a fair price. Or what say you, Mr. Highwayman? Come to town with me. Consider your night's work done, and you shall be welcome to a hundred gold pieces. I want to see you and your horse by a better light than this."

"You are better without the knowledge."

"No, by Jove! I don't think so! You fence well; and but that I am somewhat short of cash at present, I would offer you as fair a price as you could put upon your horse for it. Ah! who have we here?"

The clatter of horses' feet rapidly approaching seemed to warn Duval of the arrival of some one—although, notwithstanding he strained his eyes in the direction whence the sounds came, he saw nothing.

Colonel Jessop then laughed.

It was a cold, uncomfortable sort of laugh, without a particle of mirth in it.

"This is good!" he said. "My horse Damsel has come back again! Woa, Damsel!—woa! So you have seen something uglier up the road than a highwayman?"

The Colonel, rather adroitly, considering the darkness, caught his horse.

"Come, now, Mr. Highwayman," he cried, "I am of a social turn; and, notwithstanding your language towards me has not been of the most courtly description, I will waive all punctilios; and, giving you my word of honour as an officer and a gentleman that I will attempt no treachery against you, I invite you to my lodgings in Pall Mall; and you shall put your own price upon my ransom."

"Agreed!" cried Duval.

"Then that's settled."

The Colonel had found his sword, and, with some difficulty in sheathing it (for its sheath had got damaged by his fall), he quietly rode by the side of Duval.

"You will sell your horse, Mr. Highwayman?"

"Not for the world's wealth."

"Humph! I have nothing like that to offer you. But tell me who and what you are—for something strikes me that you are no ordinary ruffian?"

"It will be time to declare myself when we reach London."

"As you please—as you please! But, by Jove! you shall sup with me to-night! We have a few choice spirits that you will not object to."

"Perhaps."

"And here we are at the first lamps of the Oxford Road. You must, indeed, sell your horse. I am becoming viciously envious of it."

"We will talk of all these things, Colonel, shortly."

Tyburn Gate was reached, and passed.

A rattling trot of another ten minutes brought Duval and his singular companion to Pall Mall.

The Colonel halted at his lodgings, and, calling hastily to his man to hold the horses, he courteously invited Duval to enter.

"It is too soon," he said, "for our friends; but I have some sherris quite the equal of any they could offer us in St James's. Walk in—walk in!"

Duval had some reluctance to leaving Nightshade in the open street; but since he had gone so far, he would not now hesitate to follow the Colonel into his lodgings.

CHAPTER XXIX.

CLAUDE DUVAL PAYS A VISIT TO THE OPERA-HOUSE AND MEETS THE DUCHESS OF CLEVELAND.

COLONEL JESSOP opened the door of his principal reception-room with a small key he took from his pocket.

There was a scuffle, as if some person were trying to hide themselves in the apartment as they entered.

"Ah! who have we here? Andrew, you scoundrel, what is this? Who is in hiding in my rooms?"

"A—a lady, sir!"

"A light! a light! Let us look on the fair!"

Tall and gaunt, something in female garb stood behind a chair.

Andrew, the Colonel's valet, held up a light, which shone upon the mysterious female.

The Colonel lifted his hat.

"Is this possible?" he said.

"Certainly, Jessop," said the apparent lady. "knew that, at all events, I was safe here for a time. have escaped from the Tower!"

"Hush!"

"Confusion! You are not alone?"

"Hush! hush! Mr. Highwayman, excuse me! I cannot entertain you to-night."

"I cannot help that," said Duval, as he placed his hand heavily upon Colonel Jessop's shoulder.

"Ah!"

"Entertain me, or not entertain me, I do not part with you, Colonel, until I have named, and you have paid, that ransom we spoke of."

"Tush, man!—tush! Don't you see I am busy? Come to-morrow."

"No!"

"Yes, man—yes! When a lady is in the case, you know, all other things give place."

"I am quite sure," said Duval, as he walked into the room, "that the presence of his Royal Highness Frederick, Prince of Wales, need not be any bar to our proceedings!"

"Confusion!" cried the seeming lady. "I am known!"

"This goes too far!" said the Colonel. "You don't know your own danger, sir!"

"I am safe enough," said Duval. "The Prince is an escaped traitor from the Tower; and you, Colonel, aid and abet him! What if I open yonder window, and give the alarm? And yet, why should I? When I find gratitude in a King, it is time to be shocked at the criminality of a Prince!"

"What do you mean?" said Frederick. "Who is this man, Colonel Jessop?"

"It matters not," added Duval. "Give me the ransom, and let me go."

"Name it."

"Ransom?" ejaculated the Prince of Wales. "Are we in the middle ages? What is the meaning of this?"

"I have promised this man," said the Colonel, "whatever in reason he may demand of me, in redemption of this ring, which I would not willingly part with. Name your demand, sir, and leave us to ourselves."

"Hold!" said the Prince. "It is easy to say, 'Leave us to ourselves,' but he carries with him the secret of my being here!"

"That secret," said Duval, "shall be religiously kept; but, for the ransom of the Colonel, I demand—

DUVAL ESCAPES PURSUIT IN THE CROWD.

Let me see,—what shall I demand? Will your Royal Highness—providing my demand is a reasonable and easy one—see that it be complied with?"

"Faith! yes; and you must keep our secret."

"I will. I demand the Colonel's coat."

"My coat?"

"Exactly; and just as it is, without the removal of a single article from its pockets."

"Ah!"

"It's a bargain, Colonel—it's a bargain!" cried the Prince. "Give him your coat, and let him be off!"

"No, no—no, no!"

The Colonel retreated until he came to the window.

It was either his sword-hilt, or some accidental movement of his elbow, that broke a pane of glass; but Duval paid no attention to it, and still repeated his request.

"Your coat, Colonel, in exchange for mine. We are about of a height; and, after all, so fair an exchange should be no robbery."

"Give it him—I insist upon it!" said the Prince.

"But, your Royal Highness——"

The Colonel put his hand to one of the pockets of his coat.

"No!" cried Duval, in a voice of thunder. "I must have nothing removed, or our compact is at an end."

"But there may be something here of such great value——"

"That's nonsense," said the Prince, "for all the world knows you are not worth a guinea, Jessop, unless you fleece a few from some poor wretch at a gaming-table! Give him the coat, and let him go!"

"In a moment! Your Royal Highness's wishes are, of course, the laws of those devoted friends who look forward to the time when they will be your devoted subjects!"

The Colonel assumed an attitude of listening.

There came a confused, murmuring sound from the outside of the house.

Slowly, and still listening, Jessop took off his coat. Duval flung his over the back of a chair.

The murmuring noise entered the house.

There were footsteps on the stairs.

"Now!" shouted the Colonel.

The door was flung open.

"My prisoner!" cried a voice. "It is Claude Duval! I knew his horse, Nightshade!"

"Seize him!" cried the Colonel "And take that coat from him!"

"Good night!" said Duval.

Crash! went the window, as, bodily, through the frame and glass, he made his way on to the balcony in front of the house.

He vaulted over.

He hung for a moment by his hands.

One glance below warned him of his danger.

There was a deep area.

To drop into that was certain destruction.

It was a trap in which capture was certain, if he escaped broken bones by the depth of the fall.

Hand over hand went Duval, horizontally, along the parapet of the balcony, until he was over the door-step.

A man was in a bent attitude, looking through the keyhole.

Duval lit, with a thundering shock, upon his back.

The man fell prostrate, with a yell of fear and pain.

"Seize him! seize him! Stop him! stop him!" cried a voice from the window. "Stop him, Swallow—for your life's sake, stop him!"

"Good-night, Mr. Muckles!" cried Duval, as he scrambled to his feet, and was off like an arrow from a bow.

"Done brown again!" said Swallow, upon whose back Duval had alighted—"done brown again! I knowed it! I told Mr. Muckles, and he wouldn't believe it! Done brown again!"

Duval ran up St. James's Street.

He had lost his horse.

A most grievous reflection, that! But he was soon aroused to considerations of personal safety by the rapid sounds of pursuit.

"Stop him! stop him! A highwayman! Stop him! stop him!"

It was a man hunt.

The evening was yet young, and the streets were tolerably populous.

From all the various turnings out of St. James's Street people seemed to dash out, intent upon the capture of Claude Duval.

Making his way, then, down the first turning he came to on his right hand, Duval saw a prospect of safety.

A dense throng of carriages, three and four deep, was about the doors of the Opera House.

Sedan-chairs filled up every available space.

The confusion of link-boys, ticket-porters, servants in livery, idle spectators, and thieves, was very great.

In the midst of such a disorderly throng, Duval surely might look for safety

The coat he wore, and which had belonged to Colonel Jessop, was, unfortunately, to the full as noticeable an one as his own.

In fact, it nearly resembled it; for they were both scarlet, and of a military cut.

The shouts and cries of Duval's pursuers never ceased for a moment.

It was quite evident that he had been observed to take his way down the street that led in the direction of the Opera House.

Darting between a couple of footmen, who, with sleepy looks, were conversing together, Duval upset them right and left, and was soon in comparative safety among the throng of carriages and sedan-chairs.

But the pursuit was not over.

His apprehension was sought with a virulence and tenacity that showed how much angry feeling was imported into the transaction.

Muckles, the officer, clambered up on to the top of an empty coach, and, gesticulating like some furious mob orator, he shouted, "A thousand pounds reward for Claude Duval, the highwayman! He wears a scarlet coat, and is either without a hat, or wears one looped with a diamond! A thousand pounds reward! He is tall and good looking, but he's wanted!"

There was a general commotion among the linkmen and idlers—for a thousand pounds, or even half, or a quarter of that sum, seemed to them an inexhaustible and brilliant fortune.

Darting in and out carriages, and under horses, those boys and men, who were accustomed to all the noise, riot, and excitement of a grand Opera night, busied themselves in searching for Claude Duval.

Then he felt that his danger was rather on the increase—for he must either be ferreted out amid that throng of horses and carriages, or he must leave what seemed to be a good covert, and so be exposed to the observation of Muckles and the Bow Street officers.

There was another alternative, and Claude Duval embraced it.

Creeping right under a pair of tall carriage horses, he quietly opened the door of the huge family coach to which they belonged, and sprung in.

The carriage was occupied by a lady and gentleman.

The lady uttered a scream.

The gentleman uttered an exclamation, which Duval could not exactly catch.

"Pardon me!" he said. "That this is an intrusion, which looks of an impertinent character, I am free to admit; but when did youth and beauty refuse to aid the distressed?"

The lady was decidedly elderly, and as decidedly plain.

She wore a gorgeous head-dress, which looked as if she had taken flight through some tropical conservatory, carrying away, in unpleasant confusion, a great number of its products.

The gentleman was old, and decidedly clerical-looking.

He wore a white wig.

A shovel-hat.

A coat, the single collar of which came half over his ears, while the skirts nearly touched his ankles.

"Murder! Thieves! Thieves!" cried the elderly gentleman. "We shall be slain in our own coach! Thomas! Stephen!"

"I will trouble you to be quiet, sir," said Duval. "My sudden appearance is quite sufficient alarm for the young lady, without you adding to it."

"Young lady, sir!" cried the old clerical-looking gentleman. "This is no young lady, sir, but my wife!"

"Your youngest daughter, you mean?" said Duval. "Don't seek to impose upon me, sir. Madam, I am an unfortunate gentleman pursued by his enemies; and, unless nature acts by contraries, the gentleness and tenderness of your heart must be but a reflex of the beauty of your face."

"Anything the matter, sir?" inquired a footman at the door, touching his gold-laced hat, and looking in at the window of the carriage.

"Yes," said the clerical gentleman,—"yes, Thomas, this——"

"Certainly not," said the lady. "There is nothing the matter. It is a false alarm."

Thomas touched his hat and retired.

The carriage gave a sudden jerk, and proceeded onwards for a few yards in its progress towards the door of the Opera.

"This is insufferable," said the clerical-looking gentleman. "My dear, I am surprised at your conduct. This person is an utter stranger to us, and may be a criminal."

"I am surprised at you, Archdeacon," said the lady. "You should have more charity. This is evidently a gentleman, and his taste and discrimination are amazing."

"Yes," said the Archdeacon; "because he has treated you to a dose of flattery perfectly fulsome—fulsome, I say—fulsome!"

"Archdeacon, you are a brute!"

The voice of Muckles rose again upon the night air.

"A thousand pounds for Claude Duval, the highwayman!—a thousand pounds reward! Tall and good-looking, with dark hair and moustache! He wears a scarlet coat, with ruffles! A thousand pounds reward for Claude Duval, the highwayman! Ferret him out!"

"The very man!" said the Archdeacon, as he placed his hand upon the sleeve of Duval's coat.

CHAPTER XXX.

CLAUDE DUVAL RETURNS THE LETTERS TO THE DUCHESS OF CLEVELAND.

THE Archdeacon's lady uttered a slight scream.

If it had something of alarm in its tone, it likewise had something of gratification.

Who had not heard of the gay and gallant Claude Duval?

The "ladies' highwayman," as he was specially called?

The hero of the cotillion with the Marchioness of Queensberry and the Duchess of Cleveland?

"Yes," said Claude, "I am that person; and I throw myself upon the generosity of those who I am sure will not betray me. Archdeacon—for such, I hear, is your title—it does not lie within your province to betray any man to his foes; and as for you, madam, as I said before, your looks belie you if it be possible for you to do an unkind action."

"Hem!" said the Archdeacon. "My public duty as regards a malefactor——"

"Your public fiddlestick!" interrupted his lady; "don't talk nonsense."

"Exactly," said Duval; "that is the right way to put it; and I feel that I may, with perfect candour and confidence, consult with you, madam, as to the best mode of preserving me from the active pursuit of my enemies."

"Certainly—oh, dear, certainly! It's a very awkward place to get out and dance a cotillion; but the Marchioness of Queensberry and the Duchess of Cleveland make such a fuss about theirs, that if it were possible, I really——" .

"We shall meet again," said Duval; "and, in the meantime, I will suggest that the Archdeacon lend me his coat."

"My coat?"

"And why not?" half screamed his lady; "you have two on—and why not, I should like to know? I am sure this gentleman would lend you his coat on such an emergency."

"My dear," said the Archdeacon, "you talk nonsense. How can I be taken up for a highwayman? Did you ever hear of a thousand pounds reward being offered for me?"

"Certainly not, Archdeacon. I don't know any one who would offer a groat; but you must lend your coat, for all that."

"And be quick about it," said Duval; "for I am apt to be impatient."

"There, Archdeacon! Don't you know Mr. Duval is impatient?"

The Archdeacon was conquered. He slowly divested himself of his outer coat, which, after all, he could very well spare, since beneath it he had a complete clerical costume.

Duval slipped on the coat over the scarlet one he had procured from Colonel Jessop.

"Your wig, Archdeacon."

"My wig?"

"Are you deaf?" screamed his lady. "Don't you hear, Mr. Duval said your wig?"

"And your hat," added Duval.

"Take everything!" roared the Archdeacon. "Strip me between you!"

"Don't be improper," said his lady, "but do as you are told. It's only an act of Christian charity. You can go into the Opera very well without a hat; and, in fact, you look more respectable with your own natural bald head; so don't say another word about it. Mr. Duval, you had better come into our box, and stay till all the alarm is over."

"Again—once again," said Duval,—"once again am I indebted to the gentle heart of woman and the bright eyes of beauty for safety! Once again the silvery accents of pity fall upon my ears!"

Duval kissed the hand of the Archdeacon's lady, to which act of gallantry she responded with a sigh.

The carriage had jerked forward several times, and now reached the door of the opera.

The critical moment had arrived.

"What carriage?" cried a voice.

"Archdeacon Whateley's."

The door was opened, and Duval stepped quietly out, taking care that the skirts of the long coat should come as far over his boots as possible.

In the carriage he had quietly taken off his spurs, or they would have looked rather incongruous at the door of the Opera.

He handed the lady out of the vehicle, and as she hung upon his arm, he actually passed within an inch of the nose of Muckles, the officer.

The disguise of Duval was not good, and yet it answered the purpose perfectly.

Had he been alone, how much larger amount of scrutiny would have been cast upon him? But the presence of the lady of the well-known Archdeacon upon his arm set aside all suspicion.

The lobby was passed.

But the Archdeacon was anything but pleased; and in a momentary feeling of desperation, he yet thought to effect the capture of Duval.

"Gentlemen all," he said, "this is Claude——"

"I know it!" said Duval, roughly interrupting the Archdeacon, and dealing him such a thrust in the ribs with his elbow, that he had to gasp for breath instead of uttering another word. "I know it! It was an impertinent urchin at the door who clawed my coat! but it don't matter, my dear Archdeacon; come along!"

"But——" gasped the Archdeacon.

"Really!" said his lady; "don't you hear the Bishop say it don't matter?"

Duval now took care to secure the Archdeacon's arm beneath his own; and with a sense, now, of utter helplessness, that ecclesiastical personage allowed himself to be led up the grand staircase, and through the Crush Room, to the box that had been destined for the reception of his lady.

The box-keeper bowed low.

Duval slipped half-a-guinea into his hand.

The door of the box was shut as though it had been a piece of velvet.

"Who is in that box?" asked a constable connected with the theatre, of the box-keeper.

"Archdeacon Whateley and his lady, and the Bishop of—something."

"Are you quite certain?"

"Certain? Of course I am, or I shouldn't say so!"

"Oh, very well!"

"Certain, indeed!" muttered the box-keeper, as he retired. "Didn't he give me half a guinea? What can Mr. Blinks mean by asking any questions about such a real gentleman?"

The overture of the Opera commenced with a crash of majestic music.

The house was warm, and there was a general flutter of fans: and as Duval gazed around it from the back of the box—for he had insisted upon the Archdeacon and his lady occupying the front places—he saw in a box, almost immediately opposite,—radiant in youth and beauty, and covered in diamonds—the Duchess of Cleveland.

Duval looked at the gay, laughing face, with an almost painful interest.

Who could have supposed that this was the same woman who, a few short hours since, had, with tears and sobs, at that little roadside inn on the Western Road, demanded her letters of Colonel Jessop?

There did not seem to be a cloud upon her brow.

Was she a consummate actress?—or had the care that sat brooding at her heart really been chased away by the magic of the scene in which she was?

"Bishop!" said the Archdeacon's lady.

Duval paid no attention—his eyes were riveted on the fair Duchess of Cleveland.

"My dear Bishop!"

"So young, so thoughtless, and so beautiful!" murmured Duval. "If those smiles hide an aching heart, thank heaven I can convert them into real ones!"

The Archdeacon's lady followed the direction of his eyes.

She bit her lips.

She gave Duval a lightning flash of a look, which bespoke all the jealousy that had taken possession of her.

"Beware!" she said. "You are either a bishop or a highwayman, as I may choose."

"Yes, very beautiful," said Duval. "I will give a flush to that youthful brow, and a sparkle to those eyes that shall transcend all her brilliants."

"My dear Bishop, really——"

Duval rose, and abruptly left the box.

The Archdeacon clapped his hands with delight, for he had watched the whole of this little comedy, and was intensely amused at it.

But the people in the house thought he was applauding, and as the overture at that moment ended with a grand crash, the clapping of hands became general.

"Claude Duval!" screamed the Archdeacon's lady.

Duval closed the door of the box sharply.

He ran round the circle rapidly.

A box-keeper proffered his services.

"The Duchess of Cleveland's box?"

"This way, sir."

The Duchess was alone.

A couple of *beaux*, who had been paying their compliments to her, had just left.

At the entrance of Duval, the Duchess looked round with curiosity.

He bowed low.

"Duchess, excuse this intrusion. I know not if life and liberty may remain to me for the next five minutes, but while they are mine own, I acquit myself of a debt. Take this packet: it contains no less than forty letters, once written by a young and trusting heart to its betrayer."

The Duchess turned pale as death.

She was compelled to utter two faint screams, or she must have fainted.

"From Jessop?" she said. "From Jessop?"

"Exactly!"

"He relents? There is yet at the bottom of his black heart some feeling, that, like a jewel hidden——"

"Forbear, Duchess! Do not spoil a good simile by associating it with such a man. This packet of letters certainly comes from Colonel Jessop, but they were won at the sword's point."

"Ah!"

"Yes. The black heart still remains without its redeeming jewel."

"And you?"

"Do you not know me?"

"Gracious heaven!"

"Hush! Hush!"

There was a rush of footsteps in the lobby.

The name of Claude Duval resounded in the house. There was a pause upon the stage, for it was evident some alarm was growing into noisy expression in the building.

"Do you know me now, Duchess?"

"Duval!"

He smiled gently.

"And you have done this for me? Mysteriously and wonderfully done it! I had but half my life while these letters remained in Jessop's keeping! I am young again—happy again!"

"And I am repaid."

"No, no! Oh, how selfish!"

"Carry arms!" cried a voice in the lobby.

"They do me honour," said Duval. The Opera-guard has been called. Farewell, Duchess! You befriended me at the masked ball, and saved me from such a catastrophe as this. It happens now, despite all you can do or say. But if this be the last act in the drama of the life of Claude Duval, it is at least a gracious one."

There was a movement at the lock of the box-door.

Another moment, and it would have been opened; but the Duchess shot a small bolt into its socket, and nothing but force would procure admission to the box.

Duval had the scarlet coat of Colonel Jessop beneath the long ecclesiastical garment of the Archdeacon.

"Quick!" cried the Duchess. "Appear, Duval, in your new character. You are the young Prince of Leiningen, who only arrived to-day at the English Court, and is known to no one. Quick—quick! Thank heaven, the back of the box is in obscurity!"

The resource was desperate; but Duval threw off the long black over-coat of the Archdeacon, and, along with it, the white wig and the hat.

The Duchess took a diamond star from her own breast, and attached it, with trembling fingers, to his coat.

Rap! rap! rap! came a sharp knocking at the door of the box.

The Duchess panted with excitement.

She could scarcely speak; but she made a sign to Duval to throw back the bolt.

He did so instantly, and the door being dashed open, disclosed a sergeant of the guard, with his halbert in his hand, while, immediately behind him, was a file of men from the company who took post each night at the Opera.

Muckles, with his constable's staff waving ostentatiously around his head, darted forward.

Swallow dodged behind the soldiers, and this time seemed really of opinion that he would not be done brown.

"Oh!" said the Duchess; "this is well, only a little late! I have to complain of a most audacious intrusion into this box, and the more reprehensible too, because one of the foreign guests of his Majesty, the Prince of Leiningen, is here."

"Claude Duval!" cried Muckles.

"I do believe," added the Duchess, "it was the very man. I am robbed of an opal bracelet, by a man who came in here dressed in a long black coat, and a clerical hat and wig."

"Dat is var true," said Duval. "I am rob of von box-snuff!"

The sergeant looked at Muckles, and Muckles looked at the sergeant.

The diamond star upon Duval's coat glistened gorgeously.

Muckles thrust his head into the box, and glared about him.

He was here!" he said; 'he was here! He could not leave! he was here! A lady in the opposite box told us! There she is with the bouquet on her head!"

"Var true," said Duval, again; "von box-snuff is rob of me!"

"The villain escaped!" said the Duchess.

"Into the pit?" asked Muckles.

"I know not; but my impression was that he ran round to the box where the lady with the bouquet on her head may still be seen."

"Dat is true. He look now von what you call? old man's von foggy—behold!"

Duval pointed right across the house to the Archdeacon.

As he did so, both the Archdeacon and his lady rose in the front of their box, and pointed across to Duval and the Duchess of Cleveland.

The people in the pit looked with bewildered eyes from one box to the other, and wondered what was going on; while Muckles, accompanied by the sergeant, the file of men, and Swallow, ran round to satisfy themselves that the Archdeacon was not Claude Duval in disguise.

"My time has come, Duchess," whispered Duval; "I have, perhaps, two minutes in which to leave the house."

"Fly!"

"Farewell! You have saved me once more!"

"Take with you my eternal gratitude!"

"Farewell——Oh, I forgot—your star!"

"Keep it as a souvenir of this night's proceeding!"

Duval walked out into the lobby.

Calmly and serenely, as though he were quite at his ease, he slightly tapped his moustache with a cambric handkerchief.

"The Prince of Leiningen's carriage!" he said.

"The Prince of Leiningen's carriage!" shouted the box-keeper.

"The Prince of Leiningen's carriage!" roared an official in the hall.

The words were echoed from without in every variety of intonation.

There was a rush of people in the Crush Room to gaze upon the distinguished foreigner.

Duval passed through a bowing throng, whose salutes he courteously returned; and down the grand staircase he took his way, without the slightest appearance of hurry or excitement of manner.

A calm, self-possessed smile was on his lips; and still, amid all the shouts and outcries for the Prince of Leiningen's carriage, he made his way towards the entrance of the Opera House.

There was a rattle of fire-arms as the Guard saluted him, and still the shouts and outcries for the carriage rose into frantic vehemence.

Duval put on a look of vexed impatience.

A gentleman with a highly-powdered wig bowed low before him.

"Your Highness's people have made some mistake, and the carriage is not in waiting."

"Indeed!"

"But if your Highness will accept my carriage, it is quite at your service."

"Many thanks, sir!" replied Duval. "A courtesy is best acknowledged by being accepted."

In two minutes more, Duval was ushered into a handsome chariot, and respectfully asked where he would be driven to.

The hour was getting late, and he wanted to be near to Camden House.

"To the Palace at Kensington!" he replied.

Off set the carriage at the very moment that a stentorian voice shouted, "Stop him!"

Duval looked anxiously from the window, but there was no further alarm; and the carriage clearing out of the rank, he soon left the Opera, and all its excitements and all its dangers, behind him.

CHAPTER XXXI.

CLAUDE DUVAL PAYS A VISIT TO CAMDEN HOUSE.

IT was eleven o'clock.

With a feeling of bewilderment at the events of that day and night, Duval leant back in the carriage, determined to avail himself of it as far as it went his way.

The lamps in the suburbs of London were few and far between; but as Kensington was a kind of royal village, it was tolerably well looked to in that respect.

Duval had no intention whatever of allowing himself to be driven to the Palace at Kensington; therefore he pulled the check-string in the darkest part of the road before arriving at the gates leading to the royal residence.

The carriage stopped.

A footman got down from behind, and showed himself at the door.

"I alight here," said Duval. "Here are five guineas to divide between you. Whose carriage is this?"

"The Lord Chief Justice's!"

Duval smiled; and turning on his heel, he left the bewildered coachman and footman to their own reflections on the singular conduct of the Prince of Leiningen.

Camden House was not ten minutes' walk from that spot; but Duval was without a hat, and his costume was anything but well adapted for the expedition upon which he then was.

"Past eleven, and a cloudy——No, it ain't cloudy! Past eleven, and a rainy——Does it rain? I'm sure I felt a spot or two. Past eleven, and a foggy night! It's always foggy—leastways, I feel foggy; and what's more surprising is, that the more purl I take, the more foggy I gets. But eleven o'clock, and a foggy—— Eh! Who are you?"

The watchman who had been thus soliloquizing and crying the hour, held up his lantern, and glared in the face of Claude Duval.

"A gentleman!"

"I sees that, sir. Does yer honour want anybody took up?"

"No, my friend; but I want your coat and hat."

"My coat and hat?"

"Yes, for a consideration."

"Oh! that's quite another thing. Yer honour can have 'em for a consideration, and my rattle, and lantern, and pike, while I take a snooze in my box. Past eleven, and a sleepy night! That's the way to do it, yer honour! My name's Tim, and I'm called the Original Watchman, because I ain't half such a fool as I look!"

"That I can easily conceive, and I shall feel more

convinced of it upon your complying quickly with my conditions."

There was an imperative tone and air about Claude Duval which let the watchman see that he was not to be trifled with.

Upon second thoughts, however, Duval did not see the necessity of relinquishing his own coat to the watchman, inasmuch as the huge, wide, blanket-looking coat of that individual would easily go over all his, Duval's, other apparel.

The exchange, then, was soon effected; and provided with the stick, rattle and lantern, of the watchman, while his identity was completely obscured by the large overcoat, Duval made his way towards the garden of Camden House.

There was no great difficulty in effecting an entrance by clambering over the gate.

When once, however, in the precincts of the garden, Duval thought it prudent to put out the watchman's lantern.

Quietly, then, he made his way to the old historical mansion.

Remembering well the former adventure he had had within its walls, he was in a better position to effect an entrance than as though he had come perfectly strange to the place.

Deliberating, however, as to the best mode of making his way into the house, he happened by accident to press against the outer door, which, to his surprise yielded immediately.

It was at that moment that twelve o'clock sounded from various church steeples in the neighbourhood.

Duval had, at all events, the satisfaction of knowing that he was true to his appointment.

He stepped at once into the hall of the house.

A solemn stillness pervaded it, and although he paused to listen, throwing into his sense of hearing all the acuteness he was capable of, he failed to catch the slightest indication in that mansion of the presence of any living being.

A strong impulse came over him to call aloud upon Lucy.

He thought that if he shouted her name in his own well-known accents, she might, if there, be able to reply to him.

And yet again, what unknown dangers he might bring upon her by making such an appeal!

Would it not be better first to hear what the mysterious message was that had been promised him in that house, and then to shape his course accordingly?

There was but one thing that awakened his suspicions that he was observed, and that he was not so entirely alone as he had at first supposed.

Slowly and creakingly the outer door closed after him.

It was quite possible that the door might have been so hung as to close of its own agency, but something seemed thoroughly to possess Claude Duval with the idea that such was not the case.

He paused to catch the least sound of any fastening of that outer door.

Yes, there was a something.

One sharp snap, as though a lock had been set in action.

All was then still again.

Duval rather anxiously felt for his pistols, and although he still kept on the heavy watchman's coat, he let it hang open and loosely about him, so that on the impulse of a moment he could lay his hand upon his sword and possess himself of his fire-arms.

The intense darkness of the hall was puzzling and confounding, and, after advancing a few paces, Duval thought it would be imprudent to maintain silence any longer, and he spoke.

"I am here!" he said, "here according to appointment! What has any one to say to Claude Duval?"

"Ascend!" said a voice.

"Whither?"

"To the upper floor! There is no danger."

"There may be danger," said Duval; "and that, too, of a character to awaken fear."

"Fear," said the voice, "in the breast of the great Claude Duval?"

"You are not supernatural in your wisdom," said Duval; "although you would strive to make me believe you are so in your person. It is you who may fear and encounter danger. I have no such feeling."

"Ascend!—ascend!" said the voice again, somewhat impatiently.

Duval drew his sword.

He knew the situation of the staircase perfectly well, as it ascended from the great hall of the house; but he thought it prudent to keep a clear space before him in the darkness, and that could easily be done with his sword's point.

No obstruction met his weapon, and slowly and carefully Duval ascended the grand staircase of Camden House.

As he left the pitchy darkness of the hall, he seemed to find his way into a brighter region; for over the tree-tops came now the faint starlight of that precarious night, which was at times all gloom and then all brightness.

Duval, as he stood upon the large landing or corridor at the head of the grand staircase, could see dimly about him.

"Enter!" said the voice.

A door creaked slowly open, and through that opening came a faint flash of light, which fell in a broad stream, like some half intercepted moonbeam, on to the floor of the corridor.

Duval entered.

The apartment in which he now found himself was gorgeously furnished.

The walls were covered with crimson satin paper, over which glistened an intricate small network of gold, which had a most exquisitely beautiful effect even in that dim light, for the apartment was only illumined by the rays of a small hand-lantern, placed on a table in the centre of the room. The ceiling was lightly tinted, and the whole of the moveable appointments were in the most perfect keeping apparently with the decorations, and got up in the most admirable taste.

Claude Duval stood in the centre of this apartment, with his sword in hand, and a sickly feeling of despair came over him; for he began to think that the fact of that apartment being tenantless, and the mystery with which the invisible person tried to throw around himself, were mere artifices to entrap him, and so prevent his prosecuting his intended search for his lost and much-loved Lucy.

"Speak!" cried Duval; "and think not that you are dealing with one who fears aught human."

"What seek you?" asked the voice.

"Tidings of Lucy Everton—my wife. Can you give me those tidings?" said Claude.

"I can."

"Speak, then, and put an end to all this mummery or you may have reason to repent of your delay!"

"First answer me," again said the voice. "If I tell you where to find Lucy Everton, will you promise to accede to my conditions?"

"Conditions?"

"Even so."

"Name them."

"To let the past be buried in oblivion, and never attempt to discover the mystery in which the death of General Everton is shrouded."

"Never!" shouted Duval. "Never will I cease to

endeavour to discover the real murderer of Lucy's uncle; and, having discovered him, will do my best to drag him to that scaffold whence I snatched my beautiful, my innocent Lucy!"

"Ha, ha, ha!" laughed the voice.

Claude Duval's breath came short and thick. He was about to leave the room by a door he saw on the opposite side, when the voice again spoke.

"Think again, Claude Duval," said the mysterious voice. "If you accede to my proposal, Lucy Everton will be yours again; and ere you reach your sylvan home on Hampstead Heath, your bride will be there awaiting your return. Think again, I say."

"And what if I still refuse to accept your conditions?" asked Claude.

"Then Death will not again be cheated, and Lucy Everton will, ere the night be two hours older, be conveyed to Newgate, and taken thence to the scaffold. Does this arrangement suit you better, Claude Duval, than the former one did?"

"Fiend!" cried Claude. "Would that I could meet you face to face!"

Even as he spoke he dashed the point of his sword against one of the panels of the wall, behind which the mysterious voice seemed to issue.

It gave way at once, and Claude fancied he must have touched some spring; for the panel opened like a door, and he found himself in another tenantless apartment, which, from its strange construction, Duval fancied must be a secret chamber.

"Ha, ha, ha!" came again that fiend-like voice. "Fool! you cannot harm me! Now will you agree to my condition?"

"Not unless Lucy herself wishes me to do so," replied Duval.

"Lucy does wish it."

"Let me hear her voice confirm what you tell me, then I will believe," said Duval.

"Listen!" said the voice.

Claude Duval held his breath, and in far-off, wailing sounds, he heard his own name.

"Claude—my Claude!"

Duval started, and wiped the perspiration from his brow. He remained gazing around him as though fixed for life, and through his parted lips the hot breath came like the vapour of a furnace. He called out in a hoarse voice, "Lucy! Lucy! speak to me! Tell me what I ought to do—tell me——"

"Promise! promise!" came that wailing voice again upon his ear.

"You hear?" said the voice.

"Heaven help me!" said Duval, to himself. "I know not whether it be the voice of Lucy! I must be calm—calm! The door—the door! Which way to the door?"

The great object of Duval was to leave that secret chamber, and, well armed as he was, to search for Lucy in every chamber of that mysterious house. It was with difficulty, however, that he found the door by which he had entered, for the lantern he had brought from the first apartment had gone out, and he was now in total darkness—such intense darkness, indeed, that Claude stood bewildered, not knowing which way to turn, in order to find the staircase which would conduct him to the upper rooms of the mansion.

At length he touched the wall, and he thought that by following that, he should reach the landing place, just at the head of the grand staircase.

He soon reached the door of the first apartment he had entered, but it was closed.

At any other time, probably, Claude Duval would have found but little difficulty, even in that intense darkness, in finding the means of opening the door; but with his whole imagination in such a ferment, it was almost impossible for him to do so, and he almost groaned with anxiety as he grasped its handle and shook it to and fro.

Something suddenly gave way, and it opened.

Claude Duval made a rush towards the grand staircase, up which he bounded, sword in hand, calling upon the name of Lucy.

He soon came to another corridor, very similar to the one below, and on each side of which appeared doors, opening evidently to suites of rooms, corresponding to those on the floor beneath.

Claude opened first one and then another of these doors. The first one was in total darkness. The next was lighted by a silver lamp, depending from the ceiling. It was a long room, and had been most elaborately fitted up as a library.

There were book-cases upon all the walls, extending up three parts of the height, and then terminating, for the remainder of the distance, in beautiful gothic carvings.

Between each of these book-cases were pedestals with busts from the antique upon them.

The dim light from the solitary burner in the lamp gave a dreary look to the large room, but the light was not sufficient to prevent Claude from perceiving that the dawn was fast approaching.

Duval retreated from the room, for he felt certain that Lucy was not there, and hurried to the next.

Just as he laid his hand upon the handle of the next door that presented itself, Claude fancied he heard a noise in a distant part of the house.

He stood still to listen.

All was silent.

Again he was about to proceed, when the voice he had heard before again addressed him, and seemed this time to be almost close by his side.

"Time flies, Claude Duval! Are you willing to agree to the conditions proposed, or do you prefer seeing Lucy led out to die?"

Claude was about to answer, when the voice that had pronounced his name once before that night, again called out, in what appeared to his imagination, to be weeping accents, "Claude—my Claude! Save me!"

"With my life!" he shouted, as he sped along the gallery.

In this gallery there was an open window, and Claude Duval paused an instant at it. The cool morning air came sweetly and refreshingly to his fevered brow.

He was about to continue his search, when his gaze was riveted upon one of the gates of the mansion.

"Ah!" he cried, "A trap! We will see, Mr. Muckles, if you are clever enough to take me to-night."

Duval waited but one moment to ascertain if Muckles were alone or not, just as Swallow commenced a loud attack upon the gate-bell.

"It is well," said Claude. "I see that a large party is bent on my capture. Courage! For Lucy's sake, I must escape this night."

CHAPTER XXXII.

CLAUDE DUVAL MAKES AN ALLY OF A POLICE OFFICER.

CONSIDERING the extent of Camden House, and the many secret recesses and hidden chambers that there must be within its walls, Claude Duval could not but feel how hopeless it was to attempt to continue a search for Lucy in such a place.

Still, had he been alone and undisturbed, nothing would have prevented him from devoting the remainder of the night to that purpose.

The fact, however that his old enemies, Muckles and

Swallow, were at the gate, was sufficient to put an end to all considerations but those of immediate safety.

Not for his own sake, but for Lucy's.

If he were to fall into the hands of the officers, and be heavily ironed in Newgate, who would continue the search for her?

No one.

His safety was her hope.

It was with a pang that Claude Duval determined upon leaving Camden House, but he felt the urgent necessity of so doing.

He made his way to the back part of the mansion, and dropping lightly from one of the windows into the garden, he felt that he was in comparative safety.

"Take him, alive or dead!" he heard Muckles exclaim. "Take him, alive or dead. We can't waste all our time on Claude Duval."

"And besides," added Swallow, "we're always being done brown, and that's not so pleasant."

The party of officers were quite sufficiently strong that, if they were well disposed about the garden walls and gates of the old mansion, it might not be impossible for Duval to escape, but it would be difficult for him do so without observation.

At all events, he felt the necessity of pausing until he observed what the tactics of the officers would be.

The state of excitement that Muckles was in certainly got the better of his reason, for he shouted out his orders in such a voice, that the very person of all others who should not have known them, heard them as distinctly as the officers to whom they were addressed.

"Swallow, you keep the outer gate," he cried. "Post yourselves, the remainder of you, at twenty paces distant from each other round the garden, close to the wall. Claude Duval shall pass the remainder of this night in Newgate, or I will know the reason why."

"True," said Duval to himself, in a low voice, "you shall know the reason, Mr. Muckles."

A few moments' consideration convinced Duval that his best chance of escape would be by the outer gate, at which Swallow was posted.

Well he knew that Swallow had almost a superstitious fear of him, and would more easily consent to be defeated, probably, than any of the other officers.

And now Muckles having disposed of his men, with the exception of three, in the manner he had mentioned, gathered them together close to the door porch, and spoke in lower tones, although not so low as altogether to escape the ears of Claude Duval, who had slowly and carefully crept round the house to the front.

"Listen to me, my good fellow," said Muckles. "I have set my life upon the capture of this Claude Duval, and mean to do it. There is a thousand pounds reward, as you all very well know. Now, I will resign my share of it, and leave it entirely among you if you succeed in nabbing him."

"We'll do it, Mr. Muckles."

"And, mind, dead or alive will do. I hate the fellow."

"All's right, sir!"

"It is becoming a standing jest at Newgate, whenever I enter the hall, to ask me if I've caught Claude Duval. Now, come on; we will visit every room in the mansion, for, if my information be correct, he is here, past a doubt."

Without further parley, Muckles and his men entered the house.

Duval felt that his time for action had come.

The only alteration that Claude Duval attempted to make in his costume now, was to fling aside the watchman's heavy coat, and press down the hat further upon his brows.

Then he advanced quite boldly across the lawn towards the front gate where Swallow was on duty.

Among Duval's accomplishments was the great power of imitating the human voice in its various peculiarities.

Now, it so happened that one of the men who had replied to Muckles a moment or two before at the porch of the house, spoke in very peculiar tones, deep and guttural.

Duval imitated these tones to a nicety.

He approached Swallow without exhibiting the least fear of apprehension, as he said, "I think the governor's nabbed him, Swallow, for there's no end of row in the house."

It was only for an instant that he wished to throw Swallow off his guard.

He knew that a second glance from the officer would be quite sufficient to distinguish him (Duval) from one of the constables.

But the garden was dark.

The imitated voice was perfect.

Swallow hesitated.

The hesitation was fatal.

With one spring, Claude Duval reached his side, and flinging both his arms round him, held him as though in a vice, as he whispered in his ears, "One word—one cry of alarm, and you are a dead man, Swallow!"

"Ah!"

"Silence!"

"I knowed it."

"I am Claude Duval."

"In course, and I am——"

"Swallow, the officer."

"No, I wasn't going to say that—done brown."

Duval laughed.

"My dear Swallow, we may as well agree. You are a good fellow in the main, and consent to a defeat with a fair grace. Come, this shall not be the worst night's work you have ever done."

"What do you mean?"

"I mean that I will make it well worth your while to assist me."

"No, Mr. Duval—no; I may be done brown; but I'm a Bow Street runner, for all that. I'll nab you if I can, and when I can; but just now it's only man to man, and if you nab me, why I can't help it."

"Very good," said Duval; "then I will trouble you for those little barkers you have in your coat pocket."

"Take 'em."

Duval possessed himself of the pistols with which Swallow, in common with the other officers, was armed.

We have had before occasion to allude to those particular fire-arms which were carried by the officers of the police.

Short, thick, and stumpy; sometimes with brass barrels, coarsely made, and in all cases the very reverse of elegant, these pistols may still be seen occasionally, as relics of a past age, at some old iron and miscellaneous store shop, for sale at the price of a few shillings; but should the reader of these veritable pages feel inclined to purchase such a memento of the past, by all means keep gunpowder from the barrels, or an explosion in all directions than the right one may be expected.

These were the sort of weapons, then, that Claude Duval possessed himself of from the pocket of Swallow.

The officer uttered a sort of groan.

"Browner and browner," he said. "I get done browner and browner."

"Look here," said Duval; "I think you are an honest fellow, and I will take your word if you will take mine."

DUVAL DISABLES MOSSY PENDELL'S SERVANT.

"What is it?"

"I will give you back your pistols, and nobody need know that I have passed your post here, if you will give me one piece of information."

"What is it?"

Duval could not speak quite composedly as he now asked the question that had been uppermost in his mind ever since he escaped from the lodgings of Colonel Jessop, in Pall Mall.

"Where is my horse?—where is Nightshade?"

"Ah!" cried Swallow, "I have you there, then?"

"No; that is enough. You need not answer."

Swallow was silent for a few moments, and then he spoke hastily: "No; what is it to me? Your horse is at the inn, opposite the Old Bailey, where it was once before; but you won't get it out in a hurry, for, you see, it's a kind of understood thing that either I or Mr. Muckles must go and ask for it."

"Then, my dear Swallow," said Duval, as he suddenly drew the officer's arm within his own, "I shall have the pleasure of your society all the way to the Old Bailey, and if you object I shall be compelled to leave the top of your skull here in the garden of Camden House."

Duval presented both Swallow's own pistols at his head, and quietly waited his decision.

"Browner still," said Swallow. "I'm coming. I've got a child and seven wives at home! No, bless me, what am I saying? It's Mrs. Swallow, I mean, and the seven little Swallows! Come on, if you must go! In for a sheep, in for a Swallow—I mean, in for a lamb!"

With a resigned expression, Swallow permitted himself to be led through the gate of Camden House, and before they got a quarter of a mile from the spot Duval hailed a hackney coach, which, although it took them at the rate only of about two miles and a half an hour, yet secured them from observation on the route to the Old Bailey.

"Now, Mr. Swallow," said Duval, as they were within sight of the inn yard, "you get out and fetch Nightshade, and I will be in readiness to receive her."

"Oh, lor'! oh, lor'! was ever any one ever done so brown in this world?" groaned Swallow, as he alighted from the hackney coach.

Claude Duval watched intently from the coach window, and had the satisfaction of seeing the officer enter the inn yard.

In less than five minutes he beheld him leading Nightshade by the bridle.

Claude Duval sprung from the coach, giving the man a guinea as he did so.

"Thank you, my dear Swallow," said Duval.

Quick as lightning he sprung upon the back of Nightshade, leaving Swallow in a bewildered state of mind, and not knowing exactly how to account to his superior for the part he had played in the transaction.

"Stop him—stop him! Claude Duval! A highwayman! A thousand pounds reward!"

These were the shouts which greeted the ears of Claude Duval, as he put his faithful Nightshade to a hard gallop.

He turned in his saddle, and glanced behind him, and, to his dismay, he found that Swallow was not alone, but that a rather strong party of officers from Newgate had joined him.

Claude felt that life or death depended upon the next few minutes, and drawing one of the holster pistols from Nightshade's saddle, he fired it, and from the manner in which the party of officers fell back, he felt that the shot had done its deadly work.

"It cannot be helped," said Claude; "I was compelled, for Lucy's sake, to save myself at all hazards. Ah! what is this?"

Lying upon his horse's mane was a small scrap of paper, which Claude seized, feeling assured in his own mind that he must have drawn it from the holster with the pistol he had fired.

Eagerly he unfolded the mysterious note, and read the following words:—

"If you would hear tidings of Lucy Everton, be on the highest knoll on Hampstead Heath to-night, at the hour of twelve."

Twice did Claude Duval read the mysterious billet, as he asked himself whether it were worth while to attend to its invitation.

"Another trap, probably; and yet I dare not refuse to keep this strange appointment. It may be that a friend has some information; and yet, what friend has Claude Duval and Lucy Everton? Nevertheless, I will go—I will see this mysterious personage who promises to give me tidings of my lost Lucy. My heart feels lighter since reading the little billet, and I will accept it as an earnest of better success than has attended this night's search. Forward, Nightshade—forward! And yet why need I use such haste? Not till midnight—no, not till midnight is this appointment to be kept."

CHAPTER XXXIII.

THE MIDNIGHT RENDEZVOUS.—THE BEREAVED HEART.

THE moonlight streamed around Duval and his horse, as at that late hour of the evening he occupied nearly the summit of the little knoll on Hampstead Heath.

Could it be possible that the mysterious agency that seemed now to surround the very name of Lucy would at that time make to him another communication?

Patiently Duval waited, listening to the slightest sound that might be indicative of the approach of any

His patience was rewarded, for soon there came a light footstep on the heath.

Whoever was approaching kept closely under cover of the brushwood, and but for the long shadow cast by the moonbeams, Duval might well have doubted his own sense of hearing, and believed that imagination only had conjured up the light footsteps on the heath.

But there could be no mistaking that shadow.

It must necessarily have a relative substance, and Duval, as he watched it eagerly, cried out in loud accents, "Whom seek you on this solitary heath at this dead hour of the night?"

The shadow stopped instantly.

"Nay, seek not to evade me!" added Duval. "I must and will know who you are."

"Forbear!" said a voice, and it was low and plaintive,—"forbear, and do not nourish anger against the innocent. I, too, suffer, and have but one question to ask you to be assured that you are the man I seek."

"What question?"

"Is there a void in your heart? Do you feel as though the shadow of one you love only resides within it?"

"I am bereaved," said Duval.

"Yes," added the voice, with passionate eagerness,—"yes, that is the word! I, too, am bereaved; but there is this difference between us—that my heart is wrung by an unworthy object, while you garner up your affections in one whose heart is all your own."

"What mean you? Take your hand from off the bridle of my horse! What mean you by this frantic clutch upon my arm?"

A female figure had rushed out from the shadow of the furze bushes; and, clinging to him and to Nightshade, looked imploringly in his face.

The moonbeams fell upon the countenance of this unknown person, and Duval saw that along with considerable beauty there were the traces of deep anxiety and suffering.

"You—you!" she said; "I speak to you! I ask you to cast away from you the heartache, and to save me! Recover her whom you love, and do not let her cross my path, for that path is dim and dark enough already."

"Hold!" cried Duval. "I seem obscurely to divine your meaning; and you seem to have a knowledge of one dearer to me than life itself. Give me but the requisite information if you can, and enable me to save her."

"I know not what to do. I know not what to say. You will not harm him?"

"Of whom speak you?"

"Of one who should be harmed, and yet who, by the memory of former affection, I would fain save. You must promise me this, and then I will tell you all."

"And you must be more explicit," said Duval. "How can I promise not to harm one whom you will not even name?"

"His name is Pendell."

"Ah! I might have guessed as much! You speak of Mossy Pendell—the man, of all others, whom I have cause to suspect and to avenge myself upon."

"Alas—alas! I am his unhappy wife, and more unhappy still in the fact that he bereaves you of one who returns not his insane passion. Alas—alas! what am I saying? You will spare him, if you recover your own lost treasure. Do not kill him—do not kill him! I know your injury is great, but not so great as it might have been. It is I who must continue to be unhappy; but as for you, when this anxiety has passed away, there is sunshine, hope, and joy again."

The tone of acute suffering in which these words

were spoken, struck home to the heart of Claude Duval.

"Be comforted," he said. "I think you mistake. That the villain Mossy Pendell is the man who, by treachery and by violence, has torn from me my wife—Lucy Everton, that was—I never doubted; but passion was not his impulse to the deed. He has other reasons which you may know not of; and now I call upon you, by every principle of right and justice, to put me on the track for the rescue of one who, although fair to my sight, awakens more resentment than love in the breast of such a man as Mossy Pendell."

"Oh, if I could only think so! But you shall save her—yes, you shall save her! Do you know Camden House?"

Duval made a gesture of impatience.

"Too well I know it. Search there is useless."

"She was there."

"But is there no longer."

"It may be so—it may be so! My brain is vexed and disturbed, and yet I will tell you what to do. You must track him, but yet spare him. Let me think—let me think! What is the hour now?"

"Past midnight."

"At two o'clock this morning, a horseman, followed by a servant, likewise mounted, will leave the garden gate of Camden House. The horseman will be Mossy Pendell, and the servant following him is named Judge. Track them, follow them, and you will be led to the retreat of Lucy Everton, your wife."

"A thousand thanks!" cried Duval, with animation. "Unhand me now at once, and let me go."

"Nay—one moment!"

"What more would you say?"

"Spare him—for my sake, spare him! I should have made you swear by all that you hold sacred that you would spare him, before I gave you this information; but let it not be too late—oh, let it not be too late! Promise me that you will not take his life! He may yet repent—who knows? He may yet repent, and love me as of old!"

Claude Duval was painfully struck by the distress and clinging tenderness of this poor victim of Mossy Pendell.

Much cause as he had to be vengeful in the extreme upon the villain who had caused him such terrible uneasiness, and so many hours of agonized apprehension, he could not listen to that pleading voice in vain.

And yet it seemed to him so strange that such a man as Mossy Pendell could awaken in any human breast feelings of tenderness and emotion.

But that was an experience in human nature which, even young as Claude Duval was, he had often encountered.

"I promise," he said, "that if no disrespect or harshness has been used towards Lucy Everton, I will be merciful. I can say no more."

"Then I must fain be content. But were you to extend your mercy a trifle further, and take my wretched life here upon this heath, with no eyes to look upon us but those of heaven, I should be the happier, and you would be forgiven the deed, in so far as you had lifted from a human creature a load of misery almost more than she can bear."

As this unhappy wife of Mossy Pendell spoke, she turned away, and took her solitary route townwards across the heath.

Duval had no heart to follow her.

Here was one more wretched than he could be, deprived of Lucy.

One, too, more wretched than Lucy herself, notwithstanding all the perils and pangs of separation.

But Duval was far from agreeing, in his own mind, with the view taken of the affair by this wife of Mossy Pendell, although he had little doubt that, to conceal his real motives for the abduction of Lucy, Pendell had led the unhappy partner of his fortunes into a belief that it was admiration of her charms.

With a definite object, now, Duval galloped from Hampstead Heath.

Considerably before two o'clock he reached, once more, the neighbourhood of Camden House.

He posted himself within view of the garden gate, concealing both himself and Nightshade at the entrance of a narrow lane, between two cottages, a short distance down the road on the other side of the way.

Scarcely had Duval taken up this position when the garden gate was opened, and a mounted man appeared, leading another horse by the bridle.

Duval, in his impatience, would have rushed forward; and it required all his self-control and prudence to prevent himself from doing so.

Deeply, too, he congratulated himself at the speed he had made, for it wanted yet considerably more than half an hour to two o'clock; and had he paused until the hour exactly specified by the unfortunate wife of Mossy Pendell, he would certainly have been too late to intercept or follow the horsemen on their night expedition.

Probably, with his habitual suspicion and want of trust in everybody, Pendell had deceived his wife as to the precise hour at which he meant to start.

But, be this as it may, Duval fixed his eyes earnestly upon the two horses—so earnestly, indeed, that in the darkness, his fancy began to deceive him, and more than once he thought he saw the spare horse was mounted, when such was not the case.

The real appearance, however, of its rider scattered all his air-woven imaginations to the winds.

There could be no mistake, then, upon the subject; and Duval only waited long enough to see in which direction the horsemen rode off, before he put Nightshade into motion.

There was one particular pace at which Nightshade could go, which combined the qualities of swiftness and silence.

A long swinging kind of walk, which was fully equal to the trot of ordinary horses, and which, on a soft country road, scarcely produced any sound at all.

Certainly, the sound that was produced was sufficiently slight to be completely drowned and submerged in the beat of any other horse's feet close at hand.

Assuming, then, that he could keep at a sufficient distance amid the darkness not to be readily observable by any backward glance, Duval felt that he might keep on the track of the two horsemen before him with success and secrecy.

But whither were they bound?

They took a route somewhat to the left of Kensington; and after passing down a long shadowy lane, the soil of which was so soft and thick, that even had Duval put Nightshade to a gallop, his footsteps could scarcely have been heard—they emerged upon a common.

From that, they took a bridle path, which Duval knew by a short cut led across the country to the royal Palace and Gardens of Kew.

Mossy Pendell and his servant had proceeded some distance down this bridle path, when Duval perceived that the horse of Judge began to limp. The creature had either cast a shoe, or had picked up a stone in his foot.

The servant began to fall back, and Duval hoped that his villanous master would get on so much in advance, that he, Duval, would have no difficulty in disposing of Judge as he might think fit.

The man having halted, dismounted, and commenced removing the stone from the horse's foot. In the meantime, Mossy Pendell had got pretty well in advance.

Duval was not long in putting his scheme into execution, and riding within a pace of the spot where the man and the horse had stopped, Claude struck him such a blow on the back of his neck, that the man dropped senseless to the ground.

To raise him and throw him into a ditch, which ran along the side of the hedge, was the work of a moment, Duval having first taken the precaution to possess himself of the man's cloak and hat.

Duval soon recovered Nightshade, who was quietly plucking the herbage which grew by the roadside, and the riderless horse was soon started back upon the path from which it had so recently emerged.

"Now," said Duval to himself—"now we are man to man; and if that villain has subjected my Lucy to the slightest indignity, I will chastise him to within an inch of his worthless life. I have promised not to slay him, for the sake of that poor wrecked heart that still loves him, notwithstanding all his cruelty and desertion."

It was not difficult now for Claude Duval to overtake Mossy Pendel, as he no longer had the same reasons for concealing his proximity, for it would have been impossible for Mossy Pendell to recognise beneath that hat any other features than those of his man, Judge.

As Duval was now near enough for his master to address him, Mossy Pendell turned round in his saddle, and said, "Is it all right now? Was it a stone?"

"Yes, sir. I've succeeded in getting it out, and he goes better than ever."

"So I thought," said Mossy Pendell: "you seemed to fly just now."

"I was afraid I should not be able to catch you, sir," said Duval, "and so put my horse to speed."

"I see—I see! But here we are. You understand what it is I wish you to do?"

"All right, sir."

Duval trusted to his good fortune to enable him to find out exactly what it was that Mossy Pendell required of his servant; but seeing that he intended to dismount at Kew Palace, Claude rode up to him, who then threw the bridle to Duval, saying, "Wait here till I give you the signal."

"All right, sir."

Duval watched Mossy Pendell's retreating figure as he entered the grounds surrounding the palatial residence, and when he felt certain that he could not be observed, he loosened his hold of the bridle of Mossy Pendell's horse, and with a slight touch with his riding whip, Claude had the satisfaction of hearing the creature galloping at a great rate in the direction from which they had come.

"That will do," said Duval. "Now, Nightshade, I must find you some place of security, for heaven knows how soon, and under what circumstances, I may next require you."

With this intention, Duval led Nightshade by the bridle through the little gate by which Mossy Pendell had entered, and found himself in the garden belonging to the Palace.

Duval was somewhat at a loss to know what to do with Nightshade, when the moon emerged from behind a dense mass of clouds, and for the space of a few minutes illuminated all objects.

At a very short distance, Claude Duval perceived the outline of some kind of building, and made his way to it, still leading Nightshade by the bridle.

He found that it was one of the many conservatories with which the grounds abounded, and it was with a feeling of relief that he made the discovery that he could bestow his faithful four-footed companion so safely and so near to one of the gates.

Duval walked round, and soon discovered a handle which opened a door leading into the conservatory.

"Gently, Nightshade, gently."

The sagacious creature trod as lightly as foot could fall, as he followed his master into what was to be his temporary stable for the time being.

Having secured the bridle to a long pole which formed one of the supports of the building, and giving Nightshade a caressing pat upon his arched neck, Duval now left the summer-house or conservatory, and made his way swiftly across the garden towards the square old red-brick edifice, where he hoped soon to learn something of his much-loved Lucy.

He reached the Palace, and walked quietly towards the outer offices, hoping that fortune would favour him, and that either by means of a window or an unfastened door, he might make his way into the interior.

His expectations were crowned with success, for a door partially open met his touch, for it was too dark to see any object just at that particular moment.

Little did Claude Duval imagine that that door gave admission to the man of all others who had cause to dread his, Duval's proximity.

Mossy Pendell had only preceded Claude Duval by a few minutes.

Duval found himself in what he thought must be the great hall leading to some of the principal apartments of the Palace.

There was a beautifully chased silver candelabrum, held by a statue in a niche in the wall, one wax-light of which only was burning. Still, after the intense darkness from which Duval had just come, it seemed to give much more light than it really did.

By the light of this wax candle, Duval found that he was, as he at first imagined, in the grand vestibule, and that just before him was a marble staircase, the gilt balustrades of which glittered in the faint rays that fell from the wax-light in the niche in the wall.

To ascend this staircase was Duval's first determination, and he did so rapidly and quietly, until he reached a landing-place, and then he paused, for he felt certain that he heard the murmur of voices.

He immediately entered a kind of ante-room, and it was from the room just beyond, the door of which was partially open, that the voices proceeded.

"Will it please your Majesty," Duval heard a voice say—"will it please your Majesty to give an audience to one of your Majesty's most dutiful subjects?"

"An audience? An audience at this time of night, —morning, we should say? What mean you, my Lord Beacham?"

"I believe, your Majesty, that he who has ventured to intrude thus upon your Majesty's privacy has something to communicate which will not be unpleasing to your Majesty."

"We know not to what you allude; but we do not like to be kept in suspense. Admit him, my lord."

There was a silence for a few minutes, and then it appeared to Duval that the person desiring an audience was now introduced into the private cabinet of the King, by the personage named by the King as my Lord Beacham.

"Well," said the King, "what now? Ah! Mr Mossy Pendell!"

Claude Duval's heart beat quickly.

"I have the honour to be that person, your Majesty, and one of your Majesty's most faithful and obedient servants."

"Yes, yes, we know all that. What tidings bring you?"

"All is satisfactory, your Majesty; and the young lady of whom I had the honour of speaking to your Majesty is even now within this Palace, and only awaits your Majesty's pleasure to present herself before your Majesty."

"You say she is beautiful?"

"As beautiful as an angel, your Majesty."

"Tush, man! We do not want angels here. Is she young?"

"She has numbered but seventeen summers, your Majesty."

"It is well," replied the King. "It is our pleasure to receive this paragon of beauty at once."

Who can describe the feelings of Claude Duval, as he listened to this dialogue, which had taken place between the King and the unscrupulous villain, Mossy Pendell?

Scarcely could he restrain the impulse to burst into that private room, and demand his Lucy at the hands of the King; for he felt that Lucy herself had been the subject of the foregoing conversation.

Duval clutched his sword-hilt with his right hand, and had just time to draw back within the shadow of a deep bay window in the ante-room, when he heard approaching footsteps.

Those footsteps were Mossy Pendell's.

How difficult was it for Claude Duval to restrain himself from rushing then and there upon his enemy, and bringing him to account for at least some of his crimes!

"No, no!" he said to himself; "I must wait patiently. I must see if this fair girl of whom they spoke be really my Lucy. If so, what is then to hinder me from taking her from him at the sword's point? Surely, heaven itself will befriend me in such an undertaking!"

CHAPTER XXXIV.

CLAUDE DUVAL ENCOUNTERS GREAT DANGER IN THE PALACE AT KEW.

For some time Claude Duval waited anxiously listening, hoping each moment to hear the approach of her whom he half hoped, half feared, would prove to be his Lucy.

A quarter of an hour passed, and still all was silent.

Another quarter, and then Claude fancied he heard a distant door shut.

With straining eyes and beating heart, he fixed his regards upon the door through which he had seen Mossy Pendell pass on his villanous errand.

"It is well," he heard Mossy Pendell say,—"it is well you have learned submission!"

How eagerly did Duval listen to catch the tones of the voice which he hoped would reply to those words, spoken in cold, sneering accents!

There was no reply.

The footsteps approached yet nearer; and then Duval heard a voice whisper, in female accents, "If you are human—if you are a man—save me—oh, save me!"

"Save you! Have I not saved you from penury, want, and disgrace? What mean you?"

"Give me back my poverty!" whispered the voice. "Honest poverty is, at least, honourable; but——"

"You know not what you say, girl. I tell you that here you will have honour, riches, and plenty showered upon you!"

"I cannot—I will not proceed further!"

"Ah! say you so? Then our compact is at an end, and he whom you love——"

"Mercy!" cried the girl. "In mercy, restore him to liberty, and I will bless you yet!"

There was something so mournful in the tones in which those words were spoken, that they found their way at once to the heart of Claude Duval, who, with his imagination so impressed with the belief that it was Lucy's voice he heard, was incapable of restraining himself any longer, and he rushed out from his hiding-place, sword in hand, and seized Mossy Pendell by the collar.

"Fiend! Villain! Once more am I face to face with you!"

The girl had been, perhaps, more surprised than Mossy Pendell; for, with one wild shriek, she turned and fled—but not before Duval was convinced in his own mind that he had been mistaken in supposing that it was Lucy.

"Unhand me!" cried Mossy Pendell; "or, by the heaven above us, I will make you have reason to repent of this night's work the longest day you have to live!"

Claude Duval felt that in another moment it would be too late—that, whatever he intended to do must be done immediately, before Mossy Pendell had time to call for help.

Taking him up, therefore, with as much ease as though he had been a child, Claude Duval hurled Mossy Pendell to the further side of an apartment, against the door of which the contest had taken place between them.

He waited but to see that his enemy lay all huddled up in a corner of the room, and that it would be, at all events, some minutes before he could give any alarm.

But the whole proceeding had taken place too near to the private apartment in which the King was for the noise not to have come plainly to his ears, and to those of his attendants who were in waiting upon his Majesty.

"It will be a race for life now," said Duval to himself, as with one bound he cleared the staircase, knocking down in his headlong progress a personage gorgeously dressed in crimson velvet, and whose breast was adorned with many English and foreign orders.

"Bless me!" gasped this personage. "Is it a madman?"

"Yes," said Duval, as he still sped on through the vestibule, and at length reached the little door by which he had entered.

He dashed across the flower-beds, heedless of every obstruction that presented itself—for he could hear that an alarm had been given, for in various parts of the grounds could be seen lights glistening among the trees and shrubs.

"Nightshade!"

It was with almost a cry of despair that Duval uttered that one word; for, in the darkness, he had mistaken the door by which he had before entered the conservatory, and he could see Nightshade was not in the position in which he had left him.

"Nightshade!" again he repeated; and now, with an exclamation of joy, he discovered his mistake—for Nightshade was really where he had left him, fastened to a long, upright pole close to a door.

"Fly, Nightshade!" he whispered, as he rapidly loosened the bridle from its hold on the pole.

The creature neighed slightly, and followed Duval's guiding hand through the gardens.

Voices could now be heard borne distinctly upon the clear night air.

"He is in the grounds! Quick! We shall have him yet!"

"Not quite so easy a matter as you seem to suppose," said Duval, in a low voice to himself.

He had gained one of the outer gates.

Another instant, and he was mounted.

"Fly, Nightshade!—fly, my brave steed! We have work yet to accomplish before your master can allow himself to be taken!"

A great weight had been lifted from Claude Duval's heart when he found that the fair girl, who had formed the topic of the brief interview Mossy Pendell had had with the King, was not Lucy. Still, he was as far as ever from discovering the place of concealment in which his much-loved Lucy was; and when he thought upon what might be her present sufferings, and the agony of mind he knew too well she was undergoing on his account, the strong man's heart almost gave way, and it was with difficulty he could suppress a cry of anguish bursting from his lips.

But the dawn was coming.

That night of many emotions and adventures was passing away.

Again does Claude Duval seek his solitary home on what was now to him a dismal heath, unbrightened by the presence of one whose form had made it an earthly paradise.

And now he began to feel the necessity of rest.

His eyes felt dim, and he drooped somewhat upon the saddle.

Indeed, Claude Duval would soon have fallen completely into a sleep, as cavalry soldiers are said sometimes to do upon the march, when thoroughly exhausted by over-fatigue, and yet keeping on the saddle by some rare instinct.

Something aroused him.

It was the blowing of a horn.

Duval knew that some mail-coach must be close at hand; and as he reclined on Nightshade, he saw the vehicle emerge from a cross-road, with its lamps still blazing, although the dawn had made such progress that there was really no necessity for them.

"Action!" cried Duval. "In action only shall I lose the bitter pang that sits at my heart!"

Even as he spoke he dashed forward.

The old, familiar cry of "Halt! Stand and deliver!" sprang from his lips.

"A highwayman! a highwayman!" shouted half a dozen voices from the outside passengers of the coach.

"A highwayman! a highwayman!"

"Pull up your horses," cried Duval, "or you are a dead man!"

Either from fright or bravado, the coachman neglected the order, notwithstanding Duval presented a pistol at his head.

He was loth to take the life of the man, but yet he fired, making sure that the ball should pass within sufficiently close proximity to him to leave no mistake about its actual presence.

The coachman must have pulled one rein then vigorously, for the horses turned aside, and almost ran the vehicle up a bank by the roadside.

After Duval had fired the pistol shot, it was quite a sight to see how the outside passengers kept dropping off like over-ripe chestnuts from a tree.

"A highwayman! A highwayman!" was the cry.

The two leading horses began to kick and plunge, and Duval, giving Nightshade a slight touch on the flank, leaped to their heads, and held them.

"Cast down your reins, coachman," he cried; "and all will be well, unless you want another shot."

"Certainly not—certainly not, sir, if you please."

"Quick, then!"

"I'm a respectable man, Mr. Highwayman, and have druv the Highflyer for twenty years, and I don't want to be shot like a mad elephant at last."

As the coachman spoke, he threw down the reins, and rolled off the box; but where he went to, among the horses, Duval could not perceive, since he was too intent upon quieting the leaders.

When this was accomplished, and Duval could look about him, he did not see a living soul on or about the coach.

The guard had dropped down from behind, and fled, leaving his horn as a trophy on the roof.

All the outside passenges had followed his example.

And as Duval himself had, so to speak, got rid of the coachman, he was certainly master of the field and of the inside passengers.

If there were any.

That seemed a question, inasmuch as not the slightest sound had as yet come from the interior of the vehicle.

Duval had adopted the best possible means of quieting the fears of the leading horses.

He had patted and coaxed them into serenity, and feeling now perfectly certain that he might leave them in safety, he was about to turn Nightshade's head towards the side of the coach, when his progress was arrested by a loud, strange voice, apparently from some person on the other side of the hedge, calling out one word—

"Halt!"

"Who cries halt?" was the response of Duval.

"Halt but to listen;" added the voice; and the tones were deep, hollow, and sorrowful.

"To listen to what?"

"Your doom!"

"You talk to one," cried Duval, "who laughs to scorn your warning. Let my doom be what it may, and let it come when and how it may, it is not to be predicted by such as you."

"Listen!" cried the voice again—"listen! and if you have one spark of caution in your breast—if you value peace here, and serenity hereafter—if you would avoid a fearful doom in this world, and the execration of mankind—you will now pass on, making what speed you can from this fated spot, for here there is despair, here there is danger, and here there is death!"

"Take my reply!" said Duval, as, drawing his other pistol from the holster, he fired at once through the hedge, in the direction of the speaker.

"Be it so!" said the voice.

Then all was still.

A sense of loneliness came over Duval.

What could it mean?

Was there no one within the stage coach?

Had he only captured four horses and a vehicle, with blazing lights, and, apparently, all the paraphernalia of a stage coach?

The problem could easily be solved.

One bound of Nightshade brought him to the coach door.

Rather then as a thing of habit, than because he liked the words, Claude Duval repeated the old formula of the highway—"Your money or your lives!"

The glass of the coach door was up, but Duval, with a touch, let it down, and resting the barrel of one of his discharged pistols upon the door-sill, he peered into the vehicle.

He had so fully expected to find the coach empty, that it was really quite a relief to him to see persons inside it.

Indeed, it appeared to be full.

The light from the side lamps was but a reflected one, and by some means that light seemed to decrease each moment.

Doubtless the duration of the lights had been calculated to last till the dawn, and the time of their expiration had arrived.

They were gradually fading out.

But still Duval was confident, even by that dim, uncertain glimmer, that he saw six people in the stage coach.

"Your money or your lives!" he cried again.

No one replied.

No one moved.

The silence was profound.

It was something at once awful and mysterious.

"Speak!" shouted Duval. "Put an end to this mummery, or it may be worse for some of you!"

CHAPTER XXXV.

CLAUDE DUVAL STOPS A COACH, AND FINDS IT CONTAINS ONLY A GHOSTLY COMPANY.

CLAUDE DUVAL shuddered as he spoke.

The sound of his own voice seemed to awaken a strange echo in and about the spot.

He leant back over the saddle of Nightshade, and lifted one of the coach lamps from its socket.

It was nearly out, but the little flickering flame that still remained was sufficient, when the lamp was placed on the sill of the coach window, to illuminate its interior.

There were six passengers.

Duval looked with inquiring eyes from face to face, and then an awful conviction came over him that those faces all belonged to the dead.

The six passengers in that coach were not of this world; or rather, the better and immortal part of them had fled, leaving behind six pale, sad vestiges of humanity, to look with their dead, stony eyes into the face of the man who had cried out to them for their money or their lives.

Their lives were past all risk.

Would he, bold and defiant highwayman as he was, go through the terrible ordeal of rifling those still forms?

He could not do it.

"Gracious heavens!" he exclaimed. "What can this mean?"

Again he looked from face to face.

There were two females—one advanced in years, but the other still young and comely.

There was a young child.

An elderly man.

A younger one.

And up in an extreme corner, making the sixth of the dead passengers in the coach, was a stalwart, seafaring looking person, who seemed, by the convulsed look upon his face, to have suffered greatly in the brief passage from life to death.

The coach lamp went out.

Claude Duval could see no more.

He cast the lamp to his feet, and on the impulse of the moment, he shouted, "Help! help! help!"

"Thanks!" yelled a voice. "Six murders will lie at the door of Claude Duval, and not all the asseverations and all the oaths he can utter in any court of justice will free him from the cry of 'Guilty!'"

"Wretch!" shouted Duval. "Wherever you are, you are indeed the murderer!"

"Ha, ha, ha!"

The laugh that responded to these words was fearfully sardonical, and gladly would Claude Duval have sent a bullet or two in the direction of the speaker, but his pistols were discharged, and it would take him some few seconds to reload them.

A happy thought, however, struck him.

He glanced at the back of the coach, where hung the short blunderbuss usually carried by the guard.

That individual had, in a cowardly manner, deserted his trust; but he had left the fire-arm behind him.

"You dare not speak again!" cried Duval.

"Ha, ha, ha!" laughed the voice.

The sounds came from behind a particular part of the hedgerow, not many paces from the back of the coach; and now, as Claude Duval had possessed himself of the guard's blunderbuss, he levelled and fired at once in that direction.

The report was tremendous.

The recoil, too, of the piece was very great.

It nearly threw Duval from Nightshade; but, mingled with that report, and the many echoes it awakened, there came a human yell of pain that could not be mistaken.

Duval had hit somebody!

A pistol bullet might pass harmlessly enough through the hedge; but the scattering slugs, nails, and bits of old iron with which, no doubt, as was usual, the blunderbuss had been loaded, had taken in a wide area.

"Ha, ha, ha!" cried Duval, in the excitement of the moment. "Now show yourself, if you be human!"

There was no reply.

Duval threw down the guard's blunderbuss, and gazing towards the east, which was brightening into daylight, he asked himself what, under the strange circumstances in which he was placed, he ought to do.

He almost dreaded to look again into that coach of the dead.

And yet the circumstance was altogether so strange and novel, that it attracted every feeling of human curiosity in his nature.

He did look in again.

Yes, there were the six still, dead forms.

The only change that seemed to have taken place was that the hand of the stalwart, seafaring-looking man inclined downwards, resting more upon the breast.

Then, as Duval gazed upon the terrible spectacle, another change took place.

One of those mysterious movements which will, at times, occur after death, caused the young child to fall forward from the seat on which it rested.

Duval could not forbear from uttering a cry.

"Speak! Scream!" he shouted. "Let me know, even if it be but by a sigh, if any one lives!"

No.

The dead child fell listlessly.

Duval could bear no more.

For once in his life he set spurs to Nightshade—to that gallant Nightshade who never needed spur or whip—and at a furious pace he galloped from the spot.

The sky was brightening all over.

A yellow radiance shot up from the east.

The cold, grey masses of morning clouds were scattering far and wide over the sky, and between them were peeping down bits of soft, pure blue, giving promise of a morning of beauty.

Duval saw a horseman before him.

The road was long and straight at that part, and nearly half a mile intervened between them.

But what was half a mile at the rate of speed Nightshade was now going?

It was nearly passed over with a rush.

Duval slackened his speed, and brought Nightshade to a standstill.

"Halt!"

"Halt!"

The word was spoken simultaneously by Duval and the strange horseman.

Then they pronounced each other's names, for those two men recognised one another upon the moment.

"Mr. St. Ives!"

"Claude Duval!"

It was instinct that made St. Ives place his hands upon his pistols.

Duval smiled faintly.

"I am unarmed, Mr. St. Ives, except my sword."

The officer removed his hands from the pistols' stocks.

"Claude Duval, from my heart," he said, "I am always sorry to meet you! I carry on a war now with myself—a war between my duty and my inclination. I ought to arrest you, but——"

Duval waved his hand.

"You will not attempt it, Mr. St. Ives. There is a

truce between us. You will not attempt to arrest me, and, consequently, I shall not kill you in self-defence. I have something, however, to say to you now of more moment than the arrest or escape of Claude Duval."

"Indeed!"

"Yes, St. Ives. Down the road you will find a stage coach, in which, as I am a mortal man, I do believe six murders have been committed!"

"Duval!"

St Ives looked pale as death itself.

"What would you say, sir?"

"No," said the officer, as he drew a long breath, "I will not believe it. That flush upon your face, Claude Duval, is not the colour of guilt!"

Duval lifted up his right hand.

"I call upon heaven," he said, "to forbid the bright and beautiful sun ever to shine upon me again, if I have had hand or part in the tragedy of which I speak!"

As Duval spoke, a cloud burst asunder, and a long beam of sunlight fell upon him and Nightshade.

"I will swear to your innocence!" cried St. Ives. "It is my duty to see into this matter, and perhaps I guess already something more of it than I can tell you."

"Be it so!" cried Duval. "Farewell!"

"One moment."

"What would you further with me?"

"If it be necessary to call upon you for testimony in this case, will you come forward freely?"

"By heaven, I will!"

"Yet a moment. Duval, I have something to tell you. Lucy Everton lies in a cell at Newgate!"

"You give me this information, Mr. St. Ives, upon your own authority, and vouch for its truth?"

"I do."

"I thank you, then, with all my heart, but not as I would wish, for that heart is too full for ordinary utterance. I cannot ask you to help me to rescue her from death, because your position forbids it."

"It does—it does!"

"But I solemnly assure you that she is as innocent of the crime imputed to her as you can be yourself. Farewell, now; and when next you hear of Claude Duval it will be probably associated with some act that will live long in the annals of Newgate."

As Duval uttered these words, he put Nightshade again to speed, and galloped at a rapid rate to London.

What was he to do?

How was he to help Lucy now?

In the open air, let her be guarded doubly and trebly by the myrmidons of the law, there was always a chance of rescuing her by some bold stroke.

But within the thick and massive walls of Newgate, how could he reach her?

It was without reflection that Claude Duval turned his horse's head in the direction of the great prison.

A most imprudent step, certainly, because by the time he reached it the morning was sufficiently advanced for the bustle and turmoil of ordinary avocations to begin in the city.

So remarkable a figure as Claude Duval, mounted on a horse of such matchless beauty as Nightshade, could not but attract attention.

A small crowd began to collect around him, and then one voice called out, "It's Claude Duval, the highwayman! Secure him!"

"I have him!" said a man, in every respect attired as a Bow Street officer, and producing a constable's staff as he spoke,—"I have him!"

The man was mounted on a stout brown horse, and there was something about his tone and manner that at the moment struck Duval as being familiar to him.

Perhaps if Duval's brain and heart had not been so bewildered and oppressed by thoughts of the situation of Lucy, there would not have been a moment's doubt as to the identity of this person.

"Beware!" said Duval, as the seeming officer stretched forth his hand to grasp him.

"Good gracious, Captain!" was the reply in a low tone: "don't you know me?"

Duval knew him then instantly.

"Blossom?"

"Yes, Captain. I thought that this wig and false whiskers might hide me from most folks, but never from you."

"They would not—they would not, Blossom; but my mind was so pre-occupied I should scarcely have known my best friend from my deadliest and direst foe."

"Let us ride off, Captain. The mob thickens, and we shall have some of the fellows out of Newgate directly."

"Oh, that I could have one living soul out of Newgate, I would not care for all the rest!"

"Then I guess the worst," said Blossom. "Lucy Everton is captured."

"She is—she is!"

"Knock him over! Hold him by the bridle! Unhorse him! Pitch him out of the stirrups!"

These cries began to come from the crowd of people about Duval and Blossom, and it was quite evident that all the popular sympathies went with the former.

Blossom would have stood but a poor chance of escaping popular vengeance if Duval had only chosen to direct it against him.

As it was, he almost felt the necessity of showing that he was on good terms with the apparent officer who had captured him.

He held out his hand, which Blossom grasped, and then the mob seemed to see how matters stood.

"Hurrah! hurrah!—there's two of them! It's only a sell—they are both highwaymen! There's two of them, and here comes Dick Chesterton from Newgate!"

A big, burly-looking man, with a hanger in his hand, appeared at this moment at the wicket gate of Newgate.

"There is danger," said Blossom. "Let us ride off."

Both the horses were put to a gallop, and long before any of the officials of Newgate could get their steeds saddled and bridled, and themselves equipped for the road, Claude Duval and Blossom had put a good couple of miles between them and the gloomy prison.

But Duval left his heart behind him.

Behind him, in one of those old timeworn cells of Newgate, where Lucy languished, scarcely daring to hope that fate would again release her from the cruel death that menaced her.

And yet, if it were possible for human courage and human skill to save her, she would once more breathe the fresh, open air of heaven in safety and in freedom.

CHAPTER XXXVI.

LUCY EVERTON IS VISITED BY MOSSY PENDELL IN NEWGATE.

It was after a long and deep sleep, consequent upon the great exhaustion of spirits produced by the events of the last few nights, that Lucy opened her eyes, and found herself alone in one of the gloomy cells of Newgate.

So confused were the feelings and perceptions of the young girl on first awakening, that she was some minutes before she could arrange her thoughts suffi-

MOSSY PENDELL VISITS LUCY EVERTON AT NEWGATE.

ciently to enable her to comprehend what had really happened, or whether it was really only a dream that she had been rescued by Claude Duval, and afterwards made his wife.

But memory soon asserted her powers, and all that had taken place at her home on Hampstead Heath came freshly and vividly to her recollection.

Scarcely, however, had Lucy become fully awake, when the door of the cell was opened, and her cousin, Mossy Pendell, stood before her.

He carefully closed the door behind him, and placed the lantern he had brought with him at his feet.

"Well, Miss Everton, or Mrs. Duval, whichever you may be," he said, "I hope you like your present abode."

Lucy was silent; she found it would be impossible to reply to the sneering question which had been put to her by her relentless foe.

"Ah!" added Mossy Pendell, "I see—I see; my beautiful cousin indulges in the privilege of her sex, and is sulky!"

No. 12.—NIGHTSHADE.

"Leave me—oh, leave me!" sighed Lucy. "I know the purport of this visit! It is but to feast your eyes upon my despair!"

"Yes and no," slowly responded Mossy Pendell.

"Yes and no?" repeated Lucy. "What mean you?"

"I did come to see how you bore your reverse of fortune, and how the new-made bride liked her present abode; but I came also to tell you that I would set you free!"

"Set me free? Oh, say those precious words again, Mossy Pendell—my cousin, and even yet I shall live only to bless you!" cried Lucy, springing to her feet; and then, as she sunk on her knees before that man of many crimes, her tears flowed as though her heart would break.

But there was no feeling of pity at the heart of that man, as he gazed unmoved upon the misery he had caused; on the contrary, a sardonic smile played about his thin lips, as he hissed, in low tones, in Lucy's ear, "You misunderstand me, Lucy! I will save you on certain conditions."

"What are they? Speak!"

"Tell me where Claude Duval may be found; deliver him up to justice; and, Lucy Everton, you are free—free as air, to go and come whither you may please!"

Lucy recoiled from him as she would have done from the most loathsome reptile, as she cried, "Never! Wretch! Monster! Do with me as you will! Let me die; but never will I betray to you the abode of the gallant, the noble-minded Claude Duval!"

There was a long silence, broken only by the sobs of that sorely-tried heart.

"Ha, ha!" laughed Mossy Pendell. "Claude Duval will be captured without your assistance; only I thought I would do a kind action for once in a way, and give you a chance of saving yourself!"

"Oh, no, no! Oh, heaven!"

"Ha, ha! so that touches you, does it?"

Mossy Pendell opened the cell door, and banged it shut. Lucy heard him lock it, and then she heard a bar placed across it, and she felt that she was indeed a prisoner.

Then she brushed away the tears from her eyes, as she gathered strength from a feeling of resentment that began to take possession of her.

"No, no!" she said. "I should be strong, not weak! I will not be tearful! I will be strong, and I will think of him—of my husband—my preserver!"

Poor Lucy clasped her hands over her eyes, as the gallant figure of Claude Duval came vividly before her, and she could, in imagination, hear the deep, fond tones of that much-loved voice, as he said, "Lucy, Lucy, I love you!"

Then despair took possession of the heart of poor Lucy.

Gladly—oh, gladly would she have stood upon Hampstead Heath, and listened to the soft and tender tones of him who had saved her from a horrible death once before, but which now seemed to be again approaching her in long and hasty strides.

But what was she to do?

That soon became the question she proposed to herself.

Alas, poor Lucy!

Cold, weary, and sad, poor Lucy—hitherto the child of luxury—idolized by her good old uncle, the General, whom she was accused of poisoning—upon whom the very winds of heaven had not been allowed to blow too roughly—cowered down in a corner of that dark, damp cell, to try to collect her scattered thoughts, and to resolve upon some plan of action which might be the means of her escape from the terrible fate that seemed to await her.

* * * * * *

The ride to Hampstead was a gloomy one.

Duval was immersed in his reflections, and they seemed to be of so painful a character, that Blossom, athough he would fain have interrupted them, scarcely felt that he could venture to interfere.

It was not until they absolutely reached the heath, that that faithful follower ventured to speak to Duval.

He then rode up close to him.

"Captain, rely upon me and the rest of our band. If we have to pull old Newgate down stone by stone, we will find a means of rescuing Lucy Everton from within its walls.

It was somewhat strange how Blossom, and, in fact, every one else, although they well knew that Lucy was the wife of Claude Duval, still called her by her former name.

The notoriety that had accompanied the terrible charge made against her, and all the circumstances of her conviction and rescue from death, had made that name of Lucy Everton so familiar that it could never be forgotten.

And Claude Duval himself seemed tacitly to acknowledge it as the name by which Lucy was to be addressed, and even at times, in speaking of her to others, adopted it himself.

He now paused abruptly, and turned to Blossom as he spoke with emotion.

"No assurances are needed to convince me of the fidelity of yourself, or that of the band, but we are few in number, and, all counted, we are but nine."

"But we are faithful, strong, and resolute."

"Yes, Blossom, against human force, I grant it, but not against stone walls. Lucy shall be rescued, but it will be partly by finesse as well as by force."

Duval reached the now gloomy mansion, which, for so brief a space, had worn so sunny an aspect, and consigning Nightshade to the care of Blossom, he proceeded to the old faded suite of rooms, which had been so temporarily in the occupation of himself and Lucy.

Then for a time Duval paced to and fro in anxious thought.

Then he spoke in low tones to himself.

"Yes, truly, gold is the power which will open even the gates of Newgate. I will try its force before I attempt any other."

He proceeded to an ancient bureau that was in the room, and hastily flinging open the doors, he drew forth a secret drawer.

The drawer was heavy with guineas.

Claude Duval, for the first time in his life, counted them.

"One hundred and eighty," he said.

Then he sighed deeply.

"Not sufficient—not sufficient! The officers of Newgate are but men, and they have their price, but it will be a heavy one, and this is not sufficient."

Duval then remained immersed in thought for some time, and as the daylight streamed in upon him, the sense of excessive fatigue again came over him.

He felt the necessity of rest.

"Lucy!" he cried, "for your sake, I must sleep, in order that, for your sake, I may be wakeful and active. It is not while the bright sun is in the heavens that I can attempt your rescue. No, the shadows of evening must fall upon all these fair objects that I see from this window far and near, before I can act. Until then, rest—rest!"

Claude Duval was so completely overcome by fatigue that he was fast asleep in three minutes after lying down upon an immense antique couch that was in the apartment.

It seemed to him only a few minutes, so profound had been his repose, when he opened his eyes again.

During that time, however, the sun had reached its meridian, and had sunk deep down in the western sky.

The birds in the tree tops so close to the window of the room in which Duval had slept were twittering their last notes before retiring to rest.

Long, slant rays of golden light pervaded the whole landscape.

Duval sprang to his feet.

How easily he had passed those few hours that intervened between the resolution to act, and the period when it would be possible to do so with effect.

His fatigue had all left him.

He was fresh and alert, and feeling only the necessity of taking some food, he at once called upon Blossom who he knew would not be far off, to provide it fo him.

From the adjoining room the faithful follower made his appearance.

"We will eat sufficient, Blossom," he said, "to support nature and give us strength for the purpose, and then to town at once."

These were grateful words to Blossom.

What he had feared most of all was, that Duval would start on some expedition, the principal ingredients in which would be rashness and courage, and that he would go alone.

But such was not the case. After partaking of the meal, hastily prepared, Duval and Blossom were once more mounted and on the heath, just as the sun dropped finally below the horizon, and a rush of cool wind swept over the wide expanse.

"Blossom, listen to me," said Duval.

"With all my ears, Captain."

"I want a thousand pounds!"

"All's right, Captain."

"I want two thousand!"

"Better still, Captain."

"And I must have them, before another hour has passed away."

"Very good, Captain."

"Between here and Newgate lie some populous thoroughfares, and it is there that I must look for this money. You know, Blossom, that a thousand pounds are offered for my apprehension?"

"I do know it, Captain; but I don't think any one will get the money."

"I agree with you, unless I pay it myself."

"Pay it yourself, Captain? I don't understand."

"Listen to me, and you shall know my plan for to-night's proceedings. It may seem desperate; but, on that very account, I look for success. I want to take people by surprise; and, in the astonishment of the moment, to make them do things that in sober reason they would shrink from."

Blossom could scarcely conceal the feelings of apprehension that came over him, as Claude Duval spoke in this rather wild and excited manner.

"If my capture, Blossom, is worth a thousand pounds, Lucy's release should be worth as much."

"Just so, Captain."

"Officers of the police are but men; and I would ask you, Blossom, why it is they apprehend her, and hunt me to the death?"

"Of course, Captain, for what they get by it."

"Then they shall get all they possibly can hope for, by leaving us alone. I mean to gather together two thousand pounds to-night, and carry them to Newgate. One thousand shall be my own ransom—since I shall step within its walls—and the other shall be the purchase of Lucy's release."

"But, Captain——"

"Say on—you have some objection?"

"Only one."

"And that?"

"I fear treachery. The rascals will try to keep the money and the prisoners likewise."

"I must strive, Blossom, to provide against that as best I may. Have you loaded my pistols carefully?"

"Yes Captain, both pairs; those at the saddle, and the others I handed to you for your pocket."

"Then I hold four lives."

"But, Captain, let me advise. If we are to pick up these two thousand pounds on the road, let us go in force with all our men. We shall do it more safely and easily."

"Be it so. I will wait for you."

"And I would offer another piece of advice, Captain—which is, that you do not visit Newgate until the night-watch is on."

"That will be midnight."

"It will, Captain; but then there are only six men in the hall of the prison, and no one will be going in or out; so that, if there be any chance at all of dealing with them in the way you mention, that is the time."

"You are right, Blossom—you are right; and yet it will be five weary hours until that time. But I feel that you are right, and it shall be so. Go at once now, and get our men mounted, and we will ride to town."

Blossom was not slow in obeying this order.

Not only for the reason he had himself stated did he wish Claude Duval on this occasion to be accompanied by all his men, but he thought that if anything untoward happened at Newgate, it might be greatly to the advantage of Duval to have so respectable a force at hand.

In the course, then, of a quarter of an hour, the seven men who inhabited that lonely mansion in common with Claude Duval and Blossom, were all well mounted and armed upon the heath.

CHAPTER XXXVII.

CLAUDE DUVAL DETERMINES TO RANSOM LUCY EVERTON.

"Captain, said Blossom, we have plenty of time to spare."

"We have, indeed.

"I should advise, then, that we strike across the country to the Edgeware Road; and there will be a far better chance of our meeting with good booty somewhere about that part of the town where it joins to the Oxford Road, than lower down."

"Agreed—agreed! Follow me, then. We will take the long, narrow lane that leads to Kilburn."

Most persons who are at all familiar with the suburbs of London, know well the pretty, romantic, wooded lane that leads through the little cluster of houses called West End, from Hampstead to Kilburn.

That was the route Claude Duval took.

He put Nightshade to a sharp trot, and the distance appeared to be as nothing.

Upon reaching Kilburn, the party turned sharply to the left, and very soon found their way to the junction of the Edgeware Road, with the great western thoroughfare from London, then indiscriminately called the Oxford Road.

The night was a dark one.

A proper highwayman's night.

At the distance of a hundred yards, neither man or horse could be distinguished.

And, at that time, the march of bricks and mortar had scarcely extended so far; and the wretched oil lamps that lit London ceased entirely some distance before reaching Park Lane.

The inefficient watch that was likewise kept upon the public thoroughfares, made it quite possible for such a strong party of armed men to commit any depredation they proposed with almost perfect impunity.

"Halt!" cried Duval.

The band came to a stand-still.

"What is that blaze of light by Park Lane, Blossom?"

There was one house in particular, about half-way down the lane, that seemed to be well illuminated.

Lanterns were shifting about before it; and now and then, as the wind changed from one direction to another, faint sounds of music reached the ears of Claude Duval and his men.

It was not difficult to come to some conclusion as to what all this meant.

"Some entertainment is going on, Captain," said Blossom, "and here come some of the carriages."

Dashing along at a brisk pace up Park Lane, exactly towards where Claude Duval and his men were stationed, came a carriage with four horses.

It was driven by postilions in very gaudy liveries, and, altogether, looked a very pretentious turn-out.

"This shall be number one," said Duval. "Secure the horses' heads, and leave the rest to me."

"Halt—halt!" shouted Blossom, as he sprung forward, and caught the leaders by the rein.

The postilions, at first, thought it was but one man who interfered with their progress, and were quite well disposed to ride over him.

They soon discovered their mistake.

Half a minute did not elapse before a pistol was presented at each of their ears, and four of Duval's men held each one of the horses, while the remainder of the party drew themselves up in the roadway, so that the vehicle was completely secured, and its occupants left at the mercy of Duval.

Riding up to the door of the carriage, Claude cried out with a loud voice, "Toll! A toll to pay here!"

"Insolent scoundrel!" shouted a voice from the carriage, as the window was hastily let down; "what do you mean?"

"Exactly what I say!" cried Duval. "A toll to pay here!"

"A what?"

"Are you deaf? I have said a toll! and the amount is all the money you have about you, together with your watch and jewels!"

Within the carriage was a lady and two gentlemen; and the lady now uttered a faint scream, as she involuntarily put her hands to her ears, where glittered some diamond drops of great value.

"I'll see you hanged first!" said the gentleman, who had before spoken. "Thieves—thieves! A highwayman! A highwayman!"

Turning hastily from the window at which Duval stood, the gentleman let down the glass on the opposite side of the coach, and was in the act of thrusting his head from it, when he suddenly recoiled as if a blow had been struck him.

The effect was very similar.

He had come into violent contact with the pistol-barrel that Blossom, on that side of the coach, thought it prudent to present to the notice of its inmates.

"You see, my dear Duke," said the other gentleman, calmly, and who had not yet spoken, "that we are surrounded."

"I care not—I care not! I will not be robbed on the King's highway in this fashion! Help! Thieves! thieves!"

"Ah!" said Duval. "I see you put a proper value on your life!"

"What do you mean, scoundrel?"

"The repetition of that word, my Lord Duke, will be highly gratifying to your heir, and prepare your own way to the family vault of the Montroses—if they possess such a luxury!"

"Ah! you know me?"

"No one could once hear those tones, so full of passion and brutality—of mean insolence and yet vulgarity—and forget them! We have met before, my Lord Duke, on Hampstead Heath, and know each other!"

"You are Claude Duval!"

"Rightly guessed; and, knowing who I am, you likewise know what I am! Quick, your Grace, for I am getting impatient!"

"Oh, give him everything—give him everything! What is the use of contending when one's life is at stake?"

"Never!" cried the Duke of Montrose. "The rascal dare not commit murder; and I hear other carriages approaching!"

"Beware!" said Duval. "I have said before, my Lord Duke, that you put a certain value on your life; and it is evident to me that you carry exactly that sum about with you, since you prefer a pistol-bullet to surrendering it!"

"Oh, spare him!—spare him!" cried the lady. "He is my sister's husband! Spare him, Claude Duval, and take these jewels!"

"Certainly not, madam; at your entreaty, I can spare the life of this man. Blossom!"

"Yes, Captain!"

"Have him out, and take by force from him what he clings to with such pertinacity!"

Blossom blew a whistle.

The three disengaged men dashed forward.

In a few seconds, the Duke of Montrose was dragged from the carriage, and, with professional dexterity, every article of value he had about him was taken from him.

"Drive on, postilion!" cried Duval.

"Stop! stop!" yelled the Duke.

"Drive on!" cried Duval again.

The postilions hesitated a moment.

Bang! went a pistol-shot which Duval fired over their heads.

They no longer delayed, but, laying their whips over the flanks of the horses, they started off at full speed.

The Duke of Montrose, in a very undignified manner, ran after the vehicle, leaving Claude Duval and his men to their triumph.

"A lantern, Blossom!" cried Duval.

Several of the men who haunt balls and routs with lighted lanterns, to show the guests to their carriages, had strayed up Park Lane, seeing that some obstruction was made to the progress of the Duke of Montrose's carriage.

It was to one of these men that Blossom darted forward, and, giving him a blow with one hand upon the top of his hat, that sent it right down to his chin, he wrenched his lantern from him with the other, and handed it to Duval.

"Hold it yourself, Blossom. I want to see what Fortune has done for me in this my first venture."

A purse and pocket-book had been taken from the Duke of Montrose, both of which were tolerably well supplied.

At a rough computation, Duval saw that there was somewhere about five hundred pounds.

"Good!" he cried. "The night is still young, and we shall make it further profitable!"

"Another carriage, Captain!"

"Stand aside, my men! Surely those are royal liveries?"

A couple of outriders, in the scarlet livery of the royal family, dashed past Duval and his men.

At about a couple of paces in their rear, a very plain chariot, drawn by only two horses, came along at a good pace.

"Halt!" shouted Duval again; and this time he himself seized the horses by their heads.

This carriage was driven by a coachman in the ordinary way, who made some furious cuts at Duval with his whip.

There was then a short scuffle on the coach-box, and a couple of Duval's men dragged down the coachman, flinging him heavily to the side of the road.

A gentleman with a heavy white moustache put his head out of the coach window.

"Guard! guard!" he cried; "what is the meaning of all this?"

Duval was face to face with him in a moment; and as the light from the carriage-lamps fell upon the barrel of a pistol which Claude Duval carried, the gentleman drew in his head, exclaiming, as he did so, "We are attacked, your Royal Highness; but whether by thieves or assassins I know not!"

A loud voice, uttering several oaths, from the interior of the carriage, responded to this statement.

Duval, as he glanced into the luxurious equipage, saw at once who was its occupant.

It was the then well-known Duke of Cumberland, a prince of the royal family, of some military reputation, but generally disliked for the ferocity and brutality of his character.

Duval slightly raised his hat.

"A thousand pardons, your Royal Highness; but necessity banishes scruples, and I must trouble you for whatever money you have about you."

"Indeed!" said the Duke. "Do you mind whether it is in metal or notes?"

"Whichever your Highness pleases."

"Take it, then; and much good may it do you!"

The Duke, as he spoke, fired two pistols out at the carriage window, with the full intention of taking Duval's life.

One of the bullets passed so near his eyes, that he could almost be said to feel the heat of the shot.

The other touched Nightshade slightly in the neck.

Duval was certain that the noise of these shots would soon spread an alarm down the whole of Park Lane, and that the place would, in all probability, be untenable for him and his men.

"Hold Nightshade, Blossom!" he cried. "Meet me at the corner of the Oxford Road, close to Surrey House. Let one of our men mount the coach-box and take his orders from me."

"Will Armstrong, Captain, is there already."

"Good! that will do."

To spring off Nightshade and open the door of the coach, and then with one leap to make his way into the vehicle by the side of the Duke of Cumberland, was the work of the next moment.

There was a rush of many feet up Park Lane.

The tramp of armed men, and the rattle of military accoutrements.

"Your Royal Highness," said Duval, "is as safe as though you were beneath the royal canopy of your own state bed, if you please to be so; but, upon the slightest alarm, the silken lining of this coach will be spattered with your brains, and stained with your blood! My name is Claude Duval!"

"Ah!"

"Let me get out!" said the gentleman with the white moustache.

"Certainly not, sir!" said Duval. "Stir an inch at your peril! I have only fired one pistol to-night, and have three more quite at your service!"

"But——"

"Beware, gentlemen, I say! There are peculiar circumstances this night, which make it dangerous to trifle with me! Beware, I say!"

"Did your Highness call for help?" said a voice at the coach-door at this moment, as an officer of the Guard in full uniform appeared at it.

"Say 'Certainly not,'" whispered Duval. "Why should a prince of the blood royal throw away his life so needlessly?"

The Duke seemed to make two or three gulps at the words, and then he growled out, "Certainly not!"

The officer saluted, and then drew back a pace or two.

"Drive on, coachman!" cried Duval.

"What!" said the Duke; "have you suborned even my servants against me?"

"Certainly not, your Royal Highness. It is one of my servants who is on the coach-box."

"I think I'd rather get out!" said the gentleman with the white moustache again.

"I am quite sure you will do no such thing!" replied Duval. "Once more, sir, I warn you to be still; but should you persist in wishing to go out, you may, but it will be with the addition of a bullet in your brain!"

"What is the meaning of all this?" asked the Duke. "Is it a plot?"

"Certainly not, your Royal Highness; it is quite an impromptu, and you may laugh at it as a farce to-morrow, if you please, provided to-night you have the good sense not to turn it into a tragedy."

"What, in the name of all that's——Well, it's no use swearing; but what is the meaning of it all, and what do you want?"

"Money!"

"Pshaw!"

"I say money again!"

"Then you are disappointed. I have none, I never had any, and never expect to have any. Perhaps my equerry here, Colonel Mason, has some."

"Yes," said the gentleman with the white moustache, speaking with hesitation, "I think—that is to say, I feel sure that I have—hem!—half a guinea in my waistcoat pocket."

"Keep it, sir," said Duval. "I want fifteen hundred pounds of his Royal Highness the Duke of Cumberland!"

"Fifteen hundred devils!" said the Duke.

"Nay, your Royal Highness; they would not answer my purpose. I want the money, and must have it!"

"Hark you, my fine fellow—Claude Duval, as you call yourself. I admire your boldness, and from what little I saw of you and your horse, through the carriage window, I should say you would make a very good cavalry officer; but as for fifteen hundred pounds, I can assure you that my present possessions amount to seven or eight odd guineas, which I have in some of my pockets—I don't know which."

The Duke's coach had reached the corner of the Oxford Road by the time this strange conference had got so far.

"Halt, coachman!" cried Duval.

The coach stopped.

"Good!" said the Duke. "I see you are convinced, and we shall part better friends than we met."

"I hope so, your Royal Highness," said Duval; "but we do not part yet."

"I am unarmed."

"Your Highness misunderstands me. I will not doubt your royal word, that seven or eight guineas are all you have about you; but a prince of the blood must have good credit."

"What on earth do you mean?"

"I wish your Royal Highness to be so good as to raise me the sum I require."

"Insolence!"

"Nay, not so. Bethink you, Duke—bethink you of any one who will lend you the money, and we will drive there at once."

"Now, of all the impudent——"

"Beware, beware! I speak calmly; but there is a fire raging at my heart. Answer my question, and do so quickly!"

"Never!"

"Then I must try the Colonel."

"No, no!"

"Keep still, sir."

Duval placed the muzzle of one of his pistols directly in the centre of the forehead of Colonel Mason, the equerry.

"Answer me, Colonel. Who is there within your knowledge who will lend his Royal Highness fifteen hundred pounds?"

"Mr. Brydges, the jeweller, on Cornhill."

"Exactly!"

"No!" cried the Duke. "Mason, you are a coward!"

"Drive on, coachman," shouted Duval, "to Cornhill!"

The Duke flung himself back in the carriage with an execration.

"I couldn't help it," said Colonel Mason, in a rather imbecile kind of way.

"Coward!" repeated the Duke again, "This comes of making an equerry of a feather-bed soldier, instead of a man who had smelt gunpowder half his life."

CHAPTER XXXVIII.

CLAUDE DUVAL HAS TWO ADVENTURES ON THE ROAD, AND OBTAINS A RICH BOOTY.

The coach turned down the Oxford Road.

Blossom watched its progress, and, notwithstanding the order he had received from Claude Duval, he thought he could not possibly do better than keep it in sight.

That, as it happened, was just what Duval would have wished him to do; for when he named the corner of the Edgeware Road as a place of rendezvous, he had no idea of accompanying the Duke of Cumberland into the City.

As it was, the whole cavalcade went down the Oxford Road at a good pace.

The Duke of Cumberland was silent with rage and mortification.

The equerry sat in the further corner of the coach, feeling his position to be anything but an enviable one.

Then Duval spoke.

The tone in which he did so was very different from that which up to this moment he had assumed.

"Your Royal Highness," he said, "is naturally angry at this affair; but I hope that with a little explanation——"

"Peace, sir!" interrupted the Duke. "Enjoy your triumph while you may."

"Nay; hear me out. I want your Royal Highness, when you reflect to-morrow morning upon this adventure, to view it quite otherwise than in a spirit of regret."

"As how, sir?"

"I will tell your Highness. A young, fair girl was accused of a foul crime, of which she was as innocent as any child nestling in its mother's arms."

"Bah! I don't like children."

"But your Highness will like my story when you hear it through. She was brought out to die—to die in all her youth—in all her innocence—in all her beauty. Thousands of persons assembled to see her publicly strangled for a crime she never contemplated even in thought. She shrieked for help, where help there seemed to be none. Her cheeks were bloodless, her fair hair streaming in the wind, her young lips white with the fear of approaching death. Oh, your Highness, you have seen many a passing spirit on the battle-field, but perhaps you never saw a sight like that!"

"What came of it?"

"I rescued her."

"You?"

"I did. I snatched her from the hands of the executioner. I am Claude Duval!"

"Stop! I recollect something of this. She murdered General Everton?"

"No, your Highness. She was accused of the deed, but was innocent of it."

"But what is all this to me?"

"That young girl is my wife; but again he has been seized by the myrmidons of the law, and now languishes in Newgate. But police officers are but men, and they have their price. I want the money I have spoken of to bribe them to set her free."

"And the rascals are just the sort of fellows to do it. I've always said that there was no dependence to be placed upon what are called civil authorities. Troops, troops for me!"

"Let me hope, then, that now your Highness knows the use I wish to put the money to, you will no longer refuse to assist me?"

"Refuse?"

"I said refuse."

"But I am enforced. I sit, as it were, with a pistol muzzle at my head."

"But if your Highness will promise——"

"What?"

"That you will raise this money for me, or try to do so, with real good faith——"

The Duke hesitated for a moment.

"Well, what then?" he said.

"Then I will trust you."

"I promise, then."

Duval at once flung his three pistols on to the opposite seat, by the side of the equerry.

The Duke stretched out one of his hands to them.

"You are a venturesome man, Claude Duval."

The Duke lifted one of the pistols.

With a practised hand he put it on full cock.

"The tables are turned—the tables are turned!" cried Colonel Mason, as he immediately placed his hand over the other two pistols. "Ha, ha! The tables are turned, and Claude Duval is a fool! Shoot him, your Royal Highness!—shoot him at once!"

"What for?" said the Duke, as he pointed the pistol, not at Claude Duval, but right in the face of the equerry.

"What—what for? Why, because—because——"

"Because what?"

"I—I——Because, your Royal Highness——"

"Oh, I see! Because he chose to trust to my word. So that is your opinion of me, Colonel Mason?"

"No, your Royal Highness. I thought—that is to say, I thought—I thought——"

"And I've been thinking, likewise—which is, that I should be all the better without your company. You will be so good as to alight, Colonel Mason."

"And leave your Royal Highness with this——"

"Out with it," said Duval—"highwayman!"

"Get out!" roared the Duke.

The equerry had no resource but to open the coach door from within, and alight from the coach into the Oxford Road, to the great surprise of Blossom and his men, who could not see what was happening.

The coach proceeded rapidly.

A rather awkward silence ensued between Claude Duval and the Duke, but it was at length broken by Claude, who said quietly, "Does your Royal Highness happen to know General Everton?"

"Well."

"He was the uncle of that young girl of whom I have spoken, and who, being exposed to persecutions from a dissipated relative, in conjunction, likewise, with Lord Horlop——"

"Horlop? Horlop?" interrupted the Duke. "He now lies at his lodgings in St. James's Street, dangerously wounded."

"He and I fought on Bagshot Heath."

"Oh, that is it, is it?"

"It was so, your Highness; but I wish to add something more about this fifteen hundred pounds."

"Don't, for heaven's sake! for if Brydges lends that amount upon my security, it will be quite as far as he will go."

"I did not mean to add to that amount," said Duval. "What I meant to say was, that this day month I will bring the money back to your Royal Highness."

"Oh, never mind that. When once you have it,

keep it, and there's an end of it. But my opinion is, from what I can gather of the nature of your enterprise, that you will fail in it."

"I can but try; and I am in that frame of mind that, unless I try something, I shall not be able to exist for another four-and-twenty hours."

"Very well; if you do fail, let me know, and we will see what can be done."

The coach had reached Cornhill, and there the driver paused for further instructions.

"Mr. Brydges, the jeweller's!" called out Claude Duval.

The coach stopped with a jerk at the shop, which was closely barred and shut up, and appeared to be completely deserted for the night.

"Blossom!" cried Duval, as he looked from the coach window.

"Here, Captain!"

"I see," said the Duke of Cumberland, "you have your men with you."

"I heard them following," said Duval, "although I had given contrary directions, but in such cases as this they use a sound discretion. You will knock at that door, Blossom, and ask for Mr. Brydges."

"Just so," said the Duke of Cumberland. "But I warn you, Claude Duval, I am firmly of opinion that he will refuse the money, perhaps not absolutely, but he will put off the matter until to-morrow morning."

"Too late," said Duval.

"Exactly."

"Then I shall have troubled your Royal Highness in vain."

"Hem! I don't know that. It seems to me that you make very little scruple in troubling my Royal Highness after your own ordinary fashion. Pray what should exempt Brydges, the jeweller and money-changer, from the demands of Claude Duval, the highwayman?"

"Ah, I see!" cried Duval.

"Of course you do, and it will be much better; because, in that case, I shall not have to go through the troublesome ceremony of repaying the money."

By this time, Blossom had made so vigorous an appeal at the outer door of the jeweller's house, that a night-capped head was popped out at the first floor window, and a terrified voice requested to know if it were fire or thieves.

"A little of both, Mr. Brydges," said the Duke of Cumberland. "You are wanted down here."

"Bless me!" cried the jeweller; "do my ears deceive me, or is that the voice of his Royal Highness the Duke of Cumberland?"

"Exactly. Come down, Brydges," responded the Duke.

"I am at your Highness's service."

The head disappeared from the window, and the Duke then turning to Duval, said, "You must now conduct your own affairs. I have done all I can, and it won't do for me to interfere further; at the same time, I shall not contradict what you choose to assert."

"I am infinitely beholden to your Highness, and I think I comprehend fully what you mean," said Claude.

"Well, well, set about it. Here comes the jeweller."

With officious haste, having attired himself as rapidly as he could in such apparel as he could lay his hands upon, Mr. Brydges made his appearance.

"Get into the coach," said the Duke.

"Your Royal Highness does me too much honour."

"Not at all—not at all; and you will come to a contrary opinion soon, Brydges."

"It is impossible that I should ever cease to appreciate the condescension of your Royal Highness."

"Hem! We shall see."

"In what manner can I be of service to your Highness?"

"Faith! you must ask this gentleman, who at present is the master of the situation."

"The master of the—the——"

"The master of the situation, I tell you, Brydges. This is Claude Duval, the famous highwayman."

"Claude Duval? Your Highness jests!"

"Not at all. It's an awkward joke, Brydges, for both of us. He took me prisoner in Park Lane, and now has you on Cornhill. Your ransom——"

"Ransom, your Highness?"

"Yes," said Duval, "will be fifteen hundred pounds."

"Fifteen hundred drops of my blood sooner!" said Brydges. "But it's all a joke?"

"I think not," said Duval. "Time presses, Mr. Brydges; you will have the kindness to produce the money at once, or I must hand you over to my men, who will make short work of you."

"Stuff! Nonsense—nonsense! It's a jest—a mere jest, which I am rather surprised your Royal Highness should lend yourself to."

"Blossom!"

"Yes, Captain?"

"Take this man, and hang him to the nearest lamp-post."

"Hang me?" exclaimed Brydges.

"Come out, sir," said Blossom, "and don't irritate the Captain. Come and be hanged at once."

"Or pay the money," said Duval.

"I throw myself on your Royal Highness's protection," exclaimed the jeweller.

"I can't help you, Brydges. I am a prisoner myself. Claude Duval has taken from me all I possess, and consequently he has treated me much worse than he is treating you, since you are a man of large fortune, and he only asks you for fifteen hundred pounds."

"I have not the money."

"Blossom, take him out and hang him. We must go to some one else."

"Stop, stop!"

"Well, sir?"

"Will his Royal Highness be answerable?"

"That's cool!" said the Duke. "Why, I am in the same fix with yourself, Brydges!"

St. Paul's clock at this moment chimed the half-hour past eleven.

"Quick!" cried Duval. "I have neither time nor inclination to spare."

"If I must," said the jeweller, "I must. I will get it."

"No," said Duval. "You are not alone in the house. Yonder window is open, and I see a face at it. Call for the money—your voice will be recognised."

"That is my wife."

"We shall be delighted to see the lady."

"It is very well to say call for the money: but she won't bring it."

"Then, Brydges, you hang."

"My dear," cried Brydges, "bring me fifteen hundred pounds out of the iron safe."

"I'll see you hanged first!" cried a female voice from the window."

"There, there—I told you so!"

"Mrs. Brydges," cried the Duke of Cumberland, "you can have a ticket for the Court ball."

"Bless me, that's his Royal Highness! You idiot, Brydges! why didn't you mention who it was for?"

In a few moments, Mrs. Brydges appeared, attired in an immense fur wrapper, and handed into the coach a small bag weighted with gold.

"A thousand thanks!" said Duval.

"Be off," whispered the Duke.

Duval opened the coach-door on the outer side, and springing out, disappeared in the darkness.

Blossom, however, had kept a good watch on all the

proceedings, and at once galloped up to his side, leading Nightshade by the bridle.

"It is done," said Duval. "I have the money, but what success may attend the scheme I know not. Follow me, all of you. Get our fellow off the coach-box, Blossom, and let him mount his horse again."

Duval and his men swept round St. Paul's Churchyard at a canter, for he did not wish Mr. Brydges or his now aroused household to be aware of exactly the direction he meant to go in.

It was easy to get to Newgate down Newgate Street, and that was Duval's intention; and, indeed, it would be better to leave the horses with Blossom somewhere about the corner of Giltspur Street than in the other direction.

"Listen to me, Blossom," said Duval. "If you hear St. Paul's clock strike one, and I do not come or send to you, you may conclude that I cannot. It will be your duty then to take the horses and our whole party to Hampstead, and there wait until you hear something of me."

"You shall be obeyed, Captain; but I do not like to think that such will be the case."

"Nor I, either; but we must be prepared for all; so, for the present, farewell."

CHAPTER XXXIX.

DUVAL ENTERS THE VESTIBULE OF NEWGATE, BUT HIS PLANS ARE INTERRUPTED.

QUITE alone, and with the considerable sum of money that he hoped to be able to bribe the officials of Newgate, Claude Duval quietly took his way down the Old Bailey.

St. Paul's struck twelve.

Duval paused until the last sounds had died away, then he felt perfectly assured that, with the usual punctuality that characterized proceedings in Newgate, the night watch would be placed in the vestibule, and the rest of the prison be consigned to repose.

He mounted those narrow, steep steps, up which so many weary feet have conveyed so many aching hearts.

But a dim light burnt in the vestibule of Newgate; and as Claude Duval looked over the wicket-gate, he saw the officers on duty lighting their pipes and crowding round a little stove, which was the only means of warming the vestibule.

The man who was "on the lock," as it was technically called, had his back turned towards the street, so that at first he did not see Duval.

He was speaking to the others.

The words he uttered came ominously upon the ears of Claude.

"I tell you that's the way it's always done. She'll be brought up in the morning, to be identified as the same person; and there won't be a new trial, or anything of that sort, but the hanging will take place just as it ought to have done when Claude Duval took her out of the hands of the Sheriff at Tyburn Gate."

Duval tapped at the wicket.

The man on the lock gave a start round.

"Hilloa!" he cried. "Who are you when you're at home?"

"Open, open!"

"Oh, it's very well to say open; but what do you want?"

"I want to speak to you all. There is money to be earned."

"Indeed! How much? Perhaps you don't mind naming the exact sum."

The constables in the vestibule laughed, for the man who was on the lock that night had the reputation of a kind of wit; and although they could not exactly see any particular joke, they gave him credit for great smartness in his replies to the applicant for admission.

"Two thousand pounds," said Duval. "You can have that sum among you in the next ten minutes, if you please to earn it."

"Two thousand?" ejaculated the man on the lock.

"Two thousand?" cried the other officers, with one voice.

"Come in, whoever you are, and let's know more about it."

The wicket was opened.

Claude stepped into the vestibule of Newgate.

He raised his hat slightly, and stood in the full light of the hanging lamp.

"Do you know me?"

"Claude Duval!" cried the officers, with a shout that made the old hall of Newgate ring again.

"Look at me well."

"It is Claude—Claude Duval!"

That was the second shout from the officers.

Then Duval shrunk back a step.

The movement was involuntary, for there was a half kind of rush on the part of several of the officers towards him.

The man on the lock was glaring at him with all his eyes; and as Claude Duval stepped backward that pace, he came against the inner side of the gate of Newgate.

A projecting something struck him sharply in the back.

It was the key—the well-kept, highly-polished key of Newgate's best lock; that which was most used, and worked with the greatest possible facility.

Duval had but to slip his left hand behind him, and the key was secured.

There seemed safety in the touch of the cold iron.

"Yes," he cried, "I am Claude Duval; and I see that there are five of you. Be reasonable men, and let me bring you the thousand pounds myself, which you would gain by my capture."

The officers glared at each other in surprise.

"Better," added Duval, "let me go free for that sum, than lodge me in the dreariest cell of Newgate. Here is the money."

"But, Duval!"

They all spoke in chorus.

It was singular what a community of sentiment those men had.

"Hear me out," said Duval. "I offer you a thousand pounds for myself, and a thousand more for some other person."

"Lucy Everton!" cried the officers.

"The same!"

They glanced at each other.

"We should have to fly the country," said one.

"Four hundred pounds a piece!" said another.

"A little fortune!" said a third.

"Decide—decide all of you!" shouted Duval; "for there is no time to lose."

Rap, rap, rap! came a demand for admission at the wicket-gate of Newgate.

"The game's up," cried the men on the lock.

Duval turned hastily, and glanced at the face which was looking over the half-door, which was at the top of the narrow stone steps.

The face was only too familiar to him, although the eyes looked glaring out of their sockets.

It was the face of Muckles.

And if Muckles had met an apparition in the semblance of some one whom he knew to be dead long since, he could not have been more utterly surprised and bewildered than he was at the sight of Claude Duval, in the vestibule of Newgate.

DUEL BETWEEN DUVAL AND MOSSY PENDELL.

"Duval!" he yelled,

"Muckles!" said Duval.

There was a narrow arched door at the further extremity of the vestibule, and Duval made but one leap towards it.

It was not fast, and swinging it open, he darted through it as he exclaimed, "I came like a spirit, and so depart!"

He shot a couple of bolts across the door on the inner side, and then he heard a tremendous disturbance in the vestibule, and the voice of the man on the lock calling out, "My key—my key! Where's my key? Who has seen my key?"

Duval placed his ear flat to the door to listen

"Open the wicket! Open the wicket!" he heard Muckles cry.

Then a voice of authority sounded amid a sudden stillness, "What is all this tumult about? Is it not enough to have all the care of this prison on one's hands in the daytime, that I cannot go to rest without being disturbed by this outcry? What is it all about?"

No 13.—NIGHTSHADE.

"If you please, sir, a ghost!"

"A what?"

"The ghost, sir, of Claude Duval! He came into the hall, and then vanished like a wreath of smoke through the wall, yonder."

"But who is that person who is standing outside the wicket?"

"If you please, sir, it is I," replied Muckles, "and they won't let me in."

"I don't know what's become of my key," said the man on the lock.

"So, so!" said the Governor,—for it was he, who, on retiring to rest, had heard the tumult in the vestibule,—"so, so!—you have lost your key; and you know the penalty in Newgate, for that, is the loss of your situation. Come in, Mr. Muckles."

The Governor had a master-key which opened all the locks in the prison, and by its assistance Muckles was admitted into the vestibule, and the wicket-gate carefully locked again.

"Ghost or no ghost, he won't get out again; but I

beg to take the liberty of saying that I don't believe a word of it."

"Do you want to see me, Mr. Muckles?"

"If you please, sir."

"Come this way."

"Sir!"

"Well?"

"Will you oblige me with the loan of your master key a moment?"

The Governor surrendered it, and Muckles marching up to the little door through which Claude Duval had made his escape from the vestibule into the interior of Newgate, carefully locked it.

"Safe bind, safe find!" muttered Muckles.

He looked significantly at the Governor, and they both left the hall of Newgate together.

Duval was in semi-darkness.

A miserable oil lamp, that was near expiring, stood upon a stone bracket in the wall of the passage where he was.

That was not Claude Duval's first appearance in Newgate, and he had a recollection that that passage led into another at right angles to it, which traversed the whole breadth of the building, and from which cells opened right and left.

Duval knew quite well that he should not be able to go far without meeting a warder on duty for the night.

The authorities of Newgate were at that period beginning slowly to comprehend that personal surveillance was superior to locks and keys and bolts and bars.

Consequently, the passages of Newgate were no longer left to gloomy silence, but each had its appointed watchman, who, even if he went to sleep—which it is highly probable that he did—still acted as a kind of scare-crow to any of the prisoners attempting an escape.

As Duval saw a gleam of light at some distance ahead of him, he thought it best entirely to extinguish the fading oil-lamp immediately within the door through which he had passed.

He then stepped onward as carefully as foot could fall.

There was a feeling of serenity at his heart.

The terrible restlessness that had beset him while outside those gloomy walls had passed away.

At least, now, he had the satisfaction of knowing and feeling that he was beneath the same roof as Lucy Everton.

Difficult and dangerous as might be the attempt to save her from her present position of peril, he felt a kind of lightness of spirit, as though one half of that difficult and dangerous task were accomplished.

He heard an odd, croaking sort of voice, singing, or attempting to sing.

It was doubtless the warder on duty in the stone passage to which he, Duval, was slowly and silently making his way.

If, at such a time of anxiety, a smile could have come to Claude Duval's lips, it certainly would have found a place there as he listened to this warder.

"When Claude Duval was in Newgate thrown
He carved his name on the Newgate stone;
'And when in the morning for me they call,
They'll find I've wanished,' said Claude Duval."

A rapid clapping of hands, as if in applause, followed the dreary tones in which these four lines were attempted to be sung.

Then a voice spoke.

"Well, I don't care who thinks otherways; I calls Claude Duval a genus; and the more I thinks of them four blessed lines of poetry, the more I admires 'em! Capital! capital!

"'They'll find I've wanished,' said Claude Duval.

Capital! capital!—and he did wanish! It wasn't as if he hadn't wanished—but he did wanish! that was the best of it! I've tried to make some poetry myself, but can't come a-near that; it's out and out! Jerry Magsworth's last dying speech and confession was nothing to it!

"'Come all ye sinners big and bold,
And listen to my story;
I'm scragged for slitting up a wizen,
And leaving it all gory.'

No, that's nothing to it. I wonder where Claude Duval is now? He's wanished!"

A violent knocking at one of the cell doors at this moment disturbed the equanimity of the night warder.

"Will you be quiet?" he roared. "Do you want me to come in and wring your neck?"

The knocking continued.

"What now? Do you want all your bones broke? Be quiet, will you, and don't be disturbing a fellow when he's lulling himself to sleep with poetry!

"'They'll find I've wanished,' said Claude Duval.

Ha, ha, ha! Good!—good! And he did *wanish!* Be quiet, all of you—confound you! If you are in the Stone Jug, can't you be quiet? Eh?—eh? What was that? Nothing? Well, I didn't say it wasn't!

"'They'll find I've wanished,' said Claude Duval.

Wanished—wanished—wan—wan——"

All was still.

Duval crept forward.

The night warder had fallen into a profound sleep, sitting on a stool in an angle of the wall.

There was no mistaking the heavy stertorous breathing of that kind of man, who, when he was once asleep, could scarcely have been awakened by a cannon shot fired at his ears.

There was a small table close to the night warder in the stone passage.

On that lay his lantern, his pistols, his rattle, and a slip of paper.

Duval stooped over the table, and looked at the paper.

It contained a list of names, with numbers corresponding.

The numbers were those of the cell doors opening from that particular passage.

The names were those of the prisoners occupying such cells.

Number one read:—"Jeremy Abchuck. Footpad. Cast for next Monday. Dangerous."

Number two:—"Tom Weedmingle, cracksman. Booked for next Monday. Resigned and artful."

Number three:—"Nicodemus Brimmertop. Sneak. Lagged. A lifer. Bites."

Number four:—"Lucy Everton. Murder. Scragged next Monday. Sulky."

Duval uttered a cry.

The warder moved uneasily.

He muttered in his sleep.

"He did *wanish*—he did *wanish.*"

CHAPTER XL.

CLAUDE DUVAL MEETS WITH A FRIEND IN NEED.

DUVAL was as still as death.

He felt that more than one human life might hang upon the next few moments.

The sleep, mortal and natural as it was, of that warder of Newgate was the only repose that, at that time, could save him from the sleep that was eternal.

Claude Duval was not in the frame of mind to allow

a human life to interfere with the rescue of Lucy Everton.

It might be that this man, if he awakened, would have an exaggerated sense of duty, and resist all attempt to free that captive innocence from her dungeon.

How Duval watched him!

How he listened to his every breath!

With what a deep-drawn sigh of relief he felt assured that the warder slept again soundly!

Then Duval crept along the passage as softly as foot could fall, and strove to recognise the numbers on the cell doors.

The light was too dim.

It was necessary that he should be in possession of the warder's lantern, in order to see those numbers.

Softly and silently he made his way back to the small table close to the slumbering man.

He lifted the lantern as though it had been something so fragile that the slightest touch must needs dissipate it into atoms.

He shielded the light with his hands, so that no wandering ray should find its way to the eyes of the warder.

But perhaps the more intense darkness slightly disturbed the sleep of the officer.

He moved again uneasily.

"*Wanished,*" he said.

Duval crept slowly away with the light, and, holding it up to one of the cell doors, he saw the number three so dimly painted upon it that it required a strong light to distinguish it.

Claude Duval's heart beat violently, as, with a half-bound, half-rush, he made his way to the next cell door, which must needs be number four or number two.

It was four.

For a moment, life seemed almost to stand still with Claude Duval, and he was unable to decide upon what would be the best and safest mode of attracting Lucy's attention.

Any attempt to do so by tapping on the outside of the door of the cell would, in all probability, awaken the warder.

A whisper of her name, in his well-known accents, might reach her ears.

But what effect would that whisper have?

Might she not utter some exclamation full of danger?

Some scream of delight?

Where would then be the dreams of escape without taking the life of that man who kept watch and ward in the stone passage?

That was a necessity that Claude Duval shrunk from with all his heart and soul.

But time waned.

Moments were precious.

A strange sound came booming through the vast extent of Newgate.

What could it be?

A bell.

A bell at such an hour, too—past midnight, and fast approaching one o'clock.

What could it be?

What could it mean?

Boom! boom! boom! the sound came with a hollow reverberation through the old stone walls.

Then, as though a blow had been struck him, the idea shot across the heart of Duval of what that bell meant.

An alarm!

The alarm-bell of Newgate!

His presence there was declared and known; and in a few minutes all the officials who had retired to rest would be up and on the alert. Then there would be danger infinite; and all the good he would have accomplished by the efforts of that night would be to make himself a prisoner within that dreary abode as well as Lucy, and without even the consolation of being along with her.

The warder began to stir himself.

The sound of that alarm-bell reached even his slumbering ears.

Lazily he rose to his feet, and looked about him.

Duval felt that the time for action had come.

He sprung at the man, and catching him by the throat, hurled him backward against the stone wall, at the same moment that, holding a pistol to within an inch of his eyes, he exclaimed, "Life—life! surely it is precious to you as to all men! Choose between it and death! Life and wealth, or the pang of sudden extinction! Choose—I call upon you to choose—for I am Claude Duval!"

The warder was bewildered.

He was but half awake, and the light about him was dim, for Duval had cast the lantern down upon the stone flooring of the passage, where it lay half extinguished.

"Choose, quickly!" exclaimed Duval again. "Will you live, or shall I plaster this wall with your brains?"

"He *wanished,* and has come again!" gasped the warder.

"Shall I fire?"

"Bless us, no!"

"Will you have a thousand pounds?"

"Bless us, yes!"

"Listen to me well. Do you understand what I mean, and what I say? I am Claude Duval, and my errand here is for the rescue of Lucy Everton. I am prepared to give a thousand pounds to any one who will help me; and I am prepared to give a couple of bullets to any one who will hinder me. Choose!"

"I can't make *werses* like you," said the warder; "but I ain't a born fool."

"Than you decide in my favour?"

"No, I don't."

"What do you mean?"

"I decides in my own. Give us the money, Claude Duval, and keep the bullets."

"That is well said. Where is Lucy Everton?"

"Number four, sulky."

"How are we to escape? Hush! what is that?"

A sound of many voices—a clatter of feet—a combination of confused noises, still mixed up with the incessant booming of the alarm-bell of Newgate, came upon the ears of Claude Duval.

"They come!" he said; "and in another moment I may be taken, for I cannot resist a multitude."

"Get into number five," said the warder; "there's nobody there. Dick Rachell was scragged last Monday, and nobody has been put into number five since. Get in there, and it'll be all right."

"You cannot, will not betray me?"

"Take the money with you, and the bullets too. What should I get by betraying you? The thanks of the Sheriff, and half-a-crown a-week on my wages. 'Twill take a precious lot of them to make a thousand pound!"

This reasoning was rough, but Claude Duval felt that it was to the purpose, and he allowed himself to be placed in the cell numbered five, and the key turned upon him.

It was impossible, under the circumstances, that he could altogether discard from his heart a chilling fear.

The warder might, after all, betray him; and, in that case, all hope of saving Lucy was lost.

Vividly, then, came over his imagination all the improbabilities of success to the wild scheme of the night.

He held a pistol in each hand, determined to sell his

life dearly; for he felt that should an attempt be made to capture him, it must now be a matter of life and death.

The sound of many voices came from the stone passage.

There was the tramping of feet likewise; and once, somebody lurched up against the door of the cell in which he, Duval, was secreted, in such a manner that he thought it was about to be opened.

Such was not the case, however.

It was but an accident, and in a few minutes the confused noises in the stone passage died away.

The alarm-bell of Newgate had ceased to toll.

A preternatural quiet reigned in the prison.

"Come out, Muster Duval," said the warder, as he opened the door of the cell.

Duval stepped out into the stone passage.

"You have been true to me," he said; "take this." He handed to him a quantity of gold.

"I think you will find that near the sum I mentioned."

The idea of really possessing so much money seemed to take away the breath of the turnkey.

"It can't be," he said; "there isn't so much in all the world! You don't mean, really, a thousand pound, do you, Claude Duval? Why, I shall be able to set up a public-house, and be a gentleman!"

"You are a thousand times welcome to the thousand pounds, my good fellow; but where are your keys? Open number four instantly, and although still within the gloomy walls of Newgate, let me fancy that I have accomplished half my task in having penetrated to the gloomy cell which holds one so dear to me."

Even as he spoke, Duval struck with his clenched hand upon the cell door.

"Lucy — Lucy!" he cried. "It is I — it is I! Utter but one word, that I may be assured of your presence!"

There was no reply.

The turnkey looked confused.

"*Wanished*," he said.

"What mean you? You cannot — dare not deceive me?"

"I couldn't help it. They've moved her off to the Sheriff's crib."

"When and how?"

"Just now. They made me open the cell, and took her out, and I tell you she's in the Sheriff's crib. Look in for yourself."

The warder flung the door of number four cell open, and held out his lantern.

One glance was sufficient to show that it was untenanted, and then Duval turned upon him fiercely.

"Speak to me, man! Tell me, what is this Sheriff's crib you mention?"

"It's a little bit of a room up above, and close to the Governor's house. They seemed to have an idea that you was in the prison, Claude Duval, and so they moved her up to there; but that makes things ever so much easier, and my keys 'll open all the doors."

"Then you can still help me?"

"Bless you, yes! I'm not a going to take a man's thousand pound for nothin'. I'll set up a public-house, and call it the 'Highwayman's Head.' Just you come this way, Duval, and we'll soon get to the Sheriff's crib."

At the further end of the stone passage was one of those low, squat, ugly-looking doors with which Newgate abounded.

From the quantity of huge headed nails in it, that door was certainly more of iron than wood, and the lock was of enormous size.

One of the keys from the bunch the warder carried easily opened the door, and immediately beyond it there appeared a flight of steps, up which Duval and his new friend made their way.

The steps were of stone, but the passage to which they led was boarded; and each step that Duval went, he felt certain that he was approaching what might be called the unprofessional part of Newgate.

"Are we near the place?" he asked the warder.

"Hush! don't speak so loud. That door leads to the Governor's rooms, and this other one to the left opens to a little bit of a passage, at the end of which is the room we calls the Sheriff's crib."

The door to the left was opened, but immediately the warder laid his hand upon Duval's arm, and pointed to a small silver candlestick, in which a wax light was burning that stood upon the floor.

"The Governor," he whispered.

"How? What? What do you mean?"

"The Governor is in the Sheriff's crib. I can hear him speaking."

"Then I will listen to what he says," replied Duval. "I am a desperate man, and desperate remedies alone suit the present circumstances."

A kind of tremor took possession of the warder, as Duval, drawing his sword, stepped forward, and passing the light that stood upon the floor, made his way directly to the door of the Sheriff's crib.

He heard the sound of voices.

And how his heart yearned to hear the sound of that one voice which to him was worth all the world beside!

But he heard it not.

The tones were masculine, and frequently as he had heard the voice of Muckles, the officer, Duval had no difficulty in recognising him as one of the speakers.

The other was without doubt the Governor, by the manger in which Muckles addressed him.

"I'm quite certain, sir, that it was the wisest thing to do."

"It may be so," replied the Governor; "but it don't sound well for Newgate."

"Never mind about that, sir," said Muckles, "it will be give and take; and some of these days the Governor of the Compter will be only too glad to do the same thing."

"Perhaps so — perhaps so. At all events, it is done, and there's an end of it. I can sleep in peace now I know a prisoner will not be wrested from me."

"Certainly, sir," added Muckles; "and with the full conviction that Claude Duval is somewhere still in Newgate, I would advise that nothing more be done till daylight, when he must discover himself."

"Be it so, Muckles — be it so, Muckles! Take care that all the outlets of the prison are well guarded for the night."

"I will, sir. And now that Lucy Everton has been successfully removed to Giltspur Street Compter, you may indeed, as you say, rest in peace."

What words were these?

How terrible was the chill that came over the heart of Claude Duval!

Lucy removed at that dead hour of the night from Newgate to the Compter, and he further off than ever from a realization of his dream of restoring her to life and liberty!

For a few moments his brain whirled, and in the agony of his heart he forgot where he was.

The warder darted forward and shook him by the arm, as he whispered energetically in his ear, "*Wanish! wanish*, Claude Duval! They're a' comin' out!"

The door of the Sheriff's crib opened.

Duval had just time to shrink close to the wall, and the door struck against the toes of his boots.

At the same moment the warder pretended to stumble over the candlestick on the floor, and so he extinguished the wax-light.

The only illumination now that came into the passage was from a solitary candle that burnt on a table in the Sheriff's crib.

"Who is there?" cried the Governor, angrily.

"It's me, sir," replied the warder.

"Who are you? Name yourself, idiot!"

"Jenkinson, sir, if you please."

"What do you want, fool?"

"I was a looking for you, sir. I saw a strange noise in the stone passage, and heard the shadow of a man; and I think it must be Claude Duval."

"Ah! say you so? Come on, Mr. Muckles; we may unearth the fox who has so unwisely put his head into this old Stone Jug yet, before we retire to rest."

The Governor and Muckles hastily followed the warder across the short passage, and down the staircase which Duval had so recently ascended.

Then Claude Duval stepped into the Sheriff's crib; and, closing the door behind him, he shot a bolt into its socket, with a feeling that, for the moment at least, he was in security.

The room was small, and had one grated window in it, which Duval, at a glance, saw looked out into the Old Bailey.

In point of fact, it was one of the apartments properly in the Governor's house, and the window was not far distant from that well-known flight of stone steps that leads to the rather gay-looking outer door of that portion of old Newgate.

Claude Duval was in reality within twenty feet of the actual pavement of the Old Bailey.

Nothing but the iron bars at that window prevented him from gliding through it, and finding some means of letting himself securely down into the street below.

But surely that was not an insurmountable obstacle to such a man as Claude Duval?

He carried with him always a singular and complicated piece of cutlery, such as our ancestors used to delight in, comprehending some useful implements, and half a dozen others of no use whatever.

There was a corkscrew, a chisel, several different sized bradawls, a hook for taking stones out of horses' feet, and two small saws.

These latter implements were of importance to Claude Duval.

He knew that they were highly-tempered, and of the finest steel.

In less than two minutes he set to work upon one of the iron bars, through which the saw cut as though it had been a piece of wood.

But there was a grating sound, which was highly dangerous, and Duval therefore opened the door of the Sheriff's crib again, and, groping along the passage, he found the wax candle which had been over-turned; for the light that had been burning on the table in that small apartment had become exhausted to the last remnant of its wick.

A little of the soft wax from the candle completely deadened the sound of the saw, as its friction against the iron bar kept the wax melted.

The saw passed right through the obstruction; and Duval, seizing the bar by its liberated end, easily succeeded in wrenching it from its socket above.

He was slim and lithe, and although the aperture at the window was still but narrow, he felt that he should have no difficulty in passing through it. Carefully he raised the sash, and tying the end of a table-cover which was in the room to one of the other bars of the window, he flung the remainder out, and dexterously following it, he slid down with rapidity towards the pavement.

The Old Bailey was in profound darkness; for the lamps, as usual, had burnt themselves out, and Duval was not aware that he dropped bodily upon some one who was passing underneath, who uttered a shout of terror, and falling prostrate, called out in the well-known voice of Swallow, "Done brown agin! It's Claude Duval—I knowed it!"

CHAPTER XLI.

CLAUDE DUVAL ROBS THE OXFORD MAIL, AND ENCOUNTERS AN ENEMY.

AGAIN is Claude Duval alone.

Alone—his face buried in his hands, as he bent over a small table in the centre of that apartment in which he had so recently beheld his almost idolized Lucy.

Bowed was the haughty crest, unnerved the elastic figure, that had once seemed born only for majesty and command. No friends were near; but solitary and alone did Claude Duval listen to the monotonous clicking of the clock that announced the departure of hour after hour.

It may seem strange that Claude Duval fancied that he had never loved Lucy as he did now.

Was it the perversity of human nature, that makes the things of mortality dearer to us in proportion as they fade from our hopes, like birds whose hues are only unfolded when they take wing, and vanish amid the skies?—or, was it that he had ever doated more on loveliness of mind than that of form, and the first bloomed out the more, the more the last decayed?

For Claude Duval now began to think of his Lucy more as of a being who had been, rather than as still living to cheer him by her smile, and delight his heart with the treasures of her highly cultivated mind.

He had looked upon Lucy, too, as a fair, bright being to protect, to soothe, to shelter; and oh, how dear had this thought been to his noble heart!

As reflections such as these swept over the mind of Claude Duval, he drooped his head upon his hands and shed tears—tears that surely did not shame his manhood—for how sudden, how awfully sudden had been the blow that had fallen upon him!

He had left her one fair morn in health and beauty.

He had sought her again a few hours later, and she was gone—torn from him by her ruthless foe, and now she was lying languishing in a cell in the Compter.

And this being, so bright, so beautiful, loved him—oh, how she loved him!

Never on earth could he be so loved again.

The air and aspect of the whole apartment grew to him painful and oppressive.

It was full of her—the owner! For had he not given her, with himself, all that had ever been his?

Claude Duval sprung to his feet, as he dashed his hair from his brow.

"This must not be! I must not sit idly down and bewail my untoward fate; but I must think what I can do next. I will think—think—think!"

In less than five minutes Duval left the house.

It was then just on the stroke of four in the afternoon.

To him, as he walked across the heath, and the sharp winds howled on his path, it was as if a strange and wizard life had passed into and supported him - a sort of drowsy, dull existence.

He was like a sleep-walker—unconscious of all around him; yet his steps were safe and free over the uneven ground, and the one thought that possessed his being, into which all intellect seemed shrunk—the thought, not fiery and vehement, but calm, stern, and solemn—the thought of revenge seemed, as it were, grown his soul itself.

"Yes," he muttered to himself, and his voice seemed strangely changed—" yes, Mossy Pendell, we must meet again, and one of us must then die!"

Suddenly he stopped and gazed about him, and then he shook his head sadly, saying, "I must seek oblivion for a time, at all events, in action. I will return, and, mounted upon Nightshade, will go on the road this night!"

In an incredibly short space of time, Duval regained his home on Hampstead Heath, and summoning Blossom, he said, "Blossom, I'm going on the road alone to-night. Saddle Nightshade, and try not to dissuade me from doing the only thing that can bring relief to this overcharged heart—namely, active exertion."

Blossom, however, could not refrain from showing the anxiety he felt.

At all events. Captain, you will let me accompany you?" he asked.

"No, Blossom, no; remain here. Would that you had been here on that night when——"

Duval could not finish the sentence; but his faithful follower knew that he referred to that night when Lucy Everton was taken from her home.

"Be it so, Captain, if you wish it. I will bring Nightshade round in a minute or two, for he is already groomed, and has had a good feed; for I thought, in all probability, you might be wanting him to-night, Captain."

"It is well," said Duval. "You are always thoughtful, Blossom."

"You don't know, Captain," said Blossom, "how pleasant it is to me to hear you say that."

"I say it because I know it well, Blossom."

Duval was in a very short space of time mounted upon Nightshade, and might be seen galloping across the heath towards London.

Duval made his way to the Oxford Road, and there came to a halt, feeling well assured that the Oxford mail must soon pass by that spot.

A long, flourishing note from the horn of the guard of the Oxford mail came distinctly to the ears of Claude Duval.

The moon at this moment broke from behind a cloud, so that the coach was distinctly visible from where Duval had halted.

Several passengers were on it, besides a goodly array of luggage.

The coach was coming along at a great rate, drawn by four good horses, and would have swept down the road had it not come to an abrupt halt in obedience to a command uttered in a clear, bell-like voice.

"Halt! Stand and deliver!"

Claude Duval now occupied a place in the very middle of the road, and having given Nightshade a certain signal, which the creature understood, it had reared up on its hind feet, and there stood pawing the air, striking consternation into every heart.

In fact, both Duval and his horse looked something more than mortal.

"Stand and deliver!" again rung through the night air.

"Goodness gracious!" said the coachman; "why it's a highwayman!"

There was a shriek from the inside of the coach in female accents.

"Stand and deliver, or your lives be upon your own heads!" again said Duval.

Duval now, with one bound of Nightshade, stood by the side of the coach, and looking in at one of the windows, he said, "Ladies and gentlemen, I will trouble you for your money, your watches, and any jewellery you may happen to have about you!"

Two more screams came from the inside of the coach, and then a male voice said, "I never heard such consummate impudence in my life. You ask as though everything we possessed were your property."

"As it will be in a few minutes, why dispute about the way in which I demand it?" said Duval, quite politely. "Quick, sir—quick! My time is valuable!"

A couple of purses, a pocket-book, and two watches were handed to him.

Duval had just deposited these various articles in one of his capacious pockets, and had just stooped down again to demand a like compliance on the part of the other passengers to that which had characterized their companions, when he became suddenly aware of the shutting of the coach door on the other side of the coach.

To bound round the coach to the opposite side was accomplished as quick as lightning. It was then that Duval became aware of the presence of a flying figure.

Duval knew not why, but something impelled him to follow in pursuit.

On, on it sped, that dark figure, and Duval followed at an easy trot, not wishing to come up with it too soon.

Suddenly it pauses.

Duval drew rein.

Did the flying figure suppose that it had escaped the eyes of the pursuer?

It seemed as though it did, for it slackened its speed now, although it still continued its onward route.

Again he put Nightshade in motion, and about a mile down the lane he saw the figure pause at the door of a little hostel well known to Duval.

"That is well," said Claude to himself. "What is there to prevent my now satisfying my curiosity in ascertaining who that man is?"

Duval allowed about five minutes to elapse after the man entered the little inn before he drew up before the door.

He then rapped three times with the handle of his whip upon the shutter, and the door was immediately opened by a good-tempered looking man about forty years of age, who exclaimed, "Bless me, Captain, why it's an age since we saw you!"

"Hush!" said Duval. "Do not name me!" he continued, in a low voice.

"All right, Captain—I mean, sir!"

"Have you any visitors to-night?" asked Duval.

"No, sir, none to speak of; only a gentleman who said he wanted to rest awhile, having had a long walk!" he said, in the same low tone.

"That is well!" said Duval. "I know I can trust Nightshade to your care; in the meantime I will enter, for I have a particular desire to know who the gentleman is who just came in."

"Oh, Captain—sir—I can tell you at once! It's Mr. Mossy Pendell!"

"Ah!"

"Yes, Captain. Do you know him?"

"Slightly," said Claude Duval, as he made his way into the house.

"Yes," said Duval to himself, "once more have I this villain in my power, and this night will I drag from his guilty heart the name of the murderer of my Lucy's uncle!"

At this moment, a village clock struck the hour of two; and while the sound still lingered on the soft south wind, Duval made his way to an apartment which opened out of the one he had just entered, and which was the common living room of the landlord and his family.

Duval had been listening to some one who was pacing up and down that other room in hasty strides.

Duval flung the door of the room open, and stood face to face with his arch-enemy, and the would-be destroyer of his Lucy, Mossy Pendell.

Mossy Pendell drew back a step or two, as he beheld Duval, calm, quiet, and collected.

There was a pale sallow look upon the villain's

face, as though he had risen from a sick couch; and in that wan, colourless look of his face, and the terrible aspect about his eyes, Claude Duval felt that the conflict he fully intended to have with that man would indeed be a fearful one.

"Villain!" shouted Duval,—"worse villain than tongue can tell, I command you to reply to me!"

With a cry of fear, Mossy Pendell placed his hand on the hilt of a sword he wore.

The light of that outer room was so imperfect that he could not see Duval's face; but the voice he immediately recognised, and he could see also that Duval was well armed.

Recovering his first confusion, then, Mossy Pendell loosened the sword blade in its scabbard, as he said, "I think I have the honour of speaking to Claude Duval, the highwayman, and who now seems to add to his other accomplishments that of an assassin."

"No," said Duval. "If that had been so, the fair earth would not have been encumbered with a Mossy Pendell so long."

"Ah!"

He made a step forward, and Duval saw the flash of the light that came from the outer room, playing upon the bright steel of his sword, as he half drew it.

In a moment the sword of Duval was in his hand, and like a dazzling pencil of light it seemed as if it had confused the eyes of Mossy Pendell.

"In the name of heaven!" he cried, "tell me, Claude Duval, what you want?"

"I am the questioner!—I the avenger!"

"For whom? What would you question me of? Who would you avenge?"

"Lucy Everton!"

"Ah!"

"Villain! Assassin! I ask you now to clear the name of Lucy Everton! I demand of you that you proclaim, ere it be too late, her innocence of the foul crime for which she is now languishing in one of the cells of the Compter! Will you do this thing, Mossy Pendell? On your answer hangs your life!"

"My life?"

"Ay, your life! I am the avenger as well as the husband of Lucy Everton! Speak! Tell me! Will you do what I require of you?" asked Claude Duval, in a voice of emotion.

"I know not what you mean."

"False villain! you know too well!"

"Oh, that I could dye my sword in your heart's blood," yelled Mossy Pendell, "without disgracing myself!"

"Coward!"

CHAPTER XLII.

CLAUDE DUVAL HAS A DUEL WITH MOSSY PENDELL, AND ESCAPES MUCKLES, THE OFFICER.

"COWARD, say you?"

"Yes, base coward! You are brave when plotting against the life and innocence of a defenceless girl, but now you tremble!"

"Have at thee, then!" cried Mossy Pendell. "You shall rue this boastful reproach, or all skill has deserted this right arm."

"Who was the murderer of Lucy Everton's uncle?"

Mossy Pendell's only reply now was to dart forward and make a furious pass with his sword at Claude Duval, which, had it been successful, would at once have consigned to death that brave and noble heart, and deprived Lucy Everton of her only friend and protector.

But Duval was upon his guard.

From the first moment of that interview he had not taken his eyes off the hateful orbs of Mossy Pendell, and he had seen by the slight flash and quiver of them the fell purpose of his soul.

Letting the ample roquelaire cloak which he wore fall off his left shoulder, Duval gathered it by a rapid motion of his left hand into a dense mass around that hand and arm.

It was better than the best shield that ever armed warrior bore in battle; for by a half turn Duval at once and easily caught the blade of Mossy Pendell's sword in the thick folds of the cloak, while he had his own sword at liberty.

By a sudden movement, then, Duval brought his sword forward, so as to give point with it at the neck of Mossy Pendell.

"Die, then, in your crimes and iniquities, villain!" he cried.

The sword was well aimed at the throat of Mossy Pendell; but his cravat turned the point slightly aside, and although it passed through the flesh at the side of his neck, the wound was but a superficial one.

Mossy Pendell uttered a cry of rage.

"To the death—to the death, then!" he shouted. "Be it a combat to the death!"

Duval did not speak. He held his breath for the battle that was to ensue, and he saved his strength.

He saw the blood trickling down the lace in front of Mossy Pendell's apparel; but he could not tell if the wound he had given him was one that would disable him or not.

By the fury with which he now began the combat with Duval, it would seem that such was not the case.

The swords clashed together, and for a few seconds seemed each to be instinct with life, and to be twining around each other like two serpents engaged in deadly conflict.

And now Duval felt thankful for the skill he had acquired in the use of the rapier.

He had no reason to apprehend that Mossy Pendell was not a master of the weapon; and yet each moment now he began to feel high confidence in the assurance that he, Duval, could keep his antagonist at bay, and probably soon inflict upon him some new wound that would place him at his mercy.

"Die—die!" cried Mossy Pendell—"die, for your insolence, Claude Duval!"

Duval did not speak. Perfectly well he knew the wisdom of silence in such a conflict.

This silence on the part of his opponent now seemed to perplex and confound Mossy Pendell, and he made desperate attempts to beat down Duval's guard, in order that he might end the conflict by his death.

"Speak!" he cried. "Speak but one word to tell me not to kill you!"

Duval fought warily and well, but still he uttered not a word.

Mossy Pendell began to give way.

Step by step he retreated towards the outer room, and Duval could see that he was with his left hand apparently feeling for the door, which had partially closed of itself.

He thought that his object was to escape by some means, and Duval assumed more the offensive than he had done, and inflicted upon him another wound, although a slight one, on his sword arm.

Mossy Pendell had now reached the door that separated the two apartments.

He pushed it open with his left hand; and as Duval pressed him hard, taking a full step forward for every one of his backward, he could not shut him out of that outer room, which Claude Duval thought he might wish to do.

Such was not, however, the plan of the treacherous Mossy Pendell.

No sooner had he got fairly within that outer room than he made so sudden and reckless an assault on Duval that for a moment he beat down his sword blade, and the instant that he had sufficient freedom from that resistance to do so, he dashed round a table that was in the centre of the room, so as to place it between himself and his assailant before Duval could prevent him.

To throw down his sword, then, was to Mossy Pendell the work of a moment, and from that table he seized one of Duval's own pistols, which he had laid there on first entering the room, and with a shout of triumph, he pointed it full in the face of Duval.

"Die!" he said; "and in your death I shall feel that I have rid myself of the only obstacle between me and fortune."

"Heyday!" shouted a voice at this moment, and a strong hand struck up the muzzle of the pistol, which went off with a loud report. "Heyday, gentlemen, gentlemen! I can't have this unseemly riot on my premises."

"Stand aside!" shouted Duval.

There was a flash of the keen sword blade in Duval's hand, and then it was plunged into the breast of Mossy Pendell.

Mossy Pendell uttered a fearful scream.

"Fly, Captain, fly!" whispered the landlord. "Leave him to me. Your horse is ready. The house is almost surrounded. Fly, by the back."

Bang! bang! bang! came on the outer door of the inn.

"Open! open! open in the King's name!"

"For heaven's, sake, Captain," again whispered the landlord, "fly for your life's sake! The door will never hold out against such an attack."

Duval gave one more glance at Mossy Pendell, and then sheathing his sword, and hastily placing his two pistols in his pockets, he hastened from the room.

Bang! bang! bang! came again at the door.

"Good gracious me, gentlemen," said the landlord, "how impatient you be! I came as soon as ever I could."

"Rascal! tell me," said Muckles, "have you Claude Duval here?"

"Claude Duval, your worship? Yes, he's here."

"Enter!" cried Muckles to his men.

"Lor' bless me! what am I saying? You startle a poor fellow. I mean he was here a little while agone, and if so be you want him, you can easily overtake him, for he was on foot."

"On foot?"

"Yes, Mr. Muckles; he went straight ahead, and seemed to be very wild-like."

"What mean you?" growled Muckles.

"Why, Mr. Muckles, I should say he was not quite right in his mind, for he talked about burning down Newgate, and all that sort of thing."

"Ah, then, he has gone to London?"

"Exactly so, Mr. Muckles," replied the landlord. "And, if so be as you take a near cut across that there hedge, I've no doubt, in my own mind, but that you'll nab him."

"Forward!" cried Muckles. "I thought he was here, my men; but it seems we shall not have much difficulty in caging our bird this time."

"Done brown again!" said Swallow. "I knowed we should be too late."

"Silence! idiot that you are! Follow me, I say."

Muckles put his horse to a hard gallop, and was followed by five of his subordinate officers.

"He is gone," said the landlord, to himself, as Muckles, like a shadow, flitted across the threshold, leaving the door swinging open behind him.

Claude Duval, in the meantime, was at a hard gallop, putting many miles between him and Muckles and his men.

"I have distanced them this time," said Claude, to himself, as he patted the neck of Nightshade, when loud shouts came upon his ears.

For a moment Duval could scarcely believe that these cries and shouts had any reference to him, but he was convinced that such in reality was the case.

"Forward! Forward, my men!" he heard in the unmistakable voice of Muckles. "I know the horse too well to doubt it. That is Claude Duval, the highwayman. That's his horse; there is not such another in the three kingdoms. Forward! forward!"

A couple of pistol shots rung in the night air, and Duval found himself in a perilous position.

What was he to do?

Was he, after all the perils and escapes he had had, to be dragged to death without effecting the release of Lucy from her terrible fate.

Oh, the thought was maddening. He felt for a moment as though his heart would burst.

"Seize him! Seize him!" cried Muckles. "If he once gets a quarter of a mile the start of us, there is not a horse in England can reach him. Stop him! Seize him, dead or alive! A thousand pounds for Claude Duval!"

Duval tightened his hold on the rein of his noble horse.

"Fly, Nightshade, fly!" he whispered. "On, on, on! for life and liberty!"

The horse caught the contagion of his master's fears, and it darted forward at a speed that set pursuit at defiance.

"Now we have him!" cried again the voice of Muckles. "Now for it! Three of you to the right, and three to the left! Now we have him!"

The officers divided themselves in the manner indicated by Muckles, and for the space of about a minute, Duval felt that he was nearly surrounded by his foes, but he gave one touch to the neck of Nightshade, and raised a cry of encouragement to the animal, and with one leap forward, the horse cleared the grasp made at its head by a couple of officers.

"On, on!" cried Duval—"on, my Nightshade!"

"Fire!" cried a loud voice.

The sharp sound of the pistols in the night air immediately succeeded to the order, but neither Duval nor his horse were touched.

The speed of the beautiful creature rather increased than diminished; and although Duval, by a glance he cast now and then behind him, could see that the officers were in full pursuit, he did not entertain the remotest apprehension of being overtaken.

"Safe, safe!" whispered Duval, to himself. "Safe, for Lucy's sake. Had it not been for her dear sake, I would willingly have given myself up to justice and to death."

On, on he went, and still ever and anon came the cries and the shouts of the officers in pursuit.

They could have but one hope in that chase, where they went but three feet to Nightshade's four; and that was that, by keeping up a clamour as they went, some mounted and armed men—for most men in those days travelled on horseback, and were well armed—might meet the flying horseman, and so bar his progress.

Moreover, the officers knew well that they were approaching a turnpike gate—a gate which had often been a serious obstacle to the knights of the road when chased from London.

The officers had, perhaps, a hope that the five-barred gate, with its formidable row of spikes at the top, would prove an obstacle to the horse they were now in pursuit of.

And so it might, had that horse which carried the life of Claude Duval been of ordinary mettle.

The gate was in sight.

LUCY EVERTON IS CONDUCTED TO THE OLD BAILEY.

The shouts of the pursuers came hoarsely upon the night air.

There was a rushing sound—a shower of small stones and gravelly particles—and the horse had cleared the turnpike gate, with a good two feet to spare.

The turnpike keeper ran out in his night-cap with a shout, and then cried out, "By Jove! It's Nightshade and the Captain! There is not another horse I know of could do such a thing as that! Hurrah for Claude Duval!"

From that time, Claude Duval lost both sight and sound of his pursuers; but he galloped on five miles further into the country; and then, as Nightshade made his way through a hollow in the road, Duval checked the creature's speed, and finally halted on the rise of a gentle slope.

The night had nearly passed away now, and the first flash of the early dawn was beginning to make the tree tops look of a dull grey colour.

Some birds twittered in the still air.

No 14.—NIGHTSHADE.

Nightshade pawed the ground, and did not seem to be in the least distressed by his recent tremendous gallop.

And there was Claude Duval, alone on that solitary road, his heart in the gloomy cell of his lost Lucy.

What was he to do next?

Claude Duval felt sick and faint at heart. Want of rest, and want of food, together with the reaction of the violent excitement attendant upon his encounter with Mossy Pendell—then, again, his pursuit by the officers—began to tell upon his already over-tasked strength; and now, more than once, with a feeling of great exhaustion, he let his head sink low down upon the neck of Nightshade.

"Home, home!" he cried. "I must seek once more that deserted mansion, which will never again, I fear, be a home to me!"

He touched Nightshade lightly on the neck, and the creature obeyed the impulse.

In less than half an hour Claude Duval stood before the entrance to the court-yard of that house on Hampstead Heath, now endeared to him by being associated with Lucy Everton.

It was Blossom who appeared to his demand for admission.

There was a look of sympathy almost amounting to veneration on the features of this faithful fellow, friend and companion, as Duval threw the reins to him.

"Nightshade has had a hard gallop, Captain, hasn't he?"

"It was a gallop for life, Blossom."

"You don't say so, Captain?"

"Even so, Blossom; but I succeeded in distancing my pursuers—although I know not for what purpose I did so," he added, mournfully.

"Why, for happier times, to be sure, Captain. Don't be down, Captain—Lucy Everton will yet be saved, I feel certain. We will together seek this Mossy Pendell, who, if he did not himself commit the murder, at least knows who did. Together, I say, Captain, we will seek this man, and compel him to divulge the secret."

"Alas!" said Duval; "it is too late to do that."

"Too late, Captain? What do you mean? Lucy Everton is not ——"

"Mossy Pendell is, I believe, dead, by this time, with the secret locked up in his own black heart."

"Captain! Captain! You surprise me. Have you two, then, met?"

"Met and fought!" said Duval, in a strange, calm voice, that almost startled Blossom.

"Well, Captain," said Blossom, after a pause; "don't look and speak like that. Surely it is not to be deplored that you and Lucy Everton have an enemy the less."

"No, no! But his testimony, if it could have been wrung from him, might at once have put an end to Lucy's persecutions; and I should at least have been happy in knowing that she was safe."

CHAPTER XLIII.

LUCY EVERTON IS AGAIN PLACED IN THE DOCK.

It was a dreary time that poor Lucy Everton spent in the old Compter.

A dreary time to any one, whether innocent or guilty; but specially so to her, with the consciousness that she was suffering all this persecution for no fault or crime of her own, but because she had seemed good and fair in the eyes of others.

Hope, however, never deserted her.

Did she not feel assured that Claude Duval, come what come may, would hasten to her rescue; and even at the eleventh hour would cast the shield of his protecting arm about her, and save her?

Had he not done so once already?

Could any circumstances be so desperate as those from which he had once rescued her?

Certainly not.

And, therefore, was it that Lucy, although she felt acutely the irksomeness of her imprisonment, cast aside all real fears, and felt herself in security.

But it was sad to look upon those prison walls only, instead of the waving tree tops, and the bright blue sky of her happy home on Hampstead Heath.

It was sad to hear the clanking of chains instead of the melodious voices of the forest birds.

And there were times when, as hour after hour passed away, and no aid came to her, that she felt almost inclined to dash herself against the old stone walls of her cell, in her frantic efforts to be free.

Then she would press her hands upon her heart, and strive to still its tumultuous beating.

"He loves me still," she would say, "and he will not desert me. I shall see him yet, so gallant, so handsome, and so brave; and even at the moment of direst peril he will save me."

In these reflections, and in fitful snatches of sleep, poor Lucy passed the weary time.

It was Saturday morning.

Some heavy blows were struck upon the door of the cell.

She knew what the signal meant. It was that the prisoner should be up and alert to receive some official visit.

Then there was a flash of light; for in those gloomy, narrow passages of the old Compter the light of day never penetrated.

The genius of the age, at the time such prisons as that were built, was to render them abodes of madness and despair, where the innocent and guilty alike suffered a martyrdom of the senses and the imagination.

The cell door was thrown open.

A warder held up a lantern.

The broad, fanlike gleam of light fell full upon the fair but pale face of Lucy Everton; and then the Governor of the Compter, accompanied by the Chaplain and the Clerk of the prison, stood grouped together at the door of the cell.

Behind them appeared a dusky figure, dodging to and fro, and apparently striving to catch the eye of the poor prisoner in the cell.

"Lucy Everton," said the Clerk of the Compter; "you are required to answer ——"

"But she denies that she is Lucy Everton," cried the voice of the person who was dodging the Clerk and the Chaplain. "She denies that she is Lucy Everton; for if she were to admit it, according to the law, she might be led forth to execution at once, at the will of the Sheriff. Because, having been regularly handed over to him after conviction and sentence, she has never been legally out of custody—therefore, she denies that she is Lucy Everton, and is not bound to say who she is."

Lucy felt that this was advice.

Who it came from she knew not; but its soundness recommended itself to her in an instant.

She checked the words on her lips that would have self-condemned her.

"Very well," said the Governor; "the prisoner denies that she is Lucy Everton; but we have done our duty."

"Entirely so," remarked the Chaplain.

"Exactly so," said the Clerk; and he closed the book which he had held open in his hand, and put his pen again behind his ear.

"You will be brought into Court," added the Governor; "and there it will be incumbent upon the Sheriff to prove that you are the same Lucy Everton who was rescued from his custody by Claude Duval."

"Come along, Mr. Morgan," said the Chaplain.

These words were addressed to the person who had given such good and hearty advice to Lucy.

And then the cell door was closed again, and she was alone.

But she had no time for reflection.

Bang! bang! came two blows on the panel of the door.

"Don't be down-hearted," said a voice. "They haven't got you yet."

The voice was that of a turnkey, who had already, in his rough way, displayed some sympathy towards her.

"I thank you," said Lucy—"I thank you! But what did it all mean?"

"Why, don't you understand, they're forced to come and try to 'dentify an escaped prisoner, but they dont' want to do it, neither the Governor, nor the Chaplain, nor the Clerk, so they got Mr. Morgan, the schoolmaster, to come and say what he did, all for fear you should let on you were Lucy Everton."

"Yes," said Lucy, "it is kind. I comprehend it now, and it may give me some hours of life."

"I should rather think it would. If they do not 'dentify you at the Bailey, it'll be after twelve o'clock; and as this is Saturday, they can't hang you till Monday morning, so you may make yourself as comfortable as possible."

"I thank you. I am sure you mean kindly."

"In course I does. Job Spriggins is to be hung on Monday. He's a cracksman, he is, and it'll be no end o' bricks to see how game he'll die. Just you watch him. I dare say they'll turn him off afore you, so that you'll see it all as nice as possible."

The friendly turnkey, certainly friendly in his way, walked with a heavy step down the narrow passage outside the cell door.

The prospect, however, of seeing how gamely Job Spriggins would be "turned off" at Tyburn, was by no means likely to raise the spirits of Lucy.

She crouched down in a corner of her cell, and gave herself up to painful reflection.

"He will save me! He will risk his life to save me! He will strive to do so; but should he fail — should he hazard and lose all in the vain effort at my preservation, and should he only succeed in dying with me! No, no—rather let me perish twenty times over than that such should happen! Claude! Claude! Oh, that my voice might reach you, and urge you to self-preservation, rather than risk too much for me."

Bang! came another blow at the cell door.

Lucy started.

It was the turnkey.

"They're coming now. Say you're name's Poll Wilkins, or anything else you like; but don't let on who you really are, for any sake."

"I will refuse to answer. No one is bound to call upon death by the utterance of a word. I am innocent, and while heaven grants me strength and sanity, I will preserve the life it has given me."

Again the cell door was opened.

A pair of rough handcuffs were put upon the delicate wrists of Lucy Everton.

Not a word was now spoken, but according to the custom of the time, she was led through the open streets from the Compter to the court of the Old Bailey, exposed to the gaze of every heedless passer-by.

Did the consciousness of innocence support her amid that sad trial.

Alas, no!

Guilt might walk in the open streets without the blush of shame, but innocence felt the full agony of the heart's degradation.

Through many winding passages, and up some flights of stairs, hustled forward by impatient turnkeys and warders, poor Lucy was brought into the crowded court.

There was a buzz of conversation and expectation, for the judge had not taken his seat, and the criers, who so usually called for silence, were chatting in a very contented and unofficial kind of manner with their acquaintances among the throng.

And so Lucy was placed in the dock

She cast but one glance about her.

There might have been sympathizing eyes bent upon her face, but she saw them not.

Nothing but a surging sea of human faces met her gaze in all directions.

Then there was a sudden hush.

A sharp, grating sound, as some curtain was dashed aside upon its metal rings.

The ushers of the court became all activity and efficiency.

"Silence! silence!"

The judge was on the bench.

He coughed and settled his wig.

He looked drearily at some papers that lay before him, and then several more were handed to him by an official person who sat below him.

A counsel rose.

"My lord, it is my painful duty, but still a duty from which I do not shrink, to call your lordship's attention to a case of identification."

"Do you appear for the Sheriff?" said the judge, sharply.

"Yes, my lord, and it may be in your lordship's recollection that at the last sessions and gaol delivery, a person named Lucy Everton was convicted for murder, and would have suffered the extreme sentence of the law, but for a daring rescue that was perpetrated by a notorious criminal not yet in the hands of justice. I have, however, to call your lordship's attention to the fact that the escaped convict has again fallen into the hands of justice, and now stands at the bar of this court."

"Very well," said the judge; "the course in these cases is well laid down. I know nothing of who stands at the bar of the court."

"Exactly so, my lord."

"You must proceed to identification in the usual way."

"Precisely. I beg to call the Governor of Newgate."

The judge glanced up at the clock of the court.

It wanted three minutes to twelve.

If the prisoner was identified before the hour of noon, it was quite possible she might be hurried to execution within the next half-hour.

Our immediate ancestors were somewhat careless of human life.

The Governor of Newgate appeared, and with immense deliberation, took the necessary oath.

"Now, sir," said the judge, "who are you?"

There was a smile in court.

The clock struck twelve.

The judge leant back, and half-shut his eyes.

He cared little now for the identification of the prisoner, for those three minutes had, at all events, given her a reprieve until Monday.

The Governor of Newgate was then examined by the counsel for the Sheriff.

"You will be so good as to look at the prisoner at the bar."

The Governor took a long look at Lucy Everton.

Was even his worldly, cold, and obdurate heart melted by the sight of the innocent beauty of that young girl?

Did his conscience smite him at that moment that on a previous occasion he had been rough and harsh towards her?

It might be so.

His voice faltered.

He shook his head dubiously.

"Well, sir," said the counsel, "do you know the prisoner at the bar?"

"I see so many people, sir——"

The judge opened his eyes.

"Do you mean to tell me," added the counsel, "that after looking at the prisoner at the bar, you do not identify her?"

"There are such extraordinary likenesses, sir——"

The judge smiled.

"This is intolerable!" said the counsel. "Call Jonathan Thorpe."

The Governor was delighted.

Jonathan Thorpe was the chief turnkey of Newgate,

and what the Governor did not choose to recollect, Jonathan Thorpe was certain to be perfectly oblivious about.

He was duly sworn.

"Now, sir," said the counsel, "look at the prisoner at the bar."

Jonathan Thorpe shaded his eyes with his hands, screwing up his whole countenance, and half-closing his eyelids, as though Lucy had been some dazzling light, dangerous to look upon.

"Well, sir?"

"Yes, sir."

"I ask you if you know the prisoner at the bar, and can name her?"

"Never seed her afore in all my life, sir. It's a young 'oman, I suppose."

"This is too bad. Do you recollect, Mr. Jonathan Thorpe, that you are on your oath?"

"Certainly, sir. I always recollect it. We swears so many oaths during the sessions, that we can't be off recollecting it."

"Look again, then."

Jonathan Thorpe again took a curious look at Lucy Everton.

"Well, sir?"

He shook his head.

"Perhaps the young 'oman wouldn't mind saying who she is, as it might help a fellow's memory a bit."

The judge pretended to be seized with a slight hacking cough, which necessitated the spreading over his entire countenance a silk handkerchief for a few moments; and when that was removed, the judicial physiognomy was rather red.

The counsel was infuriated.

"Call Silvester Snitch—commonly known as Jack Ketch!"

There was a movement among the crowd.

A hideous, sinister-looking personage was wriggling his way towards the witness-box.

Poor Lucy Everton caught but one glance of those rat-like eyes, and the shock of red hair.

She knew the man at once.

It was the hangman, who had met with such sorry treatment in Bloomsbury Fields, first at the hands of Claude Duval, and then at those of the crowd, who had been so hilariously delighted at her escape.

No sweep, with all his sooty appurtenances about him, could ever hope to make so easy a passage through a crowded and fashionable assemblage as the hangman now made through that densely crowded court of the Old Bailey.

Every one shrunk from him.

His touch was contamination.

People shook their coat-skirts as he passed them.

And as he took his way towards the witness-box he uttered various suppressed growls and howls, which very much astonished the judge and the officials of the court.

The fact was, that Mr. Snitch was saluted by various hearty kicks on his route, for everybody knew that he came there to swear away the life of the pale young shrinking girl who stood in the dock.

And at length he reached the witness-box.

In an abject, crawling sort of manner, he took the oath, kissing the book with an unction and elaboration of sanctity that was painful to see.

He looked up then with a hideous grin.

"Now, Mr. Snitch," said the counsel.

The hangman ducked his head twice, as though the Sheriff's counsel were some idol, to whom that amount of reverence was due.

"Now, Mr. Snitch, you will please to look at the prisoner at the bar."

The hangman wheeled round upon his heels, and leered in the face of Lucy Everton.

He gave a hideous chuckle.

"Do you recognise the prisoner at the bar?"

"Certain—yes, sir."

"Can you name her?"

"If your worship pleases, she is Lucy Everton, condemned to death for murder, and rescued from off the very timbers of the scaffold, by a villain who stood upon my back ten minutes, and then kicked me down the blessed trap, as if I'd been a log of wood. I feels it now."

The hangman made a hideous contortion, and strove, with both his long arms and snake-like fingers, to rub the middle of his spine.

"My lord," said the counsel, "I apprehend that is conclusive."

The judge looked dubious.

"The evidence of the witness," he said, "is evidently tinctured by a recollection of personal injuries, and those injuries having taken place about the region of the spine, may, possibly, have impaired his recollection."

There was a general titter in court.

"No, my lord," said the hangman eagerly,—"no, my lord, my recollection isn't impaired; my back is, my head is, and one of my eyes; but my recollection isn't. The villain stood on my back, my lord, and then his horse stood on my back—a wretched beast they calls Nightshade; and before he let me go he tore a tuft of hair out of my head; and here it is, my lord, and gentlemen all—I means the bald place; and then the crowd, my lord, had a game at foot-ball, and I was the ball."

The executioner uttered three howls after this statement, in recollection of the grievous ill-usage he had experienced on the occasion in question.

"My lord," cried a young counsellor, getting up in rather a flippant manner, and speaking in sharp, clear tones,—"my lord, I appear for the prisoner at the bar, and I have medical testimony to prove that the witness at present in the box is a hopeless idiot."

"That is important," said the judge. "I will make a note of it."

The hangman glared at the young counsel as though he would gladly eat him up, at the risk of gorging to suffocation.

CHAPTER XLIV.

LUCY'S DANGER, AND A VOICE FROM THE DEAD.

IF anything could be said to be more evident than another upon this occasion, it certainly was that the feeling and the sympathy of the judge, and of every one in court, with very few exceptions indeed, were with Lucy Everton.

A more singular state of affairs could not well have been imagined, for perhaps there were fifty or a hundred, at least, persons in that crowded court, who knew her perfectly well, and could have sworn to her identity.

But they had the conviction in their minds that by so doing they would have signed, in a manner of speaking, a new death warrant for her, and consigned her again to the hands of the executioner.

No wonder, then, that they paused and hesitated, and gave Lucy the greatest possible chance of escape.

But the testimony of the hangman was, seriously, sufficient.

The young counsel in vain appealed to the judge to discredit him.

"I do not see my lord," he said, "that the testimony of this one man should be sufficient to hurry a fellow-creature to destruction."

"The position of the court," said the judge, speaking with extreme gravity, "is a painful one, but still it must not shrink from performing a duty."

"But, my lord, I have another objection to submit."

"I shall hear it with pleasure."

"In all cases of this kind, where identity has to be proved, in order that an escaped prisoner may be handed over to the Sheriff, two credible witnesses, at least, have been required."

"Is that so?" asked the judge, glancing at an old senior counsel who was present.

"Yes, my lord."

Everybody breathed again more freely.

A general glance was cast round the court, and it did not seem to be possible, amid all that crowd of faces, that there was another person to be found who would step forward into the witness-box, and proclaim the prisoner at the bar to be, indeed, Lucy Everton.

The judge began to look cheerful again.

"Well, brother Richardson," he said to the counsel for the prosecution, "what do you say to this?"

"My lord, I can only say that if the prisoner at the bar be allowed to escape, it will be a monstrous failure of justice."

"That we cannot help," replied the judge. "It may be so, or it may not. I am placed here to act according to known precedents and the law of the land."

"But, my lord, the prisoner is identified!"

"Only by one person," interposed the junior counsel, "and that not a person whose testimony will carry much weight with it."

"But, my lord——"

The judge interrupted the Sheriff's counsel.

"I may be wrong," he said, "and, of course, if I am so, I am liable to be put right; but I shall rule that two witnesses are required in cases like this."

"Another witness!" cried a voice from the crowd.

A general hiss, which deepened into a roar of execration, burst from the assembled people.

"Silence! Silence!" cried the ushers.

"Officers," said the judge, "you must preserve order. Bring any one before me who by word or act disturbs the proceedings of the court, and I will commit him."

But the officers apprehended nobody; for, in good truth, if they had attempted to do so, they would have taken the whole court into custody, for the expression of opinion was as universal as it could possibly be.

Then there was a swaying to and fro among the crowd, and it was evident that some one was, with difficulty, making his way towards the witness-box.

Every eye was bent upon this person, in curiosity to know who he could possibly be.

He was shrouded in an ample roquelaire cloak, and but little could be seen of him but the upper part of his face, and a mass of dark hair, which fell over the collar of the cloak.

And the upper part of that face was very pale.

It would seem, too, that whoever this person was, he could move with difficulty.

He even accepted the assistance of the hand of the executioner in making his way into the witness-box.

Then he let the roquelaire cloak fall from about his face, and a white, malignant-looking countenance presented itself to the judge and the court.

It was evident that the counsel for the Sheriff was taken by surprise, and had not the least idea of who this voluntary witness really was.

Nevertheless, it was his duty to question him.

"You will be good enough, sir, to state who and what you are?"

"I am known as Lord Horlop," was the reply; "and am the eldest son of the Earl of Kerrymore, an Irish peer."

Then there arose another expression of dissatisfaction, contempt, and rage from the throng in the court, for no name was better known than that of Lord Horlop, as being a disgrace to the family that owned him, and a byword for every kind of dissipation and vice which the metropolis could afford.

A sneering, malignant smile crossed the face of the dissipated young noble, and he looked with all the contempt he most probably felt at the sea of angry faces about him.

But each moment he seemed to turn paler than before, and he was compelled to hold to the rails of the witness-box for support.

"You are unwell, my lord," said the counsel of the Sheriff.

"I am so, and it is with extreme difficulty I came here; but I saw an account of the capture of the prisoner in the *Evening Courant*; and my duty to society——"

There was another yell of execration from the people as Lord Horlop made this audacious attempt to place upon the score of duty his private hatreds and vindictive feelings.

"Yes," he repeated, "I am unwell, for an attempt was made to assassinate me by the insolent paramour of the prisoner at the bar."

"It is false!" cried Lucy Everton. "The only assassin, probably, in all this court now stands in the witness-box! It is false! and I denounce Lord Horlop, in conjunction with Mossy Pendell, as the murderers of my——"

"Silence!" cried the junior counsel, in such a voice that it seemed to catch the next word from the very lips of Lucy Everton. "Silence! Let the prisoner at the bar speak! She means to denounce this man and his accomplice as the murderers of General Everton, with whom she has no relationship or connexion whatever!"

It was evident to all present that the word "uncle" was the one that was stopped from passing the lips of Lucy Everton.

If she had uttered it, it would have been at once a tacit admission of who she really was.

The judge smiled.

The counsel for the Sheriff proceeded with his examination of Lord Horlop.

"You will be so good as to look at the prisoner at the bar."

Horlop did so lightly and casually, but his eyes quailed before the steady glance of poor Lucy.

"Well, my lord, can you recognise the prisoner?"

"I can."

"And her name?"

"Is Lucy Everton."

The counsel turned towards the judge with a self-satisfied air.

"Now, my lord," he said, "I think, in conformity with your lordship's rule, we have succeeded in placing before you the two witnesses required."

The judge slightly bowed his head.

The young counsel who had assumed the defence of Lucy glanced round the court, and uttered the words, "It is time!"

There was a sort of commotion at the door of the court.

A swaying to and fro of the crowd, and then some vociferous cheering, as a wide lane was formed for the approach of two persons.

One was a tall, gentlemanly-looking man, in a complete suit of black.

The other was attired as a groom, looking good-humoured and burly, and making his way through the crowd, evidently on good terms with himself and everybody else.

"What is this?" said the judge. "Who are these

people, and what is their object in now appearing here?"

"Witnesses for the defence, my lord," said the young counsel.

Those words were quite sufficient to ensure the fullest sympathy on the part of the crowd of persons in that Court for the two somewhat mysterious personages who were making their way towards the witness-box.

But there was one person in that crowded Court who looked upon the approach of these two persons with an all-absorbing interest, which far exceeded that which the spectators could feel in their proceedings.

That person was Lucy.

She clutched convulsively the wooden bar before her.

Her eyes seemed straining from their sockets, and a death-like paleness overspread her face.

Was she the victim of her over-wrought imagination, or did she indeed recognise in the foremost of these two persons Claude Duval?

"Was he so reckless?"

That was the first word she uttered to herself.

But she soon changed it to another.

"Was he so faithful?"

But the personage in black, who made his way so quietly and so pertinaciously towards the witness-box, never turned the slightest glance towards her.

She could only see the side of the face, and that had a peculiarly cut whisker upon it, which certainly did not belong to Claude Duval.

And yet could she be deceived?

Was it possible that any disguise could hide him from her eyes? No, there was a secret sympathy of soul, which would have declared his presence to her in the midst of the profoundest darkness; and she felt that had she closed her eyes upon all the proceedings of that Court, and that then these two mysterious persons had entered it, she would have been able to tell herself that one of them was that individuality that was dearer to her than all the world beside.

And through the lane of people, Claude—for it indeed was none other—made his way to that most perilous position which he was to occupy in the witness-box.

His disguise was wonderful.

It was one of those efforts which once or twice a man may make in his life, under some powerful impulse.

No one who was not exceedingly intimate with him could for an instant have suspected he was other than what he looked.

Some respectable country lawyer, or medical practitioner—for the cut of his clothes and his general deportment would have passed for either.

And the groom that followed him?

That groom, so faultless and unexceptionable in the quiet, sober livery he wore?

Who was he?

Did Lucy fail to name him?

Could he be other than that faithful and attached follower of Duval, who was ready thus to accompany his master into what might turn out to be, figuratively speaking, the jaws of death?

A profound stillness was in the Court.

Every spectator wore an eager look, as if they expected something strange to take place, but knew not what it could possibly be.

There was a slight flush upon the countenance of the counsel for the defence, but it was soon succeeded by a fixed paleness, as, after sitting down for a few seconds he rose, and confronted the disguised Claude Duval.

"Your name, sir?"

"Mr. George Henshaw, of Cirencester."

"And your profession, sir?"

"I am a solicitor."

"Will you then be so good as to explain to his lordship the purport of your presence here?"

"At considerable inconvenience to myself, and some cost," said Duval, speaking in a low, earnest voice, "I appear in this Court to do a common act of justice."

Duval had got so far when the Sheriff's counsel suddenly rose to his feet.

"My lord," he said, "here are witnesses for the defence suddenly announced to us, and my learned friend is taking the testimony of one of them without his being sworn."

"Swear the witness," said the judge.

"I have a further objection, my lord."

The judge slightly inclined his head."

"I apprehend, my lord, it will be necessary that these witnesses—stepping, as it were, out of a crowd—should satisfy the Court as to who and what they are—not by mere word of mouth, but by some referential testimony that should corroborate their own account of themselves."

"The capacity in which I sit here," said the judge, "is a peculiar one. I can only take notice of what is sworn before me by human creatures standing in that witness-box."

"But, my lord——"

"Nay, be so good as to hear me out. In the absence of contradictory testimony to their statements, I am bound to believe them to be true; and, even in the presence of such contradictory statements, we can but weigh the probabilities on either side, and with such human judgment as we have, come to a decision."

Duval was sworn.

The next question put to him by the young counsel for Lucy was an adroit one.

So adroit, indeed, that the reader will not fail to perceive that there must have been some clear understanding between Duval and that young counsel.

What could that understanding be, but to the effect that he, Duval, would do all that lay in his power, by risking his own liberty and life, to save Lucy, but at the same time he shrank from the perpetration of a false oath?

The kind of trepidation with which the counsel spoke to him was evident to all, and the singular manner in which he framed the question was far from escaping the penetration of the judge.

"Now that you are on your oath, will you please to look at the prisoner at the bar?"

"I will."

Duval slowly turned.

His eyes met those of Lucy.

The mutual flash was more than sufficient for recognition.

She held up her arms as far as she possibly could, for the weight of fetters was upon them.

A half-suppressed cry came from her lips.

And then, as he saw those fetters, there seemed to come a rush of blood from his head to his brain, and for a moment—although only for a moment—his calmness forsook him, and he was about, in frantic accents, to call upon her by name.

By one of those great efforts, however, which men like Claude Duval can make in moments of peril and emergency, he controlled the rush of feeling that had come over him.

Duval was still.

And, to all appearance, calm and collected as before.

Lucy let her hands drop.

The fetters with which they were loaded, touched the floor with a heavy clang.

And all this, although it has taken us some time to relate, happened so momentarily, that it was only the keenest observers of that crowded Court that could notice the play of feeling and emotion between the prisoner and the witness for the defence.

"You observe the prisoner well?" said the young counsel.

"I do."

Over the heads of prisoners brought up for trial at the Old Bailey there hangs suspended a mirror, which may be adjusted to any angle, so as to reflect as much light as possible upon the face of the unhappy being who is brought there to be judged.

An officious turnkey gave this mirror a slight touch, so that it sent a whiter, brighter light upon the face of Lucy.

But Duval now had steeled his heart against any exhibition of emotion; and although that movement gave him a slight shock, he withstood it manfully, and only gazed calmly in the face of her who was more to him than life itself.

The counsel spoke again.

"To the best of your belief, can you take upon yourself to say that the name of the prisoner at the bar is Lucy Everton?"

"Certainly not."

"But, my lord," said the Sheriff's counsel, "this is absurd. Nothing would be easier than to bring a hundred persons forward who would not take upon themselves to say that the prisoner at the bar was Lucy Everton."

"If my learned friend will have a little patience," said the young counsel; "and if my learned friend will not be so anxious and so eager that this young, terrified girl now standing at the bar should be dragged forth to an ignominious and awful death——"

At these words, there arose a cry from the people.

A sort of yell of indignation.

The judge interposed.

"Let me, for the last time," he said, "implore counsel on both sides on this occasion to avoid these mere flourishes of words, which can only stir up evil passion, and by no means advance the ends of justice."

"Excuse me, my lord," added Lucy's counsel; "but I was only about to say that I feel to the full as keenly as my learned friend the absurdity of bringing forward witnesses merely to depose to a negative; and if my learned friend had not interrupted me in the way he did, I was about to ask another question of the witness that must have answered every purpose."

"Pray proceed," said the judge.

The counsel for the Sheriff threw himself back on his chair, and half shut his eyes, as if he would have said, "Oh, yes, pray proceed, and see what a pretty mess you'll make of it!"

The young counsel looked closely at Duval as he spoke again.

"You have already sworn that you do not recognise the prisoner at the bar as Lucy Everton?"

"I have."

"Do you recognise her as any one else?"

"I do."

There was a cheer in the Court, which, despite all the angry looks of the ushers, and the grave displeasure of the judge, awakened every echo within it.

CHAPTER XLV.

CLAUDE DUVAL IS RECOGNISED IN THE WITNESS FOR THE DEFENCE.

It will be seen that these questions to Claude Duval from the young counsel were most peculiarly and artfully worded.

Since Duval had been sworn, he had never asked him his name, or addressed him by the name he had given before being so sworn.

And Lucy, listening eagerly and attentively to every word that fell from Duval's lips, comprehended in a moment what he meant.

Upon his oath, he did not recognise her as Lucy Everton; but with a thousand oaths, if necessary, and deep in his own heart, he recognised her as Lucy Duval.

Was she not his wife?

Had he not, at that old church at Hampstead, made her his own with every ceremony that could sanction their union?

He had.

Lucy Everton from that moment was no more, but Lucy Duval stepped into existence, as the wife of that Claude who now stood forward to try to save her by every art and manoeuvre he could bring to bear in the cause, except blank perjury in the face of heaven.

And so the young counsel for the defence, who was doing all that was possible for a man in his situation to do in order to save the life of Lucy, hoped against his own experiences that the judge would for once in a way close his eyes to the peculiarities in the evidence of Claude Duval, and give her the benefit of it.

The judge might have done so.

There was not a spectator in Court who would not have done so.

And under other circumstances that very counsel who was acting for the Sheriff would have done so.

But a strange spirit animates barristers on these occasions.

They fight for victory.

For victory over a professional opponent; and on whatever side they happen to be engaged, they import into it a zealous partizanship that seems to engage all their feelings and faculties.

And this is abstractedly right.

The counsel must feel, or make himself feel, that the side on which he is must be right and should conquer, or he would be but a lukewarm advocate, either for the prosecution or the defence.

It was evident the young barrister who was acting in favour of Lucy did not wish to ask another question of Claude Duval.

He sat down, but the Sheriff's counsel rose.

"You say you recognise the prisoner at the bar?"

"I do," replied Duval.

"But at the same time you say you do not recognise her as Lucy Everton?"

"I have said so."

"You will, then, state to his lordship who it is you recognise her to be."

"That I decline."

"I thought so. My lord, I call upon you to deal with this witness, who is less entitled than any other to the indulgence of the Court, inasmuch as he comes forward perfectly as a volunteer to tender his evidence."

"The witness should answer the question," said the judge.

"I respectfully decline," said Duval.

"This is contumacious!" said the Sheriff's counsel.

"Probably it is," added Duval. "But still, I apprehend that I have stated enough upon my oath to make any judge pause before he hands over the innocent person now standing at the bar to death."

"Yes, my lord!" cried the young counsel, eagerly. "And although your lordship may not be quite satisfied, yet a doubt is quite sufficient to induce delay; and your lordship will probably postpone the consideration of this case for a week."

"That is the object, of course!" cried a voice.

The voice was Lord Horlop's.

"These interruptions," said the judge, "are most unseemly. It is in my power to commit the witness for contumacy in refusing to answer the questions put to him; but I think the mildest and safest course in this conjunction of circumstances will be to postpone the consideration of the case in the manner suggested."

What a weight was lifted off the heart of Duval!

A week's respite for Lucy!

How much might be done in a week!

It seemed to him as if that period of time would be almost sufficient to pull down old Newgate, stone by stone, and rescue her.

"But, my lord ——" cried the counsel for the Sheriff.

"Nay!" shouted the young barrister, in a still louder voice. "This is worse than the contumacy of a witness, because my learned friend might be presumed to know better. The Court has given its decision; and after that, to attempt to argue with his lordship is most disrespectful."

"The Court has not given its decision."

"I appeal to his lordship."

The judge spoke again.

"I intimated what was the feeling of the Court, although, perhaps, strictly speaking, the decision had not been given I shall now, however, give it in the terms of that intimation. Let the prisoner at the bar be removed to the common gaol of Newgate, and there kept in safe custody until this day week, when she will be produced again before me for identification or otherwise as the case may be; and during that period of delay let the proper officer of the Court make such inquiries with regard to the identity of this witness, at Cirencester, as are evidently desirable."

There was one look, one loving and tender look, between Duval and Lucy.

The fetters upon her young limbs again rattled, as one of the warders took her by the arm to remove her from the bar.

The young counsel gave Duval a significant glance, which meant, as plainly as possible, "Get away as fast as you can."

He turned from the witness-box, and was upon the point of stepping down amid the croud of people, when, in tones of great excitement, a man shouted out near the door of the Court, "There are two horses waiting in the Old Bailey, and I'll swear that one of them belongs to Claude Duval, and his name's Nightshade!"

Lucy uttered a cry.

She forgot all her own danger at that moment in the fearful perils she saw surrounding and hedging in Claude Duval.

"Fly, fly!" she cried,—"fly while you can! There is danger in the very air you breathe! Fly, Claude— fly!"

How fatally indiscreet might those words have been.

Perhaps they even were so now; and coming from the lips of Lucy Everton, they seemed like a trumpet sound to awaken the most ardent feelings and passions of every one in that crowded Court.

The judge said nothing, but he rose from his seat, and looked anxiously towards the door of the Court, and then at Claude Duval, as though he would have asked himself if it were possible for the daring intruder to escape.

And now the counsel for the Sheriff seemed to see that victory, after all, was within his grasp.

"Close the doors!" he cried,—" close the doors! Officers, let no one escape! And it may be that we shall catch more birds than one in this trap!"

Again, then, Lucy, with all the vehemence of alarmed affection, cried aloud to Claude Duval, "Fly, fly!—for my sake, fly!"

"Yes!" shouted Claude, in answer. "To aid you still!"

He made but one leap from the witness-box on to the floor of the Court.

"Who will stop me," he cried, "when I came here at peril of my life to try to save an innocent girl from an ignominious and shameful death? I am Claude Duval!"

At this announcement there arose such a clamour of sounds in the Court that it was impossible that Duval could fairly say if the feeling of the majority of the people was for or against him.

Quickly enough, however, he had a practical illustration that there would be no impediment to his exit from the Court so far as its spectators were concerned.

The crush was dreadful, but still a lane was made sufficiently wide for him to pass through, and Duval was not slow in availing himself of it.

Cheers, and shouts, and words of encouragement from many voices heralded his progress.

Then there arose a groan and a yell.

A man darted into the narrow lane that had been made for Duval, and hastily flinging one arm around him, shouted out, in tones of great excitement, "My prisoner!—my prisoner! I call upon you all to aid and assist me, in the name of the law! I arrest Claude Duval for felony!—felony, you hear!"

Duval did not seem to make the slightest resistance.

He only held up his arms and looked at the people, as he said, in a calm, clear voice, "Is this to be?"

The "No!" that was shouted in answer came from a thousand throats.

"You are indiscreet, Mr. Muckles," said Duval, as that officer—for it was he who had made this audacious attempt to capture Claude Duval—held a pistol at his head, threatening him with instant death.

In the excitement of the moment it is possible that Muckles might have conceived that he was only doing his duty by shooting Duval, and so hindering his escape in the most effectual manner.

If such, however, had been his feeling, he had not time to carry it into effect.

It was true he had the pistol handily in his pocket, and had succeeded in snatching it hastily from there, but it required another action to prepare it for discharge.

That action Muckles had not time to carry out.

A dozen hands grasped him.

The pistol was wrenched from his hold—he was lifted bodily off his feet, and over the heads of the people, with as little regard for his personal convenience as though he had been a bale of goods. The unfortunate officer was flung the whole length of the Court, and finally let drop in an obscure corner, more dead than alive.

Lucy then spoke again.

"Fly, Claude! fly!"

He waved his hand toward her.

A rush of a few feet more took him to the door of the Court.

"Farewell!" he shouted. "It is but for a time—we yet live or die together!"

There were other officers at hand, but the crowd had so completely taken the part of Claude Duval, and so summarily disposed of Mr. Muckles, that they stood apart too, irresolute for action.

CHAPTER XLVI.

CLAUDE DUVAL MAKES HIMSELF THE ALMONER OF THE CITY REMEMBRANCER.

THE door of the Court was gained.

One last look Claude gave towards the dock, where

NIGHTSHADE DISPOSES OF MR. SWALLOW.

still stood Lucy, straining her eyes in the direction where he had gone.

Then, as the crowd closed behind him, it seemed as if she were shut away from his gaze by a complete sea of wild, excited faces.

"Blossom!" he cried, "where are you?"

"Here! here!"

Blossom was close at his heels, and now some dozen stalwart men seized upon Duval, and for the next dozen paces, and down a flight of steps, he could not be said to feel his feet.

The immediate environs of the Court were dark and dismal, and when Claude Duval emerged into the open air, the fair light of day dazzled him.

"Nightshade!" he cried. "My horse! my horse!"

Even as he spoke, he flung from his head the strange grey wig he wore.

His long black hair, in wavy richness, fell upon his neck and shoulders.

"My horse! my horse!" he again shouted,—"my horse, Nightshade!—I am but half saved if he is lost!"

No 15.—NIGHTSHADE.

Still thus calling for his horse, Duval hastily tore open the ecclesiastical-looking coat he wore, and flung it to the ground at his feet.

He seemed anxious to justify the people who had sympathized with him, and interfered in his favour, by showing them that he was really, without doubt, the Claude Daval in whom they had interested themselves.

And beneath that coat, which had imparted an apparent stoutness to the figure of Duval, he wore the well-known scarlet clothing which sufficiently identified him as the gallant, dashing highwayman of world-wide reputation.

Hidden securely, and tucked deep down into the vest, were the ends of that lace cravat which was ever so distinguishing a portion of Duval's costume.

"My horse! my horse!" he cried again. "Will all these kind friends about me allow my horse to be filched from me? My horse! My horse, Nightshade! Where is my horse?"

Making his way with difficulty, now, through the

throng of persons that crowded about him, Claude Duval stood upon the pavement of the Old Bailey, perhaps the most popular man that had ever occupied that position.

But Nightshade was not to be seen.

A boy stood there, holding the bridle of the horse Blossom had ridden.

The boy had a bewildered look upon his face, and there was the red mark of apparently the blow of a riding whip across his cheek.

"Duval's horse! Duval's horse!" shouted hundreds of the crowd. "Who has taken his horse?"

"I left him here," said Blossom.

"All is lost!" cried Duval.

"No, Captain, no!"

"Yes, Blossom—lost for me! Make the best of your way to our house at Hampstead, and there wait until you have some tidings. Mount, and away! for there is not a moment to lose."

"No, Captain, you mount; the horse is a good one, although not equal to Nightshade."

Duval shook his head.

"The constables will muster soon, in force, from the interior of the prison;" he said, "and whether it be you or I who may remain here, capture is certain."

"Let them take me."

"No, Blossom; when shall it ever be said that Claude Duval sacrificed any one of his followers to save himself?"

"There's the horse! there's the horse!" cried the boy with such a screaming vehemency that it rose above all other sounds, and directed every eye to where he pointed.

At the further end of Giltspur Street there was seen a mounted man.

He had turned the head of the horse on which he had rode slightly towards the Old Bailey, as if to take a last look of what was going on in that interesting locality.

Now, it is well known to all who have visited that part of London, so famous in domestic history, that the ground rises towards Smithfield from the Old Bailey.

Both Claude Duval and Blossom, therefore, could easily see over the heads of the people to the higher ground at the end of Giltspur Street.

One glance was sufficient.

Their voices mingled as they cried out, "Nightshade!"

It was Nightshade—there could be no possibility of a mistake.

Partially reflected against the clear sky beyond, there was the dark, symmetrical form of Duval's horse, with its head turned gracefully towards Newgate, as though the creature knew it left its master in danger and difficulty behind it.

But who rode that sagacious and gallant steed of the highwayman?

Who had had the audacity to mount Nightshade, and ride away with him, leaving Claude Duval to his fate?

Evidently an officer of the police.

There was no mistaking the top-boots.

The heavy, broad-skirted coat—the pocket, capacious enough to hold arms and ammunition, and almost, if necessary, a complete set of felon's fetters.

There was the eternal red waistcoat, likewise, which all the officers, high and low, affected.

And this man, when he saw himself observed, raised his hat mockingly, as though he would have bidden adieu to Claude Duval, to the crowd, and to the whole of London, now that he was mounted on Nightshade, and might do so by the gallop of a few miles.

And had he galloped on, without pausing to look back, in that mocking spirit which possessed him, he might easily have escaped into the open country beyond Barbican and Finsbury, leaving Claude Duval to almost certain capture at the door of the old prison.

But he must needs pause.

A curiosity which he could not control induced him to draw bridle at that critical spot, and so the keen eyes of Claude Duval saw his horse; and it is not too much to suppose that the bright eyes and keen senses of Nightshade recognised his master, even amid the throng of persons that surrounded him in the Old Bailey.

Be that how it may, however, from the moment that Claude Duval set eyes upon his horse, although at that distance, a feeling of calmness and serenity spread over his face.

"Saved!" he said.

"Thank heaven!" cried Blossom.

Duval sprang up the steps of Newgate.

Once there, he was a prominent object; but the moment he had gained that position, a hundred warning voices arose from the crowd.

"Away with you, Duval!—away with you! Here are the traps! You'll be nabbed, to a certainty! Away with you—away with you!"

"There is time yet!" said Duval.

Even as he spoke, he saw the man who was mounted upon Nightshade wrench the creature's head violently round by a sharp tug of the bridle.

The constable who had made off with Claude's horse had satisfied himself as regarded the state of affairs in the Old Bailey, and was now willing to place as great a distance between him and the owner of Nightshade as possible.

But he was too late.

Claude Duval raised his hands to his mouth.

He placed one on each side of his face, so as to confine the sound he was about to utter into as narrow a compass as possible, and to prevent it scattering right and left among the crowd.

Something, then, after the fashion of seafaring men when they wish to hail a distant vessel, Duval, so to speak, threw his voice over the heads of the vast crowd about him, and right away up Giltspur Street, to the sharp ears of his horse.

"Nightshade! Nightshade, boy! Hither—hither!"

Then ensued a curious scene.

A scene so full of interest that it attracted unusual observation.

The crowd in the Old Bailey became hushed and still as they waited the issue of what was taking place at the end of Giltspur Street.

It was a fight.

A struggle.

A struggle between a man and a horse.

The officer who was mounted upon Nightshade, with both hands upon the bridle, strove in vain to turn the creature's head to the north.

The only effect was that Nightshade stood upon his hind feet.

It was with great difficulty that the officer could keep his place upon the saddle at all.

Then Duval called again.

"Nightshade! — Nightshade! Hither! — hither! Nightshade, boy! Nightshade, bring him along!"

The struggle was over.

The horse had conquered.

Nightshade brought his fore feet to the ground with a dash that struck sparks from the old stones in the roadway.

And now that adventurous man who had mounted him had no resource but to fling himself from the saddle, at present and serious risk to his life, or to cling still wildly to the neck and mane of Nightshade, and allow himself to be carried with the speed of the wind to the door of Newgate.

He chose the latter alternative.

It was rather by a succession of terrific leaps than by galloping, that Nightshade made his way to his master.

Then the stillness of expectation that had sat upon the crowd was dissipated, and the shouts that rose from every throat reached to the innermost recesses of old Newgate, terrifying alike the prisoners and the warders.

The people parted into two great masses like the waves of the sea.

That was to leave a route for Nightshade.

Stopping abruptly exactly at the feet of Claude Duval, the horse for a moment seemed to draw his feet from under him, as if preparing for a leap.

But that was only Nightshade's way of disencumbering himself of his rider.

A sharp movement of his back, and a lashing out of his hind feet, did the business of that officer of the police; for he was instantly dislodged over the head of the horse, and laid sprawling on his back in the roadway.

"I ought to a' knowed it," he yelled; "I ought to a' knowed it; of course I ought to a' knowed it! And here I am, done browner than ever!"

"Why, it's Swallow!" said Blossom.

"That idiot!" said Duval.

There was a roar of laughter from the crowd.

But events were thickening around Claude Duval; and during the last few minutes the authorities, both from Newgate and the Compter, had been collecting their forces to make a rush at him and secure him.

But what heeded he now that he had his hand upon the arched neck of Nightshade?

"Mount your horse, Blossom," he cried. "Mount at once! In the saddle we are in safety."

Another moment, then, and Duval was on the back of Nightshade.

He waved his hand to the crowd, and pointed down Snow Hill as the route which he wished to take.

And then the crowd parted again; and amid vociferous cheers a free passage was left to him.

There was a carriage, however, coming up the hill—a handsome, plain chariot, drawn by a couple of good grey horses.

It was the equipage of that official personage in the City, called the Remembrancer—a lawyer whose business it is specially to watch what is going on in the House of Commons, that may in any manner, nearly or remotely, affect any of the old standard abuses of the City.

It so happened that the Remembrancer's carriage had been stopped at the outskirts of the crowd; and that the Remembrancer himself, who was a short-tempered, hasty man, had worked himself into a roaring rage at the interruption.

When, however, the crowd parted to allow Claude Duval and his horse free passage, there was necessarily left a space up which the coach of the Remembrancer drove with rapidity.

Duval gave one glance at the carriage; and then turning to the crowd with a smile upon his face, he waved his right hand for silence.

"It is possible," he said, "that there may be some persons here present who still think I am not the veritable Claude Duval."

"No, no!" cried every voice. "No, no!"

He waved his hand again.

All was still.

"I thank you for your confidence, and for the service you have done me this day. It is possible, however, that some of you may never have the opportunity of seeing and hearing Claude Duval cry 'Stand and deliver!' on the King's highway."

A roaring shout from the crowd proclaimed that they divined his meaning.

And well they might do so; for as he spoke he pointed to the Remembrancer's carriage, and then turning to Blossom, had spoken a few words in a lower tone of voice.

The coachman had become a little terrified at the posture of affairs, and rather hesitated to drive on with sufficient quickness to please his irritated master, through such a throng of excited faces as he saw about him.

Then the Remembrancer looked out at one of the windows of the vehicle.

"Drive on!" he cried; "and if any one gets in your way, go over him!"

The crowd raised a yell.

A rush was made towards the carriage.

Duval again waved his arm, and all was still.

"Leave these gentlemen to me," he said; "I mean to set up a toll-bar here, on Snow Hill."

As Duval spoke, he plunged his hand into one of the holsters of his saddle.

He produced a pistol.

Some women in the mob shrieked; for they thought that murder was about to be done.

But the most ludicrous thing of all was to see the Remembrancer's coachman, who fenced in the most extraordinary and wild manner with his whip, as though he fancied it possible he could, by those means, ward off a pistol bullet, should one chance to come his way.

"Drive on!" roared the Remembrancer.

Fear of the crowd, but still greater fear of his master, perplexed the coachman.

He urged his horses forward.

"Halt!" shouted Duval.

"Drive on!" again yelled the Remembrancer.

"Halt!" Duval cried, for the second time.

The carriage still proceeded.

Duval levelled his pistol.

Expectation sat on every face.

The coachman held up his whip in so ludicrous an attitude, that a roar of laughter then arose from the crowd.

Bang! went Duval's pistol.

The Remembrancer's coachman had a very elaborate livery hat, and Claude Duval succeeded in doing what he fully intended, which was to send it flying from his head, with a pistol bullet through it.

"I'm a dead man!" shrieked the coachman; and dropping the whip, he seemed to resign himself to complete destruction by falling in a huddled-up manner on to the foot-board of the carriage.

Blossom then seized the horses by their heads, and in another moment Duval was at the carriage door, face to face with the infuriated Remembrancer.

"Your money or your life, sir!" he said; "or both, if it suit you better!"

The Remembrancer was livid with rage.

"You insolent scoundrel!" he cried. "How dare you?"

"Come, come, sir," added Duval, "it is ill work to use bad language to your master."

"Master? what master?"

"I am your master, because I am master of the situation. You have heard one pistol-shot, and you may hear another. Quick, sir, your money! I am not usually a man it is safe to trifle with, and least of all to-day!"

As Duval spoke, he produced the other pistol, and rested it upon the edge of the window.

The Remembrancer bit his lips and turned ghastly pale.

"A pretty thing this," he said, "for a principal City official to be robbed in noonday in the middle of Snow Hill!"

"Pretty or not," cried Duval, "be quick about it! My patience is oozing out at my fingers' ends, and one touch to the trigger of this pistol makes a vacancy in the City Remembrancership! Your money, sir—your money!"

"I have none!"

"A lie!"

"Ah!"

"A lie, sir—a lie!"

The look upon the face of Claude Duval, assumed though it was, awed the Remembrancer into compliance, and with the worst possible grace in the world he drew a heavy purse from his pocket, and handed it to Claude Duval.

"Take it, and my malediction with it!" he said. "I only hope that I may have the pleasure of seeing you hanged, which, however, I am quite sure to do!"

"By no means," said Duval.

He turned as he spoke, and holding up the purse to the crowd, he cried aloud, "Let all here remember that Claude Duval has given a taste of his quality to the citizens of London. I don't know if the Remembrancer be a very charitable man, but we will take it that he means this money for the poor. Let those who are well to do leave it alone; and here it goes for those that want it!"

Duval opened the purse, and began spinning the guineas right and left among the people.

The scrambling that ensued was something fearful, and, in good truth, Duval was glad when the last guinea slipped through his fingers.

He then flung the empty purse into the air, and calling upon Blossom to follow him quickly, he went at a gallop up Holborn Hill, soon leaving old Newgate, the City, and all the crowd far behind him.

CHAPTER XLVII.

NIGHTSHADE TAKES A NOVEL LEAP, AND FRIGHTENS MR. SWALLOW.

Duval's heart was heavy.

With a deep sigh, he drew rein on the other side of the Oxford Road.

He looked long and wistfully in the direction from whence he had come.

"I am here, Blossom," he said, "safe and sound; and so are you, and so is Nightshade; but my heart is yonder, and my bosom seems but like an empty casket from which its choicest jewel has been rifled."

Duval leant low down upon the neck of Nightshade.

The excitements of the last half-hour had kept him up; but now that all was still and all was safe—now that he was in a quiet suburb of the City, with green trees about him, and verdant meadows stretching right and left as far as the eye could carry, his spirits sunk, and his thoughts flew back to the dreary cell of Newgate, where pined one so near and dear to him.

"Cheer up, Captain," said Blossom. "It was a wonderful escape."

"Alas! alas!"

"Nay, Captain. Never give way; things are never so bad but they might be worse."

"I am not thinking of myself, Blossom."

"That I well know; but it seems to me that while you are free and unhurt, and while Nightshade here is all right and fit for a gallop anywhere, and a leap over anything, there can be no need to despair."

"Blossom!"

Duval looked up, and glanced in his follower's face anxiously.

"What would you say, Captain?"

"Tell me truly what you think. Will the judge alter his determination, and consider the identity of Lucy sufficiently established to—to——"

There was no occasion for Duval to complete his sentence.

Blossom understood him perfectly.

"No, Captain!" he cried; "from my heart and soul I believe there is no such danger. Did you not see all along that the feeling of the judge was all in favour of Lucy Everton?"

"It was—in truth, it was."

"Then, believe me, she is safe for a week; and in that time surely you can try twenty plans for her rescue, if necessary."

"You give me new life, Blossom. How far are we off Tyburn?"

"Not a mile. But don't think of such things, Captain. All is well; and, at any rate, everything is safe till Monday."

Duval shuddered as Blossom spoke.

He made at the same time a gesture for him to be silent, and then Blossom saw that the words were unwelcome.

It was not that Blossom wished to say anything that could by any possibility jar upon the already excited feelings of Claude Duval; but like many well-meaning people, he could only by a rude touch irritate the wound he would fain heal.

This mention of Monday, associated as it was with the possible fate of Lucy Everton, gave Duval a terrible pang.

"I cannot bear it," he cried. "I will not leave London while her fate is still in the balance."

"But, Captain!"

"Nay, it is useless to remonstrate with me. Go you to our home at Hampstead, and there, with full authority from me, take the command of our men."

"And you, Captain?"

"I will return when and how I can, but it will not be alone."

Blossom hesitated.

Then Duval spoke again.

"Do not understand me," he said "as wishing that these, my possible last words, may sound harshly in your ears; but there is a time when I must order, and it has now come. Go, Blossom. Leave me to myself. I will save Lucy, or perish with her; and the loud voice of public rumour will soon let you know which has happened. Go!"

Blossom hesitated for a few seconds longer; and then, slightly inclining his head, he turned his horse towards Hampstead.

Duval watched him.

He saw that Blossom sat droopingly upon the saddle.

Claude then gave one touch to Nightshade, and with a rush and a leap, Blossom was overtaken.

Duval held out his hand.

"We will not part thus," he said, "faithful follower, when it may possibly be for the last time."

For a few seconds, Blossom could not speak; and then it was in a voice of deep emotion that he said, " Captain, the men at Hampstead can look after themselves; and the old mansion needs no one to care for it. If there be danger, why send me from you? Rather let me accompany you, so that I may possibly ward off one-half of it."

"No, no; do not think of it, Blossom. I think there is danger; but yet I have a kind of security in my mind that all will yet go well. What is the time?"

"It is past three, Captain."

"Then, in three hours more we shall have darkness; so farewell, Blossom, and leave me—not to my fate, for that has an ugly sound with it—but to my good fortune, which I do not think will desert me even in this dire extremity."

Duval turned, and galloped back into London.

"I will visit the Duchess of Cleveland," he said to himself; "and who knows but her woman's heart or her high influence may help Lucy out of this dilemma better than I can do, were I to risk my life ten times over?"

Claude Duval soon saw, however, by the curious and observant eyes that were cast upon him in the street, that his costume was not exactly the sort of one to ensure his own safety, or in which to pay any visits.

Devoutly he wished, now, that the day was some hours older, so that he might escape observation.

That, however, could not be; and the next best thing he could possibly do was to effect such changes in his personal appearance as would enable him to pass through the public streets of London without exciting an undue share of curiosity and observation.

It was necessary, likewise, to dispose of Nightshade with safety.

Duval paused, and reflected.

"They will be only too delighted," he said to himself. "The old 'Bedford Head,' in Covent Garden, is the resort of many knights of the road; and although I have never yet crossed its threshold, my name will make me sufficiently welcome."

The ancient hostel of which Duval spoke has long since been pulled down, after being greatly injured by a fire; but at that time it presented a very antique and picturesque appearance.

It had heavy, projecting gables, and carved angels upon its door-posts.

There was a current tradition among what is called "the family"—that is to say, the thieves of London —that the old "Bedford Head" contained hiding-places sufficient to stow away at least a hundred men.

Certain it is that the officers of the police, although they frequently took drams of strong waters at the ancient bar of the tavern, never attempted to search for evil-doers within its inmost recesses.

For all practical purposes, therefore, the old "Bedford Head" was a sort of sanctuary which, when once reached, protected any one who dived beneath its ancient doorway.

Mounted men, hard-pressed by the police, or by some amateur pursuit, had been known to ride directly into the ancient hostel, and to disappear, horse and man together, as though swallowed up amid its dim and dusky shadows.

And now, as the conservation of Nightshade was a matter of the greatest possible concern to Duval, he determined to avail himself of the shelter of the great thieves' house for that purpose.

Heedless of the surmises which his appearance created, therefore, Duval went at a sharp trot towards Covent Garden.

The present market was not in existence; and the whole space now appropriated to it was occupied by a mass of ricketty old sheds.

But these old sheds had an use.

After nightfall they afforded shelter and sleeping accommodation to hundreds of houseless wretches.

Duval cast a rapid glance about him as he reached the open space, for he would have been glad to have availed himself of the shelter of the "Bedford Head" without exciting any special observation.

That was not to be, however.

The contiguity of the old house to Bow Street necessarily kept it under the observation of the "runners."

A shout was raised as Claude Duval appeared on Nightshade round some of the old sheds in Covent Garden.

"Seize him!—seize him! Stop him! The reward is still open! A thousand pounds for Claude Duval!"

An officer of the Bow Street police had raised the shout, and made a rush forward with his staff in his hand, vaguely supposing that his single strength would be sufficient to capture the celebrated highwayman.

The vociferous announcement, however, of who he was, from the lips of the officer, was far from raising up enemies to Claude Duval.

It had quite a contrary effect.

Every idle rapscallion in or about the market was up in arms immediately to assist him.

A complete shower of turnips, cabbages, and other vegetables was aimed at the officer, who, in a few seconds, was so completely stunned and bewildered by blows about the head and face with these missiles, that he stumbled and fell.

It would almost appear as if the miscellaneous mob, who had risen up with magical rapidity, intended to bury the officer beneath a vegetable mound, for in a few seconds nothing of him could be seen beneath the heap that was piled upon him.

Claude Duval had nothing to do but to look on at this scene as long as he chose.

He did so for a few seconds, and then turning his horse's head towards the "Bedford Head," he was leisurely walking up to it, when two men turned the corner of one of the by-streets.

"Duval!—Duval!" cried one of them.

"And nabbed at last!" said the other. "Keep him out of the 'Bedford Head,' and we have him!"

The semi-riot which had already taken place in the market had reached the ears of the reserve of officers in Bow Street, and some half-dozen of them came round to the spot sufficiently well armed to be decidedly dangerous.

The two men who had come out of the by-street made no attempt to capture Duval, but they ran as fast as they could to the door of the "Bedford Head."

There they stationed themselves, blocking it completely up.

They drew their pistols, and presented them threateningly at Claude Duval.

And then he felt himself between two fires, so to speak, for the officers from Bow Street were in his rear.

A glance enabled him to recognise the two men at the door of the tavern as his old enemies, Muckles and Swallow.

Muckles said nothing, but looked pale and determined.

Swallow, however, for once in his life, felt confident that Claude's career was over.

"Give in, Duval! Give in!" he cried, with a loud voice. "It's no use holding out any longer. I've been done brown often enough, and it's your turn now!"

"Not yet," said Duval.

He glanced behind him.

The officers from Bow Street had been impeded a little by the crowd of people; but, forming themselves into a compact body, they had fought their way through with their staves.

The moment was a critical one.

"Out of the way!" shouted Duval. "Out of the way, Muckles, I warn you!"

"Fire!" cried Muckles, in a voice of excitement.

He discharged his own pistol as he spoke, but Duval had seen by his looks that he intended mischief, and, bowing his head down to the saddle, he escaped the shot.

Then, amid the confusion of the discharge of the pistol, Duval took off his hat, and waved it once round his head, as he cried in a voice that rung through the whole market. "Farewell, gentlemen all! Duval is not nabbed yet; and as, when he intends to visit the 'Bedford Head' he don't mean to be baulked, here goes!"

Duval placed his hat right over the eyes of Nightshade.

There was only one thing that that sagacious and gallant steed would not do even at his master's bidding.

That was, to leap into the very face of a human being.

But the hat covered Nightshade's eyes.

The impulse was given by knee, hand, and voice.

"Forward! Leap, Nightshade! Leap!"

Swallow discharged his pistol at random.

Both he and Muckles then saw the horse and its rider coming like some catapult towards them.

They flung themselves back, each with a cry of fear.

The door of the old "Bedford Head" was free from obstructions; and, bending low down until his own raven locks mingled with the mane of Nightshade, Duval and his horse disappeared in at the doorway of the ancient tavern.

The leap carried him clear of the two officers.

It was somewhat ludicrous, then, to see both Muckles and Swallow rush out into the open air upon their hands and knees.

But it was well for them that they adopted that attitude instead of waiting to pick themselves up to the perpendicular, for the enraged and disappointed officers from Bow Street fired a volley of pistol shots at the narrow doorway of the old "Bedford Head."

"Done browner than ever!" shrieked Swallow, as he rolled into the kennel. "I won't try it any more, Mr. Muckles; you may nab him yourself! I've had quite enough of it!"

Bang! went the outer door of the old "Bedford Head," and up went a couple of heavy iron bars across it.

Duval had alighted in the narrow passage with a heavy thud of his horse's feet upon the old oaken flooring.

"Who is it?" cried a voice.

"Claude Duval!"

"No!"

"Yes. I am Claude Duval, and this is my horse, Nightshade!"

A tremendous cheer burst from the throats of several persons in the "Bedford Head," and there was a great crashing of glass, as a man, of more corpulency than activity, rolled over the front of the bar into the passage.

"Do you mean to say you are the great Claude Duval?"

"Claude Duval is my name—you may call me what else you like."

"Down with him, then, family men all! Down with him at once! Steady! Steady!"

Duval hardly knew whether to construe this into a menace or not.

But he was not a little surprised to feel the flooring on which Nightshade stood, moving under him.

"No tricks!" he cried. "Beware!"

"We must be at some tricks, Claude Duval, for don't you hear that battering at the door of the old 'Bedford Head?'"

"Am I among friends or foes?"

"Friends to the backbone, of course. They shall pull the old crib down, brick by brick, before they find you; and perhaps not then.

Duval could hardly form a conjecture as to what was about to happen.

"Steady! steady does it!" cried the corpulent man, in a thick unctuous voice—"steady does it! There we go!"

The particular part of the passage flooring on which Nightshade stood began slowly to descend.

Duval heard the creaking of the pulleys, and then he began to have an idea of what was happening.

He was being initiated into one of the mysteries of the ancient thieves' hostel.

CHAPTER XLVIII.

CLAUDE DUVAL VISITS THE THIEVES' "KEEP" IN COVENT GARDEN.

DUVAL was perfectly well aware now, however, that there was no danger; and it was no bad thing, situated as he was frequently, in the midst of many perils, that there was such a haven of safety as the "Bedford Head."

It was evidently a trap-door upon which he and his horse stood.

The space below it was about twelve feet in depth.

But that was soon reached, and then Duval heard a confusion of voices, as if many persons were conversing together, heedless of what each other said, but only intent upon giving the loudest expression to their own sentiments.

These many discordant voices were mixed up likewise with several persons singing.

But still the confusion of sounds came with a subdued murmur to the ears of Duval.

The place—be it cellar or be it kitchen—into which he had descended with Nightshade had no occupants whatever, so that when the moveable platform touched the ground, which it did with a sudden jerk, Duval found his position rather lonely.

He glanced about him with curiosity and interest.

One dimly-burning tallow candle lit the cellar-like place, and that was stuck in the rudest possible candlestick, made of a lump of clay sticking fast against a rough brick wall.

Not for many moments, however, was Duval left to his own reflections.

A voice from above called down to him.

"Move off the trap! move off the trap, Claude Duval, and let it come up again!"

A slight impulse to Nightshade was sufficient for the accomplishment of this object, and then Duval and his horse stood upon a hard-beaten earthen floor, while the moveable portion of flooring on which they had descended slowly rose up to its place again, in the passage of the "Bedford Head."

There it became fixed.

Duval heard a sharp sound, as if a piece of machinery suddenly held the platform steady.

But since it was only woodwork that formed the ceiling now above him, he had no difficulty in overhearing what took place in the passage of the hostel.

The sound of the rapid unbarring of the outer door came plainly to his ears.

"Come in! come in!" cried a voice. "What's the disturbance now, and who is wanted?"

There was a sudden rush of footsteps, and then a man spoke in loud, irritated tones.

"This won't do any longer, Simmons. We saw both Duval and his horse leap into the passage."

"You saw what?"

"Claude Duval, the notorious highwayman, and his horse Nightshade,—we saw them both disappear into the house.

"Then you are a lucky fellow, Mr. Godfrey."

"What do you mean?"

"Oh, only that you see what there is to be seen, as well as what there isn't."

"Can you deny it?"

"That would be uncivil. I deny nothing, but I didn't see it; however, if you think your man's here, take him."

"I mean to do so if I have to stay twelve months in the old tavern."

"All's right. Joe! Joe!"

"Yes, sir."

"Order a bed in the blue attic for Mr. Godfrey; he is going to stay here twelve months."

There was now a confusion of voices, and a rush of feet, combined with an imperious order from the officer that the outer door should be well guarded.

Then there was a comparative stillness in the old tavern; and Claude Duval, as he patted the neck of Nightshade, felt perfectly assured that he was in safety.

A broad gleam of light then made its way into the cellar in which he was.

The odour of tobacco—of spirits, accompanied by a rush of heated air—surrounded Duval and Nightshade.

A moment's observation of one of the walls of the place where he was, let him see that there was a doorway from which was being held aside a heavy blackened blanket, which, with its thick impervious folds, not only excluded the light which now streamed into what may be called Duval's cellar, but confused and drowned many of the noises on the other side of it.

"It is somebody!" cried the man who held the blanket on one side. "A link! a link!"

Several men rushed forward, one of whom held a link high above his head, which shed plenty of light about it, as well as a great quantity of sparks, and filled the place with stifling smoke.

Nightshade coughed.

"Why, it's a horse," shouted several voices.

"And its master," said Duval, as he stepped forward, showing himself to the astonished eyes of the men who crowded at the entrance of another and a larger cellar than that which he had occupied so briefly.

Duval had no difficulty whatever in discovering at once who and what these men were.

He had heard quite enough of the old "Bedford Head," at different times, to know that it was the special refuge of men particularly hunted by the law, and who were "wanted" by the police, with heavy rewards for their apprehension.

"A plant!" cried one.

"Nabbed and sold!" shouted another.

"Smash him!" roared a third.

"Gentlemen," said Duval, "please to have a little patience. I fancy by my appearance here you ought to be aware I am not likely to be an enemy."

"Who are you, then?" they shouted, as with one voice.

"Which do you speak to—me or my horse?"

"Both of you—both of you!"

"Then my horse is named Nightshade, and I am generally known as Claude Duval."

A shout of gratification arose from these men, many of whom had not seen the light of day for many months.

"Duval, Duval, for ever! It's the great Duval! Welcome to the old Keep! Why, who would have thought that you, Duval, would ever have had to take refuge at the bottom of the Earthen Pitcher."

Claude recollected that he had heard the cellars at the "Bedford Head" so named before.

He smiled, as he patted Nightshade on the neck, and spoke with that fascinating tone of good fellowship he could so easily assume.

"I have taken refuge here; but it will not be for long, for I have work to do to-night."

"No, no, Duval; you must not leave us. Our lives are none so bright that we can spare good company."

"It must be so," added Duval; "but I may come again, and yet spend a happy hour with you. And that you may be assured I will, I leave you the dearest friend I have on earth, excepting one."

He looked at Nightshade as he spoke.

"Let me ask of you all," he added, "in the name of good fellowship, to be kindly attentive to my horse. I may want him even in the middle of the night, or, it may be, not until the dawn of the morning; but until I do, let him remain here and have food and rest, even as you would give food and rest to me."

"That we will! that we will!" cried every voice.

Then, from a mysterious recess in one of the walls of the wine cellar, the landlord of the "Bedford Head" himself made his appearance.

"Claude Duval," he cried, "name your wishes, and they shall be attended to!"

"Look at me!" said Duval; "I want to go forth into the fading light of day, for it is nearly twilight, I reckon, and this dress is not exactly the one to suit me."

"Oh, we will soon alter all that."

"Provide me, then, with some disguise in which I may walk the streets unmolested, for I have yet much to do before rest can close my eyes. These good friends will look after my horse. Farewell, Nightshade, for a time. The hours will seem to me but weary ones until we meet again."

Duval passed his hand twice or thrice over the glossy mane of Nightshade.

"Come along with me," said Simmons, the landlord of the "Bedford Head." "There is nobody, in all London, though I say it, who can manage a disguise better than I. I'll warrant you may walk out in ten minutes, and bid the chaps at the door good evening, if you like, without their suspecting that you are the most distant cousin of Claude Duval."

The squalid, unshaven-looking men, who occupied that cellar in secret, looked disappointed that they were to be deprived of the excitement of Claude Duval's presence.

"Come! come!" cried the landlord; "drink deep, all of you, and drown care! Follow me, Duval!"

There was a long, narrow passage, dank and dingy.

The walls were merely of hardened clay.

The flooring was kept tolerably dry by a thick stratum of ashes.

Then there was a short flight of steps.

"Tread lightly!" whispered the landlord.

Duval did so, and in a few seconds he heard a creaking sound, and a long, narrow slip of a door was opened.

The warmth of a bright fire fell upon his face.

"Don't speak yet," whispered the landlord again.

Duval almost shrunk back, for it seemed to him that the place to which he was now conducted was dangerous on account of its publicity.

It was the little parlour exactly behind the common bar of the tavern.

Indeed, the only screen between it and that bar appeared to be a partition, the upper part of which was glazed.

But there were many shelves running the whole length of this partition, and those shelves were filled with glasses, punch-bowls, decanters, and bottles of every kind and description.

"Sit down," whispered the landlord,—"sit down quietly, and don't speak. You may be taking off your coat, however, and I'll soon provide you with another."

From a cupboard, in the corner of this little parlour at the back of the bar, the landlord produced a brown paper parcel.

"Now, sir," he said, "I think this will answer your purpose excellently. We keep these things, you see, in regular order, as they may be wanted at a minute's notice."

The parcel contained a long-skirted, dismal-looking black coat, which, even tall as Duval was, would nearly reach to his ankles.

A grey wig.

A common, half-soiled cravat.

A hat that had seen considerable service, and that had a decidedly clerical appearance.

There was a small bottle, likewise, in the parcel, which contained a whitey-brown looking powder.

"This is only a harmless earth," said the landlord, as he emptied some of the powder from the bottle into the palm of his hand; "but it will give you a new complexion. Just hold your head a little this way, and I'll rub it on."

Duval did so.

It seemed nothing but powdered clay, yet its effect was wonderful, and by the glance he gave at himself in a little mirror that hung over the chimney-piece, he saw how effectual was the change in his appearance.

He slipped on the long black coat.

He tied on the soiled cravat.

The landlord adjusted the wig.

And the whole disguise was crowned by the dilapidated hat.

"Capital!" said Simmons. "I should hardly know you myself. Now, we will see what Mr. Godfrey has to say to you."

"What?"

"Godfrey, the officer."

"But——"

"Oh, there's no danger; and there he comes. Well, Mr. Godfrey, any luck? Here is the Rev. Mr. Peterson, who wants to know how much of the reward you will give him if he helps you to catch Claude Duval, and whether you will divide the reward between Claude and his horse."

"Don't talk nonsense, Simmons," said Godfrey. "Give me some brandy. Your fine trade will come to an end some day."

"And where will yours be, Mr. Godfrey, then? Don't we all row in the same boat? Thieves—officers, —receivers?"

"Bah! bah! I tell you what it is, Simmons, I must have Duval."

"Take him."

Duval felt the necessity of playing the part that had been imposed upon him, and resting quite quietly, he stepped into the outer bar as he said, "I wish you good night, then, Mr. Simmons. I feel that I have been too long here already. Your liquors are strong and your tobacco good, and I am quite sure this gentleman—Mr. Godfrey, I think you call him—will be so good as not to say that he saw me here. My flock are rather particular, but we are all human—all human, Mr. Godfrey—we are all frail—frail—we are all——"

"Go to the deuce!" said Godfrey. "I don't want a sermon."

Duval stalked down the passage of the "Bedford Head," and encountered two officers, who kept watch and ward at its door.

They were Claude's old acquaintances, Swallow and Muckles.

He felt that a critical moment had arrived, and that his danger was something great.

"Who is this, Mr. Godfrey?" cried Muckles. "Did you see this long fellow coming out of the old crib? Do you know him, sir?"

"Oh, yes, yes. Let him go."

"All right, sir."

Muckles stepped aside, and Duval walked composedly out into the open air.

Then Swallow laid his finger by the side of his nose, and looked sagacious.

An indistinct vision of the glory he would achieve in capturing Claude Duval entirely by his own sagacity came over him.

"Muckles," he said.

"What now?"

"I'll be back in ten minutes, unless you particularly want me."

"Be off—I never particularly want you."

Claude Duval had got to the corner of the Piazzas of Covent Garden, and in the rapidly-increasing twilight his figure was beginning to get indistinct.

Swallow ran after him.

"Sir! sir!"

Duval paused.

Swallow placed his hand upon his arm.

"Will you be so good as to say who you are?"

Duval caught Swallow by the hand and drew his arm beneath his own, where he held it with a vicelike clutch.

"Of course, my dear Swallow, I can have no hesitation in telling you who I am, any more than telling you what you may be in two seconds. I am Claude Duval, and you will be a livid corpse, with the top of your skull blown off, if you happen to be more obstinate than prudent."

CHAPTER XLIX.

SWALLOW MAKES A COMPACT WITH CLAUDE DUVAL.

THE look with which Swallow regarded Claude Duval, under any other than the serious circumstances of the present, must have appeared to him most essentially ludicrous.

It was a look at once compounded of fear, anger, and admiration.

"You don't mean to say——"

"I have said it," interrupted Claude; "and let me add one remark, Swallow—which is, that on various occasions I have noticed you to be a very prudent man."

"Oh!"

"A man who was not disposed to run his own life into danger in order to make uncomfortable some one else's."

"But——"

"A man," added Duval, "who looked at the world with a practical eye, and when he found out that he was——"

"Done brown," interrupted Swallow.

"Exactly—he put up with it like a philosopher, and made the best of the situation."

"I don't know what's a philosopher," said Swallow, "but I do know that a fellow never was done browner than I am just now."

"My dear Swallow, there is a well-known fable——"

"About what?"

"Catching a Tartar."

Swallow made a grimace.

"I dare say you recollect it. In a campaign with the Tartars, a soldier called out that he had caught one."

"Oh! did he?"

"He did; and his comrades requested him to bring the prisoner along."

"Oh! I know—the Tartar wouldn't come; and then when they told him to come himself, the Tartar wouldn't let him."

"Exactly, Swallow. You look like a soldier."

"Don't be making game of a fellow, as well as holding his arm as if it was in an iron vice. You want me to say you're the Tartar, I suppose."

DUVAL AND LADY DOMINICK AT THE PALACE BALL.

"As you please. It is a fine night!"

By sheer strength and main force, still holding Swallow's arm with a frightful tension, Duval walked along.

They were completely out of sight of Mr. Muckles. Then Swallow spoke, with a groan.

"Mr. Duval."

"Mr. Swallow."

"What's to be the end of it?"

"The end of what?"

"You and me. How can we go on in this kind of way? I'm always nabbing you, you know, and then being done brown."

"It is diverting," said Duval.

"Oh! is it?"

"To me—exceedingly."

Swallow seemed to be considering for a few moments.

Then he spoke again, and this time in a lower tone of voice.

"Mr. Duval."

"Well, Mr. Swallow."

"If I wasn't an officer, I think I should like to be a highwayman."

"Indeed!"

"Yes, Mr. Duval; and it seems to strike me now, that as I can't nab you, let me try what I will, we may as well be friends."

"I do not precisely understand you, Swallow."

"They're always a jeering at me at Newgate, and in Bow Street, at the old Compter, and thereaway by Bridewell. Wherever I go, they've always got a joke at my expense, and it's generally to ask me if I've nabbed Claude Duval!"

"Well?"

"I was thinking, then, Mr. Duval, that if you want anybody to help you—to be a friend to you—to go about with you—and look after your horse, and do you all sorts of good offices—I'm your man."

"I think not, Swallow. You are too useful as you are—too amusing."

"What do you mean, Mr. Duval?"

"Why, my good fellow, if I take you out of the

No. 16.—NIGHTSHADE.

constabulary, there will be somebody put in your place who may be troublesome instead of amusing; whereas you are quite the reverse, don't you perceive?"

"Yes; I see."

Duval then dropped his arm.

"Nevertheless, Swallow, I am grateful for your offer of service; and if you really do me a good turn, even for the sake of those who are dear to me, and to whom my life is everything, it shall not go unrewarded."

"Very well, Mr. Duval, then that's a bargain. But I'm afraid of one thing."

"And what may that be?"

"You will never trust me."

"Indeed, will I!"

"If I thought that, and if I really had the laugh at them, and when they thought I was done brown I was in reality doing them ever so much browner, I should not mind a bit; but you'll never trust me—I'm sure you won't."

"You misjudge me, Swallow. I have always gained by trusting, and always lost by suspicion. Wait till we meet again, and you will see that Claude Duval is above petty doubts and surmises concerning the good faith of any one who professes to do him service; and so, good night."

"Mr. Duval?"

"What more would you say?"

"Tell me what you're about to-night, and I'll see if I can't be your friend?"

"I am going to visit the Duchess of Cleveland. I want to ask her advice as to which is the best course to take to rescue Lucy Everton from death, and what she advises I will do, even at the peril of my life."

As Duval spoke, he walked away.

The intellect of Swallow must have been very obtuse indeed, if he did not see that this last action of Claude Duval's was in reality trustful of him to a degree, since he, Swallow, had his pistols in his pocket, and Duval never once turned his head to see what he was about.

"I won't be done brown any more!" muttered Swallow. "They've had their laugh at me, and now I'll have mine at them; and I like Claude Duval better than I do the whole lot of them put together. He's a gentleman, he is,—a real highflier; and he shan't go to the bad if I can help it."

Duval walked rapidly down towards the Strand.

He soon forgot the little episode with Swallow, and his thoughts flew back to Newgate, and the dreary cell occupied by his Lucy.

In his frank, careless manner, Duval had spoken nothing but the truth when he said he was bound upon a visit to the Duchess of Cleveland.

"Yes," he said to himself, as he reached Charing Cross; "I will see her, and endeavour to interest her in the preservation of Lucy. There is a romantic tenderness and generosity of feeling about the Duchess, which, I am sure, will induce her to do what she can."

Duval was reasoning with himself; for he had a kind of inward conviction that the young and handsome Duchess of Cleveland would rather go out of her way to do something for him personally, than for any woman that breathed.

The young Duchess occupied a handsome house in Whitehall, which Duval soon reached.

His hand failed him as he glanced up at it, for it was in complete darkness.

"Alas!" he said. "She has left town, and that hope has died away."

He rapped, however, at the hall door.

A half-sleepy porter answered it.

"Is the Duchess within?"

"No, nor won't be till to-morrow morning."

"Is she at Kew?"

"I should rather think not, when all the world is at the King's ball at St. James's. Where do you come from, sir, that you don't know what's going on in the world?"

"In your little world, you mean," said Duval. "Mine may lie outside it, and be somewhat larger."

"Now, what does he mean by that?" said the man, rubbing his head, as Duval walked away. "Some impudence, I suppose. Howsomedver, it's something stoopid, for I don't understand it."

Duval took his way up Pall Mall; and then he soon found abundant evidences of the fact that some grand entertainment was taking place at St. James's Palace.

The desire to see the young Duchess grew upon him each moment, until he found it impossible to chase it from his mind.

But how was he to accomplish that object, unless he could make his way into the Palace?

Was that difficult?

It was.

But was it possible?

Certainly not.

Duval stood in a doorway at the corner of St. James's Street, and reflected.

What could he do?

Under what pretence, and in what guise, could he make his way into the presence of royalty?

Then he told himself that surely the following morning might answer all the purpose of speaking to the Duchess.

But would she be visible—and when?

It might be mid-day, or long past it, before she would rise, after the fatigues of that royal entertainment, and be sufficiently recovered to be even told that a visitor desired to see her.

That consideration decided him.

"I must and will speak to her this night."

There was a loud scream from St James's Street.

A trampling of horses.

A swearing of coachmen and footmen.

The crash of some carriage-pole into the panels of another.

Duval mechanically darted round the corner, and was first among the rush of people who made their way to the handsome chariot, in which sat a young lady in an extremity of terror, on account of the accident that had occurred.

The horses in the chariot were restive and plunging.

The coachman had either been thrown from his box, or had thrown himself off; and Duval, perceiving what a world of terror was depicted in the pale face of the young lady, he immediately opened the door of the vehicle, and, taking her lightly in his arms, lifted her from it.

"Oh, thank heaven!" she cried. "I am safe now!"

Duval crossed the pavement with two strides, and entered the first shop-door he saw open.

"A little water," he said. "I fear the lady is fainting. Close the door too, to keep out the rabble."

The people in the shop promptly obeyed him—for Duval had a peculiar way of giving his orders, which made them exceedingly imperative.

He placed the young lady in an arm-chair, and, for a few moments, was alone with her—as both the persons who were in the shop ran in separate directions—one up-stairs and one down—to get the water he had ordered.

"Cheer yourself," whispered Duval, "there is no danger now. All is well; and I trust you are perfectly unhurt."

The young lady looked up in his face.

Duval smiled.

He forgot that the disguise which had been put

upon him by Mr. Simmons, of the "Bedford Head," somewhat impaired his good looks.

"I think I must go home," said the young lady, faintly.

"Nay," said Duval, as he glanced at her dress, which was richly jewelled, "if you were going to the King's ball, there is no occasion to turn back, for you are within a hundred paces of the Palace door."

"But where is my cousin Dominick?"

Duval shook his head.

"I have certainly not the pleasure of knowing."

"He was to have met me; but he is so careless; and my aunt will be so alarmed. Oh, what shall I do?"

"I am hardly able to advise," added Duval; "but this packet and book that you have dropped, permit me to say you are somewhat careless of."

"They are the tickets."

"For the ball?"

"Yes; mine and my cousin Dominick's."

Duval paused for a moment.

"Is this chance," he said, "or providence?"

He glanced then round the shop.

It was a fashionable tailor's, such as abounded in that locality more at the period of our story than even at the present.

"Here's the water for the dear young thing!" cried the tailor's wife, making a frantic rush into the shop from the upper regions of the house.

But it so happened that the tailor himself at that same moment arrived from below with a huge pitcher of water, as though he expected the young lady to bathe in it.

The conjunction of events was fatal.

The tailor ran against his wife.

His wife ran against the tailor.

There was a crash of a jug and a pitcher, and not only the young lady, but Claude Duval likewise, were plentifully drenched with cold water.

"Stupid!" cried the tailor.

"Idiot!" shrieked his wife.

The young lady actually laughed.

The alarm had subsided, and this little incident, with its sudden comicality, did her more good than anything else.

With that ready adaptation, then, to circumstances, which formed a feature in the character of Claude Duval, he glanced down at his long black coat, which was dripping with the deluge that had been thrown over it.

"I think," he said to the tailor, "I must trouble you for a change of garments."

"Certainly, sir," was the immediate reply, "if your reverend worship will step into the warehouse."

Duval turned to the young lady, and spoke in those low sweet accents, which in him were not an assumption, since they were natural to him.

"May I hope that you will not be gone when I return?"

The young lady did not see the absolute necessity of the strange gentleman getting a change of clothing, because some water was sprinkled on his coat, but after a moment's hesitation she said, "No."

Duval accompanied the tailor to his wareroom.

"Here sir," said the officious shop-keeper, "is the very article that will suit you—a coat so like your own that you wouldn't know one from the other. Perhaps I have the pleasure of speaking to a gentleman in the law or the Church?"

"It is better," said Duval, "not to speak at all, unless respectfully, to a nobleman who may choose for once in a way to wear a plain garment, such as this."

"I beg your lordship's pardon."

Duval made a grimace.

"You are wrong again," he said, 'but it matters not."

The tailor bowed low.

"I ought to have said, I beg your Grace's pardon."

"That's better," said Duval.

He had retained the little card case which the young lady had dropped in the shop.

One glance had enabled him to see the names upon the two tickets of admission to the royal ball.

The Duke of Montecute.

Lady Lizzy Dominick.

The former of these cards, Duval had made up his mind should be his credential beneath the roof of royalty.

CHAPTER L.

CLAUDE DUVAL SUCCEEDS IN HIS DESIRE TO ATTEND THE KING'S BALL.

THE tailor stood rubbing his hands together, and looking inquiringly in the face of Duval.

"It is too late now to go home," said Claude.

"A great deal too late, your Grace," replied the tailor, without the least idea of why or wherefore it should be so.

"I mean too late to go home to dress for the King's ball."

That was quite understandable; so the tailor brightened up, and said, "Yes, certainly, your Grace."

"Therefore," added Claude, "if you have a very handsome Court suit, that you really think will fit me, I will put it on here."

"Twenty!" cried the tailor.

"Good! Be quick about it!"

From the well-lined shelves of his warehouse, the tailor produced a magnificent suit of velvet.

In ten minutes Claude Duval was fully attired; and, as the tailor held a small hand mirror before him, Duval saw that he only required to wash off from his face the stains of the yellow-looking clay which Mr. Simmons had placed upon it, to be himself again.

"Water."

"Yes, your Grace."

"Soap."

The tailor obsequiously held both to Duval.

The grey wig was flung into a corner—the yellow clay was thoroughly cleansed from the face and moustache of Duval.

"A comb."

One was produced, and in a few seconds Claude had arranged his really beautiful hair most becomingly.

The tailor obsequiously presented him with a Court sword of bright polished steel; and then Duval drew himself up to his full height, and felt that he was presentable in any Court in Christendom.

The young lady uttered a slight scream at sight of him.

The transformation was too complete for her yet to believe that he was the same person who had rescued her from the broken carriage.

But his voice re-assured her; and the smile with which he greeted her had already made too much impression upon her to be easily forgotten.

"Do you so soon forget," he said, "one who feels as though he had known you for an age?"

"Oh, no, no! I can never forget."

"His Grace looks charming," exclaimed the tailor.

"His Grace?" said the young lady. "Is this possible?"

"We live in a world of wonders," said Duval, "in which all things are possible. I was myself about to proceed to the King's ball, but ——"

"But what?" said the young lady, faintly.

"I was to meet my cousin."

"Your cousin?"

"Yes; the Lady Araminta."

"A lady?"

Duval sighed.

"It is very strange," added the young lady, echoing the sigh, "but, as I think I have already told you, I was to meet my cousin Dominick, as we call him, although he is the Duke of Montecute."

"Two Graces?" cried the tailor.

"Be quiet," said Duval, "and keep your distance. I grieve that I am not in possession of the name by which I may have the honour of addressing one who will need no name to live in my remembrance."

"I am Lizzy Dominick."

"Stranger still," said Duval. "The name is charming, and, therefore, well suits its owner."

"It appears to me," said the young lady, looking down while a slight flush came over her face——

She paused.

"You hesitate," said Duval, "and will not speak to me frankly."

"I was going to say, that if you are complimentary, you should reserve such speeches for your cousin, the Lady Araminta."

"There," said Duval, "is the great difficulty. The whole family on all sides are bent upon my union with her; but alas——"

"Alas what?"

"I do not love her."

"Then it would be exceedingly wrong," said the young lady, speaking with animation,—"it would be exceedingly wrong for you to marry her."

"So wrong, that I have not the slightest intention of doing so. But is it not very singular that your cousin was to meet you and escort you to the royal ball, and I was to meet my cousin and escort her?"

"But that is very different," said Lady Lizzy Dominick,—"that is very different indeed. My cousin is a gentleman, and holds high office about the person of the King. He was merely coming out of the Palace to look for my carriage in St. James's Street, and accompany me into the royal saloons, but your cousin Araminta, as a lady, could hardly meet you."

"You do not understand me. She comes from her home at Kensington, and takes me up in her carriage; but alas! I fear."

"You fear what?"

"That then the parallel between our fortunes and destinies ceases."

"I do not understand you."

Duval sighed.

"My cousin may be distasteful to me, but yours may be the embodiment of all your youthful dreams."

"I detest him," said the young lady.

There was a silence then for a few seconds between them; and then, as they were both attracted by some bustle and conversation at the door of the tailor's shop, the young lady, as if unconscious of the act, placed her hand in that of Duval.

"Your Grace," said the tailor, bustling forward, "the carriage is all right, with the exception of the broken panel, and the pole of the other coach did not come through the lining."

Then Duval spoke in a low tone to Lady Lizzy Dominick.

"Let us forget these two cousins, alike distasteful to each of us. Let us proceed to the Court ball together, and its pleasures and glittering delights will not be the less esteemed by either of us from the fact that we have reached there in pleasanter company than we expected."

"It is wrong," said Lady Lizzy.

"But so pleasant!"

"It is indiscreet."

"And yet delightful."

Duval led her to the door.

The carriage that had been so slightly injured—for a great deal of bustle on these occasions is produced by very trifling causes—stood awaiting their reception.

The coachman and two footmen looked somewhat surprised to see their young mistress accompanied by a stranger, but that stranger had so distinguished an air, and was so magnificently attired, that they never dreamt for a moment of raising the slightest question in regard to his social position.

Indeed, if they had had any scruples about him they would all have been set at rest by the incessant manner in which the tailor kept calling Claude Duval "Your Grace."

The young lady was handed gallantly into the carriage.

Duval sprang in lightly after her.

"To the Palace," he said, "as quickly as may be."

The chariot fell into the line of equipages, and Claude Duval, as he sat as far back as he could, so as to be out of the range of casual observation, made a suggestion to Lady Lizzy Dominick.

"Should your cousin, the Duke, recognise the carriage, perhaps you would not mind me answering him?"

The young lady was silent, but Duval could see that she shrank back as far as possible into the corner she occupied, so as not to be seen.

This was a practical answer, and it so happened that there was no time now for words before the event took place which Duval anticipated.

The carriage was going but at a foot pace, for those that preceded it had to set down their occupants, which, quickly as it was done, yet took up some time.

A gloved hand was laid upon the window of the carriage.

"Lizzy, are you here?" asked a voice.

"Sir!" replied Duval in a deep tone, and with excessive gravity.

The hand was removed in a moment.

"I beg your pardon, sir. I could have sworn that this was the chariot of the Lady Lizzy Dominick."

"Do not take rash oaths, young man," added Duval, in the same deep, sepulchral tones.

"Well, sir, there is no offence, I hope?"

"Not yet; but there may be. Therefore I will take the liberty of closing the window of my own coach."

With a rattle and a dash, Duval drew up the window and settled it in its place.

The carriage went on.

For a moment or two Duval was in doubt as to how Lady Lizzy would take this summary dismissal of her cousin, the noble Duke.

He turned to look at her, but that part of St. James's Street was very dark, and he could but dimly see her fair young face.

Slight sounds, however, of half-smothered laughter, as she pressed her handkerchief to her mouth, reassured him.

"That was excellent, she said. "Dominick will now go hunting up and down St. James's Street, for the next hour."

"Will he?"

"Indeed he will! And what a dreadful tone of voice you spoke in!"

"Are my tones dreadful?"

"Not to me."

At this moment the carriage reached the entrance to the Palace.

Its door was opened by a couple of the royal footmen, and an official from the Lord Chamberlain's office stepped forward with a golden salver in his hand.

There was no mistaking what that was for, and Duval placed upon it the two tickets he had, in a manner of speaking, received from the young lady.

"The Duke of Montecute and the Lady Lizzy Dominick!"

With something of a bewildered look, the young lady hung upon the arm of Claude Duval, and looked up in his face.

"You personate my cousin?"

"I pay him that compliment."

"But——"

"Are you angry with me?"

"No; and yet it is very strange."

"Stop! stop! Stop them! Something wrong! Stop! stop! I knew it was the chariot! Lizzy! Lizzy! Lizzy! Stop! stop!"

These cries proceeded from some one at the door of the Palace, who was making energetic efforts to pass the officials who were there on duty.

"My cousin!" ejaculated the Lady Lizzy Dominick.

Duval turned sharply round.

"Remove that impostor!" he said.

The word was taken up at once by the royal footmen, and they all shouted "An impostor! an impostor! Remove the impostor!"

"Fear nothing," added Duval, in his gentlest tones, as he led the Lady Lizzy along the grand corridor of the Palace, where they were preceded by a royal page, whose duty it was to conduct the guests as fast as they arrived into one of the reception saloons.

CHAPTER LI.

CLAUDE DUVAL RECEIVES GOOD ADVICE FROM THE DUCHESS OF CLEVELAND.

The scene was a brilliant one.

There was but the one drawback, which always attended the royal entertainments at St. James's.

The rooms are of considerable extent; and, in fact, by the removal of partitions, can be almost indefinitely increased.

But the ceilings are low.

The whole effect is marred by that circumstance.

Duval's eyes, however, were fixed upon the glittering throng before him; and now, anxious as he had been to associate himself with the young lady who leant so confidentially upon his arm, in order that he might make his way into the Palace, having succeeded in that object, he was almost as anxious to be rid of her, in order that he might pursue his inquiries for the Duchess of Cleveland.

There was a magnificent settee, covered with rich crimson velvet and trimmed with bullion, on which several ladies were sitting, conversing.

Towards that, Duval led Lady Lizzy Dominick.

"I have a few words," he said, "to say to a nobleman of my acquaintance. May I leave you for a short time?"

"For a short time," said Lady Lizzy, faintly.

Duval saw that she followed him with her eyes.

But the royal saloons were of vast extent, opening from one to another past gilded columns wreathed with flowers; and as numerous guests had already arrived, and momentarily others were filling the saloons, Duval had no difficulty in soon getting out of sight of his fair young companion.

He stood somewhat apart in the recess of a window, and gazed earnestly upon the throngs of elegantly dressed persons, who with all their uniforms, Court dresses, silks, satins, waving plumes, and glittering diamonds, seemed to arrange themselves before his eyes in the grotesque combinations of a kaleidoscope.

But he saw nothing of the Duchess of Cleveland.

In vain he looked for her slight figure and fair face, beneath some one or other of the plumes of feathers which it was then the fashion of the ladies to wear.

Suddenly some one strode up to him.

It was a gentleman in crimson velvet, with a star upon his breast.

"Sir, will you favour me with your name?"

"Certainly not," said Duval. "Pray be contented, sir, with your own."

"This is foolish badinage, sir. I am the Duke of Montecute."

"It may be so."

"I saw your back, sir—the side of your face, sir—and I cannot be mistaken!"

"It may be so," said Duval, with a incredulous shake of his head. "There are men in this world who think themselves infallible."

"What do you mean, sir?"

"Simply that I have not your amount of conceit; for I own to having been mistaken twice or thrice in my life."

"I will soon put an end to this!" cried the Duke of Montecute. "I don't believe you are anybody, sir!"

"Nay, your Grace. Look at me again. Am I all legs and head?"

"Oh, I dare say you think that a capital joke, but we will see on which side the laugh will lie. Be so good as to wait a few moments. The Deputy Chamberlain is in the saloons."

The Duke of Montecute ran off in a very undignified fashion.

"No," said Duval, to himself, "I will not be so good as to wait a few moments."

He glided off instantly, and made his way rapidly along the tapestried walls to the ball-room, which was a large apartment looking into the Ambassadors' Court.

This room was brilliantly lighted, and already some hundreds of persons were promenading in it, to the great detriment of the beauty of the flooring, the plain wood of which had been coloured by crayons to imitate a magnificent carpet.

But all this magnificence and lavish expenditure had no interest in the eyes of Claude Duval.

On the contrary, they only brought an additional pang to his heart, as in thought and memory he flew back to the dreary cell in Newgate, where Lucy was languishing.

Anxiously and carefully, he looked about him in the hope that the bright, fair face of the Duchess of Cleveland would meet his eyes.

But he could see nothing of her, and a feeling of heart-sickness came over him, as he thought that the scheme upon which he had set his mind, of seeing the young Duchess, would, after all the trouble and all the difficulty he had had to gain admission to that royal ball, prove a failure.

Duval retired into the recess of a bay window, there to reflect upon what he had better do under the circumstances, when the murmur of voices, not far distant, met his ear.

"I tell you," said a voice, "that she is here, and I am resolved once more to try my good fortune, by extorting from her fears what I have ceased to obtain from her generosity."

"But the letters?", asked another voice. "Surely, with such documents as those in your possession, the fair Duchess can be easily brought to terms."

An exclamation of rage burst from the lips of the first speaker, as the letters were referred to; and Duval now had no difficulty in naming the first speaker to himself, as Colonel Jessop, and the fair Duchess who had been mentioned, he had not the slightest doubt in his own mind, was the Duchess of Cleveland.

"What's the matter now, Jessop?" Duval heard the other voice say—"what's the matter, man? anyone, to see you, would think that instead of those letters giving you full power over the wilful little Duchess, that they were rather a barrier to your success."

"I have them not!" hissed the voice of Colonel Jessop.

"Have them not? What mean you?"

"I mean that they were stolen from me by a fiend —a villain!"

"Stolen from you? That was your look out, Jessop. I should have given you credit for being more careful, when so much depended upon their being in safe custody. It seems to me, that had I possessed such a key to her vast property, that I should never have considered them safe, but about my person, and then I should like to see the man who would have wrested them from me!"

"I told you that it was a fiend who robbed me of them, and sometimes I verily believe that it was the Fiend himself, and none other."

"You make me curious to hear more. We are alone here, and unobserved; tell me what you intend to do."

Duval was glad to find that his place of concealment was quite secure from the observation of those who were plotting the destruction of one to whom he, Duval, felt he owed his life, for he hoped that he might again be enabled to step between the Duchess and the arch-villlain, who, for his own mercenary purposes, was endeavouring to compass her destruction.

Again he heard the voice of Jessop.

"I came here to-night," he said, "fully prepared to meet the Duchess, and warn her that, although she had succeeded in obtaining possession of some of her letters, written years ago, when we were both younger and more innocent than we are now——"

"Younger, Jessop? Why, she must have been a mere child!"

"Not much more; but that is not to the purpose. I intend to frighten her, by telling her that I still possess two letters which I shall take the first opportunity of showing to the Duke, as having been written to me after she became his wife."

"Have you such letters?"

"Yes, I have two letters, but they never were really written by her; but they will answer the purpose, for, fortunately, just before they were taken from me, my sister, who has no difficulty in imitating any hand-writing she has once seen, made a copy of one or two of the most affectionate, and signed them so inimitably that the Duchess herself would be puzzled to detect the——"

"Forgery," said the other voice.

"Nay, McIntyre. Give it not such a name as that."

"Bravo, Jessop; I think you will be able yet to get the better of the little Duchess; and yet, what I remember of her—and it is at least five years since I saw her—she had a certain courage and strong will of her own, which kept at bay anything like——"

"Bah! you forget that she once loved me. That I was, in fact, her first love; and a woman never wholly hates one who has been the idol of her girlish affections, such as I was."

"Villain!" said Duval to himself. "Is it possible that there is so black a heart in any man's breast, who can thus systematically plot the destruction of a young and beautiful woman, reckoning even upon the mouldering embers of a love which has passed away."

The companion of Jessop, whom he had named McIntyre laughed as he said, "You are a clever fellow, Jessop, and I wish you success with all my heart; but look there, there is the very person we are talking about."

Duval, as soon as he heard these words, walked leisurely from the concealment in the window, in which he had heard the foregoing conversation; for he had no doubt in his own mind, that the exclamation of Jessop's companion alluded to the fair Duchess herself."

Duval looked eagerly and anxiously about him; and was soon gratified by seeing that the Duchess of Cleveland was seated upon an ottoman about the centre of the apartment, talking to some ladies.

"Now is my time," said Duval, "to speak to the Duchess, and see if I can interest her in favour of my poor Lucy; and, at the same time, I shall have an opportunity of putting her on her guard, respecting the little plot those two precious villains have been concocting."

Duval approached the ottoman in a leisurely manner, when the Duchess happening to raise her eyes, encountered his gazing at her.

She gave a slight start, and turned pale, but instantly recovering herself, she held out her hand to him, saying, as she did so, "This is an unexpected pleasure, and I was just looking for a cavalier to escort me to a cooler seat than the one I at present occupy; for this apartment is exceedingly warm and oppressive."

"Allow me then, Duchess, the honour of escorting you wherever it may be your pleasure to go, and I shall consider myself only too happy in being of service to——"

Whatever Duval was about to say was abruptly put a stop to by the Duchess taking his arm, and leading him as quickly as possible in another direction from the one in which he was about to take.

"This way, this way!" she whispered, nervously; "I have been looking for you to warn you that it is rumoured you are in the Palace."

"Indeed?"

"Yes. Oh, why do you risk so much for nothing?"

There was a slight quiver of the lips as the Duchess spoke; and Duval felt her hand tremble beneath his arm.

"I ventured here to see you, Duchess. Will you blame me?"

"To see me?"

"Yes; to ask your advice—your sympathy—your assistance."

"Thank heaven! Speak, Claude Duval; and tell me if there is aught within my power that will be possible for me to do, and you will see that when I told you you had my eternal gratitude they were not mere words of form, but they came from the heart that but for you would have been blighted for ever."

"I know it, I feel it," replied Duval, in his kindest accents; and, therefore, I have dared all perils. I sought you here to-night because I feared to put off till to-morrow what I wish to say to you."

"Speak quickly; we may be interrupted."

Duval drew a long breath, as he said, "I have sought you, Duchess, to ask your advice as to the course I had better pursue with regard to——"

"To whom?"

"To my dear wife, Lucy Everton."

"Lucy Everton, your wife?"

"Even so, Duchess; and, perhaps, you may have heard her sad story."

"Yes, yes; I have heard that she is accused of the murder of her uncle George Everton; but that she managed to escape even when actually on the scaffold. Some one took her away, and——"

"Claude Duval rescued that innocent girl from an ignominious death, afterwards made her his wife, and left her one fair morning in her beauty and gentleness; and when he returned, instead of finding his bride, he found only a desolate home, for Lucy had been recaptured, and thrown into Newgate, to again answer for a crime of which she was as innocent in thought even as the fair and beautiful Duchess to whom I am now speaking."

"Alas, alas! How can I aid you?"

"You have great influence at Court. Can you not devise some means by which the King may be made to interest himself in her behalf, and thereby save my Lucy, and earn my eternal gratitude and esteem?"

"And you love this Lucy Everton?"

"Dearer than life itself. Life, without her, is but a living death; and if I succeed not in saving her, I have resolved that two shall die at Tyburn instead of one the day she is murdered, for it will be a murder if she suffers the penalty of the law."

"Dearer than life itself," repeated the Duchess to herself, in a low tone, as she dropped her eyes to the floor. "Yes, I will try—I will dare all to restore happiness to him." Then turning to Claude, she said, "I must think over it to-night. Breakfast with me to-morrow at twelve o'clock, and I will then make known to you my decision."

"Thanks, thanks—a thousand thanks!" said Claude, as he pressed her hand. "You give me new life—new hope!"

As he spoke, a smile of great sweetness lit up his expressive countenance, and the Duchess wondered not that he was indeed the heart's idol of the innocent girl whom she had promised to do her best to save.

CHAPTER LII.

CLAUDE DUVAL IS IN GREAT PERIL AT ST. JAMES'S PALACE.

CLAUDE DUVAL was half satisfied.

He had accomplished what he came to the Palace for, inasmuch as had spoken to the Duchess of Cleveland, and had received the advise she had offered him.

But still the result was all mystery and darkness.

It might be that that influential Court beauty had the power, and would exert that power to save Lucy Everton.

Or it might be that an idle hour passed in his society the following morning would be the end of all his hopes and expectations in that quarter.

And yet it was hard to believe so much of the young and enthusiastic Duchess.

"No," said Duval to himself, as he made his way through the throng of courtly guests, "she surely will not play either a false or a heartless game with me."

Duval was standing near the end of one of the royal saloons.

He saw all eyes directed in one quarter, and a heavy hanging of crimson cloth slowly separated, revealing beyond it the banqueting-room of the Palace.

The hour had arrived when the royal guests were invited to sup.

Duval had no appetite for the delicacies that lay heaped up upon the tables.

He thought but of returning as quickly as possible; for the silence and solitude even of Hampstead Heath, in the dimmest hour of the night, would have been more welcome to him then than all the glare and magnificence of the Palace of St. James's.

The King's private band, and that of some of the household troops, had alternately kept up a clangour of music for the whole evening.

Those sounds had now ceased, however.

They were only to be replaced by others.

A chorus of trumpets played a royal salute.

And as these martial sounds came ringing through the assembly, each gentleman offered his arm to a lady to lead her to the banquet.

Duval would gladly have escaped, but he found it was impossible.

A light hand was laid upon his arm.

"You are here still," said a gentle voice. "Who and what are you? and what dreadful things are they my cousin Montecute has been saying?"

"What savage could say dreadful things to you?" replied Duval, evasively, as, with courtly grace, he offered his arm to the Lady Lizzy Dominick.

In two minutes more they were seated at the King's supper-table.

It was an old custom then at the Court of St. James's for the King to have a golden flagon presented to him, which he just touched with his lips, saying, as he did so, "A welcome to all present!"

Then, as the words escaped the mouth of the King, a gorgeously-attired herald, stationed in the dusky obscurity of a gallery at the further end of the banqueting-room, produced three or four loud clanging sounds upon his silver trumpet, after which he announced, in a loud, monotonous voice, "His most gracious Majesty the King drinks to the pleasure of the table!"

Then the supper began.

"You must really tell me who and what you are," whispered the Lady Lizzy Dominick.

"A gentleman."

"Oh, I see that, but I want to know what gentleman."

"Would you scream?"

"Why should I?"

Duval laughed.

"Pardon me if I say that is a lady's answer all over. You do not say yes or no, but you ask another question."

"Then answer me like a gentleman, as I have asked you the question like a lady."

"I am afraid then you would scream if I were to tell you who I really am."

"No."

"You are sure not?"

"Perfectly sure. I am strong minded, and can take physic without flinching."

"You allude to the King's canary," said Duval, "which is certainly bad. What now, if I were to tell you I am the Young Pretender?"

"You are no such thing."

"A Jesuit?"

"I don't believe it."

"A highwayman?"

"Oh, nonsense, nonsense."

"Yes, I will stick to the highwayman. Suppose I call myself Claude Duval?"

Lady Lizzy Dominick laughed.

"You had better call yourself something else more likely to be believed."

"But now, just for argument's sake, if I were——"

"If you were what?"

"Claude Duval, the celebrated highwayman. What would you do then? Denounce me, and rejoice over the possibility of bringing me to death?"

"No, I should do no such thing."

Some other court ceremonial at this moment interrupted the dialogue, and the herald in his gay apparel again blew his trumpet with sonorous blasts.

As the last of them echoed through the hall, the King was observed to grasp the gilded elbows of the chair on which he sat, and to incline his head eagerly towards some one who was whispering to him.

It was evident that there was some little dismay among the throng of courtiers immediately surrounding the chair of the King.

One of that throng then advanced a step or two and

cried in a loud voice, "It is his Majesty's pleasure that the doors of the banqueting-room be closed, and kept strictly by the Yeomen of the Guard."

There was the faintest possible flush of colour over the face of Claude Duval.

At the same moment the Lady Lizzy Dominick turned pale, for she was looking at Duval and saw that change take place.

"Does this concern you?" she said, softly.

"Perhaps."

Duval ran his anxious gaze along the table, and caught the pitying glance of the Duchess of Cleveland.

He tore hastily a leaf from a small pocket-book he had with him, and wrote the one word:

"Faint!"

A royal page immediately behind him was touched upon the arm by Duval.

"You will oblige me by placing this in the hands of the Duchess of Cleveland."

The page bowed, and took the small folded piece of paper.

The doors of the banqueting-room were abruptly closed, and a couple of the Yeomen of the Guard crossed their halberts in front of them.

Duval kept his eyes on the Duchess.

He saw her open the paper.

He saw the puzzled look with which she read the one word that was upon it.

The courtier, then, who had given the royal command to close the doors, spoke again.

"Gentlemen, draw your swords and rally round the King! There is an uninvited guest here present, who may be a traitor."

"Gracious heavens!" exclaimed Lady Lizzy Dominick, "what does it mean?"

"It means me!"

"You?"

"Yes,—and if you would save my life, faint at once and make as much confusion as you can!"

The Lady Lizzy uttered a scream, and tumbled headlong into the lap of a high ecclesiastical dignity who sat near her.

Then the Duchess of Cleveland seemed all at once to understand what she was to do, and she uttered a louder scream still, nearly shoving prostrate an old general who sat on her right hand.

The confusion in the banqueting-room was immense.

All the gentlemen rose and drew their swords.

Eight or ten ladies fainted in real earnest.

Several of the candelabra, loaded with wax lights, were upset.

In the midst of this confusion, Duval darted towards the gallery, where the herald, in his quaint, magnificent dress, stiff and ungainly with gold embroidery, did duty with his silver trumpet.

There was a velvet curtain.

Beyond that a narrow flight of stairs.

Duval gained the top of them in six bounds.

He caught the herald by the back of the neck.

"Silence!" he whispered. "A word—a cry—and you are a dead man!"

Fright unnerved the herald completely, and his legs slipping from under him, he came completely to the floor.

"Spare me—spare me! What have I done?"

"Nothing—and, if you wish to live, you will do nothing still."

"Murder!"

"Silence! Sit up."

"I do—I am!"

"Take off your tabard."

The herald was in too great confusion of mind and spirits to obey him; but Duval, with very little difficulty, took off the gorgeous overcoat of the herald.

His cravat, too, was a noticeable object, being a relic from the reign of Elizabeth.

The low-crowned felt hat, likewise,—with its particoloured ribbons—formed an essential part of the costume.

"Speak!" whispered Duval. "Is there anywhere here where you can be bestowed in safety for a brief hour?"

"The cupboard—Clareceux's cupboard!"

"Where is it?"

"In yonder corner, at the end of the gallery. Spare my life!"

"I solemnly pledge myself that no harm shall come to you if you remain perfectly quiet."

"I will—I will!"

The mystified and terrified herald crawled on his hands and knees to the cupboard he had mentioned, and getting entirely within it, closed its door with a snap.

Duval put on the tabard.

The Elizabethan cravat.

The herald's hat.

He seized the silver trumpet.

It was not an instrument on which he was an adept, and, in fact, to the best of his belief, he had never had one to his lips before.

But he was wonderfully successful.

He blew a discordant blast, which echoed through the whole of St. James's Palace, and made the King himself hold both his hands to his ears and utter that volley of bad language at which his Majesty was an adept.

All eyes were directed to the gallery.

"The King drinks to Hamlet!" cried Duval.

"The herald is drunk!" said a voice.

"I know it!" said Duval.

He blew another blast on the trumpet.

"Turn out the scoundrel!" shouted several of the lords-in-waiting. "This is most offensive in the presence of royalty."

There was a rush made up the little staircase.

Duval asked himself one question.

Was he adopting the best course, or not? If the best, he might be turned out of the Palace with ignominy.

If the worst, he might be discovered, and all lost.

The foremost person who reached the gallery was no other than the Duke of Montecute himself.

"What is the meaning of this, scoundrel," he said, "that you have besotted yourself with drink, on duty, in presence of the King?"

Duval was about to make some reply, to keep up his assumed character, when a most singular sound came upon the ears of himself and Lord Montecute.

It was evident that the real herald confined in the cupboard had found there a spare trumpet, and either was recovering his courage sufficiently to give an alarm, or was in that bewildered intellectual condition that he knew not what he did.

Faintly, the trumpet blast came from behind the wainscoting.

"Ah!" cried Lord Montecute, "there is more in this than meets the eye."

"A good deal," said Duval.

"Then you deserve the death that awaits you."

With a savage ferocity the Duke of Montecute made a pass with his drawn sword at Duval.

But Claude was not so easily taken at unawares.

He parried the pass with the silver trumpet, and then, raising it with all his strength, he brought it down with such a crush upon the head of the Duke of Montecute that that noble personage flung his legs from under him and fell prostrate on the instant.

Duval then flew to the door, flimsy and light as it was, at the head of the gallery stairs, and had just time

DUVAL SURPRISES THE MARQUIS OF HARCOURT.

to shoot a couple of brass bolts into their sockets before any one else could make his way into the place.

Practically, he was in the gallery alone.

But that frail door would not for long keep out his enemies.

Nor was it to be supposed that Lord Montecute would remain many minutes in the stunned condition that the blow from the silver trumpet had produced.

Duval felt the necessity of instant action, but in what direction that action was to develope itself he could hardly say.

He looked in vain along the wall of the gallery for some mode of exit other than that by the little staircase.

No door of any kind presented itself but that of the cupboard in which was the defeated herald.

It was almost mechanically, and not with any notion that it would assist him to escape, to do so, that Duval opened that door.

The cupboard was empty.

This was a surprise, and it was a greater one still, to see that the cupboard seemed to be of unlimited extent in depth.

That is to say, all was darkness, where the light from the gallery, faint though it was, ought to have shone upon the wall.

Duval walked hastily forward.

And it was well that he was active and agile, and well able on any emergency to call to his aid all his physical faculties, for, if such had not been the case, he would have experienced a serious fall down a flight of steps which was at the back of the cupboard, and the presence of which had produced that vacancy and darkness that had seemed so mysterious to Claude Duval.

As it was, he slipped down some half-dozen of the steps, and only saved himself from going further by stretching out his arms on either side and pressing the walls closely.

He felt convinced that he had reached some of those mysterious recesses and rarely trodden ways about the old Palace of St. James's which, since it was a religious

No. 17. NIGHTSHADE.

house, so many years ago, had been entirely neglected.

What had become of the herald he could not conceive, but he thought it very probable that there was a door at the back of the cupboard which, when closed, would make a sort of termination wall to it.

There was such a door.

Duval, the moment he found it, closed it; but, although he ran his hand up and down it several times, he could find no fastening.

Perhaps it held close of itself, by some secret contrivance, but, at all events, it interposed some sort of barrier, frail though it was, between him and his foes.

Then Duval, somewhat encumbered by the herald's tabard, which he wore, made his way carefully down the narrow staircase.

The darkness was excessive, but he had retained the silver trumpet in his hand, and, by waving it gently before him, he provided against coming suddenly upon some obstacle which might have done him a mischief.

Then the trumpet struck against some woodwork, and the sound it produced was unmistakably of that character which proclaimed a vacancy beyond.

Simultaneously with the sound of the trumpet upon the wooden panel of what no doubt was a door, Duval heard two screams in rapid succession.

The screams were decidedly feminine, and without doubt arose from some sudden alarm in consequence of the accidental blow he had struck upon the panel with the silver trumpet.

There was then a scuffling of feet, after which all was still.

Duval cautiously moved his hand over the dark panel before him.

Yes, there was a bolt.

It was difficult to move, but he worked it out of the socket, and then judging from the position of the stairs that the door must open inward to the room, he pushed decidedly but cautiously at it.

The door creaked open.

There was a gleam of light.

A feeling of unusual warmth.

The next moment Duval had stepped into a small apartment of the Palace, which was very prettily furnished, and in the grate of which there glowed a bright fire.

Upon the table a supper was laid, apparently for two persons, and by the delicate cambric handkerchief that lay upon one of the chairs, along with a lady's glove, Claude could come to no other conclusion, but that this was a private apartment of some lady attached to the household.

His only wish, however, was to escape as speedily as possible from the Palace, and he looked anxiously about him for the ordinary mode of exit from the room.

He saw a door, and was upon the point of stepping towards it, when it was pushed rapidly open, and a gentleman in elegant Court costume, with a drawn sword in his hand, stepped into the room.

It only took a second glance from Claude Duval to recognize this personage at once.

He was no other than the young Marquis of Harcourt, with whom Claude had had an adventure in the early part of this history on Hampstead Heath, and who had on that occasion been accompanied by the Duke of Montrose, who occupied so very small a place in Duval's esteem.

There was a flush of anger on the face of the young Marquis, and as he held up his sword threateningly, he cried, "What is the meaning of this insolent intrusion?"

CHAPTER LIII.

CLAUDE DUVAL ESCAPES FROM THE PALACE.

NOTHING could be further from the wish of Claude Duval then to enter into any contest with the young Marquis of Harcourt, of whose generosity and kindness of feeling he had already had sufficient proof.

"The intrusion, my Lord Marquis," he said, "is an accidental one, and the intruder is as anxious to rid you of his presence as you can possibly be to preserve the privacy of this apartment?"

There was something in the tones of Duval which evidently struck familiarly upon the ears of the Marquis, but that herald's costume, which would have been sufficient to disguise any one, completely set at nought any immediate recognition.

Duval divined that the young Marquis was asking himself if he had not heard that voice before, and he said, "I perceive that you fancy you know me, my lord, notwithstanding my disguise."

"Disguise?"

Duval raised the herald's hat which he had worn, pressed down as much as possible over his brows.

"Duval?" exclaimed the young Marquis, in surprise.

"Even so," said Claude.

"But tell me," said the Marquis of Harcourt, sheathing his sword. "I do not understand."

"I will be explicit with you," replied Duval. "I came here to-night, to see and ask the advice of a friend who has great influence at Court, as to the best means of saving my poor Lucy."

"Lucy Everton?"

"Yes, my wife."

"Your wife?"

"Yes. You probably know of the crime of which she is accused, but of which she is as innocent as you or I."

"Yes—yes. I always thought so. But tell me, I fancied I had heard she was rescued by——"

"Claude Duval," interrupted Claude.

"Well?"

"I did rescue her. I married her, and had conveyed her to a place of safety, as I thought. I left her one evening, promising to return in a few short hours, but when I did so, expecting to find my bride——"

"Well?"

"The chamber was empty. A scarf, which I remembered to have seen her wear, I found twisted in some of the shrubs surrounding our home, as though a struggle had taken place. I followed the trace of footprints as far as I could do so."

"And discovered no traces of her?"

"No. I saw her not until I again beheld her, heavily ironed, standing at the dock of the Old Bailey."

The young Marquis sighed.

"It is to save this fair, innocent girl—my wife—that I have intruded into these gay and glittering scenes this night—scenes which are so little in accordance with my feelings."

"And have you seen your friend?" asked the Marquis.

"I have; and to-morrow I hope that some means will be devised by which I may save her, or die with her."

"And now, what do you want to do now?"

"To leave this place at once. Will you help me?"

"I will—I will!" said the young Marquis. "Hush! Speak not! Retain your disguise."

The Marquis opened the door of the apartment, and disclosed a passage beyond.

"At the end of this passage," he said, "you will come to a flight of stairs, and then another passage, which will lead you to a court-yard — you understand?"

"I do—I do!" cried Duval. "But here let me thank you."

"Hush! not another word! Do I not owe you my life?" replied the young Marquis. "Follow me quickly; if we encounter no one, I will see you in safety through all these passages, but if I should be compelled to leave you for your own safety's sake, you understand the route you are to take?"

"Perfectly," replied Duval.

"Then come at once, or it may be too late."

Duval followed his young friend along a gallery, and then down the flight of stairs which the Marquis of Harcourt had mentioned, and was just proceeding to traverse another gallery, when at the other end of it two figures made their appearance, which Duval had no difficulty in recognising as the Duke of Montrose and the Duke of Montecute.

They seemed to be in deep conversation, for they did not perceive Duval and his friend.

The Marquis laid his hand upon Claude Duval's arm, as he whispered, "I must leave you now. It will not do for me to be seen with you. Go." Then, raising his voice, he said, "I will return this way; you go and keep guard at the end of the western gallery until you are relieved. Ah, gentlemen!"

"The Marquis of Harcourt!"

"Yes, my lords. I have been endeavouring to see if I could unravel the mystery of this night's doings, but have failed as yet in doing so, although I have taken every precaution, and was even now sending Summers to keep guard at the end of the western gallery."

"It is well," said the Duke of Montecute "I have my suspicions that the uninvited guest has been taking liberties with my name, and thus got admitted into the Palace. By Jove! if my suspicions are correct as to who and what he is, he shall hang before he is many hours older!"

"Whom do you suspect the intruder to be, my lord?" asked the young Marquis, looking anxiously at Duval's retreating form.

"None other than the notorious Claude Duval——"

"An unexampled villain!" interrupted the Duke of Montrose.

"Nay, my lord," said the Marquis of Harcourt; "the only occasions upon which you have met have been in my company, and then I must say that he showed an amount of generosity and self-control——"

"Ha, ha! Listen, Montecute! The most honourable the Marquis of Harcourt has taken upon himself to be the defender of one of the most notorious——"

"Hold, my lord!" cried the young Marquis, with flashing eyes, and touching his sword-hilt significantly, —"hold, my lord! I am not one to stand and hear my character aspersed without bringing the offender to task. What I said about Claude Duval was the simple truth. On the two occasions that I encountered him, I was in your company, and on both those occasions the highwayman behaved as a gentleman, and one who could be both brave and generous."

"Yes," roared the Duke,—"yes, you take up his cudgels just because he refused to receive your purse, while, on the contrary, he robbed me of all I had about me."

The Marquis of Harcourt was too anxious for Claude's safety to continue in idle parlance with the Duke of Montrose, and yet he was desirous of preventing him from following on Duval's steps; so he said, "A truce to private bickering, my lord. Let us proceed in our search for the intruder, whoever he may be; and it is my intention to go at once to the gallery, and search minutely for any one who may be concealed in or about its precincts."

"Agreed!" cried the Duke of Montecute, with flashing eyes; "for I feel convinced, in my own mind, that the fellow who has made such an impression upon my cousin, the Lady Lizzy Dominick, is none other than Claude Duval."

"Ah! say you so?" said the Duke of Montrose. "I would give my right hand to be assured of that fact!"

As he spoke, he rushed forward in front of the Marquis of Harcourt, through the elegantly-furnished room where Duval had first encountered his friend.

In the meantime Duval made his way as fast as he could without attracting undue observation from the various officials who were passing and repassing up and down the stairs which led from the corridor or gallery.

At length he reached the court-yard the Marquis of Harcourt had mentioned.

At first, Duval had some thoughts of flinging down the herald's disguise which he wore; but then, recollecting that there would be the sentinels to pass, he resolved to retain it, and walked deliberately forward towards the iron gates.

"Where are you off to?" asked the sentinel, in a familiar tone of voice.

"What's that to you?" said Duval, speaking in an assumed tone.

"Well, you might give a civil answer to a civil question, at all events!" growled the sentinel, looking after Duval, who was making his way as quickly as he could without attracting attention.

"Yes," he said to himself, "I think, now, I may say I am safe."

Scarcely had the thought shaped itself into words, when Duval became aware that there were hurried steps behind him.

He turned not to look behind him; but he felt, rather than saw, that he was pursued.

He quickened his pace, however, up St. James's Street, until he came to a little bye thoroughfare, the resort of Jews' old clothes shops and "fences," where stolen property was received.

"Now, fortune aid me!" said Duval to himself, as he darted into the shop of an old Jew, who was apparently engaged in looking over some coins which lay scattered on the floor before him.

"Quick!" cried Duval. "Do you feel inclined to make a good bargain, my friend?"

"What ish it? Solomon Josephs knows ash well ash any man how to drive a good bargain."

While he had been speaking, Duval had divested himself of the herald's tabard, and was placing it over the shoulders of the old Jew.

"Capital, capital!" said Duval. "What will you give for it?"

The old Jew's eyes sparkled at the thought of driving a hard bargain, and he said, "Well, I'll give you von crown for the old rubbish. It ish not worth so much."

As the old Jew spoke, he settled the tabard on his shoulders, and seemed well pleased with the transaction.

Duval had no time to dispute about as to the money the old Jew was to give for his bargain, for at this moment, he heard footsteps approaching, and the unmistakable voice of Montecute saying, in high, excited accents, "Now we shall have him! I saw him enter that disreputable-looking shop!"

By this time, Lord Montecute and the Duke of Montrose—for he accompanied his friend—had succeeded in getting up a little rabble of boys to join in the outcry against Duval.

"What's the row?" asked a man, at this moment turning round the corner of the street. "I'm a Bow Street runner. Can I be of any service, gentlemen?"

"The very thing! Go into that shop, and take in

charge a fellow there who has stolen from the Palace the tabard of one of the heralds, and has gone there to seek shelter!" cried the Duke of Montrose.

"All right, gentlemen," said Swallow—for it was none other than he—"all right, gentlemen. I'll have him out in a minute."

The Duke of Montrose and the Duke of Montecute waited with some anxiety outside the shop as Swallow entered it.

"Run, Duval—no, don't run—walk, I mean! Leave this affair to me. I told you I would serve you if possible; but I didn't think I should have a chance so soon. There are two grand somebodys just outside, looking for you. But never mind them; pass them, and leave the rest to me. Quick!"

There was a tone of such anxiety, and a look of such sincerity upon the countenance of Swallow, that Duval could do no otherwise than trust him; and he said, hurriedly, "If I find you are faithful. This shall not be the worst night's work you have done, Swallow."

Duval then turned, and left the Jew's shop, who had looked on half bewildered at what he heard.

Sure enough, as Swallow had said, there stood his two enemies.

As Duval passed out of the shop, they both took a step forward, expecting to see the figure they had pursued from the Palace.

They drew back, however, when they found that the approaching figure was much taller than the disguised herald, and quietly allowed him to pass unquestioned.

As the reader may suppose, Duval made the best of what really might prove his last opportunity that night of making his escape, and was quickly lost to sight.

Swallow had had the tact to keep the old Jew in conversation until he thought he had given Duval time sufficient to make his escape. Then he raised an outcry, and rushed to the door.

"Come in, gentlemen, come in!" he cried. "I've nabbed your man!"

The old Jew raised a cry.

"Mercy, gentlemen, mercy! I'm a poor old man, that wouldn't harm a mouse."

The Duke of Montrose and the Duke of Montecute rushed in, crying simultaneously, "Off with him—off with him! He is an impostor and a traitor! Off with him!"

"Come on, you old sinner," said Swallow.

The old Jew fell on his knees; and as he raised his hands imploringly, the two friends discovered that that was not the man of whom they had been in pursuit.

"Confusion!" growled the Duke of Montecute, between his clenched teeth, "the fellow has escaped us!"

CHAPTER LIV.

CLAUDE DUVAL VISITS THE DUCHESS OF CLEVELAND.

DUVAL made the best of his way to the "Bedford Head."

A feeling of excessive fatigue came over him; but, had the distance been ten times what it was, he would not have felt satisfied to take rest under any other roof than that which sheltered Nightshade.

The morning was very near at hand; but at that old hostel, so frequented by gentlemen of the road, there was no difficulty in obtaining admission at any hour to those who were properly accredited so to do.

The plan of operations was simply this.

A scout or sentinel—call him which you will—was on duty all the night through, outside the door of the "Bedford Head."

He alone knew the signal which, on that particular night, would signify that there was a friendly demand for admission; so that if any one came to the old place, and either knocked or rang, the scout had it in his power to reconnoitre them, and form his own conclusion.

If the guest were a stranger, or a suspected person, all the knocking and ringing in the world would not suffice to move the well-barred oaken door of the "Bedford Head."

If otherwise, the sentinel could easily approach, and make the requisite signal.

Immediately beneath one of the ancient bay windows of the old public-house there was a large wooden cellar-head, or flap.

Duval stood upon that, and glanced about him for a few seconds, in search of the information which he was sure would come to him in regard to the mode of letting his presence be known at the public-house.

A man lounged up to him.

"A fine evening."

"Tolerable," said Duval; "but I want to go in here. Don't you know me?"

"Ah! to be sure I do, now I look a little closer."

"I am Claude Duval."

"Of course you are, and welcome to the old 'Bedford Head.'"

At this moment the rapid sound of footsteps under the piazzas of Covent Garden came upon their ears.

It might be that those footsteps by no means concerned Claude Duval, but still, under the circumstances, they were suggestive of danger.

"Come," said the scout, "I can let you in by a short-hand way, just crouch down a little, and keep your footing firm."

"I will," said Duval.

He could very well surmise in his own mind what was about to happen; and when the scout with the thick short bludgeon he had in his hand gave four deliberate taps upon the cellar-head, and that cellar-head then began to move, Duval did crouch down, and knew that in a few seconds he would be perfectly secure in the ancient hostel.

Such was the case.

Duval leaped lightly a space of about eight feet.

The cellar-head was quickly replaced, and a couple of bolts shot into their sockets.

The scout walked slowly away whistling a tune, and Duval was in safety.

"Ah! Mr. Claude," said the landlord of the "Bedford Head," "here you are again. We have been waiting up for you, and are right glad to see you safely back again to the old crib."

"Thanks," said Duval; "is Nightshade well?"

"Bless your heart, yes, as well as can be, and sleeping as sound as a top."

"That is what his master wants to do for the next three hours."

"Come this way, then, you shall have one of the top rooms, and in case of any alarm from the grabs I will tell you what to do."

Duval followed the landlord of the "Bedford Head" to one of the attics of the house.

It was a small room with a slant roof, and a window composed of such little diamond-shaped panes of early green glass, that it was with the greatest difficulty they could be seen through even at broad daylight.

"Here is a comfortable enough bed," said the landlord, "only you must be careful how you get up in the morning, or you will knock your head against the ceiling. And now, let me show you how the window opens."

"That, then," said Duval, "will be my mode of escape if I am hard beset."

"It will; you can then get along the roofs, and take your chance of getting in at some other attic window; but I wouldn't do that except at some great extremity, which is not likely to happen."

"I think not," said Duval. "And now, good night, for I am very weary."

Duval was left to himself; and hastily removing only a portion of his clothing, he flung himself upon the bed in the attic, and fell into a deep sleep.

The sun was high in the heavens when Duval awakened, and looked anxiously about him.

His first thought was that he must have long overslept himself, and therefore unwillingly broken his engagement with the Duchess of Cleveland.

A glance at his watch, however, showed him that it was only eleven o'clock, and as he was well aware that the fashionable hour for breakfast was one, especially after a Court entertainment, he felt no uneasiness upon that subject.

There was one question, however, that deserved consideration.

What costume was he to go in to the Duchess of Cleveland's, so as to awaken no suspicion of who he really was?

Duval's first idea was, to go attired as a military officer, for at that period it was a common and usual thing for officers in the army to wear their uniforms every day, and on all occasions.

The professional costumes which are now so completely laid aside when not engaged in professional duty, were then the every-day dress of persons engaged in them.

The full-dress of a doctor of physic, with his gold-headed cane, was perfectly well known.

Clergymen went about in gown and bands.

Military and naval officers wore their respective uniforms, with the only difference, that they did so in a loose and slovenly fashion; but they never thought of putting on what were called private clothes, in which now all ranks and all distinctions are so completely confounded.

The principal objection, however, that Claude Duval had in dressing himself in military uniform was, that it was a great deal too like his own highwayman's costume.

That was a point worth considering.

He slowly descended the narrow staircase leading to the lower part of the "Bedford Head," and by the time his foot touched the last stair he had come to a determination.

"The dress of a private gentleman," he said; "will suit me best, for that I can make as plain as possible, and less likely to attract observation."

Duval's first visit, as may well be imagined, was to Nightshade, and then he communicated his intention to the landlord of the "Bedford Head" of leaving his horse yet there for awhile, since he had a visit to make.

"I have to breakfast," said Duval, "with a lady of quality. I shall want a sedan chair, and a suit of plain, private clothes, as different as possible from these I now wear."

"That's easy done, Mr. Duval; you leave all to me. But if you're going to breakfast with a lady of quality, I would advise you to lay in a good substantial meal at the "Bedford Head" first."

Duval took this advice; and by a little after twelve o'clock he was fully equipped in a plain suit of dark brown velvet, and had taken his seat in a sedan chair, to be conveyed to Cleveland House.

The Duchess kept great state, and it was said, that she contrived not only to spend her own large income, but to improve upon it by getting the same amount in debt every year.

Things equalize themselves, however, in this world, and find their level.

The Duchess's tradesmen certainly charged her forty shillings for every pound's worth of goods they furnished her with.

London, at that time, was not so large as it is at present, and the houses of the rich and noble were by no means so scattered and wide apart.

Immediately around St. James's and Westminster, within a half mile radius almost of the old Palace, were to be found the residences of the principal notabilities of the day.

It wanted a quarter to one o'clock when Claude Duval was conducted in his sedan chair to the steps of Cleveland House.

He walked into the hall, and in that quiet, unmistakable manner which characterised him, he asked if the Duchess had yet risen.

His question was met by another.

"If you will be so good as to say who you are, we will take your name to Mrs. Abigail, her Grace's own woman."

"Will you say that Mr. Lavud waits her Grace's pleasure?"

Duval fully comprehended that this transposition of the letters of his name would be understood by the Duchess.

And so, indeed, it was, for a message came down to the hall in a few minutes to the effect that her Grace waited for Mr. Lavud in her private breakfast-room.

The Duchess was attired in a very charming morning costume of sky blue silk, with very rich delicate lace trimmings.

The only jewels she wore were diamonds, and they were set in silver.

There was a harmony about her dress and general appearance which was charming to behold, and certainly transcends description.

Upon rather a small table was laid a very elegant tea and coffee equipage.

"Ah, Mr. Lavud," said the Duchess, "you are very welcome. Pray be seated. I have been expecting you for—let me see, five minutes."

"That is greatly to be regretted," said Duval. "Your grace has been in a worse condition than the French King, who almost waited one time—you have actually done so for five minutes."

"Yes," said the Duchess, "I was getting tired of myself."

"That's a sentiment that nobody else will echo."

The footman who had ushered Duval to that apartment had now fairly closed the door, and taken his departure.

The Duchess changed her tone instantly.

"Claude Duval," she said, "I am astonished at your intrepidity in coming in broad daylight even to breakfast with the Duchess of Cleveland."

"The reward is so great," said Duval, "that it covers all the danger. Nevertheless, if I might suggest, the pronunciation of my name before a third person is scarcely desired."

The Duchess burst into a peal of laughter.

"Gracious heavens!" she exclaimed; "do you call this a person?"

A black boy, fantastically dressed as an Oriental page, was attending upon the Duchess.

"Not a very dignified person," added Duval; "but we should never despise an enemy with a tongue in his head."

"Capital!" cried the Duchess, "you have just hit it!"

"Hit what, madam?"

"Come here, Columbo."

The black boy approached.

"Open your mouth."

The boy did so, displaying a couple of rows of brilliant white teeth, but no tongue.

"There, you see," said the Duchess; "he was rescued from a Barbary corsair, and that was the treatment he had received while in their hands."

"I am perfectly satisfied," said Duval; "I suppose he cannot speak a word?"

"Speak, Columbo!" cried the Duchess.

The boy made a singular sound, that more resembled "bubble, bubble," than anything else.

"That," said the Duchess, "is the extent of his resources in a conversational way; but I find him faithful and useful. Coffee, Columbo!"

The black boy did his duty adroitly, and had served both the Duchess and Duval, when he suddenly paused and pointed to the door.

It was almost immediately opened, and Mrs. Abigail, the Duchess's confidential woman, made her appearance, with an expression of fright upon her countenance.

"His Highness, the Prince, madam!"

"How provoking!"

"Prince Frederick!" exclaimed Duval, as he rose to his feet.

"Hush, Mr. Lavud!" said the Duchess; "he will only be here a few minutes. I laid a silly wager with him last night at the Palace, and I lost it."

"Indeed, madam! I thought the Prince was in such disgrace, that he was the last person to show himself at St. James's."

"That was just it; he was there in disguise, and I wagered him one of my diamond bracelets against anything he liked, that he would be discovered before the ball was over."

"Madam, you should have taken care to win the wager, and then——"

"Ah! I understand you; you think I should not have seen the Prince."

"Probably not."

"But since he is here I must see him. Get you behind that paper screen; Columbo will take care that you are not discovered; and all that you have to do is to be discreet.

Screens called Japan, but probably brought from some of the trading ports of China, were then common articles of furniture in the boudoirs and reception-rooms of persons of wealth and fashion.

The part they played in the conduct of many an intrigue, rendered them for some years exceedingly popular.

We shall scarcely find an old comedy of that period in which there are not some equivocal circumstances brought about by the agency of the screen.

This one, in the Duchess of Cleveland's private breakfast-room, was gorgeous with gilding, and oriental ornamentation, and imagery.

Duval stepped behind it instantly, and stood profoundly still.

Columbo must have been rather used to such emergencies, for the adroit manner in which he disposed of the cup and saucer which Duval had been using was something admirable to see.

Another moment, and Prince Frederick of Wales entered the room.

The Duchess rose and made an elaborate curtesy.

"Madam," said the Prince, "I have won."

"Your Highness is fortunate at the same time. I am surprised to see you."

"Surprised?"

"Yes, I thought you were in exile, or in the Tower; and, at all events, I thought your fortune partook so much of that of an owl's, that you dare not look upon the daylight."

"That is the provoking thing," cried the Prince, as he flung himself into a chair,—"that is the provoking thing. Nobody will see me."

"Nobody see you?"

"Not a soul. It seems that I am allowed to go about where I please, and show myself where I like, but it is the orders of Rex that no one should know me."

"Ah, you call the King, your father, Rex."

"I do, and he ought to take it as a compliment; for a much worse name generally rises to my throat, and only dies away upon my lips."

"Well, your Royal Highness?" said the Duchess, in a questioning tone.

"I have won."

"And there is the bracelet."

"Duchess!"

"Prince!"

"Is it possible you can think so meanly of me as to suppose I would deprive a lady of one of her jewels? I'm not a highwayman. Why, Claude Duval, that celebrated appropriator of other people's property, would scarcely be guilty of such an act."

"I am sure he would not."

"Then your Grace only does him honour, and me justice. My opinion is that when a gentleman lays a wager with a lady he always loses."

"You are gallant."

"Or he always should lose; and, since such is the case, here, Duchess, is a bracelet, which will not compare badly with the one you staked last evening."

The Prince produced a very magnificent bracelet of very beautiful emeralds.

The Duchess of Cleveland was well known as a great admirer of jewels.

"Ah!" she cried, "where did you get so splendid an ornament?"

"Stole it!"

"What?"

The Prince laughed, and stretched out his legs.

"Stole it, Duchess—stole it! There is an old cabinet at St. James's, containing Crown jewels, hoarded up and hidden by Queen Anne in her last days—they say they were the bridal presents of Prince George of Denmark; but that don't matter - this is one of them."

"It is beautiful!"

"Bubble, bubble!" said Columbo, the page, as he pointed to the door of the apartment.

CHAPTER LV.

CLAUDE DUVAL OVERHEARS A STRANGE PLOT CONCOCTED.

"We are interrupted," said the Duchess.

Prince Frederick sprung to his feet.

"Who is it?" he said, imperiously.

Mrs. Abigail again appeared.

There was more consternation upon her countenance than there had been even when she announced Prince Frederick.

"Oh, madam!"

"Hush, Mrs. Abigail; if there is anything I dislike more than another, it is needless alarm."

"But, madam, Mr. Brown——"

The Duchess turned pale, in spite of the slight tinge of rouge that was upon her countenance.

"Will you give my compliments to Mr. Brown, and tell him I shall be disengaged in five minutes."

"Hang Mr. Brown!" cried the Prince. "What on earth can such a plebeian rascal want with you, Duchess?"

"Your royal Highness has heard," said the Duchess,

"that I have put off Mr. Brown's visit for five minutes. If you have anything to say, therefore, you know the space of time in which you have to say it."

"I have something to say; and as there is nobody here but ourselves and your dumb page, I may as well say it at once."

"At once," replied the Duchess.

"Report says that you live a little beyond your income; and if such is the case, the permanent position of Mistress of the Robes and a grant of some acres of Crown land, together with a pension of ten thousand per annum, might make up even an income that would suffice the fair Duchess of Cleveland."

"And what am I to do for all these favours?" asked the Duchess, in a cold, sarcastic tone of voice.

"I have reason to believe, from information that I have received—for I have my spies and attached friend about the person of the King—that you will receive a visit from him this morning."

"From the King?"

"Yes; he will visit you under some assumed name."

"Indeed."

"I am assured of it; and you will be, perhaps, a little more surprised when you learn that it is because I have let him know I shall be here myself at two o'clock, that he will take care to be here before that hour."

"You have let him know?"

"Not seemingly myself; but I have taken care he shall be informed of the fact, as though it were an act of treachery by some one in my confidence."

"But I do not comprehend."

"Of course you do not. I am explaining."

"Does he wish to meet you here?"

"By no means; but he wishes to be here before me on the fatherly errand of helping to make me a cup of coffee."

"You speak in riddles."

"Do you not comprehend? His most gracious Majesty does not like me so near his throne. He is adroit; and although he might not propose such a thing to you, he would say nothing, but probably expressively beseech your silence, and give you a vague promise of further favours, if you handed me the cup of coffee he prepared for me at two o'clock."

"You amaze me!"

"Perhaps."

"You do, indeed."

"Well, Duchess, self-preservation is the first law of nature. I am here first. I do not make you any vague promises, but specific ones, all to be carried out when I am King."

"Ah!"

"Which I shall be, if——"

"I see—I see!"

"Of course you do, Duchess. Which I shall be, if you will only be so good as present to his most gracious Majesty the coffee which, from yonder silver urn, you will allow to trickle into this cup."

The Prince, as he spoke, took a small phial from his pocket—a phial so minute that its whole contents could not exceed above six drops.

He reversed it completely over the porcelain cup.

"One—two—three," he counted.

Three drops of a gelatinous-looking liquid fell to the bottom of the cup.

"Perfectly colourless, you see, Duchess," he said; "and easily hidden by the new-fashioned crystallized sugar."

Loaf-sugar, as it is now called, was then a great rarity, and, consequently, it was upon the breakfast-table of the Duchess of Cleveland.

She was fair, fickle, and somewhat imprudent.

Scandal at times was busy with her name; but this deliberate proposition, on the part of Frederick, Prince of Wales, to become a participator in the heinous criminality of poisoning his father, seemed completely to stun her, and deprive her of the power of speech.

"You look surprised, Duchess!"

"Good heaven! Can there be such wickedness?"

"Nay, it is retaliation. He intends just such a draught for me. It is diamond cut diamond."

"No," said the Duchess, "diamonds are pure and bright, and give pleasure to behold—for they resemble daylight, and have a thousand sparkling beauties about them; but you and your father are——"

The Duchess shuddered.

"It is needless to say what you are; but you are not diamonds."

A dark shade came over the face of the Prince.

"You refuse, Duchess?"

"With all my heart—with all my soul!"

"Be it so; but remember, what I have said is secret as the grave."

"No one would believe me," said the Duchess, "were I to relate it. There are some things so hideous—so vile and so unnatural—that human nature, with one accord, would lend no credence to their repetition."

"No," said the Prince," as he rose, "not without corroborative evidence; and since we are alone, with the exception of this dumb page——"

"Alone!" cried the Duchess. "Alas, alas! In the horror of this communication, I had forgotten——"

"Forgotten what?"

The Duchess was silent.

"Bubble, bubble," said the page, again.

Mrs. Abigail appeared once more at the door of the little boudoir.

"Mr. Brown is impatient, madam; he has already broken a mirror, and is using horrible language in the cedar parlour."

"Ah!" cried the Prince, with a half yell. "A thought strikes me!"

"And me, too," said the Duchess.

"It is a quarter to two."

"It is."

"Mr. Brown, then, is——"

"Rex, as you call him."

"A thousand fiends!"

"No, only one," said the Duchess; "for I know not which to choose between you in the deep iniquity of both your visits."

"He is coming up the stairs, madam," said Mrs. Abigail. "He has broken the image of Pomona on the landing."

"Confusion!" cried the Prince. "Where shall I hide? Ah! that screen!"

"No, no!" cried the Duchess.

"Bubble, Bubble!" said the page.

"He's in the corridor, my lady. He has pushed his walking-stick through the stained-glass window."

"All is lost!" said the Duchess.

"But not found yet!" exclaimed the Prince of Wales. "Take a better thought of it, Madam, and give him the coffee."

As he spoke, Prince Frederick darted behind the screen.

There was a slight scream.

A brief scuffle.

Then Duval had him by the throat, and all was still as the grave.

"Bubble, Bubble, Bubble, Bubble!" cried the page.

His face unusually red.

His eyes glaring, and the snarling look of some ill-conditioned cur upon his face, Mr. Brown—as he called himself—but in reality King George the Second—appeared at the door of the Duchess's breakfast-room.

His first act was to wrench from his fob a very massive gold watch, set with brilliants, and to cast a furious glance upon it.

"Eleven minutes and a-half to two," he said. "Madame, I have been kept in your waiting-room nine minutes and a quarter. Thousand devils! Madame, yes, and you knew who we were!"

"I was engaged; and as clemency is the first attribute of a king——"

"Bah! Stuff! Boo!"

The King flung himself into a chair.

It was the same that had been so recently occupied by his hopeful son.

"To what," said the Duchess, "am I to attribute the singular honour of this morning visit?"

"Business of importance."

"I presumed as much, your Majesty."

"You are right, Duchess; but in the first place let it be understood that we are not interrupted. A certain person will be here at two o'clock, but as he is not noted for punctuality it will probably be later. I suppose we are quite alone?"

The Duchess made no answer.

The King, then, partially shading his face with his right hand, continued to speak, but in a lower tone than before.

"Duchess, I very much admire the ancients."

The Duchess of Cleveland let him go on, and made him no reply.

"They possessed a stern kind of virtue" added the King; "Brutus, in particular, and he was ready to inflict justice even upon his own son if necessary."

The Duchess slightly inclined her head.

"You are generally admired, and it appears to be a kind of consequence of such admiration that you should keep up great state and dignity."

The Duchess again inclined her head.

"Those are things," added the King, "that entail expense, and we have been thinking for some time past of some means that would add largely to your income, and now, Duchess, to business."

His Majesty was not nearly so particular in the character of the bribe he offered as the Prince Frederick.

"Duchess," he added, still lower in his tone, "Frederick will be here at two o'clock. The first thing he will ask you for will most probably be a cup of coffee, and I want you to give him one."

"I shall not be wanting," said the Duchess, "in such ordinary hospitality; but while the Prince Frederick is at issue with your Majesty, I would certainly rather he did not favour me with any visits."

"Exactly," cried the King, eagerly; "but this is an excellent visit, since it is one which offers a prospect of great future advantages."

"Indeed, your Majesty?"

"Yes, the health of our son Frederick is by no means good. He looked ailing the last time we saw him, and we have taken pains to procure a medicine which will prevent him from ever looking ailing again, and after partaking of which, we feel assured he will never afterwards make the slightest complaint about his health."

The King's countenance looked perfectly hideous as he spoke.

The Duchess could not forbear a shudder.

"Now," said the King, as he took a small vial from his pocket, very similar in size and appearance to that which Prince Frederick had produced. "Now, Duchess, suppose we take this cup as the one in which you will give Frederick a cup of coffee."

The King took hold of the same cup into which the Prince had already dropped so carefully the gelatinous liquid.

He fixed his eyes on the Duchess.

She did not move.

She did not speak.

Drop! drop! drop!

That cup then contained six drops of the deadly poison.

Poison intended by the father for the son.

Poison intended by the son for the father.

No doubt they had gone to the same source for it.

There was an Italian named Nicoli in London at that period, who ostensibly carried on the business of a perfumer and a vendor of noxious compounds, which he declared, to use his own language, would make people beautiful for ever.

These cosmetics were poisonous enough.

But he dealt in subtler drugs.

It was from him, then, that both the Prince Frederick of Wales and the King his father, procured the two small vials, three drops from each of which now lay at the bottom of one of the porcelain cups of the Duchess of Cleveland.

The King carefully replaced the vial in his waistcoat pocket.

"You comprehend, Duchess?"

"I think I do."

"And you will give him the coffee?"

"Hush!"

The King turned ghastly pale.

The Duchess seemed inclined almost to laugh.

"Bubble! bubble!" said the Page.

A voice came from behind the screen.

"I will trouble you for that emerald bracelet," said the voice.

"Thieves!" was the sharp reply.

"Another word, and you are a dead man."

"Help, Duchess! Help!"

The King rose to his feet.

"Is it treason?" he said.

"Murder!" cried a half-stifled voice from behind the screen.

The King made a rush to the door of the boudoir, and he might have escaped, but that the Oriental page at that moment had dropped on his hands and knees to search for something on the floor, and the Majesty of England rolled over him in a very undignified fashion.

CHAPTER VI.

THE MAJESTY OF ENGLAND FINDS HIMSELF IN A FIX.

SIMULTANEOUSLY with the fall of the King, the Japan screen was cast down, only just falling clear of the breakfast-table, and Claude Duval appeared, holding the Prince Frederick firmly by the throat.

"Frederick!" yelled the King, as he sat on the floor with his back against the door of the room.

"Rex!" gasped the Prince.

"Gentlemen," said the Duchess; "will you permit me to offer you a cup of coffee?"

"Certainly not!"

"By no means!"

The negative came from each of the royal lips most emphatically.

The King slowly gathered himself up, and loosened his sword in its sheath.

He was not without a certain species of courage—that disreputable George the Second of England.

And he stood so near the door that the Prince Frederick, although he had all the desire and impulse so to do, could not escape.

DUVAL RECEIVES THE PARDON OF LUCY EVERTON.

He rather preferred the society of Claude Duval the highwayman to that of his father.

"Bubble, bubble!" said the Page, as he gathered himself slowly up from the floor, and strove to disarm the wrath of the King, by affecting to be seriously hurt, in consequence of the royal tumble over him.

The situation was a strange one.

The King fairly drew his sword, and stood well upon his guard.

He could not exactly come to a conclusion at that moment, in regard to whether Duval were an accomplice of his son Frederick or not.

And Duval still kept his hold upon the throat of the Prince, who fell into one of those strange, inert, paralysed conditions—real or affected—which always came over him upon the failure of any great iniquity.

He seemed then to give up all use of his legs; and when Duval dragged him forward and flung him into an arm chair, he lay in it supinely, and in exactly the same attitude in which he happened to fall.

Duval then stepped forward, and faced the King.

No. 18. NIGHTSHADE.

"I congratulate you, your Majesty," he said.

"And, who the dev—— I mean, who are you?"

"And I congratulate his royal Highness, Frederick, Prince of Wales," added Duval, without answering the King's question.

The Prince uttered a groan.

"Unless," continued Duval, " for the general benefit of society, and out of compliment to each other, your Majesty will take half a cup of coffee, and your son the other half."

"No, no!" yelled the King.

"No, no!" groaned the Prince.

"Duchess! permit me," said Duval.

He took up the cup which contained the six drops of poison, and turning down the tap of the silver urn, he filled it with coffee.

The duchess laid her hand upon his arm.

"Forbear!"

Duval smiled.

He set down the cup.

The Duchess took the cup, and flung it, with its

contents on to the bright fire of cedar-wood that burnt in the boudoir.

The King breathed more freely.

The Prince opened one eye.

"No," said the Duchess, "that is beyond a jest. So perish even the memory of the great crime."

The Prince shut the eye that he had opened.

The King looked down on the floor.

Perhaps, there was the shadow of a compunction even in his obdurate heart at the hideous assassination he had contemplated.

And it was no justification that Prince Frederick was willing to take his life.

He might defend himself, and he might punish his would-be murderer, but when he stooped to the same means of action, he placed himself upon an equality with the man who sought his life.

Keeping his eyes, then, fixed upon the face of Prince Frederick, the King slowly made his way towards the door again.

Duval did not, however, intend him to leave so easily.

"Hold!" he cried. "Not so quick, your Majesty!"

Two strides had placed Duval between the King and the door.

Claude stretched out his arm, to bar the royal progress.

As he did so, the King looked fixedly at his wrist, and then deliberately taking an eye-glass from his pocket, he looked more fixedly still.

"How came you by that emerald bracelet?" he said.

Duval had upon his wrist the bracelet he had taken from the Prince of Wales.

And then as the question was put to him, Claude remembered the answer that had been given by the Prince to the Duchess, when asked the similar question.

"This bracelet?" he said.

"Yes, that bracelet. How came you by it?"

"Stole it."

The Prince shut up his eyes tighter than ever.

"But it was in one of the royal cabinets," said the King.

"Probably," replied Duval, "and how it came out of the royal cabinet it will be better to ask his Royal Highness the Prince of Wales."

"I comprehend," said the King. "He gave it to you to assist in my assassination."

"Not so. I took it from him very much against his will."

"Help!" cried the King.

A sudden panic seemed to seize him.

"Help! help! Duchess, is it possible that you can be a party to attempted regicide?"

"There is no danger," said the Duchess. You know me well. I am the Duchess of Cleveland."

"And I am Claude Duval," said Claude.

The King looked from one to another of them doubtfully.

Duval hastily turned the key in the lock of the door, and removed it, then hastily stepping towards the Duchess, he whispered a few words in her ear.

"Excellent!" she cried. "Let it be done."

The Prince of Wales opened one of his eyes again, and the King backed to the wall, where he stood upon the defensive.

Duval put the key again into the lock of the door of the boudoir, and flung it open.

"The Duchess of Cleveland," he said, "and I, Claude Duval, are equally resolved that his Highness, Prince Frederick, shall immediately leave this house, or partake of another cup of coffee prepared by his royal father."

The Prince sprung to his feet, and bolted through the open doorway in an instant.

The King looked pleased.

"Never mind," he said; "I shall catch him another time. Duchess, I have the pleasure of bidding you good morning; and as for you, Claude Duval, why as for you, I will not betray you; you may make good your retreat, and I would advise you to live an honester life in future."

"Indeed!" said Duval.

"And, added the King, you will give me back that emerald bracelet, which is a Crown jewel."

"Indeed!" said Duval again.

"Come, sir, be quick, our time is precious!"

"It is possible," said Duval, "that I may lead an honester life, because I am a highwayman, and take from the rich for my own necessities, handing, frequently, what surplus I have to the poor."

The King made an impatient gesture.

"But I am not a poisoner!"

"Sir?"

"I am not an assassin!"

"Sir?"

"On the contrary, I have this day been somewhat instrumental in saving the King's life!"

"Oh! you want a reward, then?"

"I do."

"Keep the bracelet, and may its proceeds choke you!"

"I cannot thank your Majesty, seeing that I have the bracelet already; and I do not want a reward for saving so worthless a thing as the life of George the Second of England."

"Ah!"

"But I do threaten."

"By heaven! I thought you would."

"I threaten that the most extended publicity shall be given to the last hour's proceedings in this boudoir, unless——"

"Unless what?"

"Unless you do an act, which will be the most gracious one that you have done for many a long day."

"What act?"

"I ask of you the pardon, under the royal sign manual, of Lucy Duval—otherwise, Lucy Everton."

"So—that is it?"

"It is."

"The pardon of a convicted murderess."

"Convicted, but yet innocent. Human judgment, oh, King, is fallible; and it is not the first time in the history of the jurisprudence of this country that an innocent person has been condemned to death."

"You say so."

"I know so; and, in demanding of you the pardon of the person I have named, I give you an opportunity of doing an act of grace, and of justice, that may plead something for you when you are put upon your trial."

"My trial?"

"Yes, at that bar of eternal justice which cannot err!"

The King bit his lips.

He glanced at the Duchess of Cleveland.

"If your Majesty seeks my opinion," said the Duchess, "I should say grant this pardon at once."

"Upon compulsion?" said the King.

"There is little compulsion," said the Duchess, "in doing an act of justice."

"But I don't know it."

"I will undertake to prove it to you; and if within six months I do not bring irrefragable testimony to the innocence of Lucy Everton, I will——"

"Give her up again to the law?"

"No; but I will give myself up, and expiate my mistake upon the scaffold."

"Be it so," said the King. "Duchess, you are a witness."

"I am."

The King sat down, and the Duchess wheeled a little table towards him, on which was a desk with writing materials.

Upon the first stray piece of paper that the King caught hold of, he wrote the following words:—

"A free pardon and release to Lucy Everton, now a prisoner in our gaol of Newgate.
"GEORGE REX."

The Duchess of Cleveland took the paper, and hastily wrote her name after the words "Witnessed and countersigned."

The King gave a grim sort of smile.

Duval took up the paper.

"It may be," he said, "that I am deceived. There may be something informal about this document—something wanting or something added, which may make it a snare and a trap for me, instead of an order of liberation for Lucy Everton."

"Pooh! pooh!" said the King.

"But I warn you, oh, King! if such should be the case, that I will find a means of being free again; and let you be in the most remote chambers of your palace, shut in by thrice treble doors, and surrounded by every guard you can muster, encased in steel, yourself, and with a weapon in your hand, I will find you, and let daylight into your false heart!"

"Daylight?"

"I have said it."

"And you—you——"

"I am Claude Duval, and that is enough!"

"A light!" said the King, moodily; "a taper light!"

The Duchess made a sign to the page.

A small lighted wax taper was placed before the King.

Slowly he drew from his finger a large agate signet ring.

The Duchess divined his intention, and opening a little drawer in the desk, she produced some sealing wax, with which she made a large seal upon the order of release for Lucy Everton.

The King impressed the agate seal upon it.

"There," said he, "that is more than sufficient!"

Duval took the paper and flung the door wide open instantly.

The King cast a scowling look both upon him and the Duchess, and passed out of the boudoir.

"To Newgate at once!" cried Duval, as he seized his hat.

"And I with you," said the Duchess. "My liveries and coach are well known."

"A thousand thanks!"

"I long to see this Lucy of your's, for wonderful as you may think it, Claude Duval, I am one of those——"

The Duchess paused.

Claude Duval adroitly filled up the sentence for her.

"You are one of those handsome, gloriously-accomplished women, who do not shut their eyes to the like qualities in another."

"I did not say so," remarked the Duchess; "but I will not be such a hypocrite as to refuse such a compliment from——"

"Claude Duval, who deserves nothing but his name from the Duchess of Cleveland."

"The carriage, Columbo!" cried the Duchess.

"Bubble! bubble!" said the page.

In five minutes more Duval and her Grace of Cleveland were on their road to Newgate.

CHAPTER LVII.

LUCY IS RELEASED FROM NEWGATE.—THE CARRIAGE OF THE DUCHESS OF CLEVELAND PURSUED.

DUVAL was silent for several minutes during that auspicious ride to Newgate.

But it was not the silence of ungraciousness, but rather that he felt how inadequate would be any language to express the great obligation he owed to the Duchess of Cleveland.

Perhaps, she divined the cause of the silence.

At all events, she strove to break it, by speaking on some indifferent subject.

"These dissensions," she said, "between the King and the Prince of Wales can have but a melancholy ending."

"The ending will be death," said Duval. "But, Duchess, if I could but find words in which to express to you what I feel that I owe you."

"It is quite sufficient," interrupted the Duchess, "that you cannot find words; and if you could they are not required."

The carriage stopped with a jerk.

The high-mettled steeds of the Duchess of Cleveland had traversed the distance between her house and Newgate in an exceedingly short space of time; and the arrival of such an equipage produced some degree of excitement in the hall of the prison.

"I am still Mr. Lavud," said Duval, as he prepared to alight from the coach.

But the Duchess placed her hand upon his arm.

"No," she said, with a smile. "My principal reason for accompanying you was that you should not present this order of liberation yourself."

"You doubt my discretion?"

"No; but in the surprise of seeing you, might not Lucy Everton pronounce your name, and so, by endangering your safety, only exchange one grief for another?"

"True; that is true."

"Remain, then, here, and be content with the result. I will present the order of release."

Duval could have no just plea to urge against this mode of procedure; and he remained in the coach while the Duchess alighted, and entered the vestibule of Newgate.

Up those narrow, steep steps, which led to the interior of the gloomy prison, he saw the light, graceful form of the Duchess of Cleveland ascending.

The rich colour of her costume, and the sparkle of her jewels, formed a strange and striking contrast to the grim walls by which she was surrounded.

Then she disappeared through the gloomy wicket.

It was as if some wandering ray of sunlight had found its way to the door of that dreary region, and then had disappeared in its interior.

The moments seemed minutes—the minutes hours—during which Duval waited there for the return of the Duchess.

There was a shadow across the coach window.

Duval drew back for it was a human form.

"May I ask," said a voice, "if Claude Duval, the highwayman, is in this coach?"

What an extraordinary question?

From whom could it proceed, and what kind of answer was Duval to return to it?

He looked again at the face and then he recognised it.

St. Ives, the officer, was gazing into the vehicle.

He spoke again.

"May I ask, sir, if your name is Claude Duval?"

"I name myself Mr. Lavud," replied Duval.

"Oh, then you are not the person I seek. Private

information, direct from his Majesty, the King, intimated that it was probable Claude Duval, the highwayman, might be apprehended at the door of Newgate."

Duval understood all this now immediately.

This was a piece of treachery on the part of the King.

He had sought to have Duval apprehended, at the same time that he kept his word in regard to the liberation of Lucy.

And well for Duval was it that the duty had been placed upon Mr. St. Ives, for any other officer would, probably, have carried out the royal and treacherous intention without any compunction.

And Duval was at a loss what to say.

Fain would he have spoken a few words to signify how deeply he felt the generosity of St. Ives, but that was not a time nor a place when those words could be spoken.

St. Ives went slowly up the steps of Newgate, and he, too, disappeared beneath that narrow gloomy portal even as the Duchess of Cleveland had done.

Then the passing minutes seemed to lay heavier still; but as all Duval's senses were wrought up to a high degree of tension, he heard the rattle of the key in the wicket gate of the prison, as the warder, who was upon the lock, prepared to open it.

He saw the flutter of the blue silk dress of the Duchess of Cleveland.

Was she alone?

What an agonised moment that was for Claude Duval!

No—she had a companion with her!

Another glance was sufficient, and Duval knew that Lucy was all but free.

The coach door was reached.

It was opened.

Lucy hung back a moment, as if to give the Duchess precedence, but the latter urged her forward, and she sprung into the coach.

"Lucy!"

"Claude!"

That was all they needed to utter to each other.

There was some confusion upon the steps of Newgate.

A couple of officers hastily descended them, and reached the street.

"We have reason to believe——" cried one.

"That Claude Duval——" shouted the other.

"No!" said the Duchess.

She faced round immediately upon the two officers.

With her delicate fingers, all radiant with jewels, she grasped each of them by the wrist, at the same time that she cried out, "My servants will drive Mr. Lavud wherever he may order. That is my command to them, and my entreaty to him is that he go at once."

The entreaty was a command likewise.

"Covent Garden!" cried Duval.

Bang! went shut the door of the carriage, and in another moment it started from the gate of Newgate.

And there stood the Duchess of Cleveland, holding those two rough, burly men by the wrists with a hold that they could have shaken off with the slightest possible effort.

But they seemed like men suddenly changed to statues, and the delicate fingers held them as securely as manacles of iron.

The coach rolled away.

It turned out of sight.

Then the Duchess released the men.

"Will anybody get me a sedan chair?" she said.

"But, marm," said one of the officers, "you've obstructed us in the discharge of our duty."

"What!" exclaimed the Duchess. "Is it possible that I, frail and weak as I am, could obstruct an animal like you? The idea is absurd."

"A chair!" cried a loud voice. "A chair for the Duchess of Cleveland! Fetch a chair, instantly, one of you fellows!"

It was St. Ives who spoke.

"Oh, if you order it, Mr. St. Ives, it's all right!" cried one of the officers.

They ran down the Old Bailey, and disappeared on to Ludgate Hill.

St. Ives looked at the Duchess.

"I am inclined to be of opinion," he said, "that those fellows heard Mr. Lavud give the order to drive to Covent Garden."

"They must have heard it."

"Then he is pursued, and is in danger still."

"I think not," said the Duchess. "I mean, as regards the danger. There are but two of them, and my opinion is that Claude Duval——"

"Mr. Lavud, your Grace means."

"Exactly. My opinion is, that he is a match for twenty."

St. Ives bowed.

The evasion of the two officers was now certain, and St. Ives sent one of the warders who was off duty to St. Paul's Churchyard for a chair for the Duchess, who, with a flush of gratification on her face, notwithstanding an evident nervous anxiety of manner, was forthwith conveyed to her own house.

Duval and Lucy were conveyed rapidly enough in the Duchess's carriage towards Covent Garden.

"You are saved!" said Duval, as he held Lucy to his heart.

"Is it a dream?" asked Lucy.

"No, it is the fair and beautiful reality. Think only of the gloomy walls of Newgate as a dream, and forget them even in that aspect as quickly as possible."

"Oh, Claude! how have you succeeded in all this? It seems so incredible!"

"Partly by audacity, partly by accident; but most of all by the rare courage and kindness of the Duchess of Cleveland."

"But how did she interest herself for the poor, friendless Lucy Everton?"

"There are some natures," added Duval, "who prefer believing in innocence to guilt, and when they see, or fancy they see, that innocence oppressed, they never rest until they have done something to exhibit their sympathy."

"But my liberation? How did she procure that?"

"I procured that, Lucy, but she helped me to it."

"Ah, then, it is to you, indeed, Claude, that I owe my preservation!"

"And to her, Lucy. I cannot monopolise your grateful feelings."

Lucy was about to speak again, but Duval placed his hand upon her arm, and assumed an attitude of listening.

"Hush, hush!"

"What is it, Claude?"

"Listen! Do you hear nothing?"

There was a confused murmuring sound in the air, as if arising from the shouts of a multitude of persons afar off.

"It is danger."

"To you, Claude—to you?"

"To you, Lucy, which is of much more importance. But here we are at Covent Garden, and it shall be hard, indeed, with Claude Duval, if he cannot perfect the rescue so nearly accomplished."

The confused murmuring sound which Lucy had heard it seemed, in the very air, increased each moment in intensity.

The shouts of many voices.

The rapid clatter of horses' feet.

The quick thundering roll of wheels.

All these sounds, mingled with unintelligible shouts and outcries, made up a tumult which was evidently approaching each moment nearer and nearer to the wide open space of Covent Garden Market.

The officers from Newgate having recovered their first surprise at the heroic conduct of the Duchess of Cleveland, had given an alarm, and were soon joined by a party of their fellows.

They had lost sight of the coach which contained Claude Duval and Lucy, but the sumptuous liveries of the Duchess of Cleveland were not likely to be overlooked.

That was not a period when the aristocracy of birth and of wealth seemed to think it necessary to slink about the metropolis in the affectation of plainness and shabbiness.

On the contrary, the streets of London were rendered gay, and often resplendent, by the rich liveries and ornamental equipages of the nobility.

The Duchess of Cleveland was not likely to forget the opportunities that fortune had given her of making a grand show when she was in public.

Many a poor honest tradesman and hard-working mechanic owed the subsistence of his family to this taste for the magnificence which, of late years, it is the fashion to cry down and call vulgar, from some idea or principle that no one comprehends.

Some of the officers from Newgate hastily mounted, procuring their horses from where they always kept them, in those ancient inn-yards still remaining in the Old Bailey, opposite the gloomy prison.

Others of them pressed into their service such carts and passing vehicles as they could take possession of.

Then one took the lead, and called out in stentorian accents, "Twenty guineas reward for any one who will say which way the carriage went with the purple liveries!"

This shout was kept repeated until a disorderly rout of the rabble that infested that neighbourhood ran before the officers, and one questioning the other, it was soon discovered which route the carriage had taken.

And this assemblage of pursuers it was that made that confused and roaring sound which came upon the ears of Claude Duval and Lucy.

It was as though the waves of some raging sea were immediately behind them threatening to engulph them in destruction.

And as the mob, accompanied by the officers, came nearer, the excited shouts assumed intelligibility.

"A hundred pounds reward! A highwayman—a highwayman! A hundred pounds reward, dead or alive! Seize him! Nab him! Grab him! The yellow coach with the purple liveries! A highwayman—a highwayman! A hundred pounds reward!"

Lucy clung to Duval with terror in her eyes.

Duval smiled.

"They are afraid," he said.

"Afraid, Claude! Of what?"

"To pronounce my name! Listen. Amid all their outcries, they never mention Claude Duval."

Lucy did listen.

Duval was right.

But was there much hope in that circumstance?

She looked the question, and he replied to it.

"Yes, Lucy, there is hope in that; for see, we are just in the open space of the market, where there are some hundreds of people whose sympathies are not at all likely to go with Bow Street runners or warders of Newgate."

"Oh, no, no!"

"And the rabble that they bring with them only hear that some highwayman is being pursued. Perhaps, when they know me as Claude Duval, and you as the Lucy Everton so well known for a subject of popular enthusiasm, there will be nothing to fear."

Lucy rather hoped than believed in this sanguine state of things.

It was evident, however, that the servants of the Duchess of Cleveland were becoming alarmed.

The coachman began to drive in such a manner that he seemed to communicate some of his own fears to the horses in the carriage.

They plunged with alarm.

The two footmen dropped down from behind the coach as it began to back towards the pavement.

"It is time to alight," said Duval.

He pulled the check-string of the carriage, and the coachman with some difficulty reined in his horses.

"Open the door!" cried Duval.

One of the footmen obeyed him; and in another moment Claude had sprung out of the coach on to the pavement, immediately in front of the "Bedford Head."

"A highwayman—a highwayman! Stop him—stop him! A hundred guineas reward!"

The mounted officers came at a rough gallop among the old ricketty sheds of Covent Garden Market.

Then Duval closed the door of the carriage, keeping Lucy inside it.

"Wait," he said; "and be assured of the safety of both of us."

Then, before Lucy could reply, Duval had clambered up to the coachbox, and from thence he sprung on to the roof of the carriage.

"Yes!" he cried, in those clear, although by no means loud tones, that went so far, and reached every ear—"yes, I am a highwayman, and my name is Claude Duval!"

Bang!

One of the foremost of the officers had fired a pistol at Duval on his dangerous elevation.

The bullet struck his hat, and flung it from his head.

"Thank you," said Duval. "I was just going to take it off, out of natural politeness to all my good friends here in the market, and now you can see me better. My hair is as dark as—Nightshade!"

Duval, as he uttered this word "Nightshade," turned half round towards the "Bedford Head," and gave it such emphasis that it must have been heard in every hole and corner of the old hostel.

"Hurrah for Claude Duval!" shouted the crowd.

"Thank you," said Duval.

"And here's your hat, my darlint!" cried an Irish fruit-woman, as she handed it up to Duval.

"Many thanks! I think it is that man with the red hair who fired at me—there, upon the bright bay horse. I shouldn't wonder if the ladies of the market called him to some account for the cowardly act."

"We will! we will!"

"He is looking at me now, despite his red hair—as dark as—Nightshade!"

Again Duval called out the name of his horse in such unmistakable, summoning tones, that it was quite impossible his friends at the "Bedford Head" could be ignorant of the fact that he required the instant production of that matchless steed.

CHAPTER LVIII.

CLAUDE DUVAL AND LUCY MAKE GOOD THEIR RETREAT.

The situation of the few officers who had pursued Claude Duval and Lucy from Newgate was becoming critical.

The rabble rout that they had brought with them on their way had no feelings whatever in common with them.

And when the large open space of Covent Garden was reached, and Claude Duval announced himself by name to the multitude, the officers found themselves completely deserted, and holding a very isolated position.

It would have been well for them had they been permitted to remain apart as spectators of what was about to happen.

Such, however, was not the case.

It neither suited them nor the throng of persons that seemed to fill, as if by magic, the whole area of Covent Garden Market, to remain quiescent for any long period.

"Forward!" cried the principal officer. "We shall catch him at a rush!"

"All right!" cried the other. "You lead, and we'll be after you."

This was a bold proceeding, but it was a bad one.

It brought the officers into immediate collision with the people.

Immediately that they—the constables—made a dash towards the coach of the Duchess of Cleveland, a great body of the rather rough characters who had made their way into the Market from the courts and alleys of Drury Lane, at once intercepted them.

The officer with the red hair drew his hanger, and made a slash at a man who held his bridle.

The man adroitly avoided the sword cut, and, unfortunately for the officer, it fell upon the shoulder of a woman.

With a roar of rage and execration, those of the mob who had hitherto held aloof rushed forward.

The mounted officers were but four in number, and they were each surrounded by fifty hands, eager to pluck them from their saddles.

Three of them surrendered themselves to the mob at once, feeling convinced that it was their only chance of safety.

The constable with the red hair, however, saw all his danger.

He faced about his horse, and tried to fly, but the terrified animal stumbled upon a heap of decayed vegetable refuse.

Down went both horse and rider.

Then there was a wild commotion of heads, hands, and feet.

The horse either struggled to its legs, or was fairly lifted up on to them again, but it galloped away without its rider.

Tossed from hand to hand over the heads and shoulders of the people, the wretched officer, half buffetted to death, was at length flung bleeding and disfigured, against the railings of the church.

All this happened in three or four seconds.

Duval then again called out aloud: "Nightshade! Nightshade!"

There was a visible commotion at the door of the "Bedford Head."

Two or three startled people rushed out of the passage, as though they had been discharged from some gigantic piece of ordnance.

"He's coming up the stairs!" shouted a voice, "and won't let nobody hold him!"

"Nightshade!" cried Duval, again.

Then, with a rush, the horse bounded out of the porch of the "Bedford Head," and with distended and wide open eyes, glared about him.

The eminence on which Duval stood made him escape the observation of his horse for a few seconds.

Then Nightshade saw his master.

One leap placed him by the side of the Duchess's coach.

Duval stooped, and placed his hand upon the black silky mane.

Another moment, and he had vaulted into the saddle.

"Lucy!" he cried, as he stooped and opened the coach door again.

"Here, Claude!"

"It is time. Come!"

By the assistance of his left arm, Lucy sprung behind him on the horse.

She wound her fair arms about his waist.

"Safe and secure?" asked Duval.

"Ever so with you, Claude!"

"Off and away, then!"

There was a ringing shout from the people, a waving of hats and caps in every state of dilapidation, and a wide lane being formed for the progress of Nightshade, Duval, with a smile upon his face, galloped gaily from Covent Garden, leaving the discomfited officers to their own resources.

A quarter of an hour was quite sufficient, upon such a steed as Nightshade, to get clear of London by any of its outlets.

To be sure the great city was not a third of its present size, and after getting a little on the other side of the Oxford Road, there was nothing but open and pleasant country.

Duval had made up his mind to proceed at once to his home on Hampstead Heath, although he might not think it politic to go by the most direct path to it—considering that it was then broad daylight.

Nevertheless, he went at a sharp trot through Pancras Vale, and passing Steele's cottage, and the Load of Hay, he was soon at the hill-top, and at the entrance at the then rural village of Hampstead.

The place looked so serene and quiet, that the possibility of any danger in so peaceful and rural a spot seemed quite out of the question, so that Duval allowed Nightshade to subside to a walk.

And although the village of Hampstead has had its share in the march of extension, and is now approaching the size almost of a country town, it consisted then of but very few houses, nestled among gigantic trees.

The heath was a perfect wilderness of picturesque beauty.

"Let us alight," said Lucy, "and walk over this fair sward."

"I think we may," said Duval, "for we are near our home; and everything here looks so peaceful, so quiet, and so lonely, that my intention of taking a roundabout way to the mansion may be abandoned."

"It may, indeed," said Lucy, "for we seem to be but solitary wanderers on this heath."

It was unnecessary for Duval to hold the bridle of Nightshade.

That sagacious creature followed him with all the fidelity of a dog.

Then Duval turned to Lucy, and spoke with much emotion.

"I am not content," he said, "with this pardon of the King."

"But it has saved me."

"Nevertheless, it is irksome, Lucy, to be pardoned as though you were guilty."

"That its true, Claude; but what can we do? If my poor uncle, General Everton, be indeed no more, how are we to prove my perfect innocence?"

"That is the question, Lucy. I do not believe your uncle is otherwise than in the land of the living."

"And I, too, Claude, from what you have told me, cling to the hope that he still exists."

"There can be little doubt of it, and it is necessary that I should verify the fact."

"Is there a present and urgent necessity, Claude?"

"There is. When I wrested your pardon from the fears of the King, mainly assisted as I was by the self-devotion and generous conduct of the Duchess of Cleveland, I made a promise."

"A promise?"

"Yes; I said that within six months' time I would prove your perfect innocence, or surrender myself instead to justice."

"That was a rash promise, Claude, and may well be broken. We know my perfect innocence, and there must be no sacrifices made because others may not believe in it."

"But something tells me that I shall be able to keep my word."

"Six months is a long time, Claude."

"It is, indeed," replied Duval, with a smile. "But it seems to me that we are not so completely alone upon this heath, as we thought, for there is something moving yonder among the furze bushes."

A strange cry, like that of some wounded bird, arose from the direction Duval indicated.

He paused instantly, and, turning towards Nightshade, placed his hand upon one of the holsters and secured a pistol.

"There is something amiss, Lucy," he said. "That is a signal of danger, and made by Blossom."

Duval put his hand to his mouth, and imitated exceedingly well the croak of a raven.

Then the figure that was crouching among the bushes emerged, and, rapidly making its way from one sandy hillock to another of the heath, Blossom soon reached Duval and Lucy.

"Danger, Captain!" he cried. "It's all up at the old house!"

"What is amiss?"

"By early daybreak this morning, a party of officers assailed the place, and it was with the greatest difficulty that we escaped. Indeed, if it had not been for a white mist upon the heath, we could not possibly have done so."

"And where are our men?"

"They are hidden like so many rabbits among the furze."

Duval leant his arm upon the neck of Nightshade, and for a few moments considered the exigencies of the situation.

"We must seek a new home," he said.

"Alas!" exclaimed Lucy. "Where are we to seek that? or, seeking it, where are we to find it?"

"In Highgate Wood, yonder," replied Duval, "there is a small hut, which will afford us shelter for the present, and then, Lucy, I have other views. I think it will be safer far that we occupied a home in London. It is about the neighbourhood of the Court, in the Mall, and at the entertainments of the great and noble, that I shall be able to carry out and continue my career."

Duval spoke as if communing with himself.

"Yes," he added; "I do not say that I will abandon life upon the road, or that I shall be averse to a gallop on a moonlight night with my gallant Nightshade, but it is at the Court end of London that Claude Duval is formed to shine."

"Oh, Claude!" said Lucy; "what happiness would it be to see you taking up a position you are so fitted to adorn, alike by your talents and goodness."

Duval smiled.

"Everybody does not judge of me as favourably as does my Lucy," he said; "but, nevertheless, we will look forward to brighter days."

"Tarry not here, Captain?" urged Blossom, almost impatiently. "You may be seen; and then, heaven only knows what may be the consequence!"

"True! true," said Lucy; "let us away, Claude! The lonely hut of which you spoke will appear to me as gay and beautiful as any palace, provided you are by my side."

"Let us come, then, dear one," said Claude, as he drew Lucy's arm beneath his own.

Blossom laid his hand upon Nightshade's bridle, as he said:

"I wish, Captain, you would mount Nightshade. There is no telling; you may be seen and pursued; and then, there is no saying whether the time lost in mounting may not be almost fatal."

"Thanks, Blossom," said Duval, pressing the hand of his faithful follower. "Thanks, you are ever thoughtful, Blossom."

Duval and Lucy then mounted Nightshade, and at a quiet trot pursued their route towards Highgate Wood, where was situated the hut Duval had spoken of.

They had not, however, gone many paces, before Claude reined in Nightshade, and beckoned to Blossom.

Blossom hastened to meet him.

"Hide yourself for the present, Blossom, until nightfall, and then seek me, where we have made up our minds to pass a few hours, at all events."

"All right, Captain; but now go. I will take care of myself, never fear."

Duval gave the impulse to Nightshade, and the beautiful creature sped across the heath.

They had not pursued their way, however, for more than the space of about a quarter of an hour, before a shout broke upon the stillness of that beautiful and romantic spot.

"There they are!—stop them! Claude Duval! Take him! Fire! Take him, dead or alive! We have him now!"

These shouts and outcries proceeded from a tolerably strong party of mounted men, who were coming across the heath at a tremendous gallop.

"Hold on tight, dearest!" said Claude, as he put Nightshade to his utmost speed.

Now, it is quite certain that if Claude and Lucy had only those to fear who were behind them, they would have been pretty sure to make good their retreat, but just at this moment another party made its appearance in another direction; so that Duval and Lucy were, so to speak, between two dangers.

Duval looked calm; and there was an air of determination upon his face that would have struck terror into the heart of any two, or even three men.

"Yes," he said, between his closed teeth; "I will conquer or die! Fear not, Lucy, my beloved, I will rescue you yet, even from this peril!"

As he spoke, he took from his holster his two pistols, upon which he knew he could depend. "Now for a contest," he said.

Just as he had made this determination, he heard, or fancied he heard, a voice just beneath Nightshade's feet, utter the following words:

"Fly!—fly, Duval! Continue the direction you were first going in; keep straight a-head, and all may be well!"

"Who are you?" asked Duval.

"Don't you know my voice? I'm Swallow."

Duval felt that he was advised by a friend; and, putting Nightshade to a quick gallop, he continued the route he originally intended to take.

It was up a high hill, which declined in a rapid descent on the other side; so much so, that it was quite impossible for any one on the other side to see Duval, unless, indeed, they were on the very summit.

"That'll do," said Swallow. "I told him I'd be a friend to him, and so I will be, as long as I can."

At this moment the tramp of horses' feet was heard clattering along the little winding path, and Swallow rose hastily from his hiding place, and, going behind a tree, untied a horse which he had secured to it, mounted, and galloped to meet his comrades.

'Well, Swallow,"roared the voice of Muckles; "do you see anything of the fugitives?"

"Yes, sir, yes, Mr. Muckles. They've just turned down that lane by the church, and if we make haste we must soon overtake him, and have him snugly in Newgate in less than a couple of hours."

"Forward!" shouted Muckles.

CHAPTER LIX.

THE HUT IN THE WOOD.—THE DYING MAN.—BLOSSOM IS THE BEARER OF GOOD NEWS.

THE sky began to get cloudy.

The day was waning, and moreover a soft, sighing wind from the south was bringing up heavy banks of clouds.

A few spots of rain fell upon the hands of Lucy.

She looked up somewhat anxiously; for she thought that in the distance she heard the low rumble of thunder.

"A storm upon the heath, Claude."

"Let it come, Lucy; it will baffle our enemies more than it will distress us. But yonder lies the wood."

"And right glad am I to see it, Claude," said Lucy; "for once beneath the shadows of those old trees, and I shall believe myself safe again."

The only peril that they had to encounter now consisted in the fact that, in order to gain the wood by the shortest possible route, it was necessary to pass over a rising piece of ground, which almost might be called a hillock.

It was possible that if the officers kept a good look out they might see the two fugitives—if so they might be called—on that little eminence.

But Duval dismounted, and assisted Lucy likewise to alight.

"We will walk," he said; "probably I may be enabled to induce Nightshade to hold his head low."

There was no difficulty in this, and the little eminence was crossed over without any alarm being given from a distance, which was tolerably good evidence that they had not been seen.

If they had been, doubtless the officers would have raised some shout indicative of that knowledge.

The ground now rapidly descended, and Claude Duval and Lucy, with Nightshade, came upon the first straggling trees that formed the outskirts of Highgate Wood.

Tree by tree.

Rood by rood of land.

That little wood has disappeared almost completely.

But at the period of our story it was dense and picturesque, extending on both sides of a roadway for a considerable distance, and affording abundance of game of all kinds and descriptions.

After a few seconds, the darkness was so great in the wood, in consequence of the interlacing of the trees overhead, that Duval—familiar as he was with some of the forest paths—had to look closely, in order that he might not lose his way.

"There should be a winding path here to the right," he said, "which should lead us directly to our destination."

"I see something blacker than usual," said Lucy.

"It is the opening of the path, then. Yes; I know it now, by these two Norway pine trees."

It was with great difficulty that Nightshade and Claude Duval could walk a-breast in the narrow path.

Lucy followed; and Duval thought it was the best mode of proceeding; inasmuch as he was so enabled to clear away any obstructions that might rise in the way.

Then those threatening clouds that had arisen from the southern sky began to proclaim their presence, and their character.

A sharp flash of lightning for an instant lit up the wood with dazzling brilliancy.

Duval paused.

"Listen for the thunder, Lucy," he said; "the storm is yet some distance off. Hark!"

It was about five seconds after the flash of lightning before a crashing peal of thunder echoed from cloud to cloud.

"Nightshade must follow us," said Duval. "Creep forward, Lucy, and pass him."

She did so; and Duval, flinging one arm round her slender waist, gave her such efficient support that he might almost be said to carry her.

In this way they proceeded very swiftly, until Duval halted in a narrow, cleared space, from which the thick growth of underwood had been completely removed.

"At home!" he said.

"At home, Claude?"

"Yes, Lucy. This is the hut."

"It is a welcome shelter."

The little hovel must have belonged to some keeper of the wood, whose ideas of anything in the shape of luxury, as regarded a home, must have been of the most meagre character.

Duval by main force pushed open the door of the hut, for it was so completely rusted on its hinges as to have become almost a fixture.

And then as they stood for an instant on the threshold, they both started and clung impulsively together.

A low moan—evidently from some human being in suffering—came from the interior of the hut.

Lucy uttered an exclamation of alarm.

And Duval, too, was so completely taken by surprise, that for an instant he lost that rare presence of mind that generally characterised him.

Only for an instant, however, was Duval otherwise than calm, cool, and collected.

Then, with one step, he placed himself before Lucy.

There might be danger.

And yet the tone of the person was such as to betoken a great degree of physical depression.

"Speak!" cried Claude, "Who and what are you?"

The low moan came again.

Lucy trembled as she clung to the left arm of Claude.

"Fear nothing," he said, "it is only the darkness that puzzles me."

And that was intense.

Lucy at that moment closed her eyes, for another vivid flash of lightning lit up the wood.

And in that mysterious manner in which lightning seems to penetrate all space, there was a flash of radiance even into the interior of that miserable hut.

It was very instantaneous.

No sooner come than gone.

You might cry "Behold!" and that was all.

Duval happened, however, to be gazing into the interior of the hut, and to be straining his eyes with the hope of discovering what sort of occupant it had.

Lying apparently upon some dried fern and heath, he saw, unquestionably, a human form.

It seemed a man, but what was his appearance or condition, by that brief flash of light Duval could not divine.

"I have the means, Lucy," he said, "of procuring a light in the small haversack on Nightshade's saddle. Do you think, while I hold my post here at the door of the hut, you can get it for me?"

"Assuredly, Claude."

"Nightshade is here."

THE DISCOVERY TO LORD HORLOP.

"Yes, close to us."

It was quite evident to Lucy why Duval would not leave the door of the hut.

Whatever object of fear and mystery it contained, he was resolved to keep there until he saw who and what it was.

Lucy soon undid the haversack, and brought it to Duval, who from a secret recess in it, where they were in safety, procured some phosphorous matches.

Such things were not in common use then, although they were known, and went by the name of "Thieves' matches."

Duval likewise had in that haversack several lengths of wax candles.

One of these he soon succeeded in lighting, and keeping Lucy back with his left arm, he stretched his right, with which he carried the light, into the hut, and standing with one foot across its threshold, he looked curiously about him.

Yes.

There was a figure there.

The brief flash of lightning had not deceived him.

Lying upon a quantity of heaped-up furze and underwood, which probably, long ago, had been piled in that hut to dry, lay the figure of a man.

He wore a scarlet hunting-coat, with tall boots.

His hair and face were matted with sand from the heath, mingled with something which, in all probability, was blood.

"A wounded man?" cried Duval.

"Murdered!" moaned the voice of the stranger.

"Murdered!" exclaimed Lucy, as she stepped into the hut.

Her voice surely struck familiarly on the ear of the injured man, for he uttered a cry which had in its tones something of dismay.

Duval looked about him for some means of supporting the wax candle.

On one of the side walls of the hut were a stag's Antlers, and, on the extreme projection of one of these Duval easily secured the wax candle.

He then stooped down, and partially raised the wounded man.

"Speak!" he cried; "tell us who you are, and how this has happened?"

"He need not answer the first question," said Lucy.

"Indeed?"

"I know him."

"You, Lucy? Is that possible?"

The wounded stranger opened his eyes, and gazed upon her face.

"You too—you too!" he gasped, "have come to complete the murder!"

He closed his eyes again.

"Who is this man?" asked Duval.

"He is Lord Horlop."

Duval almost dropped the injured man, who lay heavily upon his arm; and, as he looked more narrowly into his face—in spite of the heath-sand, and the blood with which it was disfigured—he remembered his features.

"Indeed, my lord," he said, "you have more lives than an honest man. I thought the last time we met would, indeed, be the last for many a long day."

Horlop groaned.

"How has this happened?" said Lucy.

"The villain, Pendell."

Lord Horlop spoke with difficulty.

"He decoyed me to the wood, and then struck me from my horse, leaving me for dead among the tangled bushes; but I crawled in here. How long ago could it be? Has it been months? Help! Help! Avenge me!"

"Be still," said Claude; "you do but aggravate your sufferings."

"You are my enemy!"

"No!"

"And she too—she too—Lucy Everton!"

"No!" said Lucy.

"I say, yes! it cannot be otherwise! You hate me, both of you, and are sent by Pendell to finish the murderer's work!"

"We were your enemies," said Duval, "when you were able to be vicious and virulent against us; but now that you have fallen so low, we listen but to the dictates of a higher humanity than you can, perhaps, understand."

Lord Horlop looked in the face of Claude Duval, dreamily.

He seemed scarcely to comprehend the words that were uttered; and, perhaps, that want of comprehension arose, in a degree, from the fact that he, under similar circumstances, would have spoken so differently.

And then, as the light from the little wax candle fell upon the face of the wounded man, its expression changed, and Claude Duval thought that it was death he saw upon it.

"I thank heaven!" he said, "that it is not by my hands that this man has fallen."

"Is he dying?" whispered Lucy.

"I fear so."

"May I speak to him?" said Lucy, eagerly.

"Yes, if you wish," replied Claude.

"I would fain, then, ask him one question, which, perhaps, at such a moment as this, he may reply to truly."

"Be quick," said Duval, "I do not like his looks."

"Speak, my Lord Horlop!" cried Lucy, advancing a step or two. "Speak, and at this solemn moment, speak truly!"

"What would you have me say?" he asked, faintly.

"Does my uncle live?"

"Your uncle?"

"Yes; General Everton. Speak, while yet you have the power, and answer me."

"Everton—Everton—General Everton? Oh, that—all that was a thousand years ago."

Lord Horlop slipped from the arm of Claude Duval, and lay perfectly supine among the dried furze of the heath in that wretched Hut.

"Gone!" said Duval.

"Oh, this is dreadful!" exclaimed Lucy.

"Come away," said Duval, "you see it was not to be. He would not, or could not answer you."

A strange hooting noise, as of an owl, came from the wood.

"That is Blossom," said Duval, as he at once replied to the signal.

Blossom spoke from among the trees cheerily.

"Captain, all is well! The nabs have left the old house, and have gone back to London, no wiser than they came."

"Then that mansion on the heath is still our home, Lucy, and we will let it be so for a brief period, for I am very weary."

The storm had passed away, and the little party now proceeded from the wood at Highgate towards their old residence on Hampstead Heath.

Duval, as they went, related to Blossom what had occurred in the old hut.

"And do you mean to leave him there, Captain?" said Blossom.

"I think so. It is as good a tomb as he could hope for. At all events, it is not necessary that we should seek to find him another. He may, perchance, be discovered, and if not, let the night winds sing his requiem among the tree-tops."

After all the excitements they had gone through that day, how welcome was rest to Lucy Everton and Claude Duval.

And how like a dream appeared those events, so full of alarm and danger, when they looked out in the morning upon the bright and beautiful heath, spangled as were the bushes with a million dew-drops glittering like diamonds.

But the spirit of restlessness and the love of adventure belonged to the nature of Claude Duval and must be gratified.

It was towards the close of that day that Duval and Lucy walked in the gardens of the mansion they had appropriated to their own use, and fain would Lucy have persuaded him to rest for a time from the adventurous life he lead.

"Be persuaded, Claude," she said, "surely you are rich enough for some slight repose."

"No Lucy, it is a necessity of my nature, I must seek excitement; but it shall not always be on the heath, and on the road. To-morrow I will proceed to London, and there in that kind of solitude which is only to be found in a great city, we will reside in peace."

"In peace, Claude?"

He smiled.

"Well, Lucy, I must pursue my adventurous vocation, and the world has yet to hear much more of Claude Duval."

There was a shadow upon the path.

Blossom stepped forward.

"All ready, Blossom?"

"All ready, Captain."

Lucy looked reproachfully at Duval.

Duval smiled archly, and said:

"Only a canter on the heath, Lucy, and then home again; and it is principally for the benefit of Nightshade, who wants exercise."

CHAPTER LX.

CLAUDE DUVAL AND BLOSSOM MEET WITH A STRANGE ADVENTURE.

In five minutes Duval was in the saddle, and accompanied by Blossom, they trotted together down one of the avenues of the old heath.

"We shall have an adventure," said Duval, "I feel certain of it."

"And I too, Captain. Let us hope that it will be a profitable one, my purse is most uncomfortably light."

Duval laughed.

A clatter of horse's feet at some distance, as if apparently approaching from town-wards across the heath, came upon their ears.

"Listen!" said Duval.

"With all my ears, Captain."

As they listened, however, the sounds seemed to fade away.

"That's provoking," said Blossom, "he has taken one of the turnings towards Kilburn."

"Be it so," said Duval, "but now that we are completely alone upon the heath, and there are no listeners, I have something to propose to you, in which I think you, and you alone, can aid me."

"Look upon it as done, Captain."

"Among the vaults beneath the cathedral of St. Paul's."

Blossom whistled.

"You do not much like the beginning of the enterprise, Blossom."

"In truth, Captain, I do not. I was never very fond of vaults nor their inhabitants."

"Nor I, Blossom, but this is a case of necessity, I want to see one whom I never yet saw in life."

"Don't, Captain! don't! keep out of such company as long as you can."

"Nay, hear me out, Blossom, we will take a third person with us, who knew the late General Everton well; and I shall never be satisfied until such person has seen him in his tomb, and properly identified him."

"Then you don't think he's there, Captain?"

"I do not; and if I receive such a confirmation of my surmises, as finding that the occupant of the vault I mention is not the late General Everton.——"

"Hush!"

The sound of horse's feet came again rapidly across the heath.

"A chance, Captain! a chance!" cried Blossom, with a laugh, "my pockets were well nigh empty, I confess."

"And mine, too," said Duval. "Draw back beneath the shadow of those trees, and leave me to stop this man."

Blossom backed his horse against a hedge where, in the dim twilight, both steed and rider were completely hidden from view.

The horseman came on at a hand gallop.

Duval touched Nightshade on the flank.

The horse trotted into the middle of the road, and there stood perfectly still.

But the approaching horseman had evidently seen this action of Claude Duval, for he reined in abruptly.

"Halt!" cried Duval.

"No, no, stay me not!" cried the horseman in loud excited tones, " let me pass, whoever you are, a life hangs upon my speed."

"Halt!" cried Duval, again, as he dashed forward.

The horseman plunged his hand into the holster, and drew forth a pistol.

"Another step and I fire," he cried.

"You waste both powder and shot," laughed Claude, as he caught the man's horse by the bridle, and forced it back on its haunches.

Bang! went the pistol.

"I told you so," as he ducked his head, and the two bullets, with which the pistol was loaded, flew over it.

"Missed, by heaven!" cried the stranger.

He dug his spurs into his horse's sides, and tried to gallop from the spot.

Clutching him by the collar with one hand, Duval held the horse's bridle with the other, and by a great effort of strength fairly lifted the man from the saddle and flung him heavily on to the roadway.

"Blossom! Blossom!" he cried.

"Here, Captain!"

"See to this man while I hold his horse. The creature is a better one than your own, and I advise you to change with this gentleman."

"To be sure," said Blossom.

Then, approaching the discomfited horseman, Blossom said, "Now, sir, I will trouble you to hand over whatever you may happen to have about you."

"Quick!" cried Duval; "I hear the tramp of horses on the road!"

Somewhat stunned by his fall on the hard, stony roadway, the traveller allowed his pockets to be rifled by Blossom, without offering the slightest opposition.

The booty was of much value.

Struggling, then, to his feet, he said, "Claude Duval, I know you!"

Claude slightly raised his hat.

"Most folks know me by sight," he replied; "but the knowledge is sometimes dangerous."

"Not in this case," said the stranger, in tones of assurance. "I have heard that Claude Duval is ever ready to succour the oppressed against the oppressor; to punish the guilty, and avenge the innocent. This night I have need of help against one stronger than myself. Speak, Claude Duval—will you aid me?"

"In what manner?" asked Duval.

"Listen! There is a man—a bad, bold man of rank and wealth—who, casting the unhallowed eyes of passion on my child—has wooed her to be his! Baffled by her constant virtue, he has torn her from her home. I believe her to be now a prisoner in an old mansion, not a mile from here, called "The Grange."

"The villain!" cried Blossom.

"His name?" said Duval.

"The Duke of Montrose."

"Ah, I guessed as much!"

"You know him, then?"

"I do, for a disgrace to the name he bears. Believe me, sir, I will aid you with all my heart and soul to rescue your daughter from the clutches of so great a villain. Mount your horse; and as we ride on together you will give me such information as may enable me to form some plan of action."

This was no sooner said than done; and the little party had not ridden many yards ere the mounted men, the tramp of whose horses Duval had heard while Blossom was engaged in rifling the pockets of the stranger, came fully in sight.

Duval looked suspicious, and a thought of treachery crossed his mind. The stranger who had thus claimed his assistance might, after all, be some cunning emissary of Mr. Muckles, who was leading him into an ambuscade.

But he had no time for reflection.

On came the horsemen.

"There are six of them, Captain," said Blossom, in a low tone.

"See to your pistols, Blossom!"

"Pray be careful, Captain!"

A few paces only separated them from the small party of mounted men.

Both parties came to a halt.

Then a personage in the costume of a gentleman rode out from the party, and, holding up his whip, said, "Jupiter!"

"What?" cried Duval.

His companion grasped him by the arm.

"I know them," he said.

"Indeed!"

"Yes: they are friends of the Duke of Montrose. I have seen them at the Grange. I was steward to the Duke."

"Jupiter," said the man again.

"Say Europa," whispered the steward.

"But——"

"Oh, do not hesitate, for the love of heaven! Presently I will explain all. Think of my poor child! You promised to aid me, Claude Duval."

"And will do so. Be at ease."

Then, advancing Nightshade a few paces, Duval called out, "Europa!"

"It's all right, gentlemen," said the man who had uttered the word "Jupiter," as he turned to his companions; "these gallants are evidently bound on the same expedition as ourselves."

"Hurrah!" cried the others. "The more the merrier."

Claude Duval, Blossom, and the stranger rode on in company with the mysterious party of horsemen.

"Captain," whispered Blossom, "I don't like the looks of those men."

"Nor I," replied Claude. "Keep on your guard, Blossom. There is one in particular whom I seem to have met before."

Blossom started, and felt mechanically for his pistols.

The night was coming on dark and squally, and a cold, small rain caused the travellers to draw their cloaks more closely around them.

"A rough night, gentlemen," said he who had first spoken to Claude Duval. "Let us hasten to the convivial board of our noble friend the Duke."

"By Jove!" cried another; "they always used to tell queer stories about that old house of his grace being haunted, and now I believe it."

"How so, Sir Charles?"

"Why, they've found the ghost—a very substantial one of flesh and blood—a sweet little creature that might have tempted St. Anthony himself—a perfect Hebe."

"Europa, you mean," said another of the party.

There was a general laugh at this, and then he who had been addressed as Sir Charles cried out, "Gentlemen, the noble Jupiter awaits our coming."

The horses were put to increased speed, and the trees and hedges flew rapidly by.

The rain and wind beat fiercely in the face of Claude Duval.

He touched Marley, the Duke's steward, on the arm.

"Now," he said, "what is the meaning of all this? Who is Jupiter, and who is Europa?"

In a rapid whisper the man spoke.

"As I told you," he said, "the Duke of Montrose has taken my daughter Marion to the Grange, where he gives a grand supper to-night to a number of his dissolute acquaintances, at which he intends to show them my poor Marion in his power. None are to be admitted to this orgie but those in possession of two passwords 'Jupiter' and 'Europa.' It seems there was some sort of wager between the Duke and a certain great personage as to which of the two would first carry off the poor child. And now——"

The steward was interrupted by a sudden exclamation from Claude Duval, whose eyes were fixed upon one of the horsemen who rode a few paces in front of him and Blossom.

Mounted on a dark bay horse.

Closely enveloped in a cloak.

A peculiar air of command about him.

"What is it, Captain?" asked Blossom.

Duval made no reply, but advancing Nightshade a few paces, placed himself abreast of the man whom he indicated.

The horseman heard the snort of Nightshade.

He turned his head.

A puff of wind blew aside the cloak he wore.

A glance was sufficient.

The Prince of Wales!

Claude Duval, the highwayman!

Then in a yelling voice the Prince Frederick—for it was indeed he—called out, "Seize him, gentlemen—seize him! Shoot him! Cut him down! A spy—a spy!"

Although taken completely by surprise as they were, the Prince's companions uttered a shout of mingled rage and terror as they gathered round that royal personage.

There was a general flash of swords.

"Stoop, Captain—stoop!" cried Blossom.

Duval flung himself forward on the neck of Nightshade, and fired his two pistols past the creature's head.

There was a scattering volley from the horsemen, followed by a shriek of pain from some one of their number.

Duval's hat was struck from his head by a bullet, and, spinning round struck the Prince in the face.

He thought he was hit, for, with a yell of fear, he rolled from the saddle into a ditch by the wayside.

The remaining horsemen made a rush upon Duval with their swords.

"Fire, Blossom—fire!"

Bang! bang! went Blossom's pistols.

"Take that!" he said.

"And this!" cried Mr. Marley, as with a pistol in each hand, he fired over Duval's shoulder.

One of the horsemen was killed outright, and two others dangerously wounded.

The survivors were struck with dismay at the aspect of affairs.

They flung away their discharged pistols.

"Charge!" shouted Duval.

This was sufficient.

The battle was won.

Quite heedless of the fate of their royal master, the remaining horsemen dug their spurs into the flanks of the terrified horses, and at a mad pace, galloped from the spot.

"Hurrah!" cried Blossom; "we've beaten the rascals!"

"Murder! murder!" yelled a voice from the roadside.

It was that of Frederick, Prince of Wales.

Duval laughed.

"Let him lie there, Captain, it will cool his blood!" said Blossom.

"Help! help!" again shrieked the Prince of Wales.

Claude dismounted, and holding Nightshade by the bridle, approached the ditch.

"Your Royal Highness," he said, "has sought my life. But, considering who you are, I waive that little circumstance, and am willing to aid you. Will you be so good as to tell me where you are?"

"In the ditch. Oh, dear! oh, dear!"

With considerable difficulty, Claude Duval succeeded in extricating the Prince of Wales from the unpleasant position in which he found himself.

Dripping with water, covered with slime and ooze—and, take him for all in all, a most pitiable object—the Prince, after a great deal of scrambling, struggled to his feet.

"I'll have you drawn and quartered yet!" he muttered between his teeth; then, shivering in every limb from the cold immersion, he cried, "In the fiend's name give me my horse, and let me go!"

He caught the horse by the bridle.

Blossom held the stirrup.

The Prince mounted, with pain and difficulty, and, with a bitter malediction on his royal lips, galloped from the spot.

CHAPTER LXI.

CLAUDE DUVAL RELEASES A PRISONER, AND GETS THE BETTER OF MR. MUCKLES.

"AND now, Claude Duval," said Mr. Marley, who had concealed himself beneath the shadow of a tree; "may I beg of you to hasten on to the Grange? I seem to hear the voice of my poor child calling upon me for help."

"I am with you," said Duval, as both he and Blossom urged on their horses from the scene of the late encounter.

For a few moments, now, not a word was spoken, till Blossom, who had pushed on a few yards in front, suddenly called out, "Captain, I hear the sound of wheels."

They all paused; then Duval inquired, "What is it, Blossom, a coach or a post-chaise?"

"Neither, Captain; a cart, I fancy."

"A cart?"

"Yes, and here it comes."

There was a grating sound of wheels, a heavy rumbling noise, and the smacking of a whip.

As the cart neared the spot where they were, the rough tones of two men in conversation reached the ears of Claude Duval and Blossom.

"I tells you what it is, Mr. Muckles, we shall never smoke our blessed pipes in peace till we've settled Claude Duval!"

"You're too great a fool, Swallow, or we should have had him in the Stone Jug long ago."

"Muckles," said Duval.

"And Swallow," laughed Blossom.

"But what is that at the bottom of the cart?"

"Well, if my eyes don't deceive me, Captain, I should say it was a man, heavily ironed. Some prisoner of Muckles's."

"Ah! indeed, in that case, our old friend, Muckles, is in great danger of losing his prisoner. Conceal yourself on the other side of the hedge, Mr. Marley. It would be dangerous for you to be a seeming actor in what is about to take place."

The cart reached the spot.

"Hold!" cried Duval, on one side of it.

"Stand!" cried Blossom, on the other.

"What on earth is all this?" roared Muckles, as he seized a lantern, and glared fiercely about him.

He saw Duval.

He uttered a shriek of dismay.

"Drive on, Mr Muckles, drive on!" cried Swallow. "We're sure to be done brown!"

"But, I won't drive on," shouted Muckles. "Surrender, Claude Duval. I won't return to town without you."

"Certainly not with me," said Duval, as he played carelessly with one of his pistols. "Who is your prisoner, Muckles?"

"It's me!" cried a voice from the bottom of the cart; and with a great clanking of fetters, a tall, gaunt figure struggled to its feet.

"I seem to know you," said Blossom.

"Shouldn't at all wonder, I'm Hounslow Jack! I was in the blessed ken at Westminster, when we blew up St. Ives. I saw you, Claude Duval, with Nightshade. You were hard pressed by the nabs."

"Silence, wretch!" cried Muckles, as he dealt a blow at the head of Jack, but that individual dexterously slipped aside, and the blow caught Swallow about the middle of the back.

"A miss is as good as a mile," cried Jack.

"Muckles," said Duval, as he laid his hand on the edge of the cart, "Get out!"

"I get out?" said Muckles.

"Yes, at once! What say you, Jack, do you feel inclined for a gallop on the road?"

"Rather!" said Jack.

"You hear, Mr. Muckles. So get out at once, and you too, Swallow!"

"Not if I knows it, Claude Duval!"

"Then take the consequences of your own obstinacy," cried Duval, laying his hand on the officer's collar.

But Muckles, who had been fumbling in his capacious pockets during this brief colloquy, suddenly drew forth his hand armed with a large horse pistol.

He levelled it in Duval's face.

"Take that!" he said.

Bang!

With a cry of pain, Muckles himself fell back in the cart; while, to his intense surprise, Claude Duval remained calm and uninjured.

The fact was, that Blossom, who was eyeing Muckles with suspicion, had seen him draw the pistol from his pocket, and not having time to warn Duval, had fired at the same moment as the officer, who was hit in the fleshy part of the arm, and his aim thereby disturbed.

"Give in, Mr. Muckles—give in!" cried Swallow. "It's no use fighting with Claude Duval!"

Duval spoke sternly now.

"I give you one minute to decide," he said. "Either give up the cart, and release Hounslow Jack from his irons, or have your brains scattered on the roadside!"

"Oh, dear! oh, dear! Think of Mrs. Muckles and the little Muckles's," groaned Swallow.

With a considerable amount of difficulty—the pain of the wound in his shoulder, causing him to make various contortions of countenance as he did so—Muckles scrambled out of the cart, and stood trembling in the roadway.

He was closely followed by Swallow.

"Well, I suppose I must!" muttered the officer. "Claude Duval, I yield to force only! Say what you want, and let me off!"

Blossom now assisted Hounslow Jack out of the cart, an operation of some difficulty, seeing that the latter was heavily loaded with irons.

"All right, old Muckles, I shan't be lagged this time. Remember me to the Stone Jug, ha! ha!"

"Now, Mr. Muckles, I have but one thing to ask you for," said Duval.

"Well, what is that?" growled Muckles.

"The key!"

"Key! What key?"

"Why, the key of Jack's irons, to be sure!" cried Blossom.

"Take it, then!"

As he spoke, Muckles threw a large rough-looking key to Duval, who dexterously catching it, proceeded to free Jack from his fetters.

"Felony!" groaned Swallow. "Felony!"

"Come on, come on!" growled Muckles. "Let us to town at once. Duval, the game is yours, to-day, but beware of our next meeting. Help me into the cart, Swallow, and drive on."

"Not so fast, Mr. Muckles," cried Duval, "not so fast, if you please."

"What do you want, now?" he roared, in a fearful rage.

Claude turned to Jack as he said:

"Jack, you want a horse, do you not?"

"Exactly so."

"Then mount at once," added Duval, as he pointed to the stout, shaggy-looking creature in the shafts of the police officer's cart.

The rescued highwayman understood him.

With professional dexterity he unharnessed the not very lively quadruped, and jerking the reins round the neck of Swallow, who was looking with consternation at the whole proceedings, scrambled on to the creature's back.

"Good night, Mr. Muckles, good night, Swallow, pleasant dreams to you both," laughed Jack, as he trotted along beside Claude Duval.

"Confound you all," roared the discomfited Muckles, as he snatched his remaining pistol from his belt and, notwithstanding the pain of his wound, fired at the three horsemen before him.

"That makes two shots to my one," said Duval, calmly, as he fired one of his own pistols at Muckles

The officer's hat and wig flew off, and fully convinced that he had a bullet in the head, he fell to the ground, knocking down Swallow as he did so.

Duval and Blossom were now joined by Mr. Marley, who from his hiding-place behind the hedge, had been an impatient spectator of the encounter with Muckles and Swallow.

A sharp trot of about ten minutes now brought the little party, reinforced by the addition of Hounslow Jack, to a dark part of the road, where embosomed in a dense mass of stately old trees, stood the house in which Mr. Marley had reason to believe his fair child was detained by the Duke of Montrose.

"This is the place," he said, speaking in a low tone to Duval.

It was one of those old, red-brick mansions of the Elizabethan era, a maze of lordly turrets, quaint gables, and antique bay windows, so few specimens of which, unfortunately, now remain.

The Grange was one of the many country mansions of the rich and courtly Duke of Montrose, and of which many a scandal, many a tale similar to the one we are now about to relate, was whispered.

Our little party now came to a halt at the great gates of the mansion, and a puzzled look crossed the face of Hounslow Jack, for he was yet ignorant of the object of the expedition.

He turned to Duval.

"What's the little game, Captain? Is it cracking a crib? If so, I'm your man. Only say the word."

"Hold your noise, Jack, and let the Captain speak," said Blossom.

"Our object is, I fancy, to gain admission to the Grange without giving the alarm to any of its inmates. From his acquaintance with the premises, Mr. Marley, of course, will act as guide to us all," said Duval, as he glanced upward at the dark mass of clouds, which by their totally obscuring the moon's rays, made it so favourable to their proceedings.

"Then I pray you dismount, and follow me closely," said Mr. Marley.

"But the horses," objected Blossom.

The steward pointed to a dimly-seen enclosure, some few yards from the spot where they stood

"A pound!" said Jack.

"Just so, we are at Hendon."

"The very thing," cried Duval, as he flung himself from the saddle. "You, Blossom, lead the horses into the pound, and we will wait for you here."

A very few minutes sufficed for the faithful friend and follower of Claude Duval to effectually secure the horses in the pound, and placing a large stone against the gate of it, he rejoined the group assembled at the gates of the Grange.

"Now, come on," whispered Marley. "A little further on there is a door in the wall through which I would fain penetrate to the garden. Keep close to this old ivy, and above all let no one speak, for there may be persons in some of the kiosks the duke has had built about the grounds."

Creeping along like so many shadows, the little party glided past the garden wall, overhung by luxuriant masses of old ivy; and in the course of a few seconds duly reached the door before mentioned by Claude Duval's new companion.

Cautiously, Mr. Marley laid his hand upon the rusty lock.

A touch was sufficient.

The door was fast.

"I'll soon settle this difficulty," said Blossom, as he advanced; and taking from his pocket a complicated machine of twisted wire, he applied it artistically to the rebellious lock.

There was a sharp clicking sound, and the couple of bolts with which the garden door was secured were wrenched from their sockets.

"Done in a business-like manner," said Jack, as he nodded his approval at the feat.

The door now yielded to a touch, and swung lazily open; while Duval, Blossom, and Jack, preceded by the former steward of the Duke of Montrose, passed quickly through.

They were in the garden.

From what could be seen of the ornamental grounds of the "Grange" in the darkness, it was evident they were of vast extent and beauty.

"Tread softly," whispered Duval, for they found themselves on a soft gravel path, which grated ominously beneath their feet.

The precaution was needless; for a few yards further on the gravel-walk merged into a grass plot, which by its extent, and the direction it took, seemed to lead right up to the lower windows of the mansion.

"Quick across the lawn!" cried Marley. "Fortunately, the moon is down. We are sure to find a window unfastened somewhere."

The little party sped rapidly across the verdant grass, where their footsteps fell softly, crushing the white daisies as they went.

The lawn, as we have intimated, stretched right up to a flight of steps leading to a sort of terrace, on to which looked a row of tall, narrow windows of stained glass.

"A beautiful place," said Duval; "a pity that it should be in the occupation of such a man. But this should be a sort of ecclesiastical portion of the building, if I mistake not."

"It is called the 'Oratory,'" said Marley, as they all stepped on to the terrace. "The Montrose family is of the Catholic persuasion; and the Duke Reginald, they say, in order to atone for some deed of blood, caused this little oratory, or chapel, to be built. It is now abandoned to the rats and mice, I fancy."

"It seems a strange sort of a crib," said Jack, as he approached one of the windows, and tried to peer through the grimy panes of glass.

"Nothing but lots o' darkness," he said.

"Is it by one of these windows we are to make our way into the house?" demanded Duval.

"Yes. Behold!"

As he spoke, Marley flung open one of the stained glass windows with a touch; taking care, however, not to produce the slightest sound.

Motioning them all to follow him as quickly as possible, the steward clambered lightly on to the window-sell, and disappeared into the "oratory."

The little party now found themselves in a darkness almost palpable; while a confined, suffocating smell, such as is usual in places that have been a long time shut up, produced a most unpleasant effect on their nerves, coming as they just did from the open air.

A dark lantern was soon lit by Blossom; and by its feeble rays the nocturnal intruders were enabled to note the vast extent and general beauty of the old disused chapel.

There was a sort of gloomy grandeur pervading the building.

The ruined altar of polished marble, the costly vessels of gold and silver incidental to Catholic worship, a few moth-eaten banners of faded velvet, and a shattered image of the Virgin in a sculptured niche, produced a strange, saddened impression on the mind of the beholder.

As he was musing over these voiceless relics of the past, Claude Duval felt himself touched lightly on the arm, and found the pale face of Mr. Marley gazing anxiously upon him.

"Of a truth, I was forgetting the errand that brought us hither," said Duval, kindly.

The steward shook him by the hand.

"Every step brings me nearer to my dear child," he said.

"In heaven's name, let us on; and may an all-merciful providence enable us to accomplish the work we have at heart!" replied Claude, fervently.

CHAPTER LXII.

CLAUDE DUVAL SEEKS THE DAUGHTER OF THE STEWARD OF THE GRANGE.

PRECEDED by Blossom, who held the light above his head, so that its rays might the better penetrate the nooks and corners of the old chapel, our adventurers now rapidly traversed the deserted aisles in the direction of a low, arched door, that led, said Mr. Marley, into the inhabited portion of the Grange.

This door was of massive oak, and thickly studded with nails, presenting, apparently, a formidable obstacle to any one desirous of forcing an entrance.

Jack uttered a low whistle.

"It looks like the door of the Stone Jug," he said.

"Hold the light lower, Blossom!"

It was Duval who spoke.

Carefully, then, examining the ponderous door in every direction, Claude Duval soon convinced himself that it must prove an effectual barrier to their further progress, unless some key could be procured to fit the lock.

"What keys have you, Blossom?"

"Only these, Captain!"

He handed some five or six keys, of different shapes and sizes, to Duval.

Claude tried them one after another, introducing them with considerable difficulty into the lock, so choked up was it with dust and rubbish.

The others looked on in silence; and Mr. Marley turned a shade paler, as he saw key after key thrown aside as useless, until but one was left of those that Blossom had handed to Duval.

"Bravo!" cried Blossom, at this moment.

The door had yielded, and swung back heavily on its rusted hinges.

The steward uttered an exclamation of delight.

"Let us quickly leave this place," said Duval. "Time is precious to us all. Bring the light, Blossom."

With the exception of Marley, they all passed through the gloomy doorway, into what appeared to be a sort of corridor beyond.

"Mr. Marley," said Blossom; "where are you?"

Duval raised his hand.

"Hush!" he said.

He raised his hat, and pointed to a kneeling figure before that bruised and battered image of the Virgin, in the old "oratory."

It was Marley, the steward, with hands clasped in silent prayer for the safety of his dear child, more precious to his heart than the fabled riches of the golden Indies.

Instinctively, then, Jack—abandoned, rough outcast from society as he was—followed the example of Duval and Blossom, and remained silent and thoughtful to the conclusion of the steward's supplication to heaven for aid and guidance.

The steward crossed himself devoutly, and rose to his feet.

He passed through the door.

"I feel better and stronger now," he said.

The place in which the little party now found themselves was a long, narrow stone passage, evidently hewn in the thickness of the wall, which was pierced at intervals by loopholes, admitting both light and air.

A thick coating of dust on the floor of the corridor effectually prevented the sound of footsteps from being heard beyond its precincts.

Suddenly Duval paused, and assumed an attitude of listening.

"Hush!" he said, "I hear voices."

They all paused, immovable as so many statues, as Blossom closed the slide of the lanthorn he carried, leaving them in total darkness.

Duval was not mistaken.

The faint, confused murmur of voices, engaged in earnest conversation, now came unmistakably to their ears.

But where did the sounds come from?

From the "oratory" they had but just now quitted? Impossible.

That there was a room or suite of rooms immediately beyond the stone corridor, Duval felt convinced, but as to the means of arriving at the whereabouts of the speakers, he was of course quite ignorant.

"Tell me," he said to the steward, "have you no idea, as to where this old corridor leads?"

Marley considered a moment, then he said, "From my general knowledge of the mansion, I should say that we are in close proximity to a suite of rooms usually in the occupation of the Duke of Montrose. I believe that on the other side of this stone passage is an apartment called the 'King's Ease,' from the fact of King Charles the Second having there lain in hiding from a troop of Cromwell's Ironsides."

"And you think that the voices we now hear proceed from that chamber?" said Duval.

"I do; and something seems to tell me, it is there I shall find my child."

"Say you so, my good friend, then in heaven's name let us gain admittance to it. Ah! what is that?"

Hounslow Jack uttered a smothered shout of dismay, and Blossom hastily raised the slide of his lanthorn.

"What's the matter, Jack?" asked Blossom.

"Well, I don't exactly know," said Jack, gazing dubiously at that portion of the wall of the corridor against which, a moment before, he had leant his back.

"Look there," he said.

"Where? I don't see anything."

As he spoke, Blossom passed the light up and down the slimy-looking stone wall.

Placing his shoulder to what looked like an ordinary block of stone, Jack gave it a slight push, and, to the intense surprise of all present, a portion of the wall seemed to move.

Blossom intimated this mysterious circumstance to Claude Duval.

Duval had seen in the course of his chequered career more than one of those ancient mansions, in which it was by no means uncommon to discover secret passages, subterraneous vaults, or sliding panels, the secret of which had perished with the original occupants of the house.

Hence was it that Claude Duval was by no means surprised at the seeming startling discovery so unconsciously made by Hounslow Jack.

As we have said, a portion of the wall actually moved.

Claude Duval put out his hand, and, on a careful examination, found that the seeming block of stone, which had been shaken by the pressure of Jack's hand, was in reality nothing more than a piece of canvas, so inimitably painted to resemble stone, as to deceive the most critical scrutiny.

"Well, Captain, what think you?" said Blossom.

"It is an artfully contrived piece of mechanism," he replied, "a sliding panel, communicating doubtless with the chamber you call the 'King's Ease,' Mr. Marley."

"It should be so," rejoined the steward. "And in that chamber, I feel convinced, we shall find my child, my Marion!"

"Good! In the first place, let us endeavour to discover who are its occupants. Put down the light, Blossom, and listen, all of you. Ah!"

Duval had slid back the panel a couple of inches.

The slight opening revealed, as they had surmised, an apartment beyond the stone passage.

It was the "King's Ease!"

The chamber they sought.

A thin pencil of light came from it into the corridor.

The unmistakable tones of a masculine voice reached the ears of the listeners.

"So you defy me?" it said.

"The Duke!" whispered Duval.

Then a female voice of singular softness and beauty said, "I look upon you with scorn and loathing, my lord Duke. Begone, and rid me of your hateful presence!"

"My Marion!" almost shrieked Mr. Marley, as he made a movement to dash aside the panel opening into the room, but the powerful grasp of Claude Duval restrained him, and drew him forcibly back.

"Are you mad?" he said. "Would you give an alarm, and thereby ruin all? Be silent for *her* sake!"

"I will—I am!"

Very pale, and with great nervousness of manner, the steward allowed himself to be held back by Claude Duval, who waited eagerly for the next words that should fall from the lips of the Duke of Montrose.

That that unscrupulous nobleman had been much angered at the withering scorn of the young girl's refusal of his brilliant offers was evident, for he now spoke in a tone of concentrated passion.

"Girl, you know not your own danger!"

"Danger?"

"Even so. You know not the power I possess, nor the means I have of enforcing your obedience. Reflect, and let your better judgment come to your aid. I now leave, but in an hour I shall return."

The little party in the corridor conjectured that the Duke had left the room in which the conversation had taken place, for there was a sound of hasty footsteps, succeeded by the sharp banging of a door, and the rattle of a key in the lock.

Marion was alone.

"Heaven help me!" she sobbed, flinging herself on a couch by the fire-side. "What will become of me in this dreadful place? Is there, indeed, no one to help me? Oh, father, father! where are you now?"

"Here!" shouted Mr. Marley, as he at once dashed open the sliding panel, and, heedless of the danger his sudden appearance might bring about, dashed into the room, and catching his terrified daughter in his arms, clasped her to his heart,—"Here, my Marion, to save you from the snares of a villain! Look up, my darling—my treasure!"

So frightened and bewildered was the young creature at this sudden, and, to her, inexplicable appearance of her father, whom she had every reason to believe ignorant of her whereabouts, that it was some few seconds before she was capable of recognising the kindly face of the old steward.

At length, with a gush of heartfelt tears, she flung her fair arms round his neck, and wept and laughed by turns; seeming, in the joy of once more being clasped to her father's heart, to forget the trials she had passed through, and those which might yet be in store for her.

"Dear, dear father, you will save me, you will take me from this place. Oh, say that you will?"

"I will, indeed, do so, my Marion," replied the steward, gazing with the fondest rapture on the child-like beauty of his fair young daughter.

"My advice is, that we at once quit this place," said Claude Duval, as he now advanced into the "King's Ease," followed by Blossom and Hounslow Jack.

Marion uttered a cry of alarm, and clung closer to her father.

"Be calm, dearest, be calm," said Marley, "these are all good friends of mine and of yours."

Marion gathered courage at this, and gently raising her soft brown eyes, looked timidly at Claude Duval.

"Do I, indeed, behold a friend?" she said.

"A real and true friend, Marion."

The frank engaging manner, and refined handsome features of Duval, at once convinced the young creature of his sincerity and intention to befriend her.

She held out her hand to him.

A pretty little dimpled hand it was, too.

Claude kissed it, as reverentially as he would have done that of a Princess.

"Nice, that," muttered Jack, as he dodged about behind Blossom, and screwed up his lips.

Bang, bang, bang, came a furious knocking at the room door, of which Duval had fortunately secured the key on leaving the corridor.

Marion uttered a half-smothered cry, and grasped with frantic eagerness at the lappels of Duval's coat.

"Hush! hush!"

The knocking came again, and then some one tried the handle of the door.

"Open, girl; open, I say."

"The Duke!" gasped Marley.

"If it be the Duke," said Duval, "he knows not his own danger. I have an old score to settle with him as well as this one."

CHAPTER LXIII.

MR. MARLEY BY THE AID OF CLAUDE DUVAL RECOVERS HIS LOST CHILD.

THE steward turned pale.

A kind of habitual fear of the Duke took possession of him, which he could not shake off, but the young girl clung to Duval, for she felt that therein lay her safety.

"Fear nothing," said Claude, as with his disengaged right hand he loosened his sword in its sheath.

DUVAL RESCUES MARION MARLEY.

Then the steward seemed to recover from what might be called a paralysis of fear that had come over him.

"Let us have no bloodshed," he said, "I would not involve you, who have so kindly aided me in the recovery of my lost child, in the consequences that might result from even the righteous slaughter of such a man as the Duke of Montrose."

The furious knocking continued at the door.

The voice of the Duke was heard calling upon his villainous assistants to force it.

Another minute, and then affairs must come to a crisis.

Then Blossom uttered an exclamation.

"What now?" said Duval.

"All's right, Captain! I thought I should find it at last."

"Find what, Blossom?"

"Why a way out of this little crib, that, perhaps, nobody knows anything of but ourselves."

During the last few minutes Blossom had been going the round of the room, and sounding the wainscoting with his knuckles, to find where it was hollow.

By great good luck he had discovered a panel that was slightly loose to the touch.

By pressing upon it in various directions, it suddenly gave way, showing that it moved upon hinges, and constituted, in fact, a door arranged with considerable skill and secresy, in the wainscot.

But Duval was rather loth to fly.

Fain would he have met that Duke of Montrose face to face, and punished him for the various villanies of which he had been the author.

But the steward clung to his arm.

"Fly!" he said, "let us fly! I am content at present with the recovery of my child, and I will find a means of making the Duke bitterly rue the time when he attempted to rob me of her."

Thus urged Duval, considering likewise that it was not his own quarrel, consented to be led through the secret panel into the wall.

Blossom was the last to leave the apartment.

No 20.—NIGHTSHADE.

He closed the panel after him.

But not an instant too soon.

Scarcely was the concealed door in its place, so as to defy ordinary detection, when the Duke, by the assistance of his myrmidons, burst into the apartment.

His surprise at finding it empty may be conceived, and we leave him to it in order to follow the movements of Duval and his party.

The passage in which they found themselves was exceedingly dark and narrow.

The air was heavy, thick and stifling, which probably arose in a great measure from the displaced accumulated dust of many years in that secret place.

Duval went first, and with great caution.

He fully expected that they would soon reach some flight of steps, a fall down which would be anything but agreeable.

His conjecture was correct.

He reached the steps, but by his extreme caution avoided the fall.

"Halt! all of you," he said.

They came to a pause.

"Here are steps, follow me cautiously."

The steps were some twenty or thirty in number, and at the foot of them Duval became conscious of a dim mysterious kind of light pervading the spot.

That this light came from the outer air he felt convinced, and he called to Blossom to come forward, and assist him in a search for some outlet.

"There is some wood-work, here, Captain, and it's old and rotten; I think, if I were to put my shoulder to it it would give way."

"Try it, Blossom."

With a sudden rush, Blossom brought himself with such force against the old wood-work he had mentioned, that it gave way at once, and he fell forward in a rather ludicrous manner among the fragments of an old broken door.

Blossom was so completely entangled likewise with branches of ivy, that it required the assistance of Duval to extricate him.

But the whole mystery of the mysterious light was explained.

The door that Blossom had broken through opened directly upon the gardens of the Grange, but being disused, probably for many a long year, it was completely covered on the garden side by a luxurious growth of ivy.

"We are free!" cried Duval, "and since, Mr. Marloy, you choose to take further vengeance into your own hands, seek what refuge you can, and as quickly as possible, for yourself and daughter. My mission in this adventure is over, and I am contented to have thwarted the Duke of Montrose in one of his villanous enterprises."

The Steward seized the hand of Duval in both his own.

"Never," he cried, "while life remains, can I forget the debt of gratitude I owe you."

"Nor I," exclaimed Marion. "I shudder to think on what I might have been but for your courage and devotion."

"Think nothing of it," replied Duval, "I am something of a knight-errant, and it is my duty to succour damsels in distress. Away with you while you can, for danger may still lurk about this spot."

The Steward wanted but little urging to remove both himself and daughter as far from that ill-omened residence as possible.

Duval, too, now that all that was good had been accomplished, rather dreaded than otherwise to meet the Duke.

He felt that the conflict which must necessarily ensue between them, should they meet, would end in the death of that vicious specimen of nobility.

And that he now did not wish.

"Away Blossom! away!" he cried, "our shortest route will be through the wood, and then across the meadows homeward."

* * * * * *

Duval held a long conference with Lucy on the following day, the result of which was that he persuaded her, if he did not convince her, that there would be greater safety in a residence in London than in the country.

"But in what character, Claude, would you appear at a house in London, and in the streets of the city?"

"That will not be difficult to achieve," replied Duval. "Thanks to some experience in such matters, I can assume the character of a very aged man; while you, Lucy, I can present as my grand-daughter; at the same time, then, the adventures I shall carry out in my real name of Claude Duval, sometimes upon the road and the heath, and sometimes by mingling in those costly entertainments of the aristocracy, into which, by audacity, I can obtain an entrance, I shall be able to provide abundant means."

Lucy looked alarmed.

"Oh, Claude! if some other way could but be found by which to live——"

"Do not speak of it. I am Claude Duval or nothing! I have made myself a name, and it will cling to me. My lot in life is fixed, and the career that is before me I may not depart from. Be content, Lucy, and fear nothing."

"Your home," she said, gently, "is my home. Your course of life is my course of life. What am I but as one snatched from death itself to hold companionship with you?"

Claude Duval was too glad of this half consent to question it any further.

He spoke with a gay air, as though everything must, of necessity, be pleasant and easy.

"The name of Cope," he said, "belongs to my family, and, therefore, I shall assume the name of Sir John Cope. The Duvals are of French origin, and the name was adopted in consequence of a marriage in the family with an heiress of the Duval race."

"Whatever you please, Claude."

"Now, Lucy, cheer up, and look yourself again. I shall be Sir John Cope, an elderly gentleman, of large property, residing in London, and you my grand-daughter."

"Yes, yes, Claude; yes."

"Some slight alteration in the fashion of wearing your hair—perhaps, the faintest touch of rouge upon your cheek—would be sufficient to destroy your identity as that Lucy Evertom who, with all her innocence, has stood in such peril; and so you see that everything is simple and easy."

"Everything, Claude, is simple and easy when we love, and let your course in life be what it may it is not for me to throw the shadow of an obstacle in your path."

"Dearest Lucy!"

"But remember that your safety is the first and only consideration. Be not over adventurous."

"I will not. Courage and audacity, however, bring with themselves their own security. I will be careful, but not timid; and, remembering always that I have you to live for, I will guard my life as something infinitely precious."

Duval was not slow in carrying out his determination.

On that same day, a plain hired carriage might have been seen in Pall Mall.

It stopped at the door of a handsome house, which had belonged to the late Lord Farnborough.

The only heir to that title was a sickly boy, and by the advice of the family physician—as a last resource to attempt to save his life—he had been taken to a warm climate.

The town residence, then, superbly furnished, was to let.

Let us turn our attention to the plain chariot, which stood at the door of Farnborough House.

A very elderly gentleman alighted from it.

He stoops considerably, and walks with difficulty.

Who could recognise, in that well got-up disguise, the youthful, active figure, of Claude Duval?

A quiet, gentlemanly-looking man, is waiting in the hall at Farnborough House.

He salutes Duval respectfully.

"Well, Mr. Mason,—well, Mr. Mason," said Duval, speaking in the tremulous tones of an aged man, "I will take this house of you at the eight hundred guineas a-year you fix upon it as a rental."

"Most charmed to let it to you, sir."

"Well, then, that is settled."

Mr. Mason coughed slightly.

"I am the agent, sir, of the Farnborough family, and I believe you are Sir John Cope?"

"I have said so."

"If you will have the goodness, then, sir, to refer to any known person of repute——"

"Oh! I comprehend," said Duval. "Certainly—certainly. Perhaps, two references, Mr. Mason, of unquestionable respectability, will be sufficient?"

"Ample, Sir John,—ample!"

"One, then," said Duval, "is his Majesty's Ambassador, at Berlin."

"Oh, at Berlin."

"I said Berlin."

"And the other, Sir John, is, I hope—I hope——"

"You hope what, sir?"

"Nearer at hand."

"Oh, yes. In London."

"That is satisfactory."

"In Pall Mall."

"Better still, Sir John."

"At Farnborough House."

Mr. Mason started.

"Here, in this hall," added Duval, as he took from his pocket a small canvas bag, heavy with gold. "Here, Mr. Mason, is the other reference, in the shape of four hundred guineas, for one half year's rent of this mansion."

"Oh, Sir John!"

"I trust that that reference is perfectly satisfactory, and you can communicate with the Ambassador at Berlin at your leisure. To-morrow morning I take possession of this house with my grand-daughter, Pauline Cope. Good-day, Mr. Mason, good-day. Eugh! eugh! my cough troubles me a little; but I am not getting younger—not younger."

Duval got into the chariot and drove off.

It was with some degree of anxiety, not unmingled with curiosity, that Lucy met him on his return to their home upon the heath.

"Well, Claude?" asked Lucy; and then, for a moment, she stepped back, somewhat confused, for in that disguise he looked so unlike the Claude of her heart, that, for the moment, she fancied she must be addressing a stranger.

She instantly recovered herself, however, and smiling, said, "Really, Claude, I shall never know you for my husband, in that disguise."

Claude laughed, his own, light-hearted, mirthful laugh.

"You forget, Pauline."

"Pauline?" said Lucy.

"Yes, we must at once begin to practise the parts we are to play; henceforth, you must be Pauline, remember, not Lucy."

"But still your Lucy?"

"Yes, dear one, of course, no name will ever be so dear to my heart as the one by which I first addressed my bride, my precious wife."

Lucy looked up fondly into his face, and then she laughed again.

"Well, what now, Lucy? I mean, Pauline."

"There—there, Claude."

"Sir John, if you please."

"I was just going to say, that I am glad you have made a mistake. I shall take courage now, and you will see that I shall not make nearly so many mistakes as you do, *Sir John*."

With such cheerful talk they beguiled the time, while Lucy made the necessary changes in the mode of dressing her beautiful hair, so as to render her as unlike herself as possible.

"There, now, Sir John," she said, turning round gaily. "I think I have succeeded in transforming myself as completely as you have—have I not?"

"Only that you still look young and beautiful, still, Pauline——"

Claude paused, and made a comical face, as he pronounced the new name, as though he did not like the change.

"Well, Sir John?" said Lucy, demurely.

"While I am old and wrinkled——"

"Oh, never mind that," said Lucy, with one of her own bright smiles, "never mind that, dear, as long as beneath those wrinkles there is still the dear face of my handsome Claude."

"Pauline, you will really make me quite vain if you talk in that fashion; but now, come love, get ready, I wish to install you as Mistress of Farnborough House this very day, and mind you are docile and obedient to your poor old grandfather."

They both laughed merrily, and then Claude left the room, to give directions to Blossom and his other faithful followers to follow them to their new home.

"Do not forget, Blossom, that you are to personate my own personal servant as usual. A groom's livery will be the most suitable."

"All right, Captain. I'll go and apprise the other fellows of the jolly life that's in store for us all."

Duval now returned, and found Lucy ready equipped for her ride to her new home.

As he turned her round, Duval said, "Yes, Pauline, you will do now, dear," and taking her hand, he led her to the chariot, which was to convey her to Farnborough House, and which was driven by Blossom, dressed as a coachman, in a very plain but handsome livery.

"Farnborough House," said Duval, as he sprung into the carriage beside Lucy.

Blossom drove fast, and the man behind, who was attired as a footman, sprang down, and made an appeal at the hall door of the mansion, after the approved style, making an echo resound through the house, which made Lucy turn with a smile to Claude Duval, as she said, in a whisper:

"At all events, our neighbours will hear that we have arrived."

Before Duval could reply, the steps of the carriage were let down with a rattle, and Claude, after alighting, gave his hand to Lucy, and they entered the mansion.

CHAPTER LXIV.

BLOSSOM LEARNS SOME SATISFACTORY INTELLIGENCE RESPECTING MOSSY PENDELL.

WITHIN the mansion was everything to be found that could charm the senses, with rare and costly magnificence. There it would seem as though the whole world had been ransacked for the purpose of collecting into that abode the choicest products of art and beauty.

Exquisite statuary, that one might fancy almost instinct with life itself; costly hangings, blazing with gold; mirrors that made the whole scene in its endless multiplication, look inexhaustible in its beauty, reached from floor to ceiling.

"Well, dear," said Duval, as he led Lucy through a suite of five rooms, "Well, dear, are you content with your new home?"

"I am charmed, my dear—I forgot—I am charmed, my dear grandpapa."

"There is something here, love," Duval whispered, "which I wish to show you, as I think you will admire it as much as I did."

Duval led her forward, and adjoining that suite of rooms through which they had passed, was a small conservatory, filled with the choicest flowers of rarity and beauty.

They passed through a room adorned with a beautiful marble table in the centre, and then Duval opened the little glass door of the conservatory.

"Beautiful! beautiful!" murmured Lucy, as she hung fondly on the arm of Duval. "Oh, that we could spend our days here!"

"We should—or at least I should, soon tire of even this charming spot, were it not rendered doubly pleasing to me by contrast with the great world around us!"

"Ah, I forgot!" said Lucy, with a sigh.

"Forget nothing," said Duval, "but that you may remain here in peace and security. Let some of your anxieties likewise cease, for the life I may now lead, although it will be as adventurous as the past, will not be so dangerous."

"I must needs be content," replied Lucy, with a sigh.

"Come, come," added Duval, "let me see a smile upon those lips, and above all things remember who and what I am."

"You are Claude, and the dearest and the best——"

"No, no. By no means."

Duval immediately stooped in the attitude of an old man, and appeared to walk with difficulty.

"Remember," he said, "that I am Sir John Cope, and you his grand-daughter Pauline, the darling of his old age, and his heiress."

Lucy could not but smile at the successful manner in which Duval imitated the manner and appearance of an aged man.

"Let me ask, then, one thing," she said.

"What is that, Lucy?"

"It is that we should be at peace, and devoid of all anxiety for at least a few days, in this our new abode."

"Be it so. But there is still much to do."

Claude Duval held a long consultation with Blossom, in the latter part of the day, and gave him precise instructions in regard to certain matters of the greatest importance to the peace of both himself and Lucy.

"I want you thoroughly to ascertain, Blossom, what has become of the villain Pendell. I leave it to your own ingenuity to make what inquiries you can, for that he is still in existence I cannot doubt."

"Such fellows, Captain, have nine lives, like cats."

"They have, indeed."

"You may fancy you have effectually disposed of them, by means that would have been perfectly sufficient to put out of the world a dozen honest men, but these rascals like Pendell and my Lord Horlop, and the Duke of Montrose, turn up again, as though there had been very little the matter."

"It is so, Blossom, and I can only conceive that they have their appointed part to play in this great world, and it may be that out of the evil that they do springs some good, of which we can but little judge. But depart on your mission at once, and let me know the result as quickly as possible."

Blossom attired himself as a respectable serving-man, and after some consideration in his own mind, he thought the best thing he could do would be to go to the apartments of Lord Horlop, which he knew were situated in St. James's Palace, and there boldly inquire, as if with an authority, for Mossy Pendell.

Lord Horlop held one of those minor situations about the Court which form a mere verbal excuse for subsidising such men out of the pockets of the people.

He was a gold stick, or a silver stick, or some sort of a stick-in-waiting; but he had three rooms in St. James's Palace, and twice that number of hundreds a-year for doing nothing.

Blossom had the art of looking very respectable in the costume he had assumed, and there was no difficulty made in allowing him to pass into the Colour Court of the Palace.

In preference to making any verbal inquiries of persons who might not be able to direct him, Blossom knocked at the first door he saw, and boldly asked if Lord Horlop was within.

"Lord Horlop's rooms are not here," was the reply; "it is the next door."

"Oh, thank you! I thought it was this."

Blossom then applied to the door indicated, and it was opened by a footman in plain livery.

"Is Lord Horlop within?"

"No."

"Can you tell me when he is likely to return?"

"Can't say. He went out yesterday, about the middle of the day, with Mr. Pendell."

"Thank you. I must call on Mr. Pendell."

"You needn't call—for there he is!"

Blossom felt that he required all his caution, for Mossy Pendell himself came quietly down a flight of stairs immediately behind the footman, and looked scrutinizingly at him.

"This young man, Mr. Pendell," said the footman, "is inquiring for you."

Then Mossy Pendell turned very pale, and thrust his hand into the breast of his dress.

Such an action as that was not likely to pass unnoticed by so keen an observer as Blossom.

"The fellow has done something recently," he said, to himself, "and is afraid of the police."

"What do you want with me?" said Pendell, assuming a tone and manner of haughtiness and roughness.

"I am sent, sir, by Sir John Cope—no, not by Sir John Cope—Sir John Cope is my master, sir."

"Well, what then?"

"Why, sir, he is about to take a house belonging to my Lord Farnborough, in Pall Mall; and, as he said he knew my Lord Horlop——"

"Ah!"

Mossy Pendell started back.

"Yes, sir," added Blossom; "my Lord Farnborough's man of business tipped me a crown to come and ask my Lord Horlop what he knew of him."

"Bah!" said Pendell; "get out; don't trouble me with such rubbish."

Mossy Pendell turned, and ascended the stairs again.

"I don't want to trouble the gentleman," said Blossom, "but does he live here, likewise?"

"No," replied the footman, "but he is so intimate with my Lord that he comes and goes out of his rooms just the same."

"Oh! that's it?"

"Hem!" said the footman.

"What are you saying 'Hem!' about?" asked Blossom.

"Don't you think if I was to run out for a few minutes we might melt that crown-piece you talk of at the bar of the Thatched House, eh?"

There was no proposal in the world that at that moment Blossom was more ready to accede to.

He felt confident that if he once got Lord Horlop's footman to the bar of the "Thatched House," he would be able to get from him all the information Claude Duval could possibly desire in regard to Mossy Pendell and his proceedings.

"I will wait for you, then," said Blossom, "only don't be long, for I have very little time to spare."

Blossom had not long to wait, for the footman at the Palace soon succeeded in getting some comrade to take his duty while he ran the short distance to the bar of the "Thatched House" tavern, to help Blossom to liquidate the imaginary crown-piece.

And before asking a single question, Blossom took care that the footman should be thrown a little off his head, as the common saying is, by a draught of something strong.

"And so," said Blossom, "Mr. Pendell comes and goes in my Lord Horlop's rooms, just as if he were their owner?"

"Indeed, he does," said the footman; "and I can't half make it out. Of course, I'm bound not to say a word—and I do hate gossiping!"

"To be sure—to be sure!"

"And particularly to strangers, too; but I don't mind telling you that it's a very singular thing to me for Mr. Pendell to go out with my Lord Horlop and come home without him, and then stay in his rooms for two or three hours, and actually open all his private desks and cabinets with his own keys!"

"Indeed?"

"Oh, yes; and he's had such a rummage among his papers, and put so many of them into his pocket, that I can't make out what it all means."

"It's very strange. Let's have another glass of spiced Canary."

"Thank you! It is very strange, and of course I oughtn't to mention it, since he asked me not, but I don't mind telling you, as I am sure it won't go any further."

"Certainly not!" said Blossom.

"Well, then, he sent me to take a place for him in the Oxford mail for to-night, and what he's going there for I can't think."

"Then you have no notion of what has become of my Lord Horlop?"

"None at all; but as he often stays away for days together, we don't think much of that."

"Well, I must be off!" said Blossom. "One other glass, I think, and there's an end of the crown-piece."

"Oh, thank you!"

"I'm a very poor hand myself, so you stay and drink it; and I hope we shall meet again, and become better acquainted. Good day!"

The Palace footman's voice was thick and hoarse as he bade Blossom good day.

The latter then made what speed he could to Farnborough House, and at once communicated to Duval the intelligence he had received.

"That is well!" said Duval. "The servants of my Lord Horlop will wait in vain for his return, for in truth, this time, I believe he is no more."

"And what's to be done with Mossy Pendell, Captain?"

Duval considered for a few minutes, and then he said, quietly, "Go, Blossom, and take me a place in the Oxford mail for to-night."

"That's it, Captain! We shall have some sport yet, no; I say we, without exactly knowing whether you mean to take me with you or not."

Duval paced the room for a few seconds in silence, and then, turning abruptly to Blossom, he said, "I should like to have you with me. It will be dark when the mail starts, and of course it takes a guard with it?"

"Yes," said Blossom, "in a red coat, with a blunderbuss that will never go off when it's wanted, and if it did, I suppose it would knock the guard senseless."

"Blossom?"

"Yes, Captain."

"I want to have you with me, for there may be more to do than I alone can accomplish."

"Then I will take a place for myself likewise, Captain."

"Not so. You must be the guard of the Oxford mail to-night."

"I the guard, Captain?"

"Yes. How to accomplish that I leave to your own ingenuity, with a full confidence that you will be able to do it. I shall go as an inside passenger, and shall fully expect, when the occasion arises for requiring your services, that I find you on the coach, with a red coat, and the blunderbuss, playing the part of the guard."

"Captain."

"Well, Blossom?"

"Consider it as good as done."

"I know I may. The day is waning fast, so now set about your proceedings as quickly as you can."

Duval made his way to Lucy, and recounted to her what had happened in regard to Blossom's mission to the Palace.

"It is of the utmost importance," he said, "in order that we may foil the villain Pendell, and to discover what new rascalities he is about, that I should possess myself of those papers and documents which he has evidently filched from the cabinets and desks of his murdered associate, Lord Horlop."

"Yes, Claude, it may be as you say; but——"

"You are timid, Lucy!"

"I implore you to avoid danger!"

"I cannot. It is the atmosphere in which I live!"

"Alas! alas!"

"Nay, I have encountered much danger, but still you see me as I am, unscathed and unharmed. Who knows but that among those papers and documents I shall assuredly take from Mossy Pendell this night, there may not be something to throw a light upon the mysterious circumstances connected with your uncle's disappearance or death?"

This was a hope that was sure to find an echo in the heart of Lucy Everton.

"Go, Claude," she said; "and may heaven protect and prosper you!"

*   *   *   *   *   *

It is eight o'clock in the evening.

We conduct the reader to St. Martin's-le-Grand, in the City.

Not the St. Martin's-le-Grand of the present day, with the large, plain Doric building, and devoted to the purposes of the Post Office; but the old, dirty, disreputable thoroughfare which it was many years ago.

The curious range of buildings forming the old Post-office was composed of such odds and ends that it was impossible to make any design out of them.

There was a large yard, likewise, with a range of stables at the back.

And this yard, from half-past seven o'clock in the evening until half-past eight, was a scene of great bustle and animation—not to say confusion; and there was something of that.

It was from that spot that, every evening, what were called his Majesty's mails started, to traverse the country in all directions—carrying the letter-bags and such passengers as chose to travel by those conveyances.

There were very few stage-coaches, properly so called, in those days.

The mail or the waggon formed almost the only mode of reaching great distances.

People of wealth always travelled "post," as it was called.

The poor, or the economical, chose the waggon, which, at the rate of about three-and-a-half miles an hour, travelled day and night.

His Majesty's mails, well-horsed and well-appointed managed to get over the ground at about the rate of eight miles an hour.

They were considered wonderfully swift, and were accordingly popular

It is a natural peculiarity for Englishmen to wish to travel fast, and at that time this was considered a great rate of speed.

There were a few drawbacks, however, to such a mode of locomotion.

The roads were very bad.

A good coachman had not only to drive his horses with discretion, but he had to know the road well.

If he did not, it was as likely as possible that the hind or fore wheels on one side or the other would get into a dangerous rut, and over would go the vehicle.

In fact, it was well known that some coachmen prided themselves upon the dexterity with which they could upset the coach at a particular spot.

Then the roads were infested with highwaymen.

The late political troubles of the latter part of the preceding reign had thrown many gentlemen of the sword upon their wits for a subsistence.

To go upon the road, and cry "Stand and deliver!" upon the King's highway, was then considered quite a natural result of gentlemanly destitution.

Such was the state, then, and condition of travelling in England in the days of Claude Duval.

About thirty of these mail-coaches started from St. Martin's-le-Grand every evening.

The confusion then was immense.

The blowing of horns.

The cracking of whips.

The trampling of horses.

The flashing of the lights.

The tumbling about of luggage.

The oaths of the coachmen, and all the thousand and one noises, confusions, and mistakes contingent upon the starting of such a number of vehicles, each with four horses, made up a Babel of sounds which almost defies description.

It was in the midst of all this, then, at eight o'clock, that Blossom strolled quietly into the yard of the Post-office.

He had been there in the earlier part of the day, and secured a place for Claude Duval under the common name of Mr. Smith.

What disguise Duval would come in, Blossom had no idea; but that mattered not in the least, since, of course, he felt certain that he would know him under all circumstances.

Blossom looked quietly about for the Oxford mail.

It was not to start for more than half an hour, but the ostlers were busy pulling in the horses.

In a little quiet street at the back of the old Post-office, there was a very ancient public-house, called the "Sprig of Myrtle."

It was almost wholly maintained by the incessant dram-drinking of the coachmen, guards, ostlers, and others connected with the royal mails.

It was to this public-house, which he knew quite well, that Blossom wended his way.

CHAPTER LXV.

THE ADVENTURE WITH THE OXFORD MAIL.

THE bar of the "Sprig of Myrtle" was crowded.

Coachmen were there, with their huge top-coats and rubicund faces.

Guards, in scarlet, and top-boots, bearing a dirty and faded resemblance to the royal livery.

Horse-boys, passengers, Post-office porters, and all the crowd of persons incidental to starting the mails, kept pushing in and out the little public-house for the purpose of refreshment.

Blossom stationed himself by the side of one of the guards, and after ordering a glass of purl, whispered in his ear, "You belong to the Oxford mail?"

"No, I don't."

"Oh, I thought you did!"

"Jem Harris, yonder, is the Oxford mail guard; I'm the York."

"Oh, it's my mistake, thank you."

Another moment and Blossom was by the side of Jem Harris, who was rather a portly personage, and seemed as unfitted to be guard to anything but a beer barrel, as could be conceived.

Blossom whispered in his ear.

"Jem Harris!"

"Eh? Who are you?"

"A friend."

"Stuff! I don't know you. Get out! I never makes acquaintance with strangers."

"I know you don't, but as you are a respectable fellow, and I don't want to see you put out of the world, leaving Mrs. Harris a disconsolate widow."

"What do you mean?"

"Why, I'm come to warn you of what will happen to-night."

"How? To what?"

"Do you know the eighth mile-stone on the Oxford Road?"

"Rather."

"It is white."

"In course, it is."

"Would you like to see it stained red?"

"Red?"

"Yes, with the blood of Jem Harris, the guard of the Oxford mail. Ha! ha!"

The guard turned pale, and staggered back a step.

"What do you mean?" he said; "you look like a kind of decent sort of fellow. What do you mean?"

"Hush! Do not let any one hear you. It's impossible to say who may be listening."

"But, good gracious——"

"Hush!"

The guard turned completely round and looked alarmed.

"Tell me," whispered Blossom, "is there anywhere here where I can speak to you in confidence, and without fear of interruption."

"Yes, this way there's a little room, we keep some spare harness in it, and some coats and capes, come in here, and tell me all about it."

"I will."

The thoroughly-alarmed guard led Blossom into the small apartment he had mentioned, and as he went first, Blossom was able to close the door when inside the room, and then he immediately placed his back against it, and faced the astonished guard.

Blossom wore one of those wide-skirted coats common to the period, and in which there were immense pockets, capable of holding anything.

Diving a hand into each, he immediately produced a pair of pistols, and presenting them full at the head of the astonished guard, he said in cool, grating tones—

"If you raise the least alarm, or make the least outcry, four bullets will smash into your skull, for these pistols are loaded with two each."

The guard backed until he reached the wall of the room, and there he stood facing Blossom.

His eyes were preternaturally wide open.

His lips parted.

And his whole expression was that of a man overcome with terror.

"On the contrary," added Blossom, "if you are quiet and prudent, no possible harm can come to you."

"Mercy!"

"There will be plenty of it, if you deserve it."

"I will, I will!"

"Your life is in your own hands."

"My own hands?" said the bewildered guard, as he looked at them.

"Yes; you have but to obey orders, and I will inform my associates that, although they are to keep watch and ward over this room, they are by no means to do you an injury."

"Am I to be kept, then, from going with the mail?"

"Certainly."

The guard groaned.

"Say which you prefer," added Blossom, "death or submission?"

"I don't want death at all; and if I must submit, why, I suppose I must."

"Very well," added Blossom; "but, remember, I am the worst man in the world to trifle with; and if you give me cause to have even the least particle of suspicion that you are treacherous, your life will be forfeited on the spot."

"But—but——"

"What would you say?"

"If you shoot me, that will make a noise, and produce an alarm."

"Well?"

"People will run in here, and then you'll be found out."

"Will you give your life for that state of things? because if you're inclined to do so, say it at once; only let me tell you, that I have provided already against such a thing happening."

"But I don't see how."

"Then I will tell you. In a case of sudden alarm, particularly where fire-arms are discharged, people are for a few moments confused and uncertain what to do, they lose their presence of mind; but I should not lose mine, and I should have ample time, after having shot you through the head, to clasp your dead fingers round the stock of one of the pistols, and proclaim you a suicide."

The guard slid down to the floor.

"I give in!" he said.

"You are prudent."

"Say what you like, and do what you like."

"Get up."

The guard scrambled to his feet.

"Give me your red coat, and take this in exchange."

Blossom flung him his coat, taking care to remove the pistols out of his reach, and then, in exchange, he put on the red coat of the guard.

"Your hat," said Blossom, as he flung his own to the floor.

In broad daylight, probably, the change of outer clothing would scarcely have been sufficient for Blossom's purposes; but in the bustle and confusion of the Post-office yard, and the many cross lights from the coach lanterns, there was every probability of his being mistaken for the genuine guard of the Oxford Mail.

Blossom had in one of his pockets a coil of cord, by no means thick, but of extraordinary strength.

"Sit down in this chair," he said to the guard.

The man obeyed him without a word.

Blossom then scientifically tied him to the chair in a manner well known to the thieves and burglars of that period.

It consisted in tying a noose round the neck of the prisoner, and then drawing the two arms behind the chair and tying firmly the wrists together.

If this were done well, it was almost impossible for any one to escape without the risk of strangulation.

"Now, I warn you," said Blossom; "there are two of my comrades watching this room, and if you make any noise or disturbance, they will come in and despatch you. Good night!"

The guard uttered a groan.

There was a miserable little tallow candle burning upon a table in the room, but Blossom, before he left, blew it out.

Quietly closing the door, then, he made his way through the public house into the Post-office yard, and stood in a shadowy spot, from whence he could see without being seen.

"London to Oxford."

Those were the words that Blossom saw upon the bright red panels of the mail coach nearest to him.

It was the one in which he was specially interested, and he kept his eyes earnestly upon it.

It was a quarter past eight.

A man came to the door of the coach, holding up a stable lantern in his hand, and, flinging it open, he cried out, "Oxford Mail! Oxford Mail! Passengers for Oxford Mail! Here you are, Oxford Mail! Oxford Mail! Booked passengers for Oxford Mail!"

A couple of porters were busy on the roof strapping on luggage.

A lady and gentleman appeared, and what struck Blossom as particularly strange, was that the gentleman carried a bandbox, while the lady, with what might be a parasol,—but which was nearly the size of an umbrella,—dealt him several hard raps on the knuckles.

"You will drop it, will you," she said, "I should like to see you drop it."

"My dear."

"Don't my dear me, get into the coach Mr. Garrett, and if you do drop it I'll warrant that you'll hear of it in a manner that won't be pleasant."

"My dear, I never intended."

"Get in, I say, at once! and keep me one of the back seats."

"Certainly, my dear."

Mr. Garrett got into the coach with the band-box, and then the lady looked about her as she cried out:

"Here guard! coachman! somebody! where are you all? This is pretty attention for a lady who has booked two places in the Oxford Mail."

"Well, mum," said the man with the lantern, "the coachman never do come out till everything is ready, and I shouldn't wonder but the guard is in the 'Sprig O' Myrtle.' "

"Nonsense! stuff! it's very inattentive."

"Can I do anything for you, mum?"

"I want to know if any low people have taken places inside, because, if so, I positively can't go. I've been used to the very best society, and cannot travel with common people."

"Lor' bless you, mum, no—nobody but two gentlemen has took places besides yourself and the *hindiridual* with the band-box, and they is *rale* gentlemen, I assures you, mum, and here's one of 'em."

Blossom was an amused listener to this dialogue; but now all his attention was arrested by the observation of Mossy Pendell, who at that moment stepped into the sphere of light exhibited by the lantern.

He was rather richly attired.

His sword-hilt was of polished steel, and he carried in his hand a small valise, which he seemed to regard with peculiar care.

The first glance at him seemed to assure the lady who was so particular about the company she travelled with, that he was an eligible personage.

She executed a rather elaborate courtesy.

"It's quite a pleasure, sir," she said, "to find that there are respectable people to night in the Oxford Mail."

Pendell slightly bowed, and made way for her, and then followed her into the coach.

Blossom began to get anxious.

Where was Duval?

"Oxford Mail! Oxford Mail!" cried the man with the lantern, "passengers outside and in for the Oxford Mail!"

But no Duval.

"Well," said Blossom to himself, "I shall not have to play the part of guard to night."

Even as he spoke, a quiet-looking, gentlemanly man, dressed in complete black, and with a clerical-looking cravat, stepped up to the coach door.

His hair was nearly white, as was likewise the moustache upon his upper lip.

His complexion was very pale, and he spoke in a high treble kind of voice as he said:

"Is this the Oxford Mail?"

The tone was remarkably foreign in its accents, and the words were pronounced in that manner that a highly educated Frenchman or a German would speak English.

"Capital!" said Blossom, "that's Duval, but I should hardly know him myself, if I did not feel certain that he was to be the fourth person in the Oxford Mail."

"Yes, sir, this is the mail," said the man with the lantern.

"I am the passenger of the book," said Duval.

"Booked sir? all right, sir, get in."

Duval stepped into the coach, and quietly sat down in the corner.

Bang! went the door shut.

A pompous voice now sounded in the Post-office yard.

"Is all them things well strapped on?"

It was the coachman, who was slowly pulling on his gloves, and who had just emerged from the "Sprig O' Myrtle."

A mail coachman in those days was a perfect oracle; and indeed, in London, even in the present days, one would imagine that an omnibus-driver was looked upon as something preternatural, by the looks of awe and reverence with which he is listened to by the lank and sickly youths who may be seen occupying the box-seat from Paddington to the Bank.

"The 'osses all right?" added the coachman.

"Yes, Mr. Dolman."

"Their hind shoes seen to?"

"Yes, Mr. Dolman."

"Hem! where's Jim Harris?"

"Jim Harris! Jim Harris! Mr. Dolman's ready! Jim Harris!"

"Here you are," said Blossom, as he stepped forward, and began climbing up at the back of the coach.

"Hem! there you is, is you?" added the coachman, speaking sententiously. "Is the company all in?"

"Yes, Mr. Dolman."

"Then I may include as everything is ready?"

"If you please, Mr. Dolman."

"Hem! give us the ribbins."

The man with the lantern handed the reins obsequiously to the coachman, who, after carefully arranging them in a scientific manner among the fingers of his left hand, slowly ascended the coach-box.

The whip was then handed to him, and he held it aloft, pausing for a moment, as though he had been changed to a statue.

"What the deuce is the matter with him?" thought Blossom; "why don't he go on?"

But the coachman never moved.

Then the man with the lantern solved the enigma, by calling out, in frantic tones, "Goodness gracious, Jim Harris! why don't you blow the Oxford Mail out of the blessed yard. Mr. Dolman's *actually* a waiting."

Blossom at once understood what was expected of him.

By his side, at the back of the coach, in the dicky, as it was called, was a long wicker-work case, in which reposed the guard's horn.

Blossom felt very dubious about blowing a horn, but, like the Irishman who did not know whether he could play the fiddle or not, since he had never tried, he considered it possible he might succeed.

"Now, Jim Harris!"

"Coming, coming!" said Blossom.

He drew forth the horn.

He placed it to his lips.

The awful blast that Blossom produced upon the guard's horn so terrified the man with the lantern that he dropped it instantly.

Even Mr. Dolman, the coachman, so far forgot his dignity as to look round.

"James 'Arris!" he said.

"Drive on, old brick!" said Blossom.

The Post-office clock chimed the half-past eight.

The horses knew the time as well as the coachman, who mechanically tightened the reins, and produced that curious sound between a spit and a sneeze, which is popularly supposed to start a coach and horses

And so off went the Oxford Mail.

CHAPTER LXVI.

THE OXFORD MAIL PURSUES ITS JOURNEY WITHOUT THE ASSISTANCE OF THE GUARD'S HORN.

IN two minutes, all chance of pursuit from the neighbourhood of the Post-office was at an end.

It was a particular pride of the coachman always to rattle through London at a good speed.

The old Oxford Road was soon gained.

The long row of lights, which was then only on one side of the way, passed like flittering lanterns before the eyes of the passengers.

Tyburn Gate was reached.

The coachman was surprised.

Upon a near approach to the turnpike-gate—and, in fact, to any, or every turnpike-gate—it was the unquestionable duty of the guard to give notice by two or three notes upon his horn.

Blossom was remiss in this duty.

He remained perfectly quiet.

Then the coachman condescended to speak.

"James Harris."

"Here you are," replied Blossom.

The response was given in such a tone of voice that it seemed to issue from the bottom of a well.

"What is the matter?"

"A bad cold; can't blow the horn."

This was the best thing Blossom could do; because if he did attempt to blow the horn, the hideous and discordant notes he would produce, were such that some discovery must take place.

The coach rattled on.

And past Tyburn Gate, at that period, was open country.

That is to say, a few villas on one side of the way, and Kensington Gardens on the other, extended for something more than a mile.

THE CONSPIRATORS SALUTE THE PRINCE.

Then there came a little village, looking excessively quiet and rural.

One might have supposed it to be, at least, five hundred miles from the metropolis, and that its few inhabitants could only have heard by report of the great city.

There were four passengers outside the coach, but they had not yet become conversational.

The coachman was too dignified to say anything.

And so, beyond the tramp of the horses, and the rattle of the wheels, no sound whatever proceeded from the Oxford Mail.

Blossom began to get anxious.

In vain he strove to listen.

He leant his hand over the side of the little dicky on which he sat, and made futile efforts to look into the interior of the coach.

It was all in vain.

He could only wait.

Wait, with what patience he might, for what events were about to occur.

No 21.—NIGHTSHADE.

And now we turn our attention to the interior of the vehicle.

It was not quite dark, because the lights of the coach spread a kind of dim radiance about them, some reflected beams of which found their way into the inside.

And while the Oxford Mail went through the streets of London, each lamp that was passed sent its own fitful gleam of light upon the forms and faces of the inside passengers.

But this was confusing.

If those inside passengers had known each other well, such rapid passages of light would have been quite sufficient to confuse their identity.

But Mossy Pendell had not the remotest idea of his contiguity to the man who, above all others, he would have shunned and dreaded.

And Claude Duval felt perfectly easy.

From the first moment that he had seen Pendell, he had made up his mind to become possessed of the little valise which the villain carried.

But he delayed operations.

There was a reason.

Over and over again Duval had asked himself for what reason Pendell was going out of town.

He did not believe for a single moment that Oxford was his destination.

And so he waited to hear Mossy Pendell give some indication of where he meant to stop.

But the coach rolled on.

The little village of Bayswater was passed through.

The sharp descent of Notting Hill was accomplished in safety.

Then there was a movement on the part of the passengers inside.

Amid the silence that had continued so long, there came a sudden creaking, crunching sound.

"Wretch!" exclaimed the lady, who was the only feminine occupant of the seat in the coach. "Wretch! I know you are smashing that band-box all to atoms!"

"Really, my dear——"

"Be quiet, don't speak to me. I suppose you think because other persons are present, that you may tyrannize over an unoffending woman as much as you like."

"Be quiet!" cried Mossy Pendell, at this moment.

The tone in which he spoke was so authoritative, not to say insolent, that the lady's tongue was stopped immediately.

Indignation, however, glared from her eyes.

"Did you address those words to me, sir?"

"I did. Be quiet. Let me see where we are."

Pendell let down one of the windows with a sharp sound.

He leant his head and shoulders out of the coach, and attentively surveyed the part of the road which they had reached.

The unfortunate individual who carried the bandbox for decidedly his better half, gave Claude Duval a slight touch on the arm.

He spoke in a tone of great trepidation.

"I'd almost take a bible oath," he said, "that there is a highwayman in the coach."

The lady gave a scream.

"My jewellery!" she said. "My jewellery and my money! Goodness gracious, I shall be robbed!"

The screams startled Mossy Pendell, and he drew in his head.

"What's the matter now?" he said.

"Nothing sir, if you please," said the lady, in a humble tone; "but what a good thing it is, and what a mercy too, that when one travels by a mail coach instead of one's own carriage, one only brings with one threepence beyond the fare."

"What do I care what you bring with you!" exclaimed Pendell, impatiently.

He thrust his head out of the window again.

"Guard! Hilloa, guard!"

Blossom knew his voice perfectly well.

"Here you are, sir," he replied.

"Tell the coachman to pull up at the eighth milestone. I will get out there."

This was part of the information that Claude Duval required, and he was well enough pleased that his pursuit of Mossy Pendell would not carry him further than so short a distance from London.

At the rate the coach had travelled, that eighth mile-stone could not be far distant.

It was necessary at once to come to some conclusion.

Duval spoke.

"Mossy Pendell!"

The sudden start that Pendell gave, very nearly sent his head through the glass of the coach window, which he had just raised again.

"Mossy Pendell!"

Pendell uttered a cry.

"Another such shout!" added Duval, "and you are a dead man!"

The light within the coach was very insufficient for most purposes, but still it enabled Pendell to see the bright polished barrel of a pistol within three inches of his forehead.

Pendell was awed into silence.

Not so the lady.

She uttered scream upon scream.

"Two highwaymen! Two highwaymen! The coach is full of highwaymen, and I am a lost woman!"

"Woa! woa!"

The coachman pulled up.

Mossy Pendell made an attempt to leap out, and got the length of opening one of the doors.

Then Claude Duval grasped him by the throat, and flung him back into the corner of the coach.

"No!" he said; "you and I have something to say to each other before we part."

But the open coach door was too tempting to the imperious lady and her husband with the band-box.

They both immediately rolled out of the coach together, leaving the precious band-box behind them.

"James Harris!" said the coachman.

"I'm here!" replied Blossom.

"A breeze among the *hinsides!*"

Blossom immediately descended from the dicky, and approached the coach door.

"Close it," said Duval; "and say that all is right."

"Yes, Captain."

Bang! went the coach door shut again.

Blossom scrambled up into his place.

"James Harris," said the coachman again. "Is the breeze among the *hinsides* over?"

"All right!" said Blossom.

Off started the Oxford Mail again.

It was a great relief to Claude Duval that he and Mossy Pendell were the sole occupants then of the inside of the vehicle.

Duval was keen sighted, and although the amount of light within the coach was very small, he detected every movement of Mossy Pendell.

He saw him cautiously placing his right hand into the breast of his apparel.

"One word," said Duval. "My finger is on the trigger of this pistol. The lightest possible pressure will discharge it, and that pressure will be given unless you immediately place your two hands before you, and clasp them together."

Pendell obeyed him.

With a groan, he withdrew his right hand from the grasp of the, no doubt, concealed weapon he had, and assumed the attitude directed by Claude Duval.

"Mossy Pendell, you know me?"

"I think I do."

"You are sure you do. My name is Claude Duval."

"My enemy!"

"Made such by your own acts—villain that you are."

"And, I suppose," said Pendell, "that my murder is a thing determined upon?"

"I am not a public executioner, and that is the only proper person to put you out of life; but, nevertheless, so far as regards you and me, at the present moment, your life is in your own hands. I shall ask you certain questions, and if your replies are unsatisfactory and equivocal, you must take the consequences."

Pendell was silent.

"Where is General Everton?" asked Claude Duval.

"In his grave."

"I warn you. I shall now count three, and if no other answer is given to me, you are a dead man!"

"I cannot help it," replied Pendell. "It is possible

to murder any one with a pistol at his head. What other answer can I give you, Claude Duval, unless you prefer falsehood to truth?"

"One!" said Duval.

"What object can you have in killing me, unless I utter that which is false?"

"Two!" said Duval.

"Then my murder be upon your own head, and you will have to answer for it, I hope, in this world, and according to your belief, probably in the next!"

"Three!" said Duval.

Mossy Pendell closed his eyes.

Did he expect death?

No!

But he had exhibited a remarkable instance, for such a man, of that kind of courage which may be called the courage of calculation at a critical moment.

The respect in which he held the chivalrous disposition of Claude Duval, prevented him from supposing that, in this cold-blooded manner, his life would be taken.

It was a trial of the nerves.

That was all.

The only wonder is, that Mossy Pendell—real coward at his heart as he was—had sufficient presence of mind to go through with it.

Duval was disappointed.

But he lowered the pistol.

There was a dead silence for a few seconds.

Then Duval spoke in low earnest accents.

"Mossy Pendell, I am so reluctant to take life, even of the merest insect that crawls upon my path, that I spare you for the present moment, and I ask you again where is General Everton?"

"In the vault of St. Paul's, where, if you are anxious to test the accuracy of my words, you may find him."

"And, assuming that fact for a moment, although I believe it not, in what way, or by whose hands or instigation, did the General leave this world?"

"Lord Horlop——"

"Well?"

"Lord Horlop, infuriated at his rejection by Lucy Everton, and at the decisive manner in which the General forbade him Camden House, accomplished the death of that personage."

"And where is Lord Horlop?"

"I know not!"

"I do."

"You?"

"Yes, Mossy Pendell. There is a hut—a wretched hovel in the midst of the old wood at Highgate, and in that hut lies a human form still in death, and ghastly by the wound which has produced its dissolution."

"Ah!"

"You start. There is a guilty glare within your eyes, can you not name that form?"

"I cannot."

"Think again."

"Is it—is it Horlop?"

"You know it is, murderer, and none the less a murderer because he was your companion in guilt, and richly merited any death that awaited him."

The coach stopped.

"Claude Duval," said Pendell. "I have answered your questions, I have made no attempt against your life, and as you say Lord Horlop is no more, let us part in peace. I will never more interfere with you or yours, and, for your part, forget that such a person as Mossy Pendell breathes the air of life."

"Stop!"

"I alight here."

"Stop!"

"Stay me not. Good night, Claude Duval!"

"The eighth mile-stone if you please," said Blossom, opening the coach door.

"That will do," said Pendell.

He stooped, and took from beneath the seat the small valise he had brought into the coach.

But Duval placed his hand upon it at the same moment.

"Blossom," he said, "take charge of this."

"Yes, Captain."

Blossom took the valise, and then Duval leaped out of the coach.

"Come, Mossy Pendell," he said, "we do not part so easily, if this eighth mile-stone be your destination on the Oxford Road, it may as well be mine. Come out!"

Duval had forgotten some part of his usual caution.

If he had made Pendell leave the coach first all might have been well, for the villain would have been in the hands of Blossom.

As it happened, however, the moment Pendell found himself alone, he hastily opened the door on the other side of the vehicle and leaped out.

Both the doors were open.

There was a clear passage through the coach.

Bang! bang!

Pendell turned, and fired two pistols right across from door to door of the vehicle, with the hope of hitting Duval or Blossom or both.

And such would more than likely have been the case, but that Claude had taken a half turn and was out of the line of fire.

Blossom held the little valise in his hand, and at the sound of the first shot, he involuntarily lifted it before his face.

Mossy Pendell's second pistol lodged a couple of bullets right into the centre of the valise.

CHAPTER LXVII.

CLAUDE DUVAL HAS ANOTHER RECKONING WITH MOSSY PENDELL.

For once in a way, the coachman of the Oxford Mail forgot his dignity in his fears.

"Bless us and save us!" he cried, "we are beset by highwaymen!"

He set his horses in motion at once, and without troubling himself to inquire whether the guard were in his place or not, he urged the cattle forward, and the coach was soon lost to sight in the darkness.

Duval grasped the arm of Blossom.

"Don't speak," he whispered, "except to tell me if you are hit."

"No, Captain. And you?"

"All's well."

They both stood in the darkness which was now thick and dense about them, and listened attentively.

The whole place seemed preternaturally still.

Not the faintest sound came upon the night air.

The region of lamps had been long since passed, and as the night was cloudy, not a star peeped from the heaven above, to illumine even by its faint rays that rural spot.

And like two statues stood Claude Duval and Blossom.

They scarcely seemed to breathe.

Any pursuit, amid that darkness, of Mossy Pendell, they felt would be perfectly futile.

But it was possible they might hear something of him, if they only threw him off his guard by so profound a stillness that he must needs imagine they were either killed or had got into the coach again and were miles away.

Minute after minute, however, passed, and nothing was heard

The patience with which Duval and Blossom waited was not destined to go without its reward.

They heard a footstep.

It fell lightly upon the roadway, but still it was an unmistakable footstep.

Then there came a voice.

"All's still," he said, "all's still. What can have become of them?"

The voice was Mossy Pendell's.

Duval tightened his grasp upon the arm of Blossom, for he was afraid his follower might speak, or make some attempt upon the life of Pendell then and there.

Blossom understood the caution, and neither spoke nor moved.

"They must have gone," muttered Pendell, "and that they have taken with them the valise containing not only the title-deeds and papers connected with the Everton property, but likewise the plunder, in the shape of gold and jewels, I took from Horlop's apartments in the Palace, I should think this a lucky escape."

Again all was still.

"They may have dropped the valise again," added Pendell. "I will get a light."

Duval drew Blossom gently on one side.

As lightly as foot could fall, they made their way to the hedge nearest to them.

Pendell was busy getting a light by some means he had in his possession for that purpose.

He was not listening; if he had been he might possibly have detected the footsteps of Duval and Blossom.

They gained the hedge.

They crept along it.

They reached a gate.

"Over, over!" whispered Duval. "If we reach the other side before he has his light, we can watch him in security."

"But, Captain——"

"What now?"

"Let me take a shot at him."

"No, no. Not on any account. We have yet to learn why he alighted at this eighth mile-stone, and whither he is bound."

There was not an instant to spare.

Duval and Blossom had just got over the gate, and crouched down on the other side, when Mossy Pendell, with the assistance of a thieves' match, lit a small hand lantern he must have had in his pocket, and holding it up, cast its rays as far and wide as he could.

The hedges were lit up by that faint gleam, and so was the gate, and the huge stump of an aged tree that stood close to it.

And as Mossy Pendell remained in the middle of the road, holding the lantern just above the level of his eyes, Blossom could not forbear from suggesting to Duval what a capital mark he would be for a pistol bullet.

"Shall I give him one, Captain?"

"No, Blossom—no. His time will come, be assured, but for the present let him live."

Pendell looked carefully about him.

He lowered the lantern, and looked down upon the roadway, with, no doubt, the expectation of seeing some evidences of the recent conflict between him and Claude Duval.

He then muttered some words in a disappointed tone, which they could not catch distinctly, and holding the lantern carelessly by a ring that was at the top of it, he crossed the roadway, and at a leisurely pace left the spot.

"Where's the rascal going now?" asked Blossom.

"I know not, Blossom, but wherever it is we will follow him."

Mossy Pendell was quite a good guide; and the only wonder was that he carried that lantern at all, although probably he did so in order to show himself the way he wished to go.

There was a winding lane.

So shadowy, so narrow, and with a ditch running on each side of it, that no one, at that dim hour of the night, could care to venture down it, except lighted by the way.

The effect of the lantern was very curious, for it shed so few rays about it, that the appearance was exactly as if it were proceeding along the lane without any human agency.

Duval waited for a few seconds, until Mossy Pendell had made some progress.

Then he and Blossom crossed the gate again and followed in his track.

The lane was excessively solitary, and seemed to be rendered more so by the occasional cry of some bird disturbed on its roost by the passing light, or the dismal hoot of an owl taking his peregrinations.

Neither Blossom nor Duval had the slightest idea of where the lane could lead to, but they were content to follow Mossy Pendell, determined that let him go where he might, they would not be far behind him.

Suddenly the light disappeared.

"Halt!" whispered Duval.

They both came to a standstill.

And then they began to appreciate how small a quantity of light is sufficient to banish what might be called absolute darkness, and what a different thing that absolute darkness really was to the faintest twilight.

The hedges.

The tall trees.

The brushwood at their feet, and the dim black roadway, all seemed to combine together to form an indistinguishable mass of blackness.

"Gone!" said Duval.

"What shall we do now, Captain?"

"We will follow on as best we may."

"We shall tumble into some ditch to a certainty."

"That we will try to avoid, Blossom; and the next thing to seeing our way is, to try to feel it."

Duval drew his sword as he spoke.

He advanced very slowly, and before he would venture to put one foot before the other, he felt if the ground were solid in advance of him with his sword-point.

In this way they proceeded about twenty yards.

Then, a very curious phenomenon presented itself.

High up in the black and murky air, immediately in front of them, suddenly appeared a light.

It was gone as soon as they could be certain of its presence.

Then it appeared again at the same altitude, but a few yards to the right of where they had seen it at first.

And then a third time, a few yards further on, but ever keeping the same level.

"Good gracious, Captain!" whispered Blossom; "what's that?"

"Can you not guess, Blossom?"

"Not I, Captain!"

"I am surprised at your ingenuity being at fault; we are in front of some house, and that light is being carried along some room, gallery, or corridor, with a range of windows looking in this direction."

"By Jove, Captain, that's it!"

"Hush! do you hear nothing?"

A faint, strange noise came upon the night air, but neither Duval nor Blossom could make anything of it, except that they did not think that it was a human sound.

"Come on, Blossom," said Duval; "I think we are near our destination, wherever that may be."

Duval still felt the ground with his sword, and as

he raised it to do so, he became aware that some obstruction was in his way.

The sword-blade touched wood-work.

Then Duval stretched out his hands.

"A gate!" he said.

"All's right, Captain! I seem as if I saw a black kind of mountain before us."

"And I, too."

"Then, Captain, by putting this and that together, I think we may take upon ourselves to say that it is a house."

"Yes, Blossom, and one of no mean size."

Duval had been passing his hand over the gate with great care, and, at length he found that it opened with an ordinary latch.

It moved quite noiselessly upon its hinges, and Duval and Blossom passed through it, carefully closing it behind them.

Then Duval suddenly grasped Blossom by the arm, as he exclaimed: "Look! What do you make of that, Blossom?"

In the same curious manner that the other windows had appeared, as if suspended in the very darkness of the air, there now flashed into their sight, with faint radiance, a larger, Gothic-shaped window, full of stained glass.

The colours were very beautiful.

They were somewhat faint in consequence of the insufficient light on the other side, but still they harmonized well together, and the sight was pleasing and picturesque.

Then it vanished.

Vanished as suddenly as it had appeared.

All was darkness again.

These mysterious glimpses, however, of the mansion to which they were approaching, served sufficiently to point out with tolerable precision, its locality.

Then a very strange noise came upon their ears, and, for several seconds, even Duval was at fault in comprehending what it meant.

The moment, however, that he did discover what it was, he was astonished how he could have mistaken it for anything else.

"Rain," he whispered.

"To be sure it is, Captain," said Blossom. "I feel it now upon my face and hands."

Some rain-cloud was passing over, and a genial shower had come spattering down upon the leaves of the trees overhead.

Under ordinary circumstances, such a sound would have been comprehended at once; but the intense stillness of the place had given a prominence to it which made it seem unnatural.

And as this rain fell, the sky lightened.

A dim, grey kind of twilight spread over the scene, and it was no longer difficult to see the outline of the trees.

From where Claude Duval and Blossom stood likewise they could observe the shape of the roof, towers, and angles of a very large mansion immediately in front of them.

They had but to walk quietly on to reach the house.

"Here," said Duval, in a whisper, "we shall find our friend, Mossy Pendell."

"But what does he do in such a place as this, Captain?"

"That is a mystery, Blossom, I hope to solve."

"I am with you, Captain."

"It seems we are in the garden of the house," said Duval, as he looked about him.

It was no longer difficult to distinguish the path on which they were from the thick plantations and flower-borders that were on each side.

There was a flight of stone steps, and then a huge porch.

Duval was contemplating the dim outlines of the doorway when Blossom suddenly drew him on one side.

"Captain, some one is coming."

"Which way?"

"The same way we came."

They both stood aside in the deep shadow of the doorway.

A man approached with hasty steps.

The stranger evidently thought that but little caution was necessary.

Springing up the stone steps, he knocked four times deliberately with his sword-hilt at the door of the mansion.

"Who knocks?" cried a voice.

"From Versailles," was the reply.

"What have you brought?" asked the voice again.

"A lily and a lion."

"Enter."

A door was opened, but no light was emitted from within.

Both Duval and Blossom, however, heard it closed again, and then they whispered to each other.

"Blossom!"

"Yes, Captain."

"Have you any fear of this adventure? If so, I will undertake it by myself."

"You mean to get in, Captain, with the password you have heard?"

"I do."

"Then I follow you, lead me where it may."

"Come on, then, and we shall soon get at the heart of the mystery of this strange mansion, whither I am convinced the villain Pendell has made his way."

Duval ascended the steps, accompanied by Blossom.

They made neither more nor less noise than was just necessary in so doing; and upon reaching the door, Duval struck it four times with his sword-hilt.

"Who knocks?" cried the voice promptly from within.

"From Versailles," replied Duval, as promptly.

"What have you brought?" asked the voice.

"A lily and a lion," replied Duval.

"Enter."

A small wicket was opened in the great massive door of the hall.

"Two?" said the voice.

"Yes," replied Duval; "we met just through the garden gate."

"Straight on, gentlemen, and push the folding doors at the further end of the hall."

"Thanks," said Duval.

There was no light in the hall, and it seemed a perilous and nervous thing to traverse it in the intense darkness; but Duval felt that he had gone too far now to hesitate, and he walked boldly on, closely followed by Blossom.

They reached the doors spoken of.

Duval pushed one, and it yielded instantly.

There was a faint light beyond it; and it only needed a second observation to see that that faint light came through a curtain not sufficiently thick entirely to exclude all the rays that were on the other side of it.

And now Duval and Blossom paused, for they heard the murmur of voices on the other side of the curtain.

It did not seem exactly prudent to push aside that curtain, and enter a lighted apartment, where probably they would have been exposed to observation that would have at once proclaimed them to be strangers.

So they both paused, and listened.

CHAPTER LXVIII.

THE BANQUETING-HALL.—THE CONSPIRATORS' PLOT.

BLOSSOM looked about him, and, his eyes getting accustomed to the very dim light of the place in which he was, he saw to the left a narrow flight of stairs.

He whispered to Duval.

"Shall we see where those lead to, Captain? Who knows, but they may overlook this very room, which is through this curtain?"

"We will try, Blossom."

They slowly crept up the stairs, which, after a certain distance, took a slight turn to the right.

Then they came to a door.

It was easily opened, and it led them into a long narrow kind of gallery, built close to the wall of some very lofty apartment, which was dimly lighted.

A very few minutes' observation now imparted to Duval and Blossom a great deal of information in regard to the place in which they were.

It was a domed-shaped apartment, very richly furnished, and lighted by a single wax candle, in a tall silver candlestick.

Round the table on which this candlestick stood were six or seven men.

They were engaged in earnest conversation.

But at first they spoke in such low tones, that it was impossible to understand what they said.

One, at length, raised his voice, and spoke in words of authority:

"Gentlemen," he said, "I repeat to you the time is ripe for action. The plan we have hitherto pursued is an excellent one, and ought to save us one half our trouble."

"But it always fails," said another.

"It will succeed at last. We have managed so completely to set the King against the Prince of Wales, and the Prince of Wales against the King, that I will venture to say three parts of the time of both those personages is consumed by each of them in devising means for the destruction of the other."

"There seems a fatality about it," said another voice.

"You mean that they find each other out at the critical moment."

"They do."

"Well, gentlemen, we will not wait for them. Are you ready for action?"

"We are! we are!"

"I do not think there will be any difficulty on Tuesday next, at the costume ball, which is to be held in St. James's, in disposing of both the King and the Prince. The grand nephew then of James the Second, of England, and the rightful heir to the Stuart succession, can be proclaimed King."

From these words, Duval at once understood what was going on.

This was one of those famous Jacobite plots, which at that period, engaged so much the attention of the Government.

"Are we all agreed, then?" asked the first speaker.

"We are! we are!"

"Then, my Lord Montrose——"

"Hush! It is an understood thing that no names are to be mentioned here."

"I crave your pardon, but it will be your duty—just because it will be so easy for you to do it—to drop this little vial and its contents, into the gold goblet from which the King will drink, and which he will pass round to his guests."

"But, really," said the Duke of Montrose, in his own unmistakable accents.

"Can you hesitate?"

"I do not hesitate, but the difficulty to me appears to be great."

"Not at all. Here is the vial."

"Yes, it is well enough to say here is the vial, but to uncork such a thing, or to take the stopper from it, and then decant some liquid out of it, all are processes that take time and expose one to observation."

"There is no necessity—the vial is very thin—you have but to nip it in your finger and thumb, simply, when it will break; you have then to drop it into the King's goblet, bodily, and it will sink to the bottom."

"I see! I see!"

"The poison will be there and do its work."

There was a pause now, and a profound stillness, for several seconds.

Perhaps the imagination of every one there present was busy depicting the scene that might ensue, should this plan, for the death of the King, be successful.

The instigator of it then spoke again.

"You will perceive, gentlemen, how admirably this will work."

"Death! said several."

"Yes, and something more. There will be no difficulty of throwing the guilt of this transaction upon Prince Frederick."

There was a visible sensation among the conspirators.

"And in that case," added the speaker, "the horror of the crime of assassination in this country is so great, and particularly assassination achieved by poison, that the people will be disgusted with the present royal succession. A general rising, then, of different parts of the city and of the country, of the adherents of the exiled royal family, will surely meet with immediate countenance and support, and a bloodless revolution, or rather I should say, a restoration will take place."

"It is possible," said one.

"But hazardous," replied another.

"Of course, hazardous," replied the first speaker; "all these affairs are."

The conspirators, then, conversed for a few moments in whispers.

One then turned to the principal speaker, and addressed him.

"As the special agent," he said, "of that heir of the Stuarts, who is to ascend the throne of England, can you give us any certainty of what will be our position after these events?"

"I have a list here of Hanoverian noblemen, who are to be attainted and deprived of their estates; and from that list you will have your pick and choice, both of titles and properties."

A murmur of assent pervaded the little assembly.

"And now, gentlemen," said the speaker, "I must keep my word with you in another essential particular."

"One moment, sir," interrupted one of the conspirators. "The most satisfactory thing you could possibly do, would be to redeem your frequently-broken pledge of bringing over the young Prince from France, where you say he is, and introducing us to him."

"I will no longer break that pledge."

The conspirators made a hasty movement, and looked at each other.

"I will no longer baffle either your curiosity or your loyalty. The great grandson of King James the Second of England, and who is, by unquestionable descent, and the law of primogeniture, the King of this country, is here in this house."

"Here?" exclaimed the conspirators.

"Even here, gentlemen."

In the gloom and darkness of that spacious place they looked about them anxiously, as though they expected each moment to see some crowned apparition appear among them.

The agent, then, of the exiled family, lifted his hat from his head.

The conspirators involuntarily followed his example.

"Gentlemen," said the agent of the Jacobite plot, "His Majesty, King James the Third, has graciously given me his permission to announce his royal presence whenever I may think proper."

The conspirators faced about in one particular direction, where they saw the eyes of the agent were fixed.

And Claude Duval was particularly interested.

In common with all persons of any education or reading of that period, he was perfectly conversant with the fact that the struggle between the Jacobite faction and the usurping family who had seized upon the throne of England through the instrumentality of Prince William of Orange, was still raging.

Plots, and rumours of plots, were daily occurring.

And, although so many years had elapsed since the revolution in England, and the deposition of James the Second, there was always an heir to the Stuarts, who was ready to introduce turmoil and commotion into the kingdom.

Blossom, however, was not so well learned in the matter as Claude Duval.

"What does it all mean, Captain?" he whispered.

"Hush! I will tell you afterwards."

"But what are we to do, Captain?"

"Nothing, at present, but keep our eyes and ears open."

The Jacobite agent then spoke again.

"Will it graciously please your Majesty to step forward, and honour, with your royal presence, this meeting of your friends and subjects."

There was a pause.

So profound a stillness, that Duval, as he slightly leant over the rail of the gallery, could almost hear the breathing of the conspirators.

Click!

That was the sound of an opening lock.

Then there was a light footstep.

From an extremely dark corner of the spacious place, which had more the appearance of a banqueting-hall than anything else, there emerged a figure.

A slight, rather small young man, with fair hair.

A strange, set, artificial smile was upon his face.

He slightly bowed twice as he advanced.

Then the Jacobite agent cried out in a louder voice than he had hitherto used:

"Way for his Majesty the King!"

He then dropped on one knee.

The conspirators hesitated for a moment.

But the force of example was great, and they adopted the same attitude.

The young man, who had so slowly advanced, then bowed again.

He seemed upon the point of saying something.

Indeed, Claude Duval thought that he caught the first accents of his voice.

But it was only those first accents, for they were drowned immediately by one word—being uttered with such stentorian power that it awakened every possible echo in the old mansion.

"Fire!"

That was the word.

What did it mean?

A conflagration?

No.

A discharge of fire-arms?

Yes!

You might have counted four, with moderate haste, after that word was uttered, and then there came a blaze of musketry.

A roar, as of the reports of some dozen fire-locks.

The banqueting hall was full of smoke.

Then there arose a yell, partly of rage, and partly of pain.

Then all was still.

Still for about the same space of time that had passed away between the order to fire and the actual discharge of the muskets.

"Forward!" shouted a voice.

"Lights! lights!" cried another.

There was a crash of timber.

It seemed as if some panelling were being broken down.

And then there was a blaze of light, as several links were held up.

Duval could see what was going on, for the smoke had by this time curled up to the dome-shaped roof of the banqueting hall.

A party of the Foot Guard was breaking a way, with the butt ends of their muskets, through a rather slender partition, which appeared to divide the banqueting hall from some contiguous apartment.

The work was done in a few seconds.

Headed by an officer, they rushed into the place.

But the conspirators had vanished.

The young Pretender to the throne of England was nowhere to be seen, and the officer, who was accompanied by a gentleman in plain clothes, looked about him in surprise and disappointment.

"What is the meaning of this?" he said. "There is no one here!"

"But we heard the voices!" said the gentleman in plain clothes.

"Here is a candle, Major!" said the sergeant, who was with the party of Foot Guards.

"But that proves nothing. It may have been there for many a long year."

"It has been alight, Major, for the wick is warm!"

"But where are the conspirators?"

The gentleman in plain clothes looked about him with a vexed air.

He took a link from one of the soldiers, and held it down to the floor.

"It is strange," he said, "that such a volley should have done no execution."

"More than strange," said the officer. "Ah!—a prisoner, sergeant—seize that man!"

A light appeared at the further end of the banqueting hall.

It was carried by a very aged man, who advanced quite fearlessly into the midst of the soldiers.

He was seized roughly, and, by way of composing his faculties, probably, was shaken well before a question was asked him.

"Who and what are you?"

"Bless your honour, I'm the gardener!"

"What gardener?"

"The gardener at the old house. No one interferes with me, and I try to keep it as trim as I can, for who knows but the old family may come back, though they have been in foreign parts since I was a boy, and I shall be eighty come Michaelmas."

The man in plain clothes, who was with the officer, bent a keen glance upon the aged gardener.

"Come, come," he said, "I am convinced you know more than you will admit. Who were those persons that held a conference in this room—round this table, by the light of yonder candle?"

"Bless your honour, did you see them?"

"I did."

"Ah, it's the old story!"

"What old story?"

"Don't your honour know why nobody will live in the house?"

"Why not?"

"Why, because it's haunted, to be sure!"

"Haunted?"

"Yes, they do say that some Jacobite plot was got up here, and that the disaffected nobles who wanted him, who was called the young Pretender, to be the King of England, used to meet here in this very room, and had been over here from France among them. Bless you honours, they do say that once a year the ghosts of all those men, in this very room, who are long since dead, and the young Pretender with them, meet together just as they did when they were alive?"

"Ghosts!" exclaimed the officer of the guard.

"Ghosts!" muttered the civilian, who was doubtless a magistrate.

"Ghosts!" murmured the soldiers, as they huddled a little closer to each other, and glanced around them in the darkness, as though they expected each moment to be horrified by some contact with the supernatural world.

CHAPTER LXIX.

CLAUDE DUVAL BECOMES AN ACTOR, WHERE HE INTENDED ONLY TO BECOME A SPECTATOR.

But Claude Duval and Blossom knew well the reality of what had taken place.

Duval thought that Blossom was almost irritatingly obtrusive by the manner in which he pulled his arm to speak to him.

"Peace! Peace!" he said, rather impatiently.

"Sir?"

Duval started.

The voice was not that of Blossom.

"Sir!"

"Who, and what are you?" asked Duval.

"My name is James Edward, and there are those who call me King of England."

Duval understood it all in a moment.

In the confusion and general dispersion of the conspirators below, it had been a case of every one for himself.

No one had cared to look after the personal safety of that young, fair-haired, slim youth, who had been greeted with the title of Majesty.

It could easily be surmised that, in the confusion, he had found the staircase leading to the gallery, and thinking it might lead to some place of refuge, had ascended.

The probability was that he thought Claude Duval one of the conspirators.

And now the position of that descendent of exiled royalty, as well as of Duval himself, was perilous in the extreme.

"This," cried the civilian below, "may be but some absurd fable, and it will be our duty, Major Langley, to search this house?"

"A duty," said the mayor, "doubtless, but one that, at this hour of the night, it will be impossible to carry out."

"Then what should you advise, Major?"

"My sergeant here will post sentinels round the place, so that no one can escape, and will wait then till daylight."

"Be it so."

"Sergeant," said the Major, "set about it."

"It is chilly here?" said the magistrate.

"We will have a fire," added the Major. "Break up some of this old furniture, my men, and fling it on the hearth."

"Are you a gentleman, sir?" asked the young, fair descendant of the Stuarts, of Claude Duval.

"I hope so, as the word goes."

"How mean you, sir?"

"Simply, that I am a gentleman."

"I know not what your political predilections may be, but I begin to suspect you are not one of us."

"I am not one of those persons who, for the purposes of their own ambition and aggrandisement, have allured you to England, as a representative of a hopeless cause!"

"Ah!"

The young man sighed.

"Then you will betray me?"

That by no means follows.

"But the abbe always says, that those who are not for us are against us."

"The maxim is an old one," replied Duval; "and although, true, perhaps, in many instances, has its exceptions; I am not for you."

"Well, sir?"

"But I am not against you."

"This is a neutrality I hardly understand."

"I am not a much older man than yourself."

"I am only nineteen."

"Well, I admit there are some seven or eight years between us, and let me give them accumulated wisdom."

"What would you say?"

"Fly from England while you can!"

"Fly?"

"Yes, and avoid a shameful and ignominious death. The cause of which you are the representative is hopeless!"

"But if I fly, will it not look like a cowardly desertion of those who are here acting and plotting for me?"

"There are none such!"

"None such?"

"Not one. Those whom you think are doing so, only act and plot for themselves and their own selfish purposes. They will never succeed by the means they lay down, and the probability is, that there is not one of them who would not betray you to death for his own personal advantage at any moment."

The young Pretender to the Crown was silent, and sighed deeply.

"My tastes," he said, "are not those of plotters or assassins. I would rather lead a quiet life away from Courts and all their intrigues; it is by force of the will of others that I am here, and not from my own choice."

Claude Duval was particularly struck by the quiet simplicity with which this young man spoke.

He might or he might not be the real descendant of that race which claimed the crown of England through the Stuarts.

But one thing was quite clear.

He was totally unfitted for the struggle, which, were it successful, would place him upon the most uneasy throne in Europe.

A feeling of compassion came over Duval.

Was this quiet, amiable-looking lad—for such indeed he seemed—to be sacrificed, and be made the tool of the ambition of discontented men at the Court of St. James's.

But Duval was silent, he knew not what to say.

The danger was very great.

The sentinels were no doubt being posted.

Escape, then, from that house would be almost impossible.

The young Prince, if we may call him by such a title, misconstrued the silence of Duval.

"I perceive, sir," he said, "that you think differently, and belong to the other faction than that which has brought me here."

"Indeed, no," said Duval; "I belong to no faction."

"Indeed!"

DANGER THREATENS THE YOUNG PRINCE.

"Yes, there is scarcely a man in existence to whom it is so immaterial who sits upon the throne of England."

"Except myself."

"I do not comprehend——"

"I mean that as far as I am personally concerned, it is very immaterial to me. I only wish they would leave me in peace and quiet; but I fancy I shall be taken and put to death, and that the only peace I shall find will be in the grave."

The tone of deep despondency in which these words were uttered, very much affected Claude Duval.

"Why," he said, speaking in the same whispered tones in which the whole conference had been conducted. "Why, with such feeling and opinions are you here at all?"

"I was over persecuted."

"I suppose as much!"

"I was told it was a duty, and that I owed it to my family, all of whom are poor and scattered over Europe, to endeavour to recover the throne which would have altered their condition. But it is a delusion."

"I think it is," said Duval.

"Will you tell me then, sir, what I am to do?"

The utterly helpless tone in which this question was put completed, if anything was wanting so to do—the feeling of personal sympathy which Claude Duval had with the young stranger.

"I will do all in my power," he said, "to assist you to escape, not only from your present dilemma, but from England."

"I shall be only too delighted."

"Nevertheless, I can but do my best!"

"Ah, sir, I trust entirely to you; and I feel a kind of assurance in my own mind that not only will that trust not be betrayed, but that you will find some means of saving me."

"Hush!" said Duval. "Take care; keep back in the shadow."

The soldiers by this time in the banqueting-room below, had broken up some of the lightest articles of

No. 22.—NIGHTSHADE.

furniture they could find, and flung them on the hearth.

They soon set light to them.

And after a time, a bright blaze was once more in that ancient chimney, which probably for many a long year had been abandoned to damp and neglect.

That blaze sufficiently illuminated the ancient apartment to make the greatest caution necessary on the part of Duval, that neither he, Blossom, nor the young Prince, should be seen.

He spoke in a low whisper to his faithful follower.

"Blossom!"

"I'm here, Captain."

"Make the most minute examination you can of this gallery, and see if you can find any other outlet from it than that by which we came."

"There isn't a square inch of its floor or wall, Captain, that I've not sounded."

"And unsuccessfully?"

"Quite so. If we leave it, Captain, it must be as we came to it."

"Is all lost, then?" whispered the Prince.

"No," replied Duval, "we will yet make an effort to escape."

"You give me new hope?"

"Along with that new hope, let me promise you one thing."

"I have been fed upon promises all my life."

"But this is one which shall be fulfilled. It is that I will not forsake you come what may."

"I thoroughly believe you," replied the Prince, "and I place myself entirely in your hands."

"Follow me, then, as cautiously and as lightly in regard to any noise as you can."

Duval perfectly recollected that the staircase which ascended to the gallery of the banqueting-room, was outside the curtain that shut in the entrance from the hall to that apartment.

To remain in the gallery was useless.

And as there was no other mode of leaving it but that by which they had originally reached it, Duval determined to attempt it.

If once they could gain the hall in safety, they might to the right or to the left of it, get into some of the ground-floor suites of apartments, from which an easy passage might be made to the garden.

Once there, Claude Duval would be of opinion that one half of their difficulties was surmounted.

It was a perilous step.

But there was no resource.

Slowly as foot could fall, Claude Duval descended the staircase.

He was followed by the Prince.

Blossom brought up the rear.

The great danger was that some one might be passing in or out the banqueting-room, at the moment the fugitives might reach the curtain that shrouded its entrance.

A lesser danger still might be that there was a sentinel in the hall.

But with both these things upon his mind, Duval advanced.

The young Prince followed him with the simplicity and trustfulness of a child.

They reached the foot of the stairs.

They almost brushed against the curtain.

A voice sounded from the banqueting-room, and what it said was so interesting to them, that they all three involuntarily paused to listen.

"Is that a gallery above there!" asked the voice.

"It looks like it," said another.

"Sergeant!"

"Yes, your honour."

"Take a file of men and examine that place!"

"Yes, your honour. First file fall in! Right shoulder, forward! Slope arms! March!"

There was not a moment to lose.

Everything now depended upon whether there were a sentinel in the hall or not.

Duval took the young Prince by the arm, and walked hastily forward.

He opened one of those folding doors which had before yielded to his touch so readily.

They were in the hall.

No sentinel.

One had been placed at the chief entrance to the house, but the sergeant had thought it better he should be outside in the porch than actually within the building.

"Come on!" whispered Duval.

The young Prince spoke not a word.

They crossed the hall rapidly.

Duval tried two doors, but they were both fast.

A third yielded to his touch, but it creaked a little upon its hinges.

Duval was afraid to open it beyond just space sufficient for them all three to pass through singly.

Then he closed the door again.

He felt the lock carefully, to discover if there were any means within of fastening it.

There was one of those small handles which communicate with a bolt, but that was all.

Such a fastening might bewilder any one coming suddenly into the apartment, but it was not sufficiently strong to resist anything in the shape of violence.

It was a welcome sight, however, to Duval to see that there were some windows which looked directly into the garden.

He could dimly observe, apparently almost sticking against the thin panes of glass, the straggling boughs of some tall trees.

"Our worst danger is over," he said.

"I am saved, then?" asked the Prince.

"I can scarcely say so, but I hope that you are on the road to safety. Blossom!"

"Here, Captain."

"Get open one of those windows that we may emerge into the garden!"

The windows were what are called French ones, and opened inwards like doors, and in a few seconds, Blossom had succeeded in making a clear way into the open air.

They all three passed out of the room.

How grateful, cool, and pleasant was the first breath of the night atmosphere, as they stepped out into it, and felt that there was nothing above them but the waving tree tops and the vault of heaven.

"I feel that I am saved now," said the Prince.

"Do not speak for you life's sake," whispered Duval.

"More danger?"

"Listen!"

The slow, monotonous tramp of the sentinel on duty not very many yards distant from where they were, came very plainly upon their ears.

"Blossom!"

"I am here, Captain."

"I am forced to ask for you, for I cannot see you amid all these dim shadows."

"I'm at your order, Captain."

"We must pass that sentinel."

Blossom was silent.

"Do you hear me, Blossom?"

"I do, Captain, and was thinking about the best way of doing it."

"Stay!" said the young Prince. "Let no human life be taken for the preservation of mine."

"Nay——"

"I have spoken—I have spoken. I am deeply grateful for what you have done already; but I would rather surrender myself to my worst foes, and accept whatever fate may be in store for me, than that my escape from this house should be marked by the track of murder."

"I think I can manage it," whispered Blossom, "without that."

"It must be so managed or not at all," added the Prince.

"You hear, Blossom?" said Duval. "I leave the task to you."

Blossom crept forward something after the fashion of a North American Indian, and Claude Duval felt perfectly certain that if it were possible for any human being to dispose of the sentinel in a manner that would be pleasing to the young Prince, he (Blossom) was the person to do so.

The sentinel was cold.

Therefore he paced to and fro rather rapidly.

His own footsteps made a sufficient sound upon the gravel walk of the garden to drown all minor noises.

If he had stood still for ever so short a space of time he might possibly have heard the slight movement of Blossom as he approached him.

But he continued to parade to and fro, every now and then stamping to thoroughly recover the warmth of his circulation.

Blossom's task was not difficult.

All it required was coolness and courage.

Those were qualities he had in abundance.

He waited until the sentinel's back was towards him.

Then he made one dash forward, and instantly clasping his arms round the man, he secured both him and his musket with a grip that could not easily be shaken off.

And this brought Blossom so close to the ear of the sentinel that he was able to speak to him most effectually.

"Any alarm or any struggle and you are a dead man! A soldier should know when to fight and when to surrender."

"I give in," said the sentinel.

"Silence, then!" replied Blossom.

This soldier of the guard was evidently one of those matter of fact personages who easily succumb to circumstances.

He felt that he was a prisoner.

What then was the use of attempting to fight, and so sacrificing his life?

He allowed Blossom to take his musket from him, and then stood perfectly quiescent.

"Captain!" said Blossom.

Duval at once advanced with the young prince.

"All is well, Captain."

"And the sentinel?"

"He is a most sensible man, and here he stands."

"I surrender," said the sentinel, in a whining tone, "to a superior force, as I have a wife and family in Westminster."

"We don't want your reasons," said Duval. "Good night."

"If you please, sirs," added the sentinel, "perhaps you won't mind returning to me my fire-lock?"

"Certainly not," replied Blossom.

Blossom shouldered the soldier's musket, and again fell into the rear, as Duval and the young Prince made the best of their way through the garden.

In five minutes more they were in the narrow lane, and at a rapid pace—for the night was not nearly so dark as it had been—they made their way into the main Oxford Road.

CHAPTER LXX.

CLAUDE DUVAL OFFERS THE HOSPITALITY OF FARNBOROUGH HOUSE TO THE YOUNG PRINCE.

THEY proceeded some distance without breaking the silence Duval felt it was so necessary to observe while they were so near the precincts of that mysterious house.

At length he paused, and, turning to the young Prince, Duval said, "Now I think I may congratulate you upon your safety."

The young man clasped the hand of Duval, and said, in a voice of deep emotion, "Kind and generous friend, tell me by what name I may remember you in my prayers!"

"For the present," said Claude Duval, "you must think of me as Sir John Cope, who will be most happy to offer you the hospitality his house affords, if you are not quite decided where to direct your steps."

The young man eagerly availed himself of an invitation so graciously and gracefully tendered.

"Blossom."

"Yes, Captain."

"How are we to get to town? It is too far to walk."

"Why, Captain, the Wycombe coach will soon overtake us, I suspect, if it has not already passed us."

"A good thought," said Duval; "and, if I mistake not, I hear the rumbling of the wheels some distance behind us."

"I shouldn't wonder, Captain."

Bang! bang! bang! came several musket shots at this moment.

"Ah!" said the young Prince, "we are pursued! Fly! Save yourselves! I will abide my fate! I can but die!"

"Courage, courage!" said Duval. "Follow me, and I will yet protect you with my own life, if needs be!"

Duval, followed by the young Prince and Blossom, scrambled through the hedge, and lay quietly down to wait events.

"This way, this way!" they heard the voice of the sentinel shout. "I watched them! They came this way! They're hiding somewhere in the hedge!"

The sound of wheels was now heard fast approaching the spot.

"Our last hope of safety is gone," whispered the young Prince, as he grasped Duval by the arm.

"I think not," said Duval, "for it appears to me to be too small for the stage coach; but we shall see."

On came the coach.

As it came on at a slow pace, Duval raised himself to a level with the top of the hedge, and discovered that it was a private carriage, and its only occupants consisted of two ladies.

The driver was an old man, and the two horses that drew the vehicle were going at that sort of pace which showed that they had a most easy and comfortable situation.

"That's a comfort," whispered Blossom; "we yet have a chance of the coach, Captain."

"Search the hedge!" shouted a voice.

The party still advanced quickly; and as they did so, Duval, Blossom, and the young Prince receded, as it were—retracing their steps, so to speak, leaving their pursuers many paces in advance.

"That will do," said Duval. "When they find their search is fruitless, they will soon give up the pursuit."

"I hope so—I hope so," replied the young Prince; "for I am heartily tired of this dangerous life; and if ever I do get free again, I will never be persuaded again to undertake so mad a scheme."

"That is well," replied Duval; "but now I think I really hear the sound of approaching wheels. See, Blossom."

"All right, Captain! Here it comes, at a brisk pace. If there are places for us, we shall reach London yet in good time."

This time there was no mistake; it was, indeed, the coach returning to town from Wycombe.

Blossom sprang out into the road.

"Stop! Hoi! Coach!"

The coachman pulled up.

"What's the matter now?" asked the coachman.

"Two passengers—two insides."

"No room."

The coachman was urging his horses forward again, and Claude Duval and the young Prince would again have been left to their resources, had not the eyes of the coachman rested upon the two unmistakable gentlemen, who now stood almost close to the horses.

"Peter," cried the coachman to the guard.

"Well, Mr. Franks?"

"Is there two inside places?"

"Yes," replied the guard, as he dismounted, touching his hat respectfully as he looked at Duval, who certainly looked born to command.

"Enter," he said courteously to the young Prince.

The young man obeyed, and Duval sprung in after him.

"Blossom," said Duval, putting his head out of the coach window, "I dare say the guard can find you a place outside."

"Yes, sir; certainly, sir. Here you are. Jump up, or Mr. Franks will be in a awful temper at being delayed so long."

It did not take Blossom many minutes to shake himself down into the place assigned him by the guard, and again the horses were put into motion.

As they rattled along at a brisk rate, the coach soon overtook the little party which had been in pursuit of the fugitives, headed by the sentinel who had been deprived of his musket by Blossom's ingenuity.

Duval and the young Prince exchanged glances as they saw the search was still being kept up so vigorously; but neither of them spoke.

"Halt!" cried one of the soldiers.

The coachman pulled up.

"Have you seen three men on the road, going in the direction from which you are coming? They must have been running at a great rate."

"Not I," replied the coachman. "Peter, did you see three fellows a-running along the road to Wycombe?"

"No!" roared the guard. "We shan't get to London to-day if you keep on a-stopping in this 'ere fashion."

The coachman seemed to be of the same opinion, for he lashed his horses, and urged them to their greatest speed.

The young man involuntarily laid his hand upon the arm of Duval as this brief dialogue was going on.

"Highwaymen, I suppose," said Duval, in a calm voice.

"I suppose so," replied a gentleman, who had not before spoken. "These roads are infested with them, I fancy."

"So I have heard," said Duval; and then the party inside the coach lapsed into silence.

At length the coach rattled into the yard of St. Martin's-le-Grand, and our three travellers alighted.

Duval drew the young Prince's arm beneath his own, and hurried him out of the yard, closely followed by Blossom, who did not wish to encounter his acquaintance, the guard, whom he left in such an uncomfortable situation when the Oxford Mail started.

"Now," said Duval, "you are quite safe, I believe; and let me hope that happy days are yet in store for you."

"Heaven reward you," fervently ejaculated his youthful companion, "for all you have dared and braved for me to-night."

"Name it not, name it not," replied Duval; "but here we are at Farnborough House."

Duval's summons for admission was immediately answered by one of his followers, now clothed in a rich livery.

There was a glance of inquiry between this man and Blossom as the little party passed into the hall. That of the man meant to say, "Who is this stranger?" That of Blossom meant plainly, "Is all well?"

"This way, this way," said Duval, courteously, as he moved towards the grand staircase.

There was a light footstep, and in another moment, before she could see that there was a stranger present, Lucy had cast herself into Duval's arms.

"Ah, Pauline!" said Duval, with emphasis. "My grand-daughter," he continued, turning to the young Prince.

Lucy was anxious to recover from the slight confusion into which she had been thrown, and in order to give herself time to do so, she executed one of those elaborate courtesys which, at that time were made quite a part of education, and which generally took up a full minute and a half, in carrying it out to perfection.

The Prince bowed low.

And now Claude Duval felt some little hesitation in regard to what name he should give to that heir of the princely exiled house of Stuart.

The pause was an awkward one.

Duval waved his hand towards the Prince, and said, "This is——"

"Mr. Stuart," said the Prince.

"Yes, Pauline, this is Mr. Stuart; and for a short time he will partake of our hospitality."

Lucy drew aside, and Claude Duval, ascending the grand staircase of the mansion, installed his guest in one of the best apartments.

"You may remain here," he said, "in perfect safety for the present; but you must do me the favour of consenting to one thing."

"I consent beforehand. Can I refuse you, my deliverer, anything?"

"You must permit me to acquaint my grand-daughter Pauline with the real truth as regards you, and I can answer for her fidelity with my life."

"Use your own discretion, Sir John Cope, if such, indeed, be your name, and I know that that discretion will provide for my safety."

Duval was anxious to seek Lucy, and inform her of all that had taken place; therefore, he left his illustrious young guest alone, and hurried to the apartment which they had chosen in that house to call their own especially.

A very short time sufficed to put Lucy in full possession of all the facts of the case.

She was terrified at first at the idea of any complicity with those Jacobite plots, which were the common talk of the town.

But soon a feeling of profound pity took possession of her.

Duval, in a very few words, had told her how gentle and how entirely unfitted for political strife was the character and disposition of the Prince.

"Nevertheless, Lucy," he said, "for his own sake, as well as for ours, I will do everything I can to expedite his departure. And now let me look into your eyes, for I perceive that they are heavy with watching."

Lucy smiled, but it was faintl

She was, indeed, very weary.

"How am I to seek adventures," said Duval, "if during the whole time I am away, sleep is to be a stranger to your eyelids?"

"It is but the dawn of morning," said Lucy, "and there is ample time for rest."

"Fully so."

"And you, too, Claude, are but human—you likewise must sleep, so we will say nothing further of this strange adventure, until rest has better fitted us to take the necessary measures for the safety of our visitor."

There came a tap at the door of the room.

Blossom then put in his head.

"Captain, I have the little valise I took from that scoundrel, Pendell."

"I am delighted to hear it," cried Claude; "for, in truth, I had forgotten it."

"A valise, and from Mossy Pendell?" exclaimed Lucy.

"Yes," replied Claude, "and I have every reason to believe it contains papers of the greatest importance."

Lucy held out her hand for the valise, but Duval shook his head as he took it from Blossom.

"Nay," he said; "let me now be peremptory—rest, Lucy, rest. I must see your eyes looking brighter, and your cheeks not so pale, before we think of examining the contents of this valise."

* * * * * *

There was profound repose in Farnborough House.

The dim, gray light of early dawn brightened.

Long, slant rays of sunlight came from the eastern sky, on and over the house tops of London.

The busy life of the great city commenced, and the confused, subdued roar and rattle of the many vehicles parading the streets of the metropolis filled the air.

But still no one stirred at Farnborough House.

All was repose there.

It was eleven o'clock in the day, before, with a slow step, Claude Duval descended the grand staircase.

He had thrown off entirely the disguise which he had worn as a passenger in the Oxford Mail.

That disguise was as different an one as possible from that which he meant to wear under ordinary circumstances, and associate with the name of Sir John Cope.

The servants were astir, if a languid kind of life pervading the lower regions could be called such.

There was a very handsome breakfast parlour upon the ground floor into which Duval made his way, for he expected Lucy to descend in the course of a few minutes.

Strolling to the window of this room, without any fixed purpose, but merely to gaze out as any one might do upon the light of a new day, Duval observed a man on the opposite side of the way attentively regarding Farnborough House.

The experiences of Duval were sufficiently great to make him at once comprehend that this man was in some manner connected with the administration of the government of the country.

Duval suspected from his air and manner that he was what went by the name of a Secretary of State's messenger.

There were some half-dozen of such men who occupied the position of those police officers who in preceding reigns had gone by the name of *poursuivants*.

Duval felt uneasy.

He drew back into the shadow of the apartment, so that he could keep an attentive eye upon that man without being seen himself.

A Hackney coach drove up.

It stopped nearly opposite Farnborough House.

Then the man who had awakened Claude Duval's suspicions left the doorway in which he had been partially concealed, and went to the side of the coach, with the occupant of which he evidently held some conference.

The door of the breakfast-room at this moment opened.

"Come hither," said Duval, "come hither, Lucy, give me your judgment upon what is happening opposite the house."

"I regret," said a soft voice, "that I am mistaken for another."

Duval started.

It was the young heir of the Stuarts.

And he looked as surprised at Duval as any one person could look at another.

"I presume," he said, "that there is some mystery about you, for although you speak with the same voice, you do not at all represent the same person who so generously aided me last night."

Duval glanced at himself in a mirror.

The change was very complete.

He looked rather confusedly at the young Prince.

"I would fain trust you," he said, "I shall probably do so before you leave this house, but I have the consent of another to procure to enable me to inform you who and what I really am."

The Prince was about to approach the window, but Duval held him back.

"No!" he said, "it is better that you should see without being seen."

CHAPTER LXXI.

CLAUDE DUVAL MEETS WITH A SURPRISE.

THE tone of voice in which Duval uttered these words was quite sufficient to warn the young Stuart of danger.

He drew hastily back, and that faint flush, which Duval had noticed even by artificial light on the night before, came now more prominently in the daylight across his countenance.

And now the door of the breakfast-room opened again.

It was Lucy who made her appearance.

But Duval motioned her to silence.

His eyes were on the hackney coach opposite.

He saw its door opened.

A man slowly stepped out of it, and walking round it by the back, began to cross over the roadway towards Farnborough House.

Duval knew him instantly.

"St. Ives," he said.

"Then we have nothing to fear," exclaimed Lucy.

"Hush!"

The young Prince looked confusedly from one to the other of them.

"Repair to your chamber," said Duval. "Leave us to battle the astuteness of this officer of the police, or to adopt our own means of insuring his silence."

The young Prince instantly left the room.

St. Ives had crossed the road, and knocked sharply at the door of Farnborough House.

"He is lost!" cried Lucy.

"No, not yet."

"And we, too!"

"Wherefore? wherefore?"

"Under these exciting circumstances, it will be impossible that we should keep up an *incognito* beneath the keen and accurate eyes of Mr. St. Ives."

"The Prince must escape!" exclaimed Duval, "even if he go over the housetops. He shall not be taken, while I have life left to protect him, beneath this roof."

Lucy clasped her hands.

She looked the picture of consternation.

"Claude! Claude! What is to be done?"

"See St. Ives, entertain and baffle him as best you can for a few minutes. I will run upstairs and speak to the Prince and, perhaps, help him to some disguise."

"Do so in the name of heaven."

Duval darted up the grand staircase, and so rapidly did he leave the breakfast-room, that he almost upset a footman who was carrying a tray in order to lay the table.

Up to that moment, the footman had had an impression that his master, Sir John Cope, was a very aged man.

But now that he saw him going up the grand staircase at Farnborough House four steps at a time his eyes dilated with wonder.

Duval passed the drawing-room floor, and ascended the second flight of stairs.

He at once opened the door of the chamber, which on the previous night he had devoted to the use of the young Stuart.

"You must fly," he said, "and in order that you may do so with greater safety you must make some instant change in your apparel."

"I cannot."

"Cannot?"

"I have no means."

"Come with me, my wardrobe is in the next room?"

"I cannot."

"What is the meaning of this reiteration that you cannot?"

"Simply that I cannot."

"Mr. Stuart—or Prince, as I may well call you, I beg of you to take my word that the danger is imminent. I will bring you another suit of clothes instantly, and help you to put them on in lieu of those you wear."

"No."

"You say no?"

"I say no."

"Then let me tell you that one of the most energetic and keen-eyed police officials of London is at this very time in the house!"

"I will disguise myself."

"Quickly, and let me help you!"

Claude Duval seized the cuff of the coat that the young Prince wore, and, before he could be hindered, dragged the sleeve off him.

"Forbear, sir!" said the young Prince, as he stepped back.

"Good heavens!" exclaimed Duval, "is this a moment to stand upon any fanciful notions of dignity?"

"I will only consent to disguise myself," said the Prince, "if you will conduct me to the private apartment of your grand-daughter, Pauline."

"Sir!"

The Prince was silent.

"What infatuation is this?"

"It is no infatuation. I am and will disguise myself so that the generous man who has taken me beneath his roof cannot be endangered by my presence."

"But——"

"Nay, hear me out. The cunning and lynx-eyed officers of the London police seek a young prince of the house of Stuart."

"They do!"

"But not a princess."

Even as he spoke, the young Stuart lifted from his head a wig, which comprehended the light head of hair he had exhibited, and giving his head a slight shake, there fell upon his shoulders—not a great profusion of curls—but a sufficient quantity at once to stamp the feminine character of the face.

It might be, that the sudden and startling change, from one character to another, gave a romantic and picturesque aspect to the personage who, up to that moment, Claude Duval had certainly looked upon as a young prince of the house of Stuart.

Or it might be, that that feminine face and hair, combined with the masculine costume below it, produced a contrast which added much to the personal charms of the wearer.

But certainly Claude Duval thought his mysterious visitor very beautiful.

The surprise that he felt sat upon his countenance.

With an involuntary respect, likewise, he stepped back a pace.

Then a radiant blush came over the face of the young girl.

She was evidently very young.

Perhaps not exceeding sixteen years of age; and now that her secret was known to Claude Duval, and she saw him looking at her fixedly, she shrunk from his scrutiny.

"I have deceived you," she said, "and I can scarcely hope for your forgiveness."

"Say not so," exclaimed Duval, "I am only too much delighted at the incident to be able to give utterance readily to my feelings."

"Alas!" cried the young girl, as she clasped her hands. "am I for ever to be unhappy?"

Duval paused.

He could not thoroughly comprehend the meaning of this speech.

"Wherefore should you be unhappy?" he said, "when the chances of escape from your present dilemma, which a few seconds since were so poor, are now so largely increased."

The girl looked at him with a confused air.

There was evidently some misconception between them.

But then she held out her hand frankly.

"I think I was misjudging you," she said; "and I feel that I may trust you."

"You may, if you will. But tell me now, who and what you really are, since you are not a prince of the house of Stuart?"

"It is true, that I am not; but I am a princess of that name."

Duval bowed.

At this moment, the sound of voices from below came with sufficient distinctness up the staircase of Farnborough House to assure Duval that there was no time to lose."

"One moment," he said, "I will return to you instantly."

He went to the head of the staircase and listened.

He heard the voice of Lucy.

"My grandfather will be down in a few minutes, and you can speak to him, sir."

"I should prefer going up to him," replied a voice, in which Claude Duval recognised, unmistakably, that of St. Ives.

He flew back to the apartment in which he had left the young princess.

"Quick! quick!" he said, as he seized her by the arm, "this is no time for ceremony; and you will excuse a seeming rudeness, which has for its object the saving of your life."

The young girl turned pale, but it was only for a moment.

She spoke then without any tremor in her voice.

"Is the danger so great?"

"It is immediate."

"Then it must be met with courage."

"Yes, and with such finesse as we may bring to bear upon the circumstances surrounding us. Come this way, for there is one even now ascending the staircase; who, while he is one of the most generous of men, will do his duty, and that duty compromises your safety, and even your life."

The young girl suffered Duval to lead her out of the room.

They crossed the corridor at the head of the stairs with rapid steps.

Duval pushed open the door of another apartment, and almost pushed her into it, as he said, "This is the apartment of the young lady you saw downstairs. You will find plenty of means of assuming the proper costume of your sex; and I would advise you to do so with all the rapidity in your power."

"I will."

Duval closed the door.

He turned instantly to the staircase, and began rapidly to descend it.

On the landing of the first floor he met St. Ives.

That landing was a very large one.

The house was a very old-fashioned one, and peculiarly built, having on each of its floors a long gallery or corridor, running the whole depth that remained from the staircase and terminated by a very large gothic window, in which was stained glass.

The effect of these arched corridors and stained glass windows, was to give the architecture of the house quite an ecclesiastical appearance.

And as gothic windows certainly have a maximum of frame-work to the minimum of glass, the amount of light that came into the corridor at the top of the first flight of stairs was but small.

Duval, when he met St. Ives, likewise had the advantage of the window at his back.

Whatever light, then, came in through the stained glass fell upon St. Ives, while it left him, Duval, in shadow.

The officer paused, and looked fixedly at Claude.

Was it possible that his disguise was sufficiently good to withstand the keen, penetrating glance of St. Ives?

It was the worst ordeal that any disguise could have to pass through.

And for a few seconds these two men, who knew each other so well, remained silent.

It was a silence, however, which Duval broke.

"May I ask, sir," he said, "your business here in my house?"

"Certainly. My name is St. Ives."

The officer paused as though expecting an answer, which Duval gave by announcing the name he had assumed.

"I am Sir John Cope."

St. Ives inclined his head very slightly.

"The next question you will put to me, Sir John Cope," he said, "is to know my business here."

"It is, sir?"

"That business, then, is to arrest a traitor."

"A traitor?"

"Yes, Sir John Cope, a most notable traitor, and I warn you that any resistance, or any attempt at subterfuge, by which that traitor may be screened or saved from the grasp of justice will be useless."

"Do you allude to me, sir?"

"I do not, although the charge against you, Sir John Cope, will assume a serious shape."

"What charge? what shape?"

"Those who aid, harbour, or comfort traitors, are themselves guilty of treason, although in a lesser degree."

"You are strangely mistaken," said Duval, "and come here on an errand based altogether on some error."

"Not so!" replied St. Ives, "and the only reason that I waste time in conversing with you here is that I am sure of my prisoner."

"Your prisoner, sir?"

"Yes, a young gentleman slept last night in this house, who will exchange it to-night for the Tower."

"A young gentleman?"

"Oh, Sir John Cope, you are playing you part exceedingly well, and very probably you are a conscientious Jacobite enough, but when I have explained to you the exact state of affairs, you will perceive how utterly useless is any resistance or attempt at cajolement."

"I listen to you, sir?"

"Since the entrance into it by the person whom I come to arrest, this house has been closely watched."

"Indeed!"

"Yes, back and front, and two of my men are even now upon the roof. It has been impossible for th last eight hours for even a cat to leave Farnborough House unnoticed."

"Indeed,' said Duval again.

"Therefore, you perceive, Sir John Cope, I am sure of my prisoner."

"You are strangely mistaken."

"Am I!"

"Indeed, you are. I am loyal to the House of Hanover."

Mr. St. Ives smiled.

"And there is no young gentleman here what ever!"

Mr. St. Ives smiled again.

"The house is solely occupied by my grandchild, Pauline, by myself, and by a very distant relation of our's, by the name of Griselda Cope."

Claude Duval pronounced this name, Griselda Cope, in so unexpectedly high and shrill a voice, that Mr. St. Ives looked up and down the staircase to endeavour to come at some explanation of it.

He considered a moment.

"Ah!" he said, "I comprehend!"

"What, sir?"

"You have had a sudden inspiration, Sir John Cope."

"Indeed, sir?"

"Yes, I will venture to say that you never heard of Griselda Cope until this moment."

"This is insufferable!"

"It may be so, but I will trouble you to allow me to pass. I have been very patient with you, Sir John Cope—that patience is now at an end."

St. Ives clapped his hands together sharply.

A strange shadow came over the corridor as Claude Duval glanced at the stained glass window, he saw dimly outlined against it, on the outer side, the figure of a man.

"You see," said St. Ives, "I have not left even the windows unguarded at the back of the house. Resistance is useless—evasion impossible. I must, and will take with me, as a prisoner, the young gentleman who found a refuge in this house last night."

"You are strangely mistaken."

"Pooh! pooh!"

"There is no such person here."

"I can safely say there is, for I will stake my life upon the fact that no such person has left the house. So once more, Sir John Cope, I ask you to give way."

Duval stepped aside.

"That is prudent," said St. Ives, and he darted up the staircase which led to the second corridor.

CHAPTER LXXI.

THE YOUNG PRINCESS MAKES A WISE DETERMINATION.

DUVAL slowly followed the officer.

A strange scene presented itself then on that upper corridor.

The door of Lucy's chamber—

That chamber into which Duval had introduced the young Princess, was quietly opened, and attired in a pale grey silk dress, belonging to Lucy, the young Stuart Princess stepped forward.

She looked perfectly calm and composed.

Her hair was very neatly arranged in something of a French style, and, take her for all in all, she presented a very charming appearance.

St. Ives paused, and gazed at her suspiciously.

But there was no such thing as mistaking her perfectly feminine condition.

No artful disguise, or make-up of any description, could have made the youngest, or most delicate young prince in the world, so perfect a representation of a fair girl.

The first suspicion that haunted the mind of Mr. St. Ives vanished.

"Is anything the matter?" asked the Princess, as she looked from Duval to the officer, and then back again.

Duval was about to speak.

But St. Ives stopped him abruptly.

"Hold!" he cried, "one moment! will you be so good, madam, as to inform me of your name."

"My name is Griselda," replied the young Princess.

"Ah!"

"And I have the honour to be distantly related to Sir John Cope."

"Oh!"

"Who, for the present, affords me an asylum in his house, with his grand-daughter, Pauline."

Mr. St. Ives bowed low.

He walked, then, completely round the young Princess, and looked at her fixedly.

"It is impossible!" he muttered. "No disguise could be so perfect."

Then he bowed again.

"Madam," he said, "I have nothing to say to you."

At the moment he spoke, he took a small silver whistle from his pocket, and blew a shrill call upon it.

The echoes of that whistle still sounded through Farnborough House, as a violent knocking came at its outer doors.

They were immediately opened, and some half-dozen men made their way into the hall.

"Here!" cried St. Ives, over the staircase.

"Yes, sir," replied one of the men.

"You will search this house from attics to cellars, and you will do so with such vigilance that the result must be satisfactory."

"All right, sir."

"Now, Sir John Cope," said St. Ives, "I put it to you, for your own sake, whether it is not better at once to give up the person we seek, than to be contumacious in further aiding his concealment."

"I know not who you mean, nor what you mean!" said Duval.

"Very good."

"There is no person, to my knowledge, concealed in this house, and you are quite welcome to search it. Of course, I look upon all this proceeding as a kind of outrage; but I say nothing to you or to your men upon that head, as no doubt you are acting under orders, and doing your duty."

Duval then offered his arm to the Princess.

"Come, Griselda," he said, "I see no reason, my dear, why we should not descend to breakfast."

The young girl slid her arm under Duval's.

"We will leave this gentleman," he said, "if it so please him and his myrmidons to turn our house out of window, as the common saying is."

Duval and the young Princess of the House of Stuart slowly descended the staircase together, and reached the breakfast-parlour.

As they entered it, Duval placed his finger on his lips, as a signal to Lucy to be exceedingly circumspect in what she said.

But her surprise was immense at the sight of the young girl who was upon the arm of Duval.

There had been no opportunity of making her aware, in the least degree, of what was going on upstairs.

She knew nothing of the singular fact that the seeming young Prince had turned out to be a young Princess.

But still there was something about the features of the young girl which reminded her of their illustrious visitor.

But so perfect was the feminine costume, that Lucy was lost both in wonder and admiration, in the vague idea that it must be, after all, the young Prince disguised, and who came down looking so very young-ladylike into the breakfast-room.

"Is this possible?" exclaimed Lucy.

"Hush!" said Duval, in a low tone. "We do not know who may be listening."

"But——"

"You see— you see!"

The young Princess sat down, and, as she did so, she took one of the hands of Lucy in her own, and kissed her lightly on the cheek.

Lucy glanced at Duval.

He was as composed as possible.

"I am certain," said Lucy, "that——"

"Hush, hush!" said Duval again.

"But I am dying of curiosity."

"Preserve your life for a short period," replied Duval, "and all will be explained."

"But you can speak in a whisper."

"Then I made bold to show this young lady into your dressing-room, and this you perceive is——"

"One of my own dresses!" exclaimed Lucy. "I did not notice it before."

"And this," added Duval, "is the young Prince."

"So admirably disguised."

"No."

"But my own eyesight——"

"It deceives you Lucy. The young Prince was admirably disguised; but the young Princess appears in her own proper character."

"Ah!" exclaimed Lucy. "I now understand it all, and you are saved."

"It was much safer," said the Princess, "that when I did make a change of costume, it should be to this, which will bear any scrutiny; and so the Prince of the House of Stuart has disappeared, and poor Griselda Cope will be able to leave the kingdom in peace and safety, thanks to the generosity of friends, who have been surely raised up for me by gracious heaven, in this extremity of evil fortune."

The door of the breakfast-room was flung open

Mr. St. Ives appeared upon the threshold.

There was a look of vexation on his face.

"Have you found him?" asked Duval.

"No, sir."

"Ah! I thought not."

"But we shall!"

Duval inclined his head.

"And in the meantime, Sir John Cope, good morning!"

"Good morning, Mr.—what did you say your name was?"

THE RENDEZVOUS,—PLOT AND COUNTERPLOT.

St. Ives disdained to answer; but, rapidly closing the parlour door, he left the house, carrying with him his myrmidons, and slamming the outer door shut with very great vehemence.

"Thank heaven!" exclaimed the young Princess; "the danger is over!"

Duval held up his hand warningly.

"What do you dread?" asked Lucy.

"The manner in which St. Ives has left the house is so thoroughly unlike him, that I have my suspicions."

"Suspicions of what?"

"I think it more than probable that he has left one or other of his men behind him in the upper part of the mansion."

Lucy turned pale.

"Then that," said the Princess, "only involves the necessity of my carefully keeping up the character I have assumed, and never forgetting for a moment that my name is Griselda Cope."

"What is to be done?" asked Lucy.

No. 23.—NIGHTSHADE.

"Nothing," replied Duval. "If St. Ives, as I suspect, has left one of his men in the house, the best way is not to know it, or even seem to suspect it."

"True—true!" cried the Princess."

"Tell me, however," asked Duval, "have you any means arranged for your escape from England in case of an emergency?"

"There is a French fishing-boat lying off Gravesend, which will remain there until I reach it, or until it receives orders to leave its post."

"You must reach it then!" said Duval.

"Alas! alas!"

"Nay. I will almost pledge myself for your safety."

"It is not that—it is not that!"

The young Princess clasped her hands over her face and wept.

"I think I understand," said Duval.

"I am sure you do," she replied, as she dashed away the tears from her eyes. "I came here with hopes which all seem to be doomed to frustration. I was told that many of the nobility, and the whole mass of the people would be favourable to a restoration of the exiled royal family."

"A delusion!" said Duval.

"I fear so; for I find only a few men of bad character and disgraceful positions, who are willing to do anything that shall produce a change, amid the confusion of which they hope to extract fortunes."

Duval nodded.

"Their propositions are murderous, and the road by which they would conduct my family again to the throne of England, would be so stained by crime that we should be unworthy of the seat we covet."

The young Princess rested her head upon her hands while they reposed upon the breakfast-table, and she gave herself up to painful thought

Duval was deeply affected.

And so, indeed, was Lucy.

"If the exiled Stuarts," he said, "were all like you, I, too, would be a Jacobite."

"And I am," said Lucy. "Oh! that there were such a Queen upon the throne of England as you, with all your generous feelings and sensibilities, would make!"

"It is past and over," said the young Princess, as she looked up. "This shall be the last attempt of me or mine. I was resolved that I would come myself, young as I am, and look with my own eyes, and listen with my own ears. It may be that I shall still fall a sacrifice to this effort, but if heaven should permit me to escape in safety, there shall be no more Jacobite plots to compromise the dignity and the good name of the exiled Stuarts."

"In good truth," said Duval, "I am glad to hear you say so. The nation has been too long convulsed by these plots and rumours of plots; and too many brave and gallant men have already fallen sacrifices to what they have thought were the urgent calls of duty."

"True, true—too true!" exclaimed the young Princess.

"And yet," added Duval, "if all the exiled Stuart race were like yourself—the men as brave, the women as tender, beautiful, and compassionate—I repeat it—I, too, would be a Jacobite!"

"And so would I!" said Mr. St. Ives, as he suddenly flung open the door of the breakfast-room, and stood before the astonished group.

Lucy uttered a cry of consternation.

The young Princess sprung to her feet, and boldly confronted the intruder.

Claude Duval put his hand to his sword-hilt, and in a moment its bright blade was flashing forth.

Mr. St. Ives closed the door, and put his back against it.

There was an ominous silence of a few seconds duration, and then the officer spoke.

"Lilies," he said, "may not be such fair flowers as roses, but they exhale a sweeter perfume."

"Ah!" exclaimed the young Princess.

Duval stood upon his guard.

"What is the meaning of this?" he cried.

"The meaning," said Mr St. Ives, "should be obvious."

He immediately stepped forward, and knelt upon one knee.

The young Stuart Princess extended her hand towards him.

"Colonel Miravel," she said, "we are right glad to see you and greet you kindly in the name of ourselves and all our absent race."

"Is this the age of miracles?" cried Duval.

"No," replied St. Ives, as he rose; "but those who have sheltered a princess of the House of Stuart, will hardly become informers, and treacherously betray one of their most trusted adherents."

"I," said the Princess, "will answer for this gentleman."

She placed one hand upon Duval's arm as she spoke.

And Lucy, with bewildered eyes, looked from one to the other of them, as though she had risen in her sleep, and was walking in a dream.

"Do you not comprehend?" said the Princess to Duval.

"I think I do."

"This gentleman," she added, pointing to St. Ives, who had risen, and was standing a few paces aside, with a respectful air. "Do you not understand this gentleman is a faithful and trusted adherent of our cause?"

Duval sighed.

"You regret that I have such a friend?"

"I do—and I do not."

"You speak in riddles, Sir John Cope."

"Let me explain, that I would rather hear you speak despairingly, as you spoke a short time since, than see new hope springing up in your breast, for the accomplishment of that which never will be brought about."

"Never!" exclaimed Lucy.

"You, too, against me?" said the Princess.

"No," interposed Duval. "She is, like myself, for you."

"For and against?"

"No, they are your truest friends, and most for you, who would advise you to despair of ever again effecting a change of dynasty in England."

The Princess cast a mournful glance at St. Ives.

"Colonel," she said, "you hear?"

"I do, Madam."

"And what is your thought?"

"I have but one thought, and that is to do my duty to the King, my master."

"And his name?" asked Duval.

"Be satisfied with a negative answer," replied St Ives.

"A negative answer?"

"Yes—the King, My master, is not named George."

Duval slowly sheathed his sword, and as he thrust the last portion of it with a clang into the scabbard, he said, "Mr. St. Ives, you are a master of deceit, and an accomplished actor."

"Indeed!"

"Yes, you deceived me, even upon the staircase, and in the corridor, so that I thought you were fully bent upon the apprehension of this lady."

"If I were not," said St. Ives, "to seem bent upon her apprehension, and upon the apprehension of any member of the house of Stuart, who may come to this country, there are others who would be employed for that object."

"I see—I see."

"I fulfil my mission here by being the shield and safeguard—in my character of a high officer of the police of those illustrious personages whom I acknowledge to be the royal family of England."

"And still I call you an accomplished actor," added Duval.

"Perhaps."

"Nay, I am sure of it, for your manner was perfection itself when you met this lady in the corridor."

"You seem, sir," said St. Ives, "to throw these remarks at me in a reproachful spirit. But am I a more accomplished actor than he who calls himself Sir John Cope."

Lucy sprung forward, and caught Duval by the arm.

"Or she," added St. Ives, "who has rechristened herself Pauline."

"What is the meaning of this?" said the Princess.

"Simply," added St. Ives, "that in this gentleman you behold the celebrated Claude Duval!"

"Claude Duval!"

"Yes, and in this lady, his wife, whom he gallantly saved from destruction."

"St. Ives," said Duval, as he drew himself up, "you are master of the position, and I feel myself justly rebuked for finding fault with you."

"There is no fault," said St. Ives, "and there need be no reproach. You are a gallant and brave man, Claude Duval, and by virtue of the powers entrusted to me as an agent of the exiled house, the head of which should sit upon the throne of these realms. I hand you this."

St. Ives took from his pocket a long folded packet, and held it towards Duval.

"What is it?"

"A commission in blank as colonel of horse in the service of the rightful King of England."

Duval shrunk back.

"You have but to fill in the name, and it is yours."

"No!" cried Lucy.

"I congratulate you, Colonel Duval," added St. Ives, "upon your rank."

"No!" again exclaimed Lucy. "No—a thousand times no!"

Duval paused.

"You must not—you shall not take this paper! It is, no doubt, honestly intended, and proffered to you without guile or deceit; but if you accept it, Claude, I shall see the scafford—even in my fancy, upon which you will die!"

The young Princess turned pale.

"This is not a gift," she said, "to be enforced upon any unwilling hands."

"Nay," cried St. Ives, "let me speak. Duval, you have been hardly and badly used, both by the usurping King and his myrmidons."

"But that shall be no reason," exclaimed Lucy, "why he should engage in what are called treasonable practices, which would assuredly end in his destruction."

"I refuse, then," said Duval.

St. Ives bit his lips.

"Those who are not with us," he said, "are against us."

"Not so," replied Lucy. "We betray no one; and although we may not choose to actively engage ourselves in these political intrigues, we have neither sympathies nor interests that can induce us either to betray you or this lady."

"You must trust us," said Duval,—"you must trust us, St. Ives; and you, madam, I am sure will do so."

"With all my heart!" said the Princess.

St. Ives bowed.

He reluctantly put the Colonel's commission into his pocket again.

"His exiled Majesty," he said, "has lost an excellent Colonel of Dragoons."

"No," said Duval, "you only mean that he has not gained one."

"As you please," said St. Ives, with a vexed air.

He then turned, and bowed to the Princess, as he added: "Madam, I respectfully await your orders."

"They are," said the Princess, "that you do whatever to you seems most discreet."

CHAPTER LXXII.

CLAUDE DUVAL REFUSES OVERTURES FROM THE HOUSE OF STUART.

ST. IVES appeared to consider for some few seconds.

"Madam," he said, "if you will condescend to walk in the Park at about mid-day, down the principal mall from Spring Gardens towards Buckingham House, I shall have the honour of meeting you."

"It shall be so," said the Princess.

St. Ives then stepped up towards the window, and by an imperceptible gesture, he induced the Princess to follow him.

There was a whispered conference for a few seconds. Then St. Ives faced about.

"Claude Duval," he said, "would you like a title?"

"A title?"

"Yes; you may be a Lord, and you may name your own place or proper name, which you would wish appended to that title."

"No," said Duval.

"It is enough!" cried the Princess. "I cannot consent to further solicitation."

"And I," said St. Ives, "cannot help saying that such a man as Claude Duval is worth anything—aye, were it even a dukedom, to the cause of the exiled race of England's monarchs."

"You flatter me," said Duval; "but I would rather be what I am."

"Yes," said Lucy, "we know what we are, but we know not what we may be. You, Mr. St. Ives, keep secret that Sir John Cope and Claude Duval are one and the same person, and we will only see in you an active agent of the Government, and not Colonel Miravel, a Jacobite——"

"Spy," added St. Ives.

"No," replied Lucy, "if the term is offensive to you —no."

St. Ives bowed low then to the Princess.

"I humbly and respectfully take my leave," he said, "hoping for the distinguished honour of seeing your Royal Highness in the Mall at the hour of noon."

St. Ives then abruptly left the house.

It was quite evident, however, that he thought the Princess in perfect safety.

Neither had he the remotest apprehension in regard to his own personal security.

So far, he paid the highest compliment he could pay to Claude Duval and to Lucy.

He knew, and he well knew, that they must know that they had nothing to do but to betray him and the young Stuart Princess to the Government, to ensure, not only a huge pecuniary reward, but some substantial token in the shape of distinction, as well as full immunity for the past.

But such a thing never entered into the imagination of Duval.

Nor of Lucy.

St. Ives was perfectly aware of that, and so seemed the Princess.

Again and again, before the hour of mid-day, Duval urged her to abandon all idea of plotting and contriving in behalf of the exiled family.

She answered him despondingly.

"My heart echoes your counsels; and so far as I can, I will carry them out; but I am greatly in the hands of others. Forget me; but believe that I shall never forget the kindly succour and hospitality of Farnborough House."

Lucy was very much affected at the forlorn condition of the Princess.

But there was no resource but to allow her to fulfil her destiny by proceeding to the Mall, as had been arranged.

It was a perilous thing to do; but Lucy provided her fair guest with some over-apparel, by the aid of which she could walk in the open air without attracting more than a mere passing notice.

The clock of St. James's Palace struck twelve.

"Farewell!" said the Princess, as she embraced Lucy.

The latter was affected to tears.

"If happier times," added the young Stuart, "should dawn upon our house, I shall seek, as one of my best and dearest friends, Pauline Cope."

"Farewell!" said Lucy. "Heaven shield you!"

Duval was in the hall of Farnborough House.

He had his hat in his hand.

"No," said the Princess—"no!"

Lucy, in her heart, echoed the negative.

"No, Sir John Cope, I go alone."

"But——"

"Colonel Duval might have accompanied me; but I cannot, while you refuse the reward—empty though it be at present—of service, lead you into possible danger."

She left the house.

Duval stood irresolute.

"Lucy!"

"Claude, Claude, what would you say?"

"This looks cowardly."

"No, no!"

"Approve of my determination. Tell me, Lucy, if you love me, that you think it right. I shall, at all events, follow at some distance, and see that no danger threatens her."

"It is right."

Duval darted out of Farnborough House, quite forgetful at the moment of his assumed character of the elderly Sir John Cope.

"Blossom! Blossom!" cried Lucy.

"Here!"

"Quick, quick! Follow your master! You will find him in the Mall of the Park. Keep an eye on what is going on, and aid him, if necessary."

"I will!" cried Blossom. "There don't need two words to that bargain."

Blossom then darted out of Farnborough House as quickly after Duval as he had after the young Stuart Princess.

At that hour of the day, the thoroughfare by the side of Marlborough House was free to any one.

It was by that way that the Princess reached the Park.

It was by that way that Duval followed her.

And it was by that way that Blossom went closely upon the footsteps of his master.

Upon reaching the Park, Duval looked to the right and to the left.

There were not many people there; but, for a few moments, he failed to see the Princess.

Then he glanced at one of the seats beneath a magnificent elm.

There she sat.

Her forehead resting on her hand.

In deep thought?

Or in deep distress?

Duval would not approach her, but he kept on the side wall, under the shadow of the trees, and never took his eyes off her for an instant.

Blossom soon saw his master; but the manner in which he had been sent after him by Lucy, impressed Blossom with the idea that he was not to interfere unless he saw that Duval was in danger.

He therefore hid among the trees, keeping as watchful an eye upon Claude Duval as he, Duval, did upon the young Princess.

And now a man might have been seen coming with a leisurely step exactly down the centre of the grand Mall.

It was St. Ives.

In the short space of time he had been away from Farnborough House, St. Ives had completely changed his dress.

He wore an undress uniform, now, of an officer of the King's Light Horse.

Holding the high position that St. Ives did in the police of the metropolis, it was easy for him to assume any disguise, and say that it was necessary, in the discharge of his duty, that he should do so.

He was looking anxiously about him.

And soon he saw the Princess.

He did not increase his pace in the least; but walking leisurely up to the bench upon which she sat, he leant over the back of it, and began conversing with her.

The Princess started at the first sound of his voice, and turning partially round, confronted him.

The conversation soon became animated.

Little did the then inhabitants of St. James's Palace imagine that within a stone's throw of them there was a Princess of that ill-fated race which had been deposed, and one of their own active police agents in deep consultation with her.

There sense of security, and the serenity with which they were, no doubt, partaking of the royal breakfast, would have been rudely shaken, could such a communication have been made to them.

And Duval kept his eyes upon St. Ives and the Princess.

All our readers are, no doubt, well acquainted with that old historical portion of St. James's Park.

There is the great mall, and there are the little malls on each side.

At the back of the Princess and St. Ives the trees were closer together and more luxuriant in their foliage than even where Duval was hidden.

But, situated as he was, and with that keenness of sight and sharpness of ear, which were peculiarities of his, he soon began to make an observation peculiarly interesting.

A man crept up as closely as he could, with any regard to safety, among the trees at the back of St. Ives.

Another one stationed himself a little distance off.

A third soon appeared, and likewise hid himself as best he could.

Then Duval was startled by the roll of a drum, evidently proceeding from the small guard house which faces the Park by the side of the Horse Guards.

From all these circumstances, it was tolerably evident that something was about to happen in regard to the young Princess, which might call upon all her energies to use.

And it might be that if she had a friend who really had a kindly feeling for her, apart from political impulses, now was the time for him to show it.

And what was the line of conduct, which, under these circumstances, St. Ives was going to pursue?

Was he aware of the danger of the Princess?

And, after all, was he sincere?

Sincere in his attachment to her, and to the cause which had brought her to England?

Or was he, after all, playing something more than a double part, and only looking for personal advancement.

Those were times when men did such things.

Treachery and treason were rampant in the land.

Fortunes were lost and won by adherence to or treachery towards the Stuart cause.

Titles were cast about profusely among those whose only claim to them was the foulest treachery.

Duval watched the Princess and St. Ives.

Slowly and securely, but more nearly still approached the men who were making a covert of the trees.

Then Duval asked himself what he should do?

The most prudent thing in the world would have been to retire.

By staying he might mix himself up in circumstances full of danger.

The next best thing, with an eye to his own interests only, would have been for Duval to see on which side the authorities were acting, and act with them.

But he was not likely to embrace either of these alternatives.

In fact, they never occurred to him.

The only thing he thought of was how to be of service to the young Princess, towards whom he felt a kind of chivalrous devotion.

"I will save her if I can," he said.

He loosened his sword in its sheath.

He felt in a pocket in which he had a pair of pistols, on which he could depend.

And then he waited.

The conversation between St. Ives and the Princess went on with the same animation as before.

For once the active and energetic officer appeared to lose his ordinary caution.

It was always a custom of St. Ives to glance around him every now and then.

But he forgot now to do so.

The conference with the Princess was too absorbing.

And the men crept closer and closer.

There were now four of them.

Duval could not doubt for a moment but that they were bent upon the arrest of the young Princess.

Then a sickening thought obtruded itself upon him.

Was St. Ives treacherous?

Was he, after all, holding her there in conversation until his own myrmidons should pounce upon her?

"If it be so," whispered Duval to himself, "look to your own safety, Mr. St. Ives."

The men among the trees crept nearer still.

They were concentrating, so to speak.

That is to say, they had approached so closely to each other, that although they did not trust themselves to utter words, they could make signs of mental intelligence.

That they were acting in concert was evident.

It was a nervous and anxious thing for Claude Duval to feel himself alone, noticing all these things.

If that young Princess were captured her fate was certain.

Death!

Death on a scaffold!

A terrible death, with such concomitants and additions as in those days make the blood run cold to think upon.

"One—two—three—four of them," said Duval; "not counting St. Ives. Well, they shall not have an easy victory, although I am but as one to so many."

Duval sighed.

"Oh, for Blossom!" he said.

"Here, Captain!"

"Ah!"

Duval started round.

Never had the countenance of Blossom appeared to Claude Duval so thoroughly welcome as it did at that moment.

"You here, Blossom?"

"Exactly, Captain!"

"Are my very thoughts the necromancers that produce the results I wish?"

"I don't know anything about that, Captain; but I was told to come after you by you know who, and here I am."

"A thousand welcomes!"

"One's enough for me, Captain."

"Look, Blossom, among the trees yonder!"

"I've been looking there for the last ten minutes, Captain."

"Then you see four men?"

"Five, Captain."

"Then another one has joined them?"

"Yes, at this moment."

"Blossom?"

"Yes, Captain."

"Do you think you and I could give a good account of them?"

"Easy."

Duval smiled.

"Look on yonder bench, Blossom, and tell me who you see there?"

"A young lady galivanting with an officer, Captain, of the King's Light Horse; and she's the same young lady, too, that breakfasted with you at Farnborough House."

"She has to be saved, Blossom; for if she be captured, her death is certain."

"Then, of course, she shall be saved, Captain. But I wish it were night."

"And so do I."

"The Park, likewise, is one of the most ugly places for an affair of this sort that one can possibly think of."

"It is—it is!"

"You are kept so long in sight before you can get round a corer, or into anything that may be called a cover."

"We will do our best. But look at that officer again, Blossom."

"Yes, Captain: I see him."

"Don't you know him?"

Blossom shaded his eyes with his hand, and looked fixedly at the supposed officer of the Light Horse.

"To be sure, Captain. I know him well enough—it's St. Ives."

"True!"

"Then it's long odds against us, Captain; for he makes six, and we are only two."

"I don't know that, Blossom. It may be that, with him, we shall be as three against five."

"In that case, the thing is perfectly safe."

Both Duval and Blossom started at this moment partially out of their retreat, for St. Ives made a sudden movement

CHAPTER LXXIII.

CLAUDE DUVAL FINDS THAT HIS CONFIDENCE IN ST. IVES IS NOT MISPLACED.

IT would really appear—unless his acting were of the most admirable character, and unless his duplicity were even greater than his ability—that, for once in a way, St. Ives had been taken by surprise.

The start round which he gave, and the manner in which he placed his hand upon his sword, seemed to imply that for the first moment he had become aware of the proximity of the five men in the side mall.

And when those five men saw that movement of St. Ives, they seemed to consider further attempts at concealment useless.

Three of them rushed forward to the front of the bench, and drew their swords.

They were all well armed.

The other two took possession of the back of the bench, holding their swords elevated in such a manner that escape in that direction was out of the question.

One, then, spoke in a loud voice.

A voice, indeed, so loud, that it reached quite over the way, and could be plainly heard by Duval and Blossom.

"In the King's name, I arrest you both!" he said.

The Princess had hastily risen, and then she sunk back again upon the wooden bench.

St. Ives looked perfectly calm and collected.

He said something, but it was in too low a tone to reach the ears of Duval.

But further inaction now upon the part of Claude and Blossom was impossible, if they meant at all to interfere in what was going on.

"Come!" said Duval.

"I am with you, Captain."

They both left the covert of the trees.

At an easy pace they crossed the mall, making their way directly to the wooden bench, around which the interest of the scene was now concentrated.

As they approached, they saw Mr. St. Ives lift his military cap from his head, and hold it in his hand.

The look of the upper part of St. Ives' head, owing to a peculiar manner in which he wore his hair, was always sufficient to identify him to the eyes of any one who had once seen him.

"Perhaps you will say now that you don't know me, Mr. Pilkington?" said St. Ives.

The man to whom he spoke lowered the point of his sword.

"I do know you," he said.

"Then it is impossible," added St. Ives, "to misjudge my motives."

"What is the matter, gentlemen?" asked Duval, as he reached the group of persons.

St. Ives seemed to draw a long breath of relief.

The Princess clasped her hands, and an exclamation flew from her lips, which certainly had not a despairing tone about it, although it was not sufficiently articulate for any person to say distinctly what word she had uttered.

To Claude Duval's ears, it sounded like the word saved!

He was resolved that it should be truly spoken, so far as it lay in his power to make it so.

"What is the matter, gentlemen?"

The men with the drawn swords turned rather fiercely upon Duval.

"Mind your own business, sir!" said one; "and do not interfere in what does not concern you!"

"I cannot tell," said Duval, "as yet, whether it concerns me or not."

"Then take my word, sir, whoever you are, that it don't."

"Neither your looks nor your manners," said Duval, "are such as to induce me to take your word for anything."

"My looks, sir?"

"Yes. They are bad. Indeed, I may say, a more hang-dog looking ruffian I never cast eyes upon."

"Sir?"

"And as for your manners, why, they are about equal with your looks."

"This is impudence! If you were not an old man."

"Oh, don't mind that," said Duval.

"Then take the reward of your meddling; and I believe, on my soul, you're a Jacobite!"

This man, who had been named Pilkington by St. Ives, made a malicious pass at Duval with his sword.

But he little knew the person he assailed.

Duval had kept his eyes keenly fixed upon him, and was prepared for any movement.

Wearing rather thick buff leather gloves, Duval, as he stepped adroitly aside, caught the blade of Pilkington's sword in his right hand, and letting it glide through his fingers until they reached the hilt, he, with a sudden wrench, wrested the weapon from the hand of Pilkington, and dealt him such a smart blow upon the face with the hilt of it, that he staggered back.

"Treason! treason! Guard! guard!"

"Nonsense," said Duval. "It is you who commit a sort of petty treason, by brawling with a drawn sword in his majesty's park, within the precincts of the palace."

"Treason! treason! Seize him! Take him likewise! A Jacobite spy!"

"The guard is coming, Mr. Pilkington," said one of the others.

Across the wide open space from the Horse Guards, a Sergeant's guard might be seen slowly wending its way, in a direct line towards the bench upon which was still seated the Princess.

St. Ives cast a glance at Duval of peculiar intelligence, and then he spoke.

"I think I know you by sight, sir," he said. "You are Sir John Cope?"

"I am."

"You reside at Farnborough House, in Pall Mall?"

"I do."

"And this man is your servant?"

"Certainly."

"Then I am not mistaken in your identity; and I am quite satisfied that you are a staunch friend to his Majesty's government. I have reason even to know that overtures have been made to you by the exiled royal family, which you have rejected."

"Is this matchless impudence?" thought Duval; "or is it admirable finesse?"

"Allow me, then, Sir John Cope," added St. Ives, "to explain to you a little difficulty I am in. I had reason to believe that this young lady was an emissary of the House of Stuart; and disguising myself, as you perceive, in the dress of an officer of the King's Light Horse, I was carrying out my duty to his Majesty, by endeavouring to discover if such were the fact or not, when these persons interfered."

"We interfere rightly!" cried the man whose name was Pilkington. "We have been put upon the scent, and we don't mean to give up our prey."

"Scent—and prey!" said Duval, "what does the man mean?"

"He means this," cried Pilkington, "that he knows perfectly well that this young lady is a Princess of the House of Stuart, and he intends to capture her."

"Indeed?"

"Yes," added St. Ives, "but as I am perfectly well known to this same Mr. Pilkington, as an officer of the police, high in his Majesty's service, I do not choose to have a prisoner taken out of my hands by him, or any inferior official."

"But you didn't know who she was, Mr. St. Ives," cried Pilkington; "and the first who makes the arrest has the right to the prisoner."

"I deny even that proposition," replied St. Ives. "A superior officer, if he choose to do so, can, in the police service as well as in the military, take a prisoner from a subordinate, making himself at the same time, answerable for his act—not that I would do so."

"Then she is mine!" cried Pilkington. "Come on! gentlemen—come on! I shall be able yet to keep my word with you. Here is our prisoner."

"One moment," added St. Ives.

Pilkington paused.

"If you had taken this lady prisoner, I should certainly, although your superior officer, have hesitated to interfere with you, because whatever reward you look forward to, will be your right to receive, but, as I happened to take her first——"

"You?"

"I have said so."

"But—but——"

St. Ives laid his hand lightly upon the shoulder of the Princess.

"This lady," he said, "has been my prisoner for more than half-an-hour."

Pilkington uttered a groan.

The men who were with him uttered imprecations.

"And I don't choose," added St. Ives, "to give up my prisoner to anyone."

"We have your word only for that, Mr. St. Ives."

"And that ought to be sufficient, but possibly the lady herself may confirm my statement."

"I admit it," said the Princess.

There was a dead silence of about half a minute's duration, and then Pilkington spoke in a tone of savage ferocity—

"Sir John Cope, or Poke, or whatever may be your infernal name, you shall suffer for this assault upon me."

"I don't think so," said Duval, "I have not hurt my hand in the least."

"But I say you shall suffer, sir, notwithstanding all your bravado."

"I will take my chance," said Duval, "having a kind of confidence in my own ability to take care of myself."

"And now, Mr. St. Ives," added Pilkington, "you know I am an officer of police."

"Yes."

"Well sir, it's a hard case upon me, for I received information from a nobleman—actually from a nobleman, sir—in regard to this important prisoner."

"I cannot help it."

"But still, Mr. St. Ives, it is hard after I have collected a party, and actually reached the prisoner, to be baulked in this kind of way."

St. Ives shrugged his shoulders, as much as to say, these kind of things will happen.

"Therefore, Mr. St. Ives, the least you can allow us to do, is to accompany you and the prisoner to a place of safety."

St. Ives shook his head.

"I should think very meanly of myself," he said, "if I required an escort for the purpose of conveying a young girl like this to prison!"

"But the town is full of Jacobites."

"Is it?"

"You know it is, Mr. St. Ives, and a rescue might be attempted."

"Well, I won't say that that is an impossibility, Sir John Cope, will you kindly accompany me to the Gate House Prison?"

"Him?" cried Pilkington, "why ask him?"

"Ah, Pilkington, you know," cried St. Ives, "that he is not only well able to take his own part, but is likely to prove a very disagreeable opponent to any one interfering with him."

"Halt!"

The Sergeant's guard had reached the spot.

"What's amiss, gentlemen?" asked the Sergeant.

"Nothing that I know of," said St. Ives.

"But some one came and gave the alarm, and the officer on duty ordered the drum to be beaten, and sent this guard to see what it was. There was something about a Jacobite plot."

"Perhaps this person may explain to you," said St. Ives, pointing to Pilkington, "for myself, I have nothing to say!"

As he spoke, St. Ives offered his arm to the Princess.

"There they go!" cried Pilkington. "There they go! Any one would think they were great friends."

"Do you expect," said St. Ives, "that when I take a young lady prisoner—especially, too, for a political offence, that I am to drag her along by the hair of her head."

Pilkington had no answer to this, and St. Ives walked quietly away with the Princess.

He was followed by Claude Duval and Blossom.

Pilkington and the riffraff of ruffians he had brought with him commenced an eager conversation with the Sergeant of the Guard.

Affairs were still very critical.

Claude Duval and Blossom walked at the same pace, but St. Ives gradually slackened his and the Princess's, until without turning round they could converse.

"Duval," said St. Ives.

"I am here!"

"The very air is full of danger."

"Will those fellows follow us?"

"I know not, but there is treachery somewhere."

"Yes," said the Princess. "I am betrayed by some one whom I trusted!"

"It must be so," added St. Ives, "and that fellow Pilkington is a mere tool of some traitor who probably was among the party at the country-house in the Oxford Road."

"What is to be done?" asked Duval.

"Please look back and tell me what they are about."

"They are following."

"I expected as much!"

"But they come slowly."

"Is the Sergeant's Guard with them?"

"It is."

"That is provoking."

"No. The Sergeant's Guard stops. They fall to the right. They have turned in towards the Palace."

"Then we are safe!"

Pilkington and all his men, however, quickened their pace.

"Whither shall we go?" asked the Princess?

"We must reach the river," said St. Ives, "but how to do so I know not, for it is not the road to any prison where I could convey you."

"Then all is lost!"

"Duval?"

"I hear you, Mr. St. Ives."

"Can you suggest any course of action, fertile as you are in resources and accustomed to rapid and dangerous adventures?"

"I will try."

"If for five minutes you could engage the attention of Pilkington and his fellows, so that I and the Princess were for that period of time out of their sight, all would be well."

"Walk on! You see yonder clump of trees?"

"I do—I do."

"Plunge into them, and I will follow you. You need not look back to see what is doing, and you may take my word for it that I will impede Mr. Pilkington and his rascally crew for fully the five minutes you require."

"No, no," said the Princess. "I cannot allow you to sacrifice yourself for me!"

"I will endeavour not to do so, and neither Mr. Pilkington nor any of his companions shall be able to say that it was Sir John Cope, of Farnborough House, who interfered with them."

The course of action which Duval contemplated was simple enough.

CHAPTER LXXIV.

MR. PILKINGTON IS PLACED HORS DE COMBAT FOR THE PRESENT.

HE, too, wished to be for a few minutes out of sight of Mr. Pilkington and his myrmidons.

There was no place so well calculated to effect that object as the little umbrageous spot at the end of the Mall, which has now, for many a long year disappeared.

St. Ives, with the Princess, quickened his pace.

Duval and Blossom did the same.

"Forward! Forward!" they heard Pilkington cry. "He will elude us yet."

No actor, on or off the stage, was more active than Claude Duval in making any changes he desired to effect.

He was rather slender in figure naturally, so that it assisted his disguise as Sir John Cope, rather than in any way detracted from it, to wear beneath the clothing of the elderly gentleman his own complete and picturesque apparel as Claude Duval.

Blossom, too, was, to a certain extent provided for some such a contingency as the present.

He was dressed as a groom, and his coat was of that colour which went for many years by the name of pompadour.

This name was afterwards changed to claret-colour in England, when claret became a favourite drink.

The coat had white facings, and, in fact, inside it was entirely of white cloth, or that stone-colour rather, which is frequently worn as a livery.

Top-boots, and an ordinary grooms' hat, were not to be sworn to upon any one particular person.

"Quick, Blossom!" cried Duval.

He set the example of what he meant himself, by instantly taking off his overcoat, and flinging it among the bushes.

His wig and cravat followed.

A tug at his boots brought them up to the knee, and at once completely altered their appearance.

The change in Duval's appearance was immense.

He looked about half the bulk.

Several inches taller.

And, in fact, no one who had not seen the transformation take place, could possibly have believed him to be one and the same person.

Blossom quickly slipped off his coat, pulled the sleeves inside out, and put it on again.

Then, thrusting his hat a good two inches further back upon his head, he looked quite a different person, with his white coat, and claret-coloured collar, to what he had done before.

Certainly it did not take a minute to accomplish these changes.

But during that minute Mr. Pilkington and his men had reached the edge of the little wood, if it might be so called.

The time for action had come.

Duval had not time to fasten on his sword-belt.

Holding the sheath in his left hand, and the sword in his right, he made a rush forward.

"Have at you, knaves all!" he cried, in his own natural tones.

He commenced then, a furious assault upon Pilkington and his men.

Two of them were wounded before they could make any effectual resistance.

One more fairly took to his heels, so that Pilkington and only one of the desperadoes he had employed kept their ground.

That one fired a pistol at Duval, and the ball narrowly missed him.

"Help! Help! Treason!" cried Pilkington. "Guard! Guard! Help! Help!"

In the midst of these outcries he took advantage of the smoke from the pistol to rush forward and attempt inflicting upon Duval either instant death, or some serious wound.

He might have succeeded.

Duval was rather busy with the man who had fired the pistol.

But Pilkington's sword was suddenly beaten upward by another blade.

Then, with a yell, he fell backwards.

The other blade, after flashing before his dazzled eyes for an instant, had passed through his breast.

"Mercy, mercy!" cried the man who had fired the pistol, dropping to his knees.

"Fly!" cried Duval, "while you have life to do so."

The man needed no other injunction, but scrambling to his feet, he set off down the Mall at a prodigious speed.

Duval glanced at Pilkington.

"Have you killed him, Blossom?"

"I shouldn't wonder!"

"This way, this way. A fracas of this kind cannot but give an alarm."

Duval and Blossom plunged again into the little copse.

It took longer time to resume their disguises than it had taken to cast them off.

But then they were not so hurried, and that equalised the transaction.

The pistol shot and the clashing of swords, and the shouts and cries of Pilkington attracted every body in the Park towards that spot.

All those whose curiosity happened to be stronger than their fears made the best of their way to the scene of conflict.

Soldiers off duty.

Pickpockets.

Idlers, of all kinds and descriptions, to whom the park was a sort of refuge both by day and night, hastened to the spot.

They surrounded Pilkington.

"Murdered! murdered!" he cried, "I'm murdered!"

"Who did it?" asked twenty voices in a breath.

"I know the man, I saw him once before—once before at Tyburn, I know the man well."

"Who is he? Who is he?"

"Claude Duval!"

"The highwayman?"

"Yes, Claude Duval—the notorious Claude Duval—my death is at his door, and believing myself to be now at my last gasp, I charge him with my murder."

"Where is he? Where is he?"

"Search! search among the trees, among the trees."

At this moment Duval slowly stepped out from the copse.

He walked tremulously.

His shoulders were bent, and he looked a perfect picture of an elderly gentleman upon whose physical frame time had made great ravages.

Blossom followed him in his pompadour coat, looking as demure as possible.

"My good friends," said Duval, "what is the meaning of all this?"

The people separated before so respectable a gentleman, and allowed Duval to approach Pilkington.

The wounded officer glared at him with eyes of hatred.

"What is the meaning of all this disturbance," added Duval, "in his Majesty's park."

"It's a murder, sir," cried half a dozen voices.

"A murder!"

"Yes sir, and the poor man says the villains went in there among the trees."

"Then Diggory," said Duval, turning to Blossom, "I shouldn't at all wonder if those were the two rascals we saw."

"Yes, Sir John, I think they be."

"Diggory!"

"Yes, Sir John."

"Had not one of the rascals a red coat?"

"Just so, Sir John."

"And the other a white one?"

"Just so, Sir John."

"Well then, my good friend, I beg to ask you if your assailants were men of that description."

"They were, they were," moaned Pilkington, "it was Claude Duval the highwayman, and one of the scoundrels he always has at his beck and call."

"Diggory!" said Duval.

"Yes, Sir John."

"This poor fellow ought to have surgical advice."

DUVAL THROWS MUCKLES INTO THE THAMES.

"The doctor! the doctor!" cried twenty voices at once. "Make way for the doctor, here he is, here he is."

A little man scrupulously dressed in black, made his way through the throng up to where Pilkington was laying.

"Well, my friend," he said, "what's the matter?"

"Murdered! murdered!"

"Ah! oh! indeed. And where's the hurt my friend?"

"Here. Run through the body."

"Oh! ah. Run through the body, then my opinion is that it may be called a sword wound, a kind of elongated puncture, and you perceive, my friends, that this unfortunate man, is in a manner of speaking, in what we call *articulo mortimus*."

Duval had some difficulty in keeping himself from laughing.

The medical profession at that time and up to the year 1814, was infested by crowds of illiterate quacks, only profound in ignorance, and totally unqualified for the offices they assumed.

That this was one of them Duval saw at a glance.

"Diggory," he said.

"Yes, Sir John."

"I do not see that we can do any good here, and as the hour of luncheon approaches, I think I will go home, Diggory."

"Yes, Sir John."

"Be off, you old wretch," cried Pilkington, "I believe it's all through you that I've come by my wound."

"He raves!" cried the docter. "*Delirium trimmings!* He raves!"

"It looks like it," said Duval.

"Yes, sir, it's a clear case. Perhaps you wouldn't mind taking my card, sir, Doctor Blogg, at your service, but as for this man sir, it's a case of *de lunatico inquire within*."

"I don't doubt it," said Duval. "Come along, Diggory."

Duval walked slowly down the Mall, followed by Blossom.

Doctor Blogg borrowed a ramrod from the sentinel

No. 24.—NIGHTSHADE.

on duty at Buckingham House, and despite the yells of Mr. Pilkington, proceeded to probe the wound with it.

"I think, Captain," said Blossom, "we got through that little affair rather handsomely."

"I'm afraid you've killed him."

"Oh, no, Captain, not at all."

"What makes you think so?"

"Those kind of fellows, Captain, have nine lives, like cats, and it's a very hard case indeed, if this is the last of his."

"Do you recollect him?"

"To be sure I do, Captain; he was at Tyburn along with the mounted officers, when you rescued Miss Lucy Everton from the scaffold."

"I thought I had some recollection of the fellow."

"Oh, I know him well, Captain. He don't want for courage; but he's as errant a knave as ever stepped."

"I hope to heaven the Princess is safe!"

"I think we may trust St. Ives for that, Captain."

"I think so, too—I think so, too."

Both Blossom and Claude Duval had been conscious, for the last few minutes, that they were followed by some one.

They neither of them had spoken of it; but a glance from one to the other had been quite sufficient to let them both understand that each was cognizant of the fact.

The only effect it had upon Duval, however, was to impress upon him the necessity of accurately supporting his character as an elderly gentleman.

Without the least exaggeration, he walked with well-assumed infirm steps towards Marlborough House.

Then he spoke to Blossom.

"Don't look round."

"No, Captain."

"You know there is a fellow at our heels."

"Yes; he is the one who ran away when the fight began."

"I thought as much."

"What does he want, Captain?"

"Probably, only to find out where we live; but take no notice of him, and when we reach Farnborough House, come in quietly and close the door."

In pursuance of these directions, Blossom never turned to the right or to the left, nor made the least effort to obtain even a sidelong glance at the man who was following them.

They turned out of the Park, by the side of Marlborough House, as they had entered it, and soon stood upon the threshold of their own door.

Claude Duval, himself, however, did manage, as he entered Farnborough House, to glance backward.

He saw that the spy, who had dogged their heels from the Park, had crossed to the other side of the way.

Then he stood gazing at Farnborough House.

"Let him look," said Duval; "all is well."

Lucy was waiting in anxious expectation for news of the young Princess.

Claude Duval detailed to her what had occurred in the Park; and the narrative excited both her fears and her sympathies.

"What will become of her?" she said. "She will surely yet be taken."

"I think not. St. Ives is a host in himself; and, moreover, the character he holds, as a high officer of the police, gives him an immense advantage."

"It may, Claude; but it has its drawbacks."

"I admit it has."

"It has enabled, as you perceive, St. Ives to go off with the prisoner, or supposed prisoner; but how will he be able to preserve his position as a police agent, and yet not produce so important a captive?"

Duval was troubled.

He paced the room, as was his custom, in silence.

Then he spoke, with a slight laugh.

"It appears to me Lucy," he said, "that we are becoming Jacobite agents in spite of ourselves."

"It does, indeed, Claude."

"How easy it is to drift into these matters."

"Yes; and how difficult to disentangle oneself, after the slightest connexion with them."

"Well, Lucy, we must take fate as we find it. I think this Stuart cause a perfectly hopeless one; but still I cannot divest myself of the warmest sympathy with this young girl."

"And I, too, Claude—and I, too! The men in that family are cowards, or they never would have permitted her to incur the terrible danger of being their emissary."

"It looks like it; but I will save her if I can."

"What steps can you take, Claude?"

A single sharp knock at the door of Farnborough House, at this moment disturbed the conference between Claude and Lucy.

Blossom came into the breakfast-parlour in a few moments, with a rolled-up piece of paper, tied with string.

It was addressed outside.

"To Sir John Cope, Farnborough House, Pall Mall."

It was a roll of some twelve inches in length, and had all the appearance of a print or drawing.

"Take it away, Blossom — take it away!" said Duval. "It is some trash sent to the house for sale."

"Yes, Captain."

"One moment," said Lucy. "We are surrounded by so many mysterious circumstances; and there is so much happening out of the common way, that I think we should disregard nothing until we are quite assured of what it means."

Lucy took the roll of paper from Blossom, and unfastened the string.

It had evidently not been rolled up long, for it opened easily.

It was a drawing.

It was roughly, but very graphically executed in chalk.

The representation was a bridge spanning a river.

A number of small craft were in the water, and in the distance a complete forest of masts of various vessels.

At the bottom of the drawing, the following words were written:

"A view of Westminster Bridge, with a French lugger in the distance. The hour is supposed to be midnight."

"Oh, take it away, take it away," said Duval; "we have no time to waste upon such matters."

"Stop," said Lucy.

"Is it possible you have taken a fancy to this daub?"

"No, Claude. But is there not something more in it than meets the eye?"

"What should there be?"

"Do you not see, Westminster Bridge—midnight, and a French vessel in the distance? Are not these things suggestive?"

Duval started.

"What if this drawing is by St. Ives? and he has done it as a far safer mode than writing to let you know that the young Princess is to escape this night at midnight, by taking a boat at Westminster Bridge, in order to reach the French lugger in the distance?"

"By heaven," said Duval, "it must be so."

"I feel assured of it, Claude."

"Blossom! Where are you, Blossom?"

"Here, Captain."

"What manner of man was it who gave in this at the door?"

"It was merely a boy—a street boy, such as you may see many of lounging about, ready to earn a few pence by running an errand."

"It is eminently suggestive," cried Duval; "and the more I look at it, Lucy, the more I feel convinced that your view of it is a perfectly correct one."

"And I, too," said Lucy, "feel each moment more reconciled to the truth of my first supposition. It appears to me that the most elaborately-worded letter could not say more to us than this rough drawing of Westminster Bridge."

"And it means," said Duval, "that I should be there to help him, and he shall find that I will not fail."

"You will be careful, Claude?"

"I will; for how much now have I not to live for?"

CHAPTER LXXV.

CLAUDE DUVAL MAKES AN EXPEDITION TO OLD WESTMINSTER BRIDGE.

It wants one half-hour of midnight.

The night is cold, damp, and inclement.

Drifting clouds are over the face of what would have been nearly a full moon.

But there is no rain falling.

Considering the season of the year, however, the weather was anything but what it might have been; nevertheless there was nothing in it to mar any enterprise that might be on foot.

It was a matter of the very greatest importance—in fact, quite vital - to the interests of Duval and Lucy that there should be no suspicion in regard to him in his character of Sir John Cope.

Residing in the public situation he did in the midst of the town, if his identity with Claude Duval, the highwayman, were even once suspected, there would be an end of all safety.

But there was one source of danger concerning which Claude Duval and Blossom held an anxious conference.

The stabling of Farnborough House was very ample, and in that stable was Nightshade.

Now Duval was perfectly well aware that his celebrated horse, mounted on which he had performed some of his most extraordinary exploits, was well enough known to the officers of the police.

Should any accident, then, awaken a suspicion of any connection between Sir John Cope and Claude Duval, and should that suspicion be sufficient to induce a search of Farnborough House and its stables, the finding of Nightshade there would be a terrible proof.

"Blossom," said Duval, "you must find some other stable for my four-footed friend."

"I've been thinking of that, Captain."

"It is a sad necessity. I would fain have Nightshade, in a manner of speaking, beneath the same roof with me, but it cannot be."

"What will be the best plan, Captain?"

"I think it will be better to take some small private stable, to which you can make your way quietly when you please, rather than to put Nightshade at any of the livery stables in the neighbourhood."

"I think so, too, Captain; and I will seek the sort of place you mention."

This had been done by Blossom, so that Nightshade was comfortably bestowed in a stable in Westminster, of which Blossom kept the key.

Upon this occasion of Duval's determination to proceed to Westminster Bridge, at the midnight hour, for the purpose of assisting St. Ives in the escape of the Princess, he dressed himself in his own proper costume, as Claude Duval, the highwayman.

He had arranged a hat which, with the help of a pin, that made some slight alteration in the brim, suited either for the character of Sir John Cope or Claude Duval.

And now, half-an-hour before the appointed time, he wrapped himself completely up in a roquelaire cloak, which left nothing visible but his boots and his hat, and left Farnborough House.

Blossom had gone out some quarter of an hour before thoroughly to reconnoitre the neighbourhood, and make certain that no spies were watching the place.

And now feeling convinced that he might sally out with safety, Duval, after taking leave of Lucy, stepped across the threshold of his mansion.

Assuming the particular walking stoop of Sir John Cope, he went quietly along Pall Mall.

The route through the Park would have been the nearest, but at that hour of the night it was closed.

Claude Duval's way, therefore, lay down Whitehall, and Parliament Street, to old Westminster Bridge.

More than once he glanced up at the dark night sky, and was thankful that the clouds obscured the face of the moon, and so made the night much more propitious for the enterprise on foot.

In Whitehall Claude Duval quickened his steps, for he feared being late at the place of rendezvous.

More than once he glanced behind him, to be certain that the footsteps he heard following him were those of Blossom.

At length the bridge was reached.

At that time a few dreary oil lamps burnt upon it.

They shed faint, yellow streaks of light down upon the water as it surged and heaved against the piers of the old bridge.

A cold air swept over the face of the Thames.

And as Claude stood in the deep shadow of one of those concave recesses, which were a peculiarity of old Westminster Bridge, he heard the various clocks of the City begin to strike the hour of twelve.

London is five times the size it was then.

People live faster lives, and turn night more into day than did our ancestors.

In the age of Claude Duval, midnight was a quiet, solemn hour, even in great London.

Sober, quiet people had long since retired to rest.

Every shop was closed, and a stillness pervaded the City, such as is now only to be found a few hours later and then only for a very brief period.

The hour of twelve is anything but a serene one.

But then it was quiet and solemn.

And Duval, as he stood upon the bridge, thought there was something very beautiful and majestic in the sounds of those church clocks, striking the midnight hour.

The slight variations in time-keeping of the many clocks kept up a pleasant jangle, so that for the space of about a minute and a half, it seemed as if a peal of bells were welcoming in a new day.

And amid them all, came the solemn tone of St. Paul's, acting as a beautiful bass to the shriller clarion-like notes of the smaller churches.

Then all was still.

The sounds had ceased.

That midnight hour had come and gone.

Duval unclasped the roquelaire cloak from round his neck, and rolling it up carefully, he hid it beneath the wooden seat of the bridge.

He made the necessary alteration in his hat.

He adjusted his sword belt.

He placed his pistols ready for active service.

And then he stepped out of the alcove in his full costume as Claude Duval the highwayman.

A light flashed upon him.

It was but faint.

Duval glanced along the bridge, and from the Surrey side of the water, he saw one of those ancient guardians of the night who were supposed to protect the lives and properties of the citizens of London, slowly approaching.

The lantern cast a dim halo about it, which made the watchman look like some huge heap of dirty white flannel creeping over the bridge.

"Past twelve o'clock, and a cloudy night!"

Duval retired into the alcove.

He hoped to escape entirely observation from this miscalled guardian of the night.

But with a kind of perversity that, under the circumstances, was peculiarly provoking, the watchman would thrust his lantern into every one of the alcoves, as if in special search of some one.

And he had not gone above a third way over the bridge, before, from the Westminster side, there appeared another watchman.

He was on the opposite side of the bridge to that where Duval was in partial concealment, but he pursued the same course as his comrade.

With a steady perseverance, he, too, examined every alcove on his side of the way

But he walked more quickly than the other watchman; so that in reality they passed each other about the centre of the bridge.

"That is one good job," thought Duval to himself. "I shall not have the two of them to trouble me."

"Past twelve o'clock, and a cloudy night!"

Duval felt it would be quite impossible to elude the observation of this man.

He sat down, therefore, quietly upon the wooden bench, and crossed one leg over the other.

The watchman reached the spot.

The light of his lantern gleamed full upon Duval.

"Hilloa! who are you?"

"Don't you see," replied Duval.

"No, I don't. Who are you, I ask?"

"Why you must be as blind as a mole. I am a man."

"Well, I saw that."

"Then why did you ask?"

"Come, come, don't be *obstropolus*. It's my duty to know what manner of man you are, out so late upon the bridge."

"I'm merely an ordinary man," replied Duval, "of the common pattern. I have the usual assortment of legs, arms, eyes, and ears."

"Come, come, you mustn't joke with the constabulary."

"Do you call that a joke?"

"I do; and it seems to me that I shall have to take you up."

"I would not advise you to try."

"Indeed!" said the watchman, as he put his lantern down on the wooden bench by the side of Duval.

"Indeed, and in truth," replied Duval.

"We will see about that."

With great rapidity the seeming watchman flung off his huge blanket-like coat, which reached down to his heels, and disclosed beneath it quite a different suit.

"I arrest you, Claude Duval!" he cried.

"Indeed!"

"Yes, and resistance is useless. I have but to blow this whistle, which I fancy I may as well do at once, since you look mischievous, and I shall have plenty of assistance."

"Ah! I know you now," said Claude.

"I should think you did. My name's Muckles."

"It is. How is your friend Swallow?"

"He's no friend of mine, idiot that he is. But you are my prisoner, Duval; and none of your tricks can now save you, although you played so handsome a one at the old 'Bedford Head' in Covent Garden."

Muckles, as he spoke, blew a whistle shrilly.

Its echoes penetrated far and near on the night air.

Then Duval felt all his danger.

Danger not only to himself, but to St. Ives.

Danger, likewise, to that unhappy Princess whom he had made up his mind, on that night, to aid and succour.

"I am sorry, Mr. Muckles——" he said.

"So am not I," interrupted Muckles.

"To be compelled," added Duval, "to come to extremities."

Almost before the words were out of his mouth he flew at Muckles; and so sudden was the attack, and so entirely unexpected, in consequence of the previous quiet and submissive-looking conduct of Duval, that the constable was taken completely by surprise.

One well-directed blow between the eyes felled him to the ground.

Duval then stooped; and although Muckles was a rather heavy man, he picked him up bodily, and with one heave flung him over the parapet of the bridge into the Thames.

There was a loud yell.

A splash.

And surely all was over with Muckles, the thief-taker?

In a few more seconds Duval had picked up the great heavy watchman's coat, in which Muckles had been disguised, and put it on.

He held the lantern over the parapet of the bridge, and had just completed these arrangements, when half-a-dozen men surrounded him.

"Here we are, Mr. Muckles—here we are."

"He's gone," said Duval, in a very good imitation of Muckles' voice.

"Gone, sir?"

"Yes—over the bridge."

"Good gracious!"

"That's just what I said."

"But was it Claude Duval, Mr. Muckles?"

"Of course it was. And as soon as I blew my whistle, he went over the parapet like a harlequin, and disappeared."

"I heard the splash," said one.

"He shouted likewise," said another.

"Then," said a third, "he must have knocked his head against one of the piers, and was, no doubt, smashed."

"I don't see anything of him," said Duval, as he purposely held the lantern as far over the bridge as possible, in order to prevent any of its rays, feeble though they were, from falling upon himself.

There was a dead silence.

Even those officers of police seemed to regret that such a fate should overtake the gallant and chivalrous Claude Duval.

"What's to be done, Mr. Muckles?" asked one.

"Shall we run down and get a boat?" said another.

"It's of no use," said Duval. "He's gone by this time."

"Then, what's to be done, sir?"

"Go, all of you, and wait for me in Old Palace Yard."

"But about the other affair, Mr. Muckles. What's to be done in that, sir?"

"Oh! ah! The other affair!"

"Yes, sir, about the Jacobite young lady?"

"Yes, yes," said Duval. "I understand."

He wished he did.

"Because, you know, sir, after Claude Duval had taken her away from Mr. St. Ives, in the Park, it was not likely that he would be here upon the bridge, and she far off."

"Very true," said Duval. "But as I happen to know what I'm about, you will take your orders from me, and wait, as I have directed you, in the Old Palace Yard."

"Oh, certainly, Mr. Muckles--certainly, if you wish it."

"Be off with you all, at once!"

The constables retreated.

Duval was left once again alone upon Old Westminster Bridge.

He looked earnestly into the black rolling river over the parapet.

"He brought it on himself," he said. "There was no resource: it was his life or mine, and not only my life, but the lives of others as well. I would have spared him if I could, but he knew that his vocation was one of danger, as I know that mine is, so there is an end of Mr. Muckles."

"Past twelve o'clock, and a cloudy night!"

The other watchman, who had crossed the bridge, was coming back.

"Who can this be?" said Duval.

"Past twelve o'clock, and a cloudy night!"

"Provoking! I wonder if this be a genuine watchman, or not!"

Duval again sat down upon the bench in the alcove.

He knew that, as yet, his services were not required, either by the Princess or by St. Ives.

And he knew well that when they were so required, he would receive ample notice from Blossom, who was stationed at the top of the river stairs for that express purpose.

"Past twelve o'clock, and a cloudy night!"

The watchman, who had passed to the Surrey side of the river on the opposite pavement of the bridge, came back on the one where Claude Duval was waiting.

Claude had sat down on the wooden bench, and placed the lantern at his feet.

In that position it directed its light upon him in the most unfavourable manner for recognition.

The watchman came slowly up.

"Have you seen anything of him, Mr. Muckles?"

"Sit down," said Duval.

"Yes, sir."

"I am much surprised——"

"Surprised, Mr. Muckles?"

"Yes, Swallow," said Claude, in his natural voice, and suddenly grasping his arm with the force of a vice,—"yes, Swallow, I am much surprised to find you here, endeavouring to do me all the mischief in your power."

"Murder! It's Duval himself!"

"Silence!"

"Of course - of course! Oh, Claude Duval, I'm—I'm——"

"Done brown—I know what you are going to say."

"Yes, Mr. Duval, browner than ever. But let me explain——"

"Explain what?"

"Why, how it all came about. Mr. Muckles said to me, this afternoon, says he, 'Swallow, you're an ass.' 'Yes, Mr. Muckles,' says I. 'You know you are,' said he, a donkey.' 'Yes, Mr. Swallow,' said I. 'But,' said he, 'if you want to recover yourself, and get up a new character, you must come with me to Westminster Bridge at night,' says he, and help me to nab Claude Duval,' and so here I am."

"Very kind of you, Swallow."

"Bless you, I didn't mean to do it."

"What did you mean, then?"

"I would rather push Muckles into the river than raise a hand against you."

"You are very kind, but that's been done already."

"What's been done already, Mr. Duval?"

"I have flung him into the river."

"You have? Good gracious!"

Swallow shrank a little further from Claude Duval.

CHAPTER LXXVI.

MR. SWALLOW IS COMPELLED TO ANSWER A FEW QUESTIONS.

"TELL me," said Duval, speaking in a low tone,—"tell me at once, Swallow, what all this means, and you shall not go unrewarded. Hold your hand."

"Yes, Mr. Duval."

"Take that."

"A purse?"

"Yes, and tolerably full, as you may guess by its weight."

"Bless you!"

"Now tell me all you know about it."

"I have. I don't know another word."

"But how came Muckles to suspect that I should be here at midnight?"

"I don't know a bit, for I was with him all day, and I'm quite sure the only person he spoke to was a boy that asked him the way to Farnborough House, because some one had given him a groat to carry a picture there."

"Ah, I see!"

"Do you?"

"Answer me one question, Swallow."

"A dozen, and welcome, Mr. Duval."

"Did Muckles look at the picture?"

"Oh, yes!"

"Then he's a cleverer fellow than I took him to be."

"Oh, is he?"

"Yes. Hush!"

A peculiar hooting noise came from the water steps of the Bridge, and Duval knew instantly that it was the signal he had agreed upon with Blossom, which was to let him know that St. Ives and the Princess had reached the spot.

"Wait here," said Duval sharply to Swallow.

"Yes, but——"

"Ask no questions, but wait here, or it will be worse for you."

Duval hastily stripped off the watchman's coat and flung it in Swallow's face.

He then ran from the bridge to the water steps on its left hand as you come from Westminster.

Three figures stood at the top of the steps, faintly discernible in the darkness against the water.

The tide was high.

It might have been heard lapping against the steps, about two-thirds of their height.

The wherries that had been moored together heaved against each other, making a monotonous, creaking sound.

"Blossom," said Duval, in a low voice.

"Here, Captain."

"Friends all?"

"Yes," replied St. Ives. "It is too dark for you to see my face, Duval, but you know my voice."

"I do—I do."

"And mine too, I hope," said the Princess.

"Most assuredly. It is a voice that I shall never forget, nor do I ever wish to do so."

"We must have a boat at once," said St. Ives.

"Run down the steps, Blossom, and secure one."

"Yes, Captain, in a moment."

Blossom went down the steps, and they heard him splashing in the water.

"Will you come down?" he whispered. "I've got one of the wherries clear, but the tide is nearly on the turn, and I'm afraid of it drifting off if I let go of it."

"Permit me," said Duval. "I will be ceremonious upon another occasion, should we ever meet again at a time and place where it is fitting for me to be so."

As he spoke he cast his left arm round the slender waist of the Princess, and fairly lifting her off her feet, he carried her down the water steps.

She did not speak.

"Where is the boat, Blossom?"

"Here, Captain—here."

"How dark it is."

With great difficulty Duval succeeded in placing that fair young fugitive of the house of Stuart safely in the stern of one of the wherries.

"Now, St. Ives," he said, "be quick—be quick!"

"I am here. But let me caution you, Duval."

"About what?"

"My name. When you speak to me, call me Colonel Miravel, or simply Miravel."

"I will—I will."

St. Ives stepped into the boat.

"Now, Blossom."

"Here, Captain. I will row."

"We will all row."

"But there is but one pair of oars."

"Get some out of the other wherries."

"Ah, to be sure—to be sure."

"Hilloa, there!" cried a voice from the water stairs. "Who are you all of you, going off with one of the boats? Is it Jim Atkins and his boy?"

"To be sure it is," said Duval.

"I don't know that. You don't speak in his voice."

"How should I," replied Duval, "when I never heard it? Give way, Blossom—give way, and pull for your life!"

The boat shot out into the stream.

At that moment a rattle was violently sprung upon Westminster Bridge.

It might have been Swallow.

And if it were so, Duval could easily forgive him, for it was very possible he might think it desirable to spring the watchman's rattle he had with him, to save his own character, without it being at all a necessary consequence that he should give any information detrimental to Duval and his friends.

And surely had never wherry upon the Thames made swifter progress than that one upon that dreary night, loaded with so interesting a cargo.

St. Ives, Duval, and Blossom all rowed.

They were a little cramped for room, but they accommodated each other as well as they could.

There was one great advantage, likewise, which consisted in the fact that the tide had just begun to turn, and as they wanted to go down the river, that turn was entirely in their favour.

The wherry shot along with a speed that made the water rushing past its sides produce an audible sound.

The first bridge which they would come to at that period of time was Blackfriars, then tolerably new.

The water between Westminster and that bridge was very free from craft, with the exception of the coal barges, that lay thickly about the Adelphi, and the picturesque-looking corn boats at Hungerford.

"We shall succeed," said St. Ives.

"I hope so, with all my heart!" cried Duval.

"I owe you all my life," said the Princess, "and more than my life. It is not much to die, but I have begun, for the last few hours to realise how fearful a thing it is for one of my age and sex to run the risk of the terrible death that would await me were I captured."

These words were spoken with great emotion.

And if it were possible that Claude Duval could feel more urgent than ever in desiring the complete escape of that young Princess from the danger that surrounded her, the utterance of such a speech would have had that effect.

He felt convinced that that would be her last appearance in England as a conspirator and plotter.

She must, by that time, have discovered the complete hollowness and falsity of the professions of all those persons who had fed her with false hopes.

St. Ives, however, replied, in somewhat mournful tones—

"Do not, madam, make me think," he said, "that all hope is over!"

"I will not, if I can help it."

"I have clung to a fallen cause long and faithfully—the restoration of the exiled House to the throne of England has been the dream of my life, and were that to be dissipated, I scarcely know what I have to live for."

As St. Ives uttered these words, Blossom slightly touched Claude Duval on the arm.

It was evident that Blossom wished to bespeak his attention privately.

Amid the profound darkness on the river that was easy to do, and Duval inclined his head towards Blossom, to listen to his whispered words.

"Captain, look there to the right!"

As they were rowing down the river, the right would necessarily be the Middlesex side.

Duval looked anxiously in the direction pointed out by Blossom.

They were not far from Blackfriars Bridge now, and there were numerous small quays or landing-places at the end of narrow lanes and streets close to the water's edge.

At one of these Duval saw a lantern.

It was evidently moving about, as though carried in the hands of some person.

Then it became stationary for a few seconds.

And after that it seemed as if it came swiftly out on to the surface of the water.

A long black object likewise rested on the heaving tide.

The rays of the lantern were but dim, and yet they were sufficient to impart a kind of glitter to various bright points upon this black object.

The explanation of all this was easy.

A boat, crowded with armed men, in the bow of which was a lantern, had put forth from the little quay to which Blossom had directed Duval's attention.

"You see it, Captain?"

"I do."

"Then we are in danger."

"Who do you suppose those people are, Blossom?"

"The river police."

"But there is nothing suspicious about us or our boat. Surely the Thames is free either by night or by day?"

"Yes, Captain—but we don't know what information they may have."

St. Ives at this moment spoke.

"I perceive," he said, "that we are in some danger. We are closely followed by a wherry, in which there are two men, and from yonder quay a well-armed boat of the Thames Police has put forth to intercept us."

Neither Duval nor Blossom had noticed the boat that was following, for the darkness on the river was very intense, and that boat carried no light.

"What is best to be done?" asked Duval.

"We may distance them both."

"By hard rowing?"

"Even so; and if we can get through one of the arches of Blackfriars Bridge, we shall be more in the tide."

"Let us pull, then, with a will," said Duval.

The state of affairs now, in regard to the boat which was being pursued, and its pursuers, was very simple.

The wherry without the light, in which were two men, evidently had but little chance of overtaking the fugitives.

Indeed, they lost ground—or rather, we should say, lost water.

But still they rowed sufficiently quick to make that loss of trifling amount.

The police galley, however, had started at right angles from the shore.

It therefore became a question, whether Duval's boat, keeping, as it did, exactly in the centre of the river, would be able to pass the point of intersection before the police galley reached it.

If so, the chase would be a stern chase after all.

"Pull, for all our lives!" said St. Ives; "and likewise, for the life of one whom we hold as precious as ourselves."

They were all three strong men.

St. Ives and Blossom, too, were tolerably skilful at rowing.

And Duval, although he had had not much practice in such a diversion, made up for it by the tact with which he adopted what he saw the others do, and by the strength he brought to bear upon the operation.

The boat flew along with amazing swiftness.

"Hulloa!" cried a voice from the police galley. "Wherry a-hoi!"

"Do not answer," said St. Ives.

They pulled faster still.

"Wherry a-hoi! Pull up, or we fire!"

"Princess," said St. Ives, "let me implore you to lie as closely down at the bottom of the boat as you can?"

"No," said the Princess.

"But these men may fire."

"I hope not; but should they do so, I will not have the reflection in after time, should I live to see it, that I avoided the danger to which those who were risking so much for me, were left exposed."

"But our danger," said Duval, "will be none the less by your sharing it."

"Do not urge me—do not urge me!"

"I do so with all my heart."

"I cannot so far lose my self-esteem, as to lie down while you are fired at,"

Bang! went a pistol shot at this moment.

The bullet struck one of the oars that Duval was using, and the next pull that he gave with it, it broke in the water.

"Pull in!" cried a voice again from the police galley. "Pull in, or we fire upon you!"

"Not yet!" cried St. Ives, "the bridge is close to us!"

The boat that had followed them with the two men in it, still managed to keep very nearly its relative distance.

One of these men was evidently well practised in the mode of making sounds travel a long way upon the surface of water.

That consists, not in the loudness of the tones themselves, but in the prolonged character of the sound.

If a sailor wants a hail to travel far, he keeps it up without intermission, a length of time which he considers commensurate with the distance it has to travel.

One of the men, then, in this wherry, adopted such a plan, as he hailed the police galley.

"Treason! treason! Jacobite spies! Jacobite conspirators!"

He made these words last fully half a minute.

There could be no doubt but that they reached the ears of the officers in the police galley.

They redoubled their efforts to intercept Duval's boat.

But still St. Ives and Blossom bent to their oars, and rowed with all the energy they could bring to bear upon the task.

They were close to Blackfriars Bridge.

Already the dark shadow, thrown by that structure on to the water, was evident.

And as the tide encountered the piers of the arches, and was narrowed in its current, the rush beneath those arches was very swift.

Blossom could not refrain from uttering an exclamation of triumph.

The point at which the police galley would have intercepted them, was fairly passed.

There was hope, now, of escape.

Two or three random shots were fired, but no mischief was done.

"Shall I give them a bullet?" said Blossom, "in return for their's?"

"Not unless you would destroy us all?" said St. Ives.

"Then, of course, I won't do it."

The bridge was reached.

The boat was seized hold of by the tide as though it had been a cork, and carried with a rush beneath the gloomy arch.

"I think we are saved," said Duval.

"Lost!" said St. Ives.

"What do you mean?"

"Look ahead!"

Duval did so, and, to his consternation, he saw no less than two police-galleys, stationed exactly through the arch of the bridge, and apparently quietly waiting for the arrival of the boat.

The Princess uttered a sigh.

"It is proper for me to speak now," she said.

"No, no!" cried Duval; "this is the fortune of war, and we take the consequences."

"We will fight!" said Blossom.

"Not so; resistance is now useless," she added; "and since you feel so much for me, and are willing to sacrifice so much in my behalf, it is far better that you should all live for me than die for me."

CHAPTER LXXVII.

CLAUDE DUVAL AND ST. IVES ARE IN A PERILOUS POSITION.

THE tone of voice in which the young Princess uttered these words, was one of mingled depression and heroism.

"What do you wish us to do?" said St. Ives, mournfully.

"There is but one hope," she replied. "You, Colonel Miravel, occupying the position you do in the police, and being known as Mr. St. Ives, can easily state that you have me in custody."

"Alas! alas!"

"You can call upon the police-galleys to assist you."

"But, our friends, here?"

"It will be easy to say, that you procured their assistance for my capture."

"I have played such a part once," said St. Ives; "but it was under different circumstances."

"Heed not the circumstances. I know that now you will have to surrender me, or rather, accompany me to prison, escorted by these men; but whilst there is life there is hope; and the knowledge that you three live, and will do your utmost yet for my preservation, will console me in the gloomiest prison to which I may be consigned."

"I have a general order," said St. Ives, gloomily; "by virtue of which, if I capture any of the actual family of the exiled Stuarts——"

"You may put them to death, I presume," said the Princess.

"Heaven forbid! My order is to convey them at once to the Tower of London; and the sight of that order will be a sufficient warrant to the authorities of the Tower for their reception."

"The Tower!" exclaimed the Princess.

"Even so!"

"That dreadful place! The very air of it is heavy with the sighs of murdered men."

"Let me advise," said St. Ives.

"Quick, Quick!" cried Duval; "we shall have the galley upon us."

"It is easier to escape from the Tower," said St. Ives, "than from any of the ordinary prisons of London."

"And the Princess is quite right," said Duval. "It has taken me these two minutes to reconcile myself to the advice she has given."

"I thank you," said the Princess, "from my heart."

"Yes," added Duval; "it is the only true policy. If we engage in a contest with these three police-galleys, death or capture for the whole of us is certain."

"It is so," said St. Ives.

"Then it is far better for the Princess to put up with the inconvenience of, I hope, only a short incarceration in the Tower; carrying with her the knowledge that we three are unharmed, and at perfect liberty to devise means for her rescue, than that she should still be conveyed to that gloomy fortress, with the terrible reflection that there was no one to aid her or make even an effort for her rescue."

"That is what I mean—that is what I mean!" said the Princess.

"I submit," said St. Ives.

"And I too," said Blossom, with a groan.

St. Ives then raised his voice.

It had a strange, cracked sound about it, for he was struggling with his feelings.

"Police! police! police! A prisoner of State! Police! police!"

The galley that had put off from the quay reached the side of the boat with a rush.

Three or four lanterns were suddenly unmasked, and a tolerable light was at once cast upon the scene.

The crew of the police galley consisted of twelve men.

Several of them held their pistols ready for use in their hands.

They were commanded by two officers, who looked angry and suspicious.

"I claim your assistance and escort," said St. Ives.

"Who and what are you?" cried one of the officers.

"A suspicious craft, I'm thinking?" said the other.

"My name is St. Ives."

"St. Ives? St. Ives? Not the police official of the Home Office?"

"The same."

"How do we know that?"

"It matters not to me," said Sir Ives; "the value of one of these ripples on the surface of the Thames whether you know it or not."

"Indeed!"

"Yes; but if presuming upon your want of knowledge of that fact, you commit any act that shall impede me in the pursuit of my duty, you will have to answer for it at your peril."

The officers of the police-galley were somewhat abashed.

But by this time the wherry with the two men in it, who had followed what might be called the Princess's boat so pertinaciously, reached the spot.

One of these men called out at once impatiently—"Seize them! Seize them! A plot! A plot! The lady in the boat is a Princess of the House of Stuart, and, therefore, a rebel and a traitress. She is trying to escape; we have certain information of who she is, and insist upon her capture."

"My good friend," said St. Ives; "speaking quite calmly, I don't know who you are, but I dare say, in the ordinary way, you are a very energetic person."

"Never mind who and what I am, I can prove what I say."

"Pray hear me out."

"Well what is it?"

"I was only going to add that in this particular instance you were a little too late."

"Too late?"

"Yes; your information is admirably correct, but the personage you mention is already in custody."

"Yes, the police-galley."

"No."

"You fled from our boat—we have been after you all the way from Westminster Bridge."

"When I am conveying a prisoner of state to the Tower of London, by virtue of a warrant signed by the Prime Minister, I do not stop to explain to every man whom I may chance to meet, either my errand or to satisfy him as to my mode of carrying it out."

This speech, so quietly uttered by St Ives, appeared to have anything but an agreeable effect upon the two persons in the small wherry.

They looked at each other with feelings of bitterness and disappointment.

Duval took not the slightest notice of them.

And yet he felt perfectly certain in his own mind in regard to who and what they were.

They formed two of that party who had been with Pilkington, the officer, in St. James's Park, although how they had become aware of the particular mode by which the Princess was attempting to escape remained a mystery.

The idea of losing all reward, however, was an aggravation to them which they could not get over.

One of them spoke in loud excited tones.

"This won't do," he said. "This won't do. We have followed this wherry all the way down the Thames from Westminster Bridge."

"Yes," cried the other, "and almost pulled our arms out of the sockets with rowing."

"And what are we to get by it?" added the first.

"We claim half the reward," cried the other.

"I am not aware," said St. Ives, "that there is any reward to claim, and if there be it undoubtedly belongs to me, and to these two persons whom I have induced to assist me in making the important capture."

"That's perfectly true, Mr. St. Ives," said one of the officers in the police-galley; "and there can be no doubt about your authority."

"I am not quite so sure of that," remarked the other.

"What is it you doubt, sir?" asked St. Ives.

"Well, I don't know you by sight."

"That may be easily accounted for; your duty is on the river—mine is on the shore."

"But can you give us any proof?"

"I can."

St. Ives opened his coat at the breast as he spoke,

ST. IVES WARNS DUVAL OF HIS DANGER.

and showed suspended round his neck, by a very fine chain, a representation in silver, about four inches in length, of a running hound.

"This you recognise," he said, "as my badge of office as a King's Messenger."

"Exactly, but——"

"I hold that position, as well as a high one in the police, and I present this as a symbol of the latter office."

St. Ives, as he spoke, took from his pocket a small staff, likewise of silver, on the extreme end of which was a royal crown gilt.

It was so small as to be a mere toy.

Nevertheless it was well-known to the officers of the police-galley that none but the very highest officials connected with the police authorities were in power to possess and produce such an article.

"I am quite satisfied, sir."

"Then all is well."

"We shall be happy to render you any assistance in our power."

No. 25.—NIGHTSHADE.

"I do not say," replied St Ives, "that I require any assistance, nevertheless, if your other duties will permit it, I shall be very glad to avail myself of your escort with my prisoner here."

These words seemed to satisfy the officers in the police galley almost more than the production of the silver hound and the small staff.

But the two men in the small wherry were anything but satisfied.

They became absolutely clamorous.

Then St. Ives spoke again.

"I have my suspicions," he said, "that I should not have been followed with such pertinacity by these two men but for some sinister motive."

"Indeed?" cried one of the officers of the police-galley.

"Yes, sirs; and how can we take upon ourselves to say that these men may not be Jacobite agents?"

"We Jacobite agents?—we?" cried the men in the wherry.

"Why not?" added St. Ives.

"Yes, why not?" cried one of the officers of the galley; "we live in suspicious times."

"Hold on, there!" cried the other.

A couple of boat-hooks were immediately made fast to the gunwale of the wherry, and it was dragged precipitately to the side of the police galley.

"Jacobite spies, I'll wager a thousand pounds!" added one of the officers.

"It may be so," said St. Ives. "The daring audacity of these people is so well known that these two fellows may have hoped, in some secluded part of the river, to pounce upon us and rescue the prisoner."

"It's very likely, indeed!"

"Of course, they would have been mistaken, and would probably have met their own destruction in the attempt; but still the treasonable wish remains the same."

"Of course it does," replied the principal officer of the police galley. "Clap handcuffs on there, my men, and take their wherry in tow."

It was in vain that these two myrmidons of Mr. Pilkington protested against the usage they were receiving.

They were duly handcuffed and flung into the bottom of their own boat, which, being a small ordinary Thames wherry was easily taken in tow by the police-galley.

During all these proceedings Claude Duval and Blossom had not uttered a word.

They felt that silence was, in the present case, the greatest discretion.

Sitting down in the boat, likewise, the costume of Duval was not so observable as it might have been.

And the fugitive Princess never spoke.

It was evident that she had full confidence, not only in the good faith, but, likewise, in the discretion of St. Ives.

Whatever he arranged to do, she made up her mind to allow to be done, so far as she was concerned, without a shadow of opposition.

St. Ives, then, having achieved a perfect command over his voice and over his feelings, spoke again, in that calm tone of command which was habitual to him.

"I intend, gentlemen," he said, "to avail myself of the powers of the general warrant, which I hold, and convey this important state prisoner to the Tower of London."

"Very good, sir."

"For your kind and friendly escort I shall be greatly obliged."

"We shall willingly accord it."

"And you may be assured that I shall take care to represent the alacrity and efficiency of this galley in the proper quarter."

This tone, which St. Ives assumed, had all its effect upon the officers and men of the police-galley.

But St. Ives, of course, had no intention of rowing the remainder of the distance himself.

Nor did he wish to put upon Claude Duval and Blossom the ungracious task of actively exerting themselves to convey the Stuart Princess to the Tower.

"I think," he said, "that we may discharge these two rascals with an admonition."

He alluded to Pilkington's two men.

"If you think so, Mr. St. Ives, we will take their handcuffs off, and cast their wherry loose."

"It will be convenient to do so. I know them quite well by sight, and can apprehend them at any time if necessary. Moreover, I want you to take us in tow, for my two friends here are rather fatigued."

"Certainly, sir."

It was quite evident that whatever orders St. Ives chose to issue would be obeyed.

And whatever suggestion he chose to make it was equally evident would be looked upon in the light of an order.

The wherry of Mr. Pilkington's two men was cast adrift.

That which contained Duval Blossom. St. Ives, and the Stuart Princess, was taken in tow by the police-galley.

So along with the tide, and at a much quicker rate than that at which they had hitherto gone, the little party sped down the Thames.

There were sad hearts in that small wherry.

And it was no small aggravation of the disastrous situation in which they found themselves, that they dared not openly discuss any means of bettering their evil fortune.

The tow-rope of the police galley, which was attached to the bow of the wherry, was not above half-a-dozen yards in length.

The proximity, therefore, of the two boats was too close to make it safe to utter a word above a breath.

But there was nothing unnatural or unlikely in the fact of Mr. St. Ives conversing in what tones he chose with the two persons who were supposed to be assisting him in conveying his important prisoner to a place of safety.

On this supposition, therefore, he spoke to Duval in whispered accents.

"Do not despair?"

"I do not."

"Keep yourself and your man quite quiet!"

"I will."

"Speak to the Princess."

"What shall I tell her?"

"You are nearer to her than I, and I wish you to tell her, in the lowest tones you can render intelligible, that it will not be safe for a week to attempt her rescue from the Tower."

Duval communicated this to the Princess.

Her reply came in the same low tones.

"I know you will all save me if you can; but I charge you not to risk too much in so doing."

The boat sped on.

At the rate the police galley went, London Bridge was soon reached, and then the Tower Stairs.

"One of us must land here," said St. Ives, "for it is necessary that the principal warder, or the Governor of the Tower, if he be resident, should be made aware of the manner of prisoner we bring."

St. Ives spoke this aloud, so that both officers in the police galley heard him.

"Quite right, sir!" cried one. 'I suppose we shall have to pull in by Traitors' Gate?"

"We shall."

Both the boats came to a standstill, and one of the officers from the galley landed; and, after some parley with the sentinel, entered one of the posterns of the Tower.

A very chilling wind swept over the surface of the Thames.

And with all her courage, and all her indomitable perseverance, the young Princess could not help gazing, with a shudder, upon the gloomy walls of that historical building, each stone of which might have been cemented to its neighbour by the blood that has been shed within them.

St. Ives touched Duval upon the arm.

"Look yonder," he said. "I am glad you are with us."

"And I too."

"I mean, only, however, in order that you should take particular observation of everything you see or hear."

"I see; I see. You direct my attention to yonder low bowed arch."

"Yes; it it Traitors' Gate. The tide is dropping

fast, and we shall enter it. Half an hour ago we should scarcely have had space to enter beneath it.

There was a heavy dismal looking grating beneath the arch.

The tide lapped lazily against it.

And, even as Claude Duval and St. Ives gazed at it, they saw this grating begun to move upward, and finally it disappeared.

The flickering glare of a torch shed a lurid light upon the water.

"Now, sirs," said the officer, who was left in charge of the police galley by his companion.

"Ready," said St. Ives.

The two boats moved onward.

Another minute and they were under the arch, and actually within the Tower of London.

There was a rectangular space, about a hundred feet long, and half that in width, into which the tide made its way.

Gloomy walls surrounded it, and a broad flight of stone steps, from a door in one of those walls, came right down into the water.

In old times, those steps were worn by many feet, but now they were moss grown, and the lowest of them were covered with green slime from the river.

Several men stood at the head of the steps.

One was the Deputy-Governor of the Tower.

To him St. Ives presented his warrant, and in five minutes more—very few words having been spoken—the Princess was conveyed into the interior of the gloomy fortress.

It was with a pang of regret, that Claude Duval lost sight of the slight feminine looking figure, as it disappeared within the gloomy doorway.

"Gentlemen," said St. Ives, to the officers of the police-galley, "I need only give you one further trouble."

"It is no trouble, sir; anything we can do for you will only give us pleasure."

"In carrying out my duty, and by virtue of the authority I possess, I was compelled to take this wherry from Westminster Bridge, if you will kindly return it to the stairs, there is no doubt, its owner will find it."

"Certainly, sir!"

"It will be more convenient for me and my two friends here, to pass through the Tower as we have business in Thames Street."

This arrangement was acquiesced in at once, and one of the warders of the Tower led St. Ives, accompanied by Claude Duval and Blossom, through the Tower and out by the postern on Tower Hill.

Duval kept his eyes well about him in that progress.

"My heart is heavy," said St. Ives, when they were free of the fortress. "I must go home now and think over the events of this troublous night."

"Troublous, indeed," said Duval. "And must a whole week elapse before we can even attempt anything for the Princess."

"It must, by that time the vigilance of the Tower authorities will have relaxed a little; but I will see you in a few days at Farnborough House, and until then farewell."

Blossom and Duval were alone.

"A week!" cried the latter, "a whole week of expectations and waiting. How shall I pass it?"

"In action, Captain, on the road—then it will fly quickly enough. To-morrow night let us take a gallop northward, across the heath by our old quarters, who knows but we may have some sport?"

"Be it so," said Duval, "and if not, I have another plan in my head which promises both entertainment and profit, so now, Blossom, let us get to Farnborough House as quickly as we can, for the hour is late."

CHAPTER LXXVIII.

CLAUDE DUVAL ACCOMPANIES THE DUCHESS OF CLEVELAND TO THE PRIME MINISTER'S ENTERTAINMENT.

AND now once more we will turn out attention to Hampstead Heath, and with the privilege of old friends glance at the two horsemen who are quietly pursuing their way towards London, and listen to their conversation, which is carried on at intervals.

Sir John Cope, or rather Claude Duval, is the name of the first speaker—let us listen to his words.

"I tell you, Blossom, I have made up my mind to attend this soirée given in honour of the Turkish Ambassador by the Prime Minister, and I think my best plan will be to pay a visit to Her Grace the Duchess of Cleveland and get her to introduce me."

"Just the thing, Captain," replied the other horseman, whom the reader will have no difficulty in recognising as Blossom. "Just the thing, Captain, and there is no fear of any one penetrating your disguise."

"I think not, I think not," replied Duval. "Let us proceed at once to the Duchess of Cleveland, and while I present myself to her ladyship, you walk the horses to and fro, so as to be within sight whenever I may require Nightshade."

"All right, Captain!"

The two horsemen now put their horses to a gallop, and trotted briskly towards London, and any one to have seen those two men would have at once pronounced them to be a gentleman and his confidential servant.

A very short ride brought them to the mansion occupied by the beautiful and popular Duchess of Cleveland.

Claude Duval paused a moment, and turning to Blossom, he said, "You dismount and ascertain if her Grace is at home or not, and whether she can receive visitors."

Blossom looked about him, and soon espied a butcher's boy coming along looking as though he would much rather be otherwise employed than in his legitimate calling.

"Hi! Stop my lad," said Blossom.

The boy understood in a moment what was required of him, and went at once to the horse's head.

"That's it," said Blossom, as he dismounted.

In another moment he had made a tremendous appeal to the knocker on the hall-door of the mansion.

A footman in a handsome livery replied to the summons.

"Is her Grace the Duchess of Cleveland at home?" asked Blossom of this functionary.

"Haw! yes!" was the reply.

"That'll do," said Blossom, as he returned to Duval, who, at once dismounted and approached the footman.

"Tell her Grace that Sir John Cope, a friend of Mr. Lavud, wishes to see her on important business."

"Haw! yes, sir!"

The footman preceded Duval, and throwing open a door of a magnificent reception-room, intimated his intention of informing her ladyship of her visitor's presence.

Duval turned to the table which occupied the centre of the room, and amused himself with turning over some beautiful engravings.

He had not been thus engaged above the space of five minutes when the Duchess herself in a charming morning toilette entered the room.

There was a flush of expectation on her countenance as she approached Duval, but that soon disappeared and she said, calmly, "Forgive my want of courtesy sir. Pray be seated, but I feared—I thought, perhaps, that your friend, Mr. Lavud was——"

"You thought Madam," replied Duval, "that he might be here—was not that it?"

The Duchess smiled one of those fascinating smiles which was one of her powerful characteristics, as she said naively, "To tell you the truth, sir, I fancied I might have the pleasure of seeing him this morning."

"Far be it from me," said Duval, in the same tone, "to deprive your ladyship of anything that could possibly give her any pleasure;" at the same time he raised his wig just sufficiently to allow of his own raven hair being seen by the Duchess.

"Capital! capital!" cried the Duchess, clapping her hands together with almost childish delight. "Really your best friends could never recognise you now."

"I am most happy to hear it," said Duval, as he gallantly raised her small jewelled hand to his lips, "and may I now request a great favour at your hands."

The Duchess looked serious again, and raising her eyes to those of Duval, she said, with much emotion, "Ask any favour, and it is granted even before I know what it is; for what is there in all the world to which you have not the highest right to demand as your just reward for a past service."

"Pooh! pooh!" said Duval, "I had forgotten all about those letters to which you refer."

"But I never shall," interrupted the Duchess.

"But have you forgotten that that debt was more than cancelled the day you acted so nobly by my dear Lucy."

"Ah, Duval, I have been so anxious ever since that morning, but I have been afraid to make too many inquiries about you, still I have been so anxious to hear how you sped on that occasion."

"Oh, as well as could be," replied Duval, "and nothing but great events would have prevented me from seeking you long ere this, to thank you in my lady's name as well as in my own, for your great kindness and sympathy."

"Enough! enough!" said the Duchess, "but tell me what you are doing."

"I am Sir John Cope," replied Duval with mock gaiety; "Lucy is my grandchild, and I am now residing at Farnborough House, which I have taken furnished, and where, if ever your ladyship will do us the honour to pay us a visit, we will endeavour to give you an appropriate welcome."

"Believe me, I will indeed do myself the pleasure of calling upon you; in the meantime let me know what the particular favour is which you were so anxious I should grant just now?"

"Simply this. I have a great wish to attend the forthcoming reception, which is to take place at the Prime Minister's on Tuesday evening, in honour of the Turkish Embassy's arrival."

"Nothing will be easier, Sir John," said the Duchess, with a peculiar glance, as she uttered the new name by which Duval wished to be addressed. "Nothing will be easier; and if you would like to do so I should esteem it a favour if you would go with me as a friend of mine."

"Agreed then," said Duval; "and now, Duchess, I will not detain you any longer, for I perceive that you are threatened with visitors."

"Ah!" said the Duchess, glancing from behind the curtain, "it is Lady Talbot."

Claude Duval took a hasty leave of the Duchess, and resuming his stooping gait, turned and left the reception-room just as the same obsequious footman, who had admitted him, announced in stentorian accents, "Lady Alice Talbot, my lady."

Blossom was not many paces from the house, and in another moment Duval had mounted, and Blossom fell back several yards, nor did he think of shortening the distance between them until Duval drew rein, and made a sign for him to advance.

"All is well, Blossom, I am going, and hope there I may hear something more of my Lord Montrose and his villainous associate Mossy Pendell."

"It is to be hoped you will, Captain," replied Blossom, "It makes me feel more revengeful than ever, to think of those men getting off just at the moment when we fancy we have them in our power."

"Never mind, Blossom, we shall, no doubt, some day be able to make them account for all their wickedness. Let us be thankful that we were the means of frustrating, to a certain extent, their vile projects regarding one whom we will not mention."

"I understand you, Captain," said Blossom.

A short ride brought them again to Farnborough House when, as was her wont, Duval was met by Lucy in the hall of the mansion.

"You have soon returned, dear Claude," she said.

"Soon returned, Lucy? Why did I not tell you, dearest, that I should not be gone long? Since when has my Lucy learnt to doubt her Claude?"

"Never to doubt him in that meaning of the word; but I am always afraid that with your adventurous turn of mind something may occur that might lead you to forget——"

Lucy paused.

"Ah!" said Claude Duval, fondly pressing her to his heart, "I see that you are ashamed of the conclusion you intended to make to your sentence, and so——"

"And so what?" asked Lucy, archly.

"And so I will be magnanimous and forgive it."

Thus talking, they reached their favourite sitting-room, and then Lucy, drawing a chair to his side, asked him if he had contrived any means by which his wish to attend the reception of the Premier's might be gratified.

"Yes, Lucy, dear. I have been to the Duchess of Cleveland, and she——"

"Ah!" exclaimed Lucy. "I thought of her after you left me, and was vexed to think it had not occurred to me before."

"Another proof, my Lucy, of our unanimity," said Duval, stooping and kissing her fair brow. "But now tell me," he continued, "how have you been passing your time during my absence?"

"I have been quite busy in the conservatory, Claude, and have arranged the flowers much more tastefully than they were when we took possession of our nice home."

"And does my Lucy really like her new home?" asked Duval, anxiously.

"I do, indeed, Claude, but I tremble sometimes when I find myself looking with more than ordinary interest upon the various objects of beauty with which you have surrounded me—lest——"

"Lest what, dear one?"

"Lest they should vanish from before my eyes, as did those which it was the happiness of my uncle's life to lavish upon me."

"My poor love, your young life has indeed been a chequered one, but let us hope that the clouds which once hung over your horizon are now dispersed for ever."

"I do, indeed, Claude! Oh, that I could persuade you to give up this adventurous life, and spend the remainder of your days in peace and safety!"

"Nay, Lucy, do you not remember that I stand pledged to produce either the murderer of your uncle, or such facts as shall at once and for ever re-establish your perfect innocence?"

"Alas! alas!" said Lucy.

"But you have nothing to fear now, Lucy, I am merely going as a spectator to this gay assembly—not to meet with any adventures."

"Perhaps not, yet who can say?" said Lucy despondingly, "But I will not indulge in these gloomy forebodings, my Claude, or you will begin to fancy I am a coward."

"Not that, Lucy, never anything but my own brave wife—only just a little bit too anxious."

"And you do not blame me?"

"Ah, Lucy, you want me now to make a kind of admission, by which you will feel yourself justified in trying to turn me from all my purposes. I see, I see; but I will not thus arm you with weapons against myself."

Lucy smiled, and for a time peace and serenity were the occupants of her gentle heart.

At length the day arrived on which that brilliant assembly, which made such a sensation at the time, took place at the residence of the Prime Minister of England.

By ten o'clock—for our ancestors kept much earlier hours in those days—there might be seen a long line of carriages, as magnificent in their gilding and trappings, as were their occupants, some of whom wore a blaze of diamonds and precious jewels.

Claude Duval had thought it advisable not to attend this reception as Sir John Cope; he therefore had commissioned Blossom to procure for him a handsome uniform of an officer in Her Majesty's Light Horse.

When thus equipped, Claude Duval looked, to use a homely phrase, every inch a nobleman; and so thought the Duchess of Cleveland evidently, as she glanced at him with eyes of admiration when he was ushered into the room where she was awaiting him.

"Ah! here you are, Colonel!" was the greeting with which she saluted him, and when the door was closed behind him, she said, "I thought I was to have had a much graver, older companion to-night. Why have you not appeared as Sir John Cope?"

"Because, I fancied from a little adventure which I had as that same Sir John Cope only a short time ago in the Park, would render it somewhat unwise to be seen here to-night. But, come, allow me to lead you to your carriage!"

The Duchess and Claude were soon set down at their destination, and their names, the Duchess of Cleveland and Colonel Lavud, were shouted from mouth to mouth until they died away apparently in soft whispers.

They entered the gay saloons, and not long after their entrance, the band struck up a lively air, and Claude Duval selected the hand of the Duchess for the first dance.

While thus engaged, however, Claude Duval was not idle.

His keen glance had scanned the countenances of all those who were round and about him, and before many minutes had elapsed he was conscious that a pair of eyes were fixed upon him, whose hateful light was too well known to him

In the same dance the Duke of Montrose was taking part.

Duval stood his scrutiny well, but there was an undefined feeling at his heart that danger was near, but in what shape he knew not.

At length the dance was over, and Duval was handing the Duchess to a seat, when a gentleman, attired in a plain evening costume, stepped up rather abruptly, and said to the Duchess, "Your pardon, madam, but you have dropped your fan;" at the same time that he bowed low, and whispered to Duval, "There is danger here! Follow me as closely as may be, and all may be well yet."

"St. Ives!" almost burst from the lips of Duval.

But St. Ives was making his way leisurely across the room, as though he were intent on speaking to some person who was standing near the door.

The Duchess turned pale.

"What can he mean? Do you know Mr. St. Ives?"

"I have seen him often," replied Duval, evasively.

"And can you trust him?" asked the Duchess.

"I think I can."

"It is quite evident that it was for the purpose of giving you this warning—whether friendly, or otherwise, I cannot tell—that he addressed me," added the Duchess; "for see here, I have my own fan, and that which he gave me."

"There can be little doubt about that," said Duval.

"What do you mean to do, then?" asked the Duchess.

"Follow his advice, if you will permit me."

"Do so—do so at once, then, and good fortune aid you, if there, indeed, be danger."

The Duchess moved towards an ottoman, and appeared to dismiss Duval upon some trifling errand.

In the meantime, Duval, who had never, during the course of his conversation with the Duchess, lost sight of St. Ives, quietly pursued his way towards the same door to which St. Ives seemed to be making his way.

About half way across the grand saloon there was a little knot of gentlemen, who all seemed to be conversing at once.

Duval was compelled to pass very near to this little coterie, and as he did so, he recognised the voice of the Duke of Montrose, who was speaking eagerly, but, as Duval approached, he suddenly ceased.

Claude appeared not to notice this, and continued to pursue the route he had taken, when his attention was suddenly aroused by hearing some one say, "I tell you it is he- Claude Duval - I know him well. I have set Mr. St. Ives to keep watch and ward at the outer door."

"Then he will give me no more trouble," said a voice, the speaker being hidden by a heavy silken curtain.

But Claude Duval never forgot either a voice or a face he had once heard or seen; and in the tones of that voice he was at no loss to recognise that of Mossy Pendell

"If it costs me my life," thought Duval to himself, "I will not let these men escape me again."

He was about to turn and retrace his steps, when a hand was laid upon his arm.

Colonel Lavud's carriage is arrived.

Claude started, for he recognised Blossom.

"Ah! you here?"

"Yes, Captain," replied Blossom, in a low tone.

"Did you not send for your carriage?"

"I? No!"

"Mr. St. Ives——"

"Ah! I see it all now."

Duval began to think that there must, indeed, be more danger than he, Claude, suspected, or surely St. Ives would not have thus interfered.

Duval was just hesitating whether to take advantage of his advice, and get away as quickly as possible, or return and exact a reckoning with Mossy Pendell, and his vile associate, the conspirator, the Duke of Montrose, when he heard a cry of, "There he is! Seize him! Stop him! I knew I was not mistaken!"

"Quick, Captain! I have Nightshade in readiness. I will jump up on the box of the carriage Mr. St. Ives intended for you, and all may yet be well."

"Yes," said Duval; "all will yet be well."

He vaulted on to the back of Nightshade, and like lightning he sped along Piccadilly.

Again and again he heard shouts and cries, but no fear sat at the heart of Duval, for well he knew his sagacious steed could and would distance all pursuers.

He thought it advisable, however, not to appear at

Farnborough House until all the tumult had entirely subsided; and when he found he was quite alone on the high road he drew rein, and began to ask himself what he had better do next.

After some deliberation, Duval decided that he would go home to Farnborough House, and while all was quiet make sure of reaching it without being seen.

In less than an hour he rode up to the back entrance of the mansion, which now owned him for master.

One of his faithful men admitted him.

"Is your mistress up, Andrews?"

"Yes, sir."

Claude Duval hastened to the sitting-room, where he was quite sure he should find Lucy watching, and clasping her in his arms he whispered, "You see I have kept my word, dearest, and returned home without getting mixed up in any adventure."

"I see you have, dearest Claude, and heaven be thanked," ejaculated Lucy.

CHAPTER LXXIX.

CLAUDE DUVAL AND LUCY MAKE SOME IMPORTANT DISCOVERIES IN THE VALISE.

DUVAL was exceedingly anxious to ascertain the contents of that valise, which he had taken from Mossy Pendell, in the Oxford mail.

So many events of stirring interest had pressed upon his attention since that period, that although he had taken a cursory view of the papers, he had not been able fairly to set down with Lucy and examine them.

About mid-day, however, immediately following the adventure we have recorded, Duval admirably made up in his disguise of Sir John Cope, sat with Lucy in one of the drawing-rooms of Farnborough House, for that express purpose.

There was a goodly array of letters and documents, and it was with great interest that Lucy leant over Duval's shoulder as he had selected one letter from the heap, in order the better to read it with him.

The letter was short, but filled them both with surprise; and Lucy, with a strange mixture of joy and sorrow, the letter ran as follows :—

"It seems that you are quite content to leave *you know who* entirely on my hands without ever taking the trouble to come and see whether he is dead or not. Confound the fellow, although I have reduced him to the last stage of weakness and despondency, he still clings pertinaciously to life, and refuses to sign the document. Let me see you to-night, at Camden House. M. P."

Neither Claude nor Lucy were at a loss to supply the letters which were required to write the name of Mossy Pendell at the end of this heartless billet.

"Oh, Claude, Claude! surely this diabolical letter has reference only to my poor dear uncle, whom that villain, Mossy Pendell has, according to his own statement, reduced to such a fearful state. Oh! what shall we do—what shall we do?"

Lucy threw her arms round Duval, and wept.

"Hush, my Lucy! let us see what else there is; we may find something which will aid us in unmasking this fiend in human shape. In the meantime, dear one, leave me to look over these papers alone, and I will make you acquainted with their contents afterwards."

"Oh! let me stay, Claude!" implored Lucy. "I will not be weak; but this letter coming so suddenly upon me, revealing, as I cannot but believe, the continued existence of my beloved uncle, made a coward of me at first; but continue, Claude, and let me stay—oh! let me stay!"

"Be it so, then, as you wish it so much, Lucy," replied Claude, looking tenderly at her; "and believe me, dear, that I will leave nothing undone that shall lead to his discovery."

Claude Duval raised another paper, a much more pretentious-looking one. It proved to be a title deed to the estates of General Everton.

"Ah!" he said; "this, indeed, belongs to you, Lucy. See, here are the title deeds to your uncle's estates."

"No, no, not mine, Claude, they are his!"

"But were you not to be his heiress?"

"Yes, yes, Claude, after his death! but he still lives! Oh, do not deprive me of the hope—I had almost said the conviction—that I should see him again."

"True—true! I had forgotten, love. But now, what have we here? Another precious epistle from that foul fiend."

"No!" said Lucy; "the handwriting is not the same."

Duval turned to the signature and found the name of "HORLOP."

"Ah! this," he said, "may throw some light on the letter we have just read. Let us see;" and Duval read the following words :—

"I wish to goodness you would find some means of quieting that fellow, Smithers; he is continually pestering me with letters, demanding more money for the dead body he furnished us with to carry out the deception of the old general's death. He threatens to split upon us if we do not give him double what he first promised to take; but, really, I have neither time nor inclination to go and talk to this low fellow; so see to it, or it may be the worse for us both.

"HORLOP."

Claude drew a deep breath of relief, and Lucy covered her face with her hands, and wept bitterly.

"Oh, Claude, Claude!" she sobbed; "is it possible that such wickedness exists in the world. Oh, where—where is my poor uncle! In the meantime, what must be his sufferings!"

"Hush, hush, Lucy! do not grieve so, my poor dear. All this should give you consolation."

"But if he should die before we find the means of discovering where he is?"

"Let us hope that all will be well. Surely we ought to rejoice, my Lucy, to think that your uncle is still sufficiently master of himself to resist all the threatenings of these two villains; and there is no telling, he may even now be contemplating some means of escape from his cruel, heartless persecution."

"Yes, yes! Oh, heaven grant that such may be the case!"

Duval raised another letter from the packet, out of which fell a small, folded paper, which looked as though it had been an enclosure in some other.

There were but a few words in the outer paper; but the handwriting on the outside, which was addressed to Mossy Pendell, was unmistakably that of his villainous associate, Horlop. It ran thus:

"I send you another letter from that man, Smithers. It seems that you have taken no notice of what I informed you. Read, and judge for yourself."

"MY LORD.—I have been thinking that it is a strange thing for two gentlemen like you and Mr. Mossy to want a corpse, and my wife has been talking over the subject with me, and she says that I shall in all probability get into a dreadful scrape about it, some day; and I think so too, my lord.

"Nevertheless, as I don't want to pry into the secrets of two gentlemen like you and Mr. Mossy Pendell, and am quite ready and willing to believe that you required the body for the purpose of dissection for the benefit of science, and so forth, yet I have been thinking that I did not give it due consideration, or I certainly should not have let you had it so cheap.

"So I was thinking, my lord, and my wife thinks so too, that two such gentlemen as you and Mr. Mossy Pendell wouldn't mind easing a poor, hard-working man's mind, by making up to him in money some of the anxiety I have suffered ever since I let you have the corpse.

"You see, my lord, it would be much easier to make a friend of me, because if any questions are asked, I could answer more satisfactorily, *if I am well paid for so doing,*

"Awaiting your reply, I am,
"Your humble servant,
"JOSEPH SMITHERS,
"Boot-maker and Sexton."

"A most valuable document, my Lucy," said Duval, as he placed the above letter apart by itself. "A most precious document. I only regret that the fellow has forgotten to put in his address."

"Perhaps," said Lucy, "it was purposely omitted."

"Perhaps, so!" replied Duval, "but it matters not, it matters not. We will soon find out where this conscientious sexton lives, and will deal with him according to his deserts!"

There were still many other papers to look over, but both Lucy and Duval felt that they had seen enough for the present, especially as they were both expecting a visit from St. Ives, who had promised to call upon Duval at Farnborough House, as early the next day as he could.

Neither Claude nor Lucy had forgotten the Princess, who had been the object of so much interest to them both, and now that they had, so to speak, become aware of the contents of some of the letters contained in the valise, they almost simultaneously turned their thoughts to her in her gloomy abode in the Tower.

Lucy was thoughtfully gazing at the letters they had been receiving, and her tears again began to fall.

These evidences of the continued existence of her indulgent, and much-loved uncle, filled Lucy Everton with a thousand agitations and fears.

"Claude! Claude!" she cried, "can we do nothing to unravel this dreadful mystery?"

"We will unravel it, and there is but one man who can help us efficiently."

The door of the drawing-room was opened at this moment by Blossom.

"Mr. St. Ives," he announced.

"The very name," said Duval, "that was upon my lips."

St. Ives stepped into the room.

"Welcome," said Claude. "A thousand welcomes!"

"I thought you would be impatient to see me, Sir John Cope," said St. Ives.

"You may speak freely," said Duval, "there is no one upon this floor of the house but ourselves and my man Blossom, who has just shown you in."

"Nay," said St. Ives, "if you mean that I may freely call you Claude Duval, believe me it is better not to do so, if we were at Versailles or at the Hague, I should wish you to call me Colonel Miravel, but here in London, let me be Mr. St. Ives, the police agent, and in Farnborough House, you must certainly remain Sir John Cope."

"I believe you are right," said Duval, "but what news do you bring us?"

"But little."

"We have something to consult you about," said Lucy, "and feel assured that you will lend us your best assistance."

St. Ives glanced at the mass of papers on the table before them.

Duval, however, placed his hand upon them.

"No, Lucy, no," he said, "we must not be selfish. St. Ives' visit here has relation to that poor fugitive Princess, whom you pity as profoundly as I do."

"True, true," replied Lucy.

"We will let our own affairs wait awhile, important though they are, and depending upon them, perhaps, even a human life?"

"I must own," said St. Ives, sadly, "that my mind is filled up and engrossed past all other considerations, by the peril of that illustrious lady, who not only commands my allegiance as a Princess of the House to which I am attached, but who personally calls for my warmest sympathies as a man, and my constant admiration."

"You hear, Lucy, you hear," said Duval.

"I do, and have not one word to say to the contrary."

As she spoke, Lucy hastily packed up all the papers relating to General Everton, and replaced them in the valise.

Then both Claude and Lucy looked in the face of St. Ives more attentively.

They saw there the traces of great suffering.

He was pale and haggard.

"Do your despair?" asked Duval.

"No. I will never despair."

"But you suffer," said Lucy.

"I do, almost overwhelming anxiety."

"Is there any special danger!" added Duval.

"Not immediate, but I have been summoned before the Privy Council, and have been reluctantly compelled, in a manner of speaking, to give evidence against the Princess."

"She is still in the Tower?"

"She is, but she must not be there for long."

St. Ives brightened up a little as he spoke.

"No, he added, "she must not be there for long. She must be rescued. I do not ask you, Sir John Cope, for it is not fair to do so, that you should risk liberty and life in these matters."

"But——"

"Nay, hear me out. You have already rejected the rank that was offered you, if you would join the cause of the exiled family. You are not a Jacobite; and accident alone has placed you in a position to know some of our most cherished secrets, and to be of service to us under circumstances of great emergency."

"Nay," said Duval.

"Let me finish. I do not come to ask you to make arrangements with me, or to take any active part in an attempt to rescue the Princess from the Tower; but I have great faith in your ability to advise me, and being quite sure, likewise, of your good faith and honour, I wish to hold a consultation with you—that is all."

"No," said Duval, "that is not all."

Lucy inclined her head in assent to these words.

"What would you say?" asked St. Ives.

"That is not all," added Duval, "I never desert an individual, or a cause that I once advocate; and let the peril be what it may, St. Ives, I will accompany you, heart and hand, in the attempt to rescue the Princess from the Tower."

"St. Ives held out his hand to Duval.

The latter grasped it warmly.

"I should be something more or less than human,'

said St. Ives, "if I were to reject such an offer. It brings to me an assurance of success, and my mind seems lightened of half its load."

Duval smiled.

"We look upon all that, then, as settled, St. Ives," he said; "so that now we have but to consult on the ways and means."

St. Ives lowered his voice, and spoke with extreme emotion.

CHAPTER LXXX.
CLAUDE DUVAL IS RECEIVED BY THE DEPUTY GOVERNOR OF THE TOWER.

CLAUDE DUVAL had assured the police agent, or rather, the Jacobite officer, for such indeed he was, that he might speak with freedom in that apartment, inasmuch as there was not the least likelihood of their being disturbed or overheard.

Nevertheless, Colonel Miravel, or St. Ives, as we shall still continue to call him, in order that he may be the more readily recognised by the reader, spoke in a very low tone.

The vital importance of the words he uttered induced that extreme caution.

Claude Duval and Lucy listened to him attentively.

"There is but one chance of rescuing her Royal Highness from the Tower."

"One chance is enough," said Duval, "if it be a good one."

"It is a good one, and I think only requires boldness and decision in the carrying out."

"Then, it is as good as done," said Duval, "for I fancy you and I can back ourselves as possessing these qualities."

"Is the danger great?" asked Lucy.

"It is either all danger," said St. Ives, "or all safety. But you shall judge for yourselves."

St. Ives lowered his voice still more so, that although they heard him very well, he scarcely spoke above a clear, articulate whisper.

"I have already informed you, that I have been summoned before a meeting of the Privy Council, and have had to give a report of the capture of the young Princess."

"Yes—yes."

"At that Privy Council, it was determined, even while I was there, that there should be a meeting to-night in the old Star Chamber, adjoining the Speaker's House, in Palace Yard, at which she was to be brought up for examination."

"From the Tower?"

"Even so, and some of the lords of the council were pleased to congratulate me, and compliment me upon my success in effecting so important a capture. The warrant for bringing her up from the Tower was promised to be sent to me this morning."

"And you have it?"

"It is here."

"Then the Princess is saved."

"To all appearance, yes," sighed St. Ives; "but I must fly, likewise, with her, and if that could be avoided, it would be well, for I am heart and soul pledged to the cause I advocate, and would fain still preserve my reputation and position, as St. Ives, the skilful and trusted police agent."

Duval shook his head.

"I do not at the first glance," he said, "see how that is to be accomplished?"

"And yet, I have thought of a plan," said St. Ives. "It is that which I have hinted at, and which requires coolness and courage."

"What is it?" asked Duval, "we can at least discuss it."

"It is simply this. In order to bring the prisoner before the Privy Council at eleven o'clock, I must, in my own proper person, be at the Tower by ten."

"Granted."

"But is it not possible—knowing all these facts—another may reach the Tower by half past nine, or rather earlier, with a similar order, and release the prisoner."

"It can and shall be done!" cried Duval. "I catch your meaning now, and I say again, it can and shall be done!"

Lucy took up the order and read it.

"To our trusted and well-beloved Governor of the Tower.

"These shall empower you to surrender to the bearer, who is our accredited officer and messenger, the body of Elizabeth Stuart, so-called, for examination before us and our Privy Council.

"GEORGE REX."

"You will perceive," said St. Ives, "that the name of the messenger is not mentioned in this document."

"A most important and singular omission," said Claude.

"Not so—it is never the custom to name the messenger, and it is only at the last moment, sometimes, that the Clerk of the Council places such an order in the hands of the person who is to execute it."

"But in this case it has been given to you?"

"It has. And I may look upon the fact as a compliment to my trustworthiness."

"Be it how it may," said Duval, "it is a fortunate circumstance. You shall remain here, St. Ives, or meet me elsewhere, where you will, I will take this order, and release the Princess."

"No—no!" said St. Ives. "We must execute a skilful copy of it. I may be summoned, perhaps, as late as nine o'clock, to see some of the Lords of the Council, or perhaps the King himself, and if I have not the order in my possession, it will look suspicious."

"True—true!"

"And yet for all that whoever presents this order at the Tower for the release of the Princess, it must be the veritable one I now place my hand upon."

"You speak in riddles, Mr. St. Ives," said Lucy. "I do not understand you!"

"I shall be able to explain what I mean in a very few words. I am perfectly certain, although I am unable to discover it, that there is some secret sign somewhere upon this order, in some part of the writing, or interwoven in the paper, which the Governor of the Tower and the Lords of the Privy Council only, will know, and without which it will not be considered authentic; therefore whoever goes to the Tower must take this veritable order."

"But you spoke of a copy."

"I did—but that was for me."

"For you?"

"Yes—in case I am forced to show it to any of the Lords of the Council before ten o'clock, and if such a contingency should arise, the mere sight of it will be sufficient without precise examination, while at the Tower the scrutiny will be close and particular."

"He is right! He is right!" cried Lucy, "and has thought of everything. Let me make the copy, I feel assured I shall do it in a clerkly fashion, and that even more than a casual glance will not be sufficient to detect it as spurious."

Lucy set about her task, and soon produced a very creditable copy upon paper as nearly similar in colour as possible of the royal warrant.

"Thank heaven!" said Duval, "that there is now a fair chance of saving the Princess."

DUVAL RELEASES THE STUART PRINCESS FROM THE TOWER.

"There is, indeed," said St. Ives.

"I will adopt another disguise entirely, so that neither Sir John Cope nor Claude Duval shall be compromised in the affair."

"Yes," said St. Ives, gloomily.

He rested his head upon his hand.

"Come, St. Ives," said Duval, "cheer up. Do not take so sad a view of affairs. All will be well that ends well, and when the Princess is safe and at liberty we shall rejoice and smile over the adventures this night."

"I can scarcely bear it," said St. Ives. "It is too much —it is too bad, and you ought not to be put upon this task alone. I would give half my life to be able to accompany you, and yet I do not see how it is to be done."

"Think no more of it—think no more of it."

"I cannot help it, but it must be so, it would jeopardize all were I to attempt to go with you. But you may take your man."

"I would fain do so."

No. 26.—NIGHTSHADE.

"Dress him as a soldier of the King's German Legion, and then he need not speak a word of English."

"It shall be done."

"Heaven prosper you!'

"Where shall I bring the Princess?"

"I think here—here to this house, where it will be much safer to keep her concealed for a few days, after which she can get down to the coast and escape."

"It shall be done. And now make your mind easy, St. Ives. Take you the forged order, and I will possess myself of the real one."

This being determined, Duval, in order that there should be no unnecessary delays, set about procuring the disguises.

He attired himself in that same suit of black which he had worn on the occasion of so astonishing Mossy Pendell in the Oxford Mail.

There was some little difficulty in procuring a suit of regimentals for Blossom, but at last they were found at a masquerade warehouse in Covent Garden.

St. Ives had left Farnborough House, but he promised to return to it again at half-past nine, so that there would be just time for him to proceed to the Tower.

For the last few nights the moon had risen early, and the nights were fair.

There was no exception on this occasion; and it was fortunate that great secrecy and darkness were by no means elements in the success of the undertaking.

And all was ready by that half-hour after eight.

Duval looked quiet, gentlemanly, and determined.

He in every respect bore the air and manner of a man who was not to be trifled with, but who knew his duty, and would execute it.

Blossom's make up as the German soldier was capital.

And when Lucy looked at them both, many of her fears vanished, and she thought it impossible they should fail in their enterprise.

A Hackney coach was hired at some distance from the house.

In fact, they took it close to the King's Mews, at Charing Cross, so that there was nothing to identify them as coming from Farnborough House; and as a regiment of the King's German Legion was quartered at the mews, the coachman might very well believe Blossom had come out of there.

"Blossom," said Duval, as the coach lumbered along with them, "I hope you have looked carefully to your pistols."

"Trust me for that, Captain."

"We shall not require to use them; and in fact will not do so except in self-defence."

"If we are to be killed in the Tower, Captain, we will die game."

"Yes, yes; but do nothing hastily."

"Nothing at all, Captain, except under orders."

The coach went lumbering and wheezing along through the City.

But still, even at the slow pace it went, about half-an-hour was amply sufficient time to bring it to Tower Hill.

The coachman pulled up.

"Where shall I go exactly, sir?"

"To the small postern yonder, where you see the light."

"All's right. Am I to wait for yer honour?"

"Yes."

The coach in a few seconds more halted exactly at that little postern, through which now so many persons make their way, bent on expeditions of curiosity, to the White Tower.

"Who goes there?"

That was the challenge of the sentinel on duty.

"Government messenger," replied Duval.

"Pass on, Government messenger."

Duval, with Blossom following him, entered by the postern.

A Yeoman came out of the guard-room.

"What is it?"

"I want to see the Governor, or Chief Warder."

"An order, sir?"

"Yes, from the Privy Council, for the delivery of a prisoner."

"This way, sir. Is this man with you?"

"Certainly."

Blossom spoke not a word.

The Yeoman took a lantern from the wall, and in a very careless manner preceded Claude Duval and Blossom across a small court-yard, and then over a narrow bridge which spanned the moat.

Nothing escaped Duval and Blossom.

Never did two men take such extreme notice of the route they went as they did.

It was a kind of knowledge that might serve them in good stead; and if not, there was no real waste of time in acquiring it.

The Yeoman led them through the archway above, which is the darksome-looking building popularly called "The Bloody Tower."

He halted at a flight of steps, at the foot of which a sentinel was drowsily on duty.

"Follow me, sir, if you please," he said. "The soldier who is with you may wait here."

Blossom took care not to seem to understand a word that was uttered, and was about to ascend the steps after Duval.

The Yeoman, however, pushed him back, and pointed to the ground, to signify that there he was to stand.

Blossom understood nothing of German, but he made an outlandish kind of sound, which he thought might pass for it very well.

He waited, then, at the foot of the steps while Duval ascended with the Yeoman.

"Well, comrade," said the sentinel to Blossom, "how do you find duty at the old Mews?"

"Blitzen and jazzar!" replied Blossom.

The extraordinary sounds did duty for German, which fortunately the sentinel had not the least smattering of.

"What a shocking thing it is," he said, "for a fellow to be forced to speak in that way!"

"Blitzen, Blitzen," said Blossom again.

"Oh, hold your row!"

"Blitzen!"

"Be quiet, I say! What fools these foreigners must be; and what a trouble it must be to them to learn such horrid jargon, when it's as easy as opening your mouth to speak plain English."

"Blitzen!"

"Bah! bo! Hold your noise!"

"Blitz——"

"There, that'll do."

The sentinel shouldered his musket, and commenced marching to and fro at a great rate.

Blossom considered that he had managed matters well, since it was quite impossible he could have any conversation with the sentinel in the Tower without some mischief accruing from it.

Duval felt not the slightest anxiety in regard to the proceedings of Blossom.

He could fully rely upon his courage.

And what was fully as important, he could fully rely upon his discretion.

He followed the Yeoman up the stone steps—he reached what were called the lodgings of the Deputy-Governor of the Tower.

All officials of the Tower, high or low, occupy what are called lodgings.

It is an ancient word, in use there ever since different suites of apartment were devoted to the use of special persons.

In a few moments Duval was introduced into a small octagonal apartment, very amply furnished, although somewhat antique in its general appearance.

He was left alone for about a minute, and then an elderly man came to him through a doorway opposite to that at which he had entered.

Duval stepped forward.

"I have an order, sir," he said, "for the delivery of a prisoner who is to undergo an examination before the Privy Council."

"Certainly—certainly!"

Duval held out the order.

The Deputy Governor made a slight bow, and then disappeared with it through the doorway he had come in by.

Duval felt certain he had gone to give it that accurate examination which had been spoken of by St. Ives

Probably that examination was of a character so secret, that the Deputy-Governor would not even let the messenger of the Privy Council notice how it was conducted.

And Duval felt perfectly certain at that moment that if he had adventured upon this expedition with a forged order of release, the consequences might have been fatal to him.

The forethought of St. Ives, in letting him have the original one, however, had scattered that danger.

Duval felt perfectly at his ease.

The Deputy-Governor was absent nearly five minutes.

He returned, bearing a folio volume, having the appearance of an account-book.

"You will be so good, sir, as to sign a receipt here."

"Certainly."

There was not the slightest tremor about Duval as he laid his hand upon the book.

The receipt was already written, and only wanted the signature to be appended to it.

It was very simple, running in the following words:—

"Received of the Deputy-Governor of his Majesty's Tower of London the body of Elizabeth Stuart."

Duval hesitated a moment as to what name he should append to it, but he did not let that hesitation appear sufficiently long to raise any doubts in the mind of the Deputy-Governor.

He signed the name, John Smith.

The Deputy-Governor smiled slightly.

"Not a very uncommon name yours, sir," he said.

"No, indeed!" replied Duval.

The order of release lay upon the account-book, and Duval quietly took it up, and put it in his pocket.

"I am not quite sure," said the Deputy-Governor; "but you ought to leave that with me."

"Well, that's my opinion," said Duval.

"Then, perhaps——"

"But I was cautioned by the Clerk of the Council not to do so."

"Indeed!"

"Yes; upon the possibility of its getting astray, and being used by some impostor for wrong purposes. At all events, my receipt to you will be quite sufficient."

"Doubtless; and there is the order to the chief warder to deliver to you the prisoner. How do you mean to take her?"

"I have a coach at the postern."

"Oh, certainly!"

"And I shall proceed direct to Palace Yard, for the Lords of the Council are going to sit in the old Star Chamber."

"It's a serious affair, then?"

"I'm afraid it is."

"She is quite a young girl."

Duval was on the point of saying "Quite;" but he checked himself, for it might not be desirable that he should seem to know anything whatever of the Stuart Princess.

"Is she?" he asked.

"Yes, quite."

The Deputy-Governor evidently hesitated.

He still held the order to the chief warder between his finger and thumb.

Then, lowering his voice, he spoke again.

"There's something, Mr. Smith, dreadful in the idea of so young a creature coming to so terrible a death as seems to be looming before her in the future."

"There is."

The deputy-governor sighed.

He handed Duval the order, and then those two men looked at each other for a few seconds in silence.

The idea was gathering strongly about the heart of Claude Duval that if he were to say to the deputy-governor, "That young girl shall escape to-night!" the answer would be an ejaculation of thankfulness.

But the experiment was too hazardous.

And, beside, what good would it do?

Duval merely bowed and took the order.

And during all the time of this little conference the Yeoman had stood outside the door like a sentinel.

"Yeoman!" cried the deputy-governor.

"Here, your honour!"

"Conduct this gentleman to the lodgings of the chief warder."

"Yes, your honour. This way, if you please, sir."

Duval followed the Yeoman.

"Blitzen!" said Blossom, as he followed Duval.

"Go to the deuce!" said the sentinel at the foot of the stone staircase.

The lodgings of the chief warder were not far distant, and there Duval was requested to wait until the prisoner was brought to him.

CHAPTER LXXX.

CLAUDE DUVAL BEARS THE STUART PRINCESS FROM THE TOWER.

IT was a feverish thing that waiting.

Each minute seemed an hour, and, although, certainly, not more than ten of them passed away, Duval began to have a thousand wild and vague conjectures as to what was happening.

At length he heard footsteps.

A door was shut sharply.

"She comes!" he whispered to himself.

Another moment and the young Stuart Princess was introduced into the small stone chamber where Duval was waiting.

"The prisoner!" announced the chief warder.

Several Yeomen of the Guard were in attendance, and by the light of the lanterns they carried it was easy for the young Princess to see who had come to take her from the Tower.

Her air and manner had been perfectly listless when she was first brought into the room.

It was an imprudent thing to do, but the moment she saw Duval she uttered an exclamation.

It was not so marked or so loud as to attract much attention, but Duval checked any further exhibition of emotion by saying, in a cold tone, "This lady is now in my custody. I have no time to spare."

"This way, sir."

Duval laid his hand lightly upon the arm of the Princess.

There had been no possible means of communicating with her, but now her active intellect and suggestive imagination supplied all that was wanted.

She felt certain that this was an attempt to rescue her.

She felt, too, an almost perfect confidence in its success.

And so, in a kind of procession, headed by a couple of Yeomen of the Guard with lanterns, they proceeded to the postern.

Duval walked next to the Yeomen with his supposed prisoner.

The chief warder and another Yeoman, who carried one of those ancient, complicated pole axes, now obsolete, but specimens of which may still be seen in the Tower, brought up the rear.

It took about three minutes to cross the drawbridge of the moat, to traverse the small courtyard—anciently called the Lion Court, because it was in a kind of pit close to it that the royal wild beasts used to be kept.

Then the postern was gained.

The watch-word was given.

The sentinel stood at "attention."

"The prisoner returns to-night?" asked the chief warder.

"Yes," replied Duval, "but I should think not until late, for the Privy Council does not sit till eleven."

"Ah, so we heard."

The postern was closed.

Duval, the Princess, and Blossom stood in what looked like perfect freedom on Tower Hill.

And there was the coach.

But the coachman had gone fast asleep, so Blossom opened the coach door, and Duval assisted in the Princess.

"On the box with him!" whispered Duval to Blossom, as he himself stepped into the coach.

"Yes, Captain."

Blossom was on the coach box in a moment, and seizing the coachman by the collar he uttered a frightful yell in his ears.

"Murder!" cried the suddenly-awakened coachman,—"murder!"

The sentinel at the Tower postern stopped short in his walk to and fro, and looked curious.

"Blitzen!" said Blossom.

"To the Palace-yard, Westminster," cried Duval, from the coach window.

The coach rumbled off, proceeding at a slow lumbering pace along Thames Street.

Then and not till then did Claude Duval venture to speak to the Princess.

"You know me, Princess?"

"I do, and I feel I am saved."

"I hope so, even to the extent of believing so with all my heart."

Nearly a week's incarceration in that gloomy fortress, had no doubt affected somewhat the spirits and the self-control of the courageous girl.

She did not reply to Duval's last words, but she clasped one of his hands in both her own, and he heard her sob aloud.

"Courage," he said, "all will yet be well. This plan of escape has been projected entirely by St. Ives, or rather Colonel Miravel, as I ought to call him to you."

"But you are here?"

"I am but carrying out his instructions."

"And you have encountered all the danger, all the fearful peril of detention in the Tower."

"I don't think there was much danger unless I had betrayed myself, and at all events, be it much or be it little, I was quite content to brave it."

"Oh, why are you not with us? In our cause I mean. One hundred such brave hearts as your's, and I think the Stuarts would again set upon the throne of England."

"No," said Duval, "that is a dream."

"Alas! that you should think so!"

"And it will be worse than a dream if the means suggested by those men, who were a sort of council to you at the mansion in the Oxford Road, were attempted to be carried out."

"Is there anything very wrong in those means?"

"Is murder—assassination—poisoning—right?"

"What mean you? I know of no such practices."

"And yet those were the means suggested."

"I know nothing of them, and repudiate them utterly?"

"I guessed as much, but will tell you more of this when we reach Farnborough House, where Mr. St. Ives thinks it will be better for you to remain some days, until active pursuit is over."

"I will be governed entirely by you and by him."

"It will not be desirable, however, for this coach to make its way to Pall Mall!"

"No. No, certainly not."

"Do you think you can venture to make your way alone to Farnborough House, if we all separate in the streets?"

"Certainly, I can."

The coach pulled up with a jerk.

It was at the corner of Palace Yard, Westminster, and Blossom had taken good care that the stoppage had taken place at a very dark spot.

"We will alight here," said Duval, "and walk some distance together, then we will separate, and individually make our way to Farnborough House."

The coach was left, and hanging upon the arm of Duval, the Princess made her way with him along Parliament Street.

At Charing Cross they all came to a standstill.

Duval meant to keep the Princess well in sight, although he wished her to go alone to Farnborough House.

And Blossom, in his uniform still as a soldier of the German Legion, marched a considerable distance ahead, the object of which was that the Princess, who was quite a stranger in London, might not take the wrong turning and miss her way.

It would be easy to keep him in sight when he fully intended she should do so.

In this manner, they all proceeded to Farnborough House.

Blossom walked past it.

The Princess gave a single knock at its door.

For more than a hour, St. Ives had been waiting in the hall.

He opened the door instantly.

"Miravel!"

"Your Royal Highness!"

Another moment and Lucy appeared.

"Thank heaven, all is well!"

"I am saved," said the Princess, "and all is indeed well. Let my presence here be an assurance of the safety of another dearer to you naturally than the escape of a thousand prisoners."

"Hush!" said St. Ives. "I hear a footstep——"

It was Duval.

Then the outer door of Farnborough House was closed and bolted.

But Lucy asked for Blossom.

"He will go and change his clothing," said Duval, "at Nightshade's stable."

St. Ives then seized his hat.

"It is a quarter past ten," he said. "Give me the order of release, Duval. I must go and present it at the Tower and mystify the Deputy-Governor, who will tell me that the prisoner has already left in custody of a previous messenger."

"It is here!"

"I have not a moment to lose. Farewell to all. In two days I will call here. It will not be prudent to do so earlier, but should I be aware of any danger of course I will give you notice, till then. Farewell!"

St. Ives hastily left Farnborough House, and while the Princess went to the upper part of it with Lucy, Duval fell down in the breakfast-room, and felt a sensation of great thankfulness and rest come over him after the excitement of the last few hours.

In the meantime, Lucy proceeded upstairs with her interesting companion, who, no sooner found herself alone with her hostess, then she cast herself into her arms, and gave vent to the many contending emotions with which she had been struggling during the space of time which had intervened between her leaving her gloomy prison and that moment when she felt herself pressed in the affectionate embrace of her kind and disinterested friend.

"Weep not so. Oh, weep not so," said Lucy, greatly distressed. "You are safe now."

"Yes, yes. I am saved; and saved by the exertions

of your brave husband. Oh, would that he could be persuaded to join our cause."

Lucy shook her head.

"Be content," she said, "in having enlisted us among your warmest friends and best wishers; and may be we can serve you even better as we are, than as if we really professed ourselves to be Jacobites."

"I cannot think it; and then, again, you refuse all —I will not say reward—but you refuse that which you would have a right to, were you Jacobites, viz., a choice of titles and emoluments."

"Heed not that, we care not for such things. But now let me assist you to prepare for rest," added Lucy, willing to change the conversation, which was becoming embarrassing.

In a short time, Lucy had the satisfaction of beholding her guest fall into a gentle and refreshing slumber, such as, probably, she had not enjoyed for many weary weeks.

When all was still, Lucy gently left the room and sought Duval, whom she found awaiting her rather impatiently in the breakfast room.

As soon as she entered, she cast herself into his arms, as she said, "Thank heaven my beloved husband has done a good, a great, and noble thing, and without himself encountering any evil fortune."

Duval returned her caresses, as he said, "I felt all along, my Lucy, that it was the right thing to do; and with that conviction came, I may say, almost the certainty that all would be well. How is the Princess, dearest?"

"Calmer, and when I left her, she had fallen into a peaceful slumber, which I hope will last for some hours."

"Heaven grant it may!" ejaculated Duval, "for the excitement and danger she has gone through the last few weeks, has been sufficient to make fearful inroads upon a constitution apparently so unfitted for the great struggle she has had to contend with."

"But what a brave and courageous heart that fair young girl possesses," said Lucy, with enthusiasm.

"And I know of another not less brave," said Duval, fondly stroking her fair hair, "for did not my Lucy still the promptings of her own heart, which would have bade me not to meddle in this affair, and tell me to go, and look even as bravely as her words sounded."

Lucy nestled still closer to Duval, and a bright flush of gratified affection mantled to her cheek, as she listened to her husband's praises.

* * * * *

And St. Ives?

What of him?

That brave and generous man went on his way to the Tower.

His mind a whirl of confusing emotions, joy at the thought that that fair young creature, who had all his sympathies, both as a princess, as well as a fragile and gentle girl to be protected.

Admiration for that brave noble heart, who, at the same time that he refused everything in the shape of reward, still had perilled his very life to save that Princess of the House of Stuart.

And gratitude to Lucy, who had held out the hand of friendship to that forsaken and forlorn one, despite all that her heart whispered to the contrary.

At length the Tower was reached.

St. Ives was known to the sentinel, and also to the yeomen of the guard.

"The Deputy-Governor!" said St. Ives, in an authoritative voice.

"Yes, your honour, this way."

And St. Ives traversed the drawbridge, crossed the courtyard, and ascended the same stone steps which had been so recently trodden by Duval.

The yeoman of the guard opened the door of the little stone room, into which Duval had been conducted to await the presence of the Deputy-Governor.

He had not long to wait, the same elderly, benevolent-looking man soon entered the room by the opposite door, as he had done only a short time previously.

He looked inquiringly at St. Ives.

"I did not expect a visit from you at so late an hour. Nevertheless, St. Ives, you know you are always welcome."

"Thanks, my friend," said St. Ives, carelessly; "but to-night I cannot say that my visit is exactly, or rather I should say exclusively, one of friendship."

"Ah! What, then, has brought you here?"

St. Ives drew the warrant from his pocket, and placed it in the hand of the Deputy-Governor.

"What! another prisoner required?" he said, as he merely cast his eyes upon the document, and recognised in it only a warrant for the release of some prisoner.

"I know nothing about another prisoner; but this one it is necessary there should be as little delay as possible in transferring to my custody, as the Lords of the Privy Council——"

"Stop! stop!" gasped the Deputy-Governor. "Do my eyes deceive me?"

As he spoke the Deputy-Governor looked attentively at the warrant.

"Oh, you see it is all correct," said St. Ives, calmly. "Will you kindly give orders to the chief warder to place in my hands the person of Elizabeth Stuart as soon as may be."

The Deputy-Governor had sunk upon a chair.

His face was pale.

His hands trembled like a man in an ague.

"Why, what is the matter?" asked St. Ives. "Are you ill? Shall I call any one?"

The Deputy-Governor tried to speak, but words failed him, and he could only stare at St. Ives.

"Speak!" added St. Ives. "I cannot waste more time. The Council meets at eleven o'clock to-night, and it is time that we had started. Tell me what means this strange behaviour?"

At length the Deputy-Governor spoke, but it was in a hoarse whisper.

"Mr. St. Ives—I have already released the Princess once to-night. She is gone!"

CHAPTER LXXXI.

CLAUDE DUVAL AND MR. ST. IVES PAY A VISIT TO HARCOURT HOUSE.

THERE is what might be called a panic in the Privy Council of King George the Second at the extraordinary escape of the young Princess of the Stuarts from the Tower of London.

The whole affair was involved in the profoundest mystery.

Not the slightest clue to her whereabouts could be obtained, although a large reward was offered for her apprehension.

It was only privately, however, that this reward was offered.

It was sufficient, however, to hound on all the police spies and officials of the metropolis to the attempted re-capture of the Princess.

The Government was in too great a fright, in consequence of the pertinacity of the Jacobite plots, to publish the fact that a Princess of the deposed royal House was actually in the country.

The miserable newspapers of the period dared not publish anything that the authorities disapproved of.

The consequence of all this was, that although an active private search took place for the young Princess, that extensive publicity, which at present forms the element of all judicial proceedings, was entirely wanting.

At first there was some suspicion as regarded Mr. St. Ives.

But that speedily vanished.

The tale he had to tell was so simple.

The statement he made was so entirely straightforward that nothing could be made of it to his prejudice.

The most puzzling feature, however, of the whole transaction to the authorities was, that the Deputy-Governor of the Tower distinctly swore that the warrant upon which he released the prisoner was in perfect form, while at the same meeting of the Privy Council Mr. St. Ives produced that identical warrant.

And so the matter rested.

It was still thought prudent by St. Ives and Claude Duval that the first eagerness of pursuit and inquiry should be allowed to pass away before the Princess made an attempt to leave the country.

She was secure at Farnborough House.

She seemed almost happy there.

And it is to one of the drawing-rooms of that mansion that we now conduct the reader on the third night after the escape of the Princess from the Tower.

The persons in the drawing-room were Claude Duval, Lucy, St. Ives, and a young man with a very handsome curled dark wig, dressed in a plain brown suit of clothes.

This was the Princess.

It had been thought desirable that she should assume the male disguise, because St. Ives was perfectly well aware, from his intercourse with the police authorities, that their thoughts were bent upon finding her in a feminine costume.

The discourse that was taking place fell upon those extraordinary papers and letters which had been taken from Mossy Pendell in the Oxford Mail.

Claude Duval was speaking.

"St. Ives," he said, "I made a sort of voluntary promise to the King—pledging myself that I would justify his pardon to Lucy by bringing to him proofs of her innocence."

"I should be right glad to assist."

"It is not enough that an innocent person should be pardoned, for that very pardon implies a notion of guilt."

"I have thought over this thing deeply," said St. Ives, "and I have a course to suggest."

"Thank heaven!"

"It is simply this. You have frequently told me that General Everton lies entombed in a vault beneath the pavement of St. Paul's."

"Yes," said Lucy. "It is the old vault of the Evertons."

"He lies there, then, or he does not; and if not, such a fact will afford the most presumptive evidence we can possibly get of his continual existence."

Lucy shuddered.

She guessed what was going to be the advice of St. Ives.

She felt that that advice was good; but at the same time she could not but shudder at the terrible ordeal through which she might have to pass in carrying it out.

Duval inclined his head.

"I comprehend," he said.

"Yes," said St. Ives, "we must be prepared, in the first instance, with a clear and distinct statement on oath that the remains of General Everton do not, as is supposed, repose in the vault beneath the pavement of St. Paul's."

"That will surely not be difficult," said Duval.

He glanced at Lucy as he spoke.

She turned pale.

Pale at the thought of looking at those well-known features in death which had ever been turned with such kindly consideration on her in life.

"It is quite necessary," said St. Ives, "that some one who knew the General well should be present on the occasion to identify or repudiate the corpse."

Duval was silent.

"But that one," added Mr. St. Ives, "must be nobody personally interested in the result."

What a relief this was to Lucy!

"There must be no taint upon the evidence," added St. Ives. "And now tell me, Sir John Cope, do you know of any such one?"

St. Ives almost always in Farnborough House called Duval Sir John Cope.

"No."

"Do you?"

St. Ives asked the question of Lucy.

"None," she replied, "but those who are equally interested in deposing to his identity."

"Stop," cried Duval, "I have a thought. You are acquainted, Mr. St. Ives, with the young Marquis of Harcourt?"

"I am," said St. Ives, "so far as my position warrants."

"I heard him say, then, accidentally, that his father had been on intimate terms with General Everton; and that he, the young Marquis, has frequently seen the General at Harcourt House."

"It is quite impossible you could have a better witness."

"How, then, is he to be spoken to on the subject?"

St Ives considered for a few moments, and then he said, without the slightest hesitation in his tones, "Quite freely. He must be told everything."

"And implicitly trusted?" said Duval.

"Most implicitly."

"That is precisely my own thought. What say you, Lucy?"

"I hear, and receive all this with thankfulness and joy."

Harcourt House was one of those old, red-bricked mansions at Kensington, so few of which remain surviving the rage for metropolitan improvements.

The young Marquis kept a large establishment, and resided in that old-fashioned house of his father's in preference to having scanty lodgings in St. James's.

It was towards the dusk of the evening that Claude Duval, still wearing most accurately his disguise as Sir John Cope, and accompanied by Mr. St Ives, reached Harcourt House.

Duval, since his residence at Farnborough House, in Pall Mall, had set up a rather handsome chariot and pair of horses, all of which he hired at a neighbouring livery-stables.

It was in this coach, then, that the visit was made to Harcourt House.

The young Marquis was at home, and they were ushered at once into the library of the old mansion.

The walls were covered with books, and the place had a learned and scholastic air.

There was a quiet serenity about the house very different from the noise and racket which characterized in general the residences of the young nobility of that period.

The young Marquis entered the library by a door the back of which was covered with books.

It seemed for a moment as if a portion of the library was bodily walking into the apartments as that door opened.

"Marquis," said St. Ives, "this is Sir John Cope."

The Marquis bowed.

"Yes," replied Duval, "I am Sir John Cope to all the world, with the exception of a few persons in it whom I know to be so loyal-hearted and so true that I can trust them with my life."

The Marquis looked surprised.

And so did St. Ives, to some degree.

He had scarcely understood that Duval meant to inform the Marquis who he really was.

"To those persons," added Duval, "whom I have excepted from the rest of the world, my name is Claude Duval!"

"Duval!"

"Yes, my Lord Harcourt, you may have heard it." Duval smiled as he spoke.

"The disguise is perfect!" cried the young Marquis. "And knowing you, Duval, even as I do, I never could have suspected you to be one and the same person with Sir John Cope."

"Nevertheless, it is true, and you know me now by my voice."

"Oh, perfectly!"

"I come to you, my lord, to ask a great favour."

"Pray be seated, and tell me what it is; but in the first place, permit me to express one surprise."

"A surprise, my lord?"

"Just so. You trust me with this perilous secret of your identity, and you do not even ask me not to betray you."

"I would not insult your lordship by such a request, since I know it is impossible for you so to do."

"You are right, Duval; and your secret is as safe with me as though it reposed in your own breast solely."

There was a few moments' silence, and then Duval said, "You knew well the late General Everton?"

"The old General who died at Camden House, under such suspicious circumstances?"

"Perhaps."

"What do you mean by perhaps, Duval?"

"Because——"

"One moment," interrupted Mr. St. Ives. "Allow me to suggest, my Lord Harcourt, that you call Duval Sir John Cope."

"I will, although we are within secure walls."

"But the old proverb says 'walls have ears.'"

"True, St. Ives—true! I will be very cautious."

"Then, my lord," added Duval, "let me tell you that, whereas the question for some time past has been, how General Everton came by his death, it is now a very different one—viz., has he come by his death at all?"

"Indeed!"

"Yes, we have serious doubts upon the subject, and, in five minutes I shall be able to impart those doubts to your mind in the same shape and aspect that they have to ours."

Duval then rapidly detailed to the Marquis of Harcourt the strange discoveries that had been made in Mossy Pendell's valise.

"And now, my lord," he said, "what we want to do is simply this. We wish to be satisfied of the fact that General Everton does not lie in the family vault of the Evertons, beneath St. Paul's."

"And you want me to identify him or otherwise?"

"That is it."

"I will assist you with pleasure. Moreover, I think I can do so effectually. A member of the younger branch of our family, is Dean of St. Paul's."

"That smooths many difficulties," cried St. Ives; "and the investigation can be conducted with secrecy and despatch."

"When would you like this inquiry to take place?" asked the Marquis.

"As soon as possible."

"This night?"

"Most certainly."

"Let it be midnight," said St. Ives; "and we shall be free from all possibility of interruption."

"You will not object," asked the Marquis, "to my bringing another witness with me?"

"Most certainly not."

The Marquis touched a bell in the library.

"You must know that my father, the late Marquis," he said, "went through two campaigns in the Low Countries with General Everton; and I have in my service here, as gate-porter, an old sergeant of foot, named Belasis, who was perfectly intimate, not only with my father, but with General Everton. He is a man of indomitable courage, and no nerves or sensibilities of any kind or description."

"He is just the man for the purpose," said St. Ives.

The door of the library was opened, and a servant appeared.

"Send Sergeant Belasis here," said the Marquis.

"Yes, my lord."

In a few seconds, a steady, marching footstep was heard approaching.

The door was opened again, and a tall, wiry-looking veteran, with iron-grey hair, marched into the library.

"Sergeant!" commenced Lord Harcourt.

But the Sergeant marched on.

"Sergeant, I say!"

The Sergeant gained the other end of the room, and would have marched still further on but for the wall and the books.

"Your honoured father," said the Sergeant, "used to cry halt!"

The Marquis laughed.

"Halt!" he cried.

The Sergeant stopped instantly.

"Right face!"

The Sergeant faced about.

The Sergeant marched on in the new direction.

"Halt!"

The Sergeant came to a standstill, and saluted the Marquis.

"Sergeant Belasis."

"Your honour."

"Do you recollect General Everton?"

"Lieutenant-General Everton? Certainly, your honour."

"Should you know him again alive?"

"Yes."

"Or dead?"

"Yes."

"Would you have any objection, Sergeant, to go into a vault beneath St. Paul's, and look in his coffin?"

"None."

"The object is to discover if he be really the person there buried or not."

"No objection. Nothing to do with objects. Obey orders."

"Very well. We shall want you at eleven o'clock."

"Yes, your honour."

"Left face! March! Right face! March!"

By this means, the Sergeant was got out of the library again in due military order.

"What an original!" said Duval.

"He is, indeed!" replied the Marquis. "You may do anything with him; but he is a perfect machine, and it must be done in military fashion, or not at all. We will meet, then, at St. Paul's, at half-past eleven, and my relative the Dean shall either be there himself, or shall have given the necessary directions to facilitate all our inquiries and operations."

Duval was exceedingly well pleased with his visit to Harcourt House, and took care to leave home in good time to keep his appointment at St. Paul's.

He did not think it necessary to take Blossom with him, but rather felt a sense of security in leaving that faithful follower at home, in case any unforeseen danger should occur in regard to the young Stuart Princess.

A drifting rain was careering through St. Paul's Churchyard; and Duval, as he stood beneath the doorway of one of the Chapter Houses, waited anxiously for the approach of his friends.

CHAPTER LXXXII.

THE SEARCH IN THE VAULT AT ST. PAUL'S.

TRAMP! tramp! tramp! he heard a footstep approaching.

"Halt!" said a voice.

The voice was that of the young Marquis of Harcourt.

Duval then knew that that young nobleman had arrived accompanied by the Sergeant with the indomitable courage and no nerves.

Duval then emerged from the doorway.

"Marquis," he said.

"Ah, Sir John Cope, you are here. We have a squally night. Follow us, Sergeant!"

"Yes, your honour!"

The Marquis of Harcourt must have procured a key to one of the small iron gates of the enclosure of the Cathedral, for he opened it with ease, and then locked it again carefully behind him.

They crossed the courtyard in silence, and ascended the steps of the stately edifice.

The Marquis rapped with his fingers upon the small door in the panel of the real massive one of the building.

It was opened instantly.

Another moment and they had stepped beneath the roof of St. Paul's.

"You are punctual," said St. Ives, for it was he who had opened the wicket door.

"Hush!" said Duval.

They were all silent.

And amid that silence they heard a strange, scuffling kind of noise, as if rapid but light footsteps were traversing one of the aisles of the Cathedral.

"What can that be?" asked the Marquis.

"I know not," said St. Ives; "but it is a strange sound."

"Sergeant!"

"Yes, your honour!"

"Unmask your lantern."

The Sergeant flung back the slide of a dark lantern, and a broad glare of light, radiating to an immense extent, came from its lens.

The Marquis took the lantern, and moved it to and fro, so that the light should fall in various directions.

But nothing was to be seen, save the ancient tombs, with the cold stone monuments, and the noble architecture of the building.

"It was fancy," said the Marquis.

St. Ives shook his head.

"It was real enough," he said; "and yet may be something harmless enough."

"Such vast buildings as this," said Duval, "are full of strange noises and echoes. It is impossible to say through what wild noises may come, and then what echoes they may evoke beneath this wondrous roof."

"This way!" said St. Ives. "I will conduct you to the Dean's parlour, where he is waiting."

"That is well!" said the Marquis. "I am glad the Dean is here! Forward, Sergeant!"

St. Ives preceded the rest of the party, and the Sergeant brought up the rear.

The Dean's parlour, as it was called, in St. Paul's Cathedral, was a small, richly wainscoted room in which the superior clergy were wont to take refreshment during the long services which used to take place in the Cathedral.

The Dean was one of those mild spoken, timid men, who seemed to think it necessary to be always making some excuse for everything he did.

He received the party with evident anxiety.

"I cannot imagine—I cannot think," he said, as he rubbed one hand over the other nervously, "that I am doing wrong in any way in aiding and assisting in this matter."

"You are acting, reverend sir," said Duval, "in the sacred cause of justice."

"Yes, yes, exactly; and that I consider is my excuse."

"Certainly, if any were wanted," said the Marquis.

"Exactly, as you say, Marquis, if any were wanted; where can Richards be? Bless me, I don't see Richards! Oh, yes! he is here!"

The Dean had walked to the door of the little parlour in search of the man he called Richards, and who was one of the under sextons of the Cathedral.

In doing so, the Dean encountered Sergeant Belasis, who was standing bolt upright exactly outside the door of the parlour as though he were on duty at some military out-post.

"Dear me! who are you?"

"Belasis—Sergeant! Forty-fourth regiment!"

"He comes with me," interposed the Marquis of Harcourt, "and will be able to identify or otherwise the body."

"Oh, to be sure! Certainly—certainly, a most remarkable-looking man! Now, Richards, if you please, we will proceed, and as I say, gentlemen all, I feel myself perfectly excused for the part I am taking in this transaction, by the a—the a——"

"Forward, Sergeant!" said the Marquis.

"Bless me! what an extraordinary man!" said the Dean, "he has trodden upon my toes twice, and don't seem to know where he is going!"

"You must cry halt! if you want him to stop," said the Marquis.

"I will—I will. Here he comes again! Woa! no, I mean halt! He won't stop, my lord, he won't stop!"

"Not proper officer," said the Sergeant.

"Halt!" cried the Marquis.

The Sergeant stopped at once, and the Dean took the opportunity of getting entirely out of his line of march.

"Now, Richards," said the Dean, "you have the keys of the vault."

"Yes, your reverence," said Richards.

"Ah!" said the Sergeant. "Thought as much. Chaplain of the forces! Te deum, and all that sort of thing!"

The little party had to take a very circuitous route round the Cathedral to get to the entrance of the vault.

It was a low arched door in one of the aisles, and was opened with difficulty.

The Sergeant was a little in the rear of the party, and as the Marquis omitted to cry halt! and his line of march brought him right up to the door of the vault, the moment it was opened by Richards, the sexton, he continued that march down the stone steps, carrying the lantern with him, and disappeared at once before the astonished eyes of the Dean.

"A most extraordinary man! He's gone right down into the vault!"

"He thinks no more of a vault, your reverence," said Richards, "than I do of a public—hum! I mean a private house."

The whole party was left in darkness, since the Sergeant had carried the only lantern with him.

DUVAL AND HIS PARTY IN GENERAL EVERTON'S VAULT.

"Halt!" cried the Marquis of Harcourt.

The voice sounded dismal and hollow amid the silence of the Cathedral.

"Right about face. March!"

The Marquis judged rightly enough, that this would bring the Sergeant up again.

In a few seconds it had that effect.

Then he was ordered to halt again, or he would have marched right though the Cathedral and out of one of its windows if possible.

He was brought to a standstill, however, and then the man Richards took the lantern and preceded the party down into the vault.

The Sergeant had been ordered to follow last.

"Yes, your honour. Bring up the rear guard and look for stragglers."

"Exactly!"

Upon this, the Sergeant kept a sharp eye upon the Dean, who from his hesitating manner, he suspected of contemplating running away.

The stone stairs were sixteen in number, and Claude

No. 27.—NIGHTSHADE.

Duval, who followed immediately upon the footsteps of Richards, the under sexton, found that the stone floor of the vault was covered with a deep mass of sawdust.

The lantern was hung upon a hook in the wall, so that it shed a tolerable light upon the circumscribed area of the vault.

There were various coffins there, more or less dim, dusky, and decayed.

But that which was said to contain the mortal remains of the late General Everton presented a striking contrast to the others.

"I presume it is many years," said Duval, "since any of the Everton family were placed here with the exception of the late General."

"By the registry of the Cathedral, sir," replied Richards, "it was a matter of forty years since the vault was opened till this coffin was placed in it."

"Let us proceed," said Duval.

He felt well pleased at that moment that Lucy was excused from any participation in the gloomy duty that had devolved upon him and the others there present.

The under sexton had brought a few tools with him, which were quite sufficient to take off the lid of the coffin.

"I feel quite sure," said the Dean, "that we shall be excused for what we are doing."

"Upon that point we are all agreed," said the Marquis.

"But still," urged the Dean, "an appropriate prayer, don't you think——"

"I scarcely think so," replied the Marquis; "this is a purely mundane affair that we are about, and refers merely to the course of human justice."

"Precisely," said Duval, "and the sooner we get out of this place the better, for the air is noisome."

"Bad as a French prison," said the Sergeant.

Richards set to work.

The lid of the coffin was removed.

"It is only necessary that we see the face of the corpse," said the Marquis. "Hold the lantern close down, Sergeant!"

"Yes, you honour."

The Sergeant did so.

One glance was enough for the young Marquis.

"I solemnly declare," he said, "and call upon all here to witness that this is not the corpse of General Everton."

"That is important testimony," said the Dean, "and we shall all be able to aver it."

"Now, Sergeant Belasis!"

"Yes, your honour."

"Look on the face of the dead!"

"I see him, your honour."

"Is this the corpse of General Everton?"

"No."

"You are ready to swear to that?"

"Well, your honour, I've rather left off swearing since we came from Flanders, but have no objection to begin again, so here goes! May I be——"

"Stop him! stop him!" cried the Dean. "Woa! stop! halt! What is he going to say? A most extraordinary man, we don't want any swearing!"

The Sergeant paused.

He glanced at the Marquis.

"Did your honour wish me to swear?"

"Not in the sense you mean, Sergeant."

"What sense, your honour?"

"I meant that you would take your oath."

"Two dozen, your honour, in as many minutes, and each one like the discharge of a culverin. May I be——"

"Stop! stop! he's beginning again!" cried the Dean. "Woa! pull up! Hi! hi! Dear me! I always forget, what is proper to say to him. Halt! that's it! Halt! halt!"

"I think, then, we may leave this vault," said Duval.

"We have done all we can," added the Marquis, "and the important piece of evidence is gained, that General Everton is not buried here."

"It is, indeed, important?" remarked Duval, "although it is but negative evidence of his continued existence."

"But who can this be?" asked the Dean.

"Whoever it is," replied Duval, "there can be no right to the interment of this strange corpse in the vault of the Everton's."

"It is an intrusion, indeed," said the Marquis; "for although in death we are all equal, yet we have a right to our last resting-places, and that they should be kept sacred."

"All right, your honour," said the Sergeant. "Haul him out in a moment."

"Stop him!" cried the Dean. "What is he about now? The corpse can be removed with decency at some better and more fitting period."

"Let us leave this place, then," said the Marquis. "Sergeant, you will precede us with the light."

"Advance guard!" said the Sergeant. "Right shoulder forward! March!"

The Sergeant made his way up the stone steps.

He had ascended eight of them, and the little party was closely following him, when a loud clanging sound echoed through the Cathedral.

The Sergeant came to a dead standstill.

"Enemy in force," he said. "Lines of communication closed."

He faced about so suddenly that he nearly knocked down the Dean, who exclaimed:—

"Gracious heaven! some one has closed the door of the vault!"

"No!" cried Duval, as he placed his hand upon his sword.

As Claude spoke he rushed past the Sergeant, and reached the top of the steps.

The iron door of the vault was certainly closed.

Duval shook it, but it resisted his efforts to open it.

"What is this?" he cried. "Open! Open!"

A muffled voice sounded from the other side.

"A trap!" it cried.

"A what?"

"A trap to catch foxes!"

There was a long perpendicular gleam of light which came from the Cathedral through a crevice left at the hinges of the door, where it seemed never to have well fitted the stonework of the aisle.

The sword that Duval wore was a very slender one.

Instantly drawing it from its sheath, he made the experiment of whether it could pass through that narrow slit.

It did, nearly up to the hilt.

There was a sharp cry of pain, which sufficiently testified to the fact that the experiment was satisfactory.

"The enemy discomfited," said the Sergeant; "try them again, sir."

No doubt one of the enemy was discomfited, but both that one and any others who were in the Cathedral took good care to keep free of the sword blade again.

The situation of affairs, however, was anything but pleasant.

To be shut up anywhere, is not agreeable, but a family vault combines within itself a number of disagreeables in one.

"What are we to do?" said Duval; "Is this a trick, or have we some enemies in the Cathedral?"

"We are lost," said the Dean, "lost sheep."

"Found," said the Sergeant; "and if so be, your honour, it be as you say, there's no want of mutton."

"Irreverent man!"

"Silence, Sergeant!" said the Marquis. "We must hold a council of war, and see what can be done."

"Hold up," said the Sergeant, suddenly, "I didn't hear the shot—who's hit?"

The terrors of the situation had made the Dean quite limp and placid, so much so, indeed, that he lurched up against the Sergeant, and would have fallen but for his support.

"This is rather serious," said Duval. "Where are you, Richards?"

"Here, sir."

"Did you leave the key in the lock of the vault door?"

"I am afraid I did, sir."

"It was imprudent."

"But if I hadn't, sir, there's no key-hole on this side."

"Hold up!" said the Sergeant to the Dean.

"I can't; this will be the death of me."

"Not at all. I suppose you've never been in a Dutch, Flemish, French, or Austrian prison?"

"Bless me, no."

"Did you ever live six weeks on two rats and an old shoe?"

"Don't ask such questions, my good friend, it can't be done."

A loud mocking laugh at this moment resounded through the door of the vault.

"Not a word," said Duval, make no answer. "Tell me, Richards, does this vault communicate with any others."

"Oh, yes, sir, but it's through a stone wall."

"Never mind that. Here are five of us, and before we get weak from want of food or air, let us set to work."

"Pioneers," said the Sergeant.

"What?" said the Dean.

"Pioneers. Did you ever do trench work with nothing to eat but an old haversack?"

"Never, and I don't think I could."

"Your honour!"

"What is it, Sergeant?"

"I don't think the Chaplain's of much use. He's only fit to go in the hospital."

"I think," said the Dean, mildly, "if I could sit down somewhere."

"To be sure," said the Sergeant. "There you are!"

Sergeant Belasis lifted the Dean up bodily, and seated him with such energy upon one of the old coffins that, being frail and rotten with its forty years' residence in the vault, it gave way immediately with a crash.

The Dean rolled on to the sawdust.

"This is dreadful!" he said. "Who could have imagined such things. Are we in the seventeenth century?"

"What sentry?" said the Sergeant.

"Is this the close of the seventeenth century?"

"His clothes?" said the Sergeant. "What did he take 'em off for?"

"I feel my senses going!"

The Sergeant shook his head.

"Don't think they ever came. Better be quiet. That'll do, I think."

The Sergeant propped the Dean up against the corner of the vault, pulling his legs out straight before him, and wedging him up with two or three handfuls of sawdust to make him comfortable.

"Wait there," he said. "I should say you were out of line of the enemy's fire."

"Fire?" said the Dean, with a bewildered look.

"Yes, but if you get a stray shot or two don't blame me."

"A stray shot or two?"

"Sergeant!" cried the Marquis, "come here and lend assistance."

Duval and Richards, the latter of whom seemed a matter-of-fact sort of person, had commenced operations upon the wall of the vault.

It was certainly of stone, but by no means massive.

The dead were not likely to be aggressive one against another, so that the only object had been to erect a really substantial division between the vaults.

CHAPTER LXXXIII.

A LITTLE PARTY IMPRISONED IN A VAULT IN ST. PAUL'S CATHEDRAL.

THE damps of so many years since the cathedral had been built, had very much softened and disintegrated the stone from the walls of the vaults.

With the few tools the sexton had with him great progress was made, for the stone was found to be quite porous, and easy to be broken away in fragments.

"We shall be much better off," said Richards, "in the next vault, for the staircase from it leads up to one of the grated doors, and we shall have plenty of air, at all events."

The visitors of old St. Paul's Cathedral must have noticed in dim, out-of-the-way corners, small doors, the upper portion of which are composed of rectangular gratings the square spaces being rather large.

It was to one of these that the next vault to that of the Everton family would conduct the imprisoned party.

Half an hour's work was sufficient to loosen one of the stones in the wall, and by a vigorous effort it was then displaced.

The orifice was not large, but it was quite sufficient for a man to creep through.

The sexton went first, and Duval then handed him his lantern.

Then the Marquis.

Then Duval.

It was left to the Sergeant to bring through the Dean, which he did, very adroitly pushing him head foremost through the hole in the wall, where he was received on the other side by the Marquis and Duval.

"It would be much better to mask the lantern," said Duval.

This was done.

The darkness was profound.

"I can easily find my way in the dark up the staircase," said the sexton, "and the best way will be for somebody to lay hold of me, and then somebody else hold of him again, so that we may all follow each other."

This was done, but it required no little trouble on the part of the Sergeant to hold up the Dean, whose limp and dilapidated condition continued.

They reached the staircase spoken of by the under sexton.

It was a circuitous one, so that they had to ascend half way up it before, even had there been broad daylight in the Cathedral, they could come into sight of the grated door.

But there are degrees of darkness.

Each, apart from the other, would look absolute in its black obscurity; but, when contrasted the one with the other, the difference is very great.

So it was with our little party.

Emerging from the extreme blackness and darkness of the vaults, they saw, through the grated door, only the darkness of the Cathedral.

That was much less.

So much less, indeed, that the grating was plainly distinguishable.

It was quite a pleasant thing for the eyes to be able to define an outline of any kind, and to get rid of those thick, rolling, strange masses of absolute darkness that seemed to infest the vaults.

Duval spoke in a whisper.

"Let me advise no one to utter a word above his breath. It is quite necessary that we should discover who are in the Cathedral."

"A light," whispered the Marquis.

The shifting gleam of a light, probably from some lantern, shone upon and streamed through the grating.

"Pause where you all are," said Duval. "I will go forward to reconnoitre."

"Pickets in advance," said the Sergeant, in a low tone.

Duval stooped low, so that none of the rays of light should fall upon him.

He gained the grated door.

He kept himself down to the solid part of it, and listened.

"What do you make of it now?" said a voice.

"I don't know what to make of it," was the reply.

"But you closed the door."

"I did; and the trap is a good one."

"Was it you who spoke aloud?"

"I did, Mr. Pendell."

"Bah! Idiot! Why do you pronounce my name, even here?"

"Well, I thought——"

"Silence! I did not give you twenty guineas to talk, but to act."

"I've done the best I could, and there's no reason for you to be impatient, sir."

"Well, well, well! And you say you don't know any of these people, except the Marquis of Harcourt."

"I can't say I do, sir. Of course, there's the Dean. We all know him; and there's Richards, the under-sexton."

"But you told me there were five people."

"I did, sir; and one's an old soldier in the service of the Marquis of Harcourt; the other I heard one of them call Sir John Cope."

"Cope, Cope! Are you sure?"

"Yes, sir, that was the name."

"I don't know it."

"Nor I, sir."

"Well, Muckles, manage it how you may or how you will, one thing must be done before you get the thirty guineas to make up fifty."

"I know, sir."

"But I may as well repeat it. You must positively remove from that last placed coffin, in the Everton vault, the dead body you will find there. If it remains, it will afford a clue to my whole proceedings, and ruin everything."

"I understand, sir."

"I was robbed of a valise in the Oxford Mail which contained papers of vast importance; and let me tell you one thing, Muckles."

"What is it, Mr. Pendell?"

"Upon your faithfulness to me will depend your whole fortune; for I will put you in the way of apprehending Claude Duval, be assured; and then, in addition to the Government reward, I mean myself to add the sum of five hundred guineas."

"He's a slippery customer, sir; but we will try our best."

"I fear your plan will not do, though."

"Oh, yes, it will, sir. I have sent Swallow to get a good relay of constables and watchmen; and if plenty of noise is made, the whole party in the vault yonder can be taken to the Round House, in East Smithfield. When there, let them make what explanation they may to the night constable, and get released; but all that will take time, and then we can remove the body you speak of."

"True, true; but Swallow is a long time gone."

"He's a bit of a fool, sir."

"He is, he is!"

"And sometimes I think he's quite enamoured of Claude Duval."

"If you think so, it will be easy to trump up some charge against him, and get him hanged."

"We will see about that, Mossy Pendell. There he is, for I hear voices and footsteps at the door of the cathedral."

If Mossy Pendell and Muckles, the officer, had taken the greatest possible pains for the purpose of communicating to Claude Duval all that they intended to do, they could not have succeeded more effectually than by unwittingly allowing him to overhear their conference in the old Cathedral.

Situated as he was, and amid the silence of the place, not a single word that they uttered escaped him.

The only question in his mind was how they had discovered that any expedition, for the purpose of identifying the dead body in the Everton vault, was projected.

But now Duval felt that St. Ives was the proper person to give advice in this emergency.

He crept down the staircase again leading to the vault.

He spoke, then, in cautious whispers.

"Mr. St. Ives!"

"Yes, Sir John Cope, I am here."

It is a curious thing to speak to people in such total darkness as that which now enveloped the little party.

"I have discovered who is in the church."

St. Ives uttered an exclamation expressive of his interest in the communication.

"The building is beset by officers of the police."

"On what pretence?"

"No pretence at all, I fancy, except that two of them are in the pay of Mossy Pendell."

"Ah!"

"Yes; I overheard that rascal's voice."

"And who are the officers?"

"One is named Muckles."

"Then," said St. Ives, "I can name you the other, for he always associates with him—a man of the name of Swallow."

"Exactly!" said Duval.

"What could be the motive of these men?" asked the Marquis of Harcourt.

It was necessary that Duval should endeavour to state to the Marquis those motives, without, at the same time, exposing to the Dean and Sergeant Belasis his own identity.

"These men are here to defeat our object; and since that object is to prove incontestibly that the dead body in the Everton vault is not that of the late General, they wish to overcome us by finding an opportunity of removing the body altogether."

"We can defeat that manœuvre," said St. Ives; "and all I ask of you is to remain where you are."

"How do you mean?" said the Marquis.

"It will be quite sufficient for me to show myself in the Cathedral."

"True!" said the Marquis. "I had quite forgotten, St. Ives, that your position in the police gives you a certain authority."

"Let me consider for a few seconds," said St. Ives.

The silence was very profound.

Then St. Ives spoke again in a low tone.

"I do not see any difficulty in getting rid of these men in the Cathedral; if Mossy Pendell and Muckles were alone, of course they would not submit to my authority, and nothing but force would suffice; but since they have sent for assistance from constables and watchmen, I can do as I please."

"And what will that be?" asked Duval.

"I will go alone into the Cathedral; both Swallow and Muckles know me perfectly well, and must take orders from me. The door of the vault will be unlocked, and I will take care that it remains so."

"In that case," said the Marquis, "all that we shall have to do will be to retrace our steps, and emerge from this dreary region by the same way we entered it."

"Exactly," replied St. Ives. "I will go at once."

While the others all remained where they were, Richards, the under sexton, unmasked his lantern again, so as to show St. Ives the way to the door of the Everton vault.

"You can go back now, Richards," said the officer.

"I will wait here."

"Yes, sir."

St. Ives was left alone, and in darkness, at the top of the sixteen stairs which led to the vault of the Evertons'.

It was not an agreeable situation.

He leant his back against the door, and looked down into the vault.

St. Ives was rather an imaginative man.

Indeed, most of the Jacobite leaders and powerful officers were of that character.

Had they not been, they never would have clung so long and so enthusiastically to a desperate cause.

As St. Ives looked down into the vault, the shadows seemed to shape themselves into strange grotesque aspects.

And yet he knew they were but shadows.

The time seemed terribly long.

Then, suddenly the Cathedral appeared to be filled by a strange, reverberating kind of sound.

The great clock struck one.

Then St. Ives heard footsteps.

"They come!"

A confused murmur of voices.

And the footsteps rapidly approached.

How unutterably welcome is human companionship, let it be of whatever kind or description it may, under circumstances of loneliness and depression.

St. Ives knew perfectly well that they were low, rude, coarse men who were approaching.

Vulgar watchmen.

Rough, unfeeling constables.

But he was glad to hear their voices.

The tones were human, and each of them seemed to have the power to chase away some of the thick, gathering shadows that rolled before his eyes down the staircase and in the Everton vault.

A key rattled in the door.

It was flung open.

There was a glare of light.

"Surrender!" cried a loud voice. "Rascally disturbers of the dead! Surrender!"

The voice was that of Mossy Pendell.

It was quite evident that the watchmen and the constables who had been summoned by Swallow were prepared for a contest.

Some had their drawn hangers in their hands.

Others their bludgeons uplifted

Both Muckles and Mossy Pendell were armed with pistols.

Then St. Ives stepped quietly through the doorway of the vault.

"What is all this?" he said.

There was a general look of blank astonishment.

The watchmen lowered their bludgeons.

They turned the full glare of their lanterns upon him.

The constables slowly returned their hangers to their sheaths.

"I ask again," said St. Ives, "what is the meaning of all this?"

"Why, it's Mr. St. Ives!" exclaimed Swallow.

Mossy Pendell, however, was not so easily put down by a look or a word.

He advanced boldly.

"The meaning is this, that there is a desecration of the grave, and that we are determined to prevent it, and take into custody the perpetrators."

"Do you not know me, sir?" asked St. Ives, sternly.

"Certainly not."

"Then I have the advantage of you, Mossy Pendell."

Pendell shrunk back.

Muckles clutched him by the arm, and whispered eagerly in his ear.

"It's Mr. St. Ives—a high officer of the police. He can order us all at his own pleasure."

"Confusion take him!" muttered Pendell: "what does he do here?"

"I don't know."

Then St. Ives spoke in a loud, clear voice.

"To those officers of the police and the night watch who have assembled here, as they think, in the pursuance of their duty, I am much obliged; but I have myself arranged and settled this whole affair."

"Not quite," cried Pendell.

"Indeed, sir!"

"No. The vault, at the entrance of which you now stand, I suspect has more living occupants than dead ones."

"Search!" said St. Ives.

He stepped aside.

No one, however, seemed very well inclined to go down into that dreary vault.

"Let two watchmen go down," said St. Ives, "and report. You, No. 10, and you, No. 8, take your lanterns, and go."

The watchmen were not very sensitive persons, and at a slow pace, encumbered by their heavy great coats, they went down the steps of the vault.

"It is quite necessary," said St. Ives, "that there should be no doubt whatever about the proceedings of the higher officers of the police, and since this person, Mossy Pendell, has made a statement, it must either be contradicted or proved."

"Nobody here!" cried the watchmen from below.

Pendell would not believe their assertion.

He hastily descended half-way down the steps, so that he could take a glance round the vault.

That glance was sufficient.

It was evidently only tenanted by the dead.

He looked pale and anxious when he reached the cathedral again.

"Are you satisfied, Mossy Pendell?" asked St. Ives.

This repeated utterance of his name seemed to annoy Pendell amazingly.

He chafed and fumed under it, and, in the passion of the moment, he exclaimed, "Of one thing I am quite satisfied, and that is, that there is some infernal juggle or cheat in all this transaction."

"But, you see," said St. Ives, "that that vault is solely inhabited by the dead."

Pendell made an impatient gesture.

"As well," added St. Ives, "might you expect to find any living thing in a certain hovel in a certain wood north of London, where a certain man, attacked by his associates and murdered, crawled to breathe his last."

CHAPTER LXXXIV

MOSSY PENDELL FINDS THINGS DO NOT TURN OUT AS HE DESIRES.

THESE words, so clearly pointed to the murder, or supposed murder, of Lord Horlop by Mossy Pendell, that the latter was seized with consternation.

He retreated backwards step by step.

The watchmen and constables made way for him, until he was completely clear of them.

Still, then, keeping his eyes, in a sidelong fashion fixed upon the calm, steady eyes of St. Ives, he fled, from the cathedral.

"Let him go," said St. Ives.

Some of the watchmen had made a kind of movement to stop Pendell.

"Let him go. And now, as regards all the rest of you, I say, again, I thank you but, at the same time, inform you that the affair about which you come here has been taken in hand by the higher authorities, and is settled."

St. Ives, as he spoke, closed the vault door, locked it, and quietly put the key in his pocket.

"You can all go now," he said, "for you are wanted here no longer."

Without casting another glance upon the rather bewildered constables and watchmen, St. Ives then slowly paced up the aisle of the cathedral.

For the space of about a minute, they all saw his retreating form growing more and more indistinct in the darkness.

Then it mingled slowly with the shadows.

And then it disappeared entirely.

The officers and watchmen looked at each other, and wished themselves well out of old St. Paul's.

That was easy enough accomplished.

They had but to hurry out of the church as they had hurried into it.

They did so with every mark of precipitation.

Swallow then touched Muckles on the arm as they passed out into the open air.

"Mr. Muckles!"

"What now, stupid?"

"It seems to me that we are done rather brown."

"Bah!"

"Oh, it's very well to say 'Bah!' but I tell you what I think, Mr. Muckles."

"What? Something stupid, I suppose?"

"Well, I don't know, but I can't help fancying that Claude Duval has something to do with this business."

"Oh, you think so, do you?"

"Why yes; you see, Mr. Muckles, as you told me yourself, the old General who is down there in the vault, is Duval's wife's uncle."

"Oh! you've found that out, have you?"

"Well, Mr. Muckles, you told me that."

"And no more? Ha, ha!"

Muckles lapsed into a violent fit of coughing as he spoke, and had to lean against the iron railings surrounding the court-yard of the cathedral.

"I do believe," he muttered, "I've caught my death of cold from that plunge in the Thames which Duval gave me over Westminster Bridge. Luckily, I'm a good swimmer, or it would have been my last plunge in this world; but it was somewhat horrid to go right down amongst the slime and mud of the river, and stick there for a few moments before one could extricate oneself. I shall never forget it—never!"

"Yes," said Swallow, who had overheard him; "you were done uncommonly brown then, Mr. Muckles."

"Silence, wretch, and be off!"

"I'm off, sir."

The cathedral was once more left in silence and apparent desolation.

St. Ives, however, had the key of the vault in his possession.

He only waited until he was quite certain the watchmen and constables, together with Swallow and Muckles, had left the place, to proceed to the entrance of that gloomy abode, for the purpose of liberating Duval and the little party, who still occupied its darksome depths.

St. Ives unlocked the door, and descended some of the steps.

"Now—now!" he cried, "all is clear!"

"March!" he heard the Sergeant say.

In two minutes more, the whole of the party were in the cathedral, and once more the door of the vault was closed and locked.

The poor Dean was quite in a state of mental collapse; and, as weak natures, under such circumstances, have a tendency to rely very implicitly upon strong ones, he had it in his head that nothing would save him from the terrors and commotions of that night, but the cool and indomitable courage of the Sergeant.

The Dean, consequently, obeyed Belasis in every particular.

"March!" cried the Sergeant.

The Dean, in a dreamy kind of way, tried to march.

Duval and St. Ives, and the Marquis of Harcourt, were very glad to leave that Church dignitary in his own parlour to the care of the under sexton.

Then they left St. Paul's, and hastened back to Farnborough House as quickly as they could.

"The first step, Lucy, is taken," said Duval, "in unravelling the mystery connected with your uncle's disappearance, for his remains are not to be found in the vault of the Evertons'."

"Then he lives!" cried Lucy; "I feel convinced he lives!"

"He does, doubtless."

"My justification, and the declaration of my innocence will, then, come from his own lips?"

"I think," said St. Ives, "we may look forward to such an event."

"But Mossy Pendell's still active villany," remarked Duval, "may still give us some trouble."

"It may—it may," said St. Ives, as he paced the room in deep thought. "I scarcely know how to manage matters with regard to him."

"In what way?"

"As regards this murder of Lord Horlop, the particulars of which you have communicated to me. It is so unfortunate that you two are the only witnesses, along with your man Blossom, who can fix the crime upon him; and it would never do, Duval, to subject you or Blossom to the searching scrutiny that would take place at a criminal trial."

"It would be full of peril," said Duval; "but I hope the time may come when that villain will meet with his deserts. What is to be done next, St. Ives, now that we are sure the vault of the Evertons' does not contain the dead body of the General?"

"I can do nothing until the day after to-morrow."

"You are fully occupied then?"

"Yes, the grand entertainment at the Palace of St. James's, which was put off last week, is to take place to-morrow night."

"Indeed?"

"Yes—and therefore I shall be very busy, in consequence of all the police arrangements falling under my care."

Duval's mind flew back to that meeting of the Jacobites at the mansion in the Oxford Road.

An uneasy feeling crept over him.

"St. Ives," he said, "may I ask you a question?"

"A hundred, if you please."

"Were you at a certain meeting of Jacobite leaders, or emissaries, held at a mansion westward of London only last week?"

"I know the meeting you allude to, but I was not there."

"Another question?"

"Ask it."

"Is the Duke of Montrose one of you?"

St. Ives was silent.

"I perceive," said Duval, "that that is not a fair question to ask, so I will vary it, and say if the Duke of Montrose were one of you, and if he were to undertake to forward the views of the Stuarts by an act of the vilest treachery and assassination, would you consider yourself bound to support him?"

"Can you ask me such a question?"

"You assure me by that tone."

"I can answer you further, Sir John Cope, by declaring that no such assassination can be contemplated.

"I will admit to you that the Duke of Montrose is one of us, but, for reasons of State, he holds office about the person of the King, even as I do, and to-morrow he enters upon the duties of a new dignity."

"Indeed?"

"Yes—he becomes Lord Chamberlain."

"Lord Chamberlain!" mused Duval.

"The duties are not very onerous," added St. Ives, with a smile. "Indeed, I believe the principal one to-morrow night will be to hand the King a certain gold and jewelled cup, out of which he will drink to the health of his guests."

Duval started.

All that had been proposed by the Jacobites in regard to the manner in which the King was to be assassinated came with a rush back to his mind.

The little vial, containing the subtle poison, which was to be squeezed, broken, and then dropped into the cup.

The confusion that was to ensue.

The state of anarchy into which the nation was to be thrown.

All these things came vividly before the imagination of Duval, and he only asked himself one question.

Should he tell St. Ives?

The King was a bad King.

He could be no loss to any nation.

Indeed, he had behaved individually to Duval in the worst possible manner.

But still there was something revolting in allowing him to be poisoned, like some strange cur, who might be left for death without a sigh.

"I must think!" said Duval. "I must think!"

"There is something on your mind," said St. Ives, "but I seek not to penetrate it."

"A part of what is on my mind I will tell you," replied Duval, "and it is simply this. You are an honourable man, St. Ives, and there are no doubt, many other honourable men, who, like you, have linked themselves to the fortunes of the exiled royal family, but neither you nor they have the least idea of the villainous suggestions of some of your associates."

St. Ives sighed.

"It is the misfortune," he said, "of all engaged in great enterprises that they are compelled to associate themselves with unworthy persons."

"It is, indeed."

"I will not seek to know more of your meaning, Duval, at this present moment, than you choose to divulge."

He rose to leave.

"To-morrow," said Duval, "perhaps, we shall meet again."

"To-morrow be it."

St. Ives left Farnborough House.

"Where is the Princess, Lucy?" asked Duval.

"She is above."

"Summon her hither, I would fain speak to her, for I think this is a matter she should know of."

The young Stuart Princess was soon in the room, and then Duval spoke to her rapidly and distinctly.

"Will you pardon me for asking you one question, which it is both to your interest and your honour to answer."

"I will answer anything and freely."

"Are you aware that there was a proposition to assassinate the King?"

"The King? What King?"

Duval smiled.

"I forgot," he said, "that I was speaking to a Stuart Princess, and therefore, I should say, the usurper, calling himself George The Second, King of England."

"Assassinate?"

"Even so," replied Duval.

"But how came you by your knowledge, Sir John Cope?" asked the young Princess, looking alternately at Duval and Lucy. "Surely——"

The Princess paused.

"What were you going to say?" asked Duval.

"Surely Colonel Miravil is not a party to——"

"No—no! a thousand times no!" exclaimed Duval and Lucy in a breath. "He, like you, Princess," added Duval, "is quite ignorant of the base and cowardly attempt which is to be made no later than to-morrow night."

The Princess again lapsed into silence, resting her head upon her hand, and a mournful expression passed over her countenance.

Lucy laid her hand gently upon that of the Princess, as she said, "May we know the cause of your sadness?"

The Princess clasped the hand of Lucy in both of hers, as she said, with great emotion, "Tell me, oh, tell me, dear and generous friend, that neither you nor your husband thought me guilty of complicity in this dreadful crime?"

"Indeed, no!" replied Duval and Lucy in a breath, "we neither thought you any other than what you are, noble, generous, brave, and good."

The Princess smiled through her tears.

"It is well," she said; "now, may I ask you how you came by your knowledge?"

"From you, it is no secret," replied Duval. "I became aware of the attempt that was to be made to poison George The Second on the night when I had the honour of first becoming acquainted with yourself."

"Ah, at the mansion in the Oxford Road."

"Even so," said Duval.

"I see—I see," said the Princess, after reflecting a few minutes; "it was not unlikely that you should suppose I was so situated as to hear without being seen all that was said in that banqueting hall, where some of my Counsellors met on that night."

"At first I thought it just probable; but a more intimate knowledge of your gentleness showed me how utterly impossible it was for such to be the case."

"I thank you for your good opinion, Sir John Cope; and now let me hear more of this conspiracy, for I cannot call it by any other name, although it has my advancement for its object."

"I fear," said Duval, "that those who contemplate committing this crime have their own advancement alone in view."

"It may be so, it may be so," said the young Princess, sadly, "for you tell me that Colonel Miravel is not a party to it."

"Indeed he is not, for I asked him," said Duval; "and he, like yourself, was horrified at the treacherous undertaking."

"Tell me, then, all that you know of this monstrous thing; and then we may be able to think of some plan to prevent its commission."

"You have spoken my own thoughts and wishes," said Duval; "not that personally I have any feelings in common with the bad King that sits upon the throne of these realms; but I have a natural antipathy to a base and cowardly assassination of any man, be he whom he may."

"And now, tell me what is contemplated, Sir John Cope; and which of those who profess such attachment to our cause and person it is who is willing to lend himself to such a dastardly work"

"I will," said Duval. "He who is to be the seeming friend, the attached courtier, and the trusted favourite of his King, is named——"

"What?" interrupted the Princess.

"The Duke of Montrose!"

CHAPTER LXXXV.

THE STUART PRINCESS UNDERTAKES A PERILOUS ENTERPRISE.

"THE Duke of Montrose?" exclaimed the Princess.

"Even so," said Duval; "but you seem not to be so surprised as I fancied you would be, on learning the name of this would be assassinator of——"

"The usurper," said the Princess, quietly.

"Exactly," said Duval. "To you, he is of course nothing but an usurper; but tell me, had you reason to suspect this same Duke of Montrose?"

"Not in the way you think, Sir John Cope; but it is a relief to me to find that it is that man rather than any of the others, for I never liked him. I ever shrank from his hateful glance, and trembled whenever he approached me."

"You would naturally do so, for the good can have no fellowship with the base, and therefore, you and he could never be friends."

"Never!" replied the Princess, with a shudder; "and now tell me how this foul murder is to be carried out?"

"It is proposed, that at the entertainment given at St. James's Palace to-morrow night by George The Second, the wine cup, from which the King will drink to his guests, is to be poisoned."

"But how can that be accomplished," asked the Princess, "on such an occasion, when so many eyes will be fixed upon the personage they propose to assassinate?"

"In this way," said Duval. "The Duke of Montrose enters upon his new duties to-morrow night as Lord Chamberlain, and one of the duties incidental to his new dignity will be to hand to his King the cup of which I have spoken.

"Yes—yes!"

"Before doing so, however, he will squeeze between his finger and thumb a small, very fragile, crystal vial, so minute that it will be able to be dropped into the cup without pouring the liquid from it."

"And that liquid is poison?"

"Exactly so—a most subtle poison."

The Princess shuddered.

"Oh!" she cried, "how mistaken to suppose that by such means the exiled Stuarts will regain their rightful position in this country!"

"Mistaken, indeed!" said Duval.

"But can nothing be done," asked the young Princess, "to frustrate this wicked scheme?"

"I have thought of that; and if you will promise not to think I am doing anything to injure your cause, I myself would fain do what I can to prevent so dire a catastrophe, which can end only in anarchy to the nation and disgrace to the Stuart cause."

"Stay, Sir John Cope—be mine the task!" said the young Princess; and as she spoke she rose to her feet and her eyes sparkled with animation and heroism;—"be mine the task to snatch the poisoned draught from the hand of the usurper!"

Lucy was amazed.

"You know not what you ask!" she cried, as she flung her arms about the enthusiastic girl. "You know not what you say! Think no more of it—oh! think no more of it!"

The Princess gently put Lucy aside, and stood close to Duval.

"Speak—tell me," she cried; "would it be a matter of impossibility for me in a suitable disguise to go to this entertainment?"

Duval for a moment did not speak. He could not but look and admire the brave, fragile young creature who now stood before him with every womanly feeling glowing upon her expressive countenance.

"You will not answer me!" she said, sadly. "Then you, too, think the task impossible!"

"No, not quite impossible," said Duval, thoughtfully, "but I was thinking that——"

Duval paused.

"Thinking that I should not have the courage to go through with the task I had imposed upon myself?"

"No, not that—but I was thinking what a glorious thing it would be for England if she could boast of such a Queen upon her throne!"

"And you can think and say this, Sir John Cope, and still refuse to join our cause—you, so full of resources - so full of courage and high nobility of soul!"

"I may think and wish all this," replied Duval; "but, oh, that I could make you see with my eyes the utter impossibility of carrying out the views of the exiled royal family! Never—never again——"

"Stop! Say not the words that would take all hope from my heart! I believe so implicitly in all you say that I think if once you allowed the words you were about to utter to pass your lips, I should never again entertain the thought which has grown with my growth and strengthened with my strength, until it has become necessary to my very existence almost."

"It seems so now," said Duval, gently; "but believe me——"

"No more—no more!" said the Princess, waving her hand—"no more of this! Tell me—and you, too, give me your kind concurrence," she added, turning and taking Lucy's hand in hers—"tell me that you will let me go to this entertainment!"

Duval felt that there were two dangers in acceding to the proposition of the Princess.

One was to himself.

That he cared little about.

The other was to her.

That troubled him.

Moreover, these dangers ran the one into the other, inasmuch as the necessity of seeing that no evil chance should befall her would be sure greatly to increase his own risk.

But still he consented.

"Be it so!" he said; "although I know not what Colonel Miravel will say."

"My wishes will be his laws; and the only consultation I shall hold with him upon the subject will be in regard to the disguise I shall assume."

This point being settled, Duval was anxious again to see St. Ives.

He sought him about mid-day at all places where he thought he was likely to meet him, but was disappointed.

The royal assembly was to take place on that evening, and every hour of the day was one of anxiety.

Purely by accident, Duval ascertained that St. Ives had gone to the Palace, at Kew, on some business, and would not return until late.

There was no help for it but to ride there if he would see him.

"Blossom," said Duval, "you must saddle Nightshade, and get your own horse ready."

"For the road, Captain?"

"Yes; we must take a sharp trot to Kew. You will wear your groom's dress, and I my disguise as Sir John Cope. Paint a white star on the forehead of Nightshade, and whiten the fetlock of one of his legs."

"It shall be done, Captain."

"I have not the slightest doubt but that the people of London have, by this time, a full and accurate description of Nightshade."

"No doubt of that, Captain; but the white marks will puzzle them, particularly as they won't be looking for him, not seeing anybody like Claude Duval upon his back."

THE PRIME MINISTER DELIVERS A PAPER TO THE KING.

"Be quick, Blossom. I will walk down to the stable, at Westminster, and meet you."

Duval met Blossom with the two horses close by Whitehall.

He instantly mounted.

Nightshade was so well pleased to find his old master upon his back again—for no disguise could effectually hide Duval from that sagacious steed—that he gave a kind of vaulting spring into the air, to the great surprise of the passengers in the street, and then darted off at a gallop.

It was scarcely two o'clock in the afternoon, and Duval was not sorry to get out of town as quickly as possible.

He had to rein in Nightshade, however, in order to permit Blossom to approach him in anything like a reasonable distance.

But it was easier to get out of town then than now; and in about twenty minutes there was nothing on each side of the high road but tall trees and thick, impenetrable hedges.

No. 28.—NIGHTSHADE.

"Captain!" cried Blossom.

"What now?"

"Don't you think some business might be done upon the road, even in broad daylight?"

"It is possible enough, Blossom; but the risk is very much greater."

"There now, Captain; only look there! There now, there's a chance!"

A barouche passed them, drawn by two handsome horses, and driven by a postilion.

A stern old gentleman, and two elderly ladies, of enormous dimensions were the occupants of the carriage.

By the flash of the jewellery that they wore, and which gleamed brightly as the barouche passed Duval and Blossom, it seemed rational enough to suppose that they would have produced capital plunder for a highwayman.

"It won't do for Sir John Cope," said Duval, "to be robbing people on the highway; and it is quite necessary that I should keep up my *incognito*."

There was a very long, shadowy lane, something more than a mile and a half in extent, which, although it cut off a considerable portion of the road, was only adapted for foot passengers or horsemen.

Being too narrow to allow any vehicle to pass another, none ever ventured into it at either end, for fear of a dead lock.

Duval, however, plunged into this lane.

Nightshade had had a good gallop, and was rather pleased than otherwise to proceed at a rather sauntering pace upon the grass-grown way.

And the lane, by being so little frequented, was so thickly strewn with leaves, and over-run with wild flowers and vegetation, that the horse's feet made not the slightest sound.

It seemed as if they trod upon thickly folded velvet. Suddenly Duval paused.

He heard voices over one of the hedges to the left.

Blossom likewise pulled up, and they both listened.

The voice they heard was a very young one.

It was musical and sweet, although it spoke in high, excited tones.

"Had you ten times the skill you have with your sword, and were you ten times the heartless ruffian I believe you to be, I will fight you for the sake of one you have wronged and betrayed!"

"Take yourself back to school again, stripling," replied a harsh voice. "I do not fight with boys."

"You shall fight! or surrender those letters which have been obtained from a too trusting heart, but which shall never be the sport of a villain!"

"I warn you both," replied the harsh voice. "I am not a man to be trifled with. Get back to school, I say, both of you, and leave men to manage their own affairs."

"No!" was the reply. "Fortunately, I have come home along with this college companion of mine to the old Hall, and just in time, it appears, to take my cousin Anabel's part."

"Ha, ha!"

"Ah, you may laugh, Sir Charles Wilton; but you shall surrender those letters."

"Shall, indeed?"

"You are found out. You come here and partake of the hospitality of my uncle under pretence of being on a fishing excursion, and you lay siege to the heart of an unsophisticated country girl; you entrap her into writing letters to you, and then, through your own carelessness there is found, even upon your dressing-table, an epistle from a roué friend in town, which not only proclaims you a married man, separated from your wife, but asking you in ribald and unseemly language when you are coming back to London to amuse the club at the Tennis Ground with the letters of the foolish little country wench who has fallen in love with you at Halstead Hall."

"Ha! ha!"

"You laugh, sir."

"I do."

"Then it shall be my business to make you cry."

"Your business! Impertinent boy!"

"Draw and defend yourself, rascal, or give up those letters instantly."

"Indeed."

"I mean what I say, sir, and will enforce the demand."

"Beware! I, too, wear a sword."

"Yes, but you are afraid to draw it."

"Afraid?"

"Yes, afraid. You are a coward—for none but a coward would make sport of an innocent young heart, prepared by its own simplicity and want of experience to make a kind and loving response to any one who might put on an appearance of being worthy. And so I say again, Sir Charles Wilton, you are a coward!"

"This is insufferable!"

"Fight, then!"

"Be it so, since you will have it!"

"I think, Blossom," whispered Duval, "I should like to see this fight."

"And I, too, Captain."

"That's a sprightly young spark who speaks up so boldly."

Duval dismounted as he spoke, and scrambled up the hedge, from whence he could obtain a view of the meadow where the disputants were.

He not only saw the meadow, but some beautiful gardens beyond it, and beyond them again, he caught glimpses through a number of stately trees, of one of those fine old mansions fast disappearing from England for two causes.

Fire.

The wanton destruction of what is called modern taste.

But it was only a glance that Duval took of the gardens and the house.

His attention was rivetted upon the three persons who were in the meadow.

One of them was a handsome-looking man, some two or three-and-thirty years of age.

His eyes were piercing and brilliant. A short moustache shaded his upper lip, and from his dress and general appearance, he was evidently a finished gentleman.

There was, however, that indescribable something about him which marked the roué and heartless man of the world.

The other two persons were mere youths.

They did not either of them seem to be above fifteen or sixteen years of age.

The one who spoke so boldly was the taller of the two, and whatever courage he possessed was certainly not shared in by his companion, who stood somewhat apart, and visibly trembled.

The courageous youth, however, had drawn his sword.

He advanced threateningly upon the man of fashion.

"The letters! The letters, sir!" he cried, "and give them up at once."

"My young friend," said Sir Charles Wilton, "you will get into mischief. Advance another step, and I shall be compelled to draw and do you some harm."

"The letters, sir!"

"Peace! peace with your croaking!"

"Coward, as well as villain!"

The young man struck Sir Charles Wilton across the breast with his sword.

"Oh! you will have it, then," cried the roué.

There was a rapid interchange of sword thrusts for a few seconds, and then the youth reeled back.

He was wounded in the arm.

"Think yourself well off," said Sir Charles, as he slowly sheathed his sword. "Think yourself well off, malapert boy, that I do not take your life; and the next time you have anything to say to me, get a man to say it. Ha! ha! The letters of the fair Anabel will still amuse the club at the Tennis Court!"

"One moment!" cried Duval, as he scrambled through the hedge, and stood in the meadow.

All parties started at this sudden intrusion.

"One moment. The man that you advised this brave youth to get to question you, it seems has arrived."

"And who are you, sir?" asked Sir Charles, angrily.

"It don't so much matter who I am, as what I am."

"But——"

"Come, come, Sir Charles. The letters, if you please. The letters!"

The youth who was wounded in the arm uttered a cry of joy.

"Heaven sends us a champion," he cried, "although I am disabled."

"Am I to fight all the parish!" cried Sir Charles. "No, no, indeed. Settle you affairs among yourselves, and if you want any letters, ha! ha! you can write each other as many as you like, and Miss Anabel up at the Hall, who is quite a proficient in them, can join the sport. As for you, sir, I wish you a good day!"

Sir Charles turned upon his heel, and came face to face with Blossom.

"Not this way," said Blossom.

"Ah!"

"Nor this way," said Duval.

Sir Charles turned towards the house.

"Nor this way!" cried the wounded youth, holding his sword in his left hand.

"So!" said Sir Charles, "I am baited am I, and all on account of a few weeks' amusement with a country girl in her teens."

"You will be so good," said Duval, "or so bad, I don't care which you choose to call it, as to give me up those letters."

"Never!"

"Then I shall take them."

"You? you?"

"Even I."

"Beware, sir! I have already been assailed by a green youth, to whom I have had to give a lesson of blood, now it appears hoary age is about to attack me. Beware, sir, I say, beware!"

"i am not at all so old as I look," said Duval, quietly.

As he spoke he cast his hat upon the grass.

The grey wig he wore as Sir John Cope followed.

He shook his head, and his own dark locks fell down over his neck and shoulders.

He flung off his over-coat.

He gave that pull to each of his boots, which brought them up to their proper position.

"Now, Sir Charles," he said, "we will see what we can do."

"A highwayman, by heaven!"

"Yes. But do not ask my name or it may scare you."

"Your name?"

"Saved! saved!" cried the youth, who was wounded. "I know the name! for I have seen its owner before. Tell me, sir, are you not Claude Duval?"

Duval smiled.

"I fancy I must admit it."

Sir Charles turned very pale.

He slowly took from his pocket a packet of letters, and flung them on to the grass.

"Take the silly moonshine," he said, "and much good may it do you."

"Do you know how many letters there ought to be?" asked Duval of the youth.

"Oh! yes, yes!"

He dashed forward despite his wounded arm, and eagerly counted them.

"Yes, they are all here, and my heart is light again. It was an infatuation, a dream, a piece of wild, silly, girl-like romance, which never—never can happen again, and I feel that I am saved."

The youth clasped his hands over his face, and burst into a passion of tears.

Sir Charles advanced two steps.

A strange look was upon his face.

"So," he said, "this is a comedy."

The youth uttered a cry which was so expressly feminine in its tone, that Duval could no longer doubt what he had expected all along, viz., that the young champion of the Lady Anabella, was no other than that personage herself.

The manner in which she now clung to the left arm of Duval for protection, was a convincing proof if any were needed.

CHAPTER LXXXVI.

SIR CHARLES WILTON MEETS WITH HIS MATCH IN CLAUDE DUVAL.

"TAKE yourself off, sir," cried Duval, fiercely, "or the comedy you speak of, like many other comedies in this world, will end tragically."

"Confound you all," muttered Sir Charles, as he turned upon his heel. "If this story gets wind, I shall be the butt of the town. Confound you all, I say. I should like to see you all hanged, and if ever I come into the country again, may I be hanged myself."

"That might happen," cried Duval. "Let him go, Blossom!"

"All's right, Captain."

"Look to our horses, however!"

Sir Charles went away muttering vows of vengeance.

The young girl then looked up confidingly in the face of Duval.

"I know not how to thank you."

"You have thanked me already by that look and those tones. Are you much hurt?"

"I think not."

"An ugly scratch?"

Duval wound his handkerchief about the wounded arm of the girl.

"Who is the redoubtable champion," he said, "who is with you?"

Anabella laughed.

"My maid."

"I thought as much. Well, we have fairly got rid of this Sir Charles, and I rejoice that he has taken nothing with him belonging to you?"

"Nothing."

"Not even your heart?"

"That never was so free."

"Then rejoice, for what a whole volume of experience this little affair may be to you. It is not to the first comer with a fair exterior, who may say to you I love you, will you love me? that you are to give your affections."

"Oh, I have been so foolish!"

"Excellent!"

"Eh?"

"Do you know that to exclaim that you have been so foolish, is the first step to wisdom, and so now, farewell! Blossom!"

"Yes, Captain."

"Help me on with my coat. Now, my wig, Blossom—my hat. That will do. Once more, good day!"

Anabella looked with amazement upon these transformations; and, as Duval was about leaving the meadow, she sprung towards him.

"I may hear of you again," she said. "You may be in danger, and want some one to help you; and if that should happen, trust to me."

"Brave heart!" said Duval! but he smiled as he spoke.

"Nay! you remember the old fable of the mouse and the lion!" said Anabella.

"I do but doubt if the lion was ever properly grateful. I shall be, however, you may depend. Only, I exact one condition of this mouse; which is, that it never runs into any danger for this lion; and so, once more, farewell!"

In another minute Duval was mounted.

"On, Nightshade, on!"

The day was fast speeding away, and the old Palace of Kew was yet three miles ahead.

That distance, however, was speedily accomplished, and Duval alighted at the garden gate of the Palace.

The extreme respectability of his appearance, and the beauty of Nightshade, his horse, were quite sufficient to bespeak every attention to Claude Duval in his character of Sir John Cope.

Moreover, Blossom made a very unexceptionable groom, and was likewise well mounted.

The gate-keeper of the royal residence advanced, and held Nightshade until Blossom trotted up to relieve him of the duty.

"Can you tell me," said Duval, "if Mr. St. Ives is in the Palace?"

"He is walking down the garden even now," replied the gate-keeper.

"Can I seek him?"

"I think not; for I fancy his Majesty is somewhere in the garden; and we are obliged to be very careful, sir, who we admit."

Duval hesitated.

He was about to give his name as Sir John Cope, but, at the moment, he saw, about a hundred yards off, St. Ives himself, approaching rapidly in the direction of the gate.

"There," said Duval, "is the very gentleman I want to see."

"If Mr. St. Ives recognises you, sir, of course he can pass you in."

St. Ives had a keen sight, and he quickly saw who it was who stood at the gate of the royal gardens.

A feeling of alarm took possession of him; for at the sight of Duval, he feared that something serious must have happened in relation to the young Stuart Princess.

In another minute he was at the gate.

"You here, Sir John Cope?" he said.

"Yes, Mr. St. Ives," he said; "I wish to speak with you on a matter of some consequence."

The gate-keeper drew back.

"If this gentleman is a friend of yours, Mr. St. Ives, of course he can pass on."

"Oh, certainly!" said St. Ives; "this is Sir John Cope!"

The manner in which St. Ives spoke, seemed to imply that everybody ought to know Sir John Cope, and the gatekeeper felt half inclined to be ashamed of himself for his ignorance upon the subject.

St. Ives took Duval's arm, and they both walked up the gravel-path immediately within the iron gates.

"The porter says that the King is in the garden," remarked Duval.

"He is, I believe."

"Then, St. Ives, it shows what a mockery all the precautions that surround monarchs really are, when you and I are here, in the same garden with George the Second."

"How do you mean?"

"Why, you are a Jacobite Colonel of the Horse, and I am a highwayman!"

"Hush—hush!"

"Suppose we were inclined to be mischievous, now, and add a page to the history of England, in which would appear both our names?"

St. Ives faced about, and looked at Duval.

"Yes," he said, "we might, indeed, murder the King, but that is not the way in which I wish the Stuart cause to triumph. I want these German innovators to be banished the kingdom by the consent of the nobles and the people!"

"We will not talk politics," said Duval; "but I will tell you at once what brought me here."

"Do so. Although my first fright has passed away, and I am not so deeply interested as I was,"

"What did you fear?"

"That something had happened in regard to the Princess."

"No, she is perfectly safe; but I wish to ask you if the royal intention holds good in regard to the entertainment to-night at St. James's Palace?"

"I have heard nothing to the contrary; and as the day is so far advanced, I do not now anticipate any change of intention."

"But the King is down here."

"Yes; but the carriages and escort are ordered for four o'clock, so that he will be in town in good time."

"Well, St. Ives, without entering into further particulars with you, I wish you to be thoroughly aware that I intend to be present to-night at the King's entertainment."

St. Ives shook his head.

"I felt tolerably certain, Duval," he said, "or Sir John Cope, as I should call you in this atmosphere, that such was your intention."

"It is, and it is the intention of some one else likewise."

St. Ives turned full upon Duval, and slightly changed colour.

"By this time they had reached nearly to the end of the straight gravel walk, and were challenged by a sentinel.

In fact, the end of that walk might be called the real entrance to the gardens at Kew, since there was a military post which no one could pass without the watch-word of the day."

"Who goes there?" cried the sentinel.

"Crown!" replied St. Ives.

"Pass on!"

The sentinel grounded his musket, and stood at ease.

Then St. Ives and Claude Duval might fairly be considered to be within the precincts of the royal residence.

"Can you not guess?" said Duval, "to whom I allude?"

"I am afraid to guess."

"The Princess."

"Yes, my fears went in that direction."

"She has an earnest desire to be present at that royal entertainment, and my principal object in riding down here to see you, is by her request to consult you as to the best means of carrying out that desire."

"It is madness!" cried St. Ives.

"It is a fixed purpose, however, and I think even you to-morrow will not look upon it as so mad a freak as it seems to you to-day."

"I cannot countenance it, it is full of danger."

Will you take my word for it that it is not so?"

"Duval! Duval! you live in an atmosphere of adventure. Things that to other people are perilous in the extreme, are to you but the ordinary occurrences of existence. What if she were discovered?"

"I think the affair is tolerably safe; and I am quite certain she is so bent upon it that one of two things must ensue."

"What things?"

"She will either go without your assistance, and so, in all probability, really run considerable risk; or she will go with your help, and decrease that risk to its minimum."

St. Ives sighed.

They had walked over a considerable extent of the garden.

There was a shadowy walk among some trees, into which they had just turned.

At some distance off, Duval saw a man walking

alone, with his hands behind his back, and holding a walking stick in them."

"Who is that?"

St. Ives stopped abruptly.

"It is the King."

"And you are Colonel Miravel, of the Jacobite Horse."

"You do not tempt me," said St. Ives, with a smile.

"But you do me," said Duval.

"In what way?"

"If all the Jacobite emissaries and Jacobite leaders, and if all the family of the Stuarts were men like you, and all their Princesses like that one now at Farnborough House, I too should be a Jacobite'

"Duval! Duval!"

"Hush, you forget my name."

"Do not desert a cause because some of its adherents are men whom you do not approve of?"

"Don't call it desert," said Duval, "I have never joined you yet."

"Then, I mean, do not repudiate it, or hesitate to join it."

"I have just told you the conditions on which I would be a Jacobite."

"Alas! they are impossible!"

"I know it; but now, however, I will go further, and tell you what I would do if I were a Jacobite."

"What would you do?"

"I would take prisoner King George the Second, there, as he walks in his own garden. I would place his arm within mine, and frighten him into compliance, I would make him mount my groom's horse, and carry him off."

"It would be like you to try such a scheme, but it would be beset by a thousand dangers."

"Ah, St. Ives!" cried a voice, "a good-day to you."

St. Ives bowed as a couple of gentlemen in full Court costume came down another pathway.

"Who are they?" whispered Duval, as the two courtiers passed on.

"One is Lord Bute, the Prime Minister, and the other is a Scotch nobleman, the Marquis of Allendale. I suppose they have business with the King."

The two courtiers approached George the Second, bowing low every three or four steps, and then Duval saw that one of them presented a paper to him.

"What is all that about?" asked Duval.

"I know not; but I think it desirable that we should leave the gardens as soon as possible."

The King turned sharply at this moment and looked towards St. Ives.

It would seem as if one of the noblemen who had found the King had mentioned the fact that St. Ives was in the garden.

The King slightly beckoned to him.

"Wait for me here!" he whispered to Duval.

"I will!"

St. Ives hastened up to the King, and seemed to take some instructions from him.

Duval then saw him bow and retreat backward.

The King and the two noblemen turned and went up another avenue of the garden.

In another minute St. Ives rejoined Duval.

"I don't know what has happened to cause it," he said; "but there is some suspicion on the mind of both the King and his ministers that there will be an attempt to-night to make some movement on the part of the Jacobites."

"Exactly!" said Duval. "Now look you here, St. Ives. I am quite convinced that there is treachery somewhere. I do not belong to you, and have, as you know full well, refused the rank you have offered me in the name of the exiled family. But ever since that night when I was a witness to the meeting at the old mansion in the Oxford Road, I have felt convinced that among you there is a traitor!"

St. Ives turned pale.

"You may depend upon it," added Duval, "that however disagreeable such a supposition may be, the Jacobite leaders now in London are sharing their counsels with some one who is betraying them"

"If that were true," said St. Ives, "we are all lost!"

"I give it you as a caution, and bid you beware!"

"You fill my mind with uneasiness! But tell me— is it not possible to dissuade the Princess from going to the Court entertainment to-night?"

'It is not possible!—she is bent upon it'"

"Then it is better for me to assist her than thwart her!"

"Far better!"

"Be it so, then! I will be at Farnborough House by nine o'clock; and all I now request is, that she will await my coming."

"Make yourself easy upon that point."

"Then, so far, that is arranged. Good day to you, Sir John Cope—I see your horse at the gate."

"I shall be in London in less than an hour!" said Duval.

CHAPTER LXXXVII.

CLAUDE DUVAL HAS AN ADVENTURE ON THE ROAD.

IN five minutes more Duval and Blossom were on the road again.

The road from London to Kew is even now pretty and picturesque enough, but at that time it was still more so.

In the shadiest and most solitary portion of the road Blossom rode up to Duval.

"Captain," he said, "it seems a sin and a shame that we should take such a ride as this and make nothing of it!"

Duval laughed.

"You have an eye to business, Blossom."

"Indeed, I have, Captain. I don't know how your pockets are supplied, but mine are getting very empty!"

Duval paused.

"It is no secret, Blossom, to either of us that the expenses of Farnborough House must, so to speak, come off the road!"

"Exactly, Captain! Listen, now, to that sound, and only see how Nightshade pricks up his ears and snuffs at the air as though he scented an adventure!"

"You get quite poetical, Blossom! I certainly hear the sound of carriage wheels!"

"Of course, Captain! Don't they come grinding along at a good rate!"

"Let us breast this hill, Blossom; and when we get to its brow we shall be able to see what sort of a vehicle it is that approaches."

The hill was a steep one.

But Nightshade made nothing of it; and as Blossom was tolerably well mounted, they both stood upon its brow in the course of a few minutes.

At about half-a-mile distant they saw a carriage rapidly approaching.

It was an open barouche, and only drawn by two horses.

The general appearance, however, of the vehicle and the postilion and horses was aristocratic in the extreme.

As the carriage rapidly approached the foot of the hill Duval perceived that it contained two persons.

"Now, Captain," said Blossom, "what say you?

Shall we ask those gentlemen if they have anything in their pockets worth the taking?"

"It won't do, Blossom, for Sir John Cope to rob on the highway."

"But Claude Duval may. Look here, Captain: here's a little whitewashed cottage, and if there's anybody in it at all, it's most likely some old woman. Suppose you leave your overcoat and hat there, and carry out this little business in your own veritable character as Claude Duval."

Duval hesitated.

"There is scarcely time," he said.

Even as he spoke, the carriage reached the foot of the hill, and the horses subsided to a walk.

"Ample time," cried Blossom.

Duval immediately trotted up to the door of the little cottage, and dismounted.

He rapped sharply at it with the handle of his riding whip.

There was no reply.

He gave the door a sharp kick, and it flew open.

"Hilloa! within here!" he cried.

There was no reply.

The cottage was empty, and most likely belonged to some labouring family out at work in the fields.

It did not take Duval above a few seconds to get rid of his over disguise as Sir John Cope, and to appear in his true character as the dashing highwayman.

When he emerged from the cottage, too, he found that the white spot on the forehead of Nightshade had disappeared, as well as the white fetlock.

"All right, Captain," said Blossom. "I have the means with me of putting them on again when this little affair is over."

Duval sprang into the saddle.

"Wait for me here, Blossom," he said; "no one will see you among the trees."

"All's right, Captain: you won't want any help; since there are only two people and one postillion."

"Exactly," said Duval.

He trotted out on to the road.

The carriage was coming laboriously up the hill.

At its steepest part the postillion dismounted, in order to ease the horse which he had ridden.

The two gentlemen in the barouche might have done so likewise, if they had been particularly considerate.

But they were not, and they allowed the rather fagged horses to drag them up the steep ascent.

Duval did not ride on to meet the equipage.

On the contrary, he walked Nightshade slowly along the road with his back towards it.

His intention was to cry "Stand and deliver!" the moment the barouche nearly reached the brow of the hill.

He did not intend that there should be time either for the postilion to mount, or for the horse to get into a sharp trot.

And the road was very still and very solitary.

With the exception of Duval and Blossom, and that carriage with the postillion and its two occupants, there did not appear to be a living creature within miles of the spot.

Taking a sidelong glance at the progress of the carriage, Duval watched his opportunity.

He came to a standstill.

The postillion was about to mount again.

Then Duval faced Nightshade about suddenly.

He gave him that touch on the neck which the sagacious creature so well understood.

There was a rush and a leap.

Duval and his horse were by the side of the carriage.

"Gentleman," he said, "I daresay you will perceive that I am a highwayman!"

"A what!" cried both the gentlemen at once.

Then Duval recognised them as the two noblemen he had seen in the gardens at Kew talking to the King.

"A highwayman," he added; "and, as such, it is my vocation to say 'Stand and deliver!' My lords, I will trouble you for your watches, purses, jewellery, and, in fact, every article of value you have about me!"

"Insolent scoundrel!" cried Lord Bute.

"Beware, my lord — beware! I meant to take these things without making any return. They will be mostly gold, I fancy! Do not tempt me to return lead for them, in the shape of a bullet!"

The Marquis of Allendale looked vicious, but frightened.

"This is intolerable," said Lord Bute, "to be attacked in this way in the open face of day!"

"Are you so particular, my lord," said Duval, "that you must needs be robbed at night?"

"There is but one person," said the Marquis of Allendale, "who would have the temerity to commit such an act as this!"

Duval smiled.

"Do you know me, Marquis?"

"I do not; but it seems you know me. Nevertheless, if you are not Claude Duval, you are——"

"Do not trouble yourself to carry your illustration further, Marquis! I am Claude Duval!"

"I thought as much!"

A slight rustling in the rear attracted Duval's attention.

He glanced round just in time to see the postillion with a large open clasped knife in his hand approaching Nightshade.

Claude Duval, as is well known to the readers of these pages, was under ordinary, or even extraordinary circumstances usually amazingly self-possessed.

It took a great deal to move him.

Hard words passed by him like the idle wind.

A vigorous attempt upon his life he could excuse, and in the next moment he could forgive it.

But at the sight of this man with an open knife in his hand, Claude Duval appeared for a moment paralysed.

The man's eyes were fixed upon the horse — not upon its rider.

He was a fellow of most sinister-looking aspect, and to judge of him by his physiognomy, he seemed to be capable of any villany.

But what was he about?

What were his intentions?

A supposition flashed across the mind of Claude Duval.

He recollected hearing Blossom once tell a tale of how an ancient celebrated highwayman, called the Golden Farmer, was taken prisoner by his horse being ham-strung, and so effectually lamed.

Was this to be the fate of the gallant Nightshade?

Rather a thousand times would Claude Duval have had this man spring at his own throat, and aim the knife at his heart.

The state of indecision into which Duval was thrown lasted only until this supposition flashed across him.

By a peculiar touch he edged Nightshade round a few paces.

Nightshade never kicked, but Duval knew a touch that would make him do so.

He gave the touch with his heel.

Out flew the hind legs of Nightshade, and the postillion was fairly lifted off the ground by the shock of the tremendous kick he had received.

He did not speak a word.

But he rolled over and over, and the knife fell from his hand, and then he lay on the roadside, either dead or for the time being insensible.

"Villain!" shouted Duval.

All this had happened in so very brief a space of time that the two noblemen in the barouche had no opportunity of taking advantage of the abstraction of Duval.

There must have been something about the looks of Claude as he turned again towards them which was terrifying.

They made a great show of handing him their purses.

Duval passed his hand slowly across the mane of Nightshade.

"I can forgive much," he said, "but a dastardly attempt to injure this noble creature is more than I can well bear."

"We have made no such attempt," said the Earl of Bute.

"No, my lord, I do not accuse you."

"Nor I," said the Marquis of Allendale.

"Nor you either, my lord. At least, you are gentlemen, and had you treated me to a pistol shot each I should have thought nothing of it."

"We have no pistols."

Duval laughed.

"Otherwise you mean to say you would have done as much?"

"Perhaps."

"Well, gentlemen, there is no harm done. Now, be quick, if you please."

A couple of pocket-books.

Two purses.

Two gold watches and appendages.

A signet ring from the Prime Minister, and a diamond one from the Marquis.

Such was the amount of plunder which Duval was quickly in possession of.

As the Earl of Bute, however, handed him his ring, Duval caught a glimpse of some bright ornament just within his waistcoat.

"You have something there, my lord," he said, "which I think will suit me."

"I have, indeed; it is a locket, but it contains only a portrait which—which——"

"Which you wish to keep?"

"I do, indeed."

"Give me the setting then, which I perceive is enriched with brilliants."

"I have more than once," said the Earl, "tried to get this portrait out of the setting, but cannot."

"Perhaps I shall be more fortunate."

"Nay do not attempt it. The miniature is on the thinnest and finest ivory, and any attempt forcibly to remove it I feel would be its destruction."

Duval hesitated.

"You know who I am," added the Earl. "I promise you a hundred guineas to have that portrait with me."

"You shall redeem it, my lord, for that sum."

"When and where?"

"Before you are twelve hours older. I only ask of you to give me your word of honour as a peer that, when I do present it to you, you will not proclaim who and what I am; but, on the contrary, if it should be necessary to give me a name you will use the one I shall suggest to you."

"I promise."

"On your honour, my lord!"

"On my sacred word of honour as a peer and a gentleman!'

"I accept the condition; and you shall have your portrait back for half the sum you have named. So now my lords, good day!"

"How shall we get to town?"

"One of you must turn driver."

Duval, without another word, faced about to the hedge by the roadside, and encouraging Nightshade to the leap, he cleared it in good style.

The roadside was very woody, and Duval had no difficulty, whatever, in getting round to the little cottage without the two noblemen in the barouche having the least idea of whither he had gone.

"Bravo, Captain!" cried Blossom; "I saw it all."

"I have good booty."

"No doubt of that, Captain. Now my beauty, Nightshade, here goes for the white star on your forehead, again, and the white fetlock."

Duval hastily entered the cottage, and resumed his disguise as Sir John Cope.

As he was settling his wig, he called out to Blossom:

"Did you see that postillion, Blossom?"

"Yes, Captain."

"What was he going to do?"

"Hamstring Nightshade."

"I am glad of it—I am glad I was not mistaken."

"I was afraid to fire at him," said Blossom, "though I had my pistol in my hand, and raised it three times to do so."

"Indeed."

"Yes, Captain, you were all in such a line together; that if from any nervousness at the moment, I had missed the fellow, I must have hit Nightshade or you."

"I fancy Nightshade did the business for him, effectually."

"Capitally, Captain! Capitally! I know the fellow by sight."

"You do!"

"Yes, Captain. He is called Dare-all Dick, and boasts that no highwayman gets the better of him."

"I don't think he will boast that any more," said Duval, as he stepped out of the cottage.

They made their way along the meadows until they reached a narrow lane which led them out again on to the high road.

"Look back, Blossom," said Duval, "and see if you can see our friends in the barouche."

"Yes, Captain, there they come. They have lengthened the reins as much as they can, and one of them is driving from the inside."

Duval doubted for a moment whether he should put Nightshade to speed, and so easily distance the barouche, or by going at a quiet walk for about an hour, allow it to pass him.

He decided upon the latter course, for he was somewhat curious to know if the two noblemen, seeing him an apparent gentleman upon the road with his groom, would make any remark about what had happened.

The barouche came on rapidly.

Duval rode close to the hedgerow to avoid its wheels.

"I would advise you, sir," cried Lord Bute, "whoever you are, to keep a sharp look-out, for there is a highwayman on the road."

"Indeed, sirs!"

"Yes, we have been pretty handsomely robbed."

"Is he alone, sirs?"

"Oh, yes, but he is well armed, and we had no weapons, whatever, excepting our swords; and we think he has killed our postillion."

Lying across the bottom of the barouche was either the dead body, or the insensible form of the postillion.

"He must be a great rascal," said Duval.

"Well, I don't know that, exactly," said Lord Bute. "The fellow was gentlemanly enough, if it comes to that—but it is not pleasant to be stopped and robbed in broad daylight on the King's highway."

"What manner of man was he, sirs," asked Duval.

"Oh, a long, slim, wiry-looking fellow—not at all bad-looking."

"And he wore a scarlet coat," said Lord Allendalle, "and rode a horse—aye, such a horse—by-the-bye, sir, your horse, if it were not for that white star on the forehead, and the white fetlock, might do for its twin-brother."

"That is very curious," said Duval. "I have been told that there is but one such other horse as this in the kingdom, and that it belongs to the notorious Claude Duval."

"That's the very fellow who robbed us."

"I am quite delighted, gentlemen."

"Delighted!"

"Yes, for if it had not been Claude Duval, there must have been three horses such as this, and it pleased me to think that there were only two."

Duval, as he spoke, gave Nightshade a peculiar touch, and he sprung forward, stretching his limbs into a gallop which soon left the barouche and its occupants far behind him.

CHAPTER LXXXVIII.

THE FIRST SECRETARY TO THE RUSSIAN EMBASSY IS PLACED IN A DILEMMA.

It is nearly nine o'clock.

The night is very dark, but Pall Mall is lustrous with a hundred lights.

The royal entertainment has just begun—that is to say, it has begun so far, that the guests have begun arriving.

Down St. James's Street, and along Pall Mall, there are two dense lines of carriages.

Upon the footway, with great difficulty, sedan chairs make their way.

In these chairs are ladies of fashion and distinction, who will not disarrange their elaborate toilettes by getting into coaches, however roomy they may be.

Linkmen are running about in all directions.

The Palace itself, so far as its little obscure windows will permit it to be so, is brilliantly illuminated.

All is bustle and excitement.

The Palace clock strikes nine.

There is a sharp rap at the door of Farnborough House.

Mr. St. Ives is announced, and in another few seconds joins the little party who are residents of that establishment in one of the drawing-rooms.

"Welcome, St. Ives," cried Duval.

"I come reluctantly."

"Do not say so," exclaimed the Princess. "I can well understand your meaning. You do not wish me to attend the King's entertainment to-night?"

"I dread it, madam."

"It must be done. I have a motive, St. Ives, which, to-morrow I will explain to you."

St. Ives bowed.

"I have but to obey," he said; "and since this adventure must be carried out, I am, of course, desirous that it should be so with the minimum amount of risk."

"Thanks, Colonel."

"Nay, permit me to suggest it is far better to call me St. Ives even here."

"It shall be done."

"The least noticeable dress that you can go in, Princess, will be as one of the royal pages. They are all assembled on duty to-night, and there are so many of different sorts and conditions that they cannot possibly know each other."

"It shall be so, then."

"There are pages of the presence pages of ceremony—pages of the bed-chamber—of the back stairs—of the throne room—and extra pages of all kinds and degrees."

Dub! came a single knock at the door of Farnborough House.

"That," said St. Ives, "is, I fancy, a messenger of mine, with a parcel containing a complete page's costume, and, as they all wear powdered wigs, I think the disguise may be made very perfect indeed."

"And, besides, who knows me?" said the Princess. "I am but a stranger in this land, and I fancy this poor face of mine is scarcely known to half a dozen persons in all England."

St. Ives sighed.

His conjectures were right in regard to the parcel.

It was addressed to "Miss Pauline Cope."

Then St. Ives was alone with Claude Duval.

"I, too," said Claude,—"what costume do you advise that I go in, St. Ives?"

"A quiet, plain, evening dress, without disguise at all."

Duval inclined his head.

"I quite agree with you, St. Ives; but there is one question more. How are we to gain admittance to the Palace?"

"The Princess will have no difficulty, for the pages are continually running in and out; but how you are to obtain admittance, I must really leave to your own ingenuity."

"It may be difficult."

"It is sure to be so; and I, for my part, scarcely expect to see you there."

Duval smiled.

"I am rather used to encounter difficulties, and to overcome them, St. Ives."

"I know that well."

"Besides, I have an appointment there."

"An appointment?—with whom?"

"The Earl of Bute."

"The Prime Minister?"

"Yes. Are you not full of fears, St. Ives, for the safety of the Stuart Princess, and for your own life?"

"No," replied St. Ives, gravely. "I have no such fears, and that you know well, Sir John Cope."

"I do, indeed; but time presses, and I must get myself ready."

"I, too," said St. Ives, "shall be missed if I do not make my appearance quickly. Tell the Princess that when she is ready, she has nothing whatever to do but to boldly walk into the Palace."

"I will."

"And she is to adopt only one rule of conduct."

"What is that?"

"If anybody says anything to her, or impedes her in the slightest degree, she has only to be as impertinent as possible, and they will swear to her being a royal page at once."

Duval could not help laughing at this instruction, but he promised faithfully to repeat it to the Princess.

St. Ives then left Farnborough House, and Claude Duval, who was very nearly ready, soon completed his necessary costume.

He wore a plain suit of black velvet, with black silk stockings and diamond buckles.

A sword, with a cut steel scabbard and hilt, and a foreign order hanging from one of his button-holes, completed his costume.

The Stuart Princess looked charming in her page's dress.

The metamorphosis was so complete—mainly owing to the powdered wig she wore—that even Duval himself felt that he would have to look more at her, should

THE KING TAKING THE POISONED CUP.

he meet her in the royal saloons, to be certain of her identity.

He repeated to her the instructions left to her for her guidance by St. Ives.

"Alas!" she said; "my head is rather too heavy for the impertinence he speaks of; but I will do my best to put it on since it is a part I have to play."

"Do so," said Duval; "and, for heaven's sake, be careful of your safety!"

"Farewell; for the sake of those who love me, I will be so!"

The Princess left Farnborough House.

But Duval was too anxious to allow her to proceed entirely alone, and he followed her at a cautious distance.

He saw her go down by the side of Marlborough House.

He saw her turn into the Ambassadors' Court of the Palace, without being in the slightest degree impeded by the yeomen of the Guard, who were in strong force at its entrance.

No. 29.—NIGHTSHADE.

So far she was safe.

Duval had, then, to think of the best mode of effecting an entrance into the Palace himself.

By glancing into St. James's Park, he saw that by that route a long line of carriages was making their way to the palace.

The Park was darker than the streets.

There were the carriage lights, and there were the linkmen, but the latter kept in a throng near Marlborough House Gardens.

Duval strolled into the Park.

He knew that all the occupants of those carriages must have tickets.

But the difficulty was how to possess himself of one.

A bold idea came across his imagination.

He knew that his appearance would befriend him, rich and costly as it was.

He made his way along the Mall until he was so far from the Palace, that the carriages he was opposite to could not expect, at least, for a quarter of an hour, to reach the entrance.

"Tickets—tickets, my lords, ladies, and gentlemen!" cried Duval. "Show me your tickets, if you please, or you can't pass the sentinels! Now, sirs, if you please!"

Five tickets were handed to him from a large family coach.

Duval glanced at them.

They were ladies' tickets, and the occupants of the coach were two elegantly-dressed peeresses.

"Quite right, ladies—quite right!" said Duval, as he handed back the tickets. "Pass on, coachman—pass on! Tickets, sirs, if you please—tickets!"

Three gentlemen and one lady were in the next vehicle.

The whole four tickets were handed out to Duval.

"Thank you, my lords, thank you! My Lord Chamberlain feels that he cannot be too particular. Ah! all's right—all's right! This one, and this one, and this one."

He handed three back into the carriage.

"My ticket, if you please?" cried a testy gentleman from the vehicle.

"Something wrong here," said Duval; "it wants an indorsement!"

"Stop! stop!"

"I'll get it done for you, my lord—meet you at the entrance! Good night!"

"Stop! stop!—my ticket!"

Duval was off.

Light of foot, he threaded his way among the carriages, and reached the entrance of the Ambassadors' Court.

"Plenty of time," said Duval.

He knew that it would be nearer twenty minutes than even a quarter of an hour before that particular coach could get up to the entrance.

Duval walked with a quiet step towards the crowd of Yeomen of the Guard and officers of the Chamberlain, who guarded the entrance.

He presented his ticket.

It was glanced at by one of the officials, who then called out in a loud voice, "First Secretary to the Russian Embassy."

The ticket was then torn into two, and one half of it was presented to Claude Duval.

"Pass on, sir, if you please!"

"So," said Duval to himself, "I am First Secretary to the Russian Embassy."

He walked on with his half-ticket in his hand.

"This way—this way!" cried several voices.

Duval turned to the right.

He passed under a temporary portico that had been erected.

Glancing downwards he saw that he trod upon crimson cloth, and in a few seconds more he stood in one of the small vestibules of the Palace.

There his half-ticket was demanded of him.

But the demand was made in much lower and polite tones.

He surrendered it at once.

The official personage who took it bowed gracefully.

"Straight on, Chevalier," he said, "and up the staircase."

"I wish I knew my name," thought Duval. "I am secretary to an embassy, and a Chevalier, but that is all I am aware of."

Without either hesitation or precipitation, however, Claude Duval obeyed the directions given him.

He went up a staircase covered with crimson velvet.

He passed through a corridor which was a blaze of light.

At its further extremity there were two gilt doors.

About half a dozen of the royal pages, and several Yeomen of the Guard kept possession of those doors.

Claude Duval scarcely expected to see among those pages the fair face of the Stuart Princess, and yet he looked with some anxiety from one to the other of them.

"Your name and rank, sir?" asked one of the grooms of the chambers.

Duval was puzzled for a moment.

It was quite necessary to say something.

But who should he call himself.

He had a notion in his mind, correct or incorrect, that Russian names were more thoroughly Russian the more unpronounceable they were.

He spoke quite calmly, and with a most admirable self-possession.

"The Chevalier Slitzinkinoffritzvergenofen, First Secretary of the Russian Embassy."

The official looked aghast.

But he had no resource.

He must try his best; and as one of the pages maliciously flung open one of the gilt doors he cried out, "The Chevalier Slitzfitzhigintrofner!"

"That will do," thought Duval.

Another moment and he was in the royal saloon, and in the midst of an amazing scene of magnificence and grandeur.

A great number of small German potentates, with all their suites, happened to be in London at that time, and they certainly made a very brave show in the way of costume.

As Duval entered, a concealed band of music was playing a well-known Lutheran hymn, which it was well known was a great favourite with the King.

This piece of music usually heralded the royal approach; for the air which now goes by the name of the national one of "God save the King," was unknown at that period.

But the saloon into which Duval had made his way was the first of three.

It was in the second which the peculiar circle which surrounded royalty was to be found.

The third saloon was made into a banquet hall.

The doors were closed, and heavily draped with crimson velvet curtains until twelve o'clock.

The scene was a pleasant one, as all these courtly scenes are.

Whatever evil passions and jealousies may be hidden beneath the surface, that surface, like paint or painting, hides all defects.

But Duval was anxious to look for the Princess.

So anxiously, indeed, that the pages, in whose faces he gazed so earnestly, must have wondered at the interest a stranger took in their expressions.

But he could see nothing whatever of the Stuart Princess; and many fears began to take possession of him.

The saloons were well thronged, and the heat began to be oppressive.

Fresh arrivals, however, added every minute to the throng, for these Court entertainments were eminently political.

To stay away was to be suspected of Jacobite propensities.

And as it was a proof of loyalty to be present, all those who had an object in wanting to appear loyal, took care to show themselves at the King's entertainment.

Duval made his way into the second saloon.

The crowd was there more dense than in the first.

At the farther end was a kind of raised platform, not, however, above six inches from the floor, upon which no one but the Royal Family and the grand officers of state, ventured.

The King was seated there.

He was playing some dreary German game with dominoes, at a small table.

His opponent was a lady past the middle age, and

very conspicuous from the quantity and boldness of her jewellery.

A throng of courtiers half surrounded the table, towards the back of the King.

They pretended to be deeply interested in the game, of which they knew little, and cared less.

And Duval was not at all slow to perceive the wisdom of the advice which had been given him by St. Ives, viz., to make his appearance at the royal entertainment in a plain, undistinguished evening dress.

There were hundreds such.

He had but to mix with the throng about him, and his individuality was completely lost.

It will be remembered, likewise, that Duval had another errand at this Court entertainment besides looking after the safety of the Stuart Princess.

He intended to keep his word with the Earl of Bute.

The miniature, in its costly setting of brilliants, which he, Duval, had taken from that nobleman, with the promise of returning it for the sum of fifty guineas, was in one of his pockets.

But Duval did not intend to return that miniature hastily.

It was just possible that it might be of great importance to him later in the evening.

And now the dance music commenced.

The more boisterous modern dances were not in vogue at that time.

They were rather stately exhibitions of paces and deportment, than riotous twirling up and down a saloon, the only object of a couple, apparently, being not to tread on each others' toes.

Royal balls always opened with the grave, stately minuet.

It was called *La Minuet de la Cour*; it was performed to slow and appropriate music, and for many years sustained its supremacy.

Various gentlemen, connected with the Court, seemed to act as Masters of the Ceremonies.

One in particular, in a very elegant suit of white velvet appeared to give directions to the others.

Duval happened to be close to this personage, when two of the courtiers came hurriedly up to him.

"If you please, Sir Nicholas," said one, "there is quite a disturbance in the courtyard."

"A disturbance? Impossible!"

"There are high words, sir, and the Yeomen don't know what to do."

"Are they Jacobites?"

"Oh no, Sir Nicholas; but the Russian Ambassador and all the gentlemen of the Russian Embassy are in the tumult."

"Ah," thought Duval, "this concerns me."

"But what is it about?" asked Sir Nicholas.

"Why, sir, the First Secretary of the Embassy, they say, has been refused admission, in consequence of having lost or mislaid his ticket."

Sir Nicholas Grant, who was the Deputy-Chamberlain, shook his head.

"His Majesty's orders are peremptory."

"Yes, Sir Nicholas; but——"

"It's of no use to speak about it. The only persons who can be admitted without tickets are members of the Royal Family and officers in the uniform of the King's German Legion."

The two officers bowed, and left the vice-Chamberlain.

Duval was standing close to him.

"It is very strange, sir," he said, with a half bow to Duval, "that people will be so careless."

"Very," replied Duval.

The Vice-Chamberlain walked away.

Some one touched Duval's arm.

He glanced around, and saw the fair face of the Stuart Princess.

CHAPTER LXXXIX.

THE ROYAL BANQUET AND WHAT HAPPENED AT IT.

"You are here, I see," she said.

"Yes."

"Had you any difficulty it gaining admittance?"

"Not much, and you?"

"None whatever."

"You have seen the King?"

"I have seen the man who calls himself the king."

"Hush! for you own sake and for the sakes of all those who takes an interest in you. This is not an atmosphere in which to utter what are called disloyal speeches."

The Princess made a gesture of impatience.

"It is irksome to me," she said, "to see men who I know are Jacobites in their hearts, bowing and smiling round the chair of that man."

"I pray you again to be cautious."

"I will—I will! Fear nothing!"

"And at the same time I may suggest that many of those men are nothing at all at their hearts but what may turn out to their own advantage."

"It may be so?"

A man at this moment, dressed in a very quiet brown suit with a Court sword, stepped up to the Princess.

"I think you are one of the Pages of the Presence," he said.

"Well, sir?"

"This folded paper, then, ought to be placed in the hands of the King."

"Place it yourself?"

"Saucy as a page, is a proverb," said the man, "but you will not be doing your duty if you fail in this matter."

Partly curiosity and partly indecision induced the Princess to take the folded paper.

The man who had given it her immediately disappeared among the crowd.

"What is it?" asked Duval.

The Princess opened the paper.

It contained the following words:—

"Your Majesty is respectfully informed that she is here."

The Princess turned pale.

"Save me, Duval," she said.

"For heaven's sake be calm! What imprudence!"

"Forgive me! At the moment I knew not where I was."

"Hush! Let us walk along and appear to be conversing on indifferent topics."

"Yes, yes?"

"Try to laugh, and we shall, perhaps, find some corner removed from the general throng, where we can look at this paper again."

The Princess made a great effort.

She put on an air of perfect ease and composure.

A smile was on her face.

She imitated the saucy, swaggering gait, which she had seen the other pages assume.

And so, by the side of Duval, she walked the whole length of one of the saloons.

She had to keep near the walls to avoid the dancers.

"In here," said the Princess.

She pointed to one of the windows, which were so deeply set in the wall as to form almost a little apartment.

"No—no," said Duval, "that would be hazardous."

"You are right?"

"Let us talk as we walk along. We can surely manage to utter grave words with an air of levity."

"We will try."

"Did you know the man who gave you the note?"

"I have a dim recollection of him, but very dim."

"Have you any idea of who or what he can be?"

"If I have met him at all in this country, he should be a Jacobite."

"If so, then," replied Duval, "he is a traitor to your cause and, perhaps, in him you have seen the man who has been playing the spy and traitor for some time."

"It may be so."

"Ah! There is St. Ives."

"Where? Where?"

"Yonder, leaning against that porphyry column. Look with what interest he regards us."

"He has recognised us both, then?"

"Instantly."

"He is making his way towards us, let us meet him."

Without appearing to make any violent effort to do so, Claude Duval and the Princess eagerly met St. Ives half-way.

Then they all laughed, for they did not know what eyes might be upon them.

Still keeping the smile upon his face, St. Ives managed to say, significantly, "This way!"

They followed him through a small doorway, and then along a passage, which led by another route to that saloon kept closed, and in which the royal banquet was laid.

St. Ives glanced about him.

"We are alone," he said.

"I think so," replied Duval, "but I should advise that we stand as near the centre of this saloon as possible, and there speak very low."

They did so, and St. Ives then in a voice of emotion, said, "There is danger. I scarcely know what form or shape it will assume, but there is danger."

"To whom?" asked the Princess.

"We will not speak of ourselves," added St. Ives, "since I know I can speak for our friend here, when I say that our whole thoughts are of the possible danger to you."

"Do you know more than you say, St. Ives, or is this a mere suspicion?"

"I do not know more than I say, but I am so well acquainted with the looks and manners of the officials, that I am convinced of the fact."

"I fancy," said Duval, "that this is a confirmation."

He handed St. Ives a slip of paper.

The colour fled for an instant from the face of the Jacobite Colonel, as he read the ominous words.

"This is indeed a confirmation," he said, "and it is a death warrant."

"No," said Duval, as he placed his hand upon his sword

The Princess shrank back a step.

"You misunderstand me," said St. Ives, sadly, "I mean that it is the death warrant of the writer."

"You know that writer?" asked the Princess.

"I do."

"He is one of us?"

"He assumed and affected to be so, but he is a traitor."

"His name?"

"His name is Carew."

The Princess clasped her hands.

"I recollect him well now, and wonder that I could not name him; he came over to Rotterdam, and saw nearly the whole of us."

"There is only one thing that I am extremely anxious about," said St. Ives.

"And that is?"

"It is involved in the question of did he, or did he not recognise you to night."

"I think not."

"I am confident he did not," said Duval. "I watched his countenance, and it was quite impossible that any man could be so consummate an actor, as not to show by some expression, or movement of a rebellious muscle, such a recognition, if it were really present in his mind."

"You lift a load off my heart."

"Be at ease on that score, St. Ives."

"Then all may yet be well. Princess, you must fly. The same facility with which you got into the Palace, in your costume of a page, will doubly serve you to leave it."

"It is too soon," said the Princess.

"Too soon?"

"Yes, much too soon."

"Oh! Princess, beware that it be not too late! Remember, oh! remember, how many lives and fortunes depend upon your actions, and your safety. I implore you not to hesitate."

"Speak for me, Duval."

"Hush! that name again."

St. Ives looked from one to the other in a bewildered fashion.

"There is a reason," said Duval. "Trust to me; the Princess shall incur no real danger, and as soon after the royal banquet has commenced as possible, she shall leave the Palace."

Several pages and servants of the Palace, came at this moment into the banquet room.

St. Ives raised his voice and spoke carelessly.

"Very handsomely done, indeed," he said. "I never saw a prettier display."

He wished to convey the impression that they had been brought into that saloon by one of the royal pages, to see the preparations for the banquet.

The Princess took the hint.

"Yes," she said, "you see it better now than when the crowd is in."

"Far better," said Duval.

One of the pages walked up to the Princess, and looked at her steadily.

"Who may you happen to be?" he asked.

"I suppose you would very much like to know?" said the Princess.

"Yes, I should, for I never saw you before."

"You'd better walk all round me, and you'll see me in all ways."

"Oh, indeed! You're saucy enough to be a monkey's brother."

"No," said the Princess, "you and I are not at all related."

The page was discomfited.

"Just wait till after the banquet, that's all," he said.

"That's as it suits me," said the Princess. "Good bye, monkey."

"Oh, get along!"

Duval and St. Ives were somewhat amused at this short colloquy, but they were glad enough when it was over, notwithstanding the Princess had played her part so well in it.

"You're a capital page!" whispered Duval.

"I have heard several of them speaking to each other, this evening, and took some pains to catch the tone and manner of their discourse."

"You hit it admirably."

"What am I to do with this paper, St. Ives?"

"Nothing—let me have it."

There was a flourish of trumpets at this moment, which seemed as if they announced some important event in the evening's proceedings.

"Is it so late?" said Duval. "That must surely herald the commencement of the banquet!"

"No," replied St. Ives. "I saw and heard that rehearsed. It is a new dance imported from the Court of Vienna, the only music of which is a trumpet accompaniment."

"A somewhat boisterous movement."

"It is so. An Austrian galop, as it is termed."

Duval looked at his watch.

St. Ives started at the sight of it.

"Surely I have seen that before," he said.

"Like enough," said Duval, carelessly; "it was lately the property of the Prime Minister."

"Lately? Here?"

"No—my errand here is partly one of restitution, not one of robbery. The Earl of Bute and I met upon the highway, and this is one of the little results."

The Princess and Duval both looked with some curiosity upon the new Viennese dance.

It was about the first of those noisy demonstrative measures which made war against the old stately figure dances of our ancestors.

"It wants but a quarter to twelve," said Duval.

"Exactly!" remarked St. Ives; "and at the end of this dance the banquet will begin."

The dance was over.

There was a general clapping of hands.

Then the band began to play that same Lutheran hymn which had before attracted Duval's attention.

The velvet curtains were ran aside.

The doors of the banquet-room were thrown open, and the guests began to throng in to partake of the royal hospitality.

A personage, magnificently dressed in purple velvet, and sparkling with jewels, hastily passed our little party of friends.

This personage carried a gilt wand in his hand.

"His Grace the new Lord Chamberlain!" cried several voices.

It was, indeed, the Duke of Montrose, who on that night, for the first time, appeared in his new office.

At first glance, seeing that honours and distinctions were showered upon him, the Duke of Montrose would seem to have very little inducement to engage in Jacobite plots.

But he was poor and grasping.

George the Second was liberal enough of honours and distinctions to the old nobility, but he kept a tight grasp of the Crown lands.

The forfeited estates of the Jacobite nobles were not distributed with a liberal hand.

Hence the Duke of Montrose was quite willing that there should be a change of dynasty.

He was promised by the Stuart family in the event of that change being brought about, a very large accession of property."

That was the secret of his political creed.

"It is time!" whispered the Princess.

"It is," replied Duval.

"Time for what?" asked St. Ives, anxiously. "For heaven's sake tell me what it is time for?"

"Time for us to proceed to the banquet-hall."

"I had a hope that you meant it was time to go."

"No, Miravel," whispered the Princess, "it is more than ever time to stay."

"Mr. St. Ives! Mr. St. Ives!" said a voice at this moment.

Duval just succeeded in shrinking back as the Earl of Bute stepped up to the spot.

The Earl took St. Ives aside, and whispered to him eagerly.

"I will warrant," said Duval to himself, "that he is imparting to St. Ives his suspicions that the notorious Claude Duval, the highwayman, may be present at the Royal entertainment."

Duval then turned to speak to the Princess.

But she was gone.

He made no doubt he should find her in the banquet-room; and he made his way in that direction as quickly as possible, considering that he was in the midst of a dense throng of courtiers, ladies, officers, ambassadors, and general guests of the entertainment at St. James's.

The tables were very brilliantly spread.

Almost all the gold plate belonging to all the different households was exhibited.

The King sat in an arm chair, perched upon the topmost pinnacle of which was a gilt crown.

Almost immediately behind him was the Duke of Montrose with his staff of office.

A crowd of pages hovered about the royal table, at which were seated the Archbishop of Canterbury, and likewise of York, together with several of the highest ministers of state.

There was a flourish of trumpets.

The banquet began.

Duval succeeded in obtaining a seat not far from the royal table.

He ran his eye over the Pages most anxiously, in search of the Princess, but he saw nothing of her.

His heart felt sad, and full of unknown alarms.

And Duval might have looked a long while without being able to cast his eye upon that fair young face.

The fact was, she had made her way into the banquet-room with great expedition, and placed herself exactly at the back of the royal chair.

In fact, she leant her back against it, and, crossing her arms upon her chest, looked about her with apparent negligence.

But, all the while, she kept a wary eye upon the Duke of Montrose.

CHAPTER XC.

THE EARL OF BUTE IS COMPELLED TO RECOGNISE CLAUDE DUVAL AS A FRIEND.

THE Princess was so much in shadow behind the King's chair that no one took any particular notice of her.

And so the banquet proceeded.

It was more a show than a reality.

The guests partook daintily of a few dishes set before them, and the ladies demolished some of the sweetmeats.

But that was all.

Wine, to be sure, flowed freely, and then there ensued a pause.

No toast had been drunk; for it was not etiquette to do so, until the King chose to set the example.

A groom of the chambers approached, bearing upon a huge golden salver a goblet of the same metal

The new Lord Chamberlain met him two paces from the King's chair.

It was his privilege to hand the goblet to the King, who, according to custom, was to partake of some of its contents, saying, as he did so, "To all our loving subjects."

The Princess kept a wary eye upon the Duke.

Instead of turning towards the full glare of the lights in the banquet-hall, after he had taken the salver with the goblet, he turned in the other direction.

It was but for a moment.

And, narrowly, although the Princess watched him, she could not perceive that he did anything in respect to the King's wine cup.

But there was a look upon his face, when it was turned to the light again, which was conclusive.

If ever Nature painted the word "murder" upon a human countenance in legible characters, it was certainly in this instance.

The Princess shifted her position.

The Duke of Montrose had laid his long wand of office against the King's chair.

He required two hands to hold the salver.

He knelt on one knee, and held up both salver and goblet towards the King.

George the Second reached out his hand.

He took hold of the goblet, which he knew was to be the perquisite of the Lord Chamberlain.

He muttered something to himself.

The Princess could only catch the words, "jeweller," and "might have made it lighter."

It was evident that the penurious king grudged the costly character of the perquisite.

Then he rose.

Rose, still holding the goblet in his hand.

The Duke of Montrose retreated two steps, and clasped his hands so rigidly together that the knuckles stood out white and cold as marble.

"To all our loving subjects," cried the King.

The trumpeters blew a royal flourish.

The Stuart Princess had hold of the long gilt wand of the Lord Chamberlain.

She poised it securely upon some of the ornamental carvings of the royal chair.

Thrusting it forward, then, like a lance, exactly under the King's arm, she struck the side of the goblet with it.

The blow was so sudden and so entirely unexpected, that the gold vessel flew from the King's hand instantly.

It fell upon the table and rolled to the floor, spilling every drop of its contents.

"Treason!" shouted the Duke of Montrose.

The word must have been hovering upon his lips.

Why he shouted it out he would have found it difficult to tell at that moment, or at any other

"What is the meaning of this?" cried the King, angrily.

The Princess darted from behind the royal chair, and sped down the apartment.

"Stop him—stop him!" cried the other pages,—"stop him! There he goes! It's his doing! What disrespect to his Majesty! Stop that page!—stop that page!"

The Princess gained the door leading into the middle saloon.

The man in the brown coat, who had handed her the mysterious paper to give to the King, started before her and spread out his arms.

"Treason!" he cried, "and this is one of the traitors!"

"And this another!" said Duval.

As Claude spoke, he sprung upon this man, and catching him by the throat whirled him round, flinging him bodily nearly on to one of the supper tables.

The Princess fled through the doorway.

Then there came a tap of a drum.

The Duke of Montrose stood forward.

"It is his Majesty's order that no one leaves St. James's."

All eyes were on Duval, for at least a hundred people had seen that he had aided in the escape of the page.

"Seize that man!" cried the Duke of Montrose.

"Hands off, gentlemen!" said Duval, as he placed his hand upon the hilt of his sword.

"Who are you? Who and what are you?" cried a dozen voices.

"One at a time, gentlemen."

St. Ives then struggled forward.

He meant to save Duval.

He laid his hand upon his arm.

"Whoever this gentleman is," he said, "I will remove him from the royal presence."

"No, Mr. St. Ives," said Duval, "I am much obliged."

"A Jacobite!—a Jacobite!" cried twenty voices.

"You are wrong again, gentlemen, and I shall appeal against your hasty decision to a friend of mine in this assembly."

"What friend?"

"The Right Honourable the Earl of Bute."

"The Prime Minister?"

"Exactly so, gentlemen."

"What presumption! Here is the Earl."

"Ah! my Lord," said Duval, "do you not remember your friend Colonel Chevelier St. Mar, to whom you gave a ticket for this gracious assembly?"

"St. Mar?" said the Earl. "I give a ticket?"

"Down with him! Run him through! A Jacobite! A spy!"

"One moment, gentlemen," added Duval.

He stepped close up to the Earl.

"I have brought your Grace the ivory miniature in its setting of diamonds."

"Ah!"

"The fifty guineas are of no moment."

"Oh!"

"But your Grace's word of honour that you would recognise me and call me by whatever name I chose, I am sure will not be broken."

"But the miniature?"

"Is here."

Duval placed it in the Earl's hand.

"Gentlemen," said the Earl, as he slid his arm beneath Duval's, "it is an old reproach of Ministers of State that they have short memories, but I now perfectly recollect my friend here."

"Of course," said Duval.

The crowd of courtiers and guests drew back.

"Allow me to make known to you all, gentlemen," added the Earl, "Colonel Chevelier St. Mar."

Duval bowed.

He felt, however, that the Duke held his arm tightly.

And so they passed out into the second saloon which was nearly empty, except of a few serving men belonging to the Palace.

The Earl half dragged Duval into the deep embrasure of a window, and then, releasing his arm, he said, "You must explain all this to me."

"Must, my Lord?"

"Well, well, we will not quarrel about terms. I ask you to do so."

Duval was silent.

"What does it all mean? What page was that, and why did he upset the King's goblet, and why did you peril your life by throwing yourself in the way of pursuit of him?"

"My Lord," said Duval, "these are matters which are the secrets of other people. Be satisfied that I have kept my word with you, and that I freely acknowledge that you have kept yours with me."

"But all this is so mysterious!"

"It is, my Lord."

"And the King will be in an agony of curiosity."

"I cannot help it."

"I can," said a voice.

"No—no!" said Duval.

He knew the voice.

It was that of the Princess.

She stepped into the embrasure of the window, and stood by his side.

"Ah!" cried the Earl of Bute, "you are the runaway page!"

"I am."

"We shall get at the secret now."

"You shall."

At this moment there came through the doors of the

banqueting room, several gentlemen with drawn swords.

"Run round to the court-yard!" cried one.

"The Colour court!" shouted another.

"He must break his neck!" said a third.

"How strange!" cried several voices together. "The Duke of Montrose must have been struck with sudden insanity to dash through one of the windows as though he were bound to make his escape from the Palace on peril of his life!"

"The Duke of Montrose!" exclaimed the Earl.

"Stop!" said the Princess.

The Earl had been about to rush out into the room.

"Stop! you will more quickly learn the secret of this mystery by remaining here."

"You can tell me?"

"I can."

"In the name of heaven, then, what is it?"

"There was poison in the King's goblet."

"Poison?"

"Yes, and placed there by the Duke of Montrose."

"Impossible!"

"Not only possible, but true; and seeing that the dastardly attempt at assassination was foiled, he has fled."

"Indeed!" cried the Earl, "that gives a colour to the charge!"

"I saw it, and I am the page who frustrated that attempt."

"But who are you?"

"That must still remain a secret, my Lord."

"Then you are not a royal page?"

"Yes, for this night, and this night only."

"You bewilder me, both of you; but if it be true that you have thus saved the King's life, and likewise saved this kingdom from being thrown into a state of frightful anarchy and confusion, there is no reward you may not rightly claim."

The eyes of the Princess brightened.

"I do claim a reward; but first of all, I will prove the truth of my assertion. There must be still some drains of the poisoned wine in the goblet. Let them be seen to, I will stand or fall by the experiment."

"In good faith!" cried the Earl, "who will try it?"

A strange cry came from the banquet hall.

There was a noise as of the upsetting of chairs and the clashing of swords.

Several courtiers rushed into the centre saloon.

"A physician! A physician!" they cried.

The Earl would again have left the embrasure of the window, but Duval stopped him.

"Let me go, my lord, and ascertain what this means."

"As you please."

Duval walked forth.

He stopped one of the terrified attendants.

"What has happened?"

"Why, sir, one of the King's pages picked up his Majesty's gold cup, and, boy like, must needs taste a few drops of the wine that still lingered at the bottom of it, when, with a scream, he instantly fell dead."

The Earl of Bute heard these words.

"Enough," he said, "the proof is as complete as it is horrible. What would you wish me to do?"

"I want to see the King," said the Princess.

"You shall. He has retired into his own private apartments, but I can procure you admittance. Follow this way."

"And I, too," said Duval.

"You wish to see the King, likewise?"

"Not particularly; but I do not like to abandon my young friend here."

"Come along, then; you shall only abandon him at the door of the King's apartment."

All doors in St. James's were speedily opened to the Earl of Bute.

The Yeomen of the Guard made way for him at once; and, indeed, it was only with difficulty that he waved off the officious attendance of some of the Palace servants.

After traversing several corridors, and descending one staircase, and ascending another, the Earl of Bute opened a door which led into a small guard chamber.

It was well lighted, and a bright fire burnt in its grate.

Arms and accoutrements lay about it.

"Wait here a moment," said the Earl, in a low voice.

He walked through the chamber, and opened a door at its further extremity, and disappeared from before the eyes of Claude Duval and the Stuart Princess.

Then the latter sat down upon a high-backed chair, and, clasping her hands, she looked wistfully at Duval.

"Am I wise?" she said. "Or have I lost all?"

"I know not," said Duval; "but no danger shall approach you without a struggle."

"The Earl of Bute - is he to be trusted?"

"I think so. Moreover, he knows nothing of you but as one who this night did good service to the King."

"That is true, he cannot suspect me."

"And even should he do so," replied Duval, "I cannot believe there is any real danger."

The Princess sighed.

"I ought not to be here," she said; "but yet the motive will excuse the rashness."

It was quite evident to Claude Duval that the Princess had some secret motive for getting an audience of the King of which he as yet knew nothing.

That that motive was founded upon some generous impulse he was convinced.

Had Duval, however, felt inclined to question the Princess concerning it, there would scarcely have been time to do so.

The Earl of Bute was only absent about five minutes from the guard chamber.

"I have seen the King," he said to the Princess, "and you can have an audience at once."

"Do I owe that to his Majesty's gratitude?" asked the Princess.

The Earl of Bute hesitated before he replied; and then a slight smile crossed his face, as he said, "We will not be too curious in searching for motives; and whether it be his Majesty's gratitude or curiosity which prompts him to grant you an audience, you have but to accept it."

"If I still wish it."

"Nay," said the Earl, "it now amounts to a command."

"A command to me?" said the Princess.

But she recollected herself instantly.

There was danger in any such manifestation of feeling.

"I will attend you, my lord," she said, "instantly."

But Duval was uneasy.

He interposed.

"Let me hope," he said, "my Lord Bute, that as I with my life am willing to be answerable for the safety of this youth, you will not, let what may happen, allow him to be jeopardized."

"How can a person who has served the King's life be in any jeopardy?"

"That is true. I will wait here with what patience I may."

There was a something about the air and manner of the Earl of Bute which bred an innate kind of suspicion in the mind of Claude Duval that he suspected the seeming youthful page was not exactly what he affected to be.

But he could found no act upon that suspicion.

Duval, therefore, could only throw himself into one of the chairs in the guard-room, and there wait the return of the Princess.

It was quite impossible, through the double doors and thick hangings which separated him from the adjoining apartment, to hear a word that was spoken.

But the imagination of Duval was morbidly active, and he kept fancying he heard expressions which had no foundation but in his own fancy.

And now we will leave Duval to his own cogitations, while we follow the Stuart Princess and the Earl of Bute to the presence of George the Second.

At the very first substantive alarm in the banquet-hall of the Palace, the King had hastily left it, and sought refuge in those private apartments.

And it was indeed his curiosity, much more than his gratitude, which induced him to grant an audience to the strange page who had saved his life.

The King was on a couch.

He had assumed a common favourite attitude of his whenever any alarm was in the royal mind.

That is to say, he had drawn up his legs completely off the ground, and was huddled up on the couch in as small a compass as possible.

"The page, your Majesty," announced the Earl of Bute.

"Well, we said we would see him, and we will keep our word; don't go away, Bute, whatever you do; and —and Bute—come hither."

The minister went close to the King.

"Have you searched him well, for concealed weapons? Eh!"

"No, your majesty."

"No? No?"

"Your Majesty surely forgets that this is the youth who actually saved your life."

"But we can't be too cautious, Bute!"

"Certainly not, your Majesty; but we may be too suspicious."

"Well—well, let us hear what he's got to say for himself."

The Earl beckoned the Princess to approach.

"Now, Sir Page," said the King, harshly, "what is it?"

This was such an unexpected commencement of the conference, that the Princess was at first at a loss for a reply.

It was in a tone, then, that was rather contemptuous, that she spoke.

"Nothing, sir, from me."

"Nothing from you? What do you mean? What do you mean?"

"I am here first to listen."

"To listen to what?"

"To those natural expressions which might fall from the lips of any man who had stood face to face with death, and felt his heart overburthened with gratitude first to Heaven and then to its humble instrument—the person who had saved him."

The King was silent for a few seconds.

"Bute," he then said, "this sounds rather bold language. We are not accustomed to listen to such."

"It might have been," said the Earl of Bute, "your Majesty, it might have been addressed to an ear for ever deaf to all sounds in this world."

"Well—well, we pardon it."

The Princess smiled.

The Earl of Bute gave a slight cough.

"And now, Sir Page," added the King, "since that is all settled, tell us what you know of this hideous, unnatural, and frightful attempt upon our life."

"It came to my knowledge by accident, that you, sir, would be attempted to be poisoned at the banquet this night."

"By what accident? We must know all."

"No, sir! what I please to tell I tell. I will not compromise other persons by indiscreet disclosures."

"Ah! so bold!"

"I am so bold."

"But we have means of subduing such stubbornness."

"Possibly; but you will be ashamed, sir, to use them towards the preserver of your life."

The King bit his lips.

"Well—well," he said, "you heard this by accident. What did you do then?"

"I disguised myself like a royal page, as you see, sir, in order to gain easy admittance to the Palace."

"Easy admittance?" cried the King, letting his leg drop to the floor. "Easy admittance?"

"Very easy."

"My Lord Bute, you hear this?"

"I do, your Majesty."

"It must be seen to—seen to, instantly, since it appears to imply that any one, dressing himself as a royal page, might get near to our gracious person."

The Earl bowed.

"Well, Sir Page? well, sir? go on."

"I occupied a post behind your chair of State, sir, and kept a wary eye upon the Duke of Montrose."

"Then you knew it was he who meditated this fearful crime?"

"I did. Murder is a fearful crime."

"Gracious heaven! and we took the goblet from him!"

"It was at that moment I saved your Majesty's life."

The King drew a long breath.

"Yes, we are saved; and now, Sir Page, who and what are you?"

"Those are my secrets."

"More secrets?"

"Even so, sir; but rest content. I cannot be the worst of your enemies, sir, seeing that I have saved you from death itself."

"But we don't understand it. There is some mystery in all this. We must know who and what you are. How can we shape our gratitude, unless we have such information?"

"I am," said the Princess, "what your friends, sir, call a Jacobite."

"A Jacobite! A Jacobite here, in the Royal Closet! Help! murder! guard!"

The King immediately drew up his thin legs again, as though he expected the seeming page was about to fly at him like some irritated dog.

"Yes," added the Princess. "I am a Jacobite, and I give that information in order, that you, sir, may shape your gratitude to my requirements."

"We do not understand!"

"I will explain to you, sir, and to do so, I must ask a question."

"What question? What question?"

"Do you think your life worth the lives of six Jacobites."

"Sixty! six hundred! six thousand! six million!"

"I am well answered, and I have now another question to ask."

"Well, what is it?"

"Have you any desire to show your gratitude to your preserver."

"Of course we have. Eh! my Lord Bute?"

"Of course," said the Earl.

"Then!" added the Princess. "I ask, as a recompense, for what I have done to-night, six blank orders of release, and three pardons under the royal sign manual, countersigned here by the Earl of Bute, to be

THE PRINCESS PRODUCES A PARDON FOR CLAUDE DUVAL.

used at any time at my discretion, in favour of six condemned Jacobites."

"Monstrous!" cried the King.

The Earl of Bute looked grave.

"If I am refused," said the Princess, "I cannot help it."

"But really."

"And it shall go forth to the nations of Europe, that George the Second of England, refused so slight an acknowledgment of so heavy a service."

"But the thing is absurd."

"And the next time such a danger threatens."

"Ah!"

"It may not be averted."

"Bute, Bute——"

"Yes, your Majesty."

"That's the only argument I've heard yet."

"It is a very cogent one."

"Shall we consent?"

"I think so, your Majesty."

The King looked reluctant, but he slowly wrote upon six separate pieces of paper the following words:—

"Free pardon and release without let or hindrance to——" then followed a blank.

After that came the royal sign manual.

The Earl of Bute, without the slightest hesitation, countersigned the whole of these papers.

CHAPTER XCI.

CLAUDE DUVAL IS COMPELLED TO BECOME A JACOBITE FOR A TIME.

THE Princess laid her hand upon the papers rather eagerly.

And but for the counter-signature of the Earl of Bute, she would still have believed that there might have been some trick or jugglery in the transaction, by which she would have lost all the benefit of the trouble she had undertaken.

Her sole motive was now quite apparent in regard to all her proceedings of that evening.

She had no wish that the King should be assassinated.

But if she encountered the danger and the trouble of saving him, she was resolved that that danger and trouble should be the means of enabling her to interpose between death and some of those nobles, or Jacobite leaders, who might get into trouble for the Stuart cause.

It was a worthy ambition.

And if Claude Duval had only surmised for a moment, that such was the real object of the Princess, high as she already stood in his esteem, she would then have achieved a much higher position still.

The King looked vexed.

He uttered several short groans.

The idea of six detected and condemned Jacobites slipping through his fingers, and the fingers of the law, in such a way, was anything but pleasant to the royal reflection.

But a brilliant idea seemed to strike him.

"Stop!" he cried.

The Princess paused.

She was holding the six royal pardons in her hand.

"We will do better," said the King.

The Princess looked at him inquiringly.

"Are you rich?" he asked.

The Princess replied with truth, "Certainly not."

"Good," said the King, "we will redeem our royal promises of pardon."

"Certainly, at the proper time," said the Princess.

"You do not comprehend us."

The Princess shook her head to imply that she certainly did not.

"You are not rich you say, and therefore we can easily arrange this business."

"As how, sir."

"You can give us back the six pardons, and we will, so to speak, purchase them of you at a thousand pounds each. Eh? my Lord Bute, will not that be satisfactory to all parties."

The Earl shook his head.

"You hear, Sir Page," added the King. "Six thousand pounds!"

"Not for six millions," said the Princess.

"Eh?"

"I say, not for six millions."

"The boy is mad."

"I may be, sir, but there is sufficient method in my madness to enable me to speak decisively."

The King looked vexed.

"We are wrong," he said; "we are wrong. My Lord Bute, we feel we are wrong; and without the concurrence of our Council we ought not to pardon any one."

"It is too late," said the Princess. "I have the pardons and I mean to keep them. I accept them as sufficient payment—grateful payment of the service I have been enabled to do the King, and I will not part with them while I have life."

"Ah! you say so! We shall see—we shall see. Are we to be braved and bearded in our own Palace by a boy?"

"I am not so friendless as you suppose, sir," said the Princess.

As if these words had invoked it, a sudden uproar ensued in the Guard Chamber immediately adjoining the royal closet.

It seemed as if a couple of chairs were suddenly upset.

Then there was a clash of swords.

Then came loud voices in contention, and the trampling of feet.

"Guard! Guard!" shouted a voice. "Yeomen of the Guard!"

The King was terrified.

The confusion grew worse each moment.

The royal legs were already drawn up upon the couch, and could be got no further.

The Earl of Bute drew his sword.

The Princess looked pale and agitated.

Then the door of the Guard-chamber was flung open, and a scene of great excitement and dramatic interest presented itself.

But, in order that the reader may thoroughly understand what that scene portended, we must go back to that Guard-chamber at the moment when Claude Duval was left alone in it by the Earl of Bute and the Stuart Princess.

He had flung himself in a chair by the fire-side, in that anxious frame of mind to which we slightly alluded, and which made every minute of delay appear to him an age.

He was in dreamy contemplation, then, of the decaying embers of the bright fire, when the door of the Guard-chamber opened, and an officer in full regimentals came bustling in.

The officer was humming a popular air, and, without casting even a passing glance towards the fire-place, he unbuckled his sword-belt, and flung the weapon upon a side table.

The chairs were of that high-backed, rigid kind which our ancestors seemed to delight in, so that as Duval sat facing the fire, he was completely hidden from any casual observation.

After the officer, however, had got rid of his sword, he advanced towards the fireplace, rubbing his hands together.

"The nights are still chilly," he said; "and this bit of bright fire is welcome."

He gave a sudden start.

His eyes fell upon Duval for the first time.

Calm and still sat the great highwayman, confronting the officer.

They knew each other at once.

In that officer Duval recognised the Marquis of Allendale.

And the Marquis of Allendale saw in the mysterious visitor of the King's Guard-chamber, the features of the highwayman who had so recently stopped him and the Earl of Bute on the road from Kew.

The Marquis was too astonished for a few seconds to utter a word.

He then passed one hand hastily across his eyes, as if it were necessary to do so in order to assure himself that what he saw was not some mere delusion of the senses.

Duval did not speak.

If the recognition were to come he thought it was best to wait for it.

And it did come.

"Claude Duval!" cried the Marquis.

Duval rose, and slightly bowed.

"The Marquis of Allendale," he said, "I believe."

"This is matchless impudence!" he said.

"It looks like it," said Duval.

"But it will meet its just reward; and whatever may be your errand here, it shall be but a step towards the gallows."

"Not so fast, Marquis—not so fast! I am only waiting for a young friend of mine, who is in private audience of the King, accompanied by the Earl of Bute."

"Incredible!"

"And yet true. I am desired to wait here, and here I wait. Interfere not with me, my Lord Marquis, and I will be equally indulgent towards you."

"Indulgent? A highwayman? No, Claude Duval

you had the best of us on the open road from Kew, but it is now my turn."

As he spoke, the Marquis made two steps to the side table, and seized his sword.

"Very well," said Duval; "if you will insist upon fighting I can have no great objection, although this slender court rapier that I wear can scarcely be considered a match for your military sabre. Nevertheless, as I never was very particular, I waive the objection, and will indulge you—so come on, my Lord, although I am afraid we shall disturb his Majesty."

The calmness and composure with which Duval spoke, seemed in some degree to rake some of that fire and metal out of the Marquis of Allendale, which, up to that moment, had been a characterestic of his conduct.

The disparity in weapons was certainly very great.

The Marquis's sword was a real military fighting one.

The long slender rapier used only for court and dress purposes, which Claude Duval was in possession of, looked as he drew it, more like a toy than a dangerous weapon.

Perhaps the Marquis repented slightly of his precipitance,

But if he did so, he did not permit that repentance to appear.

He had himself urged on the conflict, and he dared not now, from very shame, retreat from it.

He made a furious onslaught upon Duval.

But the latter had seen, by the expression of his eyes, what he intended.

Had the Marquis's sword really struck the rapier of Duval's, it must instantly have broken it.

The admirable fencing, however, of the highwayman, saved his slender sword from such a catastrophe.

It was quite in vain that the Marquis endeavoured to get within the ground of Duval. The more he strove to do so the more he felt himself baffled.

His hand began to tremble, and he paused a moment on his guard, as he spoke in a voice of suppressed passion, "I am a fool, to waste time upon a criminal, with whom the Palace guard should alone deal."

"If you continue this conflict," said Duval, "another minute, your folly of all descriptions will be at an end, for I warn you."

"Warn me?"

"Your life has been at my disposal any time this last three minutes, and if you have just began to see your folly, I warn you that my patience is at an end, and I will be trifled with no longer."

There was a gloomy look upon the face of the Marquis. Then he suddenly brightened up, and uttered a cry of satisfaction.

Duval's back was to the door of the apartment, and as the Marquis of Allendale uttered this cry of pleasure, Duval heard that door opened.

His situation now was a critical one.

If he turned to see who was entering the room, the Marquis would surely make a rush at him, and surely succeed in inflicting a wound before he could recover his guard again.

But he was fertile enough in expedients.

With his disengaged left hand, he suddenly seized a chair which was within his reach, and flung it right in the face of the Marquis.

Then Duval was able to look round. His danger was evident enough.

A couple of officers in similar costume to that of the Marquis of Allandale, stood in attitudes of astonishment in the doorway.

Then Duval felt that his chances of escape were few, and in fact they all revolved themselves to one.

He might succeed by a sudden rush in getting out of the room, and so, perhaps, make his way from the Palace.

He made the rush sword in hand.

The two officers gave way.

Not because they were afraid to resist him, but because they were perfectly well aware of the force he would have to encounter after passing them.

Duval in a moment found himself inextricably mixed up with a strong party of the Yeomen of the Guard.

A resistance would have been useless.

He might take a life.

Or he might lose his own.

In all human probability both these things would have happened.

Duval lowered the point of his sword; and, as the halberds of the Yeomen of the Guard clashed together over his head, a pang shot through his heart at the idea that the worst catastrophe that could have happened in his pursuit of this adventure had actually occurred in his capture.

A prisoner.

Terrible word.

And more terrible to her who watched anxiously his return, than even to himself.

But Duval was equal to most occasions, let their character be what they might.

He was calm and collected in a moment.

"I surrender," he said.

He was rather roughly seized by a couple of the Yeomen of the Guard.

They wanted to show their efficiency.

And they had no means of exactly knowing of what offence this man had been guilty.

The Marquis of Allendale drew a long breath of relief.

For the last minute—and a minute is a long time on such occasions—during which the conflict with Duval had lasted, he had felt that his own life hung upon a thread.

And all this was the tumult that had reached the ears of the King and of the Stuart Princess.

The monarch was firmly convinced that treason was stalking abroad in the Palace.

He looked even with an eye of suspicion upon the Earl of Bute.

But then kings are suspicious of everybody.

That is one of the conditions of their existence.

It is part of the price they pay for the doubtful enjoyment of a crown.

The Marquis of Allendale did not behave quite generously to Claude Duval.

He must have felt and known that the celebrated highwayman had spared his life.

To spare a life may not be exactly equal to saving one; but still it is something, and deserves recognition.

On the contrary, the Marquis seemed intent upon striving to extract some popularity with the King out of the occurrence.

"Treason—treason!" he cried. "This man can have no business here, but that which is adverse to your Majesty's life and crown!"

The King made a vain effort to draw up his legs still higher.

"Treason!" he yelled.

"This way, Yeomen—this way!" added the Marquis of Allendale. "Bring the traitor this way, and let his Majesty himself issue his commands concerning him!"

"No, no!" cried the King.

"He is safely guarded."

"Are you quite sure?"

"Quite, your Majesty."

"Stand between us and the traitor, my Lord Bute!"

"Your Majesty need have no fears."

Still in the grasp of the Yeomen of the Guard, Claude Duval, although he was not brought exactly into the royal closet, reached the door of it.

He cast a glance at the young Princess.

She was pale and somewhat agitated.

Duval wanted to reassure her.

He wanted to speak ambiguously, so that she alone should understand him.

"All is well," he said, "since I alone suffer!"

Then the King uncoiled his feet on the sofa.

He had seen that there was plenty of assistance and force at hand, and likewise that Duval was unarmed.

"What notable villain is this?" he asked.

"Your Majesty," said the Marquis of Allendale, "I can explain the whole occurrence!"

"Do so," said the King, drily, "or we shall hold you responsible, my Lord Marquis, for the intrusion of this man into St. James's."

"Me, your Majesty?"

"Exactly so. Who should be responsible but you?"

"But your Majesty misconceives the whole transaction!"

"As how?"

"I beg to observe, your Majesty, that I did not bring him here, but found him here."

The King inclined his head.

"Pray explain, Marquis; we do not yet comprehend!"

"I have the singular honour, then, to relate to your Majesty that, being the officer of the guard for the night in your Majesty's private apartments, I was making the necessary round to see that all the sentinels were on duty."

"Well?"

"Upon my return to the guard-room, I thought it was empty, until, seated by the fire, I suddenly saw this man."

"What then, my Lord?"

"A second glance, your Majesty, enabled me to recognise him."

"Oh, indeed!"

"Yes, your Majesty; and I am able to name him with precision."

"And who may this notable rascal be?"

Now, the King, for the last few seconds, had been looking at Claude Duval with his eyes half-closed to all appearance, and yet with sufficient keenness of expression to be perfectly well aware of who he was.

The then royalty of England had had a previous royal interview with our hero.

And George the Second had this peculiarity.

He never forgot a face he had once seen.

Therefore he knew Duval perfectly well, but, with his usual duplicity, affected not to do so.

"And who is the traitor, my Lord Allendale?"

"His name is Claude Duval."

"Duval—Duval?"

"Yes, your Majesty."

"Surely we have heard that name before?"

Duval could not forbear a smile.

The King acted perfect ignorance of his existence exceedingly well.

"He must be some notable traitor," added the King.

"Of that there can be no doubt, your Majesty," added the Marquis of Allendale.

"Remove him."

"To the Tower, your Majesty?"

"Yes."

"Captain of the Yeomen, you hear his Majesty's commands. Remove your prisoner."

"One word, your Majesty," said the Earl of Bute.

"Well, Bute, what is it?"

"This is, indeed, Claude Duval."

"Well, well!"

"But his presence here is not in his character of the highwayman, so well known."

"For what then, my lord?"

"He comes with this Page, to aid and assist, if need be, in the preservation of your Majesty's life."

The King drew up his legs again instantly.

"Then, he is a professed Jacobite?"

"No!" cried Duval.

The Princess clasped her hands.

She looked imploringly at Duval.

He could not comprehend why, at that particular moment, she was so extremely anxious that he should not repudiate the character of a Jacobite.

And so he was silent.

He waited the issue of the mysterious circumstances in which he was involved.

"To the Tower with him—to the Tower!" cried the King.

"Still another word," said the Earl of Bute.

"Well, my lord, what now?"

"It is inconsistent with your Majesty's sense of justice to send Claude Duval to the Tower, when his real errand at St. James's has been the same as this Page."

"But a highwayman, my lord—a highwayman—a notorious highwayman!"

"But your Majesty has no such charge against him."

"I have," said the Marquis of Allendale. "He stopped me on the highway from Kew, and robbed me."

"Then, my Lord Allandale," said the Earl of Bute, "it is neither his Majesty's Yeoman of the Guard who should take Claude Duval into custody, nor his Majesty who should adjudicate upon him."

The Marquis was silenced.

"Very well," said the King,—"very well! We leave him to the ordinary tribunals, as regards a robbery upon the highway."

"Good!" said the Marquis of Allendale. "I am content to withdraw that charge."

"And I, too," said the Earl of Bute; "since I was mixed up in it."

The Princess then stepped forward.

"Claude Duval, then," she said, "is free from any apprehension on a charge of felony!"

"Be it so," said the King; "and so we revert to our original intention of committing him, as a Jacobite plotter, to the Tower."

The Marquis of Allendale smiled.

He was quite content that that major charge against Claude Duval, of treason, should take the place of the minor one of highway robbery.

"Then," said the Princess, stepping forward, and speaking with animation, "but for this charge against him of being a Jacobite, Claude Duval would be free?"

"Oh, perfectly free!" said the Marquis of Allendale, sarcastically. "Yeomen, remove your prisoner. You have heard his Majesty's commands."

"Yes, away with him!" said the King.

The Princess glanced at the Earl of Bute.

She caught an approving look upon his face, and knew that he was well aware of what she was about to do.

She darted towards the King's table.

A look of alarm was on the face of George the Second, but it subsided when he saw that she only seized a pen.

Hastily producing, then, one of the blank pardons which she had so recently received from the King, she rapidly wrote in the name.

The name of Claude Duval.

She stepped up to the officer of the guard, and handed it to him.

"There is an order for your prisoner's relief," she said; "under the sign-manual of the King himself."

An angry frown was on the face of the King.

The Earl of Bute smiled.

The Marquis of Allendale looked surprised at the mystery of the whole transaction.

But the pardon was complete. There was no disputing it, and Claude Duval was free.

CHAPTER XCII.

LUCY RECEIVES A MYSTERIOUS VISIT AT FARNBOROUGH HOUSE.

WE will now retrace our steps, in order to take a look at one who has become an interesting personage, we trust, in the history of Claude Duval—viz., Lucy—that fair young girl, who had of late encountered so many perils, but who was now, she hoped, safe at all events for the present, from all danger.

But was she altogether free from alarm, even now that she was installed as mistress in that handsomely furnished mansion, where it had been such a delight to Claude Duval to surround her with all that was beautiful in nature or in art.

It is the evening of the King's entertainment, and Lucy is seated in one of the drawing rooms of Farnborough House.

As she there sat, she raised her eyes mechanically to a tall venetian mirror which hung before her, and which had never reflected anything lovelier than herself, as hastily she passed her fair, small hand across her brow, brushing back the glossy ringlets that hung clustering over her forehead.

But Lucy was tired and pale with fatigue and anxiety for those she loved, for it was impossible for one so affectionate as the gentle wife of Claude Duval, to other than love that misguided young Stuart Princess, who had, so to speak, become a member of the household of Farnborough House.

Her eyes, too, bore the traces of tears, and with a sigh and look of dissatisfaction, she turned away from the mirror, which, like many other inventions of human vanity, as often procures us disappointment as satisfaction.

Lucy drew a chair nearer to the fire, for there was a sense of chilliness about the atmosphere of the room, as well as her own heart.

"How childish I am," she murmured to herself, "all is well. My Claude can run no risk to-night; and yet, my heart is very heavy, I will try to read, and occupy my thoughts, and the time will pass——"

The sentence, however, was never destined to be concluded, for Blossom, after knocking at the door, appeared on the threshold.

Lucy started.

"Any bad news, Blossom?"

"No; but there is a woman below, I think she is a lady by the tones of her voice; and she wishes to see you, and seems so unhappy like, I didn't like to turn her away."

"Certainly not, Blossom. Follow me, and I will see what it is she requires," said Lucy.

There was no occasion for Lucy to tell Blossom to follow her, for he seemed to think, when Duval was out, his chief duty consisted in watching over her safety.

Lucy descended to the hall, where the singular visitor was still awaiting her coming.

Lucy approached, and her visitor, laying her hand gently upon her arm, ran her eye rapidly over her face and figure, every now and then pausing for a moment, as if to impress both upon her memory.

"Well," said Lucy, gently, "have you seen me before?"

"No, lady," replied the stranger; "but I had a desire to look into your eyes, and see if I could read there treachery and dissimulation."

Lucy drew herself up.

"Who are you?" she asked, with dignity, "who dare use such words to me?"

"And who are you, lady, that such qualities should not reside in your breast, even as they do in so many others who can also boast of a beautiful exterior."

Lucy was silent, for she began to think her strange visitor's intellect was wandering.

"You do not know me," continued she, strangely "but *I know you!*"

Lucy felt a sickening feeling at her heart.

Was it possible, that her incognito was known and suspected; and if so, who was this strange woman.

The woman was not in the early spring of life, she was in the summer, but it was the early summer untouched by autumn; and her form, although it possessed no longer the lightness of youth, had acquired a degree of beauty which compensated for the softer loveliness that years had stolen away.

Her brown hair fell in a profusion of large curls, round a face which was highly pleasing; and even the sorrowful expression, from being mingled with a look of patient melancholy, produced a greater degree of interest than the features could have excited in earlier youth.

"What want you?" asked Lucy.

"Have I not told you, lady?"

"You have merely told me that you wished to look into my face to see if I were treacherous and false."

"Just so."

"But what mean you? I have never seen you, to my knowledge," said Lucy.

"But you have seen one whom I love."

There was something inexpressibly touching in the tone and manner in which these words were uttered, which excited all Lucy's sympathies in a moment.

"Ah, now," she said, "I know you are mistaken. You think I am some one else."

The woman shook her head, and approached nearer to Lucy, and whispered something in her ear.

Lucy started.

"Am I mistaken now?" asked her strange visitor.

"Mistaken in your judgment of my character."

The woman was silent

"Tell me, did you ever love Mossy Pendell?"

Lucy shuddered.

She was on the point of declaring that, as far as she was capable of hating any human being, she hated that man who had almost compassed her destruction; but she remembered that the woman who was now standing before her had said that she had loved one whom she fancied was loved by her, Lucy, so she paused abruptly.

"Well," said the woman, eyeing her fixedly—"well, can you answer my question as I would fain hear you answer it?"

"I can—indeed, I can!" exclaimed Lucy. "Mossy Pendell and I never had one thought and feeling or sympathy in common. Tell me, are you answered?"

The woman drew a deep breath.

"I am," she said; "for truth must dwell in that heart from which such words of assurance spring."

The woman turned to leave the hall.

"Nay," said Lucy, gently laying her hand upon her arm, "I have answered your question, will you not now answer one of mine?"

"Speak, lady, speak; and if I can, I will answer you as truly as you have answered me."

Lucy scarcely knew how to put the question, but she was anxious to know how the woman had discovered her at Farnborough House, and how she had associated Pauline Cope with the Lucy Everton whom she fancied to be her rival.

"Tell me," said Lucy, "how you came to know that I was residing here."

The woman gazed mournfully into Lucy's eyes as she said, "If you have ever loved with all the strength and depth of affection which alone should characterize a first all-absorbing passion, then, lady, you will understand the feeling that has prompted me never, by day nor night, to lose sight of one whom I once thought had robbed me of his love."

Lucy was about to interrupt her, for she could not endure the idea of associating that bad man's name with such high and holy thoughts, but her visitor waved her arm to bespeak silence.

"I see now," she continued, "that I was mistaken; but then *he* made me believe that it was really the case; and then I resolved to see you, and I did see you, lady, and saw that you were young and beautiful, and I thought this poor heart would break."

"Poor girl—poor girl!" sighed Lucy.

"You pity me, and call me by a name which I no longer have any right to. Look here, my hair is grey, but not with age, but with sorrow and——"

The woman paused, and clasped her hands over her eyes.

"What am I saying?—oh, what was I going to say? It is not I who will breathe to mortal ears one word that can injure him who once loved me. Forget me, lady, and all the wild things this poor, bewildered brain may have uttered, and take to your heart the consolation of knowing that you have removed a weight from off mine, for which act of mercy I will ever bless you!"

The mysterious stranger turned again to leave the hall, but Lucy again detained her.

"Will you promise me that, not even to him whom you love so well, will you breathe a syllable of what has passed between us to-night."

The woman laughed a high, discordant laugh.

Lucy shrunk back alarmed.

Fear took possession of her.

Might not this woman proclaim the knowledge she had in her possession of the whereabouts of herself and Claude, and might not she be the means of bringing the greatest unhappiness upon them both?"

"Fear not," she said, "after a pause—"fear not, *Pauline Cope*, that any harm shall accrue to you or yours from what has taken place between us this night. I will be as silent as the grave; and if I hear of danger threatening you, mine will be the self-imposed task of apprizing you of its approach; and I may perhaps be the means of warding it off. And now, lady, farewell!"

Before Lucy could reply, the mysterious visitor had hurried out into the night air.

Lucy had no difficulty in identifying her visitor as being the same who had once accosted Duval on Hampstead Heath, and extracted from him the promise of not injuring the man who of all others Claude Duval felt had most deeply injured him and his.

As Lucy turned to ascend the staircase, Blossom emerged from a small room in which he had stationed himself in order that he might be an unobserved listener to all that took place.

Blossom looked somewhat anxiously at Lucy.

"A strange visitor, Blossom?"

"Yes, Miss Pauline."

Blossom never, by any accident, addressed Lucy but by her assumed name.

"Do you think, Blossom, we have anything to apprehend from the visit?" asked Lucy.

Blossom shook his head, and looked dubious.

"For myself," added Lucy, "I fear nothing from this poor, misguided creature—and yet—and yet——"

"And yet you would rather that she had not found you out, you mean?"

"Exactly, Blossom, but yet I don't see what is to be done."

"I do, though, Miss Pauline," he said; and before Lucy could stop him, and ask him for an explanation of his words, he had darted past her, and out of the hall door into the street.

Looking to the right and to the left, Blossom soon had the satisfaction of seeing the person of whom he was in pursuit, emerge from a doorway.

A few strides, and he was by her side.

The figure paused.

"A word with you," said Blossom.

"I listen," said the woman.

"I come from the house you have just visited," added Blossom.

"I know it," said the stranger. "What would you say? Stay—let me speak, and answer the question you are about to put into words. I will keep my promise, and never mention the fact that your mistress, Miss Pauline Cope, and Lucy Everton are one and the same person."

Blossom hesitated how to proceed.

"Well," said the woman, "are you not satisfied?"

"Yes, to a certain extent," said Blossom, still at a loss how to proceed.

"You want to make my promise doubly sure," she said; "and you would threaten me with evil consequences to my husband if I break it."

"That's about it!" said Blossom.

"It was not well to doubt me, but perhaps it is natural for you, as you do not know me. Well, be it as you would say—if ever I mention the interview I have had to-night to any living soul, may the consequences of my indiscretion fall upon his head for whom I would willingly sacrifice my life. Now are you satisfied?"

"Yes," said Blossom.

"Then let me go my way, and you go yours," said the stranger; and, without another word, she hastened from him.

"Humph!" said Blossom to himself. "A strange customer, that, but nevertheless my mind is easier for having followed her."

Blossom soon rejoined Lucy, who was anxiously expecting him.

"Well, Blossom," she said, "tell me why you followed the poor creature."

"Only, Miss Pauline, to make assurance doubly sure, as the saying is."

"How so?" asked Lucy. "I felt certain that my secret was safe with her. Assurance of what, Blossom?"

"That she meant to keep her promise of not betraying you, that was all."

"Then you stood and spoke to her?"

"Oh, yes. But I had no occasion to tell her why I followed her, for she turned round and said she knew what I had come for."

"What a strange being she seems," said Lucy.

"I believe you. I could almost fancy that she's a kind of witch, for she knew what was passing in my very thoughts."

Lucy smiled, for she could readily understand that to be the case, without any great stretch of the imagination, so soon, at least, as the woman knew that Blossom came from Farnborough House.

Lucy dismissed Blossom, and again sat herself down to think, and to picture to herself what might be taking place at St. James's Palace.

Had Duval, St. Ives, and the Princess met?

That was the question Lucy asked herself over and over again.

Would danger attend the perilous expedition?

Danger to the Princess.

Danger to Claude.

Lucy rose, and she paced the room anxiously.

What would she not give to be able to go and ascertain for herself how matters stood, but then she had given Duval her word that she would wait patiently until she saw them both at Farnborough House.

"I must wait—I must wait!" she kept murmuring to herself. "Oh, how difficult is my task!"

And as she paced that room, Lucy was carried back in thought to the day she had first seen Duval.

Then, again, she beheld herself lying upon that platform which surrounded the fatal scaffold upon which her young life would have been sacrificed but for him.

She recalled the tones of love which had been his as he asked her to become his wife, if he should succeed in extricating her from the perils that then surrounded her.

She remembered her answer.

"Yours—ever yours!"

Then the fearful leap upon Nightshade.

The parted sea of upturned faces, as he bore her so gallantly from the scene of her fearful peril.

Then the release he had given her to her promise made amid so much peril.

Their subsequent union, and the many happy, though anxious hours they had spent together since that memorable day.

And again Lucy asked herself if danger were environing him she loved so well.

Would he return to her after that entertainment?

Or had his enemies lain in wait for him, recognising him through his disguise, and bore him far from her?

These thoughts chased one another through Lucy's mind, until thought became positively painful.

Then, again, she thought of that fair young Princess, who had, as it were, grown into her heart by her gentleness and beauty.

Would she return safely, or would she be betrayed? as she had good reason to suppose she might be, for had not both St. Ives and Duval expressed their belief that their was a traitor amongst her Counsellors.

"Surely," said Lucy, speaking to herself. "Surely her disguise was perfect. It must defy even the most careful scrutiny."

Twelve o'clock chimed from the various church clocks in the vicinity.

Lucy remembered that that was the hour St. Ives had mentioned as being the one at which the guests would assemble in the Banqueting Hall.

CHAPTER XCIII.

CLAUDE DUVAL AND BLOSSOM CRY STAND AND DELIVER ON THE ROAD.

IN spite of all the dangers that had beset him and the young Princess in the Palace of St. James's, there seemed to have been a protecting power over them, and they both reached Farnborough House in safety.

There was but one circumstance in the whole transaction which was calculated to weigh somewhat heavily upon the mind and spirits of Duval.

He had been compelled, in a manner of speaking, to acknowledge himself a Jacobite.

He had unquestionably received the King's pardon in that capacity.

"It seems a sort of fate, Lucy," he said, "that I should be dragged into these Jacobite plots. I have struggled against it in vain, but feel it to be almost inevitable."

Lucy shuddered.

"Claude, Claude," she said, "I was full of fears whenever I recollected who and what you were, and your reputation upon the road; but those fears were as nothing compared with the dread which attaches itself to a complicity in Jacobite plots."

"Then I cast them off at once and for ever!"

"Do so—do so!"

"In good truth, I have never engaged in them; but if I have, and if my conduct in relation to our fair young friend the Stuart Princess, could even be construed into a complicity in such matters, I have the King's pardon."

"You have, Claude! You have!"

Duval smiled.

"And so, Lucy," he said, "there is a something after all which has reconciled you to my life on the road as a highwayman."

"Of two evils, Claude, we are always only most anxious to choose the lesser."

"True, Lucy, true; and when I am on the road, and you are full of fears, fancying that my path is in the midst of danger, you will be able to think back upon what I might have been, and in the reflection, that at all events, I am not engaged in Jacobite plots, you will find consolation."

"In truth, I shall, Claude! In truth, I shall!"

"Out of evil, then, springs some good."

"It ever does."

"And so——"

"You smile. What is it you would say?"

"I have so great a dislike to the crowded saloons of the Court, and the atmosphere that there surrounds me, that I feel a kind of necessity of taking a gallop to-night on Nightshade in the free open air, on heath or road."

"Ah, Claude!"

"Shall I say, ah, Lucy?"

"I cannot stay you; these wild adventures, and chivalric episodes in your existence, have become, I believe, part and parcel of your life."

"They have. With them, I feel myself something, without them, nothing."

It was not, however, on the following evening to that on which Claude Duval had passed through such peril at the Palace of St. James's, that he started with Blossom again in search of adventures on the road.

He let a day and a night pass away, and then, just as the dusky shadows began to creep over London, he summoned Blossom.

And Blossom was well pleased, that once again, they were to go forth and cry, "Stand and deliver," on the highway.

But Claude Duval had a particular adventure in view, and it was for the purpose of explaining it more fully, that he summoned his faithful follower into one of the smaller rooms of Farnborough House.

"Blossom," said Duval, "you have often told me that we take toll on the road."

"Certainly we do, Captain; don't we cry 'Stand and deliver,' and what can a toll-keeper do more?"

"That is true, Blossom, but what I now project doing, is to commence the system more in reality."

Blossom looked as if he would like some further explanation.

"Listen to me," said Duval. "You know the house called the White Lodge in Richmond Park, or close to it?"

"Assuredly, Captain. It has been purchased lately by the Royal Family, and converted into one of their residences."

"There is a turnpike there, Blossom, at the junction of a road, one branch of which leads to Hampton Court, and the other to Richmond Park."

"I know it?"

"The pike is kept by an aged couple. There is to be a grand entertainment at the White Lodge, given by the Duke of Cumberland, and what I propose is to take toll of the guests as they go to the royal residence."

Blossom rubbed his head.

"It might do, Captain; but did you ever hear of Dick Turpin and his portable gate?"

"No, Blossom."

"Then, Captain, I will tell you. I never saw Dick and his famous mare, Brown Bess but once, and that was on the Western Road. He had a man with him, whom he used to call the skipper—a long, thin, active fellow, and he used to manage matters for Dick."

"As how, Blossom?"

"Well, Captain, I'll tell you how it all happened. I was coming home one moonlight night from Wycombe, thinking of nothing at all, and mounted on the top of a stage-coach, when suddenly the coachman pulled up.

"'Bless us, Bill,' said he, addressing the guard, 'here's a new pike!'

"Bill rubbed his eyes and so did the coachman.

"And there, sure enough, right across the road, which was not very wide just there, was a straight white bar, for all the world exactly like a pike.

"'Toll! toll!' cried a loud voice.

"'Toll,' said the coachman, 'what do you mean?'

"'It's a new gate,' said the voice, 'and you can't pass without paying.'

"'Drat your new gate,' said the coachman. 'I suppose there won't be a free road out of London in another year, but there's your sixpence. Open quickly, and let us through.'

"With that, there came something over the gate that looked like a black cloud with some red cloth on it."

"And what was that, Blossom?"

"Dick Turpin and his famous mare, and the moment he got to the side of the coach he shouted out, 'A hundred pounds toll for the Wycombe coach!'"

"And what came of it?"

"Oh, he made them pay. There was a general ransacking of pockets, and the sum was made up."

Duval laughed.

"Do you know exactly where this happened, Blossom."

"The precise spot, Captain. It was near Acton."

"Suppose we go that way?"

"With all my heart."

"I will be at Nightshade's stable in half an hour, and be sure you have all ready for the road."

"Trust me for that," said Blossom.

In good truth, the more refined and intricate adventures, which Claude Duval, from his education and admirable finesse was able to carry out, were very little to the taste of Blossom.

He did his best, but he understood crying "Stand and deliver," on the highway, very much better.

He was prompt in getting the horses ready, and within the time mentioned by Claude, they were both proceeding up the Oxford Road at a smart trot.

The night was dark, though fine.

A moon, not above four or five days old, occasionally showed her well-defined crescent through some small rift in the clouds.

But that was all.

No star showed its face, and the air was still and calm.

Some quarter of an hour's trot brought them to a shadowy, picturesque part of the road.

The ground rose considerably to the right, and all up the incline was dotted with fir trees.

On the summit of the acclivity stood a windmill, the sails of which was stationary.

On the other side of the road ran a bubbling brook, immediately beyond which was a hedge, and beyond that again, fair, undulating cornfields.

It was a pleasant, shadowy spot, when the mid-day sun was high

Dreary and mysterious at night, and well-fitted for the very enterprise that might be set on foot by a knight of the road.

"It was just here," said Blossom. "I know the place well. There is a narrow, winding lane that leads to East Acton, and another opposite to it that conducts you to Hammersmith."

"It is a gloomy spot," said Duval.

"Very!" replied a voice.

Duval started

It was not the voice of Blossom.

"Did you speak, Captain?" cried Blossom.

"No; did you?"

"Certainly not."

"And yet some one answered."

"It was I!" said the voice again.

"And who may you be?" asked Duval.

"Oh! my name is Blinks, because I blink at the sun when it shines too brightly; I blink at the moon, when its face is too fair and round. And who may you be when you're at home?"

"Whoever you may be," said Duval, "I don't answer questions."

"But it seems to me, you can ask them, master."

"My good friend," said Duval, "whoever you are, and whatever your business may be here, I would advise you to be civil, for we neither want your observations nor your company."

"That's just my case," said the stranger.

"Take yourself off," said Duval.

"Not quite yet; don't I tell you I've business here."

"Whatever it may be," said Blossom, "perhaps a pistol-shot may induce you to postpone it."

As Blossom spoke, there appeared a faint light close to the hedge.

By that faint light a man on horseback could plainly be seen for a brief moment; and then, as the light faded away, the two figures, both biped and quadruped, seemed to disappear into the darkness of the night.

"What is the meaning of all that?" said Duval.

Blossom was silent.

"Speak, Blossom, I cannot see you!"

"I don't half like it, Captain."

"Half like what?"

"To disturb him; for now I comprehend what it is."

"That is more than I do. Who is it you do not like to disturb?"

Blossom spoke in a low tone, which was not destitute of accents of apprehension, as he added, "It's the ghost of Dick Turpin, Captain!"

"Nonsense! what puts that into your head?"

"I'm certain of it!"

"But you must first make a ghost of him. Don't we all know that Turpin is alive, although it is said that he has been badly injured in an encounter on the North Road with a party of officers?"

"It's a ghost, Captain! come away!"

"Not yet, Blossom: but if you have no fancy for setting up Turpin's pike on this spot, I will do it alone."

"No, Captain, don't say that; for if all the ghosts in Christendom, and in every other part of the world beside were to make their appearance, it shall never be said that I deserted you."

As Blossom spoke, the sound of carriage wheels approaching through the high street of the neighbouring village, came plainly upon their ears.

CLAUDE DUVAL RESCUES CONSTANCE LASCELLES.

There was no time to do more than station themselves on each side of the road, and wait for the vehicle.

Mingling with the sound of the wheels, and the trampling of the horses, there were some strange, vague cries of alarm.

Duval felt interested, in spite of himself, for it was far more than probable that the approaching persons were not such as to awaken any lively sympathies in his breast.

As the carriage approached, he saw by its lamps, that it was a hired post-chaise.

The driver was one of these elderly men who are always to be found about inn yards, and who are still called post-boys, after having bidden adieu to the state of boyhood for at least half a century.

He had on a white hat very fluffy in the nap.

An old, faded, blue jacket.

Top boots, appearing very considerably too large for him.

He bent down over the horse's neck as he drove.

with every appearance of decrepitude, as though he were far past work.

Who the occupants of the chaise were Duval could not form the least idea, for whatever sounds had issued from it were now still.

There was nothing to be heard but the tramping of the horses and the rattle of the wheels.

"Shall we stop them, Captain?" asked Blossom.

"Yes: leave it to me unless I call to you."

"All's right, Captain!"

Duval trotted out into the middle of the road.

"Halt!" he cried.

There was, must have been, some singular echo about that spot; for almost simultaneously as he spoke, the word "halt" was repeated in very similar accents to his own.

And Duval felt certain that it was not Blossom who had spoken.

The elderly postillion pulled up his horses with a jerk.

"Halt!" cried Duval "or you are a dead man!"

"Halt!" cried the strange, echoing voice again, "or you are a dead man!"

A superstitious fear, that he could not wholly shake off, crept even over the bold heart of Claude Duval.

But his attention was drawn off from all these personal considerations by a cry of distress that proceeded from the chaise.

The voice in which that cry of distress was couched was young and feminine.

"No—no," it said, "I will go back—back even to my poor home, in preference to continuing with you. I am not used to blows; and from such ill-usage now, what am I to expect in the future?"

Duval trotted up to the door of the chaise.

He was about to speak, when he became conscious that another horse had made its way to the opposite door, and there paused, even as he had done with Nightshade.

"Stand and deliver!" he cried.

"Stand and deliver!" repeated another voice.

Duval shrunk back.

"Blossom! Blossom!" he cried.

"Blossom! Blossom!" repeated the strange voice.

Duval gave Nightshade the rein, and in two bounds went round the chaise and horses.

But he became painfully conscious that while he did so, the mysterious horse and rider, that echoed both his words and actions, preceded him.

They had, in fact, only changed places.

"Blossom! Blossom!" cried Duval again, "where are you?"

There was no echo that time.

"I am here, Captain."

"Alone?"

"Quite."

"Did you see any one?"

"No one."

"But you heard a voice?"

"Only yours, Captain."

Duval was puzzled, but he was soon recalled from any reflections he might feel inclined to make upon the singularity of this adventure, by a movement on the part of the people in the chaise.

The window one side was let down violently.

A man thrust his head out.

"What is the meaning of all this?" he cried. "Who dare stop me, I should like to know, on the King's highway? Get out of the way, fellow, and let my chaise proceed."

"Save me!" cried the young voice again.

Then there was a sharp cry, as though a blow had been struck.

Duval acted impulsively.

He was not aware if the man who had spoken to him so roughly had struck the blow or not.

On the chance of it, however, Duval dealt him a crack on the head with the handle of his riding-whip, that caused him to draw back into the chaise again, with all the precipitation in his power.

CHAPTER XCIV.

CLAUDE DUVAL RESCUES CONSTANCE LASCELLES FROM HER FOES.

Duval thought it desirable to strike terror into the minds of the occupants of the carriage.

He dashed the barrel of one of his pistols on to the window-sill, and, in a loud voice, he cried out—

"It is immaterial to me—your money or your life, or both together!"

"Have mercy upon us!" said a female voice.

"Yes, sir," added some one, in more masculine tones, but which were tremulous from fear—"yes, sir, have mercy upon us!"

By this time Blossom had made his appearance.

"More light, here!" cried Duval. "Get one of the chaise lamps out, Blossom, and let us see who these people are."

Blossom did as he was ordered by Duval.

He held up a chaise lamp, so as to send its rays fully into the interior of the chaise.

Three persons occupied the vehicle.

One was the man who had imprudently put his head in the way of Duval's riding-whip.

Another was a woman of very repulsive appearance.

The third, in Duval's estimation, was the most beautiful girl he had ever seen.

She was very young, and dressed with the utmost plainness and simplicity.

But with all her beauty, there was a great deal of terror upon her countenance, and her eyes showed the traces of recent tears.

Duval's first idea, then, was that his presence had terrified her.

He was anxious that she should know that there was no danger to be apprehended, and he replaced the pistol in the saddle, as he said, "Quick, now, quick! There need be no bloodshed! Your money, quick!"

"Yes, if you please, sir," said the man. "Here it is. It is only a few shillings, but you are heartily welcome!"

"Nonsense!" said Duval.

"And here is all I have, likewise," said the woman—"a seven-shilling piece, and half-a-crown. Much good may they do you!"

"This is trifling with me," said Duval. "People do not travel in a post-chaise with only a few shillings in their possession."

Duval then addressed himself to the young girl, who sat trembling and gazing at him with wonder.

"Tell me, my dear," he said, "who and what these people are, for I am sure they are of no akin to you."

"Oh, no, no!" cried the girl.

"I thought as much."

"And, indeed, I do not know them!"

"Not know them?"

"Not in the least—not in the least!"

"Oh, heavens!" cried the woman; "was there ever such ingratitude! I wonder the roof of the chaise don't fall in at once, and crush you to death, Selina!"

"Selina!" cried the girl. "My name is not Selina, and you know it is not! Why call me Selina, and why have you taken me away from the school?"

"What is the meaning of this?" asked Duval. "There is some villany afloat, I reckon."

"Indeed, you are very much mistaken, sir," replied the man, in a whining tone of voice; "and I shall be able to explain to you all about it."

"I don't want to hear," said Duval. "It is sufficient to me to know that this young lady—for such I perceive she is—repudiates all association with you."

"I do, indeed!" cried the girl, "I do, indeed!"

"Selina, Selina!" said the woman; "how can you speak in that way? My own sister's child, too, that I've brought up from an infant!"

"I am not your sister's child, and never saw you before this evening in all my life."

"Well, madam," said Duval, "how do you account for this little contradiction?"

"It's the horrid badness of human nature."

"That is precisely my opinion," said Duval; "and my only difference consists in the person to whom we attribute the badness."

"Here," said the man, suddenly holding out a purse,—"here is, in reality, all we have! You will find about nineteen guineas in that purse—take them, and be off!"

"You make things better, in one particular," said Duval, "but not in all."

"Yes, be off!" cried the woman. "We don't want to have anything more to say to you! Don't interfere in our domestic affairs!"

Duval made a slight movement, as though he were about to leave; and as he did so, the young girl in the chaise uttered such a despairing cry, that he faced about again immediately.

"What can be the meaning of this?" he said. "Speak to me, and speak freely! Do you really wish to leave these people?"

"Oh, yes, yes!"

"And whither would you go?"

"Alas! I do not know!"

The girl wrung her hands despairingly.

Duval hesitated for a few moments, and then he said, "Will you come with me?"

"Oh, yes, yes!"

"But do you know who and what I am? A highwayman?"

"But you speak kindly, and look kindly: take me with you, and I shall be more content."

"Shameless hussy!" cried the woman. "Is this to be the end of all my care in bringing you up in the paths of virtue?"

"You did not bring me up."

"Oh, Selina, Selina!" said the man, "little did I think you would want to fly into the arms of the first highwayman we met."

"My name is not Selina, and I do not comprehend what you mean."

The girl burst into tears.

"Come, come!" said Duval; "if this young creature chooses to trust me, I accept the obligation, and, with the eye of heaven upon me, will fulfil it. I am a highwayman, but I am something more, which partakes something of the character of a knight errant."

As he spoke, he stooped from Nightshade, and opened the chaise door.

"Come!" he said.

"Instantly—instantly!" cried the girl.

The woman raised her hand to strike her.

"Beware!" said Duval; "or I shall forget."

"Forget what, you wretch."

"That you bear the outward semblance of a woman."

The man, too, had partially raised his hand; but a glance at Duval's eyes made him think it prudent to replace it again.

The girl struggled to the door of the chaise, and was evidently in a state of nervous and anxious delight at the idea of throwing herself upon the protection of Claude Duval.

And Duval did not put any wrong construction upon these actions of the young creature.

He felt perfectly sure that it was not to go with him she specially wished, and that her eagerness to leave the chaise was not, as the woman had said, from any desire to throw herself into the arms of a stranger; but he felt that it all arose from that intense wish to escape, probably, the most uncongenial company she had ever been in, and to place herself under the protection of the first person who won her confidence.

But there was rather a difficulty.

It would be an awkward thing to give this young girl a seat on Nightshade.

Duval deliberated for a moment.

"To be sure!" he then said; "that will be our best plan! Here, Blossom!"

"Yes, Captain."

"Hold Nightshade!"

Duval threw the rein of Nightshade to Blossom, and hastily dismounted.

"I have altered my mind," he said. "I intended to take this young creature from the chaise, but I will no longer do so."

"Then," said the woman, "I don't grudge the nineteen guineas, particularly as I have a lively hope of seeing you hanged some day."

"Much obliged," said Duval: "but I don't think you quite understand me. I will now trouble you both to alight."

"Alight?" cried the woman.

"Get out of this chaise?" said the man.

"Certainly! Be quick!"

"Never!"

"Blossom, pull these people out!"

"Yes, Captain."

Blossom got hold of the man by the leg at once, and in another moment he was sprawling in the roadway.

The woman who had just exclaimed "Never!" seeing by what a summary process her male companion was ejected, falsified her own declaration by springing out at once.

"That will do," said Duval.

He closed the chaise door again.

"Be contented," he said to the young girl, "these people shall vex you no more; and now tell me where you wish to be driven to?"

The girl shook her head.

"Have you no friends?"

"None—none!"

"No home?"

"None, now!"

Duval was puzzled to know what to do.

He quickly, however, made up his mind.

"There is no resource for it, Blossom," he said, "this must be the beginning and ending of this night's adventures. Dislodge the old postillion and take his place. We will be off to town. I will lead your horse."

"I can manage very well, Captain, and still ride my own horse. I dare say the post-chaise horses will come along, if I keep a hand on the bridle. Now, old gentleman, dismount!"

The old postillion had been so long upon the road, that he evidently took the stoppage of the chaise by a highwayman as one of those things of course, which was sure to happen in the ordinary routine of events.

At this order from Blossom, he hastily dismounted, and, after swinging his arms to and fro for several seconds, as if he were about to perform some tremendous gymnastic feat, he cried out, in an old, cracked voice, "I'll go and tell master!"

He then set off in a ridiculous kind of run in the direction of the village of Acton.

"Off we go, then!" said Duval.

The chaise was soon in motion then again; and, with an escort that might pretty well defy interruption, this fair young creature, whose existence and connexions appeared so mysterious, was rapidly whirled on towards London.

Duval thought it better to take her at once to Farnborough House, so that Lucy should hear from her the particulars of her history, and afford her a place of refuge.

He was quite lost in conjecture on his road to town, for he could not possibly comprehend what could be the solution of the mysterious affair.

Duval did not think it prudent, however, to drive up to Farnborough House with the post-chaise.

Nor did he ever, except in a case of absolute necessity, bring Nightshade to that door.

He, therefore, made his way, accompanied by Blossom, to Nightshade's stables.

The chaise was quietly left close to the kerb-stone, on its proper side of the way, in Bridge Street, Westminster; and Nightshade being disposed of in his stable, Duval placed the young girl's arm within his own, and they walked together towards Farnborough House.

There was something very charming in the entire confidence of this young creature in a perfect stranger.

If ever perfect innocence could be its own safeguard—and let us hope, for the credit of human nature, that at times it is so—this was most truly one of those occasions.

And all the terror—all the shrinking fear of this young girl had vanished.

She hung, confidingly, on Duval's arm, as though she had known him for years.

She spoke to him cheerfully, as though the future was by no means uncertain.

And she never asked him a single question about where he was taking her, or who he really was.

But Duval, as they walked thus amicably along together, got from her some portions of her previous history.

"What is your name?" he said, to begin with.

"Constance—my name is Constance Lascelles."

"And how came you with those people, from whom you were so glad to escape?"

"I scarcely know."

There was so much simplicity about the manner of these answers to the direct questions of Claude Duval, that he could not for a moment doubt their sincerity, strange as they appeared in reply to his interrogatories.

"Tell me all you know, then, of your history," he said; "it must be a brief one, for you are very young."

"I am fifteen years of age, and I have been at a school a considerable distance down the western road for the last four years. I cannot say I was treated with kindness, but still I was content to remain, from habit; but this evening, some few hours only before you interfered for my protection, I was taken from school and thrust into a chaise with those people whom you saw, and threatened and struck whenever I attempted the least remonstrance in regard to their proceedings."

"And do you not know them?"

"No; I never saw them until this night."

"It is very strange!"

"It is, indeed," said Constance, as she looked confidingly up in the face of Duval.

"Of course, they alarmed you very much?"

"Oh, yes."

"And did the mistress of the school consent readily to your going with them?"

"She helped to force me to do so."

"I cannot comprehend it; but no doubt, Constance, we shall find a clue to this mystery shortly, and in the meantime you shall be protected."

"That I am sure of," said the girl, as she held more firmly still by the arm of Claude Duval.

Chatting in this way they reached Farnborough House, and Lucy was soon acquainted with the brief history of the young creature who had been rescued apparently from persons who certainly had no friendly feelings towards her.

And Lucy was well enough pleased that no more serious adventure had occurred to Duval on that night.

She received Constance with all the kindness possible, and that ancient mansion might be considered then as a kind of refuge for the persecuted by Fortune, and in need of the active protection of a strong arm and a willing hand.

CHAPTER XCV.

MRS. CUMBERPATCH RECEIVES SIR JOHN'S CONFESSION

It is necessary that the reader should now, in imagination, transport himself to a certain house in Bond-street—a house of some pretensions.

True, that in this unexceptionable abode lodgings were to be obtained at a high price, but no bill or advertisement was ever to be seen in the windows to that effect.

Mr. and Mrs. Josiah Cumberpatch would have thought it highly derogatory to their dignity had any one been heard to say that they had seen such a thing as a placard with "Apartments" in any of their windows.

No. Mr. and Mrs. Cumberpatch carried on their genteel profession of lodging letting by advertising their apartments in the leading journal of the day.

It was in reply to one of these same advertisements that Sir John Lascelles paid a visit to Mr. and Mrs. Josiah Cumberpatch just four years before the reader was introduced to Constance.

The drawing-floor was appropriated to Sir John Lascelles, and both Mr. and Mrs. Cumberpatch had every reason to be satisfied with the munificence of their aristocratic lodger.

In the course of time, too, Mrs. Cumberpatch began to conceive hopes that the wealthy lodger might in time turn a favourable eye upon her only daughter, who was at the time of which we are speaking just at the interesting age of sweet seventeen.

Now, whether the amiable Selina seconded her mother's views or not it matters little: but, notwithstanding all Mrs. Cumberpatch's manœuvres, Sir John Lascelles seemed much more intent upon making his life pass serenely, by enjoying himself with some choice companions, who met at his lodgings every evening, and drank and smoke most frequently until the small hours of the morning.

Time passed on; and one night Mr. and Mrs. Cumberpatch were aroused from their peaceful slumbers by the sounds of hasty footsteps.

"Good gracious, what's the matter?" almost shrieked the lady, as she started up and seized her husband by the hair. "What's that noise—thieves?"

"Hush!" replied the husband, as he hastily dressed himself; "something is the matter on the first floor."

"Oh, I shall die—I shall die! I know I shall die!" moaned Mrs. Cumberpatch, rocking herself to and fro.

Mr. Cumberpatch hastened from his room, and was just in time to encounter four men, who appeared to be carrying a dead body!

"What's the matter?"

A groan was all the response that Cumberpatch received to his question.

He pressed forward, and led the way to a sofa which was stationed near the fire.

"That'll do," said one of the men, who had helped to carry in Sir John. "That'll do, he'll soon be better."

Mr. Cumberpatch looked at the form which lay upon the sofa, and certainly thought that the person who had said "he'll soon be better," was of a very sanguine disposition, for death seemed stamped upon the pallid features.

"How did it happen?" asked Cumberpatch.

"We don't know nothing about it, we found the gentleman lying on the ground, and if it hadn't have been that we found a card in his pocket, we shouldn't have knowed where to bring him."

A knock at this moment came at the outer door.

"Ah! that's the doctor, I suppose, that I took care to send for immediately I saw what had happened," said Cumberpatch.

At this moment the servant girl, accompanied by a gentlemanly-looking man, entered the drawing-room, and walking straight up to the sofa, he laid his fingers upon the wrist of Sir John Lascelles.

"There is not much danger," he said, after attentively examining the patient's eyes, which he did by partially opening them. "It will be as well to clear the room of all intruders."

As the medical man said this, he glanced round at the group which surrounded, what they had all thought to be, the dying Sir John.

"Certainly, certainly," said Cumberpatch.

The men who had carried in Sir John looked very much as though they were not quite satisfied at being thus dismissed.

The medical man saw and understood them instantly, and taking some money from his purse, he said, "Here, my good fellows, is something to repay you for the present. Call again on this gentleman," he added, glancing at the still form upon the sofa, "and I have no doubt, he will reward your kindness and attention to your satisfaction."

The men looked at each other, and appeared quite willing now to take their departure.

In a short time, Sir John Lascelles opened his eyes, and seemed inclined to sit up.

"Ah!" he said, in a dreamy kind of way, "I thought I was still——"

The medical man held up his hand and said, cheerfully, "I must enjoin silence for a short time, Sir John. Meanwhile, with the assistance of your landlord here, I will get you into bed, and advise you to try a sleep."

"Sleep, sleep, yes—yes, I will try to sleep, but I hope I shall not dream!"

"No fear of that. Here, Sir John, take this little sedative I have prepared for you, and all will be well."

After seeing his patient in a fair way to follow his injunctions, the doctor took his leave, and the patient was left alone with Cumberpatch.

A deep sigh, almost a groan, proceeded from the bed.

Cumberpatch felt curious to know what had happened to his lodger, and thought that if he remained he might, perhaps, speak about it, thinking himself alone.

He was not disappointed.

The sick man began to mutter to himself.

"I see it all now," he moaned. "This is retribution. I have robbed the fatherless, and now I am doomed—doomed—doomed."

The sick man groaned aloud.

Old Cumberpatch wondered what it all meant, and resolved to listen still.

"My only brother's orphan child, how have I fulfilled the trust reposed in me. I have appropriated her fortune, and have neglected her these four years."

Old Cumberpatch crept still nearer from curiosity. He had no defined notion in his mind what good could arrive to him from listening to the words of what appeared to be a dying man, but still he listened, and again the sick man continued.

"But it may not be too late, I will send for her from the school where I have placed her, and where, in all probability, the heiress, as every one thought her to be, has scarcely had food sufficient, for I chose a third-rate school, in order that she should not stand a chance of seeing any of her former companions. Yes, yes, I will send for her."

Old Cumberpatch left the room as noiselessly as he could, and sought his wife, who was awaiting him impatiently.

"Well, stupid, what has happened? Is he very ill?"

"I should think he is," replied her worthy husband, "and I suspect he is raving a bit, for he is talking away for all the world as though the room were full of people!"

"What did he say? Tell me."

"Why, wife, he is talking about having robbed an orphan niece of his, whom he has placed in some third class school in the Western Road."

"Ah!"

"Yes; but it's nothing to us, you see."

"Isn't it, stupid, that's all you know about it."

"Why, how can it matter to us?"

"Why, in this way, man. What is easier, if Sir John dies, than for us to substitute our girl Selina for this niece of his, and making it appear that she is entitled to all this property."

Cumberpatch slowly rubbed his head.

"What do you mean?" he asked.

"Never you mind what I mean, but do as I tell you, that will be sufficient."

It is needless to trouble the reader with the various little details of Mrs. Cumberpatch's scheme, by which she intended to turn to advantage the late repentance of the dying man.

Mrs. Cumberpatch arranged her cap, and then slowly ascended the stairs, and quietly turning the handle of the door, approached the bed of the invalid.

"How are you now, sir?" she asked in a low tone.

Sir John opened his eyes.

"Ah, I am glad you have come," he said, "I want you to fetch my niece to me. It is time that I make restitution; and then——"

The sick man paused, and seemed exhausted.

Mrs. Cumberpatch looked terrified, it would never do for her visitor to die, until she had obtained all the information she required.

"There, you'll be better now. What were you going to say, Sir John?" she asked.

"I want you to look in that little desk on the table there, and you will find an address of a Mrs. James, who keeps a school in the Western Road."

"Yes—yes."

"Get it before I say any more. I shall be better able to give you my directions."

Mrs. Cumberpatch turned to the table where the desk indicated by Sir John was.

She opened it.

"There it is, Sir John," she said, holding up a card.

"It is well."

Another pause, which Mrs. Cumberpatch was unable to break, for she feared to appear too anxious.

"Mrs. Cumberpatch," added Sir John, "I have known you and your husband now some years, I believe you both to be very worthy people."

"Mrs. Cumberpatch merely dropped a courtesy, as she said, "We try to do our duty, sir."

"I believe it. And now, Mrs. Cumberpatch, I must tell you what I want you to do. I wish you to go to the address you see on that card, and ask for my niece, Constance Lascelles."

"Yes, sir."

"Tell Mrs. James I am either dying or dead, as the case may be."

"Oh, don't talk about dying, sir."

"Without noticing the interruption, Sir John continued.

"I wish to restore to her the property which is hers by right; and if I could do this before my death, would fain do so."

Mrs. Cumberpatch looked wistfully at her lodger.

She had sufficient experience to see that his hours were numbered, and instantly formed her resolution.

That resolution was to take her own daughter Selina to the school of which she had the address, and making it worth the while of the mistress of that school to become a party to the deception.

Accordingly, she and her husband set off, accompanied by Selina, who was nothing loath to believe that she was going to a young lady's school to finish her education.

Neither her father nor mother thought it necessary to make her acquainted with the change they hoped to work in her fortunes.

The school was soon reached, and Mrs. Cumberpatch, after beating about the bush a little, as the saying is, soon gained over the school mistress, and the exchange was effected—viz., Selina Cumberpatch took the place of Constance Lascelles in that establishment; and Constance, but for the timely assistance of Duval, would have been hurried off to a distance, where she would never have heard of her uncle, nor have known where to turn for a friend.

It was necessary to bring the events of this story to this period, in order that what followed might be the better comprehended by the reader.

It was not possible but that Duval would see at once that some foul play was intended, and he, therefore, consulted with Lucy as to the best means of unravelling the mystery.

In the first place, Duval made up his mind to go to the school in the Western Road, and there learn, if possible, something concerning the man and woman with whom the mistress had been willing to entrust her fair young charge; and accordingly, the day following that on which he had rescued Constance, he rode up to the gate of the establishment, in his assumed character of Sir John Cope.

Having been introduced into a small room, which seemed to be set apart as a kind of reception-room, Duval waited, with what patience he could, the appearance of Mrs. James, the principal of the establishment.

He had not long to wait before an exceedingly thin and repulsive-looking female, with heavy black eyebrows, appeared in the reception-room.

"I have to apologize," Duval said, with his usual courtesy, "for intruding, I fear, at an unseasonable hour, perhaps; but as I am going a journey, I was anxious to see my niece, Miss Lascelles, before I go."

"Hem! Oh, yes. Your niece, I think you said, sir?"

"Yes, ma'am," replied Duval. "I have not the pleasure of knowing the young lady personally, but I hope that will not make any difficulty to my seeing her."

"Certainly not, sir," replied the schoolmistress, much relieved. "I will send for her immediately."

"This is strange," said Duval to himself, as the door closed behind the schoolmistress. "I was expecting she would have to tell me that my niece had left her establishment; but we shall see—we shall see."

Duval had just time to make these reflections, when the room-door was again opened, and Mrs. James appeared, leading in a tall, dark girl, as unlike the beautiful Constance as light from darkness.

Duval was almost thrown off his guard; for as he beheld so very different a personage to the real Miss Lascelles, he was about to say there was some mistake.

But it was only for a moment that Duval was taken by surprise, for he said, with a smile, "I was not prepared to behold so lovely a girl; indeed, I fancied my niece was much younger."

Selina Cumberpatch—for it was indeed none other—looked composed, and Duval began to wonder if it were possible for one so young to be a party to some base deception, and whether she were merely a tool in the hands of others.

"Well, dear," said Duval, taking her hand in his, "I thought I would call and see you as I am going away early to-morrow morning, and know not when I shall return to England again."

The schoolmistress seemed uneasy, and anxious to bring the interview to a close.

"You can go now, Miss Lascelles," she said, "and amuse yourself as you think proper until the seven o'clock bell rings for prayers."

Selina made a courtesy, and left the room, after having received a kindly shake of the hand from Duval.

As soon as Selina had left the room Duval prepared to take his departure, noting, as he did so, that the garden, which was appropriated to the use of the pupils, ran round the house, and was protected from the road by a high brick wall.

"Well," said Duval to himself, "I cannot make it out. I have Miss Lascelles at Farnborough House, and come here to inquire for her, thinking that I shall have some excuse framed for her non-appearance, when, lo and behold, I am presented to a young girl, said to bear that name, and nothing is said to lead me to the belief that there is a missing pupil at all. I must, however, try to fathom this mystery; and I will, too."

Duval mounted Nightshade, and proceeded at a quiet trot to Farnborough House.

As he entered the drawing-room he looked anxiously round for his new *protegée*, almost believing that he should be told she had left; but there she was, quietly reading at Lucy's feet, and looking perfectly contented and happy.

As Duval entered, she rose and went towards him, saying, with charming simplicity, "Well, sir, did you see Mrs. James?"

"Yes," replied Duval! "and I saw the other Miss Lascelles."

"The other Miss Lascelles, sir?" said Constance, wonderingly.

"Yes. I asked for you, thinking that I should hear you had been taken away by two friends; but not the slightest reference was made to your absence. On the contrary, I tell you that when I requested to be allowed to see Miss Lascelles, not the slightest demur was made, as I previously took the precaution to say that I was not personally acquainted with the young lady."

"It is very, very strange," said Constance, looking confused and puzzled.

"It is," said Duval; "but I mean to find out who this other Miss Lascelles is."

"Do so," said Lucy, "if you could obtain a private interview with her; possibly you may discover this base plot."

"I intend to do so," said Duval quietly, as he left the room, and summoned Blossom to his presence.

CHAPTER XCVI.

CONSTANCE LASCELLES FINDS THAT SHE IS NOT FRIENDLESS.

BLOSSOM soon made his appearance, and looked somewhat inquiringly at Duval as he paced the room, as was his wont when thinking deeply upon any subject.

"Blossom, I want you."

"All right, Captain; is anything up?"

"I want, Blossom, to consult with you, as to the best means of getting at the mystery which surrounds that young girl I brought here last night."

Blossom looked as though he were ready for anything that would require skill and management.

"I'm with you ever, Captain," he said; "what's to be done first?"

"I scarcely know myself, yet," said Duval; "but it seems to me to be highly requisite that I should have an interview with a young girl whom I saw to-day at the school, from which Miss Lascelles was being carried off when she had the good fortune to encounter me."

Blossom still looked dubious.

"I am thinking that we shall have to carry this other young girl off, who, probably, knows of the scheme that has been set on foot; for the destruction, may be, of Miss Lascelles, and that I may be able to work upon her fears in such a manner as to induce her to tell me all she knows of the transaction."

"Very likely!" said Blossom; "but how is it to be done, Captain?"

"I learnt, Blossom, while I was at the school this afternoon, that the girls had the use of the garden surrounding the house from seven o'clock till nine. Now, if you and I were there, and watched our opportunity, surely, we could, together, manage, either by force or persuasion to carry this girl off.

"I should think so," Captain, replied Blossom.

"Then, have the horses ready at half-past six o'clock, and we will see what we can do, Blossom."

At the appointed hour, Blossom was ready with the two horses, and he and Duval mounted and made their way at a sharp trot towards the establishment kept by Mrs. James.

They soon found themselves beneath the wall of Bidborough House, as the school was called.

There were voices, as of numbers conversing in low tones, and Duval felt certain that the girls were in the garden.

"Now, Blossom, is our time, if we can manage it."

Blossom looked thoughtfully, then he said, suddenly, "Suppose, Captain, you look into the garden, and see if the young lady calling herself Miss Lascelles really be in the garden."

"A good thought, Blossom. Hold Nightshade!"

Duval was agile, and in a few moments had so stationed himself as to be able to command a view of the garden and its occupants.

He was gratified to find that she, for whom he was searching, happened to be seated on a bench just beneath where he (Duval) was.

"Hem!" said Duval in a low voice.

The girl started.

"Hem!" again said Duval,

This time she sprung to her feet, but her eyes were not raised sufficiently to see Duval.

Duval made a grating sound upon the wall.

Then the girl looked up.

Duval raised his finger to his lips, and said "Hush!"

Selina had had the intention of calling out; but seeing a stranger—evidently a gentleman—looking down upon her from the wall, she seemed, for the moment, unable to speak or move.

"Are you happy here?" asked Duval, in a low tone.

"Happy? No; I never was so wretched in all my life. I shall kill myself if I remain here!"

"What would you say if I liberated you?"

"You? You cannot do it."

"I have the means."

"How?"

"If you were to give me your hand, I could raise you sufficiently so that you could easily reach the top of the wall, from whence, with my assistance, you will be able to reach the roadway, and then you may be free."

The girl looked anxious, but hesitated.

"I cannot do it—no; I will remain here and wait."

"Wait? Wait for what?"

"Until my mother and father fetch me."

"Do you expect them, then?"

"Yes; when all their arrangements are completed."

"Well, as we seem now to have established a kind of friendship, perhaps you will have no objection to tell me your name."

"My real name?"

"Most assuredly. But what mean you by your real name? Have you, then, two kinds of names?"

The girl looked embarrassed.

"Do you know," said Duval, "that I have the reputation of being a conjuror?"

"You?"

"Yes; and I will tell you that you are bearing a name in this school which belongs to another, and that other has been taken away."

"Oh, hush! hush! How did you know that?"

The girl looked anxiously around, fearing that some one might overhear what was being said.

"Oh! I know all about it; but I would rather, for your own sake, hear your version of the case, so that I may feel that you deserve my good opinion and my friendship, should you ever require them."

"If you know everything, why then do you want me to tell you all this?"

"Simply as I have just told you," replied Duval; "in order that I may feel assured that you are truthful and ingenuous, and not acting the treacherous part I have been led by your father and mother to believe you are doing."

"Is it possible that they have told you that I have been treacherous?"

Duval did not answer.

The girl construed Duval's silence into assent, and then all the fiery passion of her nature broke forth.

"It is false—false! I knew nothing of their schemes except by accident, and then I overheard Mrs. James telling her sister, that my father had promised her five hundred pounds as soon as ever Sir John Lascelles was dead, if she would allow him and my mother to remove Miss Lascelles from this school and take me in her stead."

"Go on," said Duval, quietly, "that is all true."

"And they brought me here and took a young lady away with them, and since then I have been called Miss Lascelles; and when my mother left me, she told me that some day before long I should be an heiress."

"Exactly so: and now tell me, for I forget, where did your father and mother take this young lady."

"That I know nothing about. It is quite certain they would not take her to their house in Bond Street, because Miss Lascelles's uncle was living there as a lodger, and he was supposed to be dying when I left home.

"And your name, I have quite forgotten it?"

"Selina Cumberpatch."

"Of course. I recollect now," said Duval. "Well, Selina, can I be of service to you in any way?"

"No! unless you see my father and mother; and, if you do, tell them that I am heartily tired and ashamed of the part I am playing, and that I want them to fetch me home."

"And is that all?"

"That is all," replied Selina.

"Good night, then! and rest assured that you shall not want a friend when you require one."

There was a movement at this moment at the further end of the garden, and Duval thought it advisable to bring the conference to a close.

He hastily descended, and joined Blossom, who looked inquiringly in Duval's face.

"Well, Captain?" he said; "how have you got on?"

"Capitally," said Duval; "and without carrying any one off, either."

"That's well," said Blossom; "for I was beginning to think it might become a little bit awkward."

"I have ascertained that the man and woman who were carrying off Miss Lascelles, are the father and mother of the girl whom I saw to-day, and who was called Miss Lascelles by Mrs. James."

"Ah! that's something, Captain!"

"And that they keep a lodging-house in Bond Street."

"Whew!" whistled Blossom.

"I now propose, Blossom, to proceed forthwith to this lodging-house in Bond Street, taking with me Miss Lascelles, in order that she may identify her father's brother, either in death or in life."

"Then, Blossom, the path will be clear for us to act; and let us hope that that fair young creature will soon find some friends who will receive her to their homes and to their hearts."

Duval hastened to Lucy, and made her acquainted with the particulars of his visit to the boarding-school, kept in the Western Road; and also apprised her of his intention of proceeding at once to the house in Bond Street, accompanied by Constance, in order to ascertain whether her uncle still lived.

A very short time was sufficient to equip Constance for her little expedition, and there was a smile of satisfaction on her beautiful countenance as she bade Lucy adieu, and said mischievously, "I shall stay with no uncle, but return to you, mind, if you will have me!"

Lucy returned her smile; and, together, she and Duval made their way to Bond Street.

Their inquiries at a baker's shop in the immediate neighbourhood were successful, and they were directed to No. 10, as the residence of Mr. and Mrs. Josiah Cumberpatch.

Duval knocked at the door, and had the satisfaction of standing face to face with Mrs. Cumberpatch herself, whom he at once recognised as the woman he had left on the high road an evening or two since.

He was glad to perceive, however, that she did not recognise him. Perhaps, that fact was owing to the darkness of that memorable night when she and Duval had first made acquaintance; or, perhaps, it might have been that Duval, in his disguise as Sir John Cope, defied a much more accurate observer than the lady in question.

Duval had taken care to place Constance a little behind him, so that she could not be seen scarcely at first; and it was not until Duval had stepped into the hall, and drawn his fair charge's arm beneath his own, that Mrs. Cumberpatch recognised her.

The start she gave was almost as though she had been acted upon by a galvanic battery

Duval, however, pretended not to see it.

"We wish to see Sir John Lascelles, my good woman," he said calmly; "and as our business is urgent, please to show us to his room immediately."

"I do not think—that is to say—oh, lor'—oh, lor! here's a pretty business!"

"My good woman, are you crazy? Pray show us to Sir John's sick room, or I shall be compelled to find it for myself."

"He is asleep, and the doctor said his life depended upon this sleep."

"Indeed!" said Duval. "Well, I can answer both for myself and this young lady, here, making no noise, but we must go to him at once and await his awakening."

Mrs. Cumberpatch seemed ready to drop.

"And who are—you?" she gasped, turning to Constance.

"Who am I? Why, don't you know me? I have not forgotten you, although I never saw you but once, and then it was quite dark, but for the faint rays of a lantern that fell upon your handsome face, the night you were taking me away from the school."

"Oh, lor!—oh lor!" groaned Mrs. Cumberpatch, "it's all up! The cat's out of the bag!"

"Are you going to show us to Sir John Lascelles' room, or not, woman?" asked Duval, sternly.

There was that in Duval's tones which convinced Mrs. Cumberpatch that he was not to be trifled with, and, ascending the staircase like one in a dream, she led her visitors to the second floor, and opened a door, which proved to be the sleeping apartment of Sir John Lascelles.

Duval and Constance entered noiselessly, but it was needless, for the sick man was not sleeping, but tossing about on his couch, and low groans came from time to time from his labouring breast.

"Speak to him, Constance," said Duval, in a low tone.

Constance looked bewildered for a moment, for she had never before been brought face to face with what certainly looked almost like death, neither had she ever, to her knowledge, seen the occupant of that bed before, but her naturally kind heart warmed towards that poor, forsaken man, and she stepped gently up to the bedside.

"Constance!—Constance!" moaned the dying man.

"I am here, uncle—dear uncle!" said the sweet, musical voice of Constance.

Sir John started, and, as he turned, the little light which came through the partially-closed blinds, fell full upon the fair young face of Constance.

At first a look of terror passed over the features of the sick man, but Constance again spoke, and as she did so, she laid her hand upon his, as she said, "Dear uncle—you have been very ill, but now I have come to nurse you, all will yet be well.

The voice acted like magic.

"Oh, tell me that you are my niece, Constance, and that you have forgiven me, and then I shall die in peace!"

"I am your niece, Constance, and as to forgiving you, uncle, why I do not know what there is to forgive, except not letting me know how ill you were, and so now you must just show that you do love me, by making haste and getting well, as fast as ever you can."

At this moment, Duval stepped forward, and said, "Pardon what may seem an intrusion, but your niece, whom you see here, was in some trouble and difficulty the other night, from which I had the good fortune to rescue her."

"Trouble? Difficulty?"

"Yes—she will herself explain all that, when you are better able to hear it; in the meantime I should advise you to take every care of yourself, and in a few days you will be able to leave this house, where, I am quite sure, you will not be content to remain a minute longer than is necessary."

All the time Duval had been talking, the sick man had been gazing into the face of his niece, and when he ceased speaking, the invalid said, with much emotion :—

"Everything seems strange to me at present; but I must tell you, sir, that I have been unfaithful to a trust—a sacred trust bequeathed to me by my niece's father, my own brother!"

Duval was about to speak, but Sir John motioned him to be silent.

"I have appropriated her immense fortune, and sent her to a third-rate school, in order that she might never meet with any one who could tell her who she really was."

"Dear uncle," said Constance, "say no more. I know I feel that I shall henceforth be very happy with you. I was not very badly off at Mrs. James's school, but if I had been, all that is past now, so say no more about it."

THE STUART PRINCES CONVEYED TO THE TOWER.

An approving smile from Duval was a rich reward for the young, enthusiastic girl.

"But now," added Duval, "I must tell you that I do not think it prudent that your niece should remain alone with you in this house. I propose to send you a nurse, and, in the meantime, I will take this young lady back with me to Farnborough House, and there await your coming."

Constance looked all her gratitude.

"I cannot thank you sufficiently, sir," said Sir John, "for your courtesy, and will accept your proposals, all except as regards sending a nurse to attend upon me, for that I need not trouble you, as the landlady of this house——"

Duval held up his hand, as he said, "It is precisely that that landlady shall have nothing more to do in these rooms, that I propose sending you a nurse, whom my grand-daughter shall procure for you."

"Indeed, you astonish me!" and the sick man threw himself back on the bed, apparently exhausted.

"You will allow me," said Duval, "to retire for a few minutes, and I will summon my man who is waiting below in the street, and he will not leave you, Sir John, until he sees your new nurse regularly installed in your chamber."

"Be it as you say, sir," replied Sir John; "and now, my child, will you suffer me to press your hand in mine, or I shall fancy this is all a dream."

"Indeed, it is no dream, uncle!" cheerfully replied Constance; and, stepping up to the bed, she pressed a warm and affectionate kiss upon her uncle's hand.

"Farewell, dear child," murmured the sick man.

"Farewell, uncle. Make haste and come to Farnborough House—I want so much to introduce you to my dear, darling friend, Lucy Cope!"

"And this is Sir John Cope?" asked her uncle.

"The same," said Duval, with a slight inclination of his head.

"I have heard the name, sir, and will avail myself of your kind and generous offer, if heaven spares my life."

Duval, after seeing Blossom comfortably ensconced

No 32.—NIGHTSHADE.

in an easy chair in an ante-room adjoining that occupied by the uncle of Constance, now took his departure, with the fair girl clinging almost fondly to his arm.

The next few days were passed in anxious watching by Constance. It was so long since she remembered to have been caressed by any human being who could claim kindred with her, that she began to long for the presence of her uncle, although almost a stranger to her.

At length he came, and there was a manliness, and, at the same time, a tender gentleness about his every word and action towards his niece which convinced both Lucy and Duval that they need have no fears for their young friend's future happiness and prospects with such a protector.

CHAPTER XCVII.

ST. IVES MAKES ANOTHER ATTEMPT TO CONVEY THE STUART PRINCESS FROM ENGLAND.

It is night.

In solemn tones the clock of St. James's Palace had struck the hour of twelve.

And all is still in Farnborough House.

A faint light only glimmers in the hall, where Blossom, at the special request of Duval, keeps watch and ward, since the Stuart Princess effected her escape from the Tower of London, and sought a refuge in that old mansion.

St. Ives had paid a visit to Farnborough House on the day that had passed away, and he and Duval had held an earnest consultation in regard to the best means of securing the escape of the Princess from England.

The small French vessel that had been lingering in the Thames for the purpose of aiding and assisting in that escape, had taken fright.

It had made for the port of Ostend, where the Princess was to have been carried.

There the master of the little vessel gave information of the failure of the attempt, and of the committal of the Princess to the Tower of London.

A Dutch galliot, however, whose crew and owner had more faith and courage than the French vessel, immediately set sail from Ostend.

On the pretended trading excursion it slowly made its way up the Thames, until it nearly reached London Bridge.

Hoisting, then, a peculiar pennant, well known to the Jacobites, and which, for a long time, was kept secret from the Government, this vessel waited in the hope that the Princess might take refuge on board of it.

This pennant, of course, was well known to St. Ives, and as from London Bridge he looked narrowly and warily among the numerous craft assembled on the river, he saw with pleasure the little fluttering signal which assured him of the presence of a friendly vessel.

But St. Ives was now aware that he was suspected.

The whole affair of the Tower had engendered in the minds of the authorities many suspicions concerning him, and his own life hung upon a thread.

On this particular night, then, St. Ives had determined, with the assistance of Claude Duval, to rescue the Princess.

He intended, likewise, to leave London along with her.

But the whole of the day he had been painfully aware of the fact that his footsteps had been dogged.

On his visit to Farnborough House he was perfectly certain he was watched, and upon the events of the next twelve hours he was convinced depended his liberty and perhaps his life.

And now, while Blossom kept watch and ward in the hall of Duval's mansion, a solitary figure enveloped in a cloak, might have been seen walking down St. James's Street.

That was St. Ives.

And he, too, heard the clock of St James's strike the midnight hour.

He felt that the time of action had arrived.

With a sigh, he murmured to himself, "Oh, that this night had passed away, and that I saw the sunrise of another morn reflected upon the open sea!"

He looked not to the right nor to the left.

And most of all was he careful not to cast the slightest glance behind him.

He was followed.

Of that there could not be the smallest doubt, for wound up so to speak, as every sense was with a painful sense of acuteness, he heard and recognised the same footstep that had haunted him during the day.

What was to be done.

St. Ives was adverse to the shedding of blood.

He knew well that if he chose he had the means of ridding himself of this spy.

St. Ives was a perfect swordsman, and he had but to turn upon him, and in two passes the spy would have been a dead man.

But he shrunk from that mode of operation.

At the last extremity, however, if it were necessary, not so much for his own safety as for that of the Princess, St. Ives reasoned with himself that that spy had no right to count upon immunity from the dangers of his profession.

The bottom of St. James's Street was reached.

Some strange shouts and yells arose in Pall Mall.

St. Ives paused.

For the moment, so absorbed was he in his own reflections, that he was at a loss to give a name to those sounds.

It was only for a moment, however.

He then at once recognised them.

At that period, and for some years previously, bands of dissolute young men had been in the habit of parading the streets of London after midnight, and committing every species of outrage.

They went by the name of Mohocks.

Elated by their deep potations at the various taverns in the metropolis, and unrestrained by any laws, human or divine, they were in the habit of attacking indiscriminately every one they met.

The favourite occupation of these young rakes, or "bloods," as they chose to call themselves, was to propose to any chance passenger a perilous leap some six feet in height over half-a-dozen sword points.

To fall was to receive some serious injury.

To succeed was almost impossible, except with the very young and agile.

St. Ives paused, as we have said, and an idea struck him.

He was determined to know who the spy was who dogged his footsteps.

He faced about so suddenly that the spy had not time to get out of his way.

Walking then rapidly up St. James's Square some half dozen paces, St. Ives was face to face with the man who had so pertinaciously followed him.

The spy tried to dart down a side street.

But St. Ives caught him by the shoulder.

"I must know who you are!" he said.

"Not yet," replied a feigned voice.

Stepping out of his grasp like an eel, the spy ran past St. Ives into Pall Mall.

There was a shout from the Mohocks, into the midst of whom he had plunged before he could stop himself.

St. Ives was more than ever intent upon discovering the identity of the spy.

Rapidly taking off the cloak in which he was enveloped, the Jacobite Colonel flung it into a doorway.

He then appeared in that same costume he had worn in St. James's Park, viz., as an officer of the King's Light Horse.

Starting immediately in rapid pursuit of the spy, St. Ives then reached Pall Mall just in time to see the first of the scuffle between him and the Mohocks.

"A bailiff! a bailiff!" cried St. Ives.

The Mohocks raised a shout of gratification.

A glance at the uniform that St. Ives wore perfectly satisfied them that he belonged to the same class of society as themselves, and the military aspect of his clothing likewise was quite a sufficient protection.

The Mohocks were only courageous to defenceless people, or to those who, although armed, might not be presumed to be very skilful in the use of their weapons.

An officer of the King's Light Horse, however, was not to be trifled with.

"A bailiff! a bailiff!" again shouted St. Ives. "Trounce him! Trounce him!"

"Hurrah!" roared the Mohocks, "Trounce him well!"

"No, gentlemen, no!" cried the spy. "I am an officer."

"Of the Sheriffs!" said St. Ives.

"Down with him! Trounce him!"

"Gentlemen, gentlemen, one word. I hold a warrant."

"Exactly!" cried St. Ives; "that is what I tell you."

"A warrant for the arrest of a traitor."

"Fudge!" cried St. Ives.

"Jump him! Down with him! A bailiff! A bailiff!"

"Gentlemen, gentlemen, I warn you."

Yells, cries, and imprecations burst from the Mohocks.

"We hunt vermin," cried one; "and you are fair game."

St. Ives stepped forward, and tore a half-mask from the face of the spy.

Then he knew him.

Their eyes met for a moment.

St. Ives in this man recognised one of the Jacobite fraternity, who had always shown the greatest anxiety to recommend and enforce what he called strong measures against the ruling powers.

In an instant, then, St. Ives was able to understand how all the Jacobite information which the Government had received from time to time had reached it.

And the spy saw that he was recognised by St. Ives.

He stretched out his hands.

"I arrest you, Colonel Miravel!"

At these words the Mohocks grew infuriated.

The spy was loaded with cuffs and buffets; and whatever more he would have said was drowned in the outcries about him.

"Gentlemen, all," said St. Ives, "we must make common cause against fellows like this. Things are coming to a pretty pass, indeed, when a gentleman cannot owe his tailor a couple of hundred guineas but a fellow like this must be set upon his track, and dog his footsteps."

"Jump him—jump him!"

"It is false!" shrieked the spy. "I am not a bailiff!"

"Then why did you pretend to be one for, eh?" cried one of the Mohocks.

"I did not!"

"He lies—he lies!" cried several. "Here's a common fellow who has the impudence actually to lie to gentlemen."

"Jump him—jump him!"

"Well, really," said St. Ives, "I think it's the least that you can do."

A circle of bright sword-blades was around the terrified spy.

"Help, help! Watch!" he cried, in stentorian accents.

But the watchmen in the neighbourhood were much too prudent to interfere in the proceedings of the Mohocks.

Every "guardian of the night" so called upon, hearing the peculiar whooping noise which the Mohocks made, prudently retired into the recesses of his own watch-box.

And now half a dozen sword-blades were crossed in a peculiar manner, so that their points presented a kind of *chevaux de frise*.

All escape, laterally or in the opposite direction, was prevented by the remainder of the Mohocks.

"Now, Mr. Bailiff," said one, "jump for your life!"

"I cannot do it."

"Try!"

The spy uttered a yell.

The Mohock who had asked him to try, had practically backed his own advice by a severe pink with his sword.

"It is murder!" cried the spy. "Help! Watch!"

"Jump—jump!"

The spy became infuriated.

He felt that if he essayed the leap, he would be certain to fall upon the sword-points.

And the more he hesitated, the more he was goaded by the Mohocks, who cut off his chances of escape.

There must have been some latent courage in the man.

Or perhaps some access of frenzy seized him.

He suddenly turned upon the Mohock nearest him, and wrenched his sword from his hand.

His first attack was upon St. Ives.

But the furious lunge was parried with ease.

The spy then assailed the Mohocks with all the frenzy of a desperate man.

Oaths, cries, and blasphemies filled the air for a few seconds.

And then the fight was over.

Three or four of the Mohocks were badly wounded.

But the Jacobite spy was run through by two or three sword-blades from breast to back.

"Spread, and cover! Spread and cover!" shouted the Mohocks.

The Mohocks fled in all directions.

Then came the distant sound of rattles being sprung by the different watchmen.

St. Ives, still with his drawn sword in his hand, made the best of his way to Farnborough House, and knocked hastily with his knuckles upon one of the panels of the door.

"Open—open! It is it!"

Blossom opened the door, and St. Ives sprung into the hall.

The rattles of the watch were now sprung in all directions, for they always arrived on the scene of action in a strong body, after they were sure the Mohocks had dispersed.

Those words, "Spread and cover!" being the signal for the perpetrators of the outrage to separate, and bestow themselves in various places of safety, were likewise the signal for the watch to waken up, and pretend to some efficiency.

"Close the door, Blossom—close the door!" said St. Ives.

"All's right, sir! What's been the row? I heard something going on."

"I should think you did."

"The Mohocks, I suppose, sir."

"Exactly. Where shall I find Sir John Cope?"

"He was in the small room to the right, Mr. St. Ives; he went upstairs just now to see if he could look further, and ascertain the cause of the tumult in the street."

"I will go to him."

St. Ives slowly ascended the staircase.

He was met at the top of it by Claude Duval.

"Ah, St. Ives!" he said, "I see you have been in a fight."

"How did you see it?"

"You have your drawn sword in your hand."

"In truth, yes, yes. I forgot to sheathe it."

St. Ives sheathed his sword, and then taking Duval by the arm, he spoke to him earnestly.

"I think that now there is just the proper opportunity to effect the escape of the Princess."

"Then it shall be done."

"I have been dogged all day by a spy and a traitor, but he will dog no one any further in this world."

"You have killed him?"

"Not I, although I take no credit for not doing so. He fell among the Mohocks, and has been murdered twice over."

"But, St. Ives, you do not mean to continue in this dress?"

"Yes, it is a safe one; it commands respect. Hark, it is half-past twelve, and my opinion is, that now the coast is clear the Princess can be got on board the Dutch galliot below London Bridge, without any serious difficulty."

"She is ready."

"And well disguised?"

"Yes, as well as possible."

"Lend me a cloak, then, Duval, and tell her I wait for her. The next time you hear of us it will be from Scotland, I hope."

St. Ives as he spoke clasped his hands for a moment over his face.

"What is it affects you so strongly, St. Ives?"

"The conviction has been growing upon me and has now reached a certainty, Duval, that the cause in which I have embarked my fortunes, and even my very life, is hopeless."

"You think so?"

"I am certain of it; and in the wreck of all those hopes, there is another wreck still more calamitous."

"What do you mean?"

"The wreck of a human heart."

CHAPTER XCVIII.

CLAUDE DUVAL AND ST. IVES ARE ARRESTED ON BOARD THE DUTCH GALLIOT.

The tone in which St. Ives spoke betrayed the profoundest emotion.

It was an emotion, however, which Claude Duval was far from divining the cause of, and in fact he still attributed the appearance of grief that sat upon the face of the Jacobite Colonel to the gradual extinguishing of his political hopes.

"I ask you," said Duval, "to be of good cheer, although, perhaps, not in the way in which you would wish; for, inasmuch as I do not think there is any chance of the restoration of the exiled royal family, I cannot say that as yet I have come to the length of desiring such an event."

"You mistake me," said St. Ives. "All the world mistakes me."

"In what way? Can it be possible that you are not in truth a Jacobite at heart?"

"In truth, I am, as I have ever been. But another feeling has taken possession of me which rides paramount over even my political predilections."

"And what feeling may that be?"

St. Ives hesitated for a few seconds, and then, while the colour heightened somewhat upon his cheek, he added:

"It is love. The Princess to whom you have been so kind, and to whom you have done such essential service is dearer to me than a Princess.'

It was now Duval's turn to be silent, and yet it could not be said that he was surprised at this avowal on the part of the Jacobite Colonel.

The beauty of the Princess.

The misfortunes that surrounded her exalted position.

A certain heroism and grandeur of character that she possessed.

All these things combined were more than sufficient to awaken the susceptibilities of such a man as St. Ives.

The Jacobite Colonel then spoke with more animation.

"You do not know," he said,—"you cannot feel what a relief it is to me even to have said this much to you, for I can see sympathy in your eyes."

"Say more to me," replied Duval. "Does the Princess know of this passion?"

"Assuredly not. It may consume me, but I would not for worlds let her see one spark of the hidden fire."

"Then think no more of it," said Duval; "and yet there have been cases where the hidden affection, such as yours, had but to be enunciated to meet with all its adequate return."

"You make me tremble with hope and joy," said St. Ives; "but I will not entertain the delusion. It is criminal of me to have delayed even so long as I have, for by so doing I may have jeopardised the means of escape. Let me beg of you to let her know her all is ready."

"She is here," said Duval.

The Princess and Lucy came down the upper staircase of Farnborough House.

The fair representative of the Stuarts was disguised in male attire, and looked like some very charming youth.

The cloak that St. Ives had asked the loan of from Duval was quickly produced.

And then, for a moment, Lucy held the Princess to her heart, and bade her farewell.

St. Ives had run down to the hall, for he could not conceal his emotions, and wished for a few minutes to himself, in which to recover his usual calmness and serenity.

By the time Duval and the Princess reached the hall he was quite himself again, and bowed low, with his usual respectful demeanour.

"How can I ever repay," said the Princess, "all this generous devotion?"

"Speak not of it," said Duval—"speak not of it. Let us all now bend our thoughts but to one object—your escape."

"Yes," said St. Ives, "that is everything and in comparison with it all the world, and its hopes and fears, are as nothing."

"Hush!" said Duval, gently, as he pressed St. Ives' arm.

The party then hastily left Farnborough House.

Claude Duval had no hesitation in leaving that establishment only to the care of Lucy, for by taking Blossom with him, he might secure a powerful auxiliary in the event of any danger.

"Have you arranged your plan?" asked Duval of St. Ives.

"Yes," he replied—"it is to walk down the narrow lanes of Southwark, below London Bridge, until we get to some little obscure quay, or stairs, as nearly as possible to that part of the river where the Dutch galliot is lying. A minute or two will then suffice to put us on board of her, and after that all is well."

"The plan is a good one," said Duval; "and its rapidity of execution recommends it much. I think, Princess, we may congratulate you beforehand upon your escape."

"Alas!" said the Princess, "there have been so many disappointments that I shall never believe this terrible episode in my existence is over until my foot presses a more friendly shore than that of England."

"Hush!—oh, hush!" said St. Ives, "for all our sakes! The streets seem nearly deserted at this silent hour, but still we cannot be too cautious."

The little party took their way up the Strand, and without encountering any hindrance whatever, they made their way to a narrow little quay on the river-side.

There they crossed by an ordinary ferry, paying one penny each, and were landed, without one remark or suspicion being excited on the opposite, or Southwark, side of the river.

A great number of squalid, narrow lanes were there to be found close to the water's edge, down which they were much more likely to make their way in safety than as if they had kept on the other side of the stream, which would have necessitated a complete detour round the Tower of London.

The yards and little wharves that they passed were almost all receptacles of old iron, and the various component parts of broken-up ships and barges.

Now and then a ruddy light would shoot across the narrow way from some forge-fire.

The clank of a smith's hammer would break the stillness, as some artificer laboured, even at that late hour, at his vocation.

London Bridge and its approaches were passed.

The narrow ways grew narrower still.

But soon the houses began to be intermittent; and as the lights had long since ceased, bad as they were, it was difficult to see their way at all.

"I fancy we must be nearly at the spot," said St. Ives.

"Have you no ready means of ascertaining that fact?" asked Duval.

"Yes, if I discharge a pistol loaded only with so small a portion of gunpowder as will suffice to make a slight report, a green lantern will be hoisted at the mast-head of the Dutch galliot, so that we shall see its exact position."

"Fire, then!" said Duval.

"I think we are close enough to the water."

"I am sure we are; for I can hear it lapping upon some steps not far from us."

In the intense darkness, it is almost a wonder they had not fallen down a narrow flight of steps that led directly into the stream.

It was only a mercy of Providence that they saw them just in time.

"Hold!" said Duval, as he held back the Princess. "This dim kind of reflection before us must be water."

They all paused.

By straining their eyes, then, they all saw, gently rocking to and fro, the masts of numerous vessels anchored below the bridge.

"It surely is the place," said St. Ives; "and the Dutch galliot, unless it is moored further down the stream, is near at hand."

"Fire, then," said Duval, "for the air from the river is cold and chill."

St. Ives knew perfectly well that it was not for himself that Duval mentioned the coldness and the chilliness of the air, but for the Princess, who shuddered as she hung upon his arm.

He produced one of his pistols.

He fired.

The report was very slight, but the flash, as is usual with a small quantity of powder, was greater than if the weapon had been more heavily loaded.

But still, at that silent hour of the night, assuming any one to be looking for such a signal, there could be no possible difficulty in its being observed.

And now the little party, with the fugitive Princess, waited, clustered together in silent expectation, at the top of that narrow flight of little slimy stairs, upon which the river tide lapped and heaved with a monotonous sound.

"We are right," said St. Ives. "Look! look!"

As though it had come out of the very surface of the Thames, a faint gleam of light rose higher and higher, perpendicularly into the night air.

"Is it the signal," added St. Ives.

"It is certainly a green light," said Duval.

"Once on board that galliot, and we are safe."

"It seems," said the Princess, as she stretched out her arms, "as if we might almost touch it!"

"Blossom," said Duval, in a suppressed tone.

"Yes, Captain!"

"Creep down these steps, and see if you can find a boat."

Blossom made his way down the steps with great caution, returning in the same manner in a few minutes.

"There is a wherry here," he said, "but it is small."

"Never mind," said St. Ives, "the distance is so short!"

"Be careful in coming down the steps," said Blossom, "for they are as slippery as they can be with river mud!"

"We will, we will."

Duval was well aware of the state of agitation in which the Jacobite Colonel was.

"Trust me!" he whispered; "to look after the Princess!"

"With all my heart I do."

"Go down carefully, and get into the boat with Blossom?"

"Your safety!" whispered Duval, to the Princess, "is paramount to all other considerations. Permit me, therefore, to assist you in the most efficient manner I can."

Duval did not exactly carry her down the steps, but placing his left arm round her waist, he so completely supported her, as to do so very nearly.

She spoke not a word.

She was too well aware of the kindly motives that actuated him, to interpose any foolish scruples to this proceeding.

And so Duval placed her in the wherry in safety.

It was certainly small.

But the surface of the water was very still.

The movement of air upon the river was as light as it very well could be at such an hour.

And as secrecy was of more importance than speed, considering the short distance they had to go, Blossom, who had possessed himself of the pair of oars he had found in the wherry, pulled with low, silent strokes, towards the green light on the mast-head of the galliot.

"And now shall we say that all is safe?" whispered Duval.

"I think so," said St. Ives, in a voice husky with emotion.

"May heaven reward you all!" said the Princess, "for your kindness to one so forlorn as I am!"

"There are some acts," said Duval, "which bring with them, step by step, their own reward, and it is a great one."

Blossom rowed silently, and for a few seconds no one spoke on board that little wherry.

Then St. Ives, in a tremulous voice, addressed the Stuart Princess.

"I may, now, I hope," he said; "congratulate your Royal Highness upon an escape from your enemies. The moment you set foot on the deck of that galliot, its cable will be cut, its sails will be spread to the light air upon the river, and a couple of its boats will assist in towing it down the stream."

"Yes, oh, yes," said the Princess, "it has all been wisely done and ordered!"

"I have, then, only," added the Jacobite Colonel, "to ask what are your Royal Highness's orders concerning myself."

"Yourself?"

"Yes, madam, shall I remain in England still to do such humble service as I can, or shall I——"

St. Ives's voice broke down.

He could not complete the sentence.

There was an awkward silence for a few seconds in duration.

The Princess then spoke.

"Miravel," she said; "I would rather you accompanied me."

The short, sharp cry, which the Jacobite Colonel uttered, almost frightened Blossom.

"What is the matter, sir?" he said.

"Nothing, nothing," cried Duval; "pull on, pull on!"

"Yes, Captain!"

Another moment, and they were under the shadow of the bows of the galliot.

"Boat a-hoi!" said a voice from her deck.

"Lost lilies!" cried St. Ives, with an evident effort.

"That's our cargo," replied the voice from the deck.

There was a brief scramble, and the little party stood on the deck of the Dutch galliot.

"Let the wherry go down the stream," said St. Ives.

"But Blossom and I must land," suggested Duval.

"Assuredly—assuredly. You shall have one of the ship's boats as soon as we get a mile further down the stream. Where is Captain Jan Van?"

"Yar! I am here!"

"That is well. Your freight is on board."

"Yar! Ve shall make von start."

"The Dutch Captain gave some orders, in his own language, to his crew."

"Some of the sails of the galliot were hastily run up."

Then there was the sharp blow of an axe, and the cable that held her anchor was severed.

The river tide was running down, and the vessel began to move.

"Saved!" cried St. Ives.

"I congratulate you, Princess!" cried Duval.

"There is refreshment in von cabin," said the Dutch Captain. "Yar, I have great honour to say you is one companionway."

"Yes, to the cabin, to the cabin," said St. Ives. "The deck is too conspicuous a place in so small a craft."

There appeared to be a light in the cabin of the galliot, when the little party began the descent of the companionway, but before they got half way down, it disappeared.

Duval then heard a strange, rushing sound, which at first he could not comprehend.

He then heard the voice of Blossom cry out.

"A rocket? What's the use of sending off a rocket? What is is that for?"

Duval retraced his steps a few paces up the companionway, and quite by chance, casting his eyes in the direction of the Tower of London, he saw another rocket soar up into the night air, and burst into a brilliant constellation of sparks.

A pang of suspicion, and it was an absolute pang, shot across his heart as he saw this spectacle.

Added to the words he heard on board the galliot, it could have no other possible meaning than that there was some concerted action between the vessel and the shore.

"St. Ives! St. Ives!" he cried, "I do not half like this!"

"What, Sir John Cope?"

"It seems to me——"

What Duval was about to utter, was cut short by the sound of a scuffle upon deck.

"Captain! Captain!" cried Blossom, "here is treachery!"

"I suspected it."

Duval drew his sword instantly, and rushed upon the deck.

He was just in time to see Blossom strike down two or three men who had flung themselves upon him, and then leap clear over the bulwarks of the vessel into the river.

Duval had not got quite clear of the companionway, when a rush was made at him by the same men who had assailed Blossom.

He kept them easily at his sword's point, as he retreated backwards down the companionway.

Then a voice sounded from the cabin, which was that unquestionably of St. Ives'.

"Save yourself, Claude Duval!" it cried. "Save yourself! We have fallen into a trap!"

Duval turned and dashed into the cabin.

There was plenty of light in it now, and he was instantly surrounded by half a dozen officers with drawn swords, who must have been concealed in it.

A resistance would have been worse than madness.

"I summon you," cried a voice, "Claude Duval, and you, Colonel Charles Miravel, adherents of the Pretender, to surrender, on pain of death!"

CHAPTER XCIX.

THE STUART PRINCESS, WITH CLAUDE DUVAL AND ST. IVES, IS CONVEYED TO THE TOWER.

These words were terrible to hear at that period of time.

They meant imprisonment.

They meant banishment.

They meant death.

But it was a peculiarity of Claude Duval, that, in moments of imminent danger, he became calm, cool, and collected.

He never sacrificed the future to the present.

An useless struggle—a disabling wound, perhaps, and then, after all, to be a prisoner, was far worse than to be one sound in wind and limb, and able to concoct measures for his future escape.

The group in the cabin now was picturesque and singular.

There was the ex-police agent, evidently well known as Colonel Miravel, of the Pretender's army.

And there was the young Princess, still disguised in her male attire.

She looked pale and sad.

But it was not for herself.

Believing that the hour of danger, from which there would be no escape, had arrived, and that death loomed in the future, she cast off the prejudices of her sex.

She turned to Miravel.

She placed both her hands upon his breast.

"At least, my Miravel," she said, "we may die together."

There had been no love passages between those two

No tender declarations

No whispered words springing from the heart to the lips

And yet how well they loved each other.

The Princess had not been unobservant of the love of the Colonel.

But what a moment for him in which to discover that that love was returned.

Under happier auspices, what could heaven itself have offered him more full of the ecstacy of bliss than the knowledge that he had not cast away his heart upon one who heeded not the offering, and gave none in exchange.

Then one of the officers advanced.

He spoke in a voice of considerable courtesy.

"If it be understood," he said, "that the prisoners make no resistance, every possible liberty and latitude will be allowed them."

"We submit," said the Princess.

She spoke both for herself and Miravel.

"I submit," said Claude Duval, "to a superior force; but I am no Jacobite, for all that."

"You choose your company ill, then, sir," said the officer.

"That is a matter of opinion," replied Duval.

"Which we need not argue," said the officer. "Your sword, sir."

Duval surrendered his sword.

The party was disarmed, but it was a gratification to them all that they were spared the ignominy of fetters or handcuffs.

The Dutch galliot was put about, and, despite the tide of the river, it made two long tacks, and reached the shore close to the Tower.

One of its boats was manned, and Claude Duval, Colonel Miravel, and the Princess were conveyed beneath that gloomy arch which we have before described as leading to what were called the State dungeons of the fortress.

And so, the scene had changed as rapidly almost as though touched by the wand of a harlequin.

But half an hour had elapsed since Claude Duval was breathing the pure fresh air of night on the deck of the Dutch galliot.

Now he inhaled the unwholesome vapour of a dungeon.

A series of narrow passages paved with stone.

A flight of damp steps, some twenty or thirty in number.

A door, thickly studded with nails, which creaked upon its disused hinges.

And Duval was in a dungeon,

A dungeon of the Tower.

A place within the four walls of which, probably, had been enacted some of those fearful tragedies which make the whole building rife with thoughts of murder.

Can we blame him, stout-hearted though he was, that a deep depression settled upon him, and that, for a brief period, even Claude Duval gave way to despair.

He thought of his home.

Of Lucy.

Of his horse Nightshade.

Of his faithful follower, Blossom.

Of the free, open air of heath and road, beneath the pale glimpses of the moon.

Alas! was he debarred for ever from those enjoyments again.

Was he, indeed, shut up in that noisome dungeon, to wait for what?

For death!

Death in a cruel shape.

Stigmatized as a traitor for a crime which he had not at heart, and the doubtful and delusive rewards of which he had refused.

But Duval's was not a despairing nature.

There was a natural elasticity about his spirits, which soon assumed its inevitable rebound.

"I may make matters worse," he said, "by inactivity and despair, whereas by life and energy I may make them better."

As he spoke, a light gleamed into the dungeon.

It came through a grating in the door.

And the door opened.

A guard of five men appeared, one of whom carried a lantern.

A small wooden tray was brought into the dungeon, on which was some coarse bread, and an earthen jug with water.

An official personage, who appeared to be in some command, accompanied the guard.

Duval spoke to him.

"Is this proper treatment," he said, "for any one arrested merely on suspicion, and who may be quite innocent?"

"We can't help it to-night," was the reply. "Probably, to-morrow better accommodation will be found for you."

"It could not well be worse," said Duval.

"You need be under no apprehension. The tide never rises so high as the grating."

"What grating?"

"Yonder. It looks into the moat, and the cool air comes freshly across the surface of the water."

Duval hardly knew whether this was intended to let him have a knowledge of the exact locality of his dungeon or not.

"Is light forbidden here?" he said.

"You may have the lantern; it will last another hour, perhaps, and will enable you to take the supper we have brought you."

"I am thankful," said Duval, "for any courtesy meant as such."

There was something about the tone and manner of this official personage which sounded to Duval as though it were not unfriendly.

There was a look, too, as he left the dungeon, which, if looks can be translated at all, certainly meant sympathy, in the fullest acceptation of the term.

The dungeon did not appear half so gloomy to Claude Duval as it had done before.

It was not entirely that little light that was left him which made all the difference; but it was the thought that he was not friendless and completely alone in the dismal place.

In what respect the sympathy of the official person could aid him—presuming that he had it—Duval could not exactly say; but the fact of its existence lent him new strength and energy.

"About an hour," he said; "so this light is to last that time. It is ample for me to make observation; but yet not time enough to trifle away."

Naturally enough he began to examine the dungeon in all its corners.

It was a damp and gloomy place.

But there was nothing at all within it which could excite his interest or curiosity.

Duval then turned to the grating in the wall, which he had been told looked on to the moat.

Through that grating came a rush of cold air, which, in truth, was the only grateful thing connected with the place.

It was very small that opening, probably not above a foot in width, although, perhaps, three times that space in length.

It was awkwardly situated, likewise, to make any

observation through, inasmuch as it was of such a height, that Duval could only just place his hands upon the lower portion of it.

By a great effort he drew himself up.

It was an effort few men could make, and he was only just equal to it.

He was enabled to catch a glimpse of the moat beyond, and of some of the houses on Tower Hill.

It was only a momentary glimpse, however, for the strain upon his arms was too great to be maintained beyond that period of time, and he was compelled to let himself drop down again into the dungeon.

He had ascertained, however that the level of the water in the moat was not much more than a foot below the grating.

On the occasion of any extraordinary high tide in the river, or any unusual agitation of the water, it was quite clear that the dungeon must be exposed to an inundation, that, if not fatal to any occupant it might possess, would be in the highest degree alarming.

Duval considered.

What was to be done?

So near to liberty as he was.

His position was certainly better as regarded air and light, than as though he had been far away in the interior of the Tower.

But still it brought with it its own aggravations, inasmuch as it presented to him, Tantalus-like, a vision of liberty which he could not enjoy.

The gleam of light that shone out of that dungeon grating on to the black waters of the moat of the old Tower must have presented a very curious aspect to any one observing it from the hill beyond.

But the light was fading away.

The period which it was to last had nearly expired, and Duval looked forward to nothing but darkness until the dawn of the morning.

Suddenly he heard a splash and noise in the moat.

Duval again tried to pull himself so as to be able to look into the moat, but at that moment the end of candle which was in the lantern shot up one bright ray and then expired.

Claude Duval was in perfect darkness.

* * * * * *

And now it will be necessary for the reader to go back with us to the deck of the Dutch galliot at the moment that these dreadful words were uttered which made prisoners of the Stuart Princess, St. Ives, and Claude Duval.

Blossom had seen and heard enough during the last few minutes, previously to the rocket being sent off from the Tower to be well aware that there was treachery on board the little vessel, and that great danger threatened Duval.

No sooner had the officer addressed the words which we have mentioned to Colonel Miravel—or St. Ives, as we still like to call him—and to Duval, than Blossom sprung over the side of the little Dutch galliot, and plunged into the river.

It was the work of an instant, and beyond the fact that a man was overboard, all engaged in that vessel were too deeply occupied, and too much engrossed in the capture of the three prisoners to give a thought to anything else.

And it was well for Blossom that those on board were thus fully engaged, or a stray shot or two might have been sent after him, of which there is no saying what might have been the consequences.

And Blossom reached the shore, and a feeling of despair almost took possession of him.

"Here I will watch," he said to himself, in a low voice, "here I will watch. An opportunity may present itself for me to be of assistance yet. Claude Duval, when he finds I have made my escape, will not attribute my doing so to cowardice. I could not bear for him to so misconstrue what I have done; but I will think that when he finds I am nowhere on deck, he will at once look forward to my being able to accomplish something which may lead to his rescue at least."

Blossom started.

He saw a light flashing upon the deck of the Dutch galliot, and then he felt sure he was not mistaken.

There were figures busily engaged upon deck, and presently he saw four figures step into a boat and row towards the gloomy Tower.

At that moment Blossom felt as though his heart would burst with the concentrated agony such a sight produced in him.

"Lost—lost!" he groaned! "and I am safe!"

At that moment Blossom felt as though he would willingly have laid down his life for Claude Duval, whom he loved and admired so well, but the thought of Lucy restrained him.

"Oh, how shall I tell her?" he moaned to himself. "How shall I break to her the fearful news of which I must be the bearer? But I must wait a little longer; something may arise which will enable me to see some plan by which his rescue may be attempted."

And long did Blossom sit on that river side; wet, cold, and weary at heart.

He had watched the boat until it had disappeared with its little party beneath the gloomy arch at Traitor's Gate.

Then the light, which had been carried by some one in that boat, seemed to disappear altogether, and left Blossom more heartsick than ever.

Suddenly,—after waiting, perhaps, about the space of an hour, but to him that time had appeared much longer—he saw a faint gleam of light, which in reality was issuing from the dungeon appropriated to Duval.

A new hope sprung up in Blossom's heart.

"Perhaps," he said to himself, "yonder light is a guide to me where to find my beloved master. I will watch it a little longer. I may yet see something to convince me whether I am right or not.

At this moment there was a slight noise just behind Blossom; and as he turned, he saw a gentlemanly-looking man standing close beside him.

The night, which had been cloudy, seemed for a moment to clear, and the moon shone out clear in the night sky.

At first, Blossom felt that he was watched, and a sickening fear came over him that he might be recognised as an accomplice of the three persons who had just been conveyed to the Tower; and that all power of aiding in Duval's escape might be taken from him.

The new comer was the first to speak.

"This is scarcely a time of night, neither is this exactly the locality that one would have thought it likely to find a companion."

"I want no company, sir," replied Blossom; "and if you are a gentleman you will not force yours on me."

"Not if I thought it would be disagreeable," replied the stranger.

"I am company for no one, sir," continued Blossom, "and, therefore, I hope you will pass on, and forget you have seen me."

The stranger moved on a pace or two, and then he returned to Blossom's side again, saying, "I am watching that little ray of light there which comes from one of the dungeons in the Tower."

Blossom turned sharply round to look into the face of his companion; but again the moon was hidden behind a bank of clouds, and all was dark and impenetrable.

"Well, sir," said Blossom, "perhaps, you are interested in that little ray of light, and——"

"And are not you, too, interested in it?"

CLAUDE DUVAL MAKES ACQUAINTANCE WITH DICK TURPIN.

"I? Why? What matters it to me whether there be a light or not in those dreary dungeons? Although, as you speak of it, and direct my attention to it, I should like to know what unhappy being is the tenant of that gloomy abode."

"*Perhaps a Jacobite!*" whispered the stranger, as he placed his hand upon Blossom's arm. "Now have I succeeded in interesting you?"

There was no mistaking the tone in which these words were uttered.

Blossom saw at once that the stranger wished to speak to him, and he no longer thought it prudent to feign unconcern.

Blossom turned round and said, "Perhaps, sir, you can inform me of the name of the Jacobite who inhabits that dungeon."

The stranger eyed Blossom intently, and with an air of suspicion.

"Perhaps I might, if I knew whether I was speaking to a friend whom I might implicitly trust, for I, too, am a Jacobite."

Blossom grasped the hand that lay on his arm, as he said, "I am no Jacobite; but I desire nothing in this world so much as to aid in the escape of one who is supposed to be such?"

"You mean Claude Duval?" said the stranger, quietly.

"I do," answered Blossom. "But how know you so much?"

"That must remain my secret," replied the man. "But now answer me: is this brave Claude Duval really one of us? He said, on board the galliot, there, that he was not a Jacobite."

"Neither is he," said Blossom; "but he is brave, and generous, and chivalrous: and heart and soul he has tried to effect the escape of the unhappy young Princess from these unfriendly shores."

"And yet he is not a Jacobite?"

"No."

"You are quite sure?"

"I am."

No. 33.—NIGHTSHADE.

CHAPTER C.

BLOSSOM MEETS WITH AN UNEXPECTED FRIEND.

THERE was a pause, which was broken by the stranger saying abruptly, "With courage and daring, Claude Duval might be free this night."

"Ah! say you so?" exclaimed Blossom, grasping his strange companion by the hand; "say you so? Then he is free!"

"You mean that you would brave all the peril that must surround the undertaking, upon the possible chance of setting Claude Duval at liberty?"

"A thousand times! A thousand dangers would I encounter, in order to see him once more breathing the pure, fresh air in freedom."

"Brave, courageous heart!" ejaculated the stranger. "Would that our cause possessed many such!"

But Blossom was anxious to learn in what manner he might be useful to Duval, and he started up, exclaiming, "We are wasting valuable time. Tell me, oh, tell me, what I may do—"

"You must have the assistance of Nightshade."

As he spoke, the stranger smiled faintly, although that smile could not be seen by Blossom amid the pitchy darkness which now enveloped them as with a cloud.

"You see," the stranger added, "I know something more of Claude Duval than merely his name. But I see you are impatient. Go and fetch Nightshade: be on this spot an hour before the dawn, and hidden beneath that heap of rubbish you will find a crowbar."

"Yes—yes."

"Take it Plunge into the moat—reach the dungeon—you will have with you the crowbar You understand the rest?"

"I do—I do Oh, how shall I thank you——"

But Blossom found that he was alone. His strange, mysterious companion had left him, and it was too dark for him to see in which direction he had gone.

"Enough," cried Blossom, springing to his feet. "I must be up and doing. First, I will see Lucy Everton; but the tale I shall have to tell her will surely be softened and rendered much less terrible, when I have to add to it that I am going to rescue Claude Duval."

Blossom sprung up the little embankment which led down to the water's edge, and sped along Tower Hill and over London Bridge, heedless of the attention he might excite.

"Hilloa! stop! stop! stop him!" he heard a watchman shout.

Blossom turned, and faced the man.

"Why, you old fool, can't a man run to keep himself warm, without being shouted after in that fashion?"

"Come, come, come, don't be insolent, or I shall spring my rattle, and soon have you made to know who you're speaking to!"

As the watchman spoke, Blossom snatched his rattle from him, and flung it as far as he could out of his reach, as he said. "Perhaps, another time, old gentleman, you will be more careful how you threaten gentlemen who prefer running to walking. I shall not forget your conduct, and shall not fail to report it in the proper quarter."

"Oh, sir, I beg your pardon, sir; but there's such a set about, sir, that a poor fellow never knows gentlemen from——"

But the watchman found that he had no listener, for Blossom had again darted off; for, now that there was any chance of setting Duval at liberty, he felt that every moment was indeed valuable, and should not be lost.

He reached Farnborough House in safety, and let himself in with a latch-key he always carried about him.

He hastily ascended the grand staircase, and knocked at the drawing-room door, which he felt sure was occupied by Lucy.

In answer to his summons, Lucy replied, "Come in." But there was a look upon his face, and the drenched condition of his apparel, which at once sent a pang of agony to Lucy's heart.

"What has happened? Speak Blossom—tell me all —tell me quickly, or I shall die."

"The Captain is a prisoner, but——"

Lucy buried her face in the cushion of the sofa, upon which she was seated, and sobbed as though her heart would break.

Blossom approached, and the tears stood in his eyes as he gazed upon so much sorrow, in one so young and gentle.

"Nay, weep not so, lady," he said, in a voice of great emotion; "I told you the worst first."

At these words, Lucy looked up inquiringly.

"He has friends, or at least one, whose name I know not, but who has put me in the way of liberating him this night."

"Ah!" exclaimed Lucy, "and I am detaining you here when you ought to be with him."

"Not so: the same friend, who I believe may be trusted, told me not to return until near the dawn."

"Alas, alas! There are yet some hours to wait," said Lucy. "But tell me where he is. Is he in Newgate?"

"No. He, with the Princess and Mr. St. Ives, was conveyed to the Tower."

"To the Tower?"

"Yes."

"Oh, you will never find out in what cell or dungeon he is confined, and how then can you aid him?"

"The man of whom I have spoken, told me that the rays which came from a small grating, indeed, and in truth, proceeded from a lantern in Claude Duval's dungeon."

"But how will you save him," asked Lucy.

"The same mysterious personage who confessed to being a Jacobite, is interested in those three persons, and will leave me an implement with which I may force the bars of the grating."

Lucy paced the room, and then she turned to Blossom, holding out her hand as she did so, and clasping it in both of hers, she said—

"Blossom, you are brave and discreet. Tell me, may I go with you? May I not be of some assistance to you in this perilous undertaking?"

"You might, perhaps, who can tell. And yet——"

Blossom paused, for he did not like to damp the rising spirits of that brave young heart.

"And yet, what, Blossom?"

"I think the first question the Captain will ask, will be whether you are at home in safety."

"But if you tell him that I am aiding in his escape?"

"That will not make up for the anxiety he will be sure to feel, when he knows that you are encountering unknown danger. Better, far better, lady, to let me go alone, being assured that if it be possible to save him, I will do so, at the risk of my own life."

"Perhaps it is as you say, Blossom; but how shall I wait with anything like patience till you return, either to say you have failed in the attempt, or brought him home again?"

Blossom shook his head dubiously.

"I tell you what I'll do—I'll go at once. It is dark as pitch; and what is to be done can be done as well now as two or three hours hence."

"Do so—do so, Blossom!" sighed Lucy; "and heaven have you in its good keeping."

Oh, who shall describe the heart-sickening suspense

of poor Lucy as she sometimes sat, sometimes paced, the magnificent apartment in which Blossom had left her?

"Will he succeed?—will he succeed?" were the words she repeated over and over again to herself. "Or will all the plans Blossom's ingenuity may contrive be frustrated? Oh, this suspense—this suspense—it is almost more than I can bear!"

Lucy paced the room with rapid steps; and ever and anon she paused to listen—not that she hoped to hear *his* footstep in whom was centered all her affections—for she knew that Blossom had not had time to arrive at his destination, even if he put Nightshade to his greatest speed, but to listen to she knew not what—perhaps to the beating of her own heart, that was audible enough.

Still, there was a something in the heart of Lucy which supported her—a degree of faith and trust which man seldom, if ever, can attain—a readiness for the worst, whatever that might be—a full assurance that she could not, and that she would not, survive him whom she loved if death were to be his fate.

And might not death be the penalty he would have to pay for the part he had taken in regard to that fair young Princess?

In her love there was, as is almost always the case with woman's first attachment, a great difference from the passion of her lover.

It was less of the earth than his; and though Claude Duval's was pure, and true, and bright, although he would willingly have sacrificed life, and all that life can give, for her sake, yet hers was purer and holier still.

He dreamt of long days of joy and happiness with her in the midst of the warm blessings of this earth.

She might have such visions also, but they were not so vivid, and they went beyond.

Lucy thought of happiness eternal with the chosen of her heart; of joy, and peace, and sweet communion with her husband in that place where there is no change, no tears, no sorrows.

A beautiful Sevres clock at this moment chimed the hour of two.

Lucy started.

Surely they will come soon now, if Blossom succeeds in effecting his escape?

She rose, and opened the window, and gazed out into the night air.

It was an awfully dark and tempestuous night.

The wind howled in fury, and large drops of rain dashed against the casements—the panes of glass rattled and clattered in their frames.

From time to time a keen, blue streak of lightning crossed the descending deluge; and all without that palatial residence appeared like spectres of a bygone world, and sunk into Egyptian darkness again almost as soon as seen, and then the roar of the thunder was added to the scream of the blast, seeming to shake the whole building to its foundations.

"What a fearful night," said Lucy to herself, as she closed the window. "Heaven grant that I may soon have the happiness of beholding my Claude in safety once again beneath this roof!"

* * * * *

We have seen how Claude Duval was surprised, on hearing the splash in the waters of the moat just beneath his cell, and a hope immediately sprung up in his heart that his faithful Blossom was near at hand, for full well did Claude Duval know that it was not with a wish to save himself while he, Duval, was in danger, that induced him to leap into the river.

Who shall describe the all-absorbing agony of suspense which took possession of Claude Duval as he waited for a repetition of that splashing sound, or some word which would confirm him in the belief that deliverance from that dreary cell was near at hand.

He had not long to wait, for in less than five minutes there was a slow, grating noise outside his cell.

"Speak, whoever you are," at length said Duval, in as loud a voice as he dared venture to speak in—"speak, and tell me whether you be friend or foe."

"All right. It's you, Captain," replied the well-known voice of Blossom. "I'll soon have you out of this uncomfortable crib, or my name's not Blossom!"

Claude Duval clasped his hands in thankfulness.

Not wholly for himself did he wish to be free from that lonesome dungeon—for he would have entered it any day of his own free will if Lucy could have been benefited by such a sacrifice, but it was the thought of assuring that fond heart of his safety that made him almost shout for joy as he recognised the voice of Blossom.

And then, too, might he not, in turn, aid in the escape of that brave and generous St. Ives, and hear him confess that never before had life been so dear to him as it was then, when, in the anguish of her heart, that young and lovely girl had confessed her affection for him who had served her so long and so faithfully.

But Duval had not much time to indulge in these reflections, for Blossom began to make use of the crowbar which his unknown friend had not failed to place in the appointed place beneath a heap of rubbish.

"What are you doing, Blossom?" asked Duval. "What do you propose to do?"

"Only just this, Captain: I am removing the grating bar by bar, and if I can succeed in doing that, and in dislodging a stone, I think I may get you up here as nicely as possible."

"Can you do it, think you?"

"Think, Captain! Why, I've taken out two bars already; the rest will soon follow."

Bang! at the moment came the sound of a musket.

"Hush!" said Blossom. "I don't think it concerns us, Captain. Keep quiet."

Duval and Blossom listened in breathless suspense for some minutes, and no sound but that of the thunder fell upon their ears.

"Now, Captain," whispered Blossom, "if you can manage to climb up, I will give you a hand, and then you must get upon Nightshade's back, and swim to shore as quickly as you can."

"But you, Blossom—what are you to do?"

"Never mind me, Captain, I shall be all right. I know a fellow who lives about here; I can trust to him not to ask any questions; and when I have changed my wet clothes, I will join you at Farnborough House, and talk over what is to be done next. But come, Captain, we are wasting, perhaps, precious time. Climb up, and I'll give you a hand."

Claude Duval had less difficulty now in gaining the opening, inasmuch as there was a better hold for his hands, and in another moment he found himself on the back of his gallant Nightshade.

"You must give me a kind of ferry over, Captain, on Nightshade's back, for I am too tired to swim myself; and when once I reach dry land, I will bid you good bye for the present, and give Jem Sparks a call."

Nightshade only needed to hear the voice of his master, in order to take to the water again, as though it were his natural element; and in less than half an hour Claude Duval was making his way at a tremendous gallop towards Farnborough House, which he reached without any adventure, after having taken the precaution previously to leave Nightshade at his stables in Westminster.

Opening the door with the latch-key which Blossom had surrendered to him, Duval hastily ascended the grand staircase, and was soon clasped in the arms of Lucy.

"Heaven be thanked!" was all she could say, as she fell fainting into his arms.

CHAPTER CI

CLAUDE DUVAL AND BLOSSOM SEEK AN ADVENTURE ON THE ROAD.

AND so Claude Duval has escaped.

Again assuming the disguise of Sir John Cope, he was free from all the consequences of that night adventure on the Thames.

But his heart was ill at ease.

They know little of Claude Duval who could suppose for a moment that any satisfied feelings at his own escape from peril could console him for the danger of his friends.

The Tower still held within its gloomy walls the gallant and chivalrous Colonel Miravel.

It still held, too, that Princess, who was not more noticeable for her rank and misfortunes than for her beauty and many exquisite sensibilities.

How was he to aid them?

Could it be possible that, by any measures he might adopt, the dungeons of the Tower could be forced open to give up their prey?

Deep dejection came over him, from which even Lucy was scarcely able to rouse him.

He consulted long with Blossom, but could come to no conclusion.

"Captain," said the latter, "this won't do. You are getting thin, and full of grief."

"It may be so, Blossom, for my thoughts are ever wandering to that gloomy and blood-stained fortress in which lie immured those loving hearts."

"It's not a pleasant place, Captain."

"I never suspected, until he announced to me the fact himself, that along with his political predilections, St. Ives was so deeply enamoured of the young Princess."

"It's not to be wondered at, Captain. I don't think it would be very easy to look at her, and know her for long, without some such feelings."

"Perhaps not—perhaps not."

"And then you must consider one thing, Captain, which is not the lightest or least important to St. Ives. It is just this—that all these unfortunate circumstances have enabled him to discover what, perhaps, he would never have known without them."

"I comprehend. You mean that the Princess was not indifferent to his attachment, and returned it fully."

"Just so, Captain, just so. But here is the *Evening Mercury*; it is just wet from the press, and contains some news."

"What news?"

"It states that the trial of several Jacobite conspirators of the highest rank will take place by special commission next week."

"That points at St. Ives and the Princess. They must be saved, and they shall be saved or my name is not Claude Duval. I must think of it—I must think of it."

"Do so, Captain; and you may depend you will think of it far better on the back of Nightshade than by moping here at home. Take a gallop, Captain, beneath the night sky in the free open air. It will do both you and Nightshade a world of good; and who knows but something may turn up to be of help."

"I will do so. Too much thought may be fatal to any real energy of purpose I must endeavour to shake off the shadows that are about me; so saddle Nightshade, Blossom, at once, and I will come down to the stables and mount."

Blossom was not backward in obeying these instructions.

In the course of half-an-hour they were both mounted, and Duval, without any previous thought upon the matter, took, in a mechanical kind of way, the Richmond Road."

"Blossom," he said, "do you know where the Prince of Wales is at present?"

"I believe, Captain, he is at that new house they have bought and beautified, that they call the White Lodge."

"In Richmond Park it is, I think."

"Yes, Captain."

Duval drew rein, and halted.

The sound of horses' feet, coming at a deliberate pace from the opposite direction, broke the stillness of the night air.

"Now, Captain," said Blossom, "if you are not inclined for a bit of business let me undertake it."

"Be it so, Blossom; I see there are two mounted men."

"Only two, Captain. They are talking loudly, as if wrangling; but, perhaps, a common danger will make them good friends again."

"Do as you please, Blossom. I will not ride onward beyond a quarter of a mile, and then I will halt for you."

Duval passed the two horsemen rapidly. Blossom, however, wheeled his horse to the side of the road, and as they approached, he cried out to them in a loud voice, "Gentlemen, it is scarcely worth while to barter your lives for your purses and watches; therefore, when I cry stand and deliver, you will understand me, and act like prudent men."

The horsemen abruptly paused.

"A highwayman!" exclaimed one.

"It sounds like it," said the other. "I will give him a bullet."

"Beware!" said Blossom; "that is a game two can play at."

"Begin the sport, then."

Certainly, for once in a way, Blossom had encountered a man who was not likely to be robbed on the highway with impunity.

There was a rapid discharge of two pistols.

One from the mounted stranger, and the other from Blossom.

Blossom said not a word; but his discharged pistol dropped from his grasp.

He held the rein of his horse by both hands for a few seconds, without uttering a word.

Then he spoke in strange accents.

"That's over," he said, "and it's better than Tyburn."

Blossom then fell heavily from his horse, and the creature with the consciousness that something was amiss started wildly forward on the road, soon galloping past Claude Duval and Nightshade, as he stood waiting for Blossom's arrival.

Just for a fleeting moment Duval saw the riderless horse, and then a sharp pang shot through his heart, for he felt that something fatal must have happened to his faithful follower.

Then, by a touch and a word, Nightshade knew that his utmost speed was required of him, and back he dashed to the spot of the encounter at a speed that in a few seconds brought him up with the two horsemen, who appeared so successfully to have resisted the highway encroachments of Blossom.

"Hold!" cried Duval. "He who stirs is a dead man!"

"Another!" cried the horseman who had shot Blossom. "Stand aside your Highness; it seems that I am fated to clear his Majesty's way of highwaymen to-night."

Bang, went another pistol.

This man, whoever he was, did not fire at random, for even at the moment with the discharge, Duval felt the hot scathing passage of the bullet pass his cheek.

Another inch to the right, and he would have been a dead man.

"Enough, sir!" cried Duval, as he made Nightshade give a leap forward.

Seizing the traveller by the collar, Duval, by main force, bent him down towards his horse's neck, and flung him heavily from the saddle.

The other horseman was evidently not gifted with either courage or perseverance, for, seeing his comrade in danger, he turned immediately to fly.

"Another step," shouted Duval, "and I fire—I never miss!"

The horseman cowered down upon his saddle, but he reined in his steed, and seemed to wait with trembling apprehension to see if Duval would carry out his threat.

"Come back, sir! Come back, sir! or it will be worse for both you and your friend, as I am in no mood for trifling!"

The horseman reluctantly turned his horse's head back towards Duval.

He strove to put on an air of bluster and importance.

"You do not know your own danger," he said; "our well-mounted and well-armed servants are upon the road; and in giving you such information, and advising you to escape, I act as your best friend."

There was something about the tones of this man's voice familiar to Duval.

For a few seconds he was at fault, however, as to who he could be; and then, suddenly recollecting that he had heard the horseman who had made such liberal use of his pistols call him, "Your Highness," the knowledge of who he was at once darted into the mind of Duval.

This, then, was a chance encounter with Frederick, Prince of Wales, which might be of the greatest possible importance, if properly managed.

It was with a sensation of deep regret that Duval felt he had not Blossom to aid him.

Riding up close, however, to the Prince, he placed one hand on the bridle of his horse as he spoke with calm decision.

"Now I know your Highness," he said, "and you are my prisoner!"

"Prisoner! If in truth you really know who I am, I can only wonder how you dare utter such a word in connection with my name!"

"Whatever man dares that ever lived, that dare I!" exclaimed Duval; "and I repeat that you are my prisoner!"

"I comprehend," said the Prince. "Your audacity is great. Take its reward. You will find my purse well enough lined; and I suspect that in handing it to you, I may say that I am robbed by the celebrated Claude Duval? Ah!"

The Prince ended these few words with an exclamation, for the rapid sound of more approaching horsemen gave him hopes after all of discomfiting the highwayman.

And Duval more than suspected that these approaching horsemen might be the mounted attendants the Prince had spoken of.

If such were the fact, his position, without Blossom to aid him, was certainly somewhat perilous.

"Help! help!" cried the Prince. "Thieves! thieves! Help! help!"

A couple of mounted men, in the royal livery, rode up at a rapid pace.

"Seize him! seize him!" shouted the Prince. "A highwayman! a highwayman!"

Duval tried a scheme which, under somewhat similar circumstances had before succeeded.

There was a very tall hedge on one side of the road—the meadows in that direction being at a considerable higher level than the road itself, which was a kind of cutting.

Turning towards this high hedge, Duval spoke quietly, and without the least show of bustle or alarm.

"Reserve your fire, my men," he said, "until you get the word from me."

Now, as the reader is aware, Duval not only had no men there, but he had every reason to believe that in so speaking he was simply addressing the hedges and the trees, and the forest birds that might or might not have been disturbed by the little contest that had taken place.

His surprise, therefore, was very great, when he was immediately replied to by a voice, which called out, "Yes, Captain; all right."

It was not the voice of Blossom, who still lay insensible, if not dead, in the roadway, nor was it a voice, the tones of which were in any way familiar to Claude Duval.

The effect, however, was instantaneous on the mind of the Prince of Wales.

He fully believed that himself and retinue were at the mercy of some band of desperadoes, and he called out, with a desperate sort of energy, to his servants, "Don't fire! don't fire! All is well! all is well! It was only a jest."

The two royal servants stopped short in surprise, and evidently knew not what to do."

"Away with you!" cried Duval, as he waved a pistol in his right hand; "Ride onward, His Royal Highness and I have private business which will not bear disturbance. Ride onward!"

The servants looked at the Prince hesitatingly.

They naturally enough wanted an order from him as to what they were to do.

Duval then rode close to him, and whispered in his ear, "Your life is jeopardised, and the only way to preserve it, is to order your servants to ride on."

"This is a matter of ransom, I suppose," replied the Prince.

"Assuredly."

"Ride on; I will follow!"

The two royal grooms, upon receiving this order, trotted onward, and Duval, to all appearance, was left alone with the Prince.

A very curious circumstance now occurred.

The mounted companion of the Prince of Wales, who certainly had shown no lack of courage in the encounter with the highwayman, began to recover from the heavy fall Duval had given him on the road.

He was slowly struggling to his feet.

The curiosity of the affair, however, consisted in this.

At the same moment, and with very much of the same movements, Blossom, to the great delight of Duval likewise, began to get up, and to look about him.

"Blossom!" cried Duval, "is it possible that I see you still in life?"

"I don't know yet, Captain."

"But you speak——"

"Yes; but I think I'm a dead man for all that."

"No, no, Blossom; you are worth twenty dead men yet."

"I wish I could think so, Captain; but I've a conviction that there's a bullet in my brains."

"What is all this!" cried the horseman, who was the companion of the Prince of Wales. "What is all this? Surely I have not been thrown?"

"Oh, there you are!" cried Blossom. "I know your voice again!" cried Blossom.

"Ah! the highwayman!"

Blossom and the half-stunned stranger rushed at each other.

But Duval immediately interposed.

"Forbear—forbear!" he cried. "The contest is over, and I am well enough pleased to find you both in life."

With some difficulty Duval separated them.

During the few seconds it took him to do so, he lost sight of the Prince of Wales, and his Royal Highness made an attempt to escape during that brief interval.

All parties were recalled to a sense of his presence, and a knowledge of his attempt to leave the spot by hearing the strange voice again, from the other side of the tall hedge, cry out, "No, you don't! Another step, and I fire!"

It was quite evident that Duval had some strange and inexplicable ally, who had been of service to him during the whole of the adventure.

Blossom was rubbing his head about the region of the left temple.

"Captain," he said, "I begin to think the bullet was very soft, or my head is very hard. There's a bit of a trench here, but that's all."

"You are safe, Blossom; and as for you, sir," added Claude, turning to the gentleman who had fought so well, if you have as much discretion as valour, I advise you to make the best of your way from this spot."

"No; I belong to the suite of his Royal Highness, and I will not desert him, although this seems a kind of ambuscade into which we have fallen."

"And what can you do by staying?" asked Duval.

"Nothing."

"And yet you might do something by preserving your freedom and escaping unhurt."

"That is true. Rely upon me, your royal highness. These fellows dare not do you any injury, and should they keep you a prisoner it will be only to extort a sum of money, which will be easily forthcoming. My name is Sherman—General Sherman. If you are Claude Duval, as I suppose, you can communicate with me at any of his Royal Highness's residences."

"Be it so," said Duval.

General Sherman mounted his horse and rode off.

He was a man of well known reckless courage, and he looked at the whole matter in a military point of view.

He and the Prince had fallen into an ambuscade, the latter was taken, and he thought it a very good thing that he himself was allowed to escape.

"Now, your Royal Highness," said Duval, "being my prisoner, it is necessary that I should ascertain if you have any offensive arms about you."

"There is my purse," said the Prince; "I offer it you again."

"I go halves in that," cried the voice in the hedge again.

Then there was a slight rustling among the branches of the trees, and a horseman made a flying leap from the meadow on the other side of the hedge right into the roadway.

CHAPTER CII.

CLAUDE DUVAL MAKES ACQUAINTANCE WITH DICK TURPIN.

So entirely unexpected was the appearance of the horseman that both Claude Duval and Blossom instinctively recoiled and placed their hands upon their pistols.

The principal darkness of the night had disappeared, too, and they were enabled to see plainly by the clear bright light of a moon about a week old not only the surrounding scenery, but that strange horse and its rider.

A brief description of this personage will not be amiss.

The horse was jet black.

The harness and trappings, which were of the simplest and least complicated description, were likewise perfectly black.

No ornamental buckles or trappings of any description were about the horse.

There was not a single point that could attract a ray of light.

"You might have put that horse, saddled and bridled as it was, on a common, provided the night were tolerably dark, and he would have been completely swallowed up and lost amid the surrounding shadows.

His rider was somewhat different.

It seemed rather curious that such pains should have been taken to render the horse difficult to see and to recognise, while the rider presented so many opportunities of observation.

He was a man about the middle height.

He wore top boots.

His scarlet coat reached a little below his knees, the skirt being slightly thrown back, and showing the white lining.

A brown leathern belt was about his waist.

The only piece of foppery that was about him consisted of a very rich lace handkerchief which was thrust into the breast of his coat, the costly edging of which was distinctly visible.

A plain three-cornered hat, without ornament whatever, and a white cambric cravat completed his costume.

There was something very remarkable in the attitude of the horse after leaping into the road, for there it stood precisely as it had alighted, as motionless as though it had been suddenly turned into stone.

The mysterious rider then slightly lifted his hat, and holding it a few inches above his head, he again spoke:

"Gentlemen, as I have before remarked, I go you halves; for I think I've had some little share in this transaction."

That this person was a highwayman there could not be the smallest doubt.

Claude Duval, however, had no immediate means of ascertaining who he was, and he regarded him with great curiosity.

There was one distinctive feature, however, about the man which would always suffice, provided he was not disguised, to identify him.

With his hat on he looked about thirty years of age.

Indeed, he could hardly have been guessed to be so old.

But the moment he lifted his hat the change was very great.

From the forehead right over the centre of the head was completely bald.

The sides only were furnished with those thick, clustering ringlets which imparted to him so youthful an appearance.

"Halves, gentlemen—halves!"

"Who and what are you?" asked Duval.

"Need I answer the last question?" replied the stranger, with a smile.

As he spoke he looked upward.

The full beams of the moon fell upon his face and head.

Claude Duval felt certain that, let him be where he might, and under any circumstances, he should always know that man.

Then the stranger suddenly glanced towards the Prince of Wales.

"Look to your prisoner," he said.

Duval darted a glance in the direction of the Prince, and saw that he had one hand in his pocket.

There was a look of mischief in his eyes.

"Beware!" said Duval. "I have said that I would keep you a prisoner; but you are going the way to convince me it will be safest to take your life. Out of the way, Blossom!"

"No!" said the Prince, with evident alarm; "since I had surrendered to you, I thought it only fair to place in your hands the sole remaining weapon I possessed."

As he spoke, he produced from his pocket a small pistol.

It was an exquisitely-made weapon, and shone brightly in the moonbeams.

All that was usually of wood in a pistol was in that one silver.

"Take it," he said, "and do not fancy I meditated any mischief.

Notwithstanding this apparently candid declaration on the part of Frederick, Prince of Wales, Claude Duval felt certain that he had meditated mischief.

He, nevertheless, took the pistol, and then, turning to Blossom, he spoke calmly and decidedly.

"I give our prisoner into your charge, Blossom! Keep him in safety, if you can; but if you see no other mode of preventing his escape or rescue than a bullet, let him have one."

"All right, captain!"

"And now, sir," added Duval, turning to the mysterious stranger, "perhaps, you will tell me your name."

"I think not yet. You can trust me without a name."

"Trust you, I can, certainly; but yet I should like to know it."

"What's in a name? I might tell you any one. But still you shall know mine in good time, although not quite yet."

"As you please."

Duval took the purse from the Prince, and handed it wholly and bodily to the stranger horseman.

"What's this?"

"Your share of the booty."

"But I only cried out for halves."

"That is quite right. I take the prisoner, and you the money."

"Indeed? That's rather an unusual proceeding. We lads of the moon and gentlemen of the King's highway seldom trouble ourselves with prisoners. Gad's life! we're only too glad to bid good-night to any one whom we may ease of his purse, watch, or pocket-book on the highway."

"But this is an exceptional circumstance," said Duval. "I want this man."

"Very good; but I suppose it's a joke."

"What a joke?"

"You called him the Prince of Wales."

"It is true; for he is none other than that personage; and I want him for a particular purpose."

"May I imagine what it is?"

"It would be churlish not to answer you. I want a hostage."

"Gad's life! I begin to understand now. You have some dear friend laid by the heels in limbo; and your possession of this gentleman will enable you to make terms for his release."

"It is so."

"And whither," added the stranger, lowering his voice, and placing one arm familiarly upon the shoulder of Duval—"whither do you purpose taking him?"

"I scarcely know. His capture was not a premeditated act. He has fallen into my hands by accident."

"I am going townwards, and will advise you."

"I shall be grateful."

"Do you know the old Bedford Head, in Covent Garden?"

"Perfectly well."

"There is your place, then, for there could not be a better."

"It may be so."

Duval became silent in thought.

The whole party trotted on the road together towards town, Blossom keeping quite close to the Prince's horse's head, so that there was not the least chance of his escape.

"What say you," asked the stranger suddenly of Duval; "what say you to my proposition of hiding him in the Bedford Head?"

"I think well of it. My first idea was to take him to my own house."

"Your own house? A highwayman keep an own house?"

"Yes; I thought you knew me!"

"I guess; and that more by your horse than by yourself. I do not ask you your name, but if you will admit that your horse answers to the name of Nightshade, I shall have no difficulty about its owner."

Duval patted his horse's neck, and smiled.

"I think Nightshade will do as well for a name as any other."

"Then you are Claude Duval?"

"I am. And you?"

"Look at my mare."

"A sweet creature, and apparently docile as a lamb."

"She is perfectly black. There is not a white hair about her. Can you guess her name?"

"Ah!" cried Duval, as a new thought sprung into his mind; "I have heard of you. Your mare's name is Bess!"

The horseman smiled.

"And your own?" added Duval.

The stranger horseman again lifted his hat a few inches above his head, as he replied, "My own is Richard Turpin, commonly called Dick!"

Both these men now looked at each other with rather admiring eyes.

Dick Turpin was then but young upon the road, and had not obtained that great celebrity which in two or three years afterwards made his name a household word.

"Look you here, Duval," said Turpin; "if you and I choose to share the road between us, who could say nay to us?"

"Pardon me," said Duval; "I cannot, for the present accede to such a proposition. My mind is full of some anxieties that I must try to rid myself of before I commence any new complications."

A long, shrill whistle, at this moment, sounded from the meadows at the road-side.

The note varied several times with all the exquisite modulations of the song of the blackbird.

Turpin laughed.

"Is that a signal?" asked Duval.

"It sounds like it, don't it."

"Assuredly it does."

"Well, I fancy it's a friend of mine wants to know what I'm about. Leap over, Tom, if your horse will do it!"

"Coming, Dick!"

There was a rushing sound, and then a man upon a powerful bay horse leaped into the roadway.

"Fire and thunder!" he cried; "that will do! Is there anybody's throat to cut?"

"Be quiet, Tom," said Turpin; you are in genteel

company. Allow me, Claude Duval, to introduce to you Tom King."

"Flames and Brimstone!" said King; "is this the great Claude Duval?"

Duval slightly inclined his head.

He had no great inclination for the society of a gentleman who indulged in such expletives as those that rolled freely from the lips of Tom King.

"Crackers and saltpetre!" shouted King; "if I didn't think there would be some luck to-night. Sink or swim, Tom," I said to myself, "you'll meet with a surprise."

What further Tom King might have added, was cut short by Blossom, who, with his hand upon the bridle of the Prince of Wales's horse, suddenly turned round, and addressed Duval.

"There's a carriage approaching with a couple of outriders, and some more follow in the rear. It must be somebody of distinction, Captain, and, perhaps, we'd better get out of the way."

"Not a bit of it!" cried Turpin. "We have a good force. One, two, three, four of us. What do you say, Tom, shall we put up the toll-bar?"

"Ah!" said Duval, "that puts me in mind of something, and I thought I recognised your voice."

Turpin laughed.

"You spoke to me and my man on the Acton Road, close to the windmill."

"To be sure I did, and this is one of our stations. Now Tom, set about it. Look to the bar, and be quick. I'll hold your horse, woa! lad, woa! Just you do, give Bess a kick, and I'll twist your head off."

"Blazes and brimstone," said Tom King, "if I haven't all the hard work to do. Find the bar, indeed, how am I find it in a quickset hedge."

"Oh, there's space enough, Tom!"

"Yes, but every space is filled up by a bramble, five yards and a-half long. Stop my breath, and smash me in heaps if I can find it."

"Look again."

"Oh, ah! here it is."

Claude Duval, Blossom, and Frederick, Prince of Wales, looked on the scene that was now taking place with a good deal of interest.

Tom King, defending his face as well as he could from the long clinging brambles, and dashing them aside with his thick buff horseman's gloves, appeared to make his way right into the hedge.

That part of the road was very narrow.

Not, indeed, above sixteen feet in width, and on each side there were tall poplars, which gave it a pretty and picturesque appearance.

CHAPTER CIII.

DICK TURPIN ESTABLISHES HIS TOLL BAR FOR THE BENEFIT OF HIS MAJESTY.

In a few minutes Tom King emerged from the hedge.

"Blue fire and crackers!" he cried; "if I am not full of scratches and prickles."

"Never mind," said Turpin.

"Sink me! but it's very easy to say never mind; but here it is."

Tom King seemed to be carrying something from the hedge, and as he emerged into the road, it had a very curious appearance.

He lifted out of the hedge one end of a long bar of wood, and by the sweep he took into the roadway it was soon evident that the other end of it was attached to something upon which it moved hinge-wise freely.

That something to which the long beam of wood was attached was one of the poplar trees.

An ordinary staple was driven into it, and there being a hook at the end of the bar of wood, it was easily attached.

The same arrangement was connected with a poplar tree immediately opposite, so that with the smallest amount of trouble, Tom King was able to place the bar across the road.

"Whiten it well, Tom," cried Turpin.

"Yes—cartridges and bomb-shells—yes. I've all the dirty work to do. But here goes."

Tom King was evidently provided for the occasion, and with the assistance of a huge piece of chalk he took from his pocket, he whitened the piece of wood until it shone brightly in the moonlight.

"All's right," said Turpin. "Now our toll bar is established, and no one passes here without paying for the right of way."

"Look out! Look out!" shouted Blossom; "the carriage is coming up the hill, and here are the outriders."

A couple of men in the royal livery came in a straggling kind of trot towards that narrow part of the road.

There was still quite sufficient moonlight glancing through the branches of those old poplar trees to enable these outriders, whatever might be the carriage they escorted, to see plainly that there was some obstruction on the road.

Five mounted men in so narrow a space presented rather a formidable obstacle; for, counting the Prince of Wales, there were five, and they had no means of coming readily to the conclusion that one was a prisoner.

"Over!" cried Dick Turpin.

As he spoke, he faced about his celebrated mare, Black Bess, and lightly leaped over the bar.

Impulsively Claude Duval did the same with Nightshade.

Prince Frederick of Wales was tolerably well mounted, and as Blossom kept still hold of the bridle of his horse, while at the same time he put his own to the leap, there could scarcely be said to be any resource but to take it.

The Prince did so; and the consequence was, that the whole five of them were in the space of as many seconds on the other side of the bar.

The two royal outriders reined in their horses.

"Out of the way! Out of the way!" one of them cried.

"This is next thing to treason!" said the other.

"Jacobites, I'll be bound!" shouted the first.

Duval turned to Prince Frederick, and said sharply, "You are able to tell us. Who is it?"

"The King!"

"I thought as much."

The royal carriage now came up with a rush, and the postilions had considerable difficulty in reining in their horses sufficiently quickly to prevent them from dashing themselves against the bar.

The equipage came to a standstill with a sudden shock, which made it roll back upon its springs, no doubt to the great discomfiture of whoever was inside.

Then there came a loud, angry voice, "Drive on—drive on! What is the meaning of this?"

"Toll!" shouted Dick Turpin.

"Toll!" echoed Tom King.

Blossom enjoyed the joke amazingly, and joining his voice to theirs, he likewise shouted out "Toll! toll!"

One of the outriders made his way to the window of the carriage.

"May it please your Majesty, we are beset by a strong gang of highwaymen!"

THE DUCHESS OF CLEVELAND MAKES A DECLARATION OF LOVE.

" Kill them all at once, and drive on "

"Yes, your Majesty. Hem! Jenkins, his Majesty says we're to kill them all!"

"Which is much easier said than done," rejoined Turpin. "Duval, I leave these fellows in your charge, while I go to take the toll! Over, Bess—over!"

Turpin leaped the bar again; and then, placing one hand upon the window sill of the King's coach, he looked in upon the bewildered monarch.

"Now, sir, if you please, the toll?"

"Toll!"

"Yes. There's a bar on this road."

"And who dare stop me at any bar?"

"That's not the question. It's done."

"But this is the King's highway, and I am the King!"

"Nevertheless, we must have the toll."

"Insolence!"

"A thousand pounds for carriage and pair, with two outriders and two followers."

"A thousand devils!"

"Not at all; but if your Majesty has not the money we scorn to do the unhandsome thing to stop you on your road to Kew, so we will take what we can get."

"Ruffian!"

"Oh, hard words break no bones; so, your Majesty, will oblige me with those rings from your fingers and that diamond star from your breast."

"Never!"

"Oh, we shall see; and, by the by, perhaps you'll have no objection to add something handsome for the ransom of the Prince of Wales."

"Frederick?"

"Exactly. A friend of mine picked him up upon the road, and has him over the bar yonder."

"Ah! where is your friend?"

"There,—on the black horse."

"And his name?"

"Is Claude Duval."

"Take the star—take the rings, and tell that man we desire to speak to him. So, so! He has picked

No. 34.—NIGHTSHADE.

up Frederick on the road, has he, and holds him a prisoner? Bring him here! bring him here!"

The King took off the diamond star from his breast, and on shuffling some rich rings from his old, shrivelled fingers, he handed them to Dick Turpin.

"Duval," cried Dick, "you are wanted. Leap the bar, and come over here."

Duval did so; and Turpin himself went back to assist Blossom and Tom King in keeping the royal outriders in check.

Duval had no objection to say a few words to the King; and, in fact, he was quite rejoiced that chance had given him an opportunity which otherwise he might in vain have sought for.

In another moment he was at the door of the carriage.

"So," said the King, "you are Claude Duval?"

"I am."

"And we meet again? It seems to us that, by some fatality, we are compelled to be perpetually giving audiences to a highwayman."

"It looks like it," said Duval. "But there is one consolation for your majesty."

"And what may that be?"

"There is no highwayman who ever cried, 'Stand and deliver' on the high road, who can be half so bad as many of the so-called noble and illustrious personages who have ready access to your majesty's presence."

The King was silent for a few seconds.

He looked warily about him then, in a manner peculiar to himself.

That is to say, he moved his eyes without moving his head, which gave him a strange, stealthy look.

"And you are Claude Duval," he said. "I think we have met before."

"Your majesty knows perfectly well that we have."

"Our memory at times is treacherous. But how is it that you have Frederick a prisoner?"

"I want a hostage."

"Ah!"

"Yes, your majesty. Two dear friends of mine are now prisoners in the Tower of London."

"You allude to a young woman named Catherine Stuart, and her paramour,—a man who calls himself St. Ives?"

"Your majesty is either misinformed, or wilfully traduces these people. But it matters not."

"Stop! let me think. You fancy that if you hold Frederick as a hostage, no harm can come to them?"

"I hope so."

"You are perfectly right."

"I am glad to hear your majesty say as much, and hope that the price of his release may be rendered at once, by that of the persons I name."

The King put on a well-acted look of pretended surprise.

"I do not comprehend you," he said.

"The case is plain enough," replied Duval. "The meaning of a hostage seems to me that he should be exchanged for some one else, or that he should be given up upon the accomplishment of some act."

"Aye; the ordinary meaning, I grant you."

The King quite forgot, in the interest of this conversation, his regal condition, and dropped the usual "we," by which he commonly signified himself.

And Duval was so exceedingly anxious to accomplish something for the release of the Princess and St. Ives, that he answered the King with a feverish kind of anxiety, although calmer reflection must have told him how little there was to hope from such a man.

"In what does this case case differ, your majesty," he said, "from any other?"

"You are anxious for the safety of certain persons confined in the Tower of London?"

"Most anxious."

"Then let me tell you, that while you hold Frederick, our son, a prisoner, no possible harm shall come to those prisoners, let them be as deeply-dyed traitors as they may."

"I scarcely comprehend."

"Do I not speak plainly?"

"But I want their release."

"Assuredly."

"Then your majesty consents to the conditions?"

"It is for you to consent. How can you be so dull of comprehension?"

"Dull of comprehension?"

"Yes. You have not the look of a fool."

"That compliment is but a dubious one."

"Pooh! pooh! I never pay compliments. But understand me. So long as you keep Frederick a prisoner, those persons in whom you are interested, and who now lie in the Tower of London, shall not be brought to trial."

"But their release?"

"I am coming to that. You must release Frederick first."

"That is exactly my proposition, your majesty."

"But his must be a complete release."

"Assuredly."

"From all the ills of life, and all the pains and penalties of mundane existence."

Duval recoiled from the window.

The King continued to speak in a hissing tone of voice.

"Bring me such proof that he is released from existence—such proof as will not admit of the shadow of a doubt—and then, not only shall your friends be at liberty, but you shall ask of me what else you will, even if it be an earldom."

"Murder him?"

"Bah! Murder is but a word."

"Your own son?"

"How do I know that?"

"This is beyond human wickedness."

"Is it?" snarled the King, as he approached his face close to the window of the carriage, and showed that it was white with passion,—"is it? I tell you he has three times sought my life, and shall I not turn and try to sting again?"

"Your Majesty may do as you please, but I will not be the instrument either of your justice or your vengeance."

Duval, as he spoke, turned aside from the carriage.

He called out to Turpin, in a loud voice, "The toll is paid, and I think the bar may be removed."

"All's right!" replied Turpin. "Look to it Tom!"

"Blazes and crackers, yes!" said King. "It's always look to it Tom! If there's any hard work to do I am the fellow put to it. But, however, here goes. I'm too good-natured by half. Brimstone and crackers! now the road is clear."

The bar was removed.

The royal postilions took the hint, and plied their whips and spurs.

The carriage rolled onward, and in a few minutes the royal *cortége* was out of sight.

Blossom had taken good care of the Prince of Wales, so that any attempt on his part to escape would have been perfectly futile.

Duval then spoke in a low voice to Dick Turpin.

"I will take your advice, he said, and convey my prisoner to the Bedford Head."

"It's the best place, and they need scarcely know who he is. I thought, however you had made terms with the King?"

"I might have done so, but they were too terrible for me to entertain for a moment."

"Let us get to town then, for this is just the most

silent hour of the evening, and you may lodge your prisoner with perfect safety."

The whole party then started for London, and soon arrived in its suburbs.

Dick then spoke to Duval again.

"I don't think it will be prudent," he said, "to let the people at the Bedford Head know the rank of your prisoner."

"He may tell them himself."

"I think not; we will frighten him out of that."

"In what way?"

"Leave it to me. I will speak to him at once."

Dick Turpin rode up to the side of the Prince.

"It will be better," he said, "to attend to what I am saying to you, if you value your life. I'm a good-tempered fellow, and don't want any man to be knocked on the head for no object."

The Prince started.

"But," added Turpin; "there's no cause for alarm if you are but prudent."

"Prudent?"

"Yes; Duval is about taking you for safe keeping and custody, to one of the Jacobite haunts, where every man is a fanatical adherent of the exiled royal family. Now, if they should even suspect for a moment who you are, I fancy they will cut your throat upon the mere chance of being right."

"Murder! Help!"

"Don't make a noise. You have but to keep your own counsel, and neither Duval nor I will pronounce your name. Always bear in mind, then, this, that if your real name and rank are discovered, it will be your own act, and you may take the consequences."

Dick Turpin did not wait for a reply, but trotted back to Duval, and, in a few minutes more, the party diverged from the main thoroughfare in which they were, and made their way up a bye street towards Covent Garden.

CHAPTER CIV.

A SCENE OF CONFUSION AT THE OLD BEDFORD HEAD.

THE Prince of Wales was now exceedingly anxious to say some words to Duval.

He signified as much to Blossom, and Claude rode up to him.

"I have something to propose to you," said the Prince, "which will accomplish all your desires."

"That is, indeed, a wide speech."

"It means this: release for your friends, rank and wealth for yourself, and the perpetual favour of the Crown."

A sickening sensation came over the heart of Duval, and he felt half inclined to refuse any further conversation with the Prince.

He was somewhat curious, however, to know what he really had to say, and he listened in silence.

The Prince continued to speak in a low tone.

"Accident, Claude Duval, has placed in your hands a game, to play which, if you have the courage to go through with it, will place you in an enviable situation."

Duval was still silent.

"If I were King," added the Prince, "it would be in my power, not only at once to release all your friends, but to place you in so brilliant a position, that while people might wonder how you got it, they could not but look upon you with envy and admiration."

"Be more explicit!" said Duval, for he was determined to hear the worst that the Prince had to say.

"Surely to a man of your rapidity of apprehension, I am sufficiently explicit. If George the Second were no more, I should then reign."

"But he still lives."

"Life is but a fragile possession, and a man of energy, like you, might quench it."

"I do comprehend you," cried Duval; "and I am considering."

"Ah! that is well."

"I am considering whether the offers of the King to murder you, or of yours to murder him, are best worth accepting."

The Prince uttered a cry.

"His Majesty has been exceedingly liberal," added Duval.

"Name your own terms—name your own terms!" cried the Prince. "I will double whatever he has offered!"

"What's the matter?" said Turpin, riding up to them.

"Not much," said Duval; "I will tell you all about it another time."

"Very good! and in the meantime I do not think it quite desirable that this gentleman should know exactly where he is going."

As Dick Turpin spoke, he tied a silk handkerchief rather tightly round the eyes and head of the Prince of Wales.

Giving his hat, then, a sudden jerk, he pulled it very low upon his brows.

"Come on, now, Duval," he said, "our prisoner may speak if he likes, since I have warned him of the danger of so doing."

A very few minutes more brought them to the door of the Bedford Head.

The landlord was simply informed by Duval and Turpin that it was necessary to keep the prisoner they brought with them in perfect secrecy and safety for some time.

"To be sure, yes," said the landlord; "we have a strong crib on purpose. Why, we kept Mr. Lavender, the officer, there for six months, and he never knew where he was all the while; for we brought him in a sack, and took him away in one."

There was a small room, with a very low ceiling, at the top of the house, to which the Prince of Wales was conducted.

There was nothing unwholesome or disagreeable about the place, but it was made as secure as the ingenuity of such men as the frequenters of the Bedford Head could possibly suggest.

And that was likely to be secure enough, for they were well versed in all the particulars, and all the little stratagems for the detention of prisoners in almost every gaol in the kingdom.

There the Prince was left to his own reflections, which were not likely to be of a very agreeable nature.

Blossom and Tom King remained with the horses in the long, rambling range of stables belonging to the Bedford Head.

Dick Turpin and Claude Duval were conducted by the landlord into the inner sanctum behind the bar.

The diamond star was then produced that had been taken from the breast of the King, and as it was somewhat of a dangerous article to continue in possession of, Duval was anxious to get rid of it.

"It's a real beauty," said the landlord, "and should turn into a pretty round sum."

"It is, indeed," said Dick Turpin. "Such a bunch of glitter never fell to my share on the road."

"It must be disposed of," said Duval; "and that at once."

"Why, old Coles is the man," said the landlord; "and I'll send for him at once."

"To be sure—to be sure!" said Turpin; "I forgot him. The old rascal will give the most fair unfair price of any fence in London."

This man, mentioned by the landlord, and known to Dick Turpin, resided in the immediate vicinity of Covent Garden.

To look at him no one would suppose he was worth sixpence in the world.

But, in reality, he was a man of great wealth—wealth which he never had the heart or brain to attempt to enjoy.

His eyes glistened at first, almost as brightly as the diamonds composing the King's star, as he looked at it.

"My conscience!" he exclaimed; "they are beauties, that is to say if there is not a flaw in them. My conscience! it's a royal star, but it will have to be picked to pieces."

"Well, now, Coles," said the landlord; "what's to be the figure?"

"Well, my conscience! I can hardly say; but, perhaps, by this time to-morrow——"

"No!" said Duval, quite calmly; "Dick Turpin and I have quite made up our minds what we want for it, and we won't bate a farthing."

Mr. Coles changed color. "Well—well, my conscience! we shall not quarrel about price; and what may be the little sum you want for the star?"

"A nice trifle," said Duval; "we took it from a gentleman at the toll-bar, who had not money enough in his pocket to pay the toll."

The landlord laughed; but Mr. Coles began to think he was not likely to get so good a bargain as he had at first anticipated.

"What is the sum?" he asked rather impatiently. "My conscience! what is the sum?"

"There are twelve diamonds," said Duval.

"Are there twelve? My conscience! are there twelve?"

"You know there are; and the price of them is one thousand pounds."

Mr. Coles took up his hat at once.

"Good-night."

"Good-night," said Dick Turpin, carelessly. "Mind how you go, old Coles."

"I mean to mind, and no thanks to you, Richard Turpin."

Mr. Coles hurried out into the passage of the Bedford Head, and made a great clattering with his feet as though he meant to leave the house with all the speed in his power.

But he had no such intention.

He came back in a few moments and leant over the bar.

"You will get into trouble, all of you," he said, "about that star."

"Possibly," said Duval, "but if we do, we shall know to whom to attribute it."

"To me?"

"Exactly so."

"Then, the best thing I can do is to take it off your hands."

"The very best," added Turpin.

"I shall have to pick it to pieces, and send the stones separately to France and Holland; and I have not the slightest doubt but that I shall lose by the whole transaction. However, you shall have five hundred pounds."

"That will do," said Duval.

"It will?"

"Certainly—on account, and you shall have the star when you bring the remainder."

Mr. Coles this time made a fair rush out of the Bedford head, and disappeared.

Turpin laughed.

"Will he buy it?" asked Duval.

"Of course, he will. And now Simmons, let us have some of that old canary that you pretend has been in the cellars of the Bedford Head since the time of James the Second."

"Pretend!" exclaimed the landlord. "I can assure you, Dick, that every bottle has a seal upon it, with the date upon it, as plain as the nose upon your face."

"Well—well, never mind," said Dick, "the canary is good."

The wine was produced, and certainly merited every eulogium that the landlord could possibly bestow upon it.

Duval then rose.

"I will leave this star with you, Dick Turpin," he said; "And I will meet you when and where you please."

Turpin took the star, and considered a moment.

"Coles is sure to buy it," he said, "and I will meet you to-morrow night."

"That will be Wednesday," added Duval.

"And the fifteenth of the month," said the landlord.

A sudden alteration of look came over the face of Turpin.

"I had quite forgotten," he said; "it is twelvemonths since, to-morrow, since Joe Mandrake, as he used to be called, was hung in chains, on Putney Common; and I swore that I would visit him, and take a last look at him before the year was over. He was a brave and gallant fellow, and fell into the hands of the traps, through shielding me."

"Ah! that he did," said the landlord; "and he might have got free if he would only have turned sneak, and let them know that you and Black Bess, Dick, were all the time of the trial within a stone's throw of the Old Bailey."

"Don't speak of it," cried Turpin, "it drives me mad to think of him, and his poor young wife, too, but she has wanted for nothing, and never will, while Dick Turpin can cry 'stand and deliver,' on the King's highway."

"We all know that, Dick," said the landlord.

Turpin dashed his hand across his eyes.

"What's the use of grieving," he cried. "Life is short, and we ought to make it as merry as we can. It's only a kind of scuffle, and they who get out of it early, are the best off after all. What say you, Duval? Will you meet me on Putney Common, to-morrow night, at the midnight hour."

"I will," said Duval.

"Your hand upon it."

"Take it, Dick; and here I sip the last drop of the old canary to our better acquaintance."

Duval had put on his hat, and was about to sally out from the bar, when some sounds of contention were heard in the long, narrow, darksome passage of the "Bedford Head."

"What's the row?" said the landlord, looking over the bar.

"Shelter! shelter!" said a voice. "Rescue or no rescue, I've done it at last; and don't want to be trapped, and nabbed, and scragged for such a trifle."

A man, in the undress uniform of a cavalry soldier, with rather an unusually large pair of moustachios, made his way up to the bar.

"Shelter! shelter!" he said. "I know this is the proper sort of crib."

He made two or three peculiar signs with his fingers as he spoke.

"Oh," said the landlord, "you belong to the family, do you?"

"I did, and want to belong to it again. I got a drop of drink, and 'listed some three years ago; but I've granted myself a free discharge, and this is my colonel's dressing-case."

"Are you quite alone?" said Turpin.

"No, I've a comrade, who has granted himself a discharge likewise. Ah, gentlemen, you look of the right sort. I think of going on the road myself, now that I've learnt to ride. By Jove! it's a rough school to learn in—the cavalry barrack—but they do it well—they do it well, gentlemen."

The soldier leant over the bar, and kept glancing alternately at Dick Turpin and Claude Duval.

"Well, my friend," said the landlord, "if you step into the room opposite, you'll find a fire, and I will attend to you in a few minutes."

"Much obliged," said the soldier; "but, in the meantime, Claude Duval and Dick Turpin, you are my prisoners, and my name's Godfrey."

The confident look which the disguised officer wore was on the instant changed to a very different expression.

Duval executed one of those extraordinary feats of strength in which few could excel him.

Immediately dashing forward, and leaning over the bar, he seized Godfrey by both shoulders, and, lifting him clean over, he flung him into a corner of the little room, and presented a pistol at his head.

"How can you be so absurd, Mr. Godfrey," he said, "as to suppose for a single moment that such old birds as we are should be caught by such chaff."

"I will have you," said Godfrey, "or I will die in the attempt."

"A wilful man," said Dick Turpin, "must have his way. Your last moments have come, Godfrey."

"One moment," said the landlord. "Let's have his last dying speech and confession. Hold the light here, Dick. I don't want him to speak, but I want to watch his face. Now, Godfrey, was it old Coles who gave you the office?"

The officer had been staring full in the face of the landlord of the "Bedford Head," but at this question his eyes blinked, and he looked down.

"That's enough," said Duval. "Now we know all about it."

"Simmons," said Godfrey, "I call upon you in the name of the law to assist me in the apprehension of these men."

"Bless you, Mr. Godfrey, if I were to say half a word, they'd knock me into the middle of next week."

"Nonsense, nonsense!"

"I assure you I've been trying to apprehend them for the last half hour, and they've been drinking my canary, and making all sorts of game of me."

With a sudden movement, Godfrey thrust his hand into his pocket, and producing a small silver whistle, he blew a shrill note upon it.

"Look out for squalls," said the landlord; and in an instant he extinguished the light; and the bar of the "Bedford Head" was in darkness.

There was a rush of feet into the passage.

"Here we are, Mr. Godfrey—here we are! Where are the prisoners?"

"There's one," said Duval.

He had seized, even in the darkness, Godfrey again, and flung him back into the passage over the bar.

But during the brief period that had elapsed, the landlord with great dexterity had stripped Godfrey of his coat, and Duval had put it on.

The military undress cap likewise afforded a capital disguise where the light was not sufficiently strong to make accurate observations.

"Good-night, Dick!" whispered Duval. "I am going home. We meet to-morrow. Tell my man, Blossom, to take Nightshade to his stable."

Dick Turpin and the landlord retired, as it seemed, into a cupboard; but the floor of it was a trap-door, and went down with them at once.

Duval, by the light of a lantern that some one was holding up in the passage sallied out from the bar.

CHAPTER CV.

THE DUCHESS OF CLEVELAND MAKES AN UNEXPECTED COMMUNICATION TO CLAUDE DUVAL.

AMID the uncertain flickering shadows of that place, so gloomy at the best of times, all that the persons in the hall could see was that there was among them a man in military uniform.

The supposition that it was Godfrey was so natural that they scarcely gave a second glance to the figure.

Duval contrived to stoop, likewise, so as to bring himself to Godfrey's height, which was some inches below his.

"Have you nabbed him, sir?" cried a voice.

"Hush, be quiet!" was Duval's reply, in as near an imitation of the voice of the officer as, on the spur of the moment, he could command.

The four or five persons in the passage of the Bedford Head made way for him, and Duval walked composedly out of the ancient hostel.

Nobody impeded him in the slightest degree.

He crossed leisurely the market, and, passing under one of the piazzas, he went rapidly through a narrow thoroughfare that conducted him to Bow Street.

He was not without some anxiety, because he did not fully comprehend the measures taken for the safety of Dick Turpin.

Of one thing, however, he felt quite certain, and that was that the sooner he got home and resumed the habit and manners of Sir John Cope the better.

Duval, therefore, threw off the military overcoat, and, leaving it lying on the pavement, he walked rapidly in the direction of Pall Mall.

The cry of delight with which Lucy welcomed his arrival sufficiently shewed how great had been her anxieties in his absence.

And when he saw her tearful face, and heard her hysterical sobs, Claude Duval was half inclined to register a vow there and then, that he would seek no more adventures on the road.

But his career was far from over, and Duval had many a strange encounter yet in prospect.

A long and anxious consultation was held in regard to what could be done for the Princess and St. Ives; for, after all, although Duval had a hostage in the shape of the Prince of Wales, it did not seem to be one that would be likely to avail him much.

He related to Lucy his singular meeting with Dick Turpin, and it was later still in the night before they both closed their eyelids in sleep.

Duval came down stairs in the morning fully attired in his disguise as Sir John Cope.

He knew not why it was, but he felt a presentiment that there was danger, and that it would be necessary to meet it with the greatest amount of vigilance.

Blossom met him on the staircase with rather an anxious expression of countenance.

"A visitor," he said, "Captain, in the Blue Room."

"A visitor; and at this early hour?"

"Just so, Captain."

"Who is he?"

"It isn't a he at all, Captain; but a young lady, if I may gather from her voice."

"Thank heaven! Has she escaped?"

"Who, Captain?"

"The Stuart Princess."

"Oh, no; this one is a trifle taller, and altogether different looking—that is to say, so far as I could see of her, for she holds her veil so closely over her face that I could not catch the least glimpse of it."

"Is she alone, Blossom."

"It seems so, Captain, with the exception of the chairmen who carried her chair."

"Who did she ask for?"

"Sir John Cope."

"And in the Blue Room. I will go to her."

Duval cast one glance at himself in a mirror, to be sure that his disguise was as perfect as possible, and then he made his way to that room which had been set aside for casual visitors.

The veiled lady was there.

She had flung herself into an arm chair; but at the approach of Duval she arose and carefully placed herself in the room so that her back was to the windows.

Duval, too, feeling that he was disguised, and that any trifling indiscretion might expose that fact to very discriminating eyes, was also anxious to place his back likewise to the light.

But as the strange lady chose to occupy that position it was now impossible.

Duval bowed.

"You are Sir John Cope," said the strange lady.

Claude started.

It was impossible to mistake that voice, having once heard it.

His early visitor was none other than the fair, but rather fickle, Duchess of Cleveland.

What could her motive be for coming there?

Why did she preserve this kind of secrecy to him?

He spoke to her rapidly.

"Madam, do you not know me? Are you not the only one, apart from my own family, excepting one or two, who is aware of the identity of Sir John Cope with Claude Duval?"

The Duchess raised her veil.

There was a strange expression upon her face; and he thought, by the look of her eyes, that she had been weeping.

"I begin to know you, Duval," she said.

"Begin to know me, Duchess?"

"Yes. I know not what induces me to bring you a warning upon which depends your life."

"What can you mean?"

"Jacobite!"

"No, by heaven!"

"Favoured lover of a princess of the House of Stuart! And yet, what is it to me? Ha! ha! ha! What is it to me? What should it be to me? Do I aspire to the affections of a highwayman, and am I—— No, I cannot pronounce the hateful word——Am I jealous because Claude Duval has devoted himself to another?"

"Madam, you speak in riddles."

"Perhaps I do; but you can guess them."

"My devotion, madam, is but to one——"

The Duchess laughed hysterically.

"Oh, I know all about that—'but to one at a time,' you would say!"

"You misjudge me. I am willing to believe, and do believe, that some kindly motive has brought you here; but, in regard, to the insinuation that has fallen from your lips, I swear to you, by all that is sacred——"

"Don't—don't! You have heard the proverb, "At lovers' vows Jove laughs."

"This is something more than provoking!" said Duval.

"And so," replied the Duchess, with a mock curtsey, "we will say no more about it. I had a few minutes conversation with my Lord Bute, last night, and I rather think he told me, in order that I should inform you, that a warrant will be issued this day for the apprehension of Sir John Cope, whom nobody knew, on the charge of complicity in Jacobite plots. There, now—I have done my duty. They say a pretty woman never forgives. I am pretty—my glass tells me so—and yet I am magnanimous!"

"Duchess—duchess!" cried Duval.

"Highwayman—highwayman!" cried the Duchess.

"You strangely mistake me."

"How?"

"I do not love the Stuart Princess."

"Indeed!"

"She has my pity—my sympathy—some of my admiration, perhaps; but my love is another's!"

"Oh, Claude, if I could only believe you!"

Duval recoiled a step or two.

Here was another mistake, worse than the preceeding!

In repudiating a passion for the Stuart princess, Duval by no means intended to insinuate that he had one for the Duchess of Cleveland.

But how difficult it was to undeceive her!

What could he say?

What could he do?

She advanced towards him.

"Fly, Duval, and save yourself!"

She placed both her hands upon his breast.

"But you will not forget to let me know where you are. I must be assured of your safety."

"Duchess, this is madness!"

"Be of good heart—we shall meet again; and, since you have lifted this weight off my heart, by declaring that you have no passion for the fair prisoner in the Tower, I will let you see that, although the world calls me a coquette, I can be sincere."

"Forbear! forbear!"

"Claude, I love you!"

"Duchess, Duchess, you forget!"

"I do—I do! I forget all but that you are dear to me!"

She let her head droop upon his breast.

Duval felt all the embarrassment of his situation; but to cast her from him rudely and roughly was not in human nature.

It was an immense relief to him when she suddenly moved towards the door of the room, crying out, "Farewell! farewell! Make good use of the information I have given you."

"Madam," cried Duval, as he ran after her, and caught her by the arm.

The Duchess turned inquiringly towards him.

"Do you forget, madam, what I am?"

"No; but we women, when we really love, we are generous, and so farewell!"

The Duchess was gone before Claude Duval could utter another word in explanation.

But he felt that her warning was a thing to be attended to.

He paced the room with disordered steps, muttering to himself, "Infatuation, infatuation! How can I disabuse this spoilt beauty of the Court of her fancy that I am in love with her? But I suppose she imagines that of all men who come within the sphere of her attractions?"

"But all men do not resist," said the voice of Lucy, as she advanced into the room.

"Lucy!"

"Yes, Claude, I have heard all. You shall take the warning, and reject the Duchess."

"This is indeed a relief," said Duval. "I scarcely know in what words I could have related the scene to you, because, Lucy, I instinctively shrink from—from——"

"From exposing the follies and frailties of a woman. I know your generous heart, Claude."

The look of serenity upon the face of Lucy lifted all anxiety from the heart of Duval; but as he thought of the necessity of at once leaving Farnborough House, a cloud came across his brow.

"Alas!" he said. "It seems that, after all, I shall be compelled to become a Jacobite."

A tap came at the door.

It was Blossom.

"Captain," he said, "I could not help it."

"Help what, Blossom?"

"Help hearing all about it. The door was open, and I heard the Duchess's warning. I will have Nightshade at the door in ten minutes."

"No, Blossom, no! Let me think—let me think. Yes. I have it. Get a hackney-coach, place a couple of boxes on the roof, with the name of Sir John Cope upon them, and likewise the name, Southampton."

"All's right, Captain."

"Let the neighbours and any casual passers-by see the boxes prominently. I shall return within an hour in another character. Lucy, will you have a new hall porter or a footman?"

"Either, or anything, or anybody, so that it be personified by you, Claude?"

"A hall-porter, then, I will be for to-day and to-night, and then I shall see the first of my enemies as they arrive. Be quick, Blossom, be quick!"

Blossom darted off to obey the orders of Duval.

The two boxes, containing nothing of importance, were duly addressed, and placed out upon the steps.

The hackney-coach was brought, and Duval got ostentatiously into it.

Blossom rode on the box with the driver.

"Where to?" asked the latter.

"The London Docks."

"All right."

The coach drove off.

No one seemed particularly to notice its departure, but Duval saw a man run at a rapid pace from a doorway on the opposite side of the way with a piece of paper in his hand, on which he, Duval, naturally enough supposed he had taken the number of the coach.

The docks were reached.

The coach was duly discharged, and Duval and Blossom, without being questioned by any one, left the two boxes upon one of the quays, and strolled quietly away.

"Now, Blossom," said Duval, "I must get a complete suit of livery, such as will suit my new disguise as a hall-porter."

"We're in the best place of all for that," said Blossom. "We've nothing to do but to get into Whitechapel, which is not far from here, and you can buy any disguise under the sun."

Blossom was right enough in this conjecture, and Duval was very soon equipped in a suit of livery which, if it had any fault at all, was that it was a little too gaudy and noticeable.

To the jeering remarks which he met with in the street, Duval paid not the slightest attention, although they annoyed Blossom considerably.

It was a rather long walk to Pall Mall.

"I shall not be sorry, Blossom," said Duval, "for a rest in that leather chair that looks so dignified in the hall of Farnborough House."

"It's altogether very provoking, Captain," said Blossom, "but it can't be helped."

"Not a bit."

"And so long as we get the better of the Philistines, what does it matter?"

"Nothing, nothing!"

Lucy received Duval with some degree of agitation.

A man had called during his absence to ask if Sir John Cope were within.

"Fear nothing—fear nothing," he said.

Duval, as he spoke, flung himself into the large easy chair, and put on such an indolent, empty-headed appearance, that Blossom was ready to die with laughing.

The outer door had been shut about ten minutes. Then there came one sharp knock at it.

"Leave me here alone," said Duval; "I must now attend to my duties. Let our men know that they are not to interfere if they hear any knocks or rings."

"Will you open the door, Claude?" asked Lucy.

"Certainly not to a single knock, until it has at least been repeated six times. No hall-porter, I believe, who has a proper sense of his own dignity, would ever think of such a thing."

Bang! came the knock again.

Duval was left in the hall now, but he never moved.

Bang! came the knock a third time.

He let it come a fourth.

Then he opened the door a short distance, and cried out in an insolent tone—

"What now?"

"Oh, if you please, could I speak to you a moment?"

"No."

"But only a moment."

A shabby-looking man was outside on the doorstep.

He held a guinea between his finger and thumb, which he handed towards Duval.

"Oh!" cried Duval, as he held out his open palm, and cast his eyes up to the clouds—"Oh, well, if you've anything to say, you'd better come in and say it."

CHAPTER CVI.

CLAUDE DUVAL AND BLOSSOM ATTEMPT THE RESCUE OF ST. IVES AND THE STUART PRINCESS.

This alteration of tone on the part of Claude Duval was about as good a piece of acting as could very well be found.

He did the pampered domestic to perfection.

The man then quietly stepped into the hall, and closed the door behind him.

Duval took the guinea that had been proffered with a cool adroitness that was quite charming to see.

"Now, my good fellow," said the stranger, "I must see your master."

Duval shook his head.

"Oh, but I must!"

Duval shook his head again.

The stranger produced another guinea, and holding it out between his finger and thumb, he said—

"It seems to me, that you might be a very useful fellow, and I don't mind trusting you."

"You needn't mind it a bit," said Duval, "I'm always to be trusted by those who pay me best."

"Then you're exactly the fellow we want, and before I trouble Sir John Cope, I should like to have a little conversation with you."

Duval took the other guinea and pocketed it as easily as he had done the first one, and then reclining back in his easy chair in the hall, he waited for the government officer, who the stranger undoubtedly was, to say his say.

"How long have you been hall-porter to Sir John Cope?"

"Ever since he came to the house."

"Good. What visitors has he?"

"None."

"That's suspicious."

"I always thought it so," said Duval; "there isn't a chance for a fellow in this service to get a crown-piece over and above his wages from one year's end to the other."

"Exactly. And now where is your master?"

Duval looked up at the ceiling, and pretended to think.

"Well, I should say he can't be above ten or a dozen miles on his journey."

"His journey? What do you mean by his journey?"

"To Southampton. I helped to pack his boxes."

"Then he is really gone?"

"To be sure."

The stranger inclined his head towards Duval, and whispered in his ear.

"I've no doubt you think so, my good fellow, but in my idea it is only a feint."

"Faint!" exclaimed Duval—"have a drop of ale."

"Pooh! pooh! you don't understand me. I mean that it is only a pretended visit to Southampton, and, that in all probability, he will come back to the house again in some disguise."

"No!"

"Yes, I feel certain of it."

"And so do I," added Duval, "now you mention it; he is just the sort of man to do that kind of thing."

"Of course he is. And now, look you here, you may earn more money all at once than your wages will come to for a couple of years."

"Only tell me how."

"Come to the Secretary of State's office, and ask for Mr. Wilkinson, whenever you can bring news that St. John Cope has come back, and may be laid hold of."

"Depend upon me!"

"I think I can—indeed, I feel assured I can. Ha, ha! I like the man who sells himself to the highest bidder, because I am in the position to offer him the best price."

"Then you are just the man I like," said Duval; "and we are mutually delighted with each other. Rely upon me!"

"Hush! not so loud; some of your fellow-servants might overhear you!"

"That's true!"

"I will go now. Remember!"

"I'm not likely to forget."

The man stepped out of the hall again, and Duval closed the behind him.

Sinking, then, back once more into the easy chair of the hall porter, Claude Duval sighed, as he murmured to himself, "I suppose it is fate, but it seems to me quite clear that, whether I like it or not, I am getting inexplicably mixed up with these Jacobite plots. It is in vain that I endeavour to shake myself free of them; they entangle me like a chain that has become wound about me, and from the links of which I in vain struggle to free myself."

"Claude!"

The voice came from the breakfast-room.

Duval started to his feet.

"I am here, Lucy."

"I have heard all, and likewise your reflections as regards these Jacobites, and I know not which to think your greatest peril, your life on the road, or complicity with those dangerous persons."

"Life on the road!" exclaimed Duval, as a new fire seemed to flash from his eyes. "Life on the road for me! I hate these cabals of Court and Princes; I seem to live in an atmosphere of deceit and danger."

"What would you do, Claude?"

"Lucy, we will leave this place, it's very air seems to breathe of plots and counter-plots. Suppose we seek again our old home on Hampstead Heath, from which, by this time, all suspicion must have been again averted."

"Yes, Claude—yes, we were happier there!"

"Much happier. And yet——"

Duval's voice failed him.

His thoughts flew back to the gloomy Tower, where yet lingered the gallant and chivalrous St. Ives, and the young Jacobite Princess.

He paced the hall with disordered steps.

"I must save them!" he said. "I cannot desert them. It would be so easy for me to mount Nightshade, and gallop away into the quiet country, shaking off the smoky atmosphere of the town, along with it all those plots and dangers by which I am environed; but I must save them."

"And then, Claude?"

"Then, Lucy, we will make a change, and all will be well again."

Lucy sighed.

"You will encounter many dangers, and yet I have not the selfish courage to say one word to stay you."

"Do not, Lucy—do not! Accompanied by Blossom, I will make an attempt, even this night, to see what can be done for them; but, in making that attempt, I will never be unmindful of the fact that my own life shall be a thing precious to me, because it is to you precious. I will be general and prodigal of my strength and resources, but at the same time I will be just, and will not sacrifice myself, because that would be to sacrifice you."

Lucy threw herself into his arms.

"Are you content, Lucy?"

"More than content; and it is I who now urge you to do all that mortal man can do for the rescue of those two persons."

After this conversation, Duval summoned Blossom, and held counsel with him.

"I want to know, Blossom," he said, "what may be your idea in regard to the best plan of attempting the rescue of the Princess and St. Ives from the Tower."

"The best thing we can do, Captain, is to get into it."

"But how?"

"I don't think that's difficult, for two nights past there has been a white mist upon the Thames."

"What then, Blossom?"

"Why, then, Captain, when that is at its height, and everything is so confused that you can't see a complete arm's length from you, it won't be at all difficult to watch the proper height of the tide to get in by Traitor's Gate."

"It might be done."

"I'll undertake it can be, Captain. You and I will be quite sufficient, and who knows but, in the course of an hour, we might succeed in doing wonders?"

"It shall be tried to-night, Blossom, for I am anxious to leave London, and partially resume our old course of life upon the road."

After this brief conversation, it was about half-past nine o'clock in the evening when Duval and Blossom met again.

They proceeded quietly down to the river-side, and hired a wherry, stating that they were about to row themselves a mile or two down the river.

There was no difficulty then, as there would be no difficulty now, in such a proceeding.

They took an oar each, and pushed out into the middle of the stream; they pulled with even strokes quietly down in the direction of the old Tower.

"Look, Captain!" said Blossom, "it's coming now!"

"What is?"

"The white mist I spoke to you of. It seems to come up from the surface of the water, and in the course of half an hour you won't be able to see a couple of wherries' length ahead."

It was just as Blossom stated.

Owing to some peculiar state of the atmosphere at that season of the year, this white mist came over the river and all the surrounding land.

It was just the opportunity Duval wished.

They shot—as the common saying was—old Lon-

THE STUART PRINCESS AGAIN RESCUED FROM THE TOWER.

don Bridge; that is to say, they had made a successful rush through one of the arches without being swamped, which was a catastrophe rather too common at that period.

They soon then came upon the precincts of the gloomy old Tower.

They used their oars, then, very slowly and cautiously, for the Tower of London, at that time, was much more of a fortress than it is at present.

The sentinels on the walls would have thought nothing whatever of firing on any boat that they thought was suspiciously prowling about the old fortress.

But the fog favoured them, for it rather thickened than decreased; and, finally, they crept so close, that from that mere fact, they were sufficiently free from all possibility of observation.

"It should be hereabouts, Captain," whispered Blossom.

"Hush!"

They heard some sounds on the rampart above.

No. 35.—NIGHTSHADE.

Ten o'clock had struck some few minutes before, and that was the change of the guard.

Duval and Blossom kept the boat perfectly still while this operation took place.

Then they felt their way through the fog until Duval felt quite certain they were at the low archway of Traitor's Gate.

There was a kind of portcullis formed of thickly-barred wood, which defended that entrance, except, perhaps, for about the space of ten minutes twice a-day.

These periods were when the tide was in a very peculiar position.

Fortune seemed to favour Duval and Blossom on this occasion; for as the tide rolled with an idle, and heaving motion against the massive old, blackened cross-bars, it showed the termination of them at intervals, and suggested an idea to Blossom.

"I don't think there will be the least difficulty, Captain," he said, "in drawing the boat under."

"It might be done, but the tide is going lower."

"Capital!" said Blossom. "I recollect now. To-night, it is said, will show one of the lowest tides on the river. We have but to wait a little."

It was quite evident that the water was going down, for in the course of about a quarter of an hour, the spoke-ends of the wooden bars were plainly visible.

Duval tested the fact of the recession of the tide by tearing up small pieces of paper and dropping them into the stream.

The rapidity with which these pieces of paper were carried eastward, convinced him that the tide was still ebbing.

By degrees, however, the paper went slower and slower.

At length he dropped in a piece which seemed to pause on the surface of the water, as if undecided which way to float.

"The tide is at its lowest, Blossom."

"Yes, Captain; and now is our time. I think if we lie flat in the boat, we may get under the spikes."

It was rather a hazardous experiment, but they were not men to shrink from it on that account.

They both lay as flat as possible in the wherry, and Blossom paddled it forward in a very ingenious manner with his hands.

It was a narrow navigation.

But they were successful.

The boat passed under the arch, and was slowly washed forward into that gloomy recess which had heralded so many persons to captivity and to death.

But this was a great success.

One-half the battle, under such circumstances, was to get at all within the precincts of the Tower.

That once accomplished, a thousand fortunate circumstances might occur to facilitate the object Claude Duval and Blossom had in view.

The place was fearfully gloomy.

But Claude Duval and Blossom came there on an errand of chivalry and mercy, and they would not allow themselves to be daunted either by darkness or by shadow.

Thanks to former experiences, they knew sufficient of the locality to be aware of which direction to proceed in.

They paddled slowly to the left, and soon reached the slimy stone steps that led up from the water.

They spoke in whispers.

"What are you looking for?" asked Duval.

"There ought to be some means of fastening the boat here."

"Certainly there are. I noticed some iron rings."

"Here is one of them."

"Good. Fasten the boat, Blossom."

"It is done."

They carefully left the wherry, and stood upon the steps which led up to the Tower.

As high as the water laved those stone steps, in spring tides they were slippery, and covered green weed.

Above that point, the foothold was more secure, and they soon reached the low-arched door through which prisoners were usually taken.

"There is but one question now," said Duval, "and that is, is the door fastened on the inside or not?"

"We will soon see, Captain."

Blossom felt for the key-hole.

He was quite an adept at picking a lock, and, with a powerful skeleton-key, he now made repeated attempts on this door of the Tower.

There was a scraping sound.

Then the lock shot back.

It was a moment of anxiety.

Was the door made fast within by bolt or bar?"

That was now the only question.

They both pushed at it.

"No," said Duval, "it yields."

The door turned upon its rusted hinges, disclosing the gloomy passage beyond it.

"Now, Blossom, the lantern."

"It is here, Captain."

There was a gleam of light from Blossom's lantern, and then they closed the door behind them, and looked for a few seconds at the damp, gloomy stone walls of the place in which they were.

CHAPTER CVII.

CLAUDE DUVAL MAKES SOME PRISONERS IN THE TOWER.

A FEELING of sadness came over the heart of Claude Duval.

He was not much amenable to presentiments of evil, but the damp, close, unwholesome atmosphere of the place powerfully affected him.

By the gleam of the lantern, Blossom saw that he was pale.

"Captain," he said, "you don't like the Tower?"

"No, by heaven! And were it not that those in whose fate I am deeply interested were within its dreary walls, I would not inhale another breath of its pestiferous air!"

"Nor I, Captain."

"Hold the lantern up as high as you can, I will go first."

Then they reached another door.

But that was not fastened in any way, and they passed onward, hoping soon to come to a more habitable part of the gloomy fortress.

Suddenly Duval paused.

He grasped the arm of Blossom.

"Listen! What is it you hear?"

"Voices!"

"Yes, and apparently in contention."

Duval hastily moved forward, and as he did so, the sound of voices became more distinct; so that every now and then he could catch a word or two of what was said.

And, strange to say, one of the voices sounded familiarly to his ears, although, mingled with other sounds, as it was, he could not take upon himself exactly to name its owner.

Another passage of shorter dimensions was traversed with a sort of rush.

Then they reached an octagonal-shaped chamber, on the walls of which hung some faded remnants of arras.

The door was slightly ajar, opposite to that at which they had entered, and through that door came a gleam of light.

Then a voice came upon the ears of Duval, which he knew full well.

And as he heard it, he knew not whether to feel elated by hope, or cast down by fear.

It was the voice of the Stuart Princess.

"You can kill me," she said; "you can torture me. I am in your power; and you can put me to what death you please, but you cannot force from me a word which can in any manner implicate a living soul that has smpathized with me or my cause."

"Oh, we will see to that!" said a rough voice. "We will soon see to that! I suppose, Mr. Pendell, your warrant carries you to any lengths?"

At this name of Pendell Duval started.

Was it possible that even in the Tower of London he was doomed to come into contact with that arch villain who was an enemy to all that was just and right.

Both Duval and Blossom knew the voice of Pendell so well, that they waited with the most intense curiosity to hear the reply to these words.

"Yes, Mr. Lieutenant; my warrant carries me quite as far as I want to go."

It was the voice of Mossy Pendell.

Duval loosened his sword in its sheath, and prepared for action.

Then the Stuart Princess spoke again.

"I have given you your answer. I will implicate no one."

"Are you so careless of life and limb," said Pendell; "and, at your age, too? Your cause—that is to say, the cause of the Jacobites—is hopeless; and all that is asked of you is to write down upon this piece of paper the names of the persons who have aided and assisted you while in London."

"Never!"

"Your own freedom shall be guaranteed to you."

"Never!"

"Reflect!" said the other voice; "you see that Mr. Pendell has brought from the White Tower these awkward little iron instruments, which, once fitted upon a human hand, and a slight turn given to this screw, compresses it so fearfully, that no fortitude can withstand the ordeal."

"I have answered you," said the Princess.

"But think further."

"I can suffer, but I cannot betray."

"Oh, we shall see about that!" said Pendell; "and after we have done with you, we can try our luck upon Colonel Miravel, as you Jacobites call him."

"No, no!" cried the Princess; "rather let me suffer, than that one hair of his head should be injured."

"Oh! that's the game, is it?" cried Pendell, with a ferocious laugh. "I have not been long in the service of the Government, but I begin to think I shall earn my pay."

"I don't half like this affair," said the Lieutenant.

"Stuff! stuff!"

"You say your warrant will carry you through it?"

"Perfectly!"

"Then I cannot help it."

"Now, madam!" added Pendell, "will you write the names on the paper?"

"Never!"

"Then the time has come."

"It has!" said Duval, as he suddenly pushed open the door, and presented himself before the affrighted eyes of Mossy Pendell and the Lieutenant of the Tower.

The Stuart Princess uttered a cry of delight.

Mingling with it came a yell of dismay from Mossy Pendell, and darting past Duval, he would inevitably have escaped by the open door of the apartment, had he not been received by Blossom, who struck him one straightforward blow with the hand in which he held the lantern.

Mossy Pendell, as though he had been shot through a cannon, flew into the opposite corner of the room.

He fell into a sitting posture, with his back propped up against the stone wall.

"I'm afraid I've spoilt the lantern, Captain," said Blossom.

Duval had presented his sword-point at the throat of the Lieutenant, while he spoke to him in a stern voice.

"Surrender, or you are a dead man."

"I have no force here to resist you," replied the lieutenant.

"See to him, Blossom," said Duval.

Turning to the Princess then, he grasped her hand, as he exclaimed—

"I thank heaven a thousand times, that I arrived at such a juncture."

The Princess had maintained her composure up to this moment.

She had been threatened with death, and she had not faltered.

She had been threatened with torture, and she had not blanched.

But now tears rushed to her eyes, and she was not able, for some few minutes, to utter a word to her deliverer.

"Help!" cried Mossy Pendell.

"Oh, you won't be quiet yet," said Blossom, "won't you? Will that do?"

Duval turned round in time to see that Blossom had seized Pendell by the hair of the head, and was beating him against the stone wall, in no very gentle fashion.

"Murder!" yelled Pendell.

"Do you want any more of it, because only say so; this is the shop to get it at."

Pendell was silent, but the expression upon his countenance was so awfully malevolent, and so suggestive of future vengeance, if he could only live to execute it, that Blossom was half in the mind to put him out of the world at once, on the same principle that he would have destroyed the life of some venomous reptile.

Duval then spoke to the lieutenant.

"You are a sensible man," he said; "and know when you are conquered. I have, therefore, no objection to inform you, that my errand to the Tower, is for the express purpose of rescuing this lady and Colonel Miravel."

"You have me in your power," said the lieutenant, "and can kill me at your pleasure. But I will neither do nor say anything that is contrary to my duty."

"Blossom!"

"Here, Captain."

"Bind this man, and gag him, but do it as gently, and mercifully as you can consistent with doing it effectually."

The lieutenant made no resistance, and Blossom, in a very scientific manner set about the task imposed upon him, so that in a few seconds there could be no possible resistence offered by the lieutenant, but he was likewise incapable of calling out for aid, even in the faintest whisper.

Then the Stuart Princess suddenly grasped Duval's arm.

"Some one comes," she said, "I hear a footstep."

"And I, too," said Blossom.

"Hush!" said Duval, "I will see to that myself."

Duval stood quite close to the door, and in a few seconds it opened, admitting the burly-looking form of one of the Beef-eaters, as they were familiarly called, of the Tower.

The man was not aware at the moment that there was anything amiss in that little chamber.

"If you please sir," he said, addressing the lieutenant.

Then he stopped short, for Duval had quietly placed the muzzle of a pistol close against his brow.

This man had been an old soldier.

He had fought in some of those interminable wars, in the Low Countries, which, from year to year engaged the attention of our ancestors; and the consequence was, that he regarded such a little occurrence as a pistol held at his head as a very casual transaction.

"Alarm, or resistance," said Duval, "and you are a dead man."

"All right," said the Beef-eater, "I give in; better luck next time."

"You are a sensible man," said Duval, "now sit down there."

"Yes, sir."

The Beef-eater sat down with all the composure imaginable, calmly and coolly looking upon himself as a prisoner of war.

Then Duval turned to the Princess.

"I think," he said, "I may take upon myself to say that there is every probability of your rescue from the Tower."

"Forgive me," she said, "for I feel you have risked much, and may risk more in your attempt to save me, but I cannot—I dare not embrace your generous offer."

"Not escape?"

The Princess shook her head.

"It cannot be, indeed, that you are so in love with the gloom of this place, that you hesitate to fly from it."

"I hesitate to fly from it alone. I have promised."

"Another?"

"No, I have promised myself that I will not, and cannot, accept of liberty, while one who has dared so much, and suffered so much, remains in durance."

"I understand you," said Duval.

"I am sure you do."

Duval then turned to the lieutenant quickly.

"It is necessary, sir," he said, "that we should likewise take Colonel Miravel with us."

The lieutenant returned no answer.

"It is, therefore, necessary," returned Duval, "that you should inform us where he is imprisoned, and assist in procuring his liberation."

"I acknowledge but one necessity," said the lieutenant; "and that is, that I should do my duty; therefore, I refuse the information you require."

"Never mind him, Captain," said Blossom.

"Why not?"

"Because I have more tractable stuff here."

A yell from Mossy Pendell at this moment attracted the attention of all the persons in that little chamber.

Blossom had clapped on to Pendell's hands the iron instrument of torture with which he, Pendell, had had the unmanliness to threaten the Stuart Princess.

A slight turn of the screw had elicited this yell from Pendell.

Duval smiled.

The Stuart Princess, however, looked alarmed.

"I think," said Duval, "now, we shall come at the information we want."

"No doubt of that, Captain," said Blossom. "Let me ask him."

Blossom looked in the face of Pendell, and kept his finger and thumb on the screw of the instrument of torture.

"Now, Mr. Pendell," he said, "answer me. What is your business here?"

"To get a list of the names of the Jacobite conspirators."

"Then you have gone into Government service?"

"I have."

"As a sort of spy?"

"You may call it what you like."

"Very good. Now, where is your authority?"

"Here."

Pendell handed a small slip of parchment to Blossom, on which was a seal, and which contained a full authority to enable him to see and examine any prisoners in the Tower.

No doubt he had impressed the Secretary of State with a full opinion that he should be able to extract, by fair means or foul, from the imprisoned Princess, a list of those noblemen and gentlemen about the Court who were favourable to the Jacobite cause.

"I think this will do," said Blossom, as he handed it to Duval.

The latter then turned to the lieutenant again.

"In what part of the Tower," he asked, "is Colonel Miravel confined?"

The lieutenant shook his head.

It was evident he had no intention of answering.

Duval thought of asking the Beef-eater; but as he was a subordinate personage, he shrank from getting him into trouble, and he preferred asking the information from Mossy Pendell.

"In what part of the Tower is Colonel Miravel confined?" added Duval, as he fixed his eyes upon Pendell.

The Lieutenant had refused to answer, and nothing had come of it, so Pendell thought he might as well do the same.

He shook his head.

"Answer the Captain!" said Blossom.

Pendell shook his head again.

"Oh, very well," said Blossom.

Then Pendell uttered another yell.

Blossom had given the screw half a turn

"The Beauchamp Tower! the Beauchamp Tower!"

"Ah," said Blossom, "I thought we should get at it!"

Claude Duval reflected for a few seconds, and then he took the piece of parchment which was Mossy Pendell's authority, in his hand, and, turning to the Beef-eater, he spoke to him in a calm tone of command.

"You will accompany me to the Beauchamp Tower, so that it shall seem that I am properly escorted; and if you refuse, or attempt to play any treacherous game, it will be at the price of your life!"

"I am a prisoner," said the Beef-eater; "but I didn't say 'rescue or no rescue,' and I give you fair warning that I shall do the best for myself, as well as to turn the tables upon you."

"That is fairly spoken," said Duval, "and therefore I must take other measures. Blossom, you will secure all these three men; and it is necessary that you should re-adjust the gag upon Mr. Lieutenant, here, and keep them all, not only from moving, but from uttering any cries of alarm."

"That's soon done, Captain."

Blossom set about his work instantly; but when he came to the Beef-eater, Duval stopped him.

"We shall want," he said, "that man's coat, ruff, and hat."

"I understand, Captain," said Blossom. "I am to play the part of a Beef-eater for a time, and accompany you."

"Exactly."

All this was speedily accomplished, and Duval felt perfectly certain that for some hours at least these three persons would not be able to interfere with his plans or projects.

He took the hand of the Stuart Princess then in his own.

"Come," he said; "and I am not without a hope that we may rescue Colonel Miravel, and so enable you to leave the Tower in the manner you wish.

Blossom made himself up very well as an extemporaneous Beef-eater, and the little party left the apartment by entirely another door into what was called the Esplanade of the Tower.

CHAPTER CVIII.

CLAUDE DUVAL AND HIS FRIENDS REACH TRAITOR'S GATE IN SAFETY.

THE white mist from the river still continued; and, as the wind sat in the direction, it enveloped the whole of the Tower in the uncertain gloom of its waving clouds.

They were challenged by a sentinel after proceeding a few paces.

Quite at random Duval called out "Guard!" and walked onward.

That might or might not have been a proper word to say; but at the sight of Blossom, in his uniform as a Beef-eater, any scruples the sentinel had, evidently vanished.

"Pass on!" he said.

Duval knew sufficient of the internal economy of the old building to make his way easily to what was called the Beauchamp Tower.

At the foot of it another sentinel was posted.

The air of authority, however, with which Duval approached, combined with the sight of Blossom's uniform, induced the soldier to step aside, and only stand at "attention."

Duval then rapped with his sword-hilt at the oaken door of the Tower.

It was opened by a Beef-eater.

"I want the Jacobite prisoner, Colonel Miravel!" said Duval.

He exhibited to the Beefeater at the same time the slip of parchment which had been taken from Mossy Pendell.

The authority was all sufficient.

"Do you want to see him here, sir?" asked the warder; "or shall I bring him down?"

"Bring him down. I have to take him to the Lieutenant's lodgings."

"All right, sir!"

The warder ascended the narrow staircase of the Beauchamp Tower.

There was a rattling of keys.

A grating of rusty bolts.

And then, in a few moments, the gallant and chivalrous St. Ives was conducted down the stone staircase.

"Look to your prisoner!" said Duval, addressing Blossom.

Blossom laid his hand upon St. Ives' arm; and so perfectly had Claude Duval disguised his voice, that the Jacobite Colonel did not recognise him in the least, but believed that he was really in the midst of enemies, and was about to undergo some secret examination in the Tower.

Amid the white fog, too, the warder's lantern shone but very dimly, and the Stuart Princess, fearing some exclamation from Miravel, kept cautiously in the background, and out of the sphere of his observation.

"March!" said Duval.

The sentinel drew himself up again, and the warder of the Beauchamp Tower stood upon its threshold, looking after the retreating party with a dubious expression.

Then, and not till then, did Duval venture to whisper to St. Ives in his own tones

"Do you not know me?"

"Gracious heavens! Duval!"

"Hush!"

"And don't you know me, too, sir?" asked Blossom.

"Yes, now I do. What is the meaning of this?"

"It means," added Duval, "life and liberty!"

"But how? How can it be?"

"I think we can manage to conduct you from the Tower."

"No, no!"

"Do you doubt us?"

"No; far from it, for I have a kind of confidence that in any adventure, be its chances what they may, in which Claude Duval engages, has about it an element of success. I thank you with all my heart of hearts, but——"

"But what Miravel?"

"I cannot go!"

"Cannot go?"

"I cannot—I cannot!"

"And have we run all these risks in vain? Have we endangered our own safety to save you, and is this our reward?"

"No, by heaven! Hear me, Duval. You know that there is another imprisoned here, who is dearer to me than life itself. I pray you to devote your unexampled energy and rare courage to her preservation; and whatever may be my own fate, it will not be so bitter if I have the consolation that she is saved."

The Princess heard these words.

She could remain concealed no longer.

Her sensibilities were wrought up to the highest pitch of excitement.

She rushed forward, and placed both her hands upon the breast of Miravel.

"I am here," she said—"I am here, and we will live or die together!"

A cry of joy burst from the lips of the Jacobite Colonel.

"I have not, then, lived in vain," he said, "since this hour has come when the dream of my heart's best affections is a reality!"

There was a few moments' pause, which neither Duval nor Blossom were inclined to interrupt.

Miravel then held out his hand to Claude.

"You have come here to save us both," he said, "and we have abundant faith in you. Already I feel as if the free air of another clime curled round my brow."

"All that man can do," said Duval, "to accomplish that object, I will do. Who knows the way from this spot to the inner pool of water at Traitors' Gate?"

"I don't think, Captain," said Blossom, "we can find any way but just that by which we came."

"Then we had better get back at once into the narrow passages that conduct to the Lieutenant's lodge."

"That's it, Captain; and this is the way."

Blossom now led the van of the little party.

Miravel spoke to Duval in tones of deep emotion.

"I never can return to my prison-house," he said, after this. If you have any spare weapon, let me have it, Duval, with which to defend myself, and one dearer still than myself, in case occasion should arise."

"I thought these might be useful," said Duval. "Here are a pair of pistols at your service."

Blossom led the way very exactly back into the gloomy passages that conducted to the water gate of the fortress.

Then he paused.

"Look you here, Captain," he said; "the tide has been upon the turn for the last half-hour, and we shall never get the wherry under that spiked, cross-barred affair at Traitor's Gate."

"But it opens," said Duval. "It is hinged, like folding doors. I have seen it open."

"All's right, then," said Blossom. "It shall not remain closed long after I get to it."

Duval thought, for a moment, that it might be well to look into the chamber where he had left his bound and gagged prisoners, but, for all he knew, moments might be so precious that he abandoned the intention.

It was quite a relief to the whole party when they stood upon the stone steps that led down to the gloomy pool within Traitor's Gate.

Deliverance seemed so near at hand.

And yet there was danger in the very atmosphere they breathed.

They were still within the precincts of that gloomy Tower, which, certainly, by the dreary associations connected with it should, if it does not, cast a gloom over that part of the metropolis.

It was no longer necessary that Claude Duval should trouble himself to pay any attention to the Stuart Princess.

She leant upon the arm of Colonel Miravel, on whose countenance, now, there was such an expression of determination, that the danger of impeding him in his escape from the Tower would have been evident to any one who might have cast the most furtive glance at him.

Blossom ran down the steps.

He had still a lantern with him; for he had taken that which had belonged to the Beef-eater.

The wherry was quite safe where he had moored it, but there was a considerable strain upon the rope that held it, for the tide had risen above the ring to which that rope was attached.

"All's right, Captain," said Blossom, in a suppressed voice.

"Let us descend," said Duval.

The little party hastily took their way down the steps, and in a few seconds were seated in the wherry.

At that moment, a shouting noise came over the surface of the water.

"Guard! guard!" cried a voice. "Escape! escape!"

A very narrow casement was opened in an adjoining turret, and from it a man projected his head, with rather a grotesque red night-cap upon it.

"Escape! escape!" he shouted. "Guard! guard!"

"Silence!" said Duval.

"Move another step, and I fire!" cried the man.

"After me!" said Blossom.

As he spoke, Blossom levelled a pistol at the open window, and immediately fired.

The red night-capped head disappeared on the instant.

They had no means of knowing whether the shot were effective or not; but as no further alarm was made, there was every reason to suppose that it had been so.

At such a still hour of the night, however, the shouts of this man were likely enough to have been heard throughout that portion of the Tower.

The necessity of getting clear of the water-gate was more evident than ever; and Duval, seizing the oars, rapidly propelled the wherry in the required direction.

Everything now, however, depended, or seemed to depend, upon whether Blossom could unlock that barred woodwork, which, while it did not shut out the tide, either in its ebb or in its flow, was, under most circumstances, a most effectual barrier against both ingress and egress, as far as the Tower was concerned.

"Keep the boat as close as you can, Captain," said Blossom, "and I will try my hand on the lock."

This was done; and Blossom, standing up in the wherry, made vigorous attempts to pick the lock that held the two halves of the wooden portcullis together.

"Can you do it, Blossom?"

"I'm afraid not, Captain."

"That means that you are certain that you cannot?"

"It seems to come to that, Captain."

"Then we must find some other mode of getting out of the Tower."

"Not so," said Colonel Miravel. "Which way do you think these wooden bars open—inwards or outwards?"

"Inwards, unquestionably," replied Duval.

"Let me try, then. Hold up the lantern, Blossom, and show me the lock. I think this ought to do it."

Colonel Miravel fired one of his pistols right into the lock, and very much shattered it.

"Ah!" said Duval; "another shot like that, and we are free."

The other shot was freely given.

Then Blossom gave the wooden bars a vigorous shake, and the two halves of the portcullis parted in a straight line down the centre, slowly opening inwards.

"Stoop!" shouted Duval.

He had just happened to cast his eyes backward to the narrow stone steps, and at the top of them he saw several men collected, with firearms in their hands.

Hardly had the words of warning left his lips, when it was echoed by the word of command to fire.

They all crouched down in the wherry, and a rattling discharge from the fire-arms of the Tower-guard passed harmlessly over their heads.

Duval then bent to the oars which he had still retained in his grasp, and, by a few vigorous strokes, shot the wherry out into the stream.

The tide was now falling rapidly.

The wherry was heavily laden with so many persons, and was rather deep in the water; but that seemed to have the effect of making it more amenable to the tide, which, of itself, would have carried it at a rapid rate down the stream, even unaided by the oars, which Duval plied lustily.

They heard a bell tolling.

It was the alarm-bell of the Tower.

Boom! then, came the sound of one of the heavy guns from the ramparts.

That was another alarm.

But, if all the bells in London had rung, and all the cannon of the old fortress had been discharged, they would have had no effect upon the fugitives, who were each moment so rapidly increasing their distance from the ancient fortress, that they could not but feel themselves comparatively safe.

"I think, Blossom," said Duval, "you may take the oars."

"Yes, Captain, now I will."

"Why do you say now?"

"Because, Captain, you have been pulling like any two men, I am but one."

"We are saved then!" said the Princess.

"I think," replied Colonel Miravel, in a tone of deep emotion, "that we are."

"But we will recollect," said Duval, "the old proverb, of not shouting until we are out of the wood."

"True—most true!" said Miravel. "Any disappointment now would be bitter in the extreme."

"I scarcely think I could endure it," said the Princess: "my courage seems to have evaporated with the danger that called it forth."

"It would return again," said Miravel, "were that danger to recur."

The boat shot past the spires of Greenwich Hospital, and in the full rush of the retreating tide, it made its way rapidly towards the next bend in the river.

"There is a vessel ahead of us," said Duval. "Look out, Blossom!"

A strange voice hailed the boat from the vessel.

"That is a Dutch trader," said Miravel, "I feel certain."

Then there came the sing-song of sailors' voices from the deck of the vessel, accompanied by the tramp of feet, for they were hoisting the anchor, while slowly up the main-mast, bit by bit, crawled a huge square sail.

"What vessel?" cried Miravel.

"The Jongleur, of Amsterdam," was the ready reply from the deck.

"Where bound?"

"To port."

This was understood to mean the port she belonged to—viz., Amsterdam.

"Can you take two passengers on your own terms?"

"A dozen if they want to come."

"This, then, is an opportunity," said Miravel, "which may never occur again. What say you, Princess, shall it not be embraced?"

The Princess did not reply.

Her heart was too full of emotion to permit her to do so.

And all on board that wherry seemed to understand the cause of her silence, and no one, for a few seconds, disturbed the stillness of repose, which enabled her, in some measure, to command her feelings.

Then she spoke.

"I must not ask you, Claude Duval, to come with us, nor must I tempt your comrade here to forsake you; for you have nearer and dearer ties still in England to retain you, and he must not forsake his master."

"It is as you have spoken," said Duval; "but who knows that we may not meet again?"

"I pray heaven it may be so."

"Boat ahoi!" cried a voice from the vessel, "where are the passengers?"

"Here!" replied Duval.

"Farewell!" said Miraval. "It my be, that in the pursuit of my duty, I may see you again, Duval, in London; but, at present, I have a precious charge, which must be placed in safety."

The wherry grated against the side of the vessel.

Hasty adieus were spoken.

The anchor was weighed.

The square sail touched its topmost limit, and then the vessel, feeling the action of both wind and tide, glided away from the wherry, and was soon lost amid the white fog.

CHAPTER CIX.

CLAUDE DUVAL AND BLOSSOM MEET WITH AN ACQUAINTANCE.

"THAT'S over, Captain!" said Blossom.

Duval sighed.

"Yes, for the present, Blossom; but I feel assured that we shall all meet again."

"It's likely enough; but where shall we go now, Captain?"

"It will be hard work, pulling up the river against both wind and tide; so I think we had better put in at some quay as near Greenwich as possible."

"All right, Captain! If you take one oar, and I take the other, we shall soon do it."

They pulled silently.

The boat was run on to a narrow strip of beach, about half a mile below the Hospital grounds.

Duval and Blossom leaped from the wherry, and then, dragging it up high and dry, they left it with the certainty that its owner would get it on the morrow, as his name was legibly painted upon it.

"It's a long walk to town, Captain," said Blossom.

"I don't see why we should walk," replied Duval. "Let's get on to the London Road, and I dare say we shall find some vehicle which will give us a lift to the metropolis."

"That'll be the thing, Captain; if it is but a waggon."

There was no great difficulty in striking inland, until they came to the road which took its way through Deptford.

They paused at a little old-fashioned public-house, and partook of some refreshment, and they heard the clock of some rural church strike the hour of eleven.

"It's early enough, Captain," said Blossom "I wonder how far we are from Pall Mall?"

"I fancy about six miles."

"Too far to walk."

"Hush!"

They stood in the porch of the little old public-house, and both listened attentively.

A clattering sound of horses' feet rapidly approaching broke upon the stillness of the evening air.

"Who knows," said Blossom, "we may get mounted even yet?"

Duval smiled.

"That, Blossom, must depend upon circumstances. It may be cruel to take the horses from these people who are approaching."

"True, Captain; but possibly they may be just the sort of persons we shall take no heed of disobliging."

The horsemen rapidly approached; and, as chance would have it, they drew up exactly at the door of the little inn.

Duval and Blossom stepped aside into the deep shadow of the porch.

"House—house, here!" cried one of the horsemen. "Is there no one stirring? House! house, here!"

The landlord of the little roadside hostel, and the boy who assisted him in the stable, both rapidly advanced.

"Here, your honour—here, your honour!" said the landlord.

"Oh, that is well! See to the horses, for they are somewhat fatigued."

"That's a pity!" whispered Blossom to Duval; "for we want them."

"Yes, your honour," cried the landlord. "Perhaps your honour will stay for the night, for the fog is thickening on the river."

"No, no! half an hour will be quite sufficient."

"You hear, Blossom," whispered Duval. "These men are only going to stay half an hour, and then they purpose taking their horses on the road again. I think we may as well ride them as they."

"A great deal better, Captain."

The horses were taken round to a stable-yard, and the two travellers stepped across the threshold of the inn.

Only one of them had as yet uttered a word, and the other seemed to wear an air of deep dejection.

There hung a lamp just within the inn door, and as these horsemen passed it, the dim rays fell upon them.

There had been something about the tones of the one who had spoken, which sounded familiar to the ears of Duval, but he had not been able to satisfy his own mind as regarded where he had heard that voice before.

The moment the rays, however, of the little lamp fell upon this man's face, Duval recognised him.

It was no other than the traitorous and fugitive Duke of Montrose.

Who his companion was, Duval could not divine, but he saw that he was a very young man, and that his countenance looked candid and ingenuous.

"A private room—a private room!" cried the Duke, "and see that we are not interrupted."

"Certainly, your honour—certainly, your honour! This way if your honour pleases."

The landlord led the way up a rickety staircase, to the best room of the inn, into which, with many bows and compliments, he ushered his guests.

"What's to be done now, Captain," said Blossom;

"shall we just step round, and take possession of the horses and be off?"

"You know the name of one of those men, Blossom?"

"Not I, Captain; they passed before I could see either of their faces."

"The villainous Duke of Montrose was the taller of the two."

"Then we need have no compunctions at all, as to taking his horse, nor that of the other one either, since, no doubt they are friends, and one as bad as the other."

"I am not so sure of that, Blossom, and I would give something to overhear the conference they are about to have together."

"That is not so easily done as thought of, Captain. We are perfect strangers to the house, and it would be a difficult matter to manage."

"Perhaps not so difficult as it seems; the landlord is evidently one of those men who give way at once to impudence and pretention."

"It seems like it."

"Tell me, Blossom, have you that small constable's staff with you, which has been of use at times in imposing upon the vulgar and the ignorant."

"I have, it is here; I seldom stir without it."

"Give it to me, and we will soon reduce the landlord to such a state of obedience, that if there be any possible means of enabling us to overhear what the Duke of Montrose and his companion have to consult about, he will enable us to avail ourselves of it."

Duval took the staff, and he at once made his way into the house, closely followed by Blossom.

They met the landlord coming down the stairs, rubbing his hands together with a self-satisfied air.

"Richard—Richard!" he cried, "a bottle of the old wine for the Red Room."

"The elder wine, I suppose you mean, sir?"

"Idiot! have I not often told you not to call it the elder wine, but the old wine. Look sharp, for I am sure the tallest of the two gentlemen is some great lord."

"A word with you, landlord," said Duval.

"Oh, nonsense, I can't attend to anybody just now!"

"But you must, and shall, or it may, perhaps, be a hanging matter for you."

Duval had taken quite an estimate of the character of this man, and by assuming—which was very easy indeed for him to do—an air of command, he completely cowed him, and brought him to a state of abject acquiescence in whatever he chose to propose.

"Lord save us, sir, you don't mean that. A hanging matter did you say, sir?"

"I did. Step in here and let me speak to you."

Duval led the way into what was called the bar-parlour.

Holding up the constable's staff then before his eyes, Duval spoke again with the same air of authority.

"I may as well tell you at once, that all persons even suspected of complicity in Jacobite plots, are liable to be hanged without more a-do."

"Gracious powers, sir! I am not a Jacobite."

"But your house is made a rendezvous for such persons, which is quite sufficient to have you hanged, drawn, and quartered."

"My house, sir?"

"Exactly so; and there is only one thing can save you."

"Good gracious, sir, say what it is for; that is the one thing above all others I should like to know."

"Those gentlemen who have gone up-stairs are rank Jacobites, and they have come here to consult upon the best means of taking the life of the King."

"You don't say so."

"It is but too true; and upon my report to the Secretary of State, and to his Majesty's ministers, will depend whether you are taken up or not."

"My dear sir, do make the proper report; I am the father of a family, and have a helpless wife—that is to say, I'm not married yet, but I've several times thought of being so, and I daresay then I should have a helpless wife, and be the father of a family, so it comes to the same thing, you see, sir."

"Exactly," said Duval; "and therefore, if you place me and my friend here, in some favourable position, so that we can overhear the conversation that will take place between the two rank Jacobites above stairs, the favourable report will be made of you."

"A thousand thanks! a thousand thanks; This way, gentlemen, if you please. Me a Jacobite?—I hate Jacobites! This way, gentlemen, and tread softly."

The landlord led the way to a small apartment, not much larger than a moderate sized cupboard, and, placing his finger on his lips, he pointed to a green door covered with baize, as he whispered, "Through there—they are through there!"

"It is well," replied Duval, in the same cautious tones. "The report I shall have to make of you will, I see, be highly favourable. Be secret, and all will go well."

The landlord bowed himself backward out of the room, and seemed to be quite delighted that he had got off so cheaply.

Duval and Blossom kept profoundly still and listened.

They soon heard the murmur of conversation in the next apartment.

Some one was speaking in a plaintive, beseeching tone of voice.

"I assure your Grace it is the first, as it shall be the last, time, that I have ever played at a game of chance. You have had the good fortune to win from me a much larger sum than I can pay; but if you will only wait——"

"Wait?" exclaimed the Duke of Montrose, in his own unmistakable harsh, grating tones,—"wait? Who ever heard of waiting for a gambling debt?"

"Alas! what else can I say or do?"

"Of course I am very sorry," added the Duke, "to see you in such a dilemma; but I shall have to proclaim this matter to the world, and whatever discredit may attach to a defaulter in a case of honour will be yours."

"That will be my ruin!"

"Pay the money, then."

"You know I cannot."

"Then take the consequences."

"It will be more charitable to take my life. I have already given you written acknowledgments of the debt; and be assured that, in course of time, you shall receive every farthing of it."

"That will not do. And yet there is a way."

"A way to what?"

"To cancel the debt at once and for ever."

"Oh, tell me that way, and how gladly will I embrace it."

"What are your political opinions?"

"I scarcely think I have any."

"Then allow me to form some for you. Be a Jacobite."

"A Jacobite?"

"Yes. Is there anything so monstrous in that name, that you should repeat it with such accents of terror?"

"But how should my being a Jacobite cancel this debt of honour?"

"Simply by doing the Jacobite cause some service."

"What service?"

The Duke of Montrose lowered his voice.

"If the King were removed——"

"Murdered? Would you make me an assassin?"

THE DUKE OF MONTROSE MADE PRISONER.

"Pooh! pooh! You start at terms. Only say that you will attempt to do this service, and whether you succeed or not, you will hear no more of this debt of honour, which otherwise will press you down to destruction."

Long before the conversation had got to this point, Claude Duval had quite made up his mind how to act.

He whispered to Blossom, "We shall not go to town without a prisoner."

"Good."

"I intend to take the Duke of Montrose, and lodge him in the guard-room at St. James's Palace, from whence he should never have escaped."

"All right, Captain. I am with you."

Duval paused only for a few seconds more, during which the young man who was with the Duke of Montrose appealed to him in the most abject and imploring tones.

"It is needless to say that I reject the terms you propose to me. You must have known that I would do so, before you uttered them; but if you persevere in exposing me before the world as owing you this debt of honour, I shall be utterly ruined, for my uncle is implacable against gamesters."

"I cannot help that.

"I beseech you to return to me the acknowledgements of the sum in question, and to trust to my honour to pay you the money so soon as it is possible to do so."

"Your request," said the Duke of Montrose, "is as frivolous as it is absurd. Those acknowledgments of your debt at play will never leave my possession, unless, indeed, you can discharge them either with gold or by performing the service which I have mentioned to you."

At this moment, Claude Duval opened the door of communication between the two apartments, and with his drawn sword in his hand, he stepped abruptly before the astonished gaze of the Duke and his young companion.

No. 86.—NIGHTSHADE.

CHAPTER CX.

CLAUDE DUVAL CANCELS A DEBT OF HONOUR.

So completely petrified was the Duke at this apparition, as he would have called it, that he could only stagger back as far as the wall of the room, against which he leant for support

"Blossom!" cried Duval, "secure that man."

Blossom sprung upon the Duke in an instant, and before half a minute had elapsed he was securely pinioned and prevented from doing any injury.

The surprise of the young man, who, up to the previous minute had appeared to be completely in the power of the Duke of Montrose, was great.

He stepped back a pace or two, and placed his hand upon his sword-hilt.

"Do you feel inclined," said Duval, "to fight in defence of this man?"

"Heaven knows I have no cause to do so; and yet, if this be an attack from—from——"

"From whom?"

"I was going to say highwaymen."

"You judge us rightly, sir," said Duval; "and our looks do not belie us. Highwaymen we are, and we are about to cry 'stand and deliver!' to his Grace of Montrose here, in a manner which should give you the most lively satisfaction."

"Thieves!" cried the Duke; "thieves!"

"Exactly;" said Duval; "but the information is of no use. Now, your Grace, those papers acknowledging the gaming debt due from this young gentleman to you, or your life."

The Duke turned pale.

"Ah!" he said, "you have been listening."

"Precisely so. It would be an absurd stretching of the punctillios of honourable conduct to object to any means for the detection of a villain such as you are."

A look of satisfaction crossed the countenance of the young man.

"You will take those papers from him," he said; "and when you have them——"

"I shall certainly not return them to you," replied Duval. "Remember, that you have nothing to do with this affair; we are the robbers, and in order thoroughly to disentangle you from all consequences in regard to the transaction, we shall, perhaps, cry 'Stand and deliver!' to you likewise, before we leave this place."

Blossom had tied the Duke's hands behind him, so that he had it not in his power to comply with the demand to deliver up the documents in question.

Blossom, however, put an end to all trouble on that subject by adroitly emptying his pockets.

Among other papers were found three, being acknowledgments for large sums lost at play by some person who had signed the name of Horace Singleton.

Duval took these papers, and held them before the eyes of the young man.

"Are these signed by you?"

"Alas, they are!"

"Then in their ashes you shall have a receipt in full."

Duval immediately held them in the flame of one of the candles that burnt upon the table, and in a few moments they were consumed.

The young man shook his head, sadly.

"Even this," he said, "does not save me."

"How so?"

"The debt was one of honour, and it still remains such."

Duval was struck with these words, and was silent for a few seconds.

Blossom, however, soon put a different complexion upon the affair.

"Look here, Captain! here are some dice I have found in his pockets along with other things."

The young man turned his eyes away, shudderingly, at the sight of the dice.

"To them," he said, "I owe my ruin!"

"What to these?" exclaimed Blossom; "do you mean to say it was by these you lost your money?"

"Alas, yes!"

"Then I can relieve you from all anxiety about it. I don't know much about gambling and gamsters, but I know enough to be able to tell you that these dice are what is called 'loaded.'"

"Loaded?" exclaimed the young man.

"Perdition seize you all!" muttered the Duke of Montrose,

"Why, look here," added Blossom, as he flung the dice repeatedly upon the table, "you may cast them how you like, and they are sure to turn up high numbers. There is a small plug of lead in each of them which does the business."

"Convince me of that."

"It is easily done."

Blossom placed the edge of his sword against one of the dice, and striking its upper portion a sharp blow with the brass ornamental constable's staff he had, the dice flew asunder.

"Behold!"

There, indeed, was the little plug of lead.

"Your debt of honour," said Duval, "exists no longer!"

"Villain!" exclaimed Horace Singleton, as he took two steps towards the Duke of Montrose.

"Heed him not," said Duval. "I cannot understand, for the life of me, how it is that he is at large, for he is amenable to such a charge of high treason that his life must needs pay the penalty. Where have you been, young sir, that you have not heard of those remarkable proceedings which took place at the King's entertainment at St. James's?"

"I know of no such proceedings. I have newly come from Oxford."

"And whither are you bound?"

"I was riding to London with a sad heart after being compelled to meet the Duke of Montrose in the neighbourhood of Greenwich."

"And so you met with a highwayman and got robbed of your horse."

"My horse?"

"Yes; we mean to take it."

"Who can be more welcome?"

"Do not say that. Recollect that you are robbed; and now, young sir, good night! Blossom, bring along your prisoner."

Blossom conducted the Duke down stairs, and Duval again spoke to the landlord with an air of authority.

"Have you a horse in your stables?"

"Yes, sir."

"Bring it out, then, and likewise the two horses belonging to the gentleman who were above stairs. Your horse shall be left at the 'Myrtle Livery Stables,' close to the King's Mews, at Charing-Cross."

During the brief interval that had elapsed while the horses were being saddled and brought forth Duval turned to the Duke of Montrose and spoke sternly.

"Take your choice, my lord Duke; if you would prefer it, I will blow out your brains here at once, or otherwise, I will take you to town and surrender you to the Guard in the gateway of St. James's Palace."

The Duke was silent.

"Decide—and decide quickly."

The Duke spoke gloomily.

"While there is life there is hope."

"Be it so."

The horses were now brought forth, and Duval, with the assistance of Blossom, helped the Duke to mount, for, tied together as his hands were, he could not do so without assistance.

In the course of a few seconds more, the little party were on the road, and as the two tired horses had had a good half hour's rest they trotted on with tolerable speed.

The distance to London was soon traversed.

Duval drew up with his prisoner at the arched gateway of St. James's Palace.

The Duke of Montrose spoke not a word.

He felt how perfectly useless it would be to say anything with the most distant hope of ameliorating his position.

Duval dismounted, and having again, with the assistance of Blossom, taken the Duke from his horse, he held him by the arm and led him unresistingly to the Palace Guard Room.

There was quite a commotion when Duval appeared so evidently conducting a prisoner.

With one thrust, Duval shot him along into the midst of a group of soldiers.

"There!" he cried, "I surrender to your trust a most notable traitor—his Grace the Duke of Montrose."

Without waiting for a word of inquiry, Duval then turned upon his heel, and hastily left the Palace.

"Go quickly, Blossom," he cried, "and leave the innkeeper's horse at the 'Myrtle Inn,' by the King's Mews."

"And the others, Captain?"

"Let them go adrift, some one will find them—a stray horse is sure to get a home; make, then, the best of your way to Farnborough House."

In the course of another few minutes, Duval was at home.

It is needless to say with what a cry of delight Lucy welcomed him.

She was too much agitated, for a few seconds, to ask him if the Princess and St. Ives had really escaped.

But Duval replied to the question which beamed from her eyes.

"All is safe," he said; "and by this time I sincerely hope that they are both past even the risk and chance of pursuit."

"O, Claude, I thank heaven most sincerely; and they owe this happiness to you."

"We have all done our best; and shall I confess now that I am weary?"

"Who so entitled to rest as he who has laboured in the cause of others, and saved such precious lives?"

* * * * * *

The morning was very bright and beautiful when Duval, after many hours of refreshing sleep, looked out upon Pall Mall from one of the windows of old Farnborough House, and wondered what would be the next phase in his chequered existence.

He heard the role of the morning drum at St. James's.

A feeling of light-heartedness came over him in the escape, of which there could not be a doubt, of the Princess and the chivalrous Colonel Miravel, and was to him a subject of the sincerest congratulation.

"And now," he said to himself, "I shall once more be the old Claude Duval of the road and the heath. Only diversifying those exploits by occasionally making myself a welcome or unwelcome guest, as the chances may be, amid those glittering scenes of aristocratic life in the palaces and mansions of the great, where, amid the perfumes, the brilliant lights, the flash of jewels, and the soft music of flattery from mouth to mouth, I shall gather a fresh love for what is simple and beautiful in nature, and fly to the open heath and the shadowy roadway with renewed zest."

He heard a gentle sigh.

Lucy had crept close to him.

"And is this your determination, Claude?"

"Can it be otherwise?"

"Alas! I know not."

"It is my fate. I am Claude Duval, the highwayman, or nothing."

"Be it so, then. I have acquired a confidence in your good fortune; and although I may not have cause to be anxious when you are away from me on adventures of peril, I will still be ever hopeful and confident."

This was the state of mind, of all others, which it pleased Duval to find in Lucy.

He held a long consultation with Blossom in the course of the day, and at nine o'clock that night they both started for the Western Road, seeking for what adventures might befall them.

They passed through Tyburn Gate, and had not proceeded above a mile past the tall trees of Kensington Gardens and the neglected fields of Bayswater, when there emerged from a narrow lane on the right hand a solitary horseman.

The night was not a particularly dark one, and both Duval and Blossom were able to note the appearance in a general way of this stranger.

He was accurately attired in black: and from the absence of all ornament about him, and the exceeding whiteness of his cravat and ruffles, he might have been taken for some dignitary of the church.

Stopping abruptly upon coming within a few paces of Claude Duval and Blossom, this person spoke in tones of great emotion.

"If you be Christian men, I pray you listen to me."

"What would you say?" asked Duval.

"There has been murder done; and even now I leave my heart behind me as I fly for medical assistance."

"Explain yourself more fully, sir. What do you mean?"

"Do you know the house called the Myrtles, yonder?"

"Certainly not."

"Alas! that I should be compelled to leave it at this juncture; and even now my heart misgives me that I ought not to do so. Yes, I will return; for even my unskilled aid is better than the neglect of half an hour. Or stay—oh, happy thought!—perhaps, sir, you have some surgical skill?"

"In faith, not I," said Duval.

"That is unfortunate."

"At least, I have no more than what any man of experience, with his eyes open, may collect in the space of a short life."

"At all events," replied the stranger, "you have coolness and courage."

"I hope so."

"I pray you then to accompany me, and in the sacred names of Mercy and Humanity, to be of what service you may."

Without waiting for any reply, the distressed stranger turned his horse's head, and went rapidly down the lane from which he had emerged.

Duval did not hesitate to follow him, and Blossom, as a matter of course, kept close to his master.

There was an ancient house—the fore-court of which was enclosed by some iron gates, on each side of which grew some tall and stately poplars.

The clerical-looking stranger stood by one of these gates, one of which he had opened.

"Thank heaven!" he said, "the call of mercy has not been made to your hearts in vain! This way, sirs —this way."

"But permit me," said Duval, "to enquire of you some further particulars."

"Alas, you will soon know too much! This way—this way."

Curiosity, as well as sympathy, now urged Duval and Blossom forward.

They both dismounted at the foot of the flight of stone steps that led to the house, and tying their horses' bridles to the projecting iron railings, in the same manner that their mysterious new acquaintance did with his, they followed him into the mansion.

The hall door which appeared to have been open, closed with a heavy clang.

"What is that?" cried Duval.

"A current of air," said the stranger—"only a current of air—it always sets strongly through this hall."

The entrance of the house was of considerable extent, although it was but dimly lighted.

Duval could see that there were statues and paintings in abundance; in fact, the appointments of the place were such as to proclaim it to belong to persons of ample means.

"Whither do you conduct us?" asked Duval, as he paused.

"Answer me one question, sir, before I reply to you."

"What is it?"

"I would not ask it—but are you a man of honour, or merely one of those gentlemen of pleasure, who are not even moved to honourable instincts, by the sight of beauty in distress?"

"I hope and trust I am a man of honour," said Duval; "at all events, I have given a kind of hostage to fortune, in that respect, since, far from being the man of pleasure, you speak of, I am married, and have a home of my own."

"Thank heaven! Now I feel assured that all is well. This way, sirs,—this way."

The mysterious stranger rapidly ascended the grand staircase of the mansion, closely followed by Duval and Blossom.

CHAPTER CXI.

CLAUDE DUVAL MAKES A TERRIBLE DISCOVERY.

"CAPTAIN?" whispered Blossom.

"What is it?"

"I don't half like this."

"Nor I."

"I'm glad to hear you say so, Captain; for if that old villain is not a hypocrite of the first water, I'm no judge of human nature."

"Hush!"

"This way, sirs,—this way!"

The clerical-looking person had reached the landing of the first floor, which in fact, constituted the whole height of the house.

There was no time for further parley between Duval and Blossom, unless they meant to bring the affair to a conclusion, by absolutely refusing to remain in the house.

The landing was tolerably well lighted.

Duval saw the face of his new acquaintance better than he had hitherto done.

It looked mild and gentlemanly enough.

There was either a real or well put-on look of distress likewise upon it.

"Now, sir," said Duval, "since we have come so far, and know nothing, I should like to ask you a few questions."

"Oh, do not—do not! It is but a waste of precious time; you shall know all; but let it suffice for the present, that a young and charming lady has been foully assassinated, and lies in this chamber, at the point of death."

"Is that possible?"

"Alas! it is too true."

As he spoke, this mysterious man opened a door that led into a chamber, of large dimensions, but so nearly in absolute darkness, that it was difficult to see what it contained.

On a table, in the centre of the room, burnt a lamp.

It was a lamp that probably, under ordinary circumstances, would have lit the chamber well, but its flame was so near extinction, that it was only in a flickering intermittent manner, that it shed any light at all.

In a far off corner was one of those huge state beds which our ancestors so much delighted in.

Heavy plumes of feathers decked its corners, and its massive draperies were of the most ample description.

In the dim light, they could see the clerical looking person wringing his hands with all the evidence of deep distress.

"There!" he said; "she is there—so young and so beautiful! Alas, alas!"

"Is there no better light than this?" asked Duval.

"Oh, yes, I see it is going fast, ebbing away like the young life behind these curtains. Be patient for a few moments, and I will get another."

The clerical-looking gentlemen stepped out of the room.

The door closed instantly.

There was a sharp metallic sound.

"That's the lock," said Blossom.

Then there was a grating sound without.

"A bolt!" said Blossom.

"Oh, this is absurd," said Duval. "You don't mean to say we are prisoners here."

"It looks uncommonly like it, Captain."

"But—but——"

Claude Duval turned completely round twice to take the best survey he could of the apartment by the glimmering light that evidently could not last many minutes.

"I don't half like it, Captain," said Blossom.

"Nor I. But stop a bit. Are you conscious of a strange odour in the room— a faint kind of perfume?"

"Exactly, Captain. I was going to mention it."

Duval pressed one hand upon his brow.

"Either that perfume or something else gives me a pain above the eyes which is intolerable."

"Captain."

"What now?"

"I feel faint."

"Don't say that, Blossom, for I, too——"

"The room spins round with me, although I hold to the back of the chair."

"Heaven help us! What can this mean?" exclaimed Duval.

He snatched up the nearly expiring lamp from the table to assist him in looking about the mysterious room.

In doing so, it was all but extinguished.

Duval, however, saw a newspaper lying upon the table, and, hastily twisting it up so as to extemporise a torch with it, he lit it by the faint flame that still remained in the lamp.

There was instantly a blaze of light.

Then Blossom spoke.

It was but faintly.

"There, Captain, there—it is there!"

"What? Where?"

"On yonder table."

"What do you see?"

"The vapour—a faint smoke."

"Ah!"

Duval made his way towards the table indicated by Blossom; and there, in a small metallic saucer, he saw something slowly consuming, which emitted, without doubt, the sickening perfumes that were stealing away their senses.

Duval felt sick, faint, and giddy.

He had presence of mind enough, but only just strength left sufficient to seize the saucer with its contents, and rush with them both to the fireplace in the room, into which he cast them.

Then, drawing his sword by a great effort—and it had never been such an effort to him in his life – while he seemed scarcely to have the strength of an infant, he dashed its point through one of the window panes.

Then his feet sunk from under him.

The terrible sensation of fainting came over him.

Probably for about half a minute Claude Duval was really unconscious.

But the sickening, death-dealing vapour was now making its way harmlessly up the chimney.

A cool current of night air, too, was whistling through the little orifice in the window pane.

The character of the air in the room was rapidly changing.

Duval opened his eyes.

He drew a long breath.

He spoke faintly.

"Blossom!"

There was no reply.

The terrible idea that, although he had escaped the miasma of that death-dealing perfume, his faithful follower might have fallen a victim to it came with a terrible pang over the heart of Duval.

He uttered a cry of despair.

The lamp had gone out.

The room was in utter darkness, for although there were no shutters to the windows, tall, melancholy-looking trees reared their heads so close to the panes of glass, that even the dim light from without could not penetrate into that apartment.

But Duval had about him the means of getting a light.

Neither Blossom nor he were ever without those silent matches which at that time were well known, although they had not crept into domestic use.

There was a little flash.

Duval had lit a match.

But it would soon expire, and he looked anxiously about him for some means of perpetuating the flame.

There was an ancient mirror hanging upon one of the walls bearing branches for lights, in several of which were wax candles.

Duval lit one instantly.

At first the flame was very weak.

Then the wax melted, and it brightened.

Bit by bit, the whole apartment came into view.

The gloomy old state bed.

The costly, old-fashioned furniture.

The huge chimney-piece.

But Duval had no eyes for anything but Blossom.

He saw him lying on his face on the floor.

To pick him up, and to carry him to the orifice in the window, so that the cool night air played upon his face was the work of a moment.

Blossom uttered a sigh.

It was a most welcome sound to Duval, and assured him that his faithful follower lived.

His recovery was now a thing assured, although, as in his own case, Claude Duval felt perfectly certain that a few minutes more of that noxious vapour would most certainly have hurried them both to destruction.

With such force had Duval plunged the point of his sword through the window-pane, that although the glass was a little starred in all directions, the actual orifice itself was exceedingly small.

The night air made a strange sound, almost musical in its tone, as it rushed through this orifice into the room.

"Speak, if you can, Blossom," said Duval.

"Where's Nightshade?"

It was evident that Blossom was not quite himself, or he would never have asked so irrelevant a question upon that occasion.

Duval therefore let the cool air play upon his face for a few minutes longer, before he asked another question of him.

"How are you now, Blossom?"

"All right, Captain. What was it?"

"Try and recollect."

Blossom looked about him.

"To be sure. Yes, now I know all about it. That confounded perfume sent me to sleep, but how did you escape it, Captain?"

"By throwing it into the grate."

Blossom was now perfectly recovered, and every minute circumstance connected with their appearance in that place, came clearly to his recollection.

That they were in a position of extreme danger there could be no doubt.

But what was the precise object of cajoling them into that house still remained a mystery, notwithstanding one of the means by which that object was to be attained seemed to be murder.

The wax candle in the ancient mirror burnt now clearly.

And as their eyes were getting accustomed to the dim light, they saw every object in the apartment with sufficient clearness to be able to speculate upon it, and draw their own conclusion.

It was the state bed, though, in the extreme corner, which seemed the most mysterious object there.

"Is there any truth, Captain," asked Blossom, "do you think, in the story of the sick young lady in that state bed?"

"I don't think, Blossom, that any one would be sick here long, and if we find anything there it will be death."

Blossom had an evident reluctance to approach the state bedstead.

Any open danger he never shrunk from, but that which was hidden and mysterious always awakened in him uneasy sensations.

Duval approached the bed alone.

"I will unravel this mystery."

He drew aside the heavy curtains.

The bed was empty.

This was but a further proof of the delusive character of the statements that had been made by the clerical-looking personage to induce them to visit that house.

The bed-clothes, however, seemed in some disorder.

Duval had the curiosity to lift the pillow.

He dropped it again instantly.

A shuddering feeling came over him. From the under side of it were unmistakable splashes and stains of blood.

By this time, Blossom had made his way up to the side of Duval.

He had likewise looked upon the suggestive spectacle, and for a few seconds, they gazed in each other's faces in silence.

"We must get out of this, Captain," said Blossom.

"As soon as may be; but we should make further discoveries first concerning this den of murder."

"I almost think, Captain, we know too much already."

"Not so, Blossom. Help me, and we will not leave a nook or corner of this apartment unsearched."

There was a large cupboard or store-closet filling a recess in the room.

Towards that now, Claude Duval and Blossom walked rapidly.

A slight turn of the handle opened one of the doors

and indeed, for a moment, the impression upon Duval's mind was, that some one pushed it from the inner side.

So strong was this feeling, that he let go the door, and retreated a few steps, placing himself on the defensive.

The cause of the phenomenon, however, was speedily explained.

The door swung open.

A human form then fell heavily to the floor, and lay evidently in death, at the feet of Duval and Blossom.

By the horseman's boots on this dead body, and the silver spurs, which garnished them, it seemed but too evident that this was some traveller on the Western Road, who had been enticed into that house of murder even as they had been, but who had not had the good fortune to escape the trap that had been laid for his life.

"This is something more than serious," said Duval "look to your pistols, Blossom.

"They're all right enough, Captain."

"Hush!"

"What do you hear?"

"Footsteps on the stairs."

Duval stepped to the wax-light, and instantly blew it out.

The room was immediately in darkness.

Then they saw what the presence of the light would have prevented them observing—viz., a long, faint ray from some lamp or candle on the landing, which made its way through the keyhole of the door.

Duval whispered to Blossom.

"Keep profoundly still."

"I will."

Duval then crept to the door, and placed his ear flat against the panel.

He heard voices outside.

"What's the use—what's the use?" said one; "it will be a good hour yet before the coach comes."

"But we may as well take what we can get," said another voice.

"Oh! there's time enough, and the job will be all the more sure."

"It's sure enough; by this time they are quiet enough."

"Oh, no doubt about that; and if you must go in and see what they may happen to have in their pockets, of course I can have no objection; but still I say, again, there's time enough."

"Well, well! perhaps there is; I yield to you."

"Come then, and let us open a fresh bottle."

The footsteps retired.

The faint gleam of light deserted the keyhole of the door.

All was darkness.

All was silence again.

Then Duval crept back to Blossom.

"Have you found it out, Captain?"

"No; it is as mysterious as ever. They talk of some coach coming in an hour, and I presume it is for the removal of the dead bodies."

"Goodness, gracious!"

"You have your picklocks with you, Blossom?"

"Yes, Captain; but the door was bolted."

"One of your thin, small saws, which, you recollect you always carry with you, in case of having the misfortune to find your way to a round-house or lock-up, will surely overcome that difficulty."

"To be sure it will, Captain, so here goes; we shall be out of this den in three minutes."

CHAPTER CXII.

CLAUDE DUVAL AND BLOSSOM FIND THEMSELVES IN AN UNCOMFORTABLE POSITION.

BLOSSOM set to work upon the door in a very scientific fashion.

He first of all shot the lock back.

That was a very easy process.

With a fine saw that he had with him, so thin and flexible that to look at it one would think it incapable of performing any rough work, he succeeded in touching the bolt.

There was but one.

But the saw made a grating noise.

And the silence of the house was so profound, that there seemed every probability of such a noise being heard.

Blossom withdrew the saw, therefore, for a moment, and ran its exquisitely cut teeth across one of the wax candles.

When he set to work with it again, there was no noise, and in another minute, the soft iron of which the bolt was composed, was cut completely through, and there was no further opposition to opening the door.

Then Duval and Blossom both crept out on to the landing.

The light upon the staircase had been put out.

That in the hall, however, still lent a faint glimmer—for it was very low—to the statues and the pictures, and the rich furnishing of the place.

The mere suspicion of fear could never cross the minds of either Claude Duval or Blossom, but they both paused now as if by a common impulse, and made the most careful examination of their pistols, that they had ever done in all their lives.

Then they crept slowly and silently down the staircase.

They reached the hall.

Still they heard nothing.

There were several doors opening both right and left from the hall.

Duval felt that some immediate progress was absolutely necessary, and leaving his hand to be guided either by chance or Providence, he opened the first door that presented itself.

The room was empty.

But there was a faint reflected light in it.

And the moment Duval crossed its threshold he heard the murmuring sound of voices.

Where that light came from, and from where the voices proceeded, were soon apparent facts.

To the left of the doorway, that is to say, in the wall at right angles to the hall, there was a door, the upper part of which was glazed.

The glass however on the inner side was covered with a white curtain or blind, and it was through that from another room, that the faint gleam of light came.

It was from that other room likewise that the murmuring of voices proceeded.

Duval and Blossom did not now address a word to each other, but they stepped noiselessly over a soft yielding carpet, towards this glazed door.

Being now quite close to it, they heard the voices more distinctly.

It was exceedingly provoking, however, that the blind fitted so well, as to prevent them getting the slightest glimpse into the apartment.

"What has come over you to-night?" asked one of the voices; "you are full of a thousand ridiculous fears."

"I don't know," was the reply, "but I seem to have a kind of presentiment of danger."

Duval then was shocked by hearing a female tone.

"Who cares," it said, "about your presentiments; a short life and a merry one for me, and if we all get to Tyburn at last, what does it matter?"

"Ah, you've had too much wine, Poll."

"Just say that again."

"Hush! hush! Don't be screaming out in that fashion."

"Give me some more money then."

"Money, money, yes, that's always your cry."

"And do you think I am going to come here, and help to murder people, and even sell their dead bodies for nothing?"

"Be quiet - be quiet, you shall have all you can desire. But don't you see how much better it is to get together a good round sum, and then be off before there is any suspicion?"

"Yes, replied the other male voice, that is what I look forward to. The thing answers wonderfully well."

"To be sure it does; don't we get ten pounds for every one of the dead bodies from the surgeons, who can't get what they call 'a subject,' for love or money sometimes?"

"Yes, and it goes hard, but the plunder comes to as much more."

"Oh, a great deal more—a great deal more. Why, that man with the silver spurs up-stairs, had a matter of eighty guineas about him, and, if I mistake not, those two that I last brought in, will afford us a capital booty."

"Then let us go upstairs and see to it at once."

"Yes, as soon as this bottle is finished. Drink, Poll, drink."

"I want five new dresses," said the female voice, in tipsy tones. "I want a lot of jewellery, and a long chain like the Lady Mayoress."

"Oh, you needn't want for finery."

"I don't mean to want for it; but what makes you start and look about you in that strange fashion; it seems to me you are anything but happy to-night."

"I confess that I am not!" growled the man. "I keep fancying I hear strange sounds, and I'm full of all sorts of apprehensions. I don't know what it is, but I'm not happy to-night."

"Hush!" said the other.

"What do you hear?"

"The coach—the coach!"

"I'm glad of it, for I shall go to town. Things may be all right, or they may not."

Claude Duval and Blossom thought it prudent to leave their post of espial, and to bestow themselves in some place of security from observation, lest they should come into contact with these persons whose professional pursuit could not now be mistaken.

That they procured a terrible existence, and lived in luxury upon the proceeds of murder, there could be no doubt.

The grand difficulty, likewise, for the disposal of the bodies of the dead was certainly got over most ingeniously.

Hurried from the world by the insidious, death-dealing properties of an inpalpable vapour, the unfortunate victims presented no external appearances of a violent departure from this world.

Hence their disposal to medical men for the purpose of scientific anatomy became by no means difficult, for at that period there was no accredited or legal means for obtaining subjects for dissection.

"Blossom," whispered Duval.

"Here, Captain."

"I think I know all about it now."

"Well, it's more than I do, Captain," said Blossom. "What, in the name of all that's horrible, did that old hypocrite want to induce us to come into this den for? it is evident they don't want to rob, only to murder."

"Not rob us in life, Blossom; but don't you see that a gang of wretches are making a business of this sort of thing? These men suppose that we are dead, and that they will have the good fortune to pack off our bodies in company with that unfortunate man whom we saw upstairs."

Blossom's teeth almost chattered.

"Well, Captain, what's to be done?" he asked. "You don't mean to stay here longer than you can help?"

"No, certainly not; but I intend to make those two men take our places in the coach they are expecting to come for the dead bodies."

"How, Captain?"

"Hush!"

As Claude Duval spoke, he put his hand upon Blossom's arm, and drew him forcibly back against the wall, so as to enable one of the men who had been drinking in the other room to pass out.

He was immediately followed by his companion.

"You can stop here, Poll," said one of the men, "while we go upstairs and prepare our guests for their little ride to town."

The woman made no reply; probably, the deep potations in which she had indulged made her anything but conversational at that moment.

"Come on—come on! I never knew you to be such a coward before, Mike! Why, anybody would think it was you who were going to be out of the world instead of——"

"Hold your tongue!" growled the other man. "Any one, to hear you talk, would think I was the greatest coward under the sun! Why, didn't I get those two men in; and don't I tell you that, from their appearance, we shall, probably, make the best night's work we have made. I tell you they have —at least, one has all the appearance of being a man of means."

"Well, well, don't stand parleying here! You said the coach had come, and it has done no such thing: let us go up-stairs and see what booty we can find on the persons of these two last comers."

The two men now walked as hastily as they could towards the staircase, closely followed by Claude Duval and Blossom.

At the foot of the staircase Duval paused and whispered to Blossom.

"Blossom!"

"Here, Captain."

"We must follow those two men closely, and secure them."

"All right, Captain! I begin to enjoy the fun now."

"Hush! for your life's sake! Turn the key in that door, so as to make a prisoner of the woman we heard talking; if she hears any disturbance, she might become troublesome, and I would not interfere with her if I can help it."

"That's no sooner said than done, Captain."

As Blossom spoke, he gently turned the key in the lock, thereby rendering it impossible for the vile companion of the two murderers to hinder their proceedings.

Quick as lightning, Duval and Blossom bounded up the staircase after the two men, and succeeded in overtaking them just as they reached the door of the apartment at which Duval and Blossom had made their escape.

They each seized a man from behind.

"Help! Mur——"

Duval twisted his knuckles in the cravat of the villain he held as in a vice.

"Another such cry and I'll scatter your brains on yonder wall!"

The man trembled violently.

"Blossom, can you manage to secure that fellow's hands?"

"All right, Captain: it's done already!"

"That' right!"

While he was speaking, Duval was performing the same office for the man he had caught in his grasp, and in an incredibly short space of time the two companions in iniquity were securely bound back to back in a couple of chairs.

"Now, gentlemen," said Duval, "you may as well wish each other good-bye, for your time in this world is short."

The men looked ghastly with terror.

"Blossom!"

"Yes, Captain."

"Just see if you can get up sufficient of that stuff, which I threw in the fire-place, to suffocate these two fellows."

"Yes, Captain."

"Oh, mercy!—mercy! Let us go and we will——"

"Silence!" said Duval.

"All right, Captain. Why, there isn't a drop of it gone! It's all here, just as if you knew it would be wanted again. Hurrah! That's capital to let them enjoy it themselves after giving us such a dose of it."

"Place it on the table, Blossom."

"All right, Captain."

Duval examined the fastenings which secured the two murderers, and finding all was secure, he drew a match from his pocket.

The men gasped, but could not utter a word, so terrified were they at what they knew now was to be their fate.

Claude Duval walked up to the deadly vapour and applied a lighted match to the contents of the saucer.

At first a bright flame shot up, and after a second this died out, and left only a little curling vapour ascending.

At the same moment the odour, which Blossom would never forget, probably, filled the apartment.

"Come on, Captain,—come on. It's no use staying here any longer."

"I am coming, Blossom. I was only waiting to see that these two fellows were in the right way to supply our place in the coach."

Duval looked at the men, and was surprised to find that one of them had quite recovered his self-possession, and seemed quite willing to be left to his fate.

Duval at first could not understand the reason of his altered demeanour, when, happening to raise his eyes they fell at once upon the broken pane of glass.

"Ah!" he cried, "I had forgotten. Blossom."

"Yes, Captain."

"Help me to make this window air-tight."

"To be sure, Captain. Here is some brown paper, and here are some pins; we can easily pin up sufficient to keep in all the vapour we want."

A deep groan issued from one of the men.

"Then, Captain, I think that will do; but in case of an accident, I'll just put the counterpane all over the window, and then there'll be no fear."

"Murderers!" said one of the men.

"The same to you," said Blossom, as he quietly fixed the counterpane in such a manner as thoroughly to exclude all air.

"Come now," said Duval, "and let these men know what it is to die by suffocation."

As he spoke, Duval drew Blossom from the room, and closed the door.

"Help! Murder!"

Those words came at intervals, but fainter and fainter.

Duval looked sad.

"There was nothing else to be done," he said.

"Of course there wasn't, Captain."

"Let us come in here; we shall then see when the coach arrives."

As he spoke, Duval opened a door which led to one of the front rooms, and scarcely had they reached the window, when they beheld, coming at a slow pace, the coach which had been so anxiously expected.

"Now then, Blossom,—we had better let the driver go and fetch the bodies and let us take our leave of this terrible place."

"With all my heart, Captain."

There was a knock at the front door.

Duval whispered to Blossom.

"Stay, do you think you can find Nightshade?"

"Yes, Captain. I took particular notice of where that old ruffianly hypocrite placed the horses."

"That is well. Now open the door."

"Now then, what did you mean by keeping a fellow out here all this time for?" growled the driver of the coach.

"We didn't hear you knock more than once," said Blossom in an assumed tone; "but come in, and take the bodies yourself."

"Not if I know it! My orders is to fetch 'em—not carry 'em!"

"Oh, very well. I'll go and get them," said Duval, speaking so much like one of the men they had left upstairs that Blossom started.

"Come," said Duval, laying his hand on Blossom's arm,—"come and help me."

"All right."

When Duval opened the door of the room, the atmosphere was almost clear, and he began to think that there had not been sufficient of the vapour to do its work; but one look at the faces of those two men soon convinced both him and Blossom that they would never commit any more crimes.

With something akin to horror, Duval undid the fastenings which bound these two companions in iniquity together, and taking one of them in his arms, while Blossom did the same by the other, he hurried down the staircase, and placed the corpse in the coach.

He was closely followed by Blossom, who did the same by his burden.

"Any more?" asked the man.

"No."

"But I was told there were three."

"Then you were told wrong!" replied Blossom. "So take your answer and go!"

The driver got upon his box grumbling something about people not knowing how to be civil, and drove off.

"Now, Blossom, let us to town," said Duval, "for, in good truth, this adventure has made me sick at heart."

Never perhaps had Claude Duval hailed the appearance of Nightshade with greater pleasure than on this occasion.

He vaulted into the saddle, and in another five minutes was almost out of sight of that house where so many terrible scenes of murder had taken place.

CHAPTER CXIII.

CLAUDE DUVAL PAYS ANOTHER VISIT TO THE NEIGHBOURHOOD OF CAMDEN HOUSE.

ON Claude's return to Lucy, she was not slow to perceive that the adventure in which he and Blossom had been engaged had been of a somewhat painful character, for Duval was looking pale and somewhat harassed.

"What has happened to-night, Claude?" she asked, tenderly; "for I can perceive by your manner that you are not in your wonted spirits."

ALICE ASSAULTED BY MOSSY PENDELL.

"In good truth, Lucy, I must admit," replied Duval, "that the adventure of this night has been anything but pleasant—in fact, I hope it will never be my fate to encounter such another.

"What—what was it? You are not injured in any way?" said Lucy, anxiously.

"No, Lucy; but I have had a very narrow escape this time."

"Ah! Tell me all about it. No encounter with Mossy Pendell, I hope?"

"No, Lucy, not with Mossy Pendell, but with a very different kind of person, apparently. As Blossom and I were quietly trotting our horses side by side, a man in a clerical garb accosted us, and entreated that we would accompany him to a certain house, where he said a foul murder had been committed upon a young and lovely girl."

"But you could do no good if the murder had been committed; surely you did not go, Claude, you saw at once that he was an impostor."

"I am almost ashamed to admit, Lucy, that I was thrown off my guard by the apparent grief and respectability of the old hypocrite, and I did consent to accompany him to the house he designated."

"For what possible purpose—upon what pretext?"

"His excuse for getting us to enter the house was that he hoped I might be able to restore animation to the murdered corpse of which he had spoken, for that he entertained the idea that life was not extinct. Without questioning the truth of what he asserted, Blossom and I at once determined to follow him, although I must confess Blossom put much less faith in what he said than I did."

"Oh, Claude, you make me tremble! Suppose his purpose had been to murder you?"

"That was in reality his intention, Lucy," said Duval; "but you see he did not succeed in carrying out his benevolent designs, for here am I safe and well."

"Oh, if you would not be so reckless of your dear life, Claude, I might be so happy; but while you continue——"

"Nay, now, Lucy," interrupted Claude, as he bent

No. 37.—NIGHTSHADE.

down and kissed her—" nay, now I thought I should have been complimented for my cleverness and skill in extricating myself from such danger, instead of that, you only lecture me, and tell me I am reckless."

"But tell me, Claude," said Lucy, without replying to what Duval had just said—" but tell me, Claude, what danger you have really escaped."

"Merely that of being suffocated to death."

Lucy turned pale.

"Come—come!" said Duval. "If I find that to hear of my dangers after they have passed away moves you so much, Lucy, I shall keep all my little adventures to myself, and you will never know then what a courageous man you have married."

As Duval spoke, he laughed lightly, for he could see that Lucy's nerves were anything but strong.

The fact is she had suffered so much anxiety regarding the Stuart Princess, and had lived so long in the constant dread of her being discovered while an inmate of their home, that Lucy could scarcely be said to be herself.

Hence it was that Duval tried to put on a playful manner, which, in good truth, he was himself far from feeling.

"Now, Lucy, I don't mean to say another word about the affair. I intend to banish it entirely from my own thoughts, and so let us talk about something else."

Lucy smiled, but agreed to let the matter rest, provided he, Duval, would promise to be more wary in future.

The promise was soon given, and they began to talk upon other subjects.

"Claude!" said Lucy, hesitatingly.

"Well, dear?"

"I wish you would promise me one thing!"

Duval put on a look of inquiry, and said, with a smile, "Ah, I can guess what you wish to make me promise, Lucy, and I fear I cannot comply with your request, so I wish you would not make it."

"And what do you think I am going to ask, Claude?" inquired Lucy.

"Why, that I should not seek any more adventures on the road, I suppose."

"No, Claude. I would fain make the request if I thought there was any chance of your acceding to it, but, as I know there is not the remotest, I will forbear to pain you, for I know it pains you to refuse me anything."

"In good truth, it does, my Lucy. But tell me—I think I may safely promise you anything else—what is it you wish to ask me?"

Lucy rose from her seat, and coming towards Duval, she placed her arms round his neck, and the tears which had been welling up for some time into her eyes now began to fall.

Claude Duval was startled.

He began to fear that Lucy had some cause for grief, of which he was ignorant, and the thought smote upon his heart like a blow.

He twined his arms around her slender form, and said, in tones of some emotion, "Tell me, Lucy, what troubles you so much, and believe me, if I can in any way restore you to your wonted cheerfulness I will do so, even if it cost me my life!"

"Spoken like my own brave Claude!" cried Lucy, raising her head from its resting place, and looking admiringly upon his handsome countenance. "I will ask the favour, and will feel satisfied with the reply, let it be in accordance with my own wishes or not."

"Artful Lucy!" said Claude, playfully. "You know at all events, how to flatter my vanity so as to make me your slave in almost everything. Now then for the great favour. What is it?"

The smile faded from Lucy's lips, as Claude's words brought her thoughts back again to the subject upon which her mind had dwelt so painfully of late, and she spoke with deep emotion.

"Then I would ask you, Claude, not to engage in any other adventure until you have first discovered where my poor dear uncle General Everton is to be found. You are as convinced as I am that he is still in life—that Mossy Pendell has him imprisoned somewhere. That imprisonment, under any circumstances, would be irksome in the extreme to one of my uncle's temperament—but rendered still more so if he knows that I am falsely accused of his murder."

"I see—I see, Lucy," exclaimed Duval, "what you would say. You wish me to find out where your poor uncle is imprisoned, to the utter and entire confusion of your base cousin, Pendell?"

"Yes, yes, Claude, that is what I would say."

"I will do it, dear Lucy—this very night will I set about it, as much for your uncle's own sake, as for your's, dear Lucy."

"Thanks—a thousand thanks, dear Claude. My heart already feels lighter since I have your promise. Hitherto, I had thought it selfish to think or speak of what only concerned ourselves, or our own happiness, while that unfortunate Princess needed all our help; but now, Claude,—now——"

"Now all my energy—all my love for adventure—shall be directed to one object, viz.: the discovery of General Everton. But first of all, Lucy, I must seek a few hours' repose, for the fumes of that subtle vapour, to which that old clerical-looking hypocrite treated me, seems yet to be confusing my brains, and rendering me unfit for anything."

"Do so—do so, dear!" said Lucy; "and in the meantime I will watch beside you."

Duval could not repress a smile at Lucy's anxious face, and he said, "Do not look so anxious, Lucy; all will be well. An hour's sleep will restore me, and I shall be myself again."

"I hope so, dear," was all Lucy could say, as she seated herself beside the couch upon which Duval had thrown himself.

Almost before she had completed the arrangement of the pillows, and the cloak which she had thrown over him, Duval was fast asleep.

It was past mid-day when Claude Duval started up surprised to find the sun so high in the heavens.

Lucy could not suppress a smile at his look of consternation, when he found how long he had slept.

"And you have been keeping watch and ward over me all this time, dear one," he said, as tenderly he pressed her to his heart.

"Yes, dearest; for I did not feel exactly satisfied about that vapour of which you spoke, and from the restlessness which marked the first few hours of your slumber, I fancied you were still somewhat under its influence.

"Not unlikely; but I must say I feel all the better for my sleep. And now, Lucy dear, I will at once commence operations, and endeavour to ascertain where that villain, Mossy Pendell, is to be found."

After a long consultation with Lucy and Blossom, Duval determined to visit again the neighbourhood of Camden House, feeling certain, in his own mind, that Mossy Pendell might still be found there—but for what purpose, unless it were for that of keeping the General a prisoner within its walls, he could not tell."

Accordingly, about seven o'clock on the evening of the same day, he and Blossom mounted their horses, and trotted quietly in the direction of Camden House.

Their intention was not to enter the house, unless something transpired which should induce them to alter the course of action they had laid down for themselves, but to watch it narrowly, and see who came out and went into it.

In order to carry out their purpose more effectually, Duval hired a bedroom in a house opposite, from the window of which he or Blossom could, without the slightest difficulty, watch all that was taking place at Camden House, in so far, at least, as its visitors were concerned.

The first day, or rather evening, we should say, appeared to be a failure, for no one had been seen either to go or come.

"Rather a hopeless task this, Captain," said Blossom. "I seem as if I should much prefer getting over the wall, and satisfy myself that it was entirely deserted, than perhaps be doomed to watch for weeks, perhaps without discovering anything at all."

"Do not be impatient, Blossom," replied Duval. "If no one enters Camden House to-day or to-morrow, it will be pretty certain that it is tenantless; if on the contrary, we——"

"Ah!"

This exclamation proceeded from Duval, for at that very moment a female figure glided up to one of the iron gates, which she opened with a key, and closed behind her again quite noiselessly.

"You see, Blossom, we have not long to wait after all. That woman evidently carried provisions in that basket, and it is as I say, that General Everton is a prisoner in that house."

"Not at all unlikely, Captain. And now I come to think of it, that strange woman who went on at such a rate to you on the heath one night, about Lucy caring for Mossy Pendell, and said something about some strange doings that were going on at Camden House—who knows but that she might have referred to the poor old General after all. Shall we follow that woman, and make her tell us what she is doing there, and what she has covered up in that basket?"

"No, Blossom, I think I would rather wait and see if I cannot exact an account from the villain Pendell himself; for after all, this woman can but be one of his agents, and if I am not mistaken, he will not be long before he visits the house himself, if it be only for the purpose of ascertaining that his orders have been properly obeyed, whatever those orders may be."

"Perhaps so, Captain. I only hope it will not be long first."

Duval watched for two hours, in hopes of seeing the woman reappear, but was disappointed to find that such was not the case.

"Well, Blossom," he said, after watching in vain for the space of another half-hour, "you remain here at your post of observation; I will return to Lucy, as I promised not to remain all night away from home."

"All right, Captain." replied Blossom. "But if I do happen to see that Mossy Pendell, of course you will let me have the satisfaction of knocking him down."

Duval smiled.

"I would rather take him in hand myself, Blossom; however, as you do not seem to like the task of watching, as a kind of reward, I will give you leave to follow your own inclination in the matter. All I would say is, do not be rash: remember, we want to make use of him before we rid the world of such a villain.

"All right, Captain—never fear. I shall now watch with a will, and if Mossy Pendell should happen to show his ugly face, why it will be rather a bad night's work for him, I'm thinking."

Duval now made his way to Hampstead as quickly as he could, for he knew that Lucy would be anxiously expecting him, although, to tell the truth, he was somewhat disappointed at not having more to tell her.

CHAPTER CXIV.

MOSSY PENDELL MAKES KNOWN HIS WISHES.

IT is necessary that we go back a short time in order that the reader may be better acquainted with the actions of the different personages in our history.

It will be recollected that Mossy Pendell's wife had called upon Lucy, who went at that time by the name of Pauline Cope, in order to assure herself that she, Lucy, did not return the love—if such a term can be applied to any feeling that found a home in the breast of such a man—of her cousin.

We have seen that the unfortunate wife of that bad man went away from her interview with Lucy at Farnborough House perfectly satisfied that whatever might have been Mossy Pendell's feelings as regarded Lucy, hers were certainly of the every opposite description to those of affection, although, with her usual gentleness and consideration for the feelings of others, Lucy had concealed from the unhappy wife her real opinion of Mossy Pendell.

It was some weeks after her interview with Lucy, before his wife again saw Mossy Pendell, and then it was in obedience to a note, couched in words of command, that he bade her meet him one night in the neighbourhood of Kensington.

With sinking heart and trembling footsteps, Alice sought her husband, who happened to be at the place of appointment first.

"So you have thought proper, at last, to make your appearance!" growled Mossy Pendell, when his wife was within a few paces of him.

"I did not mean to keep you waiting, Pendell. I thought—that is I——"

"Hold your tongue! You came here to listen to what I have to say, not to hear yourself talk."

Mrs. Pendell waited to receive, so to speak, her husband's commands.

"Well, so now you are going to put on a fit of the sulks, are you, madam? Look up, I say! What is there on the ground to rivet your attention in that fashion?"

Mrs. Pendell raised her head submissively, and Mossy came nearer to her.

As he approached, however, his wretched wife gave a start, like a frightened hare, and half raised her arms as though to ward off a blow.

"Ah, you know you deserve it. But I have business for you to-night, and every night as long as I choose to name, and if you do not perform your task faithfully and well, remember—you know me before to-night."

A deep sigh was the only response to this brutal speech.

"Now, then, listen to me," added Pendell. "I want you to come with me to Camden House. Do you hear? Are you deaf? I want you to come with me to Camden House."

As he spoke, he clutched her savagely by the arm, and Alice uttered a half shriek.

"Beware! One more such cry, and it will be your last in this world!"

"Heaven protect me!" groaned the unhappy woman.

"Hold your noise! Don't talk any of your methodistical nonsense to me. Such as you and I have nothing to do with heaven—it is of earth I want to talk."

"You are right, Mossy," said Alice, while a bright colour tinged her usually pale cheek. "Since I married you, heaven seems to be beyond my grasp. I gave up all for you—home, friends, kindred—almost heaven itself!"

"Ha, ha, ha!" roared the inhuman monster she

called by the name of husband, "and more fool you. However, as you can be of use to me, I will not quarrel about the matter—especially as the fact of being married to you does not prevent——"

"Hold!" shrieked Alice. "Tell me what you want of me, and let me go to my lonely home, there to think over the few happy days which were too bright to last."

"But as it happens, Mrs. Pendell, I have other fish to fry to-night, and for several successive nights, so you must just put off the little romantic reflections you were promising yourself, until I give you permission to indulge in them."

Alice looked into his eyes, and said firmly, but gently, "I have ever made it a point to obey you. Hitherto your commands have not been such as I shrunk from; but you have yet to learn that I, too, have an opinion of my own. I will obey you in everything, so long as you do not require me to outrage those principles, and the duty I owe to myself, and——"

Before Alice could utter another word, her husband sprung upon her like some wild animal, and, raising his hand, with one blow felled her to the earth, as he thought; but in reality Alice had stumbled over a stone merely, in her endeavour to avoid the threatened blow.

"Take that!" he roared. "How dare you stand up before me and say that you have opinions and principles? Have we been married so long, and yet you have not found out that my opinions and my wishes are to be the sole rule and guidance of your life? Get up and listen to me, or I will find means of making you more submissive!"

"Heaven help me!" was all Alice could say, as she slowly rose to her feet.

"Now, then, listen to me! You will come with me to Camden House, there to keep watch and ward over General Everton so long as I choose! Do you hear that?"

"Yes, I hear!"

"You are by degrees to try to gain the regard and confidence of the General, so that in time he will desire nothing better than to obey your wishes."

"My wishes?"

"Yes, your wishes - inasmuch as they will be mine —do you understand?"

"I know not. Tell me more."

"There is a certain document which I wish him to sign."

Alice looked up, and said boldly, "Then why can you not ask him yourself to do this thing, you know him—whereas I never saw him in my life."

"Never you mind why I choose to employ you in this affair, that is my business. You must talk to him, as you know so well how to talk with your confounded soft woman's tongue. Make the old fool think you take pity on him—that you will use all the influence you possess in the right quarter in order to set him at liberty."

"And you will set him at liberty, Pendell?" asked Alice, gently, and looking almost as affectionately at her brutal husband as she had done in happy days gone by.

"Silence, woman! Ask me no questions, but take from me your instructions! The old man is nearly blind with grief and sorrow, and his mind is much impaired by the strong doses of laudanum I have taken care to administer to him."

Alice shuddered.

"And therefore," he continued, "it will be no difficult task for you to invent some tale, making him believe that you want him to put his name down as a subscriber to some charity."

"But if he is a prisoner for life?" urged Alice.

"Silence, again! Listen to me, woman! You are to make him believe that you have the means of setting him at liberty, if in no other way, at least by opening the door of his prison-house, when no one but yourself and he are in the house."

"But I cannot—I dare not trifle with this poor old man's feelings in this way——"

"Pshaw! Don't begin to talk your nonsense again. I say you are to do it, and you shall, too! The mode by which you induce him to sign the document I care not; but sign it he must, and that through your instrumentality!"

"Oh, spare me—spare me, Pendell! Do not ask me to commit this wickedness, and I may still be able to bless and pray for you!"

"Wait till I ask either for your blessings or your prayers, it will be then quite time enough for you to make me the subject of them. You now understand what it is I wish you to do, so come on at once, and I will introduce you to your—victim! Ha! ha! a joke that!"

As he spoke, Mossy Pendell laid his snake-like fingers on the arm of her wife and forced her to follow where he almost dragged her.

When they reached Camden House, Pendell paused and opened the iron gate with one hand, while with the other he still kept a firm grasp upon the slender wrist of Alice.

As soon as they got inside what had hitherto been the well-kept lawn - but which was now a wilderness of rank weeds - he flung her from him, and closed the gate behind him.

Alice who was but too well accustomed to such acts of brutality, had not wholly been thrown off her guard, and therefore saved herself from falling.

"Now, madam, I will trouble you to walk this way," said Pendell, with mock politeness, "and I will at once introduce you to——"

"Your victim," said Alice.

"Call him either my victim or yours, whichever you think best; for, seeing that you and I are one, it would be absurd to quarrel about terms."

Alice, more like one who was walking in her sleep, followed her relentless husband up the grand staircase of the mansion, then along a broad corridor, which seemed to extend the whole length of the building.

At a door at the end of this corridor, Pendell paused and took from his pocket a key of a peculiar shape.

He put it quietly into the lock, and it turned noiselessly.

As he pushed open the door Alice found herself in a spacious apartment richly furnished, although it was quite evident that from the accumulation of dust upon every article of the costly furniture, it had not been disturbed for some months.

Alice looked on with awe, mingled, it must be confessed, with some curiosity, for she had never beheld an apartment of such magnificence before.

When Mossy Pendell wooed and won the fair Alice Harvey she was living a life of calm contentment in one of the southern counties of England, where she was looked upon by all as a being superior to all with whom she was thrown into contact.

But her beauty was her least charm, for there was not a man, woman, or child in her native village that would not have walked a day's journey to do the fair Alice, as she was called, a good turn.

It was a sad day that beheld Mossy Pendell a visitor at the farm kept by Alice's father.

The wily villain knew too well how to captivate the heart of the innocent girl, who in time learnt to love him with all the depth and fervour of her enthusiastic nature.

In an evil hour she allowed herself to be persuaded to elope with him, for Alice felt certain that neither

her father nor her mother would give their consent to her marrying one of whom they knew nothing.

"Come," he said, in a whisper, as he closed the door of the room and locked it; "do not stand gazing about you as though you were but half awake. I tell you you are to begin your work to-night."

"Yes, yes, I come," mechanically replied Alice.

They traversed the whole extent of this vast apartment, at the further end of which was a door, draped with rich silk hangings.

The same key opened this door that had opened the last, and Alice stood within another moderately-sized apartment.

Mossy held up his finger to enjoin silence.

Alice's heart beat so violently, that she could hear every pulsation.

There was a strange feeling of awe at beholding so much grandeur, mingled with such utter solitude as appeared to reign in that deserted mansion, and Alice once or twice was tempted to ask herself if it were not all a dream.

But her husband's grasp again lighting upon her arm, soon convinced her that all was but too real.

"Stay here," he whispered, "and stir not, as you value your life, until I come to you."

"Ah! do not leave me here all alone, I beg and entreat," said Alice, as she clasped his hands in hers. "This is such a strange place. There are so many hiding places apparently."

"Stand back!" he hissed from between his clenched teeth, or you will make me dangerous."

Alice sunk to her knees on the floor.

Mossy Pendell walked to a panel, and touched a secret spring.

The panel flew back, and discovered beyond a long narrow passage, dimly lighted by a silver lamp, which hung from the ceiling.

Pendell paused on the threshold of this apartment, if such it could be called, and seemed to listen intently.

"Yes," he said to himself, "he sleeps. I have miscalculated. I hoped to have found him up and anxiously waiting for his evening meal. Ah! be this——"

From a bedstead, which occupied a rather large space in the strangely-shaped apartment, issued a sigh—which had in it more the character of a groan—came upon the ear of Mossy Pendell.

"I will enter and speak to him," he said to himself.

As he spoke, he entered the apartment, and walked straight up to the bed, on which lay the much loved and deeply-lamented uncle of Lucy Everton.

"So you are awake, uncle. How do you find yourself by this time?"

The venerable face for a moment turned in the direction from whence the voice proceeded, but immediately it was withdrawn; and a sigh was the only answer he received.

"Oh, so you are sulky to-night! This is pretty treatment after I have taken the trouble to come and see that you wanted for nothing."

"Fiend! Tempter!"

"Harsh words!—Harsh words, uncle, from lips which have but a few more words to utter in this world."

"Ah, you would kill—you would murder me?"

"No, I do not wish to hasten your death, that will come quite soon enough for me; but I should like to part friends."

"Be gone! and torment me not."

"Now, really! Here have I brought you a kind and affectionate nurse to tend you, and administer to all your wants, and yet you talk to me as though I were the greatest enemy you had."

"Where is my child—my Lucy?"

"Ah, that is what I want to find out; and am indeed doing all I can to ascertain for you, and yet, notwithstanding everything, you will look upon me——"

The old man started to a sitting posture.

But his frame had undergone so much physical suffering, that nature gave way, and he fainted.

"Alice! Come here, I say!" cried Mossy Pendell.

As she approached he pointed to the bed.

"See to your patient—your victim, if you will."

CHAPTER CXV.

MOSSY PENDELL MAKES A MISTAKE.

As soon as Mossy Pendell had uttered these words, he left the room, leaving Alice alone with the General, who was quite insensible.

Alice bent over him tenderly, and as she did so, she thought of her loving father, from whom she had fled to share with one who could neither appreciate nor understand with her, the joys and sorrows of the world.

Poor Alice! Few indeed, and short-lived have been her joys.

"Thank heaven," she said, as she chafed the aged hands—"thank heaven, that I may be the means of at least ameliorating your hard lot. So old, and yet so social a smile is playing upon his lips, I could almost fancy he was happy—instead of—ah, he stirs!"

"Lucy!—Lucy!" sighed the General.

Alice spoke not, moved not, and at length General Everton opened his eyes and gazed about him.

Alice then spoke in a low tone.

"Do you want anything. Can I assist you to rise, General Everton?"

"A stranger!" cried the old man, with a look of terror almost—who are you? I have had a dream, and methought my Lucy—the child of my affection, was standing by my side. I wake up, and find it is all a dream, and I am still helpless and a prisoner.

As he spoke, the General threw himself back again, and tears which were wrung from his overcharged heart, by a recollection of all he had suffered of late, fell plenteously.

"Sir!—sir! do not weep; let me think that you will accept my poor services, and believe in my desire to be of use to you."

For the first time the General turned his gaze full upon her, and after contemplating her for some few minutes, in silence, said—

"Is it possible with such a look of candour and kindness, you can be in the employ of that bad man, who has heaped insult and injury upon me, until my life is a burden, and I only pray for death."

"Alas!—alas! I know not of whom you speak."

"My nephew, Mossy Pendell."

Wicked as poor Alice knew her husband to be, she had not expected to hear that General Everton had received such treatment from him, but from that moment she bravely resolved to put a stop to it if possible, and she took her determination at once.

"Yes," she said, sadly. "I grieve to say that I am not only in Mossy Pendell's employment, but that he is my husband."

"Your husband? How long have you been married to him, child?"

"Nearly nine years."

"But what is your errand here? Tell me."

Alice paused irresolutely, for she knew not in what state the General's mind was, nor whether he might not, in some unguarded moment, betray her designs to Mossy Pendell. However, there was no opportunity just then of carrying on any conversation, for Mossy Pendell appeared on the threshold of the apartment.

"Well, uncle! so you have recovered from that little

fainting fit. It was a good thing I happened to make my appearance as I did, or it might have been——"

"Leave me—leave me to die in peace!" moaned the General, who had turned his face to the wall as soon as Mossy Pendell made his appearance.

"With all my heart. But before you take your leave, I want you to sign a certain little document, merely for form's sake."

"Never—never! I will not alienate my property to enrich such as you! Go—leave me—I can die."

Mossy Pendell looked ghastly with rage; and as he left the room, he made a sign to Alice to follow him.

When they were out of hearing, he turned sharply round, and whispered, in a hoarse voice, "To your work. This paper which I hold in my hand, must be signed by General Everton before sunset to-morrow. To you I consign him. Invent anything you like, but make him sign it, or tremble, for my vengeance will be sure and certain."

"But, Mossy, you have tried, and failed; and how can I——"

"How can you, idiot!" was the sneering reply. "Can you not win him over to believe that you will befriend him—that the paper is merely a form—but that, by signing it, he is saving both his own life and yours! Now do you comprehend?"

"I think I do."

"Well, then, see to it! I shall return to-morrow, and expect to find my orders obeyed!"

"Mossy, leave me not so! Husband!"

Alice flew to the door of the apartment, but it yielded not to her touch.

"Heaven help me!" was all she could say.

For a moment she crouched down upon the floor, and held her head in her hands.

"This fearful bondage must end some day! How dreadful to have outlived his affection, and yet methinks it must all have been a mistake—he could never have loved me, for my affection is still unchanged, notwithstanding all his cruelty and taunts."

Alice turned quickly round, for she heard a footstep behind her.

It was the General. He fancied that he was alone, and, as was his wont, he was making the tour, so to speak, of his prison-house.

At the sight, however, of Alice's deep grief, his kind heart was moved, and he said, gently, "Are you, too, in this man's toils? Have you been unfortunate enough to excite his anger?"

There was no reply, but Alice's tears continued to flow.

It was a long time since she had been addressed in tones of kindness, and that poor, crushed heart seemed ready to burst.

At length she made an effort, and approached the General, saying, as she did so, "Pardon me for asking the question, but how long is it since you heard of your niece, Lucy Everton?"

"Never since the night she was torn from her home and this poor fond heart. Her cousin did tell me that she had eloped with a highwayman, but I believed him not. Can you tell me ought of her?"

"Yes, I know that she is married."

"Married! Lucy married! When, and to whom?"

"To a brave and good man; one who rescued her from a disgraceful death."

The General staggered back a pace or two.

"You amaze me!" he cried. "What had she done to merit——"

"Nothing."

"But of what was she accused?"

"Of your murder."

"My murder! Merciful heavens! I begin to understand it all now! That fiend——"

Alice cowered to the floor, and her frame shook as though with an ague.

"Forgive me, I forget," said the General, laying his hand upon her head,—"I forget he was your husband. Go on—tell me all, in pity tell me all."

"It is only too true. Mossy Pendell thought that, by getting rid of Lucy, it would be quite easy, then, to appropriate your property as your next heir-at-law, therefore it was necessary that it should be thought you were no more, and that Lucy, wishing to become possessed of your wealth earlier than she would otherwise do, was supposed to have administered poison to you one evening in your arrowroot."

The General clasped his hands over his eyes, and seemed lost in thought for some few seconds.

Then there was a slight noise as of an opening door in some distant part of the mansion, and both stood in an attitude of listening.

"Retire to the inner room," whispered Alice; "footsteps approach; it is Mossy Pendell."

Scarcely had the words passed her lips, when her husband entered the room, looking anxious and somewhat flurried.

"Have you had any conversation," he asked, in a low voice.

"Not much."

"Oh! Anything to the purpose?"

"No."

"Well, you have plenty of time; but I forgot to leave you a soothing potion, which it will be as well for you to give him as soon as he has signed the paper, as he is sure to become excited. And Alice——"

There was an unwonted tone of kindness in his words which went at once to Alice's heart, and made her think of by-gone days.

"Alice," he continued; "I'm afraid I have been somewhat harsh to you lately, but forgive me."

"Oh, do not ask me to forgive you; all is forgotten —all is forgiven!"

As she spoke, Alice threw herself into her husband's arms, and burst into tears.

She saw not the fiendish smile that sat upon his lips, or she would have fled from his embrace as she would have done from that of a serpent.

But she saw it not, and for a few seconds, at all events, she was happy.

"There now, that will do. I must leave you now. Don't forget the sleeping draught, but do not administer it until after the paper is signed. You understand: as I must have that to-morrow evening, and he may not wake in time. Now, good-bye, Alice! Why, I declare, you look quite pretty!"

In another minute Alice was alone.

Mechanically she looked at the little phial which Mossy had put into her hand on parting with her.

"Do not forget the sleeping-draught; but, remember, it is not to be administered until after the paper is signed."

The words recurred to her again and again, together with the caressing manner in which he had spoken to her, and a shade of deep dejection passed over her features.

"I would rather it were so. I have heard him speak once more in tones of kindness; my life is weary; this little phial may, indeed, prove a friend. I will conceal it; but he, that good old man, shall never taste it—heaven guide me!"

She tapped gently at the door of the inner room.

The General made no reply.

"General Everton, may I come in?"

"Ah! is it you? Enter! Enter! Welcome, a thousand times welcome; for it is dreary watching alone!"

* * * * * *

Again Claude Duval is at his place of observation.

Blossom had had a weary time of it, for no one had been seen to enter Camden House.

The fact is, Blossom had only left his post of observation to drink a draught of porter, for which the "Blue Lion" was celebrated. But, during that short interval, Mossy Pendell had both entered and left the house unperceived.

The next afternoon, however, Claude was gratified to see a woman approach the iron gates from the house, and, after looking carefully to the right and left, she put a key in the lock and let herself out.

The instant she was clear of the house, Duval followed her at a distance, so as not himself to be seen; and, at the corner of Kensington Gardens, she again paused, and looked about her.

She had not long to wait, for Mossy Pendell, who was evidently expecting her, soon joined her.

Claude Duval quickened his steps, so as to be in time to listen to their conversation.

He had no difficulty in secreting himself behind one of the tall trees, just within ear-shot.

"Well?" he heard Mossy Pendell say; "have you succeeded yet?"

"No."

"No! but you will?"

"Perhaps; but you are changed again. You were kind and affectionate to me yesterday, and to-day——"

"Nonsense! A man with his hands full of business cannot be expected to be always making love speeches to his wife. Go! and remember the—the——"

"Poison?"

"Who said that it was poison, woman? You know not what you are talking about!"

"Perhaps not. But will you not kiss me before we part."

The latter part of the sentence was unheard by Mossy Pendell, for he walked at a sharp pace along the side of Kensington Gardens.

Alice turned from the spot with a sigh.

"I would rather that yesterday had been our last interview; for then he was kind to me."

Duval allowed her to reach Camden House before he accosted her, and just as she was about to enter the iron gate, which she had unlocked, he stood before her.

There was a look of terror at first upon Alice's face; but when she looked attentively at Duval, that feeling seemed to give place to another of a totally different character.

"You here?" she cried—"the person of all others who will be able to advise me."

Duval was completely taken by surprise.

"What mean you? Who are you?"

"Never mind who I am. Suffice it to say that I can give you tidings of Lucy's uncle."

"Ah!"

"Follow me."

As she spoke, Alice led the way into the house, and when she had closed the front door, she threw back her hood, with which she had hitherto concealed her face, and Duval had no difficulty in recognising the woman he had once encountered on the heath, and who had really given him valuable information respecting Mossy Pendell's proceedings.

"Is it possible," he exclaimed, "that we meet again? Tell me if I can serve you in any way."

"Trust to me. I will guide you to General Everton. I know not what is to be done; but you are wise and brave. He is a prisoner here. I am to get him to sign some document, and after that I am to poison him."

"Merciful heavens! Are you in earnest? Do I hear aright? Lucy's uncle here?"

"Come and see."

In another minute Duval stood in the presence of General Everton.

With the courtesy for which Claude Duval was almost celebrated; we may say he explained in a few words to General Everton the relation he stood in to Lucy—his unavailing search for him—Lucy's grief at his disappearance.

The General looked first at him and then at Alice, with bewildered eyes.

"What do I hear? I am free, you say?"

"Free as air," replied Duval; "for I fancy the man is not born who would dare to dispute my right to claim you as my wife's uncle."

"And you are?"

"Lucy's husband, and Claude Duval."

"I will trust you," said the General, giving him his hand; "and you—what are you going to do—not remain here alone, surely?"

"Yes," said Alice, in a quiet tone of voice. "I shall remain here to receive my husband, who will be here a little after sun-set. Leave me—I would be alone."

There was something so melancholy in the tone of her voice, that both the General and Duval would fain have persuaded her to leave that house with them. But Alice's resolution was taken.

"No. If you would show that you are grateful to me for the slight assistance I have afforded you, you will leave me at once. Let me implore you to go, while there is yet time."

These last words reminded the General of the risk he ran, and he turned to Duval, and begged him to lead him to his niece.

But Duval could not, without one more effort to induce that unfortunate woman to fly from her wicked husband, and leave the spot.

He approached Alice, and said, "Tell me, at 'east, that you have nothing to fear from your husband's anger, when he finds his prisoner has escaped."

"I have nothing to fear. Now go, and tell Lucy——"

She paused abruptly.

"No; do not mention me to her: it is better not. Go, and heaven bless you and yours! Here is the key of the outer gate—take it."

"But shall you not want it yourself? We can do without it."

"No, take it; I shall not require it. Go—go before it is too late."

In another moment Claude Duval and General Everton were going at a swinging gallop towards Hampstead, for Blossom had his horse, as well as Nightshade, in readiness at a moment's notice.

"Managed much quieter than I expected, Captain," he whispered, as he held the stirrup for Duval to mount.

"A great deal quieter, Blossom. You'll find your way home somehow, I suppose."

"Never fear for me, Captain; you'll see me some time to-morrow morning."

As soon as Alice caught the last glimpse of the two horsemen between the trees, she ran towards a table, on which were writing materials, and wrote the following words:—

"Farewell! The sleeping potion has done its work. I could not kill the old man, he has still those who love him. I was alone and unloved. Farewell!"

She placed the paper beside her, and then she drained the contents of the phial which Mossy Pendell had given her for a very different person.

Gradually her head sunk upon her arm, and it drooped lower and lower; and in less than two hours Alice was deaf alike to words of love or anger.

CHAPTER CXVI.

GENERAL EVERTON IS LIBERATED.

THE meeting between Lucy and her uncle was, indeed, a joyful one.

As Duval and General Everton, however, neared the deserted mansion on Hampstead Heath, the latter drew rein, and, turning to Duval, he said, "Do you not think it advisable to go on and prepare poor Lucy for seeing me?"

After a moment's pause, Duval determined upon following the General's suggestion; "for although," he said. " joy never kills, yet Lucy has of late gone through so much—and the very fact that her own life might be forfeited at any moment so long as you were hidden from those who could and would have served you,—I must confess, I should be afraid of the shock which it must be, under any circumstances, to her to see you again in life. Wait at this small door, and I will alone dismount, and speak with Lucy."

Scarcely, however, were the words passed his lips, than there was a cry of joy, and Lucy herself sprung forward, and was clasped in her husband's arms.

"Look up—look up, Lucy, for I have a companion!"

There was one start, one half-shriek, and Lucy was clasping her uncle's hand, which he stretched down to her from his high elevation on Nightshade's back.

Duval gently disengaged her from her uncle's saddle, and almost carried her into the house.

In another few seconds all was tumultuous joy. Questions were asked in quick succession, without any one thinking, apparently, that it was at all necessary to wait for answers.

Oh, how much was there to tell of the events that had happened during the last few months.

And Lucy—what was not the fact of her uncle still being in life worth to her, in addition to the joy which must ever be experienced when near and dear friends meet, after a long and painful separation!

It was life itself to her, for up to that time was she not in danger of at any moment being dragged forth to expiate by her death the awful crime of which Mossy Pendell had accused her—namely, compassing her uncle's death?

The love of life is strong in all, both old and young; but surely to the latter, who have but just passed the threshold of existence, so to speak, it must be immeasurably dearer.

Perhaps it was the thought of her own exculpation from guilt which now gave a deeper hue to her cheeks and an additional sparkle to her eyes, for her uncle, who had been gazing at her fondly for some moments, at length exclaimed, "And so, dear one, I find you married?"

"Ah, uncle, I would fain have waited for your consent, could I have believed it possible that we should ever meet again on this side of eternity; but as it was——"

Lucy paused, and a shudder, which always crept over her whenever her thoughts reverted to that fearful scaffold from which Claude had rescued her with so much peril to himself.

"Go on, dear: what do you want to tell me?"

"He—my husband—my Claude—took me, I may say, from the very hands of the hangman. He then told me that he loved me, and asked me to be his own. Oh, uncle! ought I—could I refuse so generous an offer? Me, a disgraced girl, actually about to perish upon the scaffold!"

"Enough, enough, Lucy! And how shall I ever be able to repay the debt of gratitude we both owe to our generous preserver?"

"By saying no more on the subject, General," replied Duval, in a light tone. "And now I think it is high time for us to consult as to the best means of making it known that you are still alive."

"That must be the first step, unquestionably," replied the General; "and until that end is accomplished, it is necessary that I should remain concealed somewhere."

"No place fitter for such concealment than the house to which I have brought you," replied Duval. "Let me, therefore, advise you to rest in peace for to-night, and then to-morrow we will together, or separately, take steps for your reintroduction into that world from which you have been so barbarously withdrawn."

There was a look of weariness and exhaustion upon the face of General Everton, which filled Lucy with anxiety.

The tears rose to her eyes many times during the course of that evening, as she marked the ravages grief and suffering had made upon what she had only known as the handsome and manly countenance of her beloved uncle.

"Come dear uncle," she said, "let us defer all discussions till to-morrow; but to-night seek that repose, I beg of you, which is so needful to you."

Nothing loath, the good General rose and followed Lucy, who led the way to a spacious chamber she had prepared for him.

A fire was burning in the grate, and there was an air of comfort and home-like serenity pervading everything upon which his eye rested, that the General looked almost like his former happy self, as he turned to bless the child of his affections.

Placing his hands upon her shoulders, he looked at her steadfastly for a few minutes without speaking.

Lucy met that gaze, even as she had done in childhood, with fond affection.

"And so my Lucy is a wife?" he began, as he smoothed her beautiful hair.

"Yes, dear uncle, the happy wife of one of the best of husbands. I wanted but your blessing, uncle, to make me supremely blessed."

"You have it now, darling," he said, as he placed his hand upon her head. "May God bless and have you in his holy keeping."

Lucy bowed her head; and the remembrance of that blessing was in after years a comfort to her, when sad and cast down, and there seemed not a ray of hope or gleam of sunshine in her earthly path.

When she left her uncle, she sought Claude, who was pacing to and fro the apartment they had been sitting in, talking over the past.

He seemed so occupied with his own thoughts, that he did not at first perceive Lucy, indeed, not until she had reached his side.

"Ah! dear Lucy, are you here? You see I have kept my word as regards your uncle."

"Yes, dear. But you look troubled. Tell me, is anything amiss?"

"No no. I was merely thinking that now I might seek a real adventure upon the road—such an one as I have not indulged in for a long time. What say you, Lucy? Will you consent?"

Lucy looked sad; but she strove to speak cheerfully.

"I promised you, Claude, that I would not fetter your actions in any way. Go, Claude, but be careful of yourself; and never forget your Lucy."

"No fear of that, dear one. You have lifted a weight off my head, for I feared you would oppose my wishes."

"That would be of no use," said Lucy, trying to smile. "But you do not think of going to-night, do you?"

"No time like the present, Lucy. So do you return to rest, and by the dawn you will see me again."

CLAUDE DUVAL ACCOSTS THE OLD LADY AND HER NIECE.

Duval sought Blossom, who had just arrived.

"I suppose, Blossom, you are too much fatigued to accompany me on the road, to-night?"

"Not a bit of it, Captain. I got a lift home the greater part of the way, so you see there is nothing I should like so well as a downright highwayman's adventure."

"Well, then, I want you to get a sedan chair, and be one of the carriers yourself, and you can easily select one of our men to be the other."

"Nothing easier; for Ben Stringer knows me well, and will not have the slightest objection to oblige me with a chair for as long as I like."

"That is well; but now attend to my instructions, Blossom."

"You must have in readiness no less than four different costumes, which, if necessary, I can change in the chair."

"All right; I see, Captain. What dress do you intend to start with?"

"An officer of the King's Light Horse, I think," replied Duval.

"All right, Captain; and now what other dresses shall I look out."

"Well, in the first place, I think my highwayman's costume for one, for I may find it advisable to appear in my proper character, as Claude Duval."

"Yes, Captain. Go on."

"Then, I shall want a clerical-looking dress—a suit of plain black."

"All right, Captain; you've got a suit that you have never put on."

"Then I think, I must leave the rest to you, Blossom."

"What do you say to a Quaker's suit, for the fourth, Captain?"

"I've not the slightest objection."

"And the fifth can be the uniform of a naval officer, eh, Captain?"

"As you will, Blossom."

A slight noise made Duval turn sharply round, and he beheld Lucy.

"Ah, Lucy," he said, coming forward, and taking her by the hand, "what now? You have not surely repented of the permission you gave me to go on the road to-night?"

"I have, indeed, Claude. Do not leave me to-night, for, in good truth, I feel nervous and despirited."

"It is nothing, dearest," was his reply. "It arises from the excitement of again seeing your uncle, whom you looked upon as dead."

"Perhaps so, Claude; but do humour me to-night, and stay at home."

"Well, then I will remain, since you seem so much set against this expedition. But, remember, Lucy, you must let me begin my old life to-morrow."

"I will—I will! Thank you, Claude."

Duval turned to Blossom, who looked anything but gratified at the turn things had taken; but he contented himself with merely saying, that he supposed the ladies always had their own way.

"Then, when will you want the sedan chair?" he asked.

"To-morrow morning, Blossom, directly after breakfast."

Blossom gave a long whistle.

"Well, Blossom, will not that suit you?"

"Capitally, Captain! But is it to be a day adventure, then?"

"Precisely so! Why not?"

"I know no reason in the world, Captain, why we should not have as much sport in the day-time as at night; so I'll just go and give a look-in at Ben Stringer's, and ask about the chair."

"Do so—do so! Now, Lucy, dear, I am at your service."

There was a look of deep joy and thankfulness upon Lucy's face, as Claude led her from the apartment; and balmy sleep stole over all the inmates of that strange, deserted-looking house as sweetly as though they had been the lawful possessors of it.

The morning sun rose bright and beautiful, and awakened General Everton from his refreshing sleep, such as he had not known for many weary months.

At first he gazed about him in some bewilderment, for he found he had been dreaming only of his escape from that fearful imprisonment; but as he gazed about, the different objects in that room, soon recalled to his mind the various incidents of the last few hours previously to retiring to rest.

The business of the toilette was somewhat tedious to him, for General Everton had been in the habit, before his imprisonment in his own house, to submit himself to the hands of a valet; and while he was shut up in Camden House, he had contented himself with merely washing his hands and face, each morning hoping that it would be the last.

But, on this day, he was anxious to make as good an appearance as possible; for his quick eye had detected at a glance, that Lucy thought him changed for the worse.

He had just given the last touch to his dress, which was that of an officer in a military undress uniform, when Duval knocked at the door.

His surprise was great as he perceived the General had risen without any assistance, and the greeting was more like that between old friends, than between two persons who had only seen each other for an hour or two the previous night.

"Up and dressed!" was Duval's exclamation, as he seized the General's hand.

"Aye, up and dressed!" was the reply; "for I am anxious to look again upon my Lucy's fair face, and to hear her say again that she is happy; for you love my child?" asked the old man, with emotion.

"Better than life itself!" was Duval's answer; and there was something in the tone in which these words were uttered, that left no doubt in the General's mind of their truthfulness.

They descended together to the breakfast-room, where Lucy was busily engaged in arranging the table.

No sooner did she hear their voices, as they approached, than she advanced to meet them; and taking her uncle by the hand, was about to lead him to a seat, but the latter folded her in his arms, saying as he did so, "Heaven be praised that I again behold my darling!"

Lucy had some difficulty in restraining her tears, for she had began to think that that voice was lost to her for ever; so that now that she heard it again, it was only with deep emotion.

The breakfast passed off cheerfully; and then Duval asked the General if he had decided upon any steps to take with regard to his restoration to the world?

"I have," he replied. "I see by the newspaper, here, that the King holds a levee next Wednesday."

"I understand," exclaimed Duval; "and you intend to be present."

"Precisely."

"Oh, uncle, how happy we shall all be now!" said Lucy.

"I hope so, Lucy. In the meantime, I think it will be desirable for me to remain here until I have shown myself at Court and confounded that arch-plotter, Mossy Pendell."

"Do so—do so!"

"And after that I see no reason for our staying away from Camden House, for I need not say that I have no desire to leave you and your husband, if you can make room in your home for a feeble old man like myself."

"Most joyfully do we accept the bargain!" said Duval; "and it will give Lucy a companion when I am forced to be absent from her. Business this morning calls me away; but I have no doubt by the time you and Lucy have talked over the past I shall rejoin you."

"Be it so. Farewell!"

One parting embrace to Lucy, and Claude Duval, accompanied by Blossom, set off to the appointed spot where a sedan chair was to be in waiting in charge of one of his men.

CHAPTER CXVII.

CLAUDE DUVAL SEEKS EXCITEMENT IN THE PARK.

At the corner of Welbeck Street was a sedan-chair, and against a post lounged a man who appeared to be the owner of it.

Duval, however, had no difficulty in discovering that the pretended chairman was none other than one of his own trusty followers.

"Here we are, Captain!" said Blossom; "and the different packages are all labelled, so that you will have no difficulty in laying your hand upon whatever dress you wish to wear."

"I think the best way will be for you and Blossom each to carry a parcel; it will facilitate my getting in and out of the chair, if the other two are placed under the seat."

"All right, Captain! Now, where will your honour like to go?"

Blossom put on the air and manner of a chairman to perfection, much to his own satisfaction.

"To St. James's Park," said Duval.

"All right, yer honor!"

Blossom and his companion hoisted the chair, and went at a brisk pace towards the Park.

At the entrance to the Park they paused for further directions.

"Make towards that clump of trees, and then I will alight," said Duval.

"All right!" replied Blossom.

At the appointed spot the pretended chairmen came to a standstill while Duval alighted.

He emerged from it, dressed as an officer of the King's Light Horse.

"Wait for me here."

"All right, Captain!"

Duval made his way towards the more populous part of the Park, and at length seated himself upon one of the benches.

"I will wait here," he said to himself. "Perhaps kind fortune may place something in my way."

Scarcely had he uttered the words than a shadow fell upon the pathway, and a young officer threw himself on the bench beside Duval.

"Aw! a fine day, sir—aw!"

Duval at a glance saw he had a coxcomb to deal with; but the same glance also discovered to him the presence of a large amount of jewellery.

"A chance!" thought Duval to himself. "I will humour this young fop."

The young man, in the meantime, had stretched his legs out to their furthest extent, and had just adjusted his eyeglass so as to make it serviceable with the least amount of trouble to himself—viz. by fixing it permanently in his eye.

Duval, however, had not yet spoken.

The young man turned the eyeglass upon Duval, and looked at him as though he had been some natural curiosity.

"A fine day, sir!" he said again.

Duval inclined his head.

"Aw! I see, deep in thought. I am sometimes deep in thought, now would you believe it?"

"Scarcely," said Duval, quietly.

"Ha, ha! That's very good, now—'pon honor, that's good! You mean that I, Lord Adolphus Freeman, does not look like a thoughtful man?"

"Not exactly."

"Now, 'pon honour, I admire your impudence, it's so good! Aw! Are you ever thoughtful?"

"Only when I meet with something curious. I am thoughtful now, for instance."

Duval had succeeded in transferring from the young officer's pocket to his own a very handsome snuff-box, and also a cigar-case richly mounted.

"And do you come into the Park to think?" asked the young man. "I come here, I will confess, to look at the pretty girls."

"You might do worse," was Duval's reply.

"Aw! yes, I suppose I might; but you know it isn't all on my side. The girls come here to look at me."

"So I suppose."

"Now—aw!—really I don't know whether to think you are laughing at me or not. You do say such deused queer things. By the by, do you know Lady Alice Vargrave?"

"But slightly; in fact, I doubt whether I should know her now if I were to see her, for it is some years since we met—when she was a child."

"Oh, indeed! Well, I don't mind telling you, but it is quite a case with her."

"As how?" asked Duval.

"Why, she loves me, sir—loves me to distraction!"

"I dare say. And are you waiting to see her ladyship?"

"Of course! What else should bring me to the Park do you think?"

"Oh, to see the pretty girls, you know!" said Duval, as he playfully struck the young officer lightly on the breast, and at the same time displaced a very handsome diamond pin, which, of course, found its way to the same pocket as the snuff-box and cigar-case.

At this moment, another gentleman came towards the bench upon which were seated Claude Duval and the young officer, and the former began to think it high time to beat a retreat, as he had every reason to be satisfied with the little adventure.

He therefore rose slowly to his feet, and, with a slight inclination of the head, turned in the direction of the spot where he knew that Blossom had the chair in waiting for him.

The young officer, without appearing to see him, put his glass in his eye, and accosted the new-comer.

"Ah, Beecham!" he cried; "it does one's eyesight good to get a look at you so early in the day! Sit down, and—aw!—take a pinch of snuff!"

The exquisite started to his feet, and let the eyeglass drop in the excitement of the moment.

"Good gracious!" he cried. "I have lost it!"

"Lost it! Lost what? What are you talking about? Don't look so scared, man?"

While the gentleman who had been addressed as Beecham was looking on evidently much amused at the bewilderment of his friend, the young officer was making frantic efforts to plunge both hands into all his pockets at once.

"What on earth is the matter with you?" again inquired his friend. "You look like a man beside himself!"

"What is the matter? Why, didn't I tell you that my snuff-box and cigar-case had both disappeared from my pocket—the snuff-box worth I don't know how much; it was given to my great grandfather by the late King; and, look here—by Jove! my breast-pin has disappeared also! It must be that fellow who was talking to me when you came up!"

"Nonsense! he was an officer of the King's Light Horse!"

"I don't care! I'm sure I had them all right when he came and sat down beside me—no, I make a mistake, I was fool enough to come and sit down beside him. Look—there he goes!"

"Let us give him chase, then. There can be no harm done. If he be a gentleman, we are mistaken: it will be easy to make matters right with him. Come on, Caxton, and we will make him disgorge if he have your property about him."

During all this time Claude Duval was making his way, as quickly as he could without attracting observation, towards the sedan-chair, the door of which Blossom held open.

As soon as he was sufficiently near to be heard, Duval said, "Quick, Blossom, the Quaker's suit!"

"Here you are, Captain! Is there any danger?"

"No; only a little sport. Don't move from this spot; and if two gentlemen speak to you, just keep them talking until you think I have had time to change my dress."

"Trust to me, Captain! Hilloa! why here they are, coming at a brisk rate across the Park! Now for it!"

Blossom was delighted to think that he had a little "business" to do in the affair, and rubbed his hands and chuckled merrily, just as the infuriated Caxton and his friend Beecham reached the spot.

"Halt!" shouted Caxton.

"Who are you?" asked Blossom, indolently; "and what do you mean by telling us to halt? Ain't we a halting as hard as we can?"

"Insolent vagabond! tell me who is your fare? No, I'll see for myself!"

"No, you won't though! What's it to you, young

jackanapes, who my fare is? Get out of the way, or I'll spoil your brilliant plumage for you."

Young Caxton, however, strode past Blossom, just as Duval put his head out of the sedan-chair, looking a very different individual to the one who had entered it.

"Friend," he said, addressing Caxton, "I fear thou art creating a disturbance. I regret to say, that I shall require this chair for the remainder of the day, and if thou wantest one thou must even go and hire one, as thy betters have had to do. Proceed, my friends!"

The young officer had been so unprepared to meet with the particularly close-shaven, mild-looking individual, that he literally started back in amazement, treading upon Blossom's toes as he did so.

"Now then, stupid!" said Blossom, as he gave him such a blow in the middle of the back as sent him almost through the window of the sedan chair,—"now then, stupid, mind where you're a driving to! Don't you see you've nearly crushed my foot with your ugly carcase?"

Caxton, however, rallied instantly, as the thought flashed across him that there must still be hidden somewhere in the chair the man who had robbed him.

"Well, friend?" asked Duval, in the mildest of mild voices,—"well friend? thou hast evidently been taking too much wine, early as it is, and fanciest that thou seest what is not to be seen. I pray thee, impede not the progress of my chair, but allow me to go on my way in peace."

"Villain!" roared Caxton, quite beside himself with rage; "tell me where you have hidden your accomplice?"

"Poor man!—poor man!" murmured Duval; "he is evidently an escaped lunatic. Don't be harsh to him, but pinion him."

"Silence!" shouted the young officer. "Tell me where he is, for I saw him get into this chair with my own eyes."

"Well, and what if thou didst? I know not of whom thou speakest, friend, but all I can say is, that no one has got into this chair but myself since I engaged it this morning."

The young officer looked first at Duval, and then at his friend Beecham, who seemed to be enjoying his friend's dilemma amazingly.

"Why, Caxton, what a fool you are making of yourself this morning. I really begin to think that it is as this gentleman says—you have taken too much rum and milk at breakfast."

"Do you suppose I don't know whether I have a snuff-box or not?—whether I have a cigar-case or not? And then my diamond breast-pin! Where are they?—I ask you, where are they?"

"Really, my young friend," replied Duval, "it seems to me that the police would be the best authority to apply to in thy case, not to me, who am but a simple, quiet citizen, on my road to see my daughter Ruth and her——"

"Confound your daughter Ruth! Where's the man—the highwayman—the robber—the——"

"Hush, hush, friend! Thy cries and frantic gestures will collect a crowd, and thou must bear in mind that I am a man of peace. Farewell, and keep thyself out of evil company, and then thou wilt not lose thy worldly property in this fashion. Chairmen, proceed I beg."

Blossom and his companion raised the chair so suddenly upon receiving this order from Duval, that it was a miracle that the young officer escaped only with having his toes dreadfully trampled on.

"Did you ever see such savage, blood-thirsty villains in your life?" he asked of Beecham, as he looked after the retreating sedan-chair; "and that old hypocrite inside aided and abetted them in all they did and said."

"Well, I must confess that you were being very provoking to insist that the old fellow, who looked as though butter would not melt in his mouth, nor cheese choke him, had stolen your property. I only wonder that he did not lay his silver headed walking stick about your shoulders."

"By Jove! I should have liked to have seen him try to do any such thing; and, say what you will, Beecham, I still think that old wretch knew the fellow who robbed me."

"Stuff, nonsense, man! Don't talk such ridiculous rubbish! Do you suppose the long-legged fellow I saw talking to you could be hidden anywhere in a sedan-chair and not be found out."

"But where are my things?" demanded the young officer. "Don't I know that I had them all about me when that fellow came and sat down beside me, and that as soon as he took himself off I missed them? Perhaps you will try to persuade me next, that I don't know what I am saying."

"Never mind it, man, now. Come to the Club; young Escott is to meet us there, you know, at one o'clock to-day, and it is past twelve now."

With an uncomfortable feeling in his mind that he had not only made a fool of himself somehow, but that he must put up with the loss of his property, young Caxton suffered himself to be led by his friend, Lord Beecham, once more across the Park towards St. James's Street, where they were to meet and play billiards.

"Halt!" said Duval, as having assured himself that there was no chance of again encountering the young officer and his friend, he wished to give directions to Blossom where next to take him.

The sedan chair came to a standstill.

"Well, Blossom," said Duval, as the former came close to the window; "this promises to be not only a profitable, but an amusing day's work."

"I think so too, Captain. But I was sorry to think you let that up-start young blade off with that diamond ring, he wore so ostentatiously displayed."

"You are a cormorant, Blossom!" replied Duval, laughing. "I think I eased him of quite enough for once; but now let me have my highwayman's uniform."

"It's under the seat, Captain."

"That will do. Wait here while I put it on."

"All right, Captain!"

It never took Claude Duval many minutes to effect any change which he wished to make in his dress. Therefore, in the space of five minutes, he was fully equipped as a knight of the road.

"Ah! that the dress after all, Captain, that I like to see you in best! Now you look like yourself! Where are you going now, Captain?"

"Merely to take a walk across the park, Blossom, in search of another adventure; but mind you have another dress in readiness for me when I come back, as I may be known better in this costume than in the uniform of an officer of his Majesty's Light Horse."

"Trust me for that, Captain. Is the chair to remain here?"

"I think you might follow at a short distance; and when you come to yonder clump of trees, there halt, for I may want you."

Duval stepped lightly across the bright green turf, and there was a look of enjoyment upon his handsome countenance, which was particularly fascinating at that moment.

"I wonder how long I shall have to wait in search of an adventure," he said to himself. "Ah! not long, I fancy, for the park is beginning to grow quite populous."

Duval walked up to a seat, just as an elderly lady and a young girl reached it.

Duval drew back cautiously, as if to pass on, and allow them to take possession of it; but he had no such real intention, for the glance he had had at the two ladies, told him at once that one was beautiful, and the other vain, and richly dressed.

"Pray, sir, do not allow us to prevent you from being seated, if such were your intention," said the elder lady, addressing Duval, "for we are always very glad when we meet with a gentleman who knows what is due to ladies."

"Oh, aunt!" whispered the young girl.

"Silence! Children should be seen and not heard," was the rebuke conveyed in the same low tone.

Duval heard, and was highly amused both with the remonstrance, and the rebuke; and courteously raising his hat, he said, in his most winning accents, "With such kind permission, I cannot tear myself away from so much grace and dignity without availing myself of the unexpected pleasure of conversing with one who must thoroughly appreciate the beauties which surround this lovely spot."

"Quite the gentleman, evidently," whispered the old lady, turning to her niece.

"And so handsome!" was the rejoinder.

"Silence, miss! How dare you look to see whether he is handsome or not. When I was your age, I never allowed myself to raise my eyes to gentlemen's faces. Look down instantly, Adele."

Adele did look down, but not before she had looked up into Duval eyes, and there caught such a merry twinkle, that she was forced to bend down to pat a tiny dog, which was attached to her aunt's wrist by a blue ribbon.

Duval stooped down at the same moment, and whispered into the young girl's ear, "Oh, why did you not come alone."

CHAPTER CXVIII.

DUVAL HAS REASON TO REPROACH HIMSELF.

These words brought a bright accession of colour to the cheeks of the beautiful girl to whom they were addressed, and Duval thought, at that moment, that he had never beheld any one so lovely.

Adele was still a child at heart, yet somewhat more than a child in mind.

Duval was not slow to perceive this, and it was with something like a qualm of conscience that he resolved to win her young affections.

The old lady made room for him by her side, which kindness Duval was not slow to avail himself of, as he perceived that upon one of her plump, fat, little wrists she wore a magnificent bracelet, ornamented with diamonds and emeralds.

"Do you often thus come alone to commune with nature, my dear madam," asked Duval.

"Oh, no!" she replied. "It is seldom that I can escape from callers or company, and thus enjoy a quiet stroll in the Park. Down, Fido! down."

These last words were addressed to the dog, which, at this moment, was making frantic efforts to make friends with Duval, much to the amusement of Adele.

"Nay, do not chide the playful animal, my dear Madam," said Duval, as his hand descended simultaneously with that of the Dowager's, upon the head of her favourite.

This accident, however, was not without a corresponding result, for when Duval withdrew his hand, the beautiful bracelet he had so much admired, was no longer to be seen on the wrist of its possessor, for Duval had transferred it to his own safer keeping, without the lady being at all aware of the fact.

"I hope this will not be the last time I shall have the pleasure of meeting you here," at length he said.

"I cannot make any appointments, sir, that would indeed be indiscreet; but should we have the opportunity of renewing our acquaintance, began in so strange a manner, it will not be displeasing to me, for I flatter myself that I can read physiognomy, sir, and your face speaks much in your favour."

"I feel much flattered, and will make it my duty to deserve the compliment," replied Duval, raising the old shrivelled hand to his lips, with great gallantry.

Adele, at this moment, happened to catch Duval's eye, and the look of unmistakable glee that he there encountered was well nigh sufficient to make him lose his presence of mind.

But her aunt at that moment happened also to glance in the same direction, and a frown gathered upon her face instantly.

"Adele," she said, sternly, "take Fido, and walk him to and fro there, where I can see you. It is too warm for me to walk to-day."

Adele gave another glance at Duval, and then proceeded on her errand.

When she was gone, Mrs. Eldridge said, "I have not the pleasure of knowing your name, sir. May I inquire to whom I have the pleasure of speaking?"

"My name? Would it not be more romantic to remain in ignorance of it, think you, madam?"

"Oh, sir! certainly not. We are not to be strangers henceforth, are we?"

"I trust not. But——Allow me! There!"

These exclamations proceeded from Duval's lips, as he pretended to take a wasp from beneath the veil of the old coquette, bringing with the offender, however, a magnificent brooch.

He watched his opportunity; and soon that lay side by side with the bracelet that had at first attracted his attention.

"That is the worst of sitting beneath trees," began the dowager; "but yet it is so sweet to listen to the carols of the birds, and to contemplate nature from this sweet spot, that I cannot resist the temptation."

"I quite agree with you, madam," replied Duval. "Would that I might ever be by your side to defend you from this disagreeable though harmless insect."

But Duval had no intention of protracting the interview, now that his object was gained. He had a magnificent bracelet and brooch in his possession: surely he had no intention of flirting with that ancient piece of humanity?

Not the remotest; but he thought he should like to look again upon the beautiful girl who had been so abruptly dismissed, in order that she might not be any drawback upon the gratification which Duval's attentions were affording to her aunt.

"Allow me, madam," he said, "to fetch your niece, as I must, for the present, bid you farewell, as I have an appointment at my club in half an hour's time."

Mrs. Eldridge said something, but Duval had already gone too far to be able to hear that something distinctly.

He had a dreamy recollection of hearing something about "troublesome children—and so much trouble;" but he was too intent upon carrying out his self-imposed duty to care to listen.

He soon found himself beside Adele, who seemed anything but displeased at beholding him, for she half ran to meet him, exclaiming, "Oh, I am so glad I've seen you! You look like a real live highwayman! I have read so much about that dear, delightful Claude Duval, and how he dances with the ladies he robs, that I quite longed to see how somebody would loo' dressed just like him; and you are, for I read a description in the newspaper of his dress, and it is just like yours."

"And do you really mean to say you would like to see the real Claude Duval?" he asked, much amused by her simplicity.

"Oh, indeed, I should," she answered, clasping her hands together. "Where is he to be seen? If I could but get my aunt to come out late some night, I shouldn't be at all afraid, for I know he would not do us any harm."

"But what if he should make you fall in love with him, this same Claude Duval? For, I can tell you, I have heard he is a very dangerous fellow."

"Oh, but I am in love with him already. I don't mind telling you, because you look good-natured and kind. But, do you know, I keep a kind of journal, and I am constantly writing letters to him, just as if I knew him."

"And what becomes of these letters?" asked Duval, more and more interested in the strange girl.

"Oh, I write them in my journal, and then——"

"Well, what then?"

"I don't like to tell you."

"Oh, you need not mind telling me. Fancy I am Claude Duval."

"Oh, no, I can't do that," said Adele, shaking her head. "He is so very handsome, you know."

"And am I not handsome? But tell me what you were going to say you did, after writing these letters to Claude Duval in your journal?"

"Well, then, the next day I write an answer to my letters."

"An answer? I do not understand."

"Why, I mean that I sit down and write myself just such a letter as I fancy Claude—I never call him anything but Claude, to myself—would write to me, if he really received my letters."

"A capital plan, upon my word," said Duval. "I shall see him to-night."

"You will see him?"

As she spoke, the young girl advanced a few paces, laid her hand on his arm, and looked earnestly into his face, as she said, "Do you really know him, then?"

"Most intimately. We are like two brothers. Don't you see we dress alike?"

Adele looked at Duval with admiring eyes.

"Adele! Adele! Adele!"

"Oh, there is my cross old aunt calling, just as I was going to hear something about your dear, dear brother."

"Will you send him a message by me?"

"No."

"No? Why not?"

"Because I am sorry that I have allowed myself to talk about him to a stranger. If ever I were to meet him now, I should be——"

"Very dear to him," whispered Duval, as he possessed himself of one of the little hands.

Adele, however, snatched it quickly away, and flew on before him like a graceful young fawn, followed by Fido.

"I am no match for your niece, my dear madam," said Duval, when he reached the old coquette. "She runs like a hare."

"Highly improper behaviour. So often as I have told her to cultivate dignity in her carriage and bearing, I shall be only too glad when her cousin Adolphus takes her off my hands."

"Aunt!"

There was so much sweetness, mixed with grief and remonstrance, in the utterance of that one little word, that Duval, in spite of himself, felt deeply interested.

"I say it again: I shall be only too glad to be rid of the charge of you, for you sit and mope all alone in your room, scribbling from morning to night, and there is no doing anything with you."

"I shall never scribble any more, aunt."

There was a tone of dejection in Adele's voice which went at once to Duval's heart, who wished now to bring this scene to an end, so raising the hand of the old dowager to his lips, he said:

"Madam, I must thank you for the trust you have reposed in me, and now that I am about to take my leave of you, I will tell you that my name is Claude Duval."

With a shriek, Adele heard him pronounce the words, and but for his sustaining arms, she would have fallen to the ground.

"Be not alarmed, madam," he said, turning to Mrs. Eldridge, "I always keep about me all kinds of specifics for such emergencies as this."

As he spoke, he bore the insensible girl a pace or two from where her aunt was sitting, and, unperceived by her, pressed upon her lips and eyes such passionate kisses, mingled with such words of endearment, that at another time he would have thought himself incapable of.

Adele slowly opened her eyes, and seeing his gazing upon her, and hearing her name pronounced in accents of affection by those beloved lips, she threw her arms round his neck, and sobbed as though her heart would break.

"Poor child, poor child," murmured Duval, "I meant not to have distressed you thus. I did not think you loved me; I fancied it was a girlish freak."

The twining arms were loosened, and Adele now began to shrink from the arms in which but a moment before she had nestled in all the joyful bliss arising from the thought that the loved one is near.

"Leave me, oh leave me, and try to forget that we have ever met. Oh, why did you deceive me, and let me talk as I did? It was cruel—so cruel!"

"Why cruel, Adele? Do you think I do not love you?"

There was the quick, inquiring, upturned glance which eagerly sought his, but Duval's was averted.

Perhaps at that moment another face, another form, still dear, started up before him, and filled him with disquietude.

"No. I say no, you do not love me. False, bad man, you would have led me to believe that you loved me with a love so deep, and pure, and lasting as my own; but I know by your looks that you love me not. Perhaps you love another? Oh, heaven!"

"Adele, Adele, do not make me hate myself."

"I would make you hate yourself, even as you have made me detest and loathe myself. How dare I, foolish, vain, love-sick fool that I was—how dare I encourage a feeling that I ought to have known would end in nothing but misery insupportable?"

As she spoke, Adele wrung her hands, and rocked herself to and fro, unmindful of all surrounding circumstances, but intent only on shutting out the presence of Claude Duval.

Then she raised her head proudly, and refusing Duval's proffered aid, she rose to her feet, and approached her aunt.

"Are you ready, dear aunt?" she asked, in such an altered voice to the one her aunt was accustomed to hear, that the old lady fairly started.

"Are you well enough, child, to go home?"

"Quite well enough, aunt."

"May I trouble you then, sir, to give us your arm till we find our carriage, which is waiting at one of the gates?"

"Allow me to go in search of it, and when I have found it, I will return."

"Thank you—a thousand thanks!"

Adele and her aunt were left alone together.

"Well, now, come, cheer up, child! Quite a romance, I declare! Now, who would have thought of our meeting Claude Duval?"

A shudder, accompanied by a sigh almost resembling a groan, was all the reply.

"Come, come, you will soon be at home now. Try to get well. Should you have thought that a highwayman could be so polite and so handsome, too? I declare it will be something to talk about. I don't know what to do about inviting him to the house. I have heard that he visits the Duchess of Cleveland, the Marquis of Harcourt, and many of our highest nobility. But what is the matter, dear? Are you cold? You tremble. Lean upon me."

"Dear aunt!"

"Yes, yes. There, you will soon be well again. But here he comes. Come, come, don't let him think you can't walk without his assistance. Young men are so vain."

Adele needed but this incentive to her pride.

She drew herself up, and coldly declined Duval's arm.

The old lady, however, made up for what she considered her niece's want of courtesy; and when she was seated, she leant from her carriage, and said, with what she considered to be one of her most fascinating smiles, "I shall be most happy to improve our acquaintance, Mr. Duval. There is my card."

As she spoke, the old lady handed to Duval a card, on which were the words:—

"*The Honourable Mrs. Eldridge,*
"*7, Brooke Street.*"

The carriage drove off, leaving Duval more like a man in a dream than aught else.

"Poor girl—poor girl!" were the first words he uttered; and then, with a haggard look, thoughts of Lucy made him quicken his pace, and he sighed, "Wretch that I am! would I break my Lucy's heart?"

CHAPTER CXIX.

CLAUDE DUVAL FLIES FROM TEMPTATION.

CLAUDE DUVAL bent his steps towards the spot where he had told Blossom to wait for him.

Blossom had been too long accustomed to study the different expressions upon Duval's countenance, not to see in a moment that something unusual had happened.

But Blossom was too discreet to make any comment upon his master's haggard looks; he contented himself with merely saying, "What next, Captain? Have you had enough for one morning's work, or do you intend to do anything else?"

Duval was too deep in thought at first to hear Blossom's words, but he made an effort to put on an air of indifference.

"In good truth, Blossom, I have reason to be content with this morning's work, so far as the plunder is concerned."

"I'm glad to hear that, Captain; at all events," said Blossom, "I began to think——"

"To think what, Blossom? That I, Claude Duval, have come out in the new character of villain?"

Blossom looked petrified.

He began to entertain doubts as to Duval's soundness of mind.

"Don't talk so, Captain. For heaven's sake, what has happened?"

"Nothing—nothing! But never, as you have a regard for my feelings—never refer to this day as long as you live!"

"I give you my promise, Captain, if that will be any consolation. Perhaps, if your were to talk over what troubles you, it might not be so bad."

"It will do no good. Say no more, Blossom, about it, and I will try and be myself again."

"Then what do you say, Captain, to a little bit more business in the Park?"

"As you will; I care not to return to Lucy yet?"

Blossom was at a loss to guess the reason of Claude Duval's altered tone.

"Well, well!" he said to himself, "if it were not that I know such a thing to be impossible, I should say he had gone and fallen in love with somebody in the Park, only I know he is too fond of Miss Lucy for such a thing as that to happen. Well, well! this is a funny world we live in. I hope he'll come round after a little while, and be himself again."

At this moment Duval stepped out of the sedan chair, equipped in his clerical suit.

"Wait for me here, Blossom; methinks I shall have had some strange adventures before the day is over."

Without waiting for any reply, Duval made his way towards the broad walk, and took a seat upon one of the benches.

Scarcely had he done so, when, happening to glance around him, his eyes encountered those of the young officer named Caxton, whom he had robbed only about two hours before, fixed upon him as though endeavouring to recollect his features.

Duval began to think that his disguise was not so good as he could have wished; but it was too late to retreat—he must have recourse to other expedients.

Presently the young officer approached, and stood close beside Duval.

"Pardon me, sir," he said; "but, if I mistake not, we have met before."

"Indeed, sir," replied Duval, "it is possible, but I do not remember having seen you in my life."

"It is very strange," continued the young officer, speaking as though to himself, yet regarding Duval steadfastly,—"It is very strange, and yet I may be mistaken."

"There may be something strange in the fact, sir, that you should obtrude yourself upon me thus," said Duval; "but nothing strange in that, at some time, you may have seen me before."

"But your voice!"

"You may have heard my voice many times in the pulpit, young sir, if you are in the habit of attending divine service."

The young man made a gesture of impatience.

"Pshaw!"

Duval rose and turned as if to leave the spot; but at this instant he became aware of the fact that he was being hemmed in by at least a dozen persons.

The reader is aware that Claude Duval was great on emergencies—his presence of mind did not forsake him on this occasion.

Without appearing to notice the glances which were being directed towards him, he made towards a number of carriages which were at that moment entering the park.

His quick eye at once detected the carriage of the Duchess of Cleveland among the number.

His determination was taken on the instant.

Quickening his pace he reached the carriage, and was only too glad to find that its only occupant was the Duchess herself.

"Ah! Claude!"

His hand was on the handle of the door. He opened it and sprang in.

"Are you in danger?" she asked.

"I fear so. Say that I am a friend of yours, if you should be questioned."

"That I can with truth," she replied, as she turned and calmly surveyed the passers-by.

Duval had seen that the young officer, whose name was Caxton, was making towards the carriage.

The Duchess turned to Duval and said—

"I see young Lieutenant Caxton approaching this carriage, apparently—have you anything to fear from him?"

"Yes."

"Then, fear nothing. He knows me well, and lives only on my smiles—foolish boy! I see you are personating a clergyman," continued the Duchess, as she glanced at Duval's dress.

"Exactly. Do you know any clergyman?"

"I have as many on my list of admirers as of any other profession. I shall call you—what name shall I give you?"

Before, however, the Duchess could make up her mind as to what name she should give Claude, the young officer stood by her carriage window, and was exchanging bows and compliments.

At first, so much engrossed was he with regarding the Duchess, who was looking exceedingly beautiful, he did not perceive Duval; but, happening to cast his eyes upon him, he gave a sudden start.

"Oh! never mind, my friend, the Rev. Courtenay Evelyn, he can talk nonsense quite as fast as any of the officers in his Majesty's service."

The young officer and Duval continued to regard each other with looks of distrust.

Lieutenant Caxton was the first to speak.

"This gentleman, you say, is a friend of yours, Duchess?"

"I did say so. Is there anything extraordinary in my taking an airing in company with my friend?"

"Your friend!"

"My friend! But what ails you to-day? You echo my words like a man in a dream. Surely you are not going to be jealous?"

"Jealous? Me jealous of——"

"Take care, Henry," whispered the Duchess, "I will not have my friends insulted, and in my presence, too! I have spoilt you by according you already too many favours, I fear."

Lieutenant Caxton looked amazed, for the Duchess had never treated him to anything but her most fascinating smiles.

At that moment he forgot everything. His suspicions—his convictions that the man seated beside the Duchess was the one who had robbed him in the park only a short time since—all, everything was forgotten in the thought that the man seated in the Duchess's carriage had him at a disadvantage; for he was, as it were, sheltered by the woman he loved.

The young man made a low bow and said, in a hoarse whisper—

"I will not intrude longer, Duchess. My company, I see, can be dispensed with to-day."

As he spoke he darted a furious glance at Duval, who returned it with interest.

"Yes, Caxton—dispensed with to-day, and every day that you forget what is due from you to me," calmly replied the Duchess, as she gracefully inclined her head and ordered the coachman to drive on.

The carriage was soon in motion.

An awkward pause ensued, which was broken by the Duchess.

"And why have you avoided me since my visit to you at Farnborough House, Claude?"

The Duchess spoke with some emotion, and Claude was at a loss how to reply, for well he knew that she was thinking of those words which had fallen from his lips when her head was stung with maddening jealousy at the thought that Duval loved the Stuart Princess.

"I have been much occupied since then."

"But she—the Stuart Princess, as she called herself—she has not occupied your time and thoughts, for I heard she had left England."

"No, duchess, I have not been occupied in her affairs. I have been seeking General Everton, Lucy's—my wife's—uncle."

The Duchess made an impatient gesture.

"And is it to talk of another that you have sought me?" she asked.

"I sought you, Duchess, because I required a friend. Have I been mistaken in supposing that you claimed that title?"

"I would fain be all that you could wish to find me; but am I to understand that you refuse to accord me a dearer title?"

"Do not tempt me, I entreat of you?" cried Duval, in accents full of grief, for he was still reproaching himself—not only with causing pain and sorrow to the young and tender heart of the fair girl he had just left in the park; but also for his infidelity at least in thought, to his devoted Lucy.

There was a look of triumph in the eyes of the beautiful Duchess as she heard these words fall from his lips.

"You are afraid then of being tempted and falling a victim?"

Duval was silent.

Then she said, quickly:—

"But I had forgotten. Where do you wish to go? My carriage is at your service."

"Anywhere."

There was so much despondency in the tone in which these words were uttered, that the Duchess was touched, and laying her hand upon his arm, she said, tenderly:—

"Would it not be as well to go home with me—take a cup of coffee, and talk over your difficulties—might we not be able to find a way out of them all?"

Duval could not resist the syren's voice.

He seized her hand, which still lay on his arm, and pressing it to his lips, he said:—

"Do with me as you will. I will be led entirely by you to-day. I cannot—I dare not think for myself—much less act."

The Duchess of Cleveland was a woman of too much good sense not to see just how far she might go with impunity.

The passion—for we will not call it love—which she had conceived for Duval was fierce and uncontrollable, and she determined to lose no time or opportunity of imparting to him the same feelings that had reigned in her own breast.

So she sat silent, and contented herself with merely now and then turning her eyes to his, and caressing the hand which lay so passive in her own.

At length she reached her mansion in Park Lane and ordered coffee to be brought to her boudoir, where Duval, on a former occasion, had been a witness to the visits of both the King and the Prince of Wales, when each had so earnestly desired the life of the other.

"Now, Claude Duval," said the Duchess, gently, "you will, at least, give me credit for being silent when you have no desire to talk—and let me hope that you have something now to say to me—now that we are alone, and you free from danger."

"Yes, free from danger—but believe me, Duchess, the danger from which you rescued me was not nearly so painful to me as the one which new threatens me?"

"Danger?—danger threatens you now? What mean you, Claude Duval—dear Claude—speak and tell me what you fear?"

As she spoke, the Duchess drew nearer to him, and

DUVAL EXCITES THE JEALOUSY OF THE DUCHESS OF KINGSTON.

apparently unconsciously, half embraced him with her arms.

"The danger of loving you!"

There was a shining light in the eyes of Claude Duval as he gazed upon the beautiful woman half kneeling by his side, and yet he did not love the Duchess at that moment; but he seemed impelled against his will, to do and say things from which at another time he would have shrunk in horror.

"And is that danger, as you call it, so much to be dreaded?" asked the Duchess. "Do you know, Claude Duval, I have never asked before for any one's affection, and am I to be spurned—shrunk from now?"

As she spoke the Duchess rose to her feet in all her majestic beauty, and stood some paces off, as if awaiting Duval's answer.

"Speak again!" she cried. "Do you spurn the love of one who has never loved before; or will you accept that love, and make me the happiest of women. Speak, Claude Duval, for your silence kills me?"

No. 39.—NIGHTSHADE.

"Live: Live! For this heart bids you live to comfort what, but for your affection, must be indeed a dark and dreary life."

"Yours—yours for ever!"

As he pressed her to his heart Duval, in the frenzy of that moment, forgot all that had made life bright and beautiful. Lucy was forgotten!

But forgotten only for a moment. It was not in the nature of a man like Duval long to be oblivious of a love so pure, unselfish, and devoted as hers had been, and would continue to be as long as life lasted.

He gently withdrew from the embrace of the Duchess, and retreated backwards until he reached the door.

The Duchess looked at him bewildered. A minute before, and she believed that he was all her own—but what was she to think now?

"What mean you by this behaviour?" she asked. "Do you mock me?"

"Alas!"

"Do you not love me, then?"

"My love has been long since given to another, and I hate myself to think that in a moment of weakness I have caused you pain."

The Duchess raised herself to her full height.

"You shall repent of this conduct, Claude Duval," she said, "as surely as you are a living man. Nay, let me not hear the tones of your voice again—that voice which only a few short minutes ago, bid me rise to comfort you; and when you, in all the power of your man's vanity and pride, believed this heart all your own, you must need trample upon it, and probably go away and smile at the weakness of the Duchess of Cleveland."

She paused, overcome by her own emotions.

Again Duval made a step towards her, but again she repelled him.

"Hear me—at least, hear from my lips, that I had no intention of paining you."

"No intention of paining me? Ha! ha! ha! Go! Leave me, Claude Duval, or you may not find it so good a thing to have me for an enemy as for a friend."

As she spoke, the Duchess pushed open a door, and left Duval to take his departure.

CHAPTER CXX.

CLAUDE DUVAL MEETS WITH AN ADVENTURE.

"AH, Claude! how jaded you look," were the words with which Lucy greeted Duval, after his adventures in the Park, on the eventful day with which we closed our last chapter.

"I am tired, I believe," he replied; but he did not meet her eyes, as was his wont, for he felt at that moment that he deserved not the devotion of such a heart as hers.

"Rest, dear, rest, and I will get you a cup of coffee, and then we will have a nice long evening, for my uncle has not told me half he has to say."

"Ah! I had almost forgotten him, Lucy dear, in the pleasure of seeing you. How is your uncle, and where is he?"

"He is quite well, dear, and has only just stepped out for a walk on the heath. He promised to be back about this time, and—here he is. See, Claude?"

At this moment General Everton could be seen approaching the house, and Claude Duval was struck with the improvement which had already taken place in his appearance.

"Ah, my young friend," he exclaimed, as Duval stepped forward to meet him. "I am so glad you have returned. Lucy has been telling me how happy you have made her, and I was anxious to thank you from my heart—but what is this?—you turn pale, and avoid my gaze."

"Oh, it is nothing, dear uncle," said Lucy, taking Duval's hand, and pressing it to her lips, "it is nothing, Claude is tired, and needs rest."

But General Everton still regarded Duval narrowly. At length he said, "I trust that I am not mistaken, sir, and that you do really love my Lucy."

"Heaven knows I love her only too well."

As he spoke, he let his head drop upon his hands, and a deep groan burst from his lips.

"Then what means this strange conduct? Speak and tell me, am I to think that; no, no, I will not believe it. My Lucy is your wife."

"My true and loving wife. Let me beg that you will not question me further."

"Well, be it so, then. I will believe you, sir, for I think she believes that you love her as dearly as she loves you."

General Everton spoke slowly and clearly, and without giving Claude an opportunity of replying to him, he quitted the room, and Duval was left alone.

"Oh! of what was I thinking?" he said to himself, as he paced the apartment to and fro—"of what could I be thinking to be induced to forget my Lucy even for a moment?"

"And for a woman no more to be put in competition with her than day is to night. Fool, fool! vain fool that I was! When shall I feel myself again, I wonder?"

"In a quarter of an hour from this time," said Lucy, who happened to enter the room at this moment, heard Duval's the concluding words.

He turned quickly, but one glance at her face convinced him that she had not heard more than he could have wished.

"Are you there, dear Lucy? I see you have brought the coffee. Set it down—I will take it presently."

"No, Claude."

"No, Claude? What do you mean?"

"I mean that I shall not set it down, and that you will not take it presently; for I intend to make you take it at once, and to remain with you while you drink it, in order to watch the effect of my prescription."

Poor Lucy was in her highest spirits, and it was fortunate that it was so, or she might have perceived that something else was the matter with Duval besides being tired.

"As you will, Lucy, dear," he replied, trying hard to assume the same tone of badinage. "I suppose I must do as I am told, or you will cease to love me."

"Oh, Claude!"

It was all Lucy could say. She turned pale, and hastily placed the cup on the table by her side, for his words had made her tremble.

"Why, what is it, you little goose?" asked Duval. "Surely you do not suppose that I think you ever will cease to love me."

"No, Claude; of course you do not think that could be possible; but it sounded—oh, so terrible! Even in jest such words should never pass our lips."

As Lucy spoke she leant her head against Claude's shoulder, and tears fell from her eyes, which but a moment before had been dancing in glee and merriment.

"It was foolish and thoughtless, dear one," he replied; "but I did not think you would take it so much in earnest. Come, cheer up!"

"Ah, Claude, you never—do not—cannot understand love as we women do. If I thought that you could for one moment fancy you loved another, however much I might feel convinced to the contrary, the thought that you had at some time forgotten me would break my heart, I think."

"And make you hate me, Lucy?"

"No, no, Claude; I could never love you less, but I should hate life and light, and seek refuge in the dark grave."

As she spoke she twined her arms about him, and

Duval felt then that the resolution he had taken to tell her all, and ask her forgiveness was not a wise one.

"Fear not—fear not, my Lucy. Be ever gentle, tender, and loving, as you are, and I shall never stray from you."

At that moment Claude Duval felt that he was strong, and could promise anything to the fair being who regarded him as her idol.

It was not long that one with so sunny a disposition as Lucy possessed should give way to an imaginary sorrow, and one which in her pure devoted confidence believed the slightest word spoken by her husband to be truth itself, was soon able to throw off every trace of sorrow, so that when next she looked into Claude's eyes he read nothing in their depths but love and confidence unbounded.

"Lucy," said Claude, after a pause, "shall you think me very exacting if I ask permission to go on the road to-night?"

"To-night, dear Claude? Have you not had enough adventure to-day? Stay at home to-night."

"Do not urge me, Lucy, to refrain from going to-night. I feel restless, and a good gallop on the back of Nightshade will put me all right."

"Go, then, Claude. I promised not to thwart you, whatever my feelings in the matter might be."

"And you will not be alone, either, dear."

"No; my uncle is with me, but his society does not make up for the loss of yours, you know."

"Flatterer!" exclaimed Claude, gazing fondly at her. "Then to-night, at nine o'clock, I shall leave you, dear; and rest assured I will get into no unnecessary danger."

"I trust not, Claude. Would that you were less adventurous!"

"It cannot be helped, Lucy; but if I were less courageous I should be in greater danger. Believe me, it is audacity that gets the better of danger in the sort of life I lead."

"I believe it is. But here comes my uncle."

General Everton glanced at Duval, but seeing Lucy smiling and content, he was only too glad to believe that his suspicions had been erroneous with regard to Duval.

But the fact is, the old General was a man of the world, and was nearer guessing the truth than he, Claude, suspected.

"Your niece, General, has just given her consent that I should try what fortune has in store for me to-night, on road and heath," said Duval; "and seeing that I leave her in your company, I am doubly anxious to avail myself of the opportunity which offers."

The old General did not seem exactly at his ease, and yet, after all that Duval had risked for his sake, was fully appreciated, he almost accused himself of ingratitude towards the man who had more than saved his life.

Blossom had watched Duval enter the Duchess of Cleveland's carriage, and as he recognised it, he felt quite certain in his own mind that there would be no occasion for him and his companion to wait about in the park any longer.

"Gray," he said, to the man who was with him, "we need not stay here any longer; we had better make good our retreat while we may, for we may attract notice."

"All right!"

So it was that Blossom was at home in time to hear Duval's determination of going on the road that night.

"I am glad to hear it, Captain," he said; "for it was neither one thing nor the other to-day in the park. Did you get much plunder, Captain?"

"Much more than I expected, Blossom; so you must not be dissatisfied."

"Not I, Captain! so long as it brings grist to the mill, it matters not what sort of adventure it is. What time shall you start, Captain?"

"Be ready with Nightshade at nine o'clock."

"All right, Captain!"

At the hour named, Duval and Bolssom, well mounted, started, and took their way towards the Oxford Road.

"What do you mean to do, Captain? Rob the mail?" asked Blossom.

"If nothing better offers itself," replied Duval. "I'm with you at any rate."

Duval and Blossom separated, and stationed themselves on each side of the road.

They had not long to wait before the sound of wheels was heard coming at a swinging pace down the road.

"Here's a chance, Captain," whispered Blossom.

"Is it the coach?"

"No, I think not; but I cannot see until it gets to the top of the hill."

The vehicle had no sooner reached the summit of the hill, than, crash! crash! bang! came to the ears of Duval and Blossom.

"A spill, as sure as I'm alive," cried Blossom; "let us push on, Captain, and see what's the matter."

Duval and Blossom put their horses to a gallop, and soon came up with the shattered vehicle.

"Halloa! coachman," shouted Duval; "what's the matter here?"

There was no answer to his enquiry.

Duval, with a spring, was by the side of the coach in a moment, which was lying on its side, while the horses were kicking furiously.

"Here, Blossom, lend a hand," said Duval; "let us right the carriage, and make these creatures stand on their legs again, and then we shall know what to do."

It did not take long, for two men, so accustomed, as Duval and Blossom were to horses, to restore them to something like tranquility, after having done which, the former proceeded to reconnoitre the persons inside the coach.

All was so still, that at first Duval began to think the carriage was empty, until happening to throw the rays of light which came from one of the carriage lamps, about in every direction, he distinctly saw the prostrate form of a man, clutching a small valise.

At first Duval thought the man must be seriously hurt, as he made no effort to stir; but thinking probably that he was alone, the prostrate man held up his head, and gazed about him, as he muttered to himself—

"All right—all safe, so far—the gold—the jewels, are all safe within this little leather receptacle, while I am in reality the richest men in London."

"Don't be too sure of that, friend," said Duval, stepping up to the man, who clutched convulsively at the valise; "there are two words to be said to that bargain. Do you not know who I am?"

"Good gracious, me! I think I do—I fancy I have the pleasure, no—yes, the pleasure of conversing with ——"

"A highwayman!" interrupted Duval, as he leapt from Nightshade's back on to the ground, and strode up to the prostrate figure.

"What is there in this valise?" he asked of the crouching figure.

"Oh, nothing—nothing, sir! but merely a change of linen. I am on my road—or rather I'd say, I was on my road to visit my sister; and as I thought I should like to look nice— -"

"There, that's quite enough," replied Duval; "tell me who was in the coach beside you?"

"Oh, only my cousin, who is going to be married next week to Grace Ireton."

"Indeed! Then I don't think I need detain you

any longer, for you have a long job before you, if you intend to mend the chaise in order to proceed to town to night."

"Oh! I shall leave my cousin Pendell to do that. I intend to walk, good sir, if you will give me a hand to raise my valise on to my shoulders."

"What did you say your cousin's name is?" asked Duval.

"Pendell, sir—Mossy Pendell! A strange name, is it not, sir?"

As he spoke, the man scrambled to his feet, but Duval soon made him crouch down lower than ever, as he pointed a pistol just between his eyes.

"Attempt to move from this spot until I give you permission to do so, and you are a dead man

"Yes, yes—I mean no!—that is—oh, Lor', oh Lor'! what will become of me?"

"Nothing at all, if you obey my orders."

"Anything you please sir, certainly."

"Well then, call out to Mossy Pendell, and tell him where you are.

"But, to tell you the truth, sir, I would much rather be alone than in his company; for you see, sir, a man that talks to himself in such a fashion as Mossy Pendell has taken to do of late, is sure to bring bad luck wherever he is."

"Do as I tell you," said Duval, in a low tone, still keeping the barrel of the pistol in uncomfortable proximity to his listener's eyes.

"There—there! pray take that thing away, sir. Suppose it were to go off, now? A pretty sight I should be!"

"Yes, certainly!" replied Duval; "such a sight that your dearest friend would not care to look upon you again; for your brains would be scattered to the winds."

The teeth of the man chattered audibly as he thus temporised with Claude Duval.

"Now, then, call to Mossy Pendell, I say, and make haste, or I will first blow your brains out, and then I will call to him myself."

"I'll do it!—oh, I'll do it! But be merciful to me, if you please, sir; for I am willing to do whatever you tell me."

"Show your willingness, then, by doing as I bid," said Duval.

As he spoke, he allowed the cold barrel to touch the man's forehead.

"Oh, Lor! oh, Lor! Mossy Pendell! Mossy Pendell! A gentl——"

"Silence! Who told you to say a gentleman wanted him? I wish you to tell him that you are quite alone and unhurt."

"Yes, sir! Mossy Pendell!"

"Hold your confounded tongue, or it will be the worse for you," roared Mossy Pendell, in his own unmistakable voice. "Hold your confounded tongue, and don't be shouting out my name in that fashion, or I shall be tempted to silence you for ever. Where are you?"

"Here, close to the hedge."

"Then why don't you come here when you know we must contrive to get this confounded chaise to rights, or we shall never be able to keep our appointment."

"Lie where you are," whispered Duval; "and you, Blossom, see that he does not escape."

"All right, Captain!" said Blossom, in the same low tone.

Duval then strode up to Mossy Pendell.

"At length, villain," he shouted, "we have met for the last time. Do you not know me?"

Mossy Pendell gave a half shriek.

"Cries and shrieks will avail you nothing now, wretch that you are! This night is your last on earth!"

"But what if I make a full confession, Claude Duval, and tell you all—you would not wish to murder me?"

"I want no confession now, it is retribution only that I seek—revenge only that will satisfy me. Rise, villain, rise, or you will tempt me to fire at you as if you were a dog. Your life, villain, I say—your life alone must expiate your crimes!"

"Be it so, then," said Pendell, as a ghastly smile passed over his face, and he slowly rose to his feet.

CHAPTER CXXI.

DUVAL ROBS THE OXFORD MAIL.

CLAUDE DUVAL stood only a couple of paces from Pendell when the latter rose to his feet.

"Now, Mossy Pendell, draw at once, or I will soon make an end of this encounter by running you through with my sword."

"Have at you, then," shouted Pendell, "since you will have it!"

As he spoke, he made a sudden rush at Duval, and it required all his skill to parry the blow.

The fight became furious; but each succeeded in defending himself against his adversary for some time, and then Duval made a lunge at Mossy Pendell, which seemed as though it would prove fatal, for his sword-arm dropped powerlessly by his side, and he gradually sunk to the ground.

"You have killed me!" he gasped.

"And cheated the gallows!" replied Duval.

"The gallows—the gallows? Who talks of the gallows? I tell you she did not die on the scaffold! No, no, that, at least, is not on my conscience! Claude Duval, you know you saved her! Help, help! I am dying!"

Mossy Pendell rolled over and over, clutching at the very stones on the roadway.

Duval looked on calmly.

More calmly than he could have believed it possible; but the man before him had stained his soul by so many crimes that he, Duval, felt that he had in reality done society a benefit by ridding the world of such a monster.

He sheathed his sword, and then he walked up to Blossom, who was still keeping guard over the man who was grasping the valise with both hands in a most frantic manner.

"This is my property!" said Duval, as he stooped down and possessed himself of the little leathern receptacle.

"No, no! It is mine—mine! It contains nothing but——"

"Peace, I say!" cried Duval. "Blossom, follow me, and bring the valise with you."

"All right!" said Blossom. "But what am I to do with this fellow, Captain?"

"I care not! Leave him where he is!"

"Yes, sir," whined the man, "if you please, sir, leave me where I am."

"Not until I have made you a little more secure!" replied Blossom; "and another time you will know better than to attempt to kick and scratch as you have done to-night."

As Blossom spoke, he dexterously made the man incapable of further action, by pinioning his hands behind his back, and then tying him to a tree.

"There, Captain, I think that will do! Now I'm ready! What's to be the next job?"

"I don't exactly know; but I think I hear the mail coach coming down the hill. Suppose we stop that, Blossom?"

"I'm your man, Captain!"

"Then let us stand aside under the shadow of the trees, Blossom, and we will see what we can make in the shape of plunder."

The sound of the coach wheels came nearer and nearer.

At length it passed close to Duval and Blossom.

They each came out of their hiding-place, and stationed themselves on either side of the road.

"Halt!" shouted Duval.

The coachman almost rolled off his box with fear.

"Halt!" echoed Blossom, as he, following the example of Duval, presented a pistol full in the face of the driver.

"Hold hard, there! Who are you?" he gasped.

"Don't ask any questions! Be quiet, and you have nothing to fear!"

"Oh, lor—oh, lor! he's a highwayman!"

"Exactly!" replied Duval. "And now I cry, stand and deliver!"

Duval rode round to one of the doors of the coach, and, putting his hand, in which was a pistol, he was received with various expressions of terror, according to the character of its inhabitants.

"Murder!"

"Thieves!"

"Oh, what will become of me!"

"I'm not afraid of a highwayman, just because I've nothing to lose!"

"How can you tell such a tale when you know you have that cask——"

"Hush! It isn't true, Mr. Highwayman!"

"Settle it amongst yourselves, ladies and gentlemen!" replied Duval, "so that you do not keep me waiting here much longer, or I shall be obliged to discharge this pistol and help myself—whereas, I am quite willing to receive your property from your hands without making any noise!"

"Exactly, sir! That old lady in the corner, sir, has, I believe, quite enough to ransom us all out and out!"

"You wretch!"

"Don't quarrel, I beg!" replied Duval, calmly. "I will begin with you, madam, first, as you seem to be a lady, and a young one, too!"

The old lady looked somewhat mollified, as she said, "Really, I was never in company with a highwayman before, and I thought they were a set of ruffians; but I find that they can behave like gentlemen."

"I am a gentleman, madam. Would you like to know my name?"

"I think I can guess it; for I have heard that Claude Duval is handsome—hem! I don't mean to say handsome—but——"

"Never mind what you have heard, madam. Claude Duval has the honour, now, of addressing a beautiful woman."

"Really, he does say beautiful things!" said the old lady, glancing triumphantly at a female to whom she did not appear to be particularly gracious. "There, sir, is my card-case; it is silver, and was given to me by one who—who——"

As the old lady spoke, she looked almost tenderly at the handsome card-case she tendered to Duval.

"And you value it for the giver's sake, I suppose?" he asked.

"Yes. But perhaps it is better to part with it to you, than leave it to strangers when I die, for I have no one to care for me now!"

"Keep it then, madam," replied Duval; "and when you make your will, do not forget to bequeath this card-case to Claude Duval."

"Thank you—thank you! But you shall have this bracelet. It is only fair that I should pay 'toll.' That is what you gentlemen of the road call this sort of thing, is it not?"

As she spoke, the old lady laughed merrily; and Duval could scarcely find it in his heart to accept anything from her, but a second glance convinced him that she could well afford to part with some of her beautiful jewellery, so he took it gracefully, and bowing, said, "This, madam, will never leave my possession. I shall retain it as a remembrance of the most interesting robbery I have ever committed."

"Now, sir!"

As he spoke, Duval suddenly brought down his hand with such force upon the sill of the coach window, that the gentleman whom he addressed jumped nearly off the seat, to the great amusement of the old lady.

"Oh, dear me! I am suffering from an attack upon the nerves, and you have nearly frightened me to death! I told you just now, sir, that I had nothing—literally nothing."

As he spoke, he dived his hand into one of his pockets, and brought out a latch-key.

"Here is a very useful article to some people, now; but I doubt whether you will care to have it."

"No nonsense, sir, if you please," said Duval. "I want that casket you have."

"Me?"

"Yes, you. Hand it out directly!"

"Not true, sir—not true. I tell you I have nothing but this latch-key, and just enough money to pay my fare."

"Very well; we will pass by you for awhile, and in the meantime you will oblige me, madam, by handing over your purse."

"Yes, sir, that is right," cried the gentleman whom Claude had "passed by," for a time,—"that's it. I have no doubt there is a good round sum in it, for she told me she had just received her rents from her agent."

"Now, then, madam!" said Duval.

The purse was duly handed to him.

"Take it, thief that you are! I'll expose your conduct as soon as ever I get to town!"

"Now, sir, it is your turn," said Duval, addressing a jovial-looking old gentleman, who had not uttered a word all the time. "Now, sir, be quick, for I have already lost too much time."

"Then you had better take your leave at once."

"When I please; but your watch and rings, sir—and be quick."

"You are an impudent, but not a bad fellow, so take my pocket-book and be content."

"Your rings, sir."

"I have only this mourning one."

"But there is a diamond of some value in it."

"There is. But I would fain redeem it at some future time, if you will allow me."

"Agreed," said Duval.

The gentleman drew the ring from his finger, and as he gave it to Duval, he said—

"Take it, sir. I will trust to you."

"You may do so, I assure you."

The rest of the passengers each handed to Duval something of value, and then he turned from the coach, raising his hat, he said—

"Good evening, ladies and gentlemen. I will detain you no longer."

The gentleman who found that he had escaped, laughed hoarsely, as he said—

"Well, this is a rich joke, to think that you should be robbed of your valuables, while I, who in reality, possess sufficient in this little casket, to buy you and the coach and horses all up in a heap; are allowed to go scot free."

"Take care—take care," said the old gentleman; "it is not too late yet; perhaps he may return."

"Not at all likely," I should say. "Hilloa, coachman, drive on as quickly as you can!"

"All right, sir! Has any one been robbed?"

"Everybody!" cried several voices.

"Except me," said the man who had escaped; 'and it was all owing to my good management."

Again the coach started.

While this little parley and congratulation was going on between the passengers of the coach, Claude Duval was not idle.

He made a sign to Blossom.

"Here you are, Captain."

"There is a man in that coach with a casket of jewels."

"Then let us have them in our possession, Captain, for we can do with them."

"Yes, Blossom."

"But the coach is off."

"I see it is. We must stop it again."

"All right, Captain!"

In a moment Duval and Blossom had made their horses leap the hedge, and in much less time than it took the coach to travel, they reached a dark part of the lane, through which it was forced to pass.

"Quick, Blossom, the rope!"

"There you are, Captain!"

With Blossom's assistance Duval attached it to a stake in the hedge, then, throwing the other end to Blossom, he said, "Quick, Blossom, make the other end fast, and the coach will be effectually stopped without our interference."

"I see—I see, Captain! You mean to stretch the rope across the road?"

"Yes."

"It's as good as done, Captain."

In less than five minutes Duval was waiting for the coach.

Slowly it wound up the hill, and, as a natural consequence, no sooner had the leading horses come to the rope, than they stumbled and fell.

"Woa! woa! Confound it! there is something in the road!"

The coachman rolled off the box, and went to the horses' heads.

"I don't care for nothing but highwaymen," he said, speaking as much to himself as to any one who might be listening; "but hang me if they don't make me all of a tremble, them sort of gentry, for you never knows whether they ain't a-goin' to blow your brains out. Ah! Oh! Murder! It's one of them!"

"If you open your lips you are a dead man! for I am a desperate man!" cried Blossom, as he held the coachman by the throat.

"Yes, yes, I see! Oh, I won't speak! Don't fear me, dear Mr. Highwayman; only don't strangle me, that's all!"

"Tell your passengers that all is right!"

"Yes, Mr. Highwayman, if you please. Oh, lor! oh, lor! if it only was all right, how glad I should be!"

"Do as I tell you!"

"Yes, sir—yes, sir!"

The coachman went to one of the windows, and, putting his head in, whispered, "Don't be alarmed, gents and ladies, it's all right—only the 'osses has fallen down, that's all! You didn't think it was another highwayman? Ha, ha, ha! What a joke if it had been!"

"It might have been a joke for you, you idiot," growled the man with the casket; "but not for us who have anything to lose. Why didn't you mind your horses, eh? Are respectable people's lives to be endangered because you can't drive, I should like to know? Get up on the box, I say and drive away as fast as you can, or I'll do so myself!"

"Yes, sir—directly, sir! Only I thought you would be——"

The coachman was prevented from indulging either in self-justification, or in endeavouring to console his passengers, for at that moment Duval laid a hand on his shoulder, and dragged him to the horses' heads.

"Give me your coat."

"My—my coat?"

"Yes, your coat. Do I not speak plainly?"

"But——"

"Do not trifle away valuable time, if you have any regard for your wife and family."

"Well, I can't say as Mrs. Wiggins is the best of tempers, Mr. Highwayman; but nevertheless, England, you see, expects every man to do his duty."

"Cease your foolery, and give me your coat."

"Yes, sir."

The coachman divested himself of his coat as quickly as even Claude Duval could wish.

Duval put it on.

"Now, your hat!"

"Oh, but——"

"Now, your hat!" repeated Duval, as he made a sign as though he intended again to sieze the unfortunate coachman by the throat.

"Yes, sir, here it is; but perhaps——"

"Now, then, give me that neck-handkerchief you wear, and my dress will be complete."

"Mercy on us! if he isn't a going for to act a coachman. Oh, lord! What will become of us?"

"Now, then, out of the way! Here, Blossom!"

"Here you are, Captain!"

"Just dispose of this fellow, so as to make it impossible for him to interrupt us."

"Oh, no fear, sir, if so be you'll just make it known as I had no hand in the affair."

"That depends upon your own discretion. Now, stand aside."

"Yes, sir."

Duval whispered a few words to Blossom, and then, having seen that the horses were all right, he mounted the box.

Before, however, he set the coach in motion, a head was projected from one of the windows.

"I say, coachman, whatever is this all about? Do you intend us to get to town to-night or not?"

"I hope so," replied Duval, in a feigned voice; "but the fact is, it was another highwayman, who was going to attack you all, only I've given him something to remember for a short time, at all events."

"Another highwayman! I dare say now it was the same one come back for my casket. But I'm in luck's way to-night, coachman. Would you believe I was fortunate enough to persuade him I had nothing, when in reality I had in my possession ten thousand pounds' worth of jewellery of one and another."

"Glad to hear it," replied Duval, assuming the voice of the coachman.

"Glad to hear it! Glad to hear what? The man must be drunk."

"Glad to hear you were fortunate enough not to lose it, that's all, sir," replied Duval, as he put the horses to a gallop.

CHAPTER CXXII.

CLAUDE DUVAL ATTACKED BY A HIGHWAYMAN.

SUDDENLY Duval pulled up.

"Well, what now?" asked the man with the casket.

"Nothing; only I thought I heard a horse's feet."

"Well, what if you do? Why don't you go on?"

"Another highwayman, by Jove!" said Duval, as he perceived and recognised Blossom.

"Stand and deliver!" shouted Blossom.

The man with the casket rolled off the seat.

"Now, then, sir," said Blossom, opening the door of the coach—"now, then, sir, I have just parted from Claude Duval, and he told me he had left me my share of the plunder, for that I was to claim for my share the casket of jewellery you have. So give it me at once, if you please."

"I'm glad of that," shouted the lady, who had been so piqued at being obliged to surrender her purse—"I'm glad of that. I thought your boasting would come to nothing."

"Are you glad of it? I'm sorry for you, for your joy will be but of short duration; for I say to you, sir, as I said to that other scoundrel, that I have nothing but a latch-key, and just enough money to pay my fare."

"Then I will just look for myself," said Blossom; "and if I do find it, mind, I'll blow your brains out for trying to deceive me."

"Oh, dear! oh, dear! was ever anything so unfortunate? Here, take it, and welcome."

As he spoke, the jeweller, for such he appeared to be, handed to Blossom the casket, having, however, previously taken from it much of the jewellery it had contained.

"That's right," said Blossom; "but as I do not think you look quite like an honest man——"

"Sir!"

"But as I do not think you look quite like an honest man," repeated Blossom, "I shall take the liberty of examining this casket. Ah! It is as I supposed—some of the jewellery is gone."

"That is all I had."

"It isn't—it isn't!" cried the old lady, who had made such a favourable impression upon Claude. "He has done nothing but call Claude Duval the worst names he could lay his tongue to, and then he took out of the casket no end of rings and watches, and hid them away in all sorts of out-of-the-way pockets, in order, he said, that no highwayman should be able to find them, let them search ever so closely."

"Did he say so? Thank you, madam. Now, sir, if I must take them for myself, I will begin at once."

Blossom made no more ado, but, in another second, he had dragged the unfortunate man out of the coach, and was quietly rifling all his pockets, having first, in a most scientific manner, secured his hands behind his back.

By this means it became quite an easy matter to possess himself of everything that was valuable about the person of the refractory jeweller.

"Now, then, sir," said Blossom, "as I do not consider you a gentleman for giving me so much trouble, I shall not allow you to take your place amongst this respectable company, so stay there until some one passes who may be willing to release you."

"Drive on, coachman," said Blossom.

Crack! went the whip, and off started the coach, but scarcely had it gone a couple of miles, when a mounted man sprung out of a thick-set hedge, and, levelling a pistol full at Duval's head, cried out, in a clear ringing voice—

"Halt!"

"A highwayman, by Jove," said Blossom, in a whisper to Duval; "what shall we do? Show fight?"

"Leave him to me. If I mistake not, I recognise his mare—it is none other than Black Bess."

"And her master is Dick Turpin."

"Exactly, Blossom."

While these few words were passing between Duval and Blossom, Turpin—for it was, indeed, none other—rode to the side of the coach, and cried out—

"Your money or your lives—which you please. If I take your lives, why I have both, for I shall help myself after I have shot all, every one, so be quick and decide. Coachman!"

Duval took not the slightest notice of the tone of command which Turpin assumed.

"Coachman!"

Still no reply.

"You won't answer, won't you?" cried Turpin. "I'll soon find means of making you."

As he spoke, Turpin spurred his mare up to the side of Duval, and, presenting a pistol close to his eyes, said—

"Now, will you answer me?"

"Not while you act like a madman."

"What do you mean?"

"By robbing, or trying to rob a coach which has already undergone that little process."

"What?"

"Claude Duval has been here already."

"Nonsense."

"But I say he has!"

"And robbed the passengers?"

"Every one."

"How did he succeed?"

"By audacity and courage."

"And you speak well of him?"

"I ought to do so."

"Because he spared your worthless life, I suppose."

"Well, not exactly."

"Speak plainly."

"I will. Finding that one of the passengers would not deliver to him a certain casket he had in his possession, he resolved to make the coachman dismount from his box and take his place."

"As coachman?"

"Yes."

"And you are Claude Duval?"

"I am."

"Hurrah! I'm glad we have met. And, then, there is no business to be done here?"

"I think not. Hush! what was that?"

A noise as of a number of persons making their way through the hedge attracted the attention of both Duval and Dick Turpin, and, in another moment Duval recognised the voice of Muckles the officer.

"Now, then, my men. Be brave and resolute, and we shall make a good capture to-night."

"Ah!" said Turpin, "I must make a bold leap, or I am lost. Claude Duval, your disguise is complete—they will never know you. Try to put them on a wrong scent, if you can."

"All right."

There was no time to say more, for at that moment Muckles and four of his men rode up to Turpin.

"Black Bess! Black Bess! It's Dick Turpin after all, and not Claude Duval! But never mind, seize him! Seize him! A hundred pounds reward to whoever secures Dick Turpin!"

"Done brown again, Mr. Muckles," Duval heard Swallow say, "you told us we were going to take Claude Duval."

"Fool! Idiot! What if I did? Never mind as long as we take somebody! Now, Mr. Turpin, I beg to inform you that your career is at an end. Surrender, or it will be the worse for you."

"Not if I know it," was the reply, and with one desperate leap Black Bess was past the little group.

"It's no manner of use, sir," said Duval, in a feigned voice. "That fellow will never be taken alive. They do say as his mare Black Bess, as they call her, is possessed."

Muckles made a bounce and shouted, and, whether

it was that the mare which Turpin rode was nervous or made a false step, was not certain; but, in trying to leap the hedge, she stumbled and fell, of course, bringing Dick along with her.

In an instant, and with a shout of triumph, Muckles and his men rushed forward.

"Give in Turpin—it's of no use fighting against five men," cried, Muckles, "we came here to capture a highwayman, and, although you are not exactly the one we wanted, still you are better than nobody, so just get up and come along with us."

"It's a done job this time I think," said Turpin; "but lead the way, I'm ready."

Muckles now gave directions to some of his men to secure Turpin, which they did by fastening his hands behind him, and then placing him upon his own mare, were about to leave the spot, when Muckles addressed Duval:—

"Coachman."

"Yes, sir."

"Have you seen Claude Duval to-night?"

"Yes: and he's robbed us of every farthing."

"Which way did he go?"

"He went towards London I fancy."

"How was he dressed?"

"In his scarlet coat and horseman's boots."

"That'll do. We may not now be too late. Forward my men."

Muckles and his men, with their prisoner, Dick Turpin, put their horses to a gallop, and Duval soon found himself alone in charge of the coach.

"Blossom, where are you?"

"Here, Captain."

"Is Nightshade all right?"

"Yes, Captain."

"Then I will mount and leave the coach to take care of itself, for it seems to me that we have got as much out of this adventure as we can hope for."

"I think so, Captain. This casket seems a tidy little bit of plunder. I don't know what else you got out of the coach, Captain?"

"Quite sufficient, Blossom, to repay me for the risk I ran. I'm sorry for Turpin; but I could not see any way of helping him."

"Because there was none, Captain: except at the risk of your own life; and, after all, I don't think he's worth throwing that away upon."

"Still, I sorry for him, Blossom."

"That may be; but don't let us waste any more time here, Captain. There's no telling what that fellow Muckles may not take it in his head to do."

"True, Blossom. Let us go."

Duval and Blossom now mounted their horses and galloped down the road, leaving the coach and passengers to themselves.

It is not to be supposed that those passengers left apparently to themselves would long remain inactive.

The jovial old gentleman, after sitting quietly smiling, and pondering in his own mind over the events which had taken place at length spoke:—

"I wonder how much longer we are supposed to be obliged to sit here looking at each other. Where, in the name of wonder, can the coachman be?"

The old gentleman put his head out of the window to reconnoitre.

All was still.

All was dark.

"I can see nothing," he said, addressing his companions; "but hark, what is that?"

Most unmistakably upon the night air there came cries of distress from a little distance.

"It sounds like a man in distress."

"Help! Help! I'm the driver of the Oxford Mail. I am bound hand and foot, and cannot use my limbs. Help! Help!"

"Why, its our own coachman most likely," said one of the ladies; "who'll go and see?"

"Not I, in faith," said the jeweller, who had managed to get into the coach again. "That fellow gave me such a blow on the back of the head that I feel as though I had no senses left."

"I will go and see," said the old gentleman who had just spoken.

He had not been gone many minutes before he returned, bringing with him the veritable coachman whom, it will be remembered, Claude Duval had displaced.

"Now, then, you are a man again," said the jovial old gentleman as he gave the coachman a push. "Get on the box and drive as fast as you can, for I am heartily tired of this night's adventure."

Nothing loath, the man mounted his box, and once more the Oxford Mail was in motion.

But Claude Duval's adventures for that night were not at an end.

He and Blossom had not gone very far before their attention was directed towards a tall house in the distance.

A strange effect was produced by the reflection of a bright red light, which seemed to move from window to window, without the slightest interruption apparently, which the opening of different doors must have produced; but the light seemed, so to speak, to glide stealthily up and down the whole front of the house, as though it had been a beacon out at sea, and had been placed there for the purpose of guiding to the land those who happened to be out at sea.

"That looks strange, Captain," said Blossom.

"It does, and I feel very much inclined to see what it really is."

"Oh, I wouldn't I interfere with it, Captain," said Blossom, still having a vived recollection of what passed at the lonely house, when he had had so narrow an escape of his life.

"You wait for me here, Blossom, and I will pursue this adventure by myself, but be within call of my whistle, and if I blow twice upon it, you will know that I am in danger, and want Nightshade."

"All right," Captain.

Duval dismounted, and pursued his way on foot towards the deserted-looking mansion, which presented so strange an appearance.

But by this time the light had disappeared, and Duval was enveloped in perfect darkness.

While Duval was asking himself whether or not it was worth while to pursue this adventure, he became conscious that there were two persons on the other side of the hedge holding a whispered conversation.

"Listen to me," he heard a female voice say.

"I shudder—my blood turns cold. Oh, sister give up this project. Do not venture to that house? Did we not try it once before upon the occasion of the breaking down of the chaise. Did we not then think of going to see—to see——"

"For the body!"

"Hush! hush! Oh, sister! sister!"

"Fool! if we are frightened by words, what may we not be by deeds. You know that we both felt uneasy about where the body was secreted, and wished to make some change in that particular."

"Under pretence of a general visit to look over the place," she continued, in a lower tone, "we wanted to make the necessary change, but the breaking down of the chaise, and the inclemency of the weather, which had been calm and serene enough before."

"It was a judgment upon us."

"Nonsense, man; it was your utter prostration of all physical energy, that induced me to yield to your solicitations, and give it up; but now it may as well

JABEZ OVERWHELMED WITH TERROR.

be done—for it must be done at some time, I tell you, and no time like the present."

"But, sister, why must it be done at all? Are we not going to fly from England for ever, and why now should we terrify ourselves by going—going to—to——"

"Hill House!"

"Well, well, I was going to say it, sister. You are so quick—so very quick and sharp upon me."

"I will tell you why it must be done, brother. If we do escape, as we have every hope to think we shall, Jennings will be sufficiently furious against us to do us all the harm he can.

"But he does not know for certain that—that—we——"

"He said quite sufficient to convince me that he knew enough of the affair to be able to rouse up against us the vengeance of the law, and then no country would protect us. If the body is found we shall be lost to a dead certainty; and, therefore,

brother, you see that that part of his evidence, if he ever gave any, must be deficient."

"Deficient?" shuddered the man. "But how?"

"The body must be removed?"

CHAPTER CXXIII.

CLAUDE DUVAL MAKES A TERRIBLE DISCOVERY.

CLAUDE DUVAL listened to the conversation which was carried on between the man and the woman on the other side of the hedge with an all absorbing interest, and he determined, if possible, not to lose sight of them.

There was a silence for a few minutes, and then Duval heard the man again speak; and, as the moon at that moment burst from behind a cloud, he could see both the speakers.

No. 40.—NIGHTSHADE.

The man approached his companion, and laying his hand upon her arm, he hissed out the words, "Do not say that again? Do not mention that one word again?—Do not? There is a limit to all things, my reason included. I cannot bear it! Do not say it. Do not mention the—body."

The man got the word out with a spasm.

"Very well, very well," replied the woman. "I am not so particular about mere words. Understand, though, that it must be done."

"I don't see that it need," persisted the man.

"I tell you it must and shall be done. Whether we were about to leave England or not, it would have to be done after what we know; so that if this man Jennings should ever choose out of revenge or caprice to tell the tale, he may be proved wrong in the most essential particular. You understand me without me speaking plain."

"Oh, yes—yes—but yet——"

"Go on. What now?"

"I was not going to say anything, sister; only it struck me as you were a strong-minded woman—yes, a very strong-minded woman."

"I might do it by myself, I suppose?"

"Well—I—no—that is—should you have any objection? Eh?"

"No. I will not go without you. In every act of the drama of blood I will have you. Do not suppose for one moment, that I am going to allow you to shrink from it."

The man groaned.

"No! you shall go with me," continued the woman, without noticing the interruption; "even if it so appal your coward spirit, as to drive you to madness. I will have you with me."

The man held up his hand as if imploring silence, but the woman went on.

"Do not interrupt me! To your good profit the deed was done."

"But you, sister—you too——"

"I know what you would say; I shared in the results—I know I did. What then?"

"Well—well—you need not be so passionate. It is done."

"No doubt about that."

"Oh, would that time could be pushed back to the day before that deed was done! True, I was a man even then, who did not stand fair and bright in the world's esteem. They called me crafty and unscrupulous; ruin was laid at my door; and they said I fattened upon the spoils of hearths and homes."

"But they could not say that there was — was — blood upon my hands. I was a villain then, only I—I——"

"You are about to say, brother, that you are a little worse now. Come, there is nothing like candour and sincerity. Open confession, they say, is good for the soul, and you seem to be in the humour, to-night, of confessing a great deal more than I care to listen to—so be quiet!"

The last words were uttered in a tone of command, which seemed to strike terror into the poor cringing, abject wretch to whom they were addressed, for Duval could see that he was bending low—almost touching the ground, as he whined out.

"Yes, sister—yes. I will be quiet. I am silent. What did I say to make you speak so angrily?"

"Nothing to the purpose, idiot. You were beginning to rave again, as is your custom, that is all."

There was a silence for some few minutes, which was broken by the man, who said, in tremulous accents—

"Sister!"

"Well, what is it?"

"I was thinking, that perhaps it would be better, after all, for me to go to Hill House, although I dislike the job so much. I will do all that is necessary and spare you the trouble, for you have convinced me that it must be done by one of us."

"No, brother," said the woman, calmly; you would just wait long enough about the neighbourhood, to induce the belief in my mind, that you had been to the house, and you would come back to me and say it was all done. Oh, no, brother, I know your coward heart, and so I will go with you!"

The man groaned, and muttered something about his sister being a wonderful woman.

"We understand each other," added the woman. "Do not try any foolish tricks with me, for it will not be good for you if you do. I shall be sure to find them out, and then——"

"No doubt—no doubt!"

"Beware! Past experience ought to have taught you a better lesson. Do not try to deceive me, and all may be well yet."

The man shook his head. The last hope of escaping, the, to him evidently frightful visit to the Hill House, the scene of a great crime committed by him and his sister, was fast fading away, and without daring to assert a will not to go, Duval could believe he was preparing himself for the worst.

"I see the moon is rising," said the man.

"You really think so?" Duval heard the woman say, without the slightest attempt at the concealment of the contemptuous tone in which she spoke to the contemptible wretch before her.

"Well, sister, you need not snap one up so. I am quite willing to do you bidding."

"Why do you shake in that way? Come on at once—I say."

"Yes, sister—yes—Why do I shake so? I think it has turned colder; the air is damp and chill. The moon is really rising."

"Come on, then. The signal that all is quiet within the house, has been given by Jessie."

"Poor Jessie!" Duval heard the man sigh.

"Have a care—have a care, Jabez, or you—you will——"

"Share her fate? Not for the world. How bright the moon is!"

The man and his vile companion now made their way at a brisk pace towards the house, from which Duval now believed a signal had been given for some purpose, in order to enable these two to carry out their nefarious plans.

Duval had no difficulty in following them without being heard, for so engrossed were they in their conversation that it was not likely that they would detect the fact that they were not alone.

But how to get into the house without being seen by either the man or his companion in iniquity was the question.

But Duval trusted to fortune, and was not disappointed.

"Here we are, sister," said the man, as they both paused at some iron gates.

The woman looked fixedly at the house for a few minutes.

"Are there any lights in the lodge?" she asked.

"Yes, one of the windows sends out a faint gleam. Jessie has not gone to bed yet; doubtless she is waiting for us."

The woman now rapped with her knuckles on the door of a little thatched lodge, nestled by the side of a huge, old-fashioned iron gate that led into the broad drive to the house.

The door of the lodge Duval could see from his place of espial was opened by a pale young girl. She held a light above her head, and looked curiously at her visitors.

"I scarcely know you," she said, in a strangely mournful tone of voice.

"They have not returned yet?"

"No; not till next week."

"That is well. You see my brother and I want to take the measure of one of the rooms for a new carpet, and he is so much occupied during the day that we are forced to come at this late hour."

"Shall I go with you?" asked the girl.

"No, thank you; if you will be good enough to wait here for us, we can do better alone—I know the house so well."

"Very well," said the girl.

The door of the lodge closed upon the man and his sister.

"Now, fortune befriend me!" said Duval to himself. "I must follow those two if it costs me my life."

He waited patiently for some minutes, until he had seen the two persons who had entered the lodge leave it again with a lantern, and proceed towards the hall-door.

The man opened it with a key, and closed it after him.

Then Duval's resolution was taken.

He advanced to the lodge, and rapped gently upon the door with his knuckles as the woman had done.

There was no response, but he could see that the young girl had started to her feet, and was listening in an attitude of fear.

He knocked again.

The young girl came to the window, and tried to peer out into the night, to ascertain who this visitor could be.

Duval made a sign to her to open the door.

The girl opened the door with trembling hands.

"Fear nothing," he said. "Are you employed by those people who have just entered?"

"Alas! alas!" cried the girl, "Unwillingly."

"And would you be free from the bondage in which they seem to hold you?"

"I shall soon free myself from it, for I cannot live such a life much longer—but I am so young to die."

As she spoke, the young girl clasped both her hands over her face.

"Weep not. I am a friend sent by Providence to befriend you. Can you tell me how I can follow those two without myself being seen?"

"I know not unless some of the lower windows are unfastened."

"I will try—but you will not betray me."

"No, I will not; you look good and kind, and I will trust you."

"You may," was all Duval would trust himself to say, for he feared that he might yet lose sight of the two murderers, for such he had no doubt they were.

He quickly traversed the space of ground between the lodge and the house, and trying the first window he came to, he had the satisfaction of finding it yield to his touch.

He leapt lightly into the room just as the man and woman were passing the door of the apartment.

Duval placed himself close to the wall.

The lantern which the man carried cast a sickly light upon his ghastly face. He trembled violently.

The woman appeared to pay no attention to these symptoms of sinking fear upon the part of her brother, but amused herself with the key that had been given her by the young girl at the lodge.

All within the house to Duval looked like some vast cavern, into which the light of day had never shone.

"Come in," he heard her say to the man, as they reached another room.

The man sunk on his knees, and the lantern which he carried rolled from his grasp.

The woman only just saved the light from being extinguished.

For a few minutes the man's lips moved, but he spoke not—in fact, he did not seem to have the power of articulating a single syllable.

At length, with a sharp beseeching cadence, he addressed the woman.

"Sister, sister," he said, "spare me this one act, and I will do anything else you may ask me. Do not force me to cross the threshold of that dreadful room, and you shall find me as obedient as a child to all your other wishes."

"Fool! Idiot!" was all the reply he got.

"It is true—true that *she*—the spirit of that murdered child, walked with me up the avenue. I did not see her, but I felt that she was by my side all the way. I wonder I did not go mad mad—mad. Yes, yes, she is with us now. I tell you, Sarah, she is with us now!—She is with us now, I tell you sister!"

"Come on!" said the woman.

"No, no! Anywhere but there! Let me entreat, implore of you to ask me not to cross this threshold. The air of that room will kill me! The scent of blood is in it yet! Spare me—spare me!"

The woman laid her hand upon his arm.

"Come in, I say! You shall! Come in, I say! We have our work to do, and it shall be done. Listen to me."

Claude Duval felt deeply interested, and yet he knew not why. What terrible sight was he about to gaze on? he asked himself over and over again.

But he had not much time for reflection; for, at that moment all his senses were merged into that one of listening.

"Are you listening to me?" asked the woman, in a firm voice.

"Yes, yes, I will listen!" replied the man.

"There is in the garden an old well."

"Yes, to be sure! An old well, did you say?"

"Well, then, that must answer our purpose. A grave in some unfrequented spot would do better; but we have neither time nor tools to make one; and, if we had, you are such a trembling coward, that you would be unequal to perform your part of the task."

"Yes; quite unequal; that is——"

"But if we remove all that remains of her whom we must not mention, the well is the next best thing to the grave in an unfrequented spot. Now, do you understand? The well will for ever hide those remains from every eye."

"Yes," replied the man; "that is just what I was going to say, sister; hide them from every eye."

"Get up—get up, I say! Do you wish to remain here in the hearing of we know not who, with a light glaring out into the darkness of the night, until, perchance, we draw upon ourselves the observation of some busy spy who will share with us our dreadful secret, as he whom we are already slaves to shares it with us? For our own sakes, take courage and get up, I say."

The man who all this time had been crouching down to the ground, now rose slowly to his feet.

The woman seized a favourable opportunity for thrusting him across the threshold of the, to him, dreadful apartment.

Duval perceived that a little further on was another door, which, if it did not really lead into the room, must, at all events, lead to an adjoining one.

It turned out to be an adjoining one, and communicated with that in which the man and woman were, by folding doors.

They were a little ajar, and Duval had no difficulty in both seeing and hearing all that took place within the next apartment.

CHAPTER CXXIV.

CLAUDE OVERHEARS A FEARFUL DISCLOSURE.

As soon as they were fairly within the apartment, the woman slammed the door, which shut with a force that awakened a dismal echo in the house.

The man uttered a shrieking cry, and then he clung to his sister with such a frantic eagerness, that all her efforts to shake him off were vain. His voice sunk to a hoarse whisper as he said, "Did you hear that—did you hear that?"

"Hear what, you coward?"

"That cry—that strange, terrible, unearthly cry! Did you hear it? Do not try to persuade me that it is merely the effect of my imagination; you must have heard it. I tell you, sister, you did hear it or I am mad!"

"Yes, I heard a cry, but it was from your blanched lips."

"From my lips—my lips, did you say?"

"Yes; you in your abject fear cry out, and then you listen to the echo of the sound you have yourself made, and convert it into one of terror to yourself. Shame! shame! this cowardice is worse than even I, who know you so well, could have believed possible. It is most dastardly. When I do a deed I will not live in horror of that which I have done. Come on, I say! We have not yet reached room we want—this way—this way!"

The woman placed the lantern, which she had taken from her brother, on a bracket in the hall, while she went back to bolt and bar the door.

The man, while she did so, stood a few paces from her, utterly bent double, his hair straggling over his face, wet and clammy with the dew of fear, and his hand up to his ear in an attitude of intense listening.

At this moment, Duval incautiously moved too quickly, fearing to lose sight of them, and in doing so, threw down some light article of furniture.

The woman turned pale, while her brother, with a howl of horror, fell to the marble flooring of the hall.

At this moment, Duval was rejoiced to see a bat start from its hiding place, and whirl through the hall; and, ever and anon as it did so, it flapped it wings against the sides of the lantern.

The woman at once concluded in her own mind that the bat alone had been the cause of all their alarm.

She now ran towards her brother.

"He has fainted!" she cried.

She stooped, and lifted up his head, he was sensible, but the most abject fear was in his eyes and in every feature.

"You have been frightened by a harmless bat," she said, soothingly. "Get up, and you shall see it."

"A bat?" grasped the man, evidently not comprehending her.

"Yes, a bat. Did you never in the country see a bat before, man? Get up, I say! You will be the destruction of me as well as of yourself, by this fearful waste of valuable time. If you had had ever so little courage, we might have done all by this time."

This argument seemed scarcely to reach the man's perceptions, but he staggered to his feet, and looked about him with a bewildered kind of gaze.

"Oh, if it were but done!" he whispered. "If it were but over."

"It will be, if you will but make a beginning. Follow me, I say!"

She took the lantern from the bracket in the hall on which she had placed it and was followed by the man, who was wringing his hands, and uttering deep sighs as he went.

There was an old, wide staircase, with broad, shallow steps, and a rich old oaken balustrade, and up that, they went. Duval following, and hiding ever and anon behind some one of the many statues which adorned the staircase.

It took a wide sweep to the floor above, terminating in a kind of corridor, from which opened several rooms, and it was towards one of these that the woman, without a pause, made her way.

The door of that room was locked, but she had a key which easily opened it.

The man placed both his hands over his face, as he said, in a strange, hollow voice—"Lead me in, if I must go. Lead me in."

There was a wailing pathos in which these words were uttered which excited the pity of Claude Duval, much as he felt that the guilty pair before him deserved the execration of their fellow men.

Perhaps the mournful tone in which the man had spoken touched even the hard heart of that woman of many crimes; for, instead of applying to him harshly as was her wont, she merely took him by the hand, and led him into the apartment.

No sooner had he entered it, then he raised his arms above his head, and cried out in frantic accents.

"Here—here we did it! Here we caught her, after chasing her along the corridor! We did not mean to do it here, but we did! Here she was struck down after clinging to me with the warm blood streaming from her wounds, and shrieking for mercy!"

"Hush! oh hush!" gasped the woman, now looking almost as terrified as her brother.

"Here it was that the last crushing blow was given!" he continued, not heeding his sister's altered looks. "I saw the fair hair dabbled in blood! I saw the blue eyes close for ever, and the little hands grasp at nothing in the vacant air, before the pure spirit fled to accuse us of murder!"

The woman strove to silence him, but in vain.

"It was here that she gazed for the last time upon my face. That look was enough, for it was the fiat of the Almighty! Here—here she fell——"

"Peace! Silence!" cried the woman, striking him a blow on the chest with her clenched hand.

"No! No! Save her! Save her! She flies to me for protection! She is hurt, but she is not killed yet! Not another blow! Help! Help! Murder! Murder!"

He fell upon the floor, and the woman stood over him, trembling partly from fear, and partly from rage.

"If I had only known it would come to this. He will go mad, he will surely go mad."

She placed the lantern upon the floor, and for a few seconds she pressed her hands upon her eyes.

In a few moments she looked up, and Duval could see, by the rays of the lamp which fell upon her face, that it was as pale as that of some statue upon a tomb.

"I must do it all now—all by myself," she muttered.

In the centre of the room was a large square table. The floor was covered with a rich Turkey carpet, which had long since faded to one uniform tint of brown.

She next drew the table, and placed it against one of the walls of the apartment, and upon it now placed the lantern.

Then she took off a large cloak she wore, and from underneath she produced a large sack, or bag, that seemed to have been made out of some old article of wearing apparel.

While she had been making these arrangements, Duval had crept noiselessly into the room, and hidden himself under the table.

This sack she placed upon the table, and then she crept to the door of the apartment, and projecting her head out on to the landing-place, she listened intently for several seconds.

"All is still," she said—"very still."

She then returned, and began to roll up the carpet from a large portion of the room; and in doing so she threw a quantity of it upon her brother.

Then she took from her pocket a short gimblet.

With this she worked away at one of the boards in the floor.

This board was loose, and when she had a firm hold of it, she raised it with ease.

She raised it about a couple of inches; but then a sickening feeling seemed to take possession of her—she turned ghastly pale, and let it fall again into its place.

For once, even that woman was overcome.

She had knelt upon the floor by that loose piece of board because that was the most convenient attitude in which to raise it; but now she flung herself as far back as possible; and with clasped hands, and with eyes that seemed almost starting from their sockets, she gazed at it in horror.

There was something of woman's nature yet clinging to even that dreadful person; and as she knelt by the side of the unhallowed resting-place of the murdered child—for such, indeed, it was—she shook with a strong convulsion.

She was then glad, probably, that her companion in guilt was not up and moving, to notice her in her hour of weakness and agony.

She remained about five minutes in this state; then she slowly moved, and spoke.

"There is nothing to fear. The dead are but loathsome likenesses of the living, without being half so dangerous. I breathe, and am myself again. What was it that for the first time came over me, and seemed to grasp my heart, as though the cold hand of death were upon it?"

She drew her breath in short gasps, and then continued.

"What was it that made my blood come and go from my bosom in frightful gushes, and caught my breath, as though it were flying away to the winds for ever? What have I to fear? I am alone."

She cast her eyes upon the recumbent form of the man.

"Alone, but for such companionship as that!"

She gazed around her, and Duval could see that she cast a scrutinizing glance into every corner of the vast apartment; and then she drew a long breath again, and her hand nervously wandered to the temporary hold she had contrived to have of the board in the floor.

Beneath that board she and her brother had, years before, placed the warm and bleeding body of their victim.

"What," she gasped "what does it look like now, I wonder?"

The woman evidently felt that she had proposed to herself a fearful question—one which was suggestive of a thousand hideous fancies. Truly, she peopled that small space, beneath the orifice of the plank, with a world of horrors.

At this moment the man, terror-struck, uttered a faint groan.

The woman rose to her feet, and stepped over to where he lay. A large fold of the damp, discoloured carpet lay on his face.

She dragged it off, and looked at him.

"What now? What did you say, brother?"

"The Lord have mercy upon us!"

She spurned him with her foot.

"Lie where you are. I can do better without you. Lie still, coward, that can neither face the living nor the dead. I do not now ask you to rise. It shall be sufficient that you are here—that this night's work is not done without you. Lie still, and pant your coward heart to death, if you will; I have nothing more to say to you now."

"Hush! Is—is she quite dead?" he whispered.

"Dead?"

"Hush! I would not have her scream again for worlds! Hush! Tell me is she quite dead?"

"Are you dreaming, or are you mad?"

"No—no—no! We chased her here, you know. Wipe up the spots of blood that fell by the way. Hush! Not a word! Be still as death—yes, as death! She fell; but she is quite dead. Who would think a child—a mere child was so hard to kill? Hush! Did you hear her then?"

"What—what?"

"I thought I heard a voice say, 'Mercy!'"

"I could find it in my heart to take from you that coward life that I one day fear will be the destruction of us both. Rouse yourself from the past, and bring your thoughts to the present! You speak of what happened long ago, brother. We are here upon a very different errand."

"So that she is quite dead," whispered the man—"so that she is really quite dead, I—I can breathe! But she clung to me - me—me! Oh, heaven, yes, she clung to me, and said, 'Save me!'—in all her beauty and innocence she clung to me to save her! The little fingers got locked about me! There—there she cries again for mercy! I tell you, sister, she is not dead yet! We cannot kill that child, the spirit of God is in the room and stays our hands! We cannot do the deed! Where is the hammer?"

The woman clenched her right hand, and for a moment it seemed as though passion would have lent her strength to do her companion some serious mischief: but by a great effort she seemed to control herself, and merely tossing her hand slightly she left him to rave or to be silent as he chose.

Once more she knelt by the side of the loose plank, beneath which she had seen placed the body of the murdered child years before, and beneath which imagination had painted such a sight of horror, that even she, with her iron nerves, had lingered there long before she could work herself up to sufficient courage to gaze into the depth beneath.

The man sat up and looked at her.

His perception of the present was coming back to him.

His intellect seemed to be fighting with the vapours of the past, and more than once he pressed his hands over his eyes, as though they presented him confused images which, perchance, might vanish if he could only continue to shut them out of his brain for a little time.

"It must be done, and it shall be done!" muttered the woman.

Again she placed her hand upon the board.

With a sudden wrench she raised it.

One glance sufficed.

She sprung to her feet.

"Gone—gone!" she cried.

"Gone?" shouted the man, as he dragged himself to the spot upon his knees—"gone, sister?"

The little bit of candle that was in the lantern at that moment expired, and Claude Duval was alone in the darkness with the two murderers.

What should he do?

What ought he to do?

These were the questions Duval asked himself

CHAPTER CXXV.

CLAUDE DUVAL OBTAINS POSSESSION OF A CASKET.

It was not possible but that the fearful scene to which he had been a witness should make a most painful impression upon the mind of Claude Duval.

It was quite evident to him, that a terrible and cold-blooded murder had been perpetrated, and that the victim of these fiends in human shape was none other than a young and defenceless girl.

For what object had these people sought her death?

He resolved to wait, perhaps he should hear more.

For a few minutes there was a profound silence between the man and woman; probably, the removal of the body had suggested to their minds what might be the dreadful consequences to them from such an unlooked-for result to all their plottings and schemings.

At last the woman spoke.

"Look, Jabez—look and see if the casket is also removed!"

There was no reply.

"Speak, I beg of you; it is fearful to feel alone in this frightful place, and without a light, too! Try to rouse yourself, Jabez, and help me to search for the casket, for we must take that with us somehow!"

The man uttered a deep groan.

"There, that's right; now you'll soon be yourself again, if you will but make an effort. Speak to me."

Duval fancied he could hear a movement, as though the woman were shaking her brother in order to rouse him from his state of imbecile terror.

At length he spoke; but his voice came in strange spasmodic gasps.

"What is the use of searching for the casket now—it is of no use to us?"

"Of no use to us? What then did we kill her for, if it were not in order to possess ourselves of all her wealth?"

"We might have had it upon easier terms," moaned the man, "than in taking her young life. Oh, if I could but bring the dead to life!"

"It's of no earthly use talking in that way now; let us see if the casket has been taken away. I will feel myself for it if you will only talk to me the while; but it is so dreadful not to feel that there is any kind of companionship in this dreadful place."

"Yes, yes! I will talk to you; but make haste, and let us leave this place, or I shall go mad."

The woman appeared to be groping about beneath the flooring for some minutes, and then Duval heard her draw a long breath.

"Here it is! Here it is, Jabez. I tell you no one, at all events, has found the most valuable thing we placed in this strange resting place of the dead. I tell you the casket is here, and even now I have my hand upon it; but I cannot raise it myself. Help me!"

With some difficulty Duval could hear that the man and woman dragged what sounded to be a good sized box out of the orifice in the floor, and with a heavy sound they dragged it between them until it reached the upper air.

"That's it," he heard the woman say. "Now let us open the box, and when we have the casket in our possession, let us not delay a moment in seeking some other country, where we may forget the past, and live in luxury for the future."

All this time Duval had been turning over in his mind various plans for the frustration of the evil designs of the two unscrupulous persons before him.

It was now time to begin to act.

He would fain have confined his designs to the woman, who certainly appeared to be the worse of the two; but as it was not likely that they would separate, he resolved at once to try and play upon their already over-excited imaginations, and so thoroughly to scare them that he would have no difficulty in appropriating the casket.

Duval made a slight noise.

They evidently thought that the other had made some movement—and therefore neither of them spoke.

Finding that they took no notice of the noise he had made, Duval emerged from under the table and stood up as near as he could venture to do in the dark to the spot where the man and woman were crouching upon the floor.

Duval did not think it prudent to speak until he had produced a certain impression upon the eyes of the two persons whom he was now quite resolved should be punished as much as he (Duval) had it in his power of punishing two such unscrupulous wretches.

Drawing from his pocket as quietly as possible a small hand lantern, which he fortunately happened to have with him, and then a match, which he made it a rule never to be without, Duval calmly ignited the match and lit the candle in the lantern before either the man or woman could muster courage to utter a word.

Then the woman gave a half start, as she said this:

"Don't light the lantern again; I can find the way out without a light."

"Oh! Look!"

The man fell flat on his face as he uttered these words, in such a tone of agony and terror that it was terrible to hear.

"Who is that?" asked the woman, evidently fancying that it was some one from the lodge, who had been sent to see if they could be of any assistance.

Duval only replied by raising the light to his face, so as to make every feature distinctly visible.

With a harsh, strange cry the woman fell back upon the floor.

Her lips turned livid with fear, and she grasped at vacancy with both hands, while the heavy drops of perspiration stood upon her brow, and her eyes glared like metallic plates.

"I have found the murderess at last," said Duval, in a deep voice. "Listen! Listen! Listen!"

"I do!" gasped the woman. "Spare me!"

"Even as you spared her!" said Duval, in the same tone in which he had already spoken.

"Oh, mercy! mercy!" groaned the man. "I have repented long and bitterly of that dreadful act."

"I believe it," said Duval; "and therefore your punishment shall not be so great as that of your accomplice. Rise, and answer the questions I am about to put to you."

The man slowly succeeded in rising to a sitting posture.

"Now tell me the name of the murdered girl?"

Duval could hear the very teeth chattering in the head of the terrified wretch before him.

"Answer me quickly, what was the girl's name?"

"Netta."

"Netta what? What was her surname?"

The man looked at the woman as though to receive some intimation from her, as to what answer to make to this last question.

"Netta what, I ask you," said Duval, and as he did so, he presented the barrel of a pistol full in the face of the man, who shrunk back close to the wall with dilated eyes.

"Speak, and that instantly," again said Duval: "or your life shall pay dearly for your obstinacy."

"It's of no use!" cried the man, appealing to the woman; "it is the fiend himself sent here to torment us before our time!"

The woman neither moved nor spoke.

"I can wait no longer!" cried Duval.

As he spoke, he strode up to the abject wretch, and seized him by the throat.

The man fell to his knees, and shrieked out.

"Mercy! Mercy! Help!"

"It is of no use calling for help here, as you well know," replied Duval, still keeping his grasp on the man's throat. Tell me all, or I will shake the life out of you, and leave you to rot in the same grave which you made years ago for one good, and pure, and innocent."

"Yes, yes, she was all that—Good, pure, and innocent."

"Tell me her name?"

"Nella Vargrave."

"Who was she? What was she?"

The man groaned, and shook convulsively.

"What was she, I ask?"

"An orphan. Oh, heaven, she was an orphan, confided to the care of myself and my sister!"

"That wretch there?" asked Duval, pointing with his disengaged hand to the crouching figure of the woman.

"Yes."

"And you murdered her?"

"Alas! alas!"

"For what purpose?"

"For gain. She possessed a fortune I robbed her first; and then—and then——"

"And then you found it in your heart to murder this young creature, who clung to you, and implored you to have pity on her."

"Hush! Oh, hush!"

Duval now released his hold of the man, and went towards the woman, who had never moved.

"Give me that casket you are endeavouring to hide beneath you?" said Duval.

"Never!"

"Ah!"

Duval was just in time to prevent her from striking him in the face with the pointed end of the gimlet she still held in her hand, and with which she had raised the board in the floor.

He wrenched it from her grasp with some difficulty, and spurning her from him, she fell backward with a shriek.

Duval raised the casket from the floor.

"I leave you both now to your own reflections," he said, as he moved towards the door, which he opened and closed after him.

When Duval reached the hall, and had opened the door, he was surprised to find that the dawn had made some advance.

It was a very sweet sunrise, at least, so Duval thought, as he stepped lightly across the lawn, which surrounded the mansion. Those who professed to be weather-wise, however, might have detected something about the look of the sky rather peculiar as to colour, from which they would have predicted something in the shape of storm or tumult.

A dull, metallic kind of tint seemed to pervade the whole sky, and to be reflected on the earth.

The trees had a strange aspect with that glistening light upon their leaves, and the forest birds flew low, and uttered notes of fear, as they sought darksome recesses, into which that preternatural light did not penetrate.

For about ten minutes this lasted, during which time, Duval had taken to reach the spot where he had left Blossom.

"I began to fancy all sorts of things, Captain," were the first words he said as Duval reached him.

"I have had a strange adventure, indeed," said Duval; "but we are going to have a storm, Blossom, can we find shelter about here?"

"None better than what the trees afford, Captain," replied Blossom, "for I was just thinking as you came up, that I was in for it."

At this moment a creeping, sighing wind swept over the land, and large drops of rain began to descend.

Duval and Blossom thought the wisest plan would be to gallop as fast as they could towards London.

Suddenly the rain ceased, and the clouds begun to move quickly over the sky.

"We shall have a fine day after all," said Duval, as he and Blossom trotted side by side.

"So it seems," said Duval, absently, for his imagination was still busy with the fearful scene he had witnessed in the deserted-looking house.

"Are you going home now, Captain?" asked Blossom.

"Yes."

"Well, Captain, I may as well tell you: I have done a little business on my own account while you have been in that house yonder."

"Ah!"

"Yes; I cried 'Stand and deliver!' to two horsemen at once, who were so much afraid of losing their worthless lives, that, upon consideration of my sparing them, they were only too willing to give me all they had about them that was valuable."

Duval laughed.

When he reached the mansion on Hampstead Heath, Duval was pleased to see that the General and Lucy were looking much more serene and happy than when he had left home.

The fact is, the General had decided at length upon the steps he meant to take in order to reinstate himself in his former position.

"Lucy and I have been talking over the matter," he said, as soon as they were alone, seated at breakfast; "and I have decided this very day to present myself at the Palace, and to crave an audience of the King."

The rest of the time between breakfast and the hour at which the General felt he might, with propriety, claim an audience of royalty, was spent by the General in preparations for the undertaking.

Fortunately he had on, on the day that Duval released him from Camden House, a complete military Court suit, for it was the only pastime the poor old man had to dress, and undress, arrange and re-arrange the various suits of wearing apparel which had been left free to his disposal; not from any desire which Mossy Pendell had to amuse his dull and monotonous life, but simply because it had never occurred to him to remove them from his reach.

The sun shone brightly, as, mounted upon one of Claude Duval's best horses, the General waved an adieu to him and Lucy.

They watched him as far as they could, until the trees hid him completely from their view.

Lucy sighed.

"Why that sigh, dear Lucy?" asked Duval.

"I am sorry, and yet I suppose it could not be avoided, to think that we could not all live happily and quietly together, without taking the great world again into our every-day life."

"But, Lucy, think of the brilliant position your uncle occupies in society. I should have thought that even my Lucy's heart would have beaten with something akin to exultation when she thought of taking her proper place in society."

"But, as your wife, Claude!"

A cloud passed over Duval's face.

"True!" he said: "I forgot, at the moment, that you were tied to me."

"Forgot!—tied to you! Why, what mean you Claude?" asked Lucy, looking greatly distressed "Surely you do not regret that tie?"

As she spoke, she looked into his eyes, but he did not meet her gaze, as was his wont.

The fact is, a quiet, domesticated kind of life was not exciting enough to one of his disposition; and perhaps he did begin, just a little, to regret that he had made the gentle Lucy his wife.

But he hastened to relieve her mind of any misgivings she might entertain on the subject, by saying, "But if it were not for me, Lucy, you might, by to-morrow, take your proper position in society, as the niece and heiress of one of the bravest and wealthiest men in England."

"But am I not the wife of one of the bravest men in England?" urged Lucy, looking affectionately at Duval.

"Yes, yes—that is——"

"And one who deserves my heart's best affections?"

"At least, I will try to do so, dear one," replied Duval, as he gazed fondly upon the upturned face, and thought that such a heart was indeed worth possessing.

"Let us go in-doors, now dear," he said, not desiring to continue a conversation which had taken rather a different turn to what he expected, and which was now rather irksome than otherwise to him. "Let us go in; I want to examine the casket I was telling you about."

CHAPTER CXXVI.

PREPARATIONS FOR THE EXECUTION OF DICK TURPIN

About a fortnight after the events which we have just recorded, Blossom encountered Duval just as he was preparing to ride over to Camden House to take a survey of the place before taking up his abode in that mansion, as General Everton strongly recommended him to do.

"Well, Blossom," said Duval, "what now? you look as though you had news of some sort to communicate. Speak; what would you say?"

"Of course you've heard, Captain, that Dick Turpin is to be hanged to-morrow morning' at Tyburn."

"Yes. I suppose you want to go and see the execution? Well, go Blossom, if you wish. Those things are not to my taste."

"Nor are they to mine, Captain, unless I think I can do any good by going."

"Why, what good can you do, Blossom?" asked Duval.

"I—that is you and I, Captain, might contrive to save him."

"Ah! say you so?"

"Yes, Captain, if you feel inclined to try. He is to be hanged in chains, and left."

"Good! I will think of it."

"Do, Captain; for he is a brave fellow after all."

"No doubt about that, Blossom."

* * * * *

At Tyburn such an assemblage of persons was collected, that when you looked from an elevation at the monster gathering, it seemed to extend for miles into the open country, while from every road and lane, fresh reinforcements were each moment arriving to swell the concourse.

The best elevation to look at the monster crowd from, was a scaffold that was erected some short distance from the place of execution—Tyburn.

There was that day a man to be hanged.

A man well known to the world, no less for his handsome exterior and gallantry, than for his many crimes and depredations.

A sharp north-east wind, that brought with it an army of frosty particles, that cut like knives, careering over the immense space. But the curiosity of thousands there assembled on that day of storm and wretchedness, as it turned out, was proof against all inclemencies of the season; and the great mob swayed to and fro with excitement, while now and then the fierce roar of many voices would rise upon the air, or some melée took place amid the assemblage from some real or fancied cause.

Yes, there was a man to be hanged.

A fellow creature was to be strangled according to the law, at Tyburn, and it was not likely that human nature, in its ordinary variety, could resist the attractions of such a show as this.

What to them was the cold and biting air from the frozen regions of the north?

What to them were the icy particles that hung upon their beards, and cut their faces as though millions of little needles were dashing through the air?

What to them was the fact, patent to them all, that the clouds were gathering over the sky, and that a snowdrift or a torrent of hail might be expected soon?

There was a man to be hanged, and that was such a grand attraction, that it outweighed all events that might be encountered in the course of seeing such a sight.

Now, it will be remembered that all this happened many years ago, and that many things took place then which would not take place now.

To be sure now, as then, crowds collect to see a fellow-creature sent to his long account, with all his sins upon his head, but the affair, as regards the authorities, is conducted rather differently.

We shall see how they did those things in the old times—in the "good old times"—as they are called.

It wants a quarter to twelve, and the sky is getting darker and darker each moment.

The dense clouds are coming up from the south, and they would bedew the earth with plentiful showers, if that north-east wind did not meet them and trip up the soft drops into hail and snow.

Many feathery particles of snow are already in the air, floating hither and thither, as if enjoying a gambol before they plunged down upon the sea of upturned faces that crowd around the fatal beam.

And now a cry arises from ten thousand throats.

"They come!—they come —here they are!"

Oh! what a striving, and trampling, and pushing there was now for a better place, than those who strove and pushed fancied they had already!

The mob seemed to be having, throughout its length and breadth, a fight of its own, for no other earthly purpose than to celebrate the arrival of the malefactor, who, then and there, upon that spot, and on such a day, was to make reparation with his life, for the evil he had done to society—that society that had come roaring and shouting to see him die.

Poor wretch!

But there is the scaffold.

It is worth a word or two.

It was the custom to hang criminals on what was called the gallows-tree.

That gallows-tree consisted of an upright piece of wood, stuck firmly in the ground, with the traditionary piece at right angles from the top of it and the slanting strengthening band of timber beneath.

On this occasion, however, an attempt had been made to construct a scaffold.

It was, to be sure, a very rude attempt.

A quantity of planks had been brought from London, and placed on the tops of some half-dozen carts, as nearly of a height as possible, so that a kind of platform was made, loose and shifting, certainly, but still tolerably secure.

THE REMOVAL OF DICK TURPIN'S BODY.

In the middle of this platform, where the boards were left open for the purpose, rose up the awful gallows with its cross-tree at the top, and the rope dangling from it

The hangman, who must have been a bit of a genius, in his way, had so managed, that by the removal of one board the victim of the day would be suspended in a tolerably satisfactory manner, and, from underneath, he could remove that board with ease.

A black cloth was laid over a portion of this extemporaneous platform, so that the erection looked something like the proper sort of thing, and had more of a professional look about it, than the ordinary rough mode of shuffling poor mortals into eternity.

That ordinary mode was to bring them in a cart under the gallows, and when they were suspended, to remove the cart from under them; so that the last words the criminal usually heard were from the carter to the horse, and consisted of, "Come up!"

Well, we have spoken of the gallows, and now we will say something of those who were upon it.

No. 41.—NIGHTSHADE.

By the by, it was reached by a flight of steps that were lashed firmly to the wheel of one of the carts, and formed the substructure of the whole concern.

Upon the platform there was one of the Sheriffs, conversing with a gentleman who had come from a distance to see the sight.

Around the scaffold was a company of mounted yeomanry, with their heavy jack-boots and huge bear-skin helmets, and drawn swords.

They shook again with the cold.

A small knot of some eight or ten officers of the police stood close to the steps that led up to the platform.

The Sheriff took out his watch—about the size of an ordinary saucer,—and as his nose turned bluer and bluer from the cold, he said to his companion, "Confound them, they are late. It is only a quarter to twelve now. Why don't they bring him and hang him as once?"

"Ye—es!" stuttered the gentleman; "if they don't

come and turn him off quickly, we shall not have a bit of feeling left."

"Not a bit," said the sheriff.

What sort of *feeling* did they mean? Was it for themselves, or for the unhappy mortal who was about to meet death at their hands on that day?

"They come!—they come!"

"Ah, there they come!" said the Sheriff.

A shout from the crowd now prevented any one from holding anything like a discourse upon any subject whatever, for the cavalcade, with Dick Turpin, was close at hand.

First of all, there came several mounted officers of the police, with cutlasses in their hands, and pistols in their belts. Then there came the Governor of Newgate; and then there came an open cart, in which sat the chaplain of the prison, and the coffin, and the hangman, and Dick Turpin.

Another troop of yeomanry followed this cavalcade, and on each side of the cart rode a mounted police-officer.

This was rather a brief procession, but it was terribly significant.

The executioner had his coat off, but he had tied it round his neck by the arms, for he felt very cold.

The clergyman was bare-headed, and appeared to be much more affected at the situation of the prisoner than at the cold, which must have cut him deeply, or the piercing wind which played through his thin, white hair.

There was a look of firm and dogged resolution about all the officers; and the Governor of Newgate was as pale as death itself as he rode along.

But now for the prisoner, the hero of the day.

As the cart moved slowly forward on its way to the place of execution, Dick Turpin bowed to the spectators, with an air of the most astonishing indifference and intrepidity.

When he came to the fatal tree he ascended the ladder, and on his right leg trembling, he stamped it down with an air of assumed courage, as if he was ashamed to be observed to manifest any signs of fear.

Having conversed with the executioner for half an hour, he threw himself on his knees, and seemed to be making violent efforts to say something.

He then rose and shook hands with one of the police-officers, and then the crowd raised another shout.

What it was they shouted at though, it is highly probable not one of them could have told satisfactorily.

Now, the sheriff, who at some risk of his neck tottered along the unsteady platform, to that end of the platform which was the nearest to the approaching cavalcade, stood with his huge watch in his hand, and shook his head at the governor who, as he wiped the sleet and the snow from his face, just said:

"I could not help it, sir; there have been all sorts of delays."

"Well—well, be quick now, we shall have a snowstorm as sure as fate."

"Not a doubt about that, sir—with a little hail, too, to keep it company."

"Yes; yes; no doubt. Now, Mr. Scraggs!"

This was to the hangman, who jumped from the cart on to the scaffold.

A howl of execration burst from the mob at the sight of that unpopular functionary of the law, and several stones were cast upon the platform.

The sheriff got alarmed, and turned round three or four times, as if he did not know what to do under the circumstances.

The yeomanry looked fierce.

"Down with Jack Ketch!" roared a hundred voices.

"Oh, go along with you!" growled the hangman, as he sidled along the projecting gallows, and began to adjust the rope.

"Back! Back!" said the governor, as the crowd now swayed to and fro, and pressed the yeomanry closer each moment to the scaffold. "Keep the mob off, Captain Appleby."

The captain of the yeomanry gave the necessary orders, and the heavy lumbering horses began to tread upon the toes of the foremost of the people, and for some few minutes a scene of great confusion arose, all of which the hangman looked at with quite a grin of satisfaction, for several stones had struck him, and he was glad to see the people harassed by the burly yeomanry.

But, after all, the hearts of the bluff farmers, who composed the troop of county cavalry, were not with the business they had in hand, and the people knew it, so they did not much heed the demonstration of the horses after all.

In fact, every man in that vast multitude seemed to be much affected at the fate of this man, who was about to pay the penalty of his crime, and who had the good fortune to be possessed of great personal attractions. They looked upon him as a hero, and as a man of great courage and generosity.

"Hats off! Hats off!" suddenly was the cry that arose from many throats, and the multitude at once uncovered as Dick Turpin reached the scaffold.

"Now, sir!" said the executioner.

"I am ready!" said Dick, in an audible voice.

It was frightful now to hear the shouts of the mob.

The governor of the prison got alarmed, and caught hold of the Captain of the yeomanry by the shoulder, as he said:

"You will have to charge!"

The Sheriff in dumb show urged the hangman to more expedition in his proceedings.

"Now, sir," again said the hangman, "if you please."

"Hear him! Hear him! Hear Dick Turpin, he is going to say something! Hear him, if you hurry him afterwards! Hear what Dick Turpin has to say!"

The rage of the vast multitude terrified the hangman, who crouched at the feet of Dick, looking much more like a culprit himself than did that man who was brought there to die.

"Are you ready?" shouted the Sheriff.

"Yes, sir!" said the hangman, as he dropped from the scaffold to go underneath it, having previously adjusted the rope about the neck of Dick Turpin.

"Now, Scraggs!" called out the Sheriff.

Dick Turpin, however, threw himself off, and in another moment was dangling by the rope.

CHAPTER CXXVII.

DICK TURPIN IS NOT DESERTED BY HIS FRIENDS.

To and fro swayed the body.

Horrible—oh, most horrible! What potent spell can restore motion and sensation to those limbs again?

What medicament—what skill of learned men—what subtle secrets of science will open those eyes again upon the world?

All—all is over.

The snow-drift and the north-west wind came on savagely now; and amid a whirl of snow, sleet, and misty vapours, the dense multitude took its way from Tyburn.

To and fro swayed the body.

The carts and the temporary platform had all disappeared.

The hangman alone kept watch beside the hideous spectacle.

The body now presented a strange appearance in the irons; but it hung much more steadily as the additional weight resisted the keen air that before had driven it from side to side.

It was to complete the job—viz., to put on the irons, for which the executioner had been waiting.

And now his work was done.

The body now only occasionally swayed to and fro, and then the irons would jingle together with a terrible significance

The snow-drift that seemed for a while to have paused, came on afresh now with such a fierce and mad vehemence that the hangman's horse could hardly stand against it, and, setting his teeth, he muttered a few hearty curses, and said to himself, " It is done; now I'll go home !"

Even as he spoke, and turned his horse's head, the sky darkened.

Dense masses of clouds, fringed with an ominous yellow-looking edge, covered up the southern sky, and seemed to pause over the place of execution.

For a few minutes the air was so still that the cutting wind which had made itself so manifest only a little time before seemed to be completely stopped in its progress.

Then there was a strange, rushing sound, and down came the snow like a white mantle over all things.

Tyburn was devoted to the dead.

The snow piled itself up a foot high at the foot of the gallows tree.

It piled itself up upon every ridge and inequality in the dress or the chains in which the mute figure was hung.

Into a conical shape it heaped itself on the cross tree of the gallows, and gradually, then, as minute after minute passed the strong upright piece of wood, to which hung the body, appeared as though it were slowly sinking into the earth.

It was the snow which was piling itself up round it.

A few frightened birds screeched round the dismal spectacle.

The dense shower of white flakes hardly permitted the sound to vibrate through the air, and so for the space of four hours the snow came down upon Tyburn Common till the shrubs were all but concealed, and the trees looked short and stunted, as they rose, black and wiry and dead-looking, from the pure white surface around them.

As for the swinging figure upon the gallows, it seemed as though there would have been no difficulty in standing below and touching it with your hand, so much lower had it seemed to drop to the earth.

And now the dim twilight of that winter's day had come.

The brief sun had set, and though the snow storm had abated, still great quantities were caught up by a fierce wind that had risen and dashed hither and thither with mad violence.

Oh, that was a fearful night!

The wind was now high enough to swing the body to and fro upon the gallows tree, and the chains rattled and jammed against each other.

A carrion bird hovered round the head of the hanging man.

It was the eyes of the victim of the law that it wanted as a delicious morsel ere it tried to roost.

But as often as it flapped its wings, almost to the touching of the face of the hanging man, it flew off again with a scream of disappointment.

There was some strange instinct which prevented the bird of prey from touching Dick Turpin.

The twilight died away quickly, and a dark night shrouded the face of nature.

There was quiet for a time, a strange, reflected radiance from the snow, and then all was gone, like a dream, and earth and sky appeared mingled together in one black confusion.

A faint light showed itself at some distance off in the intense darkness.

It moved along some two feet from the snowy surface, casting a strange halo around.

After a time it stopped, but it was not far from the gallows when it did so.

There was a faint murmur of voices, and then the light came on again, and suddenly the voice of one well known to the reader cried out, " Here it is—here it is, Captain !"

" I see—I see," replied Duval, as the beam of the lantern—for that is what it was—fell upon the hanging man.

Blossom, from a belt that was round his waist, took a woodman's axe, and casting a glance up and down the upright beam of wood, he said, " Let him come gently down, Captain. Lay hold of him when you see the wood giving way."

" All's right, Blossom."

" There you are, then," said Blossom, as he swung the axe once round his head, and then sent its blade deep into the solid timber.

Another such blow, and the gallows slowly bended over, crackling into splinters at the spot where the axe had made its deep indentation.

Duval with difficulty caught it, and in another moment Dick Turpin lay upon the ground, half hidden by the snow.

" Hold the light nearer, Captain," said Blossom, as he knelt by the body, and, by the aid of a knife, cut away the rope. " A little closer with the light, Captain. I hope we're not too late."

" Not a bit of it," said Duval, in a decided tone of voice, which seemed to inspire Blossom with fresh courage.

A very few minutes sufficed to free the body from all the insignia of the gallows ; and then Duval and Blossom opened a kind of hammock which they had brought with them, and laid it in it, and lashed the sides together with cord, so that the body was completely hidden.

" I wonder where Ben can be ?" said Blossom, as he peered far away into the thick darkness. " I told him to meet us here half-an-hour ago."

" Are you sure you can depend upon him, Blossom ?" asked Duval.

" Not the slightest doubt of it, Captain : he's as true as steel. But I hear a footstep now ; be quiet for a moment—it may be somebody we don't wish to see just now."

Duval and Blossom were silent for a few minutes, and then they heard a long, low whistle.

" There he is," cried Blossom. " That is the signal we agreed upon. But I wonder what makes him so late ?"

" Never mind, Blossom," replied Duval, " as long as he has come at last. Pray be quick, or all may yet be lost."

Blossom answered the whistle by a similar one.

A big, burly-looking man now made his appearance, who, as soon as he saw Duval, removed his hat, and stood as if awaiting his orders.

" Why didn't you get here sooner, man ?" asked Blossom. " You must have known that we were not in such pleasant quarters, or in such good company, as to wish to prolong our stay in this place."

" I was obliged to go round out of the way ever so far," said the man, " for I fancied I was being dogged."

"Ah! Are you sure that you have not been watched to this place?"

"Quite certain of it—for I did not attempt to turn in this direction until I found the man, who had evidently been watching me, had given up the pursuit."

"That was well," said Duval, speaking for the first time.

"If you'll just carry the lantern, Captain, we will follow with Dick. You know the nearest way to the coach we were to have in waiting to convey us to London Bridge?"

"I do," said Duval; "but if either of you get tired, I will take a hand at it in a moment, remember that."

"All right, Captain! Now let's be off."

It was a strange-looking procession, that.

There was the tall, powerful-looking figure of Claude Duval, sliding along at each step, up to the knees in snow, and turning back now and then to hold up the lantern for the others to follow him without losing a step by any deviation.

There likewise following him were Blossom and his companion, bearing between them the hammock and its terrible burden, and the lantern which Duval carried shed a sickly halo over them all, and as their footsteps in the snow made no noise they looked like ghostly spectres.

They had not far to go before they saw the coach which Duval had hired to convey them to London Bridge, where they intended to take a boat and drop quietly down the river to Greenwich, where Dick Turpin's mother lived, who had already by the thoughtfulness of Duval been apprised of the ghastly vision she was to expect.

We will pass over the intermediate space, and arrive just before the sad cavalcade reached at the widowed mother's cottage.

It is some hours yet ere the dawn can be expected.

Most of the inhabitants of the little village are still slumbering; but the little household with which we have to do is up and alive.

The mother had prepared a good fire, and ever and anon she went to the little casement and peered out into the darkness.

"Does he come? Does he come?" asked a young girl, who was arranging some pillows in an easy chair, close to the fire.

"Yes; here he is!" was the joyful exclamation as the mother flew to the cottage-door and admitted a young man of prepossessing appearance.

"I am in time, I see," said the new comer, glancing round. "It is impossible for them to arrive for two hours yet, so let me entreat of you to be patient."

"Ah! you know not a mother's feelings, sir," said the woman, as she hid her face in her hands.

"Yes—yes! I know all that you must suffer; but I would urge on you the necessity of trying to control your emotions, so as to be able to give me your assistance when the hour of action arrives."

"Fear not—fear not!" said the young girl, whom we have before mentioned.

As the tones of the girl's voice fell upon the ear of the visitor he started, and turned somewhat paler than was his wont.

"You here? You here, Alice?" he said, in a voice of deep emotion.

"Where should I be, if not to watch and tend him who is dearer to me than life itself?"

The young man shaded his eyes with his hand, and yet it could not have been that the faint light emitted from the poor candle which stood on the table, in the centre of the room, distressed him—some other feeling must have actuated him, as could be seen by the heaving of his broad chest, and the half-uttered sob which burst from his lips.

"What infatuation!" he sighed; "to think that one so good and pure should cling to one——"

"No more, sir! No more!" said the girl, as the colour rose to her cheeks, lips, and brow. "I know that he I love is an outcast; but he is good, generous, brave, and true——"

"Alas! alas! alas! that you should so deceive yourself, Alice," said the young man, looking steadily at her.

"I do not deceive myself as regards *him*, Richard—my Richard; but I fear that I have deceived myself——"

The girl paused, and then the old woman spoke:

"Nay, dear Alice, do not let your grief make you unjust, ar ungenerous. Remember all that we owe to this our benefactor, to say nothing of his coming here to-night to restore to life one——"

The poor woman could say no more, she trembled violently as she remembered the spectacle she was about to behold.

"Forgive me!" cried the girl, as she now fell at the feet of the young man. "Forgive me, and save him!"

"I have promised to do all that mortal man can do in such a case, and I renew that promise, although it may be the means of raising me up so dangerous a rival in your affections."

"Nay, say not so. He can never have a rival in my heart—it is his wholly and entirely, now and for ever!"

"Oh, Alice!" continued the visitor, not seeming to hear her, "how often have I promised to myself a bright and happy future with you, my dearest, by my side!"

"Forbear!—forbear!" cried the girl.

"I should have been so proud of your gentleness and your beauty, and now—now—to have my hopes all shattered!"

"I never gave you any!" said the girl, in a low voice.

"Perhaps not, in reality; but I used to fancy, Alice, that I was not indifferent to you till one night."

The girl raised her head.

"You mean the night I first met Richard Turpin?"

"Even so."

"You are right. Perhaps I was to blame. I was vain, and pleased with your attentions and the notice you bestowed upon me—a poor sempstress."

"But a lady in every sense of the word," urged the young doctor.

"By birth, yes; but working for my living in the family of one of your aristocratic patients."

"I saw and loved you then, Alice; and you——"

"Fancied that I returned your love; but the real feeling I knew not until I first saw him whom you have promised to save for me."

As the girl spoke, she seized the hand of the young man, and pressed it to her lips.

There was a look of ineffable love upon his countenance as he gently withdrew his hand, and placed it upon the girl's rich brown hair, which fell in luxuriant masses upon her beautiful neck and shoulders, saying as he did so, "By all my hopes of happiness, here and hereafter, I promise that I will watch over Richard Turpin with all the tenderness of her who gave him birth; that from this moment I will regard you only as his destined bride."

As he uttered these words, there came a gasping sob.

The girl again took his hand, and pressed it to her lips.

"I promise to regard you as his destined bride," he again repeated, "and my much-loved sister. Are you satisfied, Alice?"

"More than satisfied, dear, brave, generous heart!"

exclaimed the girl, as she gazed up into his face, and read there only lofty aspirations.

At this moment there was the sound of footsteps.

"They come—they come!" cried the girl, flying towards the door, then pausing, and turning deadly pale, she leant for support against the wall of the cottage.

"Oh, heaven give me strength," she ejaculated, "to look upon him!"

"Allow me to go first," said the young doctor, as he opened the door quietly, and stepped out into the darkness.

He was not absent long, and he and Duval entered the cottage together.

He must have taken that opportunity, brief as the time had been, to make Duval acquainted with the fact of the girl's affection for the object of his care—for as soon as he entered, after speaking a word to the afflicted mother, he passed quickly on towards Alice, and taking both her hands in his, said in his gentlest accents, "You will be brave for the sake—for the life's sake—of one who is dear to you?"

Those few words had their desired effect upon the girl, and she answered steadily, "I am prepared to do anything to show my gratitude to his preserver. Command me—I will obey you in all things."

By this time Blossom and his companion had deposited their burden on the rug before the fire, and were awaiting further orders.

CHAPTER CXXVIII.

THE DEAD RESTORED TO LIFE.

Two hours have elapsed, and still the mother, the doctor, Duval, Blossom, and the girl are watching anxiously by the couch on which lies Dick Turpin, whom every one had supposed had been hanged on that bitter winter's day at Tyburn.

And now there is an anxious movement among those silent watchers; but the doctor holds up his finger to command perfect silence.

The man who has engrossed so many of their thoughts breathes audibly, but is still sleeping.

Now he mutters in his sleep.

Evidently he is dreaming of the terrible events of the morning, for he moves restlessly, and raises his hand to his throat.

Alice is kneeling very near, and with difficulty restrains herself from throwing her arms round him, and imploring him to wake.

But again the Doctor interposes.

"Not for worlds must this sleep be disturbed. Get some warm gruel ready."

The girl flew to obey the order.

Anything was preferable to inaction.

In less than ten minutes the cordial was brought, into which the Doctor dropped a small quantity of a bluish-looking mixture.

"He is about to wake; give him a spoonful when I make a sign for you to do so."

The patient groaned, and then a few articulate sounds came from his lips.

"Alice! dear Alice!"

Alice almost uttered a scream of delight; but the warning finger of the doctor again besought her to control her emotions.

"You will blame me when you hear me spoken of as a murderer," continued Dick; "but I did not mean to kill him. King told me to fire, and I hit the wrong man. Poor King!"

The old woman sobbed aloud.

"Alack!" she cried. "He'll never be himself again!"

"Hush!" said Duval. "It is merely the result of fever. He is better—much better than we could expect, is he not, Crawford?"

"Much better," replied the Doctor, calmly. "But see, he is waking."

Dick Turpin slowly opened his eyes, and looked bewildered as he gazed around on the different familiar objects by which he was surrounded.

At length his eyes fell on the kneeling figure of Alice, who had been afraid to address him until she had received permission to do so either from Mr. Crawford or Duval.

"You, too, Alice?" he said, in a dreamy kind of way. "No, no, this is a dream! You could never come to such a place as this. Yet—and yet, methinks, that—that——"

Dick had all this time been trying to raise himself, so as to get a better view of surrounding objects, and he now sunk back exhausted.

The Doctor pointed to the gruel, and made signs to Alice to give him some of it.

She managed to pour a teaspoonful down his throat, but as she did so her hands trembled so violently that Duval had to assist her.

Turpin seemed somewhat revived as soon as he had swallowed even that small portion, and then he opened his eyes again.

"Speak to him," whispered Duval.

The girl looked inquiringly at the doctor, who nodded assent.

"Do you know me, dear Richard?" she asked, as, with one of her small hands, she stroked back the dark hair from his brow.

Turpin started, and looked bewildered, but did not answer.

Duval made a sign for her to say something else.

With a great effort, Alice succeeded in controlling her emotions; and then she said, gently, "Dear Richard, do not try to remember anything; but touch my hand, and feel assured that I—your Alice am with you."

The right cord was touched.

There was a heaving of the broad chest, and then the strong man, twining his arms around the fragile form which now clung so lovingly to his breast, burst into tears.

"He is saved," whispered Mr. Crawford, as he turned away his eyes—for although he had fancied that no love but that of a brother remained in his heart for that beautiful girl, he could not bear to see her in the close embrace of another, and that other a robber, perhaps a murderer.

Claude Duval saw and understood it all in a moment as the young doctor turned to him, and said, "I leave him in good hands, I see. There is no occasion for me to stay. Avoid all exciting topics, and all will be well."

At this moment Turpin spoke in low tones, so different to his usually clear, ringing voice.

"What is it, Alice? Where am I? Was I not——"

A spasm passed across his face, and he fainted.

Alice uttered a cry of despair.

"Nay, nay; do not be alarmed," said Mr. Crawford. "This was sure to happen as soon as the memory began to assert her sway. There is nothing to apprehend—indeed, there is nothing to apprehend."

These few words, spoken as they were, went further towards restoring poor Alice to her wonted calmness and decision than anything else could possibly have done; and she now busied herself in carrying out Mr. Crawford's orders with a firmness of purpose which astonished him.

In a short time Turpin revived, and again gazed

about him in a bewildered kind of way, and then his eyes fell upon Duval.

"Ah!" he exclaimed. "I see it all now!"

As he spoke, he feebly stretched out his hand, which Claude took, and clasped between both his own.

He saw the necessity of at once speaking in an off-hand kind of way about the whole transaction.

"All right, old fellow!" said Duval. "I thought I would just stay to see you look a little more like yourself, but now I must go."

"And it was you—you, Duval, who—who——"

Dick Turpin could not bring himself to name the service which Duval had done him, but he still retained his hand in his, and looked fixedly into his eyes as though he would know more.

Duval merely nodded.

"You saved me?"

"So it seems," said Duval, trying to smile.

"But why should you do this thing for me? I thought I had lots of friends who would have perilled their lives for me, and yet you, of whom I know so little—you have dared all this, Duval, for me?"

"No," said Duval.

"No! What mean you?"

"I have saved you, it seems, for *her*."

As he spoke, Duval pointed to Alice, who was still kneeling by the side of the couch, but whose presence Turpin seemed entirely oblivious of, in the contemplation of the fearful death he had escaped from.

"Ah, Alice! Yes, dear, I will try to make you happy, and be more worthy of your affection."

"You do make me happy, Richard, and I do believe you worthy of all this heart's fondest affections."

As the girl uttered these words, he saw the usually pale face of his friend Crawford turn a shade paler, as he quietly lifted the latch of the cottage door, and went out into the darkness.

There was something so touching in this manly struggle with an all absorbing love, that Duval resolved to hasten after him, and, if possible, engage him in conversation, which might have the effect of weaning his thoughts from his great sorrow.

Taking a hasty leave, therefore, of the humble inmates of the little cottage, Duval, after making a sign to Blossom to follow, soon followed on the steps of Mr. Crawford.

He had not gone far before he found him leaning against a tree, utterly heedless of the nipping wind, and the frozen particles which were still falling.

"I am glad I succeeded in overtaking you, Crawford," were the words which fell upon the sorrow-stricken man. "A walk with a friend on such a night as this is much more pleasant than a solitary one. What say you? shall we join company, or have you any particular engagement?"

Without waiting for an answer, Duval put his hand through the arm of his friend, and soon had the satisfaction of engaging him in conversation.

They soon reached Mr. Crawford's house, surrounded by trees, which, in the pale moonlight, looked beautiful, covered with snow.

"You will stay with me to-night, Duval; I can accommodate both you and your men."

"Thank you, but I have only one, for I see Blossom has dismissed his companion."

"Then come in and rest, for this must have been an exciting night for you."

"Well, I confess," said Duval, "it is not exactly to my mind, these kind of affairs, but as it has to be done——"

"But I don't understand; that man—Dick Turpin, I mean—seemed to speak as though you were almost strangers to each other."

"So we are, comparatively," replied Duval; "but you see, he was taken in an affair in which I also had a hand—namely, robbing a coach. I had the good fortune to get off scot free, while poor Dick was surrounded, and made prisoner."

"Then was it only a robbery, in which he was concerned?" asked Mr. Crawford, with some interest.

"So far as that affair was concerned, yes."

"But how did you contrive to escape?"

"Merely because I had taken the precaution to dress myself in the coachman's coat, hat, and boots, and take his seat on the box."

Mr. Crawford could not help laughing.

"Then you saw Turpin made prisoner?"

"Yes, and would have helped him then, but did not see my way clear: the chances were that I should only have implicated myself, without doing him any good."

"So you resolved to save him at the least?"

"Well, I cannot take credit to myself for having been the first to think of that, for my man, Blossom, there, suggested the idea which you carried out?"

"Which you carried out?"

"Exactly."

"It was a nervous thing to do."

"Not a pleasant thing, I am free to admit!" replied Duval.

And thus for two hours, the two friends beguiled the time, and Duval had the satisfaction of seeing that the young doctor had regained his usual looks and manner before he, Duval, retired to rest.

By six o'clock the next morning, Duval was prepared to take his departure; but he thought he should like, as he was so near to Turpin's house, just to look in and see how he was.

Accordingly he descended, and, opening the front door as quietly as he could, he stepped out on to the sloping lawn, which now, however, was covered with snow, which glistened in the morning sun.

"Beautiful!" escaped from the lips of Claude Duval, as his eyes fell upon the scene before him.

A very brisk walk soon brought him to the cottage door, where he had spent so much time the previous night.

He rapped gently on one of its panels.

There was no answer.

Again he knocked, and this time he heard a window opened cautiously, and the face of Alice from above took a survey of the visitor.

Duval looked up, but did not speak.

In another minute he was admitted, and had the satisfaction of seeing Turpin dressed and sitting by a cheerful fire, looking very much as if nothing had happened.

"Why, where on earth have you sprung from, Duval?" he asked, as he pointed to a chair by his side, which Duval took. "I thought you returned to London last night."

"No. I spent the remainder of the night at Crawford's."

"At Crawford's? Ah!"

There was a look of thoughtfulness upon the face of Turpin as he uttered these words, that Duval was rather surprised at.

Then Turpin spoke again.

"It's a bad job, Duval!"

"What?"

Turpin approached nearer to Duval, and then he said, "I would to heaven that Alice had returned his affection; he is much more deserving of her than I ever was, or ever can be."

"But if you make her happy, that is all that is necessary, Dick."

"But she is not the sort for me, I tell you, Duval! She is too pure, too innocent! Why, if she thought I robbed a bird's nest, even, she would learn to hate me, I believe; but when she comes to know that robbery and even murder do not come amiss to me, why what do you think she will say then—eh?"

"Dick, you are making yourself out to be worse than you really are. Tell her the kind of life you lead, and then be guided by her answer."

"I can't do it—I can't do it! When she looks at me with those innocent blue eyes of hers, and I feel her gentle touch upon my hand, I feel a very villain! But I would fain release her if I knew how!"

"Release yourself, you mean, Dick!" said Duval, gravely.

"Well, perhaps it is a little of both!"

At this moment the door communicating with the next room gently opened.

A fair form entered the apartment.

The silence which had ensued between Turpin and Duval had deceived her; she believed that Turpin was alone.

Then she heard their voices again, and, not wishing to intrude upon them, she was about to withdraw, when her own name arrested her attention.

"But I would fain release her if I knew how."

"Release yourself, you mean, Dick!"

"Well, perhaps it is a little of both!"

She had entered the room with her heart upon her lips—hopeful love in every vein, in every thought—she had entered, dreaming that across that threshold life would dawn upon her afresh, that all would be once more as it had been when the common air was rapture.

Thus she had entered, and now she stood spellbound, terror-stricken, pale as death, life turned to stone; youth, hope, bliss were for ever over to her! Richard—her Richard anxious to find some means of releasing her and himself from vows which he now regretted! For this she had been faithful and true amid storm and desolation, for this had she hoped, dreamed, and lived!

Neither Turpin nor Duval had seen her.

But the words she had heard were enough for the listener; she turned noiselessly away.

The door closed on her.

What matter what became of her?

One moment, what an effect it produces upon years! One moment! Death itself is but a moment, yet eternity is its successor!

CHAPTER CXXIX.

DUVAL AND LUCY TAKE UP THEIR ABODE IN CAMDEN HOUSE.

It was on the evening following the events we have just detailed, that Duval encountered Blossom, looking anything but cheerful.

"What's the matter, Blossom?" asked Duval.

"Why, Captain, if you ask me, I must say that I am beginning to get a little weary of this quiet sort of life."

"But, surely, Blossom, you had enough excitement last night to last, at all events, for some little time."

"That's not the kind of excitement I care for, or wish for, Captain; it is life on the road which has such charms for me."

"Well, Blossom," said Duval, "your desire shall be gratified this very night. I intend to seek a real highwayman's adventure on the road, and to cry stand and deliver the first chance that presents itself."

"All right, Captain; now I'm happy again."

And certainly the change in Blossom's countenance was truly surprising.

"Then at nine o'clock, Blossom, you will be ready to accompany me?"

"Never fear me forgetting the appointment, Captain; but I suppose you mean to take Nightshade?"

"Yes, I intend to ride her."

"All right, Captain; you'll find us both ready and up to the mark."

At the appointed time, Blossom was at the rendezvous; and scarcely had he reached it before Duval, too, made his appearance, in his scarlet coat and horseman's boots.

"Which way, Captain, do you intend to go?" asked Blossom.

"The Western Road, I think," replied Duval.

They both put their horses to a gallop; and when they had fairly entered the Western Road, Duval pulled up close to the hedge, telling Blossom to follow his example.

And then they sat and waited.

All was quiet, and the air was not so cold as it had been by many degrees.

True, the snow still lay thickly imbedded in some parts, but the trees were black, and stood out in the moonlight like so many disreputable birch brooms, instead of the luxuriant objects they had been only a few months before.

The air was nevertheless frosty, and every sound made itself distinctly heard in the locality Duval had chosen for his scene of action.

Presently there came a rumbling kind of noise upon the night air, and, in a few seconds, both Duval and Blossom detected the sound of wheels coming at a leisurely pace up the hill.

"Ah! some one who has been to dine at the Palace, probably," said Duval, as he continued to listen to the advancing vehicle.

The coach approached nearer, and Duval could see that it was a carriage, and that the coachman wore a handsome livery.

"A rich prize, probably, Blossom," whispered Duval. "I wonder how many there are inside!"

At this moment a man's head was thrust out of the window, and a voice said, impatiently, "What are you creeping along like this for? We shall never get to London Bridge to night, you scoundrel, unless you drive faster than this!"

"Shall we stop it now, Captain?" whispered Blossom, ever impatient to begin an adventure that promised anything like success.

"Hush, hush! wait a little longer!"

Then they heard the coachman say, "If you please, Sir John, the road is slippery just here; and if I drive any faster the horses will never keep their footing."

"Stuff! zounds! I'll discharge you, if you don't get to London Bridge in time for the Dart."

"What's that?" whispered Blossom to Duval.

"A vessel, probably, by which the occupant of the carriage wishes to leave England. But I'll stop him now."

As he spoke, he touched Nightshade on the flank, and in another moment he was by the side of the carriage.

Duval was about to use the usual formula, "Stand and deliver!" but the exclamation from the only occupant of the vehicle arrested his words.

With a half-stifled cry the man said "I am lost!—too late—too late!"

"Oh, you are not too late, Sir John; I have been expecting you, though, for some time!"

"Alas! alas! he knows me! Oh, have pity on me! Let me go, and I will deliver everything up to you, for I can see you are the officer sent to arrest me!"

Duval now began to understand that the occupant of the carriage mistook him for an officer who was commissioned to arrest him; on some pretext, therefore, he resolved to keep up the delusion.

"Resistance is vain, Sir John," he said. "I am

resolved to do my duty unless, indeed, you make it worth my while."

"And what would you consider worth your while? I am sure I would gladly give you up all the jewels contained in this casket, if you would promise me that when you searched me you found nothing upon me."

By this Duval fancied that the personage he had stopped must be some official, who supposed that he, Duval, had been sent after him in order to arrest him for some real or supposed robbery of jewels from one of the royal palaces, and, accordingly, he determined to humour the mistake.

While Duval was engaged in these reflections, the personage in the carriage had been looking earnestly at him, and again he spoke.

"Tell me, I beg of you, what terms will satisfy you, sir, and I am willing to accede to anything you can demand in reason."

"Nothing, sir, will satisfy me," returned Duval, "but doing my duty. I therefore, apprehend you."

"Apprehend me? But, good heavens! did you not lead me to understand, but just now, that for a consideration you would—you would——"

"But I have thought better of it, sir,; so at once hand to me the jewels, and then I will summon my men to take you prisoner, and——"

The man fell on his knees as he tendered to Duval a beautifully inlaid casket, containing jewels of considerable value.

"Now, sir," said Duval, taking out his pocket-book, "your name in full, if you please."

"But you know it—you know it!"

"Of course I know it; but it is a matter of form which cannot be dispensed with."

"Sir John English."

"And your official title?"

"Lord Chamberlain."

Duval wrote both these pieces of information down in his pocket-book, then having done so, he blew a note on the silver whistle, which he always wore, and which at once brought Blossom to the side of the carriage.

As soon as Sir John said that another man made his appearance, he gave up all for lost, and threw himself down on the floor of the carriage in an agony of terror.

"Now, Sir John," said Blossom, who had been instructed by Duval what to say. "Now, Sir John, step out, you are my prisoner!"

Sir John uttered a cry of despair.

"Hold!" said Duval; "retire for a few seconds, I would speak again with this gentleman."

"Yes, sir," said Blossom.

As soon as he was alone with the Lord Chamberlain, Duval said:

"I see but one way to help you out of your present dilemma, Sir John; and that is by our being candid with each other."

"Yes—yes! Oh, yes—I will be candid!"

"Then I will begin by telling you that I am not the person you took me for."

"Not—the—person—I—took—you—for?"

"No!"

"Who then? The dev——?"

"Not exactly; but I am a highwayman!"

"A highwayman; and I have been——"

"Robbed," said Duval, quietly.

"Ha, ha! Then it is not such a serious matter after al'," said Sir John, in quite a different tone of voice to the one he had hitherto used.

"I don't know that," replied Duval; "that depends."

"I do not understand you. You have robbed me; go your way, and let me go mine."

"Not so fast. You must remember that I proposed making my own terms."

"Yes, but I then thought that you were acting in an official capacity."

"I cannot help what you thought," said Duval. "You will either accede to my terms, or I will go at once and deliver you and this casket in the right quarters, and leave you to take the consequence of your acts."

There was such a decided tone about Duval that Sir John felt he was not a person to be trifled with; so he said, doggedly, "Well, what are your conditions, Mr.——, I have not the pleasure of knowing your name."

"Claude Duval."

The name acted like a talisman upon Sir John, for he instantly dropped his dogged, sullen tone, and assumed one of great deference.

He even inclined his head slightly, as he gazed upon the handsome highwayman, of whom he had heard so much but had never seen before.

Then he said, courteously, "I am in your power, Claude Duval, but I am happy to think that I have a gentleman to deal with. Name your conditions."

"Simply that you will give me some token—a ring, for instance—by showing which I shall be able to obtain ready access to the Palace, whenever I choose."

"But—but——"

"The alternative, if you refuse, has been already presented to you."

"Alas! what am I to do?"

As he spoke, Sir John looked helplessly about him.

"Do as I request; no one shall ever know from me by what means I obtain access to you."

"But if you show some token from me; and then —and then, if——"

"And then something should take place at the Palace which would not be pleasant, you mean, it might be easily traced to me, as having been admitted to see you—eh? Is that your objection?"

"Exactly."

"Then you must contrive to admit me yourself whenever I choose to demand it, under such disguise as I may think proper to adopt."

"Be it so."

"You agree to my terms?"

"I agree to your terms."

"It is well," said Duval. "So long as you keep faith with me, I will keep faith with you; but so soon as I detect the slightest disposition to deceive me, then beware."

"And the casket?" gasped Sir John.

"The casket I shall keep as a kind of hostage for your good faith."

"It is a hard bargain, I think," urged Sir John.

"But a just one," replied Duval. "And now listen to me. At twelve o'clock to-morrow morning you may expect my first visit. I shall be disguised as an officer in his Majesty's Light Horse."

"Be it so. I am your servant now!" sighed Sir John.

"Or my coadjutor, whichever term you prefer," laughed Duval. "Au revoir, Sir John."

As Duval spoke, he touched Nightshade, and galloped past the carriage, leaving Sir John English in no very enviable frame of mind.

"Come on, Blossom," cried Duval. "I have not only a valuable booty, but I have made a still more valuable stipulation."

Blossom was delighted.

"Have you looked into the casket, Captain?" he asked.

"No; but by the weight of it, I should say it contains an immense quantity of jewellery."

"Shall you sell them, Captain?"

DUVAL CONCEALS HIMSELF IN THE CORRIDOR.

"I do not yet know. I may do so. But who have we here?"

At this moment two horsemen appeared, and from the tone in which they were speaking, Duval thought that they were disputing.

He whispered to Blossom to get on the other side of the hedge, as he had done, and to keep pace with them, but so concealed by the brushwood that there would be no chance of their being seen. The sound of their horses' feet, too, was completely lost, while those of the two horsemen echoed far and near on the frost-browned road.

Duval could hardly believe his ears.

"To think that the old fellow should turn up just at such a crisis as this," Duval heard one say; "just as Pendell had matured all his plans, too."

"It's most provoking," replied the other voice; "but there's one thing, we dogged him well, and we shall be able to pounce upon them all before to-morrow's dawn; and when it is discovered that that girl Lucy and her husband are nowhere to be found, the thing may die out, and the King will forget all about it."

"By Jove! what a rage he was in, though, when General Everton had had that private audience with him."

"He was, indeed. But do you know how many men this Claude Duval has on Hampstead Heath?"

"Eight, I believe, besides himself and the General."

"Then we shall beat them easily, even if they show fight. But I fancy, if we play our tactics well, this Claude Duval will be absent, and the capture will be easier."

"Undoubtedly, for he would fight like a lion."

Duval had heard enough.

"We must return to Hampstead at once, Blossom." he said, laying his hand upon the bridle. "Quick, or we may be too late!"

A sharp gallop soon brought Duval to the deserted house on Hampstead Heath.

As he approached the house, a peculiar starlike light illuminated one of the upper windows.

"Push on, Blossom, my presence is required."

Another moment, and they were at the gate which led into the court-yard of the ancient mansion.

Lucy met Duval in the hall.

"There is danger Atkins thinks," she said.

"Where is he?" asked Duval, hurriedly.

"Here!" replied a voice, and, descending three stairs at a time, a tall powerful-looking man stood before Duval.

"What is it, Atkins?"

"Nothing, perhaps, Captain; but my suspicions were aroused this afternoon by two men prowling about the grounds, and when I warned them off, they certainly went away, but I heard from the boy Richard that they had questioned him as to the number of men you had."

"Why, Captain, it's best for you to know the worst—he was imprudent enough to tell them."

Duval turned somewhat pale.

"Where is the General, Lucy?" he asked.

At this moment General Everton made his appearance, saying, in a off-hand kind of way, "I am glad you have come, Duval; I cannot persuade your man to take no notice of some low fellow or other who was prowling about these grounds some hours ago. Why we are enough to hold a thousand such at bay. You try to use your influence now. Why they have even succeeded in dispelling the roses from Lucy's cheeks."

But Lucy's eyes were fixed upon her husband's face ever since the man Atkins had spoken; and, for the first time, she began to apprehend danger.

"There is more in this than meets the eye," said Duval, in a low tone to General Everton. "Come with me and I will enlighten you. In the meantime, Blossom, summon all the men to be ready to leave this house in half an hour."

"It shall be done, Captain."

CHAPTER CXXX.

CLAUDE DUVAL PAYS A VISIT TO THE LORD CHAMBERLAIN.

As soon as Duval had closed the door, he spoke to General Everton.

"My reason for returning at this moment, General, was dictated solely for the purpose of hastening our departure from this house."

"Indeed!"

"Yes," replied Duval. "Riding along the Western Road, to-night, I overheard two horsemen in close conversation, and they seemed to speak of a large force invading this house before the dawn and taking us all prisoners."

"Taking us all prisoners?"

"Yes; that was the purport of their conversation. I can now understand how it is that they know, exactly the number of men they would have to encounter. The boy Richard, as you have heard, not knowing—or rather, I should say, not thinking—of the consequences of his imprudence, told the man who questioned him."

"Ah! I begin to understand. What do you propose doing then?"

"I propose that we go to Camden House, and take possession of it as our home, at all events, for the present."

"With all my heart," replied the General; "but remember, I shall remain here to see who are the assailants of your home. I have nothing to fear."

"On the contrary," replied Duval; "it is on your account solely that this attack and capture are to be made. It is proposed to get you out of the way again, in order that Mossy Pendell may be enabled to get back to Court, and worm himself into the King's good graces again."

"But he has been expelled!" cried the General. "I never saw the King in such a rage as he was when I told him all that villain had made me endure. I have nothing to fear, I tell you, and, therefore, I shall remain."

"For my sake, uncle," pleaded Lucy, laying her hand upon his arm; for she saw that Duval was far from being convinced by her uncle's arguments.

"Well," he said, "if you so much desire it, Lucy, I will submit. I am an old man now, and have fought battles enough in my life without seeking one now with men who have no claim upon my consideration. I will go with you. When do you start?"

"Immediately."

Duval left the room, and in a few minutes returned, saying that all the arrangements were completed.

It was decided that Lucy should ride upon Nightshade, and that Duval should mount one of the next best horses his stables could produce.

Then were to follow, at some distance, Blossom and the General, and, lastly, the few men who formed what Claude Duval called his band of men.

Lucy could not leave the old mansion without a sigh of regret; for it was there that Duval had taken her as a happy bride, after rescuing her from a death, that even now never failed to make her shudder whenever she thought of it.

Their progress over the heath was soon accomplished, but, as they neared London, they thought it prudent to slacken their horses' speed.

When they reached the Oxford Road, their attention was attracted to a party of mounted men.

"Keep close, Lucy," whispered Duval. "If these men speak leave me to answer them."

Lucy obeyed, just as the men rode up to them.

At first the foremost of them seemed inclined to address Duval, but his appearance had nothing in it to excite remark—for he was attired in a plain black suit—that the man seemed to change his mind, and let him and Lucy pass by without taking the slightest notice of them.

There was a look of sadness upon the face of General Everton, as he entered the neglected garden which had once been his pride.

The snow still lay thick upon the bushes and trees, and there was a look about the whole place of desolation and coldness.

Lucy glanced up into her uncle's face, and understood his thoughts.

"Grieve not, dear uncle; we are together again, and the dear old house will soon be itself again."

When he had seen Lucy and her uncle fairly within the mansion, Duval felt comparatively easy, and began to turn his thoughts to the visit he had promised Sir John English, he would pay him at the Palace.

He had fixed noon-day in order to be convinced that Sir John did not mean to play him false; but this, his first visit, was not to secure to himself any advantage. A much later hour Duval, in his own mind, had fixed upon for what he called to Blossom his *professional* visit.

The clock of St. James's Palace was just striking twelve as Duval presented himself at the Palace, and asked for Sir John English.

A young man of prepossessing appearance, stepped forward, and said, "Sir John is expecting you, I believe, sir. Will you be good enough to follow me?"

Duval was glad that his first visit was stripped of everything that could make him in the least degree uncomfortable; and when he saw a door thrown open, and beheld the Lord Chamberlain himself seated at a table on which breakfast was laid, all doubts as to the good faith of that personage vanished.

"Good morning, Colonel!" cried Sir John, as soon as Duval entered the room. Then addressing the young man who had conducted, he said, "Order some more hot coffee, Mr. Spenser."

The young man bowed, and left the room.

As soon as the door was closed, Sir John looked somewhat confused.

"Well?" he said.

"It is well," replied Duval; "and if you give me no cause to feel dissatisfied, I may have it in my power to advance your interests at the same time that I am looking after my own."

The Chamberlain smiled.

"It is a strange compact for an official to enter into with a——"

"Hush, Sir John! There may be listeners, to whom the knowledge that Claude Duval is an inmate of the Palace would be welcome news."

At this moment a footman appeared with the coffee.

"You have not breakfasted yet, Colonel?" said Sir John, addressing Duval, as the man was arranging the breakfast equipage.

During the meal, the conversation turned upon indifferent subjects; and no one to have seen those two men would have supposed them to be other than they seemed—the one, high in office; of strict integrity, and gentlemanly bearing—the other no less polished and courtly, but in reality the notorious highwayman.

As the clock of the Horse Guards chimed, Duval took out his watch, and saw that it wanted only a quarter to two o'clock.

"I must be going, Sir John," he said, rising from the table; "and at half past ten o'clock you must meet me in Palace Yard."

"Impossible!"

"Nay, that is a word which is to be struck out of our vocabulary. Who would have thought it possible that I, Claude Duval, the highwayman, upon whose head a price is set, would be here this morning, taking breakfast with his Majesty's Lord Chamberlain—eh?"

The Lord Chamberlain made an impatient gesture.

"How long is this connection to last, pray?"

"Nay, that is scarcely courteous," replied Duval,—"just at the commencement of our acquaintance, too! Probably, I should say—as long as we live!"

The Chamberlain heaved a deep sigh.

"Oh, if I could but have foreseen what the folly of indulging in avarice would lead to——"

"You fancied it would lead to death!" laughed Duval, "or you would not so easily have fallen into the mistake, that by making friends with the officer who was sent to arrest you you would save yourself."

"No more!—no more!"

"I am quite willing to drop the subject," said Duval, "if it is unpleasant to you; but do not be continually talking as though you were a pattern of honesty and uprightness, when in reality you are no better than Claude Duval, the highwayman, and with few temptations to be dishonest. And now, adieu! until half-past ten o'clock to-night."

"Be it so," said the Chamberlain.

Duval was shown out with the same ceremonious attention which had characterised his entrance to the palace, and altogether was far from being dissatisfied with his visit.

As Duval was making his way across the park, seated on one of the benches a figure caught his eye, which he recognised at a glance.

"Mrs. Eldridge," he said to himself. "I will speak to her, and perhaps learn something of that infatuated girl, whose innocent love makes me almost hate myself."

As Duval approached, the old dowager raised her eyes, and met his fixed upon her.

There was a flutter, Duval could see, of the fan she carried, and then the exclamation for which he had been waiting, came—"Ah!"

"I am too happy to-day," said Duval, as he took a seat by Mrs. Eldridge. "I am too happy, madam, to have this pleasure. Each day have I returned to this spot, and yet have I been compelled to leave it again without beholding her for whom my eyes longed."

"Really, sir, you do say such things, that I scarcely know what reply to make," simpered the ancient dame. "But I am full of trouble. I ought not to speak as I did, or think as I did."

The old lady now covered her face with her handkerchief, and Duval believed she really was weeping.

For an instant his thoughts flew to that gentle girl who had spoken so heart-brokenly only a few days before, and while he longed for, yet he dreaded to ask the cause of Mrs. Eldridge's grief.

"May I know the cause of your grief?" he asked.

"Adele! Adele!"

"Good heavens! What has happened to her?"

"Sir?"

"Such grief as yours, madame, alarms and pains me. Oh, speak, and say if I can do aught to assuage this sorrow?"

Duval could scarcely restrain his impatience, but he felt quite certain in his mind that any show of interest as regarded the fair girl, who really occupied so many of his thoughts, would be fatal to his intercourse with her aunt.

"She was taken alarmingly ill as soon as we reached home, and before night delirium seized her."

"How sad!"

"But that is not the worst, for the doctor assures me that she will soon be herself again; but she has done nothing but rave about that notorious highwayman, Claude Duval. Have you heard of him? but why do I ask, of course you have. For my part, I cannot think what the women can see in such a disreputable fellow, and to think that my niece—my niece, sir, should go on talking and raving as though she had seen him."

"Perhaps she has," suggested Duval.

"How could she? I never let her out of my sight—indeed, it is my belief that I owe all this trouble in some measure to you!"

"To me?"

"Yes. The day you first met us in the park, I remember now that Adele was absent for some little time, and during that time she must have seen this vile man."

"Oh, impossible, madam!" said Duval; "he dare not trust himself in the broad, open face of day in this park, with a large reward set upon his head. You must be mistaken, some one has probably been talking to her about him, and thus the whole affair may be accounted for."

"But she continually utters whole sentences, such as might have taken place between herself and some other person."

"Oh, let me beg of you not to give heed to the fancies of an overwrought imagination. The delusion will soon pass away, and your niece will neither talk nor think of a highwayman."

"I hope you may turn out to be a true prophet, sir," said Mrs. Eldridge, whose mind seemed much more at ease since her conversation with Duval.

At this moment Duval perceived, coming at a sharp pace across the enclosure, no less a personage than Muckles, the officer, with his attendant shadow, Swallow.

It was too late for Duval to attempt to leave the spot without attracting the attention of these two men, so he resolved to remain where he was, and be guided by circumstances.

When they were within a few paces of the bench

upon which Duval and the old lady were seated, Swallow happened to encounter the gaze of Claude Duval fixed upon him.

Swallow's first impulse was to cry out "There he is!"—but the next was less disastrous to Duval, for he said,

"It's no use, Mr. Muckles, a goin' on a scouring the country in this fashion. Claude Duval is a ghost, I believe, after all; or he must have been taken long ago."

"I tell you I saw him enter the Park disguised as an officer of His Majesty's Light Horse—and have him I will, if it costs me my life. Eh? What?"

These words were caused by Muckles happening to raise his head, and discovering that he was face to face with the very man whom he was in search of.

With a cry of joy he leapt almost into Claude Duval's lap.

"Now I've got you!" he shouted, "and hang me if we part again, Claude Duval!"

"What does this fellow mean?" asked Duval, with imperturbable coolness, looking towards Swallow, who stood with open mouth and distended eyes watching the whole proceeding.

"Only this, sir, that Mr. Muckles is an officer of the police; and as such, occasionally makes a mistake. Mr. Muckles! Sir!"

Mr. Muckles still held on to Duval, who, however, never stirred an inch; but merely said in a low voice to Mrs. Eldridge, who was trembling violently:

"Fear nothing, madam—this gentleman is a most efficient and gentlemanly officer in his Majesty's police service. He has merely made a mistake, and supposes me to be some one else."

Muckles slowly turned and regarded Swallow.

"Come away, Mr. Muckles, before he gets into a passion. Why, bless me, can't you see there is no resemblance between Claude Duval and that gent. Why he's as tall again—Duval, I mean."

Muckles began to look puzzled.

"Do you mean to say that I did not see you come in at the gate over there," he asked, looking at Duval steadily.

"I dare say you saw me enter by that gate, for now I come to remember, I did so."

"Then you are Claude Duval!"

"This is really too absurd. Do you know, sir, to whom you have the honour of speaking?"

As Duval uttered these words, he rose from his seat and glared so fiercely at Muckles, that that officer was only too glad to take refuge behind Swallow.

"Begone, sir," continued Duval, following up his advantage—"or this will be the worst day's work you have ever done in your life!"

Swallow twitched his superior by the coat.

"Come away, Mr. Muckles, it isn't Duval. We are done brown again, and if you stay here any longer, you will most likely get into some trouble, for that fellow looks as though he would as soon run us through with his sword as look at us."

"In truth, I think you are right, Swallow," whispered Muckles; "I believe I am at fault this time."

"Well, sir?" asked Duval, assuming an authoritative tone of voice.

"I beg your pardon, sir, I confess I have been mistaken."

"That is sufficient. Now take yourself off, sir, and another time, be more careful when you make an assault upon a gentleman."

Muckles looked crest-fallen; and Swallow, after giving Duval a glance of intelligence, withdrew with his superior from the spot.

CHAPTER CXXXI.

CLAUDE DUVAL FINDS HIMSELF IN COMFORTABLE QUARTERS.

As ten o'clock was striking by the Palace clock a solitary figure might be seen slowly pacing up and down Palace Yard, as though expecting to meet some one.

Ever and anon, as this figure moved to and fro, he kept muttering to himself disjointed sentences.

"Fool—idiot that I was to allow myself to be drawn into such a compact! What, if he did proclaim all he knows? Would his word be believed when contradicted by me?"

The Palace clock chimed the quarter

"Only another quarter of an hour, and then it will be too late. What is to be done? Ah!"

This exclamation was caused by the fact that at this moment Duval stepped up close to the side of Sir John, and whispered in his ear,

"No treachery, if you value your life. See here!"

As he spoke, Duval produced a loaded pistol, and presented it full in the face of Sir John.

"Have a care! have a care!" the latter almost shrieked. "Who thinks of treachery?"

"You contemplated ridding yourself of me to-night, and for ever. But I tell you, Sir John, that the compact must be fulfilled. You and I must pass a good deal of time in each other's society. But we are losing time. Is the King at St. James's?"

"Yes."

"Then lead me to the suite of apartments set apart for his majesty's service, and show me a place where I may conceal myself."

"You surely do not contemplate——"

"What? Speak, I shall not be offended!"

"Murder!"

"Well, certainly not! Do you not know that it was I who saved his life when my Lord of Montrose contemplated putting his Majesty out of the world?"

"Ah, to be sure, I forgot! But tell me, did his Majesty reward you for that service?"

"No: his Majesty was too anxious to forget the circumstance to be able to remember what he owed me on that occasion; and, as I think, saving a man's life, and that a King's life, is deserving of some gratitude or some token, I intend to help myself, perhaps, to-night to some of his Majesty's jewellery."

"But—but——"

"But the honesty of the affair strikes you as being rather—equivocal, eh?" laughed Duval.

The Lord Chamberlain winced.

"Come," said Duval, "time presses. Let us go into the palace."

"And you really mean that I must lead you to the King's apartments?"

"Even so. Now lead the way."

Duval followed his guide, looking warily about him from time to time, for he still entertained suspicions as to the good faith of the man whose guidance he was trusting.

Through several corridors, and up flights of steps, across passages and vestibules, at length Duval found himself in a handsome picture gallery.

A profound silence reigned around

"Fiend," lightly whispered the Chamberlain, as he pushed open a door at the end of the gallery.

There was a feeling of warmth and comfort about the temperature of this apartment, which was particularly grateful to the two almost benumbed men who entered its precincts.

It appeared to Duval to be a kind of vestibule—or more particularly speaking, an ante-room to the apartments beyond.

Rich velvet drapery covered the walls of this room, and fell in massive folds over the door and windows.

"What room is that beyond?" asked Duval, over which the velvet curtains were drawn aside, as if for the purpose of giving ready ingress or egress to another apartment.

"That is where his Majesty occasionally stops when he has only one or two friends with him—or——"

"Or a lady, you would say?"

"Just so."

"Let us enter."

"But——"

"Let us enter, Sir John English. His Majesty is not there?"

"No."

"Then lead the way."

The Lord Chamberlain opened the door nervously, and in another moment he and Duval stood within the beautiful apartment, known at that time as the King's refectory.

The supper was laid for two.

"Good!" said Duval. "Now show me his Majesty's sleeping apartment."

"I dare not open the door. I know not who may be there; but that is the door of it."

"I am satisfied," said Duval. "Now you may leave me. But stay; you have not yet shown me where I may conceal myself, if I have occasion to do so."

"Occasion to do so? Why, what do you mean? You must conceal yourself, or it will be certain death if you are found here."

"Oh, I'll look after myself, don't you fear!"

The Chamberlain looked very much as though he would rather hear him say he could not take care of himself.

"Quick!" added Duval. "Tell me where I may hide."

"What, in his Majesty's bed chamber?"

"Well, I did not mean that, but I think I would prefer those quarters to these; so tell me exactly where I can hide within that chamber."

"At the bed-head there is a marble statue, holding a lamp; you will have no difficulty in secreting yourself behind that."

"Thank you. Now I would be alone."

The Chamberlain, looking the picture of misery, walked quickly from the room, and Claude Duval found himself alone with his hand upon the handle of the door which led into the King's sleeping apartment.

There was a moment's indecision on the part of Claude Duval, whether to enter the sleeping apartment or secret himself in the room in which he then found himself.

The sound of approaching footsteps, however, determined Duval to seek refuge in the first mentioned apartment.

Scarcely had he done so and closed the door behind him, leaving, however, a small crevice through which he might see and hear all that took place in the apartment, in which it appeared his Majesty intended to sup on that night; then the door of the apartment opened from a kind of corridor, and three gentlemen appeared, preceded by an official richly dressed in purple velvet.

Duval had no difficulty in recognizing in the foremost of the three gentlemen his Majesty, King George, but the other two seemed perfect strangers to him.

The King looked hot and flushed, and was speaking in an angry tone of voice as he entered the supper room.

"It is ever thus," he said. "Foiled at every turn: Frederick has friends who never fail to report to him all that takes place within the privacy of our own circle. There is treachery somewhere. and if I do find out who the traitor is let him tremble."

The two gentlemen exchanged glances, but uttered not a word.

The King threw himself into a chair, after having, by a wave of the hand, dismissed the high official, who then noiselessly withdrew, and closed the door behind him.

After the lapse of a few seconds the King spoke again.

"I would be alone, my lords."

The two personages thus addressed backed towards the door, and in another moment the King was alone.

Duval slowly opened the door of communication, but as the King's back was towards it, he could not see Duval, unless he had actually turned round.

Duval waited for a few minutes and then he coughed slightly.

The King started up, and turning round, perceived that he was not alone.

Duval spoke calmly.

"There is no danger, your Majesty. I wished to have some conversation with you, and have taken this means to secure my object."

"Impudence! Traitor! Gua——"

Duval stepped forward with a loaded pistol in his hand, the muzzle of which, however, he was careful not to direct towards the King.

"Do not give an alarm. I intend no injury to your sacred person, as I told you before. I came here to talk, not to murder."

"Mur—murder?" echoed the King, turning pale.

"Yes, your majesty, would it not be murder if I were to take the life of a man who was unarmed?"

The King looked somewhat more re-assured.

"What is it you want to say, sir?" asked the King, "that you come here dressed and armed as a highwayman, as you are."

"As I am," said Duval, gracefully inclining his head; "but now to the purport of my visit. I came here to remind you that I had fulfilled my promise of freeing Lucy Everton, as she was called, from the stain cast upon her by the accusation which was brought against her for murder."

"Lucy Everton? Murder?" mused the King. "Really, a—yes—there are so many murderesses, that we cannot take upon ourselves to remember this one in particular."

"Indeed, your majesty. Not when the person said to be murdered happens to be one of your majesty's bravest officers, and a member also of your Privy Council?"

"Oh—ah! Yes—you refer to General Everton?"

"I do, your majesty."

"Well, then, we can only say, that we were glad, very glad, to find that the reports which had been so ingeniously circulated respecting that gentleman, are entirely without foundation."

"Exactly," replied Duval; "but is the young girl, who was accused of the foul crime of murdering General Everton, to meet with no redress at the hands of justice?"

"Well, a—really—we—we do not wish to enter into a discussion upon the injustice that was done—suffice it, that she is now cleared from the slightest imputation."

"That is scarcely sufficient, your Majesty. I must have a more substantial proof than mere words, of your Majesty's desire to see justice done to the innocent."

"But what would you have?"

"I would have a fortune, your Majesty, to lay at Lucy Everton's feet, by which she may be enabled, as long as she lives, to purchase consideration from those in power; and to begin, I may as well state that this circlet of diamonds which I saw lying on your Majesty's dressing-table will make a suitable offering to one who has great pretentions to beauty."

"Hold, sir!" shouted the King, turning very red in the face. "That circlet of diamonds you so impudently appropriate is already disposed of."

"But they are still in your Majesty's possession?"

"Yes, sir; but they are no longer mine to give."

"Then I shall be under the necessity of taking them. I would have preferred receiving them from your Majesty, but if you will not accede to the request, there is no other mode left to me."

"This is infamous!" cried the King; and he made a movement as though he would have passed Duval, and rush towards the door.

But Claude was much too quick.

He passed quietly but dexterously between the King and the door of the apartment, so as to effectually bar any attempt at escape.

"Do you presume to stop us?" almost gasped the King.

"I regret exceedingly that your Majesty should make such a proceeding necessary."

"I will summon the guard!" forgetting, in the excitement of the moment, to use the pronoun we, as is usual when royalty is speaking of himself or herself.

"I will summon the guard, Claude Duval!"

"No, your Majesty will not," calmly replied Duval, as he gave a slight movement to the hand which held the pistol.

"What! you would assassinate us in our own palace?"

"I might be compelled, for my own safety's sake, to have recourse to this little weapon. But, as I said before, I came not here for the purpose of putting you out of the world, but in order that I might receive from your Majesty a compensation for all that Lucy Everton has suffered."

"But I did not accuse her."

"No—but I have a fancy that some sort of compensation shall come from you, so I must trouble your Majesty for those three diamond rings you have on, the breast-pin, and likewise any money or valuables you may happen to possess that can be easily carried."

"Upon my word, Claude Duval, you are an impudent thief!"

"An epithet which scarcely sounds well, coming from your kingly lips. But we will say no more about it; give me what I should be sorry to take by force."

"Take—by—force?"

"Yes—why not? When I cry 'Stand and deliver!' on the high-road, does your Majesty suppose that the person or persons I think fit to rob, can evade me, just because it may not be convenient to them to hand me their property? No—I follow 'Stand and deliver!' up with 'Your money or your life!' and generally get the former without the latter."

"But you have never really murdered?"

"Oh, I have been obliged, you see, when those I have accosted have preferred the latter alternative in that case, your Majesty perceives I get both their money and their life."

"Good heavens!" gasped the King.

Claude Duval appeared neither to see nor hear the effect his words had produced upon the King; but it was exactly what he wanted, for he commenced taking off his rings immediately, and handed them to Duval.

"That will save a vast deal of trouble to your Majesty,' he said, as he coolly put them on.

"How save us trouble?"

"I meant, it would save me trouble, your Majesty."

"I don't understand you," said the King, looking from side to side, as though he would assure himself, by that, that he was awake. "I don't understand you."

"I mean this, then, if your Majesty commands me to be more explicit, that it is not what I like exactly to rifle dead bodies, I would much rather take what I want, and then let the persons I rob go cheerfully on their ways."

"Cheerfully?"

"Well, that is as their dispositions may urge them," laughed Duval. "Now for that watch and seals, if it please your majesty."

"This watch? Why, it is worth—worth—I don't know how much."

"For that very reason, I will trouble your majesty to resign it to me."

As Duval spoke, without seeming to approach one step nearer to the king, he skilfully transferred it from his majesty's pocket to his own.

CHAPTER CXXXII.

CLAUDE DUVAL FINDS HIMSELF IN A PERILIOUS SITUATION.

THE King looked perfectly aghast; but just at this moment a slight scraping was heard on the panel of the door.

Duval knew in an instant that the slight noise meant that some one was about to enter the royal presence.

The King gave a smile of satisfaction and relief, for he fancied that Duval would not understand the signal; but he was not long left to enjoy his apparent triumph, for Duval laid his hand on the lock of the door, and turned the key.

As he did so, he whispered, "You must admit no one until my interview is over. You understand, your Majesty?"

The King, who had been standing ever since Duval had first made his appearance, now sunk down into an easy chair, and gazed about him with a helpless, inane kind of stare, as though he were not certain, exactly, who he really was.

The scraping on the panel came a second time.

"What is the signal your majesty makes when you do not wish your privacy intruded upon?" whispered Duval.

The King shook his head, but did not utter a word.

The scratching came a third time; and after listening for some few minutes, Duval fancied he heard the sound of retreating footsteps.

The King heard them likewise, and turned deadly pale.

"It is well," said Duval. "Now, your majesty, we are alone again."

"Yes—alone again," sighed the King.

"Then, now I will trouble you for whatever money your majesty may happen to have about your royal person."

The King mechanically put his hand in his pocket, and handed to Duval a pocket-book. Saying, as he did so, with a ghastly smile, "Mr. Highwayman, you seem to have been made well aware of the best time to pay us this visit; it is not often we have so well filled a purse as that we have just now handed to you."

"Nor such a diadem of diamonds," said Duval, as he held the magnificent circlet of brilliants up, so that the rays of light from the silver lamp which depended from the ceiling fell upon it."

The king stamped with rage.

"They cost me — "

"Forget what they cost, your majesty, remember what they might have cost you, if you had not been wise."

The King was silent.

"Now, your majesty, I want to leave the palace; but I must have your word of honour that I shall do so unmolested."

"Go; and may — —"

"Hold, your majesty!" said Duval, raising his hand, and drawing himself up to his full height. Let us not part with words of anger and defiance. I have treated you with all respect and deference."

"Yes, with a loaded pistol in your hand, to enforce all your extortionate demands."

"Nay, your majesty, I am disappointed to find," replied Duval, "that you give such harsh terms to arts which were not invented to excite your majesty's indignation."

"Go, sir—we would be alone."

"By which door?"

"We care not, so that you rid us of your presence."

"But your promise, your majesty."

"Promise? I have promised nothing."

"No, but you must do so."

"What, now?"

"Promise me that you will give no alarm—that what has passed between us this night shall remain a secret."

"But the circlet of diamonds, I wanted it to-night. We must speak of the shameless manner in which we have been robbed."

"Your majesty may speak of it, then," replied Duval; "but not until I have had sufficient time to leave the Palace."

"Go, sir," again said the King.

"No."

"No? Do you beard me to my face?"

"Not until I have your Majesty's promise that I shall leave the Palace unmolested will I stir from this spot."

"Go; you shall not be molested."

"But—but pardon me, I have on two other occasions had cause to know that your Majesty's memory is somewhat treacherous. Give me a pass which I can show, and which will secure me against all suspicion."

"What would you have of us now, sir?"

"Merely a few words, under your Majesty's sign manual, to say that I am to be allowed to pass through all the doors which are between me and the open air. See, here are writing materials, your Majesty".

Duval drew towards him a small desk, inlaid beautifully with mother of pearl and gold, and seizing a pen, he wrote the following words on a sheet of paper.

"Allow the bearer, Joseph Spencer, to pass out unquestioned. Given under our hand, this 3rd day of January, 17—."

When Duval had written the above words, and approached the King, and falling on one knee, presented it to him to sign, the King could not forbear a smile at the cool impudence with which Duval had transacted the whole affair, and taking up the pen which Duval held in readiness, he signed hastily,

"GEORGE REX."

"That will do, said Duval, as after glancing hastily at the signature, he folded it, and put it in his pocket."

"I now humbly take my leave of your gracious Majesty."

With a low bow Duval left the room by the very door at which he had heard the strange, scraping noise.

Duval found himself in a long corridor, from which opened doors on either side.

He walked leisurely, asking himself which one he should open, when he thought, suddenly, he heard the trampling as of many feet.

He paused for an instant, and then he became aware that the footsteps issued from the direction he had just left; and a conviction that the King had repented of having given him the paper which would ensure him leaving the Palace in security, came over his mind.

The gallery or corridor, in which Duval found himself, was ornamented with statues, and behind one of these he resolved to hide himself until he should have ascertained whether or not he was the cause of the sudden tumult.

Scarcely had he made his way behind a figure of large dimensions, than the door leading into the first of the suite of apartments in the occupation of the King was burst open, and a number of men, Yeomen of the Guard Duval fancied they were, but the light was so dim which issued into the corridor, that it was impossible to form an exact idea on the subject.

"Treason!—treason!"

Yes those were the words which came unmistakably upon the ears of Claude Duval, as he drew himself close to the wall.

"He cannot have got far!" he heard the King say; he must be hiding behind one of the statues. Search every nook and corner."

The situation of Duval was perilous in the extreme.

It would have been madness to have attempted to fight his way throught a body of armed men; and yet, if he remained in his present place of concealment, discovery was inevitable.

Unconsciously, Duval drew himself still further back—still nearer to the wall - while he thought.

But he felt that his situation was one of too much peril even to admit of thought—that is to say, all thoughts were merged into the one of escape.

But how was he to escape?

Even now, were not those Yeomen of the Guard—for such, indeed, he had no difficulty in discovering them to be, for they had lighted a lantern, and one of their number was carrying it high above his head, in order to light his companions in the task of searching that corridor, by command of the King himself.

By the merest accident, Duval leant against the wall, and, at first to his surprise, and then to his great joy, he discovered that it was a moveable panel against which he was leaning.

To any one less versed than Duval in such ingenious contrivances, this fact would have only given rise to another cause of terror and uncertainty.

But upon Duval the effect was quite of another character.

He hastily moved his hand up and down, and had the satisfaction of seeing that the part of the wall against which he had been leaning turned upon a pivot, and that there was a sufficient opening for at least a man as big again as himself to pass through.

He was not long in taking his determination.

In another moment, Duval had stepped into the space beyond, and had shut the panel after him.

It was well for him; for at that very moment a couple of the Yeomen of the Guard advanced to look behind the very statue which had formed his temporary hiding-place.

Duval kept his ear close to the panel, in order that he might hear what was said; for suddenly the thought took possession of his imagination that perhaps the sliding panel was no secret, and that after the search in the gallery they might pass into the very place in which but a moment before he had congratulated himself upon being so secure.

But he was not kept long in suspense, for he heard one of the men say, "He must have got as far as the picture-gallery, which he might easily do without encountering any one at this time of night; but as soon as ever he attempted to leave that, he will be challenged by the man on guard.

"It's quite certain," replied the other, "he is nowhere in this corridor, so we may as well give up the search in this direction."

"Quick, my men," said another voice, "no time is to be lost. Every one must be warned that Claude Duval has a paper in his possession, signed by the King, authorizing his departure from the Palace. That paper must not be attended to."

"All right, sir," replied some of the men, as they withdrew from the gallery in different directions to fulfil the orders of their superior.

"So this pass will not avail me after all," said Duval to himself, as he placed his hand in his breast-pocket, and felt that the pass, if it may be so called, was secure.

Yes, there it was; but of no more use to Duval than a blank sheet of paper.

Still he was thankful to think that he had acquired so valuable a piece of information; as, of course, now, he would never dream of presenting it.

Duval waited until all was quiet again, and then he began to contemplate his present situation with anything but a pleasant feeling.

His first step was to furnish himself with a light, the means of doing which he was never without.

The light from the noiseless match, known only in those days as thieves' matches, but so common in our own, was so feeble that at first it only made the intense darkness in which he found himself visible.

But soon he became accustomed to its feeble rays, and, by the time he had lighted another from the expiring remains of the first, Duval could see that he was on the top of a perpendicular flight of steps.

The feeling of thankfulness arising from the thought that, twenty times during the space of as many minutes he must have been just on the point of precipitating himself down those steps, at first overpowered every other.

He now lighted another match, and holding them both up high above his head, he saw that the steps amounted to about twenty.

They were steep, and nearly upright.

From the look of the thick layer of dust and damp upon them, Duval felt certain that no one had descended those steps for years, so he was under no apprehension of pursuit from the direction from which he had come.

His own footsteps were plainly visible; and as he slowly descended, great lumps, so to speak, of dust preceded him, and fell with a dull thud upon the step beneath.

To any one less courageous than Duval, that descent into what had evidently been an unexplored region for so many years, would have been a serious thing.

And perhaps Duval himself, at that moment, would have preferred something less mysterious. But still it must be done—some outlet must be found, or he felt that he must look forward to death—death the most painful, most lingering—that of starvation; for, as far as he was concerned, he was buried—entombed, so to speak.

Duval paused, and again felt in one of the pockets of his apparel.

"Now," he said to himself, "I can brave anything. At least, I shall have the means of discovering the kind of place I am in."

As he spoke, he drew from his pocket a square box, about six inches in length.

From this box he took a small wax candle, which he lighted, and carrying it in one hand, he slowly began to descend the steps again.

CHAPTER CXXXIII.

CLAUDE DUVAL SUCCEEDS IN ESCAPING FROM THE PALACE.

AT first, Duval had fancied that it was a flight of stone steps he was descending; but he found, when he removed with his foot the thick coating of dust which wholly concealed the material of which they were composed, that they consisted of large square blocks of oak, with nothing but a rope to steady the steps.

He counted twenty-five, and then he found himself in a wide corridor below, flanked on one side by tall windows like those of a church, and on the other, by numerous small doors.

The darkness was so profound, that at first the rays of the candle which he carried only served to dissipate the obscurity immediately around it, while the rest of the corridor beyond looked like the mouth of a yawning cavern, or interminable vault, filled with gloom and shadows.

But, as Duval began to get accustomed to the darkness, and the rays issuing from the newly lighted wax candle became stronger, he saw here and there an old suit of armour; and the grotesque figures on two large antique stone benches seemed to grin and gibber in the flame.

Still he walked on, pausing only for a moment at a door on the left hand.

At the end of the corridor on the left, he came to a larger staircase than that which he had just descended, and going cautiously down and through some other passages, Duval found himself in a large vestibule with two doors on either hand.

They were of various dimensions, but all studded with lage nails, and secured by thick bands of iron; and, turning to the largest of the four, he quietly lifted a latch and pushed it open.

Duval then closed the door carefully and quietly behind him; and thinking that he would be more secure and certain from all interruption, he turned the key in the lock.

He now entered a spacious hall; but it had evidently been untrodden by human footsteps for many years.

There were manifold green stains upon the stone pavement, which testified to it having been long disused.

A number of torn and dusty pennons and banners, on the lances which had borne them to the field, waved overhead, as the wind, which found its way through many a broken pane of glass in the casement, played amongst these shreds of departed glory.

A whispering sound in Duval's active imagination seemed to proceed from them, and they seemed to say, "Whither, whither?" and others to answer, "To dust, to dust!"

In the middle of the hall, Duval paused and thought.

A degree of hesitation came over him, and then he murmured to himself:

"It must be done. I must find some means of egress from this fearful place; or I will return and retrace my steps, and meet the death which awaits me in the upper air, as all brave men should do."

He then walked forward, and discovered another door at the far end of the hall, much smaller than that by which he had entered.

Apparently, it had not been opened for a long time, as a pile of dust lay thick against it.

There was no key in the lock, and it seemed fastened from the other side.

DUVAL SEEKS THE SHELTER OF THE ASTROLOGER'S ROOM.

After pushing it for some time to see if it would give way, Duval drew forth from a pocket in his coat a bunch of skeleton keys, which he was seldom without.

After trying three or four keys without success, he at last had the satisfaction of finding the lock yield.

It grated horribly on its hinges; but still Duval was enabled, by exerting great strength, to throw the door back.

Then holding up the candle he carried, he gazed attentively into the space beyond him.

It appeared to be a long narrow passage in the stonework, with no windows that he could see; and yet, Duval could scarcely account for the damp slime which was glistening on the walls, unless there were some opening of some description.

The pavement, for such he believed it to be, was covered with a damp, black coating of mould, from which here and there sprang up a crop of pale, sickly fungi, covered with noxious dew, spreading a sort of faint, unpleasant odour around.

No. 43.—NIGHTSHADE.

So foul, and damp, and gloomy looked the place, that it required an effort of resolution on the part of Duval to enter; but, after pausing for a moment, he did so, and closed and locked the door behind him, as he had done the other.

Then, turning round, he looked about him, still holding the candle high above his head, as though expecting to encounter some fearful object in the way.

All was vacant, however; and as the faint rays of light dispersed the darkness, Duval perceived another door at the end of the passage, some thirty yards in advance.

Duval approached, and found that it yielded readily to his touch, and on drawing it back, for it opened towards him, he discovered another flight of stone steps, descending, apparently, into a well.

It was no faint heart which beat in the bosom of Claude Duval.

He did, certainly, feel awe, for he was going in solitude and the midst of night, into places where mortal feet evidently had not trodden for years.

He paused for some moments at the head of the flight of steps, and gazed down into the dark void below, but the next instant, with a slow and careful foot upon the wet and slippery steps, he began the descent.

The air felt stifling above, but gradually grew cold and chilling, as he descended, and the candle burned dimmer and dimmer from the impure vapours that seemed congregated in the place.

Each step he took, too, produced a hollow, unearthly sound, both above and below, till it seemed that voices were whispering behind and before him.

Twice he paused to listen, scarcely able to persuade himself that he did not hear voices speaking; but as he so paused, the sound ceased, and again he proceeded on his way.

The square cut stones forming the shaft in which the staircase turned, with the jointings only more clearly discernable from the mortar having dropped out, soon gave way to the more solid masonry of nature; and the rude, roughly-hewn stones were all that was left around him, with the steps still descending in the midst.

At length Duval came to the termination of the stone staircase, at the foot of which a door was half open.

All was darkness beyond, and although there seemed a freer air as he pulled the door back, and the end of candle burnt up somewhat more clearly, yet the vast, gloomy expanse before Duval lost scarcely a particle of its gloom as he advanced, bearing the light in his hand.

Laying his left hand on his sword, he turned suddenly, and looked behind him, but there was no one there, and he saw nothing but the heavy stone walls, and low groined arches, which seemed spreading out interminably on each side.

Duval again listened, for again he fancied he heard a whispering near him.

But he could see nothing.

The next moment a frightened bat fluttered across the passage, and nearly extinguished the light he held.

Again he fancied he heard a voice, and he took a few steps forward, and asked, in low voice, "Who are you?"

Still Duval listened, for he could not divest himself of the uncomfortable feeling that he was not alone in that solitary place, and he asked, but this time in louder tones, "Who is here?"

"Here!"

Duval felt sure, in his own mind, that the utterance of that one word was in human accents, and not the echo produced by his own voice.

Again he demanded, "Who speaks?"

There was no reply, but the echo of his own voice among the arches; and holding the candle before him, he turned to the side from whence the voice had seemed to proceed, and thought he saw a figure standing in the dim obscurity, at a few paces' distant.

"Who are you?" Duval cried, stepping forward.

But there the figure stood, growing more defined as the rays of the candle fell upon it, and the eyeless, grinning head, and long mouldy bones of a skeleton appeared, bound with a rusty chain to a thick column.

Instinctively he recoiled, as the ghastly figure met his gaze; but after a minute had so elapsed, he advanced boldly, and confronted it.

It was the figure of a Catholic priest, in his full vestments, which fell about their fleshless owner in strange, suggestive folds.

Duval was horror-struck.

Nothing having, however, showed itself, and ashamed of the fears which had taken possession of him, he drew his sword out of its sheath, and walked quickly past the fearful object.

His path soon became encumbered; and first he stumbled over a slimy skull, and then trod upon some bones that crunched under his feet.

It was with a feeling of joy that Duval saw the further wall of the vault, with an open arch leading out into some place beyond.

When he reached it, however, the scene which met his gaze was no less sad and gloomy, for he seemed now in a vast building, like a chapel, where, ranged on either side, were sepulchral monuments, covered with the dust of ages apparently, and between them long piles of mouldering coffins, with overhead a banner here and there, gauntlets, and swords, and tattered garments, the hues of which could scarcely be distinguished through the deep stains of mildew which covered them.

Here frowned the figure of a warrior in black marble.

There lay another, hewn in plain stone.

Here stood a pile of coffins, with the velvet which once covered them, and the gold with which they were fringed all mouldering in shreds, and offering a stern comment on the grossest of human vanities, that tries to deck the grave with splendour, and serves up the banquet of the worm with finery.

When he had half passed through the solemn avenue, Duval thought he heard a sound behind him, and turned to look, but there was nothing near, except three small coffins, and the marble effigy of a lady kneeling in an attitude of prayer.

"By heaven! this is all very strange and horrible!" he could not help exclaiming.

But yet he resolved to continue his steps, in hopes of finding some means to reach the outer air; and he hurried quickly forward till he reached the door at the opposite side.

It was bolted within, but not locked; and pulling back the iron bar from the staple, he was about to rush out, when he stumbled over something in which his feet had become entangled.

Stooping down, he beheld that the object which had impeded his progress was a quantity of long, fair hair, and that it belonged to the body of a skeleton which lay at his feet. Evidently, from the length and beauty of the hair, it must have belonged to a very young girl.

Duval put his hand to his brow with sensations in his bosom which he had never felt before, and which he felt almost ashamed of feeling now.

Hastily gathering up the hair, and a couple of curious rings which lay on the pavement at his feet, he rushed out at the open door, and, with a cry of joy, beheld that he was once more in the open air, and beneath the canopy of heaven.

He followed the path which was just before him, being guided by some trees and bushes, which, no doubt, in summer time, grew in wild luxuriance.

But still it was in vain that Duval looked about him for some mode of leaving the palace.

The walls were high, and he had just resolved to attempt to scale them, when he felt certain that, at a very short distance, he heard voices in altercation.

He turned round twice, but could not make up his mind from whence the voices came.

Sometimes they appeared above his head, high up; and then again the sounds seemed to proceed from beneath the ground upon which he was standing.

While still engaged in listening attentively, in order to catch some of the words of the invisible speakers, his eyes fell upon what at first looked only like a well, but, upon a closer examination, Duval found the water it contained to be very shallow, and that to the left, after descending a short flight of steps, there was a low-arched door.

Duval was only too glad to have made this discovery.

He had often heard that there were communications between St. James's Palace and Marlborough House, then in the occupation of the Duke of Cumberland; and he had no doubt whatever in his own mind that he should now be able without any difficulty to make good his escape.

He was just congratulating himself upon his good fortune, when again the voices which had before attracted his attention fell upon his ears.

It was quite evident now that two men, and from the sound of their voices, Duval had no doubt but that they were both young, were at high words.

He stepped noiselessly along a stone passage, at the end of which he perceived a door, which seemed to lead into the very room in which the quarrel was taking place.

The door was partially open, and as Duval looked through a crevice, he found that the two disputants were in a room beyond that in which he had at first supposed them to be.

His determination was formed instantly.

He entered the first room, and found that it was only separated from the adjoining one by a heavy curtain.

The voices of the speakers were now distinctly heard, and Duval resolved to watch the adventure to the end.

All his own peril was forgotten, while listening to what was going on in the adjoining apartment.

He had so contrived, that by slightly moving the curtain, he could see as well as hear all that was taking place.

The young men seemed to be nearly of the same age, both handsome; but one, with all the charm of youth and intellect indelibly stamped upon the the pure high brow—while there was something even repelling in the sinister expression of his companion, which, for the time, obscured all pretensions to beauty. It was about the eyes and mouth that this expression was to be seen.

"Cousin," Duval heard the one say whom he considered the handsomest of the two. "Cousin, until this moment I believed that you were my dearest friend."

"Friend!" scornfully replied his companion.

"Yes. I would have trusted you with my life. I would have sacrificed my life for you."

"Pshaw! I ask not for your life."

"What then? Why this appointment in so strange a place? What can you have to say that must be said in so lonely a place as this?"

"Something, Henri, that touches your life or mine."

"But how? Forgive my hasty words just now? Speak to me. You have incurred some debt of honour. I am now richer than you; but we were brothers once in affection, let us be so still. Take my hand, Adolph."

The one named Adolph, Duval could see only placed both his hands behind him, as he hissed between his clenched teeth.

"Never; but on my own terms!"

CHAPTER CXXXIV.

DUVAL BECOMES A SECOND IN A DUEL.

"And what are these terms, Adolph?" demanded Henri.

"That you resign all claim to the hand of your cousin Emily de Clare."

"Resign Emily? You are jesting, Adolph. We are to be married to-morrow, and her heart is mine."

"But she shall be mine, I tell you—or death's!"

The young man named Henri, stepped back a pace or two, and then he said, in a tone of deep emotion—

"I am sorry; but henceforth, we are strangers. I will not reproach you. I am your fortunate rival."

"Yes, rival——"

"Nay, that is a wrong word. There never was any rivalry between us; for, from childhood, Emily and I have loved each other; and, now that I find her, after an absence of six years, a loving and trusting girl——"

"And your affianced bride, you had better add," sneeringly suggested Adolph.

"And my affianced bride, then, since you will have me speak the words. I know you to be generous, Adolph, I forgive you; but never more can we be as we were."

"By heaven! we never will be, if I can help it!"

As he spoke, Adolph drew from his pocket a small whistle, and blew a low note upon it.

In an instant, a door at the other end of the room, and which Duval had not perceived before, opened, and a page in the royal livery advanced towards the two young men.

"Ah," exclaimed Henri, "there is treachery intended!"

"No, not treachery. This gentleman has come here for the purpose of seeing fair play. Draw, Henri Deschappelles!"

"I was not prepared for this; and, therefore, refuse to fight, as I have no second."

"Coward!"

Henri grasped his sword, as he said,—"From you such a name falls harmlessly. It is you, rather, who are the coward!"

"Come, gentlemen," said the gentleman who had been summoned by Adolph. "We are losing valuable time here. A truce to such epithets. Draw, gentlemen, draw; and I will see fair play on both sides!"

"Down with him, then!" shouted Adolph, making a desperate lunge at Henri, who was quite unprepared for so sudden an attack.

His sword-point had been levelled at Henri's heart, and but that the arm which had dealt it was struck up by Duval, who, unperceived, had approached nearer and nearer, the life-blood of that young, brave heart would have been sapped.

The three actors in this strange scene all turned towards Duval, who stood motionless, but with his drawn sword still outstretched.

Adolph was the first to break the silence.

"Who are you, sir, who dare thus intrude on the privacy of your betters?"

But Duval took not the slightest notice of the words addressed to him, and turning slowly round, he addressed Henri.

"Is it your desire, sir, to fight this man?—this coward! who would have murdered you but for my timely interposition?"

"I know not who you are, sir," replied Henri, with a courteous inclination of the head, "but I feel that I owe my life to your kind interference. Probably you have heard the conversation which has passed between us, and can understand that if you will kindly undertake to be my second, I shall have the greatest pleasure in life in chastising that false-hearted villain as he deserves. Yes, sir, I do now wish to fight that man."

"Spoken like a man!" said Duval. "Now, sirs, if you are ready, let the duel begin."

Adolph was ghastly pale.

He had not, evidently, anticipated such an accession as Duval made to the party, and would fain have shrunk from the task before him.

He turned and whispered something to the gentleman who was to act as his second.

The latter seemed to make some objection.

"Come, sir," shouted Henri. "You not long since hurled at me the name of coward! It looks as though that term might with greater propriety be applied to you. I am ready."

As he spoke, Henri drew his sword from its sheath, and made a step or two towards his adversary, striking him lightly on the shoulder.

In another moment their swords were clashing, and Duval could see that Adolph had the advantage as far as skill and dexterity went.

Henri was hard pressed; and Duval, who had never taken his eyes of Adolph, saw him take from his breast a small dagger.

"Hold, craven!" cried Duval, as he rushed in between the combatants, and snatched from Adolph the dagger which Henri had not perceived.

Adolph made another desperate lunge at Henri, but the sword of the latter had fallen from his grasp, and, but for Duval, he would have perished.

At this moment, a piercing shriek rang through the gallery or passage leading to the room where the duel had taken place, and a young girl, beautiful as an angel, ran forward, and threw herself into the arms of Henri.

"Oh, Henri, dearest! was this kind? Am I too late?" she cried, glancing first at Duval and then at Henri.

"All is well," replied Duval.

"All is well, you say?" repeated the girl; "but why this unseemly strife? I thought, and hoped, and believed, that you and Adolph were friends. Oh, Henri! what is this all about?"

Henri did not answer, but he looked at her with the fondest affection.

"Tell me, Adolph, what is this? Have you quarrelled?"

"It is better that you should wait and hear what your cousin here can tell you of this sad affair," said Duval. "Suffice it to say, now, that he whom you call Henri is all that is good, generous, and brave."

A look of intense joy lighted up the expressive features of the lovely girl to whom these words were addressed, and putting her hand into that of Henri's, she said, gently, "Forgive me, if I have said anything that sounded unkind. I am ignorant of these things which men call affairs of honour. Come with me—come!"

Henri drew her hand within his arm, and turning to Duval he said, courteously, "May I have the honour of being of any service to one to whom I have twice owed my life this night. Speak, sir, can I serve you in any way?"

"You may be of service to me," replied Duval. "If you will lead the way, I will follow."

While all this conversation was going on between Henri, and his cousin, and Duval, Adolphe had risen to his feet—for Duval, when he had snatched the poniard from his hand, with which he intended to put an end to the life of Henri, had cast him to the floor by one of those tremendous throws, if such a term may be used, for which he, Duval, was so remarkable when occasion required.

There was a look of hatred upon his countenance which seemed entirely to alter the character of his face; and Duval wondered to himself how he could have thought him handsome.

As he rose to his feet, and lifted his sword from the ground, he said, "I hope we shall meet again, sir, whoever you may be. If before that time I can, upon inquiry, find out that you are a gentleman, and that I shall not be disgracing myself by measuring swords with you, I shall look forward with great pleasure to the day when I shall rid the world of a meddler and a——"

"Silence, sir!" shouted Duval, "or you will compel me to chastise you on the spot. I am now at your service," he added, quietly turning to Henri.

Without deigning to look at his discomfited cousin, Henri, still holding his cousin's hand in his, advanced towards a low door, from which Emily had issued.

"This way, sir," he said, courteously; "and allow me once more to thank you for your timely aid this evening."

"Oh, Henri, what mean you?" asked Emily, pale as death. "Have you been in such peril?"

"Indeed I have, dearest; and but for the unexpected appearance of this gentleman, I should most assuredly have been murdered."

Emily burst into tears, and it was some moments before they could proceed.

Then Duval thought it would be better for all parties to turn their thoughts into another channel.

"And," interrupted Duval, addressing the young girl, "if it were not for the accident which has introduced me to this gentleman, I should be in great peril."

"You sir?"

"Even so. For the present, my actions must be veiled in some degree of mystery. Suffice it to say, however, that my principal object was to find some means of leaving the Palace, when I found myself drawn into a quarrel, which I was fortunate enough to put an end to without the cowardly deed which was intended being put into execution."

Emily shuddered, and looked up into Henri's face with tears glistening on her long eyelashes.

"Having accomplished this, may I now beg of you, sir, to show me some means of leaving this place without being questioned?"

"Nothing is easier. But stop! Perhaps your dress might be known. Come with me, and I will give you a large military cloak, which will entirely conceal the dress you wear."

"Thanks — thanks! — a thousand thanks!" exclaimed Duval.

The young lovers led the way to a large and luxuriously-furnished apartment, and closing the door behind them, Henri requested Duval to follow him, saying quickly as he did so:

"Go to my mother, Emily dear, but say not a word of the sad scene which has taken place to-night. Thanks to our kind friend here, all is well."

"Yes," cried the young girl, as she placed both her hands in those of Duval, "to your noble conduct do I owe the gratitude of a life. You said just now you were in danger, and that your actions must for a time be shrouded in mystery. We will not ask for your confidence, but we will hope — we may hope — that one day it may be given to us unasked."

"You may, indeed," said Duval, as he pressed the tiny hands in his.

"We are wasting, perhaps, valuable time," suggested Henri. "Follow me, and I will then put you in the way of leaving Marlborough House, for you are no longer in St. James's Palace, sir, as you seemed to think a short time ago."

"I guessed as much," replied Duval; "but I could not be certain. Adieu, fair lady! I will go now."

Duval and Henri quickly came to another room, which was evidently the sleeping apartment of the latter.

He opened a large, old-fashioned wardrobe, and took down from one of the pegs a large military cloak, which would effectually conceal the whole of Duval's dress.

"There. I think if concealment be your object, you will succeed in obtaining it. Now follow me."

Enveloped in the cloak, Duval stepped lightly after his guide, who led the way up several flights of stairs, along corridors and passages, which were almost bewildering from their numbers, and then down another flight, along another passage, and thence into a courtyard.

"There," said Henri, pointing to a gate on the right-hand side, "through that gate you must go. The pass-word is 'Rex!' Do not forget it. And now, adieu!"

"Adieu! But tell me when I may see you again?"

"Whenever you feel inclined to pay me a visit, ask for the Honourable Charles Henri Deschapelles, and I shall be delighted to see my preserver."

The young man uttered the last word in a tone of deep emotion, which sensibly touched the heart of Duval.

With a warm pressure of the hand, Henri turned and left the spot, leaving Duval to pursue his route alone.

There were some doubts in his mind whether he had done right in not telling Henri his true position.

Perhaps he was running the greatest risk in trying to leave his present quarters alone.

But it was too late to draw back now, so he walked briskly up to the gate, and in another instant he stood face to face with a sentinel on duty.

"Who goes there? The word?"

"Rex!" replied Duval, in an assumed voice. "Quick, I am in a hurry!"

"Yes, yer honour," replied the man, as he proceeded to open the gate.

"Good night!" said Duval.

"Good night, yer honour!"

Duval experienced a feeling of relief when he heard the gate closed behind him.

He was once more free.

Duval pursued his way taking the route towards Westminster, when, just as he was turning a corner, two mounted officers of the police made their appearance.

"There he is! Seize him—seize him! Caught at last, Claude Duval!"

These were the words which fell upon Duval's ears, but for the moment he heard them as though he heard them not, so sudden and unexpected had been the encounter.

Unfortunately, however, for them (the police-officers) from being mounted, and seeing that Duval was on foot, they placed too much reliance upon their own powers of success.

Duval certainly, to them, appeared to be in a very perilous position, so they relaxed their vigilance somewhat, because they felt that they had only to stretch out their hands in order to capture him.

One glance showed Duval that one of the officers was his old enemy, Muckles, the other was Mr. Pilkington.

"Resistance is vain, Claude Duval; we are a strong party, and most of us are mounted, so give in, without any more ado," said Pilkington.

"Much obliged to you for your advice," said Duval.

This was to give himself time, for Duval felt that his situation was perilous, but not so terrible as it would have been to one less accustomed than he was to such adventures.

But, strong, active, and clear-headed as he was, his plans were soon matured, and with one bound he cleared a space of several yards, and before the officers could turn their horses' heads, and get the animals in motion, Duval placed several yards between himself and his enemies.

CHAPTER CXXXV.

CLAUDE DUVAL MEETS UNEXPECTEDLY WITH AN OLD FRIEND.

Duval could hear the clatter of the horses' feet in pursuit, and he began to entertain doubts as to whether it would be possible for him much longer to keep up the race.

He made his way in the direction of Westminster, as there were several courts and by-streets in that neighbourhood perfectly well-known to him, and which would be very difficult for his pursuers to enter, mounted as they were.

In the hope of reaching one or other of these thoroughfares, Duval kept up the chase; but in the race he had lost his hat, which circumstance he knew well would make him an object of observation to any persons who might be abroad at that early hour.

Duval leant for a few seconds against the railings of the Park, and his breast heaved as he drank in the frosty atmosphere.

The dawn could scarcely be said to have come, and the dim oil lamps shed but a sickly lustre, for, owing to the low temperature, the oil was in a half-state of congelation, but never had Duval thought the mere fact of being in the open air one-half so pleasant.

His heart beat so violently for a few minutes, that he felt it would be impossible to proceed, and it was evident that his pursuers had lost him for a time, at all events.

"This will not do," he murmured to himself. "I must walk if I can't run."

Just as Duval emerged into George Street, however, a man darted out upon him from a doorway.

"Hilloa!" he said. "Who are you without a hat?"

"Who are you with one?" said Duval.

"I'll let you know when I get you to the lock-up! You are my prisoner, now, my fine fellow. I've been on the look-out for you these three nights."

"And you are going to take me to the lock-up just because I have no hat?" said Duval.

"Just so, my fine fellow."

"Then I'll take the liberty of supplying the deficiency by borrowing yours," said Duval.

With a well-directed blow, which caught the officious officer—for such, indeed, he was—in the neck, Duval sent him right across the road, and, with a heavy thud, against a shop-door.

The man's hat fell off into the snow, and Duval picked it up, and put it on, saying, as he did so, "Good night, my friend! I don't look so suspicious now, I hope! Mind nobody comes and takes you up because you have no hat."

At this moment Duval became aware that he had thrown away valuable time, for there was a tumultuous noise at this moment borne upon the wind, and he felt that he had no time to lose.

Again he gathered himself up, as it were, to begin the race—a race, probably, for his life.

"Stop him! stop him! There he goes! The highwayman! A highwayman! A thousand pounds reward! Stop him! Kill him! Take him dead or alive!"

Duval knew how much depended upon the next few minutes, and still he ran until he came to one of the many narrow streets which are to be found in the neighbourhood of Westminster, and feeling unable to continue the race any longer, he paused before the door of a dingy-looking house.

The door yielded to his touch.

What a feeling of relief took possession of Duval at that moment, only those who have been in a like situation alone can know.

With one bound he cleared the first flight of stairs, without encountering any one.

Higher up, and higher still was his determination to ascend, for if he could but make his way into an attic, he had no doubt but that he might finally escape over the roofs of the houses.

"Claude Duval—Claude Duval!" was the shout which came up to his ears. "Stop him! That's the house! After him!"

Duval had entered one of the attics, and had just opened one of the windows to look what his chances of escape might be, when he suddenly became aware of a light grasp being laid upon his arm.

For a moment all hope vanished from his mind, for, in the darkness, he could not see to whom the hand belonged; but he soon heard a voice which reassured him.

"Quick! quick! Claude Duval! I am a friend! This next attic is mine! If you succeed in reaching it, you will be safe, for no one interferes with Surdoni, the astrologer."

Duval felt that, at all events, he would be as safe in the next attic, if not safer than where he was, as it was evident that the officers had watched him enter the house.

To jump upon the narrow parapet, and to crawl along that, and then, by taking a leap, Duval found himself face to face with an aged man, of venerable appearance.

The attic was a study to behold.

Upon the walls hung massive black velvet curtains, on which were embroidered silver stars.

The room, small though it was, had an imposing look.

In the centre of the ceiling was suspended a small silver lamp, which emitted a red light.

It was vivid enough to cast a tolerable radiance over the room, which had its atmosphere loaded with a sickly, enervating perfume.

A chair, covered with black velvet stood by the table, and the floor itself was covered with the same material.

On another table, by the door, was a crocodile, and several dried fishes, a skull, and various other articles, which to Duval only conveyed the idea of a system of mummery which, probably, had all its effect upon those who were weak enough to consult the wise man, for such he supposed his unknown friend to call himself.

"Sieze him! sieze him! Catch him! A thousand pounds!" yelled now the voice of Muckles. "A thousand pounds' reward! Sieze him! sieze him! A thousand pounds!"

Duval looked at the old man, who merely placed his finger on his lips, to make him understand that he was not to speak.

"Done brown, by Jove!" Duval heard Swallow say. "He's escaped! I knowed he would!"

"Hold your tongue!" replied the voice of Muckles; "he is hiding on the parapet, I tell you, he has not had time to get far."

Duval could hear the attic window in the next house opened violently, and then voices shouting his name.

"Quick!" whispered the old man. "They will visit my attic. Conceal yourself behind those hangings, and be not alarmed at anything you may hear."

Duval obeyed implicitly the directions which had been given him; but not a minute too soon, for the window of the old man's attic was burst open, and Muckles, the police officer, thrust in his head.

"Now then, old man, give up our prisoner, or it will be all the worse for you. In fact, I think, my men, we may as well take the fellow with us, for he practises the black art against the laws."

"Yes, yes. We will take him!"

"Gentlemen — gentlemen," remonstrated the old man, "be not hard upon me. I thought you would pay me a visit, and, therefore, I sat up later than is my won't."

"How should you know that we were going to visit you, you old fortune-teller?"

"You ask me a question, and then answer it yourself."

"What do you mean? I ask you, how you knew we should visit you to-night?" asked Muckles.

"By the art which you a short time ago called the black art."

"Ha! ha! ha! Well, what did your art tell you we should want?"

"To know where Claude Duval, the highwayman, was to be found."

"Eh? What?"

Mr. Muckles turned somewhat pale, as he glanced at the old man, and then at the table containing the heterogeneous mass upon it.

"Is it your pleasure, gentlemen, that I should tell you where to search for this notorious highwayman?"

"Yes, yes. We are losing time. But you cannot do it—you are false—you are merely detaining us here, for all we know, in order that he may have time to escape. Forward, my men, forward!" shouted Muckles.

As he spoke, Muckles withdrew his head from the window, through which he had thrust it, and took his departure.

For some minutes, the old man sat in silence, and then he rose gently and closed the window.

Then he put a shutter up, and placed across it a strong iron bar.

"Come forth," he said. "Claude Duval, come forth, your enemies are gone."

Duval emerged from his place of concealment, and stood before the aged man, who had afforded him such timely succour.

"I owe you my life," said Duval, as he advanced towards the old man; "and can never repay the debt."

"On the contrary, it was I who was endeavouring to show that I was not ungrateful for past services."

"But——"

"We have never met, you would say, Claude Duval?"

"Not to my knowledge," said Duval.

"Do you remember once saving the life of a police officer?"

"A—police—officer—merciful heavens!" exclaimed Duval. "Can it be possible——"

"Hush, no names!" returned the aged man; but, as he spoke, he raised his hand, and partially removed the wig which he wore, in such a manner, as to conceal most effectually his black hair.

"You know me now?"

"My dear friend, said Duval," in a voice of deep emotion.

That one glance was sufficient. Duval no longer doubted the evidences of his senses, St. Ives stood before him.

"You would ask," said St. Ives, "my reason for adopting such a disguise; and I will tell you."

"There are so many others," said Duval, with a smile, "which I should have thought would have been more germain to your feelings."

"Exactly; but the cause I serve requires that I should become acquainted with the nobility in this country."

"But such——"

"You would say that I cannot succeed in carrying

out my wishes in this place; but wait, and you shall see. Even as you entered, I was expecting a lady of the court, who has great influence with the King; and who I shall endeavour, either by promises or by threats, to win over to our cause."

"You surprise me. But tell me of the Princess, is she well?"

"She is both safe and well," replied Duval.

As he spoke, a look of melancholy, which seemed to have become habitual, passed across his face, and St. Ives shaded his eyes with his hand.

At this moment, a footstep was heard on the attic stair.

"Hush," said St. Ives, grasping Duval by the arm, "you must retire behind that curtain, my visitor approaches."

Even as he spoke, a rap came at the door of the attic.

"Enter," said St. Ives, in a deep voice.

The door opened, and Duval could hear a light footstep upon the soft velvet carpet.

"Surdoni! Surdoni!" whispered a low, sweet voice, which Duval at once recognised as belonging to the beautiful Duchess of Cleveland.

"What would'st thou?" demanded St. Ives, in the same deep voice he had assumed.

"Appear! This dreadful place oppresses me. Let me see you face to face"

"You must be content, fair lady, to have the future revealed to you as I please, and not as you choose to dictate. Again, I ask, what would'st thou lady?"

"I would know where to find—to find——"

"Whom? Speak."

"Ah, if you knew—if you can read the future, as you pretend—can you not tell who it is that I would speak of?"

"May be I can; but it does not suit me to do so. Tell me whom you want to inquire about?"

"If I must do so, I will."

"That is well; speak."

"I would wish to know where Claude Duval is at this present moment, and whether—whether——"

The Duchess paused.

"Well?"

"Whether he loves me?"

"Lady, I have the means of bringing the spirit of Claude Duval into communication with yours—would you prefer to have the answer from his lips?"

The Duchess trembled violently as she said, "You are sure that you can do this thing?"

"Test my power if you will."

"I will, then. Let Claude answer my question himself."

"I will, upon conditions."

"What conditions?"

"That you join the Jacobite cause; and from time to time you give me all the information I may require respecting the movements of the English Court?"

"I cannot—impossible!" exclaimed the Duchess.

"Then our interview is at an end."

"Stay—let me think."

"Time presses."

"It is impossible. I cannot—I dare not—betray my friends. He would not ask it of me."

"But if he did?" asked St. Ives.

"Heaven help me! I know not what I should do!"

"Think again, Duchess of Cleveland. Is the King who sits upon the throne of these realms so estimable a personage that you should sacrifice yourself for him or his?"

"No, no, it is not that; but it is so difficult to give up one's thoughts and opinions—prejudices you will call them, perhaps - in which from our cradle we have been brought up. No, I cannot do it—at least, not to-night. I must think."

"Be it so," replied St. Ives. "Our interview for to-night is at an end."

"But, Surdoni ——"

St. Ives made no reply.

"Surdoni, hear me. You promised that I should hear *him* speak."

St. Ives was still silent.

"Ah, I have offended you," said the Duchess, with some emotion; "and I must leave you without the information I sought."

"Without the information you sought."

These words were in such a low tone that they seemed but the echo of the Duchess's own words.

The Duchess rose from the velvet chair, and putting a fee on a side table, which seemed placed there for that purpose, left the room.

No sooner was she gone than Duval came from his place of concealment.

"You have heard all?" asked St. Ives.

"I have."

"You see, that you might induce her to join our cause if you would. What say you?"

"Can you ask me such a question, St. Ives?" said Duval —"you who know Lucy so well?"

"But the cause—the cause I have so much at heart. Methinks any means taken to incline the wealthy and influential to join us righteous and noble."

"I cannot do it, St. Ives. I can neither deceive the Duchess nor Lucy. I shrink not, as you well know, from danger, so long as that menaces only myself, but——"

"But there can be no danger to you in using your influence with this vain woman, and certainly no danger to Lucy."

"What do you mean, St. Ives? Is there not the certainty that if I were to do as you seem to hint at, is there not the certainty, I would ask, of making Lucy's life miserable—a living death, in fact? No St. Ives. I can sacrifice much to friendship, as you know, but not my wife's peace and happiness."

"Forgive me, Duval. I looked not at a flirtation in so serious a light as that in which you put it. My desire to see the rightful Sovereign upon the throne of these realms prevents my seeing any obstacles to the consummation of my wishes. I was wrong. You will forgive me?"

"I will – I do!" said Duval, grasping his offered hand, as he rose to depart.

CHAPTER CXXXVI.

CLAUDE DUVAL ROBS AN OLD GENTLEMAN, AND BECOMES POSSESSED OF SOME VALUABLE PROPERTY.

DUVAL was surprised and gratified to find that at the end of the street, in which the house was situated where he had seen St. Ives, Blossom was waiting, holding Nightshade by the bridle.

"You here, Blossom?"

"All right, Captain. I thought, maybe, you'd like a gallop in the road to-night."

"Nothing I should like better, Blossom. But what made you come? I never gave you any orders to that effect."

"No, Captain; but I had what they call a presentiment that Nightshade might be wanted; so here she is, you see."

Duval vaulted into the saddle.

While they were talking, the sound of carriage-wheels was heard approaching.

"A chance, Captain, a chance!" cried Blossom.

"I hear it. Stand aside, Blossom, and do not show yourself unless I call you."

"All right, Captain."

The carriage which had been heard advancing was now near at hand, and it turned out to be an open phaeton, in which were two ladies, and a gentleman, who was very red in the face.

When the phaeton was within about thirty yards of the spot where Duval had stationed himself, he trotted up to its side, and bending low in the saddle, he said, "The ladies need be under no apprehension; all I require, sir, is your money!"

"Sir, what did you say?" roared the red-faced gentleman.

"Your money!"

The next sound the old gentleman made was quite inarticulate from rage.

"And your watch!"

The old gentleman stamped, for he was unable to utter a word.

"And that diamond ring you wear; it appears to me to be a very fine one!"

The old gentleman, after two or three efforts, at length succeeded in roaring out, "Murder! murder! Thieves!"

"Oh, no, I do not intend to murder you, unless you drive me to extremities," replied Duval, calmly.

"Thieves! thieves!" again shouted the old gentleman.

"No, there is only one. Do not exaggerate, I pray. It does not become a man at your time of life, my dear sir!"

"You villain! you wretch! you highwayman!"

"Right again, old gentleman!" said Duval. "Why, I begin to think you are not so stupid, after all, as I took you to be."

"I won't be robbed! Be off!" roared the old gentleman.

"Ladies," said Duval, addressing the old gentleman's two companions, "allow me to suggest to you the propriety of using your influence with this irascible old fool, so that he may surrender to me whatever property he may have about him, or it may turn out to be a serious affair if it comes to a trial of strength."

"Oh, give him all he wants!" cried one of the ladies.

"Oh, do, dear uncle," said the other.

"I won't—I shan't do anything of the kind!" roared the uncle. "I'm ashamed of you both being such cowards!"

"Quick, sir! I am not accustomed to be kept waiting in this manner!"

As he spoke, Duval drew a pistol from the holster, and put it with a sharp click on full cock.

At sight of this deadly weapon the two ladies began rifling their uncle's pockets in a most expert manner; and in an incredibly short space of time succeeded in possessing themselves of the old gentleman's well-filled purse and pocket-book, both of which they handed triumphantly to Duval.

"There, take them; that is all he has!" they cried, in a breath.

"But the ring—the diamond ring, ladies, which sparkles so magnificently in this half light. I have set my heart upon becoming its possessor."

"Oh, but it won't come off," said one of the ladies. "I tried to get it off, but could not."

"But I must have it, nevertheless," said Duval, in a decided tone of voice.

"We can't get it off, sir; but he can himself. It was only yesterday that we both tried to do so, and he showed us that no one but himself could take it off."

"Now, old gentleman," said Duval, rattling the pistol on the side of the carriage, "you hear that. I must and will have your ring. Will you give it to me yourself, or do you prefer my cutting your finger off, and so possessing myself of it? For I have said that it shall be mine, and I always keep my word!"

"Oh, do not be so cruel, sir!" cried one of the ladies. "He is not so cross as he seems."

The slight smile that Duval answered her with reassured her, and she said:—

"Uncle, give him the ring, you have plenty more. Give it him, and let him go about his business."

"I can accommodate you with a pen-knife, sir, you do not happen to have one about you," said Duval. "And you will find that, if you pare your finger towards the point in the same manner in which you would cut a pencil, it will come off without your absolutely cutting off your finger. I have often had occasion to do this when rings fit too tightly."

The old gentleman took off the ring as he roared out, "Take it, you murderous villain!"

"You are a sensible man, sir, but somewhat abusive in your language. But I am generally considered to be a good-tempered man when everything goes as I wish, so I will not take any notice of the names you have called me since I first introduced myself to your notice and to that of your lovely nieces."

The two ladies simpered, and looked down.

"I have other business to-night on the road, so I regret to say that I must tear myself away from such charming society."

Raising his hat gracefully, he added, "Good morning, ladies—good morning!"

"Go the devil ——!" roared the old gentleman.

"Hush! hush!" said Duval. "Such language in the presence of ladies, and those ladies your nieces, too, is highly reprehensible; but you are agitated—irritated, I fear. By the bye, if it will be any consolation to you, old gentleman, allow me to say that the diamond ring fits as though it had been made for me. What should you say, now, is its value?—upon a rough calculation, now?"

"Be off with you, you scoundrel!" roared again the old gentleman. "Of all the impudent thieves——"

"Highwaymen, if you please," suggested Duval. "Highwaymen—it sounds so much more aristocratic. What were you about to observe?"

"I hope I shall see you hanged, that's all!"

As the old gentleman spoke, he seemed to shake himself down into a corner of the carriage with such vengeance that the vehicle lurched quite on one side.

"Gently—gently, sir," said Duval. "I shall begin to think you are a very violent man in a minute, and shall be forced to accompany these ladies home, in order to protect them from any sudden outburst of temper you may choose to indulge in."

"Will you take yourself off?" roared the irascible old gentleman again. "Or do you intend, after robbing me of all my money and jewellery, to drive me mad, mad, mad?"

"By no means would I be the cause of such a catastrophe! Ladies, your servant!"

Duval gracefully raised his hat, and trotted off, leaving the discomfited old gentleman to be consoled by his nieces as best he might.

Duval had not gone far, however, before he became aware of the unpleasant fact that he could hear shouts and outcries.

And very soon these shouts and outcries shaped themselves into distinct words and sentences.

"There he is! There he is!" roared out some half-dozen voices.

"I'm a made man! The reward is mine! Stand back! I will myself capture him, and get the thousand pounds reward!"

Duval was at no loss to recognise, in the tones of that voice, Muckles, the police officer.

ST. IVES WELCOMES HIS BRIDE.

Muckles rushed up to Duval, and seized Nightshade by the bridle, as he cried out, "The reward is mine!"

"Take it, then," said Duval, "since you will have it!"

There was a sharp sound, and the butt-end of one of Duval's silver-mounted pistols descended upon the officer's head with such force that he fell prostrate to the earth.

"Seize him! seize him!" cried several voices. "Help! help! help in the King's name! A highwayman! a highwayman! Seize him! Brain him! Stop him! A large reward to whoever captures Claude Duval, the highwayman! Down with him! Cripple his horse!"

Up to this moment, Claude Duval had been calm and collected—his face even wore a smile; but those three last words which had reference to his horse changed the whole expression of his features as suddenly as one may see a cloud, with the quickness of thought, shoot over and obscure a shining summer's sky.

There was a flushing look from the eyes of Duval as he looked round almost fiercely, and said, "Who said that? Who said that my horse was to be crippled?"

The tone in which he spoke was so suggestive of danger that the officers and stragglers who had joined them all shrank back appalled; and the man who had really uttered the words ran away, and took refuge in a shop.

But Duval saw him, nevertheless.

He touched Nightshade, and with one bound she was inside the little shop.

Several females, who happened to be in the shop making purchases, screamed at the sight of a man and horse entering the shop.

The man who had sought refuge there was making frantic efforts to scramble over the counter. But in vain; for Duval stooped from the saddle, and grasped him by the collar.

Duval then gave the impulse to Nightshade, who turned round; and Duval, Nightshade, and the unfortunate man, who was still held tightly by the collar, made their exit from the little shop quite as quickly as they had entered it.

At this moment one of the officers fired a pistol-shot at Duval. The man he held by the collar uttered a fearful yell, and Duval could see that blood was flowing from his face.

In an instant he let go his hold of the man's collar, and he fell at once into the roadway.

The shot intended for Duval had struck the man who had suggested crippling Nightshade.

Then there was a rush of several officers at Duval, but it was too late.

One word to Nightshade—a peculiar pressure on one side of her neck—and she was off like an arrow from a bow.

There was only one man who had the temerity to rush forward, and succeeded for a moment in getting hold of the creature's head; but the next he was dashed, stunned, and bewildered, some yards off, and the highwayman was free.

Free, and his faithful Nightshade unharmed.

Dashing up a narrow street, Duval made his way towards the Oxford Road.

A couple of horsemen were quietly trotting along the road, and they pulled rein at sight of Duval dashing along at such speed.

"Hoy! Hilloa! Stop! Who in the name of wonder are you?"

"Stop him! stop him! Seize him! seize him! A highwayman!" shouted the mob, some members of which began to emerge from the narrow streets that led to the Oxford Road.

Duval still gallopped on, but the two gentlemen put spurs to their horses, which were hunters, and one called out to him, "Stop! stop! I want no reward for your capture, man, if you be a highwayman! But I will make a bargain with you for your horse. I will give you five hundred guineas, and that will be a good night's work, even for you. Stop! stop!"

But Duval still kept up his headlong speed.

"By Jove, what a beautiful creature! I will make t eight hundred, if you get to Tyburn Gate before I do!"

"I can't do it, my lord," replied Duval. "Tyburn is out of my way."

As he spoke, Duval reined in Nightshade so suddenly, that the gentleman's horse actually passed him some paces, and had to be brought back.

"I can't do that, my lord," said Duval; "but I will race you for the money."

"'My lord?' Do you know me?"

"Yes, you are Lord Sefton. Are you willing to race?"

"Oh, dear no!—certainly not!"

"Good day, then, my lord!"

Three mounted police-officers at this moment emerged from a bye-street; but when they saw the rate at which Nightshade was going, they drew up.

"It's no use!" said one.

"None in the least," said the other. "We are sure to be done brown."

"I don't care," said Lord Sefton, turning to his companion. "I gave two thousand guineas for this hunter, and it is believed to be capable of beating anything on four legs; so I will try and win the wager."

The other gentleman smiled, and shook his head, as he said, "If that be the celebrated Nightshade, I will not give much for your chances of success in that quarter."

"Nevertheless, I will try," said Lord Sefton.

As he spoke, he put spurs to his horse, and set off after Duval at a rattling pace.

"Ah," said Duval to himself, as, looking round, he saw immediately what was the intention of Lord Sefton; "be it so, then, if he will have it."

Duval had not the slightest intention of running races with Nightshade, so he only kept just sufficiently a-head of Lord Sefton to prevent him from overtaking him.

A beautiful green lane stretched away to the right; and into this lane Duval turned, and soon perceived that he was still closely followed by the nobleman.

Duval went on about half a mile down this lane, and then, glancing over his shoulder, he saw that Lord Sefton was making signs for him to stop.

Duval drew up. A smile lighted up his face, as he said, "Well, I am a highwayman; and now I will pursue my calling."

"Hilloa! hilloa! sir!" shouted Lord Sefton, as he rode up; "hoi!"

"Well, sir?" said Duval.

"As I came along, I have been thinking that—that——"

"What, my lord?"

"I am quite sure you stole that horse!"

"Indeed!"

"And so I intend to take him and you both to town. Come, sir, I am not a man to be trifled with!"

"Nor am I," said Duval. "Your money, my lord! And quickly, for I am apt to be impatient."

As he spoke, Duval presented one of his pistols calmly and deliberately at the head of the nobleman, looking more like a bronze statue than a living man.

"A highwayman!" shouted Lord Sefton, evidently somewhat alarmed.

"Just so."

"To be sure! fool that I was, I heard people shouting as much, but was thinking so much about that horse you ride, that every thing else was forgotten."

"May be so. Your money, my lord!"

"By jove. You are not wanting in courage."

As he spoke, Lord Sefton bit his lip.

"Quick, sir—quick," said Duval; "you have sought me. I did not molest you."

"Well, well; I am unarmed. I have about a couple of hundred pounds in my pocket-book. My life is worth a larger sum, so—so—well—take it! You are a bold rascal."

"My Lord, it is not wise in this lonely place to use hard words. What I am, I am. Go in peace now, and let me go mine. No, stop!"

"What now?"

"I must have that diamond ring you wear; it is a valuable one apparently."

"It is. Fool that I was to wear it to-day. It is worth another couple of hundred pounds—but—but—it belonged to my mother, and I—I love to look upon it; I fancy I can see her lovely eyes in the sparkle of the stones. Well, well; you have me at a disadvantage; it is useless talking sentiment with a loaded pistol at one's head. Take it."

"No, my lord, keep it; and when you fancy you see your mother's eyes looking at you from the facets of the diamonds, remember that even a highwayman can respect the most cherished emotions of the heart, and bow to their influence. Keep it, my lord, with many welcomes."

"Can this be possible?" said Lord Sefton.

Duval bowed, and calmly put his pistol in the holster of Nightshade's saddle.

"Stay!—stay!"

"Well, sir?"

"One word—who are you?"

"Claude Duval."

"I thought as much," said Lord Sefton.

"Farewell, my lord."

As Duval spoke, he turned his horse's head, and waved his arm.

CHAPTER CXXXVII.

A WEDDING AT THE CHAPEL ROYAL.

It is now time that we return to one of whom we have lost sight off too long.

We mean the Stuart Princess.

It was the evening of the day on which Duval had taken refuge in the attic occupied by St. Ives, in his new disguise as an astrologer, that a man enveloped in an ample roquelaire cloak, might have been seen waiting at the water's side, close by Richmond.

He was evidently expecting some one to join him, for ever and anon as he paced to and fro the slippery embankment, he looked anxiously across the river.

"Will they never come? Will they never come?" were the exclamations that burst from his lips more than once. "Ah, here they are!"

As he spoke, a small boat containing three persons might have been seen to shoot out of a little alcove, and come swiftly across the water in the direction of the watcher.

"She comes! She comes!" the figure murmured to himself. "All is well! She is safe—safe—safe!"

Even as he spoke the little boat grated against the flight of steps, upon which the man had been standing the last few minutes, watching so intently the progress of the little bark.

In another moment a young and lovely girl had thrown herself into his arms.

"At last—at last I clasp you to my heart, my beautiful one—my own," whispered the tall stranger. "Is all well?"

"Quite well, dear Miravel," replied the girl, as she clung confidingly to his arm.

"Any further orders, yer honour?" asked one of the men who had rowed the boat.

"None. Here, take this."

As he spoke, Colonel Miravel, or St. Ives, for he will be better known to the reader by that name, handed to the man who addressed him a well filled purse.

"Thanks, yer honour!" cried both the men; and in another instant St. Ives and the Stuart Princess were left standing alone upon the banks of the Thames.

"This is but a poor reception, my Mary," said St. Ives, sorrowfully, "but it could not be otherwise."

"Nay, apologies to me, Miravel?" exclaimed the Princess, as she looked lovingly up into his face "have you not brought me yourself, and do you think I require any other escort than your brave arm and true heart?"

"Blessings on your trusting heart," replied St. Ives, in a tone of deep emotion; "how shall I ever repay you for all this trust and confidence."

"By continuing to deserve them; as I am quite sure you ever will," replied the Princess.

One fond embrace was all the reply St. Ives could make to this, and then drawing her hand gently within his arm, he said—

"I have but poor accommodation to offer you. In order to defy detection, I have rented an attic floor, where I carry on the mummery of fortune-telling."

"You, Miravel?"

"Yes, dear one; and you will be surprised to hear that I have been visited by some of the first people in this great city, who, for a glimpse of the future, are ready and willing to coin almost their heart's last drop of blood."

"But you cannot."

St. Ives smiled.

"You would say I cannot read the future? No, certainly not, dear one. The future has been hidden from mortal eyes, by an all wise and good Creator; and it is in vain that any one dare attempt to raise the veil, placed by Providence between the present and the future."

"Then why have you chosen such a vocation?"

"Have I not already told you, that by that means I succeed in learning all that I wish to know in reference to Court matters."

"True—true, I had forgotten. But where are we?" asked the Princess, gazing about her anxiously.

"At my temporary house, for which I was endeavouring to prepare you."

"Your home, Miravel? Then I am ready to follow you. Lead the way."

Miravel opened the door of the house in which he had taken his abode, and having closed it behind him, he commenced ascending the narrow flight of steep stairs that led up to the attic.

Fearlessly the young Stuart Princess followed him, nor did she pause until they reached the attic door, which St. Ives opened with a key, and threw open, making a sign for the Princess to pass in before him.

Unhesitatingly she passed into the room, and a slight smile passed her lips as she beheld the various, and to her incongruous articles which lay strewed about in such disorder.

"And that is the dress you wear," she said, pointing to the long robe and the wig, which were thrown upon a chair in a corner of the apartment.

"Yes, dearest; but we will not talk about that now. My own!—my beautiful!—mine, and mine only!—first, and only love!—treasure of a heart that never no never for one moment swerved from its loyalty to you. Do I really feel that I can call you mine at last? Is there no doubt, nothing still to step between me and the sunlight of this happiness?"

"Nothing, dear. I am yours; and by to-morrow this hand will be yours. I shall be your loving wife then."

"Is it; can it be possible? That after so many years of silent love all my despair is swept away, and that I can gaze into your dear eyes, and read there the confirmation of all my hopes—you have no doubts, no fears, now all is happy—happy, so happy. Nay, why do you weep? All sorrow has passed away."

"Yes, dearest; but——"

"Ah! I understand you. This is no place for you to-night. I was thoughtless; at least, I thought only of the near approach of that hour which is to make me the happiest of men; but I will take you to Duval's house, at least, the house which is his for a time, and where you will have the companionship of Lucy."

"Thanks, dearest."

"Then I read your wishes aright, dear one?"

"Yes."

"Then come—come at once. How could I have been so forgetful of what was you due? To-morrow, and you will share with me this humble dwelling."

"Indeed I will, most joyfully."

While the Stuart Princess had been speaking, she had been resuming her walking dress, and then they left the apartment together, St. Ives locking the door behind him.

They had not far to walk to reach the Strand, where St. Ives hailed a hackney-coach, and giving the driver directions to drive to Kensington, they soon had the satisfaction of finding themselves in the neighbourhood of Camden House.

Having discharged the coach, St. Ives rung the bell at the iron gates, and as he did so, Blossom happened to be on the point of coming out.

"Ah! who are you, sir?" said Blossom. "What want you here?"

"Do you not know me, Blossom?" asked St. Ives.

As he spoke he slightly removed the wig, which so effectually disguised and concealed his hair and features, that Blossom exclaimed—

"Mr. St. Ives, by all that's sacred. What can we do for you, sir?"

"Is Duval at home?" asked St. Ives.

"No, sir."

"But your mistress?"

"She is at home, and will be only too glad to see you, sir, and the lady too, for the matter of that, for she has talked about you often, and often since that dreadful night when——"

"Hush—hush, Blossom, do not talk about that night! Show us to your mistress; and tell her that we want shelter here until to-morrow."

"And no one will have a more joyful welcome, I know," said Blossom, as he hurried off to find Lucy.

It was with feelings of no ordinary pleasure with which Lucy embraced her fair young friend, and as she glanced from her to St. Ives, it was quite evident that only natural delicacy prevented her from asking the question which was uppermost in her thoughts.

"I understand you, dear friend," said the Stuart Princess, answering the look of mystery. "I have come to ask your hospitality till to-morrow, when another will alone have the right to claim my presence, viz., my husband."

As she spoke, the young Princess placed her hand upon the arm of St. Ives.

"I am so glad to hear it! May you both be happy!"

"With love, such as ours," replied St. Ives, in a tone of deep emotion, "there need be no fears."

At this moment Duval entered the room; and his surprise and astonishment were great, as the Princess stepped forward and took his hand in both her own.

"This is, indeed an unlooked-for pleasure," he said, as he extended his other hand to St. Ives, "Welcome—welcome; and if I can ever be of service to you, you have only to claim it, and it is yours."

"I know it and feel it," replied St Ives; "and it is for that reason that I sought you here to-night."

Duval made a sign to Lucy, and then she withdrew with the Stuart Princess, in order to have some further explanation of what was about to take place.

"Oh, tell me!" exclaimed the Princess, as soon as she found herself alone with Lucy,—"tell me that you do not think me forward or unmaidenly in what I have done."

Lucy smiled as she said:

"Before I know even what you have done, I shall have no hesitation in saying that I am quite sure you could not do anything that might come under such a name. Do you not love St. Ives? and does he not love you, and are you not both worthy of the other's affection?"

"Yes, but——"

"But what? Speak freely to me, for I can see that you are perplexed about something."

"Will he—Miravel, I mean—will he at some future time in looking back upon the past, think that I was to blame in thus coming to him alone and friendless? Will he blame me? Can he think me wrong?"

As she spoke, the young girl clasped her hands over her eyes, and a sob burst from her lips.

Lucy was by her side in an instant, and as she drew the weeping girl towards her, she said in her gentlest accents:

"St. Ives—or Miravel, as you like to call him best —is the very soul of honour."

"Yes, yes; I know it and feel it."

"And therefore he has shown you upon more occasions than one that he is deserving of all your trust and confidence. Therefore, you have done right not to disappoint his hopes. You have trusted him, and he could not betray you."

"But I came over here alone. He took me to his lodgings, and, weak girl that I was, so happy was I when I heard his dear voice and felt how dearly he loved me, I forgot all but the happiness of the present."

"Well?"

"When suddenly I rememberrd that I had but one female friend in this great city, and that—that——"

"That it would be better to seek the shelter of her roof until you became the wife of the man who, while he loves respects you, you did well."

"And I have done nothing that was not justifiable under the circumstances?"

"Nothing."

"I am happy, then; and to-morrow I am to become the wife of Colonel Miravel."

"And where is the ceremony to take place?" asked Lucy

"At the Chapel Royal. Colonel Miravel has spoken to a priest who knew me in childhood, and he has consented to unite us."

"I would fain go with you."

"It is the wish of us both that you and Duval do us this act of friendship."

The morning came, and the young Stuart Princess saw the bright sunshine with a feeling of deep and heartfelt joy.

So much as she had gone through lately had shattered her health somewhat, and made her look upon the outward aspect of nature as bearing some reference to her future life."

If, therefore, instead of sunshine and blue sky, the morning had been ushered in by clouds and rain, she would have gone through that eventful day with far different feelings to those which really filled her heart with joy and gladness as she stood beside her lover at the altar.

The good old priest was waiting within the altar rails when the bridal party entered the church, attended only by Duval and Lucy.

The short impressive ceremony, according to the rites of the Catholic Church, was completed, and St. Ives, as he clasped his almost adored bride to his bosom, looked supremely happy.

"Mine now through weal or woe," he whispered.

"Through weal or woe," repeated the Princess.

"And you are happy and content?"

"Quite. So long as your love remains to me I can defy the shafts of fate."

The little party returned to Camden House till towards evening, when St. Ives, after expressing to Duval and Lucy his own thanks and those of his bride for the many acts of kindness they had received at their hands, took his departure, accompanied by the Stuart Princess, who was henceforth to become his partner in all his joys and sorrows.

"Farewell! we will meet again soon," were the last words the Princess whispered into the ears of her friend Lucy at parting.

"A happy couple," sighed Lucy as she and Duval watched them as far as eye could reach, "if they would but give up all thoughts of the Stuarts ascending the throne of this country."

"That they never will," replied Duval. "St. Ives seems more bent than ever on the restoration of the exiled royal family.

"Alas, alas! to what dangers will not such aspirations lead? But you, Claude—you will never be tempted to join any plots against the Government?"

"I know not, Lucy. I cannot say what I may be induced to do. I have not had much reason to be loyal to the present royal family of England."

"That is true; but I do so dread your being mixed up with these Jacobite plots, Claude."

"Well, I am free at present, dear Lucy; let that suffice."

"I will."

Duval and Lucy together entered Camden House, where the latter began to feel herself thoroughly at home.

CHAPTER CXXXVIII.

CLAUDE DUVAL PLEDGES HIMSELF TO UNRAVEL A MYSTERY.

THE day following the marriage of St. Ives with the Stuart Princess was warm and genial comparatively with the severe weather which had just preceded it, and Claude Duval could not resist the temptation of a ride over hill and dale on such a morning.

Taking, therefore, an affectionate leave of Lucy, he mounted Nightshade, without well knowing, indeed, what route he would take.

At last he determined to make his way towards Richmond; and, at a hand gallop, he and Nightshade pursued their way, both apparently well satisfied with the scenery which met their view.

At a short distance stood a little church in those days, although now it has given place to a fine gothic building; at the time of which we are writing it was one of those Norman structures calculated to accommodate some fifty people—a humble house of prayer, with its one grand pew, and its half-dozen little pews, its ivy-covered porch, its barn-like aspect, its square tower, and gloomy chancel, where a huge chest of oak kept the records of the parish.

Brasses and tablets spoke eloquently, if not truthfully of defunct generations, and an old font, which many fingers, in old times, had dipped in to bring forth a portion of the holy fluid which was to form the sign of redemption on the brow of the faithful, stood prominently in the little aisle.

The church door was open, and Duval thought that probably some of the villagers were being married or christened, and an impulse—a presentiment of he knew not what, induced him to linger at some short distance from the little church.

Scarcely had he made up his mind to witness at a distance what was taking place within that little rustic church, embowered, as it was, among old ivy and sweet clematis, there came a joyous peal of bells, and from a cottage close by trouped a number of young people, all in holiday costume, and merry peals of laughter made the very atmosphere of the place seem joyous and sunny, although heavy clouds had now obscured the sky, and a cold wind blew across the meadow which the little wedding party had to cross to reach the church.

Duval watched the little party trip lightly over the meadow, and saw many a wondering look from distant cottage windows, and from a high road near at hand turned upon the happy little party, and he felt that he, too, would like to look upon the face of the bride and bridegroom.

Duval rode up and took his station close to the old porch, and soon the bridal party approached. Friends of the bride, friends of the bridegroom, young smiling faces and old pleasant ones, and such a chorus of voices, too, and such laughter as is to be heard only at a wedding—for this was a wedding; and when Duval saw that it was a true love affair—no marriage of convenience—no got up match with interest on one side and indifference on the other, but a real love match between two tender and gentle hearts, who thought more of each other than of all the world beside, he felt glad that he had waited to see them.

And then the little party entered the church, each one making a bow or a curtsey, as the case might be, to so distinguished a looking personage as Duval appeared to their eyes.

The little party had been within the little church perhaps a quarter of an hour when cries of surprise and terror burst from within the sacred edifice.

Then there came a crashing sound, as of broken glass, and Duval saw that the bridegroom, whom he had seen, as it were, but a few minutes before gazing so lovingly into the eyes of her who was about to become his wife, force the window of the vestry outwards. He beat with his clenched hands upon the stone walls, and the church itself echoed with his frantic cries.

"Help me, all of you! Seek her with me! You look amazed all of you! Are you mad, as I shall be but too soon if I do not see her? Speak to me, and give some solution to this mystery!"

Duval instantly dismounted, and as the distracted bridegroom was about to rush past him, he caught him in his arms.

"Stay!" he cried, "Speak, and tell what has happened.

The young man gazed at Duval with a bewildered look, as he said, "Who are you, sir?"

"I would be a friend. I will assist you if I can.

"Tell me, then, have you seen a fair girl, beautiful as an angel, pass this way? But it is useless asking. Nina! Nina!"

"Be more explicit, I beg," said Duval. "I saw that girl."

"You saw her?"

"Yes; but when she was leaning on your arm."

"Alas! alas!"

As he spoke, the young man held up a small crumpled glove, and a flood of tears came to his relief.

Duval was puzzled.

He felt quite convinced that no one had passed him while he had been waiting to see the wedding party leave the church. Then where had the bride gone?—by whom could she have been carried off? It was quite certain that there was treachery somewhere.

"Stand aside," said Duval, in an authoritative voice. "I must speak to the clergyman who united this couple."

"Do so, do so!" shouted several voices.

Duval strode into the little church, but he could scarcely believe the evidence of his senses, for the church was empty.

"Where is the clergyman?" he asked.

"In the church—in the church!" replied two or three who happened to be standing close to the bereaved young husband.

Duval entered the church once more, but soon returned.

There was a look of deep commiseration upon his face as he approached the bridegroom, and took his hand in both of his.

"Look at me, all of you," he said, as he drew himself up to his full height. "I do not appear like a man who would undertake what he was not able to perform. I give you my word of honour that I will leave nothing undone to sift this matter to its foundation. Will you accept my offer, or not?"

"We do! we do!" cried every voice.

"And you?" he asked, speaking gently to Charles Lennox. "Will you give me leave to aid you in your search for her you love?"

"Most gratefully—most willingly!" gasped the sorrow-stricken man, as he clasped one hand over his eyes, while with the other he grasped that of Duval. "O you know not the sorrows I have gone through, nor how happy I was only a short time since, when I thought that all my cherished wishes were fulfilled! But now——"

"Then tell me, now," said Duval. "exactly what happened within the church, for I was outside the whole of the time."

"I will. Scarcely had we entered the church, when the rapid flight of a carriage, and two half-maddened horses, which sprung from no one knew where, but which ran past the end of that rural lane close to the church, and which communicated with the high road, made us all turn our eyes in that direction."

"Well?"

"They passed like a vision: the tramp of the horses, the grinding sound of the wheels, and then all was over."

"Was this before the ceremony had taken place?" asked Duval.

"Yes, sir."

"What then happened?"

"Then we stood side by side at the altar, and the words were spoken which made me her husband."

It was with a gasping sob that the young man pronounced these last words.

"Go on. What followed?"

"After the ceremony was concluded," continued Charles Lennox, with difficulty, "the clergyman touched the clerk on the back with an impatient gesture, who then advanced towards me, and said, "The register, sir, if you please—in the vestry, if you please, madam," he added, turning to Nina.

As he pronounced her name, another burst of grief almost overpowered him.

When he had sufficiently recovered himself to be able to speak again, he continued:

"I was about to follow this man into the vestry, for the purpose of signing the register, and had, in fact, taken Nina's hand in mine, to lead her in, when the clerk stopped abruptly, and said, 'One at a time, if you please, sir; it is a rule, sir. You see, one at a time—the lady first, and then the gentleman. It's only a little rule, you see, sir, after all.'"

"Proceed!" said Duval.

"I know not whether my Nina suspected treachery in any shape, but she clung closer to me, and seemed to ask me not to let her go alone."

"And did you allow her to go alone?"

"I was unwilling to do anything that might look like an infringement of the rules of the church; but, as it seemed a strange one to me, I turned towards the clergyman, and asked him if it were really the rule that the lady should sign the register first?"

"And what did he say?"

"I scarcely know; but at all events his manner implied that it was the custom."

"And then you told your wife to go into the vestry alone?"

"No; I do not think I should ever have consented to such an arrangement, had not Nina herself said, 'Let me go, Charles?' No sooner had she spoken the words, than the clerk again advanced, and with great obsequiousness, led the way to the little vestry."

"Well?"

"Nina lingered on the threshold, and there was such a look of wonder upon her countenance, that again I stepped forward a pace or two to accompany her. But I was too late—the door was closed between us, and she was gone."

"And then?"

"I scarcely know what happened between her leaving me and a strange, feeble cry, suggestive of stifled agony—a world of gasping and suffering. It seemed, however, to find an answering echo in this poor heart."

"Alas!"

"I sprang forward, and laid my hand upon the arm of the clergyman, who had also been startled by the sound. He shook me off, as he was endeavouring to leave the chancel, and said, haughtily, 'What do you wish to say to me, sir?'"

"What reply did you make?" said Duval.

"I asked him what the noise was?"

"And what did he say?"

"Say? Why, he almost drove me to madness, for he replied, with a half-sneer, that I must be more explicit before I could expect him to give me an answer to my question."

"Is it possible?"

"Again I asked him the meaning of the smothered cry he had heard, as well as I and my friends here."

"What did he say to that?" asked Duval.

"I know not what he might have said, had I given him the opportunity of replying, for I made two steps towards the little oaken door through which my Nina had passed, in order to satisfy myself, when he (the clergyman) stopped, and, speaking in a more courteous tone than any he had yet used, he said, 'Pardon me, but your impatience is not seemly. I will send the lady out, and then, if you will oblige us with your signature to the register, this strange affair will, I hope, be at an end.' Even as he spoke," continued Charles Lennox, "the clergyman passed on, and reached the oaken door which led into the vestry. At the door he turned, and, addressing the beadle, he called out 'Richards!' The clergyman immediately passed through the doorway into the vestry, as it was called, followed by the beadle Richards."

"What did you do then?" asked Duval.

"A strange feeling took possession of me, that the clergyman and Richards were in the plot—if plot there were—and this conviction was impressed more deeply upon my mind, as I fancied I could detect a peculiar sidelong glance from the eyes of the beadle, as he bowed to us all, when he followed the clergyman, and closed the door with a loud bang behind him."

As the remembrance of all the suffering that had been condensed into those few minutes came back vividly to his recollection, the young man was compelled to lean against the church porch to prevent himself from falling.

"You now know all, sir; will you—can you help me to find my Nina—my bride for a moment?"

Duval looked thoughtful, and then he said, addressing himself to Charles Lennox, "And did none of you go into the vestry?"

"Oh, yes, yes. I turned the handle—or, rather, I should say, I raised the latch of the door, calling upon Nina; but no answering voice replied to my cries. All was still the room empty!"

"It is very mysterious," said Duval. "Come with me; we must examine this vestry more minutely."

The young man availed himself of Duval's offer to lean upon his arm, and thus together they, followed by the friends who were so joyous but a hour before, entered the vestry.

It was a small apartment; low, groined arches supported its roof; a few rushes showed its floor of stone; an old oaken table; the parish chest, with its ponderous clasps and locks; a mediæval chair, and some mouldy hassocks; a clergyman's gown, hanging against the old wall, completed the contents of the apartment.

As soon as he entered the room again, the agony of Charles Lennox burst forth afresh.

"Nina, Nina!" he cried. "Speak—oh, speak! Heaven, she is gone! Nina—wife—darling of my broken heart! Lost, lost, lost!"

"Hush, hush! Calm yourself, I beg of you!" said Duval, drawing the young man aside. "This immoderate grief will render you totally unfit to render me any assistance. You must help me to discover this mystery."

"Have you any hope, then?" he asked, glancing up into Duval's face, as he uttered these last words.

"I feel quite certain that this mystery, whatever it is, is capable of being unravelled, therefore be brave, and heaven itself will assist us."

"Amen!" said the young man, in a different tone of voice. "Yes, Nina, my grief must not unfit me for prosecuting this search. I am with you, sir, and am willing to be led by you in all things."

"Courage, then," said Duval, "and all may yet be well."

CHAPTER CXXXIX.

TREACHERY AND THE IRON COFFER.

It is night—a white mist is in the valleys, a chill wind is sighing and moaning under the night-clouds—not a star is visible in the murky sky. It is high tide in the Thames, and the view presented is at once blank and desolate.

A solitary wherry, propelled by two rowers, nears a landing-place, and as the boat touches the shore, one of the rowers springs hastily to land, and with a gesture of command to his companion, points in a particular direction, where a narrow path lay along the skirt of some gardens slightly diverging from the banks of the sham island.

"Oh, you're a mighty great man now, ain't you, William Steel?" growled the man in the boat, as he secured the wherry to some rolling timbers, that had once formed portions of a little landing stage at that spot. "You're a mighty great man now, since my lord took to you. I'll be even with you one day, my fine fellow, though, or my name ain't Jacob Browne. Well, I'm a coming!"

These latter words were bellowed forth in reply to an impatient gesture from his companion, who now, with a few strides, returned round to the water's edge, and, in a hissing whisper, between his clenched teeth, he said—"You scoundrel, how dare you transgress my injunctions, by raising your voice in that fashion?"

"How? What?"

"Silence, knave?"

"Oh, now I understand you. You speak such plaguy fine long words at times, Master Steel, that a poor, plain fellow like me, don't always know what you mean."

"You know well enough. Follow me."

"Aye—aye—all right!"

Master Steel, as he was named by his companion, set off at a fast walk, which rather tasked the powers of Browne to keep up with.

"Master Steel! Master Steel!"

"What would you?"

"Not so fast—not so fast, I ain't used to it; and can't tear along like Sam Vale that wins the wagers—not so fast."

"Be it so."

Steel slackened his pace, which enabled Browne to keep tolerably close to him. After a pause of some duration, the latter, who was evidently of a loquacious turn, said again.

"Master Steel."

"Well, what do you want?"

"Oh, I may go on, may I?"

"Yes, if you speak low."

"Well, then, Master Steel, where may we be going to now?"

"To him. For our reward."

"Oh!"

"I suppose you want it."

"Certainly I do; and you too, Master Steel, eh?"

"Mind your own business."

"Oh, very good, I only spoke out of fellow feeling, you know; and, as the job is done, and the blessed reward is due, may I ask what it is to be?"

"Anything in reason."

"Humph, people's notions about what's in reason do differ so."

"Well, you need not be too modest. But that is a needless counsel, you are not apt to fail in that particular."

"No," said Browne, "we are not apt, as you say, to fail in that particular."

His companion felt the retort, for he quickened his pace a little, and walked on in silence.

"Master Steel."

"Well, well!"

"Where are we going?"

"To the old place. The old house."

"What, the Pal——"

"Hush, fool. Trees and frogs have ears. I would not that a night bird or a marsh frog heard you."

Browne trudged on in silence, save an occasional grunt of dissatisfaction at the distance he had to walk. After a somewhat lengthened period, they reached a park paling, which seemed to enclose a plantation of considerable extent. Steel climbed the obstructions with more ease than his companion, who fell rather heavily on the other side.

"What now?" exclaimed Steel, impatiently. "Upon my faith, Browne, you get worse and worse. Time was, when you were fit for anything; and now——"

"I am getting old, Master Steel, and stout."

"Bah! Come on."

"Yes, it's all very well for a fellow like you, that's as tall as a may-pole, and without an ounce more flesh on your bones than just does to hold them together, to say, bah! but I can tell you——"

"Silence, once more. Silence, I say. You don't know who may be listening. I suppose, now, you know where you are?"

"Well, I rather suppose I do. Yonder's the place."

"Yes, tread lightly."

Some few shades only darker than the night sky, and looming large in the misty air, was evidently a building of considerable extent, nor many paces in advance of these strangely assorted companions. A tall and dense hedge divided, what seemed to be a flower garden, from the plantation in which Steel and Browne were walking. They skirted this hedge for a considerable length, until a very narrow opening, only fenced by a gate, tall, but simply composed of three spars, presented itself. However, as this gate was, it had a lock and hinges. By the aid of a small key, which he took from a canvas bag, Steel opened the gate, and motioning to his companion to pass through, he followed him, and carefully closed it again behind them.

"Steel, Steel," whispered Browne.

"Well?"

"Do you think I may ask him fifty?"

"What guineas?"

"Aye!"

"You may ask what you like, Browne; what you get is quite another affair; oh, yet I don't know! If he is in full feather, you know, he don't take much account of fifty guineas."

"That's true. I'll ask that much at all risks."

"Hush!"

With stealthy steps they proceeded through the

garden, apparently little heeding the havoc they made of the flower-beds over which they trampled. To deaden the sound of their feet, appeared to be to them a much higher consideration than any mischief they could otherwise do. As they approached the house, a faint gleam of light began to make itself manifest in the dull radiance that fell on the trees and bushes, and now and then a sound as of voices came on the night air.

Steel paused.

"Who is with him?" he muttered.

"Oh, the old precious lot, I'll be bound!" said Brown.

Stooping so low that his head was below the top of the tall shrubs in the garden, Steel, now followed by his companion, whose shortness of stature did not with him render such a precaution at all necessary, made his way to some marble steps leading to a terrace, on to which opened a row of windows, from behind the blinds of which, there came sounds of feasting and enjoyment. Steel laid his hand on the arm of his companion to enjoin him to be silent, and he then carefully ran his eyes over the crevices of the window opposite to which they were, to see if, through any accidental opening, a view of the apartment within could be obtained.

Nothing could be seen.

Passing along the terrace, then, to another window, and going through the same process, Steel was more successful. A crevice between the blind and the edge of the casement presented itself sufficiently large to enable him to obtain a good view of the room within.

Browne was silent, for he, too, at the same moment, had satisfactorily placed himself at a crevice, so that his curiosity was gratified.

The room was large and handsome. The ceiling was dome-shaped, and painted in the style of florid allegory, which is to be observable in so many of our palatial residences of the sixteenth and seventeenth centuries—heavy draperies hung on the walls, and by the windows, and the floor was carpeted with the richest fabric that the age could produce; mirrors, bearing wax lights, graced the walls, and at a table in the centre of the apartment, on which a profusion of wines and fruits glittered in their glass and porcelain receptacles, sat a party of six persons. Their dress, although the period was not one that admitted much bravery of costume, was costly in the extreme, and about two of them there was a certain style of uniform, compounded of a Court and a military costume, to which was added the long, slender sword, which, as an adjunct to the present Court dress, has survived so many changes of fashion.

There seemed to be plenty of mirth at this table, but it was of a sparkling, rather than of a noisy character. All laughed at times together, but still the sound was gentle, and there was that indefinable something about the tone which bespoke the Courtly polish of those present, and that constant restraint upon the louder and coarser ebullitions of animal spirits which is acquired among the highest and the noblest.

By listening attentively, Steel could pretty well hear every word that passed.

A tall, thin man, with grey moustache and long hair, that hung in wavy masses nearly to his shoulders, spoke.

"You are all mistaken," he said; "the place is too dull and formal for him. He would die of *ennui* in a week. I don't mean for a moment to say but that one of the Princesses may not choose it."

"In that case," said another, "I suppose we shift our quarters at once?"

"Why yes, I fancy so."

"A pity."

"Oh, a thousand pities. There are so many advantages here. Come Four, you don't drink!"

"Thank you, Six, I am doing well."

It seemed that these men, be they whom they may, addressed each other by numbers instead of by name, some mysterious bond of union held them together, which appeared to make it indiscreet for them, even in the presumed privacy of their secret counsels, to name each other.

And now the tall man with the grey moustache rose, and with one of those slender ruby-coloured glasses in his hand, which now are never to be seen but in the cabinets of the curious, but which were at one time so much in use to give a lustre to the light wines of the Continent, he spoke in a half-savage, half-jeering tone.

"I don't know, my noble numerals, what may be your notions or ideas of our progress; but, if you think as I think, that out of the confusion and the chaos of what may happen by our good aid, an old and a good cause may look the brighter. I give you a health—'The King! who is coming.'"

"The King! who is coming!" repeated the others; and then a man with black, sparkling eyes, long raven hair, a handsome, but dissolute countenance, and one of those charming and seductive smiles upon his lips, which seem to have been lent to such men by the bad angel for the beguilement of a weaker sex, rose and spoke.

"Another toast yet," he said. "I drink to the fairest flower earth ever owned or heaven ever looked down upon. Be it tapering and slender as a willow wand, or gorgeous in its refulgent beauty as the guelder rose. Be it fair as the water lily, or lustrous as the deepest-hued flower that ever bloomed—be it coy to the breeze of love, or amorous as the south wind—I drink to woman!"

A gesture of impatience escaped from him who wore the grey moustache, but the toast was drank in that cold serenity and absence of bustle or undue excitement in which these men seemed to do everything.

Steel, who had watched all these proceedings attentively, now turned to Browne, and spoke in a whisper.

"Browne!"

"Aye—aye! What now?"

"Not so loud. Go round by the old fountain, and see if the boy, Hatcham, be there with a horse."

Browne, with the reluctant and grumbling air which characterised all his movements, lounged from the spot, and then a sudden gleam of light shot over the terrace on which Steel stood, as one of the French casements was opened outwards, and the man with the grey moustache, accompanied by him who had proposed the toast of woman, stepped out. It was by far too late for Steel to attempt to escape, and he stood convicted of eaves-dropping.

"Ah, indeed!" said the grey-moustached cavalier, as his hand seemed mechanically to wander to his sword-hilt.

"Master Steel, by all that's—hem!" said the other, with a louder laugh than any that had been yet indulged in by the party.

Steel's self-possession appeared to desert him for a moment or two, and he stammered, rather than said, "Noble sirs, I—I—that is your grace, I—but this moment—I——"

With a look of ineffable disdain, the grey moustache waived his hand.

"Not a word—not a word! You have been listening! What then? There is no treason in a few old friends drinking a social glass together, although it be in his Majesty's palace at Kew."

"Oh, no, no! and I assure your grace——"

"Grace me no grace! Have not I over and over

NINA RESTORED TO CHARLES LENNOX.

again, Steel, told you to drop that mode of address to me when we meet thus in private? Come, now, speak! Your news?"

"It is done!"

"Ah!"

"Yes, it is done, your gra——I beg pardon—it is done!"

"And well done?"

"Well done! As well as could be wished! No alarm, no scandal, no noise! The storm helped us famously!"

"Providence is good!" said the man with the dark hair, sarcastically. "I suppose, Six, this is some little affair of your own—eh?"

"Entirely, my dear Four."

"A thousand pardons, then! You join us soon?"

"Very soon. Come, Steel, follow me!'

There was a strange look about the eyes of this man who was called your grace by Steel, and number Six

No. 45.— NIGHTSHADE.

by his friend, as he preceded Steel down the little steps of the terrace into the garden. Number Four returned into the room again, and closed the casement after him, so that a darkness, all the more intense for the transient gleam of light that had dissipated it, fell on the air without.

Steel, not without some feelings of uneasiness, followed his conductor for about twenty paces in silence, and then the grey moustache turned, and, grasping him by the arm, said sharply, "Now, Steel, quick—all about it! The whole particulars—quick!"

"Yes—I——"

"Speak low—lower still!"

Steel made, in rapid, whispered accents, a communication that took up about two minutes of time.

"What do you say? The carriage gone?"

"The horses took fright!"

"And so that was foiled. Of course you could not take her to town."

"No, but—but——"

"Well—well?"

"We thought it best to do as we have done. Nobody goes to the Corinthian Temple. Here is the key. She is still as a Dormouse."

"'Tis well—well! Perhaps better!"

He passed his hand over his brow, and but for the darkness around, a flush of guilty joy and excitement might have been observed upon that usually impassable cheek. After a moment's pause he spoke again.

"Steel, you have done this well!"

"Oh, your grace, I——"

"Yes, yes; and you have done for me many things well. It is time you should have your full reward. Follow me!"

There was a strange equivocal sound about these words, which went with a sort of chill to the heart of Steel—perhaps in his own full knowledge of his abundant wickedness he knew what his reward ought to be. Without, however, more than the pause of a moment, he followed number Six, who led him through rather an intricate shrubbery, and completely round one of the angles of the house. Pausing, then, at a low, arched door, which seemed by its plainness as though it led to the offices of the building, he took a key from his pocket, and, forcing the lock back with some difficulty, he passed through the doorway.

"Come on, Steel!"

"I follow. But whither are we going?"

"Stop!"

Steel paused, and the man with the grey moustache, by the aid of a chemical preparation then rare, and all but unknown, procured a light, and, placing his hand in a nook behind the door, produced a small lantern, which he lighted. The rays it sent forth were but feeble; nevertheless, they sufficed to shew that the two men stood in a small hall or vestibule, from which ascended in one direction a flight of stone stairs, while to the left there branched off a rather narrow passage paved with different coloured slabs of marble placed lozenge ways by each other.

"Come on, Steel."

They traversed the passage for about twenty yards in silence; and then placing the lantern on a bracket some height from the floor, the mysterious man with the grey moustache spoke slowly and distinctly.

"Steel, I am poor. Don't interrupt me. I say that with all my large revenues I am poor. I cannot reward you as I wish, because I think you have acted for me so long, that you ought to take a journey."

"A journey?"

"Yes, a long journey. Why do you tremble, and draw back? I want you to go well provided; and it is to point out to you how you may go well provided that I have brought you here, my excellent Steel."

"Oh! ah!"

"Yes. Now, listen. It is known to me, although but to one other besides, that in an iron coffer—a kind of iron safe built into one of the inner walls of this place—there is a plate and jewel chest, in which James the Second, some weeks or so before his flight, placed a large store of wealth in a small compass."

"Ah!"

"It is so. Now, Steele, since I cannot myself reward you, I have thought of showing you this treasure."

"And letting me have it? Oh, my lord——"

"Nay, not so fast. You shall help yourself from it—you shall take almost what you please from it, but not all. You comprehend? No greed, Master Steel; moderation in all things, if you please. If I introduce you to this iron coffer, will you be satisfied, and look upon that as a receipt in full?"

"Oh, yes, yes!"

"Agreed. Come on, then."

Ten paces further on, and they stopped at the door of a small room, the walls of which were of polished oak, and in which there were a couple of ancient-looking couches and some chairs. A very large chimney-piece for the size of the apartment nearly filled up one side of it; and over a recess in one of the walls was a niche, which appeared as if designed for some image of a devotional character. Immediately opposite to this was a massive-looking door, with a long, narrow slit of not more than one inch in width in the upper portion of it.

Number Six pressed upon a small iron knob in a corner of the floor, and a square piece of the flooring rose by a spring, disclosing beneath a little cavity, in which lay a large key. Possessing himself of this, he approached the massive door, and tapping upon it with the key, he said, "Iron, you perceive, my dear Steel."

"Yes, iron; and that is——"

"The iron coffer I mentioned."

"And within it——"

"Are the plate and goods. Well, my friend, your fortune will be made at last; and I shall hear no more complaints from you, I feel assured. Ah, how hard to turn. This lock is rusted. Ah!"

By a great effort he unlocked the iron door, which opened heavily upon its massive hinges, presenting a thickness of at least six inches at its edge. The cavity within was about six feet by four or five, and at the back were several handles of drawers, apparently let into the wall.

"There, Steel?"

"There?"

"Yes, there is your fortune in those drawers. I will hold the lantern for you, or you can take it yourself. Now, be moderate, man. I would not, were I you, encumber myself with any of the plate. Jewels will be your best market, you know."

"Oh, yes, yes!"

Steel took the lantern, and paused a moment on the threshold of the iron coffer, as though some suspicion haunted his mind.

"And you, my lord, you——"

"Well?"

"You will not want any yourself? Shall we divide?"

"Bah! no. I can come when I like."

"True, true; so you can. I, I——"

"Good gracious, man, do you want to keep me here all night! Take what you will, and be off. I pray only there is a cross of brilliants in your left-hand corner drawer, which do not take. Here, just by this drawer. Out of the way! Good night, my dear Steel!"

As Steel stood in the very doorway of the iron coffer, and as Number Six uttered these words, he placed his hand on his shoulder, and, with one vigorous effort, pushed him in. Another moment, and the huge iron door was slammed, shut, and the key turned in the ponderous lock.

Steel uttered a shriek that vibrated through the room; and for the moment, by its despairing, awful, agonized sound, made the man with the grey moustache stagger backward a pace or two. Through the narrow slit in the door there came a gleam of light from the lantern Steel had in his hand; and on the opposite wall it shook to and fro in a hue of light that reflected a dim kind of twilight throughout the room. For a moment, it seemed as though that first shriek had smothered him, and burst his very brain, for all was still. You might have counted ten in quick accents before another cry, something between the roar of some caged wild beast and the scream of a human being in his last agony, again appalled the ear!

CHAPTER CXL.

NINA ENDEAVOURS TO MAKE HER ESCAPE FROM THE CORINTHIAN TEMPLE.

"HELP! Oh, help! Where am I? Charles! Husband! Is it all some frightful dream of the imagination; and yet, I thought——Ah, yes, there is the ring he placed upon my finger. I am Charles's wife, and who has dared to tear me from him? I remember it all now—the sickening sensation at my heart when I was told to go into that vestry alone to sign the register!"

The young girl, who uttered these unavailing cries, was none other than Nina, to whom the reader has so lately been introduced. As she spoke, she raised her hands to her fevered brow, and gazed about her like one bewildered.

The room in which she found herself was of spacious dimensions, and appeared to have been fitted up at some time as a kind of chapel.

"Where am I? Oh, heaven, who will release me from this dreadful place? I shall go mad! Charles! Charles! Oh, what agony of mind you are suffering at this moment on my account. I will try and find some outlet."

Poor Nina, with a feeling of great exhaustion, slowly rose to her feet. As she did so, she clasped her head with both her hands, and moaned.

"Oh, this dreadful pain, it recalls everything to my mind again. The fearful, but ineffectual struggle with those two masked men—the effort I made to call upon Charles, and then the cloak in which my head was enveloped, which effectually prevented my cries from being heard. Oh, what is the meaning of it all? I, who thought I was going to be so happy!"

A gush of tears came to her relief, and after another effort or two, she succeeded in walking round her prison walls, for such, indeed, they were to her.

As Nina commenced an examination of her prison-house, her attention was attracted by a crevice in one of the panels, as though it were an ill-fitting door.

Hope sprang up in her bosom, she knew now why, but anything seemed better than staying in that place, in which she had been left by the two ruffians, who had torn her from happiness and love.

She pressed the panel slightly, and it yielded immediately to her touch.

The room into which this door led Nina, was one that, in any other less pre-occupied time, might have arrested her attention; but now, "Escape! escape!" was all she could murmur to herself.

The apartment in which she now found herself was a long room, that had been most elaborately fitted up as a library.

There were book shelves upon all the walls, extending up three parts of the height, and then terminating for the remainder of the distance, in beautiful gothic carvings.

Between each of these book cases, were pedestals with busts from the antique upon them.

An immense lamp of bronze depended from the ceiling, in which a solitary candle was lodged in some manner, so that it gave a dreary kind of light over the vast apartment.

The carpet felt soft as the driven snow, and strewed about the room there were couches and chairs of the most repose-inviting character.

A table covered with magnificent purple velvet, occupied the centre of the room.

Nina rushed towards one of the windows of the room, and her heart beat high with expectation as she beheld that it was surrounded by a garden.

"May I not now hope to attract the attention of some passer-by, and so I shall be free. I shall yet escape—escape—escape!"

Yes, those were the words that sounded so musically to her ears, and she kept repeating them to herself in all kinds of different intonations, as if, by so doing, she could bring them to effect sooner.

The garden upon which she looked had been some one's pride and pleasure at one time, evidently, although now, like some poor faded beauty that finds her admirers disappear with her more youthful charms, it appeared to Nina to be now a deserted spot.

The trees had spread their branches in all directions, entangling the one with the other in wild confusion; and many a rich and dainty plant, that in the time gone by had been tended with exemplary delicacy, had grown rollicking, and bold, and wild, upon finding itself at liberty to do so, and had gained in strength and size what it had lost in beauty and gentle elegance.

A greenhouse had, metaphorically speaking, burst its bounds, and gone out of doors, for every pane of glass was gone, and the long dancing tendrils of the vine seemed delighted to dance to and fro in the fresh open air of the spring.

A sun-dial, upon what had once been a sweetly, artful spot of rare vegetation, was choked up with tall weeds, and absolutely did not care for time, or how the world wagged.

A statue of plenty, with an urn overflowed with sculptured produce, afforded shelter to a nest of bold sparrows, who made a home within the urn and there defied wind and weather.

And yet there was something beautiful in that place.

A garden is about the only work of man that even in its decay presents to those who really love such spots a world of beauty.

The struggle between nature and art, has in its results much that is mysterious and delightful. It was no bad idea of the sage of Melos, to plant a garden and shut it up for three seasons with a seal upon its gate, and then with all due reverence to open it and wander in it, to see what the trees, and flowers, and birds, and insect things had made of it.

But as we said before, poor Nina had no heart to look at any of these things.

Her one thought, her one hope, was to leave that place; but how was the task to be accomplished?

The walls which enclosed the little garden were high,—too high for her ever to hope to reach the top —and door or gate there seemed to be none.

With an aching heart she turned again towards the house, and began to examine it afresh.

But now, why does she start and turn pale?

Why comes her breathing so laboured and quick? her eyes seem starting from her head, as she gazes about her in search of some hiding place!

"I must hide! They come!—come perhaps to kill me—ah no! that would be merciful! and they know not the word. What shall I do!—ah! here is a place of concealment."

As she spoke, Nina darted behind a huge screen, just as she heard a hand on the handle of the door.

* * * * *

It is necessary now, that we return to Claude Duval, whom we left vainly endeavouring to comfort Charles Lennox.

"I must leave you for a short time," said Duval, turning to Charles Lennox, "but believe me, I will not forget the vow I have taken, to trace your lost bride."

"But sir—sir——."

"What would you say," asked Duval.

"If you can find her, surely I—I can do so—tell me where to search for her? Did I only know where to seek her, brick by brick would I demolish the place that separated me from my Nina!"

"Where to look for her, I cannot tell you;—but I have my suspicions."

"Oh! What are they sir?—what are they?"

"Did you notice a carriage in the lane, as you entered the church."

"A carriage?"

"Yes!—try to remember?"

"Alas! I was so happy, that I noted not what was passing around me.—And yet,—and yet—I do recollect a rushing of horses' feet——"

"Exactly!—and I not only heard the tramp of the horses' feet, but I had the good fortune to notice the livery of the coachman and footman belonging to that carriage."

"Merciful heavens! you do not think that my Nina was in that carriage, that was being whirled along at such a frightful speed?"

"No; you forget. The carriage rushed up the lane while Nina was yet with you."

"Yes, yes, I think it was so!"

"I know it was; and it is to ascertain what business that carriage had in the lane at that hour, that I am about to leave you."

"Whose carriage was it?"

'Nay, do not ask me. It may not have anything to do with the abduction of your bride. It is to assure myself of that fact that I must leave you."

"When will you return?"

"Be assured that you shall either see me or hear from me by this time to-morrow."

"I will endeavour to do my best, too, in that time. Oh, Nina, Nina! this is, indeed, a cruel fate!"

Claude Duval turned from the spot, and mounting Nightshade, who was quietly grazing in the meadow which skirted the little grave-yard, he galloped towards London.

Then, drawing rein, he came to a stand-still, for it occurred to him that the best plan to pursue, would be to watch about the neighbourhood of Richmond; for he could not divest himself of the idea that the hapless girl was to be found not far from the spot from whence she had been abducted.

But how to set about the investigation?

True, the lover and friends of the girl, had made known the affair to the police authorities; but well Duval knew, that if she had been carried off by any of the officials of the palace, in order to pander to the sensual fancies of the King, or his dissipated son, the Prince of Wales; well he knew that they had means of, if not defying detection, at least, they had those which would at once put a stop to all inquiry.

As Duval thought, he turned his horse's head in the direction of Kew, where he was aware the King was at the present time.

His first impulse was to see Sir John English, and force him to pass him into the Palace at once; but upon second thought, Duval made up his mind to secret himself somewhere in Kew Gardens until night, and see if any information regarding this most mysterious affair would offer itself.

Accordingly, he rode back again, nor drew rein until he was beneath the garden wall of the Palace at Kew.

Duval knew the Palace and gardens so well, that he had no difficulty in affecting an entrance by a little gate, known as the "Gardeners' Gate."

Then he dismounted, and, climbing the wall, opened the gate, in the lock of which the key was left, and admitted Nightshade.

Just within the gate, was a thick growth of briars and underwood, a perfect wilderness, in fact: and notwithstanding that there were no leaves, there was ample room for concealment, both of himself and his horse.

"Lie down, Nightshade, we will wait."

As he spoke, Duval placed his hand upon the obedient creature's neck, and, in another moment, he and Nightshade formed part and parcel of the surrounding blackness, for darkness had set in, and all was still.

He had not been in his hiding-place long, when the little gate by which he had entered, opened, and a man, closely followed by another, entered the garden.

Duval made a signal—which the creature well understood—to Nightshade, to lie perfectly still, for the least movement must have been fatal to all his plans.

These two men were Steel and Browne, who have already been introduced to the reader, and going to ask for their reward for having done something for which they were to be well paid.

That conversation threw some light upon the mysterious disappearance of the young girl—at least, Duval was only too anxious to believe that the reward was in some way connected with her.

As the two ruffians trod lightly across the flower-beds, in order that their footsteps might not be heard, Duval quietly emerged from his place of concealment and followed them.

He saw Steele looking into the room from whence voices could be heard, and then he saw him send the man Browne to see if the boy was there to his appointment.

For a moment Duval felt that he had that man in his power, and his first impulse was to rush forward and force him to confess what he knew of the affair that had taken place in the little church at Richmond.

But upon reflection, he resolved to wait yet a little longer, and even then, would there not be ample time to get all the information he required from this man, if, by waiting, he found that he did not arrive at the desired knowledge.

While these thoughts were passing rapidly through the mind of Duval, the French casement opened, and the man with the white moustache stepped out on to the lawn, and encountered Steel.

Of what took place between these two men the reader is already aware.

But Duval did not think it necessary to follow them when "his Grace" as Steel called him, led him to his destruction.

"The Corinthian Temple—the Corinthian Temple!"

Those were the words Duval kept repeating to himself.

"It should be close by this spot," said Duval to himself. "Ah! there it is!"

A bright moon at this moment shone out from the dark sky, and, for a few seconds, illuminated every object.

Making Nightshade understand that he was to remain perfectly still, Duval strode on, regardless of where he trod, for he felt, that in all probability. much misery, or great happiness, hung upon the result of the next few minutes.

He soon reached a Gothic-looking structure, with high mullioned windows of stained glass.

To any one less active than Duval, it would have been impossible to scale those walls; but he was accustomed to such feats, and, in less than five minutes he had pushed open one of the windows, and let himself drop down into the temple, or chapel, in which Nina had first awakened from her death-like swoon.

CHAPTER CXLI.

CLAUDE DUVAL RESCUES NINA AT GREAT PERIL TO HIMSELF.

DUVAL produced a light, shading its rays carefully with his hand, lest they should be seen by hostile eyes.

A glance told him at once that the object of his search was nowhere in the apartment in which he now found himself.

A feeling of anxiety took possession of him, as he pictured to himself the terror of that fair young creature when she found herself in such a place.

The door through which Nina had passed now met his eyes, and through that Duval passed into the little wilderness of a garden we have already described.

For one moment a feeling of shuddering horror took possession of him, as Duval cast his eyes up the wall and asked himself if it were possible that she could have climbed so high?

The terrible suggestion that forced itself upon his mind, that if such had been the case, she must now lie a mangled corpse on the other side, made him clasp his hand over his eyes as a groan burst from his lips.

Then he turned from the garden, hoping and believing that it would have been impossible for her to have accomplished such an ascent unaided, and a feeling of relief and hope again sprung up in his bosom.

But where now should he seek for her?

At this moment he fancied he heard a slight, creaking noise, as of a door opening or shutting with difficulty.

His heart beat violently with expectation.

Was it Nina?

He made his way towards that part of the apartment, and, to his great joy, discovered another door.

As he entered this second room, Duval felt certain that he was not its only tenant, and yet he could see nothing to induce him to believe that any one else besides himself occupied that room.

"Nina! Nina! If you are here, in Heaven's name do not seek to hide yourself from me," he whispered in a low, but audible voice.

No reply.

"I have come from Charles Lennox, your lover, your husband! Speak to me, and let me befriend you."

And Nina, did she hear those consoling words?

Yes. With a thrill of agony and joy those words went to the heart of the young girl, who was still crouching down behind the screen.

Oh! the irresolution of that moment!

What torture was it to that young and gentle being to think that, perhaps, this might be a friend to take her back to him who is all the world to her; or the dread alternative would force itself upon her, and she resolved that nothing should induce her to leave her hiding-place.

Happily for her, Duval's eyes at this moment fell upon the screen.

In another moment he had darted round it.

With a shriek Nina sprang up, to fly she knew not where—she cared not where; but overpowered with exhaustion, and want of food for so many hours, she would have fallen to the ground, had not Duval caught her in his.

It is better that it should be so, poor heart-broken girl,—the fresh air will soon revive her, and then, when she finds herself clasped in the arms of him who loves her, s e will be happy.

There was a feeling of tenderness in the breast of Claude Duval, as he raised the slight form of the girl-wife in his arms, to bear her from that spot, which resembled those of a brother.

Beautiful she was, and wholly in his power as she was, Duval bent over her with as much reverence and respect, as though she had been some queen surrounded by her court.

Carrying her as easily as though she had been an infant, he made his way again into the Corinthian Temple, and thence again through a doorway, across a kind of lawn, from where he soon gained the spot where he had left Nightshade.

"Up, Nightshade!—up! I have work for you to-night!"

In obedience to his master's voice, the faithful animal stood erect.

"Where am I?—Oh, heaven, have mercy on me?"

"Fear nothing!—did I not tell you just now, that Charles Lennox had deputed me to help him search for you.—I am but doing his bidding."

"But,—but—I do not understand.—I never saw you?"

"No—but I have seen you.—I saw you this morning enter the little village church at Richmond, to give your hand to the lover of your choice."

"Ah! yes—yes. But then I was torn from him. And you too, may be.—But yet—yet——"

"Ah! I see you do not think I would harm you. That blushing look would be quite sufficient, even if I had so base an intention. Besides, do you not see that I am taking you away from this place, which was to be your prison."

"Ah, yes—I will trust.—You said that my Charles sent you to me."

"He did not send me to you, for if he had had the least idea where you were hidden, nothing would have prevented him from coming himself, to rescue you. He is searching for you elsewhere."

"Oh, take me to him!—take me to him at once, I beg of you!"

"I will—I will! Now, then, give me your hand, I will place you behind me, and in less than half an hour from this time, you will be safe in your own home."

Nina seemed to have no misgivings now, as she gave her hand willingly to Duval, who assisted her to mount behind him.

"Forward, Nightshade!—forward!"

Ever obedient to Duval's voice, Nightshade, with one spring, bounded forward at a tremendous rate.

"Fear nothing!" said Duval to Nina, who clung terrified to him. "In less than a quarter of an hour I tell you, you shall be with Charles Lennox."

At this moment, emerging from a lane that ran along the side of the hedge, came a number of mounted officers of police.

So near were they, that Nightshade reared at their sudden appearance, for it seemed as if they had risen out of the earth.

"Halt—Claude Duval!" shouted Muckles.

"Halt!" repeated another voice, the tones of which, were equally familiar to Claude Duval.

The second voice was that of Swallow.

"Now, Claude Duval, surrender for you are my prisoner—or I fire!"

As he spoke, Muckles levelled a pistol at the breast of the young girl, who was trembling in every limb.

"Yield, I say!" shouted Muckles, "or I fire!"

"No, don't fire," cried Duval, "I yield, for I see the chances are against me!"

"They look so! Ah! Ah!"

"But if this poor girl were not here, Muckles——"

"Well, if she were not here, what then?"

"I would defy you yet, and grappling with you. I would see whether you or I, Mr. Muckles, were the better man."

"But since she is here, you think it best to be discreet."

"As you say, I think it best to be discreet."

As he spoke, Duval gave Nightshade the impulse, and clasping Nina round the waist, off he started again, scattering such a shower of stones in the faces of the officers as he did so, that for a moment they were blinded and bewildered with the suddenness of the whole transaction.

"Forward, my men!" shouted Muckles, as soon as he had sufficiently recovered to be able to realise all that had taken place. "After him! A thousand pounds reward for the capture of Claude Duval! Catch him! Stop him!"

But Claude Duval and his fair companion were nowhere to be seen.

Nightshade had been put to his utmost speed, and Swallow was the most reasonable of the number, for he cried out, addressing his superior.

"What's the use? It'll take a cleverer man than you or I, Mr. Muckles, to catch Claude Duval. He is always doing us as brown as possible; it's no use, I tell you! It's no earthly use in the world trying to catch the likes of him. Hasn't he got a charmed life, and neither bullet nor sword blade has the least effect upon him. I daresay, now, if we could just see him, he is sitting down quite calm and collected, talking no end of nonsense to that pretty girl as he had behind him; and——"

"Silence, fool, idiot!" roared Muckles; "if it had not been for you and your comrades being afraid of him, nothing would have been easier than his capture to-night!"

"Perhaps so, Mr. Muckles," replied Swallow; "but why didn't you try to catch him yourself as he passed you?"

"Silence!"

In the meantime, Duval and Nina had reached the neighbourhood of Richmond; and then, as the well-known scenes burst upon her view in the early dawn, Nina tried to utter a few words expressive of her gratitude to her brave protector.

But words failed her, and a gush of tears came to her relief.

"Hush, hush," said Duval, as he strove to calm her, "you musn't present yourself to your husband with tears in your eyes."

But she could not restrain them.

What a world of anxiety and desolation was at this fair young girl's heart, now consequent upon the events of the last four and twenty hours.

She had seen more of life, and had sufferd more during that short time, than in the whole of her previous existence.

But, as the thought crossed her mind, that she was so near to the home of him she loved, her heart beat quickly, and something like the shadow of a smile passed over her face, as she said—"Dear Charles! How little he thinks that his Nina is so near to him!"

"Do not be disappointed if you do not see him at home; for it was his intention to commence a rigorous search for you, aided by the police."

"Oh, I hope he is at home!" exclaimed Nina, as Duval paused at the door of a pretty gothic cottage, which Nina had pointed out to him as being that of Charles Lennox.

There was no need for Claude to rap for admission, for at that moment the door of the cottage was opened suddenly, and Charles Lennox, pale and haggard, stood before Duval.

From the position of Nina behind Duval, Charles had not perceived the idol of his heart, and in frantic accents, he cried out.

"You have had no better success than myself. I saw it by your looks!"

"Charles beloved! Look at me!"

Nina was stretching out her arms, and had he not rushed forward and caught her, she must have fallen to the ground.

"My own, my beautiful! My wife! My treasure!" almost screamed Charles, in the wild excitement of the moment. "Do I again hold thee to this heart, and gaze into your gentle eyes? A life of gratitude to Heaven will be too short to testify what thankfulness is in my heart. Oh, Nina—Nina—I thought you dead, worse than dead!"

"It was worse than death," whispered Nina; "for I feared that death would not come, and that the remainder of my life would be a living death, separated from you."

Again she clung lovingly to that manly breast.

"Dear, dear Charles, we are selfish, we have neither of us thanked the brave and generous man who has rescued me from such peril, I believe, at the risk of his own life."

Charles Lennox looked up at Duval, and holding out his hand, he said, with deep emotion—

"Pardon me, sir, the joy you have been the cause of, made me for the moment forget to whom we owed our happiness. Pray dismount, it is yet early morning, and some hours must elapse before the dawn appears."

Duval felt half-inclined to accept the hospitality so heartily and kindly given, but ever mindful of others, he thought that, under the circumstances, the presence of a stranger might not be welcome to the two lovers, much as they felt they owed to his exertions.

"Thank you, my friends," replied Duval. "Not to-night; but soon I shall certainly do myself the pleasure of paying you a visit."

"And no one will be more welcome than yourself," replied Charles Lennox, as he passed his arm round the slender waist of his now happy bride.

"Adieu, then," said Claude, as he courteously raised his hat.

"Sir, allow me?"

"What would you say?" asked Duval.

"May we not know the name of him to whom we owe so much?"

"Most assuredly, if you desire it."

"We do—we do!"

"Claude Duval."

"Claude Duval!" exclaimed both Nina and Charles, in a breath.

"Even so. Is the service I have been able to render of less value now?"

"Oh, no, no!" said Nina. "But that explains all! Those men who attacked you——"

"Were officers of the police," replied Duval, with a smile.

"Then you are still in danger?"

"I am always in danger," replied Duval, lightly; "but I seldom come to any harm, as you percieve by to-night's little adventure."

"Heaven protect you!" said Nina. "And if ever we can be of service to you, remember that to you we owe more than our lives."

"I will remember," said Duval, as he stooped from Nightshade, and shook the hands of Nina and Charles.

"Adieu!"

"Farewell!"

The lovers lingered on the threshold of the little cottage until the sound of the horse's feet had died away, and then they looked into each other's eyes in silence, for their hands were too full of love and thankfulness for their feelings to find utterance in words.

CHAPTER CXLII.

CLAUDE DUVAL ROBS THE PORTSMOUTH MAIL.

"So, ho, Nightshade!" said Duval, as soon as he had left the cottage and its happy inmates far behind; "we will have some spoil to-night, for I hear the sound of wheels."

A dull, rattling sort of noise came upon the night air.

"It comes—it comes!" said Duval. "And if that be not the Portsmouth mail, I am no judge of sounds, that is all. Why, let me see, I have never yet had the pleasure of stopping that coach. The last time a highwayman stopped it, a Government bag containing ten thousand pounds was taken from it; but I fear there is no such good luck as that for me and you, Nightshade."

Nightshade made that peculiar noise which was customary with him when Duval repeated his name more than once or twice.

Then the rushing sound of wheels, and the tramp of horses' feet, came so plainly upon the ears of Claude Duval, that he began to fancy the coach was much nearer than he had at first believed it be.

He gave Nightshade a slight touch upon the neck, and in a few minutes he was as immovable as a statue by the side of the roadway.

Then came the notes of the bugle.

That was to advertise the man at the toll-bar that the coach was near at hand, so that he might open the gate with as little delay as possible.

The lights of the coach were now clearly discernible to Duval, and he could even hear the deep breathing of the leading horses, as the coachman urged them to increased speed.

"Now, Nightshade!" said Duval, in a quick, sharp tone, which the creature understood perfectly well.

Nightshade made but one leap over some furze-bush, and then planted himself so firmly on the roadway, that it would seem that the creature expected to be called up to stop the mail coach of his own mere strength.

Flashing onwards came the lamps, and as the moon was obscured by a dense mass of black clouds at this moment the only light which shone upon the scene came from them.

Edging off just a little from the centre of the roadway, Duval watched his opportunity, and then, in a loud clear voice, which had something monotonous and chaunt-like in its tone, he cried out—

"Stand and deliver! Pull up, or I fire!"

As if by magic, the coachman, on hearing these words, pulled up, and drew rein so tightly, that the horses reared on their haunches.

Dashing up then to the horses' heads, Duval turned the leaders aside by the bridle, and they at once commenced trampling on some furze bushes by the side of the road.

The fore weeels of the vehicle were turned very much from their onward course by this stratagem of Duval's, and the coachman lost all presence of mind, as he dropped his whip, and cried out—

"A highwayman! A highwayman, by George! Get out of the way, you villain, or I'll—I'll——"

What more he might have been going to say was lost in the screams of some one in the interior of the coach.

"Where? Oh, Where? A highwayman, did you say? Where is he?"

"Here," said Duval.

"I'll have him down in a brace of shakes," said the guard, who, at that moment scrambled from behind the luggage, and levelled a blunderbuss right at the head of Duval.

Had the blunderbuss done its duty in a proper Christian-like manner, it is probable that the reader would never have heard any more of the doings of Claude Duval—but it merely flashed in the pan quite harmlessly.

"You had better have another try, my fine fellow," said Duval; "that was a failure."

"I knowed how it would be when I let Jim Skylark load it; the booby knows as much about loading fire-arms, as——"

"Ah! not so fast, my man," said Duval, seizing the coachman by the arm, who was making frantic efforts to get sufficient length of reins in his hand to give Duval a cut across the face with them.

"You won't get the better of me, nor fifty highwaymen like you. I'm Job Stapleton, and you don't stop my coach without remembering it the longest day you have to live."

The horses now became restive, and began to kick and plunge furiously.

"Here you go, then, Job Stapleton!" said Duval, as he fired a pistol, which he took from the holster.

The coachman's hat flew off, while he himself rolled off the box.

"Oh, I'm shot! I'm dead! I mean I'm dying! Oh, lor! Oh, lor!"

"Now, it's your turn," said Duval, turning to the guard, who still held the useless blunderbuss as though he intended to take aim. "Now, it is your turn, my fine fellow."

"Murder! Murder!"

"Now, then, get ready," said Duval. "Have you any last wishes? Are you ready?"

"No, I ain't ready. Don't be a stupid; I'm not a-going for to shoot you, and why can't you let me alone, I should like to know."

"For the best of all reasons, because you cannot. You did your best to kill me; and if your blunderbuss did not go off, there is no blame attached to you," said Duval, calmly.

"I didn't try to shoot you, I tell you, I only made believe. I knowed as how it wasn't loaded properly; who ever heard of Jem Skylark ever doing anything properly but eat his dinner. Do you think for a moment, that I could go about with a thing like this if it was likely to go off? Of course I shouldn't. Why I should be afraid of doing either myself or some of the outsiders a mortal injury if I did."

Duval could not help laughing,

"Mr. Highwayman!" said one of the "outsiders."

"At your service," said Duval.

"Go your way, young man, and let us go ours, and do not get yourself into trouble. Do you know this is his Majesty's mail?"

Duval left the outside passengers and the guard to settle some disputes which seemed to be taking place, and rode up to the side of the coach.

"Your money, watches, and trinkets, if you please, gentlemen and ladies!" he said, as he laid a pistol on the side of the window.

An old lady and a young lady now began to scream vigorously.

"Silence!" said Duval.

The tone of command in which he spoke had the desired effect. Then, all was still as death.

"Now, sir," said Duval, addressing a gentleman, who had one hand concealed beneath his cloak. "I want that pistol you have."

"Pistol?"

"Yes. Be quick, sir, or I shall lodge the contents of mine in your brains."

The old gentleman at once handed to Duval a beautifully inlaid pistol.

"That is wise; you were scarcely justified in throwing away your life."

"Have mercy upon us all, good Mr. Highwayman!" whined a man in one corner of the coach. "Take our lives but spare our money. I mean, take our money but spare our lives! I am but poor. Sixpence halfpenny is all I possess."

"Then I will begin with you, since you desire it," said Duval.

"Certainly—certainly, sir, that is but fair, then! There, take it all. I will never, no never, appear against you."

"What is this," asked Duval, "which you have handed to me?"

"My purse—my purse, if you please, good Mr. Highwayman! I always admired highwaymen, they are so good-tempered."

"But there is nothing in your purse!"

"Come, come!" said the old gentleman; "this is only wasting time. It is quite certain we must consent to be robbed. Here are my rings, and there is my purse. Now go, sir."

"Good night, ladies and gentlemen!" said Duval; "you will all remember Claude Duval."

Off into the night air went the victorious highwayman; and Nightshade, whose sense of sight was most acute, leaped lightly over the furze-bushes that were in the path.

And then Duval knew, by a sound he uttered, that some other horse was near at hand.

Coming, apparently, exactly in the direction that would face him, was a single horseman, at a sharp trot.

The blood was curling warmly in the veins of the highwayman, and he resolved that that night should be one of adventures; so, without a moment's hesitation, he advanced towards the horseman, and called out, "Stand, sir!—your money or your life—or both!"

The moon, which up to now had been hidden behind a dense mass of black clouds, burst out in all its beauty through a long crevice, and sailed slowly and sweetly, with the deep blue sky behind it, and one small star in its wake of vivid brightness.

The horseman drew in his horse as he said, "And so, sir, you are a highwayman?"

"I am; quick sir!"

"And if I don't choose ot be quick, what then?"

"Sir, I have neither time nor inclination to parley with you; you have guessed rightly, I am a highwayman. I stop you; you know my purpose; so be quick, I say again, and let us part."

"You are bold?"

"I should be."

"And young?"

"I am so. Come sir, your money!"

"Take it, then," said the horseman, handing him a purse but indifferently filled.

"And that leather case strapped behind you."

"Only a change of linen, sir, I assure you," replied the man. "I am very poor."

"Indeed!"

As he uttered this one word, Duval cut the straps with a large clasp knife, and possessed himself at once of the leather case.

The man uttered a yell of rage and despair; but the sight of Duval's pistols at his head, seemed entirely to prostrate him, as he groaned out—"They were for my Lord Mansfield—jewels of price! Oh, dear! Oh, dear!"

As he spoke, the man sunk down low on his horse's neck, and striking his spurs deep into the steed's flanks, he flew rather than galloped off.

"Not a bad night's work, by my faith," said Duval, as he felt the weight of the casket, for such he had no doubt it was. "Come, Nightshade, we may do a little more business yet, before sun-rise. Forward!"

The night was now rapidly passing away; and, as Duval felt himself once more alone, that chilly feeling, that precedes, by perhaps one hour, the dawn, swept over him.

The wind was light, but it made its presence manifest by a low, half whistle, and half sighing sound, which died away mournfully in the distance.

Duval felt weary, and Nightshade, at this moment, gave a shudder, as the morning air swept over him.

"It is cold, my Nightshade," said Duval. "Come, then, we will have a canter over the heath. It will warm us both."

Nightshade seemed only too willing to fall in with this arrangement.

The young moon looked down, and cast a long shadow of Duval and Nightshade on the frosty ground.

The rapid speed at which they had come, aroused the spirits of both Duval and his steed; and, as he patted his horse's neck, he said, almost affectionately—"Here we are, both ourselves again now, Nightshade. That little canter has done us both good."

Duval was about to add something else to his four-footed friend, when the crack of a whip came upon his ear, together with the unmistakable tramp of horses' feet.

"A post-chaise, I fancy, by the sound," said Duval, speaking as much to Nightshade as to himself. "We shall, perhaps, yet have another adventure before the dawn."

On came the post-chaise at a rapid rate, and ever and anon you could hear the sound of a human voice, mingling with the cracking of the whip.

It was evident that the postillion was urging his horses to their greatest speed.

But, in addition to these sounds, Duval fancied he heard another voice, in high tones of expostulation.

Duval stooped low in the saddle, as, by that means, he hoped not only to prevent himself from attracting observation, but also to enable him the better to listen to what was going on in the post-chaise.

There was a mass of furze close to the road-way, which was some six or eight feet in height.

Behind this breast-work of furze and brushwood, Duval had no difficulty in concealing both himself and Nightshade, and waiting patiently for the approach of the chaise.

He now clearly heard a voice call out something, but the distance was yet too great to enable him to make sense of the few words which fell upon his ear.

In another minute, the chaise had reached the spot where Duval had concealed himself, and then an angry voice shouted out—

"Stop! stop! Confound you! Pull up here! Stop, I say!"

"I couldn't stop before, your lordship, at the rate we've been coming, it was quite impossible to do it."

"Silence!" roared the voice. "Speak when I speak to you!"

"But I thought, your honour——"

"You have no business to think, low fellow. You are here to do my bidding, whether it be impossible or not!"

Duval now ventured from his hiding place to take a view of the vehicle; and he soon came to the conclusion that it was a private carriage. The lamps were of silver, and the wax candles within them cast plenty

DUVAL SAVES THE YOUNG WIFE FROM OUTRAGE.

of light upon the carriage, and upon the roadway, and the hedge behind which Duval and Nightshade had found such good accommodation, where they could see all that was taking place, without themselves being seen.

An old gentleman, evidently the person who had been shouting so furiously to the postillion, now got out of the chaise.

He wore an ample cloak lined with fur, and upon his breast, there glittered, what appeared to be, several foreign orders.

"Get out! Come out, I say!" he shouted, as he held open the door of the chaise.

"Willingly, oh, most willingly, if you will only let me go in peace."

"Go where you will, after you have given me those papers you stole from me."

"I did it in self-defence."

"Self-fiddlestick!" shouted the old man. "Come out, and I will tear you limb from limb, but I will find them!"

"I have them not about me," answered a youthful voice; and, at this moment, a young girl, not above sixteen, leapt lightly from the chaise.

"I have them not about me, and if I had, you should never have them, for you have killed my brother—my poor brother."

"As I intend to kill you, if you keep me parleying here much longer!"

As he spoke, the old man darted forward, and seized the young girl by the wrist.

"Help! Murder! Remember I am your wife!"

"Yes, I do remember it, madam, to your cost. I remember that you are mine to keep, or to kill, or to do what I like with. Did I not buy you?"

"Alas! alas! that such should have been the case; but you shall not trample on me as you have done. The murder you have committed on my poor brother has roused a spirit and a feeling within me which I knew not of before, I will revenge his death, monster that you are!"

CHAPTER CXLIII.

CLAUDE DUVAL STOPS A POST-CHAISE, AND RELEASES A PRISONER.

"You avenge his death!" sneeringly replied the old man. Have you never heard of the story of a nobleman who tied his wife to the wheel of his carriage, and when he reached her father's house, left the mangled corpse at his doorstep?"

"There may have been such a monster, as there is such a monster as yourself," replied the girl; "but——"

Before the girl could utter another word, the old man rushed towards her, and in a skilful, business-like manner, confined her hands behind her back.

"Now, madam. Tell me where the papers are, and who that fellow was I found you with?"

"I will not tell you where the papers are; and as for the gentleman with whom I was flying, I have told you already, that he was my brother."

"Oh, your brother? I was under the impression that your precious brother was in Paris, and all of a sudden I find him springing up in my path here, in England."

"Exactly so. I make no secret of having written to tell him of your cruel treatment; and begging him to come and take me back again to my once happy home."

"Ha, ha!" laughed the heartless wretch; "then your little plans have been all disarranged by my unerring skill in using fire-arms. Ha, ha!"

The young girl shuddered, and as the light from the lamps fell upon her face, Duval could see that it was as pale as death.

"Release me, I say," said the girl; "and let me leave you. I would rather beg my bread from door to door, than live any longer beneath the same roof with you."

"But you shall live with me. I like these little excitements, they make me feel young again. You are my wife, my slave; and as long as I choose it, you shall live with me, and when I am quite tired of you, why, then you shall share the same fate, your brother, as you called him, suffered half an hour since at my hand."

With a cry of despair, the young girl made a step or two forward, and glancing up at the postillion, she said, in a voice of touching emotion—

"James — James! You are human, surely you will save me from this bad man, although he is your master?"

A grunt was all the response she met with to that touching appeal.

"Heaven help me, then, sighed the poor girl, as her head dropped upon her breast.

"Tell me where the papers are?" again shrieked the man.

"Never, you may kill me, but I will not give them up to you!"

"Very well, then, your doom is fixed. James!"

"Yes, my lord."

"You go and search the dead body I left in the roadway, about half an hour since, and see if you can find any papers. No matter what they are, bring everything to me."

"Yes, sir—yes, my lord."

The young girl made a step towards the postillion, as though she were about to follow him.

"Not so fast," said her husband, as he cast his arm about her slender form. "Not so fast, madam—he is not your brother too, surely."

"Wretch! What would you?"

He placed his mouth close to her ear; but he was so near to where Duval had stationed himself, that the latter could hear distinctly.

"I intend to murder you, as I murdered your brother!"

"Oh, help! help! Murder!"

"It's of no use calling for help. No one can hear you but James; and you see, that as he happens to be in my power, he could not, if he felt inclined to do so, help you."

"No!" shouted Duval, as with one bound, he leapt over the hedge. "No, villain; but I will help this unfortunate young lady, whose life you have made miserable!"

Duval had seized the monster by the back of the neck, and held him in such a tight grip, that his eyes seemed to be starting from their sockets.

The young girl dropped upon her knees at Duval's feet.

"Now, sir, what have you to say for yourself, before I shake the life out of you?"

"Mur—mur——"

"It is of no use calling out murder here, as you told your poor wife just now, there is only your villainous servant to hear your cries, and one honest man is a match any day for two such dastardly villains as you both are."

As he spoke, Duval shook the man to and fro; and from the tight grip in which he still held him, the old man had become almost black in the face.

"Now, sir, perhaps you like that."

"Murder! murder!"

As he spoke, he plunged his hand into the breast of his apparel, and but for the timely interference of the young girl, would in all probability have plunged it into Duval's heart.

But she, probably knowing of the concealed weapon, rushed forward and struck up his hand.

"Ah!" said Duval, "I might have expected as much. Nightshade!"

In obedience to the call, Nightshade reared, and her two fore feet were dashed against the chest of the old man, and he fell.

"Hold him, Nightshade," said Duval.

Nightshade held him down by placing one of his fore-feet on his chest.

Then Duval sprang from the saddle, saying, as he did so—"Still hold him, Nightshade," then turning to the young girl, he said—"To you I probably owe my life; and now you are free, tell me how you can proceed to save yourself?"

"I know not—I know not. My poor brother told me that at Kew he was to meet two friends; but he is killed—murdered by the man who calls himself my husband."

"Are you sure he is dead?"

"Oh, quite sure. We left him lying a short distance from here, covered with blood, caused by a pistol shot, fired by him."

As she spoke, the young girl pointed to her husband, whom Nightshade was holding down still.

"Perhaps it may not be so bad as you imagine. A pistol shot does not necessarily kill because it brings blood. Come with me, and I will see if he be really dead."

"But what is to become of my husband," asked the young girl.

"Never mind. Leave him to me," replied Duval. "You surely cannot feel anything like pity for one so utterly devoid of feeling as he is?"

"You will not hurt him?"

"I will be less cruel to him than he was to you," said Duval.

Then approaching the old gentleman, Duval said to Nightshade—

"Let him go now, Nightshade."

Nightshade lifted up his feet, and the old man, after several ineffectual attempts, at last succeeded in struggling to his feet.

"Now, sir," said Duval, "your money and whatever other valuables you may happen to have about you."

"Ah! now I understand you!" exclaimed the old man. "You will take a ransom? Yes—yes that's it. I am poor, but still I have a tolerably well-filled purse about me—here, take it—it contains about five hundred pounds in notes and gold."

Duval took it and put it in his pocket.

"Now your ring and breast pin."

"No—no. I think five hundred pounds quite sufficient for one night, my young spark; and you will get nothing else out of me, I can tell you."

"Indeed!" said Duval.

As he spoke, he levelled a pistol, and made an ominous sound with the trigger, so that the old man believed it was going off there and then.

"Be quick, I say," said Duval, "give me that ring and breast-pin, or I fire!"

"There! take them; and now leave me in peace."

"Not till I have possession of your handsome watch," said Duval.

"Well, well, take it! Now are you satisfied?"

"Not quite."

As Duval spoke, he adroitly caught both the old man's hands in his, and tied them together securely, with the same scarf he had used for the purpose of fettering his wife.

"What is this?" exclaimed the enraged old gentleman. "What do you mean by tying my hands in this fashion?"

"I had some thoughts of fastening you to the wheels of the carriage, as you threatened to do by your wife, if I had not fortunately overheard your resolution."

"No—no! You do not mean to do any such thing, it would be cruel."

"No, I shall not do that."

"I thought you would not have the heart to tie a poor old man like me to the wheel of the carriage."

"Not from any regard to your feelings, mind," said Duval, "do I abstain from doing so; but simply because I think you might slip, and so escape the punishment you deserve."

"Eh? What?"

"No, I intend to fasten you behind the carriage, and make you run perhaps faster than you ever thought it possible."

"Me run? I can't run at all, my dear sir. Ask my wife, and she will tell you I never have run. Have I, my dear, since you knew me?"

The young girl, however, was not likely to hear this appeal, for she had entered the chaise, and had drawn up the windows.

"It makes no difference in the world to me," replied Duval, "whether you can run or not. If you do not run, all I can say is, it will be all the worse for you —almost dangerous, indeed."

"Murder! Help! Mercy!"

"As much you were inclined to show that poor girl whom you call wife."

While he was thus talking, Duval had securely fastened the old man to the frame-work at the back of the carriage, and having satisfied himself that he would not easily get loose, he jumped at once on to the back of one of the horses.

"Nightshade, follow on—follow on! Off and away, Nightshade!"

Duval turned the carriage round, for he was anxious to go and search for the wounded man, whom he devoutly hoped to find still alive.

He urged the horses to their greatest speed, both by whip and his heels; and, from the roaring cry which issued from the back of the carriage, Duval felt quite certain his prisoner was still secure.

This continued for about three-quarters of a mile, when the silken scarf tore asunder, and sent the old man with such violence to the ground that he rolled into a ditch by the roadside, where, for a time, he lay insensible.

"Stop! In heaven's name, stop!" shouted a voice from the other side of the hedge.

Duval drew up, and then he discovered two persons making frantic gestures to attract his attention.

"What now?" said Duval, when he was near enough for them to hear him.

"Tell me," asked one of the gentlemen,—"tell me if you have met a carriage, driven by a postilion, on the road?"

"I expect it is this carriage you mean," said Duval.

"How? What do you mean?"

At this moment the carriage window nearest the hedge was let down, and the young girl put out her head, crying:

"Oh, Edward, Edward! are you still alive?"

"Sophy!"

The young man sprang to the side of the carriage, and clasped both of the young lady's hands in his.

"I fancy I leave the young lady in good hands now," said Duval. "So, with your kind permission, I will now take my leave."

"Oh, Edward! thank this gentleman; he has saved me from a dreadful death."

"Nightshade—Nightshade!" said Duval.

Another moment, and he was in the saddle.

"Gentlemen," he said, "that lady's husband—or rather, I should say, persecutor—is somewhere lying in a ditch by the roadside. Make good the opportunity which now presents itself, and fly while he is yet unable to do you any harm. Adieu!"

As Duval spoke, he raised his hat and gallopped away.

CHAPTER CXLIV

LUCY MAKES A STRANGE COMMUNICATION TO CLAUDE DUVAL.

"WE have had enough adventures, my Nightshade for one night, at least," said Duval, as he patted his steed on the neck. "We will return now to Camden House, and rest awhile, for I am weary, and I have no doubt a few hours' repose will not come amiss to you."

But little Duval suppose that the adventures of that night, exciting as they had been, were to be surpassed by what was to follow.

He put Nightshade to a gallop, and hedges and trees quickly flew past him. Nor did he draw rein until he came within sight of Kensington Gardens.

There he pulled up suddenly, for a female figure darted from beneath the shadow of the wall, and placed itself directly in his path.

"Claude, Claude!"

"Lucy?"

"Yes, yes. Do not return to Camden House. There is danger."

"What mean you, Lucy?"

"Yesterday morning, I was awakened by a loud knocking at the outer gate; the bell also was violently rung, and upon looking out at one of the upper windows Blossom saw a carriage surrounded by a detachment of soldiers. He came to me instantly, and said that it would be much better to let them suppose that the house was still vacant, especially as it had the repute of being haunted since the supposed death of General Everton.

"He thought that if you desired it, you might take advantage of this rumour if you choose, by letting it be supposed that you were one of the spirits said now to inhabit it."

"I see,—I see!" said Duval, laughing.

"But in the meantime, I made my escape, hoping to meet you long since, while Blossom is gone in another direction in search of you."

"Well, Lucy, you did quite right, both of you, and now that I am prepared for it, and know what I have to encounter, I anticipate a great deal of sport from this adventure."

"But be careful, Claude."

"I will, dear—do not fear for me! But I think you had better return to our house on the heath, with Blossom, and remain there till I join you."

"As you will, Claude—but I would much rather be with you!"

"Believe me, it is better that you should not, until, at all events, I understand the meaning of these people appropriating Camden House."

"Oh, I had forgotten," said Lucy, "but now you mention it, I recollect that Blossom said the government had taken possession of it, and that the Dutch envoy, his neice, a girl about seventeen, and his secretary, with their attendants, were the persons who are henceforth to occupy it."

Duval laughed heartily.

"I see it all now. A Dutchman!"

"Oh, what a fright I will give him! What a man that Blossom is, for finding out everything; he is quite a loss to the secret police. But here he is, to speak for himself."

"Ah, Captain, I thought I should be the one to tell you the news first, but it don't signify much, who tells, so that you know it. I say, Captain, shan't we have a spree with the old Dutchman?"

"It is my intention, Blossom, to extract as much amusement as profit out of this adventure, so I think I shall begin at once by frightening the sentinel, who looks as though he would be only too glad of an excuse for running away."

"I don't know, for the matter of that, Captain, what he might be if he were doing duty for an Englishman, but the idea of being obliged to keep guard over a Dutchman?"

"Hush! Hush, Blossom, you forget that this same Dutchman is to be made profitable to us. You go with Lucy, to the old house on Hampstead Heath, and wait there till you see or hear from me."

Blossom looked somewhat disappointed, for he too had laid his plans; but the habit of obedience had become a second nature to him, and accordingly, without a word of remonstrance, he consented to accompany Lucy to Hampstead,—she riding Nightshade.

"Farewell, Claude," said Lucy, "remember, I shall be anxious, until I hear from you!"

"Fear not that I shall keep you in suspense, one moment beyond what is necessary, Lucy!" was the reply, as he kissed her cheek, and turned his steps in the direction of Camden House.

Sure enough there was no mistake about it. His home, as he believed it to be, had been taken possession of, and there were sentinels marching to and fro before every door and gate.

Duval paused a moment, wondering in his own mind how he should effect an entrance into so well-guarded a citadel.

He had not long to wait, however, for the sentinel at the back entrance went into his sentry-box, and from the heavy breathing, Duval soon divined that he had fallen into a deep sleep.

"Come, that is better than I expected," said Duval to himself, "I must make good use of this opportunity, or I may lose my chance of getting in."

Duval had had sufficient time during the few days that he and Lucy, at General Everton's wish, had taken up their abode there, to explore the different rooms in that extensive mansion, and when once within it, he had no difficulty in making his way to a large apartment, where suits of armour which probably had not been in use for half a century, were hanging against the walls.

"The very thing," said Duval, as he immediately commenced putting on a suit of steel armour. "The very thing! My first object must be to get rid of the sentinels."

As soon as Duval had equipped himself to his satisfaction in one of the suits of armour, he stole down noiselessly again into the garden, and there listened; for he heard voices in conversation.

"I say, Jim," said one, "I don't half like this berth. They do say as the place is haunted!"

"Haunted? You don't say so?" replied another voice."

"But I do, though! My brother, as keeps the public-house up yonder, told me yesterday that the strangest noises have been heard, and——"

The speaker paused in the middle of his sentence, for Duval at that moment made a strange, hooting kind of noise, which startled the two men dreadfully.

"I say, I don't half like it!"

"Nor I! But we must not budge from here, that is quite certain, until we are relieved!"

Duval gathered from the foregoing conversation that he was listening to two of the sentinels, and he resolved to make his way to a sentry box, which was a few paces off, in hopes that one or other of the men would take possession of it.

Scarcely had he ensconced himself in it, when he heard the regular monotonous tramp of the sentinel, and he had no doubt in his own mind that it was one of the two he had heard conversing.

This was just what Duval wanted.

Duval drew himself up to his full height, and held one arm outstretched before him, so still, so statue-like that a stronger brain than the sentinel possessed might well have been imposed upon.

Tramp, tramp, tramp! on he came; but so lost in thought was he, reflecting upon all that his companion had told him about the ghosts, that his foot was actually upon the sill of his box before he perceived Duval.

"Help, help! A ghost! Fire!"

Those were the words that sprung to his lips as he turned and fled in the direction from which he had come.

Duval still remained immovable in the sentry-box, never doubting but that he would have a visit from the other sentinel.

He was not mistaken.

In less than five minutes he heard their voices.

"I tell you I've seen one of them for myself, and no Dutchman shall be the cause of my exposing myself to such danger again! I'm not a coward! I don't care for flesh and blood a bit; but when you come to ghosts and hobgoblins——"

At this moment Duval made a low, guttural sound, which, to the excited imaginations of the two sentinels, appeared to be of a most unearthly description.

"Come away—come away! I am quite willing to believe you!" said one of the men.

"No, no! I would rather you saw for yourself, in case I get into trouble."

"Oh, very well! Come on, then!"

At this moment the two sentinels approached. One look at Duval was sufficient.

The one who was a little behind his companion fairly sunk to the ground with clasped hands and glaring eyes, while his companion intent only on making his own escape, shrunk back just as his companion had fallen, and so rolled over him.

As soon as their presence of mind returned to them, they scrambled up, and Duval could hear them running away as fast as their legs would carry them.

"So far I am successful," said Duval, as he prepared to emerge from the sentry-box; "and now for the Dutchman!"

Duval had no fear of encountering any sentries now in that part of the garden, and he was therefore enabled to effect an entrance without molestation of any kind or description.

Knowing the situation of all the apartments so well, Duval at once made his way towards the secret chamber which had for so long been the prison-house of General Everton.

There, he knew, he should be perfectly safe from detection; while, at the same time, it communicated with the suite of apartments which he had no doubt was set apart for the accommodation of the Dutch envoy and his suite.

Duval now began to look about him for something to beguile the time with, for it was yet early, and he scarcely expected the envoy to be stirring before midday.

There were several books scattered about the room with which the General had endeavoured to solace his weary hours, and therefore Duval was quite content to wait the envoy's pleasure.

At twelve precisely the sound of footsteps was heard by Duval, and he sat up and listened, for he had thrown himself upon a luxurious, repose-inviting couch.

"Monsieur van Burg! Monsieur van Burg!"

"Yes, yes, your Excellency."

"What for you keep me waiting for von cup of chocolate? Send my niece to me in the instant, I say!"

"Yes, your Excellency," replied another voice.

"Oh!" said Duval to himself; "that is the secretary, I suspect, who is to send his niece to him. I am fortunate to be so well situated as to be able to hear all that takes place."

"Ah! you have come at last!" Duval heard the Dutch Envoy say. "Vat for you have been so long?"

"I knew not that you were up," replied a low, musical voice, in which there was the faintest possible foreign accent.

"Then you ought to have inquired, dat is all I have to tell you."

"But, uncle, tell me why you have brought me to this house. I was so happy in my dear home?"

"To make your fortune, girl, if you are not von fool."

"I have a fortune, more than sufficient for all my wants."

"Ha, ha! have you? I know more about your little fortune, I tell you girl, than you fancy."

"Of course you know all about it, uncle, since you are my guardian, and the only friend I possess."

"Yes, I know—I know all that; and I know, also, that you have lost all your fortune, and that you have not one farthing that I do not give you."

"You give me? It is my own!" replied the voice of the young girl.

"All a dream—all a dream, I tell you. I put it out to make it more for you, and the—what do they call him?—speculation failed, and so you have got nothing in the world but vat I give you."

"Oh, uncle!"

"But mind vat I say, if you are von good girl, and do as I tell you, I shall be able to make a good arrangement with a high personage, and you may be richer than ever you would have been with your own fortune."

"But what do you want me to do, uncle?"

"I don't know myself yet. I am going to see a gentleman to-day who will help me."

"But what gentleman can help you to make any arrangements for me, uncle?" asked the soft voice. "I know no one but you in this large City, and I do not desire any new acquaintances."

"That is as I may think proper. But hush! I think I hear somebody speaking in the next apartment."

At this moment Duval heard the voice of the man whom he supposed to be the secretary of the Dutch Envoy, say, "Mr. Mossy Pendell, your Excellency!"

"Ah! what villany is on foot now?" said Duval to himself. "I am glad I have such a good opportunity of hearing all that takes place."

"As soon as Mossy Pendell was announced, Duval heard the Dutch Envoy say to his niece, "This is a gentleman who comes to speak to me on business. You may go, niece—you may go!"

"I go, sir; but let me request that as soon as you have dismissed him, you allow me to speak to you on my future prospects."

"You shall—you shall—ha, ha! you shall!"

Duval heard the door closed, as he supposed, upon the niece, when another admitted Mossy Pendell.

"Well, sir!" said Mossy Pendell, as soon as the door was closed upon them. "Well, sir, have you considered my proposition?"

"I do not know yet whether you may be able to make it worth my while. My niece has a most beautiful presence—what you call it here, in England, and might hope to captivate the fancy of the most fastidious."

"I know all that. Have I not seen her, and told her that she is the very girl that will suit a certain person?"

"Vell, vell, vat vill you give?"

"That must all depend upon a certain person. If he is generous, of course I will not be niggardly."

"No, no—all right! I see you are von gentleman. But when are the final arrangements to be carried out?"

"That I know not—perhaps this very night. But you shall hear further from me," said Mossy Pendell, now that I know you entertain my scheme."

"Exactly so; and now good morning! Let me see you to-morrow, at this hour."

"Be it so, then, to-morrow at this hour."

"A precious pair of villains!" said Duval to himself; to be laying their heads together for plotting the destruction of that innocent girl. But I am happy to think that I have it in my power to thwart them."

Duval resumed his book, which he had thrown down at the commencement of the conversation between the Dutch Envoy and his niece, and resolved to wait till night before he began his operations.

The hours seemed to pass slowly, but night did at last come, and Duval roused himself for action.

The supper was served in the same apartment in which the first conversation, overheard by Duval, had taken place; but, as Duval felt lost to terrify that young and gentle girl, he forbore his ghostly visitation until later in the night, when he intended to frighten the Envoy.

About eleven o'clock the Envoy rose to retire to his sleeping apartment, attended obsequiously by his secretary, who was received with a torrent of abuse and invective as soon as he entered the presence of his superior.

"Well, White Fever, what's the matter with you? You look as though you had seen something, or somebody worse than yourself. Speak, man, what's the matter with you?"

"Nothing—oh, nothing, your excellency—only—only, I don't exactly like this house—that's all. They do say who ought to know that—that——"

"That what?" shouted the Dutch Envoy.

"That ghosts walk in the middle of the night through all the principal apartments, and that murder has even been known to be committed here."

"Stuff! Nonsense! Do you think to terrify me—the Dutch Envoy, by a parcel of old wives' fables. Lead the way, and don't let me hear any more of your foolery. Ghosts, indeed! I should only like to see one, that's all!"

"Don't, now—don't—there's no telling what might happen if they were to hear."

"If they were to hear? Who do you mean?"

"Why, the ghosts and hobgoblins if you must know."

"If you repeat such nonsense, I will be the death of you!" roared the Dutchman, now almost beside himself with rage.

"I won't! I won't! I wish your excellency good night and pleasant dreams."

"Of course, I shall have both! I always have! Ha! ha!"

The echoes of the laugh died away on the stillness of the night, and after the secretary, who was also officiated as valet retired, the Dutch Envoy threw himself into a chair, and indulged in a long low chuckle, at his own adroitness, in having deprived of her fortune the only child of his only brother.

"Yes," he said to himself, "To-morrow morning I shall know the exact terms for which I am to—ha! ha! to let my niece to—but hush—walls have ears, and some persons names are never mentioned, even in whispers. Now to bed—to bed—for I am weary."

As he spoke, he threw himself back on the luxurious pillow, and in a few minutes was lost in forgetfulness.

CHAPTER CLXV

CLAUDE DUVAL SUCCEEDS IN FRIGHTENING THE DUTCH ENVOY.

HELP! Help! Murder! Who are you? What are you? A ghost! a real live ghost! No, I mean a dead man's ghost!"

"Prepare! Prepare! Prepare!" said Duval, assuming for the occasion, as ghostlike a voice as possible.

"Prepare? What do you mean? For 'vat am I to prepare?"

"For death!" said Duval, in the same sepulchral accents.

"Help, Victorine! Victorine! Come to your dear uncle, Victorine! Murder!"

Duval approached a step nearer to the terrified Envoy, and laid his hand heavily upon his arm.

"Another such cry, and you are a dead man. Get up, and come with me."

"With you?" gasped the Envoy.

"Yes."

"Waere to?"

"Never mind where to—that you will know quite soon enough. Make haste, or I will find some means of making you obey me."

"Yes!—yah!—Mr. Ghost!"

The unhappy envoy slowly rose to a sitting posture—never, however, for an instant taking his eyes off Duval, whose gaze seemed to fascinate him.

Duval, in the meantime, was not idle, but was quietly putting on the dress of the Envoy, which was scattered about on various chairs and ottomans in the apartment.

"But, Mr. Ghost," commenced the Envoy, "me cannot come to you if I have not my clothes—impossible!"

"You will not want your clothes where you are going."

"Not vant my clothes? Oh, murd——"

"Hush!" said Duval. "What did I tell you about making a noise? Do you think I will not keep my word. Rise, and come with me."

Duval had, during the whole time of his interview with the Dutch Envoy, assumed a deep, guttural tone of voice, which went very far in persuading the unfortunate man that he was visited by one of the spirits from another world.

"My vig—my vig! I shall get you big cold in my head!"

"I want your wig," said Duval, as he took that important article of dress off a stand on the toilette-table, and put it on, having first taken off his own.

"Good gracious! Mien Got!"

"Come along," said Duval, grasping him by the arm—" come along. I have no time to lose; but first of all, give me whatever jewellery or valuables you may have about this chamber."

"I have nothing—nothing worth speaking of, good Mr. Ghost—nothing at all."

"We will begin with the diamond ring you imprudently went to bed in. It is a pity—it does precious stones a great deal of harm."

"Exactly, Mr. What's your name; he is quite spoilt by this time, you see."

"Oh, never mind the slight injury your neglect has done to the ring; give it to me all the same."

"I won't!"

"You say that to me?"

"I do say it to you! Help! Mur——"

"Ah!"

Duval seized the old man by the neck, and shook him to and fro several times; after which little performance, he said in a calm tone, "Remember my commands to keep quiet."

"Yah!—yes, Mr. ——"

"Now your watch, and that diamond pin."

"Yes, kind sir."

"It is well we understand each other better now. Now, give me whatever money you may happen to have."

"Here—here is all I possess in this pocket-book."

"Very good. Now, come with me."

"Yes, Mr. Ghost; but in consideration of the valuable things I have given you, you will not let me come to any harm."

"That depends entirely upon yourself," replied Duval. "Come!"

Duval laid his hand on the arm of the Dutch Envoy, and led him by the same route which he himself had taken in leaving the secret apartment, known to no one in that house but Duval, and Mossy Pendell, and General Everton.

As soon as he had thrust him far into the apartment, Duval closed the door upon him, upon which the Envoy raised such a shout, that Duval began to fear his cries might reach the ears of his attendants.

He again opened the door, and presented full in the face of his prisoner a loaded pistol, which he had never put out of his hand since he first made his presence known to the Dutch Envoy.

"Hark you," said Duval, in a tone which could not be mistaken, "I am not going to waste any more breath in threatening you. The next time—the very next time, mind, that you raise your voice—that minute will be your last."

Duval then closed the door; and after listening for some little time, felt quite certain that he had nothing more to fear from his prisoner.

Duval's next object was to get back again to the sleeping apartment in which he had first made acquaintance with the Dutch Envoy, and so arrange his dress as to pass himself off as that personage.

A short time sufficed to make the necessary disguise; and then, as the morning light penetrated into the room, Duval made such a disposition of the drapery at the windows as to cause as little light as possible from entering into the apartment.

His object in holding so long a conversation with the Dutch Envoy was wholly and solely for the purpose of acquiring the exact tone and pronunciation of the Dutchman.

Duval smiled to himself when he was fully equipped for the part he meant to play, and ventured on practising a few phrases, so as to make sure of the tone of voice he had to assume.

"Now, Mr. Mossy Pendell," he said to himself, "I shall be ready to receive you, and hear the villanous proposition you may have to make, which has for its object the destruction of the peace and happiness of that fair young creature who has the misfortune to call yonder scoundrel uncle."

Duval looked at the Envoy's watch, which he now wore instead of his own.

"Time to ring for chocolate, I fancy; but I had forgotten one thing. I shall have to search for the niece. Will she take me for her uncle, or will she penetrate my disguise?"

"I must trust to my usual good fortune, and hope for the best. If she is not imposed upon, I can but tell her that I am willing to befriend her, and no doubt she will entertain my proposal, as it is quite evident she and her uncle are not on the best of terms."

Duval placed his hand on the bell, and rang it violently.

Scarcely had he removed it, when the door was opened by the secretary, a tall, thin, fair-haired young man, with pale grey eyes, and a stupid expression of countenance.

"Chocolate!—chocolate, I say!" roared Duval, imitating exactly the tone of voice of the irascible Envoy.

"Yes, your Excellency——"

"Don't answer me, idiot!—but go at once, and bring me von cup of chocolate, and my niece!"

"If you please——"

"Go at once, scoundrel!" cried Duval, throwing a book in the direction of the Secretary's head. "Go at once, I say. I vant my niece!"

"May it please your Excellency——"

"No, it von't please me, at all, I say. Go- bring me chocolate, and my niece!"

The Secretary withdrew just in time to escape another missile.

"Well," said the Secretary, as he put up his hand, probably to feel that his head was on his shoulders - "well, of all the fiery vagabonds I ever came near, he beats them all to atoms. Why, I do believe he's getting worse and worse. Oh, he's mad—mad—mad! No doubt of that—and how am I to send that sweet Victorine—that angel of beauty—into that wild lion's den! Why, he'll be the death of her! I can't, and what's more I won't—Eh?—What?"

Another peal at the bell showed the Secretary that his master was getting impatient, and would allow no delay.

"Oh, lor!—oh, lor!—what shall I do? If she would but marry me right off hand, we might go away, and never see him again. Good gracious, how he is roaring at me now! Oh, I must go to Miss Victorine. I suppose he will tear me to bits, if I do not take her as well as the chocolate."

ting-a-ding—ding—ding—ding—ding! "What, the bell again!"

The Secretary sped along a corridor, and knocked nervously at a door opening on the right.

"Well, Mr. Van Burg," said a young girl, as she opened the door; "is my uncle up?"

"Oh, yes, if you please, Miss, he is up, and no mistake! He's in such a fury this morning, that——"

"What, worse than usual?" said Victorine, smiling sweetly.

"Oh, a great deal worse. He wants you to go to him while he takes his cup of chocolate. But I say, Miss Victorine——"

Here the Secretary stopped short, but whether to take breath, or from some other cause, we will not stop to inquire.

"Well, Mr. Van Burg, what were you going to say?"

"Only, Miss Victorine, if—if——"

"If what? Go on."

Ring-a-ding—ding! ding! ding!

"There's the bell again, Miss; but I was only going to say if you knew how I loved your sweet face——"

"Hush—hush, Mr. Van Burg. I have already told you that I feel grateful for your many acts of kindness, but you must not talk of loving me, or I shall be afraid to speak to you."

"But I can't help it. Oh, if you would but be Mrs. Van Burg——"

But Victorine had not stopped to hear the last sentence; the sound of her uncle's bell had been quite sufficient to warn her that it was no time to stand parleying with the weak but good-natured Secretary; therefore she had fled past him in her simple white dress, with her golden hair floating in luxuriant curls over her back and shoulders, looking, to the eyes of the Secretary, like some beautiful being from another world, so etherial did she look in her lovely innocence.

Ring-a-ding—ding! ding! ding!

"There's that awful bell again, enough to deafen one —and she—she, the sun-beam, as I love to call her, has gone alone to beard the lion in his den. I must be quick, for I never leave her alone with him unless I am close at hand."

Mr. Van Burg flew to the regions where the cholo-late was being prepared, and in another moment he advanced, with a trembling step, towards the easy chair in which Duval was lounging.

Victorine was seated at a table a short distance from her supposed uncle, and, shading her eyes with her hand, seemed to have given herself up to the most painful reflections.

"So you have come at last, you villain!" were the words that greeted the Secretary as he entered the room.

"Oh, do not scold him, uncle, I detained him."

"No you didn't, miss, it was all my fault, if you please."

"What do you both mean by telling such untruths? I'll have you locked up, minx, if you dare to take that scoundrel's part. Get out of the room, and rid me of your presence. Yah!"

The secretary gave another glance at the drooping head of his idol, and then left the room.

"Vat you mean by taking his part?"

"Oh, uncle," said Victorine, looking up into Duval's face, "he is not deserving of such treatment as he meets at your hands. He is so good—so kind—so——"

"Indeed," said Duval. "Since ven have you found out so many good qualities in von scoundrel like that?"

"Ever since he has been in your employ," bravely

replied the beautiful girl, whom Duval, for a minute, wished would speak as highly of himself; for there was something particularly winning and graceful about that fair young girl, that could not fail to take captive the heart of the fastidious Claude Duval.

"But you do not love him?" said Duval, assuming her uncle's foreign accent.

"Uncle!"

"Vell, vat now?"

"You know that my hand and my heart are both pledged to one whom I have long loved; and if it were not so, the question you just put to me is an insult."

"And why, pray?"

"Mr. Van Burg is a good man; but he is not a gentleman, and my father's daughter could not love excepting in her own station."

"Vary well — vary well. I will make von good marriage for you, and then you will be rich and great."

"I am rich now, great in your sense of the word, I never wish to be."

"Ha, ha, ha! you mistake—you mistake, you are not rich—you have lost all your moneys."

"Uncle," said Victorine, rising slowly. "You said words like those, or similar to those, yesterday. What do they mean?"

"I will tell you when it suits me. Now you may go, I expect von gentleman here presently."

"I go, sir."

Victorine rose to leave the room but Duval had no intention of bringing the interview to so speedy a close, so he said, still in the tone of her uncle—

"Vill you not give your uncle von kiss before you go?"

There was a quick, upward glance of the clear blue eyes, a glance that made even Duval wince a little, for he feared that she had penetrated his disguise.

But a moment more, and his mind was at ease; for, with a firm step, Victorine approached the chair on which he was sitting.

At that moment, Duval regretted that he had made such a request, for it seemed as though he were taking an undue advantage of her.

Instead, therefore, of stooping forward to kiss her, he merely held out his hand, and drew her towards him.

"Forgive me," he said, assuming his natural tone, "for imposing so long upon you—believe me, I am here to protect, not to harm you. Let my present conduct towards you prove the sincerity of my feelings."

Victorine had shrunk back, as soon as Duval spoke in a different tone.

"Then—then—you are not my uncle?"

"No; but in order that I may be able to put you on your guard, will you promise to keep my secret; and, in the presence of your attendants, address me as your uncle?"

"I know not what I ought to promise; but your voice sounds kind—yes—I think I will promise."

"Do so. Tell me, am I to have that kiss now?"

But Victorine was gone.

At the door, she encountered Mr. Van Burg, who, in reality, had been vainly endeavouring to catch the last few sentences; but she heeded him not, but sped on to her own chamber, where, closing the door, she threw herself on an ottoman, crying out—

"Oh, mother! mother! Look down upon your unhappy child, and shield her from the many dangers and trials which seem to be surrounding her."

CHAPTER CXLVI.

THE TWO PLOTTERS DEFEATED BY CLAUDE DUVAL.

As the clock struck twelve, Mossy Pendell was announced.

"Show him up, idiot!" said Duval, again shouting out, in the manner usual to the Dutch Envoy.

Mossy Pendell looked round the apartment to see if they were alone.

"How dark it is here," he said, addressing the supposed Dutch Envoy.

"You vill soon get accustomed to the darkness. I have von bad English cold on my head."

"Humph!" said Mossy Pendell. "I hate talking in the dark. One never knows whether there may not be some one hidden behind some of the draperies."

"Ha! ha! I understand you—you have some time done the like. Ha! ha!"

"Perhaps I have, when there was aught to be got by it. But now to business. Have you considered my proposition?"

"Your proposition? I forget. Let me see," said Duval, wishing to gain time, for he really had not heard sufficient of the conversation the day before between the Dutch Envoy and his unscrupulous companion to be able to enter into it.

"Yes, how dull you foreigners are," said Mossy Pendell, impatiently.

"Vary," said Duval; "but perhaps it vill save time to speak it all over again."

"Well, then, listen. A certain person——"

"Frederick, Prince of——"

"Hush—hush! on your life, do not mention names; it is treason, and you will be hanged, to a surety!"

"Ah! I did not know! Go on, von certain person——"

"Has deputed me to find him a young and lovely girl."

"For von wife, of course you means?"

"Of course—of course!" replied Mossy Pendell, impatiently.

"And he, the Prin——I mean the certain person, is willing to pay down a large, big sum of moneys for this pretty girl?"

"Yes; but he, of course, wishes to see her first."

"Yes, yes! Then he will come here to look at her —my niece? I mean ——"

"No, no! She must go into the Park."

"Yah! Yes!"

"In the carriage, you understand?"

"Yes, yes, I understand!"

"And the certain person will give me full authority to bring her to him."

"Yes, yes!" said Duval; "but she—my niece, I mean—is so obstinate—obstinate like what, do you say? von donkey—no, von mule!"

"Never mind that. I will manage all that, fast enough; only you mind that she is in the Park by four o'clock this afternoon."

"But she vill not get out, I am sure," said Duval, anxious to know beyond a doubt that violence were indeed intended.

"Then, my good friend, I shall have the pleasure of taking her out myself. You understand now?"

"Quite vell—quite vell! And how much moneys am I to be paid?"

"A hundred pounds now, and another hundred as soon as a certain person has seen and approved of your niece."

"Capital—capital!" shouted Duval. "I vish I had two nieces instead of von! She vill be there, Mr. Pendell—she vill be there, I says!"

"Then I take my leave of your Excellency."

MOSSY PENDELL ENTERS THE TRAP.

"Stop—stop! You have not given me the von hundred pounds!"

"Oh, I had forgotten!" said Mossy Pendell, as he took from his pocket-book a note for the amount.

"It is right—quite right! Now I vill go and order my niece to be ready. Good morning, my dear friend—good morning!"

"Remember four o'clock!" said Pendell.

"I am not likely to forget," said Duval, as he watched Pendell out of sight. "And so once more I have it in my power to frustrate your villanous schemes. But I must think—I must think!"

Duval paced the room in deep thought.

"I must see her and warn her!"

He placed his hand on the bell; but this time it did not ring violently.

"Hilloa! The lion's rage is over! I never heard him ring so gently before. I dare say, if the truth were known now, that angelic little creature, Miss Victorine, made him feel ashamed of himself. However, I must not stand talking here; he shall see that the bell is answered much more expeditiously when he rings like a gentleman than a wild savage."

The surprise of the secretary was complete when, upon answering the summons, Duval spoke quite kindly to him, instead of addressing him as he had done before in imitation of the Dutch Envoy's tone.

"Will you be kind enough to send my niece to me at once, Mr. Van Burg?"

The secretary stood aghast. He could scarcely believe that he heard aright, but, nevertheless, he hastened to obey.

"Well," he said, as he retired, "wonders will never cease! Why, here have I been for more than six years in his service, and never till now have I been spoken to like a man and a christian.

No. 47.—NIGHTSHADE.

Oh, it's all a dream. I shouldn't wonder at all now if I were to find Miss Victorine—that dear gentle little angel—stamping and tearing with rage—just on purpose to prove to me that I am mad. I will just go and see."

The Secretary walked rapidly until he reached the door of the suite of apartments which had been set apart for the use of the niece of the Dutch Envoy, and then he stood still and listened.

All was still.

"No, she seems all as usual," said the Secretary to himself. "I will knock and apprize her of the change in her uncle's manner. Poor girl, it will be welcome news to her—so lonely as she must find it with no one to talk to but him—and me. But she will not have a good long talk to me. Perhaps, I was too precipitate to tell her all of a sudden that I loved her. I must be more on my guard, and then—and then who knows?"

The Secretary tapped lightly with his knuckles upon the panel of Victorine's door.

"Come in!" said her sweet voice.

Mr. Van Burg gently turned the handle of the door, and entered what was properly the sitting-room of Victorine.

"Well, Mr. Van Burg," said Victorine, without raising her head, which was bent over a well-coloured drawing, in which she seemed to take an all-absorbing interest—at least, so thought the Secretary, who would at any time have given the thing he valued most for one glance of her eye,—"well, Mr. Van Burg, I suppose you have come to tell me that my uncle has gone out?"

"No, Miss, not that; something ever so much better than that!"

"Why, what do you mean, Mr. Van Burg?" said Victorine, now giving the much wished-for upward glance.

"Oh, Miss Victorine!" began the embarrassed Secretary, "if you would but look upon me as a friend, I——"

"I do, and ever shall, kind Mr. Van Burg," said Victorine, as she held out her hand towards the Secretary; "I do think of you as a friend, and should be so glad if—if——"

The Secretary had clasped the tiny hand in both his and was devouring her with his looks of deep devotion.

"Go on—oh, go on, if you please, Miss; tell me what you would like me to do, and what would make you look upon me really as your friend?"

"Well, then, if you would believe that while I can give you only friendship in return for your love, you would strive to conquer a feeling that—that can never be reciprocated!"

"Be it so, then!" gloomily replied the enamoured young man. "I call heaven to witness that from this day forth you shall never hear one word of love pass my lips. If I find that to live in your presence, and yet not inspire you with the same feelings which have become a part of my very being, I have another recourse open to me."

"And what is that, dear Mr. Van Burg?" asked Victorine, looking up ingenuously into his face.

"I can die, Miss Victorine."

"Oh, do not talk about dying. I cannot spare you, you see, Mr. Van Burg. I want you—you may be of the greatest assistance to me, so promise me that you will banish all the vague hopes you may have formed and let us be friends—dear friends for the future. Now tell me why you sought me here, for surely it was not to tell me this?"

"Goodness gracious me, Miss! what have I been thinking about to keep his Excellency waiting all this time! Why, Miss, he is quite a different being to what he was."

A slight smile crossed the face of Victorine as the Secretary said this.

"Why, Miss, he sent me to tell you he wanted to see you, and here am I keeping you from going all this time. But I say, Miss——"

The Secretary made a sign to Victorine to approach nearer.

"Well, what now, Mr. Van Burg?" said Victorine, coming close to him. "You look so mysterious! What is the matter?"

"Well, Miss, it's my belief that——"

The Secretary looked all round the room, apparently to assure himself that they were alone.

"Well, Mr. Van Burg, do not keep me waiting. What is it you have to tell me about my uncle?"

"Why, Miss, he's changed."

Victorine gave a hasty glance into the eyes of the Secretary, to ascertain if he had any meaning for his words beyond what he intended to convey to her. But the way in which he stood her severe scrutiny convinced her that he could not have penetrated Duval's disguise.

"Yes, Miss, he's changed."

"Changed, Mr. Van Burg? What do you mean?"

"Why, miss, do you think for one moment that we could have been talking here all this time when he sent me to fetch you all in a hurry, like, without ringing his bell down twenty times? I tell you, miss, he is changed.

"Well, I am very glad to hear it. I will go and see if your report be correct. Farewell! Mr. Van Burg; remember our compact—we are to be friends not lovers."

"Anything—anything—so that you will but smile upon me thus!" replied the enchanted Secretary, as Victorine flitted along the corridor in the direction of her uncle's apartments.

But as she neared the door, which led into the first of the suite, she paused, and placed her hand on her heart, to still its beatings.

"What am I doing?" she said to herself. "Am I not conniving at a fraud? True, my uncle was violent and overbearing; and of late hinted at my making a good match, as he calls it,—although he knows I love another. But still, he is my uncle—my dear father's brother—and I ought to shrink from deceiving him. Yes, my resolution is taken. I will tell this—this gentleman—for I believe he is a gentleman—that I cannot, and will not, aid him in carrying on this masquerade, even if it be innocent. And I will demand to know where my uncle is. Yes, I am resolved to put an end to this at once."

As she spoke, Victorine turned the handle of the door of the apartment in which she was wont to seek her uncle whenever he required her presence.

As soon as she entered the room, she saw Duval, who was seated at a table, his head resting upon his hand, and in such deep thought, that her light footstep had failed to arouse his attention.

Victorine coughed, slightly.

"Ah!" said Duval, starting up and coming forward, he took her hand and led her to a seat on the opposite side of the table.

Then he resumed his own, and for a moment there was an embarrassing silence.

Duval had never before been at a loss to find a subject for conversation when in company with the young; but now he felt that his task was no easy one, for how could he make that fair and beautiful girl aware of her danger, without at the same time shocking her delicacy, by detailing the vile schemes which were being set on foot for her destruction.

And then, again, he was a perfect stranger to her. Would it be possible, without detailing the whole of what had come to his knowledge, to make her believe that her uncle was to be distrusted, while he, Duval, was to seek to make her trust him implicitly.

Something akin to these thoughts, were chasing each other through the mind of Duval, when the silence, which was becoming exceedingly embarrassing, was broken by Victorine herself.

"Sir," she said, in a calm, firm voice, which, at first, astonished Duval; "you have sent for me: had you not done so, it was my intention to seek you before another hour had passed over our heads. I demand to know what all this means, and where my uncle is?"

"In reply to your first question I will say, that circumstances, the knowledge of which came to my ears by accident, made me aware that in this house resided a young lady whom I had never seen, but who was the subject of a conversation between two bad men. They plotted together to make her life one of wretchedness, and I resolved that if I could prevent this foul crime, I would. That is why I assumed the disguise of your uncle.

"But I do not understand, sir——"

Duval held up his hand. "Hear me out, I beg of you. Your uncle was one of these two men——"

"Good heavens!" exclaimed the young girl, starting to her feet.

"Be calm! be calm! no harm shall happen to you if you trust me—but you must do that, or I cannot save you."

"Go on sir!" said Victorine, as she clasped her hands over her face.

"Do you not know, that yesterday morning your uncle expected a visitor?"

"Yes—oh, yes!"

"Exactly! Well, that visitor was your uncle's accomplice in plotting your ruin."

Victorine uttered a cry of distress.

"Once more let me beg of you to be calm," said Duval, in his kindest accents. "But to continue:—

"The visitor who came here yesterday morning was to come again to-day at twelve o'clock, to finish all the arrangements of their villanous plot."

"He did come—he did come! I was here when he entered the room."

"But have you forgotten that it was I who received him, and heard all the details of their plans, instead of your uncle?"

"Oh, sir, how shall I ever be able to repay you?"

"By being brave now. Before this man came I conveyed your uncle to a part of this house which is only known to myself. There I made him a prisoner until such time as it will be proper to release him."

"Then he is not in danger?"

"No! on the contrary, he is far better lodged than he deserves to be. And, now let me ask you if you are inclined to be led entirely by me?"

"Yes—oh, yes!"

"Then drive into the Park at four o'clock to-day, and leave the rest to me: or, stay, I see you are not equal to the task. I have imposed upon you. I will go instead."

"You?"

"Even I; but, in order to do so, I must borrow some feminine attire, which, perhaps, you can accommodate me with."

"Most willingly," replied Victorine, with something approaching to a smile, at the idea of the handsome man before her personating a lady.

"You will find that I can be very ladylike when it suits me. The only difficulty will be with the servants."

"Oh, leave them to me. They will be deaf and blind too, if I order them to be so."

"I am delighted to hear it. Perhaps you will send me some clothes directly, as it will take me some time to dress, unaccustomed as I am to the costume."

Victorine sped along the corridor, at the end of which she encountered Mr. Van Burg.

CHAPTER CXLVII.

CLAUDE DUVAL ENCOUNTERS MOSSY PENDELL ONCE AGAIN.

"COME here! Come here! Mr. Van Burg, I want you! I want you! Quick!"

The Secretary stared with astonishment, as he prepared to follow the young girl, saying to himself as he did so:

"What now? what now? Has everybody gone mad to-day?"

"Mr. Van Burg! Mr. Van Burg!"

"Yes, miss—yes miss."

"Come here and take this dress, and this shawl and hat to my uncle. You were quite right, Mr. Van Burg, he is changed."

"Yes, miss. But what am I to do when I go into his room with all this female toggery?"

"Why, Mr. Van Burg, may I trust you with a great secret?"

"To be sure you may! Oh, if you would always tell me all your secrets, how happy I should be."

"Don't talk nonsense, then, there's a dear Mr. Van Burg, and I will tell you this secret to begin with. My uncle is going to dress himself like a lady and take a drive."

"What? Eh? Miss Victorine, what do you mean? You are not changed are you, Miss Victorine?"

"Of course I am not! But you see if my uncle has taken it into his head to go out, dressed like a lady, why who is to hinder him?"

"Oh, no one! But why? That's what I want to know, miss?"

"Never mind that, as long as he is changed, as you yourself said. Don't let us try to thwart a little harmless amusement, especially as he seems so much kinder."

"Far be it from me, Miss, to do anything to bring back the old state of affairs; so give me the things and let me go."

Victorine loaded the Secretary's arm with all kinds of female wearing apparel, and then pushed him towards the door.

She thought he was gone, but again the door opened, and the Secretary thrust in his head.

"Well, Mr. Van Burg, what now?"

"I say, miss, you are not playing me a trick, are you? Because he would murder me outright, I do believe if——"

"Of course I am not! How could you think I would be so cruel? Make haste, or he may get impatient."

"All right, miss; I would take your word against all the world." Then, turning in the opposite direction, the Secretary hurried to the apartments of the Dutch Envoy.

"That will do, Mr. Van Burg," said Duval, as the Secretary advanced towards him. "Lay them on that sofa, and withdraw."

The Secretary obeyed, and then he returned to Victorine, who had expressed a wish to see him again, after he had carried the wearing apparel to her uncle.

"Now, Mr. Van Burg, I am going to put your friendship to the test," said Victorine, as soon as the Secretary entered the apartment.

"Do so—do so, and you shall find that I am ever your most willing slave."

"Then are you willing to become my uncle's coachman for to-day?"

"Me?"

"Yes. You see, dear Mr. Van Burg, I should be much more comfortable if I thought you were with him in his present state of mind."

"But you—don't think—that—that——"

"I do not think that there is anything to fear, Mr. Van Burg; but this strange desire to appear as a lady certainly looks rather eccentric; do you not think so?"

"Yes, yes; I understand."

"Of course you do; but I am anxious to humour him, especially as he seems so much better-tempered than we have ever known him to be."

"He does — he does; and if you had heard how kindly he spoke to me after I had kept him waiting so long and all——"

"That is why I think we ought not to try and thwart his little peculiarities, you see, Mr. Van Burg; but I do not wish to enter into all these details with the servants, so if you would be so very kind——"

Victorine paused, and gave the Secretary, as he thought, one of her brightest looks.

"To be sure I will, miss; and I will also undertake to make the coachman understand that I am going to take his place to day, and I will do it in such a manner that he shall not feel offended."

"Thank you — thank you!" exclaimed Victorine, holding out her hand to the Secretary; "and you can say that the footman will not be wanted."

"I will see to it—I will see to it. Have you any more commands?"

"No. Oh, yes! you might say that I do not intend to receive any visitors to-day."

"Very well. I will not forget."

The Secretary retired, but it would be expecting too much of human nature to say that he did not feel considerable curiosity respecting the strange arrangements about to take place in reference to the drive which he supposed the Dutch Envoy was about to take.

"I don't care," he said to himself. "Miss Victorine has confided in me, and I will do my best to carry out all her wishes, although I do think she might have told me a little more if there be, indeed, anything to tell; but perhaps it is but a mere whim. However, time presses, and I must go and see James, the coachman."

The Secretary found that functionary in the full enjoyment of a pipe and a flagon of foaming ale.

"Ah, James!" said the Secretary; "the very person I wanted to see."

The coachman half rose, not knowing exactly what to say or do under the circumstances, as he was aware that the Secretary possessed extraordinary influence, not only over the Envoy himself, but also over his beautiful niece.

However, Mr. Van Burg did not keep him long in suspense, and was glad to find that, far from feeling annoyed at the novel arrangement, he seemed rather pleased to think he might consider himself off duty.

"Perhaps, then, sir," he said, "you would not mind giving me permission to join a little family party as is going to have a sort of pleasure trip to-day?"

"Go by all means, my good man," said the Secretary.

The man soon disappeared.

"That is done," said the Secretary, as a bright smile passed over his countenance. "Surely, she must believe that I love her?"

Victorine, when she was left alone, threw herself into an easy chair, and gave herself up to the most gloomy reflections.

"What am I doing," she asked herself, "in thus being led by a perfect stranger? And yet—and yet I cannot distrust him, there is something so truthful in the expression of his countenance. I—I do know that my uncle has of late striven to possess me with the idea that I have lost all my property. Surely, surely, he has not himself appropriated it? He has told me more than once that I have lost everything, and—and that I must make a rich marriage. Heaven help me!"

In the meantime, Duval had put on his own apparel; the garments which had been sent to him by Victorine; and it must be confessed, he had great difficulty in accomplishing the feat, in such a way as to make a very respectable appearance.

A large cashmere shawl, however, effectually concealed any defects in the misfitting dress; and the large hat and feather concealed his features tolerably well.

But where were the floating curls, which formed almost the only ornament of the fair young being whom he wished so much to personate?

Duval thought for a moment; and then, having written a few words on a scrap of paper, he rang the bell.

When the Secretary made his appearance, Duval handed to him the paper.

"Take that to my niece, and wait for an answer."

The Secretary, as soon as he saw Duval, could not forbear a smile, which, however, he endeavoured to suppress as quickly as possible.

"Here Miss Victorine," he said, as soon as he had obeyed the order to enter; "here is a note your uncle has just given me for you, and he says I am to wait for an answer."

Victorine tore open the little billet, and then laughed outright.

"What now, Miss Victorine?" said the Secretary.

"Why he wants a wig! One with fair curls, to resemble mine as nearly as possible."

"But you have not got such a thing, Miss. What does he mean? There never was, nor never will be a wig half so beautiful as your lovely hair!"

"Not so fast—not so fast, my good friend!" said Victorine, still smiling. "I do happen to have such a thing; for when my cousin was staying with us, do you not remember that he disguised himself so well, that no one could say which was Victorine—him or me?"

"Yes, I remember something of the sort," gloomily replied the Secretary.

"Well then, you must know, that he had a wig made to resemble mine, so closely, that not the best judge could detect the counterfeit."

"I could, always!" replied the Secretary.

"And here it is," said Victorine, "rummaging in a drawer. I always carry it about with me, wherever I go, in remembrance of those happy, happy days."

As she spoke, the eyes of Victorine filled with tears.

"There, Mr. Van Burg, give that to my uncle, but ask him to take great care of it, as I set a value upon it.

With a much heavier heart than he had sought the young girl's presence, did the Secretary retire.

"Infatuation! Infatuation! What can she see in his baby face to admire? I do believe she loves him! I always was afraid of their being so much together— but he will soon forget her, and then—and then,—oh, the thought of ever being able to call her mine, makes me almost wild with joy."

"The idea, too," he continued, "of calling this an imitation of her glorious hair,—it is a libel!"

As the Secretary spoke, he dashed the wig down on the floor. Then hastily stooping to pick it up, he proceeded to the apartment now in the occupation of

Duval, and whom he still believed to be the Dutch Envoy.

"Ah! you have succeeded," said Duval, imitating the voice of the Dutchman, but speaking in very different accents to what he—the Envoy—was in the habit of addressing the Secretary,—"you have it. Now I think my disguise is complete."

As he spoke, Duval put the wig on so quickly, that there was not time for Mr. Van Burg to notice whether or not he was indeed the veritable Envoy.

"It is indeed complete, your Excellency. May I retire?"

"Yes; and remember at a quarter to four I want the carriage. It is now just half-past three."

"Your orders shall be attended to, your Excellency," said the Secretary, as he bowed himself out of the room.

"I must just see her again, to know if she has any further orders to give me, before I take my place on the box."

Mr. Van Burg passed quickly along the corridor, and knocked on the panel of the door of the outer apartment, known as Victorine's own.

"Come in!" was the immediate reply.

The Secretary opened the door, and stood before the young girl.

"Well, Mr. Van Burg, was my uncle satisfied with the wig?"

"He said nothing could be better."

"That is well. And now, Mr. Van Burg, I am going to ask a particular favour of you."

"Yes, yes—what is it?"

"That you will be ready and willing to do anything—no matter what strange request it might be—that my uncle may tell you."

"Certainly."

"And if—if any danger seem to menace him, you will—you will afford him all the assistance he may require, and that you can give? Have I your promise?"

"I promise most faithfully to guard him—even as I would you, were it really you instead of your uncle disguised as you."

"I am satisfied, then, Mr. Van Burg, and have only one more request to make."

"And that is?"

"That you will come to me as soon as ever you return, and tell me what has happened to my uncle."

"Why, Miss Victorine, whatever can happen to him. No one will detect the difference Any passer by glancing in at the carriage would suppose it to be occupied by a lady, and you know no one who could be likely to accost you."

"No, that is true," replied Victorine.

"You have nothing more to say," asked the Secretary, still lingering.

"Nothing, but to thank you, dear Mr. Van Burg, for all your kindness to an almost friendless girl."

The Secretary seized the hand Victorine extended towards him, and pressed it respectfully to his lips.

"At least he is faithful,' said Victorine, when she found herself once more alone, "and I shall ascertain from him, in a very short time, whether he who says he wishes to befriend me is sincere or not."

CHA'TER CXLVIII.

CLAUDE DUVAL ENACTS A NEW CHARACTER.

EXACTLY at a quarter to four o'clock Duval stepped into the carriage which usually conveyed the niece of the Dutch Envoy for a drive in the park.

The Secretary mounted the box, and it may be said that his disguise was almost as perfect as that of Claude Duval.

The carriage, with their splendid horses, drove rapidly in the direction of the park.

Duval, who kept his eyes upon a carriage, which was standing a few paces from Camden House, when he entered the Envoy's chariot, saw that it followed almost close upon the one in which he was seated.

"Mossy Pendell, I suppose, is the occupant of that carriage," said Duval, to himself.

The part of the Park in which they now found themselves, seemed almost deserted, and Claude Duval having a great desire to make assurance doubly sure, that he was not mistaken in conjecturing that his old enemy, Mossy Pendell, was seated in the other carriage, ordered his coachman to pull up for a short time.

Scarcely had he done so, than what he expected did happen.

The other carriage pulled up also, and Mossy Pendell alighted from it.

He passed the carriage in which was Duval, probably to satisfy himself that it contained no one but the helpless girl, who was that day to be carried off to serve for the plaything of an hour to the dissolute Frederick, Prince of Wales.

Having assured himself that there was only one occupant in the carriage, and that occupant none other than the fair and lovely Victorine, Mossy Pendell—who was by nature a coward—took courage, and boldly approached the carriage.

The Secretary, who had not been unobservant of all that had taken place, and remembering the caution which Victorine had given him to look after her uncle's safety, turned sharply round on the box, and looked inquiringly at Mossy Pendell, who, at this moment, raised his hat, and approached his head close to the carriage window, saying, as he did so, "Have I the pleasure of addressing the lovely niece of His Excellency the Baron Von Schneider?"

Duval bowed.

"Then, if you will allow me, I will present my wife to your notice, and hope that we may have the happiness of becoming great friends."

Again Duval inclined his head.

"You may have heard your uncle speak of Mr. Pendell, high in the favour of his Royal Highness the Prince of Wales."

"I have," replied Duval, in a low voice, which so well resembled that of the beautiful Victorine, that Mossy Pendell at once fell into the trap.

"Then, will you alight, or shall I bring Mrs. Pendell to your ladyship?"

"I will do myself the pleasure of accompanying you to your carriage," replied Duval; "and, if you please, I will send mine home."

The look of astonishment upon the countenance of Mossy Pendell, as all the obstacles he had apprehended were thus cleared away by the unlooked-for compliance of the young lady, to aid him, as it were, in his diabolical schemes, did not pass unnoticed by Duval.

He gave his hand to Mossy Pendell, and entered the other carriage, in which was a female of the most forbidding appearance.

"Her ladyship desires me to say," said Mossy Pendell, turning to the secretary, "that she will not require her carriage any longer."

"Very well," said the supposed coachman—he then added to himself; "but if you expect I am going to leave *her* uncle in the power of such a hang-dog-looking scoundrel as yourself, you are greatly mistaken."

The carriage containing Mossy Pendell, Duval, and the repulsive-looking female drove off at rather a rapid pace in the direction of Pall Mall.

"Fred! Fred!" cried the secretary, to a youth of about sixteen, who had kept the Envoy's carriage in view ever since it had left Camden House."

"Here, Ralph!"

"Be quick, jump up on the box, while I follow that carriage!"

As he spoke, the secretary dropped from the box, and his place was taken by his young brother Fred.

Swiftly as feet could carry him, the secretary followed the retreating carriage, which, as he supposed, contained the Dutch Envoy.

He had no desire to save that wicked and passionate man from harm; but inasmuch as he had promised his fair neice to watch over his safety, Ralph Van Burg was resolved to carry out his promise to the letter.

The carriage stopped at a magnificent house in Pall Mall, and the door was opened by a footman in a showy and somewhat gaudy livery.

Mossy Pendell gave his hand to Duval, and as the latter alighted, he happened to perceive the secretary.

He thought it strange that he should have followed him, as he supposed he was in perfect ignorance of the whole transaction; and was not even aware that he was the person who had driven him, Duval, from Camden House.

But Duval took no apparent notice of the fact, but feeling that he was not quite alone in an unknown situation, gave him a greater feeling of security than he would otherwise have possessed.

Mossy Pendell led the way up the grand staircase, and then into a small, but magnificently furnished apartment.

"I will leave you here, fairest of the fair," said Mossy Pendell, "while I to apprise my wife of the pleasure that awaits her."

For another moment, Claude Duval was alone.

He went to the window and looked out.

On the opposite side of the way, was the Secretary.

"Good!" said Duval. "Now, Mossy Pendell, I am ready for you."

As he spoke, Duval was hastily divesting himself of the feminine apparel, and stood arrayed in his full highwayman's costume.

Scarcely had he had time to conceal the female-garments, when he heard hasty footsteps approaching.

In another instant, a hand was laid on the handle of the door, and Mossy Pendell entered the room alone.

Duval had concealed himself behind the door of the apartment, so that it was not until Mossy Pendell had fairly got into the room, that he perceived who was its tenant.

With a look of affright, almost terrible to behold, he gazed upon Claude Duval, as the latter slowly closed the door of the room, turned the key, put it into his pocket.

"Where —where is," he gasped, – " where is she?"

"Where is the young girl, you would ask, villain, whom you decoyed hither? I will answer you! I am here instead to call you to account! Have you a weapon? If so, draw!"

"I have no weapon," said Mossy Pendell; "and if you fight an unarmed man, you will be a coward and a murderer!"

"You shall not have that excuse," said Duval, coolly. I will ring, and when your servants answer the summons, tell them that you want a sword, or a pair of pistols—either will do. The weapon we fight with is perfectly immaterial to me!"

"But—but——" stammered Mossy Pendell.

Duval heeded him not; but with two strides he reached the fire-place, by the side of which hung a silken bell-rope.

As soon, however, as he touched it, the rope came down in his hand.

"Ah! villain!" he exclaimed, "your plans were well laid, even the bell-rope has been tampered with; but a second thought is sometimes the best. This room shall be your prison, instead of that of the helpless girl whom you intended it for."

As he spoke, Claude Duval dexterously threw Mossy Pendell on to his knees; and, with the aid of the bellrope, he contrived to pinion his arms behind him, bringing the end through the bars of the grate, to which he securely fastened them.

"Help! Murder!" shouted Mossy Pendell.

Duval presented a loaded pistol at his head.

"Remember," he said, addressing Mossy Pendell in a low tone of voice. "I do not look upon you as I do upon other men. I should shrink from committing murder; but in your case, if I hear you raise your voice above your breath, I shall consider that I am doing society at large a service by ridding the world of such a villain. Another such cry, and without further warning, I fire."

Mossy Pendell was silent.

"Now," continued Duval, "I shall help myself to whatever you may have about you, and when next we meet we will fight."

"Malediction!" growled Mossy Pendell.

Duval had no difficulty of course in rifling the pockets of his prisoner, and he was glad to find that he had a well-filled purse to begin with.

"This, I suppose, is the price you received from your villanous employer for the fair young girl you brought here?"

Mossy Pendell maintained a dogged silence

In the meantime Duval transferred from the pockets of Mossy Pendell everything that was in any way valuable, and then he made his way to the door, but scarcely had he placed the key in the lock before Mossy Pendell, in a voice between a shriek and a shout, called out,

"Help! help!"

In an instant Duval closed and locked the door again, and striding up to him, he said:

"I would have contented myself with mere fettering your limbs, but since you will drive me to extremities, it is not my fault.

"Mercy! mercy!" shrieked Pendell. "I am silent —silent as the grave. Spare my life, and I will not utter a word."

"Yes," said Claude Duval, "I will spare your life, because I will not soil my soul with the reflection that even you were taken at an unfair advantage; but I intend to take steps which shall effectually prevent you from calling for assistance again."

As he spoke, Duval took from his pocket a silk handkerchief, and so adroitly placed it about his mouth, that it would be a matter of impossibility for him to make himself heard.

"Now, Mossy Pendell, I leave you to your own reflections, and take my leave of you. Have you, by the by, any message to send to your friend, the Baron von Schneider, for I am now going to see his niece, and put her on her guard against her uncle and his dear friend, Mossy Pendell."

Mossy Pendell turned livid with rage.

Duval now opened the door again, and after listening attentively for some minutes, returned to the apartment in which he had left his prisoner.

On a chair Pendell had thrown an ample roquelaire cloak he usually wore, and on a table was his hat.

"The very things I want," said Duval, as he put on both the cloak and the hat.

Pendell watched him; but, of course, could do nothing to prevent his taking them.

"With these," said Duval, "I shall find easy egress from this house probably; and, if I find it necessary to do so, I dare say I can contrive to imitate the air and gait of Mossy Pendell.

Wrapping the cloak about him, Claude Duval strode down the stairs, at the head of which he encountered the hag-like-looking female Mossy Pendell had taken with him to aid in the capture of the beautiful Victorine.

The woman did not look up, but merely curtseyed low as Duval passed her.

"My disguise is not so bad, after all," said Duval to himself, as he continued his way to the hall.

The porter was asleep in his leathern chair, and Duval passed out at the outer door without the slightest difficulty.

Scarcely had he gone twenty paces, however, when he became aware that he was being quickly pursued, and turning round, he beheld the Secretary.

Duval had felt all along that this young man was only acting in the interests of Victorine, so he gave himself no anxiety about the fact of his following him, until at the corner of the street he saw the carriage in which he had come disguised as the niece of the Dutch Envoy, and the boy Fred on the box.

Then Duval made up his mind to speak to the Secretary, for which purpose he paused abruptly, and as he had been previously walking very fast, and the Secretary had been keeping up with him at the same pace, it necessarily brought them almost close together before either of them was well aware of the fact.

"My friend," said Duval, speaking in the tone he had assumed when disguised as the Dutch Envoy,—"My friend, I have every reason to believe that you would serve your young lady?"

Mr. Van Burg stared with astonishment, for the voice, while it was precisely that of the irascible Baron von Schneider, the face and figure were totally different.

"You look surprised," continued Duval, in his own natural tones now; "but you can have no doubt left in your mind now as to who I am."

"Who you are, sir?"

"Yes. Do you not perceive that I am the person to whom Miss Victorine leant some of her wearing apparel this morning, and whom you drove into the Park?"

"Is it possible? Then where——"

"Where is the Dutch Envoy, the Baron von Schneider, you would ask? I will tell you, my friend. I have the means of entering Camden House when I please."

"You, sir?"

"Even I; and it pleased me yesterday to enter, and fortune directed my footsteps to an apartment from whence I overheard a conversation between two of the greatest villains on the face of the earth."

The Secretary looked inquiringly at Duval.

"The names of these two scoundrels I will tell you. The Baron von Schneider was one, and Mossy Pendell was that of the other."

"Indeed."

"And now shall I tell you what led me to enact the little masquerade of which you have been a witness? It was simply that I might be able to convict these two men to their faces of endeavouring to compass the ruin of that fair and lovely girl who has the misfortune to call one of these same scoundrels uncle."

"What, Miss Victorine?"

"As you say. When I alighted from the carriage, he—Mossy Pendell, I mean—thought that I was Victorine.

"You look surprised," said Duval, smiling, "to think that any one with half an eye could be deceived into the belief that I and she were one and the same person."

"Well, I must confess that rather puzzless me," replied Mr. Van Burg.

"But I will let you into the secret: Mossy Pendell's eyes had been blinded by a large sum of money, which had been given him to bring your young lady to a house in Pall Mall."

"I see—I see now," replied the Secretary.

"Of course you do," said Duval. "Now I will again enter the carriage, and once more I will request you to drive me, but this time let it be to, instead of from, Camden House.

"Willingly," replied the delighted Secretary. "Wonders will never cease."

CHAPTER CXLIX.

CLAUDE DUVAL SUCCEEDS IN BAFFLING MOSSY PENDELL.

A VERY short time sufficed Mr Van Burg to drive Claude Duval to Camden House.

As soon as he entered the apartment in which the Dutch Envoy was wont to receive his niece, Duval turned to the Secretary, who had followed him, and told him to acquaint the niece of the Baron von Schneider that he desired to speak to her.

Mr. Van Burg did not require a second bidding to hasten to the presence of the young girl whom he looked upon with so much affection; for the thought of the danger from which she had escaped seemed to add to his impatience once more to look upon her, if it were only to assure himself of her perfect safety.

The gentle "come in," in reply to his rap for admission, sent the blood coursing madly through his veins.

"Oh, Miss Victorine, heaven be praised!" was all he could say when he beheld her.

"Why, what is the matter, dear Mr. Van Burg? Why that exclamation of thankfulness?"

"Do not ask me—suffice it to say, you are safe. But I am forgetting what I came for. A gentleman—the gentleman who dressed himself up in some of your clothes this morning—is waiting to speak to you."

"Then you know all?"

"No, not all; but sufficient to feel quite satisfied that he is a gentleman and a man of honour."

"It is now my time to be thankful," said Victorine, as her eyes filled with tears. "Oh, that I could return to my kind friends' protection."

"I wish you could, miss; but let me advise you to speak to that gentleman about all that sort of thing—he is just the man to advise you."

"You think so?"

"Most assuredly, I do. If you only knew what he has saved you from—but there, you had better not know—only this I will tell you: your old uncle is no longer a proper guardian for you; he is a ——"

"Forbear, Mr. Van Burg. I must not listen to anything disparaging of him. Remember, my dear father, who loved me so fondly, committed me to his care on his death-bed."

"And nicely he has fulfilled the trust!" exclaimed the indignant Secretary. "Why, is he not continually telling you that, if it were not for him, you would be a beggar, when I know your father left you sixty thousand pounds. Was I not one of the witnesses to his will?"

"Yes, yes, I know all that. But, after all, what is money? Besides, he says he has lost the will, so——"

"Pray do not talk in that way; nobody loses a will

unless it does not suit them to produce it; and then you talk like an innocent child, as you are, in reality. You say, what is the use of money? Why, everything. It gives you power, wealth, influence,—all that can make life happy."

"I would rather receive all I possess from my uncle, if he would but love me a little, than be the possessor of all this wealth, and feel so lonely as I do."

As she spoke, the young girl drooped her head on her hand, and large tears forced their way through her fingers.

"Oh, don't cry—don't take on! What a fool I was to say anything to make you cry! Oh, forgive me!"

"You have said nothing, dear Mr. Van Burg. I was crying, but it was at my own thoughts, not at what you said."

"Well, I do not like to see tears in such eyes as yours, so try and be more cheerful, and go and see what the gentleman has to say."

"I will—I had forgotten."

As she spoke, Victorine rose from her chair, and after removing the traces of her tears, she made her way towards the apartment in which the Secretary had told her Duval was awaiting her.

And it must be confessed that Duval was not sorry to have some time left him to reflect upon how much it would be best to tell, and how much to keep from the innocent girl whom it had been his happiness to serve.

The traces of tears were still visible as Duval advanced and led her to a chair.

After a short pause he said, "You have thought me long?"

"No, sir—that is, yes—at least, I do not know!" stammered the young girl, blushing and looking down.

"Well," added Duval, "I will not trouble you with details, which could only shock you; but believe me, when I say that this house—any house in which your uncle resides, in fact—is not a fit home for you."

"But, sir, my dear father, on his death-bed——"

"Was deceived—basely deceived—by his false brother."

"Oh, sir!"

"Tell me," continued Duval, taking the young girl's hand in his, "does not your uncle speak of your fortune as being lost?"

"Something of the kind; but I never took particular notice of what he said on that subject, as money cannot purchase happiness."

"But if it cannot purchase happiness, it is a great incentive to it."

"Perhaps so; but unfortunately my uncle lost my father's will, and so——"

"Does he say that it is lost?"

"Yes."

"It is respecting that will that I wanted to speak to you. Supposing the will to be still in existence, have you any relative or friend to whose protection you could be confided?"

"Yes, oh, yes! My school-friend, Mrs. St. Clare, with whom I resided so happily after my poor father's death."

"Then I understand you to say that if the will of your late father be not lost, and you are assured that the vast wealth he bequeathed to you is really your own beyond a doubt, you would not only be willing but glad to reside with the lady you have mentioned?"

"Oh, yes; but my uncle?"

"Believe me, he is in every way unworthy of your regard?"

"Alas! alas!"

"Now, follow me, and, together, we will seek your uncle."

Victorine looked wonderingly at Duval as he walked towards the wall of the room, and lifted the ancient tapestry which covered the walls.

"This house," said Duval, smiling at the young girl, "has many secrets, known only to very few persons, and I am one of those."

As he spoke, Duval touched a small brass knob, and pressed it slightly inwards with his thumb, and in a few minutes the sliding panel which led into the room in which he had shut the Dutch Envoy opened.

Victorine gazed about her in a bewildered kind of way, as Duval said courteously, "I am going to lead you to your uncle. Allow me to assist you."

With some hesitation, the young girl gave her hand to Duval; and in another moment they stood in the presence of the Baron Van Schneider.

"Ah, you have come at last to release me!" he cried, as he made a step towards Duval.

"That is as the case may be, Baron," said Duval, calmly. "I come now——"

"Not to rob me?"

"No, not to rob you, but to force you to make restitution."

"Restitution! What mean you?"

"Oh, sir," said Victorine, laying her hand upon Duval's arm, "let me speak, and ask my uncle one question."

Duval courteously inclined his head.

"Oh, tell me, uncle, you did not — you could not——"

"I tell you that the will was lost, girl—quite, irrecoverably lost."

"Oh, uncle, uncle, I am not talking—I am not thinking—about the will. But tell me that you had no hand in what was to have been my abduction this afternoon in the Park."

The Dutch Envoy turned ghastly pale.

"Allow me," said Duval, "to inform you, as far as it is necessary to do so, of the villanous plot concocted by your uncle and his companion, Mossy Pendell."

At the mention of this name the Baron turned, if possible, a shade paler, and Duval continued:

"It was purposed that when you went out for your drive this afternoon in the Park, as usual, that Mossy Pendell should stop your carriage, and carry you away by force to a house in Pall Mall."

"It is false—false!" shrieked the Dutch Envoy. "The fact that you are standing here in my presence, Victorine, shows that what this man says is false—for, instead of being carried off as he so insolently asserts, you were to be, your drive was not interrupted."

"But I did not go, uncle," said Victorine, looking into his eyes.

"You did not go? Maledictions!"

"No, sir, I went instead."

"Indeed; and perhaps, sir, my friend, Mr. Mossy Pendell, did himself the pleasure of carrying you off, when he was disappointed in not finding my niece. I doubt not you will assert this interesting little fact next?"

"Mossy Pendell did carry off one whom he supposed to be this young girl, and did take her to the house in Pall Mall."

"What?"

"I say—or, rather, I now tell you for the first time—that I fortunately overheard the vile plot against this young lady's peace; and accordingly I dressed myself in some female wearing apparel, and trusted to Providence that the deception would not be detected."

The Baron was about to speak, but Duval, in an authoritative voice, commanded him to be silent.

"Knowing how much depended on this Mossy Pendell's success in obtaining possession of your niece, I was not wrong in supposing that a few incongruities in regard to my outward appearance would be over-

DUVAL IN THE HOUSE OF MORNING.

looked, so anxious would he be to carry out the villanous instructions of his vile employers. I was not wrong in my conjectures: he did overlook these incongruities, and I was fortunate enough to take this young lady's place."

"You?"

"Even so. I alighted from your niece's carriage, and entered one which this scoundrel Mossy Pondell had in waiting. I was conveyed to the house in Pall Mall, where I had the great satisfaction of leaving your friend bound hand and foot, gagged in such a manner that no one will be disturbed by any cries he may try to give utterance to."

"Fool! Dolt! Idiot! not to look and be assured of her identity."

"You see," said Duval, turning to Victorine, "you see that he inadvertently admits that his friend is a fool, a dolt, and an idiot, for not assuring himself that the person he conveyed to the house in Pall Mall was indeed you."

No. 48.—NIGHTSHADE.

"Alas alas!" said Victorine, as she sunk upon a chair.

"Courage! courage!" whispered Duval, "you ought rather to rejoice."

"Yes; I know I feel I ought, but yet——"

Duval turned again to the Baron Von Schnieder, and in a serious tone, said:

"Now, sir, I have candidly told you the condition in which I have left your friend. It only remains for me to assure you that your fate will be a similar one, unless you at once tell me where the will of this young lady's late father is to be found."

"I know not. I cannot tell you."

"Then I will find some means of making you, that is all. May I request you to retire," added Duval, turning to Victorine.

"No, no!" shouted her uncle, as he made a rush towards her, but was met by Duval, who hurled him against one side of the apartment. "No, no! Do not leave me. He will murder me! murder me! I see it in his eyes. Come here! come here! I command you, girl!"

But Victorine left the room, for Duval took the opportunity, while her uncle was raving, to whisper to her that she need be under no apprehension, as it was not his intention to do more than frighten her uncle out of the will, which he felt sure he had hidden for his own purposes.

As soon, therefore, as the door was closed, Duval drew a pistol from his pocket, and levelled it at the Dutch Envoy.

"Now, sir," he said, addressing the Baron, "you have seen enough of me by this time to know that I am fully capable of carrying out my intentions. Those intentions at present are to scatter your worthless brains upon that wall, unless you instantly tell me where to find the will."

"In a secret drawer in my escritoire," doggedly replied the Envoy.

"Enough! Wait here until my return."

"But you cannot find it. You cannot open the drawer unless I show you how."

"Then you shall show me how."

As he spoke, Duval placed the arm of the Dutch Envoy beneath his own, and dragged, rather than led him to the apartment in which stood the escritoire belonging to the Dutch Envoy.

"Open it!" said Duval, as he led the Baron to the escritoire.

The Baron opened it.

"Now the secret drawer," said Duval, keeping his eyes fixed upon him.

The Baron touched a secret spring, and a small drawer flew open.

Duval instantly grasped a sheet of parchment, on which were endorsed the following words—

"The last will and testament of Count D'Able."

Duval advanced towards the door of the apartment, and made a sign to Victorine to enter.

"Here," he said, holding up the parchment, "is your late father's will, which makes you his heiress. You can have no desire to remain an inmate of the same home as that man, whom you unfortunately call uncle; therefore, if you have any friend you can trust to escort you to the lady whom you mentioned to me yesterday, I will gladly be of what service I can to aid you in seeking her protection."

"Oh, how can I ever repay the debt of gratitude I owe you?" exclaimed Victorine, as she clasped Duval's hand in hers.

"I am repaid already in having baffled those who would first have robbed, and afterwards destroyed you."

It was next agreed that Mr. Van Burg and Victorine's favourite maid should accompany her back to Ghent, where she had spent so many happy days with her friend, Mrs. St. Clare—a widow with an only son—whom Duval shrewdly guessed was far from being distasteful to the fair girl to whom he, Duval, had been of so much service.

CHAPTER CL.

CLAUDE DUVAL ENTERS A HOUSE OF MOURNING.

IT was easy for Duval to effect a departure from Camden House, for as yet the sentinels had not recovered from their fright, and he walked rapidly in the direction of Westminster.

As he was passing the end of a lane in the Oxford Road, however, in which were situated a few cottages, inhabited by the very poorest of the population at that time, a loud voice broke upon his ear—broken, though loud and harsh, but Duval had no difficulty in detecting in its tones that it was the voice of some one doing battle with a mighty grief.

"Dead!" cried the voice, "dead! God of Heaven, no! It cannot—it shall not be! Let me look upon her face! I tell you, woman, she was my child, she is not dead!"

Duval paused a moment, in hopes of learning more, or at least of understanding better the cause of such lamentation.

Then he heard the snuffling tones of a woman's voice, reply in dejected accents—

"No, no! Don't go to her. It's not such a beautiful sight to look on the face of the dead. Indeed, indeed, she is dead!"

Without another moment's hesitation, Duval turned down the lane, and directed by the sound of the voices, he paused before the open door of a miserable-looking habitation, from the interior of which came the tones of expostulation and lamentation which had first attracted his attention.

Duval hesitated a moment whether to enter or not; for, to a refined mind, there is ever something sacred about grief which represses all curiosity.

"This is absurd," said Duval to himself, "I will enter, perhaps, I may be of service."

Duval at once entered the miserable dwelling, but the room in which he found himself was untenanted.

Facing the door of the hut—for such it was—was a dark, dilapidated staircase, and it was only by the sound of deep grief and convulsive sobs which smote his ear as he ascended, that Duval was enabled to guide his footsteps in the right direction.

Duval knocked gently with his knuckles on the panel of the door to his left hand.

"Who's there? Who's there?" demanded a voice from within the chamber. "Has death returned to give me back my child?"

"Hush, hush! Oh, what heathenish talk!" Duval heard a female voice reply, as the speaker, an old woman, opened the door of the room and peered inquiringly at him.

Duval passed into the room, which presented an appearance of the most abject poverty.

The walls were bare, and dripping with unwholesome moisture.

A miserable truckle bed occupied one corner, and that, together with a table and two dilapidated chairs, completed the furniture of the room.

Scarcely had he time to make the most cursory observation, when Duval found himself confronted by a tall, soldierly-looking man, in whose countenance anger was struggling with deep grief.

His eyes were bloodshot and swollen, his dress disordered, and his pale, haggard face showed that either sorrow or want, or perhaps both, had sapped the springs of life.

"Well, sir," he said, addressing Duval, as he evidently made a strong effort to suppress his feelings, "well, sir, you have come at last."

Duval looked at him, at first, supposing that grief had disordered his reason, then the poor man continued.

"You are too late, sir, too late, I say. Death has been here before you. God forgive you! God forgive you! God forgive you!"

The bereaved father covered his face with his hands, and heart-rending sobs burst from his almost broken heart.

"Sir," said Duval, kindly, "there is some mistake."

"Mistake! mistake!" shouted the man, looking up, and pushing his long hair back from his fevered brow. "Oh, would that there were! Would that there were! But no—no!"

He turned his eyes to the miserable tuckle bed and a shudder passed through his frame.

"That," he said, pointing to the bed, "is too terrible a truth, I tell you, sir. There is no mistake, it is too —too real. Go away, sir. Your presence is not needed now, and my poor heart is too bruised to quarrel with you. There was a time—but no matter now—go, sir! I command you!"

He sunk down upon a chair, and covering his face with his hands, sobbed audibly.

Duval was still at a loss to understand the meaning of what the man said, when he kept insisting that he, Duval, was too late. He looked towards the old woman, who was seated beside the fire, rocking herself to and fro, to see if she were inclined to give him any explanation.

"I know something of medicine," said Duval, softly, as he approached the old woman.

"No doubt — no doubt," was all the reply he got.

That was not at all explanatory, so Duval said, "If I can be of any assistance, I shall be very much pleased to do all I can, if you will only tell me in what way I can serve you."

"Pleased!" cried the man, starting up so suddenly, that Duval involuntarily took a step towards the door. "Pleased, do you say? Can you dare to talk of pleasure here? Fiend! fiend! When—when can I know pleasure more, I ask you? Look on that still, silent form! Look! look!"

He pointed to the bed, and Duval saw what he had before surmised, that beneath the sheet, which lay completely over it, was a body.

Duval was silent, and, after a few moments, the man spoke again.

"You are in danger here, I tell you, sir. There is something struggling within my breast which tells me that you are. In my poverty and bitter destitution, while—while my child, my Agnes still loved, I sent for you—for you, sir; but you came not until all was over!"

"Indeed—indeed you are wrong," replied Duval, seeing at once that the poor man had all along taken him for a doctor. I was merely walking past the lane when I heard lamentations issuing from one of the houses. A feeling of curiosity at first, but afterwards a better motive, prompted me to enter and offer my services."

The poor father looked in Duval's face for a moment, then turning to the old woman, he said—

"Neighbour, is not this Dr. Snell?"

"Indeed, no. At first I thought he was, but when I came to take a good look at him, I saw that he was quite a different person."

"Pardon me, pardon me," said the man. "Grief has blinded me. I sent—I sent for aid to my dying child, my pretty Agnes, and it came not—now—now it is too late—too late,"

Duval made no reply.

"Come—come," he continued. "I—I will show her to you; or—or you would never believe how beautiful she was."

He then took Duval by the arm, and led him towards the bed, then gently turning down from off the face of the dead the sheet, he pointed to the calm features of a child, apparently between eight and nine years of age.

The beauty of that face, even in death, exceeded anything Duval had ever seen in life.

There was still a faint tinge of colour on the damask cheeks, the beautiful lips were slightly apart, and through the long silken eyelashes a glimpse of the clear blue eyes could be obtained, a flood of golden hair hung over her breast and the pillow on which she lay.

Duval felt quite fascinated by the picture before him. She looked like some beautifully executed piece of waxwork.

For two or three minutes there was a deathlike silence in the room, and then Duval said, almost unconsciously—

"I can scarcely believe that she is dead."

The father's feelings could bear no more, and with one bitter cry, he fell to the floor in a swoon.

Duval raised him in his arms, and with the assistance of the old woman, did all in his power to restore him.

Then leaving him to the care of the old woman, Duval again approached the bed, and laid his ear to the heart of the dead child, to assure himself by that test that all vital action had fled.

"Alas!" he said to himself; "it is too late—too late!" then, turning to the old woman, who was still occupied in chafing the hands of the bereaved father, he said—

"What was the matter with the child?"

"Indeed, sir. we none o' us know; she seemed ailing and moping like, and then she went off as you see, sir."

This was anything but a satisfactory answer to his question; but Duval felt that no better one was to be obtained in that quarter. The father might be able to give him more information; put to question him in his present state seemed to Duval unjustifiable cruelty.

"Ah, sir! she was a bright, beautiful angel, too good for this world; and now a superscription is going about."

"A superscription?" said Duval, not at the moment understanding what his informant meant.

"Indeed, yes; for the purpose of placing the dear child in a decent grave in the churchyard, you know."

"Oh, a subscription, then, you mean?"

"Well, well, anything you like to call it. It's all one and the same thing, you know, sir."

"And when will she be buried?" whispered Duval.

"Next Sunday, please God, sir."

"And where?"

"In the little churchyard yonder, sir. You can just see the spire through the trees, if you please, sir."

Duval looked at the man, and found that he was slowly returning to consciousness.

Leaving behind him something towards the subscription, Duval now took leave of the grief-stricken father, and left that house of mourning with his mind full of the strange adventure.

"I must see more of that unhappy father," said Duval to himself, as he made his way towards Westminster, at a little public-house in the neigbourhood of which Blossom had had directions to put up Nightshade, after he had taken Lucy to the house on Hampstead Heath.

Duval's mind was so depressed by the scene of sorrow he had witnessed at the little cottage, that the face of Blossom was quite a treat for him to gaze upon.

"Blossom," he said, as soon as they were alone, "I have had some singular adventures to-day, but I have just come from a scene of sorrow that almost unmans me."

"Why, what was it, Captain?"

"A child's death-bed," said Duval, mournfully; "and I must confess I have a strong desire to see more of the unhappy father, so, on Sunday next, we must both find ourselves in yonder churchyard; something seems to whisper to me that my presence may be of service to him."

"All right, Captain! You know I am always with you."

"I know it—I know it! Now let us to Hampstead Heath."

"With all my heart, Captain," replied Blossom. "Nightshade looks as fresh as a daisy, notwithstanding the trot he has had this morning."

Thus beguiling the time with conversation upon indifferent subjects, Duval and his faithful follower soon arrived at the house on Hampstead Heath, which had so long been a safe asylum for him and his band.

"Safe home again, dear Claude!" were the first words that met the ears of Duval, as Lucy met him at the head of the stairs as was her wont. "Tell me, what have you done with the Dutch Envoy? Have you succeeded in frightening him away from Camden House?"

"I fancy he will not be willing long to remain there now, after what has taken place between us, especially as he knows that I have means of entering and leaving it of which he is ignorant."

"Oh, I shall be so glad to return to it, Claude," said Lucy. "I do not like this lonely house now."

"Why not?"

"Because—because I am in constant fear lest I should be again dragged from you, as I was once before."

"Ah, I had forgotten that at the moment, dear Lucy," replied Duval; "or I would not have left you alone so long. In a few days, at the most, I hope we shall be able to return to our old quarters. To-night, dear one, I will leave Blossom, and then you will be under no apprehensions, will you?"

"To-night? Must you go out again to-night, Claude?" said Lucy, looking up sorrowfully into his face?

"I must. These jewels are of no use to us. I must turn them into a more marketable commodity, and then, my Lucy, we will talk about our future proceedings.

CHAPTER CLI.

THE DEAD RESTORED TO LIFE.

It will be remembered that Claude Duval felt irresistibly drawn to look upon the little grave, in which were to be deposited the remains of the child whose father had so deeply interested him.

It was a bleak and rainy night, as Claude Duval, wrapping an ample cloak about him, entered the little church-yard, to take a last look at the little mound which contained all that was mortal of Agnes.

The wind blew in fitful gusts, and the dashing cold rain in a short time penetrated every article of clothing.

Still he did not feel inclined to turn back, although it would have been difficult for him to assign any reason for persisting in what many would have called a whim or fancy.

The night, however, was not very dark, for the rain seemed to beat down all the vapours of the air.

Duval pushed open the little wicket gate that led to the churchyard, when suddenly he paused, and listened attentively, for he fancied he heard, at no very great distance from the spot upon which he was standing, a low moaning sound.

"It must be the wind among the tombs," said Duval to himself.

Again, however, came that low, moaning sound.

At this moment, a heavy, slow footstep, approaching from the churchyard side of the wicket gate, came distinctly upon Duval's ears.

He crouched down behind an old tombstone, and waited to see if the strange, moaning sound proceeded from the same person who was now making his way through the churchyard.

Nearer and nearer the footsteps came, and now in the dim light, Duval could trace the outline of a human figure.

He instantly recognised the father of the dead child, as the figure paused at the gate, and spoke in a low tone, as if communing with himself.

"Yes, a good thought—a happy thought," said the poor father.

Again he paused, and laid his hand upon the gate, as he said, "Oh, Agnes! My Agnes! My own blue-eyed prattler—oh, heaven! oh, heaven!"

"Yes, yes!" continued the sorrow-stricken man. "My Agnes shall not lie here alone, I will bury her myself by the side of her mother."

Duval now began to feel glad that he was so near, for he had no doubts in his own mind about the poor man being mad.

Duval raised himself somewhat, and a feeling of horror took possession of him, as he got a better view of the soldier.

He had the dead child in his arms.

Duval was so taken by surprise, that he started up before he very well knew what he was doing, and confronted the broken-hearted father with his horrible burden.

He did not seem at all startled by the sudden appearance of Duval. On the contrary, in a calm tone of voice, he said, as he gently waved his arm above his head, "Away spirits, away! Stay me not! Stay me not! It is a holy duty I am performing this night. The mother and child must sleep together."

"Sir, sir," cried Duval, laying his hand upon his, "for Heaven's sake, think of what you are doing!"

"Yes, yes!" he cried, "It is for Heaven's sake she shall sleep by the side of her mother. It is a long way to carry her I know, but then the burden is light, and my poor heart will be much lighter when this duty has been performed. Yes, yes!—she shall sleep by the side of her mother, sir—by the side of her mother, I say! Hence! Away! Stay me not, I tell you, for I may be dangerous."

Duval had now no doubts as to the poor man's insanity.

"Go back to your grave, spirit!" he repeated, speaking in a tone of command—"back to your grave, I say She is not one of you yet. Away with you, she is my child—my Agnes!"

In his arms he carried the body of his child, wrapped in the long winding sheet of the grave. It was an awful-looking sight.

"Stay! Stay an instant," said Duval.

"Yes," he cried. "What want you with me."

"For Heaven's sake, tell me," said Duval, speaking slowly and distinctly, "What you mean to do with your poor child, who is beyond human grief or pain."

He smiled faintly, as he said more composedly, "You are not one of the bad spirits. Sit down here —here on this grave. Hush, Agnes, hush!"

Duval humoured him, and sat down upon the grave he had indicated, but before doing so he took a lantern from his pocket, and having lit it, he placed it on the head of a gravestone, with the hope of attracting notice in the little village, and bringing assistance to the evidently-deranged father.

The man, however, seemed to take no notice whatever of the light, but seated himself on the green turf, and deposited the dead Agnes at his feet.

Duval was undecided what to do, but then he thought

it best to sit down beside him and engage him in conversation until some one could come to his assistance.

Suddenly the man stretched forth his arm and again clasped his child in his arms, at the same time as he uncovered the face.

"Look, sir," he said,—"or spirit, if such ye be. You never saw this child's mother, but look at this cherub face—it is the miniature image of her, by whose side I would place my darling."

For a few minutes he gazed upon his child's face, and then an overpowering burst of grief shook his whole frame.

Duval was glad to see the tears flow so freely, as he felt that they would give relief to that already overcharged heart and brain.

Those tears, as Duval hoped they would, seemed to relieve him, for he suffered him to take the dead child from his arms, and the wild glare subsided as he became calmer.

The rain, which had partially ceased at the moment, came on again with redoubled energy, and their half-dried garments were wet through again.

The father was weeping bitterly, with his head buried in his hands.

Duval touched his arm, and strove to rouse him.

"Be calm—be calm," he said. "Let us restore your dead child to her resting place again. I will assist you. Look upon all this night's proceeding but as a dream. Come, come, be a man."

"I—I will," he murmured. "Thanks—thanks. I am better—much better now."

As Duval turned to raise the child from the ground where he had deposited her when he was speaking to her grief-stricken father, he could scarcely prevent himself from giving utterance to a cry—for there, at their very feet, sat the child, the grave-clothes huddled up around her, and her eyes wide open, staring at him and at her father.

Duval heard a cry from the poor father, as he held his hands to his head.

"No, no, Agnes!" he gasped.

A gush of blood came from his mouth, and the heart-broken father fell dead on the mound at his child's feet.

A glance told Duval but too plainly that all human assistance would be in vain for the poor father; he therefore turned his thoughts and attentions to the newly-risen, so to speak, Agnes.

"Speak, Agnes," he said, gently. "Can you speak to me?"

"So cold—oh, so cold!" was all she murmured, as she nestled close to Duval, who had folded her in his cloak.

Duval darted from the churchyard with his burden, and delivered the child to the first female he encountered.

"A warm bath immediately, my good woman, and some weak wine and water. Here is gold to pay yourself for any trouble you may take."

"That's him! Seize him! Take him!" were the words which met Duval's ears at this moment.

With one bound Duval cleared the threshold, knocking down Swallow, who as usual was in close proximity to his chief, Muckles.

"Not so fast, my fine fellow! Here you are!" cried one of Mr. Muckles' myrmidons, as he made a dash at Duval; but in the next moment he reeled on one side, and rolled in the mud, half-stunned.

It was a man hunt now. On through the open street—sometimes in the roadway, and sometimes on the pavement went Duval, with Muckles and his men not a hundred paces behind him.

On—on they went, now through mud, mire, and kennel, amid shouts, cries, and oaths.

Windows were thrown open in all directions.

Dogs yelped, barked, and joined in the chase; and the confusion was most intense, and seemed to be increasing as little bye streets and lanes disgorged their little knots of idlers.

Some people sought refuge in shops and under doorways.

But Duval still distanced his pursuers.

His great object was to make for some of the thoroughfares that led in the direction of Stratford.

And then, too, there was a hope in his heart that perhaps he might meet with some place of refuge on that road, so on he still sped, leaping over obstacles.

Once he began to fear that his capture was certain as his strength was now well-nigh spent; and a big, burly man ran out of a shop, and spreading out his arms, said, "Now, then, surrender!"

"Stand aside, or the consequences be upon your own head!" cried Duval, rendered almost desperate as he looked over his shoulder, and found that his pursuers were gaining upon him rapidly.

"Stand aside, I say!" again he shouted.

"Ha, ha! I have you now!"

Duval suddenly dashed into the roadway, and half-passed the man, who made a kind of snatch at him.

By one of those sudden efforts of strength, for which Duval was always remarkable, he caught up the man fairly off the pavement, and flung him through the window of the shop from which he had issued, and which happened to be filled with crockery.

The crash was something never to be forgotten, any more than was the howl of the unfortunate, but over-officious man.

But all this had taken time, and Duval found that the officers had gained on him sufficiently for him to distinguish the words:

"Stop him! stop him! Seize him! seize him! A thousand pounds reward to whoever captures Claude Duval, the notorious highwayman!"

A smile passed over the features of Claude Duval as he heard these cries.

"A thousand pounds! Just now it was but five hundred; and, at starting, it was only one hundred. Good! I am worth a good deal yet."

"Hoy! Stop! It's no use, Claude Duval!" he heard a voice cry. "You are my prisoner, and so there's an end of it!"

"Not yet," said Claude Duval, as he put more speed into the race he ran close to the pavement's edge; but seeing that his pursuer was gaining fearfully upon him, he made up his mind to a different course of action.

Suddenly, as though he had been struck down by a bullet, Duval fell flat on his face, and his pursuer, who was coming on at a tremendous rate, flew over him without being able to stop himself.

There was a fearful kind of crack as the man's head came into contact with the kerbstone, and when Duval sprang up and run on, he could just see him lying on his back, and opening and shutting his hands, while his eyes stared wildly at the sky.

Yells and shouts rose from the officers and from the crowd of idlers who had joined in the race.

Again Duval gave a rapid glance over his shoulder, and a new fear seized him, for he saw that Muckles and several of his men had mounted horses.

"Lost! lost!" said Duval, as he felt giddy and distressed. "Lost! lost!"

He was at the foot of a steep hill, and he began to feel the impossibility of attempting to run up it, spent and weary, as he was, when suddenly from the other side—now on the summit, so to speak,—appeared a man on horseback.

"Saved!" almost shrieked Duval, as Blossom trotted up on Nightshade.

"Here you are, Captain!" said that faithful follower. "Courage for a moment, in another instant all will be well."

Duval made a last effort, and placed his hand upon Nightshade's saddle.

One more leap and he was in the saddle.

"The pistols, Blossom?"

"All right, Captain; you'll find them in the holsters all ready for use."

"Blossom, you have saved me."

But Blossom had disappeared.

"Forward, Nightshade! Forward, Nightshade!" cried Duval.

Then, clear upon the night air, came the shouts of the mounted officers.

"Seize him! Take him! Let him not escape! A thousand pounds reward for any man who captures Claude Duval, the notorious highwayman."

"Forward, Nightshade—forward! We need not fear now. There are not six horses in England that can overtake us."

Bond Street was passed through quickly, and the Oxford Road gained.

Duval swerved to the left, and crossed the road, and took a road that he knew would lead him to the back of the village of Kilburn, to the open country about Hampstead.

The north side of the Oxford Road was but thinly built upon; you could soon get into the open country if you went down almost any of the turnings west of what is now the busy and populous Regent's Circus.

The road, or lane, rather, down which Duval took his way, had tall trees on one side of it, and garden-walls on the other.

The soil was rather heavy, and in places there were heaps of stones which straggled right into the roadway.

If this irregular character of the road, however, was a disadvantage to Duval, it was also a similar one to his pursuers, so that he heeded it not, but rode on at a rapid pace right out into the open country.

Duval looked over his shoulder, and found that he was distancing the mounted officers rapidly.

"Well done, Nightshade!" he said, as he patted the creature on the neck; "our enemies will now soon give up the pursuit."

But, suddenly, there was an odd clicking noise, and in another moment, Duval was aware that Nightshade had cast a shoe.

The horse could no longer make speed.

"Seize him! seize him!" yelled now the voice of Muckles. "A thousand pounds reward from the King for whoever captures Claude Duval! Seize him! seize him!—a thousand pounds reward!"

Muckles appeared in sight, but he was alone; his men were far behind.

"You are mad, Mr. Muckles," shouted Duval, as he took a pistol from one of the holsters, and halted his horse. "You are mad to try to take me unassisted."

But scarcely were the words out of his mouth, when another horseman appeared in sight, just as Muckles fired one of his pistols at Duval.

The bullet grazed the neck of the horse, but did no further damage.

Muckles then fired, and Duval returned the shot with one of his pistols.

"Missed!" said Duval.

"I have him!" shouted Muckles.

He sprang forward; but as he did so, there was a report of a pistol from the road-side, and he reeled back in his saddle with a yell of pain.

The horse turned round twice in a circle, and then dashed off with his wounded rider at a mad gallop.

The horseman who was so close to Muckles, seeing how affairs were going, thought that discretion was evidently the better part of valour, so he quietly turned his horse's head towards London again, and trotted back.

"Now I am safe!" said Duval to himself. "Let me see, Nightshade, if you are lame?"

He dismounted, and finding that his horse had not sustained any injury beyond the graze in the neck, he hoped that by leading him by the bridle the lost shoe would prove to be merely a slight inconvenience.

Duval was gratified to find that he was approaching a small village, as he had no doubt that he would soon be able to have the lost shoe replaced.

His expectations were not disappointed, for the ruddy glow of a forge, and the monotonous clank of an anvil soon came upon his ear.

The blacksmith was whistling a merry tune as Duval halted before the door of the smithy.

"Ah! Jack," said Duval, as he addressed the blacksmith, "it is long since you and I met. I want you to put a shoe on my horse's foot."

"Claude Duval, by all that's glorious!" shouted the man as he flung up his cap in the air. "Well, to be sure, wonders will never cease. I never expected to see you again, Captain!"

"Nor I you, honest Jack; but be quick, for time presses."

"No danger, is there, Captain?" asked the blacksmith, as he looked up and down the road.

"Not that I know of," replied Duval; "but as I have just had to run for my life. I do not feel quite anxious to court attention just now. So be quick, my good friend."

The blacksmith set to work with a good will, and in a short time Duval mounted Nightshade, feeling quite certain that he could now defy his enemies.

CHAPTER CLII.

CLAUDE DUVAL AND DICK TURPIN STOP THE OXFORD MAIL, AND MEET WITH A STRANGE ADVENTURE.

THE evening following the events detailed in the last chapter Claude Duval might have been seen mounted upon Nightshade, and lingering about one of the green lanes, that at the time of which we are writing intersected the Oxford Road.

There was a look of impatience upon his countenance, as he looked to the right and to the left, as though expecting to be joined by some one who was late in keeping their appointment.

At length the clatter of a horse's feet was heard, and at the same moment a mounted figure appeared, who made directly for the spot where Duval had been waiting.

"You are late, Dick," were the words uttered by Duval, as the horseman joined him.

"I know I am; but it couldn't be helped. And now to business."

"With all my heart," said Duval.

"Do you feel inclined, then, to drive the Oxford Mail to-night?" asked Dick.

"I have no objection," replied Duval, "provided it promises to be profitable."

"Come on then," said Dick; "I have arranged the matter, and we have nothing to do but assume our proper places, you as coachman, and I as guard."

At a small inn, not far from the place of starting, Claude Duval and Dick Turpin put up their steeds while they proceeded on foot to the coach office.

"This is the person of whom I spoke," said Dick Turpin, addressing a red faced man, and who Duval rightly supposed to be the driver of the Oxford Mail. "I can recommend him, so you can give yourself a rest to-night."

"I should like it amazingly," replied the coachman; "so, upon your recommendation, I am willing to give up my duty for a night."

"All right," replied Dick, "when shall we start?"

"Not later than ten o'clock, remember—it is now a quarter to nine, so you will have plenty of time to come in and taste mine host's ale before you start."

At the appointed hour, Duval and Dick Turpin, in their disguises of coachman and guard, were duly mounted on coach-box and dicky, as it was called.

There were already several inside and outside passengers—the bell rang—Dick Turpin blew a furious blast upon the horn, and off started the Oxford Mail.

"I say, coachman," said an old gentleman, who carried a travelling bag, which seemed to contain a number of small, square boxes—"I say coachman, I don't think there is any fear of encountering that fellow Claude Duval to-night. The last time I travelled by this coach I was robbed of some valuable jewels."

"Indeed, sir?" said Duval. "I wonder if any body has any fire-arms about them—nothing like a bullet for such gentry."

"You are right, Mr. Coachman," said the old gentleman, who was evidently gratified by the thought that he was about to become an interesting person, as every one bent forward to listen to his experience of the highwayman; "but this time, Mr. Coachman," he continued, "he will not make me his dupe so easily, for I have taken care to provide myself with this pair of pistols."

As he spoke, the old gentleman handed a pair of beautifully mounted pistols to Duval,

"That is indeed fortunate," said Duval; "but the great danger is in the nervousness of the moment: you may miss your aim, and then he is so cool, so I have heard, that he would think nothing of making you discharge the second pistol, and then beginning to fire away at you."

"Ye—yes; I—I know, and I do get nervous, Mr. Coachman! Now, if you——"

"I; I?" exclaimed Duval. "I fire a pistol, unless —unless I were compelled to do it in self-defence. I don't think I could; but I don't mind trying just to oblige you, sir."

"That's a good fellow," said the old gentleman, his face brightening as he saw that another was willing to ease him of the risk he had imposed upon himself. "You take the pistols, and then they will be handy whenever you may require them."

"All right!" said Duval, as he handed them to Turpin.

"All right, Coachy!" said Turpin, as he secured the pistols.

"What's all that talk about pistols?" asked a female voice at this moment.

"Nothing amiss," said Turpin, "only we were taking stock of the fire-arms."

"Fire-arms! Goodness me, you don't think we shall be stopped by highwaymen, do you?"

"Can't say, miss; but think it's very likely. Thought I heard a horse's feet just now."

"So did I, miss; but, you see, we can muster a pretty strong force against one man. Why, here's the coachman, and myself, and that gent sitting beside him with the black leather valise."

"Oh, yes; he's my uncle, and he's got a pair of pistols, so he can fire them both off at once, you know, and frighten all the highwaymen."

"Oh, yes, miss, nothing can be easier. But I wonder if any of the insides has got fire-arms?"

"I have not! Nor I! Nor I!" were the replies Turpin got to his question.

"Then, we must do the best we can, with what we have got," he said.

At this moment Duval pulled up.

"Eh? What? What do you see, Coachman?" asked the old gentleman at Duval's elbow.

"Nothing," was the reply; "but I thought it was no use getting on any further."

"Not go on any further? Why, what do you mean?"

"I mean that I may as well be candid, and tell you at once that I am Claude Duval, and that I have a fancy for robbing the Oxford Mail in a new fashion."

"Mercy! mercy!" shrieked the little old gentleman.

"What are you making that noise for?" asked Duval, calmly. "I am not going to shoot you."

"Oh, he's got my pistols!" groaned the old gentleman.

"Yes; but I do not intend to use them, unless you compel me to do so, by refusing to deliver to me that little leather bag which, I have no doubt, contains something of value."

"It contains nothing—nothing, I assure you, but children's workboxes, which I am going to dispose of as soon as I find a customer. They are valueless, I assure you! Mere toys—mere toys, sir, I assure you!"

"Indeed," said Duval. "I have a slight suspicion that you are under-valuing your commodities, so allow me to be the judge."

As he spoke, Duval adroitly transferred the bulky-looking bag from the hands of the old gentleman to his own, and then he handed it to Turpin.

"Here, Dick," he said, "put this with the pistols, and just see what there is worth having inside."

As he spoke, Duval went round to the door on the other side of the coach and looked in.

To his surprise, he beheld a lovely young girl in a crouching attitude, as though she had fallen from the seat.

"What is the meaning of this?" asked Duval, as he laid his hand upon the young girl's shoulder. "You have nothing to fear."

"That's just what I have been telling her, Mr. Highwayman," whined a voice, close to the door. "I tell her, that if she sits quiet you will not interfere with her, will you, Mr. Highwayman?"

"And who may you be, sir?" asked Duval, as he glanced fiercely at the man who had addressed him.

"Oh, nobody, sir! Only the uncle of my niece, here, if you please, sir."

"Is that so?" asked Duval, addressing the young girl.

"Oh, no, no! I never saw him before to-night, when he came to my lodgings, and told me the lady who had given me some work to do wished to see me particularly."

"Oh," said Duval.

Then, turning again to the snuffling, whining personage, who had said he was the uncle of the young girl, he asked, "Where are you going to take this girl?"

"Oh, do not ask me—do not ask me! I give up the job from this moment, if you will only let me go unquestioned!"

"Come out," said Duval, as he opened the door of the coach.

The man got out of the vehicle.

"Here, Dick," said Duval, addressing Turpin, "help me to search this fellow, and perhaps we shall then get at the heart of this mystery."

In a few minutes the man's pockets were rifled, but nothing of much value was found about him, except a small piece of paper, on which was written, "Bring the girl you mention to —— House one Monday evening, and you may be sure of your reward."

"Villain," said Duval, "tell me instantly where you

were going to take this girl, or I will blow your brains out!"

"Mercy! mercy!" whined the man. "I was only acting under orders."

"It matters not! Tell me instantly the name of your employer."

"The Earl of Montrose, then, if you must know," replied the man, doggedly.

"Where is this Duke of Montrose?" asked Duval.

"I know not; but I believe he was to have been at Epsom to-night."

"And you were going to take that young girl to him?"

"He wanted to see her."

Duval seized the wretch by the collar, and shook him to and fro until he was black in the face; then, turning to Turpin, he said, "Dick, to your care I commit this young girl. You will see her safely to wherever she may wish to go."

"Certainly," replied Dick Turpin. "Can you ride, miss?" he asked, addressing the young girl.

"Oh, yes, yes," answered the girl, looking from one to the other. "Give me but an opportunity of returning to my home, and I care not how I reach that destination, so that I am free again."

"Never fear," said Duval; "you shall be safely escorted. Dick, we may as well leave this coach to its fate, and make use of as many of the horses as we may require. What say you?"

"The very thing I thought of doing," replied Turpin.

As he spoke, he took from his shoulder a kind of valise, in which were to be found two or three bridles.

"You commence to unharness the horses, Duval," said Dick; "and then we will take possession of three of them, and to town at once."

"But what is to become of us?" whined the old jeweller.

"Oh, you must stay here until some one passes by, to whom you can tell your tale," laughed Dick Turpin.

"What! leave us here to our fate?" asked the female.

"To your fate. Now, miss, are you ready?"

"Quite, quite!"

The young girl was soon placed in the saddle, such as it was; and with Duval and Dick Turpin on each side of her, she went at a good pace down the lane in the direction of London, where she soon found the means of directing her preservers to her lodgings

"Now you are once more safe," said Duval, kindly, after he had assisted her to dismount. "Never again be tempted to leave your home under any pretence whatever, unless you know where you are going."

"No—never again," said the young girl, as she gave her hand to Duval, and looked up into his face with a look of deep gratitude.

"That's over," said Duval, as the door of the humble tenement closed upon the young girl. "What are we to do now, Dick?"

"Look at our spoils, to be sure," said Turpin.

When the spoils of that night were examined, Duval and Dick Turpin came to the conclusion that their business on the road had been far from unprofitable.

"Now, good night, Duval," said Dick. "Before long I hope to do a little more business on the road with you."

"Agreed," cried Duval, as the two separated to seek their respective destinations.

Duval now began to wish for Nightshade, as he had no desire to return to Hampstead at so early an hour, as he felt that there was yet time for another adventure on the road.

While he was debating with himself what he should do, his attention was drawn to the clattering of horses' feet.

He drew on one side, to enable the rider to pass without being himself observed, when he saw by the light of the moon, a riderless horse making furious speed.

"Ah!" said Duval to himself; "if I can but succeed in capturing him my wishes for a horse will be fulfilled."

The creature came on; but seeing Duval, probably swerved somewhat to one side of the road, and there stood perfectly still.

"Fortune favours me to-night," cried Duval, as he made his way towards the creature, who seemed by no means to shun him.

Duval patted the animal on the neck, and, after speaking a few words to it, as he was in the habit of doing to Nightshade, he had not the slightest difficulty in mounting it.

The moon, at times, was entirely obscured, and an uncomfortable moaning wind was making itself heard among the giant trees as Duval again made his way towards the Western Road.

In a few minutes, a tremendous clap of thunder, multiplied by the echoes of the forest into something grand, suddenly broke upon the stillness that had seemed like a living thing to creep around him.

Duval was at first startled, as was also the horse upon which he rode; in fact, the creature stumbled, and then stood still, and shook with fear.

He used all the usual modes of re-assuring the horse—he coaxed, he threatened, but move it would not until there came a flash of lightning, so vivid, so beautifully alarming, that, for a moment, Duval thought his sight was injured by the purple glare. Then off the creature sped as though it had been the fabled steed in the "Wild Huntsman," and Duval its fabled rider.

Duval thought that he kept the high-road pretty well, although, notwithstanding that he was a perfect master of horsemanship, he found it very difficult to keep anything like control over the headlong gallop of his steed.

Before him was an incline of some half a mile or so, and then Duval knew that the road wound round to the right, avoiding the forest, or, at least, only partially straggling through its outskirts.

Duval felt a sort of presentiment that his horse would keep upon that right-hand road, until upon reaching the point where the curved turn should have been taken, he was at once convinced of the contrary by his at once dashing right into the forest.

Duval pulled and fought with the creature in order to induce it to turn upon its track, but to no purpose —on—on he went.

And now he felt what true darkness was in a forest of trees; and the wonder to Duval was that the horse did not dash its own head as well as his against the trunks of some of the trees; but by some rare instinct, even in the midst of his fright, the creature steered clear of every obstacle, going at the mad pace at which he had started about three miles, without showing any signs of flagging.

During that period the storm had not been idle. It was for some time one of those threatening, grumbling sort of storms, which you may expect will go off altogether, but which, on the contrary, may come to something very serious; and, in this case, the elements embraced the latter alternative, for by the time the horse had galloped off some of his panic, and was beginning to manifestly slacken in his pace, the roar of the wind and the rain, the lightning and the thunder began.

The noise among the trees could be compared to nothing else but a storm at sea; and Duval could not help being struck by the kind of analogy there is be-

DUVAL ALARMED BY A SPECTRE IN THE FOREST.

tween the operations of nature under widely different circumstances.

To have shut his eyes amid the tempest in the forest, Duval had no difficulty in imagining that the hurricane among the trees was the wind upon the water, while the rustle of millions upon millions of leaves resembled the dash and the roar of the impetuous waves.

The horse suddenly stood still. Duval could not see or hear him panting, but he felt that the creature did so.

The rain began to come down in torrents, and Duval could hear it fuming and gushing round the trunks of the trees in wild eddies; so that what with one thing and another, the tumult around him was beyond description, and even that lion heart wished himself beneath the covert of some friendly roof.

"A night in this confounded forest," he said to himself. "I did not bargain for such an adventure; but it must be endured now; let us hope that something will come of it.

No. 49.—NIGHTSHADE.

Duval thought that if he could but find shelter beneath the shade of some gigantic tree, he might manage till the morning; "or, perhaps," he said to himself, "I may find some human habitation near at hand."

Full of the latter idea, Duval waited until there was a lull in the wind, and then he raised his voice, and shouted, "Hilloa! hilloa!"

He waited a moment, but the war of the tempest among the tree-tops was his only answer.

CHAPTER CLIII.

CLAUDE DUVAL MEETS WITH A SPECTRE STATUE.

DUVAL then dismounted, intending to grope his way to the trunk of some tree, and there tie his horse, and wait until morning dawned; but the idea of wandering amid the mazes and intricacies of what seemed to him to be an unknown forest was anything but an agreeable task.

As soon as Duval placed his foot on the ground, he found himself ankle deep in a mass of dead leaves, wetted almost to a consistency with the rain; and through them he struggled on some half-dozen paces or so, with the bridle of his horse upon his arm, keeping his hands before him, so that amid the darkness, he might not come into contact with the trunk of some tree,

As he did so, however, Duval drew back with a precipitancy that had no slight effect upon the horse, for he nearly upset him by getting quite into a tangle with his fore feet.

At the same time, Duval could not refrain from uttering a cry which, for the moment, rose above the tempest.

He had felt something cold and wet—very cold and wet; but it did not feel like the trunk of a tree.

Duval passed his fingers carefully over it, and then he felt assured it was a hand.

"Who are you? What are you?" he cried. "Merciful heavens! why do you not speak? Off!—keep off—keep off!"

He fancied, in the darkness, that something terrible came looming on towards him. He thought it was within six inches of his face—in fact, he began to fancy that he could feel the hot breath of some horrible thing upon his face.

With a feeling of desperation, Duval drew a pistol from his pocket, and fired right in front of him.

The flash of the pistol showed him, for a moment, the surrounding trees, and the sloppy earth, and it convinced him, at the same time, that nothing of the character he had in his imagination pictured was before him.

Indeed, Duval began to think he had got into some little cleared part of the forest, for he saw a kind of circle of trees, as it were, around the spot on which he stood.

So momentary, however, had been the glance which he had been able to take, that he could not, when gloom came again, take upon himself to say if he had turned from the direction in which he had fired the pistol or not.

He was still a prey to all sorts of doubts, and fears, and perplexities.

When once the idea, however, had fairly taken possession of Duval's mind that he might, in his terror, have changed his position, he no longer gathered any hope from what that transient flash from his pistol had revealed to him, and he turned rapidly round several times, as though he had been playing at blind man's buff.

At length he paused again.

Notwithstanding the coldness of the night air, Duval could feel the heavy drops of perspiration standing upon his brow, as he tried to reason himself out of the superstitions that were each moment like shadows creeping over him.

"Was it really a hand?" he asked himself; "or was it some gracefully-shaped piece of the bough of a tree, which, suggesting the idea, induced the fancy for the moment to fill up the delusion.

Duval tried to persuade himself that such was the case, and partially succeeded in doing so, for he resolved upon once more feeling his way to the shelter of some tree.

After proceeding onward about six paces, again his hand touched something cold and wet.

Duval was rooted to the spot; but rallying himself he said, half aloud:

"This is foolishness."

As he spoke, he stretched out his hand again, and passed his fingers over the object, and felt convinced in his own mind that he was touching a face.

But there was no shrinking from his touch; the fearful object seemed immoveable.

"Help, help, help!" shouted Duval, as loud as he could, in the hope of attracting the attention of some human being who might bear him company in the anything but pleasant situation in which he found himself.

"Hilloa!" at length replied a voice. "Who are you? and where are you?"

What a relief was it to Duval to find that he had, at all events, human companionship so near at hand,

In a few minutes, a sturdy-looking man stood before him.

"Where are you?" again asked the voice. "Speak again, for the lantern I carry only serves to show me the path just before me."

"Here, here! straight on!" cried Duval.

Duval could, of course, see his guide—or, the person whom he hoped would become such—from the darkness in which he stood, better than the man could see him.

When he approached nearer to Duval, the man held up the lantern, and examined him most minutely.

"You'll excuse me, sir," said the man; "but at times there is gentry about these parts such as one would not wish to meet with; but, as I see that you are not one of them, why, I shall be glad to either show you the way, in order that you may pursue your course, or offer you a shelter for the night."

"Thank you, my friend," replied Duval. "I will willingly avail myself of your kind offer, for I am fatigued."

"All right, yer honour, the storm is not yet over, so you had better rest at the big house up yonder. It is the only night of the year that I could ask you to take shelter there, for all the family are absent."

"Indeed?"

"Yes, sir. Why, you see the house is haunted, sir; and on this night the ghost of my young master, who was murdered, wanders through every chamber, driving every one mad that sees it."

"But you, my friend," said Duval, "are not you, too, afraid of seeing this ghost?"

"Yes, sir; but my poor daughter is ill at the house there; and I have been afraid to have her removed, being anxious to put it off till the last minute, when this fearful storm began. I know not what we shall do, for to allow her to remain all night in that house, to-night of all nights in the year, would be impossible, while to take her away in the storm seems fraught with almost equal danger to her in her present state."

As Duval and the man were thus conversing, they had walked a few paces in advance; and then the man paused, raising the lantern as he did so, so that its rays fell upon what appeared to be some person in a sitting posture.

"There it is, sir," he said.

"What?"

"Why, the statue as they say walks through the mansion up yonder once a year."

Duval advanced towards it, and touched it — while the man fell back a pace or two.

In his own mind, he felt perfectly convinced that this statue, which was made of iron, was the same he had come so suddenly upon in the dark.

Of course he did not say a word to his companion of the terror he had already felt, when accident led him towards that statue; but he merely remarked that it was a strange place for a statue.

"Not so strange after all, sir, when you come to see that we are actually within the grounds of Ackland House."

After casting one more glance at the statue, Duval followed his guide to the house, and even in the dim and uncertain light of the lantern, he could see that it was of immense extent.

He was, however, too well pleased to get under shelter to waste any time in examining the exterior of the building, and in the course of a few minutes, Duval had the satisfaction of snugly esconcing himself in the chimney corner of the old kitchen.

The old man volunteered to take the horse, which had, as it were, been sent to him so mysteriously, and which Duval now remembered had brought him to his present abode almost in that furious headlong gallop, which he, Duval, notwithstanding his skill as a horseman, had found himself wholly unable to control.

While the old man had gone to find shelter for the horse, Duval had time to look about him at the family, which consisted of the old man's wife, two boys, and a young girl about eighteen or nineteen years of age.

There was a look of terror upon the countenances of each, as they continued to turn their eyes upon a large eight-day clock, which ticked solemnly behind the kitchen door, as though they feared that the hands might point to the hour of midnight before they had had time to remove from that house which was so soon to witness the annual visit of the spectre statue.

The homely repast was spread, and they invited him to partake of it with them. The fare was not exactly what Duval would have expected beneath that stately roof; but such as it was, he partook of with a good appetite.

As the hands of the clock moved round, Duval could see that the whole family began to experience great fear and trepidation.

"Let us go now, father," said one of the boys; "it is near the hour of midnight."

"Yes, yes, let us go!"

"One minute!" said Duval, speaking in his persuasive accents. "I would give so much to reason you out of this superstitious fear!"

"Superstitious fear?—reason us out of it?" cried the man. "Impossible, sir! You know not what you say!"

"But tell me one thing," said Duval. "Have you, any of you, seen this apparition?"

"No, sir! Heaven forbid that we should see such a sight! No, no, sir, we all leave the house before the hour of midnight, and take shelter in a little wooden hut, where we will make you welcome, sir, if you will deign to put up with the poor accommodation."

"But how do you know, then, that the ghost makes its appearance, if there is no one in the mansion to see it?" asked Duval.

"We can hear dreadful noises going on in this place, sir; and then we know the ghost is here. We leave all the doors open for it to come in and go out. But let us talk no more about it—suffice it to say, that it drives to madness all who behold it."

Duval made no reply to this, but merely asked the man if he had not understood him to say that one of his children was ill.

"Ah, yes, sir, poor Mary! My poor child, who is ready for heaven, and whom the good angels are ready to carry from this earth. Have you seen her lately, wife?" he added, turning to the mother.

"Not for the last hour, Paul," replied the woman

"Then I will go to her; and if this gentleman will be so good as to accompany me, he will say at once that she is not in a fit condition to be left to brave all the horrors of this night within these walls. We must remove her, if it cost us her life."

Duval signified his ready acquiescence to accompany the father to the bed-side of his suffering child.

He took with him the same lantern he had had when first Duval had attracted his attention.

Duval could not but look round with interest at the remains of former state and magnificence which that mansion exhibited, as the man led him up the grand staircase and through a suite of rooms that must at one time have been perfectly regal in their decorations.

The light flashed upon painted ceilings and rich gilt cornices, some of which appeared most wonderfully to have withstood the withering hand of time and neglect, and from the walls, the panels of which, round their edges, were exquisitely carved, looked forth grim portraits of a past age, the eyes of which, at times, as the light flashed upon them, seemed to be following them through the gloomy spacious rooms.

As they occasionally passed a casement, Duval could hear the storm raging and tearing without like a wild animal plunging about to find an entrance.

Duval counted that they passed through five rooms before they reached a little chamber which completed the suite, and which, from the light, airy, and somewhat fantastic character of its ornaments, he guessed had been the favourite resort of the lady of the house.

In this chamber, lighted by a little flickering oil-lamp, placed upon the floor, was an antique couch, upon which lay a girl of about twelve years of age.

Duval was struck with the purity and delicacy of this fair young creature, so fragile that she seemed like a being of another world.

Her hair, which fell in clustering ringlets about her neck and shoulders, was of that rare golden tint only seen in paintings, and her soft blue eyes, which she half closed at the additional glare of light that came into the room were exquisitely beautiful.

"Father, is that you?" she asked, as the man approached the bed. "How good of you to come so often to see your poor little Mary!"

The plaintive sweetness of that voice Duval felt that he should never forget.

Duval had purposely kept in the background, and it was not until her father said gently that he had brought a gentleman to see her that she perceived he was not alone.

The slight accession of colour to the pale cheek, and the start, showed Duval that she was too weak to bear the excitement of a stranger's presence and he would have withdrawn, but it was too late, for her father made a sign for him to approach.

Duval did so; and taking the tiny hand in his, said in his gentlest accents:—

"You have been ill, Mary, they tell me; you are better now, dear?"

"Oh, yes, yes—better now!" was the feeble reply. "I am cool, and so happy now—so happy!"

The child passed her hand across her brow, and as Duval still retained the other in his, and felt the moisture on the skin, he had no difficulty in at once surmising that she had passed through the crisis of a fever, and was now recovering

"Have you had medical advice for your child?" Duval asked, turning to the father.

"Yes, sir, Doctor Sterling came to see her, but the last time he was here he shook his head, and told us she was not long for this world. She knew no one, sir, and raved all day and all night."

"Well," said Duval, cheerfully, as he gently patted the little hand, which lay on the white coverlet, "Dr. Sterling will not shake his head the next time he pays your little girl a visit, for he will be able to tell you that the danger he anticipated has passed away."

The rough peasant's eyes glistened with pleasure, as he bent over his child, and kissed her tenderly.

"Ah, my Mary, this is good news indeed; you must try and make an effort, my child, to get up and come with us to the old hut yonder, for this is the night, you know, that the ghost walks through this house, and——"

"Good heavens!" cried Duval; "you surely do not contemplate removing this young creature in her present state? It will be certain death if, in her condition, she meets with a chill, such as she cannot fail to experience, if she leave her bed. Would you peril your child's life for the sake of an idle tale about a ghost?"

The father looked at Duval with his eyes almost starting out of his head, and his mouth wide open, while the young girl half rose from her couch, and looked eagerly first at him and then at her father, as though her life —which indeed it did—depended upon the result of their conversation.

"Would it destroy my child? Oh, sir, do not tell me so!"

"I do tell you so," replied Duval, solemnly. I swear that that would be the result were you to attempt to take her out of this house—out of this room even to-night."

"You terrify me," said the father, sinking on to a chair as he rocked himself to and fro, "what shall we do—what shall we do? To take her home or leave her here, seems as though it would be alike disastrous."

"Save me—oh, save me, my father!" said the young girl, as she looked imploringly at him. "Do not let me die yet!—do not let me die yet! I thought I was willing—but oh, I feel better now, and this world is so beautiful—do not let me die yet!"

She wept as though her heart would break.

At that moment the clock struck the hour of eleven.

CHAPTER CLIV.

CLAUDE DUVAL EXORCISES THE GHOST.

"ELEVEN o'clock!" sighed the unhappy father, just as the voices of his wife and children were heard from below, begging of him to hasten their departure before the fatal hour of midnight.

As they entered the room, the peasant made known to them what Duval had said, and they all shrank back aghast at the idea of leaving her, their darling, to encounter the perils of that fearful night.

As Duval stood there, the young girl clasped both her hands round his arm, as she said, almost shriekingly:—

"No, no, do not let me die in the forest. Let me stay here."

"Listen to me," said Duval, speaking with great emotion. "I do not think that accident brought me into your neighbourhood this night, but the hand of Providence, I believe, guided my horse's footsteps, in order that I might be the means of saving this fair young creature from death. The time for God to summon her to heaven has not yet come. Go; leave me. I will protect her life with my life. I look upon it as a sacred duty. Go, all of you, and fear nothing."

The little family looked upon Duval as though he had been a being from another world who thus addressed them, while their tears fell abundantly.

Seeing the impression which he had made upon them, Duval was anxious to work as much good to these simple people out of the adventure as possible; so, turning to them once more, he said, "Do not leave this house, but fasten the doors as usual. All will be well, believe me. I will watch beside your child, and to-morrow morning you will all thank me for having been the means, not only of disabusing your minds of this horrible superstition, but also of preserving your child's life."

"Margery, Margery, what shall I do?" asked the man, turning to his wife.

"Let us remain, William. What is the value of our own lives, compared with that of our child? If she dies, let us die with her."

"Be it so, then," said Duval. "Now, go; bolt and bar the doors, and rest in peace, being assured that I will fight to the last drop of my blood for this helpless girl here."

They each took an affectionate and affecting leave of the sick girl, and then Duval was left alone with his charge.

He could hear the doors and windows being barricaded, as though a siege were expected to take place.

The light which still remained upon the floor cast odd, grim shadows upon the walls and ceiling, of the various articles of furniture in the room.

The wind, now that all other sounds were hushed, dashed sometimes in fitful gusts against the casements; and at others, after rattling the loose framework of the windows, passed on with a wailing sound, as though it would, with almost an inarticulate voice, tell of woe and of horror that was to come.

Duval raised the lamp from the floor, and with it in his hand, looked about in the scantily-furnished apartment for some place upon which to put it where it would cast pleasanter shadows than the upward ones that spoilt the face of the lovely child.

He found a portion of what had once been a richly-gilt cornice, which would just hold the lamp, about eight feet from the floor, and there he placed it.

The improvement in the look of the apartment was immense, although it was but a dim light, after all, that the little lamp shed around it.

The sick girl had watched with her full blue eyes all these movements of Duval.

Her wasted face made them look preternaturally large; and as he turned his gaze upon her, now that all was still, and the transient glow of excitement had passed away from her cheeks, he began to tremble for his prediction concerning her recovery.

"Sleep, Mary," he said, gently, as he approached her bed-side—"sleep in peace, dear child, and fear nothing; all will be well."

The child reached out her hand to him, and for the first time Duval noticed how thin and fragile it was. It seemed as though the light might have shone through it.

She smiled faintly as she laid it in that of Duval, and said, "The good God will bless you; and I will tell heaven how kind you have been to poor Mary!"

She then folded her hands upon her breast, and from the movement of her lips, Duval thought she was lifting up her pure heart in prayer to heaven for protection for herself and those so dear to her; and he was pleased to think that his name, perhaps, might ascend to heaven from those childish lips.

After a few minutes had elapsed, she again turned, as though to look once more upon Duval before she closed her eyes in slumber.

Then he spoke to her, and asked her if she were warm.

"Yes."

"And has all pain left you?" he asked, bending tenderly over her.

The young girl replied with a sweet smile, that she felt much better, and taking Duval's hand, placed it upon her brow.

"It feels moist and calm," said Duval, speaking more to himself than his little patient.

She closed her eyes, and murmuring some words, the import of which Duval could not catch, she composed herself to sleep, and by her deep breathing, he felt that she had, indeed, fallen into a healthful slumber.

Duval felt that there was something holy in the trustfulness of this young creature in one who was a perfect stranger to her—a trustfulness that sufficiently bespoke the fact, that as yet her young heart had not tasted of that knowledge which comprehends in its bitter fruits more evil than good; and the thought forced itself upon him as he gazed upon the pure countenance, that it would not be a thing so much to be regretted if she were now in her innocence and purity to be summoned to that land where there is no sin, no grief, and no pain.

A sudden dash of rain against the casement, roused Duval from these reflections, and he rose quietly, laying the little hand, which still rested in his upon the coverlid.

He stepped to the window and tried to look out. He could see nothing but the faint images of trees dashing to and fro in the passing gale.

Then he went to the door to see what available fastenings there were, and found only an old rusted lock which had evidently not done duty for many years, and a little bolt, which, although it would give way before a tolerably vigorous push, was yet a something. This he pressed into its rusty socket.

An odd feeling of dread began to creep over him in spite of himself, and Duval set it down as an infirmity of nature which no education, no reasoning will entirely divest the imagination of, and he rather smiled at it than endeavoured to do useless battle with it.

Taking, then, from his pocket, a small pair of pistols, which he was never without, he carefully examined them.

They were both ready for service at a moment's notice, so that Duval felt tolerably free from any natural or human terror.

He then sat down upon a huge high-backed old Flemish chair, with a wilderness of cushions in it, by the bed-side of the sleeping girl, and determined to keep watch and ward over her until the morning light came to relieve him of his task.

"A spectre statue!" said Duval to himself, as he settled himself in the arm chair. "Impossible! It is too absurd! The idea of a statue walking, and with its feet of bronze tramping to the bed-side of any one, to glare at them with its iron eyes. Stuff! The disembodied spirit appearing upon the spots of earth it was familiar with during its long pilgrimage, and to people whom its has cause to love or to hate, may be matter for argument: but a statue—an iron statue, to do this—I never heard of such a thing in tale, legend, or song."

The wind moaned gloomily through the trees, and around the house.

Duval turned and looked at the sleeping girl.

"At all events," he continued, still speaking in a low voice; "*she* has no more fears of this spectre, or ghost, or whatever it may be."

There is a sound that breaks the stillness of that now silent house.

The old wooden clock below is striking the hour of midnight.

One—two—three—four—five—six—seven—eight—nine—ten—eleven—twelve! It is twelve o'clock.

It is twelve o'clock.

* * * * * *

With a cry Duval awoke.

A soft gleam of morning sunshine was coming through the casement, and at the door of the apartment stood the peasant and his family.

The child, evidently awakened by the cry of horror that had burst from the lips of Duval, looked up in amazement, as he stood in the middle of the floor, looking the picture of astonishment and amazement.

"The night has really, then, passed away?" at length he asked, looking upon the astonished faces of the peasant and his family.

"Yes, sir, and the morning is bright and beautiful. Heaven bless you, sir, we have had a quiet night, and we shall now ever laugh at the spectre horseman."

"Ah, my dear friend!" said little Mary; "let me kiss you for being so good to me. I am quite well now. You have had a bad dream, for I woke once, and was so glad to see you sleeping in the old chair!"

"Sleeping?" repeated Duval. "Sleeping? Then, after all, it was only a dream!"

"You must have been dreaming, sir," said the father, as he made a sign to Duval to say no more on the subject.

"Yes—yes," said Duval, "I was weary with watching, I suppose, and so fell asleep."

"Just so—just so, sir—now, if you will partake of the morning meal with us, sir, I shall be most happy to conduct you on your road."

Duval, still thoughtfully, turned towards the young girl, who was looking so much better from the long sleep she had had, that he could scarcely persuade himself that she was the same person he had beheld the day before so attenuated and feeble.

"Good bye, dear Mary," he said, as he left a kiss upon the pure brow, "remember me in your prayers."

"Indeed—indeed, I will," replied the child, as she looked up lovingly into Duval's face.

The father, however, drew him aside into a small apartment, before he descended the staircase, saying, as he laid his hand upon his arm——

"I am sure you have seen something; tell me what it was before you leave, I implore you?"

"All a dream, a wild imagination of the brain, I assure you," replied Duval, "do not ask me to tell you. I was in a state of strange and unwonted excitement when you left me, and those thoughts were strengthened rather than obliterated when I unfortunately fell asleep."

"Still, I should like to know your dream," urged the father.

"Then you shall have it," said Duval, as he seated himself at a table.

"Methought, then, that I heard a steady tramp—tramp—tramp—soon after midnight. My blood ran in icy coldness round my heart, and with a hissing sort of gush it seemed for a moment to stagnate there. I could not move. I could not speak. I felt my hair moved like coiled snakes, as, far away, I heard that steady sound in the old house—tramp—tramp—tramp!"

"Did it sound like an iron footstep on the oaken floors?" asked the peasant.

"It did—it did; but remember, it was after all only a dream."

"Yes—yes, sir; but please go on. What next took place?"

"Nearer—nearer still it came," continued Duval. "The tread at each footstep went through my brain. Oh, if I could but have spoken! If I could but have uttered one prayer. I would have given worlds had they been mine to give; but there was I, spell-bound and horrified, my inmost soul crouching with fear."

"Go on—go on!"

"Tramp—tramp—tramp. I still thought I heard the sound," continued Duval. "On—on it came. I heard it in the first room of this suite of apartments. I heard it in the second. I heard it in the third. I heard it in the fourth."

"And then?"

"And then I fancied I heard it in the fifth. Tramp—tramp—tramp—that foot of metal and the hand so cold and wet, which I had touched in the forest."

"Yes, sir, go on," gasped the peasant, as he drew quite close to Duval.

"It reached the door of the room in which I was with the sick child."

"But it did not enter—you did not see it, the horrible thing?" cried the father.

"The footsteps ceased there," said Duval; "but I thought the iron hand was dashed against the panel of the door. But I know now that the noises I heard were caused by the efforts you were making to awake me."

"Perhaps they were—perhaps they were," sighed the man.

"I am quite sure of it now, my good friend; for do you suppose that so redoubtable a visitor would have been prevented from making its entrance into a room where it expected to find only a sick child. No, no, believe me, that the spectre exists only in your own imaginations, for do you think if any living being from another world had really made his presence known to me, that you would not likewise have been made aware of it?"

"It may be as you say, sir, nevertheless I am glad you have been so candid with me as to tell me all. I shall be in less danger now, of believing in the existence of this terrible ghost."

"Then I am content," said Duval, as he grasped the rough palm of the honest peasant, and took his leave.

"Never shall I forget the adventures of this night," said Duval to himself, as, mounted upon the horse which had come just at a time when he was wishing for Nightshade, he galloped out of the forest, and took the nearest road which led to the house on Hampstead Heath, where he found Lucy and Blossom anxiously expecting him.

CHAPTER CLV.

AN OLD ACQUAINTANCE MAKES HIS APPEARANCE.

A DRIZZLING rain had set in the night succeeding the events which had happened to Claude Duval at the mansion which was said to be haunted; and we must now introduce our readers to an old acquaintance, viz., to Colonel Miravel, or rather, St. Ives, for by that name he is more familiar to us.

He is seated with his gentle bride, that heroic Stuart Princess, who having given him her best affections, had not withheld her hand, where she had given her heart.

The night was cold, and snow had been falling at intervals during the day.

There was a look of serene happiness upon the face of the Princess, who, with her gentle smile, and mild swimming eyes, and delicate cheeks, and long auburn hair, looked all that one could wish a bride to be.

She was regarding her husband with a look of fond affection, as she told him that, now for his dear sake, she was only too willing to relinquish all thoughts of future pomp and splendour, and live quietly with him in some quiet cottage, far removed from the noise and turmoil of every day, and find her greatest happiness in loving and in being beloved by him.

At this moment, however, and just as St. Ives was about to make some reply to her, a loud crash, and a wild waving to and fro of the crimson curtain at the bay window, proclaimed that some portion of the ancient casement had yielded to the violence of the storm.

St. Ives hastened to the window, and when he drew aside the curtain, the scene that presented itself without—for it was not yet quite dark—was most curious.

The whole aspect of the landscape was changed from what it had been only a few hours before.

Tall trees looked dwarfed by the accumulation of snow at their roots, and the palings which enclosed the little garden looked ridiculously small—their black heads only just peeping above the snow here and there, while many small trees and plants in the garden were completely covered up.

The snow was still falling thickly and in large flakes, but the wind did not appear to be so boisterous, although a cold current, loaded with particles of snow, poured in at an upper corner of the bay window where a few of the small latticed panes had been blown in by the violence of the wind.

While St. Ives, and his young wife lingered in the bay window, the storm gave more than one indication of a changeful character, for a shower of hail and sleet came with a sudden splash against the window once; and, at another time, when the snow seemed upon the point of ceasing to fall, there came a sudden wind, creeping, as it were, insidiously upon the ground, and tossed up such a quantity of it into the air, as to make another mimic snow-storm.

The cold, too, was evidently intense, for the breath of St. Ives and his wife was fast frosting in rich and rare devices upon the glass of the window.

St. Ives temporarily secured the broken portion of the window, and once more he led his gentle bride to the warm fire-side they had just quitted, and the hail, the sleet, the snow, and the wind, were alike forgotten by those two loving hearts.

"Would that we could ensure always being as happy as we now are, dear Charles," said the Princess, as she laid her hand upon his shoulder, and gazed fondly into his eyes.

"And what should hinder us, dear one?" was the reply, "so long as we continue to love each other as we do now."

"I can answer for myself," said the Princess, half playfully; and yet, as she spoke, a pained expression passed across her face. But, hark! what is that, Charles?" she asked with a look of alarm.

"It is the baying of the old hound, that is all."

"Hush! hush!" said the Princess; "what does it mean?"

There was a profound silence between the husband and wife, and then the hound's voice, in a long low melancholy wail, came fully upon their ears.

"Something is amiss, dear Charles," cried the Princess. "Can there be danger to you?"

"Do not alarm yourself, dear one. No one knows us here. I will go out and see what it is. Stay here, I will be back directly."

"Oh, no no!—do not go!" said the Princess.

"Nay, nay, dear! do not alarm yourself! No harm will happen to me; who knows, it may be some one lost in the snow-storm."

"Then they will see the lights. Stay here, I implore you," said the Princess, turning pale as death, and placing her hand upon her heart as if to still its beating.

"Be it so, then," said St. Ives; "since you are so urgent upon my remaining here, and let us——"

Before St. Ives could finish the sentence, the door of the apartment was burst open, and a female, with one wild shriek, bounded in.

Bewildered, no doubt, at the moment, by the sudden transition from darkness to light, she paused and shrunk back.

During that time, St. Ives and the Princess had an opportunity to see what sort of a person the intruder was.

She was particularly tall for a woman, and instead of the ordinary covering for the head, some dark-coloured mantle or shawl seemed to be fastened to her hair, falling thence in ample folds below her waist.

The lower part of her garments were completely draggled in snow, and, indeed, in every crease of the mantle she wore partially upon her head, the snow lay in thick masses.

Her arms were bare and her face was wan and haggard, and painful in its expression.

Still there was a kind of beauty still lingering upon it, like the spell of grandeur round a ruin, speaking eloquently of what it once had been but could never be again.

She quickly recovered from the first dazzling effect of the light, and advancing, with one arm outstretched to within a pace of where St. Ives and his wife were standing, she cried, "He is coming! He is coming! The despoiler is coming! Shun him! Flee! flee from him while there is yet time! His smile is a decoy! His hate—and he hates all that God has made—is destruction! Flee—he comes! He comes! Through the snow-drift he tracks me! He comes! He comes!"

"She is mad," whispered St. Ives.

The Princess clung to him.

"Come, come," said St. Ives, "my poor woman, you have done wisely to come in here out of the storm, sit down by the fire, and you shall have some hot wine and water."

The poor woman passed her hand across her brow, as though to clear away the cloud from her intellect, and then stepping towards the door, again she listened attentively.

St. Ives and his wife could only hear the baying of the hound, all else was silent as the grave.

"He comes!" again shrieked the woman in gasping accents. "He comes! Do you not hear him? Save me!"

As she uttered these last words, she clung to the Princess, and taking both her hands in hers, sank at her feet.

With a cry, she started up, pointing to the plain gold ring which St. Ives had so recently placed upon her finger at the altar, where he had promised to love and cherish her so long as they both should live.

"You—you, too, are a victim!" she cried; "and you are another!"

As she spoke, she turned and pointed to St. Ives.

"Stop her! Stop her!" shouted a voice. "She is mad!"

The moment the accents of that voice reached her ears, the poor creature darted forward, and flinging aside the curtain which covered the bay window we have already mentioned, she, with a shriek of despair, plunged right through the casement, before either St. Ives or the Stuart Princess could divine what were her intentions.

Simultaneously with her exit, a tall, thin man in black made his appearance at the door of the apartment, in which the transaction had happened.

He was in the worldly acceptation of the word, a gentlemanly-looking man. His hair was parted in the middle of his forehead.

But it was his forehead itself that attracted the most attention.

When he frowned—and he did so as he advanced to the middle of the room—by some arrangement of the muscles, the shape of a hoof was fairly and legibly marked upon his brow.

"And pray, sir, who are you?" asked St. Ives, as he stood between him and the window, through which the unhappy woman had made her dangerous leap.

"Who am I?" slowly repeated the stranger.

"Yes, sir, who are you?"

He turned sharply round, and after regarding St. Ives fixedly for a moment, he said—

"I am a stranger to you, sir."

"Yes; but——"

"Come away Charles," whispered the Princess, "he looks—I do not like his looks."

The stranger heard these words.

"You do not like my looks," he said, as he turned his gaze full upon her. "We shall meet again."

He made a low bow that was full of courtly grace; and then, with one bound, disappeared through the opening in the casement that the female had made when she took that mode of leaving the house.

"This is too much!" cried St. Ives. "Fear nothing, I will return in a minute."

"No, no, no!" cried the Princess.

"Release me, I will not go far."

St. Ives at once darted out into the night air after the stranger, and by the same means, too, viz., through the open window.

It seemed as though he were under the influence of some sort of fascination, and was forced to go, so hasty had been his manner.

The effect produced upon him at first by the sudden transition from heat to the cold without, with its drifting snow, its hail, and sleet, was at first completely prostrating.

His frosted breath seemed to congeal in his very lungs, and he paused to accustom himself for a moment or two to the new climate in which he was.

He then looked round for the strange man who had preceded him.

He had not to look far.

Some one stepped before him.

St. Ives sprang forward, but the figure eluded his grasp; and the same voice that had before spoken to him only a few moments previously, again addressed him.

"What would you with me, Mr. St. Ives; or rather, Colonel Miravel?"

"I would know who you are, whether man or fiend. Are you human? Speak to me."

"I am mixed up with your future destiny, your wife——"

"Ah! what would you say of her?"

"Ha, ha, ha!"

The figure turned and darted through the snow and sleet, and when St. Ives would have followed him, he heard a low, wailing cry as from afar off.

In a moment, the mysterious man was by his side again.

"Do you hear that?" he asked. Follow it. That is your path. Then you will see the eyes that dictate your fate. Go, go!"

The cry came upon St. Ives' ears again; and while he, for a brief moment hesitated whether he should follow the stranger and demand a brief explanation of his mysterious words, or proceed in the direction whence the cry for assistance—for such it was by its tone—proceeded, the man was gone again.

By this time, the old man and his wife, who were

the only domestics St. Ives had, had sallied forth, and it was the sound of the man's voice that recalled St. Ives to himself.

"Master! master! Sir! Where be you? Missus sent us after you! Did you catch that man, sir? I thought he would have knocked me down when I told him he could not come up-stairs. Did you catch him, sir?"

St. Ives was silent for a moment, and then he said—

"No, Thomas."

He could not have given a reason had he been asked for one, for suppressing the truth regarding that man. He could not tell why he shrank from giving an explanation, he had none to give to the strange and mysterious words he had uttered.

By some most strange, unaccountable impulse, St. Ives said, "no," when he felt that he ought to have said "yes."

Perhaps the evident hesitation and confusion of his manner might have betrayed him, and even induced the simple-minded Thomas to think there was some concealement, had not his attention and that also of St. Ives been suddenly arrested by the passage past them of a horse at headlong speed, dragging after him, what seemed by the uncertain light of the lantern, a portion of a chaise.

Then there came again the wailing cry, which could be translated into nothing else but a call for help, rendered inarticulate by the storm of snow.

"There, there!" said St. Ives. "Some one is in peril, let us go, Thomas, and see if we can be of any assistance."

"That will we, master," replied the man, "never let it be said that we leave our fellow creatures to perish in such a night as this, without lending them a hand. This way, sir. This way, sir."

St. Ives and his man proceeded as fast as the many obstacles which they met with would allow them, to the spot whence they believed the cries to come.

What a fight it was to get through the snow drift.

CHAPTEL CLVII.

THE BROKEN CHAISE

The snow dashed in their faces, blinding and bewildering them as to their route, and how oddly hollow places were filled up to their level, into which those who had not known the road as well as St. Ives and the old man would have fallen, to emerge again completely covered with a white mantle of snow.

But they pushed on until they reached a roadside meadow, and from this spot the cries seemed to have proceeded.

Skirting the road, and under ordinary circumstances, even in the darkest night sufficiently defining it from the fields, was a row of trees; but even they had lost their significance in the snow drift, and close under them, in a little hollow, where a huge chestnut spread its broad arms far and wide, a black mass of something appeared projecting from the snow.

Neither St. Ives or the old man dared hazard a conjecture concerning it. There it was, huge, black, and indefinable. A thing to dread amid the winter's storm, upon that night of evil omen.

"This way, sir. This way," cried the old man, holding the lantern high above his head, which, well protected from the cold blast in its house of horn, allowed some feeble rays of light to fall upon the object that had attracted the attention of them both.

It was a post-chaise lying upon its side. One horse was still struggling faintly in the snow to free itself from the traces—the other had galloped past them some minutes before.

"Light me, Thomas!" cried St. Ives. "Light me!"

St. Ives flew to the door of the carriage, and forced it open. A hand—it was as soft as a child's—was held towards him, and a low, soft voice said—

"Help! Save me!"

"Yes, yes!" he cried, "give me your other hand."

Another of the little hands, so exquisitely soft, so beautiful, was extended.

St. Ives dived into the chaise, and drew out a young girl.

To get her out he was compelled—it was a pleasant compulsion that—to clasp her round the neck and waist, and then she fainted.

But by the light of the lantern, St. Ives had seen her face.

It was one to dream of, one to haunt the imagination in solitude, one to prove a curse or a blessing to those who gazed upon it.

The sweet mouth, the peach-like bloom of the cheeks, the delicate tenderness of the soft blue eyes, the wavy golden hair, parted over a brow full of genius and ingenuousness.

St. Ives had looked upon beauty — the Stuart Princess, his wife of a few days only, was exceedingly lovely—but he now gazed upon the *magie* of loveliness and fascination.

He held the young creature to his heart, he sprang with her from the side of the carriage, he forgot even to see who else there was to save,—he had helped, he had saved her.

At that moment he felt as though she had been created for him, and that envious Fate only had kept her from his arms. From that moment he felt that she was his destiny, his evil or his good spirit as it might be; and he said, as he still held her to his beating heart—

"She is mine—mine—my own!"

"You may call it madness if you like. You may call it the wild enthusiasm of a false spirit, with more of imagination in its disposition than reason; but love is no plant of slow and meagre growth.

It is a flash, a passion, an explosion. It lights the heart like the red lightning gleam; but unlike it, it does not come and go; but it comes to stay for weal or for woe. St. Ives loved, as man can love but once in a lifetime, he loved, adored, worshipped madly, doated upon a being whom he knew not by name even; whom he had only heard speak two short words, but whom he now held to his heart—whose lips he covered with burning kisses.

And he had been a husband but four short days.

An eclipse even of the fair beauty of the night seemed to creep with a shuddering earnestness over all things.

In double darkness the sky looked down upon a moment which decided the fate of the lovely and the loved.

The lull in the tempest was over, and with a shout and a whirl, as though millions of demons held wild contest in the upper air, the roar of the elements commenced anew.

The lantern was dashed from the hands of the old man, and all was darkness—the darkness of darkness—the night of night!

But in his arms St. Ives held what was henceforth to be his world, his heaven, his idol, his good and evil genius in one.

There was no such thing as darkness to him while he held *her* close to his heart. When she was not with him he felt that gladness would leave sunshine, joy

ST. IVES RESCUES EVA ST. CLAIR.

would bid farewell to music, and fragrance would no longer dwell in the soft petals of the rose.

She still lay in a state of insensibility in his arms. She was dead to the world, and all its joys, and all its woes.

She knew not that she was in the arms of her destiny. She felt not his warm caresses. His kisses were upon her lips, but she knew it not. Oh, what a moment of joy that was to him. Amid the intense darkness of that dark night she seemed wholly his, and as he held her to his heart, he said, "Oh, that the sun would never come again! Oh, that it were ever thus!"

St. Ives must even then at that moment of wild and frenzied passion, have had some perception of his position, or he could not so have spoken. He must have felt that he and daylight were at war. He must have drawn some analogy between truth and daylight, and as he henceforward felt that he could not bear the one, so the other became obnoxious to him

No. 50.—NIGHTSHADE.

But he could not for long there remain in the tempest with her in his arms. And other voices now came upon his ear.

"Captain Granville! Captain Granville! where are you? Captain Granville! How confounding this darkness is to be sure!"

St. Ives passed his hand across his fevered brow and listened.

For a moment he had forgotten the meaning of that name, Captain Granville, and yet it sounded familiar to him; it was the name he, St. Ives, had assumed when he took the house in which he thought he was going to spend the remainder of his existence in love and happiness with that heroic girl who had consented to share with him life's joys and sorrows, the poor Stuart Princess.

"Captain Granville! Thomas!" Again the names were shouted upon the night air. "Thomas, Thomas! Why don't you speak man?"

"He has gone back to the house, perhaps, for a light," said a voice.

"But where is Captain Granville? I should like to know where Captain Granville is?"

Would St. Ives speak? Would this dissolve the charm that held him to that spot? No—no. The light would soon come he thought, and then—but not till then, it would be time to do so. Then it would be time to step from heaven to earth; then it would be time to try and look, and speak, and move as though no avalanche of passion had come upon his heart, crushing out all that was there enshrined.

A confused chorus of voices calling for help came upon the night air.

The other occupants of the carriage, whoever they might be, were still in durance, for the light had been extinguished too soon, for any one, if they had been on the spot—which, at the time St. Ives rescued the young girl, they were not.

One of the new comers who, from his speech was evidently a sailor, advised them to hold on and fear nothing, and while he spoke, a dim, moving star appeared, coming from the houses.

It was Thomas's re-lighted lantern as it moved its tiny rays around it, and St. Ives began to feel that it was time for him to surrender his fair burden, which he still held in his wild embrace.

Nearer, nearer still came the light.

It was surrounded by a kind of halo of frosted air.

St. Ives felt that in another moment he should be within the sphere of its influence, and then he laid the young girl quietly down on the snow, and then springing to his feet, he shouted, "Hilloa! Hilloa! This way!"

"Aye—aye!" cried the voice of the sailor. "Who speaks? What cheer, mates? Speak again!"

"It is I—Captain Granville—Don't you know me? Don't you know my voice?"

"By all that's good, I didn't! and there's something uncommon strange about it, still, for the matter of that—but mayhap its only the night air, after all. But don't let us waste time; there's a ship in distress—I mean a carriage broken down, somewhere a-head."

"Here, Thomas, this way with your lantern, man—this way. Heave to!"

"Help! Help! Murder—I am suffocated—choked! Help! Help! Good people, help me out, for mercy's sake!"

This was a female voice, but in a moment or two that of a man joined the cry, and in this latter case, more oaths were uttered than were at all necessary upon the occasion.

St. Ives, to cover the state of confusion he was in, and to get rid of any awkward questioning concerning his silence when he was so recently called to by his friends and neighbours, made him affect to be greatly occupied in assisting the people still in the carriage, but they were so wedged in, that he found it quite impossible to get them out.

"Avast, there, my hearties!" cried the sailor. "We shall be able to right the craft if we mind how we set about it; and so we need not be trying to drag the folks through this starboard port-hole in that fashion. Give her a heave with a will, and up she must go. Now then—a hoi!—a-hoi!"

This was evidently the most rational way of extricating the travellers from the vehicle, and it was at once put into execution by the sailor.

St. Ives and several men hoisted up the post-chaise to its proper position—an operation, which, amid the snow, they found was a much easier task than they had at all imagined.

The vehicle was soon as Thomas said, "on its feet again;" and then as the old man held the lantern, there issued from the open door of the post-chaise, its terrified occupants.

The first person who stepped out, was a woman of a certain age. Her tall and somewhat gaunt form had got in some way fixed in the vehicle in a most extraordinary position, so that if it had not been "righted," or "set on its feet again," it would have been next to impossible to have got her out at all.

As it was, she looked a most deplorable figure Some species of head-dress, which no doubt she thought particularly fascinating before the accident, had now, squeezed flat as it was in some places, and extraordinarily elongated in others—a very remarkable appearance, to say the least of it.

It was as much as St. Ives could do to lift her from the topmost step, for either with fright or with cold, she appeared to be too much paralyzed to descend herself.

"Oh, Gracious! I do believe Jacob is no more—Jacob must be no more—much as I hate him, and ugly as he is, I cannot help being dreadfully shocked. Good gracious, what an escape I have had."

"Are you talking about your husband, ma'am?" asked old Thomas, "because, perhaps, this is him, all huddled up at the bottom of the chaise."

He was without a hat, his head was partially bald, and his small eyes were so deeply sunk in their orbits that they were scarcely visible at all.

The skin of his face was pinched and yellow as some old parchment deed, his dress was the plainest of plain black, and a white neck-cloth tied so tight to all appearance, that he looked to be within an hair's breadth of strangulation.

From the attitude of this man, and the uneasy glances he cast around him, one would have thought him some fugitive from justice, who expected in each face to see an enemy; but, perhaps, it was only a manifestation of a constitutional suspectfulness, so to speak. But this appearance either passed away very quickly, or it was one of those expressions to which our eyes so soon become accustomed as to lose perception of it in any great excess with much rapidity.

"I really am very much obliged," sighed, rather than said, the aforesaid Jacob, as he descended the steps of the carriage. "Gentlemen, accept my thanks. My wife is, I presume, in safety. Humph! Mrs. Joyce! Mrs. Joyce—how do you feel now, Mrs. Joyce."

"What?" said the sailor, stepping forward, "is there any one else in the ship?"

"It's roomy," said the clerical-looking personage. "Yes, it is roomy—remarkably roomy, warranted to hold six."

"Six? Why how many more of you is there packed in the hold?"

"My sister, Mrs. Joyce, and the young man we allowed to ride with us, whom we picked up on the road, on the express condition that he paid his equal share of the expenses."

"A lawyer, I'll be bound," muttered the sailor to himself. "If he does not look his calling, at least he spoke it plain enough. What cheer there? Oh, here you are, ma'am."

A small vivacious-looking female made her appearance. Her sparkling black eyes and olive complexion, could hardly have been supposed to belong to a native of our cold, northern region.

As she appeared, she said "I am really afraid the young man we gave a lift to, is killed; he has not spoken one word since the chaise was upset."

"I have not had a chance, yet," said a cheery, youthful voice from inside the chaise. "The fact is, I thought it best to remain passive, seeing that I was so jammed in that I could not be of any assistance; but now that I have a chance of leaping out, why, here goes!"

He leaped from the chaise, and in a moment, with a shout of joy, the sailor sprang towards him, and clasped him in his arms, crying out, "Charles, Charles —my boy!"

"Yes, father—yes, father," cried the lad,—" yes, I—I heard your voice—heaven bless it!—and so I was well content with the break-down, as I guessed we must be near home. Are—are you well, father?"

It was evident that the joyful feelings of the lad were too much for him. He caught his breath as he spoke; and by the light of the lantern, his eyes glistened with unwonted moisture as he warmly returned his father's embrace.

"This is a happy night!" cried the old sailor. "Hurrah! my boy has come! Captain Granville, this is my boy, Charles—my—my boy—my brave, darling boy; and he has come, you see, so—so unexpected, that—that——"

The delighted father could keep the farce of calmness up no longer, but, falling upon the breast of his son, he sobbed aloud, while he inarticulately blessed him in the name of that God to whom such a scene is well pleasing.

There is a sacredness in tears, which, whether they be shed in joy, when the surcharged heart must relieve itself of its abundance of bliss, or in sorrow, when Nature kindly provides that with each pearly drop there shall flow from the heart a fragment of its grief.

No one spoke for a few moments.

Jacob Cuthbert—for such was his name—was rubbing his hands together with a slow and oily motion, and apparently not attending to Mrs. Joyce, who was whispering in his ear.

His wife still sat upon a snow-heap, as though the rapidity of the incidents we have described had changed her into part and parcel of the frozen mass.

"Come, father, all's right!" said Charles, affecting an indifference he was far from feeling,—" all's right! You don't know what a scramble I've had to get here, so let us come home."

The old sailor wrung his son's hand, and laughed through his tears. How he did laugh! "Thomas, you rascal," he said, "here's Charles! Of course, I am well, Charles—quite well! Here, come and let me show you to Captain Granville! I am proud of you, my boy! Where is he? Captain Granville—Captain Granville! Why, where the deuce has he got to now!"

"Here!" said St. Ives, in a strong, sharp, shrill voice, and he hastily came forward from the side of the young girl whom he had rescued first from the chaise.

"Why, what's the matter with you, sir?" cried the bluff old sailor. "You look half-scared like, as if you had seen a ghost! This is my boy, Charles, Captain Granville!'

St. Ives stretched out his hand in an absent kind of way towards the young man, and was muttering something about being glad to make his acquaintance, when the attention of all was attracted by Mrs. Joyce suddenly calling out, "Where is Eva—where is Eva?"

"Is that her name?" almost screamed St. Ives, suddenly breaking away from the old sailor and his son. "I mean—I mean—is that the name of the young lady who—who is close by here?"

They all followed him to the spot upon which he had laid the young girl whom he had helped from the chaise. He felt inwardly tempted to fly before them all, and stand over her to prevent any one from touching, and so polluting, his new-found treasure; but he had reflected enough, though only just enough, to prevent himself from committing so mad an act.

At this moment he happened to encounter the eye of old Thomas, who had been a faithful and tried friend to the Stuart Princess and her family, and there was that in his glance which made St. Ives tremble.

While the others gathered round her who had been named Eva by Mrs. Joyce, St. Ives clasped his brow with both his hands, while he asked himself what he had said or done for Thomas to make anything of. He was interrupted in this retrospection by hearing what Mrs. Joyce was saying to the young girl.

"Why, Eva, you are not hurt, surely?" she said. "Speak to us, Eva St. Clair! You are not hurt. Do you not know us? I am your aunt, you know!"

"Her aunt! That woman her aunt!" gasped St. Ives.

"Come, come, Eva; rouse yourself up, girl! Here is your uncle, Mr. Cuthbert, and your aunt Cuthbert; and here am I!"

"Her uncle," said St. Ives, to himself.

"She must be hurt," said Mrs. Joyce; "only look how she draws her breath, and how her colour comes and goes. Oh, she is dying!"

"No, no—a thousand times no!" shrieked St. Ives, as he bounded through the circle. "Dying? No! She dying, why do not you all die? I—I—heaven help me!"

He caught up two handfuls of snow, and pressed the frozen particles to his brow.

Again he encountered the glance of the old man, Thomas, fixed upon him, as though it would read his heart.

"Pardon me—pardon me! In the confusion, I thought they said my wife — yes my wife I I thought! But who is this? Is this young creature, who, after all, is little more than a child in years—is she to die here, with the warm blood congealing in her young heart, while there is light, and warmth, and comfort indoors! To the house—to the house! Who will carry her? Well, well, I will! Indeed, I thought you said my wife was ill! Ha! ha!"

Lifting Eva St. Clare in his arms, St. Ives sped with her towards the house, where poor Mary, the Stuart Princess, was so anxiously awaiting his return.

CHAPTER CLVII.

ST. IVES RESCUES EVA ST. CLARE FROM IMMINENT DANGER.

MRS. CUTHBERT, as her fright decreased, and as her assurance of having fallen into comfortable quarters increased, became rather voluminous in her remarks.

She attached herself with frightful pertinacity to the sailor, and was so voluble and discursive in her gossip, that he was fairly bewildered by her, and at last took refuge in absolute silence.

Mr. Cuthbert hovered over the outskirts of the party, as though it had been a hostile force and he some scout duly commissioned to mark the course they took, while Mrs. Joyce kept not far off St. Ives, notwithstanding the speed he made with his fair burden. She seemed as if she could have said, "This way mischief lies!" and the congeniality of her disposition for anything of that character kept her upon the scent like some ill-omened bird of prey about the dying.

Had there been no snow upon the ground, had the dripping sleet not half blinded him at times, and had the roaring wind not now and then seized him as though with a gigantic hand that would not be resisted, St. Ives, in the then state of his feelings, would soon have reached the house with the young girl, whom he clasped so wildly in his arms, and Mrs. Joyce might have been distanced; but it was a night upon which the weak could make as much way as the strong, and she kept close to him.

Suddenly, to shorten the road, St. Ives dashed aside into a narrow garden-path.

In the summer time, this pathway was so closely sheltered by trees that a dim, religious kind of twilight reigned within even at high noon; but now the trees, denuded of their leaves, only made faint music to the storm, as they slightly cut the passage of the howling wind.

A few steps brought St. Ives, most unexpectedly to him, into a broad beam of light.

The eagerness of the Princess to see what was taking place without, and her endeavour to catch a glimpse of him who had become a part of her very existence, had induced her to draw aside the thick curtains before the large bay window, and to press her pale face against its frost-encrusted panes, to penetrate the night air, and so the light of the blazing fire went out boldly to the tempest in a broad halo of crimson light through the chequered panes of the casement, tinging the snow flakes with a strange beauty, and lighting up with a preternatural lustre the naked branches of the whistling trees that bent and shivered in the gale.

It was within the sphere of this steady glare of light that St. Ives suddenly stopped.

He paused a minute with a feeling of confusion, and then from the trunk of a large sycamore tree there glided a figure.

It was that of a man, and he laid his hand on the shoulder of St. Ives.

He did not speak, but, with his lips close to the ear of St. Ives, he uttered a fiendish, yelling laugh.

St. Ives recoiled a step or two, and the cry for help came from his lips.

But the figure had sped away, favoured by the darkness.

"I am mad!" said St. Ives. "I know that I am mad! I feel a fire raging in my brain! I am mad—mad—mad! Ha, ha, ha! Has it come to this, that I, who prided myself upon my rare intellect, my learning, my many mental endowments, my reputation among those who own no majesty but that of mind? Has it come to madness? Ha, ha, ha! Yes, I am mad! Help, help! Blow on ye wintry winds! Is there no sharp wedge of ice that can be plunged into my heart? Help, help! This is not winter; there is no coolness in the snow flakes, they fall like sparks fresh from the anvil upon my brow, and I am mad! Off, off! Why do you crowd upon me thus? Off, I say! Who laughs—who laughs at a madman? Make way—make way! There, touch her gently! How beautiful she is! Radiant artizans of heaven, which of you all fashioned this fair being? You? you? or you? No, no, you are a fiend! Back, back, I say! Touch her not! I know you by your glittering eye! Eva! do they call her Eva? Angels, why did you send her here to drive me mad? Look up, darling, and tell me that you return my love!"

Mrs. Joyce called aloud for help.

But there was another at that moment who required help more than did even St. Ives.

The party that had been distanced in the brief walk from the overturned carriage to the house by St. Ives, now pressed forward, impelled by the cries of St. Ives himself, and the loud calls of Mrs. Joyce for help.

In another moment he would have been surrounded, when, after staggering in a circle for a moment or two, as though by some more than earthly power, he was kept within its radius, he suddenly clasped the young girl tighter to his heart, and rushed onwards round the angle of the outer wall of the house.

The lad Charles was quickly on his track, believing that he was indeed pursuing a madman who might possibly do some injury to the fair girl he held so tightly pressed against his heart; but it was very difficult for any one to make much progress now, for old Thomas had fallen down and crushed the lantern he carried, and the broad beam of light from the bay window made everything without the sphere of its immediate influence doubly dark and uncertain.

Those who followed St. Ives, or tried to follow him in the dark, seemed to have taken a nearer route than he to the house, for they all reached it before he had done so, and the only person they saw as they entered was the young wife.

Old Thomas was the first to enter the room, and there he found her kneeling upon the floor, her face buried in the recesses of a large chair, and resting upon her hands.

It would seem as though she were making frantic efforts to shut out the sounds from without—those sounds that in the voice of her husband came to tell her that henceforth her young life must be a living death.

She had heard him say those words that had filled her heart with such intolerable anguish—"Look up, darling, and tell me that you return my love."

What could ever obliterate the recollection of those words addressed to another.

Old Thomas availed himself of the privilege long years of service and devotion had given, and laid his rough but honest hand upon his mistress's arm.

"Rise, your royal highness," he said, "and let not these strangers witness the secrets of your heart."

"Alas! alas!" moaned the Princess; "I can remember only that I am a woman and a wife!"

"Hush, hush! I am an old man; call all your strength of character to your aid; you will want it all."

"I want only to die."

As she uttered these words, the Princess again buried her face in her hands, and wept so bitterly that even old Thomas was forced to turn away; but as he heard voices below, he returned to his mistress's side.

"Your husband is ill."

"Ah! say you so? Tell me—oh, tell me that it is illness—madness—anything but inconstancy, and I will bless you!"

"Believe that it is so—he cannot love another."

"Ah! then you know all?"

"What an old fool I am! What am I thinking about? Of course he cannot; but I was vexed to see him carrying that girl. But, after all, what else could he do? She was faint and could not walk, and all those people who were with us were rough fellows, and she seems gently born."

"Yes, yes! Then you think Thomas, that—that——"

"What—what, dear heart—what would you ask?" said the old man, taking both the Princess's hands in his.

"Then you think he is only mad?"

"Hush! hush! do not talk of such things!" said the old man, glancing uneasily about him.

"Ah! leave me—leave me, and I will remove the traces of these tears, and show myself, perhaps he does not love her!"

With one long look, in which were equally blended love, respect and admiration, the old servitor left the unfortunate Princess to her own sad thoughts.

She rose from her recumbent position, and began pacing the room.

Oh, that he may indeed be mad—even that fearful calamity I would hail with joy, for his heart would still be mine!" she cried. "Oh, Charles, Charles! your mind is my treasure, and if it be broken, it will be my treasure still! If you rave, my arms shall confine you—your grasp, even in fury, would have a charm for me – if you flew at me, I would receive you in an embrace at least as fond as it would be restrictive! In your quiet moments you should have no watcher, and no nurse but me—and I would hang over you with untiring tenderness, though you gave me no smile in return, and I should be never weary of gazing into your eyes, although they had no longer a ray of recognition for me! Oh, Charles, Charles!—husband—lover! My all in life—love me, or I die!"

Again the youthful head was bowed upon the clasped hands, while heaving sobs came from the labouring heart.

"But I must rouse myself for his sake. I will win back his love. I must see this girl, whom he thinks so beautiful—he used to think me beautiful once. But I must not think any more, I must act!"

The Stuart Princess did all she could to remove the traces of tears from her face, and smoothing back her luxuriant hair, she, with a slow step, descended to the room below.

CHAPTER CLVIII.

A NIGHT OF TUMULT AND ANXIETY.

IN the confusion of feeling which every one was labouring under, no one found themselves introduced to the beautiful girl—for such indeed she was—who entered that room, not so much to offer hospitality to so many intruders, as to make inquiries as to what had become of her husband.

At first there was a look of satisfaction upon her sweet face, as she saw only Mr. and Mrs. Cuthbert, Mrs. Joyce, the sailor, and his son, there was a feeling of thankfulness at first, to think that she had not the onerous task imposed upon her of welcoming her rival to what had, until within the last hour, been to the Stuart Princess such an abode of love and peace.

But as she gazed around, and missed also the face which, above all others, she longed to gaze upon, her heart sank within her, especially as the interrogatory which burst from all lips, took the form of "Where is Captain Granville?" The words were echoed by the sailor and his friends, who had been into the night air with him, and "Where is the Captain? Where is Captain Granville—has he not been here?" were the eager questions by all.

A dozen voices answered that he had run towards the house with a young girl, who had fainted.

Just at this moment, old Thomas rushed into the room in which the unbidden guests were assembled.

His eyes just encountered those of the Princess, fixed upon him with a meaning look.

Terror was in his looks—his eyes glared, and his voice was strange and unnatural, as he cried:—

"He's coming!—he's coming! He's as mad as a March hare! The Captain is coming, with the young lady! He is mad, and we shall all be mad!"

The Stuart Princess looked up for a moment, and then she sunk down upon her knees, as she gave one heart-rending shriek.

There was a pause—a lull amid the confusion of voices—one of those mysterious lapses of all sound, that will at times, as if by common consent, take place in both large and small assemblages of persons.

You might almost have heard the Princess's heart beating.

All eyes were turned towards the open door, at which Mrs. Joyce was standing, with her dark eyes flashing, and her whole attitude and demeanour showing how powerfully the startling events of the night had enchained the attention, and taken hold of her imagination.

There seemed to be a sort of perception that St. Ives would enter by that door before the lapse of another minute.

In another moment his voice, thick and husky, called out "A light!—a light!—a light here! She shall not die! I tell you she shall not die! No!—no!—no! Just as I have found her too! I tell you all she shall not die! I have saved her—and I will save her yet! Help!—help I say! Are you men, and can you see the fairest flower of earth fade before your eyes, and not do aught to save her?"

He staggered across the threshold—the young girl was still in his arms. Both his attire and hers were torn by the reckless manner in which he had dashed through the garden, heedless of regular paths. His face was flushed, and his eyes had about them a wild and unnatural brilliancy.

"Help! help!" he cried again. "Help and aid for her! Do you see that she recovers not—speaks not—moves not—and yet I tell you Death has not yet claimed her for his own. The evil spirits clutched at her as we passed them, but I held her close to my heart—yes, I held her tightly, mine—mine—my own! Ha, ha! She has come to me at last, my beautiful one! She has come to fill the void in my heart which nothing else could fill!"

He pressed his lips to the brow and then to the lips of his fair burden. He wept like a child, as he frantically called upon her to look upon him—to speak to him—to smile upon him; and all there present, and who looked first upon him, and then upon the pale face of his beautiful wife, seemed spell-bound and unable to utter a word.

At length the Stuart Princess tottered to her feet, and approached St. Ives She turned towards him with a sweet smile, but her smile vanished at once, as her eyes met his changed and working countenance. Cold drops stood upon his rigid and marble brow—the lips writhed, as if in bodily torture—the muscles of the face had fallen, and there was a wildness which appalled her in the fixed and feverish brightness of the eyes.

"You are ill, Charles—dear Charles, you are ill! Your look freezes me!"

"Nay, Mary," said St. Ives, recovering himself for a moment with a great effort, of which only such men as he are capable,—"I have been ill—very ill—but I am better."

"Ill, and I not know it!" She attempted to take her husband's hand as she spoke.

"It is fire—it burns! Avaunt!" he cried, frantically. "Oh, heaven, spare me—spare me!"

The Stuart Princess was now seriously alarmed; she seemed to see nothing but her husband; she saw not how fondly he enfolded her fragile form which lay so passively in his arms.

Strange as it may seem – despite her agony, despite her grief, despite the evidence of her own senses of the unfaithfulness of her husband—he was dearer to her in that hour, as she believed, of gloom and darkness, than in all the glory of his majestic intellect, or all the blandishment of his soft address.

But old Thomas could bear the sight no longer.

"Captain Granville—Captain Granville!" he cried: "are you mad? Who is this that you hold to your heart, false man? Unhand her, I say, and she shall be cared for, but not by you."

The still insensible form of Eva St. Clare was torn from the arms of St. Ives by the old man, whose feelings lent him the strength of youth for the time, but the exertions of those present were not sufficient to hold St. Ives.

He broke from them with a cry, and apparently fancying that she who had fired his blood with so wild and overbearing a passion, had fled to the snow-storm again, he made for the still open door

He would have passed out at it, but a face appeared there, and once more repulsed him. He turned, and made two or three wandering steps across the room, then, before any one could support him, he fell heavily to the floor.

Nature had done her utmost.

The physical powers could no longer uphold themselves against that frightful strife of the mind, and St. Ives laid as still as though the hand of death were upon him.

Alas! alas! what are we in our hour of pride and strength, but the frail toys of passion.

The Stuart Princess sprung forward, and, kneeling by his side, imprinted one long kiss upon his unconscious lips, murmuring, as she did so, "The last—the last! Yes, the last!"

Then she rose up. True, she was of a deathlike paleness, but her step was firm as she stood by her faithful servant's side, who, with his wife, and Mrs. Joyce, was trying to restore the unconscious girl to her senses.

"She is very beautiful!" she whispered, still in the same strange, far-off kind of voice. "Who is she? how came she here? It is a mystery!"

"Not at all, ma'am, if you please," said Mrs. Joyce, suddenly looking up, and encountering the Princess's gaze. "This is my niece, ma'am. The carriage broke down, and we are all here."

The Princess bowed, and giving one more long, lingering look at St. Ives, she slowly quitted the room.

* * * * *

It is midnight.

The bustle and turmoil consequent upon the strange events which had taken place during the last few hours had subsided.

A few hours had elapsed only, but what changes had taken place in the minds and hearts of some of the characters with whom the reader has become so familiar.

While in fitful gusts, like the storm upon an angry ocean, wild insanity spoke its insatiate ravings from the vexed brain of St. Ives, they who had congregated beneath that roof—some from curiosity, others from some of the best motives that actuate human nature—had left it.

St. Ives, however, continued to rave of all those disjointed strange thoughts and feelings, that lie like caged spirits at the bottom of every man's heart, and which only struggle into freedom when the cloud of partial insanity is upon the sterner reason that combats them.

He lived for a time the king of a fantastic realm, and saw what others saw not.

He had no regrets just then, and no affection for any one.

In another room, kneeling, with clasped hands and a world of suffering expressed in every feature of her sweet face, was the Stuart Princess.

She was striving to forget all but her love for her husband; and yet, ever and anon, his voice, calling upon another, met her ear.

Twice she strove to rise to her feet to go to him, but her limbs refused their office, and then she sank down again passive and helpless as a child.

There is a gentle tap at the door of the apartment, and then the handle is quietly turned, and the faithful old servitor makes his appearance.

At the sight of his mistress's grief, the old man turns aside, and dashes his hand across his eyes.

"Come in, Thomas, you have something to say."

The Princess was, at first, almost as much startled as Thomas had been at the changed tone of her own voice, it sounded so strange, so hollow, so lifeless.

"Yes, your Royal Highness; that is, I thought I would just come to see if your Royal Highness wanted anything."

The old man evidently thought that his mistress would be soothed by some reference to her rank, for he never, since her marriage with St. Ives, had so often addressed her by the title of Royal Highness as he had done during the last three hours.

But she to whom he gave the title either heard it not, or heeded it not. Her thoughts were busy upon other subjects.

"Sit down, Thomas," said the Princess, in the same hushed voice. "Sit down. Do not weep and shake your head. There are few evils that may not in some way be remedied. Sit down and tell me all—all you know."

It was with difficulty that the Princess could finish the sentence.

"Yes, your Royal Highness. Heaven bless you, I will sit down and talk to you, as I have done many a time to amuse you when you were that high."

The old man tried to speak cheerfully, but it was a terrible failure.

"You were always kind to me, Thomas, and—and faithful; but now tell me all you can about—about to-night."

"Do not ask me—oh, do not ask me! All must come right again, dear mistress!"

"Yes, yes! But tell me, I beg of you, if you love me, tell me all you know that I may be the better able to act judiciously."

"Well, then, if your Royal Highness commands me," replied the old man, "I will speak. Your Royal Highness must know then——"

Again the old man paused, for well he knew that whatever he had to tell respecting that night must be a stab at the heart of the gentle being to whom he was speaking. The Princess divined his scruples, so she took the initiative by saying as calmly as she could, "Tell me, Thomas, did you see the meeting between—between your master and the young lady he had in his arms?"

"I—I did, your Royal Highness."

"And what did he do, Thomas?"

"I rather think—I fancy—but I should not like to speak positively—but I fancy he—he kissed her."

"Have you heard anything about these people whose arrival has been the cause of so much unhappiness. Tell me, and speak freely."

"Well, your Royal Highness, my wife, as she said she was sure you would not like to turn even a dog out in such a storm as this, has put the young lady and the other lady, whom they call Mrs. Joyce, in the blue room."

"Yes; well, go on."

"In the blue room, with her aunt, you see——"

"Her aunt?"

"Yes, your Royal Highness. You see, I have found out all the relationship between them, and I'll just tick them off to you on my finger ends. Who knows, said I to myself, but that it may be useful some day or other. So I got it all out of the post-boy, who was, so to speak, dug out of the snow; but he is all right now, your Royal Highness, and he's fast asleep before the fire in the hall, and——but I was forgetting. let me see, the odd-looking gentleman dressed all in black, is a Mr. Cuthbert, and he is a lawyer, or some such thing. The lady, as was so frightened, and wrapped herself up in all the shawls she could get, and then sat down on a heap of snow, is his wife; and Mr. Joyce is the sister of Mr. Cuthbert, and she's a widow, and an uncommon knowing one, too, I should think!"

"Yes, yes!" said the Princess. "Now, tell me who the young lady is?"

"Ah, your Royal Highness, I'm coming to her; and have left her till the last, because she seems too good to belong to any of them; leastways, she is very beautiful!"

"So I suppose. But you have not told me who she is!"

"I was just going to tell your Royal Highness," replied the garrulous old man, "that the young lady, by name Eva St. Clare, is the daughter of a sister of Mr. Cuthbert who is dead, and her husband likewise."

"You mean that the young lady is an orphan, and lives with her uncle and aunt?"

"Just so, your Royal Highness."

"Thomas, I have not asked you all I wished. Have you heard why these people came to this neighbourhood?"

"They were going to a place called Wingfield Hall, where Mr. Cuthbert has come into possession of the estate they say; and, as ill luck would have it, the post-chaise broke down just a few yards off this house."

"Thank you, Thomas," said the Princess, in the same hushed, hollow tone, that had first startled her humble follower, but to which he seemed to have become almost accustomed by this time. "Thank you, Thomas. You may go now, and I will take your place in a short time beside your master's bed."

"Don't—don't do that! You may trust him to me, for have I not learnt to love him since he has become your husband? Wait till he comes to himself a bit; he don't know what he says now, your Royal Highness, and it's not fair, like, to—to——"

"Be easy, Thomas. I can have but one object in life, and that is to be kind to—to my husband. Now leave me."

Thomas made a step towards the door, but he quickly returned, as though he had something to communicate which could not fail to bring comfort to his much-loved mistress.

"The Cuthberts talk of continuing their journey early in the morning, and when they are gone, let's hope that all will be well."

"Go, go, I implore you!" said the Princess.

The old man crept to the door, his head bowed in grief, and the Princess thought she might have spoken too hastily to him, and she called him back, saying, "Thomas, my old and faithful friend, I thank you with all my heart for all your kindness to me and mine."

She held out her hand, which the old man clasped between both his, but his heart was too full to allow him to speak, and he went hastily from the room, leaving the Princess a prey to a thousand conflicting feelings and emotions.

CHAPTER CLIX.

THE INNOCENT ARE MADE HAPPY AGAIN.

HOWEVER she viewed the events of the last few hours, there seemed to be nothing but misery in store for that brave but gentle heart.

What if the wild passion which now seemed to fill the heart and brain of St. Ives, was only the *consequence*, and not the *cause* of the insanity with which he was afflicted?

Could anything more terrible befall one so dear to her—as madness?

The princess trembled as she told herself that that masterly intellect—the sparkling conversation—the brave, courageous heart that had won her best and deepest affections, was henceforth to be eclipsed. But even that thought was more bearable, than the dreadful alternative that he loved another, and because she was the barrier between him and happiness—madness had seized upon him and struck him down.

The most profound stillness reigned in the house. It seemed to the Princess, as though all but she slept. As if the loved and the loving, the injured and the injurer, alike had dropped into repose, and that she alone watched the slow progress of that faint dawn, in all its cold beauty.

A sudden crash of glass alarmed her, and she sprang to her feet. A pane of glass was broken, and something lay on the floor, which appeared to be the missile by which the mischief had been done.

It was a jagged stone.

The princess stooped and picked it up, and found, that tied round it was a folded paper.

Full of curiosity, she opened it, and found that something in the form of a letter, was written upon it.

The first words would have removed any scruples with regard to the propriety of reading it—if she had been in a state of mind to have any—for those first words showed that the letter—if such it may be called, was addressed to her.

With a mixture of curiosity and anxiety, she read the following words:—

"To Her Royal Highness, Princess Mary, of the house of Stuart, and wife of Colonel Charles Miravel.

"The drama has opened—the play has begun.

"You by accident are one of the performers.

"What think you now, of your marriage with the ex-police officer, known as St. Ives—the highly intellectual and much be-praised Colonel Miravel? What think you now, of your prospects of happiness with such a man? You are not a stock or a stone; you have human feelings, and human affections, and will you tamely stand by and submit to seeing yourself the slave of the caprices of a man whose affections are as inconstant as the winds. Will you allow him one day to swear unalterable affection to you, and almost the next, to breathe such rank perjury in vows to another as might make angels weep, to see what perfidy there is on the face of God's fair earth? I warn you, Colonel Miravel—St. Ives, will scorn you. If you love him, your heart will be blighted. Look to it, Princess; there is one who would peril his life, to obtain one smile from you. Your husband loves already *another?*"

There was no signature to this epistle.

The Princess read it over twice, and her uneasiness increased each time.

"Treacherous, treacherous fiend in human shape!" exclaimed the Princess, as she crumbled the billet in her hand. "I see now, that it is the work of some disappointed, grovelling wretch, who fancied he loved me, but of whose very existence I was ignorant. My Charles is not himself; he still loves me. I will go to him. I will not care what words he gives utterance to in his present state. The first person his eyes shall encounter when returning consciousness asserts her sway over his mind and intellect, shall be his Mary—his wife."

The Princess hastily threw around her slight form an ample cloak, and hurried to the apartment where Thomas had told her he had had his master conveyed.

The morning had made its appearance with a sombre gloom. The snow had lost some of its pure beauty, and thick, threatening clouds were in the south. It was day, but the light looked only like the waning of sunshine.

The Cuthberts rose early, and after a brief conversation with Mrs. Joyce, Mr. Cuthbert announced his intention of giving up the further prosecution of his projected journey to Wingfield Hall.

The inclemency of the season, he said, which in London had not shown itself in all its terrors, was the sole reason.

He was more than profuse in his thanks for the hospitality that had been awarded to him and his family.

He left his address, saying how pleased he should be to see any member of the family who had rendered them such timely assistance in their hour of need, at his house in London, and then they left in the post-chaise that had been repaired.

And Eva St. Clare embraced the Stuart Princess, and seemed as though she would have said something —a something which trembled on her lips, but yet could not give utterance to it. Tears were in her eyes, and her long, silken eyelashes drooped heavily over those orbs of heaven's own blue.

The Princess was too kind, too generous to seem cold to her, although she knew that she was the subject of St. Ives' delirium. She kept telling herself that it was no fault of hers—Eva's—that she was beautiful, and that at that inopportune moment, when fever, with its wild impulses, was in the heart and brain of her Charles, she should have crossed his path, and had so become the chance subject of his wandering thoughts, for that poor wife tried to make herself believe—and perhaps succeeded somewhat that the illness of her husband was not in consequence of Eva's advent among them, but that he would have been ill at any rate.

And so the Stuart Princess, with her sweet gentleness of spirit, submitted to Eva's parting kiss, although a cold chill struck to her heart as her lips touched hers.

It seemed to her at that moment as though she were enfolded in the glittering embrace of a serpent.

She shuddered.

"I am an orphan," whispered Eva, "and my life is so lonely. I could love you so dearly, if you would let me. I seem as though I had seen your face in my dreams. I hope we shall meet again."

"Yes," said the Princess, and the cold shudder came once more over her, leaving her of a deathlike paleness, as if a hand of ice had been placed upon her heart.

"Farewell!" said Eva. "I hope when we meet again, your husband will be restored to you, and then you will be so happy—so very happy!"

The Princess glanced up quickly into the face of the young girl to see if she were trying to wring her heart; but the ingenuous, candid look, in those innocent eyes, rebuked her for the thought, and she felt that she had been unjust.

"I should like to hear that you were happy," added Eva, still loth to leave one whom she felt she could love; "if your husband were not ill you would be happy."

Eva bent down, and looked into the tearful eyes of the Princess, who made an effort, and then replied, "Yes, very happy!"

She smiled faintly, as she said these words, and then Eva kissed her cheek; she, too, tried to kiss the beautiful girl, but she could not: she only succeeded in preserving the set smile she had assumed, and during the unswerving lustre of which Eva went away.

And then there was stillness in that old rambling-house—such a stillness that even in the most distant rooms, at times, the high and fevered voice of St. Ives, as in his delirium he spoke strange things, might be easily heard, and she, the young wife—the wife of a week—the young mourner—for mourn she did—sat by him, and heard him say how madly he loved another, and saw how his soul was in his eyes when he looked for that other.

Was this all delirium? she asked herself.

But the man of skill came from the large city, and the battle between life and death began.

The strange fire was banished from the brain of St. Ives.

The blood coursed calmly in its wonted channels, and the words "he is saved" went forth in the house.

These words fell upon the heart of the suffering wife like words from heaven.

She retired to a small chamber St. Ives had set apart as her own particular little sanctum he had said, and where he should only consider himself a visitor.

By a couch she knelt, and prayed, and wept—by that couch, where a few hours before she had knelt, and bade adieu to that haven of hope, that harbour of refuge for her shrinking, foreboding spirit—where the future rose up before her, gloomy and spectral.

"Oh, heaven!" she cried, as she clasped her hands over her eyes. "Shall I, too, go mad? No, no! Why do I feel as though the daylight of my life had passed away?—why do I feel that I and happiness no longer walk smilingly together? For what have I exchanged what I was? Is it for a doubt that in itself is madness? Does my Charles love another? Heaven, heaven help me! Does Charles love another? How long shall I ask myself that fearful question? Oh, if he loved me not as he should have loved me—if he had a doubt of the truth of the seeming sentiment, why did he make me his, but to kill me with the knowledge of the doubt? If his soul was waiting until it met the congenial spirit that could bind him ever in the bonds of true affection, why did he make me his victim in the passing time, and ask heaven to be an accomplice in his guilt?"

She wrung her hands and wept still. Her deep sobs found an echo in that room.

Oh! how desolate she felt.

And then she rose and strove to calm herself.

She washed from her fair and gentle face the traces of her tears. Would that she could as easily have washed from her heart and brain the cause of them.

She looked in the tall mirror which had often told her she was beautiful, and practised a faint smile which she was to wear to her husband when he should know her. She felt she had a duty to fulfil, and so, with her hands crossed upon her bosom to keep down the rising sobs that strove to make themselves heard and seen, she left that little apartment in which she had passed many happy hours with St. Ives.

Noiselessly she glided into her husband's room.

As she entered, he turned his languid gaze upon her in a furtive kind of way, as though he would ascertain before hazarding a remark what were her feelings towards him.

The Princess looked at him with a sad smile that sank into his heart, and, after a time, she laid her hand upon his breast, and said in her own soft accents, "My poor Charles, you have suffered much."

He tried to shrink back, for he felt he had no right to receive so much affection from her.

"It was a dream—a dream only," he said.

She held one of his feverish hands in hers, and looked fondly at him.

"All was a dream," he went on. "I was mad, Mary—mad!"

He looked at her, tears were falling from her eyes; and, as he looked at her, the memory of all her love, all her generosity—all her heroism came back to him —he recollected how on that night of peril, when she thought death awaited them both, how she had spoken from the dictates of her heart, and had placed her hand in his, saying, "at least, my Miravel, we shall die together." He remembered also the thrill of delight that had passed through him when he heard those words, which convinced him beyond a doubt that her happiness was in his keeping. He saw in her the pure and beautiful being who had trusted all to him, and at that moment his heart returned to its old allegiance, and he held out his arms to her, and, with a cry of joy, she, who could love but once, and that for ever,

EVA ST. CLARE IN DEEP MEDITATION.

fell upon his breast and clung to him. Who else had she to cling to? He was her plank amid the surging waters—her oasis in the desert—her sun in darkness. Oh! what joy that he should open his arms to her and smile as of old upon her, and clasp her to his heart, and smooth her glossy hair, and kiss her eyes, and smile again, and look and speak in the rich, sunny manner which, to her, was a whole universe of delight.

"Charles! Charles, we must ever love each other as we now do!"

"Yes, yes! Oh, can you forgive me, dear?"

"Forgive you Charles? oh, do not speak to me of forgiving—I have nothing to forgive! I have been foolish, but now I will only let my heart sing for joy that you love me; and as the ivy twines its soft tendrils round the lordly oak, and can only give the unfading verdure of its foliage for the protection it receives, so will I, so do I, creep to your bosom, my

No. 51.—NIGHTSHADE.

Charles—my brave Miravel and cling around you. You are great, and gifted, and noble, in that nobility of nature which has heaven's patent for its own distinction, while I can but love, and smile, and weep, and love again. My Charles, you will ever remember that I am your own dear Mary, and that I love you."

Half smiling, half sobbing in the fullness of her joy, she clung to her husband—to her recovered treasure.

Who but he and heaven were now the arbiters of her destiny?

And then he would have spoken, but with one of the little childlike hands she stopped his mouth, and, shaking back the clustering ringlets through which her beauty was in glimpses only beaming, she spoke to him again, and as she spoke her soft cheek rested upon his, and he could see tiny images of himself in her lustrous eyes.

"Shall we not be ever happy, Charles," she asked, after a short silence.

"Yes, my Mary,—yes. I am unworthy of you—I know and feel that—but I will endeavour to preserve your affection. I do not think such a dream as that which has passed will come again. In your society I shall find a dearer charm than ever I can find in the flatteries of another. The events—if events they were, and not the mere spectres of a troubled brain—of the last seven days and nights shall be forgotten. I will try to separate the real from the unreal —yes, we will be happy."

"Happy, happy, happy!" said the Princess, as she rested upon the bosom of her husband,—if you love me ever thus! But oh, Charles! when I thought your love another's, I cannot tell you how dark and dreary the bright sun became to me! Oh, Charles! tell me that it was indeed madness with which you were seized when you called so wildly upon another to look and smile upon you."

St. Ives groaned; for too well for his own peace did he feel that, notwithstanding all his desire to return the deep, devoted affection of his wife, that a chord had been struck in his heart which had never before vibrated there, and a hidden chamber in his heart had been invaded, the existence of which he never dreamt of until Eva had entered there, and taken his very thought captive against his will and better judgment.

"Mary, dear, never let us speak of that terrible illness which nearly deprived me of my life. Let the future convince you that you are my much cherished and dearly beloved wife."

"Be it so!" was the soft reply. "Let us banish it and ever from our recollections."

CHAPTER CLX.

ST. IVES ENCOUNTERS TWO OLD ACQUAINTANCES.

The next day the sun beamed cheerily into the sitting-room, where were seated St. Ives and his happy bride.

There was a look of quiet happiness now upon the face of the Stuart Princess, as she there sat, and ever and anon turned her eyes upon her husband, who was busily engaged reading and sorting papers.

At length he pushed them all back, and looking at the Princess, he said—

"To-day, dear one, I shall go to London, and seek Claude Duval; he must already, in his own mind, have accused us of ingratitude for allowing so long a time to elapse without seeking him."

The Princess looked up.

There was a look of sadness upon the fair face which it was evident she tried hard to combat, as she said—

"Go, Charles, if you wish it; but do not stay away long. We are very happy; still, it is very natural that you should wish to mix somewhat in the world."

"Spoken like a wise woman!" replied St. Ives, half-laughingly and half in earnest. "I intend to go to the house on Hampstead Heath, and if he is from home, I shall, at all events, see your friend Lucy."

"Dear Lucy," exclaimed the Princess, "my mind has been so occupied with other things, that I had almost forgotten her. When do you go, Charles?"

"At once, I think. The day is fine, in half an hour I shall be ready to start."

As he spoke, St. Ives left the room, and the Princess, after several ineffectual efforts to repress them, burst into tears.

And yet she could not have said why she wept. There was a strange, undefinable feeling at her heart which told her that the freshness of her husband's love had departed from her; and then the agonizing question rose to her lips "Did he love another still, and had he only spoken to her as he did yesterday because he felt that he was bound in honour to make her as happy as he could do? Oh, heaven!" she sighed, "let me not become a burden to him for whom I have sacrificed everything! Rather let me die while he still loves me, than live long enough to know that he regrets having made me his wife!"

She had just time to dry her tears, when St. Ives entered the room, looking happy but absent—at least, so he seemed to the eyes of affection.

"Farewell, my Mary," he said. "Expect me home about six o'clock this evening. I shall call at the club as I go along; it is better that no one should miss me."

"Farewell, dearest," said the Princess, as she clasped her arms round his neck, and a choking sob, which she could not suppress, startled herself no less than her husband.

"Why, what is the meaning of these tears, Mary?" he asked, and there was a slight tone of annoyance as he spoke. "You surely do not wish me to retire altogether from the world?"

"No, no, Charles—you are great, and gifted, and noble—take your place among men, but when you are sated with the commendations of those who praise you for what you do, come to me and know and feel that I love my Charles—my brave and faithful Miravel—and we must always be happy."

"Of course—but why are you constantly repeating the same thing, as though you doubted the probability of our being always happy? Come, let me see a smile before I go, or that unhappy face will haunt me the whole of the day."

There was a bright upward glance of the blue eyes, and St Ives, as he imprinted a parting kiss upon his wife's lips, felt quite certain that he left her cheerful and contented.

* * * * * *

The morning had become dull, and cold, misty, and marrow-piercing in its intense chilliness, a morning not to linger at corners.

No doubt on the rich uplands of the far-off country it was bright, and cheering, and beautiful, but London was a region of damp frigidity, and the icy atmosphere, like a dome of frost-work kept down the smoky vapours of the huge city, and horses steamed through the streets carrying with them a portable fog, and frosty people chafed their hands, and chattered, while their teeth and their breaths made misty halos around them, inducing an appearance of every man being his own steam-engine, and boys fled hither and thither frantically, and soon got glowing hot to the immense envy of gouty old gentlemen, and elderly ladies, whose bustling days had long since passed away, and who had fallen back from the "robustiousnes" of former days upon the flannels and linsey-woolseys of the present, and Mr. Cuthbert blew upon his finger-ends, as he and his sister, Mrs. Joyce, pursued their way to the west end of the town, where the former had an appointment, and where the latter was to dispose of herself with looking at the shops until her brother joined her again.

But it must not be supposed that the brother and sister were so much attached to each other that the one could not keep an appointment without being accompanied by the other for the mere pleasure of each other's society, they had other motives for their proceedings which we will lay before the reader.

Mrs. Joyce, who was the recipient of all the scandal and all the gossip of the neighbourhood in which she lived, had, the day before, picked up the information that a Captain Granville and his wife had taken a house at the West-End, and it was supposed that the said Captain Granville and his wife intended to astonish their neighbours by the magnificence of their establishment and the grandeur of the balls and parties they intended to give.

Now, as is often the case, Mrs. Joyce had been misinformed, for Captain Granville was only in treaty for a house and had not actually taken it; but it was true that he had the intention of coming to reside in London as soon as he could make the necessary arrangements.

Now, we have had occasion to show how clever Mrs. Joyce was in—to use one of her own favourite expressions—putting things together, and making up a something which, if it did not really come to pass, at all events, served to while away some of the tedious hours of her existence. Hence it was that she had tormented her brother into taking her into the neighbourhood of the West-End almost every day since she had heard of the advent of Captain Granville, in order that they might encounter him—"quite accidentally, like"—and so strike up an acquaintance with one who would, perhaps, be of service to Eva, as she told her brother.

This is the reason she had given to her brother, but she had another which she kept to herself.

Mrs. Joyce had not been a witness to the strange events which had taken place on the night of the accident, and heard the wild ravings of St. Ives for nothing. As we have said before, she rejoiced in evil, and she had laid her own plans in order that Captain Granville and Eva St. Clare might meet again.

She had every reason to believe that Captain Granville was rich, and what, she asked herself, would one who loved so passionately not be induced to give for the sake of passing some of his spare time with the idol of his heart. Money was the end and aim of Mrs. Joyce's existence; to obtain that she thought no obstacle too difficult to surmount.

And so the brother and sister had walked on morning after morning, in the hope of meeting St. Ives, but hitherto they had been doomed to disappointment.

"Will he come—will he come, think you?" asked Mr. Cuthbert.

"Never fear—have patience!" At the same moment she caught him by the arm, St. Ives at that moment turned a corner of the street. His eyes were glancing up at the clouds, as though, for that day, he was taking his first look at the open air.

"Come, come!" whispered Mrs. Joyce, "let us accost him, or he will escape us now."

She placed her arm within that of Mr. Cuthbert, and they walked on so as to encounter St. Ives.

With what a careless air they trod the street. How engaged in conversation they were, and how little they looked as though they expected to meet Captain Granville; and, when they did see him, what looks of pleased surprise they bent on him to be sure. At least, Mrs. Joyce did all that boldly and unshrinkingly, while her brother was only a faint reflex of her manner.

"Why, brother, this is Captain Granville, the gentleman who was so kind to us all when the chaise broke down. My dear sir, how do you do. What a happy, unexpected meeting this is, to be sure; and how is your charming lady?"

"Ha, ha!" laughed Cuthbert. "How delightful! Beautifully warm—I mean—that is to say, what cold weather we have still! I and my sister, Mrs. Joyce, were out for a morning's walk. We come out in this season for the purpose of relieving objects of charity."

St. Ives shook hands, per force, with both of them. He said he was very glad to see them—that his wife was quite well, and he hoped that they were all well—all—all!" What an emphasis he placed upon the "all!" and Mrs. Joyce was not slow to remark it.

"Why," said she, with a slight, tremulous shake of the head, and a shivering kind of closing of the eyes, as though she could say much more than she would. "Why, I'm afraid of poor Eva. Perhaps you recollect her slightly, sir. She is our niece, and was with us upon the occasion of our having the pleasure of making the acquaintance of yourself and your amiable lady on the night of the accident. A slight-looking girl, sir, rather pretty—blue eyes, long, glossy curls, and teeth, as I often tell her, like little pearls. But, perhaps, you did not notice her. She fainted, or something of that kind. But, my dear Captain Granville, how we do bore you about our family matters. You see, we look upon you just like a friend. Never mind what I have been running on about—girls are strange creatures, you see, sir. I hope you are not vexed with me?"

"Oh, no, no! And so she—that is, the young lady—she is, you say—she is—I mean the young lady of whom I think I have some slight recollection——"

"I really hardly know what to say about our Eva. It's a pretty name, is it not? But, as I was going to remark, I scarcely know what to make of her since that night; she seems so dreadfully out of spirits, like. You don't think, do you—for I fancy you know everything—you don't think that—that she received a shock in any way, do you?"

"Do you mean she is suffering from any hurt she may have received?" asked St. Ives, in agony.

"Oh, no, not in the slightest degree! But, to tell you my candid opinion, she seems to me like one who was suffering from something saddening—one would almost think connected with the affections; but that cannot be, you see, because she knows no one—in fact, I think you were the first gentleman who ever said so much to her in her life."

St. Ives turned deathly pale, but, rallying himself, he said, with an effort, "Oh, let us hope it is nothing! As you say, it cannot be any hidden grief. The fine weather is coming, then it will be impossible for one so young and so beau—I mean that——"

"Exactly," said Mrs. Cuthbert. "My sister alarms herself unnecessarily. That is just my opinion, eh? We shall be so glad to see you in Ivy Lane."

"Delighted!" cried Mrs. Joyce; "and as for Eva—let me see, I don't think she has mentioned Captain Granville, has she, brother?"

"I I think not."

"She would scarcely recollect me," said St. Ives, smiling a faint, sickly smile. I hope she—that is, I am sure we shall be very happy to see you and your amiable niece, and my wife also. We intend taking a house in Park Street, and then I hope we shall often meet. I fancy I do recollect your niece."

"I thought you would, Captain Granville," said Mrs. Joyce, with a meaning look, "just a little, when you came to remember how you carried her from the postchaise into the house, and seemed so anxious for her to revive. What number in Park Street? Depend upon my calling upon Mrs. Granville. I do think I never yet met with such an amiable lady, and in her case, gentleness and amiability are so apparent. As we were saying only yesterday, my brother and I, what a difference there is between our Eva and your good lady, both so pretty, but yet so different. Ah! there is a glimpse of sunshine at last! We shall have a fine day after all, do you not think so, dear Captain Granville? You will remember us at home. Ah! I'm afraid you handsome men think too much of yourselves. We poor women are like moths—we don't know our own danger until our wings are scorched; but when they are, you can do anything with us,

Good day; we will call—No. 12, I think you said Captain Granville?"

St. Ives bowed. Mr. Cuthbert laughed, and stamped upon the pavement, and said how happy he was at having met Captain Granville, and hoped that it would not be long before he graced his humble home with his presence.

"And who knows," chimed in Mrs. Joyce, "perhaps a little excitement might be most beneficial to our poor Eva, who reminds me of a drooping flower, while, before that accident, she was as gay as a bird. But we are detaining you, Captain Granville; but when once I begin to talk about our Eva, I forget everything else. Good morning, Captain Granville – good morning!"

And so they parted.

St. Ives wandered on with some faint, dreamy consciousness of where he was going. He reached his club, and in a shaded corner of the reading-room, where a massive curtain might be so disposed as to hide him from prying eyes, he gave himself up to a whirlwind of thought. His lips at times moved very slightly, but he uttered no sound. Surely, if the invisible world sends its spirits of good and of evil amid the hearts and homes of men, to whisper heavenly suggestions, or to fan the smouldering fire of unholy passion, the air around St. Ives, as he sat in that dark recess, must have been heavy with shadowy shapes.

The war between the principles of good and evil had begun in his heart and brain.

To say that, previous to this meeting with Mr. Cuthbert and his sister, Mrs. Joyce, he had forgotten Eva St. Clare, was without the range of probability. The tempest of wild passion that had swept across his soul on that night of the accident must needs leave traces of its path. From amid the chaos of former serenity some fair flower of peace and goodness might struggle into life, but such a tumult of the passions was not to be forgotten. Shadowy and ethereal, like an aerial something that the imagination might fashion out of dancing atoms in the sunbeams—a thing of ideality—a vague principle of beauty and delight, rather than anything corporeal and life-like. The form, the face, the smile of Eva St. Clare had haunted him, but time might have faded the remembrance. The high-souled and generous woman he called his wife must, in time, have wound herself around his heart, and he would have admired her more and more as he found out, day by day, some new virtue and sterling quality.

But St. Ives was of the world, worldly.

Alas, for that poor Stuart Princess! little did she think, as she sat in her now lonely room—lonely, because *her* sun, as well as the natural sun, had left it all in shadow,—little did she think that, at the moment she was inventing new modes of showing how dear her husband was to her, and how entirely she had forgiven that sad episode of their existence, when she had sat beside his sick couch, and heard him call upon another in accents of love—little did she fancy that, at that very moment he—her Charles, her light, her life—was thinking of another.

CHAPTER CLXI.

ST. IVES LISTENS NOT TO HIS BETTER ANGEL.

"SHE is not happy—she is not happy! They who see her day by day have found out that there is something between her pure spirit and the light of its accustomed joy. They asked me if I remembered her? Remember her? Oh! she is memory—she is thought. Do they speak to me of eyes, form, and feature. Remember her! Oh, heaven, when shall I remember that I ought to forget her? And she will cross my path again —! know it—I feel it, and I shall look into her eyes, and I shall listen to the sweet music of her voice, and watch the shadowy grace with which she moves before me. I shall, perhaps, touch the little hands that I have kissed and held in mine; and I shall see the lips move gently to the utterance of words of customary greeting—the lips that I have kissed! I shall again live in the light of her beauty; but I must be cold and calm. I dare not look as I would look—I dare not speak as I would speak—I dare not wrestle with the world as I would wrestle with it for her love. She knows not—she will never know that I have held her to my heart, and I felt the soft flutter of her own, like an imprisoned bird. She knows not that fervent kisses have dashed the lilies from her cheeks. She will come before me, and with feigned courtesy I must speak to her. We shall meet, and we shall part again. In linked companionship with her shadow I shall follow her; but I must not tell her that I love her. No—no! that would be base. I did yield to the weak impulse of a moment, when I saw her first. When heaven and earth seemed to say, 'Take her, she is yours.' I yielded for a time, but reason has come back again, and I shudder while I tell myself that I adore her. And she, whom I have taken and sworn to love at God's holy altar—she whom I have made think that I shall, in my affection, be father, mother, kindred, all the world—she must not be desolate. She loves me. I thought I loved her. Oh, fatal error! I shall see you again, Eva! At once my blight and my blessing, and I must play a part, and seem to be happy. I must smile upon the ruin of my heart's affection, and feel that all is lost—while the world thinks me happy. Shall I fly? There is safety in that; but no—no! I dare not, I will dissemble; but—but if she should become another's. No—no! I could not bear that. I should go mad!"

St. Ives started. He heard a general movement in the room, and when he rose suddenly and looked around him, he was surprised to see the half-dozen persons it contained gazing upon him with looks of amazement.

He had spoken the last few words aloud, unconsciously.

"Are you ill?" Captain Granville; asked one.

"Ill? Oh, no—no! I am—I am not ill, I thank you; I am quite well. I am going home."

He staggered as he left the house.

"Am I deserted by my better angel?" he said, "that my feelings thus grapple, and get the better of me. What have I said? What have I said to attract attention? Oh, Eva, Eva, my fate—my fate. I totter on the brink of such a precipice, that my brain grows dizzy as I look into its awful depths. Home—home—home—yes, I have a home and *a wife!*"

It was late when St. Ives reached his home. He had wandered, heedless of where he directed his steps, and it was raining fast as he let himself into his house.

The Princess met him with a smile of welcome, saying, as she flung her arms around him, "So you have returned at last, wanderer. You have seen Duval, I know; or, you could not have stayed away so long."

"Seen Duval?" said St. Ives, looking up with the air of a man who has just been awakened from a sleep. "Seen Duval? Has he been here then?"

"No; but did you not see him when you called. Come, sit down dearest, and tell me all about Lucy, and how she is looking, and what she said; but——"

"Well?" said St. Ives, in a sharp voice.

"You are ill?" my Charles. "How blind I was not to see that at your first coming in. You are not well, Charles; there is fever on your cheek—there is a strange fire in your eyes. My Charles, you are suffering!"

"No, no! I am well—too well!"

"No; do not try to deceive me. I know you wish to spare me; but what eye so watchful as that of affection. There, lean your head upon my bosom, dearest, and I will not talk—perhaps if you sleep——"

"Leave me to myself. I wish to be alone!"

The Princess wound her arms about him, as she said gently, "Nay, do not fear for me dearest. I am strong and brave, as you have often told me; but do not treat me like a child, Charles. Do let me stay with you, dearest?"

As she uttered the last words she looked into his face as no one can look, unless the soul of a pure affection glistens in the eyes, and St. Ives lifted up his arms, and after one inefficient struggle with his "worser angel," he said slowly and distinctly, "Mary, your caresses are irksome, and to-day unwelcome to me."

The arms of the Princess relaxed their hold. A devotee clasping an idol in mad worship might so have shrunk back upon the whisper of some angel, of "That is not the true God." She released him from the best and purest caress that man can hope for. Her arms fell listlessly by her sides, and as she still knelt, she said faintly, "Charles! Charles!"

"It is spoken," said St. Ives.

"Charles, Charles! You do not—you cannot mean what you have just said. It is a jest—a very cruel jest - but no more, Charles. Speak to me."

Swaying back still upon her bended knees, so that she could hold out her hands clasped together, and yet not touch him, she waited to hear him speak again. She watched for some breaking smile amid the stormy cloud of his face.

In an agony of woe, she paused for him to raise her and press her to his heart, and tell her how he had jested with her holiest feelings, and how he hoped she would forgive him—but she waited in vain.

The madness of wild passion grew upon the face of St. Ives, until in the fair being he saw before him, his distorted imagination pictured the glittering barrier that kept him away from happiness—from Eva! The angel with the flaming sword that forced him out of Eden.

"Enough! Enough!" he cried, in a voice that echoed through the room. "You now know that I was mistaken when I fancied that I had given you my heart. That heart, I tell you—all the best affections of that heart, at least, were hidden and covered up until—until—oh, heaven! Touch me not!—Touch me not! I know not what I would say!"

"Charles! Charles! Husband?"

"Leave me! Leave me! While I can yet pity, and be sorry for you; but do not try to reason with me. The torrent of my passion is even now working with lashing fury at the frail bulwarks that keep it from, at one fell swoop, overwhelming all reason. Even now there is war within my heart and brain. I tell you, Mary, I am nearly mad, and would you make me worse by your caresses? Banish me from your thoughts. Live, eat, drink, and sleep. I will work for you—you are fair; but in me you have but a casket without its jewel. Why do you look upon me in that accusing aspect. I tell you I am mad enough already."

"Mad—enough!" gasped the Princess, and then, with one look of concentrated love and grief, she fell forward on her face at the feet of him who had sworn to love, cherish, and protect her—a wreck.

At the sight of the desolation and anguish he had caused that heroic girl, who had braved fearlessly so many dangers, St. Ives was almost beside himself.

He knelt by her side, and raised her head as he cried, "What have I done? What have I said? What busy fiend has been at work at my heart and brain to prompt me to kill my gentle Mary—my loving wife. heaven! Is she dead? Mary! Mary!—Speak to me, or I shall die."

But no sound came from those pale lips. The eyes were closed, and a slight spasm only shook the long lashes a little.

St. Ives pressed his hands upon his eyes, and tears at length came to his relief.

"And this is death," he almost shrieked; "and she died without one word of forgiveness, but I ought not to have expected it. I who have outraged every holy feeling. Alas! alas! Why did I know too late that I had not found in her my other self. Why, oh why, Eva, did you beam upon me in all your loveliness, when to love, to adore you, would be a sin. Farewell, dear Mary, we shall meet again in that land beyond the grave, but we shall not recognise each other, but you will pity me—you will be happy then, while I——"

He sprang to his feet, and elevating his hands above his head, he cried out, "In mercy, heaven, tell me if I be mad."

The Princess at this moment, with a shudder, looked up. She saw St. Ives dimly, and stretched out her arms to him. With a staggered step he tottered towards her. He knelt by her, and folded her in an embrace—she sobbed shriekingly.

"Hush—hush! oh, hush! Mary! Mary!"

"It—was—a dream!" she gasped; "a dream! Charles you did not, you could not, tell me that you did not love me? It was only a dream, Charles. Tell me it was only a dream."

"Only—a—dream? Let us try to pray, dear one! Pray for your wretched husband!"

* * * * *

We must now follow Mr. Cuthbert and his sister to their dreary house, in the upper part of which was situated what may be called the domestic part of the establishment; for on the ground floor Mr. Cuthbert carried on business, but up, up, far up the dark and gloomy staircase, encased in the rough ceiling of a dark and dismal room, and casketed as never such a jewel was before, was that priceless pearl, Eva St. Clare.

To Eva's room the affectionate aunt, then Mrs. Joyce, first directed her steps, to tell her fair niece the news that she hoped would give her much pleasure: viz., the meeting with Captain Granville, who had been of so much service in general on that night of the accident, and to her, Eva, in particular.

Eva had not been, to use Mrs. Joyce's own words, quite herself since that night. She had grown listless and silent, and she used to be a perfect sunbeam about that old dingy-looking house.

Eva was lost in thought when her aunt entered, and as she caught up her work, a radiant blush suffused her countenance.

Of what was she thinking? Perhaps, she had not asked herself the question, or probably she had asked it, and hence the cause of her unaccountable depression.

"Guess whom we met, Eva, this morning; a great friend of yours?" began her Aunt.

"A friend of mine, Aunt?" said Eva: "oh, you are joking! You know I am friendless and an orphan; but for you and my uncle Cuthbert."

But why did the little hand tremble, and refuse to hold the dainty piece of work? Did Eva guess by some intuitive impulse who her Aunt alluded to.

"Well, my dear, to judge from appearances, I should say that he wished to be a friend to you, for when I told him you were dull and out of sorts——"

"Oh! aunt, you did not say that to - to Captain Granville?" said Eva, with a distressed look upon her sweet face.

"Well, now, that is the very first time you have mentioned his name! I must confess that for the first time in my life, I was beginning to think you a wee bit ungrateful to Captain Granville; but, to be sure, you could not see how lovingly, I may say, he carried you from the broken chaise to his house, and how wildly he called upon you to open your eyes and speak to him; but, of course, all that only arose from the tenderness of his disposition: I have no doubt if I had fainted, he would have been quite as much distressed about me."

There was just the shadow of a shade of a smile around Eva's lips, as her aunt said these few words; but it was only like the lightning flash, it was soon gone, and again the old look settled about the mouth and eyes.

"Well, my dear," continued Mrs. Joyce, "you don't seem to care much whether we saw him or not, and here was I saying to myself, perhaps her life is dull shut up here with these old people—at least so much older than herself—I will ask Captain Granville to call, and——"

"Oh, aunt, aunt, he is not coming here?"

As Eva spoke, she sprang to her feet and looked about her, as though seeking some place of refuge to which to fly.

"And why not, my dear? Your uncle has business with him, and, in common gratitude, I think, we ought to be civil to him."

"Yes; but——"

"But what? Oh! I see, you feel ashamed to think that he carried you in his arms, and was so kind to you; but do not let that trouble you. I believe he has forgotten all about it by this time; so don't make yourself uncomfortable about such a trifle as that. Why, any man would have done the same."

"And—and his wife, aunt, is she also coming?"

"Well, my dear, I can hardly say. You see this is a business house, and we cannot expect a lady to come here; but Captain Granville said she would be very happy to see us all. But it is twelve o'clock, my dear; I must run away, and leave you to your own devices for a short time."

Mrs. Joyce left her niece, and as she did so, a well-pleased smile passed across her forbidding-looking face.

"The bait will take. Mischief is brewing. All goes as I would wish. I shall have some sport yet to enliven my dull life."

CHAPTER CLXII.

THE DESOLATION OF A YOUNG HEART.

WITH a staggering step, Eva made her way towards the door of the apartment as soon as she felt sure her aunt had descended the staircase, and locked it.

A strange mist seemed to gather around her.

She wrung her hands and wept. Her sobs came thick and fast. It was the very tempest of affliction, and more than once she called upon heaven to aid her; and why she so called she knew not; for what had she to fear?

Again the strange mist seemed to gather around her. She fought with it with her hands; she called once for help; and then the world seemed to step from her and to leave her for a moment a whirling atom in the vast realms of space.

"Oh, heaven! what is this that fills my head and brain," she sobbed. "What misty image of one whom I dare not name is this that sits at my heart in sullen majesty. Help me, heaven!"

Eva sunk down beside the chair on which she had been seated, and then she knew no more.

When Eva awoke from that trance, which had followed immediately upon the interview with her aunt, Mrs. Joyce, she, for the first time in her brief existence, knew the full significance of that word *alone*.

Solitude had ever to her had a loving charm; but now, as she rose and tottered to a seat, the very spirit of desolation seemed to be about her.

Yes, she was alone; and why was she alone?

Why did bitter tears course each other down her young cheeks? Why did she, like one upon whom the heavy hand of some sore affliction had been laid, sit like desolation personified, and weep? She knew not. Why she felt so lonely and depressed she could not tell; and she, with throes of anguish and many tears, had given it a tongue, and that was all.

"Alone—I am alone!" she cried. "No one loves me! No mother, with a quiet earnest smile, to tell me that she lives for me! No father, to call me his darling as he holds me to his heart! No brother—no sister! All alone—alone!"

And so she wept long—long and bitterly, until exhaustion crept over her, and she lay down upon her little bed and slept.

The shadow of St. Ives' spirit was upon her, but she knew it not, in he guilelessness and her innocence.

Sleep—sleep, poor spirit—sleep! Who would raise a hand to awaken thee to the rude world and all its shocks! Sleep—sleep gently.

* * * * *

Another week rolled by, and added its events to the muster-roll of the past.

Heaven only knows how many tears had been shed in that brief period, but there were some that angels might have caught and carried to their own starry home to set as gems in the blue firmament. They were shed by the Stuart Princess. Each drop was hallowed by a prayer—not a prayer for some boon from generous heaven—not a prayer dragged up from the depths of a selfish heart, lest some of the choice luxuries of this world should slip away in the fulness of time. No, the prayers of the Princess were that she might have strength to suffer. Could a purer aspiration reach the throne of Grace.

St. Ives, after that brief prayer, in which he had solicited the aid of his wife, had asked her to leave him to himself awhile, and had gone to a small room on the floor above, where he thought he should be quite alone.

As hour after hour passed by, and St. Ives did not rejoin her, the Princess rose, and made her way to the room which she knew her husband had sought.

She laid her hand upon the handle of the door, and then she pressed her other to her beating heart.

"Will he be himself again? Oh! will he love me?" were the questions she asked herself.

Then she turned the handle and entered.

St. Ives was seated at a table, apparently engaged in reading.

He looked up as the Princess entered, but there was a cold look about his face, and he seemed to have forgotten the sad scene that had taken place before he sought the privacy of that apartment.

The Princess advanced towards him, and laid her hand upon his shoulder.

There was an impatient gesture as St. Ives said:

"Well, what now? Am I never to be at rest? What would you? I am busy!"

There were writing materials on the table before him, and she could see that he had been sketching a face, lovely as a dream.

"Oh! Charles—Charles! is it thus that you have been employing your time?"

As she spoke, the Princess pointed to the female heads.

Instantly St. Ives gathered them under his hand and

pressed them to his heart, as though even her glance had polluted his idol.

"What then," he said, looking up into her face, "do you deny me even this simple pastime?"

"No, Charles! Henceforth you shall not dread my approach. You shall be happy in your own way."

As she spoke, she stooped down and imprinted upon his lips a kiss of pure and ardent affection.

And then she left the room with a hurried step.

St. Ives' first impulse was to follow her, for it struck him that her action was a strange one. He had expected reproaches, and met with love; but his evil angel must surely have been at his elbow at that moment, for, in imagination, he saw Eva holding out her arms to him, as she told him she was alone in the world.

"She has thought better of it! Mary has grown wise! She sees it is of no use to do battle with such a love as mine; and she is content to eat, drink, sleep, and enjoy life as I wish her! Yes, heaven knows, I will grudge her nothing, nothing but my love; and that is given to Eva."

The Princess sped down the stairs, how she did so she could never tell, nor stopped not until she reached her own room. Then she locked the door, and there was a look of unutterable despair upon her countenance, as she clutched at a glass of water.

"No, no! I must not faint! Heaven, is this death that I feel? No—no; I must not die yet! I must live; for he will one day want me to comfort and console him; but I must never meet him again beneath this roof! I must leave it and him! Heaven! that I should ever have to utter such words! To think that I, whom he has known so long, through so many perils and dangers, should be cast aside for the sake of a young girl, beautiful certainly; but what opportunity has he had of knowing whether her mind is capable of appreciating such a heart as his? She looked innocent—she looked sad—and she told me she was lonely. Oh! with what pleasure would I have extended my hand to the poor motherless girl, under other circumstances! But I cannot forgo his love, and still live beneath his roof."

The Princess rose and paced the room.

The rain was beating heavily against the casement, and the wind was making a mighty moaning, like the agitated sea afar off on some storm-beaten beach.

She strove to pray. To pray for guidance in the future, which, to her, was henceforth to be so dark, so dreary; but words seemed impossible, excepting to give utterance to her woe. To be sure, often and often had she repeated to herself these words, "Oh, how I have loved him! Oh, how I have loved him! And now he loves another, even as I loved him!"

"Yes, yes; I must leave him!" she continued, gazing round upon the different objects in the room, and which only served to remind her of him who was henceforth to be a stranger to her.

Then, in the confusion of her thoughts, for a few minutes she could scarcely make up her mind how she was to carry out her determination of leaving her husband's home. But that she must do so seemed an imperative necessity.

As she gazed around her chamber, the idea of taking some small collection with her of such things as she might justly call her own crossed her mind.

In a drawer she had a miniature of St. Ives, set with diamonds; a medal for services in the field, belonging to some of her ancestors; and there was her purse, too, of which, till now, she had never cared to count the contents. There were, too, some letters which she had from time to time received from St. Ives, in which he had breathed vows of unalterable affection. These she put by with a shudder.

"No, no; I cannot call those mine now!" she murmured; "he knew not his own heart when he said he loved me!"

Having put the things together, she intended to take with her, she made them up into a small parcel, and then she approached a table, on which were writing materials, and, drawing a small desk towards her, she wrote a few lines to her husband. They were as follows:—

"I release you from the consequences of, probably, the only error you have ever committed. No longer shall my presence annoy you. I will never again force my unwelcome caresses upon you; but should the day ever come when you long for the affection you have cast from you, we may meet again; but under no other circumstances will you behold her whom you call wife. Farewell!"

Having sealed her billet, the Princess rose, and took one more fond look at the miniature of him she almost worshipped.

Then she replaced it on the toilette table, and, taking the little parcel she had made in her hand, she once more looked round the room she was about to leave—it might be for ever.

Her eyes filled with tears, and she could see nothing distinctly, until she had dashed them away.

Again her eyes fell upon the miniature.

"I cannot leave it—I cannot leave it! it is all that is left to my widowed heart!" a tear fell upon the little gem, and she pressed it to her lips.

"Who knows—who knows," she whispered, "he may return to me!"

As she spoke, she placed the miniature upon her heart.

Then she opened the casement, and the rough night wind extinguished her light.

Still in the darkness she could still see the outlines of the various articles in the room which St. Ives had, with such apparent affection, had so elegantly adorned for her own particular use.

There were the tall mirrors and the chaste vases, where flowers of the costliest and rarest variety were ever kept blooming.

All these objects, so familiar to her, she saw more by the aid of memory than by the night-light about them; and then they seemed all to fade away like images in a dream, as she opened her door, and stepped softly down the stairs and reached the hall, and thence the little garden she had hoped to spend so many happy hours in.

The rain fell in scattering showers, for the storm was nearly over, and the wind, although it blew now and then in a wild, gusty fashion, was far from being so steadily violent as it had been.

The Princess shrunk a little from this contest with the elements, but she had made a determination; and it was not rain, it was not wind, nor the utmost that the tempest could do that would suffice to shake it.

No, it must not be supposed that the Princess, even in the affliction of her heart and the agony of her feelings, was wholly without a plan or idea of action.

It was a vague one, to be sure, but still it was one, and it saved her from the feeling that she was quite a homeless wanderer in the wide world.

No, she had resolved to seek those friends who had stood both her and St. Ives in such good stead, when they were being hunted by their enemies.

Wrapping closely around her a large cloak, the Stuart Princess almost flew across the meadows which divided her from the high road.

"Lucy, Lucy!" she kept saying to herself. "Yes, she will give me shelter until I can mark out some course for myself! Yes, she and her high-souled husband will give me protection without asking any questions, for they will see that I am broken-hearted.

A deep sob burst from her lips, which she tried hard to stifle.

"It is a long walk, but I can rest on the road; but I hope my departure will not be discovered until I am some miles on my journey."

Here the sound of horses' feet broke upon her ear, and the Princess, in fear, crept close to the hedge-row, in hopes that the traveller, be he whom he might, would pass her unnoticed.

Tramp! tramp! came the horse's feet; and just as the rider reached the spot where she had secreted herself, he pulled up.

"Who is there?" asked a voice. "Speak!"

For a moment the heart of the unhappy Princess beat so violently, that she thought it would burst its confines, and lay her a corpse at the feet of her interlocutor.

"Speak, whoever you are," again said the voice, in kindly accents.

There was no mistaking the tones of that voice once heard, they must ever be remembered.

They were those of Claude Duval.

For a moment or two there was a feeling of relief in the breast of the Stuart Princess to think that at the very commencement of her journey she had fallen in with the person who, of all others, she would wish to encounter; but, simultaneously with this reflection, came another, which took away all powers of speech —what was she to tell him? Was she to be the first to make Claude Duval despise her husband and his friend? She resolved, therefore, if possible, to so disguise her voice that he would not recognise her."

By this time Duval had dismounted, and stood close to the trembling Princess.

"Speak, I beg of you," he said, "and tell me if I can be of any assistance to you."

"You can, Claude Duval," replied the Princess, in an assumed voice.

"Ah, you know me?"

"For one of the sincerest friends of that unfortunate Stuart Princess, who visited your country only a short time."

"She is not ill, or in danger?" asked Duval, anxiety marking his every tone.

"She is not ill, neither is she in danger; but for her sake, I would beg of you shelter and protection for a few days."

"You could not have named a service more congenial to my feelings than in claiming my aid in the name of her you have mentioned. Can you ride?"

"Yes."

"Then you shall mount Nightshade, and in less than two hours you shall be beneath a roof where its inmates are only too glad to receive tidings of one whom they loved so well."

Duval first mounted, and then, assisting the Princess, she soon sprang up behind him, and both were cantering along the road at a brisk pace.

CHAPTER CLXIII.

CLAUDE DUVAL AND LUCY ENTERTAIN THE STUART PRINCESS.

IT was sufficient for Lucy that their new guest seemed to be intimately acquainted with that unfortunate Princess, with whose interest she and Duval had become so intimately mixed up, for her to receive a hearty welcome.

Lucy at once led her guest to her own room, where she intended to assist her in making those necessary changes in her apparel, for her clothes were draggled with mud, and she was cold, and appeared scarcely able to walk.

Lucy had removed the cloak, and was about to leave the room to give instructions for a meal to be prepared, when the Princess herself removed the veil which had so effectually concealed her features from Duval, and, with a cry full of anguish, she stretched out her arms, and but for Lucy's timely support, would have fallen to the floor.

"Merciful heavens!" exclaimed Lucy; "do I see aright! It is she herself! What brings you here and alone? Where is St. Ives—your husband? Has aught befallen him? Oh, speak—speak to me! Do not keep silence! What is the meaning of all this?"

Lucy gazed into the pale face of the Princess, but all was calm and still—she had fainted.

The cries of Lucy soon brought Duval to the apartment, who was as much at a loss as she had been to understand the meaning of the Princess's actions.

"Hush!" said Duval. "She is recovering. Take my advice—ask no questions. Of her own accord we shall know in time what all this means; for myself, I am at a loss to conjecture the cause of the Princess's conduct."

"Be assured her conduct arises from good motives, Claude. I fear that some calamity has fallen St. Ives, else why is he not with her?"

Duval held up his finger in token of silence, and then pointed to the Stuart Princess.

A flood of tears came to her relief, and then she placed her hand in that of Lucy, saying, "You think my conduct strange; but do not condemn me unheard; but, to-night, I cannot talk. I must rest and think.

"Be assured," replied Lucy; "that we are both convinced of the purity of your heart and intentions—only one question would we feign ask you to-night, and that is, is St. Ives well?"

"He is well?" replied the Princess, in a hoarse whisper.

"It is sufficient—our fears are now at rest. Tell us what you please. Keep from us what you please—we are and ever shall be your royal highness's devoted servants!"

"I know it—I feel it, and it was because I felt assured of that, that I sought you."

"Sought us?"

"Yes. I was on my road to walk to Hampstead when Providence directed your husband's course."

"Heaven be praised that I encountered you. I will now leave you to seek that repose you appear to stand so much in need of."

Lucy now assisted her guest to undress, and after seeing her comfortably reposing, she left her and sought Duval.

There was a look of inquiry upon Duval's face as Lucy entered the room, which she replied to by saying, "I fear me that there is some misunderstanding between the Princess and St. Ives."

"Let us hope that such is not the case," replied Duval; "and yet appearances favour the supposition, I must confess."

"We shall see—we shall see!" replied Lucy. "How thankful I am that she sought us. Even if it be as we suppose, who so likely as you to bring about a reconciliation between them, for St. Ives has the greatest esteem and friendship for you."

"Let us hope for the best. Probably, to-morrow, the Princess will be equal to talking over her affairs with you, and then we can see what is best to be done."

* * * * * *

Some hours after the Stuart Princess had left her home, St. Ives made his way to his wife's apartment.

He was not sorry, at first, to find that she was not

MRS. JOYCE PLAYS THE EAVESDROPPER.

there, for he feared to encounter the quiet, upbraiding of her eye.

He then set about trying to convince himself that she would soon recover from the shock and disappointment she had received, and that with ample means she might yet be very happy.

At length his eyes fell upon the little billet she had left on the toilette-table.

He tore it open, and read the contents; and as he did so, a look of indignation grew stronger and stronger upon his face, and at last he gave utterance to his wild fancies.

"I suspected as much; this is only a ruse. I knew she would soon console herself for the loss of my affection. She, too, in all probability, loves another, or why should she leave her home thus." How pleased he was; how he gloated over the idea that the Princess could not present quite such a contrast to him, and by fancying that the lustre of her character was somewhat dimmed, he thought that his own rubbed off some of its moral rust.

Had she not left him, he would have felt his spirit rebuked by her better presence; but, although he thus tried to reason with himself, a sense of his own littleness would creep upon him, and he could not but feel that all he was saying was merely an attempt to ease his own conscience, and that his wife really stood upon a pinnacle his grosser spirit might vainly hope to reach.

But still he was delighted to be able to tell himself that his wife had acted unwisely, to say the least of it, in withdrawing herself from the protection of her husband's home; and then he nursed his wild passion for Eva, and, with a false philosophy, called it the romance of his existence, and even stultified himself to the thought that it was the will of heaven.

And now, if we take but a passing glance at St. Ives, we shall see, how by regular gradations, he came

No. 52.—NIGHTSHADE.

to a state of mind that calmed itself down to a contemplation of what he knew was indefensible and unjustifiable.

We have seen how, at the first sight of Eva, on the night of the accident, one of those electric sparks of passion that come we know not how, lit up his heart, and how upon the impulse of that new-born but gigantic feeling, he spoke, and looked, and acted wildly. Then came the reaction, and even he, selfish as he was, from philosophy, walked back again from the flowery path of sinful dalliance, and yielded to the spell of goodness that encompassed his wife.

Serenity and peace had almost come back to him, and the image of Eva, although it was rivetted in his heart never to be displaced, was becoming more dreamlike and spiritual, and, if such a state had continued for a length of time, and he had not seen or heard of her until the charming freshness of youth had left her, St. Ives would have, perchance, smiled at some of the recollections of the past. But busy fiends were at work to hold him to his ruin.

He was not permitted to shake off the spell of fascination that a happy home would, after a time, well have borne comparison with, and so, when he met Mr. Cuthbert and his sister in the street, and he was all but told that Eva thought of him with some feelings akin to those with which he thought of her, it was as if the invisible spirits of mental commotion had suddenly waked up a whirlwind in his heart and brain.

Then ensued his strange abstraction at the club.

Then followed his still stranger scene with his wife—that scene that looked so like high-wrought insanity, and yet was not.

And then, again, he yielded to the charm of goodness, when he asked her to pray with him. But when he found, after brooding alone for so many hours over all that had taken place, that the Princess had left him, the halo of perfection which her moral character had around it, faded, and he began to try and convince himself that *fate* had much to do with his condition, and with a spurious kind of logic, he tried to persuade himself that what heaven permitted, heaven sanctioned; and so, from one step to another, he began to think of Eva more systematically than he had hitherto done, and in his mind the whole affair began to shape itself more and more into the aspect of a delicious and soul-entrancing intrigue.

"I will strive to see her," he said. "Why should I strive to shut out the daylight from my soul."

Such, then, was the state of mind in which we find St. Ives after having had a week in which to think.

And Eva—what of her?

She, too, had had a week in which to think.

Her first gush of sorrowful feeling had silenced down to one of deep melancholy.

Was this deep melancholy caused by the fact that she had met St. Ives on that fatal night—fatal both to herself and to him?"

The purity of Eva's heart would not permit such a question to suggest itself.

We will now, with the privilege accorded to us in our capacity of reader and writer, look in at the breakfast meal of the Cuthberts, where we shall find Eva looking paler than usual.

Mr. Cuthbert has got his favourite position with his back to the light—that is to say what little light found its way through the begrimed windows,—and Mrs. Joyce is stealthily looking at Eva, and Mrs. Cuthbert is fussing about, pressing everybody to eat until they wish her at Jericho.

"Now, Cuthbert, you really have eaten nothing, as one may say. Mrs. Joyce, take some more watercresses. You Eva—won't you?"

"There, there, that will do!" cried Cuthbert, pettishly. "I think, sister, Captain Granville left a card yesterday, it would be but proper to pay him and his wife a visit."

"Captain Granville?" cried Mrs. Cuthbert; "why that is the extraordinary gentleman everybody thought had gone out of his mind on the night of the accident. Don't you remember him, Eva?"

"Yes."

"Of course you do!" said Mrs. Joyce. "Poor fellow, he carried you into his house, and afterwards had brain fever, or something of the sort. Dear me, yes, to be sure, and a nice-looking man he is, too, but rather flighty! I mean, not very strong in the brain, you know; for, after all, who would have thought of anybody going crazy just for helping a young girl out of a post-chaise? I certainly think' however, as he has been so polite and condescending as to leave a card, we certainly ought all to go—all!"

"Yes, I think we ought all to go," said Cuthbert.

As he repeated the word "all," he looked stealthily from face to face to mark the effect that it had upon them.

Mrs. Cuthbert only elevated her eye-brows a little.

Eva placed her hand upon her heart, and looked a little paler. She did not know why she looked a little paler.

"I expect," continued Cuthbert, "that Captain Granville will become a client of mine, and therefore I hope none of my family will refuse me the favour of accompanying me to pay this visit—which is merely one of ceremony, and—and——"

"And by all of us going," said Mrs. Joyce, "it will not look particular upon the part of any *one*."

Eva spoke in a rather strange, agitated voice, catching her breath as she did so.

"Do you really wish me to go, uncle?" she asked.

"Yes, my dear, I should certainly like you to accompany us."

"Yes—oh yes, I will. I should like to see Captain Granville's wife again. She seemed so kind and gentle, and there was a sadness about the tone of her voice, which—which——"

Mrs. Joyce rose with vivacity. "Well I declare," she said, "it is nearly ten o'clock. How late we get up at this gloomy season of the year. But never mind, Eva, we don't care about the gloomy weather, as long as we know that in a few short months flowers and sunshine will soon be here."

"Yes," said Eva, faintly, "flowers and sunshine will soon be here."

"Now, brother, mind you are not late as usual," said Mrs. Joyce, as Cuthbert was leaving the room, "*we* shall all be ready in half an hour."

Mrs. Cuthbert descended to the lower part of the office for the purpose of giving some final instructions to a boy who revelled in the title of clerk, and then he went back again, to await, in the common sitting-room for the appearance of the ladies.

When St. Ives left his card at Jacob Cuthbert's, he had no idea then that his wife was about to leave him, and he believed that he merely wished to see somewhat of Eva as a friend, and that he and his wife could both make themselves useful to the young girl in the way of rendering her present dreary life more happy and contended.

Nothing more than this at that time entered into the imagination of St. Ives.

Now, however, it would not do for the Cuthberts, and possibly Eva, to return the call, and find him alone, so St. Ives resolved to put an end to such a visit, by himself calling upon Mr. Cuthbert, ostensibly upon business, but really to say that his wife had gone away to the south of England to visit some friends.

———

CHAPTER CLXVI.

ST. IVES' FIRST INTERVIEW WITH EVA AFTER THE ACCIDENT.

"I WILL call upon these people," said St. Ives to himself, as he walked rapidly in the direction of Cuthbert's house. My wife has left me to follow the bent of my own inclinations—it is her fault—yes, I will call, and perhaps I shall see Eva."

Hover around her, guardian seraphs!—whisper your better counsels in his ear! Leave him not to the devices of his own vain imagination. Is there no bright minister of human happiness to whisper to St. Ives, and prevent him paying that visit to Mr. Cuthbert's office.

Alas! there is not. He is there!

The murky house, with all its dingy accessories is to him a palace—a shrine—for is it not the dwelling-place of the idol of his heart—the divinity of his affections. Is not Eva there?

The boy, or rather the "clerk," is in the outer office. He has never seen St. Ives, and therefore does not know him. He thinks he is merely a chance visitor of Jacob Cuthbert, and he showed him into the private room, while he went upstairs to announce to his employer that Captain Granville wished to see him.

Cuthbert rose hastily, and at two steps at a time, descended the narrow staircase.

"My dear sir," he said, "this is indeed a pleasure. I and my family were thinking of doing ourselves the pleasure of calling upon you and your lady this morning."

"We should both have been most happy to see you and your amiable family, Mr. Cuthbert; but my wife, whose health, I am sorry to say, is very indifferent—has gone into Devonshire on a visit to some friends."

"Indeed!"

What a convenient little word that is; it commits us to nothing, and yet is considered to be a reply.

"Then I hope, my dear sir," continued St. Ives, "I may have the pleasure of seeing your family this morning all the same."

"Certainly, certainly; but really we are all so pleased with the great kindness of yourself and your amiable lady that we shall quite quarrel among ourselves, I fear, as to how to amuse you when you do us the honour of visiting us, which, as you are alone, we hope will often be the case."

St. Ives' face flushed a little, in spite of him, as he made answer that it was quite dangerous to invite so idle a man as he was to visit them, lest he should come too often.

"Come as often as you can, my dear sir, and we shall only be too happy and too grateful, for, after all, we are but humble people.

"Come often!" Those were the words that had the effect upon St. Ives. He was to be there, in the same house with Eva, very often; he was to become an *habitué* of the house—a familiar visitor, to see her as a privileged person.

The silence was broken by Mr. Cuthbert putting the apparently irreverent question to him—"Captain Granville, what do you think of investments in general?"

"Investments?"

"Yes, my dear sir! Now, as you have nothing to do, you had better come here very often, indeed, so that you can see and understand for yourself how with a small capital a large fortune may be made in no time."

How strangely the judgment succumbs to passion, and becomes at times but the poor slave of those sorcerers of the imagination that mar our choicest blessings.

St. Ives knew nothing, saw nothing, heard nothing, but that Mr. Cuthbert, a solicitor and a man of business, proposed some advantageous knowledge to him that had attached to it the rare advantage of looking into Eva St. Clair's eyes some half-dozen times a week, if he chose to do so. Could anything be more delightful?

"My dear sir," said St. Ives, "consider it as settled. I can easily come often."

"That will be a great point; but we will talk it over another time. And now let me hope that you will do the ladies the pleasure of walking up stairs, if it be only for a few minutes. This way, if you please; Mrs. Cuthbert and Mrs. Joyce are probably in the drawing-room with my niece—the young lady, you probably remember, who was with us——"

"Yes, yes, I remember," said St. Ives, almost impatiently. Why would this man and his sister persist in supposing that there was any doubt about his remembering that beautiful girl?

Mrs. Joyce, with such a wreath of smiles as she seldom wore, bustled forward, and taking both St. Ives' hands in hers, said, "How glad I am to see *you*, and how well you are looking! Well, this is an unlooked for pleasure. We were thinking of calling upon you and your amiable lady this very day. My dear sir Eva—bless me, Eva, where are you?"

St. Ives could not see Eva, but he knew, by the throbbing of his heart, that she was hidden behind Mrs. Joyce's voluminous drapery.

Mr. Jacob Cuthbert sat down on the nearest chair to the door with what he intended to be a smile upon his countenance, and rubbed his hands together.

Mrs. Cuthbert seated herself by the fire-place; she was always rather chilly, and St. Ives looked into Eva's eyes.

They stood together close to a window. The crimson drapery lent a glow to Eva's cheek.

St. Ives was compelled to hold by his left hand to the back of a chair, with the hope of composing his nerves and controlling the too evident agitation of the moment.

The right hand he held out to Eva.

For a moment only—a brief moment—there was a pretty hesitation, and then the little hand was quietly placed in his, and then the room, and everything in it, swam for a moment before the eyes of St. Ives; but his recovery was too rapid for the sudden delirium of feeling to be perceived by those present, and the little hand slowly slid from his, and he tried to speak—he tried to say some of the little ordinary common-place courtesies usual upon such occasions, but he could not. He could only look at Eva, and his soul was in his eyes.

A new light was in the eyes of the impassioned man—a flush was upon his face.

He was in the presence of his heart's idol—she whom he loved with a passion so pure and so spiritual—for so he called the feeling to himself—that he had at length persuaded himself that heaven would hallow it.

He breathed the same air that she breathed—he heard her voice at times in soft, murmuring music. Content—rich, measureless content, for a time, sat on the heart of St. Ives, and during that time he was happy—something more than happy.

And gently he drew closer to Eva, and joined in the conversation that was going on. Like a flood-gate he opened the stores of his mind, and in the full tide of rich eloquence, he talked of all things.

And so an hour passed, and the visit ended; but Eva had drunk in the poison of an eloquence, the clinging charm of a manner that was to influence her whole future life. Admiration, dread, respect, were struggling together in her breast, as she thought of St. Ives.

Eva did not shake hands with St. Ives when he rose to leave. She was *afraid now;* but she looked at him, for she wanted to preserve the look of that glowing countenance, so full of the spirit of genius, and she bade him good day gently, and forgot even to make inquiries about the gentle wife of his for whom she fancied she had such a kindly feeling.

* * * * * *

The morning was bright and fair; the sun shone with a ruddy radiance upon the Serpentine; and a south wind had tempered the keen air, that else, with a wintry chill, would have made rude holiday through the tall trees of Hyde Park.

There was a spring-like look about everything, early as it was in the new year. It seemed as if the young and jocund summer had, in passing mirth, knocked at the door of the huge world to give promise that it was coming soon. Some of old winter's icy chaplet buds had fallen before that soft south wind which, in fairer climes, had been visiting banks of violets, and gently straying where "the wild thyme grows."

A screen of light fleecy clouds cowered between the world and the deep blue heaven, and the small lambent flame of joy that the spring-time was coming, was lit up in the heart of many a shivering piece of poor, suffering humanity who had battled long with the dreary season.

And so St. Ives reached the little bridge, and leans upon it, and a lonely man he is.

He and the great world never had much in common, and now they have less, for he knows and feels, that of all the myriads of human beings whom he sees floating down the stream before him, there is not one to whose faintest perceptions he could justify himself.

He is cheating his own intellect as he there pauses and reflects.

How he hugged to his heart that one conceit, that the Princess, his wife, had left him to gratify some wish of her own—perhaps to seek some former discarded lover.

But now he ceases to gaze upon the water, and he paces up and down the walk with anxious steps. "Will she come? Will she come? She told me, when last I saw her, that her life was lonely, and that she had not a single friend to turn to for advice, and I promised to be a friend—a brother."

These were the words that came from the lips of St. Ives as the climax of his hopeful cogitation that she would come.

On the evening previous he had contrived to slip into her hand at parting, a little billet, asking her to meet him on the spot where he now was, as a friend; and it was because he thought she was guileless and innocent that he thought she would come. Yes, St. Ives based his hopes, not upon any proneness to wrong-doing in human nature, but upon the god-like sincerity—unsuspecting innocence, of Eva St. Clare. And so, as to and fro he paced, he kept telling himself that she would surely come.

The hour that St. Ives had named in his brief note had come and gone, and yet Eva had not made her appearance.

His heart sank within him, and he paled as with a sickness of the soul as he told himself it was a mad hope. She will not come! A very—very mad hope, indeed, - she will not come!

He buried his face in his hands for a moment, to shut out the glare of the daylight.

Suddenly he raised his head, determining to return to his lonely home.

But how his heart beat! How his colour fled! She was standing a few paces from him!

Gently and slowly, like some fair being from another world, upon some mission of tenderest charity, she moved towards him, and there he stood, unable to approach her even by one step. Her evil angel!

How beautiful she was!

She came near to him and spoke.

"Against my judgment, Captain Granville, but with faith in the honour of a gentleman, I am here. You wrote to me—you said you were unhappy—you promised to be a brother to me—and I am here to comfort you."

He looked into her eyes. Oh, what a world of witchery to him was there! Honour, remorse, all were forgotten as he so gazed.

The bright flush came to his cheek; the sunny lustre beamed from his eyes, even as it had done upon his first visit to Jacob Cuthbert. Some kind spirit lent him music for his tones, and St. Ives was, once more, the brilliant and eloquent speaker.

"How good, how kind of you," he said, gently, as he took her hand. "How trustful, indeed, it was of you to come!"

"You told me in that letter, which I thought afterwards I ought not to have taken," said Eva; "that you were unhappy; and I thought that your wife, whose health, you say, is so indifferent, might be worse, and that you were sad; and so——"

"And so you came to comfort me, dear Eva?"

He called her Eva now.

"But I did not want to speak about my wife, Eva," St. Ives continued. "She has—has deserted me!"

"Deserted—deserted you?"

Eva, in her innocence, scarcely understood the meaning of the words; but, in a moment, all her kindly sympathies were enlisted in St. Ives' behalf; and indignation, as far as her gentle heart could experience the feeling, rose up against the already too much injured Princess.

"It is a sad story, Eva, for youthful ears to listen to; but, when I tell you that I am lonely, you will, perhaps, learn to pity me. My wife never loved me, Eva!"

"Oh, impossible!" said Eva; and then checking herself, she added, while a deep flush overspread her countenance, "if she had not loved you, she would never have married you."

St. Ives, out of his rich imagination, soon converted a romance, which he hoped would meet with the full credence of the young girl; and, while he hoped to enlist her pity, preserved to himself the joy of transforming that feeling into love.

"Alas, alas!" said St. Ives, "we neither of us knew our own hearts! I, too, was mistaken!"

"Sir! But let us not talk of these things. I knew not that you wanted to speak to me on such subjects. I must leave you now. I did wrong to come."

"No! No, Eva, stay! You told me you have neither father, nor mother, nor friend. I, too, may say the same thing; let us be to each other true and sincere friends! I do love you, Eva, but it is with a pure and holy love, such as the angels in heaven have for one another! Let us meet—meet often, and commune with each other, and forget the world, with all its troubles and disappointments! Tell me, Eva, will you be to me my better angel—my sister?"

"It cannot—it must not be, Captain Granville!" said Eva, in a choking voice. "Heaven forgive you for the sorrow you have caused me—the joy you have robbed me of! Farewell! We never meet again in private!"

Eva St. Clare turned and fled, nor paused not until she found herself amid the bustling multitude, who scarcely heeded her, as she passed by them a prey to the most agonizing thoughts and reflections.

CHAPTER CLXV.

ST. IVES INDUCES EVA TO WRITE TO HIM.

HALF maddened with himself for his precipitancy, heart-stricken by the recollection of the agonized look upon Eva's face when she turned and fled from him, St. Ives could not sleep until he had written to her.

How he reached his home he knew not, neither did he observe the curious gaze of the passers by, as they made way for him to pursue his onward course.

He did, however, reach his home—now so desolate, where there was not one heart to whom he could turn for sympathy; for she, who would ever have been a power of strength, and who would have loved him through good and ill, had he not broken her heart, and forced her, as it were, to seek another home.

How dreary and silent everything seemed to St. Ives, as he crossed the threshold of his home.

He went at once to his little dressing-room, where he knew he always kept writing materials; and, drawing them towards him, he sat down, and wrote the following letter to Eva:—

"EVA,

"It matters not that I simply place your name at the head of this letter. I would fain have written dearest Eva; but, even that term of endearment, appears no more affectionate than does the one little one; for, to me, it is surrounded of itself by a halo of endearment.

"Eva, did you part from me in anger? Oh, if you had but stayed a few minutes longer, you would have known then that there was nothing to fear—nothing to shrink from in my love! You misunderstood me, dear one! Have I not already told you that I have nothing in common with my fellow men; and, therefore, when I told you I loved you, I meant not that I loved with an earthly love! Mine is an affection which is—must be—hallowed by high heaven! It was that word 'love' which misled you, Eva! Let me be to you a dear friend—one who wills only your happiness—could I then be so base as to seek to make you other than you really are good, pure, and trusting?

"In mercy answer this,
"CHARLES GRANVILLE."

This wild, and somewhat incoherent letter, St. Ives despatched by a special messenger; and, in a state of mental anxiety, amounting almost to frenzy, he awaited the answer.

He believed, then, what he wrote. He fancied that he was *not* trying to deceive Eva St. Clare. He tried to believe—nay, he did believe at that moment, that the feeling he had for Eva was pure and holy!

Alas! clever as he was, intellectual as he was, how little did St. Ives know his own heart!

In the meantime poor Eva received St. Ives' letter.

At first there was a feeling at her heart which prompted her not to open it—but then she thought to herself that perhaps it was only an apology for his strange and startling confession, and she could not but tell herself how much happier she should be to think of him kindly than with anger.

Poor Eva had no friend to whom she could turn, and say "what ought I to do under these circumstances?" No mother who, if she had been a wise counsellor, would have at once shown her the impropriety and the danger of answering such a letter; but having no one but her own innocent and gentle heart, and her small, very small experience of the world to guide her, she did sit down and answer it.

There was a tumult at her heart, as she penned her note in the following words:—

"CAPTAIN GRANVILLE,

"You ask me if I parted from you in anger. Such a term cannot apply to the feeling of sorrow which I experienced when I found that one whom I hoped and believed it would be safe to admire and esteem, must henceforth be a stranger to me. You say that I misunderstood you. I am glad to think that I may have done so; but I cannot reconcile my mind to accept the love you offer me. I am very young—and may be wrong—but being so friendless, I must try to keep the straight, onward path that is clear before me, and neither wander to the right nor to the left."

"EVA ST. CLARE."

After she had written this letter, Eva felt much more light-hearted. The thought certainly did suggest itself, once or twice, that perhaps she had better not have answered the letter; but then again she fancied that it would at once put an end to a correspondence which her own innate delicacy told her was not a desirable one.

With what a feeling of delirious joy did St. Ives press the little billet to his lips—even before he perused it!

And then he read the letter—and, strange to say, he was not disappointed to find that there was no sign in it to show that he was other than a friend to that friendless girl.

"I would not have her other than she is," he said again, pressing the letter to his lips and heart; and never from my lips shall she hear one word that might not be whispered to a seraph in paradise. My Eva, my worshipped idol, you shall still be my pure, my better angel. I will speak to you only about all that is excellent and beautiful in art and nature, and all will be well—yes, all will be well!"

St. Ives rested his face on his hands, and gave himself up to the exquisite joy of living over in anticipation the happy hours he intended to spend with Eva, in storing her young imagination with some of the treasures of knowledge with which his own intellect abounded.

Old friends, old pursuits were abandoned—even the Princess, his wife, whom, at one time, he fancied he loved so devotedly—all, all was forgotten in the one bright perception that he loved Eva St. Clare!

The bright and beautiful temptation no longer looked like one. He had passed all that, and the love that he had at one time shuddered at, and scarcely dared to whisper to his own heart, was now the only, and the cherished companion of his thoughts.

Again he resolved to write to Eva.

"EVA,

"Thanks, a thousand thanks for your reply—cold and measured though it is. You seem to censure me, dear one, and for what? I have frightened you by telling you that I love you, but when I explain to you that love is not incompatible with your innocence and purity, surely it will become a blessing to you, and not a source of unhappiness. There are so few joys in this life, dear girl—do not let us refuse the one—which heaven itself, in its mercy, has given to us —to love one another, even as the angels love in heaven. God's blessings hover around you, and may gentle dreams and happy days be yours, ever and ever!

"From your own
"CHARLES GRANVILLE."

Eva read this letter with fear and trembling.

She read, and she wept—wept long and bitterly.

There seemed, even to her inexperienced mind, to be a wild incoherence about it, which, while it spoke of sincerity and honour, said little for the endurance of the calmness of mere feeling.

She looked up, half-blinded by her tears, and in a soft voice, she communed within herself—

"Oh, if I could but think," she said, "that Captain Granville might be to me the dear friend he says he will! What is this dread feeling? Of what am I afraid? Where does friendship end and love begin?"

Eva St. Clare little knew the extent of the intricacy of the questions she had, in her innocence, propounded to herself; for who shall tell us—who can tell us—where the ever-placid stream of friendship ends, and mingles with the turbulent ocean of passion? Alas, Eva! subtler brains than ever yours or St. Ives' have been submerged in that torrent, and in the confluence of those waters have sunk to rise no more.

Eva did not answer this last letter of St. Ives'. It did not require an answer, and so she did not intend to frame one.

If she had been less pre-occupied, Eva would have noticed that her aunt, Mrs. Joyce, left her much more alone than she had hitherto done; but as Eva had so much else to think about that was so new and strange, and yet, it must be confessed, so delightful to her, she did not notice many things which she might otherwise have done.

At first she thought that she should like to carry that letter about with her; but then she feared that, by some mischance, it might perhaps fall into the hands of some one for whose eyes it was never intended; so she took from her bosom a small key, which was attached to a chain, and unlocked her little writing-desk, where reposed that other note which St. Ives had written, so incoherent, yet so full of sophistry.

Eva read that other letter again; and this time, although she knew every word of it previously by heart, it did not seem so impossible, she thought, to love as he, St. Ives, said he loved her.

Alas, alas, Eva! what would not have been one hour of a mother's love and counsel to you now?

But Eva was friendless and alone, and so she failed to detect all the danger which lay in those few glowing words.

In the meantime, Mrs. Joyce had not been idle, or an unobservant spectator of the progress of events.

Since the night of the accident, she had been fully aware of the feeling which actuated St. Ives, and she determined to make that knowledge profitable to herself.

She did not start with the idea of standing by, and seeing her orphan niece made the sport of an idle hour, then to be cast aside and forgotten. No; she was too well-versed in such matters, not to know that the feeling St. Ives had for Eva was an all-enduring one, and that, perhaps, woman was never loved so well as was she by St. Ives. But still, she had another reason for permitting the affair to go on, and that was the hope of making money by the transaction.

She had every reason to believe that St. Ives, or Captain Granville, as he called himself, was a rich man, and that if she helped him as far as she could in getting Eva to return his love, gratitude for such good service would undraw his purse-strings, and she should, after all, make a good thing of the transaction.

And then, again, she reasoned with herself, would not Eva be well cared for as long as she lived; and as virtue and honour were things unknown to Mrs. Joyce, excepting as names, she had no qualms of conscience on the subject.

So Mrs. Joyce resolved to wait, and watch the progress of events, determining, in the meantime, to make the meetings between St. Ives and Eva as easy as possible, to strip them, in fact, of everything that looked like difficulty.

Hence the many and pressing invitations to St. Ives to call upon them at all times, and the understanding that if one member of the family was out, another would be at home, and equally pleased to see him.

And St. Ives, superior as he was to these people, fell quickly into the trap, and did call frequently, and on one of these occasions, at parting, as we have seen, he slipped the first little billet into the hand of Eva.

He thought, and Eva thought, that no one saw the action; and it was fear that made Eva conceal it, although at the time her better angel whispered to her that she was doing wrong by so concealing it.

But there was another person who saw the little clever manœuvre, and that was Mrs. Joyce.

"A letter," said that lady to herself. "I must read it. I did not think they had got to that length yet."

We have seen with what mingled feelings of pleasure and pain poor Eva read that first billet from St. Ives; and how she, in her innocence and goodness, answered that letter, which answer she went out herself to post, having previously taken the precaution to lock up St. Ives' letter in her little writing desk.

Mrs. Joyce met her niece, as she was going out, with quite a radiant smile—or at least what she intended and thought was radiant, but, in reality, it was merely a distortion of her usually plain features.

"Oh, she has written a reply," was the mental observation Mrs. Joyce made to herself; then, addressing Eva, she said:—

"So you are going out, my dear? I am glad of that, for I think you spend too much time in the house; and you see, dear, I can't manage to go with you, as often as I feel I ought. But never mind; perhaps I shall have more time some day. Why, what is the matter now? I declare you look, for all the world, as if you were going to cry. There, go along, and mind you bring back a happy face with you!"

Mrs. Joyce bustled away, for it was no part of her plan that Eva should make a confidante of her in any way. That would ruin everything; and so she turned away from Eva, who at that moment, softened by her aunt's unusually kind manner, would have told her all her perplexities, and asked her to guide her in her present difficulties.

But her aunt was gone; and then poor Eva felt that the few words she had written to Captain Granville would be sure to put a stop to anything like a renewal of the same subject between them; and so she resolved to post her letter, which was to be the means of placing her friendship for St. Ives upon a very different footing.

Mrs. Joyce watched Eva out of sight, and then she put on a look which she thought full of penetration and discernment.

"Now for the letter," she said to herself. "Silly little fool, to suppose that no one has a key to her desk but herself!"

Mrs. Joyce hastened up to the sitting-room, and taking from her pocket a small key similar in every respect to the one Eva had attached to a chain she wore round her neck, she saw the letter St. Ives had written asking her to meet him on the bridge which crosses the Serpentine, in Hyde Park.

Thus it was that Mrs. Joyce had really been a witness to that short, and, on St. Ives' part, passionate, interview on the bridge; but neither St. Ives nor Eva had seen her.

When Eva, on that occasion, had rushed from the detaining grasp of St. Ives, Mrs. Joyce was close to the spot, only concealed by the trunk of a tree.

"A fair beginning—a very fair beginning!" she said to herself. "This will not be their last meeting, or my name is not what it is."

CHAPTER CLXVI.

THE STUART PRINCESS MAKES A CONFIDANTE OF LUCY.

THE sun shone brightly through the casement of the chamber in which Lucy had left her guest the previous night, in order that she might seek that repose of which she seemed to stand so much in need.

It is late in the day, and the two friends—for such indeed they are in the highest acceptation of the term—are seated in that same apartment.

It is the Princess who is speaking.

Her voice is still soft and musical, but she is pale, and there is a look of suffering about the sweet mouth that may well fill Lucy with anxiety.

They have been sitting in silence for some time, and Lucy is making vain efforts to concentrate her thoughts upon the needlework before her.

The silence is broken at length by the Princess.

"Lucy, dear; I have a sad, sad tale to pour into your ear; but it must be told, or you will think that I do not deem you worthy of my confidence."

"Oh, no, no!" replied Lucy, casting her work from her. "Do not so misjudge me. I would fain hear the cause of your seeking us—not from idle curiosity; but so that I might be able to comfort you, dear friend. Nevertheless——"

The Princess shook her head sadly.

"No one will be able to administer comfort to this broken heart. The idol I had set up in it has shattered it, and left me the fragments to live over again the remembrance of the past."

"Alas! alas!"

"A few words will be sufficient. I cannot speak upon the subject at any length. When I tell you——."

The Princess paused, and a paleness as of death overspread her countenance.

"Hush! hush! Oh, do not speak of it. It moves you too much. I was wrong to require it," said Lucy, thoroughly alarmed.

But the Princess recovered herself with an effort, and then she said gently,—

"Yes, I must tell you. St. Ives—my Miravel—my husband—loves—another."

As she uttered these words, the Princess sank apparently lifeless to the floor.

* * * * * *

If a cannon shot had suddenly been fired at Lucy, the effect would scarcely have been more startling than had been those few words spoken by the unfortunate Stuart Princess.

Lucy raised the pale face and gazed with sorrow upon the ravages which grief had in so short a time made upon that sweet face.

"Alas! alas!" she murmured to herself, "ought I to desire to bring her back to life, when her existence henceforth must be but one living death?"

The Princess moaned faintly.

Lucy flew to a table on which was a glass of water, and sprinkled a few drops upon her face.

The cool drops seemed to revive the Princess, and in a few minutes she opened her eyes and gazed about her.

"Ah! I remember," she whispered, as she clasped her hands over her eyes. "I remember—I told you—that—I told you why I had sought the shelter of your roof."

"Yes, yes, dear; but do not think now. Try to sleep, and something may be done to make you happy again."

"Never—never!" was the low-spoken reply. "He can never be to me the perfect idol he once was; for my trust—my faith are gone. I may—I must love him while life remains; but, oh, Lucy, I never knew till now that there was as much reverence and respect as love for him in this poor heart; but now only love remains—that, I suppose, never dies!—respect, reverence, esteem, can never return, I fancy, when once they are lost."

"Oh, do not talk so despondingly, dear friend," sobbed poor Lucy, now altogether overcome by the tale of wrong she had listened to. "Who knows but that there may be some mistake. You may have been misinformed. The world is only too ready to separate loving hearts; and St. Ives——"

"Hush! no more," said the Princess, and as she spoke there was a look of command about her which Lucy had never before seen. "Hush! no more. No living being could have made me think *him* faithless. I know it of my own knowledge—know that he thinks and dreams, and lives but for another."

"And that other?"

"A fair and gentle girl, apparently. One whom I would have loved and trusted as a sister."

"Alas! alas!"

At this moment a footstep, which Lucy knew to be Duval's, was approaching the room in which the two friends sat, and the Princess raised herself from the floor, and sank into a chair which Lucy placed for her.

"I do not ask you, Lucy, to have any secrets from your husband. You may—you ought to tell him, perhaps, as much as I have told you. But, remember, I want no one to interfere between me and Colonel Miravel."

Lucy had just time to assure the Princess that her wishes should be obeyed, when Duval entered the room.

In his hand he carried an open letter, which he held towards Lucy without speaking, fancying that the Princess slept, as she was perfectly still.

Lucy took the letter without speaking, and found it contained only a few lines.

"If Claude Duval will seek the death-bed of one who has injured him, and accord his forgiveness to a penitent, let him follow the man who is the bearer of this epistle, and he will, while imparting comfort to the dying, receive valuable information which will benefit one he loves."

There was no signature to this mysterious billet, and Lucy, after she had read it, looked up uneasily into Duval's face as she said,—

"You will not heed this mysterious billet, Claude?"

"Indeed, Lucy," he replied, "I feel very much inclined to do so. What harm can there possibly be. You know, Lucy, dear, fear is not one of my failings; and who knows, it must be of you, too, that I am to hear—something connected with you—so you will consent to let me go?"

"As you will, Claude," was the reply; and she took that opportunity of leaving the room with Duval, to impart to him as much as she herself knew of the Stuart Princess's affairs.

"Impossible! I will not—cannot believe it," were Duval's first exclamations—and then a bright flush of shame tinted his cheek, as he called to mind that he, too, had forgotten the fair and loving wife for a few minutes, when dazzled by the blandishments and beauty of the captivating, but frail Duchess of Cleveland.

But there was no time to waste. The man who had brought the mysterious billet to Claude Duval was showing signs of impatience by every now and then kicking the palings against which he leant a violent blow with his heavy horseman's boots.

Claude Duval descended to the court-yard, and after speaking a few words in a low tone to Blossom, to the effect that nothing was to induce him to leave the old mansion on the heath during his absence, signified his intention to follow his guide.

The man made no reply, but prepared to walk at a brisk pace towards the metropolis.

"Stay," said Duval, addressing his unknown companion. "Stay; I prefer riding. Wait here for me. I will join you again in a few minutes."

A kind of grunt was all the reply his silent companion vouchsafed to this remark of Duval's.

Claude was as good as his word; and in less time that appeared necessary, he was seen issuing again from the courtyard of the mansion, mounted upon the gallant Nightshade.

The man took a keen glance at rider and horse as they approached; and if Claude Duval had been only a few paces nearer to him, he would have heard the words,—

"Just what I wanted! I shall make a profit upon the horse, and no mistake."

Oh, what a beautiful morning it was on which the gallant Claude Duval thus rode along a rural lane leading from Hampstead Heath!

A thousand birds seemed to follow him along the shadowy road, each straining its little throat to produce the more melodious music.

The sweet perfume of the hawthorn and the wild honeysuckle loaded the air, while in the far distance the lowing of the cattle made up a kind of bass to the songs of the birds.

There was a turn in the lane at this moment, and strange to say, for the moment Claude Duval became entirely oblivious of the fact that he had a destination, and that his guide was only a few paces in advance of him.

A coach—a London hackney-coach, now became clearly discernible, and Claude felt tempted to do a stroke of business then and there on the spot, especially when he perceived that the vehicle was driven by a man who was evidently not an ordinary coachman.

The two miserable horses seemed to be very tired; but the man who was driving plied them with the whip, and they were dragging on as quickly as they could possibly go.

Some sound came to the ears of Claude Duval as he neared the vehicle, which he at the time almost fancied was a cry for help from the inside of the coach; but he was not quite certain of the fact.

The moment the man who was driving saw Claude Duval on the road, he urged the horses to a still quicker pace, and made them take quite the side of the road, so as to pass Duval as quickly as possible.

But this was a little manoeuvre which Duval was by no means willing that they should carry out.

Keeping as much as possible in the very middle of the road, Claude Duval now very leisurely trotted on, and as the coach came at speed, it was soon within about twenty yards of him.

"Out of the way—out of the way, will you?" shouted the man who was driving.

The man who was, so to speak, Duval's guide, turned sharply round, and blew a blast upon a silver whistle which was suspended from a chain he wore round his neck.

"Ah!" said Duval, "what is the meaning of this?" as another note of a similar sound came upon his ear.

For an instant it flashed across the mind of Duval that the man who had undertaken to lead to some place where he was to have an interview with some person or persons who were to give him some kind of valuable information, was, in reality, in the employ of perhaps his bitterest foes.

He set himself firmly on his gallant Nightshade, and patting that faithful creature almost affectionately upon the neck, he said, in a low tone, as though he thought the animal could understand what he was saying—

"Courage, Nightshade—courage! There is work for us to do to-night!"

Claude Duval continued to advance towards the coach.

"Halt!" he cried, in a loud voice, when he was near enough to be heard.

"Halt, indeed!" was the reply. "What do you mean by that?"

"What I say!" replied Duval. "Halt!"

Duval drew one of the pistols from the holster of the saddle, and presented it at the head of the man who was driving, who, as soon as he saw the formidable weapon so directed, stopped the horses, and called out loudly, "Hilloa! hilloa! What's the meaning of this? Stokes, where are you?"

"Here!" shouted the man who had constituted himself Duval's guide. "It's all right!"

"Not as far as you are concerned," replied Duval, drawing another pistol from the holster, and presenting it at the head of Mr. Stokes. "Move another inch, and you are a dead man!"

This threat had the desired effect, for the man Stokes sunk to the ground in a state of abject helplessness.

A scream then came from some one inside the coach, and a female voice called out aloud, "Help! help!— oh, help!"

"It is at hand!" cried Claude Duval. "Be you whom you may, help is at hand!"

He darted, with several bounds of the horse, up to the window of the coach which was the nearest to him. It was closed, but in another instant some one from within opened it, and an angry face projected from it.

"Who dares stop this coach on the highway?" shouted the owner of the angry face.

An exclamation of surprise burst from the lips of Claude Duval.

He recognised, in a minute, that it was no other than Mossy Pendell who was in the coach.

For a few seconds these two foes inveterate gazed at each other in silence.

The recognition had been mutual.

"Mossy Pendell!" said Claude Duval.

"The highwayman!" said Mossy Pendell.

Claude Duval was so much surprised and confounded by the unexpected meeting with a man whom he believed to be dead, that for a moment he was thrown off his guard, as he said—

"How, in the name of all that is strange, came you here, Mossy Pendell?"

"To meet you. Ha! ha!"

"To—meet—me?"

"Yes, to be sure."

"And what for?"

"To rid myself of you at once and for ever!"

Even as he spoke, Mossy Pendell levelled a pistol at Claude Duval; and so certain did he seem to feel, that he had Duval's life in his hands, that for a moment he felt an evident pleasure in protracting the scene, as some epicure might dally with the cup at his lips.

He rested the pistol on the coach window, a baleful look was in his eyes, and he added, in tones of concentrated hate—

"Die at last, bane of my life! Danger to more than life itself, die now at once!"

END OF VOLUME I

ST. IVES AT THE FEET OF EVA ST. CLAIR.

CHAPTER CLXVII.

CLAUDE DUVAL AND MOSSY PENDELL MEET NEAR HAMPSTEAD HEATH.

Mossy Pendell pulled the trigger of the pistol; there was a sharp click of the lock—a bright flash of the ignited powder in the pan—but no explosion followed; and for once again that marvellous good fortune, which so often preserved the life of Claude Duval, stood him in good stead.

It was by no means, though, an unusual thing for fire-arms, at the time of which we write, to miss fire. The old flint and steel locks alone were in use, and the construction of the weapons were altogether crude and barbarous, and the powder bad.

The modern percussion lock, with all its elegance and excellence of finish, was undreamt of; and the only pistols that had any pretensions to elaborate finish, were those used for duelling, and this finish simply

No. 53.—NIGHTSHADE.

consisted in the fact that the slightest touch would let them off.

It would be difficult to paint in words the rage which burnt in the heart of Mossy Pendell when he found that the man whose death he so much wished to compass, stood before him unscathed; and for the moment, perhaps, a feeling almost of dread crept over his coward heart, as he contemplated the countenance of Claude Duval, and saw only in it the evidences of serenity and peace.

And Claude Duval was thinking at that moment of what Mossy Pendell's fate might be if he chose to fire one of his pistols at him in return for the attempt he, Mossy Pendell, had in such a dastardly manner made upon his life.

Claude Duval's pistols happened to be highly finished ones—even such as we have described above as used only for duelling. If he did but touch the trigger, he knew that death would follow with the slightest touch.

Hence they were called "hair triggers," because a

horse-hair over the tigger would discharge the pistol before breaking.

Claude Duval, strange to say, made no active movement to escape even the chances of the shot, consequently, as it was, if the pistol had gone off, he must have been killed.

A yell of rage burst from the lips of Mossy Pendell, as he flung the useless weapon from him.

Then it exploded on the roadway, quite harmless.

It had what is called "hung fire," only.

Had Mossy Pendell held that pistol another moment at the breast of Claude Duval, it would have killed him.

"You are lucky, Mossy Pendell," said Duval.

"Lucky! Lucky!"

"Yes; you have been saved a great crime."

"Then I will commit it still."

"No!"

With a brutal laugh, Mossy Pendell turned towards the interior of the coach, evidently in search of another pistol; and, in so doing, he liberated a hold which, with his left hand, he had of a silk handkerchief, which was twisted tightly round the neck of some one who was with him.

That was, probably, the person who had screamed for help.

Now, as even Mossy Pendell could not do two things at once—viz., open a pistol-case to search for another pistol, and hold the ends of a silk handkerchief, which had already half-strangled some one who was with him in the hackney-coach—he let go the latter, and that person recovering breath enough to do so, called out aloud— "Help! help! murder!"

Claude Duval made an effort to look into the coach, but, from the position which Mossy Pendell occupied, he was unable to see the person from whom the cries proceeded.

"Help! help!"

Claude Duval plunged his left arm into the coach, and seized Mossy Pendell by the collar.

"Hold!" he cried; "my forbearance will pass away on another attempt upon my life. Who is it you have with you in this coach?"

"Drive on—drive on—drive over him!" shouted Mossy Pendell.

"Yes, sir," said the man on the box, and immediately he began to lash the poor jaded horses, who had been quite delighted, no doubt, at the rest they had had.

The wheels of the coach began to grate in the sandy road, and Claude Duval's horse, through being touched on the flank by one of them became a little restive.

"I see I am not equal to this adventure by myself," he said; "and, therefore I will get some help."

Still keeping his hold by the collar of Mossy Pendell with his left hand, Claude Duval drew with his right, one of his pistols from the saddle, and fired it in the air.

Now, the driver of the coach came at once to the conclusion, when he heard the report of this pistol, that it was fired at him, and he at once believed that he was shot, for, with a cry of dismay, he let go his hold of the reins, and rolled off the coach-box, and thence on to the roadway.

The horses stopped again on the instant.

Then there was a rush and a gallopping of feet, and Atkins, one of Duval's men, with four others were, in half a minute, on the spot.

"Hilloa!" said Atkins, "what sport, captain?"

"The other door, Atkins—go to the other door!" cried Claude Duval, who had slipped his grasp of Mossy Pendell from the collar to his right arm, in the hand of which he had now a second pistol.

This reinforcement, however, altered the whole aspect of affairs.

Atkins went to the other side of the coach, and tore open the door in a moment, when the first person that presented herself was a young girl of about fourteen or fifteen years of age, who was kneeling among the straw at the bottom of the coach, and who was evidently in a swoon.

The man, Atkins, at first, thought she was dead.

"Why here is murder done!" he said.

"No, she has only fainted," said some other person, in a firm tone of voice from the coach. "Lift her out, and then help me. My arms are tied behind me, and I have been nearly strangled by this ruffian."

Atkins had lifted out the young girl, and given her in charge of one of his companions, and then he sprung round the coach, to the side of it where Claude Duval was, and he opened the door at the moment that Mossy Pendell fancied himself free from Claude Duval's grasp.

"The first man who lays a hand on me has a bullet in his brains!" cried Mossy Pendell.

"Oh, nonsense!" said Atkins, and he closed with him at once on the coach steps.

Bang went the pistol, at this moment, that Mossy Pendell had possessed himself of, but the bullet fortunately lodged harmlessly in a tree, and Atkins dragged him out of the vehicle into the road.

"I have him, Captain—I have him!"

"Seize this fellow, Thompson," said Atkins.

"Aye, aye, Atkins, I have him."

Thompson treated Mossy Pendell with very slight ceremony. He twisted his hands behind his back, as if they had been the fins of a turtle, and tied them together by the wrists with a piece of whipcord, which was much too sharp and secure to be pleasant.

"You are too handy by half, with your popguns!" said Thompson.

"Thieves!—thieves!—murder!"

"Oh, you need not make all that noise. It's all up with you now, my fine fellow, and you can bellow as much as you like, while I get a nice little gag ready, which will effectually put you to silence."

Claude Duval had dismounted, and hastily approaching an elderly lady, who had spoken so resolutely from the inside of the coach, he took her hand, and said, in his kindest accents:—

"I am only too well pleased to have been the means of delivering you from the power of that bad man, although how you and that young girl came to fall into his hands, is a mystery I cannot hope to solve."

"Is not your name Claude Duval?"

"It is."

"And did you not marry Lucy Everton?"

"I did."

"Then you must know that I was well acquainted with her mother, and knew her also as a child. The young girl you see with me is the daughter of an old and faithful servant, and lived in the family of that man, from whom you have rescued us, Mossy Pendell."

"Go on, I listen," said Duval.

"Stop him!" shouted Atkins at this moment.

"Who is it?" cried Duval, sharply.

"Ah, yes! Stop him, indeed! Bring him back at once, he must not be let escape on any account!"

One of the men gallopped after the unfortunate driver, and soon brought him back with every appearance of so much fright about him, that it was tolerably clear that he would answer any questions that might be put to him.

"Continue your narration, my dear madame," said Duval, turning again to the aged gentlewoman.

"I will. It appears that the girl's mother had an interview with Mossy Pendell, at which they had some words, and the girl heard part of the conversation, which so alarmed her that she ran out of the house, and came to me, for her mother, as I told you before, had once been in my service, many years ago, and this girl was quite familiar with my name, and my friendly feeling towards her mother."

"Yes, yes. Did she hear anything that concerned Lucy?"

"Yes.—The villain had contrived a plot with another man, whose name the girl did not catch, to carry off Lucy, in order that he might, by leading you to think that he could give you information about her, get you into his power, and put an end to your existence."

A smile of contempt passed over the expressive countenance of Duval, as he said, "I should despise myself, if I thought I should meet death at that man's hand!"

"Be not rash, but listen," continued the old lady.

"I at once hired this hackney coach, in order to drive to Hampstead Heath, where I knew, from General Everton, I should find Lucy, when all of a sudden the vehicle came to a standstill, and Mossy Pendell got into the coach,—while the driver I had engaged was replaced by another, and the coach turned in an opposite direction."

"Did he say where he intended to have you driven?"

"No; all he said was—'Now the principal danger will be over, and this troublesome old woman shall be taken care of for the rest of her days.'"

"I see · I see!"

"Of course, I was soon overpowered, and when you so happily came to our rescue, I had given up all hope of ever looking again into the face of a friend."

"And that is all."

"All I know."

"Captain," said Atkins, at this moment, "this fellow is ready and willing to tell everything that he knows, and more too."

"Oh, yes, yes!" said the man, who had been the driver of the coach. "I will, indeed, tell his honourable worship anything he may wish to hear. I am a poor, hard-working man."

"If you do," said Mossy Pendell, "you shall be hanged; not that you know much."

"If you don't, you shall be hanged!" said Claude Duval.

The man looked with blanched cheeks from one to the other.

"Look here, old fellow," said Atkins, "Mossy Pendell promises to hang you if he can, but he cannot, at all events, just now, as, perhaps, we shall hang him. Now, as regards us, if you don't make a clear breast of it, and tell all, you will be hanged by us off hand."

"Oh!—no, no!"

"But I say, yes. There is a convenient bough of a tree yonder, I fancy, isn't there Thompson?"

"Ay—ay!"

"Have you a cord with you?"

"To be sure."

"Stop! stop!" cried the driver. "The cord will not be wanted. You shall know all I know. You see, sir, I can't possibly help it, for your promised hanging is far off, while these gentlemen have both the will and power to hang me at once."

"Spoken like Solomon," said Atkins

"Peter?" said Mossy Pendell.

"Well, sir."

"I will give you a hundred pounds to be dumb."

"A hundred pounds?"

"Yes; on my honour."

"The cord!" said Atkins.

"Sir," said Peter, "it is very kind of you, but I don't see what good all the money in the would be to me when I am dangling to the end of a rope. Now, gentlemen, I am ready and willing to tell all I know."

Mossy Pendell muttered imprecations, and Duval turned towards Peter, saying, "Who and what are you?"

"Keeper at Mr. Markham's asylum."

"Asylum?"

"Yes, for lunatics at Croydon."

"Go on! go on!"

"Well, gentlemen, I don't know that there is much more to tell, but you may see for yourselves."

"What do you mean?"

"Why, when I, a keeper of an Asylum, am on the coachbox, and driving in the direction of an asylum, with somebody who is being taken care of inside, why you see they can but be going to one place—that is, to Mr. Markham's asylum to be taken care of."

"In fact, to be kept out of the way."

"Well, you may call it so if you please."

"You know it is so. And now, Peter, if that be your name, your candour has been the means of saving your life, for most assuredly you would have dangled by yon bough of a tree if you had not been as explicit as you have been. As for you, Mossy Pendell——"

A deadly paleness—the paleness of intense fear now came over the features of Mossy Pendell, for he could not believe for one moment but that the man whom he had striven so often to injure, and to whose wife he had shown himself so deadly a foe, would now retaliate upon him.

Without allowing Claude Duval to conclude what he was about to say, Mossy Peddell cried out, in a loud voice, "I take you all to witness that I am a murdered man, and I offer a thousand pounds to any one who will interfere to save my life. You, too, Mrs. Martin, I ask you if you can stand by and see a cold blooded murder committed."

"I do not see anything of the sort, as yet," replied the old lady.

"Nor any one else," said Atkins.

"But," added the old lady, with a severity of tone, which showed how very low Mossy Pendell had sunk in her esteem. "But I see and hear a man, who knows well, by his own wickedness, he is deserving of death, and is full of fears that retribution may overtake him."

"And that is all," said Claude Duval. "Mossy Pendell, since I have no intention of taking your life, I scorn of keeping you in fear."

A remarkable change immediately ensued upon the countenance of Mossy Pendell, so soon as he heard these words from Claude Duval, and much of his old and ordinary insolence came back to him, as he looked about him with confidence; and then he cried out, "And why, I ask, am I stopped on the King's highway in this fashion?"

"Insolent!"

"Well, Mr. Highwayman," he continued. "I do not know which you may consider the most insolent act, that of stopping a gentleman on the King's highway, or his protest against it?"

"Look to that man, Atkins," said Claude Duval, "and prevent his escape," pointing to Mossy Pendell as he spoke.

"Man, indeed! That is an insolent way of speaking of me, who am a gentleman, and high in favour at Court."

"Well, then, you are no man!" said Atkins. "And, indeed, you can't be much of a man, or you would not be such a cowardly rascal as you are. But keep quiet now, or it will be the worse for you."

Atkins placed a pistol so close to the eyes of Mossy Pendell, that intense alarm once more took possession of him, and he called out, "Come, come, my good fellow, keep that pistol the other way, if you please."

"What for?"

"Why, it might go off, and surely you would not murder me?"

"It might go off, certainly, but never mind that; you make yourself easy if it does—I dare say it will if you move."

"But I cannot be quiet—I cannot. It would kill me."

"And of what consequence would that be, I should like to know? What's that to you? It would not be all your fault, you know? Be quiet, will you."

A slight tap on the head with the barrel of the pistol, enforced the request to be quiet, and, as Mossy Pendell thought that that mode of action would only increase the likelihood of the pistol going off, he was silent accordingly, and looked under his bent brows all the rage and fear that was in his heart.

Claude Duval was now only too anxious to put a stop to an adventure which could result in nothing but bloodshed, probably.

He had heard all that he wished to hear respecting Mossy Pendell's scheme to get Lucy once more in his power; so, turning to Mrs. Martin, he invited her again to enter the coach with the young girl, and ordered the man Atkins to drive her wherever she might wish to go, while he gave Mossy Pendell, and the man who had been sent to conduct him, Duval, to certain destruction, into the charge of Thompson, to guard them strictly until the coach was safe from the possibility of pursuit.

Duval took leave of the old lady amid a profusion of thanks; and, turning Nightshade's head, quietly trotted back to Hampstead.

CHAPTER CLXVIII.

EVA ST. CLARE AND ST. IVES HAVE ANOTHER INTERVIEW.

WE left Eva St. Clare a prey to such conflicting emotions, that she scarcely knew what was real, and what was only the effects of her own lively imagination, in the world around her.

She was alone one evening, or, at least, she knew not in what part of the old rambling house her aunt Joyce was to be found, when she was startled from her reveries by a hand being gently laid on the handle of the door of the common sitting-room.

Did her heart at that moment whisper to her that he who had been the cause of the calm of her existence passing away so early, was even then close at hand.

A sudden catching of the breath, and a half-cry, announced the surprise of the moment, and then she saw St. Ives dimly in the twilight.

He had taken advantage of the general invitation he had received to come and go whenever he pleased; and so, this evening, he had sought the dingy abode of Mr. Cuthbert, little dreaming that he would find Eva alone.

St. Ives advanced, tremblingly, as he heard the half-cry that burst from Eva's lips.

"Eva!" he said—"Eva!"

She rose, but she did not take his proffered hand; perhaps she did not see it.

"Captain Granville, this unexpected visit— Mr. Cuthbert is—I think at home—I will go and see! Let me pass!"

"Ah, Eva! I do not wish to see any one but you! When you are here, all else fades in the great world for me!"

"Sir!—Captain Granville— do not—I must not stay to listen to such words! Let me go!"

"Eva—Eva, will you kill me?"

"Kill—you—oh, heaven!"

He crept close to her; he tried to take her hand, but she shrank back. He then reeled a pace or two from her, and then he nervously clutched the back of a chair, and spoke to her. There was a strange fascination in his tones. Eva might then have left him. He might not have tried to prevent her doing so, but she did not. She stood spell-bound.

"Eva, you do not mean to cast me from you? Tell me, if I have ever, by look, word, or gesture, said one word that should make you thus seek to shun me! You are young and alone—no brother, no sister, no mother!"

Eva clasped her hands over her eyes.

"I ask you only to take me to your heart as a dear, loving brother! But if you cannot, will not, let me be that dear friend, I will leave you, and pray for your welfare and happiness, although you will not allow me to be what I would fain be to you! Eva, could I speak to you thus if my affection for you were not a pure and holy thing? Oh, no, no!"

Eva trembled.

"Do you not believe that there are many kindred souls walking upon this earth who may seek each other's sympathy, and yet be innocent and pure, even as the angels in heaven?"

Eva's tears began to flow, and she sank upon the nearest chair.

St. Ives knelt at her feet.

He took both her hands in his, and placed them gently upon his face, kissing them as he did so.

They were unresisting now, those little hands, and St. Ives smiled in his delight, and softly whispered, "How good is heaven to bless its creatures thus!"

Eva looked at him through her tears.

"Captain Granville," she said, "this must not be!"

How her voice shook, and with what catching spasms her words came through her parched lips. "This—must—not—be! Let this be our last meeting! Had we met earlier, all might have been different; but it is too late now! I feel this ought not to be."

"No, no, no! do not say that it is too late!"

"Yes; it is too late now!"

"No, no, I say again, not too late to lead a life of dear companionship!" whispered St. Ives. "Why can we not be what we may be, because we cannot be what we might have been? Oh, do not say that it is too late for the fire of pure friendship to burn brightly on the altar of our hearts!"

"No, no! Forget me!"

"Eva, you deceive yourself! You do not mean what you say! If you thought that I could really forget you, the words would never have been uttered by those lips! Forget each other we never shall, and the time will come when you may be in difficulty and in danger, when you will feel all the happiness arising from the thought that there is one heart which beats truly for you! Henceforth, Eva, you will feel that you are not alone! Do you hear me, dear?"

"Yes, yes!"

"And—and you feel with me?"

"It may be as you say; but, Captain Granville, if you really only desire my happiness, surely you must see that this—this feeling, of which you speak, must be trodden down!"

"Kept under, Eva, but not quenched."

She looked into his face again now. It was a mirror of bright thoughts; there was no unholy passion upon his broad, intellectual brow.

"I will believe all you say," she murmured; "but yet let me entreat of you not to let us meet often!"

There was a look of love—of a young girl's first, pure, devoted love upon Eva's face, as she said this that sank like sunlight into the heart of St. Ives. He did not speak, but he folded his arms about her, and kissed her brow so gently, and looked so serenely happy; and she, too, was happy: she forgot, at that moment, that it was too late.

And so they looked into each other's eyes, his arms were around her, and her head reposed upon his breast. An hour flew past them upon easy pinions, and they were very happy; and all that time Eva forgot still that it was too late for them to be so happy; but in the delusion of their mutual innocence—and innocent they both were—they spoke of how kind it was of heaven to make them so blessed.

And now Mrs. Joyce bustled into the sitting-room, and from the start she gave no one could have supposed for a moment that she was aware of the presence of St. Ives, although, in reality, she had heard every word, and had been a witness to every action which had passed between Eva and him.

"Oh, Captain Granville, is that you?"

St. Ives started, and Eva dropped a book she had just taken up to ask St. Ives the meaning of a passage in it.

They were both confused, but it was not the confusion of guilt; and so it passed off very quickly, and St. Ives was able to make a few commonplace remarks, and to express his regret that Mr. Cuthbert was not at home.

"Dear me, no! He's gone, I think, to make somebody's will, or something of that sort; but you are not going, Captain Granville, before Mr. Cuthbert returns?"

St. Ives made some incoherent speech about not wanting to see him at all, and then corrected himself, and said it was on business of importance he had called, or he should not have intruded so long.

"Oh, don't mention that, pray, dear Captain Granville; I am sure it is quite a charity to drop in sometimes to enliven us; and Eva, you see, can understand you better than I do, for my education was——Oh, he's gone!"

St. Ives backed out of the room. He took leave of Eva with a look; and when he found himself in the street he gave himself up to a sense of his happiness.

Did no thought of her, who had once been the idol of his mind, cross him at that moment?

Did he picture her to himself, heartbroken and sorrowful, yet loving him still, as woman can love but once, through good and ill?

He did think of her.

St. Ives was not a man ever to forget one whom he had loved; but he determined, in his own mind, to believe that she had left him to seek consolation elsewhere, and he laboured to tell himself that had she acted otherwise— i short, if she had remained with him, and endeavoured, by gentleness and affection, to win back his love, she might have succeeded.

And then his thoughts reverted again to Eva.

"She loves me—yes, she loves me, and I am happy! I will not be to her the blight that I might be! Angels shall walk with us, and listen to us! I would not, for worlds, sully her mind by one unhallowed thought! No, no; she shall never regret loving me, and she does love me— she does love me!"

* * * * * *

Could St. Ives be long now without seeing Eva again? Ah, no! She was the sunshine of his life—his sun, his joy!

And now that he felt confident that his love was returned, he looked a different being.

He wrote to her to meet him again by the side of the Serpentine.

Eva trembled at the message, for she thought there had been some sort of understanding that they were not to meet often, and yet she hardly knew.

But it was sufficient for her that he told her she was to meet him by the side of the Serpentine, and it was such a delicious thing for her to feel that now she had one whom she could love and trust as a dear *friend*.

Alas, poor Eva!

St. Ive's note did not require an answer, only her presence at the desired spot, and so she went.

He advanced with rapid steps to meet her, and the delirium of joy which shone in his eyes as he gazed into hers made Eva almost regret that she had yielded to his request to grant this interview.

"Ah, you are angry with me!" said St. Ives, looking all the sorrow his words were meant to express.

"No, not angry, Captain Granville; but——"

"But what, dear Eva?"

"A little—I mean, that I think I am doing wrong. What if your wife could know of my meeting you thus?"

St. Ives laughed scornfully, as he said, "Do not allow your brow to be clouded with thoughts of one who does not, and never did, love me!"

A bright flush rose to St. Ives' cheek as he uttered this falsehood; for he knew only too well that the Stuart Princess had loved him better than man was ever loved.

"Never loved you?" said Eva, incredulously.

"No! Ah, I see by your looks that had we met earlier, I should not have been able to make a similar charge against you. Your gentle and affectionate heart could not have withstood love's claims! But enough of this—let us talk of other matters."

"Then why did you marry her!"

"For reasons—and good ones, too, dear Eva, which I will tell you some day, but not now; let us talk of ourselves and our new-found happiness, dear one!"

Poor Eva glanced up into his handsome face, and wondered how it was that all the world did not love—almost worship—one so gifted morally and physically.

"And you will never doubt me, Eva?"

"My friend, my brother—why should I doubt you?"

"Yes, I am your friend. How we ought to bless the good angel that brought us together! There was always a void in my heart until I knew you. I could not give it a name, but now I know what it was."

"What?"

"I wanted somebody to love—to understand me—to enter into all my joys!"

"Hush, hush! You promised me that you would never speak of love—it terrifies me!"

"But that is the only word which is applicable to the feeling I have for you, dear; and you see there is nothing to fear from me, dear one."

As he spoke, he took one of her hands gently in his.

"But—but——" persisted Eva.

"Dear little trembler, why should we shrink from the contemplation of love—one of God's best gifts to man. Love is divine!"

"Captain Granville!"

St. Ives started.

He had persuaded her, of late, to call him by his name, Charles; and the way in which she now pronounced Captain Granville, made her seem thousands of miles away from him.

"Captain Granville, you terrify me. In purity of thought and intention, I have consented to meet you; but do not—oh, do not, Charles, talk of love!"

St. Ives breathed again.

"I breathe again," he said. "Let me be always Charles to you, and never Captain Granville; and if you do not wish me to talk of love, we will converse on some other subject. Oh, Eva! it is because you do not trust me that you forbid me to speak of love. Do you suppose in those bright realms above the sky, that the blessed inhabitants talk not of love, and cannot our love be as holy as theirs?"

"It may be so—I know not—but let us talk of other things."

"Oh, Eva! look up, dearest, gentlest love. I do not wish that through another's death you could be mine; but, oh! the heart-pang to think that we did not meet one little year since."

"Again—again!" said Eva, and her eyes filled with tears. "Again you speak in that strain!"

"Well, well!" he said, mournfully, "we will not look back at the past, and sigh for things that might have been, but are not. Hand in hand, in purity and joy, we will walk the sunny paths of the future. You are happy with me, are you not."

"It is great happiness to have a dear friend."

"Eva, do you remember when first we met?"

"But vaguely, Charles. It seemed like a dream when I tried to think of it. Did I not faint?"

"Yes, dear one! I held you to my heart, and carried you into the house through the snowdrift. It was then that I first saw you—it was then that I first loved."

"Ah! you will say, loved."

"You will let me say it? We will append to it a pure and holy memory. Ours is a sentiment and not a passion, and so we may smile at our fears, and be very happy."

Eva turned aside her head, to conceal the deep emotion his words conjured up.

"Ah! do I pain you by these sad confessions?"

"Oh! no, no, no."

"Well, then, Eva, we may meet you see, and love, and be great; and rise above the common prejudice of the world, and love deeply and truly, and yet feel no pang—no remorse."

"Yes, Charles, yes."

"Eva, if you and I only were in the world, should we lack company?"

"I think not, Charles."

"If we could end our days in some island?"

"Do not—do not wound my heart to think of what might have been."

He folded his arms round her, her head rested on his heart and she sobbed bitterly.

"Eva, Eva, listen to me. Let us fly away from England, and live but for each other."

"Charles, Charles—peace!"

"No, no; it is a blessed thought."

"Your wife?"

"She loves me not, I say.

"Charles! Charles!"

"Yes, we will fly far—far away—we will——"

"Charles, unhand me! Captain Granville!"

Eva sprang from his side, and looked, in her purity and innocence, as some offended angel might have looked when crossed in its radiant path by one of the impure spirits expelled from association with the spotless seraphs who look on the Immortal.

"Captain Granville, this is our last meeting."

"Eva?"

"Our last meeting, I say. Attempt not to cross my path again. Do not haunt my path, for I love you not. I thought in you I had found a friend, but heaven has punished me for my presumption."

"Eva, Eva, spare me."

"Henceforth," continued the heroic girl, "we are strangers to each other. I should hate myself if I thought now it could be otherwise. Your wife, your gentle wife doubtless loves you still, and heaven grant that she may never know what has passed between us."

"Eva, Eva, you are innocent and pure, and you magnify the meaning of a few empty words."

"Enough! I will now be guided by the dictates of my own heart, and flee your dangerous presence."

As she spoke, Eva turned and fled from the spot; and so paralyzed was St. Ives by sorrow and remorse, that he attempted not to follow her.

On, on sped the young girl through the park, nor did she pause until she reached one of the gates, and then she asked herself what she was to do—where she was to go.

CHAPTER CLXXIX.

SHEWS THAT ST. IVES FORMS A GOOD RESOLUTION.

WE must now return to the Stuart Princess, whom the exigencies of our story have compelled us to leave so long.

It would be a mistake to say that the quiet and unobtrusive attentions of Lucy had been wholly without a happy result; but still there was a settled paleness upon her face, which resembled more the pallor of death than aught else.

And at times, there was a catching of the breath, as though a sigh were smothered in its birth, that told how ill at ease the heart was—that pure, gentle, loving, forgiving heart, that should have throbbed out its allotted span of existence amid the smiles of happiness, and the perpetual summer of its own affections.

Who shall say what she suffered? but she prayed for strength, and, like a wounded angel, she only sought to forgive.

It happened to be in the evening of the very day on which poor Eva had resolved never to meet St. Ives again that the Princess and Lucy found themselves alone.

Silence had fallen upon the two friends.

It was broken by the Stuart Princess, who said, in a tone of deep emotion, "Dear friend, I am about to make a proposition to you."

"Speak!"

"Last night I had a dream."

"A dream?"

"Yes; I dreamt that he—my husband was in danger—that he was lonely and forsaken—that he turned his throbbing eyes from side to side, in the vain endeavour to behold the face of a friend."

"Well!"

"I have been wishing this morning that such might really be the case."

Lucy looked inquiringly at her friend, for she began to think that grief had unsettled her reason.

The Princess continued.

"I intend to make my way to what I thought was to have been a house of wedded happiness, but which was so cruelly destroyed. There I will seek him—my Charles—my Miravel—my husband, and if he be sick, I will tend—if he be lonely, I will cheer him, and perhaps—perhaps he——"

The pale face was bent down upon the thin, small hands, and sobs alone finished the sentence of the broken-hearted, but still loving wife.

Lucy was not likely to seek to deter her friend from carrying out any project which was likely to lead to such happy results, and she, therefore, entered into the Princess's plans with warmth and energy.

It did not occupy much time for the two friends to make the needful preparations for the intended visit of the Stuart Princess to the house which St. Ives had taken soon after his marriage, and where, under the assumed name of Captain Granville, had spent so short a time with his happy bride, when Eva St. Clare unfortunately appeared upon the scene, and innocently was the cause of so much desolation and misery.

And St. Ives? What became of him after Eva turned and fled?

"Eva! Eva!" was all that he could say, and as he saw her slight form rushing away—away from him who loved her so well—and seeing her, as he thought, passing from before him for ever, he gave one wild cry, and fell to the ground in a swoon.

When he returned to consciousness he found himself in his own lonely home. Some passer by probably had known and recognised him, and had him conveyed home.

He gazed about him, thinking he was still in a land of dreams, when he became conscious of the presence of an old woman, who was sleeping soundly by the fireside.

"Alone!" said St. Ives. "Quite alone now," and then he rose from the couch upon which he lay. "Oh, yes, I am alone now!—alone in all the world. The sun has gone out—quite out!"

He staggered to a chair, and sinking into it, he shut out the world from his perceptions by covering his face with his hands, and remained for more than two hours in intense thought.

When St. Ives removed his hands from before his face, few who had seen him that morning in all the bright joyance of his feelings, telling himself that he was beloved by her whom he prized so highly above all other treasures, would have known him, he was so very much altered. He did not rise, but he spoke tremulously, and from what he said may be gathered in some measure what he had been thinking about during those two hours.

"Now welcome death in any shape it may will to come," he murmured. "Here, for once, is a victim who will not shrink from the fiat of the fell destroyer. Welcome, now, any fate, for I am tossed upon such a sea of undue calamity, that to loose myself in losing my life is to gain much if I gain the bliss of oblivion. She is mine no more! That dream has fled, and I am desolate. I have no home—no resting place in all the world now! All is blank despair and wretchedness! She loves me not! Death! death! Come to me!"

He was silent, then, for a few moments, and from some itinerent organ, placed just beneath the window, he heard a strain of music.

"No, no," he said. "Vanish music's strain. What have I to do with sweet sounds? I have no home—I had one. I might have had one still, but I destroyed what might have been an earthly Paradise in grasping at a heavenly one, and now I stand repudiated by God and man! I have no one to love me—my wife! Heaven! she loved me!"

As the recollection of the Stuart Princess crossed his mind, St. Ives again covered his face with his hands.

Who shall say what direful images crossed the brain of that misguided man during that brief space of time in reality, but long to him. Who shall say that some good angel was not at work at his heart to bring him back to duty and affection.

Then he rose with a strange look upon his face, and paced the room.

He trembled so violently that he was forced to seek the support of a chair, and there he stood looking, in complexion, more like a corpse than a living man.

He told himself as yet how far his years had been—how far from all bodily ailment he was—what a long future might lie before him—how his wife might yet look back with compassion, and a loving forgiveness upon the past, and be yet to him all that she had been before that blow which had awakened her to grief.

St. Ives clasped his hands together, and for the first time the strong man wept.

Wept not so much for himself and the loss of Eva's love, as for the sorrow he had brought upon his young wife.

From the moment that he shed those tears, a vast revulsion of feeling seemed to come over him.

All his interests in the world and its doings appeared to revive in him with tenfold force and certainty, he became much more rational than he had been for many a day.

It seemed as though suddenly, and as for the first time, he saw his conduct both to Eva and to his wife in its proper light, for although he still loved Eva, it was with a quiet brotherly love, which now sought only her good. There was no passion now mingled with his affection—it had been this young and inexperienced girl's task to show this man of high intellect and refinement what was right.

Again he paced the room with hasty strides.

"Yes," he said, " I will seek her— my poor Mary. Yet she will, if her heart can be warm towards me, forgive my sin against her. She will smile upon me again, and all the past will vanish from our memories like the image of some feverish dream!"

St. Ives now turned his footsteps to his chamber, and, with a dreamy kind of look, threw himself upon the bed.

He never gave it a thought to inquire what had become of the faithful old man-servant and his wife; had he done so, he would have felt that he was not quite deserted, for they were waiting and watching, and expecting each moment to be summoned to the presence of their master, who, until the last few weeks, they had looked upon as something too good, too generous and kind, to mingle with the world in general.

Alas! that so much goodness should have been led away by too fervid an imagination!

That night the blood bubbled through the veins of St. Ives, and his vexed brain, in all the delirium of fever, suggested wondrous things.

It was an awful thing for those two faithful servants to linger by the bed-side and listen to the ravings of such a mind.

"Oh, would that Lucy had not gone away!" sighed the old woman. "I understand all now! They might yet have been happy!"

"Ay, ay, dame; but all my inquiries have been fruitless, as you know. I believe he loved her; it was only his fancy, like, that made him care for——"

"Hush, hush! he may hear us! Leave me to watch him, while you go for Dr. Marshall."

"I will—I will!"

At this moment the two servants were startled by a gentle tap at the outer door.

"Who can that be?" they both exlciaimed in a breath.

They must have been very intent upon watching their master, or surely the very gentle rap could not so have startled those two.

"I will go and see who it is," cried the old woman; "you wait here."

She hastened from the room, and as quickly as her agitation would permit her, she hurried to the outer door, and opened it.

There was a suppressed cry of surprise, and then all was silent.

"Is your master at home, Hannah?" was all that the Stuart Princess could trust herself to say.

"Yes—yes, ma'am—my lady; but he is ill—very ill!"

A paleness as of death overspread the countenance of the broken-hearted wife.

"And who is tending him, Hannah?" at length she summoned courage to say.

"My husband, my lady, was even just now going to fetch Dr. Marshall, and if you will allow me to return to him, he will go at once."

"Do so, Hannah, and I will return with you; but remember, I do not wish him to know that I am present. You know, as you say he is so ill, perhaps it might do him harm."

"Alas! he is not likely to know, my lady; for he does not recognise us in the least."

With a beating heart the Stuart Princess sought the chamber of her husband, with a heart overflowing with gentleness and forgiveness.

Heaven speed her on her mission of mercy, and guard her ever in this world, and reward her for all her goodness!

CHAPTER CLXXX.

A HAPPY RE-UNION.

"THIS will be a battle between life and death," whispered the kind-hearted physician to the Stuart Princess, "and heaven only knows which will be the victor. The reaction of the great excitement which Captain Granville has gone through lately has commenced, and if the frame battles through it, all will be well. The next three days will decide the contest."

Between life and death St. Ives hovered for three days, gently tended by his still loving wife. Day and night she watched by his side, and only withdrew when she fancied that he might recognise her; and till she knew with what feelings he thought of her, she was most anxious to avoid being seen and recognised by him.

On the dawn of the fourth day as the physician sat by the bed-side, and the faint grey light of a new day peeped into the chamber, the sufferer awoke from a long sleep. The physician bent over him and looked into his eyes.

"Saved!" he said.

St. Ives would have spoken, but the low "Hush, hush!" of the physician silenced the desire to do so. The proffered medicine in a cup was taken, and with a deep sigh he closed his eyes to sleep again.

In two days more St. Ives was up, and seated in an invalid chair by an open window.

The world without seemed happy in the soft breeze that bore upon its wings the odours of millions of fair flowers—sweet children of the sun who smile in beauty only when it looks gently upon them.

Some early fruit had been spread for him while he slept, by the loving hands of his wife; and, pale and wan, poor St. Ives tried to smile faintly—very faintly, as the physician talked cheeringly to him of the future.

'Now, my dear fellow, you must try to get up your strength, you know, and then all will be well, you know."

St. Ives pressed both hands upon his head, as he said, faintly—

"No, no; all cannot be well. But I am content to suffer, for I deserve to suffer. When none of you thought of it or dreamt that I was sane enough to know the past, there were pauses in my brain-sick fancy, and with a clear mental vision I was able to see my late career."

"How? What do you mean?"

"I mean that when I ought to have wrestled with the promptings of unholy passion, I yielded to the soft seduction. I had won a heart—a priceless treasure that was all my own, and in the gentleness and the purity of that affection I should have looked for that happiness which my restless spirit cast from it."

As he spoke, St. Ives covered his face with his hand and sunk back in the chair in deep thought.

"Oh, heaven!" he continued in a few minutes, raising both his hands; "if the past could only be erased from life's facts—if the fair and suffering wife could only see how penitent I am, I could then resign my breath to the Great Being who gave it to me, without a sigh. But—it may not be! No, no; oh, no!"

"Calm yourself," replied the physician, who had known all the events of the past few months,—"calm yourself, and tell me, can it be possible that your wild mad love for Eva St. Clare has left you?"

"Yes; that which you call the wild, mad love has left me, but the better love, which only seeks the happiness of one dear by respect and friendship, still remains, and will remain. Like a divinity I have, as it were, held that young pure spirit in my grasp for good or for evil—and it came to evil."

"Not wholly so. You spared the innocence that had no other safeguard but your latent sense of honour."

"I meant to do so. Heaven knows I meant to do so! Oh! is it not now a blessed thought. Now that I have cast away the worst portion of my heart, and could I but see my poor Mary once more in life, I could be happy—happier and better than I have ever been—before I die."

"Do you know that I can give you news of your wife?"

"Oh, no, no! Let me look into your face, doctor. You do not—you will not deceive me?"

"Not for worlds would I deceive you."

St. Ives sank back in the chair again, and looked very faint.

"Ah, my friend!" said the physician, "I am afraid that you are not fit to hear further news that I have to tell you. You are not strong enough to bear such shocks."

"What?—oh, what? Tell me! is it bad or good? I cannot be crushed more than I am. If you move my heart at all you must lift it up from the profound abyss in which it now lies panting."

"The news is good, and yet I fear——"

"Fear nothing. Good news never kills. It may send the life blood coursing through my veins in quicker currents, but that is nothing. Tell me—oh, tell me quickly! Already fancy is in arms, and with a thousand incredulities, battles at my head."

He fell back with a deep sigh.

"Hilloa!" cried the physician, "I am the worst hand in the world at breaking news to any one! Here! Come here!"

The door of communication between the two rooms opened, and the Stuart Princess tottered forward. She could not see her way for tears; but, with a shriek of joy, she flung herself at the feet of St. Ives, and clasped him round the waist.

CLAUDE DUVAL IN THE DUCHESS OF CLEVELAND'S OPERA-BOX.

Then the two faithful domestics both entered the room; but St. Ives could not speak, and the sobs of his wife was the only sound that could be heard in that chamber.

But in a little time St. Ives was able to raise that drooping wife, and to hold her to his heart; and then, at one glance into her eyes, he could see that she was happy, and that the past was forgiven.

"Oh, heaven!" he said, "if I could only die now!"

"Nay, dearest Charles!" replied the Stuart Princess, with one of her old bright smiles. "Nay, rather wish to live, that you may make me as happy as I hoped to be when I gave you this hand and heart!"

"And how have I fulfilled your expectations, dear one?" exclaimed St. Ives, gazing sorrowfully at the pale face that was turned so confidingly towards him.

"Do not mention the past! Let us forget it; or, at least, remember it only to contrast it with the happy present!"

St. Ives covered his face with his hands, and swayed to and fro upon the chair, but did not speak

No. 54.—NIGHTSHADE.

The Stuart Princess crept closer to him; and, again kneeling at his feet, she lifted both his hands off his face.

A radiant smile now played upon his expressive features. Heaven, what a change was there! The weight of twenty years seemed to be lifted off his eyes! They sparkled with a new joy. The long lost colour had come back again to his lips. He stretched out his arms; and, as he clasped his wife to his heart, he burst into such a passion of tears, that the physician, and the two faithful domestics, were too deeply affected to remain on the spot.

He walked towards the bed, and then kneeling, he tried to pray.

For full five minutes he wept; but at last the tears ceased, and the first words he said were, "It is morning again!"

"Morning?" said the Stuart Princess.

"Yes, dear one! It is the morning of my soul! The night of my affliction has passed away, and it is a delightful morning! The morning of spring, when all the world is fresh and beautiful from the hand of God! Oh, when was I ever so happy as now? Oh, can you—have you forgiven me?"

"Oh, hush!—hush!" said the Stuart Princess, as she saw St. Ives' face was flushed, and he was getting fearfully excited. "Not another word, if you love me!"

He shuddered and was still.

"You are not quite yourself yet," she said, gently. "This excitement is too much for you."

We cannot describe the scene which, for the next half-hour, was being enacted in that once lonely apartment. Let us fancy that St. Ives is a little more composed, and that the Stuart Princess is sitting upon a couch holding both his hands in hers, and that she is looking into his face—it is still pale from recent suffering—while tears of joy are streaming from her eyes.

The physician had left the house, strange to say, without even taking leave of his patient.

St. Ives spoke.

Oh, how those tones fell like the murmuring of blissful music, long gone into the dim past, upon the heart of the Stuart Princess!

"Mary," he said, "how much you have to foregive and forget!"

"No, no, nothing!"

"Yes; but, indeed, you have! My cruel neglect! All my wild and wilful conduct! Oh, Mary—my Mary, can you indeed love me again as once you did?"

"Again?"

"Yes, again! Is it possible that you can?"

She sobbed upon his breast.

"From first to last, in affectionate intercourse, or in estrangement, I never ceased to love you, Miravel! I cannot love you better—I never loved you less!"

"Then you are an angel, and the greater is my fault that I cast from me for a time the joy of such a treasure!"

She still wept, but they were tears of joy.

"Tell me," she said, "if you can, dear Charles—tell me where the young girl, Eva St. Clare, is, and whom I will now receive and love as if she were a child of our own."

"Ah! that is well thought of!" said St. Ives. "How selfish we all are, after all; when we are happy, we forget all the pains and vexations of others. I am glad that you mentioned to me the name of Eva."

"Let us seek her, dear. You say that her uncle and aunt are uncongenial spirits for her to associate with; there is no reason, is there, why she should not become an inmate of our home?"

As she said this, the Stuart Princess looked confidingly and earnestly into her husband's face, as though she would, by such scrutiny, read his heart.

And she seemed well pleased with what she read there, and still more so, when, as he folded her in his arms, he whispered, "As a dear sister—even as you, yourself, will love Eva St. Clare, will I love that innocent and gentle girl."

"And will she love me, too, Charles?" she asked, as a shade passed over her face, when she remembered the different footing upon which their affection would henceforth be placed.

"Most assuredly, she will, dear one—she cannot fail to do so—in fact, my darling, I suspect that it was the affection with which you inspired her which enabled her to withstand ——"

"Hush, hush! We must never allow our conversation to touch upon the unhappy past. Let us seek Eva; and from what you say, we shall have no difficulty in persuading her relatives to part with her."

"We will go to-morrow morning; and heaven bless you, my Mary, for your goodness!"

It is necessary that we should take a passing glance at affairs in the house of Eva.

We left that heroic girl—so strong in virtue, running with the speed of lightning across the Park, without being able to determine, in her own mind, whither she was to direct her steps.

Where, in her wild, excited state, she might have fled, heaven only knows; but it was not left to her to choose, for, as she turned a corner, who should she encounter but Mrs. Joyce, who affected to be quite surprised to meet her niece, but who, in reality, had been a witness to the interview which had just taken place between St. Ives and Eva, and who felt no small amount of chagrin at the turn affairs had taken.

"Heighday! Why, where on earth are you running to, at such a pace as this?"

These words recalled Eva to herself somewhat, and she gazed in her aunt's face in a dreamy kind of way, but made no reply.

Her aunt saw that she was in no state to walk even the short distance that they would have to traverse to reach their home; so, hailing a hackney coach which happened at that moment to be passing, poor Eva was soon within the precincts of the chamber, which she had been wont to call her own.

As soon as she reached that room, however, with one gasping sob, she fell to the floor, and lay insensible.

"Help, help!" shrieked Mrs. Joyce. "She is dead! Help! some one!"

Perhaps, as she looked upon that young face, and saw the suffering about the sweet mouth, even her conscience smote her, and she would have given worlds that her part in the said drama could have been undone.

The cries of Mrs. Joyce alarmed the whole house, and all with one accord rushed up to Eva's room.

A medical man was soon in attendance, who seemed to consider the case as one of extreme gravity.

With the strictest injunctions concerning her being kept quiet, he took his departure.

Poor Eva remained in a kind of semi-trance for some hours. It was a condition which the medical man did not think it prudent to adopt any energetic means of rousing her from.

He preferred that Nature should for a time have her course, knowing well that she would do more remedially than Art could ever hope to accomplish. He hoped that the state she was in would lapse into sleep, and if it should not, he gave orders that he was to be sent for again.

Another hour passed away, and then Eva, after moaning, sadly awoke.

The difference in her breathing aroused Mrs. Joyce that the mourner was again in the land of realities, and no longer slept that distracted sleep which took her spirit to the land of dreams for transient happiness, or for greater misery as it might chance.

Days, weeks passed, during which Eva hovered between life and death.

At length a change for the better took place in her symptoms, and one morning she turned gently on the pillow, and said faintly, "Aunt! Aunt! Where are you?"

"Here, Eva—are you better?"

She stretched out one of her little hands—it was moist and calm. The flush of fever had gone from it.

"Oh, yes, I am well now, and wise," she added, with a sigh. "I feel calm, and as happy as I can ever hope to be now. Hark! what was that? I thought—I fancied I heard *his* voice."

Eva was right. St. Ives was in the room below—but he had come accompanied by his wife this time;

and they were, in fact, making the necessary arrangements for the invalid's removal, as soon as that could be accomplished with the consent of the medical man.

"I will go and see who is below, Eva," said Mrs. Joyce, in good truth nothing loath to escape from the sick room where she had been compelled to pass so much of her time of late.

As she descended the stairs, she became convinced that it was the voice of St Ivves she heard speaking to her brother.

A well pleased smile flitted across her face, as she thought to herself that only the first part of the drama had been enacted.

"My dear Captain Granville," she exclaimed; but she got no further, for she did not expect to see that he was accompanied by a lady, and that lady his wife.

CHAPTER CLXXXI.

EVA ST. CLARE RECEIVES THE REWARD OF VIRTUE.

TREADING lightly lest she should disturb the gentle girl to whom she was about to impart comfort and consolation, the Stuart Princess entered the chamber of Eva.

There was a bright flush upon the face of the invalid, as her visitor advanced towards her, but there was such a look of goodness and gentleness on the countenance of the Stuart Princess, that Eva instantly stretched out her hand towards her, as though she had been expecting her.

"This is kind," she said gently. "I have so often thought about you during my tedious illness, and wished so much that I could see you, and hear you say before I die that you forgive me all—all the sorrow of which I have been the unhappy cause."

"Hush, hush! dear Eva; do not talk of dying. I have come to ask you to be my sister—my friend—my constant companion."

Eva raised herself, and looked steadfastly into the eyes of her visitor, as though she doubted whether she had heard aright.

At length she said, "Be your sister?"

"Even so—you once wished to think of Charles as a brother—will you not extend the same affection to me?"

As she said this, the Stuart Princess drew the bowed head towards her, and when it rested on her bosom, she whispered, "Dear Eva, I know all your goodness—all the temptation to which you have been subjected; and I know, also, how bravely you withstood temptation, and can guess how great was the sacrifice you were willing to make rather than sacrifice me."

"Has *he* told you all?" murmured Eva.

"Yes, dear Eva, and I am here now to ask you for both our sakes, to get well and come and live with us."

"Dare I—ought I?"

Eva saw not the flush that rose to the brow of the Princess, as she unwittingly asked a question which would seem to imply that she feared the influence she, Eva, had possessed over St. Ives might not entirely have passed away.

But the reply was gentle.

"Fear not to accept our offer, dear Eva. My husband henceforth will regard you as a much loved sister—with an affection, in fact, which, while it will satisfy your heart, will not take one iota of the love he has for me as his wife—away. Will you consent?"

"Most willingly—most gratefully," was all poor Eva could say, as a flood of tears choked her utterance.

Again the slight form was pressed to the heart of her who had so nobly adopted that friendless orphan, and feeling that the interview had been rather an exciting one, the Princess took her leave, promising to return again the next day.

And Eva was left alone.

Who shall attempt to describe the tumult of thought which whirled through the heart and brain of that young and innocent girl, as she reflected on all that had passed in the brief interview with the wife of the man whom she could not but tell herself had made her feel the intoxicating influence of first love?

And well was it for Eva that her very innocence, instead of making her an easy prey to one so well calculated as St. Ives was to awaken love,—well was it for Eva that virtue became her lover, her pride, her comfort, her life of life!

She felt sure now that he would never seek to rob her of that treasure, and she no longer feared danger.

She looked forward, with a feeling akin to ecstacy, to, in time, being his firmest, truest friend. She felt that she would henceforth be a nobler and a better being. She saw life through the medium of purifying admiration for a gifted nature and a profound and generous soul.

Nay, she now contemplated with pleasure the prospect of seeing his affection for his devoted wife manifested in a thousand different ways.

The Princess did not fail to visit her young friend the next day, according to her promise; and every day for more than a week she might have been seen talking cheerfully to Eva, who was beginning to feel the benefit of her refined conversation, and to look forward with impatience to her visit.

At length it was agreed that Eva should bid adieu to her uncle and aunts, and take up her abode with St. Ives and his now happy wife.

Mrs. Joyce shed abundance of tears at parting with her "darling niece," as she designated Eva for the first time in her life; while her uncle wished her all kinds of happiness; and his wife quietly acquiesced in every arrangement that was made, as was her wont in general.

Eva's heart was too tender not to feel somewhat sad at parting with those who, although they had never shown her any particular kindness, had yet had allowed her to go her own way, and amuse herself in her own fashion.

At length the adieus were finished, and in a hackney coach Eva, accompanied by the Stuart Princess, reached her new home.

St. Ives received them, and there was something so fraternal, yet so solicitous in his behaviour for his young friend's comfort, that Eva felt the dread she had all along of their first meeting depart, never to return.

* * * * * *

The reader is too well acquainted with the affectionate interest, if we may use the word, which Claude Duval had ever taken in the welfare of the Stuart Princess, not to be fully aware of the anxiety with which he waited to hear some tidings of the result of her journey to her home where she had known so much happiness and so much sorrow.

Lucy, indeed, could scarcely control her impatience to go and seek her, for might she not encounter St. Ives, and would the meeting be a welcome one to him, and if it were not, "Oh, Claude!" she exclaimed, "what will become of that poor heart-broken wife? Let me go!"

"Nay, nay, Lucy," replied Duval; "I know not why, but I have felt a kind of conviction that all will yet be well."

Lucy shook her head doubtingly, as she said—

"I thought that all would be well with them; little

did I ever suspect that that heroic girl would ever have such a trouble as this to battle with."

"Nor I—nor I!" said Duval. "But I promise you, if you do not receive tidings in the course of to-morrow of your friend, I will go and seek her myself."

Lucy seemed much better satisfied now, and the day passed happily to her; for was not Claude with her, and did he not seem the same loving husband that he had been when he first took her to that deserted mansion, and called her his precious wife—his priceless treasure?

Towards the end of the third day there came to Lucy a little billet, containing the following happy intelligence:—

"DEAR FRIEND,—

"Do not be uneasy about me any longer. I have found him whom my heart pined to look upon again, and am happy—oh, how happy no one can tell. I am now going to visit my dear *sister*, Eva St. Clare, but was anxious to send you these few words, as I knew you would be glad to hear from

"Your affectionate friend,
"MARY MIRAVEL."

Lucy wept for joy as she read the above, and Claude Duval seemed greatly moved.

"Thank heaven," he exclaimed, "that she is happy!"

"Yes," said Lucy, "heaven grant that it may continue! I think—I hope it will."

"And now, Lucy," added Duval, "that I see your smile has returned, and you are no longer anxious about your friend, I will tell you what my plans are, for, in good truth, I have led but an idle life lately, my Lucy."

"But we have been so happy, Claude," pleaded Lucy.

"Yes, dear one; and we are not going to bid adieu to happiness because I am going to carry out an adventure or two."

"No, Claude."

"Then do not look sad, dear Lucy, for I am going into the very best society—as far as wealth goes, at least, for I intend to go to Court."

"Be careful, Claude."

"Indeed, I will, my Lucy; but it is some time now since I saw my friend the Chancellor, and he will think I have forgotten him."

"I almost wish, dear Claude, that you had never seen him."

"Nay, do not wish that. Think how I may be able to do good in some way or other. But do not look alarmed, I am merely going to a masquerade at the Opera House, and if it will be any relief to your mind, Blossom shall accompany me, so that if I should get into any scrape, you may hear from him exactly what is the matter, and not be fancying it worse than it is."

"Thank you—thank you, Claude! I always feel more content that you should have some one with you."

"To take care of me, Lucy?" said Claude, in a tone of pique.

"No; but as you say, the probability is, that if, at any time, anything should happen to you, it is not likely but that he will be able to make good his escape to apprise me of your danger, and let me know if anything can be done for you."

"Exactly. Then you are now content to let me gang my own gait?"

"If you wish to do so—yes."

"Then I do most assuredly, dear Lucy."

Duval now went to his chamber, and in a few minutes, in answer to his summons, Blossom made his appearance.

There was a look of expectation upon the face of Blossom as he entered the room as he said—

"Shall I get Nightshade ready for a canter to-night, Captain? It is a long while since he had one over the heath."

"Not to-night, Blossom," replied Duval. "I have other plans."

Blossom looked somewhat disappointed, but he did not express his disappointment in words.

"I intend," continued Duval, "to be present at the masquerade to-night."

Blossom looked interested.

"And," added Duval, "if you would like to accompany me, you can do so."

"All right, Captain! I should, indeed; but how is it to be managed? How shall we dress?"

"I think we had better both be dressed in suits of plain black; but we will each be provided with three dominoes."

"I see—I see, Captain! So that if we get into any scrape, by throwing off a domino, we shall then present a totally different appearance."

"Exactly. Now go and make your preparations?"

When Duval and Blossom reached the neighbourhood of the Opera House—now called Her Majesty's Theatre—it was as much as they could do, after alighting from the coach which had conveyed them to the scene of action, to elbow their way through the dense crowd which had congregated even about the very vestibule of the Opera House.

The usual Babel of sounds was there—shouts, cries, and groans—as carriage after carriage drove up to set down their occupants, among whom were some of the highest and noblest in the land.

Duval had, during the day, taken care to provide himself with two tickets, so that he had nothing to do but to present them, and pass on; instead of - as many had to do who had not had the forethought to procure them early in the day—to purchase them of an individual who was selling them in a kind of pigeon-hole to the right.

"We shall have some sport, Captain, to-night," whispered Blossom—"that is to say, if you intend to do a little business as well as pleasure."

"Hush," said Duval, "you know not who may be behind us in this crowd."

Blossom took the hint, and was silent.

Laughter—loud, shrill, hysterical in its vehemence, prolonged beyond all power of cessation—rang through the house with a million of echoes.

Music that, with its clashing sounds—only now and then made itself heard above the wild rout of noises.

Now and then, the angry tones of quarrel—the screams of those entangled in some brawl—those of the softer sex, who were so well represented, so far as numbers went, in the busy scene.

Whirling, dancing figures, half-mad with excitement.

The blaze of lights.

The aroma of rich wines.

The sparkle of jewels.

The clash of swords.

All made up a scene of confusion and of riot, that, up to the hour of three in the morning, shewed no signs of flagging or abating.

Many of the maskers had changed their costumes twice or thrice in the course of the evening, so that the confusion in false recognitions, and the jests and disputes consequent thereon, kept up that strange roar of sounds which could be heard, like the subdued murmur of the sea, at some streets' length from the busy scene.

CHAPTER CLXXXII.

CLAUDE DUVAL IS BETRAYED BY THE DUCHESS OF CLEVELAND.

Duval and Blossom made their way as quickly as they could into the very centre of the scene of action, and not until they had reached that position, could Duval be said to have looked about him to notice any individual in particular in that moving mass.

The scene was brilliant.

The tier upon tier of boxes were filled with fashionable company.

Mad, whirling dances were going on in the smallest possible space, and under the most difficult conceivable conditions.

Duval had now began to take a survey of the company filling the boxes, and he was not long before he recognised the fair Duchess of Cleveland, looking, perhaps, more radiantly beautiful than ever.

"Stay here, Blossom," he said. "I am going to speak to some one in the boxes."

"All right, Captain!" said Blossom. "But be careful."

Duval made his way with some difficulty through the crowd of officers—Turks, Indians, French—grotesque animals, dominoes, all mingling up together in one dense mass, with an army of dancing-girls, flower-sellers, ballet-posturers, mythological divinities; and, in fact, every possible and impossible representation of real or supposed costumes in the, or above or below the world.

At length he reached the Duchess's side, who happened, at that moment, to be leaning back in her chair with a look of thoughtfulness upon her fair face which was scarcely in keeping with the riotous scene she had come to witness.

"You are thoughtful, Duchess!" whispered Duval behind her. "Are you thinking of absent friends?"

The Duchess started.

"Claude—Claude Duval—you here?"

"And why not? Are not you here?"

Duval said these few words in his most winning accents; and instantly the face of the Duchess was lit up with a smile of gratified vanity.

"You repent, then," she whispered, "of your obstinacy, and—and——"

"And what?" asked Duval, smiling.

"And do you love me?"

"To see you is to love you."

The Duchess looked down, and played with her fan, but her heart beat quickly, and she could have fainted with over joy at hearing the admission Claude Duval had just made.

And the reader must not be too severe upon him, for thus speaking.

It was a part of the evening's entertainment, to talk occasionally sentimental nonsense, and Claude Duval was just the man to do the kind of thing, without in the slightest degree, even in thought, being unfaithful to his Lucy.

He knew that the Duchess was weak enough to be very fond of him—but then he knew perfectly well at the same time, that she would easily be consoled for the loss of his friendship, or affection—call it what she might—whenever he saw that the fitting time had come to withdraw it from her, and so he resolved to enjoy her society for that evening, at least.

Whether such a resolution were wise or not, will be shown in the course of this true history.

"Well," said Duval, "Well Duchess, have you nothing to say to me, after wishing so much to see you?"

"If I thought—if I could believe that my affection was returned, and that you would——"

"Would what, Duchess?"

"Forsake her, whom you were mad enough to marry on the impulse of a moment, but who can neither understand nor appreciate your talents."

Duval did not reply, but looked fixedly at the Duchess, who went on.

"Oh, Claude, Claude! I knew not how dear you were to me, until I thought we had parted, never to meet again."

"But here I am," quietly replied Duval.

"Yes, and I am happy."

The Duchess laid her small jewelled hand upon his, and looked lovingly up into his face.

Duval gently withdrew his hand. At that moment, he felt that Lucy—his Lucy, was worth ten thousand such women, young and beautiful as the Duchess was —But it was no part of his plan at present, to bring the interview to a close, for he had looked upon a face which he recognised.

The face of Muckles, the police officer.

"You have sought me then to night, Claude?"—she called him only Claude now—"you have sought me then to night, Claude, to tell me that you love me, and me only.

"Scarcely that, Duchess—My hand is another's——"

"Pshaw!"

"My heart——"

"Your heart, you would say, is mine. Then why go on deceiving that young girl, and making her believe that you love her, when in reality you love another?"

"Pardon me, Duchess, you interrupted what I was going to say. I was about to say, that my heart was hers long before I gave her my hand, and——"

The Duchess shrieked.

All eyes were instantly turned towards the box occupied by the Duchess, and before Duval could effect his retreat, some half dozen gentlemen surrounded him and the Duchess.

"Help! help!" shrieked the Duchess, "a highwayman! Claude Duval, gentlemen! Seize him! seize him!"

"Here you are, gentlemen," said a voice at this moment at the back of the box, and Muckles, the police-officer, with half a dozen of his men, made their way up to Duval.

"Now, Mr. Duval," said Muckles, "if you please, sir —No mistake this time—I've got you tight enough."

As he spoke, Muckles, with the assistance of one of his men, slipped a pair of handcuffs over his wrists, and Claude Duval was indeed a prisoner.

The Duchess during the time, had studiously avoided Duval's eye for she felt how treacherously she had behaved, and if she could at that moment, have undone what she had done, she would willingly have laid down the whole of her wealth, to have accomplished such an object.

"I am ready," said Duval, in a clear, calm voice. "Lead the way, Mr. Muckles. Duchess, whenever you want *a friend*, do not forget, Claude Duval."

"Stay! oh, stay!" cried the Duchess.

But the police officers, either heard not, or heeded not the entreaty, and as soon as the door of the box was closed with a bang, the Duchess fell to the floor in a swoon.

In the meantime, Claude Duval was jostled and hustled by the officers in no very ceremonious manner, through the house, and down the stairs, at the foot of which stood Blossom.

A sign from Duval probably had the effect of checking an exclamation of sorrow and surprise which was about to escape from his faithful follower, who then remembered that it was in order to convey intelligence to Lucy that he had been chosen as the companion of that night's adventures.

Blossom heard the order for a hackney coach, given in vociferous language by all the officers at once, he saw the coach driven off.

He had heard the direction given by Muckles to the driver.

"To Newgate!"

Blossom reeled against the wall as he heard the ominous words.

"How shall I break the news to her? Oh, how shall I tell her?" he kept repeating to himself.

"Now, sir—move on, sir—you're on my foot, sir; and if you don't move on, I shall take you up for being drunk and disorderly."

Like one in a dream, Blossom obeyed the injunction to "move on."

"Whatever is to be done, must be done quickly," said Blossom to himself, as he walked at a brisk pace from the opera house.

At first, he had some idea of hiring a hackney coach, but he soon discarded the thought, when he found that he did not encounter any of those crazy vehicles—the truth is, Blossom had more faith in his own powers of sharp walking, then he had in a dozen of the poor hacks, which, at that period, were even worse than the cab horse of the present day, at going a distance.

So Blossom walked on, pondering in his mind the best means of telling Lucy of the capture of Duval.

The first person he encountered on entering the mansion on the heath, was Lucy herself.

A strange, undefined kind of fear had crept over her—a fear of, she knew not what; and when she saw Blossom was alone, she guessed at once the true state of the case.

"Tell me—tell me at once, Blossom; for I know you have evil tidings."

"Just so; but we must see what we can do," stammered Blossom.

"Where is he?"

"In Newgate, by this time, I fancy."

Blossom expected that Lucy would either faint, or shriek, or do something that would be productive of no good results to him whom they were both so anxious to serve. It was, therefore, with no small degree of satisfaction that he saw her merely sink into a chair, and, covering her eyes with her hands, give herself up to reflection.

"Better than I expected," he muttered to himself. "I might have known that she would do the right thing. I, too, must think."

Blossom was about to leave the room, when Lucy removed her hands from before her eyes, and arrested his steps.

"Stay, Blossom," she said, "we must lay our plans together. Are you quite sure he is in Newgate?"

"I can't say. Those were the words, 'to Newgate,' that I heard Muckles say to the driver."

"Blossom, you must find out where he is, and let me know. I will go with you to London, we must not lose time going backwards and forwards."

"You?"

"Yes, Blossom, who but I should risk even life itself, if that be necessary, for Claude Duval?"

There was a look of heroism upon the face of the young wife, as she uttered these words, that made her look surpassingly lovely.

"I have hopes now," he said, as he looked at Lucy, "that we shall be able to find out some means of serving the Captain, so as soon as you are ready, let me know, and I will take you to a friend of mine in Newgate Street, where you can wait while I go and make inquiries."

In less than a couple of hours from that time, Lucy was seated in a little room, at the back of a little dark shop in Newgate Street, waiting for Blossom to bring her tidings of one dearer to her than life itself.

She had not long to wait, for Blossom returned in less than an hour.

"It's all right. I know pretty well the very cell he is in."

"That is something, Blossom, that is something. Now, how are we to proceed?"

We must now leave Lucy and Blossom discussing their plans for his deliverance, while we, with the privilege of readers, pay a visit to Claude Duval in his cell.

How desolate he felt.

With what a feeling of anguish did he think upon Lucy and all her loving ways. For did not her pure affection stand out brightly before him now, as contrasted with the passion which the Duchess of Cleveland had professed for him?

What would not his Lucy suffer when she heard of the sad incident of his arrest?

Claude Duval strode up to the wicket which was in the door of his cell, and by putting his fingers through the bars, was enabled to push back the little panel.

This the prisoners in their cells were quite at liberty to do, for the opening in the door was too small, even if he had succeeded in removing the iron bars to admit of anything larger than a cat.

Claude Duval now, with the heel of his boot, hammered lustily at the door of his cell.

"Well, what now?" said a turnkey, who had heard the noise, and whose duty it was to come and see what was the matter.

"I want to see Mr. Muckles," said Duval.

"Then you won't," replied the man; "for he's gone away, and won't be back again for a day or two."

"But he has——"

"Who are you?"

This exclamation proceeded from the gaoler as some one, apparently by accident, stumbled against him.

"A visitor to the prisoner."

A tall, gentlemanly-looking man, dressed in a suit of black, now showed himself as he turned to the warder by whom he was accompanied, and said,—"Thank you, my friend, I will not trouble you further. When I have a desire to leave this unhappy man, I will rap at the wicket."

"All right sir—your reverence, I mean."

"Oh, a parson!" said the other turnkey.

"Hush, Bill! I think he's a bishop, or a curate, or something of that sort—mind what you are at."

Claude Duval had taken no part in the conversation; indeed, his mind was so full of other thoughts, that he scarcely understood that the clerical-looking personage had referred to him when he spoke of the "unhappy man."

The turnkey closed the door of the cell with a loud bang, and Claude Duval and his mysterious visitor were left alone together.

"Hist! be quick, Captain, and tell me what is to be done."

"Blossom!"

"Of course! I knew I should be able to get in if I put on such a dress as this, and you see I am not mistaken. Will bribery do, Captain?"

"I scarcely know as yet; Muckles will not be here for two or three days, and the governor is ill; so that if we could make it worth their while, we might be able to buy the services of these men."

"That's what I was thinking, Captain, and Miss Lucy, too, for the matter of that."

"Ah, poor Lucy! how does she bear up."

"Capitally, Captain; she's in Newgate Street, waiting for you."

"Waiting fer me?"

"Yes, Captain; so you know you must be quick, and decide as to what you will do."

"Now then, gentlemen," said the man who had shown Blossom into the cell. "Now then, gentlemen, if you please, time's up." Then he added in a low voice, so as to be heard only by Duval and Blossom,— "Make it worth my while, and I'll tell you how to escape, Claude Duval."

"Ah!"

"Hush! I will speak to you again. Now, sir," speaking in a loud voice; "if you please, sir, this way."

Blossom hastily whispered to Duval the name of the man at whose shop Lucy was staying in Newgate Street, and withdrew.

"I wonder if that man is to be trusted?" said Duval to himself, when he was left alone. Ah!——"

"Here I am, Captain! what will you stand, now, if I tell you how you may get out of the stone jug?"

"I would give you twenty guineas to-night, and ten more when I am free."

"Thirty guineas! Well, it's cheap; but I like and admire you. Claude Duval, and so I'll do it."

"You will?"

"I will; but you must understand that I shall have to leave myself, as well."

"You?"

"Yes; because they would be sure to know that I had aided in your escape, and the consequences are not pleasant."

Claude Duval reflected for a few moments, and then he said,—"If you really are able to set me free, and are willing to become one of my band——"

"Oh, Captain, Captain! the dream of my life would be realized. Let me serve you, and I shall be only too happy."

"Agreed, then! Now tell me your plan."

"It is soon told. The gaolers are now making merry, and I alone am on duty in this part of Newgate. I will get Jim Taylor, a friend of mine, to visit you."

"To visit me?"

"Yes; and you shall change clothes with him; he is about your height; and you shall go out in his."

"But your friend may not be willing?"

"Lor' bless you, he's only half-sharp, Captain, and will do anything if you do but promise him a glass o' purl. So you see the thing is quite easy."

"We shall see—we shall see!" said Duval. "I must confess I am not very sanguine."

"You just will see, Captain. In two hours' time from now, I will bring my friend to see you."

How long did those two hours appear to Claude Duval; but at last his patience was rewarded by hearing the sound of voices approaching his cell.

"They come—they come!" said Duval to himself.

"An extra glass of purl, did you say, ah! you are good——But what are we going in here for?"

"Be quiet and you shall see."

At this moment the warder opened the cell-door, and Jim Taylor stared at Duval, who returned his look with a smile

"This is the gentleman, Jim, I told you would give you an extra glass of purl."

"Ah! Thanks, thanks!"

"But he has a fancy to go and fetch it himself, so as he has neither wish nor inclination to go out without a hat such a night as this, why you must just lend him your's."

"Oh, the gentleman may have the loan of mine in welcome if he pleases," said Jim, as he tendered to Duval the article in question.

"And you may just as well lend him your cloak, too, Jim," said the warder, "for he can conceal the purl beneath that, or otherwise those fellows, who are drinking there, may ease him of it before he gets here!"

"To be sure, to be sure they may. Here, sir, take the cloak also—it is a large one, and will effectually conceal the purl."

"I see—I see," said Duval, as he clasped the cloak round his neck.

"Now then, follow me," whispered the goaler, "and you wait here till we return," he added, turning to his friend.

"All right - all right, don't be gone long!"

The warder led Duval through several stone passages and up a steep flight of steps, and at length they reached the vestibule, where several of the warders were making merry, while some were fast asleep, overcome with the deep libations of which they had been partaking.

"Oh, here is Job Miller!" shouted one; "won't you join us, old fellow," as the warder made his appearance, closely followed by Duval.

"Yes, yes—but I have promised this gentleman, who has made it worth my while to call with a message in the Old Bailey for him."

"Made it worth your while, eh? Then you'll stand treat!" shouted two or three in chorus.

"The very thing I mean to do," whispered the turnkey, "but don't let on, we don't know who he is."

"All right, all right! He doesn't seem to have much to say for himself, at all events!"

With this opinion, the men betook themselves to their tankards again, and Claude Duval stood free as air in the Old Bailey by the side of the gaoler, who was thenceforth to share his good and evil fortunes.

"Thanks, friend," said Duval, as he grasped the man's hand. "Here are the other guineas."

"No, Captain, I don't want them now, it is share and share alike, now that I am one of Claude Duval's men. Hurrah! I am free of the Stone Jug!"

CHAPTER CLXXXIII.

CLAUDE DUVAL MEETS WITH A STRANGE ADVENTURE.

As the reader may suppose, Claude Duval and Lucy had no intention of remaining longer than necessary in the neighbourhood of the Old Bailey.

Therefore, in less time than it has taken us to write, he, Lucy, and his new ally, the ex-warder of Newgate, were on their way to Hampstead.

They had not, however, proceeded very far, before Blossom joined them with Nightshade and another horse.

Claude assisted Lucy to mount Nightshade, and he himself intended to ride the other one, leaving Blossom and his new companion to follow on foot.

But Duval was deep in thought, and that fact accounted for his going so slowly, that Blossom and Miller, as the new man was named, had no difficulty in keeping pace with them on foot.

They had gone some distance at this pace, when just as they were passing one of those pretty suburban villages which abound in the neighbourhood of Hampstead, a young woman suddenly opened the garden gate, and as soon as she saw Duval, she raised her hand, as if by so doing she could force him to come to a standstill.

Simultaneously the party came to a halt, and then they heard the young woman say in a whisper, almost addressing herself to Duval.

"Oh, sir, are you a doctor?"

"No," replied Duval, "but I have some medical knowledge. Can I be of any assistance."

"Oh, pray come in, sir, I am so alarmed, and dare

not leave the house to fetch a medical man—but I dare say, sir, as you understand doctoring, you will do as well as any doctor."

Duval smiled at the young woman's unconscious bad compliment to the medical profession, but thinking, probably, that he might be of some use, he turned to Lucy and told her to go on with Blossom and Miller, and not expect him till she saw him.

Lucy felt anxious but not uneasy, as Duval, waving her an adieu, entered the well-kept garden, replete with all those prettinesses which make our suburban abodes so charming.

"This way, sir!" said the servant, as she preceded Duval up-stairs.

Duval fancied there was an air of mystery and secrecy rather than of quiet, which he expected to find; but he had no time for reflection, for the young woman opened a door on the top of the first flight of stairs; in which, by the aid of a dim light which burnt on the table, Duval was enabled to see a female figure, leaning her head on the arm of a sofa.

"Here's a doctor, ma'am," said the servant, addressing the female on the sofa.

There was no reply, and the words were twice again repeated before the female betrayed consciousness of them.

Then, however, she started up suddenly—so suddenly, indeed, that even Duval was thrown off his guard, and stepped back alarmed towards the door.

The female sunk back into a seat in a moment, and said, in a tone of exquisite anguish, "Leave the room, Martha. I will ring for you when the doctor is going."

The servant left the room, and then Duval turned towards the lady, and said, "I hope, madam, you are suffering from no serious indisposition?"

He had just got thus far, when she interrupted him by saying, "Doctor, tax you skill. Think of some drug—some potent means of banishing sleep for ever from my eyes. I must not, dare not sleep again."

"Then," she added, in a low hollow voice, "The reason is a simple one." Then she shuddered as she pronounced the words, "When I sleep I dream."

"Oh, is that all?" said Duval quietly; "Then we will get rid of the dreams without depriving you of your necessary sleep."

"Never! never!" she almost shrieked. "Oh, heaven! Never! never! Too well I know that dreadful vision will ever come to me! Oh, spare me!—spare me, heaven! My brain must sink, and then—then madness will ensue, and in the wild delusion I shall tell all, and while I blast the happiness of many others, bring upon myself disgrace and infamy. Oh, heaven! What awful sufferings do not some of thy creatures undergo! Spare me! Spare me! Mercy! Mercy! The dream! The dream!"

All this was uttered with such a wild vehemence of tone and manner, that Duval was perfectly astonished, and said hastily, "Pray be calm, my dear madam. Some freak of the imagination in a dream has distressed you, but you will soon forget it."

She fixed her eyes upon Duval, as she said slowly and distinctly, "This morning a beggar came to the gate—she was trembling with cold—fainting with hunger—her face was pinched and wan with want and misery—the scanty rags that covered her were shaken by the slightest wind—tears streamed down her sallow cheeks, and she prayed for the hardest crust, the merest offal to allay the pangs of hunger. Doctor, I envied that poor creature!"

"You envied her," said Duval, as he glanced round the luxuriously-furnished apartment.

"Oh, heavens! how I envied her!" she repeated. "But time is flying! There—there, sir, is your fee. Write me a prescription that will banish sleep for ever from my eyes. I must never sleep again!"

Duval shook his head, as he said, "Madam, you ask an impossibility. There are no means of banishing sleep, except by producing the sleep of death. All the energies of the medical profession are frequently directed to procure sleep for their patients but never to banish it."

"But mine is a different case!" she said, impatiently, and, as her eyes flashed with resentment, she added,—"You are an imposter, and no doctor!"

"I am sorry, then, that I came," said Duval, rising. "I had hoped to be of service, but I find I was mistaken."

The lady then clasped her hands together convulsively, and cried, "Sir, I implore of you to save me! You appear to be a gentleman by your conversation and bearing. I cannot endure existence. It is too frightful! Have mercy on me!"

"I really cannot comprehend you," said Duval, still keeping up the delusion in her mind that he was an accredited medical man, for he now began to feel certain that there had been some foul play at work—of what kind he could not tell—but he hoped before he had done with this strange adventure to be able to do good to some injured individual—perhaps to restore to calmness the agitated being he saw before him, and whom he still hoped he should find innocent of the great crime she seemed to impute to herself. "Come," he said, speaking gently, "you are anxious to consult a doctor, and yet you have not told me of any tangible indisposition. Tell me what it is that so distresses you?"

"For five nights," replied the lady,—"for five nights now in succession I have had a dream!"

There was a tone of plaintive misery in her accents that went at once to Duval's heart.

"Well?" he said, gently.

"A dream that has made me start raving from my slumbers. Oh, how I have striven to keep awake—but all in vain!"

"You have allowed this dream," said Duval, "to take too strong a hold of your imagination. I will write you a prescription, not to keep you awake, but to make you sleep sounder."

"Oh, no, no! Sleep is horrible! Oh, sir! do you think it possible that there is any mercy for—for——"

She paused, and Duval said, "For whom?"

"No—no matter; not now! There may come a time, but not now not yet. The dream will come again, and then I shall go mad! I know it too well—too well!"

"May I ask if you are married, madam?" asked Duval, for he was anxious now to speak to some one concerning her who would be a little more rational than herself; and then he fully intended to apprise that other person of the fact that he had no right to pretend to be a member of the medical profession, but had merely gone in at the earnest entreaty of the servant girl.

Again Duval repeated the question.

"Are you married?"

"Married?" she repeated; "I am—I am; and, as you see, childless. You know my child died—died in its infancy; and I put up with the dispensations of Providence. But now I am tormented by dreams—frightful dreams—that drive me mad. What do you suspect?"

"Suspect!" said Duval.

"Aye; you look so suspicious, man! What do you suspect, I ask?"

This was so strange a question that it was a moment or two before Duval could reply to it, and then all he said was, "Madam, I must leave you, for I fear our further conversation is not likely to benefit you. I will write you a prescription which cannot harm you,

MRS. MAURICE RELEASES DUVAL FROM THE CLOSET.

although I must say I know too little of the case to fancy it will do you much good."

Duval turned to write the prescription—which he was well able to do in the style and manner of the medical profession—when the lady started up suddenly, and before he was aware of her intention, she caught up a small phial, which was by her side, and applied its mouth to her lips.

In a moment, however, Duval had wrested it from her grasp.

"Are you mad?" he cried; "and if so, why send for me to be your keeper? I will call for assistance."

She threw herself on her knees at his feet, as she spoke, and looked up in his face with such an expression of abject fear, that Duval was much moved, and said to her, in a kinder voice than he had hitherto used—

"Will you confide in me, and tell me frankly the cause of your evident great mental distress?"

The same shudder he had noticed before came over

No. 55.—NIGHTSHADE.

her, and she rose from her knees, saying, in a voice a little above a whisper—

"No, no, I dare not—I cannot! Go now—go now at once! You have been here too long!"

CHAPTER CLXXXIV.

CLAUDE DUVAL FINDS HIMSELF IN AN AWKWARD POSITION.

AT this moment a loud appeal to the bell at the outer gate echoed through the house.

At the sound of that bell the mysterious invalid, with a scream, sunk into a chair, exclaiming, hysterically—

"My husband—my husband! All is lost!"

"Your husband!" exclaimed Duval. "Then I am only too glad, for he may be enabled to give me some explanation of the strange interview we have had together."

"No, no, not a word—not a word—on your life, not a word to him of what has passed between us! If you would avoid the curse of a dying woman, I implore you to speak not to him! Go in peace, as you have come, but oh! speak not to him!"

"I do not see how I can avoid doing so," replied Duval. "How can I account for my presence here, otherwise than by telling him why I am here?"

"Oh, you must hide—you must hide!"

"I beg your pardon," said Duval; "but I shall do no such thing."

"This closet!" she muttered, not heeding what Duval had said, "this closet will be your hiding-place!"

As she spoke, the lady flung open the door of a large cupboard which was at the end of the room.

"But, madam——" began Duval.

"Silence, sir!" she said, as at the same time she presented a large pistol at his head.

For the moment, Duval was so surprised that he could not utter a word.

There the two stood, confronting each other in silence.

The lady was the first to speak.

"Choose, sir," she said, with flashing eyes,—"choose between a few minutes' concealment, until I can get you out of the house without my husband's knowledge, or instant death! The weapon is loaded."

Duval felt the awkwardness of his position, for he was unarmed, even if he had had any intention of defending himself against the attack of what he had no doubt, in his own mind, was a mad woman.

He was in hopes that either the husband or the servant girl would again make her appearance, and therefore he strove to gain time by parleying with his antagonist.

"That closet?" he said. "Why, really, madam, your conduct is altogether extraordinary."

As he spoke, Duval approached a step nearer to her.

"Keep off, sir!" she cried, as she deliberately presented the pistol. "The slightest attempt on your part to take this weapon from me will cost you your life! As I told you before, the pistol is loaded."

At this moment a step was heard upon the staircase, and the lady immediately whispered, in frantic eagerness—

"The closet—the closet—or death!"

There was something in her looks and tone which convinced Duval she was quite capable of putting her threat into execution; and not, at the moment, being able to see his way out of the affair, and, moreover, being somewhat curious to learn more of the story of the mysterious female, he entered the cupboard

The lady immediately closed the door, and, to Duval's consternation, he heard her fasten it on the outer side.

He had not much time, however, for reflection, for almost as soon as the cupboard was fastened, Duval heard some one enter the room, and a man's voice said—

"My dear, you should not have sat up for me, in your delicate health."

And then he heard the lady reply, in quite a different tone of voice to that in which she had all along addressed him—

"I could not sleep; you know that I am afflicted with terrible dreams."

"What dream is it that troubles you so?" said the husband. "You never would tell me."

"An idle, fanciful dream, not worth the relation," replied the wife, in a high, hysterical tone of voice. "Some day you shall know all!"

"Know all! All what?"

"Nothing, nothing!—a mere nothing! I am much better now. You go to bed, and I will come very soon. I have a few things to put to rights in this room."

"Then leave them till to-morrow," said the husband, in a kind tone of voice. "You look feverish and unwell, and had better retire to rest. I declare I will, in spite of all you can say to the contrary, send for a physician to-morrow if you are not better."

"No, no!" she replied; "physicians can do nothing for me! Time may obliterate—!"

"Ah! you have ever been unhappy since our great loss. If our dear child had but lived——"

"Hush, hush! you will drive me mad!" said the wife. "Never—ah, never allude to her, unless you wish to see me some day drop a corpse at your feet. I cannot bear it! She is lost—lost to us for ever! There is—there cannot be the least hope!"

"Hope!" echoed the husband. "Of course there is no hope on this side the grave! I myself live but with the consolation of again meeting my beloved child in heaven."

The wife gave a loud scream, and she shrieked rather than said—

"Then I shall never see her—never—never! unless heaven has more mercy upon me than it is possible to conceive."

"What do you mean?" said the husband. "You alarm and afflict me by those strange hints! Oh, wife, wife! if there is anything pressing on your mind, let me know it, and what consolation one human being can give another, you shall have."

The wife moaned audibly.

"If it be only that you continue to grieve for the loss of our dear child, believe that I feel as acutely as you do, although I will not allow myself to be entirely beaten down by a domestic calamity, however terrible it may be."

She only replied by an agonizing burst of hysterical weeping. Her deep sobs were dreadful to hear, and Duval never in his life was so awkward and uncomfortable in a position in his life.

"Good heaven!" said the husband, suddenly, "why have you this pistol on the table? My dear, you should not meddle with these things, for they may pinch your fingers, although they are not loaded."

"Not loaded!" said Duval to himself. "What a confounded fool I have been, to be frightened into a cupboard for nothing!"

"Leave me—leave me!" cried the wife. "I shall be better soon. Leave me!"

"No, indeed, I shall not leave you any more to-night," was the reply. "You need comfort and society, so come away to your own chamber. I have some letters to write, which I will do at the dressing-table, while you endeavour to get some sound refreshing sleep."

"Sleep—sleep!" she cried. "I would not sleep for worlds! No, no! Such another dream would kill me!"

"Always harping upon that dream!" muttered the husband. "It is very strange—very strange, indeed!"

"It is—it is awfully strange; but leave me now— oh, leave me, I pray you!"

"Well—well!" said the husband. "I will write my letters in my own study, if you wish it, but I will send Martha to stay with you. Bless me, whose gloves are these?"

Duval remembered that he had flung down his gloves on the table as he entered the room.

"Whose gloves are these?" repeated the husband.

There was no reply, and he again said, with a tone of some asperity, "Whose gloves are these, I ask?"

"Gloves?" repeated the wife. "I told you they were thrown in at the window, and I took the pistol out of the closet to defend myself!"

"You never told me anything of the sort!" said the husband suspiciously. "This is the first I have heard of it, Mrs. Maurice!"

"Oh, their names are Maurice," thought Duval to himself. "I wish to goodness, Mrs. Maurice, you had been a thousand miles off before you drew me into such an adventure."

"I care not whether you heard of it before or not!" she replied, carelessly.

"I have my suspicions, ma'am!" he said.

"You are welcome to them!" was the reply.

"Woman!" said the husband, after a pause, "there is guilt upon your soul! Your manner, your trepidation, and your dread of sleep, all tend to prove that some secret cause of disquietude is ever present to you!"

"Good heavens!" she said, "there wanted but this to fill my cup of misery to the brim!"

"In heaven's name, explain yourself!" cried the husband.

"Will you kill me?" she said.

"Kill you?"

"Yes; will you—will you do me so much grace as to take my life? Oh, I could worship the hand that would take my life!"

"I cannot understand you! To-morrow we will talk more at large concerning this affair; but, for the present, I will keep these gloves, with the hope of finding an owner for them!!"

With these words, Duval heard him leave the room, and he had scarcely been gone a minute when the wife opened the closet door, and, clasping her hands, she said, in a tone of wild entreaty, "Fly, fly! You will easily find your way! Leave this house instantly!"

"Upon my word, madam," said Duval, "you are complimentary as well as considerate; but I will not fly!"

"You will not?"

"Certainly not! Why should I?"

"To save one who is innocent from despair! To light up for the remainder of a life the flame of joy! To restore the parent to his child!"

"Explain yourself!" said Duval.

"Meet me to-morrow night at eight o'clock, by the corner of Spring Gardens, and you shall hear a tale which, in the telling, may kill me!"

"Thank you, I would rather not!" said Duval.

"Then hear me now swear, as I believe there is a heaven above us, I will destroy myself this night without repairing the evil I have done!"

"You had better tell your husband," said Duval.

"No, no, no! Some stranger alone can act in such a manner as to restore what is lost!"

"You speak in riddles," said Duval; "but I promise to meet you as you propose, but I do not bind myself to keep any secrets!"

"I do not wish you," replied his strange companion. "When I tell you that it is with the wish that you should be the medium of divulging what has been kept locked in my own heart for five years now!"

"Is it possible," said Duval, "that you could succeed in concealing a secret from your husband so many years?"

"Yes—yes, it is! The other person who knew it is dead—gone to that dreadful account which I shall soon go to! Oh, horror—horror! Is there no hope? Oh, heaven, have mercy!"

Claude Duval gazed in wonder and astonishment upon the mysterious person with whom he had become, so to speak, mixed up; and as she sunk back into a chair, he resolved, then and there, to end the adventure, which was anything but in accordance with his taste.

With this intention, he reached the door and crept down the stairs as noiselessly as he could, in hopes of reaching the street unseen by the husband, for he had no desire to rouse his suspicions either against himself, or to direct his attention to the fearful secret he now had no doubt his wife carried in her heart.

However, the Fates decreed that it should be otherwise, for just as Duval got to the foot of the stairs, a door immediately opposite opened, and a gentlemanly-looking man appeared, carrying a lighted candle in his hand.

They stood for a moment confronting each other, those two men, and then Duval said, in as calm a voice as he could summon on the circumstances, "How do you do, Mr. Maurice?"

The husband seemed to be so astonished at what he considered Duval's cool impudence, that he said nothing for another minute; then he darted back again into the apartment he had just left, and returned to the hall, armed with a bright steel poker.

"Mr. Maurice," said Duval, "you are labouring under an error! Pray be calm!"

"I think it is you, you scoundrel, who are labouring under an error!" he replied, with a face as white as a sheet with passion; "and you shall be labouring under this! Pray, sir, may I so far presume in my own house as to ask you if these are your gloves?"

"They are, sir," said Duval; "but——"

"None of your buts, sir."

"I will explain."

"I want no explanation," cried the enraged husband, as he aimed a blow at the head of Duval with the poker, which, however, he was fortunate enough to step aside and so avoid.

The blow, however, took effect upon a plaster cast in the hall, which it smashed to pieces.

Duval now watched his opportunity, and closed with the infuriated husband, and being the stronger man of the two he soon pushed him, poker and all, into the parlour; and the key luckily being on the outside of the lock he fastened him in, and then rushed from the house, pursued by a little yelping terrier, who held on by the leg of his trousers, and would not let go until he knocked him off with a great piece of cloth in his mouth.

Duval now ran across the garden, clambered over the gate, which was locked, and found himself in the Hampstead Road, without his hat and gloves, in a mizzling shower of rain.

Duval had scarcely ever been out in so persevering a rain.

It came down in perfect lumps of water, as it were, and ran into his neck, splashing and dashing a trickling stream down his back of an intense coldness.

However, as he was not inclined to "stand the pelting of the pitiless storm," he shrank under the friendly archway of a neighbouring stable-door, with the intention of waiting till the weather should moderate.

But it was something like waiting for a legacy to wait until that rain should cease—on—on it went, with a provoking calmness, that looked very much as if it had made up its mind to continue for an indefinite period.

There was no bullying, no blustering about the weather—as in the case of a thunder-storm, when the more noise there is, the more bluster, like human passions, we know it will be the sooner over. But this was a steady, easy-going, cautious rain—if we may use the term—one of those rains that go steadily pelting on, as if they knew they had lots to come.

After waiting about twenty minutes, Duval began to feel very cold, for he had been in the rain quite long enough to get very damp, although not wet through, and he reluctantly thought of moving.

"I must walk on," he thought to himself. "There is no other resource, and ring them up at the first public-house I come to."

It was far from pleasant to be without a hat on such a night, and all that Duval could do was to wind his handkerchief round his head, in the manner that old women do on the continent, which, however, was far from an effectual repulse to the rain.

He was, then, upon the point of leaving the shelter of the gateway when the welcome sound of wheels came upon his ears.

CHAPTER CLXXXV.

CLAUDE DUVAL BEFRIENDS MR. MAURICE.

Some vehicle was evidently coming from London towards Hampstead, and that at a pretty smart pace, too.

"Here is a chance, at all events," said Duval to himself; and he sallied out into the road, and cried, "Hilloa!"

"Well, what now?" said a man's voice, as a gig pulled up abruptly.

"I have lost my hat," said Duval, "and I thought I might get a lift by paying for it; but I see, I am speaking to a gentleman."

"Lost your hat?" said the gentleman in the gig.

"Yes."

"Ah! I should know that voice among a thousand," said the gentleman, who had been driving the gig, as he sprang out and seized Duval by the collar.

"You are the man who was at my house, to-night!" he shouted.

"I am," said Duval.

"Then, sir; I have a question to put to you."

"Have you," said Duval; "and I, Mr. Maurice, have a great many to put to you."

"Confound your impudence!" said the enraged husband. "Do you know, I shall horsewhip you, sir, in case you refuse me the satisfaction of a gentleman."

"Mr. Maurice; you are a fool!" said Duval.

"What, sir?"

"A fool, sir!" replied Duval; "for you do not look before you leap. You want me to fight a duel without asking the least explanation of my appearance at your house."

"I want no explanation, sir; the circumstances explain themselves to any reasonable man."

"Which you are not. But nevertheless, I am willing," continued Duval, "to look over your very intemperate conduct, and to explain to you the cause of my appearance at your house, if you will listen to me."

"Answer me but one word!" shouted the husband. "Will you or will you not, meet me when and where our respective friends may appoint?"

"No!"

"You will not?"

"No!"

"Then you must take the consequences."

So saying, Mr. Maurice began to flourish his whip about; but as Claude was young and agile, and very strong, he was enabled to spring upon him in an instant, and brought him to the ground, when he instantly wrestled the whip from his grasp, and flung it over the hedge.

"Mr. Maurice," he said, "you are making yourself exceedingly ridiculous, and I am sorry to see you in that situation. I can satisfactorily, as far as your honour and my own are concerned, explain to you the cause of my presence in your house."

Duval then related to him all the circumstances of which the reader is already aware, and concluded by saying. "Now, sir, I have given you an explanation of my conduct, which ought to satisfy a gentleman; now, let us part better friends, than we met."

"Sir," said Mr. Maurice, "I beg your pardon."

"Granted," said Duval. "Good evening."

"But, sir—sir," continued the husband, "will you allow me the pleasure of making your acquaintance."

"Certainly, Mr. Maurice, if you desire it."

Mr. Maurice sighed deeply, and said, "I was on my way to fetch a medical man to see my wife; but from what you have told me, I fear that hers is no malady his skill could touch. Will you return with me, and let me make you acquainted with some passages in my past life?"

"Most willingly," replied Duval, "now that you can converse like a man of sense."

"Get into the gig then, and I will drive you to my house."

Half an hour's drive was sufficient to bring the gig to the garden-gate, which Duval had entered under such very different circumstances, only a few hours previously.

A lad took charge of the gig, and Mr. Maurice at once led Duval to the apartment in which he, Duval, had made the master of that house a prisoner.

Mr. Maurice closed and locked the door of the apartment, and motioning to Duval to be seated, he rested his elbow on the table for a few minutes, and shaded his eyes with his hand, as though he were nerving himself to speak of things that he knew, would move him much.

"At length," he said, looking at Duval, with a sad expression; "I am the unhappiest of men. Fourteen years ago, I married a woman of my choice, and in every way worthy of such a choice. We lived a life of uninterrupted happiness together."

"Let us hope," said Duval, "that such may be the case again."

The husband shook his head, and went on.

"We had one child—a girl—and then as she—the child, I mean—fell into a very bad state of health; indeed, we were—much against our inclination—compelled to send it to nurse with my wife's sister—a woman I never liked."

Duval began to feel deeply interested.

"Well, sir," continued Mr. Maurice; "the child seemed to thrive, and do well, for some time; when, one day, I found my wife was in tears."

"Yes."

"The reason was soon told; our child had died suddenly in some of those spasmodic complaints incidental to infancy.

"I was inconsolable.

"For a week, I scarcely eat or drank; but time at length assuaged the violence of my grief, and I began once again to mingle with my fellow creatures, and to feel an interest in the affairs of the world.

"My grief, however, remained, although it had calmed down to a more sober feeling.

"But the most remarkable circumstance connected with the whole affair, was the conduct of my wife, who seemed to forget the loss of her child completely; and, with the exception of occasional fits of gloomy despondency, she was ever in good spirits.

"I often spoke to her about our loss; but she always answered in such words of resignation, as I never yet heard come from the lips of a mother, however unreasonable they may be.

"Well, sir; time wore on. We had no more children; and it seemed, as I recovered, in some degree, from my grief at the death of my child, and resumed my usual habits, my wife gradually sank beneath the pressure of some hidden grief.

"She scarcely ever sleeps, as she told you; and when she does, she is sure to start awake with cries for mercy.

"She remains, for whole hours together, weeping as though her heart would break; and as yet I have not been able to induce her to tell me the reason of her strange conduct."

"Your situation is a distressing one, Mr. Maurice," said Duval, kindly; "but your wife's behaviour may arise from some incipient mental disease, which might yield to medical treatment, if taken soon enough."

"I do not think she is insane," he replied; "I have a dreadful fear, from her muttering in her sleep the name of her sister, that she has been induced by her to engage in some transactions, which now, in her stings of conscience, are bringing with them their own punishment."

"Have you any idea, in your own mind, of what those transactions can be?" asked Duval.

"None."

"What is her sister?"

"She has a small property, which she ekes out by taking a child to nurse. At the time she had ours she likewise had a very sickly little thing, who was the heiress to an earldom."

"Indeed?"

"Yes. The Earl and Countess de Clifford were advised to send their child to some cottage in the country in preference to the costly nursery they would have provided for it."

"And this child went to your wife's sister's cottage?" asked Duval.

"Yes. They let her, at a very large salary, have the care of the child, which was the same age as our own little one, within a week or so."

"And did both the children die?" said Duval, now deeply interested.

"No. Ours, the healthy child, died. The weak young scion lived to bless her parents."

"That frequently happens," said Duval. "There is no counting upon the lives or constitutions of very young children for a day."

"But now," said Mr. Maurice, "that I have imparted to you this old grief, can you advise me what I had better do in this new sorrow which has overtaken me?"

"You mean with regard to this secret which is preying upon your wife's health?" said Duval.

"Yes. What do you advise me to do?"

"Why, the best thing you could do," replied Duval, "would be to get a clear statement from your wife as to what troubles her, and then take some measures therefore. Of course, you must be guided by circumstances. It may be, after all, some mere trifle, acting upon a nervous system, and dressed up in imaginary horrors by a diseased fancy."

"Heaven grant it may be so. But I fear she will not confide in me. Will you do me the favour to call again?"

"Well, I do not much mind," said Duval.

"You may rely upon nothing disagreeable occurring," said the husband, "because I look upon all that ensued before as arising from her extreme nervous terror at my finding you. She believes you are a doctor, you say; now, if you will call when I am out, as if you had made the visit from your own thought, she may possibly be induced to put confidence in you."

"Very well," said Duval; "you can tell me what hour you will not be at home, and I will call upon Mrs. Maurice."

"This afternoon!" he said. "Any time before six o'clock."

"I will call, then," said Duval, "at three o'clock, and meet you where you please after I have had an interview with your wife."

"If you walk down the road," he said, "I will meet you between this house and Camden Town."

With this understanding Duval and Mr. Maurice separated; the former, it must be confessed, with no small degree of curiosity concerning what could cause the mysterious and inexplicable conduct of Mrs Maurice.

As may be supposed, Claude Duval took Lucy into his confidence, respecting the extraordinary scene at Grove Villa, the residence of Mr. and Mrs. Maurice, and the whole of the time which intervened till three o'clock was spent by them both in conjectures as to what could be the cause of Mrs. Maurice's singular conduct.

Three o'clock was, however, near at hand, and Duval walked to the Hampstead Road to pay the promised visit to Mrs. Maurice, during her husband's absence.

A little distance, however, beyond the turning which leads up to Chalk Farm, Duval met Mr. Maurice, and he could see by his countenance that he had no good news to tell him concerning his wife.

After they had exchanged civilities, Mr. Maurice said, "Mrs. Maurice remains shut up in her own room, and will scarcely speak to any one. I fear much that her mind is affected."

"Well, well," said Duval, "do not torture yourself by conjectures. I will do my best to get the secret cause of her deep melancholy from her, and I think I am likely to succeed."

"My mind misgives me very much," said Mr. Maurice, "that something terrible will arise from all this, for she has occasionally repeated the name of her sister, and of our own lost child, evidently with so much mental agony, that I cannot but think that the key to the mystery will be found in connection with them."

"When shall I see you," said Duval; "my visit cannot be a very long one, as I have business this evening; but if you will wait anywhere about here for me, I will call for you as I come back."

Mr. Maurice pointed to an inn in the vicinity, saying that he would take a private room there, and leave his name at the bar, and they parted, on the understanding that Duval should call on his return from his visit.

Duval, it must be confessed was not over pleased at the task he had undertaken; but as he had promised, he determined to go through with the adventure.

In answer to his summons for admission, the same servant who admitted him on a former occasion, made her appearance at the gate of Mr. Maurice's villa, and upon Duval telling her that he had called to see her mistress, she showed him into a little waiting-room while she went to acquaint Mrs. Maurice with his visit.

In less than five minutes she returned to say that her mistress would be glad to see him, and Duval was conducted up-stairs to the same apartment in which the first interview had taken place.

"I have called, madam," said Duval, "to make a friendly visit, and hope I find you better?"

"Better! better! Oh, no!" she replied, in a wailing voice. "I shall never be better; but tell me, have you brought me a drug to make me sleep?"

"Yes," replied Duval, for he had taken the precaution to prepare some pills, made of bread rolled in magnesia, in order to see if her imagination would make her sleep after taking them, supposing them to contain an opiate.

"Then I may know some peace; but tell me, will they make me dream, because you know that would be dreadful?"

"They will not, Mrs. Maurice; but, even should they, why cannot you expect pleasant dreams."

She shuddered as she said, "I expect pleasant dreams! No, no! there are no pleasant dreams for me; All I hope for is a temporary oblivion for thought."

"Nay, Mrs. Maurice," said Duval, solemnly and seriously, "listen to me."

Mrs. Maurice raised her eyes inquiringly to Duval's face as he continued.

"We physicians can do a great deal when we really know what is the matter with our patients. We can restore the mind to its healthy functions frequently as well as the body; but there is one condition with which we are as likely, and, in fact, more likely to do good than harm, and that is, unreserved confidence on the part of our patients."

Mrs. Maurice was silent for some moments, and sat with her hands clasped before her, glaring at Duval in a truly fearful manner.

Then she spoke in a low voice, saying, "You would have my secret; but I dare not tell it to you. No, no, heaven have mercy on me, but man can have none. I am nearly mad now; but to tell that fearful tale would unsettle my reason for ever—for ever!"

"I think you are wrong," said Duval, calmly and quietly. "Confidence in any one relieves the mind, and you must be assured that what is told to a physician is kept sacredly secret."

Duval felt some qualms of conscience as he uttered this last sentence; but he had promised, if possible, to extract the fearful secret from Mrs. Maurice, and he felt that he was justified in thus keeping up in her mind the delusion that he belonged to the medical profession.

"No, no!" she shrieked. "Tempt me not to my ruin—to shame—to disgrace—to—the scaffold?"

Duval was totally unprepared for such an admission as this, and started to his feet as he repeated the word, "Scaffold! Surely I misunderstand you, Mrs. Maurice. You cannot mean that——"

"Hush! oh, hush!" she cried. "Another word of suspicion, and I will take your life or my own. Am I not sufficiently punished? Oh, heaven! am I not punished enough? Where is my child, that would now be so great a joy to me; save me from the fiend that even now is gnawing at my heart."

"Mrs. Maurice, you will make yourself seriously ill if you go on in this way," said Duval.

"Man—man, you know not what you say," she shrieked.

"I can do you no good. I must really take my leave at once," said Duval, "if you do not become calmer."

He rose as he spoke, and with a grave air, Duval walked to the door of the apartment.

She saw him place his hand on the lock before she spoke again, and called him back, saying,

"I will be calm, sir; do not desert me now, or I shall do myself some violence. If you have one spark of pity for the most miserable creature that ever drew the breath of life, aid me to procure some trifle and forgetfulness of my sorrow.

CHAPTER CLXXXVI.

CLAUDE DUVAL TRIES TO GAIN THE CONFIDENCE OF MRS. MAURICE.

As Mrs. Maurice uttered these words, Claude Duval returned; as, indeed, he intended to do upon the slightest possible excuse, or none at all, for his only object was to alarm her, if possible, into a confession of what was the secret cause of grief that prayed upon her spirits, and drove her to the wretched mental state she was in.

"Well, Mrs. Maurice," said Duval, "I trust you will confide to me then, fully and unreservedly, your grief, whatever it may be. By so doing, you will make a confidential friend, who will not only advise you to the best of his power, but keep your secret, if it be necessary to do so inviolate."

"I dare not! I dare not," she moaned. "Sir—tell me—did you ever commit a crime which, in the ignorance of your heart, you fancied would contribute to your happiness, and then found, when too late, in its results naught but misery?"

"I cannot say that I ever did," replied Duval.

She sighed deeply, as she muttered, "Then die soon and be happy—die soon—die soon!"

"You will confide in me," said Duval.

"Not now—not now," she replied. "I will think—let me sleep first—let me know the dear comfort of rest, and then, in my thankfulness to you, I may tell all. Give me, first, the means of rest."

"Well," said Duval, "there are the pills which I believe will produce that effect, and I will call again upon you to-morrow."

"Thank you—thank you," she said. "For heaven's sake avoid my husband!"

"Be at rest upon that head," said Duval. "Good day to you, and remember your promise of to-morrow, communicating all your griefs to me."

"I will think—I will think!" she muttered.

Duval then left the villa, and made the best of his way to Mr. Maurice, who was very anxiously expecting him.

To him Duval related the particulars of the very unsatisfactory interview he had had with Mrs. Maurice, and when he concluded, he said, "Now that you have had a second interview with my wife, what do you think is the cause of her mental disquietude?"

"Why, Mr. Maurice," said Duval, "my opinion may not please you; but since you ask me, I cannot help thinking that Mrs. Maurice has really something on her mind of a serious character."

"Gracious heavens!"

"And," continued Duval, "from a review of her past life, I should say you are much more able than I to come to some conclusion—at all events with regard to the nature of it."

"There is nothing in her past life," he replied, "that I am at all aware of which could induce any criminality."

"Her sister was a scheming, immoral woman, and at one time, to my regret, had considerable influence over my wife's mind, but that was years ago, and I never knew of any circumstances which could have embroiled Mrs. Maurice in anything disagreeable."

"She is not insane," said Duval. "There are no symptoms that I can see that would at all lead one to suppose she is."

"And yet," said Mr. Maurice, "does it not strike you that her strange and anomalous conduct on the death of our child strongly savoured of insanity?"

"To what do you allude?" asked Duval.

"Why sometimes, when open to observation, she would appear to be involved in the deepest grief, and at others, I have entered the room suddenly and unexpectedly, and found her apparently at her ease, and even amused by some trivial thing which would have passed by a mind really oppressed with grief, quite unheeded."

"It does seem strange, and would almost lead one to think that she is insane. At all events, let us watch her a little longer before calling in medical advice, and see whether she does confide in me."

"How shall I ever be able to repay you for all the trouble you seem willing to take?" asked Mr. Maurice, with evident emotion; "and now that I think of it, I do not even know the name of the man to whom I am under such vast obligations."

"Seek not to know my name at present," said Duval, "it can do you no good, and I would rather not tell it you; you see I am candid, nothing would have been easier, than for me to give a false name."

"Just so—just so. At all events, I am convinced that I am dealing with a gentleman, and so I will no press you further as to your name. And now, may I beg the favour of your meeting me here again, after your interview with Mrs. Maurice to-morrow?"

"Most certainly," replied Duval, "and I shall be not a little anxious to know whether her imagination will really cause her to sleep to-night under the impression that she has taken a powerful narcotic."

With this, Duval and Mr. Maurice parted, the mind of the former being very much engrossed with the really singular adventure, so little in accordance with his usual pursuits; but it had taken such a strong hold of his imagination that he anticipated his visit to Mrs. Maurice, on the morrow with considerable interest.

At length the appointed hour arrived at which Duval intended to present himself at the villa, and this time he had no occasion to name his business, for the same servant he had seen on the two former visits, opened the garden-gate, and without uttering a word, led him to the little parlour on the ground floor, while she went upstairs to apprise her mistress.

In an incredibly short time she returned and requested him to be kind enough to walk upstairs, when she ushered him into the same room in which I had before seen Mrs. Maurice.

She was sitting by the table, her head leaning on her hands.

As Duval entered the room, she looked up and regarded him with a glance of awful dejection.

"Ah!" said Duval, cheerfully, and kindly. "I am glad to see you looking somewhat better. Now tell me if I can be of any service to you."

Mrs. Maurice saw that he wished to soothe her, and with an impatient gesture, she said, "Peace! peace, I say! Am I a child, or a maniac? Tell me what friend put it in your head to give me those pills?"

"Do you mean the sleeping pills?" asked Duval, wishing to lead her mind back to the fact that they were given for the specified purpose of inducing sleep.

"Yes — yes!" she exclaimed with sudden vehemence.

"Did they make you sleep?"

"Yes, yes! they did, but what awful drug was there to drive me mad with dreams of blood."

"Hush! hush!"

"Oh, such dreams, that I would not sleep again for the universe, I am nearly mad—nearly mad."

"Indeed - indeed, Mrs. Maurice," replied Duval, you are much mistaken. There was nothing in those pills to produce the effect you speak of, I solemnly assure you."

"It is false! it is false! I tell you," she screamed with vehemence, "even now the images of the dream haunt me. It was a dream of retribution—I saw the face of a corpse plainly, I saw it as I now see you—oh, spare me such another awful dream."

"I will—I will. Calm yourself."

"Let medicine now work its utmost to save me from ever again closing my eyes in slumber. No more sleep —no more sleep!"

"Hush! hush!" said Duval, who was beginning to feel somewhat alarmed, and to think that after all, this was really a case for a medical man. "Hush! hush! I will get you something to do you good."

Duval rose from the chair upon which he had been seated, being anxious now, as far as he was concerned at least, to bring this adventure to a close.

With this intention he went to the top of the stairs, and called to the servant, whose name he remembered was Martha.

The servant soon made her appearance, and in a hurried whisper, Duval told her where to find her master, and to say that he was to return to his house immediately, as Mrs. Maurice was evidently very unwell.

"Dare to send for him!" exclaimed Mrs. Maurice, suddenly seizing Duval by the arm — for she had followed him, unknown to Duval, out of the room, and had heard sufficient to let her know that her husband was being sent for.

"Dare to send for him!" she cried, "and I will do more murder."

Duval was, it must be confessed, alarmed by her vehemence; but, as was always the case with him, in an emergency, he never lost his presence of mind; and he knew that the only chance of subduing her was by expressing great firmness; so, turning to her, he said,

"Madam, I will send for whom I like; and if you talk in that outrageous manner about committing murder, I will have you placed immediately under restraint."

Mrs. Maurice looked aghast at the turn affairs were taking, and Duval continued,

"Do you imagine that I am to have my actions controlled by you?"

Duval's manner seemed to awe her; for she went back to the room, muttering to herself, in a low, melancholy tone.

"The dream—the dream—the awful dream of retribution! Oh, save me from sleep!"

"Now, Mrs. Maurice," said Duval, calmly; "listen to me. I have nothing to do with your past life; I do not wish to pry into your secrets, if you have any. When I asked you to confide in me, it was not from idle curiosity, but ——"

"What for, then? what for, then?" she asked, clutching convulsively at the table-cloth.

"For hopes of being able to be of service to you—to soothe you—to make you see things in their proper light, instead of through the medium of your own diseased imagination."

"Then you think that it is all fancy?"

No; I do believe that there is something on your mind, which, from being nursed up, has grown into a something terrible. However, our acquaintance ends now, and for ever."

She looked in Duval's face, with a strange expression, then, clasping her hands, she said, in a hoarse whisper,

"I will—I will tell you all—I will place my life in your hands. Yes, I will tell—you—all!"

"Your life, Mrs. Maurice?"

"Yes—yes! Oh, heavens, yes!"

"Stay!" said Duval, a strange fear, so to speak, now creeping over him.

"Do not interrupt me," she said; "I seem just as if I were compelled to tell you all."

CHAPTER CLXXXVII.

MRS. MAURICE MAKES A STARTLING CONFESSION TO CLAUDE DUVAL.

IT was only for a moment that Duval wavered in the task he had imposed upon himself, and then he sat down, prepared to listen to the fearful tale, he felt convinced he was about to hear.

"I am all attention, Mrs. Maurice," he said.

The unhappy woman gave one gasping sob, and then she said,

"My child, my beautiful child! how I doated on it! I was sinful in my love for it; made me forget heaven. My sister had it to nurse at the same time that she was nursing the young Baroness de Clifford—the infant heiress to untold wealth."

For a moment, Mrs. Maurice seemed totally incapable of proceeding with her story, but at length she said,

"My child was healthy, but the young Baroness was a weak, sickly thing, and her noble parents never hoped to rear her."

"Well?"

"Oh, heaven! it was my sister who started the dreadful idea."

As she uttered these words, Mrs. Maurice shuddered and clasped her hands over her eyes.

"Come, come," said Duval; "try to compose yourself. Remember, you are speaking about the past."

"Yes, yes; the past—the irretrievable past. You did well to remind me that what is done cannot be undone."

"Nay, nay!" said Duval; "take comfort. You may magnify the evil you may have been the cause of. Try to be calm."

"I will—I will; for you are kind, and do not spurn me from you.

"My sister—it came to my knowledge some time afterwards—had been promised a large gratuity if she succeeded in rearing the young Baroness well."

"Go on," said Duval, gently.

"Can you not guess the awful truth?"

"Indeed; no."

"The eyes and general appearance of the children were both alike! Oh, can you not spare me the dreadful recital, and guess my dreadful crime?"

"Indeed," said Duval, "I would not hazard a guess in such a case. I might do you some grievous injustice."

"No, no, no!" she shuddered; "that is impossible. You cannot think me worse than I am, for I—am a murderess!"

A cold chill ran through the heart of Duval, as Mrs. Maurice uttered these words, but he said not a word, and, after a moment's pause, she continued—

"One day I went to see my child, and found that the young Baroness de Clifford was dying, or appeared to be so. Her noble parents were to visit her that day, but her severe illness had come on so suddenly that they did not even know of it."

"Yes, yes!"

"Then my sister whispered an awful suggestion to me to the effect that if the scion of nobility were dead, and my child could be passed off upon the parents as their own, it would reap all the benefit of its noble and wealthy connection, while she could say that the other child had died."

"I see," said Duval.

"She painted to me in glowing colours what a delight it would be to me to know that my child, upon whom I doated so fondly, was one of England's richest ladies, loaded with honour—the theme, perhaps, of a nation's adoration.

"She pointed out the likeness between the two children—a likeness which dress would perfect; and—and I was cruel enough to listen."

"Go on, Mrs. Maurice," said Duval, as she paused, —"go on. Depend upon it, you will never regret having made this confession, terrible though it be."

"Ah, you do not guess all—you cannot guess all," she moaned.

"Never mind. Take courage; all may yet be well," whispered Duval, gently.

"We—we, my sister and I—placed a pillow over the face of the sick child—we murdered it!"

Duval rose from his chair, and looked at Mrs. Maurice in perfect horror, for all along he had thought from the tenour of her story that after all it would turn out that she had merely been a party in making an exchange of the children.

"Yes," she cried, "shrink from me! I knew how it would be—loathe me, for I am indeed a wretch to be detested."

As she spoke, Mrs. Maurice cowered down to the floor, as though she would avoid the gaze which Duval bent upon her.

Then she continued, with great vehemence—

"Yes, I tell you, we killed the child, and clothed mine in its rich apparel.

"The Earl and Countess came; they were overjoyed to see their child—as they supposed mine to be—looking so well, and the Countess even said that but for the eyes she should not have known it."

"Poor mother!" said Duval.

"Yes," continued she, "and I—I was foolish enough to feel pleased when I heard her say that."

"And have you kept this fearful secret all this time from your husband?" asked Duval, scarcely believing such a thing possible, and yet hoping to find that he, too, was not implicated in the crime.

"I have—I have!" she replied. "He was imposed upon by being told the child was dead. I knew he never would for one moment sanction the fraud."

"Unhappy woman!" sighed Duval.

"Time passed on," she continued, "and then conscience began to upbraid me of my crime.

"I became restless—unhappy—agonised.

"I could not sleep—my solitude was ever peopled with frightful shapes."

"And where is your child now?"

"Ah, that question almost maddens me! What I had never anticipated happened. My child was taken away by the Earl and Countess, and I have never seen her since. You now know all. Heaven help me!"

Duval was quite at a loss to know what to do; and even when Mrs. Maurice had concluded her frightful narrative, he continued gazing at her for some moments in silence, thoroughly astonished and bewildered.

She trembled now so excessively that Duval became seriously alarmed at her condition.

"Mrs. Maurice," he said, solemnly, "repentance may yet open to you the gates of that heaven whose mercy is boundless."

"Heaven for me!" she shrieked. "No, no; my crime is too terrible for hope—I shall be lost for ever!"

"Tell me," said Duval, anxious to turn her thoughts from herself,—"tell me—is your sister still living?"

"She is—she is! Heaven help her! It was she who tempted me! Oh, tell me—tell me, if I can yet make any reparation! Oh, tell me how to fly from myself!"

There came at this moment a loud ring at the gate bell.

"Stop, stop!" she cried, as Duval made a movement towards the door. "That may be my husband! Swear by all you hold sacred! by all your hopes in a hereafter! that what I have told you shall remain locked in your own breast."

"I cannot — I dare not," replied Duval, "take such an oath as that. I pray you to be calm! Your story has so amazed me, that I know not what to say to you. I heard, now, Mr. Maurice's voice, in anxious accents, inquiring if I had left the house."

"It is he—it is he! My husband!" she gasped. "Oh, save me from him! One word will kill me! Save me—save me!"

"Hush, hush!—for heaven's sake, hush!" said Duval. "I will return to you in a few moments. Remain here quietly."

He with some difficulty released himself from her hold, and went down into the hall, just in time to take Mr. Maurice by the hand and lead him into the parlour.

"My wife!" he said. "What of her? I could not contain myself any longer! Ah! I see that she is worse, by your looks! Good heavens, she is dead!" he cried, alarmed at Duval's tone and manner. "Suspense is terrible—tell me at once!"

DUVAL AND BLOSSOM OBTAIN SEATS IN THE MAIL COACH.

"I will! Be calm, and you shall know all!" You are wrong, your wife is no worse than when you left her. Ah!"

Bang went the front gate at this moment, and Duval flew into the hall, and then up the stairs into the room in which he had left Mrs. Maurice a few minutes before.

It was empty!

"Good heavens!" cried the almost distracted husband, "what has happened? Give me some explanation, or I shall no mad!"

"Your wife was here; but she has just left. Follow her if you will, or remain here, and I will tell you all that she has told me."

"I will return—I will return!" he cried, as he rushed from the house.

What to do, or how to act, in the peculiar situation in which Duval now found himself, quite puzzled him, and he wished, over and over again, now that it was too late, that he had never attempted to gain the confidence of Mrs. Maurice.

No. 56.—NIGHTSHADE.

Hour after hour passed by, and still Mr. Maurice did not return.

It was getting late, and Duval had just rung the bell, to tell the servant to say, when her master returned, that he, Duval, would call upon him early on the following morning, when there was a violent ring at the gate bell.

The ring was immediately repeated.

"Open the gate, immediately," cried Duval, and the girl flew to obey the summons.

Pale, haggard, and exhausted, Mr. Maurice staggered, rather than walked, into the room where Duval was, and sank, with a deep groan, into the first vacant chair.

"She is dead—she is dead!" he cried.

"Mr. Maurice!" exclaimed Duval.

"Yes, yes—she is dead! Her body was picked up at London Bridge!"

"Mr. Maurice," said Duval, slowly and calmly, "you are, I see, full of grief at the loss of your wife. Be consoled—I have that to tell you which will make you thank heaven that she is no more."

"Alas, alas!" moaned the unhappy husband. "Had I but taken precautions, this would never have happened! I tell you, sir, her body was picked up at London Bridge! In some frantic moment she has drowned herself! Oh, heavens! that it should come to this! My poor Annie!"

Duval saw that he had not heard what he said, so he resolved at once to proceed with the story his wife had told him, never doubting but that it would soon attract his utmost attention.

He listened, at first, listlessly, then with growing interest, and by the time Duval had concluded, his feelings were wrought up to the highest pitch of intense interest and excitement.

"Can this be true?" he exclaimed, at length.

"I believe every word of it," said Duval. "You may now do just what you please."

"My child—my child!" he cried. "My child lives! My beautiful child!"

Duval felt that his mission was accomplished, he could do no more. Doubtless the heartbroken father would find means of retracing his long lost child, and might yet be happy.

"Farewell," he said, as he held out his hand to Mr. Maurice. "Farewell! I do not leave you so lonely as I might have done."

But his words fell upon an ear alike insensible to joy and grief.

The bereaved husband and father fell to the floor in a swoon.

Duval rung the bell for the servant, and then gave orders that she should remain with her master until the arrival of a medical man, whom Duval went immediately to seek.

A few doors from Grove Villa, he had the satisfaction of beholding the ruddy glow of a surgeon's lamp.

He pulled the bell sharply, and was instantly confronted by a small boy, all glistening with buttons.

"Tell your master," said Duval, "that Mr. Maurice, of Grove Villa, just above here, is dangerously ill, and requires his services."

"Mr. Maurice?" said a gentlemanly man, who, unperceived by Duval, had entered the garden. "I will go at once."

"Thank you," said Duval, as he watched the surgeon, until he had disappeared within the garden gate of Mr. Maurice's residence.

"That's over," said Duval to himself, with a sigh of relief, "I hope never to have another such adventure as long as I live. Now for Lucy."

A sharp walk brought Duval into the neighbourhood of what was usually called the "Haunted House."

Lucy was deeply affected at the tragical termination of the adventure, and shed many tears over the sorrows and ultimate death of the weak, fond mother, who had grasped at wealth as a means of securing the happiness of her child.

"Well," said Duval, as he and Lucy were chatting quietly at breakfast, the morning after the death of the misguided and erring Mrs. Maurice, "I shall be careful, in future, how I am entrapped into playing the part of a medical man."

"Yes, Claude; but surely this sad event is not wholly without its compensating comfort?"

"As how, dear Lucy?"

"Why, have you not been the means of poor Mr. Maurice arriving at the knowledge that he still has a child; and will not that, think you, be some consolation to him in his loneliness and sorrow."

"It may be," said Duval; "but it is a very questionable kind of comfort, I fancy; for he will ever be thinking of the terrific crime his wife committed to compass the welfare, as she thought, of their child."

"And it will be a sad thing, too," said Lucy, "for the Countess de Clifford to have to part with one whom she has for so long looked upon and treated as her own child."

"It will, indeed, Lucy; but let us now dismiss the subject from our minds. I declare, you look quite pale this beautiful morning. You have thought too much already about it."

"Yes, dear Claude, I will strive to be myself again, if you promise to be more careful of yourself in future?"

"Careful, Lucy? I was careful enough. You mean, I must be on my guard against treachery; for was it not through the treachery of the Duchess of Cleveland, that I was made a prisoner this time?"

"And yet this woman says she loves you?"

"Do not, Lucy, dear, desecrate the name of love by applying it to the feeling she has for me. Could you, Lucy, however I might sin against you, could you betray me to my enemies?"

Lucy threw herself into the arms of Claude Duval, and the only reply she could make to his question, was a flood of tears.

"Hush, hush, dear one. I pray heaven that I may never be tempted to put your affection to such a test."

"I do not fear that, my Claude," said Lucy; "but the very thought of such a thing seemed for the moment to almost break my heart."

"The thought of what? You betraying me?"

"No, no, that would be quite impossible; but——"

"But what then?"

"That you should ever in thought do anything that could pain me."

"Never fear—never fear! And now listen to me. This evening, dear Lucy, I am going out on the road for an adventure."

"So soon?"

"Even so; for do you know our exchequer is low. Have I your consent?"

"Yes, dear Claude; but always remember that I am anxious until your return; so let your absence be as short as possible."

"I promise—I promise! I will now seek Blossom and talk to him about our new follower, Miller, the gaoler from Newgate."

CHAPTER CLXXXVIII.

CLAUDE DUVAL MAKES ACQUAINTANCE WITH MR. KNIGHT, ATTORNEY-AT-LAW.

CLAUDE DUVAL'S idea now was to disguise himself as a bluff country gentleman, or, we should say, farmer, and to take Blossom with him as a servant to London, where he intended to take a place in a coach, and trust to Fortune to place at his disposal either money or other valuables belonging to his fellow-passengers.

One of the effects which the depredations of Claude Duval's band produced, was that they had become possessed of various portmanteaus, valises, and all sorts of travelling boxes, which had contained clothing of all kinds and descriptions.

There was one apartment in the deserted mansion on the heath well-stocked, then, with disguises.

It was a period, too, when persons of any means thought it rather the thing to wear a wig, so that this appendage rendered it very difficult to recognise even the most intimate friend, if that friend did not wish to be known.

Behold, then, Claude Duval, on the evening following the sad catastrophe which terminated the existence of Mrs. Maurice, fully equipped as a country farmer.

He had found the means, too, of imparting to his cheeks a much more ruddy glow than they usually wore.

His moustache, which was naturally small and silken, and which made him look at once handsome and *distingué*, he showed off entirely; and, attired in top-boots and a large coat, with huge lappels, a cravat, as was then the custom with persons whom he was anxious to personate, wound several times round his throat, Claude Duval looked the perfect country gentleman.

He took care to be well armed, however, although he wore no sword. He placed his pistols handily about him, so that they could be got at at a moment's notice.

The change in Duval's appearance was so complete that even Blossom, for a moment, failed to recognise him; and the unmistakable start he gave, while it highly amused Duval, at the same time put him quite in conceit of his disguise.

Blossom was attired in a suit of livery, which, together with the broad country dialect he knew so well how to use, completely transformed him from the neat, smart-looking man, he was naturally, to the country lout.

As Duval had already taken leave of Lucy, and given what directions he had thought necessary to the band, he turned to Blossom, and said, "Follow me, Blossom, we will strike into the high road, and probably we shall be overtaken by a coach, into which we can get without let or hindrance."

Duval walked a little in advance of Blossom for some time, and then he glanced behind him, and made him a sign to advance.

"Yes, Captain."

"Do you know what you have to do?"

Blossom shook his head.

"Well, then, you must remember the character you have to enact, and, therefore, you must say and do as little as possible. You understand?"

"Quite, Captain," said Blossom.

"Hush!" said Duval. "I think I can see, some half a mile off, a four-horsed mail-coach coming along at great speed."

"You are right, Captain!" said Blossom; "it is one of the north mails."

"Yes; I will stop it. But stay, I have not yet given myself a name. I have one! I am Squire Brightwell, of The Grounds, Warwickshire."

And my name, Captain, is?"

"Thomas."

"Yees, measter!" said Blossom, in country dialect.

The coach, as it approached, appeared to Duval to be heavily laden with luggage, and he began to entertain fears that if the passengers were as numerous as the boxes outside of the coach, that there would not be two places vacant.

"It's no go," said Blossom. "There's no room in that one."

"I fear not," said Duval; "but nevertheless I will chance it."

As he spoke, Duval hailed the coach and, to his surprise, the driver drew up with alacrity.

"Going to town, sir?" asked the Coachman.

"Yes: if you have room for me and my servant."

"All right, sir; there's one vacant place inside, and your man can find room on the roof."

The guard got down from his seat behind the coach, and opened the door for Duval.

The moment the door was opened, however, a sharp-faced, sinister-looking man, attired in a suit of rusty black, cried out:

"Eh? what? What do you mean? I thought you said I should have the inside all to myself, eh? Didn't I promise you an extra shilling on that condition, eh?"

"It's quite true, sir.'

"Well, then, what do you mean, you scoundrel, by putting people in upon me in this fashion; I've a great mind to—to——"

Claude Duval contorted his countenance into a broad kind of grin as he said,

"Oh, never mind me, sir; I'm a harmless sort of person! Don't fear, I'll not step on your toes! I am Squire Brightwell, of The Grounds, Warwickshire! Everybody knows me. Mind your toes, sir."

"Oh, murder! you beast! you elephant! What do you mean by crushing my toes in that fashion, eh, sir?"

Duval had purposely come with all his force upon the toes of the quarrelsome personage, who wanted the whole of the coach to himself.

"Bless my soul," sir," he said, "I am very sorry; was that your foot?"

"You know it was."

"I know it was?"

"Guard! guard! Here guard!" shouted the irascible man. "I cannot suffer this person to ride inside with me, you know I was to have the inside all to myself.

"Beg pardon, sir," said the guard. "I didn't not promise no such thing. You asked me if it was likely that you would have any fellow passengers, and I said no, because I thought we shouldn't have any more; but as this here gentleman——"

"Hold your tongue, blockhead!" roared the passionate man. "I tell you he shall get out."

"Ha! ha! ha!" laughed Duval.

"Do you hear what I say? Make him get out immediately."

"Are you willing to pay for all the inside places then, sir?"

"If he is," said Duval, "it is too late to do so now. Ha! ha! ha! I am Squire Brightwell, and I won't budge an inch!"

"But I'll make you."

Duval turned round, and placed his face almost close to that of the violent old gentleman, and said,

"Now look here, my little fellow, if you think you can put me out, do so. Try now, will you?—only try!"

The guard could not help laughing at the idea of the little wizen-faced old man putting the burly farmer out.

"Now then, Jack," said the coachman, "look sharp and settle matters quickly, we can't stop here all night."

"Go a-head! all right!" cried the guard, as he slammed to the coach door, and blew one shrill blast upon his horn.

Off set the coach, Duval inside with the irascible old man, and Blossom outside, amongst the luggage on the roof.

The passionate little man got as far away from Claude Duval as the very limited space would allow, and ever and anon as he shuffled about his feet he uttered low groans.

"Why what's the matter with you?" said Duval, putting on a jovial expression.

"Nothing—nothing particular!"

"Then keep quiet, and don't be so fidgetty."

"I will be fidgetty, if I like! I have a right to take care of my property, I suppose, without asking you."

"Oh, it's your property you are so fidgetty about is it?"

"No, it isn't; and if I were, what's that to you, I should like to know?"

"I tell you what it is, my ill-tempered friend," said Duval, "if you are not more civil, I'll just open the coach-door and drop you into the road as easily as I would a kitten."

"You—you drop me into the road?"

"Yes, you to be sure! Who else is there to drop?"

The strange passenger made a sudden dive with both his hands under the seat of the coach, and brought up a black portmanteau, which he placed on his knees, and then, looking defiantly at Duval, he said—

"Did I understand you to say that you would drop me into the road?"

"I did."

"Do you know who I am, sir—eh?"

"No; and I must add that I don't care."

"Then my name is Knight, sir."

"It may be Night or Day, for all I care."

"I am an attorney, sir—an attorney, I say."

"I thought so."

"And therefore, I advise you to be very careful of what you say, or what you do."

"I mean to be."

"Then, sir, you are wiser than you look."

"Thank you, Mr. Day, attorney-at-law, I am sorry I cannot return the compliment, for you, on the contrary, are quite as stupid as you look."

"Beware, sir—beware!"

"Well, what's the matter now?"

"Nothing, sir—nothing! Don't speak to me—I beg you will not address me again."

"That is as I please. If I think proper to do you the honour of speaking to you, I shall do so."

"Bah!"

"I shall begin at once by asking you what you have cuddled up in that portmanteau, Mr. Day, attorney-at-law?"

"My name is Knight, sir—Knight."

"Well, Mr. Blight, what is it?"

"Go and be hanged."

"Oh, that's it, is it?"

"No, sir; that's not it."

"Come, now, if you go on in this way, you will lose a good client, for I was on my way to seek an honest lawyer, for I have thirty thousand pounds I want to put out in some way."

"Eh? What, sir?"

"Sir to you!"

Mr. Knight put on a bland look—or one which he intended to be such; but it made his face look more repulsive than ever.

"Hem! I am sure, Squire Brightwell, of 'The Grounds,' that, as a man of the world——"

"What?"

"As a man of the world, and a man of business, you will excuse any little—what shall I call it?—caution, or what you might think unpoliteness, in my manner."

"Oh, don't mention it!"

"You are very good, sir."

"Not at all; you couldn't help it."

"Sir, permit me to apologise."

"Don't; it is nature."

"But, sir—Squire Brightwell—I think you named something about thirty thousand pounds. I am a lawyer, sir, and——"

"Sir?"

"And an honest one, too."

"Now, you don't mean that?" said Duval.

"I do—indeed, I do!"

"Then give me your hand."

"Oh, sir, you are too kind, too condescending, after what has passed."

"Oh, don't say a word about that!" cried Duval, as he took the proffered hand of the lawyer, and gave it such a squeeze that he roared out—

"Hold hard—hold hard! Your grasp is like a vice. But let us talk of business! If you entrust me with your thirty thousand pounds, be assured that I am in the way of making first-rate investments for you."

"I am delighted."

"And so am I," said Mr. Knight.

"Your hand again, friend," said Duval.

"Mind, don't squeeze it—quietly, mind!"

"As quiet as a dove."

"Murder—murder!" roared Mr. Knight again.

"Hilloa, there!" cried the guard. "There's something amiss inside, Bill; put up a moment, and let's see what it's all about."

"Woa! woa!"

The mail-coach came to a stand-still, but Mr. Knight attorney-at-law, was in such a state of mental agony lest he should have irretrievably offended his rich client, and lost his patronage, that he put his head out of the window, and said—

"Oh, it's nothing—nothing at all, Mr. Guard! I was only telling this gentleman a story I heard last week, and spoke too loud. It is nothing more."

"Then I wish you to keep your stories to yourself," grumbled the guard, as he again mounted to his seat at the back of the coach, "and not make us pull up the 'osses for nothing."

The coach drove on again, and Mr. Knight looked as pleased as the crushed state of his hand would allow him, and he spoke blandly, as he said—

"My dear sir, if you really have no destination, will you honour me so far as to make my house your home while you are in town?"

"Ah, but how do I know that you are what you say? An honest man, and an attorney-at-law—how do I know——"

"My dear squire, stop, stop! I will soon convince you of all that!"

The attorney hastily produced a huge bunch of keys, and proceeded to unlock his portmanteau, which was upon his knees.

He then took a letter from it, and, giving it a kind of flourish before his eyes, he said—

"There, sir, you will see by this letter that I am the confidential agent of one of the first noblemen in the land."

"What nobleman?"

"The Duke of Montrose."

"Ah!"

"You—you know him perhaps?"

"No; but I had a fancy that I heard the name before, and that somebody said he was imprisoned for high treason; or, no, I make a mistake—was he not executed for attempting to take the King's life?"

"Ah, my dear sir, I know to what you allude; but that little affair all blew over nicely."

"Indeed!"

"Yes, my dear squire, you heard some rumour, but the whole truth is this, there is an outrageous, murderous scamp and villain who is named Claude Duval——"

"Really!"

"Yes, one of the greatest scoundrels unhung—although, thank heaven, that won't be for long."

"Then you mean he is reforming—amending his ways?"

"No, no! I mean, he won't remain for long unhung."

"Oh, I beg your pardon, I misunderstood you, Mr. Knight."

"Well, squire, this unmitigated scoundrel, who I only wish I could see face to face, had the unparalleled impudence to take the Duke into custody himself, and deliver him up to the guard."

"So I have heard."

"You have?"

"Oh, yes. But somebody down our way told me something about this rascal, Claude Duval."

"Oh, he must, and will, be hanged before long! I only wish, as I said before, I could take him by the collar myself, he should remember it as long as he lived."

"I dare say," said Duval, "you would make him feel."

CHAPTER CLXXXIV.

MR. KNIGHT, ATTORNEY-AT-LAW, DOES NOT SEEM DISPOSED TO CARRY OUT HIS THREATS.

"I just would," replied the little attorney; "but I am afraid there is no chance of that, for of course he would take good care to keep out of my way."

"I should think so."

"I see you are a sensible man, squire; and now that I know who you are, I will prove to you my respectability, by showing you the trust the amiable and excellent Duke of Montrose reposes in me."

"I should like to hear," said Duval.

"Well, then, this good Duke of Montrose became very short of money, and so I have been to some of his estates, and, partly by threats, and partly by great tact—great tact, indeed—have induced the tenants to pay six months' rent in advance."

"I am glad to hear that," said Duval.

"I thank you, squire, for taking an interest in my doings."

"And how much have you succeeded in collecting?"

"Four thousand pounds, sir—four thousand pounds in hard cash! What do you think now, sir, of my tact?"

"I am perfectly astonished," said Duval, "and am only too delighted to think I should have encountered so clever a lawyer."

"And just to think our acquaintance commenced almost with a quarrel!"

"Yes; and who would have thought that we should have been so friendly in so short a time?" said Duval.

"Who, indeed! One would almost think we had known each other for years."

"Yes, indeed! Is the money in that portmanteau?"

"Every farthing of it."

"Then I will trouble you for it, as I, too, happen to be short of money just now!"

A slight paleness came over the countenance of Mr. Knight, attorney-at-law, as he said, "Eh? What? Ah, I see you are fond of a joke, squire! Ha, ha, ha! Very good—very good, indeed! Admirably done!"

"I never was more serious in all my life!"

"But—but——"

"I want the money!"

"You—want—the—money?"

"To be sure; do I not speak plainly enough?"

"Oh, you are mad!"

"Come, sir, be quick! I am not used to be trifled with! Where is the money!"

"Help, help!"

"Be quick, sir!"

"Murder, Murder!"

"Ah!" growled the guard, at this moment. "You don't catch us pulling up the 'osses again for nothing, old fellow, and then to be told it's some story you are telling! Do you hear the old ape, Bill?"

"Ay, aye! I hear him! All right! Gee up!"

"To be sure, it's all right; he does it to spite us because we let that gentleman in!"

"That's it! Play a 'hair' on the horn to drown his noise!"

"I will!"

The guard began to play a deadly lively kind of air on his bugle, which, if it had no other effect, certainly put an end to all Mr. Knight's efforts to draw attention to his critical situation.

While the above conversation was being carried on between the guard and the driver of the coach, Claude Duval had placed the muzzle of a loaded pistol exactly between the eyes of Mr. Knight, attorney-at-law, as he said to him, "I do not wish to make too much noise, Mr. Bright, or Fright, or whatever your name may be, and, therefore, I will trouble you to be quiet. If it will be any satisfaction to you, I will tell you that you now have your wish, and are setting face to face with Claude Duval!"

It would be impossible for any language to describe the look of consternation depicted on the countenance of Mr. Knight on hearing Claude Duval name himself.

A kind of paralysis seemed to come over all his faculties, and he sat, staring with eyes that looked as though they would come out of their sockets, in exactly the same position in which he happened to be at the moment that Claude Duval announced his name and intention of possessing himself of the portmanteau.

Duval also fixed his gaze steadily on the eyes of the attorney, and the silence which now reigned in the stage-coach was something profound and strange.

Mr. Knight then let the portmanteau slip from his knees to the bottom of the coach, and then he slid down after it, uttering, as he did so, a succession of low groans.

"Don't make that noise," said Duval, "or I will throw you out of the window!"

"Mercy, mercy!"

"Why, you cowardly hypocrite," said Duval, "what do you mean by asking mercy of me, when it was only a few minutes ago that you were wishing you only had the chance of shaking me by the collar?"

"Alas, alas! My life is not worth a moment's purchase!"

"You never spoke a truer word, if you are not discreet!"

"Oh, do let me go—do let me go!"

"Of course I will let you go. I would not be troubled with such a cowardly rascal as you; but I mean to have the money!"

"Oh, pray do not take the money from me! You don't know what a savage the Duke of Montrose is when he is crossed! He doesn't mind——"

"Why, what do you mean, you lying scoundrel," said Duval, "by saying that, when you have just been trying to persuade me that his lordship was the very incarnation of everything amiable?"

"Oh, but I didn't mean it, you see, kind sir! I was obliged to say something!"

"And so you thought you would tell a parcel of lies, did you?"

"Oh, let me go—let me go, and I will always pray for your welfare!"

"Silence! Answer the questions I am about to put to you, and do so truthfully, or it will be the worse for you!"

"Yes, sir."

"Do you mean to tell me that you were really conveying to the Duke of Montrose four thousand pounds in that portmanteau?"

"Well, not exactly that. You see, we were to go halves."

"I see. Then you were to have two thousand as your share?"

"Yes."

"And do you know how you may make another thousand?"

"Another thousand?"

"Yes."

"How? tell me how, for I am poor and——"

"I will tell you. There is about a thousand pounds offered for my apprehension; so that if you succeed in giving me up to justice, as you talked of doing a little while ago, why the thousand pounds reward will be yours."

"Yes; but I am afraid you will not let me!"

"I certainly should resist," said Duval; "but as I wish to give every man a fair chance, and as even you shall not say that I took an unfair advantage of you in a stage coach, I shall hand you a pistol well primed and loaded."

"Hand me a pistol? Me?"

"Yes; why not?"

A slight flush came over the face of the attorney-at-law, as the thought crossed his mind that the advantage might be in his favour, owing to what he called the romantic generosity of Duval.

But it was not for long; for, as soon as Claude Duval produced the fellow pistol to the one he handed to him, the notion of getting the advantage over the highwayman vanished in a moment.

"Now, sir," said Duval, "we are equally armed; and if you like to fight the matter out, even in the narrow precincts of a stage coach, I am perfectly agreeable."

"I beg your pardon, sir, but I would rather decline your request to fight. I have never fired a pistol in my life, so you see you would have me at a great disadvantage."

As he spoke, Mr. Knight laid the pistol down upon the seat of the coach, and folded his hands across his chest.

"You won't fight?"

"No. But I have a proposition to make, which you ought to consider an equitable one."

"Well, what is it?"

"Simply this: that you will be content with the half of the four thousand, and——"

"And let you have the remainder?"

"Yes; that is what the Duke of Montrose intended to give me."

"Yes," replied Duval, "because you were employed by him to lie and bully his tenants as you pleased; but I have not employed you, you know."

"I am lost! I am lost!"

"Not at all, my good friend," said Duval; "if you look from the coach window you will see the streets of London, which must be quite familiar to you."

"Ah! yes—I see! Constables! An outcry now, Claude Duval, would be fatal to you!"

"Perhaps."

"Certain death!"

"I think not."

"But I say, yes! You have been short-sighted, Claude Duval; you should have carried out your little attempt at robbery while we were on the country road, and not have delayed until we reached London."

"Not at all. I wished to go to London, and here I am."

"But don't you see your danger? Why, here we are in Bishopsgate Street."

"I see we are."

"I cannot help thinking, then, Claude Duval, that you are in great danger. You, a notorious highwayman, with a price set upon your head,—alone—in London—for you have no one with you but that country bumpkin on the roof. I shall now make my terms, Claude Duval, and ask you what sum you will give me to make it worth my while to keep quiet."

"Is that all you have to say?" asked Duval, quietly.

"It is, and what answer do you make to my proposition?"

"Simply this—that it is you who are in danger, and not I."

"How so?"

"Why, if you attempt now to give the slightest alarm I will blow your brains out. That is all."

"But you seem to forgot, Claude Duval, that to blow my brains out you must make a noise."

"No, I do not."

"Then you would soon be surrounded, and apprehended for murdering me."

"But I shall have murdered you."

The lawyer seemed to have forgotten what would inevitably be his own fate until reminded of the unpleasant fact by Claude Duval.

Mr. Knight shrunk back aghast, for there was a look of resolution upon the countenance of Duval which said, most unmistakably, "I can carry out my threats to the utmost."

"Now, Mr. Knight," said Duval, as the coach drew up at a well-known inn,—"now, Mr. Knight, we will alight together, and proceed arm-in-arm for some distance."

"But the portmanteau?"

"My portmanteau do you mean?"

"No, mine—this one."

"Well, we will call that mine, now, since it contains my property."

"Your property?"

"Of course. Have I not yet succeeded in beating it into your stupid old brains that I intend to have the four thousand pounds it contains."

"Murder! Thieves!"

"Silence!"

As he spoke, Duval just touched the forehead of the attorney with the cold muzzle of the pistol.

This action on the part of Duval had the desired effect of reducing the attorney to silence.

"Listen to me," continued Duval. "My country bumpkin of a servant, as you were pleased to call the young man who is on the roof of the coach, will take charge of the portmanteau."

The attorney was silent.

"I see you agree to the proposed arrangements, and it is fortunate for you that such is the case."

Pale and haggard, the attorney alighted from the coach, closely followed by Duval.

Mr. Knight, with a groan, paid his fare, and Duval likewise paid his, adding, at the same time, so liberal a gratuity, that the coachman and guard were both ready to swear, on the slightest provocation, that he, Duval, was the most respectable passenger it had ever been their good fortune to fall in with.

Duval slid his arm beneath that of the lawyer, and took care to hold him tight; and then he called to Blossom on the roof of the coach.

"Come down, Tom!"

"Yees, measter," said Blossom.

"Take charge of my portmanteau, and follow us."

Blossom looked amused, as he said to himself, "That accounts for the Captain going off arm-in-arm with that ill-looking little man. He's been doing a little business, as he said he would. I wonder what's in this portmanteau."

Blossom shouldered the portmanteau, and while Mr. Knight eyed his proceedings with a look of anguish difficult to describe, Duval and he proceeded arm-in-arm towards the heart of the city.

"You might let me go now," whispered the affrighted attorney. "You've got the money, what more do you want? I can't do you any harm now."

"I am not so sure of that," replied Duval. "If I were to let you go now, it is just possible I might have a mob at my heels before I knew where I was to avoid such a disagreeable state of things. Mr. Knight, I think we had better keep each other company a little longer. Blossom."

There was no longer any need to keep up the delusion in the attorney's mind that the "country bumpkin" was really what he appeared to be, so Duval called him by the name he went by usually.

"Yes, Captain," said Blossom, in so different a voice that Mr. Knight looked perfectly amazed.

"Come here; I have some directions to give you concerning my portmanteau."

"His portmanteau!" sighed the attorney.

Duval placed his lips close to the ear of Blossom, and whispered a few words.

"All right, Captain!" was the reply. "It shall be done."

CHAPTER CXC.

CLAUDE DUVAL AND BLOSSOM SUCCEED IN DISPOSING OF A TROUBLESOME PERSON.

THERE were but few pedestrians at that hour, but still there were quite sufficient to make Duval perfectly aware that, unless he could dispose of the attorney in some way until such time as he and Blossom might make good their retreat from that neighbourhood, there would be danger to him.

The few words he whispered into Blossom's ear, notwithstanding all his efforts to catch them, escaped the attorney entirely, and it was with no small degree of nervousness that he awaited to know their result.

All Blossom replied, however, to those few words, was merely a nod.

"You quite understand, Blossom?"

"All right, Captain!"

Blossom strode on more quickly now, and Mr. Knight made a vain attempt to disengage his arm from that of Duval.

Duval made no remark whatever, but continued to follow Blossom, who sometimes stopped, and looked down a street, as though he were in search of some particular one.

At length he came to a standstill, and Duval then made Mr. Knight walk somewhat more briskly.

When Duval came up to him, Blossom said, merely, "I began to think I had mistaken the street, Captain; but it's all right: here's the street, and there's the house. Shall I knock?"

"Yes, Blossom."

Blossom went up to one of the houses, and gave three taps on the street door with his knuckles.

There then came a similar knock from the inside.

Then Blossom repeated the three raps again, and then the door was opened by a powerful-looking man, with a jovial expression of countenance.

"Ah, Sleekman," said the man, addressing Blossom, "you are only just in time, for I was going out for a stroll."

Blossom laughed.

Duval, at this moment, stepped up to the door, and the man closed it somewhat abruptly, as though his presence were not desirable.

"Why, don't you know me, Ralph?" asked Duval.

"Ah, I had forgot!"

Duval had forgotten, since he had not been compelled to act the part of the gentleman farmer, that he was so admirably got up as to deceive even those who knew him best.

As soon, however, as he spoke in his natural voice, the man whom he had named Ralph knew him instantly, and threw open the door wide.

"Welcome—welcome at all times, Captain! I didn't know you, or Ralph Purkiss is not the man to forget all he owes to you."

"Enough! No more in that style, Ralph! I want you to do me a favour."

"Right willingly will I serve you, Captain!"

"Then I want you to keep this man a close prisoner."

"Murder!" cried Mr. Knight.

Duval drew him into the passage, and presented a pistol at his head, while Ralph shut the street door.

"Another such shout, and it will be out of your power, friend, to give an alarm," said Duval.

"Mercy! mercy!"

"No one will hurt you, so long as you remain quiet; but as soon as ever you make the slightest outcry——"

"I shall despatch him, Captain," said Ralph.

"Just so, Ralph," said Duval.

"Come along, my fine fellow," said Ralph, as he put his arm within that of the terrified lawyer,—"come along, my fine fellow! I've got the Captain's orders, and they must be obeyed."

"Stay," said Duval; "you understand that I do not want you to take this man's worthless life!"

"Worthless life!" sighed the attorney.

"Unless," continued Duval, "you find him troublesome."

"In which case, Captain?"

"I leave him entirely in your hands, to do with him as you will."

"All right, Captain! How long am I to keep him—a week, or a month, or a year?"

"Only one hour, if he is tractable."

"Oh! that's soon accomplished," said Ralph, as he prepared to lead, or rather carry, the terror-stricken attorney from the passage.

"Good night, Ralph! I am off at once. Now, Blossom, proceed."

Blossom once more shouldered the portmanteau, and he and Duval again made their way back to the inn.

Blossom preceded Duval about a hundred yards, therefore he reached the door of the inn at which they intended to stop, some little time before Duval.

Just as he was about to deposit the portmanteau on the ground, to wait for Duval to come up to him, Blossom gave a start, for not many paces from where he stood, he saw Muckles, the police-officer, accompanied, as usual, by his shadow, Swallow.

Blossom saw instantly that there was no time to be lost if Duval was to escape the peril which menaced him, therefore, leaving the portmanteau to take care of itself, he darted back to Duval, and whispered eagerly in his ear—

"Muckles is standing outside the door of the 'Blue Boar,' Captain!"

If Blossom had announced that an earthquake was about to take place, the announcement could not have been received with greater surprise by Claude Duval.

"No, Blossom—you must be mistaken!" he said.

"Not at all—not at all, Captain! He's there, and no mistake, and Swallow, too!"

As Blossom spoke, Duval, with an almost involuntary movement, plunged his hand into the bosom of his apparel, to feel for the butt of one of those pistols to which he had so frequently owed the preservation of his life.

But, as it happened, there was not the slightest occasion for any violence.

Muckles had not the slightest idea that he was anywhere in the vicinity of Claude Duval; and his presence in that particular neighbourhood, at one and the same time with Claude Duval, was one of the accidental circumstances which are out of the sphere of all calculation.

The ostler, who happened to be near the spot where Duval and Blossom carried on their hurried conversation, must have thought them a little distracted, at the celerity with which Blossom again shouldered the portmanteau, and darted from the inn yard, as swiftly followed by Duval.

As soon as they had got a sufficient distance, to render open conversation at all safe, Duval turned to Blossom, and, with surprise and incredulity in his tones, exclaimed—

"You must have been mistaken, Blossom. Surely Muckles is not there!"

"Oh, he was there, Captain, fast enough," said Blossom, in a decided tone of voice.

"Well, Blossom, then I do not think I will venture to return to Hampstead Heath until to-morrow—so you go home, and explain to Lucy that she is not to expect me to-night."

"All right, Captain. Shall I take the portmanteau with me?"

"No, I will take charge of that."

"Then I shall come back to you, Captain."

"Yes."

"Where shall I find you?"

"At the Golden Cross. As Squire Brightwell, I think I may venture to take up my quarters there, and wait for you."

"Yes, Captain."

"Do not be later than mid-day to-morrow, Blossom."

"All right, Captain. Shall I call a coach for you."

"Ah, yes, I had forgotten my luggage."

As Duval said this, a smile came over his countenance, which looked so like his old self, that Blossom became reconciled to the arrangement of leaving him alone, while he returned to Hampstead, a proceeding which at first he did not at all seem to relish.

Blossom, therefore, hailed a coach in Piccadilly, Duval got into it, and having given the driver directions to convey him to the ancient hostel at Charing Cross—which was at the time of which we are writing, one of the oldest houses in London for the accommodation of travellers, although it is now so modernised, that it presents nothing of the appearance it did those days.

There, it was, that Duval found himself soon comfortably situated in a small apartment, that, for the time being, at all events, he could call his own, and he proceeded to make an examination of that portmanteau, which had strangely enough, fallen into his possession.

He found the amount as stated by the attorney and agent of the Duke of Montrose, to be perfectly correct.

Duval was re-packing the portmanteau, and considering the desirableness of making some alteration in his apparel, when there came a slight rap at the door of the apartment.

"Come in," said Duval.

The handle of the door was turned gently, and then the rap was repeated.

Duval remembered that he had taken the precaution to turn the key in the lock, before he began to examine the contents of the portmanteau.

This fact now seemed to impress Duval with the idea that he must use caution; so, instead of at once unlocking the door, he said, merely—

"Who's there?"

"Me, sir."

"And who is me?"

"Peter, sir."

"I am as wise now as ever. Who may Peter be? Peter who?"

"Peter Simpkins, if you please, sir, I'm the head waiter."

"Well, what do you want?"

"If you please, sir, you've been put into the wrong room."

"The wrong room, what do you mean?"

"You are in number eight, sir, and you ought to have had number seven, sir."

"Why?"

"Because number eight was engaged by another gentleman, sir, before you came; and it was by mistake, sir, as you were put in here. Perhaps, sir, you won't mind going in number seven."

"Not in the least—wait a moment!"

Duval threw the things into the portmanteau pell mell, and turned the key of it before he opened the door of the room.

"Very sorry, sir," said the waiter, as soon as Duval made his appearance.

"Oh, never mind—never mind," said Duval.

"It's just as good a room as this, number severn is, sir."

"My good man, you need make no more apologies, it makes not the slightest difference to me which room I occupy for so short a time."

"All right, sir!"

Then the waiter faced about, and calling down the stairs, he called out:

"Now, sir, you can come up, sir, if you please, your room is vacant now."

Some one from below now began slowly to ascend the stairs, and Duval, as he stood upon the threshold of his new apartment, was somewhat surprised to hear the new comer uttering groan after groan every step he took.

"Is the gentleman an invalid?" then asked Duval, as he continued listening.

"Oh, no, sir, he's a lawyer!"

"A lawyer,' said Duval, smiling, "but what is he giving utterance to those hideous groans for?"

"Why, sir, if you please, sir; the gent has been robbed and nearly murdered by that rascally, blood-thirsty villain of a highwayman, Claude Duval."

"Indeed? when?"

"To-night, sir."

"What, just now?"

"Oh no, sir; after he had beaten him—I mean after the murderer had beaten Mr. Knight, attorney-at-law, all over the head with the butt-end of one of his pistols, he then took him out of the coach, and had him taken to a house, sir!"

"Peter, Peter!" groaned the lawyer, half-way down the stairs, at this moment.

"Yes, sir—here, sir?"

"Fool! Idiot! give me your hand. What are you standing up there for looking like a stuck pig. Help me up, I say."

"Yes, sir!"

Duval just advanced sufficiently close to the stair-head to see and recognise his late companion of the mail-coach, Mr. Knight.

Duval made a hasty retreat into number seven and closed the door, as he had no desire that the recognition should be mutual.

Another moment, and the lawyer was safely deposited in number eight.

"Now, Peter," he said, "go at once to the Duke of Montrose's house in St. James's Square, take the note, and say the messenger is to have half-a-crown."

"Thank you, sir, I won't forget, sir No fear, I'll deliver the note."

"Make haste—make haste, I must see him before I sleep. Oh, dear, oh, dear—every bone in my body aches."

Duval now thought the wisest plan would be for him to leave the Golden Cross at once, and yet when he thought there was, perhaps, a chance of encountering the villainous Duke of Montrose, the desire to remain became irresistible, and so he resolved to wait and see what would come of the note.

THE DISCOVERY OF AGNES IN THE MEADOW.

CHAPTER CXCI.

CLAUDE DUVAL HAS A NARROW ESCAPE.—HE MEETS WITH AN OLD FRIEND.

WELL would it have been for the peace of mind as well as for the safety of Claude Duval, if he had left the Golden Cross, as his first impulse prompted him to do, instead of waiting to see if the Duke of Montrose would visit his vile agent and accomplice in many deeds of darkness.

But his destiny would not have it so.

Duval had to pass through a very great danger, which was gathering round him.

Ever and anon Duval applied his eye to the keyhole of the door of number seven, to see if the false and wicked Duke of Montrose would arrive.

Half an hour—three-quarters—an hour passed away, and Duval began to think he had kept watch in vain, when suddenly he heard the sound of approaching footsteps ascending the stairs, and in another moment, he saw the Duke of Montrose appear.

The Duke paused at the head of the stairs, as if in doubt which room to go into; and it was a wonder—quite a chance—that he did not apply to the very room where the man he had so often tried to injure had taken refuge.

There was, however, a kind of timidity about the Duke of Montrose, which prevented him from opening any door at random, so he called out down the staircase, "Which is his room?"

"Number eight, sir— my lord!" replied a voice. "I will come, my lord, if your lordship wishes."

"No, no! never mind, I see the number painted on the panel."

The Duke of Montrose turned the handle of the door of the apartment in which the attorney-at-law awaited him, and went in.

All that Duval could hear was a loud exclamation from some one; and then another voice, as if in entreaty or supplication.

No. 57.—NIGHTSHADE.

The old panelling was thick between the two rooms, and Duval sought in vain for some place in it by which he would be enabled to hear what was going on in number eight.

None such, however, presented itself; and all he could make out was, that the interview was too noisy an one for him to suppose, for one moment, that it was a harmonious one.

Then there was a sharp, sudden cry, and the door of number eight opened quickly.

"Very well, sir!" said the Duke of Montrose, as though addressing his lawyer; "very well, sir, I will send to you!"

There was no reply to this speech, and it looked rather suspicious to Claude Duval, that the Duke of Montrose should take the trouble to close the door of the apartment very carefully, making several rattling efforts at the lock before he fully succeeded in doing so.

Duval saw that proceeding through the keyhole, and as he did not think it worth his while to show himself just then to the Duke, he allowed him to descend the staircase without making his presence known to that personage.

The Duke of Montrose, indeed, descended the stairs with such haste, that if Duval had desired to speak to him, and renew their old quarrel, he would have had to call after him.

As it was, however, he let him go.

But the intense stillness in number eight was suspicious—nay, it was something more than suspicious—coupled with the extraordinary conduct of the villain who had just left that apartment.

A terrible idea took possession of the mind of Duval.

"Had the Duke of Montrose, influenced by rage and disappointment at the loss of the four thousand pounds, actually murdered his agent and man of business?"

This was an idea which such a mind as Duval's could not long support without seeking to arrive at the truth.

The corridor was silent and deserted.

There was no one on the stairs.

It would but be the act of a moment to put an end to all doubt on the subject, by looking into number eight.

Duval, with three long strides, was at the door.

He rapped at it gently.

There was no reply.

He pulled the handle of the latch and looked in.

What a sight then met his gaze!

A sight that even he, lion-hearted as he was, would not look at a second time if he could avoid it.

Partially propped up by a chair, was the dead body of the Duke of Montrose's professional agent.

The aspect of the dead face was a terror to be remembered in dreams.

A thin stream of black blood was slowly oozing from a wound in the dead man's chest, and collecting on the floor.

"It is murder then!" said Duval to himself, as he closed the door of number eight, and stood for a few seconds on the threshold in a state of doubt and irresolution as to what it would be best to do.

Then his impulse was to fly from the ill-omened house, and seek for any other shelter which, until the morrow might present itself.

This was a resolution which grew in strength every moment, and Duval at once fetched the portmanteau from number seven, and as hastily descended the stairs as the Duke of Montrose had already done before him.

It cost him a painful effort of self-control to hinder his voice from making itself heard in startling accents throughout that hostel from crying out murder!

But Duval was peculiarly situated.

How could he put himself into contact with the police and the magistrates, as he would be compelled to do if he tendered the information he had it in his power to do if he became the accuser of the Duke of Montrose.

No. His reason told him that there was no resource for him but flight from a house which would surely soon be full of peril to him if he lingered.

Nay, who should say that if he remained he might not himself be suspected of the crime?

And how could he clear himself from that suspicion by avowing who and what he was.

"No—nothing but flight," he murmured to himself; "nothing but flight. *He*, the victim is past all human aid now, and I must fly, perhaps for my life and for Lucy's sake."

And so Duval reached the hall.

The waiters looked surprised, and the head waiter who had been so communicative to him when the change of rooms was being effected, bustled up to him, and asked if he wanted anything.

"Nothing, thank you," replied Duval, as calmly as he could; "but I find I must leave. I have an appointment I had forgotten until just this minute."

"Indeed, sir! I am very sorry, sir," said Peter; "but I hope you are not offended, sir, at being asked to change rooms?"

"Not in the least. Here is a guinea; keep the change. It will pay for my short stay."

" h, yes, sir. Very sorry, sir."

"Good day."

"Good day, sir. Glad to see you again, sir."

It was with a feeling of exquisite relief that Claude Duval felt himself once more breathing the open air.

But he hastened onward.

The very air of that neighbourhood seemed to his excited imagination to be tainted with blood.

But he was now at a loss to know where to go, and the idea at length came across him that he would spend the remainder of the night at Camden House, and ascertain if the Dutch Envoy had left it.

Without hesitating for another moment Duval turned his face in the direction of Kensington.

Once only he paused in his progress, because he heard, coming through the white fog which, for the last half hour had been gradually settling over London, shouts and cries as if either some accident had happened, or if some excited pursuers were on the track of some fugitive.

Duval paused, and bent his ear to listen.

"Stop him! Stop him! Murder! Murder!" were the cries that came distinctly to his senses.

But, strange to say, those cries had no disturbing power over the heart and brain of Claude Duval.

He in no way connected them with himself, and he stood within the arch of a doorway, listening with a vague curiosity to the cries until they died away in the distance.

"Some crime has been committed," he said, "in the streets, perhaps, of nearly as black a dye as that which the Duke of Montrose had been guilty within the last hour."

"Stop him! Stop him! A thousand pounds reward for Claude Duval!"

Duval's heart stood still for a moment, and an icy chill passed through his frame as he now for the first time understood the meaning of those cries.

He was the supposed murderer of the attorney!

He shrunk further back into the shadow of the friendly doorway.

What was he to do?

Which way was he to turn?

He looked to the right and to the left, and fancied that he might have time yet to distance his pursuers.

"But from what am I flying?" he asked himself.

From a false accusation.

An accusation, however, which he (Claude Duval) —because he happened to be that person—would have great difficulty in freeing himself.

He slowly emerged from his hiding-place.

As he did so, he was surprised to find that he had not been alone.

A tall figure, enveloped in a cloak, laid his hand on Duval's shoulder.

"A word with you, friend," said the figure, in a familiar tone.

"With me? But do I not know that voice?" said Duval.

"As I know yours, *Claude Duval.*"

"Dick Turpin!"

"The same. What's the game to-night? you are hiding."

"Stop him! Seize the murderer!"

"Is that you?" asked Turpin.

"Yes, and no," replied Duval.

"What mean you?"

"I am accused of a murder I never committed," said Duval, in an agitated tone.

"Then never heed their cries. Follow me, and I will lead you to a safe refuge."

As Turpin spoke, he turned, and, passing his arm beneath that of Duval, he strode out into the open street.

The crowd were still coming on at a good pace, but it was only by the sound of their voices that their presence could be detected; for the fog had thickened so that you could not have seen your hand before your face.

"Here," said Dick Turpin,—"here, Duval, throw this cloak over you, in case your disguise should be recognised."

"Thanks," said Duval; "I had forgotten."

At this moment, the excited mob surged past the two highwaymen, who were apparently pursuing their course, little heeding the tumult around them.

"Seize him! stop him! We saw him come down this street; search the doorways. Down with the highwayman! down with the murderer! A thousand pounds reward for Claude Duval!"

A sickening feeling, in spite of himself, took possession of Duval, as he thus heard his name associated with the dastardly murder of Mr. Knight

And to think that he could so easily have fixed the guilt upon the right person!

And yet, who would take his unsupported testimony against one of the wealthiest nobles in the land?

No, no; he must keep silent.

A man brushed rudely passed Duval and his companion, and then he looked back, and said,

"Why don't you help us to capture the murderer of a respectable lawyer?"

"Faith!" said Turpin; "we are peaceable men, and have no desire to meddle with what does not concern us."

"Catch him! stop him!" shouted the multitude, as men and boys rushed pell-mell passed the two friends, who in time were left alone.

"Now you are safe," said Turpin.

"Yes," said Duval, gloomily.

"Come, cheer up, man," said Turpin, "or I shall begin to think you really did commit the deed."

"Dick!"

"Well?"

"Do not jest upon such a subject. If such a spectacle had met your gaze as I looked upon, only a short hour and a half ago - so far from jesting upon the matter, you would do your best to banish it from your recollection for ever."

"Very well, then; don't let us say any more about it; but let us, on the contrary, seek an adventure to-night, and drive all sad thoughts from our minds by crying, 'Stand and deliver!'"

"Oh! a highwayman's life for me;
A life on the turnpike road,
Where all is——"

"Hush!" said Duval laying his hand upon Dick's arm. What was that?"

"What? I heard nothing but my own voice."

"There! there!"

Turpin now heard a low groan, which seemed to proceed from the other side of the hedge.

"Did you hear that?" asked Duval.

"Yes, let us see what it means."

CHAPTER CXCII.

CLAUDE DUVAL AND DICK TURPIN CHASTISE A VILLAIN, AND GAIN A RICH BOOTY BESIDES.

DUVAL and Turpin soon made their way over the hedge into the meadow beyond, and there, lying on her face, they beheld an object which excited both their sympathies.

A young girl scarcely eighteen, and beautiful as an angel, was lying in a swoon in the foot-path which conducted to the high road.

A crumpled letter was clutched in one of her small hands.

Just as Duval reached her side, she raised her head, and stared about her, saying in an absent kind of voice, "I shall be too late to prevent it! I shall be too late! What has happened to me?"

"You fainted, madam," said Duval, in his gentlest accents.

"Ah! Good heavens! Who are you, sir? What has happened? Oh, speak!"

"Don't alarm yourself—you have only fainted; but you will be better soon."

"Fainted?—fainted?" she repeated. "Why did I faint? Ah, I know!"

As she spoke, her eyes had fallen upon the letter which she held in her hand.

"The letter! the letter! Yes, where is the letter?" she asked. "Ah, here it is!"

She tried to read it, but it was much too dark for her to see anything written on the paper.

"I must go, I must go, or I shall be too late, I tell you!"

"Whither would you go?" asked Duval, seeking to detain her. "Tell me; I may be of assistance to you."

"I go to prevent murder!"

"Murder?"

"Yes."

"My cousin is this night to die by the hand of his dire enemy, Sir Philip Lonsdale."

"You mean that he is to fight a duel?"

"Yes, yes! But do not detain me, or I shall be too late."

"But what can you do? you, a weak, delicate girl!"

"I know not. Yes, I can die—die, shielding my Henry's heart from his adversary's ball!"

"Brave girl, I will not seek to detain you; but will you grant me a favour?"

"What would you of me, sir? I know you not."

"Will you accept my escort, and, if needs be, my assistance, in this affair?"

"Will you help me?"

"Most assuredly."

"Then come, oh, come! Lose not a moment. A precious life hangs upon the events of the next quarter of an hour!"

"And where is this duel to take place?"

"In the next field. Ah, I can hear voices even now!"

True enough, there were voices in deep conversation; but the words were spoken too low to reach the ears of the listeners.

"Stay here," said Duval, to Turpin, "with this young lady, while I go forward and ascertain who the speakers are."

Duval crept along the soft turf until he came to the trunk of an oak, behind which he had no difficulty in concealing himself, and in such a position as to be enabled to hear all that was said.

"I am glad, Gerald, to find that we are first in the field—at all events, he shall never call me coward again."

The voice evidently belonged to a very young man, and there was a sweetness about it, which reminded Duval strongly of that of the fair young girl who had accepted his services.

"Her cousin," said Duval to himself; "but Sir Philip Lonsdale does not seem inclined to make his appearance."

Duval now made his way back to the young girl, who he doubted not, would be suffering from a thousand needless, fearless, anxieties.

"Your cousin is there, and the gentleman, who is to act as his second, but no Sir Philip."

"Henry, there!"

"Yes. Then I must speak to him, and tell him not to meet this man who is known to be a most skilful swordsman."

As she spoke, the young girl darted forward, and threw herself upon Henry's breast.

"Agnes?"

"Yes, yes, Sir Philip wrote me a note."

"Wrote you a note, Agnes?"

"Yes, dearest Henry, one which he thought would break my heart, in which he told me that at this hour you would fall by his hand."

A scornful laugh was all the reply that Henry made, and after a moment's silence, he said:

"Sir Philip seems to have thought better of the threat, for it is past the hour, and he has failed to keep his appointment."

At this moment, shouts of "Murder! help!" came upon the night air, and Agnes clung to Henry, in an agony of terror.

Duval turned to speak to Turpin, and found that he had left the spot where he believed he was standing.

"Dick," said Duval, in a low voice.

There was no reply.

All was still.

Duval advanced gracefully towards the young lady and the two friends, and raising his hat, he said, courteously:

"My services I think, will not be required to-night, therefore I beg to take my respectful leave."

"Sir!" said the young man, who drew the young girl still closer to his side.

"Oh, Henry, I had forgotten to tell you that—that——"

"That what, dear one."

"That this gentleman was kind, and gave me his assistance——"

"When—where?"

The young girl did not reply, and Duval answered for her.

"I scarcely can say I have been of any assistance to this young lady, but I happened to be passing on the other side of the hedge, when I heard a groan——"

"A groan?"

"And upon leaping the stile, I found this young lady just recovering from a swoon."

"Dear Agnes!" whispered the young man, fondly; "it was too much for your gentle heart."

"And he—this gentleman," said this young girl, "promised to aid and assist me in any way in his power, should I require a friend. Thank him, Henry—thank him for us both!"

The young man turned, and gave his hand to Duval, who grasped it warmly, as he said—

"You owe me nothing, sir, and I can see that this young lady will now certainly not require my services."

"It seems that Sir Philip has thought better of it, and does not intend to meet me," replied the young man; "so we will return, dear Agnes; we will leave you at your father's house, and then I can pursue my journey to London."

With mutual feelings of courtesy and kindness, the little party took their leave of each other: Henry and the young girl walking apparently in confidential conversation, and the friend bringing up the rear.

Claude Duval found himself alone.

"Where on earth can Dick have hidden himself?" thought Duval; "and why did he leave us without saying a word?"

As he thus thought, Duval then remembered hearing the noise which came upon the night air, while he and the little party were conversing in the meadow.

"Ah, I see now!" he said, half-aloud. "Dick had an eye to business, and finding that his presence was not required, quietly left us."

Thus thinking, Duval continued to pursue his way down the green lane, but he had not gone far before he became conscious that he heard footsteps behind him.

At first he began to imagine that those who had pursued him a short time before for the murder of Mr. Knight, the attorney, had discovered him, and were again upon his track.

It must be confessed that this was no very agreeable thought, and Duval continued to walk on as quickly as possible, in hopes of soon coming to a turn in the road, which would serve to conceal him from hostile eyes, and give him a chance of distancing his pursuers.

"Hoi! hilloa!" shouted a voice.

Claude Duval took no notice, but pursued his way.

Then there came a long, low whistle.

"Ah, Dick Turpin!" cried Duval. "Now I know my man."

"Of course you do!" replied Dick, coming up to Duval considerably out of breath. "Why, what on earth made you give me such a chase as this?"

"I did not know you."

"But when were you afraid of meeting one man—or two men, even, Claude?"

"Never!" said Duval; "but I knew not whether there might not be a mob at your heels, and so I thought the better part of valour was discretion."

"I see—I see!"

"Now, tell me, Dick, why you left us so suddenly?"

"Simply because I was not wanted."

"Not wanted?"

"Not wanted there; but I knew that my presence was required elsewhere."

"Elsewhere?"

"Why, of course! Do you suppose, Claude Duval, I was going to let that girl's lover be murdered before her eyes?"

Duval looked inquiringly at Turpin.

"Don't you see, I went to prevent him keeping his appointment."

"Ah!"

"Of course I did! But he made such a confounded row, he and his friend together, that it was almost more than I could do to silence them both; but I did succeed."

"And where are they?"

"Oh, if you have any wish to see them, they are tied back to back against a large oak tree."

Duval laughed.

"But how is it they are so quiet?"

"Because they think I am there, and fancy that the first one who dares to raise his voice to speak will receive a bullet in his brains."

"Capital! capital!" cried Duval. "Now let us make the best of our way to Hampstead Heath, Dick, for I told Blossom to meet me at the Golden Cross early to-morrow morning, and as I am suspected of having committed that horrible murder, it would be better to prevent his going there, or he may get into trouble."

"As you please," said Dick; "but there is yet time for an adventure, if you like. What say you?"

"Not to-night, Dick," said Duval,—"not to-night! I must get home."

"Very well. Good night to you, then; but I wanted to ask you one thing—don't think me a fool, will you?"

"What is it, Dick?"

"Have you any idea—have you ever heard anything about—about——"

Dick paused, and Duval instantly remembered that young girl who had loved him too well for her own peace of mind, and he said—

"That young girl to whom you were engaged to be married?"

Dick nodded.

"No, Dick; I have never seen her nor heard of her since that night at the cottage."

"It is strange," said Dick, "but she mysteriously disappeared."

"Dick."

"Well?"

"Do you know, I am afraid," said Duval, "that she overheard our conversation on that night."

"Oh, no! And yet—and yet——"

"It would seem like it. Ah, well, I must not think about her, or I shall get down-hearted. She might have made me a better man, Claude; but it wasn't to be, seemingly. Never mind, a gay life—I mean, a short life and a merry one is what I want! Ha, ha! Good night, Claude Duval! The road is clear, I think, now!"

With a light-hearted laugh, Dick Turpin struck across the fields, while Duval continued to pursue the lane that led to the high road.

Duval buttoned the cloak, for which he was indebted to his friend Dick, tight up to the chin, and pulled his hat low down upon his brow, in order the better to face the sharp north-east wind that had, as it were, suddenly got up.

But, in spite of all these precautions, the wind would creep down his neck, and up his coat-sleeves, and round his ankles, according to the usual habit of such winds.

Duval had by this time reached the outskirts of London, and the houses were few and far between.

Pedestrians there were none, so that the rumbling noise of a crazy-looking hackney-coach made quite a pleasing variety in the landscape, as the driver endeavoured to lash his jaded horses into something like a trot.

All was so still that Duval began to think his own footsteps unusually loud as he came nearer to the hackney coach.

More from curiosity than he chose to admit, he trolled up towards the coach which had just stopped at the corner of a bye-street.

At first he thought he might have an opportunity of levying toll upon the occupants.

A man and a woman alighted from the coach, and the latter was carrying something that was either a child or a bundle strongly resembling one in shape.

Perhaps Duval would have passed these people, as they were poorly clad, had his steps not been arrested by hearing the woman say, "Hush, Cato—hush! don't you see somebody has just passed?"

"What an odd name!" said Duval to himself. "Cato!"

Duval strolled on, however, and after he had gone some distance, something tempted him to look back.

The man and the woman had crossed the road; the woman was certainly without the bundle which had attracted Duval's attention, and the pair were making off at a great rate.

A few moments sufficed to bring Duval to the spot they had just left, and there, sure enough, placed at the corner of the street, was a child, apparently about two years old.

The child was not asleep, but was looking about in a bewildered, but not an alarmed manner.

Duval's first impulse was to run in pursuit of the man and woman, but they had got out of sight by this time, and Duval, when he returned to the child, began to ask himself what he had better do under the circumstances.

The child at this moment made a little, wailing sound and Duval's heart bled for its cheerless prospects.

At first Duval felt very much inclined to take the child home to Lucy; he had, indeed, raised it in his arms with that intention, when he heard the sound of a watchman's voice.

"Past two o'clock, and a windy night!"

"The very thing—the very thing!" said Duval to himself. "I will give you into the care of the guardian of the night, little one; at least you will be better off than lying here exposed to this biting wind."

"Hoi! watch!"

"Who calls watch, now? Can't ye be quiet, wid ye, and let a man do his duty! Past two o'clock, and a —eh? what?"

Claude Duval strode up to the watchman, having thrown open the cloak which had hidden his disguise as a country squire; and he now stood revealed in that character to the good-humoured son of Emerald Isle.

"Did you hear me call you just now, my man?"

"Sure enough, yer honour; but I didn't know as it was yer honour!"

"Then I will look over your inattention upon condition that you take that poor child at once to the workhouse."

"Workhouse, yer honour? What child? Whose child? Your child, yer honour?"

"No, man, but a poor little creature who has been left to the pitiless winds on this bitter night."

"Deary me—deary me! The hearts of flint as we do come across in this brave counthree!" said the Irishman. "Where may be the little creature, yer honour?"

"Yonder," said Duval.

"May be, yer honour, you'll just give me your card now, to make it right with the authorities."

"I'll do better my man; here is a guinea!"

"Hurrah! to your honour! Come here, my beauty! Where are you?"

The watchman had no difficulty in seeing the little friendless child, and taking it, with the tenderness of a woman, in his arms, he strode off, no doubt, to the workhouse with it.

"Well, it is the best thing I could do with it, poor little thing!" sighed Duval; "at least it will be cared for now, and if it has been stolen, its parents will surely advertise for it, and all may yet be well."

The incident made a great impression upon Claude Duval, and a feeling of sadness crept over him as he pursued his solitary way.

CHAPTER CXCIII.

IN WHICH CLAUDE DUVAL OVERHEARS A PRIVATE CONVERSATION.

CLAUDE DUVAL soon found himself in St. James's Park, and as he was crossing the Mall he heard, or fancied he heard, voices.

At such an hour, such a circumstance was, to say the least of it, unusual, so Claude thought he would ensconce himself behind one of the trees and listen.

"Hilloa! There he is!" cried a voice not far from Duval, and a couple of gentlemen approached one of the benches in the Park, upon which reclined, even at that late hour, a rather young man.

He was rather stout and tall in appearance, with hair inclining to be sandy in its colour, and a certain floridity of complexion which in youth was very well, but as years increased, was likely to degenerate into the look of the voluptuary.

The dress of the young man, although carelessly enough put on, became him well.

"Yes, by Jove, it's he!" replied another voice.

That voice Duval knew too well to belong to the Duke of Montrose.

Frederick, Prince of Wales rose, and, extending his hand, said, "What Duke, and you Colonel, were you looking for me?"

"By Jove, yes," said the Duke.

"'Pon honour, we were, your royal highness," said the Colonel.

"Yes, by Jove! yes. Come, now; what news of the mysterious and the fair—for we suppose her to be fair—wanderer of the Mall?"

"Ah! what news? 'Pon honour," said the one who had been addressed as Colonel.

"But little," said Prince Frederick. "She has not been here to-night."

"Now, really—'pon honour——"

"Hush! Hide somewhere! She comes! Last night I spoke to her, and she answered me. I must speak to her again to-night."

Agreeably to the expressed wish of the dissolute young Prince, his two companions hid themselves behind a tree, even as Duval had done.

Duval strained his eye in every direction to catch a glimpse of the approaching "Wanderer of the Mall," as she had been designated by the two dissolute friends of the young Prince; and he was so fortunate as to be behind the tree nearest to the spot where the Prince of Wales stopped and accosted the figure.

He had no difficulty in deciding, not only from the walk but from the voice of the speaker, that the Wanderer of the Mall was a young girl.

But what could she be doing in the Park at that hour, and what would be her bearing towards the Prince of Wales?

"And so you have come at last, fair wanderer of the night!" Duval heard the Prince say.

"Yes. Did you expect me?"

"If you had not come, I should have died of——"

"Of what?"

"Of despair! For I love you!"

"Love me?"

"Passionately—fondly!"

"What, after an acquaintance of about ten minutes?"

"Indeed—indeed, I do! Is it possible to do otherwise?"

"I don't know."

"How long a time would you give me to see that you are beautiful?"

"That I cannot answer."

"Well, are you satisfied?" asked the Prince.

"Of what?"

"That I love you—that I adore you!"

"Oh, yes!"

"You are?"

"Why not?"

"Well, I should say why not, because, knowing the truth of my great affection for you, it is very painful for me to think that for a moment you could doubt it!"

"I am glad to hear it," said the young lady, with a slight tone of badinage, Duval thought, "because I have the less hesitation in bidding you good night, or rather good morning!"

"Oh, no, no! Why, would you leave me to despair?"

"To despair?"

"Yes; the greatest despair!"

"Why, I thought that you told me just now that you were happy, indeed!"

"Yes; and so I am when you are here!"

"And so you would have me stay?"

"Oh, yes, in good truth, I would!"

"How long?"

This question seemed rather to puzzle Prince Frederick, for he repeated the words, "How long?" twice or thrice without being able to append anything to them.

"Ah!" said the lady, "I see; you never thought of my happiness at all in the matter. So long as you felt supremely happy, you were quite contented."

"Alas! love is ever selfish!"

"Granted; and so I now leave you, because I love myself, sir!"

"No, no! I implore—I entreat you to stay! Beautiful and mysterious being, I beg that you will not leave me! Tell me who and what you are, and the cause of the mysterious conduct that I saw take place for four nights in succession in this Park! Oh, do not leave me to cruel conjectures!"

"Mysterious conduct, sir? To what, pray, do you allude?"

"Ah! now you are angry with me!"

"No; not if you are candid!"

"Then I will tell you all that I know!" said the Prince.

"I am all attention! Proceed, sir!"

"Well, then, about this time on the evenings, or rather the early mornings, in question—about this time you came and seated yourself upon one of the seats in the Mall, not far from this spot."

"Well, sir?"

"After a moment, a man came and said a few words, after which, you rose and left the Park, taking your route out of it by Spring Gardens."

"Is that all?"

"Is it not all true?"

"It is."

"Well, then, last night I followed you and spoke to you, but you repulsed me."

"I did."

"But, love," continued the Prince, not heeding the interruption. "But love, however,—for indeed I do love you—got the better of all such feelings, and again I spoke to you to-night."

"Well, sir, and what inference do you draw from my mysterious conduct to-night, then?" asked the young girl.

"I am convinced that you are not cruel. That is all I know."

"It is all, sir, you should seek to know."

"Nay, do not say that; I——"

"Hold, sir! You are a gentleman, I hope?"

"I trust so."

"Well! you love me, you say. What are your intentions, then?"

"My—my intentions? Oh, I—that is—my intentions?"

"Yes, sir, your intentions?"

"Strictly honourable."

"Then you will marry me?"

Prince Frederick, Duval could see, rather started at this abrupt question, and he stammered out something in reply that was certainly not very intelligible; and then the young girl, gathering her cloak more closely about her, said in a voice that seemed struggling with wounded pride,—"Spare yourself further speech, sir. I know you—farewell!"

So saying, she disengaged her hand, which the Prince had got hold of, and darted from him along the Grand Mall.

For a few moments he stood in a state of consternation, and then he darted after her, and quickly overtook her.

Duval was at too great a distance to hear the conversation which ensued after the Prince had overtaken the mysterious wanderer, as she had been called; but could see—for they were standing just beneath a lamp which happened to be burning very brightly, for a wonder—that the young girl suffered the cloak she wore to fall away so far from before her face, that the Prince had a good view of it.

And even from where Duval had stationed himself, he could see that by a slight action, which might have been accidental, or otherwise, on the part of the young girl, that as she put up her hand to dash the dancing ringlets of her hair from before her eyes, or it might have been some sudden gust of wind; but the little light hat she wore fell back from her head, and only hung round her neck by its strings.

It was but for a moment that that vision of beauty bewildered the Prince, and then all was over.

The hat was hastily replaced, the cloak was drawn close, and the young girl fled with the speed of lightning through the narrow passage that led to Spring Gardens.

The Prince of Wales walked with a dreamy look back to the seat he had occupied, when his two friends first addressed him.

When he had flung himself down, he uttered with a deep-drawn sigh, the not very poetical ejaculation,—"Oh dear!"

Loud, deep-drawn sighs, Duval could hear, came from his breast, and after a time he spoke.

"She is decidedly the prettiest creature I ever saw in my life. Why, she can't be above fifteen or sixteen at the outside; and such eyes—such a form—such a face—such——"

At this moment the Duke of Montrose and the Colonel, as he was called, emerged from their hiding-places.

"Ah, your Royal Highness!" said the Colonel; "what news? 'pon honour!"

"But little," replied the Prince, despondingly.

"I told you both how I had watched her, and how, last night she spoke to me in answer to my solicitations. Well, she did the same to-night."

"Yes, 'pon honour!" said the Colonel; "It made me feel I don't know how, to think you had her so long all to yourself."

"Yes, yes! she spoke to me again to-night!" and he sighed again.

"Good, by Jove!" said the Duke of Montrose.

"A thriving wooer, 'pon soul!"

"Not so!"

"Ah! what means your Royal Highness?" asked the Duke.

"What do you think, she plumply and plainly, and in as many words, without any circumlocution about it, asked me something. Guess what it was she wanted to know?"

The Colonel shook his head, and the Duke tried to look wise but, of course, that was a complete failure.

"I see that you are both puzzled," added the Prince; "but, in a word, she asked me if I would marry her!"

"By Jove!"

"'Pon honour!"

"Yes, she did! and then finding that I hesitated to know what to say to her, off she started, and left me here to despair, after letting me get one bewildering look at beauties that have made me nearly mad."

"Yes, by Jove!" said the Colonel, "she did."

"Well, I tell you she did."

"Ah, yes! but by Jove! we saw her, too, from where we were hiding, and just as you parted with her, your Royal Highness, she dropped this card which I picked up."

"A card! let me see it! Oh! let me see it! There may be hope in that!" cried the Prince.

"By Jove! there you have it; you can just manage to read it by the light of this lamp."

The Prince of Wales eagerly took the card, which was of very thin and fine texture; and, by the light of the lamp, which was not far from where he had been sitting, he read the name, but in so low a tone that Duval could not catch it.

"I breathe again!" cried the Prince. "Oh! I breathe again! My Adelina! oh, my Adelina!"

"By Jove! its a pretty name; and——"

"Romantic, 'pon honour!"

"My good friends," said Prince Frederick, with emotion. "I love this girl to distraction. I never saw such eyes—such teeth—such hair—such——"

"Stop—stop! By Jove! your Royal Highness forgets that we too admire a pretty girl!"

"But in a word, I tell you, she must and shall be mine. I shall become ill—mad—anything you like, if I do not see her again. Will you aid me? May I put your friendship to the test, so far."

"Depend upon me," said the Colonel, "to the death, by Jove!"

"And upon me," said the Duke; "I will do anything in the world for your Royal Highness."

"Then follow me to the address written upon this card, my friends, and Adelina will be mine."

CHAPTER CXCIV.

IN WHICH A SINGULAR PERSON IS INTRODUCED TO THE READER.

PRINCE FREDERICK, and his two dissolute companions now made their way towards Spring Gardens, and as soon as they were sufficiently removed from him, Duval followed, scarcely knowing why he did so; but he felt that he might, perhaps, be of some assistance to that young girl—perhaps a protector.

But we must now introduce the reader to a very different scene, while we leave Claude Duval following hard upon the tracks of the three debauchees.

All the world knows the Adelphi Terrace

You go down Adam Street, in the Strand, and disregarding the portion of John Street, on the right hand—a street which is getting now too well known as the resort of that questionable portion of society that is supposed to live upon its wits — the word wits in that case being convertible to roguery—you go straight on till you are stopped by an iron railing from walking into the river, or, rather, on the roofs of some singular buildings, which seem to be so mingled with coal, and barges, and huge waggons, that one would suppose that there was some strange affinity between the two classes of objects.

Then you turn to the right, and the row of houses on your left hand, comprises the Adelphi Terrace.

The inhabitants of that Terrace are sufficiently removed from the roar and bustle of the Strand only to hear its echoes, in a continuous kind of murmur, shaking the air, and the view they have from the windows is of the river—ever teeming with life, but of a much more quiet order, for the liquid highway makes no noise, and beyond an occasional 'ease her," and "stop her," from the captains of the steamers that go bubbling and hissing and whistling by, all is tolerably still.

It is hard to say, at the date of our story, what class of people inhabited the Adelphi Terrace, but we are inclined to think that the place has fallen off from its fashionable celebrity since then.

All we have to do though, is with number sixteen and that was, to all appearance, an empty house.

To be sure, there was a bill in the parlour window of number sixteen, to the effect that the house was to be let, and there was a name and an address given where people might apply for further particulars.

But the name was Smith, and the address was somewhere at Fulham, and when, as sometimes happened, a persevering and adventurous person went in search of the Mr. Smith, who was supposed to know all about No. 16, Adelphi Terrace, they always failed in finding such a person.

And so the house remained for years "to let."

But yet such was the address which was written upon the card dropped by the mysterious lady near Spring Gardens – which card, as the reader is aware, was at that moment in the possession of Frederick Prince of Wales.

Whether the card had been dropped purposely, or by accident, remains yet to be seen.

But now let us enter, in imagination at least, that deserted looking house, and enter a very large room upon the first floor, in which there are three windows —opening, if they were ever opened, to the street.

Imagine the shutters to be closed, and imagine the room to have been furnished in the most costly style, some twenty years before that night, and imagine all the dust and soot of all that time to have been allowed to settle and have its own way in the apartment without the shadow of a disturbance.

Spiders had taken possession of the elaborately gilt cornices and frame work of the mirrors and glasses.

Bullion tassels that at one time, no doubt, had glittered in beauty, hung thickly coated with black dust.

Mice ran about the dark corners of the room in all the freedom of long absence from molestation.

The glass chandelier which hung from the ceiling with its thousand of drops looked like some mysterious conglomeration of spider webs, with here and there a diamond sparkling in the midst of them.

A tiger's skin was upon the hearth, and in the low grate there dimly burnt a log of wood.

A kind of settee, covered with old faded velvet, was upon the very verge of the hearth, and upon that, crouched rather than lay, a human figure; but so aged and so decrepid was he, that it was difficult to say if a corpse did not there rest to make the strange sights and desolation of that room more manifest.

Long white hair streamed from the back of the old man's head, and his eyes looked lost beneath the mass of thick overhanging white eyebrows that hung over them.

Thick white moustaches, and a beard of the same hue, concealed the lower part of his face.

This aged man spread his thin attenuated hands over the fire, and now and then rubbed them together with a shivering nervousness.

At times, too, he would take a keen glance round the room, and once in a sharp, querulous voice, he called out, "Adelina!"

There was no answer.

"Enough! enough!" he half ejaculated, half coughed, "They don't attend to me now—they don't attend to me now! I am getting old—old, and they think me a trouble!"

"No, grandfather," said a voice, "you wrong us all by such a thought—indeed, and in truth you do."

The speaker was a young lad, rather richly dressed but in something of a continental fashion, and who came with a slow and rather timorous step from another room.

"Ah, my Catherine," said the old man, "is it you my child?"

"Yes, grandfather."

It scarcely required a second glance at the young lad to see that, notwithstanding the male apparel, he belonged to the softer sex.

"And where is Adelina?—where is she?"

"On her mission, grandfather."

"Her mission! her mission! Yes, good child— good child. You are all good children, and you will be so rich—oh, so rich! Where is the—the—no, I ought not to call him the king yet—not while I live. Where is James?"

"Oh, grandfather, never call him king—never call yourself king. It is the title to care—to sorrow— to suffering. Oh, who would envy the circle of sovereignty now. Try to disabuse yourself of the delusion, dear grandfather, and——"

"Silence!" shrieked the old man, as he rose to his feet,—"silence, girl! Treason—I say this is treason I am the lineal descendant of King James the Second! Monarch of England, who was hunted from his crown, and died at St. Germains, in France! I—I am a poor, weak old man!"

He sunk upon the settee with a deep sigh, and shook with palsy, which was an affection which had long stricken him.

"Ever thus!" said Catherine, as the tears gushed from her eyes,—"ever thus upon this subject. James, James—oh, where are you, James?"

A quick step sounded in the next apartment, and a young man appeared with an expression of alarm upon his countenance.

"What is it, Catherine—what is it?"

"Grandfather is worse, James."

"Alas, yes! I fear——"

"You fear?" cried the old man, raising his hand with momentary energy. "Let me never hear that word. It is by fear we lost our crown! We lost all by fear! No, no, not quite all—some by treachery and evil counsellers; but much by fear—very much, indeed! Oh, my poor children, what can I say to you? Your father should have been king, but he is dead; and so you, James, are King of England! I salute your Majesty—I—I commend myself to your Majesty —I—I——Oh, heaven!"

The old man fell back on the settee in a state of total and deathlike insensibility.

Catherine clasped her hands in despair, and looked at her brother James, who, with a bewildered look, cried—

"Oh, Catherine! ought we not, in defiance of all his injunctions to the contrary, call in medical aid to him?"

"Alas! I know not, James."

"I will—it is a duty."

"Oh no, no! Get some of the cordial from the adjoining room, James, and the ammonia! Quick! If

THE MYSTERIOUS FAMILY IN THE "HOUSE TO LET."

we can restore him, he may be much as usual; but if we once call a stranger into the house, it will kill him with grief and anger."

"It will, indeed! Hush!"

"What do you hear?"

"Is not some one at the door?"

They both listened, and distinctly heard the street door open, and then close again, and various fastenings being put up on the inside.

"Thank heaven!" said Catherine; "it is Adelina. She will know what to do. She is more equal to these emergencies than we are, James."

"It is true—it is true!"

The door of the vast apartment at this moment opened, and the young girl we have already introduced to the reader as the "fair wanderer" entered the room.

In a moment she cast off her cloak and hat, and, approaching the settee, she said—

"Fainted again?"

"Yes, dear," said James. "He has been talking

No. 58.—NIGHTSHADE.

again of his right to the throne, and it has overcome him."

"Alas! alas!"

"We thought—that is, it just occurred to us to get some medical aid for him."

"Not for worlds!" cried the young girl. "Do not suppose that it is from any indifference to our poor grandfather's health or life that I speak thus; but I know that the sight of any one here, in his present weak state, but those whom he expects and wishes to see, would kill him."

With ready tact, Adelina set about endeavouring to restore the old man to consciousness, and in about a quarter of an hour they had the satisfaction of seeing him open his eyes, and look about him.

"Where am I?" he said.

"Here, in your own house, grandfather," replied Adelina; "and surrounded by those you love."

"At St. Germains?"

"No, no!"

"In Rome?"

"Oh, no, grandfather—in London! Look about you."

The old man feebly raised himself on his elbow, and glared about him with a strange, startled look.

Then his eyes fell upon Adelina, and he said, more gently—

"Ah, my Adelina, are you returned?"

"Yes, grandfather—yes."

"And did you see him?"

"Yes."

"Heaven be praised!" ejaculated the old man. "And my Mary—what of her?"

"She is happy with the husband of her choice."

"Foolish girl—foolish girl!" sighed the old man, "to wed with one beneath her, when she might have aspired to the hand of a prince!"

"But, grandfather," urged Catherine, "surely our experience of princes is not such as to induce us to wish that our sister had chosen otherwise."

"Tush, girl! you know not what you are prating about,"

"But Miravel is good and great."

"But he is not of the blood-royal; and Mary should not have allowed herself to be led away—dazzled by his intellect."

"But surely such an adherent, grandfather, to our cause——"

"Silence, girl! Was he not an adherent before this marriage with your sister took place? But tell me, what said he of our plans?"

"He said to-morrow would be the time."

"To-morrow—to-morrow!" whispered the old man. "Well, I am glad—I am delighted! My children, if there be any one who, in all the world, can give you back your crown, it is he! Ah! what's that?"

"It is nothing, grandfather, but the wind," said Adelina. "Try and compose yourself to rest now, for heaven only knows what you may have to go through to-morrow."

"You are ever wise, Adelina," said the old man, as he fondly stroked the sunny ringlets of his favourite grandchild; "you are ever right! I will try and get some repose. Leave me now, dear ones, and seek each one your chamber, and, like me, prepare for the morrow."

CHAPTER CXCV.

CLAUDE DUVAL DETERMINES TO WATCH OVER ADELINA, AND ENCOUNTERS AN OLD FRIEND.

WE must now return to the Prince of Wales and his two wicked associates, whom we left on the point of going to search for the house, the address of which was written on the tiny card now in the possession of Prince Frederick.

Duval, too, had a great desire to find out where that young girl lived, but from very different motives to those of the Prince.

Duval was determined to watch over her and protect her from further molestation, if needs must; while the Prince was determined to ruin that fair young creature body and soul, if such a thing were possible.

Duval therefore continued to follow in their wake, until they all three arrived at, and stopped before, No. 16, Adelphi Terrace.

There the Prince and his companions stopped, and looked up at the house in wonder and amazement.

"Why, the house is empty," said the Prince, in a tone of vexation.

"'Pon honour, so it seems!"

"A sell, your Royal Highness—nothing but a sell, by Jove!"

"Confusion!" said the Prince. "But I'll knock, at any rate."

At this moment the Duke of Montrose came close up to the Prince, and whispered something in his ear, which Duval rightly divined was a suggestion to go no further into the affair just then.

"Perhaps you are right—perhaps you are right," said the Prince aloud. "We will come again to-morrow night, much earlier—much earlier."

"Oh! that is your determination, is it?" said Duval to himself. "I too will return, and warn her, you would fain get into your power, of her danger."

The Prince of Wales now left the spot, accompanied by the Colonel and the Duke of Montrose.

Duval, however, did not leave the neighbourhood so quickly.

He was wondering in his own mind what he had better do, for he felt convinced from all he knew of the dissolute young Prince and his vile associates, that mischief was intended.

Then he asked himself who that beautiful young creature could be, and what she could be doing in the Park at so late an hour alone.

He could not bring himself to believe that she was other than what she appeared to be, for had he not heard sufficient to convince him that she was too pure and innocent to understand even half that the Prince would have implied by his pretended confession of love.

"At all events," said Duval to himself, "I will take counsel of Lucy; I have often found her judgment worth all my reflection put together, especially where one of her own sex is concerned. I will to Hampstead at once."

Lucy was as much at a loss, however, as Duval could be in coming to any conclusion as to the conduct of the young girl.

"At all events, Claude, you can but go to the Park to-night," said Lucy; "and if you happen to get an opportunity, speak to her yourself, and tell her that—that——"

Lucy paused, for she shrunk, even as Duval would have done, to open the eyes of a young and innocent girl to the intentions of the dissipated Prince of Wales.

"I understand you, Lucy. I will manage to point out to her the impropriety of coming unattended to the Park at such a late hour; and I will, at the same time, tell her who the Prince is."

"Do so, Claude—do so!"

At eleven o'clock on the night following the events we have just detailed, Claude Duval sat and watched upon one of the benches in the Park for the approach of the young girl he so much wished to befriend.

He had not long to wait, however, before he saw her making her way towards a tall figure, wrapped in a cloak.

Duval felt conscious that he had seen that figure somewhere before; and yet at the moment he could not recall it to mind.

He felt quite convinced that it was neither the Prince of Wales nor his companions; and he, therefore resolved to watch the conduct of the young girl, and be guided by circumstances, as to whether or not he would show himself.

On, on came the young girl, and now the cloaked figure advanced to meet her.

As they neared each other, Duval could see that the young girl held out both her hands to the figure, as though it were a relief to her to find him on the spot.

Duval was at too great a distance to hear the conversation which ensued, but at its conclusion he could see that the man bent his head, and imprinted a kiss upon the hand of the young girl.

"More mysterious than ever," said Duval to himself.

"He is not a lover: what, then, can he come here to meet that young creature for night after night?"

Duval's curiosity was now fairly roused, and he resolved, at all events, to address the man before he left the Park.

The young girl now walked swiftly towards the narrow passage which led to Spring Gardens, doubtless anxious to get home before the Prince should make his appearance.

As soon as the figure had watched the young girl quite out of sight he turned to leave the Park, and in doing so found himself face to face with Claude Duval.

"Sir!" ejaculated the man in the cloak.

Duval stepped backward a pace or two, and then he exclaimed—

"Do I see aright—St. Ives?"

"Duval!"

The two friends grasped each other by the hand, and looked inquiringly at each other.

Then Duval said—

"Who is that young girl?"

"The young girl who has just left me?" asked St. Ives.

"Yes."

"A jacobite—a descendent of——"

"Stay—I do not wish to hear more now. I am satisfied. I intended to have watched over her, but I leave her in as good hands as mine."

"Nay, stay, and hear me, Duval. Give us your assistance, for we want a few good men and true to accomplish our object."

"Oh, St. Ives, is it possible that you are still willing to peril life, and the lives of those dear to you, in carrying out projects which can only end in your destruction."

"Hear, before you condemn, Duval. We are anxious to get possession of a casket of rare jewels concealed in St. James's palace."

"For what purpose?"

"To raise funds by which we hope to bribe the King of France to aid us in setting on the throne of these realms its rightful monarch."

"I will think—I will think, and let you know," said Duval, "whether I will join you or not in your adventurous enterprise."

"Then you will consent, I know. No harm is intended either to the man they call King, or to that dessolute young Prince. Farewell—meet me here tomorrow night at this hour, and tell me your determination."

"I will, I will!" replied Duval, and the two friends parted.

We must now return to the "house to let" in the Adelphi Terrace.

It is night.

Eleven o'clock has sounded from all the church steeples in the neighbourhood.

The Prince of Wales has had a lovely evening.

He has watched in vain for the approach of the young girl to whom he was so enamoured, and he now resolves to go and satisfy himself whether or not she lives in that house which looks so dark and deserted.

At length Prince Frederick found himself standing on the ample step, and held the knocker of the door in his hand, irresolute, at first, whether to make his presence known or not.

All was dark, and in addition to the shutters being closed, there were heavy curtains of cloth, or of velvet drawn over each window, so that the possibility of a ray of light from the interior of the mansion being seen was out of the question.

The Prince could hear that the sound of the knocker, when he did make up his mind to use it, produced a hollow, reverberating sound, as if the house were just what it purported to be—namely, empty.

He began to entertain now serious doubts as to whether it were possible that such a piece of loveliness as the young girl whom he had seen in the Park could reside in such a place.

But he had the card, and there was the number of the house, and the name of the terrace quite distinct and clear, so there could be no possible mistake about it.

"I am quite right," said Prince Frederick, as he knocked a second time; "and I am very glad to have got rid of the Duke and the Colonel, for they would only have been in my way. I will carry out this adventure single handed, let the consequences be what they may, for on my life I never did see such a piece of loveliness as that young girl."

The Prince knocked a third time.

"Well," he said to himself, "this is the third knock, and perhaps there is a kind of magic in that number, and I may get some answer"

"You will," said a voice.

The voice followed so quickly upon his own half uttered words, and seemed to him to be so close at hand, although the door had not moved, that the Prince gave a start, and uttered an exclamation of surprise at the moment.

"Be not alarmed," added the voice. "Speak freely —what want you here, noble sir?"

"What want I here? Oh, I—that is, who are you?"

"Your good genius," said the voice.

"My good genius? Well, I am much obliged to you, but I should be more so, I fancy, if you would be so good as to make yourself visible to me."

"I cannot."

"Does that mean inability or unwillingness."

"Never mind which. Suffice it to say, that it is conclusive. You seek one in this house whom you should not seek—the innocent should remain innocent."

"I do not know what you mean by that," replied Prince Frederick. "If you know my errand here, and in good truth you speak as though you did, and if you are as you say my good genius, you will aid me in carrying it out."

"But, what if there be danger?"

"A little I don't mind."

"But, if there be much?"

The Prince was silent.

"You are right to pause," said the voice again; "but make up your mind quickly."

There was a silence, and then the voice added,—

"Will you enter the house in search of her you so much admire, or, will you go from its portal and forget that you have ever seen her. The latter is the safer plan, but the former is more in accordance with your own wishes."

"She is so beautiful!" sighed the Prince.

"She is. Decide!"

"I will seek her—open the door."

As he spoke, Prince Frederick laid his hand upon the door, and it gently gave way before his touch, and went creaking open apparently to its full width, showing him the passage beyond, looking intensely dark, like the mouth of some hideous cavern going far into the very bowels of the earth.

A braver man, and one more accustomed to perilous and turbulent life, venturing escapades by flood and field, might well have paused before entering that passage; and had it not been for the master passion of the human mind—Love—had become the uppermost feeling in the breast of the Prince at that time, he too would, no doubt, have shrunk from the darkness and the mystery of that abode.

For about half a minute he tried to pierce with his eyes the obscurity of the place, and then he crossed the threshold.

"Lovely girl! beautiful being! in search of you I will run every risk. For your sake I will exchange life and liberty. Oh! if my reward be but to hold you to my heart, all will be well. I promise you the gratitude—the love—the devotion of——"

Bang! went the street-door.

The Prince found himself alone in that dark and dreary passage. With his arms extended, he turned slowly round, but nothing met his touch. The darkness was like that of the grave, and the most intense and profound stillness, too, reigned in the house.

"What strange place is this?" he said in a hoarse and anxious whisper. "I hear no one—I see no one. Where am I? Speak, you who spoke to me before—speak now again!"

"Advance!" said the voice.

"Ah, welcome! I am glad to hear your voice again. Did you say advance?"

"I did."

"But which way? To the right, or to the left, or straightforward?"

"This way."

At that moment, a very small, starlike light appeared to the right hand of Prince Frederick in the air, about, as far as he could guess, some fifteen feet from the floor of the hall, or, rather, passage.

"Yes, yes—I see!" he cried. "I am advancing."

"Come, then!"

"I come!"

With his hands stretched out before him, he slowly, step by step, went onward in the direction of the star; and then he touched, as he thought the wall, but it must have been a door, for it gave way beneath the very slight pressure he subjected it to, and in another moment, he felt that he was treading upon some very thick and soft carpet.

"Where am I now?" he asked.

"Where you wish to be," said a sweet, low voice.

"Ah!" he cried; "that is the voice of—of Adelina! Dear girl, are you not indeed, and in truth, her?"

"I am."

"Speak again—oh, speak again! and at greater length, that I may know which way to run, in order to reach the spot where you are?"

With a sudden noise the door of the room closed; and then a strange, high-cracked voice cried out,—

"Yes, master, in a moment."

"What is it? What is the meaning of all this?" said the Prince. "What is to be in a moment. Ah! the place grows lighter and lighter still. Tables, chairs, cushions, mirrors,—yes, I see now. Who, on earth, sir, are you?"

A gradual, soft light had, from some unknown source, crept over the room, and disclosed its furniture to the Prince, and along with that furniture a man in a long cloak edged with crimson, who was bending over a charcoal fire that was on the hearth, and stirring, or seeming to stir, something that was in a small ladle.

Close to this man was a table, covered with what strongly resembled a funeral pall, and upon it was a number of strange-looking astrological implements and apparatus.

Upon the man's face was a mask of green glass which, of course, effectually concealed his features from Prince Frederick, and made him look ghastly and unearthly.

As all this became apparent to the Prince, his surprise, as the reader may suppose, was very great, and he retreated as far as he could, until the door stopped him, and then, with his back against it, he glared at the strange man before him.

"Humph!" said the man with the mask, as he cast something into the ladle that sent up for an instant, a bright green flame. "It don't work well! There is some sort of distracting influence! What says the circle now, I wonder."

All this was uttered as though the speaker had been entirely unconscious of the Prince's presence.

"Sir," said the Prince of Wales, "who and what are you?"

"Silence for a moment!" said the astrologer. "I will attend to your Royal Highness in a minute or two."

"Ah! you know me?"

"Silence, I say!"

The Prince sunk into a chair which happened to be standing near him, and with his eyes fixed upon the astrologer, for such he took him to be, he regarded him in silence.

"Yes," said the mysterious man, "that makes the conjunction surely."

He cast something into the ladle which he had wrapped up in a piece of tinfoil, and, after hissing for a moment or two, it sent up such a shower of beautiful green sparks, that they were dazzling to look upon.

Then, taking the ladle from the fire, the astrologer crossed his arms upon his breast, and turning the strangely-hideous face upon the Prince of Wales, he said—

"What want you with the child?"

"The—the child?"

"Yes; the fair child whom you met and spoke to in the Park, and whose place of residence you have by accident discovered?"

"Oh, the—a—the—a—young lady, you mean?"

"Well?"

"Why, a—I—that is——"

"You seek her ruin!"

"Sir!"

"I say, you seek her ruin—body and soul you would destroy! You would make her the plaything, the toy of an idle hour, and then cast her off to ruin and to shame!"

"Nay, hear me——"

"Oh, sir, shame—for shame! Is this a fitting position for a Prince?"

"But——"

"Shame—oh, shame upon the world!" continued the masked figure; "that calls the lapses of heaven's first laws venal errors! Shame upon the man who can so still his conscience that to ruin and destroy the best and the fairest of heaven's creatures shall give him no pang! Oh, shame—shame!"

The Prince—a glow of crimson stealing over his face—half rising, said, in a hesitating voice—

"Sir, I have the pleasure of bidding you good evening. Our interview is at an end."

"Stay—oh, stay! This child—for she is but a child—this beautiful girl, with all her loveliness and all her warmth of heart, has seen you, and she—she——"

"Go on. What would you say?"

"She loves!"

CHAPTER CXCVI.

THE PRINCE OF WALES BECOMES ACQUAINTED WITH SOME OF THE MYSTERIES OF THE "HOUSE TO LET."

A STRANGE thrill of delight shot through the heart and brain of the dissolute young Prince as he heard these words fall from the lips of the mysterious individual. He advanced towards the speaker, and, holding out his hands imploringly, said, with great emotion—

"Does—oh, does she love me?"

"Even you."

"Oh, joy—oh, joy! This is greater happiness than I ever dreamed of attaining! Does she indeed love me, or are you deceiving me?"

"She does—she does; and yet you will desert her."

"No, by heaven, I will not!"

"You will—you must."

"No!"

"Yes, I say. After a time, if she were to become yours, you would see other eyes you thought brighter, and perhaps they would be, not yet dimmed by the tears that would swim in hers, as she bethought her, with agony, of her shame, and then you would desert her."

"No. I swear to you that I will not do so! In what way can I make it manifest to you that I will not? You know who and what I am, and therefore you know that I cannot, in the open face of day, make her my wife, but that she shall be such in all honour. I mean that I cannot make her the Princess of Wales, but yet I can and will marry her."

"Oh, let me think—let me think!"

The astrologer clasped his hands over the strange, ghastly-looking green mask that he still wore, and for several minutes appeared to be in deep thought. Then, withdrawing his hands, he said—

"I am about to make some statements: if I am wrong, you will be able to correct me."

"I fear not."

"Yes; they are about you, and therefore you can have no difficulty."

"Then I will answer your questions to the best of my ability."

"You have a suite of rooms in St. James's Palace, commencing on the ground-floor of what is called the Queen's Court?"

"I have."

"This suite of rooms extends three storys in height, do they not?"

"Yes."

"And there are five rooms upon each floor?"

"Yes, yes"

"Those rooms, fifteen in all, are peculiarly you own, although you do not occupy them to any very great extent; and at all times and at all hours you have access to them, or you let any one else, by your orders, have such access to them?"

"That is true; but——"

"Well, then, if the child whom you say you love so well—but I see that the term child displeases you, so I will call her a young lady,—if, then, she should come to you at that suite of apartments, how would she get admittance to you?"

"Come to me—come to me! Oh, what joy! I will give an order for her to be admitted!"

"But will you marry her?"

"I will—I will!"

"But you do not know anything of her. You do not know who or what she is. Her very name you are ignorant of—that is to say, her family name."

"I know enough of her," replied the Prince of Wales, "to be quite certain that she is very beautiful! I know enough of her to feel assured that she is the fairest of human beings; and the sound of her voice assured me that she is gentleness itself! Do not say that I know nothing of her!"

"And will you marry her?" again asked the astrologer.

"I will—I will!"

"Nowhere else but to St. James's would she come to you."

"Be it so, then; I will write an order."

"They will say it is a forgery, if unaccompanied by some token that it is correct and true; besides, others may have orders, and may most inopportunely arrive at the same time."

"Yes, yes—that is true! I will stop all orders on the evening you tell me she will come to me. I will take such means as shall most completely and effectually stop the possibility of any other order coming in, so that when she comes all may be well."

"Ay, but there should be something more. Suppose you date from the third night from now, the order that you give to the young girl to visit you, and give command to those about you that on that evening no other order was to pass?"

"I will—I will."

"And do you mean to say that you will be provided with a clergyman on that night who will perform the ceremony of marriage between you and the fair young creature whose misfortune it is to love you?"

"Not misfortune, surely. But to answer your question, I will be so prepared in all respects."

"And will you swear to keep secret all that has passed in this house?"

The Prince was silent.

"If you do not," added the astrologer, "you will never see her again; and if, after swearing you break your oath, you will never see her more, for we shall know of it be assured."

If the Prince had not been so assured as he was that there was something like supernatural prescience on the part of the astrologer, his passion for the young girl was so great, that, doubtless, he would have sworn, as he now did, for he said:

"I swear by all that I hold most sacred, that I will divulge nothing, except so far as is necessary to get a priest to perform the marriage ceremony."

"That will suffice. And now you would like to see her whom you love, would you not?"

"Oh, yes—yes!"

"Write the order first. There is paper and writing materials."

"Oh! I had forgotten. There—there!"

"And, if you do not marry her you forfeit——"

"Forfeit what?"

"Should it not be a large forfeit, think you?"

"My life—my liberty!"

"No; you have a valuable watch about you. It was supposed to belong to James the Second, and to have been worn by him when he died at St. Germains."

"How know you this?"

"Never mind how I came by the knowledge, suffice it to say that what I assert is the fact. Before James the second died, he handed it to one whom he loved, and from whence it got to the possession of the present royal family of England."

"I have heard as much," said the Prince.

"Will you leave that watch here, with the order you have written, as a pledge of your sincerity, and the young lady will bring it to you, and give it to you when the affair is completed."

"Oh, yes! I can have no possible objection to such an arrangement," replied Prince Frederick.

As he spoke, the Prince took out of his pocket the magnificent old gold watch, studded with diamonds, and placed it on the table.

"It may occur to you," said the astrologer, "that the whole affair may end just in the loss of a watch of the value of some thousands of pounds, or so; but in order to disabuse you of any such idea, here is a diamond of the full value, which you are at liberty to keep until you get your watch returned to you."

The Prince was about to speak, but the man in the mask held up his hand to intimate that he wished to finish what he was about to say, and continued:

"The watch, as being a family one, will be of more

importance to the young lady as a proof of who you are to whom she is about to be married than a hundred diamonds."

"I do not want the diamond as a pledge of sincerity," replied the Prince. "I am quite satisfied without it. I have no such suspicion as you seem to think."

"Nevertheless, take it."

As he uttered these words, the astrologer dealt the table a slight blow with the flat part of his hand, and the Prince's watch, and the order for admittance to the Palace, that lay one upon the other upon it, both disappeared through it in an instant.

"Now you shall see her whom you love," said the astrologer, and holding up his hands, he cried out something in a language that the Prince of Wales did not understand, when gradually, even as it came, the strange white light that had pervaded the apartment, slowly disappeared, and all was impenetrable darkness again.

"Hold! hold!" cried Prince Frederick. "I can see nothing now. Keep your promise with me, and let me look in the sweet face of her whom I love so tenderly. I implore you to let me see her. No—no, she does not come! I cannot hear even her voice—I cannot see her—all is dark and dreary!"

"Patience!" said a voice.

"Yes, yes! who spoke?"

"Be still!"

The Prince stood in an attitude of expectation in the room.

He dared not move in the intense darkness that was about him.

He dared not speak for fear of losing the sound of something that might be said to him.

The moments seemed like hours as they lagged lazily by; but just as anxious and eager expectation had become almost too painful to last longer, a faint light appeared upon one of the walls of the room.

"Behold!" said a voice.

It seemed as though the wall sunk from before the vision of the Prince, leaving a kind of light in the form of an oval in its place, and some four feet in height.

The oval kind of halo settled itself after a few moments into a clearer outline, but still the centre of it was but dim and obscure; but that was fast clearing, and then Prince Frederick was certain that he saw something in the shape of a human form.

Suddenly, with an exclamation of joy, he saw the dim, vapoury condition of the interior of the oval of light become quite clear, and then, as if some life-like picture in a frame, he saw the young girl who had so enchanted him in the Park, and for whose love he was willing to do so much.

"Beautiful vision!" he cried, "come to me—oh, come to me!"

The girl smiled sweetly upon him, and then the roseate lips opened, and she said in a voice of gentle melancholy, "Be true, and I will come at the appointed time!"

Gradually the mist gathered over her, and the oval of light began to disappear.

"No—no!" cried the Prince; "do not leave me thus. Speak to me, I implore you! You do not know how truly and fondly I love you!"

"Come!" said a voice.

At that moment a hand grasped his arm and led him from the room, as he soon found; although at the moment, in the intense darkness that had come over all things, he could not tell where he was going, and conjectured that it might be to the presence of the girl.

A rush of cold air came suddenly upon his face.

Something like a heavy piece of drapery seemed to be suddenly drawn from before his eyes, and the Prince found himself in the Adelphi Terrace, with a drizzling rain pouring upon him, and a cold wind whistling from the river.

* * * * *

Let us shift the scene to another room in that deserted-looking house.

Crouched, rather than sitting, upon an ottoman of crimson velvet, her face buried in the cushions, and sobbing as though her heart would break, was that young and lovely girl whom we have introduced to the reader as Adelina.

The door of the room was opened gently, and the young man, whom we have heard addressed as the King of England, by the old grandfather, entered the room.

He was very pale, and as he laid his hand upon the sunny curls of the sobbing girl, it trembled violently.

"Hush, hush, Adelina! do not weep so! I thought you were braver, or I would not have subjected you to this ordeal."

"Oh! it is cruel—it is cruel!"

"What is cruel."

The young girl raised her head, and tossing back the luxuriant curls from her brow, she said—

"It is cruel—it is treacherous to make him think that—that I love him."

As she said these words, the young girl sunk again upon the cushion, and convulsive sobs burst out afresh from her overcharged heart.

"Have a care, Adelina," replied her brother; "or I shall begin to think you really do love this enemy to our house."

"Leave me, James—leave me to myself. I must think—I will be brave—I will remember that I am a descendant of the Stuarts; but leave me now—leave me now, I pray you!"

"But you know what you have to do?"

"Yes, oh, yes!"

"Yours is the mission to enable me and some of our trusty friends to enter the Palace, where we have been informed there lies hidden a casket of jewels of enormous value, sufficient for all our purposes; for with the money which the sale of these precious gems will produce, we shall be enabled to offer such a bribe to the King of France, that he will no longer withhold his support, and then—and then——"

The young man's eye kindled, and he looked almost superhuman, as he contemplated, no doubt, his bright future."

"And then?" said the girl.

"A life of regal splendour in exchange for this poverty and obscurity, and——"

"And what of me?" asked the girl.

"You? you, Adelina? Why, you will marry a Prince, and your beauty and gentleness will receive the homage they deserve."

"Never, never, James! Never shall I be able to enjoy life after playing so treacherous a part to one who—who——"

"Fancies he loves you."

"Go, James—go, I beseech you!" urged the girl. "You shall not find me wanting in my part. But now let me rest."

"Do so, dear Adelina, and believe that your brother loves you fondly."

"I know he does, or I could not do what I have promised to do," was the girl's reply.

CHAPTER CXCVII.

FREDERICK, PRINCE OF WALES, TAKES COUNSEL OF HIS TWO ASSOCIATES, THE DUKE OF MONTROSE AND COLONEL JESSOP.

IN a state of great bewilderment at what he had seen and heard at the "House to Let," on the Adelphi

Terrace, the Prince of Wales reached St. James's Palace, just as the clock over the old gateway struck ten.

The whole affair had taken so strong a hold of his imagination, that, as he entered the Palace, he began to entertain the most serious doubts as to the reality of the adventure.

The clank of the muskets of the guard as they saluted him, recalled him a little to his senses, and having reached his own apartments in the Palace, in that very turret portion of the old building that had been mentioned to him by the astrologer at the Adelphi Terrace, he cast himself upon a couch, and tried to reason with something like coolness regarding what had taken place.

The more Prince Frederick thought over the affair, the more thoroughly he was troubled to know what to do; for, upon cool reflection, he fancied that he had committed himself to such an extent that the difficulty, if not the impossibility, of disentangling himself from the adventure was immense.

But did he wish to disentangle himself?

Oh, no! The more he thought of the beauty of the young girl who had so enchained his faculties—the more he admired, loved, adored her, and the more ready he was to go through with the adventure at any cost, and at the prospect of any further peril.

"Let it come to the worst," he said. "There can but be a disturbance about it, and I am so used to those that I don't care much about them."

"The King will storm and the Court will laugh, and so there will be an end of it. What do I care?"

This was just true. What did he care so long as his own passions were gratified.

After a time, then, his Royal Highness fully succeeded in relieving his fears; and then a new difficulty presented itself to him; and he said—

"Am I, indeed, though, to marry this girl? Am I really to make her my wife? Is it not possible for me to carry out this little affair without quite committing myself so far as that comes to? To be sure! Surely it can be done; I have heard and know of such matters being very differently managed.

A slight tap at the door of the apartment at this moment attracted the Prince's attention, and he cried out—

"Come in!"

A servant in plain clothes appeared, and, in a soft, bland voice, said with a low bow, "The supper is served, your highness, and the gentlemen are there, if you please."

"Supper? Gentlemen?"

"Yes, your highness."

"Oh, I recollect I did ask the Duke of Montrose and Colonel Jessop to supper. Why, what is the time?"

"Half-past eleven, your royal highness."

"Very well, I am coming."

The servant again perpetrated a low bow, and then left the apartment; and the Prince, before he followed, paused at the door of it, and seemed lost in thought for a few moments, and then he said, "These fellows who sup with me to-night are just the ones, of all others, to be able to advise me what to do in this affair. It is true I have given my word, and, in fact, I suppose I have made a kind of oath of secrecy in the matter; but that is all nonsense, for how can I make any arrangement for the wedding without telling some one? So I will just let the Duke and Jessop know all about it."

With this resolve, the Prince repaired to an apartment on the ground floor of his portion of the Palace, and in which he occasionally met some of his dissolute companions before sallying out into the streets, and behaving as "gents" now-a-days would do, if it were not for the police.

The Duke and Colonel Jessop were both there, and the supper was instantly served.

During the repast, the Prince was unusually silent, so that his two rascally intimates could see that there was something on his mind.

It was not until the cloth had been removed that the Prince of Wales, putting on a look half of fright, half of importance, said, "I have something to tell you both!"

"Indeed!" said the Colonel. "What about?"

"What about?" cried the Duke. "How dull you are? Pray, what can it be about but the old subject, woman's bright eyes?"

"That's true!"

"It is true!" said the Prince; "but how you came to guess that, I don't know! However, as I say, it is true!"

"Of course!"

"Well," said Colonel Jessop, "all I can say is that I am here at all times and in all ways to aid your highness in anything you may command me!"

"And I, too!" said the Duke, "Pass the wine!"

The Prince of Wales took a bumper glass, and then he said, "You saw the girl who was in the Park, did you not? I mean the girl who dropped the card."

"Yes, yes!"

"Well, I—I have had a little adventure with her!"

"Oh, oh!"

"Now—now, really, gentlemen, hear me out! Do hear what I have to say, and then you will see that there are difficulties in the affair that you don't think of just at present, but which I have no doubt you will be able to help me to get rid of."

"No doubt at all!" said Colonel Jessop.

"None in life!"

The Prince then told them all that had happened, pretty much as it is known to the reader, only that he very much exaggerated the sense and supernatural power of the astrologer. At the conclusion, he said, "Now I have told you all, and I have to desire you that you will be perfectly secret upon this occasion, as I don't know what the consequences may be both to myself and to others."

The Colonel and the Duke listened with attention, for, to tell the truth, it was rather a strange story which the Prince had made them acquainted with.

There was a silence of some minutes after the Prince had done speaking, and then he spoke again.

"You don't know what to think of it. You are both puzzled now, are you not? But still it must be met in some sort of way."

"Of course it must!" said the Duke; "and as your Royal Highness has told us all about it——"

"Upon my life, I have!"

"I did not doubt that for a moment! I was going to add, it was quite a point of honour with both of us to get you nicely and comfortably through the affair!"

"I am really very much obliged! How can it be done, think you?"

"Why, of course, you must not think of really marrying her—that would be absurd; but if she is particular on that matter, what so easy as for myself or a friend here to perform the ceremony to her satisfaction, and your Royal Highness's also?"

"My dear Duke," said the Prince, "will you be so good as to play the part?"

"With all the pleasure in life. That is to say, for your Royal Highness I will."

"I don't know how to thank you—upon my life I don't, for I feel—oh, dear, I really do think I love the girl! She is so lovely, so—so——"

The Duke and Colonel Jessop could scarcely forbear laughing at the seeming sentiment of the Prince, but they did manage to control their mirth, and then they set about making their preparations for carrying out their plans.

It was agreed then, that upon the evening in question, when the young girl was to visit the Palace, the Duke should be ready, in full canonicals, for the purpose of uniting the Prince and her in the bonds of matrimony, and that Colonel Jessop should be ready in one of the rooms, ready to be called upon as a witness to the act, if such should be required.

The Prince, when all this was explained to him, drew a long breath and seemed much relieved—but, after a little time, he said, with some appearance of doubt, "I trust all will be well."

* * * *

Leaving the Prince of Wales and his companions to their own devices as regarded the passing of the time that hung, no doubt, rather heavily upon their hands, we once more enter that mysterious house in the Adelphi Terrace, where resided the strange family of which the young girl, who had so smitten the Prince, was one.

The reader will please to imagine himself again in that large apartment on the first floor, where the white haired man who had proclaimed himself a descendant of James the Second of England appeared to reside.

In that room, then, was the same old man, sitting upon a sofa, partially only it would seem, recovered from the state of collapse into which he had fallen.

In the room, likewise, was the young man of the mild and noble bearing, whom we have seen conversing with his sister immediately after the departure of Prince Frederick.

There were likewise present, the two girls, one of whom exercised such an influence over the heart of the Prince.

All eyes were bent upon the old man, who, with the Prince of Wales's watch in his hand, was muttering something to himself that they strove in vain to catch the purport of.

The young man at length stepped up to him, and said, "Grandfather, what are now your commands?"

"Your Majesty, for I abdicate in your favour, shall hear," said the old man.

"Do not call me by such a title!" said the young man. "Call me son, it will be more pleasing to me."

"No, no!—you are a king."

"Alas, I fear not."

"You fear not!" cried the old man, with fury in his looks and gestures. "You fear not, and why fear you?"

"Be calm," said the young girl.

"Calm, calm, oh, yes; I am calm."

"Dear grandfather," said the young man, "we know that all you have told us about our rights is true, but what of that watch which you were so anxious to obtain?"

"Alas, I know not."

"You know not, sir?"

"Listen; Sir John Allwood, whom I expect will soon be here, gave it as one of his instructions that the procuring of this watch from the Prince of Wales was a great object, and when he comes he will doubtless tell us what the object really is."

"Hark!" said one of the girls, "There is the bell."

They all listened, and the bell sounded thrice, so that they knew that it was a friendly hand that rung it.

"It is Sir John Allwood," said the girl, "I will open the door for him."

The girl reappeared in a few minutes, followed by a tall lank man, who wore large moustaches that met the coarse black whiskers he had in abundance.

At the entrance of this man there was a general salutation, and he, stretching out his hand, grasped that of the old man cordially.

"Good evening, old friend," he cried. "Have you succeeded in taking the first step towards reinstating the rightful king upon the throne of these realms?"

Then, in a lower tone, he continued, "What news? What cheer? What have you all done for the cause?"

"Here is the Prince's watch," said the young girl, as she pointed to it as it now lay on the table before the old man.

"Ah!" cried their visitor, "That is well."

"What Prince's watch?" cried the old man, springing to his feet. "What Prince do you mean, girl?"

"Hush, hush," said Sir John, soothingly, "She means Prince Frederick's."

"I do," said Adelina.

"Now," said Sir John Allwood, in a low soft tone of voice, "Permit me to draw your attention to the reasons why this watch became a matter of great moment."

Expectation sat upon every face, and the speaker continued—

"When his majesty King James the Second was, partly by force and partly by fraud, driven from England and his throne, he left behind him many very important papers. Among the important papers was one of very small dimensions, being described by him as not being larger than the palm of your hand, which, he says, was at the last moment given to him by one of the ladies in attendance upon the Queen, and which contained an account of where she (the Queen) had hidden jewels to the value of a million of money sterling.

"That small piece of paper had not been read by either the King or the Queen in the hurry of departure, but the King, in order to take special care of it, hid it."

"Where?" said the old man,—"oh, where? For if we can but obtain possession of such a sum of money, it will aid us much in the recovery of our rights."

"Not a doubt of it," said Sir John Attwood,—"not a doubt of it! But, listen. When his majesty James the Second died at St. Germains, amongst other matters, he stated that the jewels were hidden somewhere in the turret now in the occupancy of the Prince of Wales, as they call him here, and which adjoins the court called the Queen's Court at St. James's."

"But the paper of instructions, where is that?"

"You shall hear. The wardrobe lady was drowned in the process of escape from England, but the King in order to conceal the paper, and to have it safe, bethought him, about half an hour before his departure from St. James's, of hiding it in a secure place."

"Yes, yes; and that place?"

"Patience! He had a watch, the exterior case of which was so artfully contrived that it was seemingly of only one plate of beaten gold, whereas, in reality, it was of two, and they would part one from the other with ease to those who knew the secret of causing them to do so. Within these two plates of gold was kept a holy relic that the Pope had presented to him, and it was there that he placed the slip of paper given to him by the Queen's attendant."

"I see it all," cried the old man.

"Nearly all you do. Our spies in England soon ascertained that that watch, which before his departure was taken from the King, had passed from hand to hand of the usurping family, until it came into the possession of the man who calls himself the Prince of Wales."

"This, then, is that watch?" said the old man.

"I believe that it is. Now let me examine it."

The watch was handed to Sir John Attwood, and

THE DUEL IN THE PALACE.

the family of the Stuarts crowded round him with deep interest depicted on their countenances.

"Yes," he said. "Here, you see, are the royal arms, and I make no doubt in the world but that this is the watch of his majesty King James the Second."

"But has it the double case?"

"It ought to have it. I will, with what art I can bring to bear upon the matter, see to that part of the affair. I have tools with me for the purpose."

Sir John then took from his pocket some small tools of exquisite workmanship, and in the use of which he appeared to be quite a proficient.

In the course of two or three minutes snap went something by the side of the gold case of the watch, and then gently upon a concealed hinge the case divided.

A small piece of paper fell out, and a little splinter of dark coloured wood.

Sir John Attwood let the wood fall, but grasped the paper, which was faded and yellow-looking with age, but the wording upon it was perfect.

No. 59.—NIGHTSHADE.

"Listen!" he said.

They all listened with intense eagerness as he read.

"The casket containing the jewels is hidden behind the back of the grate in the oval room."

A smile of triumph came over the face of Sir John Attwood.

"The game is almost won," he said. "If all goes on as well as hitherto the jewels will be ours."

"Yes," cried the old man, lifting his hands above his head, and pointing to the youth who called him grandfather,—" yes, and there stands the King of England!"

CHAPTER CXCVIII.

CLAUDE DUVAL IS MADE ACQUAINTED WITH SOME OF THE JACOBITE PLOTS.

IT is eight o'clock in the evening—that evening when that fair young creature had promised to go to the

Prince of Wales, that St. Ives and Duval met to talk over the plans of the dethroned family.

As we have before seen, Duval had no desire to mix himself up with Jacobite plots and schemes. Not that he had any reason to admire either the King or his dissolute son, Prince Frederick, but simply because adventures of this kind were, so to speak, out of his line.

But St. Ives was anxious to secure his co-operation.

"But tell me," said Duval, after they had been conversing for some time,—"tell me if—if any crime—if, in fact, the life of the King or the Prince of Wales is to be attempted, for in that case I wash my hands of the whole affair."

"Indeed—at least, so far as I know—nothing is further from our thoughts than the crime of regicide."

"Are you sure? Do you remember the dastardly attempt made only a short time ago upon the King's life by the Duke of Montrose?"

"Ah, I had forgotten!"

St. Ives seemed lost in thought.

"Is he to be of the party?" asked Duval.

"No, no; he knows nothing of our plans this time!"

"And are you sure of those who do know them?"

"I think—I hope so!" said St. Ives. "There is only one man I distrust."

"And who is he?"

"Sir John Attwood. He is morose and vindictive."

"Then——" began Duval; but St. Ives stopped him.

"But then, Duval, may you not aid me in frustrating this man's schemes—if, indeed, he have any which he has kept to himself?"

"I may—I may be able," said Duval; but there was no cheerfulness in his tone. It was evident that he did not like the proposition of St. Ives; but hoping that he might, perhaps, be instrumental in saving the stain upon their reputation which must accrue to all of them if only one of their number went to such lengths as to jeopardize the life of any member of the royal family.

"I will be with you, St. Ives," he said, "by half-past eleven to-night"

"Thanks—thanks!" cried St. Ives. "Would that you could be persuaded to take some rank amongst us!"

"I care not for rank nor titles," said Duval, with a smile. "I prefer a gallop on the highway upon my trusty Nightshade, to all the luxuries of St. James's."

* * * * * *

By appointment, Prince Frederick met in his own apartments the Duke of Montrose and Colonel Jessop about one hour before that at which they expected the young girl to make her appearance at St. James's.

"Well, Frederick," said Colonel Jessop, who always affected much more familiarity with the Prince when there was something to do for him,—"well, Frederick, you're a lucky fellow, upon my life."

"Do you think so?"

"Do I think so? Oh, I am sure of it! Don't you think so, my lord?"

"Decidedly!" replied the Duke.

"Well, then, I suppose I am," said the Prince, smiling.

"You are," added the Colonel, "in more ways than one. But are all the domestics got rid of?"

"All."

"Good. And we three alone, then, occupy this suite of apartments?"

"Precisely so; and I have even led every one to believe that I am not in London at this time, so that if any inquiry should be made for me, it will end in that supposition."

"Good again; and the fair one is to come at the hour of midnight, I think you said?"

"Yes."

"Well, then, I act the part of parson, and the Duke here will act as my clerk, who is to be the sole witness of your Royal Highness's marriage."

The Prince was about to make some reply, but such a gust of wind, accompanied by such a dash of rain, at that moment came against the window, that they all three sprang to their feet.

"What a night!" said the Prince. "Surely she will not come."

"Oh, yes, she will!" replied the Colonel.

"To be sure she will," said the Duke; "for what will not love go through, eh? There is no doubt the girl loves you."

"Well," said the Prince, "there is something in that, certainly. But as it is now so near the time, I think it would be but civil for me to be by the door opening from the court to receive her when she does come."

"Do so; and we will go and prepare ourselves for the parts we have decided to play. By the by, which room will your Royal Highness take her to?"

"The next room to this."

"Well, perhaps it will be better to do so; but yet I should have thought the room that looks upon the garden the most private."

"No, no; lights can be seen through its windows—but that, to be sure, would not matter much. Hark!"

"It is the old clock."

St. James's clock chimed three-quarters past eleven, and the Prince left the room to stand at the gate to receive her whom he fancied he loved.

Imagine the Prince sheltering himself from the rain just a few paces under cover of the little doorway that opened from the Colour Court, and then let the reader accompany us into the Park.

From half-past eleven to twelve o'clock, four persons had entered the Park by the entrance at Spring Gardens, and four by the entrance at Bird-cage Walk.

The eight persons all slowly, and not appearing to have the least knowledge of each other, made their way towards the garden-wall of the Palace.

It was at ten minutes to twelve that a ninth person entered the Park by the Spring Gardens gate.

This person was attired in a long cloak of blue cloth, but the head-dress was evidently feminine, and the reply made to the challenge of the sentinel was in a female voice.

This person was Adelina.

There was so much grace about the walk of the young girl, and there was such a world of melody even in the two words "A friend," that she pronounced in answer to the soldier's challenge, that the sentinel looked after her with undissembled admiration before he resumed his solitary walk.

"A pretty young creature, that," he said, "I'll be bound! Ah, it strikes me she won't get further than the Palace!"

Adelina walked very rapidly after she had passed the sentinel, and would soon have reached the garden-gate of the Palace, whither she seemed inclined to take her way, but just at this moment a tall man emerged from rather a gloomy spot, and cried out—

"My love, where are you going?"

Adelina still pursued her way.

"Come, come!" said the stranger; "why so coy?" as he reached her side again. "Come, come! you cannot evade me, you know."

"Sir, I do not desire your company."

"Well, but I desire yours."

"Sir," said Adelina, in a calm, firm voice,—"sir, for your own sake—for your safety's sake—I beg you to leave me."

"Thanks, my pretty one."

"Sir, I—I——"

"I have made up my mind to bear you company, and therefore——"

Again the stranger made an attempt to catch Adelina in his arms, but she evaded him, and ran across the Mall towards the enclosure of the Park.

"Help!—oh, help!" she cried.

In a moment, from the shadow of some trees, there darted out a tall man, who intercepted the stranger.

With the a speed of thought he plunged a poignard up to the very hilt into his bosom, and, with great strength, he caught him in his arms, and carried him to the enclosure, and cast him over in a moment.

He who had stabbed the stranger as he passed Adelina merely said to her, "Go on and prosper, you will not be interrupted any more."

Adelina recognised the voice of Sir John Allwood, and shuddered.

Terrified at the interruption to her progress, and more terrified still at the summary way in which it had been set aside, Adelina ran in the direction of the garden-wall to the Palace.

By the time she got near to where the two sentinels were on duty, she was compelled to pause for breath, and as she leant against a tree, a man stepped up to her, and in a low voice said, "The jewel casket!"

"Yes, yes! you are a friend!"

"I am Number One!"

"Right! You are to take this pass, then, and when in the garden, you are to wrap up a stone in it, and cast it over the wall to me, are you not?"

"I am. Give me the pass, quick!"

Adelina handed to this man the written pass, which the Prince of Wales had left at the house in the Adelphi Terrace, and, in a moment, he disappeared in the gloom with it.

The young girl watched the gate, at which were two sentinels, and by the light of the lamp that was close to it, she soon saw a third figure was upon the spot.

This third figure she knew to be the man to whom she had given the pass.

She just paused long enough to see that, after a brief parley, the gate was opened, and the man admitted; and then she ran along the Mall, parallel with the garden-wall, and then she paused and listened.

Then she heard some one say, "Hist!"

"Yes," said Adelina.

Another moment, and something struck her shoulder, and then fell at her feet.

"It is the pass," said Adelina.

"Caution!" said a voice, somewhere behind her; but she could see no one; but she knew that it was intended to warn her not to speak so loud.

After a few moments of anxious search, she found the pass.

"Safe—safe!" she said; "I have now but to proceed."

Adelina now made her way to the two sentinels, who had just before admitted Number One, and presented the pass.

"All right!" said one of the men; "shall I show you the way to the Prince's apartments?"

"No, thank you!" replied Adelina, "I will go alone. Give me back the pass, if you please."

"You require its return?"

"Certainly."

The man handed it to her, with a bow; and Adelina hastily concealing it in the folds of her dress, crossed to the little doorway, where the Prince himself was waiting to welcome her.

"Charming girl!" he cried; "how can I sufficiently thank you for coming to-night!"

"Do not thank me."

"Yes but I will—I must—I ought—it is so good and so kind of you.

"No, no!"

"You may say no, no! but I think it is for all that, my dear girl—this way."

Adelina allowed the Prince to lead her up a small staircase to the corridor; and then she said in a low, sweet voice, "Prince, do you remember?"

"What, oh, what?"

"Your promise."

"To love you for ever and ever?"

"Yes; and to marry me'"

"Oh, yes—yes! Do you think I could by any possibility forget? I have a clergyman in my own apartments, dear girl."

"Indeed!"

"Why do you say 'indeed?'"

"I only thought that—that I did not think that you really would marry me. At least so soon. Is the clergyman alone?"

"Oh, yes! replied the Prince, with the exception of his clerk, and those two and myself compose all the inhabitants in this portion of the palace."

"And is this portion so well shut out from the others, that nothing can be well heard of what passes here?"

"Not a sound, believe me."

"Lead on, Prince, I will follow you. You doubtless have some room looking on to the garden. If you have, I—I——"

"What mean you, dear one—why do you tremble so?" Do I not love you?"

"I am a little faint, and would be glad to sit at some open window for a while.

"To be sure! This way—come this way. There, lean on me. The gayest and prettiest apartment I have looks on the garden."

Rather alarmed at the faint tone in which the young girl had spoken, the Prince led her at once to the apartment that looked on to the garden by a French window, which was not above six feet from the ground.

A dimly lighted chandelier hung from the ceiling.

The Prince led Adelina to the window, which he flung open.

"Are you better," he asked.

"Yes, I—I think I am. The air revives me."

"Oh! what joy to hear you speak again in your own sweet accents!" cried the Prince. "I do love you—indeed I do!"

"Silence! silence! you distress me!"

A sound came from the garden like the faint note of some forest bird.

"Bless me! what is that?" said the Prince; "shall we have more light?"

"Yes, yes!"

The Prince got upon a chair to light some more of the wax candles in the chandelier; and while he was so engaged, Adelina dropped from the window the written pass that she had retained, and a figure seized upon it, and then glided away.

CHAPTER CXCIX.

CLAUDE DUVAL CONSENTS ONCE MORE TO TAKE PART IN JACOBITE PLOTS.

"TIME—time!" gasped Adelina, as she clasped her hands over her face. "All I want now is time; and then I shall have performed the dreadful task of treachery which has been imposed upon me."

"Did you speak, dear girl?" said the Prince, as he stepped off the chair. "Did you speak?"

"No—no!"

"Oh! I thought you did."

Adelina gazed out into the darkness; and a feeling of relief crossed her mind as she saw another dark figure cross the line of her vision.

"Come, come!" said the Prince, "you are agitated."

"I am—indeed I am?"

"Well, I'm quite sure you need not be, for you know how entirely I love you."

"Do you really love me?" asked the young girl with emotion.

"Indeed, and in truth, I do! Let me hope that you feel better than you did."

"Oh, yes, I am fast recovering, and a little more time, Prince, and all will be well. Have you kept your promise not to tell any one of what passed at that house in the Adelphi?"

"I have, dear one; except, you know, I was obliged to say something to a clergyman; but I merely told him that a lady was coming here to-night between whom and myself he would have to perform the marriage ceremony."

Adelina now began to engage the Prince in conversation, in order to give her friends time to enter one by one into the precincts of the Palace.

But now let us go and be married, urged the Prince, and then we shall have all the time to ourselves, you see——"

"Yes—yes, in a minute—Ah!"

Adelina sprung to her feet just as a low, plaintive note, as if from some forest bird, sounded from the garden.

"What is it? What is that?" cried the Prince.

"Silence!" said a voice, at this moment, "or you are a dead man!"

"Dead? Murder!"

Before the Prince could say another word, a hand was upon the back of his neck, and then a couple of men sprung into the room, through the open window; and one placed a dagger against the throat of the Prince, saying,

"Be silent and discreet, and no harm shall happen to you."

"Have mercy upon me!" groaned the Prince.

"Silence!"

The point of the dagger just pricked the skin above the cravat of the Prince; he then sank back into a chair, and looked as if he were at his last gasp.

With her arms folded across her breast, and her head lent forward—somewhat so that her face was sunk in shadow, Adelina stood by the window.

She seemed to be ashamed, and full of regret, at the part she had played in this singular drama.

Four more men had by this time clambered into the room from the garden; and one of them was masked, but, placing his hand upon the arm of the young girl, he whispered to her,

"You have done well for the cause."

The tones of this voice could not, by any possibility, be mistaken.

They were those of Sir John Allwood, who seemed to be the leader of the Jacobite party.

Adelina looked up, and shuddered.

"I hope I have done well," she said.

"Make no doubt," replied Sir John Allwood, as he passed on, and stood opposite the Prince of Wales, with his arms folded across his chest.

The Prince gazed at him, but uttered not a word.

"Frederick!" said the leader.

The Prince was silent.

"Frederick! Do you hear me?"

"Yes—yes; I—oh, yes!"

"By order of King James the Third of these realms, I command you to obey me in all things!"

"Eh?"

"Silence!"

"Oh!"

"Speak a word—move a limb—cough—laugh—cry or do anything, or cause anything to be done, which can in any way give an alarm, and you are a dead man!"

"I won't——"

"Silence!"

"Yes—yes!"

"Bind him!" said the leader, after a pause; and then one of the five men who had made their way into the room, stepped up to the Prince, and, with considerable dexterity, bound him to the chair. He made not the slightest resistance.

"Hush!" said the leader; "his Majesty approaches."

In another moment, the tall, thin young man clambered in at the open window, and the whole of the little party took off their caps to him, and made low bows.

Adelina sprung towards him, and clung to his arm.

"Dear brother!" she said; "I am so happy to see you."

"Hush! hush!"

"Yes, brother, yes! Did I do well?"

"You did, dear Adelina—you did. Gentlemen, have you performed your mission?"

"No, sir," said Sir John Allwood; "but we now go about it, if your Majesty pleases."

"We do, and the sooner we are free of the atmosphere of this place, the better pleased we shall be; the very air seems filled with treason."

"It does, your Majesty; but the time may come when its walls will echo with the cry of 'Long live King James.'"

At this moment, the room door was opened, and the Duke of Montrose put his head in, saying,

"I thought I heard a noise. Goodness gracious! Who? What?"

Duval's hands were about his throat in an instant, as he said,

"Murderer! we meet at last!"

At the risk of the utter annihilation of the Duke of Montrose—around whose throat the fingers of Duval were placed, we will, for the due understanding of our story, relate some few little matters, which it is necessary that the reader should know in full.

Of course, the reader has had no difficulty in perceiving that the family, which occupied the house in the Adelphi Terrace were, without doubt, descendants of the fickle and weak James the Second of England.

Sir John Allwood, he who had constituted himself the leader of this night's drama, had really only his own advancement to wealth and honour in view, hence his desire to obtain possession of the casket of valuable jewels said to be concealed at the back of the fire-place in the oval chamber.

But the Stuart family believed that his object in securing these magnificent gems, was in order to raise funds by which they hoped to secure the co-operation of the French king in their favour.

How much they were mistaken in this supposition will be shown hereafter.

The manner in which Sir John Allwood proposed to get possession of the Prince of Wales' watch, in which it was believed the precious document was concealed, which would give the necessary directions for the finding of those jewels, was just this—

That Adelina should throw herself in the way of Prince Frederick, and try by all possible means to inveigle him into a marriage with her—which he, Sir John, justly enough considered, would very much complicate the question as between the Jacobites and the Hanoverian dynasty.

But should this scheme fail, he had another plot by which he hoped to obtain possession of the casket himself, and the utter destruction of every living being within the precincts of the Palace.

But we must not anticipate.

We have already stated that eight men entered the Palace, by availing themselve one after the other of the written pass which Adelina had thrown out of the window. Two of those men are well known to the reader—viz., Duval and St. Ives.

The other five men were totally unknown to Claude Duval, and but partially known to St. Ives, excepting, in so far, that he had every reason to believe them to be close adherents to the Stuart cause.

The young man, whom we have heard so frequently spoken of by the old man in the Adelphi as the future King of England, was, of course, regarded by St. Ives - or Colonel Miravel, as we ought to call him—as his future sovereign.

We now return to the chamber in the palace, where such a strange sight presented itself, and where so singular and terrified a group of persons was assembled.

The Duke was getting black in the face, from the grasp that Duval had of him, and he had ceased to struggle, his legs had ceased to support him, and it was tolerably clear, that for the time being, at least, he was not likely to be mischievous.

Duval flung him into a corner, and drew a long breath of relief.

Adelina at this moment now rose from her chair, on which she had sunk, and cried out—

"There must be no violence! There must be no murder! Remember that, all here present. It is a part of the thorough understanding that there should be no bloodshed!"

"Be calm, sister," said the young man, whom she called James.

"Nay, but I must know that that point remains unchanged; does it not so, brother?"

"Yes, said the young man, with me it does. In good truth, I would not owe even my crown to a midnight murder."

"Then all is safe," said Adelina.

Claude Duval now approached Prince Frederick, and motioned to the man who stood over him with a poignard pointed at his throat, to stand aside; and then, while the others looked on, Duval pointed to the prostrate body of the Duke in the corner, and said, in a stern, clear voice:

"Was that man to perform the marriage ceremony between you and this young lady?"

"It's all a dream," said the Prince.

"I ask you, is that the man who was to have performed the marriage ceremony?"

"Eh?"

It was quite clear, from the appearance of the face of the Prince, that suspense and terror had, for a time, deprived him of all power of reasoning, and the look of abject fear with which he regarded Duval was both ludicrous and painful.

"You will get nothing from him," said Sir John Allwood. "Question the fellow himself."

"There is no occasion to do that," said Duval, "for I happen to know him well; and I wonder that none of you gentlemen have not recognised the vile and treacherous Duke of Montrose."

"The Duke of Montrose?" burst from every lip in amazement.

"The same," said Duval.

"Oh, have mercy upon me at this moment," moaned the duke; "and I will tell you all. I adopted these robes for the purpose of conducting a false marriage between the Prince of Wales and a young lady, whose scruples it was thought, would only yield to such a course. But I am very sorry now, I assure you."

The young man turned slowly and looked at Adelina, as he said, in a low voice—

"You hear, sister. Did I not tell you that that man was not worthy of your compassion? Did I not tell you he was quite willing to make you a victim?"

A flush of shame and anger came over the face of Adelina as she thus found how the Prince had intended to sacrifice her to his evil passions, while he had pretended to love her so well; but she made no reply.

Then her brother stepped up to the Prince, and said, in a stern voice—

"Did you, sir, plan this?"

"Eh? I plan? Eh?"

"I say, sir, did you, in your wisdom or your wickedness, plan the destruction of the pure spirit who was so much better protected than you thought her to be."

The Prince did not reply.

"I take your silence for an affirmation to my question," said the young man; "and I can only say that you are too base for the treatment of a gentleman."

"Let him be," said Sir John Allwood. "That part of the enterprise is over. I never thought it would succeed."

"But, although this enterprise has failed, Sir John," replied the young man, "the other yet remains to do."

"True, true; bind them."

Sir John Allwood made a motion with his hand to indicate the Prince and the Duke.

His companions understood him at once, and placing the Prince's chair to the back of one into which they forced the Duke, they with stout cords bound them back to back, in such a manner that to stir was out of the question.

"Now, gentlemen," said Sir John, "I purpose still to ask a question of this person."

He indicated the Prince of Wales as he spoke, and the brother of Adelina bowed his head, in assent to the proceedings.

"Tell me," added Sir John Allwood to the Prince,—"and tell me truly, are we who are now in this room the only persons in this part of St. James's Palace."

"No," said the Prince.

"What other persons are there?"

"One only, a gentleman of my acquaintance, a colonel in the army. He is not far off."

"Not far off? Where is he?"

"In a room close to this, down the corridor," said the Duke.

A sallow tinge came over the face of Sir John as he heard this, and he glanced round him rather narrowly for a moment or two, before he said—

"This is worth seeing to. The person mentioned may have given an alarm. Follow me a couple of you. No, no; let me think."

There was something about the manner and bearing of Sir John Allwood that was anything but satisfactory to Duval, and he turned aside to St. Ives, and whispered in his ear.

"Be sure not to lose sight of that man; there is mischief and treachery in his every look."

"You are right," said St. Ives, in the same low tone, "I have watched him narrowly, and feel certain he is not what he appears to be."

Sir John during this whispered conversation between Duval and St. Ives had been standing with one hand clasped over his eyes, and then he said rapidly to the Prince:

One more question, and remember, that your life depends upon your answering it properly, and with truth. Is there a chamber in the Palace called the oval chamber?"

"The oval chamber?"

"Yes—answer me quickly."

"I really——"

"Yes, yes," interrupted the Duke of Montrose, "I dare say your highness don't know it, but it is the second room after you pass through the old tapestry chamber, and it is now used as a sleeping apartment, by the lord in waiting."

"Oh yes,—I have heard it called the oval chamber."

"Has it a fire-place in it?" asked Sir John.

"Yes, a very large old-fashioned one."

"Ah!" cried Sir John, "then it is the chamber we seek."

"Then I will proceed with number two to the oval chamber, gentlemen, and leave you here in attendance on his majesty."

As he spoke, Sir John Allwood bowed to Adelina's brother.

The man whom Sir John designated as number two, had a strange sinister scowl upon his face, and more than once he had caught the gaze of Sir John during the time they had been in the room, and each time that he had done so, he had significantly, with his thumb, pointed over his shoulder to what looked like a small round bundle of clothing, but that its weight refuted the idea of its being anything of that sort.

Whatever it was, though, he evidently took great care of it, and the pressure of the belt that supported the cloth in which the unknown object was wrapped was evidently rather great on his chest, for at intervals he had to shift its place.

As soon as Sir John, and the man with the mysterious bundle had left the room, Duval and St. Ives made towards the door, in order to follow on their track.

CHAPTER CC.

FREDERICK, PRINCE OF WALES, IS CHALLENGED TO SINGLE COMBAT.

LEAVING, therefore, Sir John Allwood, and the sinister-looking man, followed by Duval and St. Ives, to prosecute their search for the oval chamber, we will return to the room in which the Prince of Wales, the Duke of Montrose, and the rest of the Stuart party were assembled.

That Adelina all along had shrunk from the part she had to play in the transaction now so nearly brought to a close, there can be no doubt; and that she had felt that it was a degradation to her to play such a part, was tolerably apparent by all she said, and all she did. But she was certainly not quite prepared for the diabolical mode by which her moral destruction would have been accomplished.

The confession of the Duke that a mock marriage was intended, had filled her with horror, and as she sat half fainting in the room, she shuddered to think of the danger she had unwittingly ran, in the part she had been prevailed upon to play.

"You are faint, Adelina," whispered her brother.

"I am—I am," she replied.

"Then let me advise you to leave this room, and go out into the open air."

"No—no."

"Why not? You will be quite safe in the garden."

"I know that, James."

"Then why do you hesitate?"

Adelina was silent for a few moments, and then she looked up into her brother's face, and said gently, "Do you wish me to go?"

"Wish you?"

"Yes. Have you any reason for wishing me to go, apart from the fact that you think it will be good for my health that I should do so? oh, brother, tell me truly!"

The young man leaned his head aside but he did not speak.

"Ah! then," said Adelina, "there is some reason."

"There is."

"And will you not confide in me?"

"Yes, Adelina, so far, that it is a reason that concerns my honour, and, therefore, I hope that shall be sufficient for you to act upon."

Adelaina looked puzzled for a few moments, and then she appeared to make up her mind on the subject, for she said, in a low and distinct tone, "That is enough, James; to whom should your honour be so dear as to me. I will walk in the garden, and try to recover my spirits."

James now gave his sister into the charge of one of the party, whom he strictly enjoined to take special care of her in the garden, and by no means to wander far from the direct route to the gate opening near St. James's Park.

It was strange that Adelina did not suspect that something was about to occur in her absence from the room, that she would fain have put a stop to, but she did not suspect any such thing.

It will be remembered that Prince Frederick and the Duke of Montrose, sat in two chairs, the backs of which were close to each other, and that they were then tied together so that they could neither of them move.

When James had made sure that his sister had reached the garden, he stepped up to the Prince of Wales, and looking him sternly in the face, he said to him:

"Sir, I request you to answer me truly and distinctly, what I am about to ask of you."

The Prince looked at him rather vacantly.

"Do you understand me," said James, "I wish you to reply to me with clearness and with truth, if you have any pretensions to be a gentleman."

The Prince only looked still more puzzled, but the Duke, whose fears were more lively, nudged him with his elbows, saying:

"Answer him, your highness. It is much better to answer him what he shall ask. It is of very little consequence what information you give to him now."

The familiar voice of the Duke must have reached the ear of Prince Frederick, for he managed to reply to him.

"Yes, I will answer—of course. Oh, anything you like. I will answer directly and quite truly."

"Be it so," said James. "Now, sir, did you or did you not promise to wed the young girl who has just left the room."

"Eh? Promise to wed her?"

"Yes; answer me at once."

"Say, yes!" prompted the Duke, "say, yes!"

"Yes!"

"Well, was that marriage, with your connivance, to be a mock one or a real one."

"I could not marry her, it would not be legal," said the Prince.

"That is sufficient, sir, I am answered," replied James. "You intended to deceive my sister by having the union performed by a sham clergyman. I am content now to sink the fact that I am a king, and only to recollect that I am a man, and that my sister has been insulted by you, I therefore challenge you to single combat with me."

"Single combat?"

"Yes, here upon the spot."

"Oh, no—no," said the Duke, "that must not be."

"And why not, sir?"

"Because the precious life of his highness must not be so lightly ventured. I say it cannot be."

"Certainly not—oh, certainly not," said the Prince.

"It shall be," said James, "and I tell you how it shall be, I will fight you either with swords or with pistols, as shall seem to you most fitting. If you choose swords, I will release you, in order that you may meet me upon equal terms, and here, foot to foot you can decide our wrongs; if, however, you will not choose, I shall decide upon pistols."

"Indeed?"

"And in that case," added James, "I will have only one of a pair of pistols loaded, and they shall be placed under the green cloth upon yonder table, and you shall take your choice of them in the dark, or I will; so that one of us must fall."

"Oh, dear, no!" said the Prince. "A mad Jacobite, evidently, eh, my lord? You know I might chose the wrong one, and then he would have the right one, and I should decidedly get the worst of it. Oh, dear, no! I won't fight at all; so I don't want to hear any more of your abominable plans."

"Be quiet," said the Duke, as he gave the Prince a nudge with his elbow. "Will you, sir, listen to my plan."

"I will," said James.

"Hem! It is that the Prince meet you to-morrow morning on Plumstead Common, with me as a second, and that you should come there too with any particular friend you like to bring with you."

"Hold, sir!" cried James. "No more! I now have the advantage, and I mean to keep it. Do you suppose that I am not perfectly aware of the fact that I should, if I followed your suggestion meet, instead of this man, a party of the Guard? You shall fight!"

"Me?"

"Both of you. When I have despatched one I will begin with the other!" said James.

"Then you will oblige me, sir," said the Prince, "by beginning with the Duke of Montrose."

"No, no! I could not think of taking precedence of your royal highness. I won't—indeed, I won't!"

"I am sorry," said James, "to have got up this contest between you gentlemen, but it shall be decided by lots who shall fight first."

As James spoke, he stepped up to a side-table, upon which there were writing materials, and tearing two little slips from a sheet of paper he found there, he wrote upon one "Frederick," and on the other "Montrose." He then folded up the pieces of paper, and approached the Duke with them.

"Now, sir," he said, "your own name is upon one piece of paper, and your friend's upon the other. If you draw your own name you fight me first; if his, he fights me first."

"Oh, good gracious, I protest!" cried the Prince,— "I protest! Murder!"

"If he speaks again so loud as that," said James, to one of the party in the room, "you will be so good as to run him through the body at once with your rapier."

"Yes, sire."

"Come, sir," said James, to the Duke, "I will trouble you to draw the lots at once."

"Oh, dear! I—I——"

"Draw, sir!"

"But allow me to say——"

"Draw, sir, I say!" repeated James.

"It is murder!"

"As you please, but draw!"

"I won't! I tell you, I won't! and there's an end of it! I won't fight!"

"You won't, sir?"

"No, I won't!"

"Sebastian!" said James.

One of the men stepped forward.

"You hear this man?"

"Yes, sire."

"Finish him!"

Sebastian took from his pocket a small dagger, and after examining the point of it, he approached the Duke; but, before he got close up to him, Montrose cried out, "I will fight!—I will fight!"

"It is well. Choose!"

The young man again held the two pieces of paper before him, and, with evident reluctance, the Duke stretched forth his fingers to the papers.

He dallied with them for a few minutes, just taking hold of one and then of the other of them, and seemed quite incapable of deciding which to take.

"Quick!" said James.

He took one.

"You chose that?"

"Yes, I—that is—no—the other!"

"Take it then."

The Duke took the other, and then James, opening the one he retained in his own possession, and read upon it the name of "Frederick."

The Duke uttered a deep groan. After all he had drawn the one which had his own name inscribed on it, and he felt as though he were a dead man already.

"Which has he chosen?" asked Prince Frederick.

"His own name," said James. "He has to fight me first." Then, turning to one of his followers, he said, "Unbind the Duke of Montrose, and give him a sword."

"Oh! it's to be with swords, is it?" said the Duke.

"Yes, if that suits you."

"Oh, dear, yes!" said the Prince; "it will just suit him, he is a first-rate swordsman."

"Is he so?" said James.

"No, no," said the Duke; "I only know a little — a very little about it. Do you fence, sir?"

"A little."

A gleam of satisfaction passed over the face of the Duke. He was, as the Prince had said, a good swordsman.

"Now, see," said James, "are you quite ready?"

"Oh, quite, if it must come to this; but stop one moment, I have something to say."

"Say it quickly."

"If I am the victor, I suppose your friends, out of revenge, will fall upon me and kill me?"

"No," said James; "that would be unfair, and they will not. Listen to me, now, all here. It is my order, that if the Duke of Montrose should be the conqueror in this duel, he be allowed to leave this room in freedom. Now are you satisfied, sir?"

"I am."

"Then come on at once, for we run the risk of being interrupted."

The swords clashed against each other.

"You fence well," said James.

"And you," faltered the Duke, "I think you fence more than a little, sir."

"Oh, no!"

The Duke's face looked like the face of a fiend as he all at once put forth all his power and skill in one vigorous attack upon James; but for once in a way he had met with his match, for fencing had been the passion of James, and there was not a swordsman in the whole of Europe to compare with him.

With all the coolness and judgment of a master, he parried every impetuous thrust of the Duke, and as if a cold hand had been laid upon his heart, the conviction began to creep over the mind of the Duke that he was but as a child in the hands of such an opponent, and that his life was not worth a moment's purchase.

The sight of the Duke began to grow dim, and his knees shook under him. The sword of his opponent gleamed before his eyes for a moment, and then he felt it piercing into his breast, and with a cry, he fell weltering in blood to the floor.

"That's over," said James,—with all the coolness and *sang froid* in the world—"Now, sir, it is your turn."

"No, no!" cried a voice at the window, and Adelina rushed into the room. "Oh, heavens! what is this? What have you done, James?"

"Avenged mine honour!" said James; "and yours, sister."

"No, call it by the right name—you have had your revenge."

"Revenge, sister?"

"Yes, it is—it is! Oh, was it for this I was persuaded to leave the room? No, no; put up your sword—there must be no more of this. For my sake, there must be no more of this."

"It is for your sake I have done what I have done, Adelina—I must fight that man."

He pointed to the Prince of Wales as he spoke, but at that moment Prince Frederick tumbled on to the floor, chair and all, and it was evident that he had fainted.

"Behold!" said Adelina, "can you wreak your vengeance on such a coward as that?"

"Is he dead?"

"No, but he has fainted. James, I tell you he is not worthy to cross swords with one so brave as you."

"You are right, Adelina—he is not. Sebastian, see to the man who has fallen."

Adelina wrung her hands.

"Murder done already!" she said.

"No," said her brother; "he will recover. I am skilful enough to wound without killing. Be calm, sister—be calm."

CHAPTER CCL.

ST. IVES PERSUADES THE STUART FAMILY TO QUIT THE PRECINCTS OF ST. JAMES'S PALACE.

WE must now return to Sir John Allwood and that sinister looking man whom he had selected from among those who had entered St. James's Palace by means of the Prince Frederick's written pass.

It will be remembered, too, that Claude Duval and St. Ives—feeling anything but satisfied with Sir John's conduct generally—had followed him and his companion, but so noiselessly that they believed themselves to be alone.

Upon hearing that the lord in waiting slept in the oval chamber, Sir John felt that he was called upon to use the utmost caution in his proceedings, so he turned and whispered something to his companion, but in so low a tone that it was impossible either for Duval or for St. Ives to catch a word of what he said.

The reply, however, was given less guardedly, and Duval heard the man say, "I will obey you, Sir John —for such a reward I would even go to the brink of the abyss that leads to death."

The light was so dim that it was only now and then that either Duval or St. Ives could catch a glimpse of the faces of either of the speakers; but it was quite sufficient, however, to enable them to see that the man who accompanied Sir John Attwood was very anxious still to conceal something which he carried in the breast of his apparel.

"Now, come on," said Sir John.

Leading the way, with such a noiseless step as one might almost attribute to an apparition Sir John at length reached the door of the room in which the Colonel had waited so long the return of the Duke of Montrose.

At that door, the leader of the Jacobite party came to a pause.

Above the door there was a little gilt bracket, and upon it a small lamp that seemed to be of silver. It shed a faint and a rather sickly light about the spot.

That faint and sickly light fell upon the countenance of Sir John Allwood, and showed that he was much paler than usual, and that around his eyes were strange livid-looking circles that betrayed the intense conflict of the soul that that bold, bad man was engaged in.

The fact was that this man, who had on this occasion constituted himself the leader of the Jacobite party, had motives and intentions in his appearance in old St. James's Palace that those who aided in getting him there, and who thought that the discovery of the hidden treasure of James the Second was the grand object, little dreamt of.

Holding up one hand as a signal to his companion to stop, Sir John placed his ear close to the panel of the door of the room, and listened intently.

For a few moments no sound came upon his ears, and then, just as the leader, with a puzzled expression, was about to move his ear from such close proximity to the panel, there came an odd sort of laugh from some one in the room.

That one could be none other than the Colonel.

Sir John slightly started.

"Hush!" he said, as the man was about to speak— "hush!"

All was still again for a few seconds, and then the odd laugh broke out again.

Duval and St. Ives instantly recognised in it the tones of merriment of a tipsy man.

The fact was Colonel Jessop, never a temperate man at the best of times, had commenced wine-drinking to wile away the time till the Prince should come to him and the Duke; and when the Duke left him, it seemed that he had taken it into his head that he must do double duty with the decanter, and drink both for the Duke and himself.

The effect of this was that the Colonel, while affairs were taking so serious a turn in the room that looked on to the gardens of the Palace, drank himself into a very complete state of intoxication, and then he sat in an easy chair, with an insane sort of look upon his face, laughing at nothing.

He had forgotten the Duke of Montrose, and Prince Frederick, the occasion of his being there, and everything else in the maudlin condition of mind to which he had reduced himself.

Sir John was not slow in coming to a correct conclusion with regard to the state of the Colonel, who was in the room, at the door of which he and the man with the cadaverous-looking countenance paused, and after a few moments' thought, he pushed open the door and entered.

There was a cry of surprise from the Colonel, and then Duval heard the leader say, "Gag and bind that man!"

"It will be easier," replied the man, "to shut up his faculties with the remainder of the brandy in this decanter."

"Do so, then."

The man took the decanter of brandy in his right hand, and stalking up to the side of the astonished Colonel, he grasped his hair with his left hand, and drew his head back in a moment.

He then began deliberately to pour the brandy into his mouth.

The Colonel tried to shriek—he tried to rise—he fought with his hands and feet - his face deepened in

THE MURDER OF THE LORD IN WAITING.

colour—it then began to assume a purple tinge, and his hands fell powerless—a faint gurgling sound in his throat was all that could be heard, and then he fell heavily to the floor, as the man released his hold of the hair of his head.

"He will die!" said his superior.

"He may recover!" said the man.

"It does not matter," was the reply. "Come on now, and with caution. Have you the necessary implements?"

"Yes—yes!" replied the man, as he stooped and picked up the bundle from the floor, where he had left it while he operated upon the Colonel.

"Keep close to me," said his leader, "and be ready to act upon a word or a look."

"I will."

Sir John gave but one parting glance at the Colonel, as he lay strangely huddled up upon the floor of the room, and then he passed on.

At the extremity of the apartment, opposite to that which they entered, there was another door similar in size and appearance, and this Sir John opened without hesitation.

All was darkness beyond it, and he then paused for a moment.

"Franz!"

"Here!" was the cold reply.

"One of the lights!"

The man, who still carried the bundle so carefully, took from the table one of the wax lights, and brought it to Sir John.

On his route, he had either to step over the prostrate form of the Colonel, or on to it.

He preferred the latter alternative, and so trod upon him without the slightest appearance of compunction, or apparent care to know that it was a human form that was under his feet.

Sir John took the candle, and held it above his head.

"It is well," he said; "I know the place now. Carry this candle, and be ready to extinguish it if I give you the word to do so."

"I will."

No. 60.—NIGHTSHADE.

The narrow sort of passage in which they were was very richly carpeted, and the walls were hung with silken drapery.

St. Ives touched Duval on the arm.

"Duval!"

"Well!"

"Remain here—that is, do not lose sight of that villain—while I make my way back to the future King of England."

"For what purpose?"

"This is no place for him. As soon as that scoundrel has got possession of the hidden casket of jewels, he will decamp, and every one here will be blown to pieces."

"What mean you?"

"Hush! Do not speak so loud. Do you not see that bundle which that ruffianly-looking man is carrying so carefully?"

"Yes, yes!"

"Can you not guess, then, Duval, what are the intentions of that man, who has by some means won over the Stuart family to entrust him with the conduct of this business?"

"Gracious heavens! can it be possible?" said Duval, horror depicted in every feature.

"I am sure of it."

"Go—go, then, at once! but do not leave me long. I shall rush upon him single-handed, and tear his false and treacherous heart from his bosom."

With the same noiseless step, St. Ives returned to the apartment where James and his sister were looking on, as one of their followers was doing his best to recover Prince Frederick from the death-like swoon into which he had fallen.

Upon seeing St. Ives alone, James looked inquiringly at him.

Scarcely noticing any of the other persons assembled in that apartment, St. Ives at once made his way to James, and falling upon one knee, he said, with some emotion, "Fly—fly, my Prince—fly from this place ere it be too late! Tarry not! Death—certain death awaits you if you linger here!"

James drew himself up proudly, as he said, "What mean you, Colonel Miravel? We do not know what fear is!"

St. Ives struggled with his emotion, and then turning to Adelina, he said, "You—you, at least, were not deceived—you ever distrusted him who calls himself Sir John Allwood."

"Ah! what of him?" asked Adelina.

"He is a traitor, and even now he has in his possession means of destroying every one in this place, so soon as he has obtained possession of the hidden casket, and has placed sufficient distance between his own worthless life and danger. Now, my Prince—my King—will you follow the advice of one of your most devoted servants?"

"But you, Miravel?" said James.

"I shall still watch this villain, and, perhaps, be the means of bringing down a righteous retribution upon himself."

James turned to Adelina, and said, "What say you, sister?"

"Let us fly, dear brother; but—but there were seven of you—I see but six!"

"The seventh will keep guard with me, and watch over the safety of the descendants of King James."

"Be it as you will, Miravel. Our honour is safe in your keeping. I know," said James, as he grasped the hand of St. Ives.

The reader will remember that St. Ives left Duval to watch the movements of the man calling himself Sir John Allwood just as the latter, upon holding up the candle which had been given him by the man named Franz, discovered the door over which the royal arms were so richly carved.

As he did so, Sir John pointed to the door with the royal arms in bold sculptured relief upon the panel, and in his low, deep voice, he said, "Behold the oval chamber."

"Yes," he added to himself, "that is the goal of my hopes—my dreams!"

Then, apparently fearing that his follower may have overheard his words, he said, addressing him, "I say that we shall soon, I hope, and fully expect, have accomplished the mission which brought us here."

"I am ready," replied the other man.

"Worthy Franz, it rejoices my heart to think that you will unflinchingly perform your part."

"Is not my reward to be great?"

"It is—it is! Do you think that I would not enrich you beyond all your hopes for having gone hand-in-hand with me in this dangerous venture?"

"Ay, ay!" replied the man; "but time flies; let us on!"

"Yes, yes; let us on, and all will be well!"

Half a dozen of the long, noiseless strides of Sir John Allwood sufficed to bring him to the door of the oval chamber, within which apartment—so said the paper, at least, which was concealed so artfully within the case of Prince Frederick's watch—was to be found the treasure hidden by order of King James the Second.

There was a calm and exultant expression upon the countenance of the leader of the Jacobites, as he paused at the chamber door; and then, placing his finger upon his lips to indicate to his follower, and we may say accomplice, that silence was necessary, he took the candle from him, and carefully examined the lock of the door for about the space of a minute.

"Take it out of sight," he said, as he gave the candle back again to the man; "so that it may throw no light here."

The man Franz took away the candle to the further end of the passage, and further stopped its rays from reaching the door by interposing his body between them and it.

The object of the leader was to discover whether there was a light in the room or not.

Placing his eye to the keyhole, he managed to detect, although there was something on the other side of the door that very much obstructed his vision, some faint rays of light.

"Shall we seize him now?" asked St. Ives of Duval, "before he does any more mischief?"

"No, no; he can do no mischief now that we cannot easily prevent," replied Duval. "What I want is to let him have all the trouble of getting the hidden treasure, and then to deprive him of it."

"True, true."

The leader of the Jacobite party now turned towards his villanous associate, and said, in a low tone, "There is a light in the room."

"That's true," said the man, in a sullen voice. "What's to be done now?"

"Silence," said Sir John, in a hissing whisper—"silence, on your life! Think you I was not prepared for this emergency?"

There was such a look of concentrated rage in the glance that he cast upon the man, that it was truly awful to see him, and, ruffian as he seemed to be, he shrank back aghast.

"Fool!" added Sir John. "Did you think, for one moment, that it was necessary to suggest to me to recollect information I had received, and not one word of which has escaped me?"

"I know that some one sleeps in this chamber; and I know, too——But never mind."

"Pardon," said the man; "I meant not to offend."

Again, without heeding the imploring tones in which the man had uttered these few words, the arch villain placed his hand cautiously on the lock of the door.

The lock seemed to be perfectly right, and to decline moving in any direction.

After a trial of a few moments' duration, and finding that the door would not move, Sir John turned, and said in a low tone to the man, "Give me the light."

The man fetched the wax light from a bracket upon which he had placed it a few minutes previous, and presented it to his master—for such, indeed, seemed to be the relative positions of these two men—viz., that of master and servant.

Sir John seized the candle, and immediately placed it close to the lock of the door, with the hope of finding out apparently what had hindered it from opening.

Still he saw—at least, so Duval and St. Ives conjectured—no reason why the handle should not turn, although another trial proved that it was perfectly rigid.

Sir John Allwood looked puzzled.

Casting his eyes in the direction of his man, who stood a few paces off with the bundle still slung round his shoulder, he spoke to him in a whisper, but not in so low a tone as to prevent Duval from overhearing his words.

"You are skilful, Franz. What think you of this task?"

The man stepped forward, but before he could say a word in reply to his master's question, a sharp, clear voice from the room within the doorway called out, "Who is there?"

CHAPTER CCII.

CLAUDE DUVAL AND ST. IVES WITNESS A HORRIBLE MURDER WITHOUT BEING ABLE TO PREVENT IT.

THE start that Sir John gave was very great, and both he and his man recoiled a step or two from the door.

"Who is there?" cried the voice again, from within the oval chamber.

The man, who at this moment took the candle from the hand of his master, shook perceptibly.

Sir John's face had a slight accession of colour upon it, and his brows were knit.

He held up his hand to enjoin total silence on the man's part.

A creaking noise now came from within the chamber, and Sir John guessed right.

The lord-in-waiting, who slept in that chamber, had sprung out of bed.

"Hilloa!" said the voice again. "Did any one knock just now?"

The wax candle shook more than ever in the hands of the man now, but the face of Sir John resumed its ordinary sallow complexion.

His eyes, though, seemed to be preternaturally bright, as he said in a whisper such as, but for the intense stillness round, could not have possibly been heard by the man.

As it was, however, the purport, more than the words themselves, were understood by him, as we shall see.

Duval and St. Ives, however, were totally in the dark as to what the directions were Sir John appeared to be issuing to his man.

Those words were as follows:

"Franz!"

Two noiseless steps brought the man to his master's side.

"Here I am," replied the man, in as low a whisper as his master had used in summoning him.

"It is time," said Sir John.

"To strike?"

"Ay."

From under the short cloak that he wore, Duval and St. Ives could see the man, at this moment, produce a hammer.

The head of it was not very large, but the handle was a good two feet in length, and a glance at it showed that it was made with amazing strength—for, connected with the steel head, there were two long pieces of the same metal that went down the whole length of the handle.

A strange sort of shudder passed through Duval's frame as he saw this formidable weapon, and, seizing St. Ives by the arm, he whispered, "What are they going to do with that hammer?" asked Duval, in a whisper.

"Hush! Break open the door."

A long breath of relief came from Duval.

Again they watched those two men, who believed themselves to be entirely alone in that dimly-lighted corridor.

Sir John Allwood's eyes sparkled with more than their wonted animation after the brief conversation he had with his man.

At this moment there was another movement in the room, as though the occupant of it had stumbled over some chair or piece of furniture within it; and the impression upon Sir John and his follower was that whoever slept in that apartment was hastily dressing himself, and therefore probably taking longer time in the process in consequence of that haste than as if he had proceeded more deliberately, and without any alarm at all.

Sir John took hold of his man by the collar, and whispered eagerly in his ear.

"You comprehend me?"

The man nodded.

The man then took up his station by the side of the door, and freeing his arm from all entanglement of the cloak that he wore, he held the hammer in both hands, and raised it above his head, and there kept it, as Duval and St. Ives thought in readiness to give a blow to the door as soon as his master should give the order.

Then Sir John stepped up to the door of the oval chamber, and rapped gently at it with his knuckles.

Upon the instant a voice from within answered him, crying out with precipitation, "Who is it?"

Sir John rapped upon the door the second time, but he uttered not a word in answer to the inquiry.

"Who are you? what do you want?" cried the voice from within the chamber.

Again he rapped at the door.

"Coming! I'm coming!" cried the voice; "but you might just as well answer me. What is amiss? Is it fire?"

The door was flung open, and a man half dressed stepped half a pace over the threshold.

"Now!" said Sir John.

Duval and St. Ives, believed that by the word "now," Sir John meant the man who had just come out of the room was to be seized and made prisoner to prevent his being mischievous.

But that little word had a more terrible signification than either of them dreamt of.

Almost simultaneously with the word "now," which issued from the lips of Sir John Allwood the hammer descended.

There was a crash!

One smothered shriek!

The occupant of the oval chamber lay a corpse upon its threshold.

A cry of horror at this cold-blooded murder, burst from the lips of both Claude Duval and St. Ives, but so much occupied were the actors in this horrible crime, that fortunately it passed unnoticed by them.

St. Ives had some difficulty in restraining Duval from rushing forward and wreaking summary vengeance on the actors in this terrible scene.

But it was only for a few moments.

Too well he knew that the lord-in-waiting—for doubtless that was the rank of the murdered man—was past all human aid, and Duval remembered that the Prince of Wales had said that he and the Colonel were the only two persons who were in that portion of St. James's Palace on that particular night.

Therefore he felt assured that no other murder could be committed—at least if they were able to prevent that wholesale slaughter which the villain Allwood meditated.

For some seconds—nay, for some minutes, both Allwood and his man looked aghast upon the awful spectacle before them.

It seemed as if the dead body upon the threshold of the oval chamber was doomed to constitute a barrier, over or past which neither Sir John nor his man would have the power to go.

It is more than probable that if Sir John himself—that arch fiend who was the very head and substance of the whole plot—had not been of a sterner temperament than his companion in iniquity, the enterprise might then and there have been abandoned.

But he was not of a mould to shrink from any transaction he had chosen to carry out, because bloodshed happened to stand between him and his object.

With a gesture towards the oval chamber, he stepped over the body, saying, "Follow me."

The man hesitated still, for a moment.

The dark, bloodshot eyes of his leader, flashed fire.

"Do you hesitate?" he asked. "Have you forgotten the reward?"

These words seemed to have the desired effect upon his man, for he moved at once after him into the oval chamber.

When they had both got into the oval chamber. Duval and St. Ives left the station they had occupied behind a piece of statuary, and stood just inside the door of the apartment into which the murderers had entered.

They could see that a night lamp burned on the chimney piece—but now that Sir John no longer dreaded interruption, he ordered his man to light a couple of wax candles that were upon the table.

Those candles in a moment or two burned clear, and shed a bright cheerful light through what, till then, had appeared to be a gloomy apartment.

With the eagerness of a falcon swooping upon its prey, Sir John now turned to the fire-place in the apartment, behind which he hoped, according to the information given on the piece of paper he had taken such pains to procure, he should find the treasure hidden by King James.

"Franz!" he called, and his voice, as it shook, betrayed the eagerness of his soul to grapple the bright jewels which he hoped would soon be in his possession.

"I am here!" said his rascally associate.

"Behold!" he said, pointing to the grate,—"behold, at last the spot where there is every reason in life to believe King James of England hid the magnificent gems he spoke of! Franz, you are a skilful and handy workman—be yours the task to wrench the grate from its fastenings, and you will be rewarded by half the profits arising from the sale of those costly jewels."

The ill-looking rascal plumped down upon his knees before the grate, and with one of the candles in his right hand, and with his left held up so as to shield his eyes from its rays, Claude Duval and St. Ives could see, from where they had stationed themselves, that he proceeded to examine, by what simple or complex means he could contrive to get the grate away from its fastenings.

Sir John raised his hands with exultation, and cried, in tones of frantic enthusiasm, "Oh, Franz, Franz! you will have reason to bless me for this night's work, for henceforth, instead of toiling for your daily bread by the sweat of your brow, you will be able to keep servants, and carriages, and horses, and go where you please, and no one will ask you a single question as to how you came by your vast wealth!"

"Those will be jolly times," Sir John," grunted the man, who was still on his knees before the grate.

After a pause he continued, as if speaking to himself, "Only screws, after all!"

"What?"

"Only screws."

"Take them out—take them out as quickly as possible; my eyes long to look upon the gems."

The rascal now took from his pocket a strong, well-made screwdriver, and commenced taking out the long screw that alone appeared to hold the fire-grate in its place.

As screw after screw came away, he cast it on the floor, and when the twelfth was removed, he wiped the perspiration from his brow, and, looking up to his chief, he said, "It is loose."

"Joyful news—joyful news!" said Sir John. "Remove it now, and be quick, good Franz!"

The man laid hold of the grate by the bars, but with all his strength—and that was rather considerable—he could not move it from its place.

A groan came from Sir John.

"It is tight still," said Franz.

"But you removed all the screws?"

"Yes, yes!"

"The walls shall come down," said his master, "but I will see behind the grate."

"But—but——"

"I will listen to no remonstrance. I tell you I came here to carry off the jewels, and no earthly power shall prevent my doing so. Perhaps our united strength may enable us to move it. Let me get hold of one of the bars, Franz."

"No, no! Stop!"

"What for?"

"Oh, fool, fool that I have been!" now cried the man. "It is at the back of the grate that you expect to find the treasure, is it not?"

"Assuredly!"

"Then I see that the back lifts up in a groove, and can easily be removed. Behold!"

As he spoke, Franz laid hold of the back plate of the grate, and, without much difficulty, slid it up, disclosing an aperture behind it that looked as if it were full of some kind of black, gritty dirt.

From the very midst of that dirt there fell something forward into the grate about the size of a jewel-case—that is to say, about eight or nine inches in length, and about half that in width, while the depth of it seemed to be as nearly as possible its width, and the upper portion of it, or the lid, was semicircular.

By the sound that this box made upon the bars of the grate, it was evidently of metal.

Sir John, with a cry of joy, sprung towards it, and clutched it in his bony fingers.

"It is gained—it is gained! All the trouble has not been in vain! This is the great prize! There is probably within this little casket wealth enough to enrich me and fifty Franz's! The prize is won! Ha, ha! I am, indeed, rejoiced."

He clutched the casket to his heart, and then, snatching one of the lights from the table, he closely examined the exterior of the treasure-box.

"Silver, richly chased!" Duval heard him murmur to himself; "but blackened, of course, by time, and by the influences of the situation in which it was placed! Ha, ha! All is well—all is well!"

"Can't you open it?" growled Franz.

"No, no! it is locked, and there is no key! But it can be opened at leisure, good Fraz, when you and I are safe beyond these walls. There is is no time to lose. Ah! what is that?"

"A clock!" replied the man.

"Hush, hush!" cried Sir John.

One—two—three—sounded by the turret-clock of St. James's, and the leader strode towards the door of the oval chamber, exclaiming, as he did so—

"By heaven! I thought it was not so late by an hour! Quick—quick, good Franz! Let us leave this spot, and when next we come to it, let us hope that it will be in the train of the King of England! Ha, ha! What a farce you and I, have carried out to-night?"

"Don't laugh like that; and what have we to do with kings of England, or any other country? Did you not say that we were to divide this treasure, and seek our fortunes beneath brighter skies?"

"I did—I did! It was but the force of habit. Do you suppose that any earthly power should make me give up this costly treasure?"

As he spoke, Sir John Allwood clutched the precious casket in his hands, and left the room, quickly followed by his associate.

CHAPTER CCIII.

CLAUDE DUVAL AND ST. IVES VISIT ST. GERMAINS.—CONCLUSION.

SIR JOHN led the way back to the room, where the prostrate form of Colonel Jessop still lay on the floor, and it was quite evident from the constrained attitude in which he lay, that he had not moved since falling under the powerful dose of ardent spirits that had been administered to him.

"He sleeps soundly," said Sir John.

"So sound," said the man, "that he will never wake any more."

"Ah! say you so?"

"Even so. If you step this way, and take one look at the face, you will agree with me in that."

"I will take your word for it. I would that half a dozen other we know of, good Franz, lay as still as he does."

"Ay, ay!"

Out of the room they both now passed, and then Sir John paused a moment, and said to the man who had the mysterious bundle in his cloak and still carried the hammer—

"My friend, go back a moment, and I will wait for you here. Put everything in train, and be sure and put out all the lights but one."

It was only by a gasping sort of effort that the man replied—

"Yes—I will!"

As he spoke, his face looked perfectly livid from fright and agitation.

The man turned and retraced his steps, which were again arrested by Sir John saying again carelessly—

"Leave the hammer with me. Do not encumber yourself unnecessarily—you will be more at liberty to perform your part of the undertaking."

The man, without uttering a word, threw down the hammer at the feet of his master, and, with a hesitating step returned to the room to perform his appointed task.

Sir John watched his retreating steps, and then, with the quickness of thought, he raised the hammer from the floor, and rushed after him.

As he entered the apartment noiselessly, the man had no idea that any one was watching his movements, as he placed the heavy weight he had carried so long on his shoulder on the floor

Neither Duval nor St. Ives were at a loss now to know what that bundle had contained.

It was an iron shell, and was, no doubt, full of such awfully combustible compounds that when it exploded would bring St. James's Palace down in one common ruin, and destroy every one within its walls,

The man was now engaged in lighting a fusee, which, it was supposed, would burn about half an hour—time, in fact, for Sir John to make good his escape with his treasure.

Slowly he glided up to the man whom he had made his tool.

Unseen by him, he took his station almost close behind him.

And then, while a fiendish smile lighted up his face, he raised the hammer even as it had been raised once before that night when the lord-in-waiting had fallen a victim.

He was poising a moment in mid-air in order to make sure of his aim.

It had even begun its awful descent when a pair of strong arms dashed it aside, and Duval held the would-be murderer in a grasp of iron.

With a shriek of terror both Sir John and the workman sank to the floor.

"Fiend! traitor! murderer!" cried Duval, as he grappled with him, and struck his head several times upon the floor. "Quick, quick, St. Ives! Help me to bind this ruffian that he do not escape us."

St. Ives looked at the man he had been holding.

He had nothing to fear from him, for he lay at his feet in a swoon.

With the assistance of St. Ives, Duval succeeded in so pinioning the arms and legs of Sir John Allwood that there was no difficulty in making him quite secure to the bars of the very grate which he had been so anxious to have removed, in order to secure the costly casket of jewels.

The wretch seemed so panic-stricken, that all this was done without his giving utterance to a single word either of remonstrance or defiance.

Having secured him most effectually, Claude Duval now directed his attention to the man, who began to give some signs of returning consciousness, for he raised his head and glared about him.

Duval and St. Ives spoke not a word, but at once commenced pinioning him in the same manner as they had already done his master.

Having secured his arms and legs they tied him to a heavy, antique-looking piece of furniture, which happened to stand nearly opposite to the fireplace.

"That will do!" said Duval. "Let us leave these two villains to their own resources. It is fortunate for them that there are others in the Palace, or they should suffer the horrible fate they had prepared for those others. As it is, another death shall be their's."

Neither of the prisoners spoke as Duval blew out the death-dealing fusee, and poured a decanter of water, which happened to be standing on a side-table, over the shell.

And then he prepared to leave the apartment, when St. Ives said—

"But the casket, Duval—have you the casket?"

"Indeed, not I," replied Duval. "I had forgotten all about it. Ah, here it is!" he added, as he raised it from the floor.

With a shriek of dismay, Sir John tried to make a rush at Duval.

But the attempt was a failure.

"Why, you don't suppose for a moment, do you," said Duval, "that we are going to save the Prince and all within the Palace from such a terrible fate as you had prepared for them, and not expect something as a reward for our trouble?"

With a cry more like that of an enraged animal, Sir John Allwood sank back, and a livid hue overspread his countenance.

"Let us make the best of our way now to the Adelphi Terrace," said St. Ives. "There is danger here."

"I come—I come!" replied Duval.

They quickly left that room, which had been the scene of so much riot and confusion.

They just paused as they passed by Frederick Prince of Wales, but neither of them thought it worth their while to set him at liberty, so they left him still bound to the chair to which one of the followers of James had tied him.

To reach the garden of the Palace, and from thence the Park, was the work only of an incredibly short space of time.

In silence they threaded their way down the Strand, and at length reached number sixteen, where they gave the three knocks on the outer door.

Adelina opened it.

The young girl was pale, and her voice trembled as she said to St. Ives, "You are safe, Charles—is all well?"

"All is well, Adelina." Then, turning to Duval, he added, "Follow me!—we must adopt some plan for leaving this country as early as may be to-morrow."

St. Ives proceeded at once to the large apartment in which assembled those members of the Stuart family with whom they have lately been made acquainted.

The elderly man, as usual, was seated on the settee, close to the fire; and grouped around was the young man who had shown so much bravery and coolness, when dealing with Prince Frederick, the young girl, Catherine, and one or two of the faithful adherents of their fallen fortunes.

As St. Ives entered the room, followed closely by Claude Duval, and the young girl, Adelina, the old man raised his head, and said, somewhat excitedly, "Well, have you succeeded? What is this these children tell me of treachery and deception the part of Sir John Allwood?"

"It would have been murder on his part, too," replied St. Ives, "If I and this brave Claude Duval had not been too many for him."

"Is it possible? But the treasure—the hidden casket—have you secured that?"

"We have," said Duval, as he advanced, and placed the silver casket on the table in front of the old man, who instantly caught it up, and endeavoured to raise the lid.

"Stay—stay!" cried Duval; "I will open it!"

As he spoke, Duval took from his pocket a bunch of skeleton keys, which he always carried about him; and after trying, first one and then another, at last found one which opened the casket.

The sight that met the eager gaze of that little group, was sufficient to make their hearts beat with joy and triumph; for the casket contained jewels and precious stones of great value and magnificence.

"At last!—at last! My son," cried the old man, "I shall see thee seated on the throne of your ancestors—long live King James!"

There was a flush of excitement upon the face of the young man, James, as he heard these words, and turning to Adelina, he said, "And it is to you, my sister, I am indebted for this costly treasure, which will enable us to carry out our schemes for the restoration of our family to the throne of these realms."

Adelina looked up with a smile, and said gently, "Yes, brother; and now that we have seen how utterly unworthy the Prince of Wales is to wear the crown of a great kingdom like this, I have no regret when I think of him being deposed."

"That is well," said James; "and now, Miravel, I would ask you what is best to be done? We are certainly no longer safe in this house, it is known too well. Where can we seek a refuge until we can leave this country for awhile to mature our plans?"

St. Ives looked at Duval, who said, "I would suggest that you all return with me to Hampstead. The house I occupy will afford every accommodation for a few hours. It is not what I would wish to offer, but it is the best I can."

The old man gazed at Duval for a moment in silence, and then he said to St. Ives, "Miravel, who is this gentleman, to whom we owe so much, and whom we seem to have forgotten to thank for the services he has rendered to us and our cause?"

"He is, nevertheless, well known to you," replied St. Ives, with a smile, "as Claude Duval, who——"

"What he who refused to receive rank in the Jacobite cause — who so nobly protected our Mary, at the peril of his own life?"

As he spoke, the old man grasped the hand of Claude Duval in both of his, and his voice shook with emotion, as he continued:

"Oh! refuse no longer to become one of us. We will heap honours, and wealth, and distinction upon one so great, and noble, and self-sacrificing. Speak, and tell me that you will become one of us!"

Duval was silent.

He was thinking of Lucy, and wondering what she would wish. For his own part, he had seen so much of the weakness, treachery, and dissipation of the reigning royal family, that he had no feeling of respect left for them; and, on the contrary, all that he knew of the Stuart family, excited his warmest sympathy and admiration.

"Speak, Duval," said St. Ives. "Can you refuse to join your fate with ours?"

"I will think about it," replied Duval; "but be assured, whether I am one of you or not, my heart and sympathies go with you."

"We will not press you further to-night, sir," said James, courteously; "and we will gladly avail ourselves of your kind offer to take up our abode with you for a few hours, and then we will leave England for France, where we have every reason to believe we shall meet with powerful and influential friends."

It was decided, then, that the old man and his three grandchildren should accompany Duval at once to Hampstead Heath; and that St. Ives would follow with his wife and Eva, who was still a happy inmate of their home.

The little party was soon ready to leave that house, which was no longer a safe refuge for them.

As the hour was still early, they met no pedestrians, and Duval hailed two hackney coaches, and himself mounted to the box of one of them, gave the necessary directions to the driver.

A short time brought the little party in sight of the Heath, and here they all alighted, with a handsome gratuity to the two drivers, who took care not to be curious to learn where their "fares" were going.

Lucy was soon made acquainted with all that had happened, and we need hardly say, that she waited impatiently for the moment when she should again behold her friend, the Stuart Princess.

She had not long to wait, for St. Ives, with his wife, and Eva, soon knocked at the outer door.

The meeting between the two friends was, indeed, a happy one, and Lucy thought she had never seen the Stuart Princess looking so happy as she did on that morning.

No one knew the arguments she had used to induce Lucy to accompany them to France; but, certain it is, that she told Duval that she no longer had any scruples about his becoming a Jacobite, and that she was quite willing to share the perils and pleasures of life with her dear friend, the Stuart Princess.

"Be it so, dear one," said Duval, as he folded Lucy in his arms. "I will become a Jacobite—for, at least, the Stuarts are not ungrateful."

At midnight, that eventful day, our little party took their departure from Hampstead Heath; but there was an addition to it in the shape of Blossom and Nightshade

A cutter was lying in readiness at Westminster Bridge, which was to convey the Stuart party to the vessel which was bound for France.

Already the old man and the two girls, with their brother James, and Eva, had taken their seats; and she whom the reader has followed through so many of these pages by the name of the Stuart Princess was the last to be handed in by Duval and St. Ives.

"The boat must return for you, Blossom, and Nightshade," whispered Duval; "you can make him lie down, quietly enough."

"All right, Captain—be quick! I feel nervous, to-night," replied Blossom.

Duval leaped into the boat, and the little cutter sped along the water.

The French vessel is reached, and the party congratulated each other upon their success, when a loud firing was heard from the shore.

The Stuart Princess turned pale.

"There is danger!" she said.

At this moment the wind arose, and dashed the ship about—the whole fabric shudders from stem to stern.

The Stuart Princess clung to her husband, and James clasped Eva to his heart.

All was confusion, and the boat which was following them, neared their vessel.

"Lost—lost, Charles!" said the Princess.

"Hush—hush! Mary, dear one—all may yet be well!"

There was now a cry from the boat, and the unmistakable voice of Mossy Pendell broke upon their ears.

"Claude Duval and St. Ives! It is of no use—you are our prisoners—Mr. Muckles is with us!"

"Ah!" cried Duval, as he threw his arms around Lucy's slight form—"either that man or I must fall to-night!"

"Do not be rash!—oh, do not be rash, dearest!" cried Lucy.

"Hark!" said Duval.

There was a shout from the boat that had been pursuing the fugitives, and then all was still.

The boat, and all who were in it, perished in the deep waters.

* * * * * *

A month after the events we have just recorded there was a ball given at the French Court, and if the reader will enter one of the reception-rooms with us, he will see amongst the guests all those whose fortunes we have followed through the pages of this history.

There was Claude Duval, who had accepted, after much persuasion, high rank from the Stuart family, and his gentle Lucy; there, too, might be seen St. Ives—or, rather, Colonel Miravel, as we should call him—and the Stuart Princess, looking serene and happy; and James, likewise, is present in that brilliant assembly; and, if one may judge by looks, he evidently thinks Eva St. Clare the most lovely of the many lovely girls by whom he is at that moment surrounded.

The look of affection and admiration which James bestowed upon the young girl at his side was seen and understood also by the Stuart Princess, for she slid her hand under the arm of her husband, and said, softly, "If my eyes do not deceive me, dear Charles, our brother James fully appreciates the gentle worth of my dear Eva!"

St. Ives started, for he, too, had been contemplating that youthful pair; and it was with a feeling of unutterable thankfulness that he had perceived, day by day, springing up between them a pure and holy affection.

"Yes, dearest!" he replied, as he pressed the hand which lay so confidingly on his arm. "Yes, dearest, and I am now happy!"

"Now happy, Charles?" said the Princess. "What mean you by now?"

"Because I feared that I had, perhaps, madly wrecked the happiness of that innocent heart; and until I saw that she loved another, there would ever be bitter remorse and anguish for me!"

"Hush, hush! Speak not thus!"

"And you forgive me?"

"Nay, now — have you any doubts?" she asked. "Are you not now all my own?"

"And I ever was, I do believe, my dear! It was but an infatuation which must have vanished as I became more and more impressed with the beauty of your mind!"

"Nay, now, you must not turn flatterer again, Charles! That misunderstanding did us both good, I believe; and, therefore, we will not continue to nurse any recollections of it—at least, no unpleasant ones. But I must go to Eva, she seems in doubt whether to run away, or stay to reply to something her companion is asking her."

As she spoke, the Stuart Pincess glided across the room, and making her way to the youthful couple who had formed the subject of her conversation with her husband.

Eva, with a bright flush upon her fair cheek, instantly placed her hand in that of her friend; and, as he did so, she whispered, "Let us leave this scene as soon as may be, dear friend! The lights and the music somehow seem to bewilder me to-night."

The Princess smiled archly, as she whispered, in the same low tone, "Is it not rather that you would meditate in solitude over the confession of love you have this night heard, my darling? Nay, I did not mean to pain you," she continued, as she felt Eva's hand tremble, and something very bright sparkled on her long eyelashes.

At this moment James joined them. He had been detained in conversation by an old friend, who had not seen him for many years.

"I confide her to your keeping, dear sister!" he said, addressing the Princess, "for I see you have done it better, much better than I could have done; and, believe me, nothing could have given me greater happiness than to welcome as a sister one who has been such in affection ever since I have known her! Come, dear Eva, we will leave these scenes, as you wish to do so! Good night, James!"

The young man bade adieu to his two fair companions, very reluctantly, it must be confessed, for he had hoped for a few more last words with his Eva; but at that moment one of the members of the French royal family accosted him.

The Princess and Eva, however, had no difficulty in finding Duval and St. Ives, who at once escorted them to their carriage.

"Oh, my kind friend and sister, I do not deserve to be so happy!" were the first words Eva uttered, as she found herself alone with the Princess.

"Nay, darling," was the gentle reply, "if you do not deserve happiness, I know not who is to expect it in this world!"

"But—but——"

"But what, dear? What would you ask?"

"Have you forgiven me?"

A fond pressure to that faithful and affectionate heart was sufficient reply; and then Eva, pressing back the mass of sunny ringlets from her intellectual brow, looked smilingly at her friend, as she said, "He does love me! Oh, I think he loves me!"

"Well, dearest," replied her friend, with a smile, "to judge from appearances, I should say he does! Shall I ask him?"

"Oh, no, no! Not for worlds! I would not let him think I doubted him!"

"A wise resolve, dearest! But now to repose, or we shall have pale cheeks to-morrow!"

The ball is over; the lights are extinguished; each one has sought his pillow; no, there is one yet threading his way towards the stables of a lordly mansion in the Rue St. Germains.

Blossom!

"Here, Captain ;—I beg pardon, I mean Colonel!"

Duval smiled as he followed Blossom, who was carrying a hand-lantern.

A stable-door is flung open, and Duval, as is his wont every night before he retires to rest, throws his arm round the beautifully arched neck of his noble steed, as he says "Good night, Nightshade!"

THE END.

Milton Keynes UK
Ingram Content Group UK Ltd.
UKHW030245011224
451916UK00011B/85